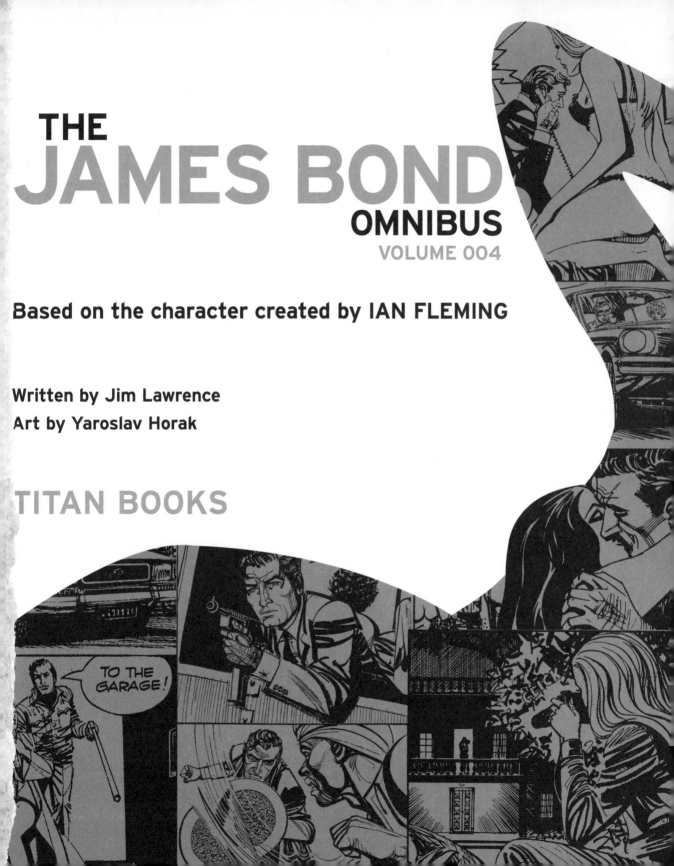

# THE JAMES BOND OMNIBUS
## VOLUME 004

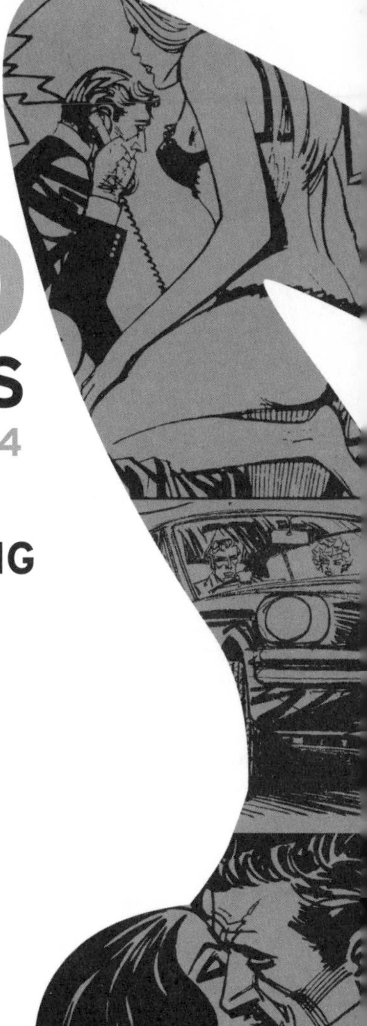

**Based on the character created by IAN FLEMING**

**Written by Jim Lawrence**
**Art by Yaroslav Horak**

TITAN BOOKS

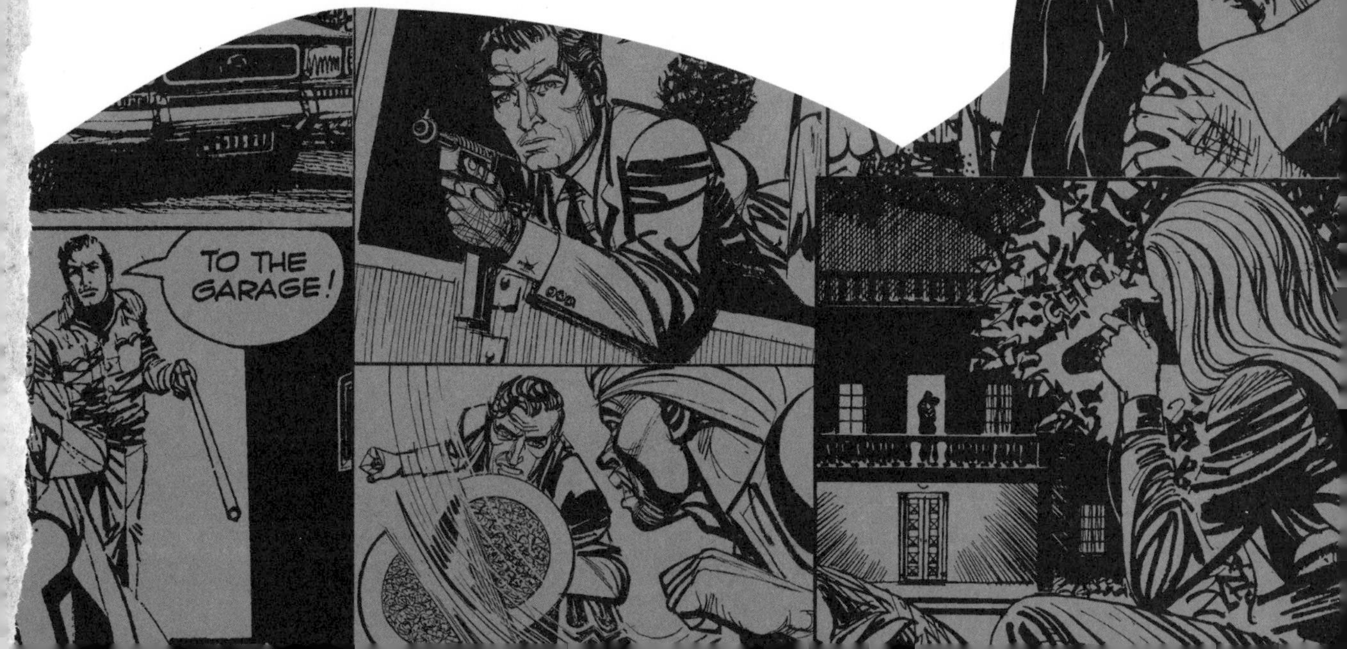
TO THE GARAGE!

THE JAMES BOND OMNIBUS
VOLUME 004
ISBN: 9780857685896

Published by Titan Books,
A division of Titan Publishing Group Ltd.
144 Southwark St.
London, SE1 0UP

Trouble Spot is © Ian Fleming Publications Ltd./
Express Newspaper Ltd. 1971-72
Isle of Condors is © Ian Fleming Publications Ltd./
Express Newspaper Ltd. 1972
The League of Vampires is © Ian Fleming Publications Ltd./
Express Newspaper Ltd. 1972-73
Die With My Boots On is © Ian Fleming Publications Ltd./
Express Newspaper Ltd. 1973
The Girl Machine is © Ian Fleming Publications Ltd./
Express Newspaper Ltd. 1987
Beware of Butterflies is © Ian Fleming Publications Ltd./
Express Newspaper Ltd. 1987
The Nevsky Nude is © Ian Fleming Publications Ltd./
Express Newspaper Ltd. 1987
The Phoenix Project is © Ian Fleming Publications Ltd./
Express Newspaper Ltd. 1974-75
The Black Ruby Caper is © Ian Fleming Publications Ltd./
Express Newspaper Ltd. 1975

James Bond and 007 are trademarks of Danjaq LLC, used under licence by
Ian Fleming Publications Ltd. All Rights Reserved. No portion of this book
may be reproduced or transmitted in any form or by any means, without the
express written permission of the publisher. Names, characters, places and
incidents featured in this publication are either the product of the author's
imagination or used fictitiously. Any resemblance to actual persons (living or
dead) is entirely coincidental.

A CIP catalogue record for this title is available from the British Library.

First Edition: October 2012
10 9 8 7 6 5 4 3 2
Printed in China.

Huge thanks to Simon Trewin and Ariella Feiner at United Agents, and Corinne
Turner and Sarah Fairbairn at Ian Fleming Publications Ltd. without whom
this book would never have happened.

www.ianfleming.com
Cover Image © Shutterstock 2012

What did you think of this book? We love to hear from our readers.
Please email us at: readerfeedback@titanemail.com, or write to us
at the above address.

To receive advance information, news, competitions, and exclusive
offers online, please sign up for the Titan newsletter on our website:
www.titanbooks.com

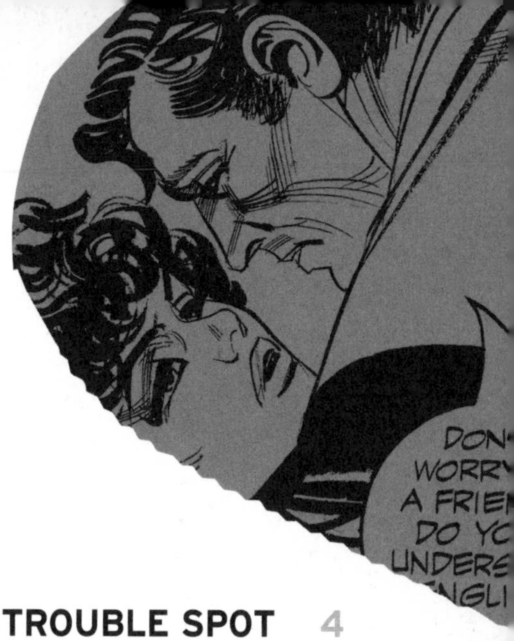
DON
WORRY
A FRIE
DO YO
UNDERS
NGLI



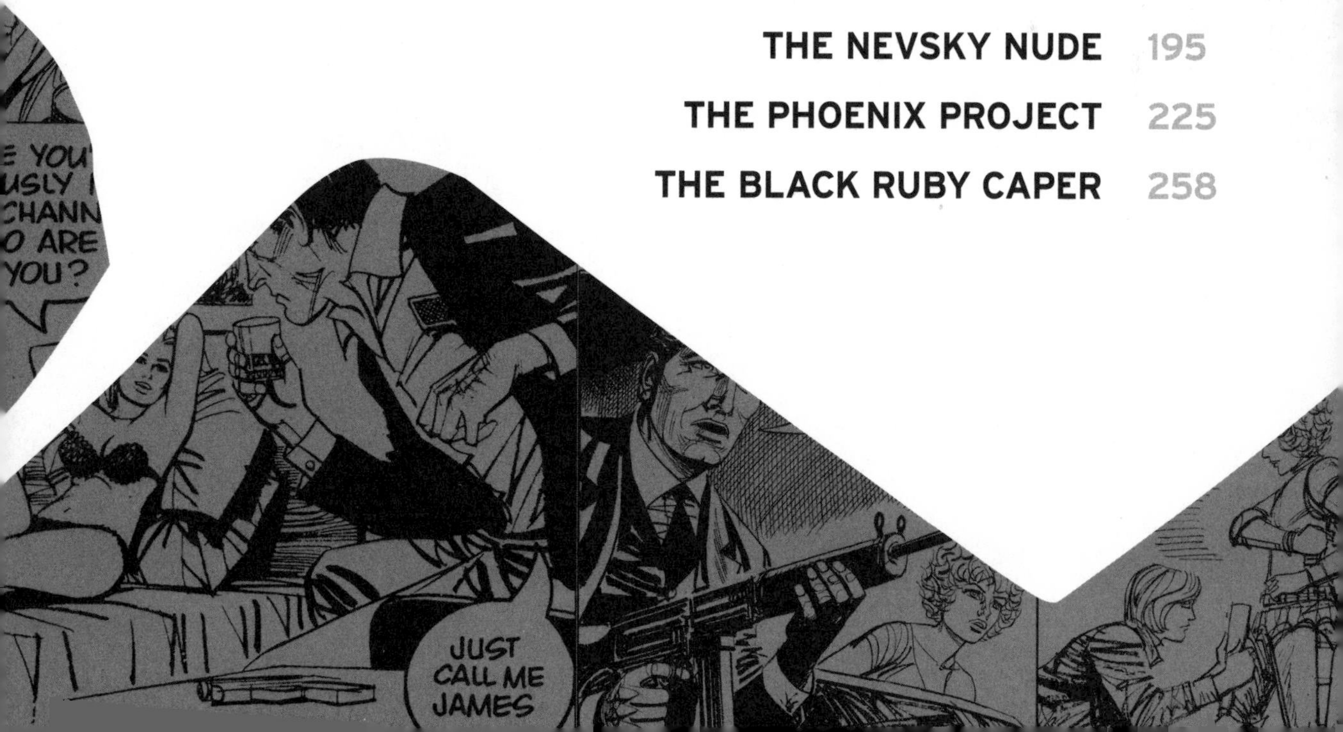
E YOU
USLY
CHANN
O ARE
YOU?
JUST CALL ME JAMES

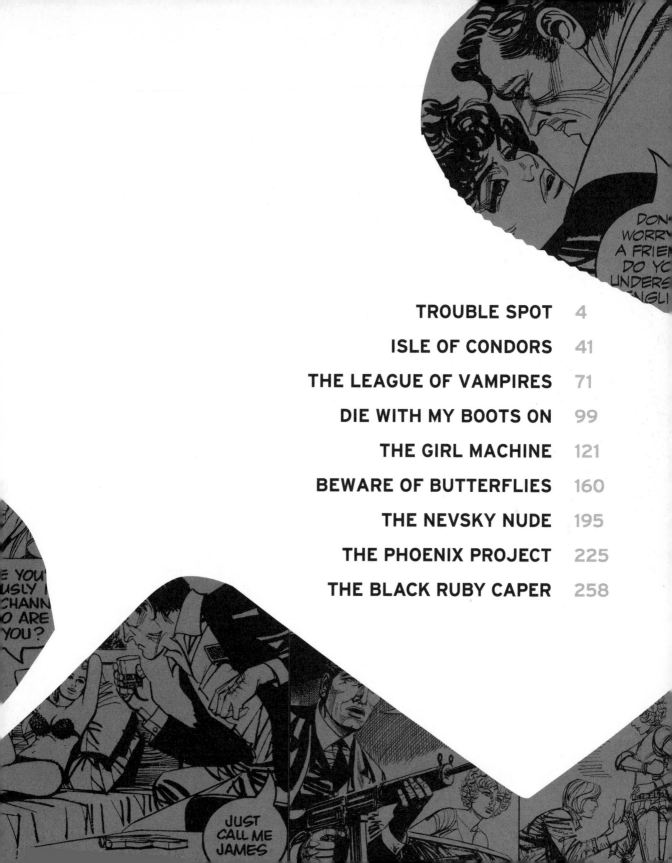

# TROUBLE SPOT

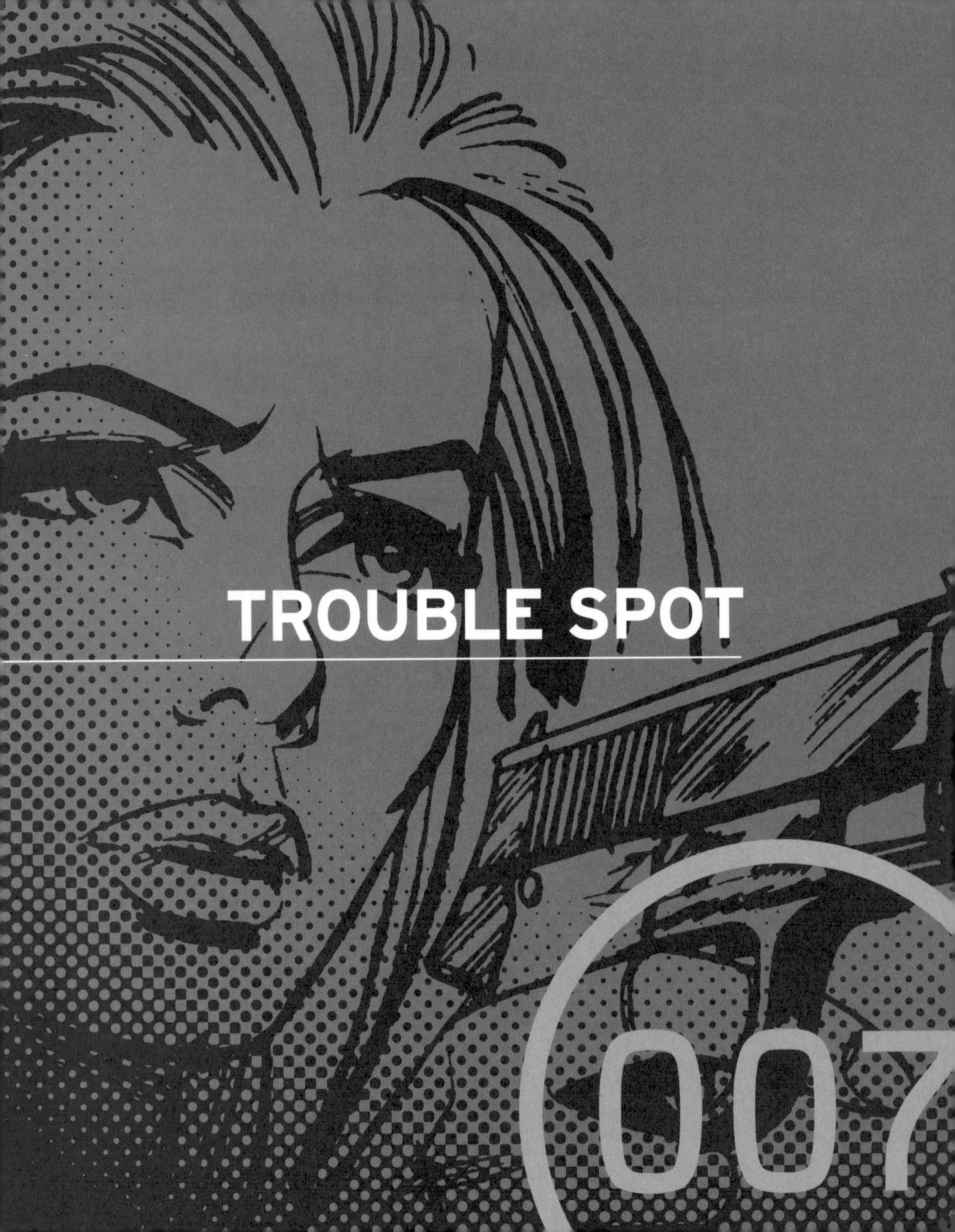
007

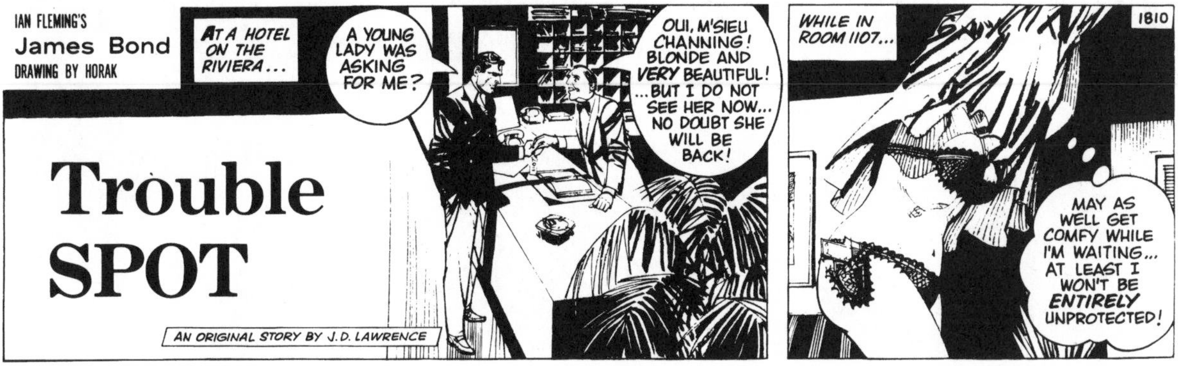
IAN FLEMING'S
James Bond
DRAWING BY HORAK
Trouble SPOT
AN ORIGINAL STORY BY J.D. LAWRENCE
AT A HOTEL ON THE RIVIERA...
A YOUNG LADY WAS ASKING FOR ME?
OUI, M'SIEU CHANNING! BLONDE AND VERY BEAUTIFUL! ...BUT I DO NOT SEE HER NOW... NO DOUBT SHE WILL BE BACK!
WHILE IN ROOM 1107...
1810
MAY AS WELL GET COMFY WHILE I'M WAITING... AT LEAST I WON'T BE ENTIRELY UNPROTECTED!

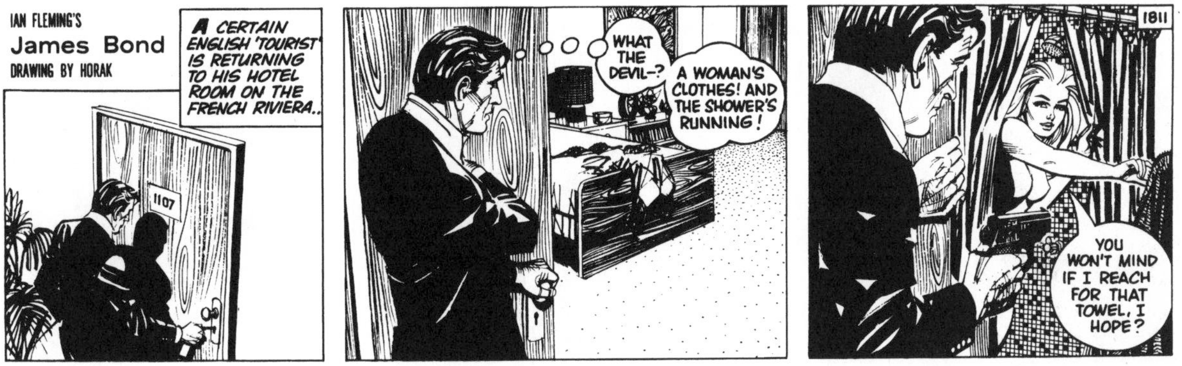
IAN FLEMING'S
James Bond
DRAWING BY HORAK
A CERTAIN ENGLISH 'TOURIST' IS RETURNING TO HIS HOTEL ROOM ON THE FRENCH RIVIERA..
1107
WHAT THE DEVIL-?
A WOMAN'S CLOTHES! AND THE SHOWER'S RUNNING!
1811
YOU WON'T MIND IF I REACH FOR THAT TOWEL, I HOPE?

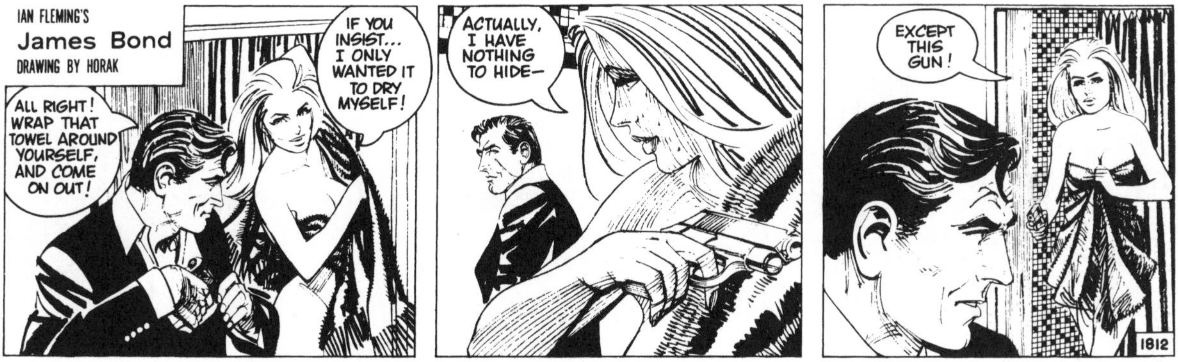
IAN FLEMING'S
James Bond
DRAWING BY HORAK
ALL RIGHT! WRAP THAT TOWEL AROUND YOURSELF, AND COME ON OUT!
IF YOU INSIST... I ONLY WANTED IT TO DRY MYSELF!
ACTUALLY, I HAVE NOTHING TO HIDE-
EXCEPT THIS GUN!
1812

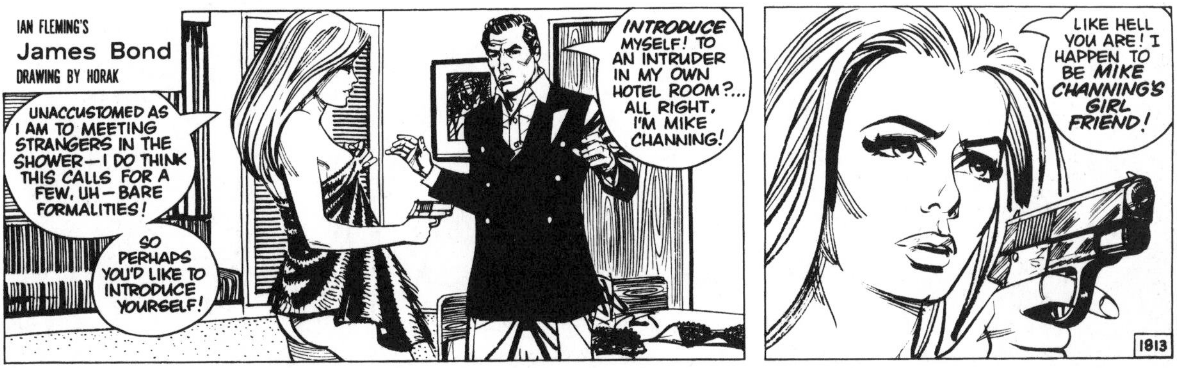
IAN FLEMING'S
James Bond
DRAWING BY HORAK
UNACCUSTOMED AS I AM TO MEETING STRANGERS IN THE SHOWER—I DO THINK THIS CALLS FOR A FEW, UH—BARE FORMALITIES!
SO PERHAPS YOU'D LIKE TO INTRODUCE YOURSELF!
INTRODUCE MYSELF! TO AN INTRUDER IN MY OWN HOTEL ROOM?... ALL RIGHT, I'M MIKE CHANNING!
LIKE HELL YOU ARE! I HAPPEN TO BE MIKE CHANNING'S GIRL FRIEND!
1813

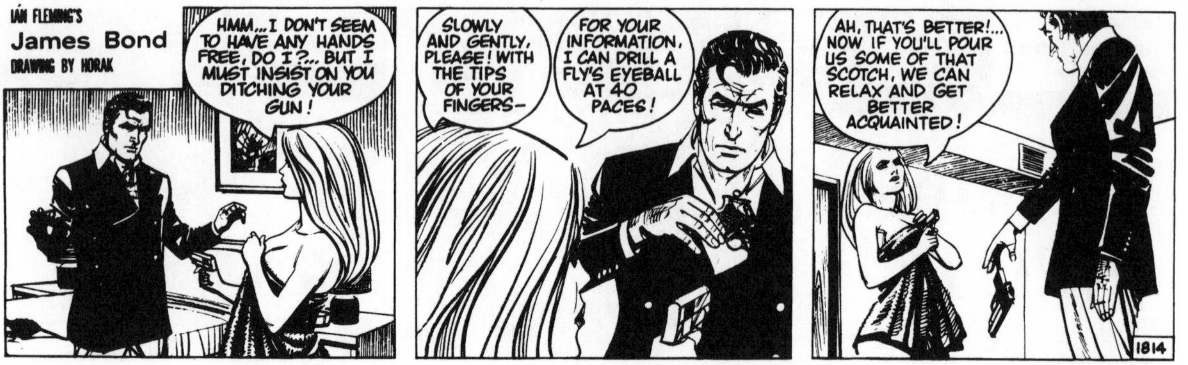
IAN FLEMING'S
James Bond
DRAWING BY HORAK
HMM... I DON'T SEEM TO HAVE ANY HANDS FREE, DO I?... BUT I MUST INSIST ON YOU DITCHING YOUR GUN!
SLOWLY AND GENTLY, PLEASE! WITH THE TIPS OF YOUR FINGERS–
FOR YOUR INFORMATION, I CAN DRILL A FLY'S EYEBALL AT 40 PACES!
AH, THAT'S BETTER!... NOW IF YOU'LL POUR US SOME OF THAT SCOTCH, WE CAN RELAX AND GET BETTER ACQUAINTED!
1814

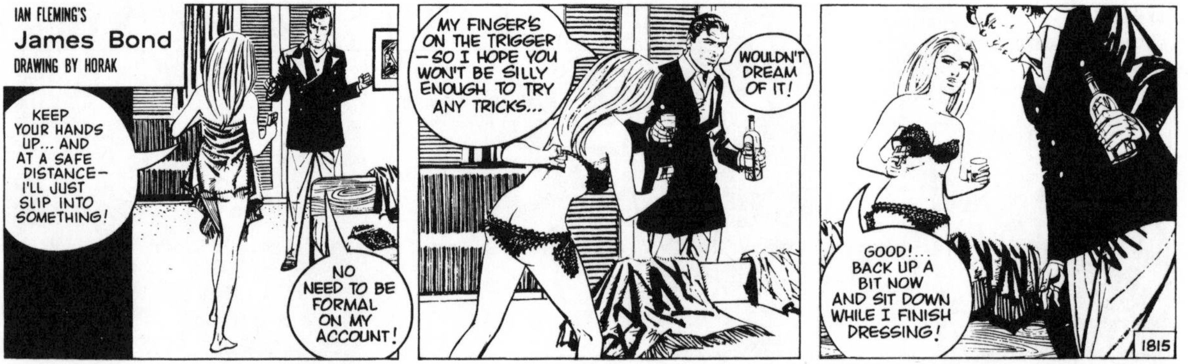
IAN FLEMING'S
James Bond
DRAWING BY HORAK
KEEP YOUR HANDS UP... AND AT A SAFE DISTANCE– I'LL JUST SLIP INTO SOMETHING!
NO NEED TO BE FORMAL ON MY ACCOUNT!
MY FINGER'S ON THE TRIGGER –SO I HOPE YOU WON'T BE SILLY ENOUGH TO TRY ANY TRICKS...
WOULDN'T DREAM OF IT!
GOOD!... BACK UP A BIT NOW AND SIT DOWN WHILE I FINISH DRESSING!
1815

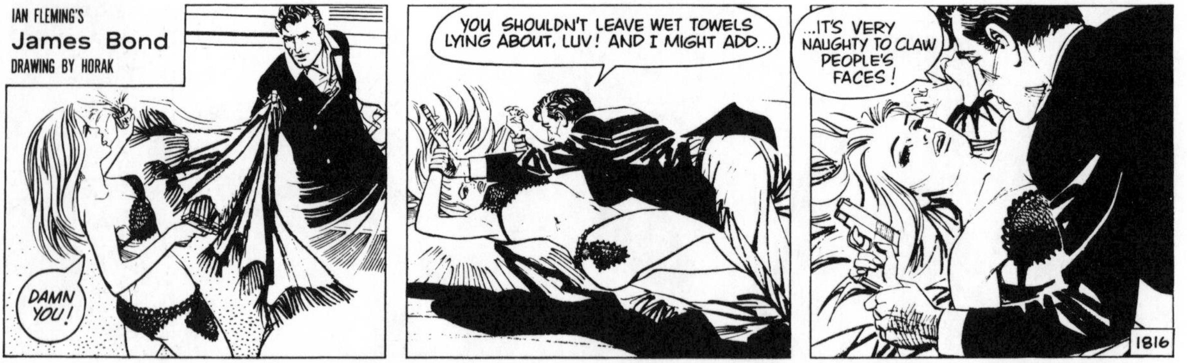
IAN FLEMING'S
James Bond
DRAWING BY HORAK
DAMN YOU!
YOU SHOULDN'T LEAVE WET TOWELS LYING ABOUT, LUV! AND I MIGHT ADD...
...IT'S VERY NAUGHTY TO CLAW PEOPLE'S FACES!
1816

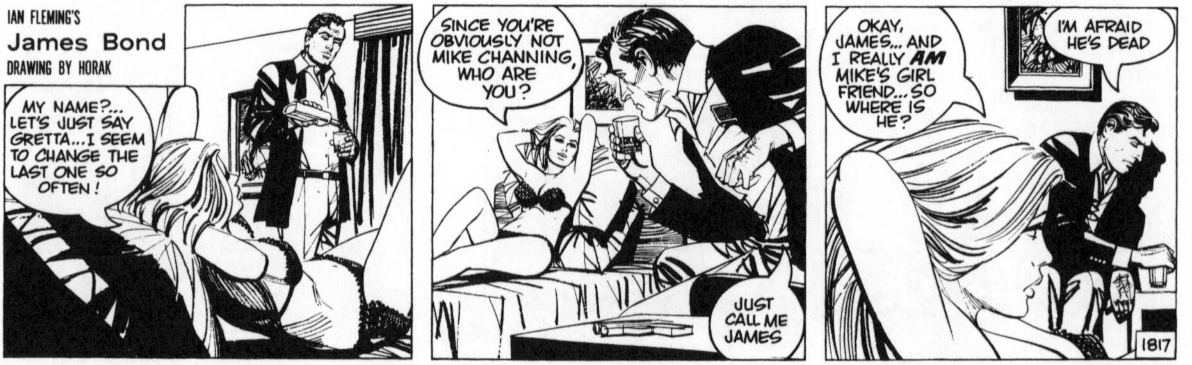
IAN FLEMING'S
James Bond
DRAWING BY HORAK
MY NAME?... LET'S JUST SAY GRETTA... I SEEM TO CHANGE THE LAST ONE SO OFTEN!
SINCE YOU'RE OBVIOUSLY NOT MIKE CHANNING, WHO ARE YOU?
JUST CALL ME JAMES
OKAY, JAMES... AND I REALLY AM MIKE'S GIRL FRIEND... SO WHERE IS HE?
I'M AFRAID HE'S DEAD
1817

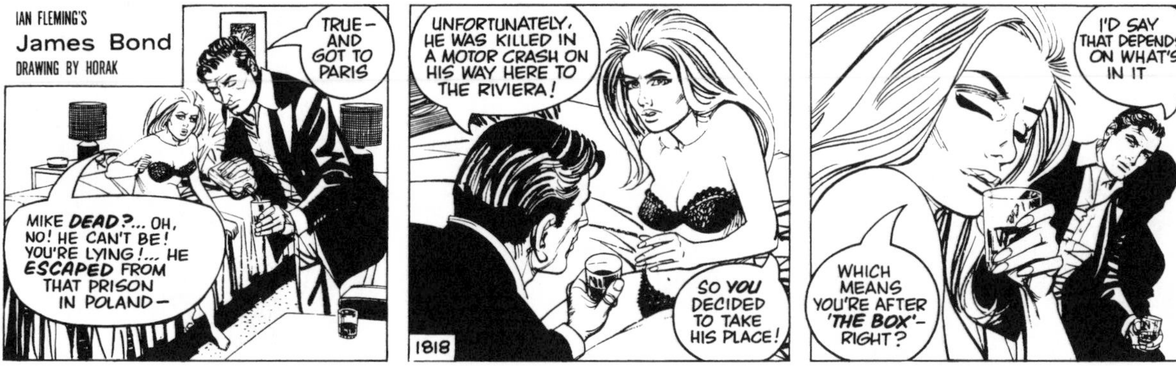
IAN FLEMING'S
James Bond
DRAWING BY HORAK
TRUE— AND GOT TO PARIS
MIKE DEAD?... OH, NO! HE CAN'T BE! YOU'RE LYING!... HE ESCAPED FROM THAT PRISON IN POLAND—
UNFORTUNATELY, HE WAS KILLED IN A MOTOR CRASH ON HIS WAY HERE TO THE RIVIERA!
SO YOU DECIDED TO TAKE HIS PLACE!
1818
I'D SAY THAT DEPENDS ON WHAT'S IN IT
WHICH MEANS YOU'RE AFTER 'THE BOX'— RIGHT?

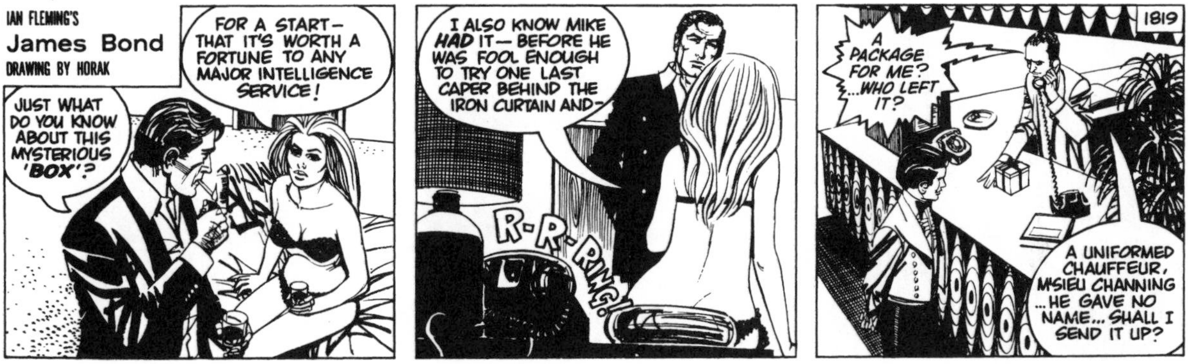
IAN FLEMING'S
James Bond
DRAWING BY HORAK
JUST WHAT DO YOU KNOW ABOUT THIS MYSTERIOUS 'BOX'?
FOR A START— THAT IT'S WORTH A FORTUNE TO ANY MAJOR INTELLIGENCE SERVICE!
I ALSO KNOW MIKE HAD IT— BEFORE HE WAS FOOL ENOUGH TO TRY ONE LAST CAPER BEHIND THE IRON CURTAIN AND—
R-R-RING!
1819
A PACKAGE FOR ME? ...WHO LEFT IT?
A UNIFORMED CHAUFFEUR, M'SIEU CHANNING ...HE GAVE NO NAME... SHALL I SEND IT UP?

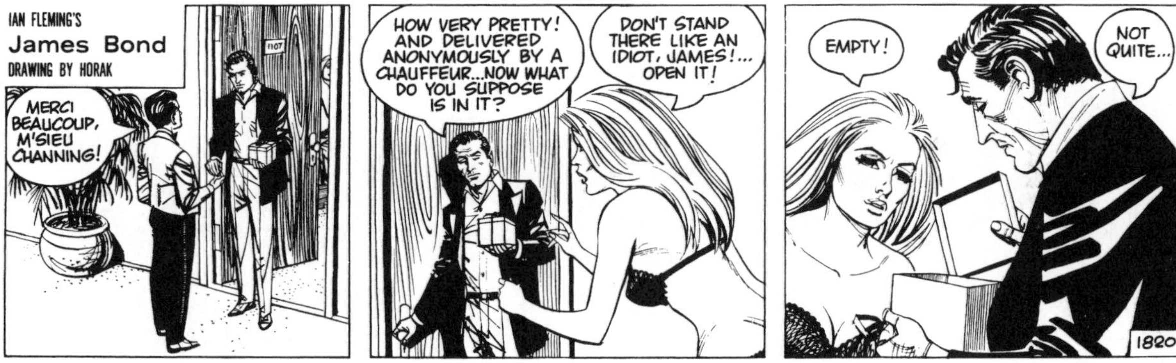
IAN FLEMING'S
James Bond
DRAWING BY HORAK
MERCI BEAUCOUP, M'SIEU CHANNING!
HOW VERY PRETTY! AND DELIVERED ANONYMOUSLY BY A CHAUFFEUR...NOW WHAT DO YOU SUPPOSE IS IN IT?
DON'T STAND THERE LIKE AN IDIOT, JAMES!... OPEN IT!
EMPTY!
NOT QUITE...
1820

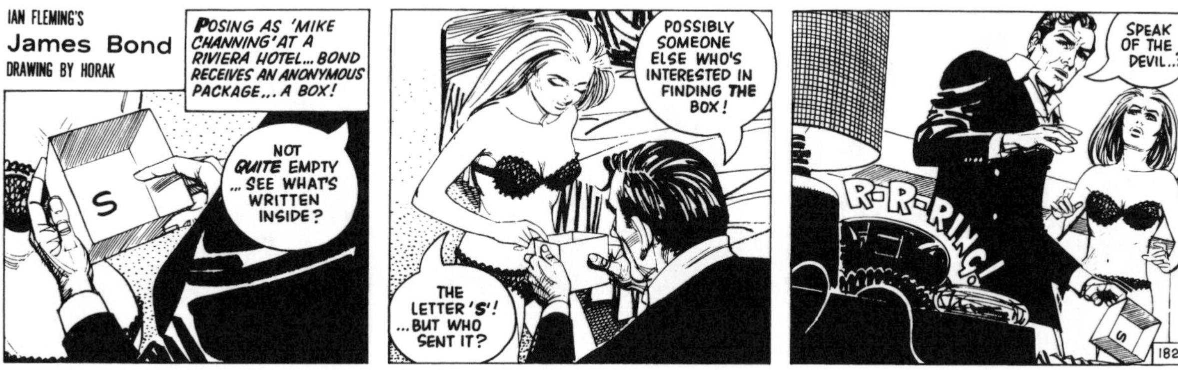
IAN FLEMING'S
James Bond
DRAWING BY HORAK
POSING AS 'MIKE CHANNING' AT A RIVIERA HOTEL... BOND RECEIVES AN ANONYMOUS PACKAGE... A BOX!
NOT QUITE EMPTY ... SEE WHAT'S WRITTEN INSIDE?
S
THE LETTER 'S'! ...BUT WHO SENT IT?
POSSIBLY SOMEONE ELSE WHO'S INTERESTED IN FINDING THE BOX!
SPEAK OF THE DEVIL..?
R-R-RING!
1821

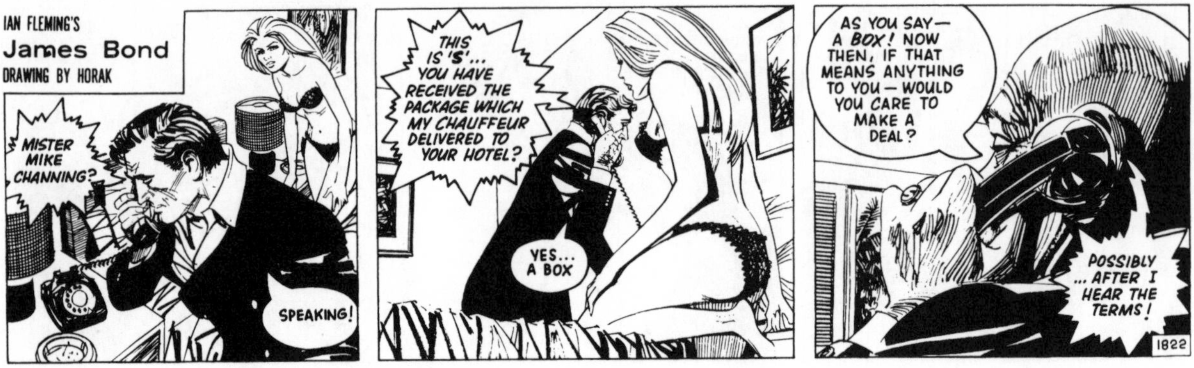
IAN FLEMING'S
James Bond
DRAWING BY HORAK
MISTER MIKE CHANNING?
SPEAKING!
THIS IS 'S'... YOU HAVE RECEIVED THE PACKAGE WHICH MY CHAUFFEUR DELIVERED TO YOUR HOTEL?
YES... A BOX
AS YOU SAY— A BOX! NOW THEN, IF THAT MEANS ANYTHING TO YOU — WOULD YOU CARE TO MAKE A DEAL?
POSSIBLY ...AFTER I HEAR THE TERMS!
1822

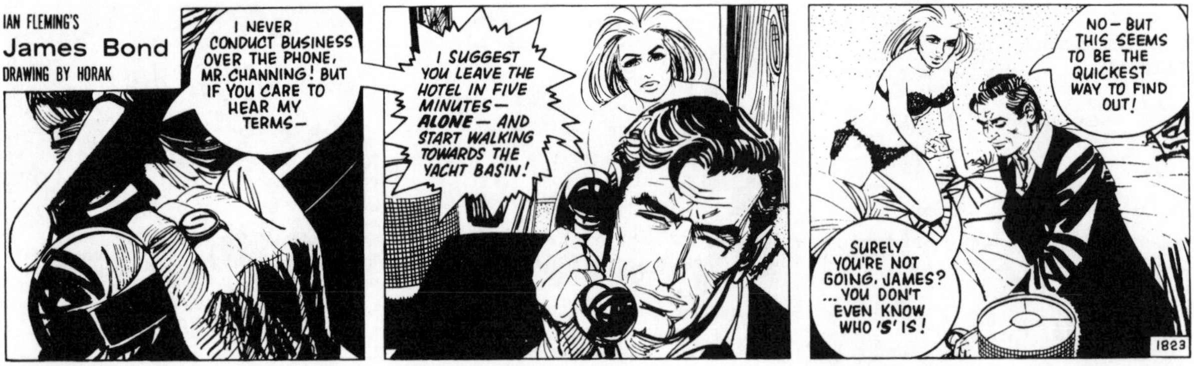
IAN FLEMING'S
James Bond
DRAWING BY HORAK
I NEVER CONDUCT BUSINESS OVER THE PHONE, MR. CHANNING! BUT IF YOU CARE TO HEAR MY TERMS—
I SUGGEST YOU LEAVE THE HOTEL IN FIVE MINUTES— ALONE— AND START WALKING TOWARDS THE YACHT BASIN!
NO— BUT THIS SEEMS TO BE THE QUICKEST WAY TO FIND OUT!
SURELY YOU'RE NOT GOING, JAMES? ...YOU DON'T EVEN KNOW WHO 'S' IS!
1823

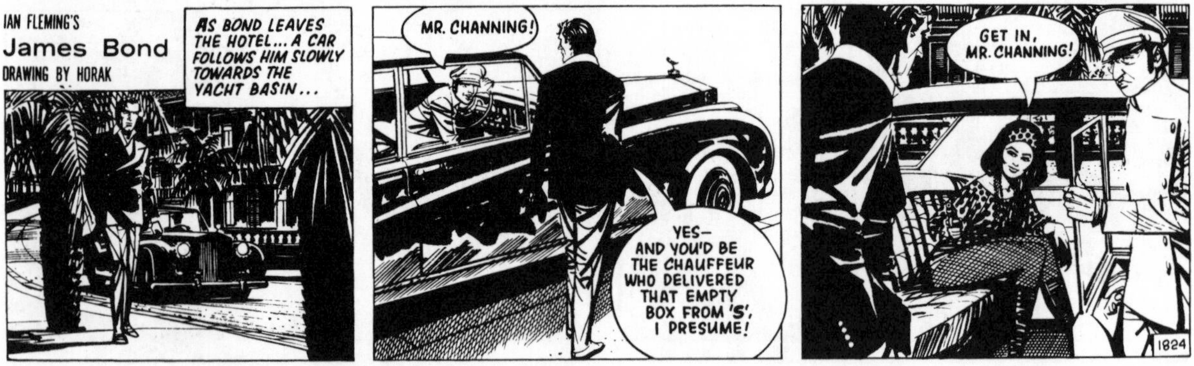
IAN FLEMING'S
James Bond
DRAWING BY HORAK
AS BOND LEAVES THE HOTEL... A CAR FOLLOWS HIM SLOWLY TOWARDS THE YACHT BASIN...
MR. CHANNING!
YES— AND YOU'D BE THE CHAUFFEUR WHO DELIVERED THAT EMPTY BOX FROM 'S', I PRESUME!
GET IN, MR. CHANNING!
1824

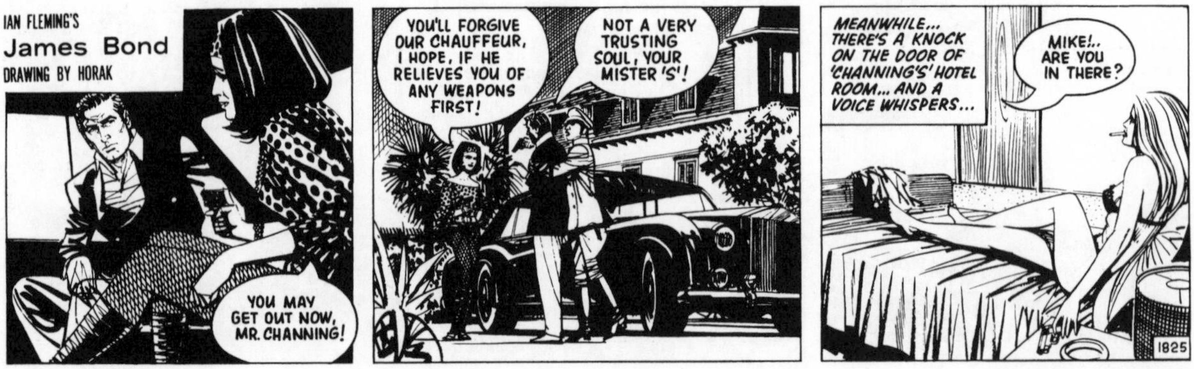
IAN FLEMING'S
James Bond
DRAWING BY HORAK
YOU MAY GET OUT NOW, MR. CHANNING!
YOU'LL FORGIVE OUR CHAUFFEUR, I HOPE, IF HE RELIEVES YOU OF ANY WEAPONS FIRST!
NOT A VERY TRUSTING SOUL, YOUR MISTER 'S'!
MEANWHILE... THERE'S A KNOCK ON THE DOOR OF 'CHANNING'S' HOTEL ROOM... AND A VOICE WHISPERS...
MIKE!.. ARE YOU IN THERE?
1825

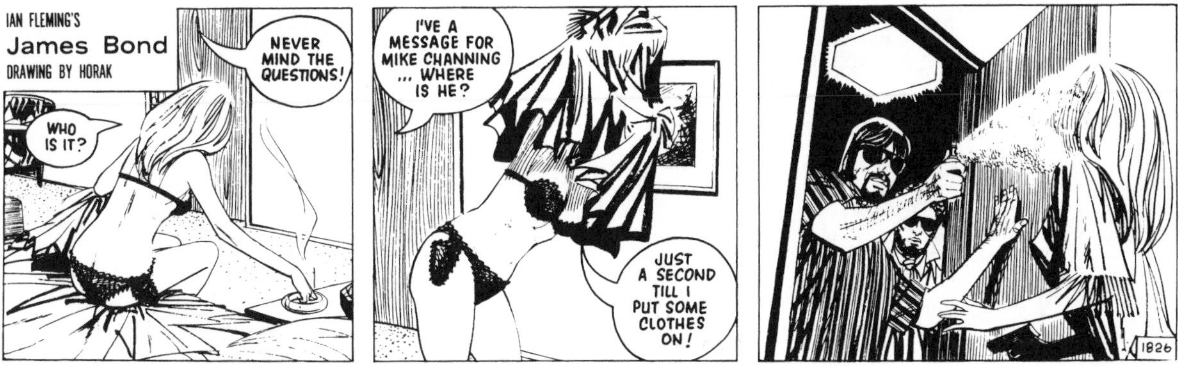
IAN FLEMING'S
James Bond
DRAWING BY HORAK
WHO IS IT?
NEVER MIND THE QUESTIONS!
I'VE A MESSAGE FOR MIKE CHANNING ... WHERE IS HE?
JUST A SECOND TILL I PUT SOME CLOTHES ON!
1826

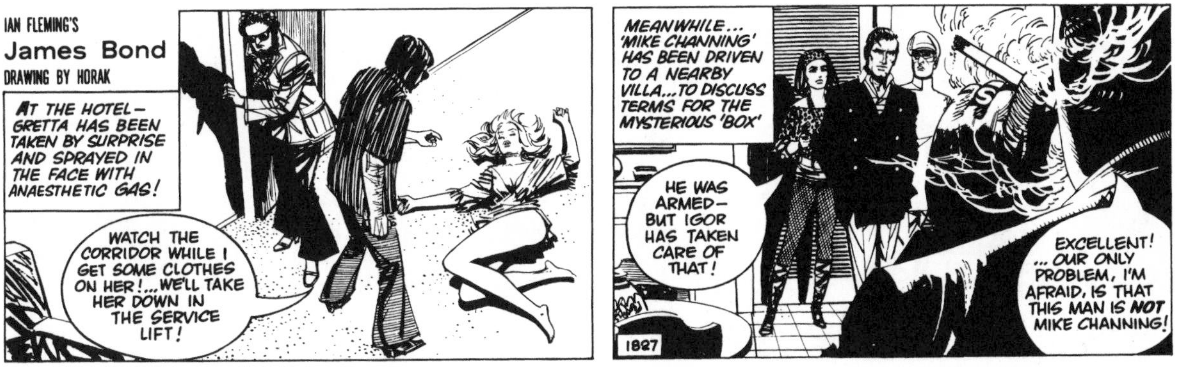
IAN FLEMING'S
James Bond
DRAWING BY HORAK
AT THE HOTEL– GRETTA HAS BEEN TAKEN BY SURPRISE AND SPRAYED IN THE FACE WITH ANAESTHETIC GAS!
WATCH THE CORRIDOR WHILE I GET SOME CLOTHES ON HER!... WE'LL TAKE HER DOWN IN THE SERVICE LIFT!
MEANWHILE... 'MIKE CHANNING' HAS BEEN DRIVEN TO A NEARBY VILLA... TO DISCUSS TERMS FOR THE MYSTERIOUS 'BOX'
HE WAS ARMED– BUT IGOR HAS TAKEN CARE OF THAT!
EXCELLENT! ... OUR ONLY PROBLEM, I'M AFRAID, IS THAT THIS MAN IS NOT MIKE CHANNING!
1827

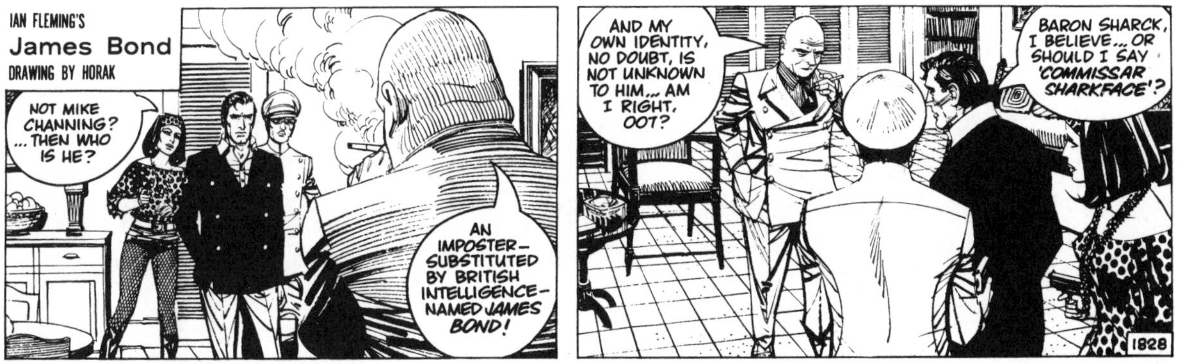
IAN FLEMING'S
James Bond
DRAWING BY HORAK
NOT MIKE CHANNING? ... THEN WHO IS HE?
AN IMPOSTER– SUBSTITUTED BY BRITISH INTELLIGENCE– NAMED JAMES BOND!
AND MY OWN IDENTITY, NO DOUBT, IS NOT UNKNOWN TO HIM... AM I RIGHT, 007?
BARON SHARCK, I BELIEVE... OR SHOULD I SAY 'COMMISSAR SHARKFACE'?
1828

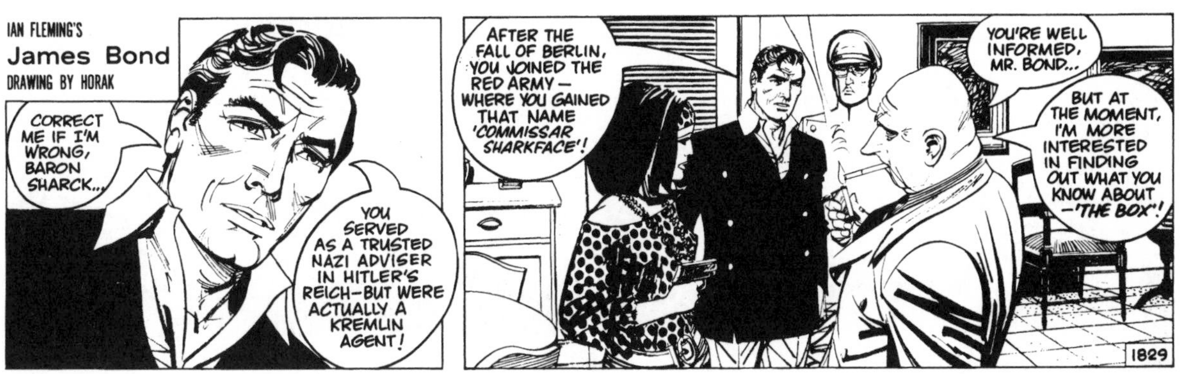
IAN FLEMING'S
James Bond
DRAWING BY HORAK
CORRECT ME IF I'M WRONG, BARON SHARCK...
YOU SERVED AS A TRUSTED NAZI ADVISER IN HITLER'S REICH–BUT WERE ACTUALLY A KREMLIN AGENT!
AFTER THE FALL OF BERLIN, YOU JOINED THE RED ARMY– WHERE YOU GAINED THAT NAME 'COMMISSAR SHARKFACE'!
YOU'RE WELL INFORMED, MR. BOND...
BUT AT THE MOMENT, I'M MORE INTERESTED IN FINDING OUT WHAT YOU KNOW ABOUT –'THE BOX'!
1829

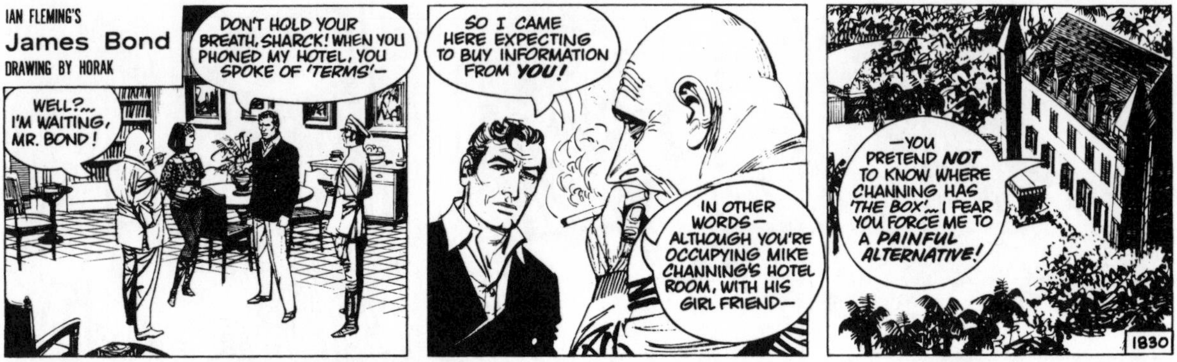
IAN FLEMING'S
James Bond
DRAWING BY HORAK
WELL?... I'M WAITING, MR. BOND!
DON'T HOLD YOUR BREATH, SHARCK! WHEN YOU PHONED MY HOTEL, YOU SPOKE OF 'TERMS'—
SO I CAME HERE EXPECTING TO BUY INFORMATION FROM YOU!
IN OTHER WORDS— ALTHOUGH YOU'RE OCCUPYING MIKE CHANNING'S HOTEL ROOM, WITH HIS GIRL FRIEND—
—YOU PRETEND NOT TO KNOW WHERE CHANNING HAS 'THE BOX'... I FEAR YOU FORCE ME TO A PAINFUL ALTERNATIVE!
1830

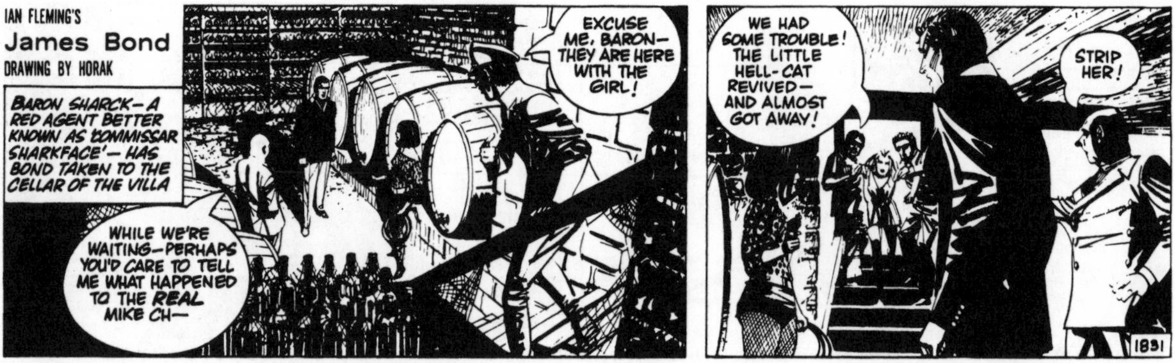
IAN FLEMING'S
James Bond
DRAWING BY HORAK
BARON SHARCK—A RED AGENT BETTER KNOWN AS 'COMMISSAR SHARKFACE'—HAS BOND TAKEN TO THE CELLAR OF THE VILLA
WHILE WE'RE WAITING—PERHAPS YOU'D CARE TO TELL ME WHAT HAPPENED TO THE REAL MIKE CH—
EXCUSE ME, BARON— THEY ARE HERE WITH THE GIRL!
WE HAD SOME TROUBLE! THE LITTLE HELL-CAT REVIVED— AND ALMOST GOT AWAY!
STRIP HER!
1831

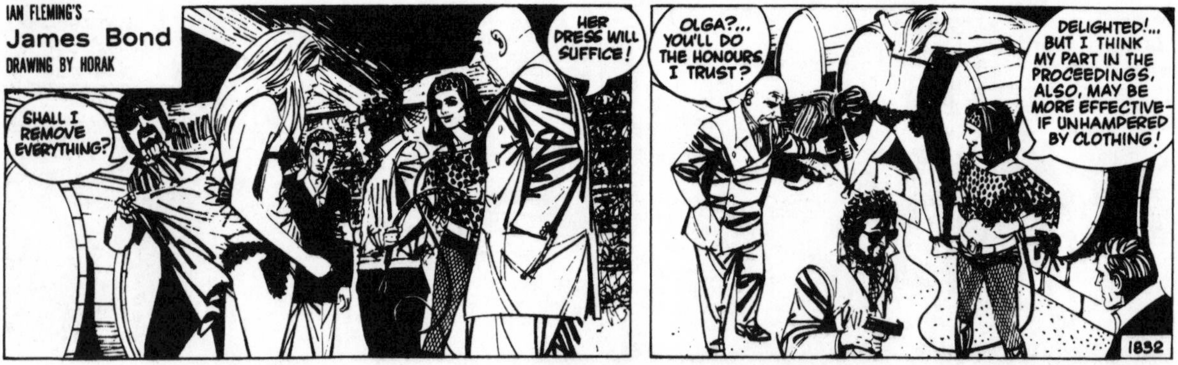
IAN FLEMING'S
James Bond
DRAWING BY HORAK
SHALL I REMOVE EVERYTHING?
HER DRESS WILL SUFFICE!
OLGA?... YOU'LL DO THE HONOURS, I TRUST?
DELIGHTED!... BUT I THINK MY PART IN THE PROCEEDINGS, ALSO, MAY BE MORE EFFECTIVE IF UNHAMPERED BY CLOTHING!
1832

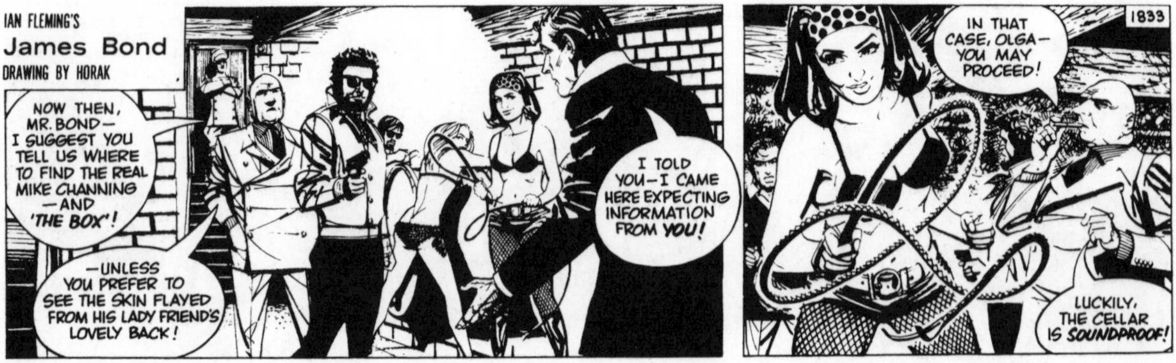
IAN FLEMING'S
James Bond
DRAWING BY HORAK
NOW THEN, MR. BOND— I SUGGEST YOU TELL US WHERE TO FIND THE REAL MIKE CHANNING —AND 'THE BOX'!
—UNLESS YOU PREFER TO SEE THE SKIN FLAYED FROM HIS LADY FRIEND'S LOVELY BACK!
I TOLD YOU—I CAME HERE EXPECTING INFORMATION FROM YOU!
1833
IN THAT CASE, OLGA— YOU MAY PROCEED!
LUCKILY, THE CELLAR IS SOUNDPROOF!

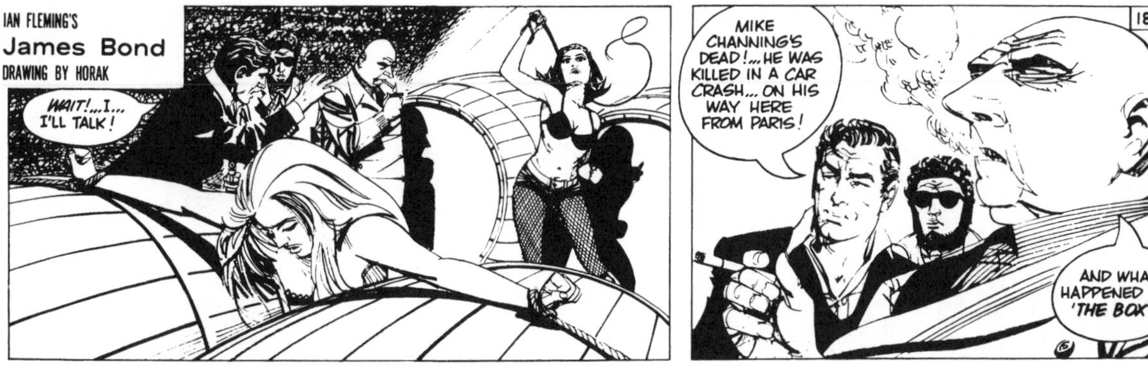
IAN FLEMING'S
James Bond
DRAWING BY HORAK
WAIT!...I... I'LL TALK!
1834
MIKE CHANNING'S DEAD!...HE WAS KILLED IN A CAR CRASH... ON HIS WAY HERE FROM PARIS!
AND WHAT HAPPENED TO 'THE BOX'?

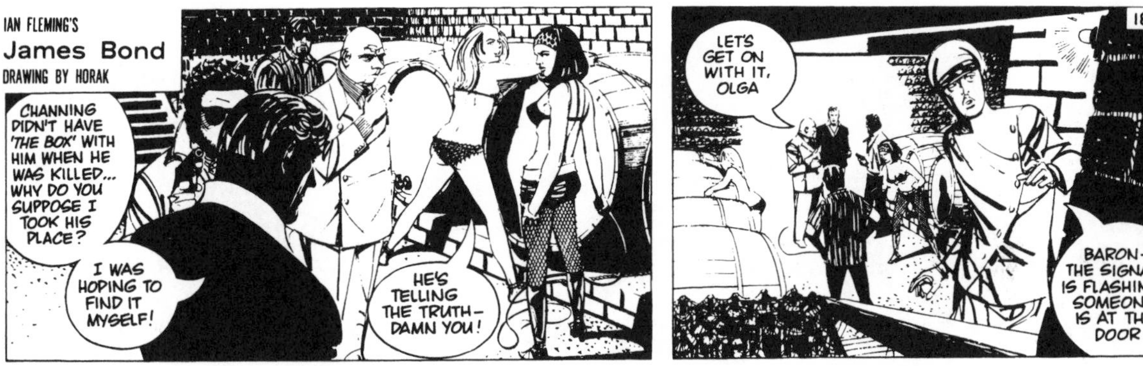
IAN FLEMING'S
James Bond
DRAWING BY HORAK
CHANNING DIDN'T HAVE 'THE BOX' WITH HIM WHEN HE WAS KILLED... WHY DO YOU SUPPOSE I TOOK HIS PLACE?
I WAS HOPING TO FIND IT MYSELF!
HE'S TELLING THE TRUTH—DAMN YOU!
1835
LET'S GET ON WITH IT, OLGA
BARON—THE SIGNAL IS FLASHING! SOMEONE IS AT THE DOOR!

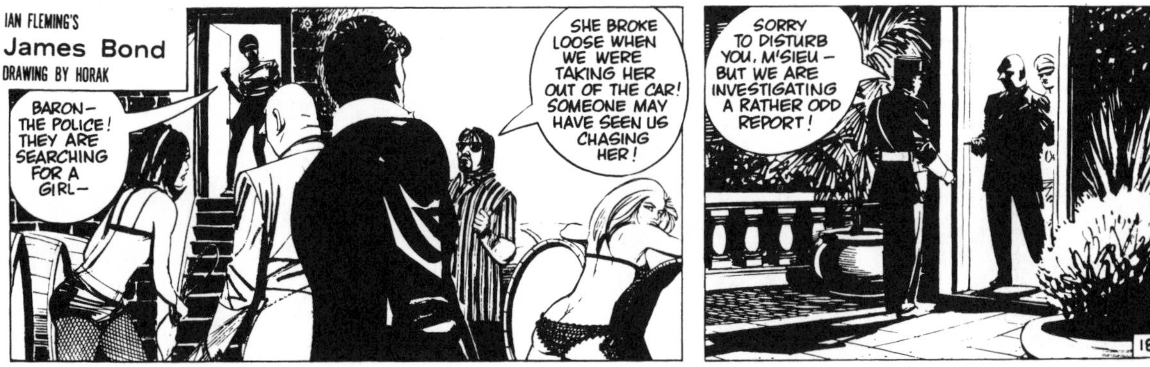
IAN FLEMING'S
James Bond
DRAWING BY HORAK
BARON—THE POLICE! THEY ARE SEARCHING FOR A GIRL—
SHE BROKE LOOSE WHEN WE WERE TAKING HER OUT OF THE CAR! SOMEONE MAY HAVE SEEN US CHASING HER!
SORRY TO DISTURB YOU, M'SIEU—BUT WE ARE INVESTIGATING A RATHER ODD REPORT!
1836

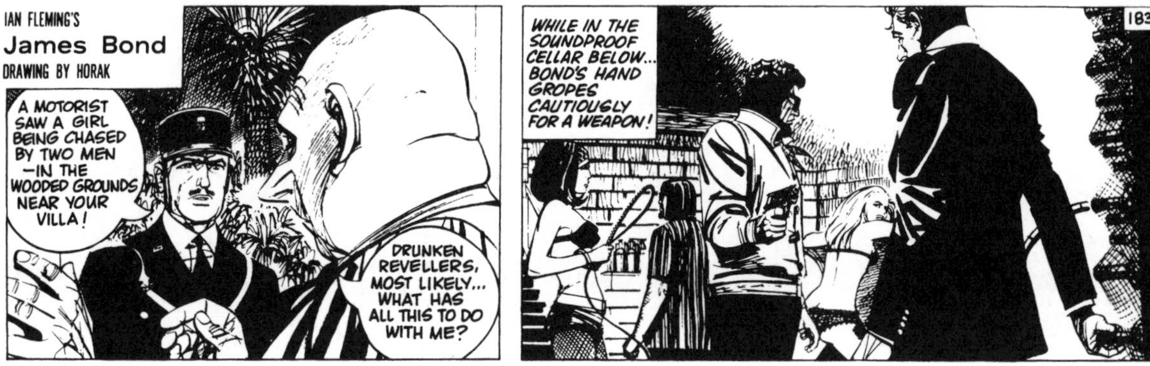
IAN FLEMING'S
James Bond
DRAWING BY HORAK
A MOTORIST SAW A GIRL BEING CHASED BY TWO MEN —IN THE WOODED GROUNDS NEAR YOUR VILLA!
DRUNKEN REVELLERS, MOST LIKELY... WHAT HAS ALL THIS TO DO WITH ME?
1837
WHILE IN THE SOUNDPROOF CELLAR BELOW... BOND'S HAND GROPES CAUTIOUSLY FOR A WEAPON!

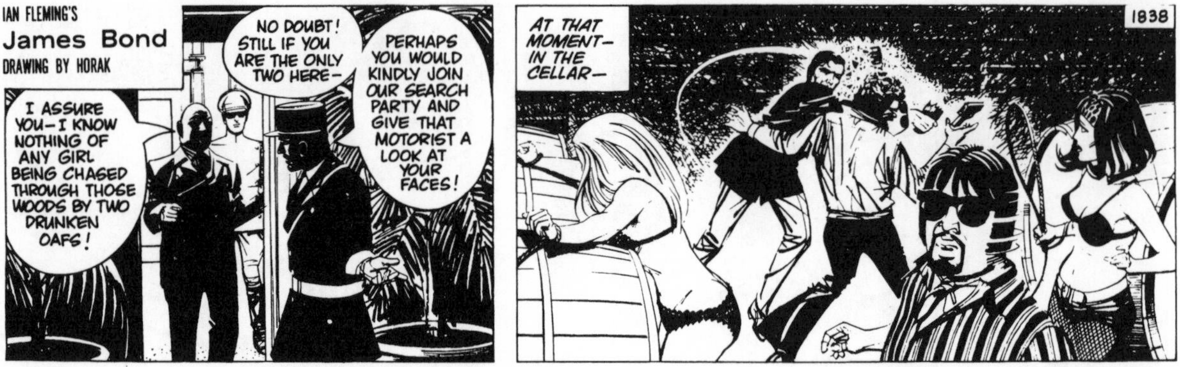
IAN FLEMING'S
James Bond
DRAWING BY HORAK
I ASSURE YOU—I KNOW NOTHING OF ANY GIRL BEING CHASED THROUGH THOSE WOODS BY TWO DRUNKEN OAFS!
NO DOUBT! STILL IF YOU ARE THE ONLY TWO HERE—
PERHAPS YOU WOULD KINDLY JOIN OUR SEARCH PARTY AND GIVE THAT MOTORIST A LOOK AT YOUR FACES!
AT THAT MOMENT—IN THE CELLAR—
1838

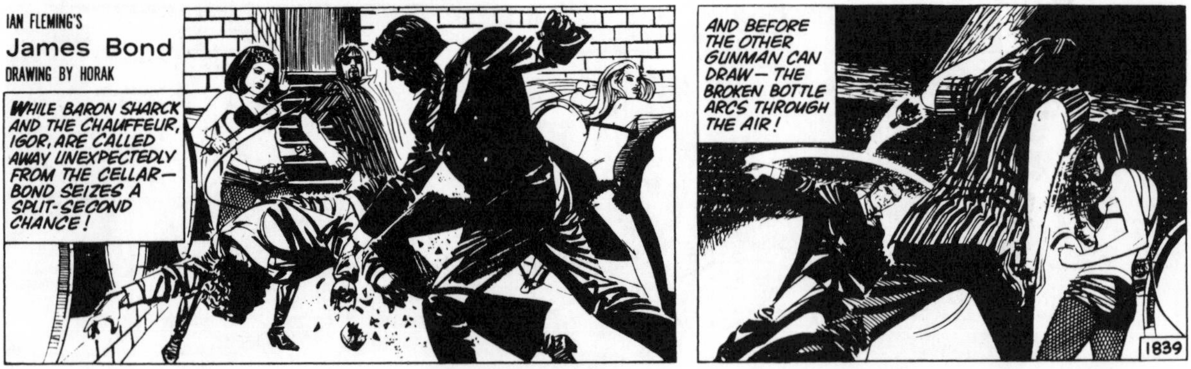
IAN FLEMING'S
James Bond
DRAWING BY HORAK
WHILE BARON SHARCK AND THE CHAUFFEUR, IGOR, ARE CALLED AWAY UNEXPECTEDLY FROM THE CELLAR—BOND SEIZES A SPLIT-SECOND CHANCE!
AND BEFORE THE OTHER GUNMAN CAN DRAW—THE BROKEN BOTTLE ARCS THROUGH THE AIR!
1839

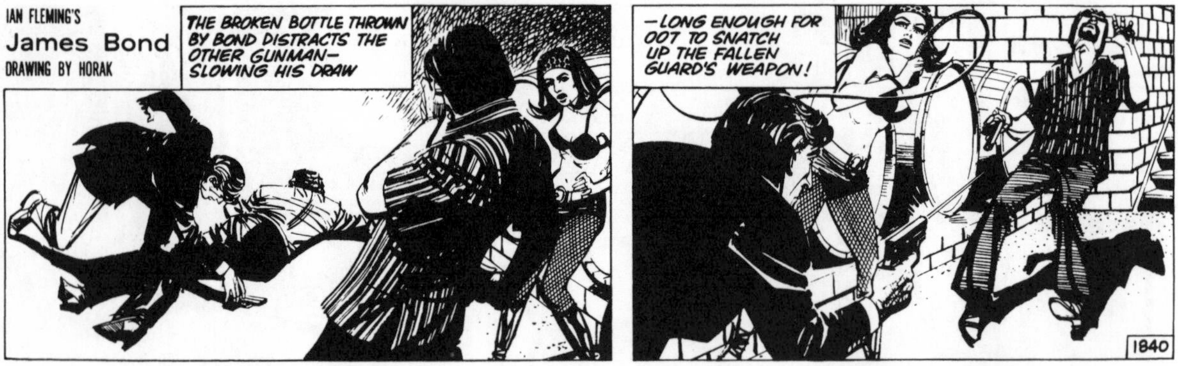
IAN FLEMING'S
James Bond
DRAWING BY HORAK
THE BROKEN BOTTLE THROWN BY BOND DISTRACTS THE OTHER GUNMAN—SLOWING HIS DRAW
—LONG ENOUGH FOR 007 TO SNATCH UP THE FALLEN GUARD'S WEAPON!
1840

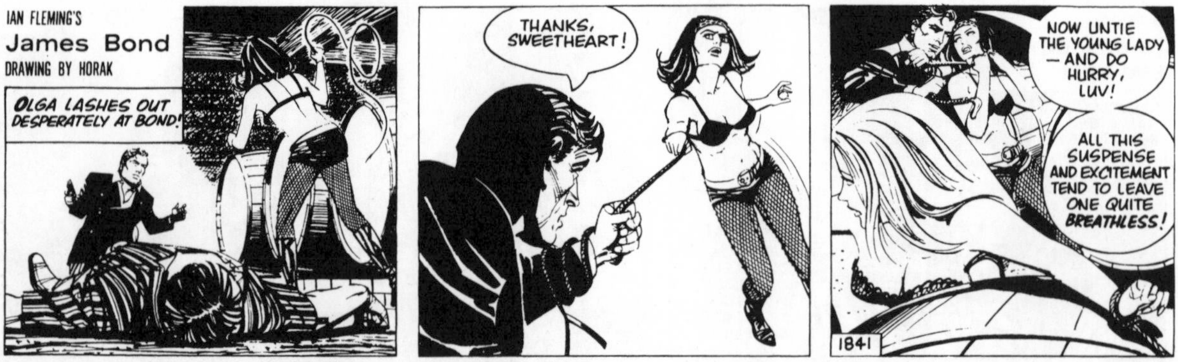
IAN FLEMING'S
James Bond
DRAWING BY HORAK
OLGA LASHES OUT DESPERATELY AT BOND!
THANKS, SWEETHEART!
NOW UNTIE THE YOUNG LADY—AND DO HURRY, LUV!
ALL THIS SUSPENSE AND EXCITEMENT TEND TO LEAVE ONE QUITE BREATHLESS!
1841

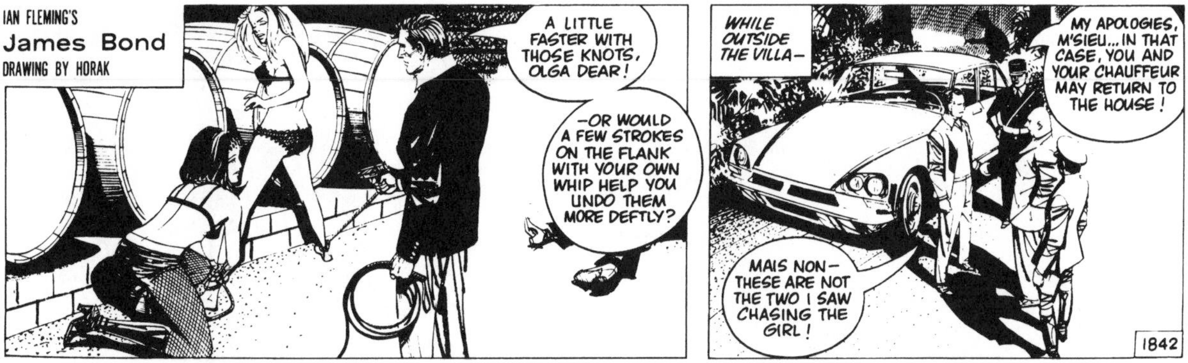
IAN FLEMING'S
James Bond
DRAWING BY HORAK
A LITTLE FASTER WITH THOSE KNOTS, OLGA DEAR!
—OR WOULD A FEW STROKES ON THE FLANK WITH YOUR OWN WHIP HELP YOU UNDO THEM MORE DEFTLY?
WHILE OUTSIDE THE VILLA—
MY APOLOGIES, M'SIEU... IN THAT CASE, YOU AND YOUR CHAUFFEUR MAY RETURN TO THE HOUSE!
MAIS NON— THESE ARE NOT THE TWO I SAW CHASING THE GIRL!
1842

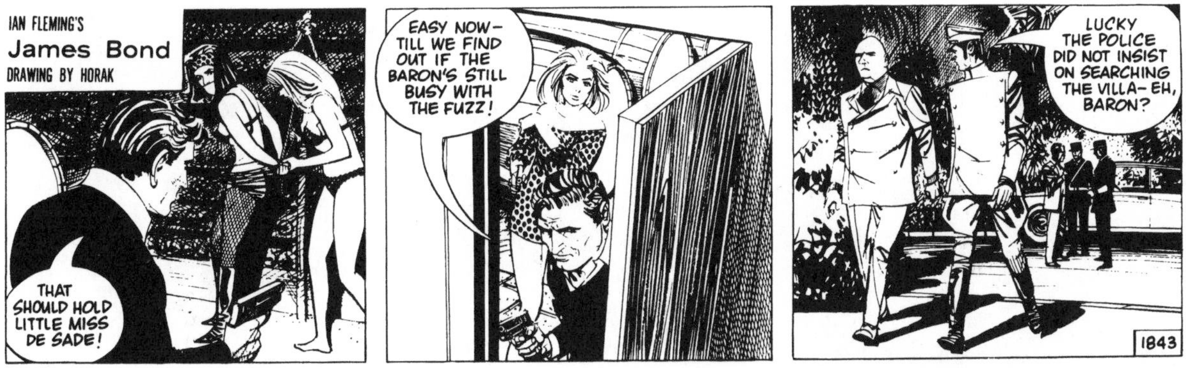
IAN FLEMING'S
James Bond
DRAWING BY HORAK
THAT SHOULD HOLD LITTLE MISS DE SADE!
EASY NOW— TILL WE FIND OUT IF THE BARON'S STILL BUSY WITH THE FUZZ!
LUCKY THE POLICE DID NOT INSIST ON SEARCHING THE VILLA— EH, BARON?
1843

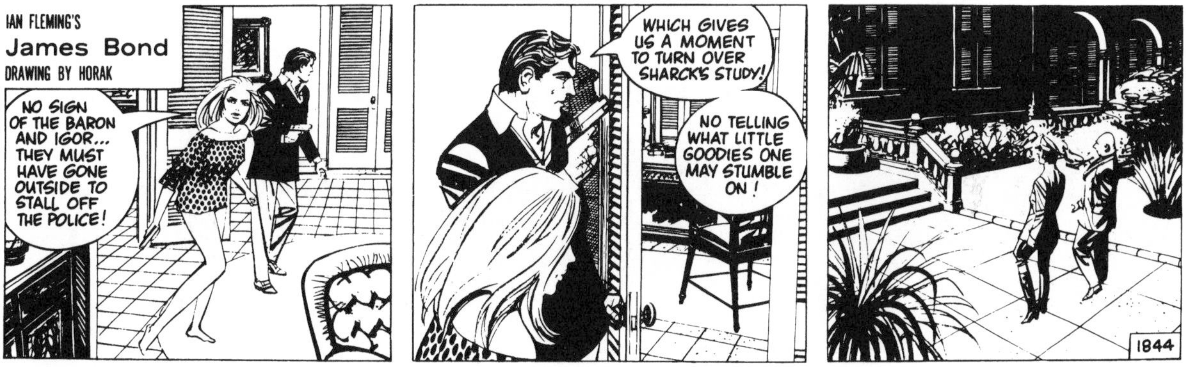
IAN FLEMING'S
James Bond
DRAWING BY HORAK
NO SIGN OF THE BARON AND IGOR... THEY MUST HAVE GONE OUTSIDE TO STALL OFF THE POLICE!
WHICH GIVES US A MOMENT TO TURN OVER SHARCK'S STUDY!
NO TELLING WHAT LITTLE GOODIES ONE MAY STUMBLE ON!
1844

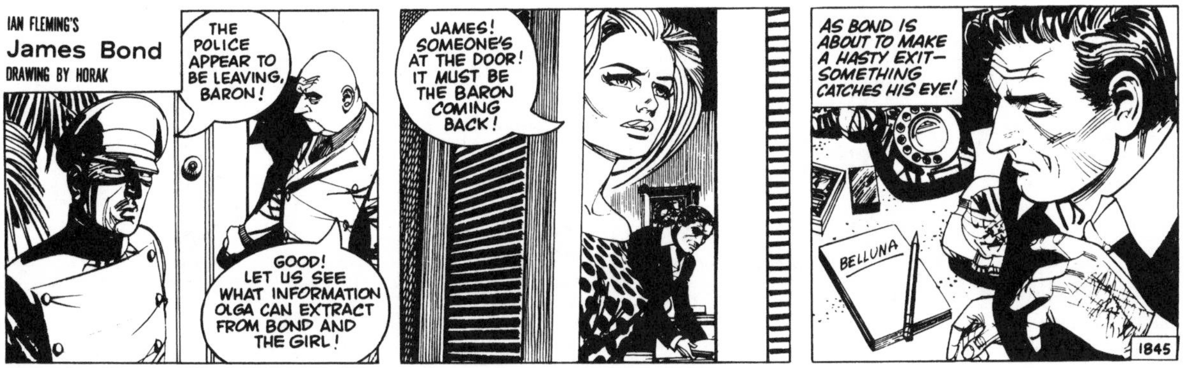
IAN FLEMING'S
James Bond
DRAWING BY HORAK
THE POLICE APPEAR TO BE LEAVING, BARON!
GOOD! LET US SEE WHAT INFORMATION OLGA CAN EXTRACT FROM BOND AND THE GIRL!
JAMES! SOMEONE'S AT THE DOOR! IT MUST BE THE BARON COMING BACK!
AS BOND IS ABOUT TO MAKE A HASTY EXIT— SOMETHING CATCHES HIS EYE!
BELLUNA
1845

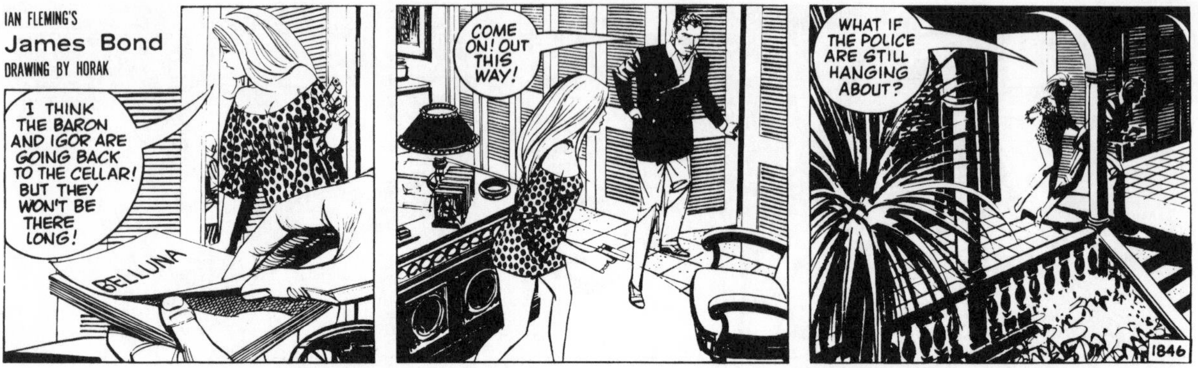
IAN FLEMING'S
James Bond
DRAWING BY HORAK
I THINK THE BARON AND IGOR ARE GOING BACK TO THE CELLAR! BUT THEY WON'T BE THERE LONG!
BELLUNA
COME ON! OUT THIS WAY!
WHAT IF THE POLICE ARE STILL HANGING ABOUT?
1846

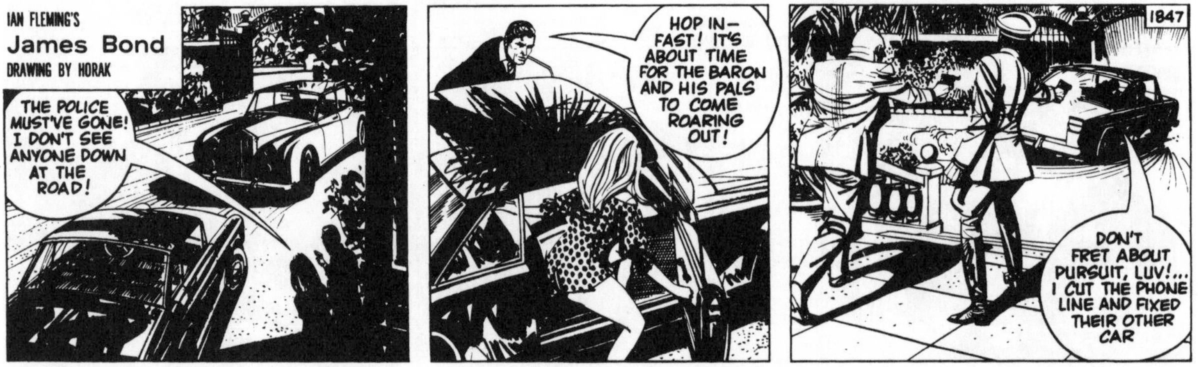
IAN FLEMING'S
James Bond
DRAWING BY HORAK
THE POLICE MUST'VE GONE! I DON'T SEE ANYONE DOWN AT THE ROAD!
HOP IN— FAST! IT'S ABOUT TIME FOR THE BARON AND HIS PALS TO COME ROARING OUT!
1847
DON'T FRET ABOUT PURSUIT, LUV!... I CUT THE PHONE LINE AND FIXED THEIR OTHER CAR

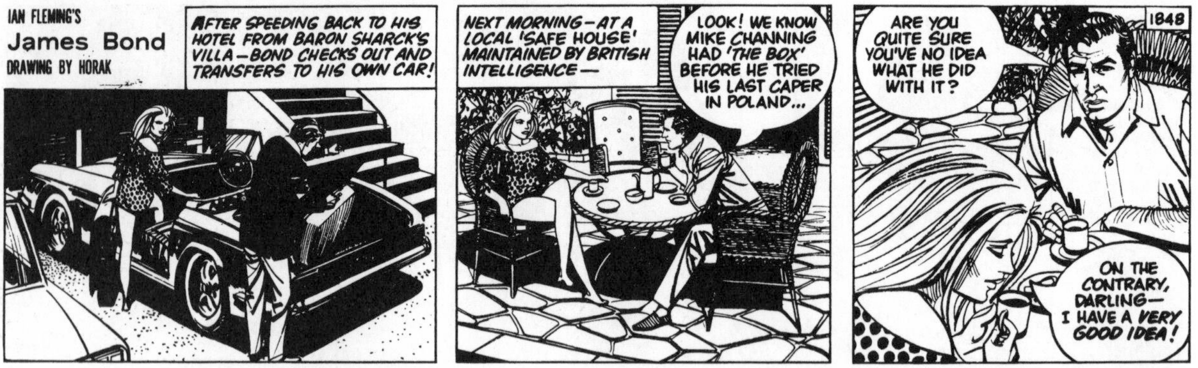
IAN FLEMING'S
James Bond
DRAWING BY HORAK
AFTER SPEEDING BACK TO HIS HOTEL FROM BARON SHARCK'S VILLA—BOND CHECKS OUT AND TRANSFERS TO HIS OWN CAR!
NEXT MORNING—AT A LOCAL 'SAFE HOUSE' MAINTAINED BY BRITISH INTELLIGENCE—
LOOK! WE KNOW MIKE CHANNING HAD 'THE BOX' BEFORE HE TRIED HIS LAST CAPER IN POLAND...
1848
ARE YOU QUITE SURE YOU'VE NO IDEA WHAT HE DID WITH IT?
ON THE CONTRARY, DARLING— I HAVE A VERY GOOD IDEA!

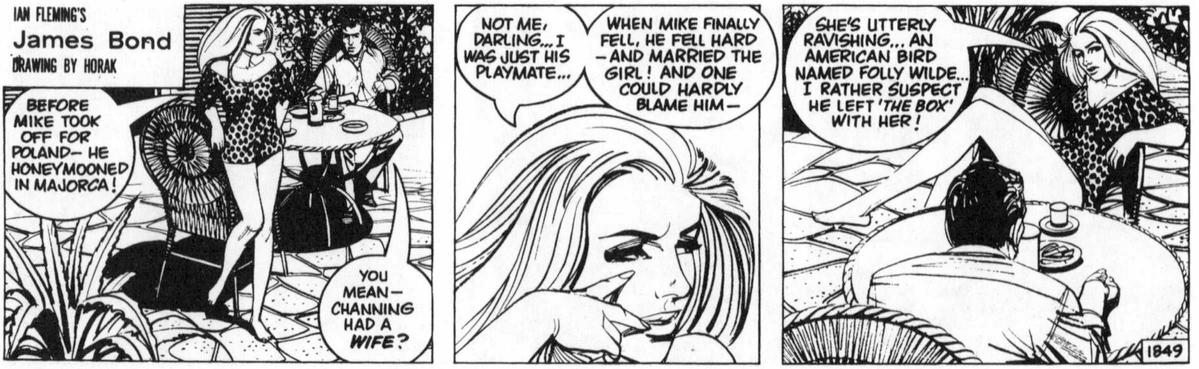
IAN FLEMING'S
James Bond
DRAWING BY HORAK
BEFORE MIKE TOOK OFF FOR POLAND— HE HONEYMOONED IN MAJORCA!
YOU MEAN— CHANNING HAD A WIFE?
NOT ME, DARLING... I WAS JUST HIS PLAYMATE...
WHEN MIKE FINALLY FELL, HE FELL HARD —AND MARRIED THE GIRL! AND ONE COULD HARDLY BLAME HIM—
SHE'S UTTERLY RAVISHING... AN AMERICAN BIRD NAMED FOLLY WILDE... I RATHER SUSPECT HE LEFT 'THE BOX' WITH HER!
1849

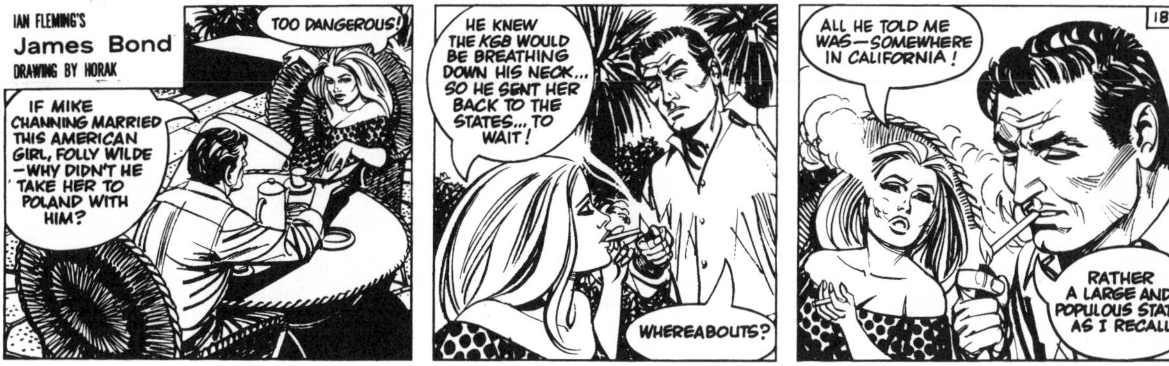
IAN FLEMING'S
James Bond
DRAWING BY HORAK
IF MIKE CHANNING MARRIED THIS AMERICAN GIRL, FOLLY WILDE —WHY DIDN'T HE TAKE HER TO POLAND WITH HIM?
TOO DANGEROUS!
HE KNEW THE KGB WOULD BE BREATHING DOWN HIS NECK... SO HE SENT HER BACK TO THE STATES... TO WAIT!
WHEREABOUTS?
1850
ALL HE TOLD ME WAS—SOMEWHERE IN CALIFORNIA!
RATHER A LARGE AND POPULOUS STATE, AS I RECALL!

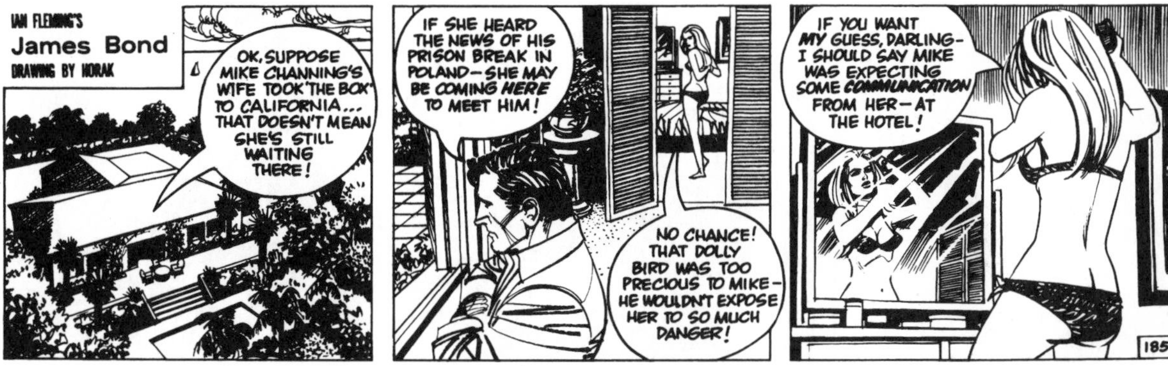
IAN FLEMING'S
James Bond
DRAWING BY HORAK
OK, SUPPOSE MIKE CHANNING'S WIFE TOOK 'THE BOX' TO CALIFORNIA... THAT DOESN'T MEAN SHE'S STILL WAITING THERE!
IF SHE HEARD THE NEWS OF HIS PRISON BREAK IN POLAND—SHE MAY BE COMING HERE TO MEET HIM!
NO CHANCE! THAT DOLLY BIRD WAS TOO PRECIOUS TO MIKE—HE WOULDN'T EXPOSE HER TO SO MUCH DANGER!
IF YOU WANT MY GUESS, DARLING—I SHOULD SAY MIKE WAS EXPECTING SOME COMMUNICATION FROM HER—AT THE HOTEL!
1851

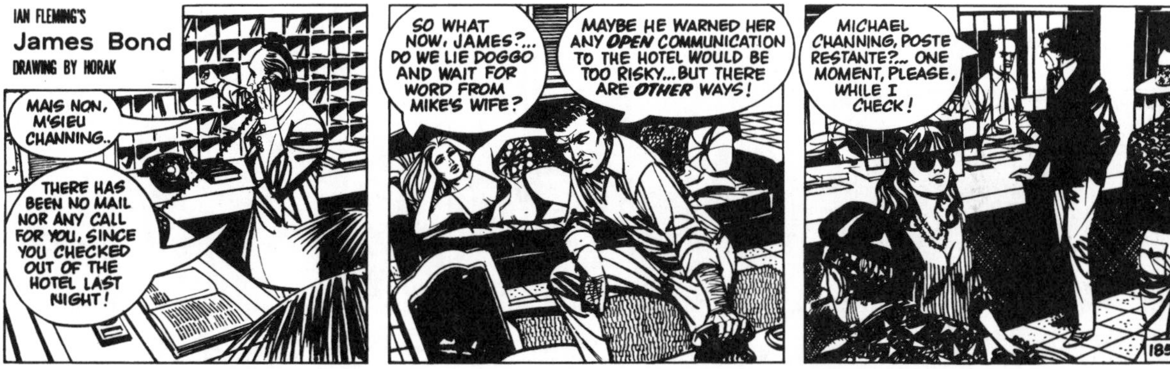
IAN FLEMING'S
James Bond
DRAWING BY HORAK
MAIS NON, M'SIEU CHANNING..
THERE HAS BEEN NO MAIL NOR ANY CALL FOR YOU, SINCE YOU CHECKED OUT OF THE HOTEL LAST NIGHT!
SO WHAT NOW, JAMES?... DO WE LIE DOGGO AND WAIT FOR WORD FROM MIKE'S WIFE?
MAYBE HE WARNED HER ANY OPEN COMMUNICATION TO THE HOTEL WOULD BE TOO RISKY... BUT THERE ARE OTHER WAYS!
MICHAEL CHANNING, POSTE RESTANTE?... ONE MOMENT, PLEASE, WHILE I CHECK!
1852

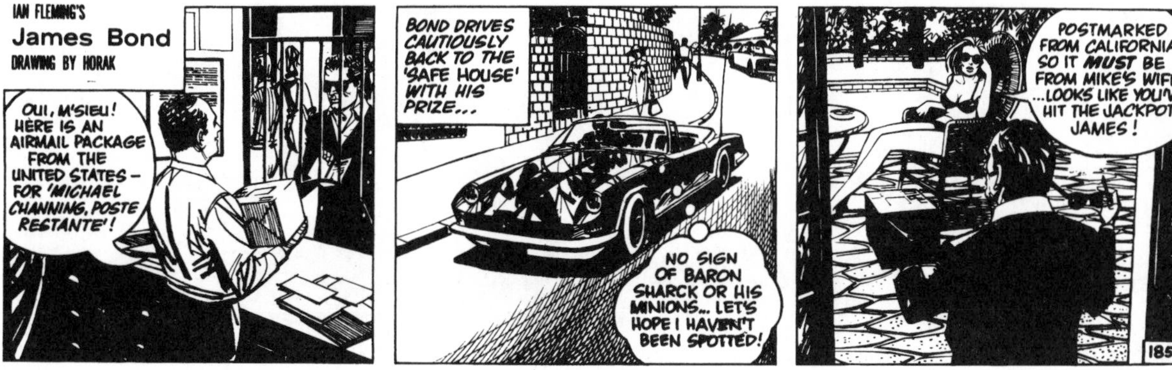
IAN FLEMING'S
James Bond
DRAWING BY HORAK
OUI, M'SIEU! HERE IS AN AIRMAIL PACKAGE FROM THE UNITED STATES—FOR 'MICHAEL CHANNING, POSTE RESTANTE'!
BOND DRIVES CAUTIOUSLY BACK TO THE 'SAFE HOUSE' WITH HIS PRIZE...
NO SIGN OF BARON SHARCK OR HIS MINIONS... LET'S HOPE I HAVEN'T BEEN SPOTTED!
POSTMARKED FROM CALIFORNIA! SO IT MUST BE FROM MIKE'S WIFE! ...LOOKS LIKE YOU'VE HIT THE JACKPOT, JAMES!
1853

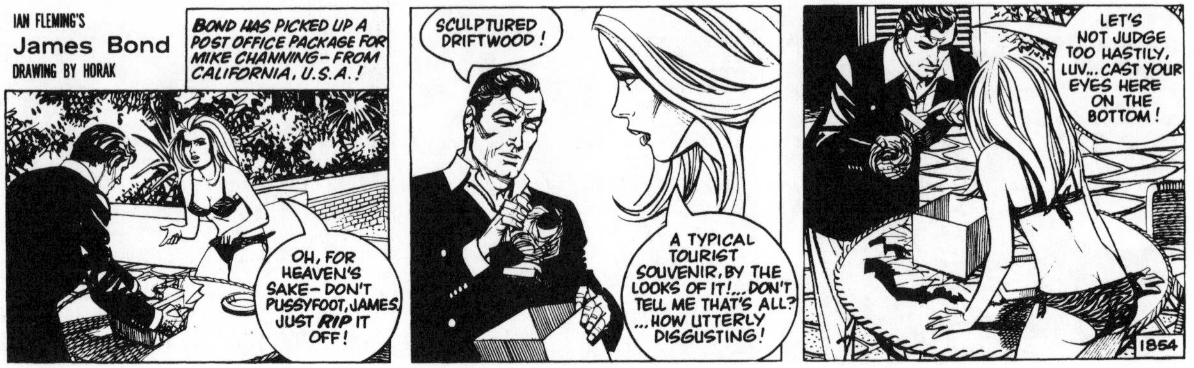

IAN FLEMING'S
James Bond
DRAWING BY HORAK
BOND HAS PICKED UP A POST OFFICE PACKAGE FOR MIKE CHANNING—FROM CALIFORNIA, U.S.A.!
OH, FOR HEAVEN'S SAKE—DON'T PUSSYFOOT, JAMES. JUST RIP IT OFF!
SCULPTURED DRIFTWOOD!
A TYPICAL TOURIST SOUVENIR, BY THE LOOKS OF IT!...DON'T TELL ME THAT'S ALL? ...HOW UTTERLY DISGUSTING!
LET'S NOT JUDGE TOO HASTILY, LUV...CAST YOUR EYES HERE ON THE BOTTOM!
1854


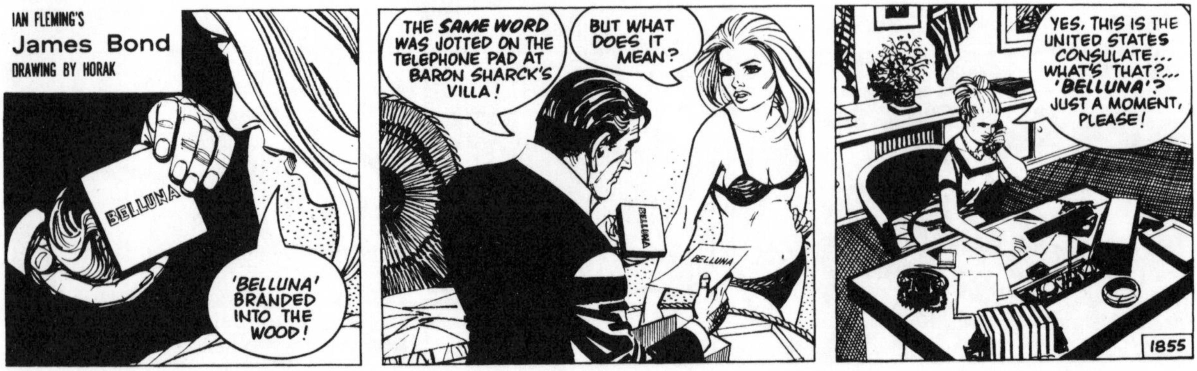

IAN FLEMING'S
James Bond
DRAWING BY HORAK
BELLUNA
'BELLUNA' BRANDED INTO THE WOOD!
THE SAME WORD WAS JOTTED ON THE TELEPHONE PAD AT BARON SHARCK'S VILLA!
BUT WHAT DOES IT MEAN?
BELLUNA
BELLUNA
YES, THIS IS THE UNITED STATES CONSULATE... WHAT'S THAT?... 'BELLUNA'? JUST A MOMENT, PLEASE!
1855


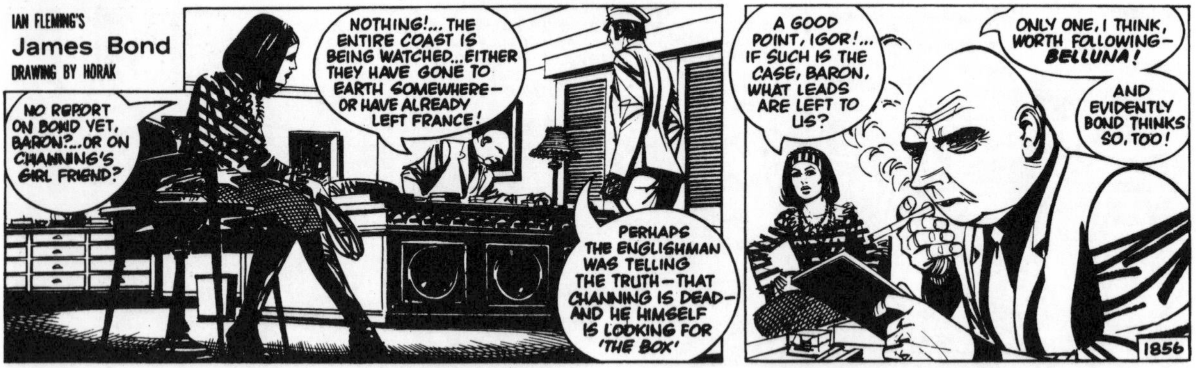

IAN FLEMING'S
James Bond
DRAWING BY HORAK
NO REPORT ON BOND YET, BARON?...OR ON CHANNING'S GIRL FRIEND?
NOTHING!... THE ENTIRE COAST IS BEING WATCHED...EITHER THEY HAVE GONE TO EARTH SOMEWHERE—OR HAVE ALREADY LEFT FRANCE!
PERHAPS THE ENGLISHMAN WAS TELLING THE TRUTH—THAT CHANNING IS DEAD—AND HE HIMSELF IS LOOKING FOR 'THE BOX'
A GOOD POINT, IGOR!... IF SUCH IS THE CASE, BARON, WHAT LEADS ARE LEFT TO US?
ONLY ONE, I THINK, WORTH FOLLOWING—BELLUNA!
AND EVIDENTLY BOND THINKS SO, TOO!
1856


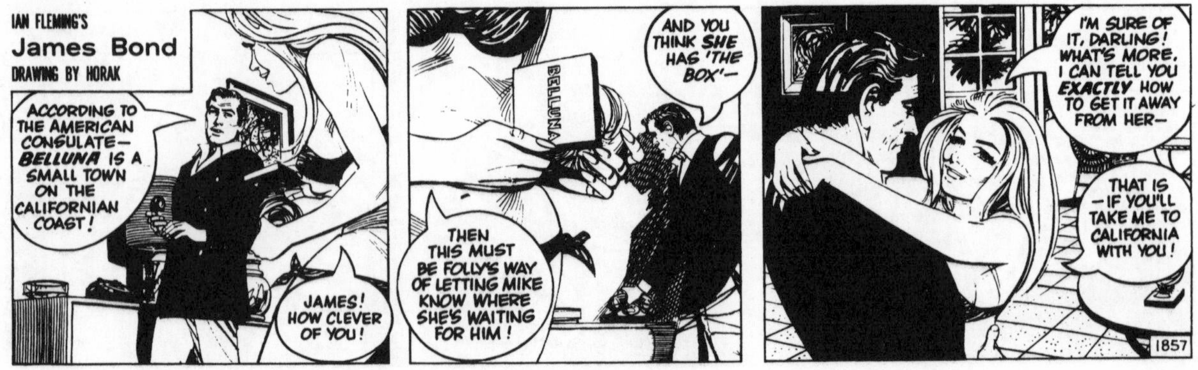

IAN FLEMING'S
James Bond
DRAWING BY HORAK
ACCORDING TO THE AMERICAN CONSULATE—BELLUNA IS A SMALL TOWN ON THE CALIFORNIAN COAST!
JAMES! HOW CLEVER OF YOU!
BELLUNA
AND YOU THINK SHE HAS 'THE BOX'—
THEN THIS MUST BE FOLLY'S WAY OF LETTING MIKE KNOW WHERE SHE'S WAITING FOR HIM!
I'M SURE OF IT, DARLING! WHAT'S MORE, I CAN TELL YOU EXACTLY HOW TO GET IT AWAY FROM HER—
THAT IS —IF YOU'LL TAKE ME TO CALIFORNIA WITH YOU!
1857

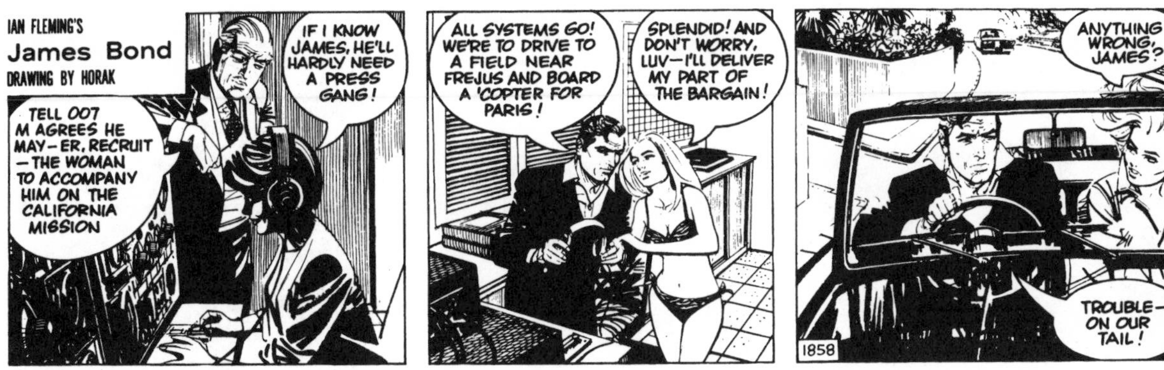
IAN FLEMING'S
James Bond
DRAWING BY HORAK
IF I KNOW JAMES, HE'LL HARDLY NEED A PRESS GANG!
TELL 007 M AGREES HE MAY-ER, RECRUIT —THE WOMAN TO ACCOMPANY HIM ON THE CALIFORNIA MISSION
ALL SYSTEMS GO! WE'RE TO DRIVE TO A FIELD NEAR FREJUS AND BOARD A 'COPTER FOR PARIS!
SPLENDID! AND DON'T WORRY, LUV—I'LL DELIVER MY PART OF THE BARGAIN!
ANYTHING WRONG, JAMES?
TROUBLE—ON OUR TAIL!
1858

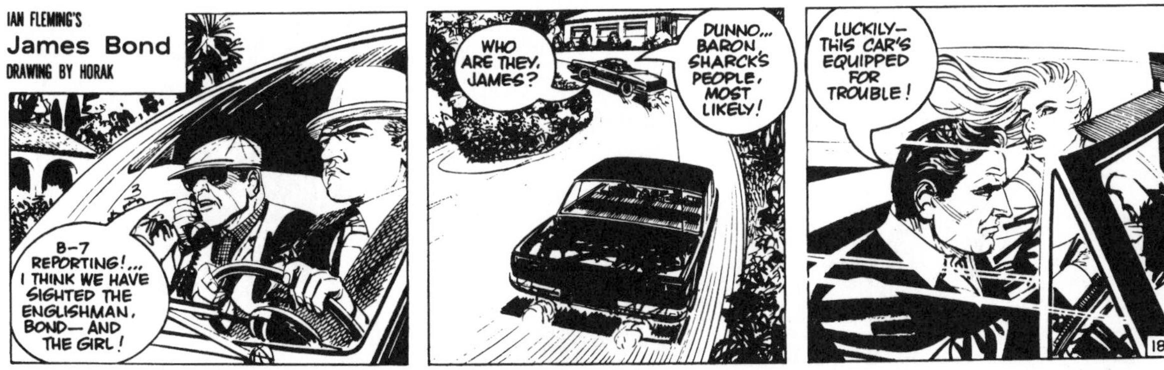
IAN FLEMING'S
James Bond
DRAWING BY HORAK
B-7 REPORTING!... I THINK WE HAVE SIGHTED THE ENGLISHMAN, BOND— AND THE GIRL!
WHO ARE THEY, JAMES?
DUNNO... BARON SHARCK'S PEOPLE, MOST LIKELY!
LUCKILY—THIS CAR'S EQUIPPED FOR TROUBLE!
1859

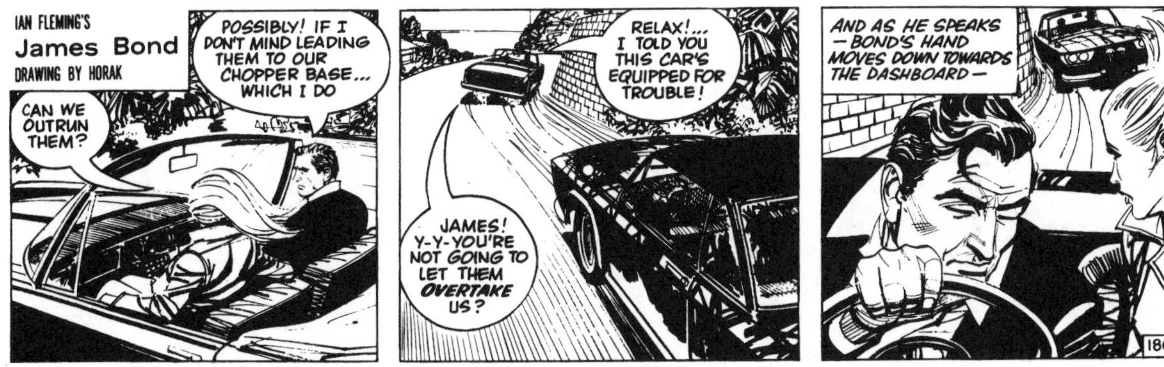
IAN FLEMING'S
James Bond
DRAWING BY HORAK
CAN WE OUTRUN THEM?
POSSIBLY! IF I DON'T MIND LEADING THEM TO OUR CHOPPER BASE... WHICH I DO
RELAX!... I TOLD YOU THIS CAR'S EQUIPPED FOR TROUBLE!
JAMES! Y-Y-YOU'RE NOT GOING TO LET THEM OVERTAKE US?
AND AS HE SPEAKS —BOND'S HAND MOVES DOWN TOWARDS THE DASHBOARD—
1860

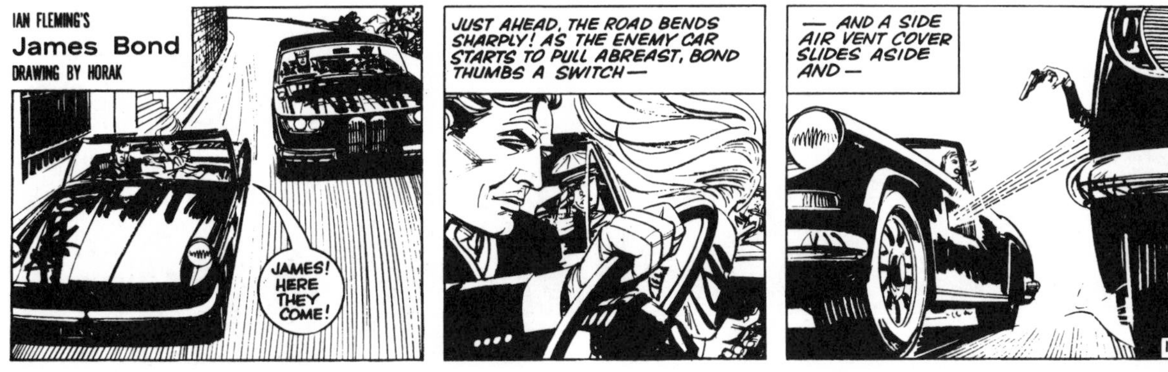
IAN FLEMING'S
James Bond
DRAWING BY HORAK
JAMES! HERE THEY COME!
JUST AHEAD, THE ROAD BENDS SHARPLY! AS THE ENEMY CAR STARTS TO PULL ABREAST, BOND THUMBS A SWITCH—
— AND A SIDE AIR VENT COVER SLIDES ASIDE AND—
1861

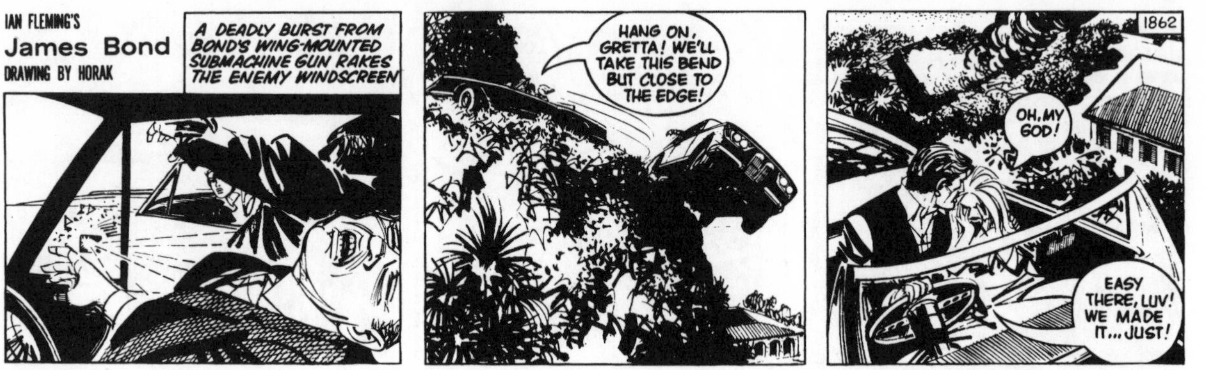
IAN FLEMING'S
James Bond
DRAWING BY HORAK
A DEADLY BURST FROM BOND'S WING-MOUNTED SUBMACHINE GUN RAKES THE ENEMY WINDSCREEN
HANG ON, GRETTA! WE'LL TAKE THIS BEND BUT CLOSE TO THE EDGE!
1862
OH, MY GOD!
EASY THERE, LUV! WE MADE IT... JUST!

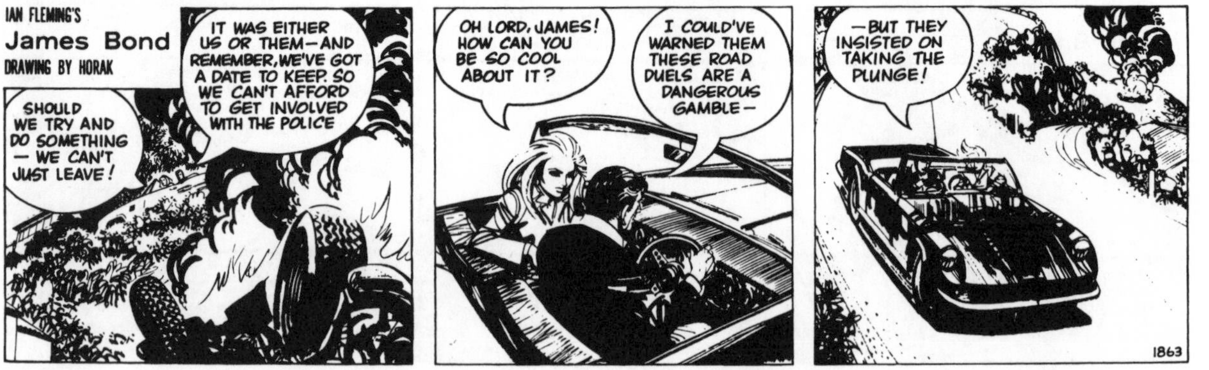
IAN FLEMING'S
James Bond
DRAWING BY HORAK
SHOULD WE TRY AND DO SOMETHING — WE CAN'T JUST LEAVE!
IT WAS EITHER US OR THEM—AND REMEMBER, WE'VE GOT A DATE TO KEEP. SO WE CAN'T AFFORD TO GET INVOLVED WITH THE POLICE
OH LORD, JAMES! HOW CAN YOU BE SO COOL ABOUT IT?
I COULD'VE WARNED THEM THESE ROAD DUELS ARE A DANGEROUS GAMBLE—
—BUT THEY INSISTED ON TAKING THE PLUNGE!
1863

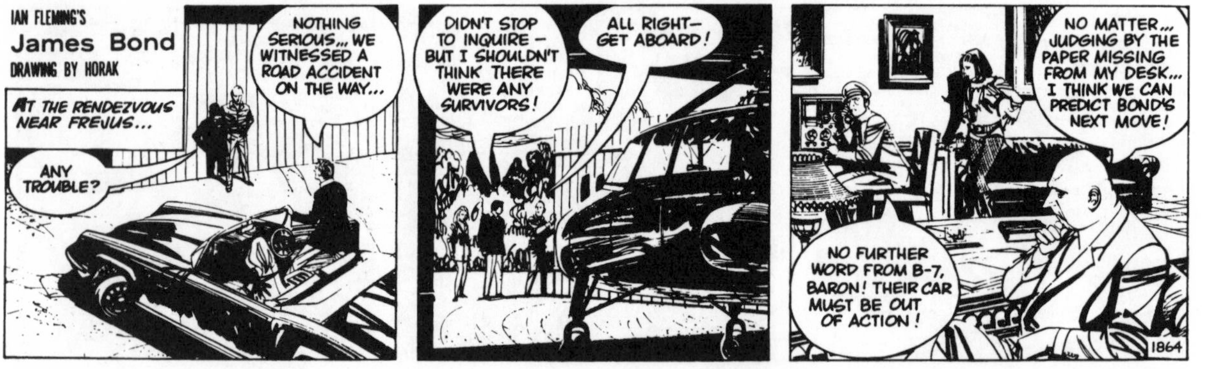
IAN FLEMING'S
James Bond
DRAWING BY HORAK
AT THE RENDEZVOUS NEAR FREJUS...
ANY TROUBLE?
NOTHING SERIOUS... WE WITNESSED A ROAD ACCIDENT ON THE WAY...
DIDN'T STOP TO INQUIRE — BUT I SHOULDN'T THINK THERE WERE ANY SURVIVORS!
ALL RIGHT— GET ABOARD!
NO FURTHER WORD FROM B-7, BARON! THEIR CAR MUST BE OUT OF ACTION!
NO MATTER... JUDGING BY THE PAPER MISSING FROM MY DESK... I THINK WE CAN PREDICT BOND'S NEXT MOVE!
1864

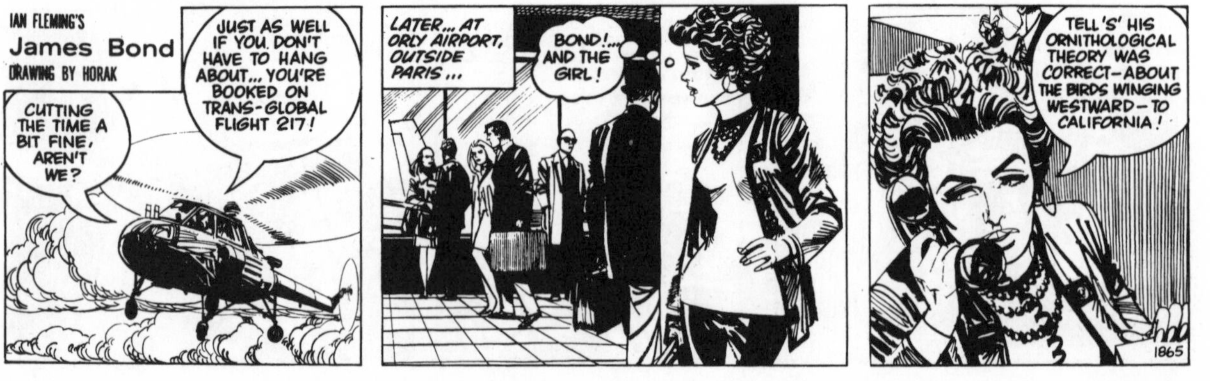
IAN FLEMING'S
James Bond
DRAWING BY HORAK
CUTTING THE TIME A BIT FINE, AREN'T WE?
JUST AS WELL IF YOU DON'T HAVE TO HANG ABOUT... YOU'RE BOOKED ON TRANS-GLOBAL FLIGHT 217!
LATER... AT ORLY AIRPORT, OUTSIDE PARIS...
BOND!... AND THE GIRL!
TELL 'S' HIS ORNITHOLOGICAL THEORY WAS CORRECT—ABOUT THE BIRDS WINGING WESTWARD—TO CALIFORNIA!
1865

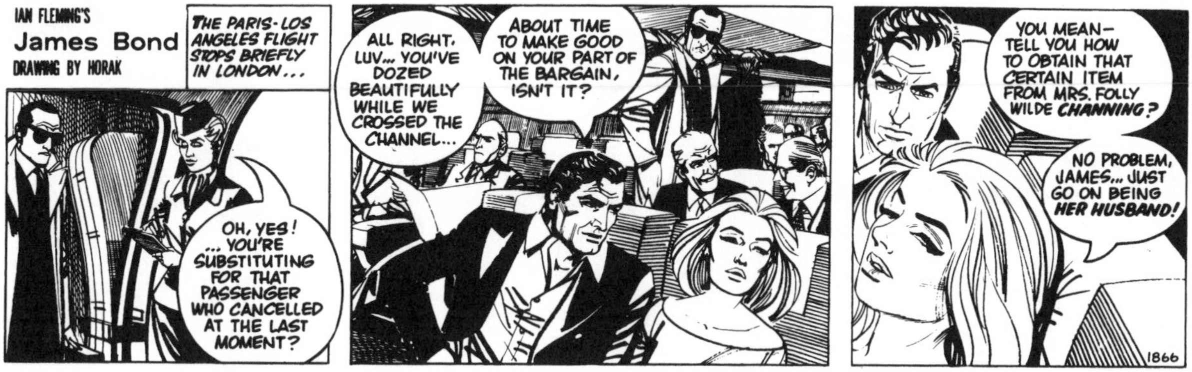
IAN FLEMING'S
James Bond
DRAWING BY HORAK
THE PARIS-LOS ANGELES FLIGHT STOPS BRIEFLY IN LONDON...
OH, YES! ... YOU'RE SUBSTITUTING FOR THAT PASSENGER WHO CANCELLED AT THE LAST MOMENT?
ALL RIGHT, LUV... YOU'VE DOZED BEAUTIFULLY WHILE WE CROSSED THE CHANNEL...
ABOUT TIME TO MAKE GOOD ON YOUR PART OF THE BARGAIN, ISN'T IT?
YOU MEAN— TELL YOU HOW TO OBTAIN THAT CERTAIN ITEM FROM MRS. FOLLY WILDE CHANNING?
NO PROBLEM, JAMES... JUST GO ON BEING HER HUSBAND!
1866

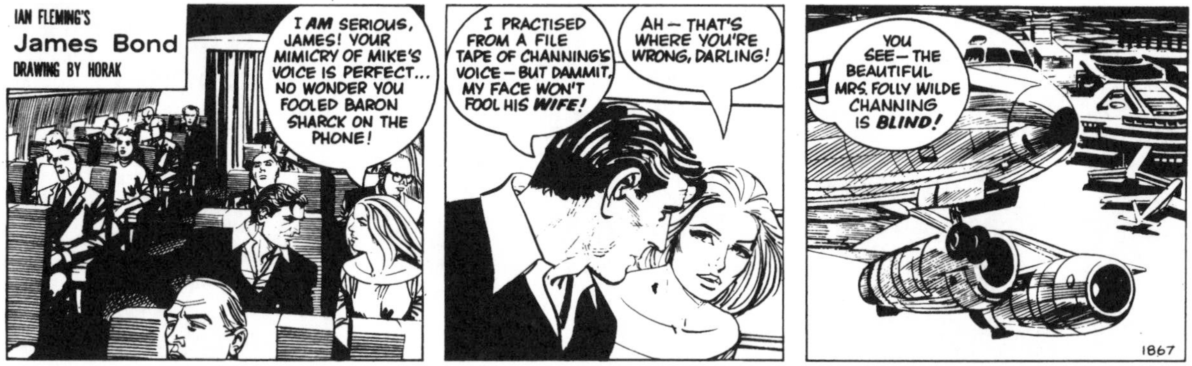
IAN FLEMING'S
James Bond
DRAWING BY HORAK
I AM SERIOUS, JAMES! YOUR MIMICRY OF MIKE'S VOICE IS PERFECT... NO WONDER YOU FOOLED BARON SHARCK ON THE PHONE!
I PRACTISED FROM A FILE TAPE OF CHANNING'S VOICE—BUT DAMMIT, MY FACE WON'T FOOL HIS WIFE!
AH—THAT'S WHERE YOU'RE WRONG, DARLING!
YOU SEE—THE BEAUTIFUL MRS. FOLLY WILDE CHANNING IS BLIND!
1867

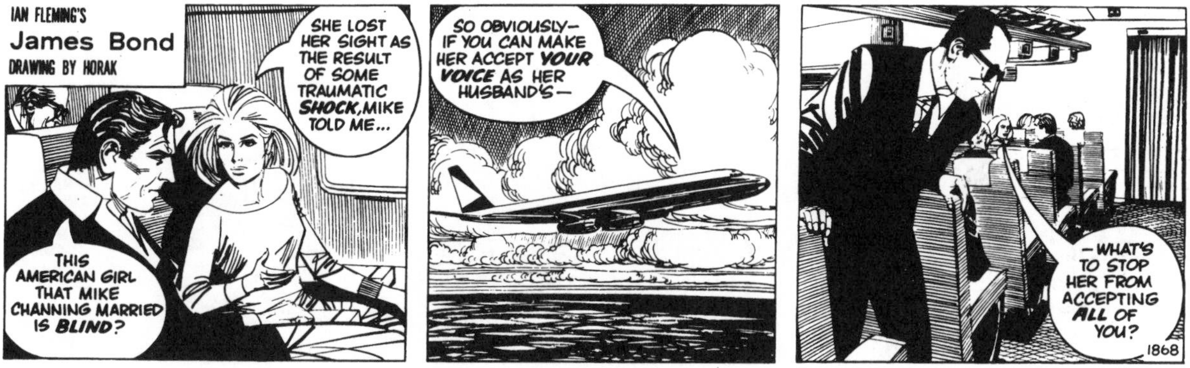
IAN FLEMING'S
James Bond
DRAWING BY HORAK
SHE LOST HER SIGHT AS THE RESULT OF SOME TRAUMATIC SHOCK, MIKE TOLD ME...
THIS AMERICAN GIRL THAT MIKE CHANNING MARRIED IS BLIND?
SO OBVIOUSLY— IF YOU CAN MAKE HER ACCEPT YOUR VOICE AS HER HUSBAND'S—
—WHAT'S TO STOP HER FROM ACCEPTING ALL OF YOU?
1868

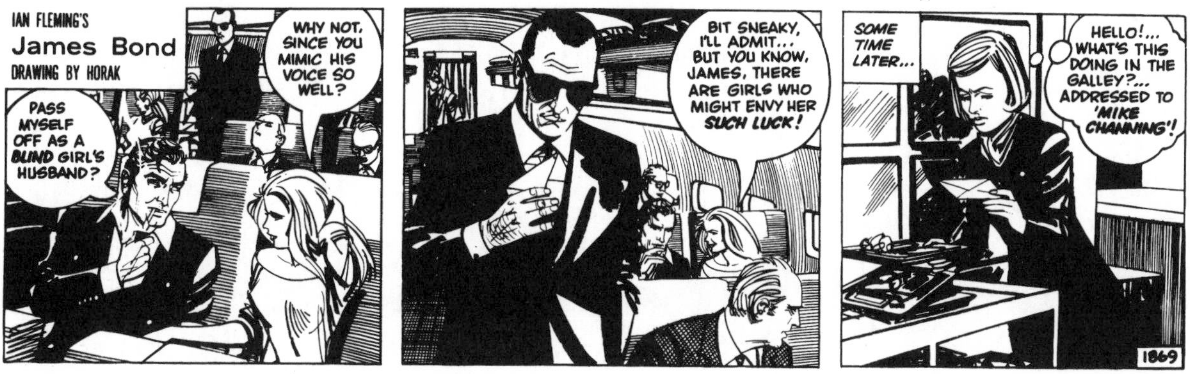
IAN FLEMING'S
James Bond
DRAWING BY HORAK
PASS MYSELF OFF AS A BLIND GIRL'S HUSBAND?
WHY NOT, SINCE YOU MIMIC HIS VOICE SO WELL?
BIT SNEAKY, I'LL ADMIT... BUT YOU KNOW, JAMES, THERE ARE GIRLS WHO MIGHT ENVY HER SUCH LUCK!
SOME TIME LATER...
HELLO!... WHAT'S THIS DOING IN THE GALLEY?... ADDRESSED TO 'MIKE CHANNING'!
1869

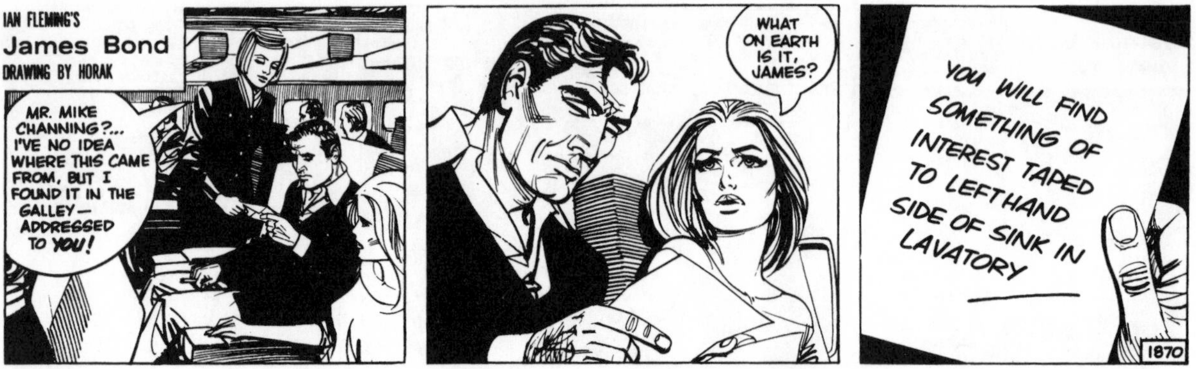
IAN FLEMING'S
James Bond
DRAWING BY HORAK
MR. MIKE CHANNING?... I'VE NO IDEA WHERE THIS CAME FROM, BUT I FOUND IT IN THE GALLEY— ADDRESSED TO YOU!
WHAT ON EARTH IS IT, JAMES?
YOU WILL FIND SOMETHING OF INTEREST TAPED TO LEFTHAND SIDE OF SINK IN LAVATORY
1870

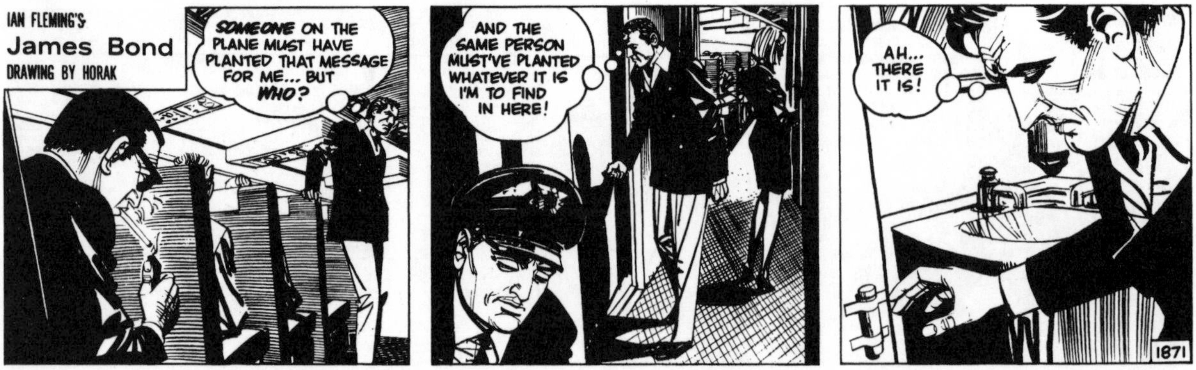
IAN FLEMING'S
James Bond
DRAWING BY HORAK
SOMEONE ON THE PLANE MUST HAVE PLANTED THAT MESSAGE FOR ME... BUT WHO?
AND THE SAME PERSON MUST'VE PLANTED WHATEVER IT IS I'M TO FIND IN HERE!
AH... THERE IT IS!
1871

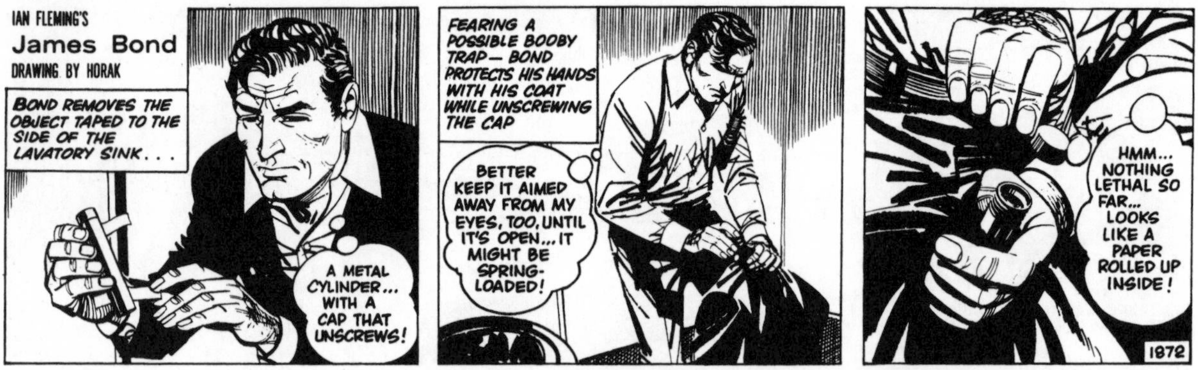
IAN FLEMING'S
James Bond
DRAWING BY HORAK
BOND REMOVES THE OBJECT TAPED TO THE SIDE OF THE LAVATORY SINK . . .
A METAL CYLINDER... WITH A CAP THAT UNSCREWS!
FEARING A POSSIBLE BOOBY TRAP— BOND PROTECTS HIS HANDS WITH HIS COAT WHILE UNSCREWING THE CAP
BETTER KEEP IT AIMED AWAY FROM MY EYES, TOO, UNTIL IT'S OPEN... IT MIGHT BE SPRING-LOADED!
HMM... NOTHING LETHAL SO FAR... LOOKS LIKE A PAPER ROLLED UP INSIDE!
1872

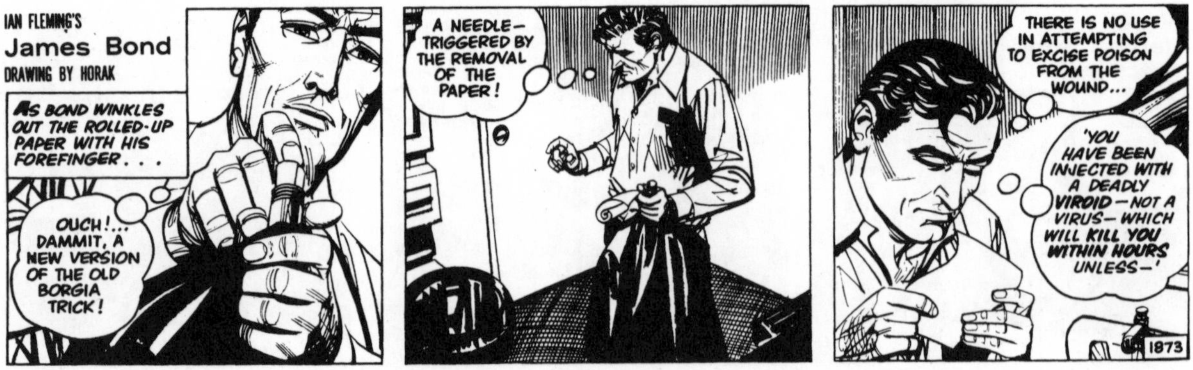
IAN FLEMING'S
James Bond
DRAWING BY HORAK
AS BOND WINKLES OUT THE ROLLED-UP PAPER WITH HIS FOREFINGER . . .
OUCH!... DAMMIT, A NEW VERSION OF THE OLD BORGIA TRICK!
A NEEDLE— TRIGGERED BY THE REMOVAL OF THE PAPER!
THERE IS NO USE IN ATTEMPTING TO EXCISE POISON FROM THE WOUND...
'YOU HAVE BEEN INJECTED WITH A DEADLY VIROID— NOT A VIRUS— WHICH WILL KILL YOU WITHIN HOURS UNLESS—'
1873

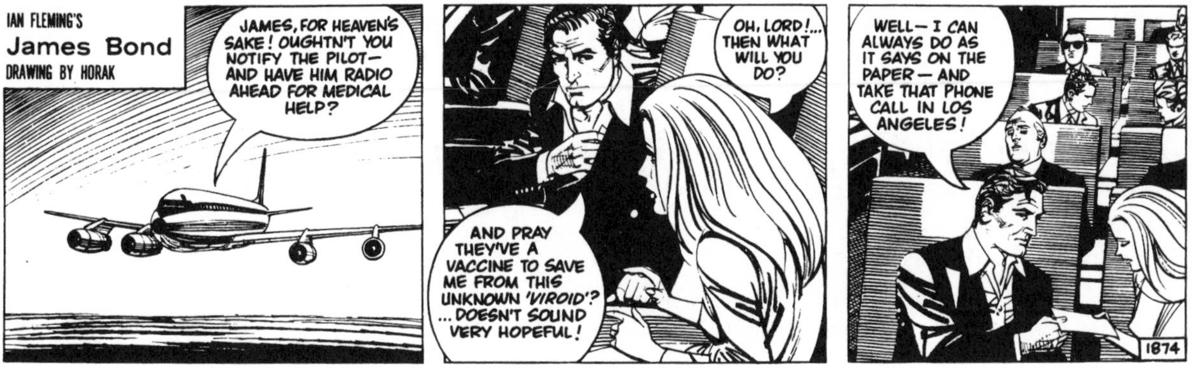
IAN FLEMING'S
James Bond
DRAWING BY HORAK
JAMES, FOR HEAVEN'S SAKE! OUGHTN'T YOU NOTIFY THE PILOT—AND HAVE HIM RADIO AHEAD FOR MEDICAL HELP?
OH, LORD!... THEN WHAT WILL YOU DO?
AND PRAY THEY'VE A VACCINE TO SAVE ME FROM THIS UNKNOWN 'VIROID'? ...DOESN'T SOUND VERY HOPEFUL!
WELL— I CAN ALWAYS DO AS IT SAYS ON THE PAPER — AND TAKE THAT PHONE CALL IN LOS ANGELES!
1874

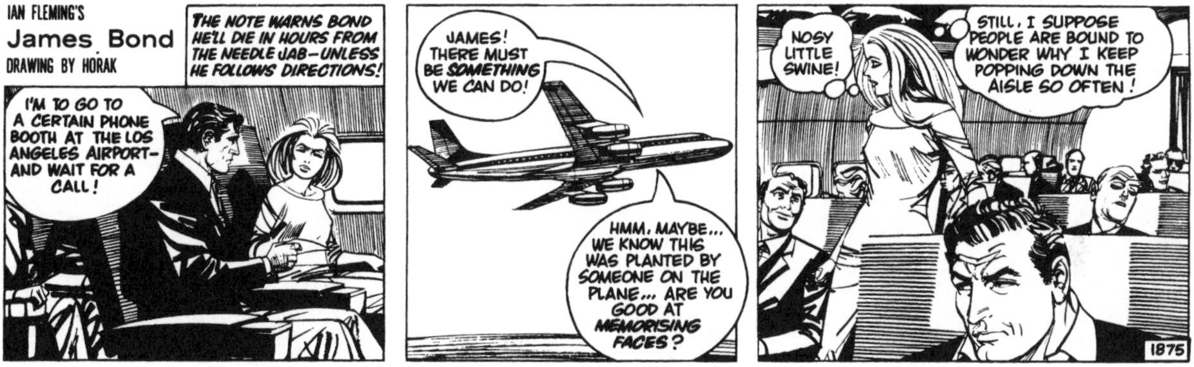
IAN FLEMING'S
James Bond
DRAWING BY HORAK
THE NOTE WARNS BOND HE'LL DIE IN HOURS FROM THE NEEDLE JAB—UNLESS HE FOLLOWS DIRECTIONS!
I'M TO GO TO A CERTAIN PHONE BOOTH AT THE LOS ANGELES AIRPORT—AND WAIT FOR A CALL!
JAMES! THERE MUST BE SOMETHING WE CAN DO!
HMM, MAYBE... WE KNOW THIS WAS PLANTED BY SOMEONE ON THE PLANE... ARE YOU GOOD AT MEMORISING FACES?
NOSY LITTLE SWINE!
STILL, I SUPPOSE PEOPLE ARE BOUND TO WONDER WHY I KEEP POPPING DOWN THE AISLE SO OFTEN!
1875

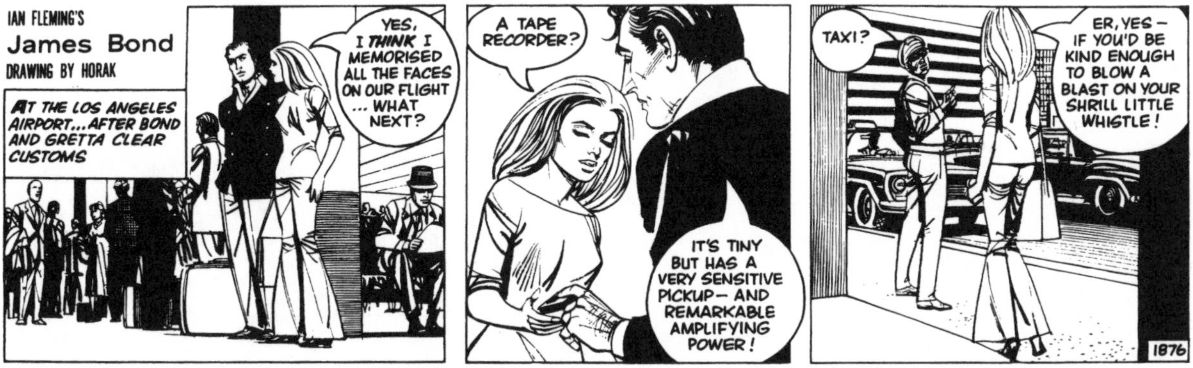
IAN FLEMING'S
James Bond
DRAWING BY HORAK
AT THE LOS ANGELES AIRPORT... AFTER BOND AND GRETTA CLEAR CUSTOMS
YES, I THINK I MEMORISED ALL THE FACES ON OUR FLIGHT ... WHAT NEXT?
A TAPE RECORDER?
IT'S TINY BUT HAS A VERY SENSITIVE PICKUP— AND REMARKABLE AMPLIFYING POWER!
TAXI?
ER, YES— IF YOU'D BE KIND ENOUGH TO BLOW A BLAST ON YOUR SHRILL LITTLE WHISTLE!
1876

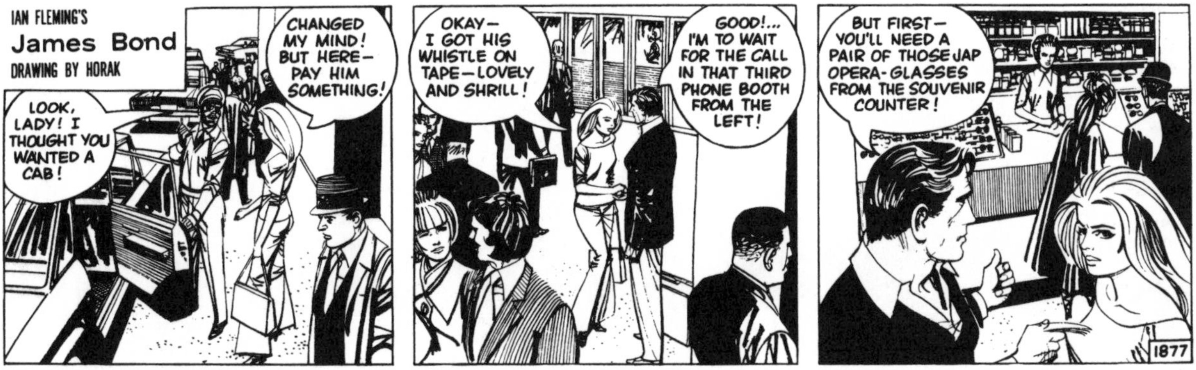
IAN FLEMING'S
James Bond
DRAWING BY HORAK
LOOK, LADY! I THOUGHT YOU WANTED A CAB!
CHANGED MY MIND! BUT HERE— PAY HIM SOMETHING!
OKAY— I GOT HIS WHISTLE ON TAPE—LOVELY AND SHRILL!
GOOD!... I'M TO WAIT FOR THE CALL IN THAT THIRD PHONE BOOTH FROM THE LEFT!
BUT FIRST— YOU'LL NEED A PAIR OF THOSE JAP OPERA-GLASSES FROM THE SOUVENIR COUNTER!
1877

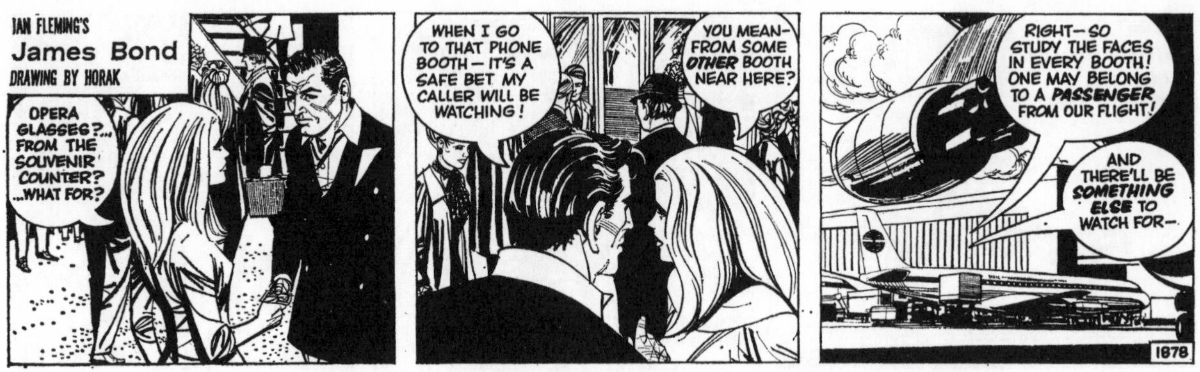
IAN FLEMING'S
James Bond
DRAWING BY HORAK
OPERA GLASSES?... FROM THE SOUVENIR COUNTER? ...WHAT FOR?
WHEN I GO TO THAT PHONE BOOTH — IT'S A SAFE BET MY CALLER WILL BE WATCHING!
YOU MEAN— FROM SOME OTHER BOOTH NEAR HERE?
RIGHT—SO STUDY THE FACES IN EVERY BOOTH! ONE MAY BELONG TO A PASSENGER FROM OUR FLIGHT!
AND THERE'LL BE SOMETHING ELSE TO WATCH FOR—
1878

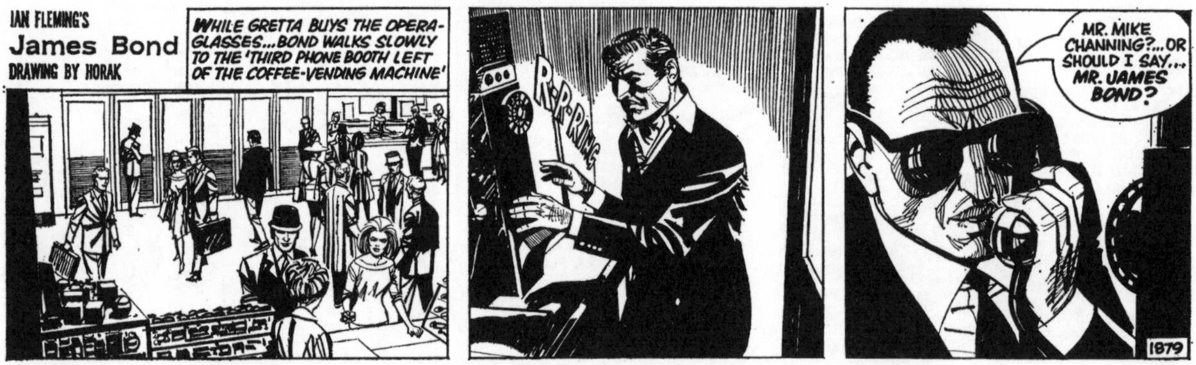
IAN FLEMING'S
James Bond
DRAWING BY HORAK
WHILE GRETTA BUYS THE OPERA-GLASSES...BOND WALKS SLOWLY TO THE 'THIRD PHONE BOOTH LEFT OF THE COFFEE-VENDING MACHINE'
R-R-RING
MR. MIKE CHANNING?...OR SHOULD I SAY... MR. JAMES BOND?
1879

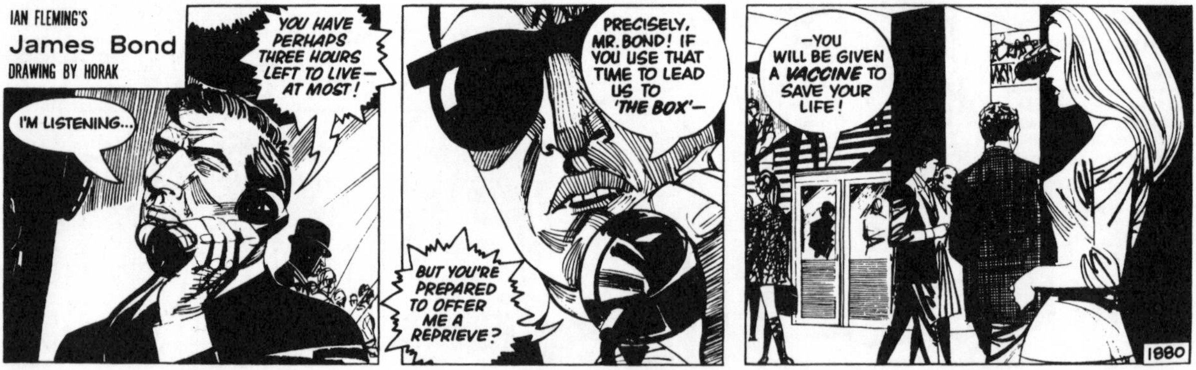
IAN FLEMING'S
James Bond
DRAWING BY HORAK
YOU HAVE PERHAPS THREE HOURS LEFT TO LIVE— AT MOST!
I'M LISTENING...
PRECISELY, MR. BOND! IF YOU USE THAT TIME TO LEAD US TO 'THE BOX'—
BUT YOU'RE PREPARED TO OFFER ME A REPRIEVE?
—YOU WILL BE GIVEN A VACCINE TO SAVE YOUR LIFE!
1880

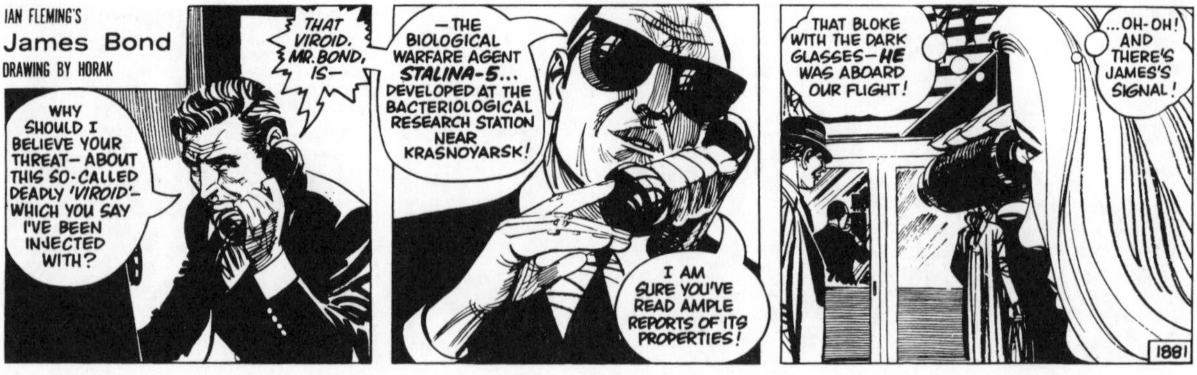
IAN FLEMING'S
James Bond
DRAWING BY HORAK
WHY SHOULD I BELIEVE YOUR THREAT— ABOUT THIS SO-CALLED DEADLY 'VIROID'— WHICH YOU SAY I'VE BEEN INJECTED WITH?
THAT VIROID, MR. BOND, IS—
—THE BIOLOGICAL WARFARE AGENT STALINA-5... DEVELOPED AT THE BACTERIOLOGICAL RESEARCH STATION NEAR KRASNOYARSK!
I AM SURE YOU'VE READ AMPLE REPORTS OF ITS PROPERTIES!
THAT BLOKE WITH THE DARK GLASSES—HE WAS ABOARD OUR FLIGHT!
...OH-OH! AND THERE'S JAMES'S SIGNAL!
1881

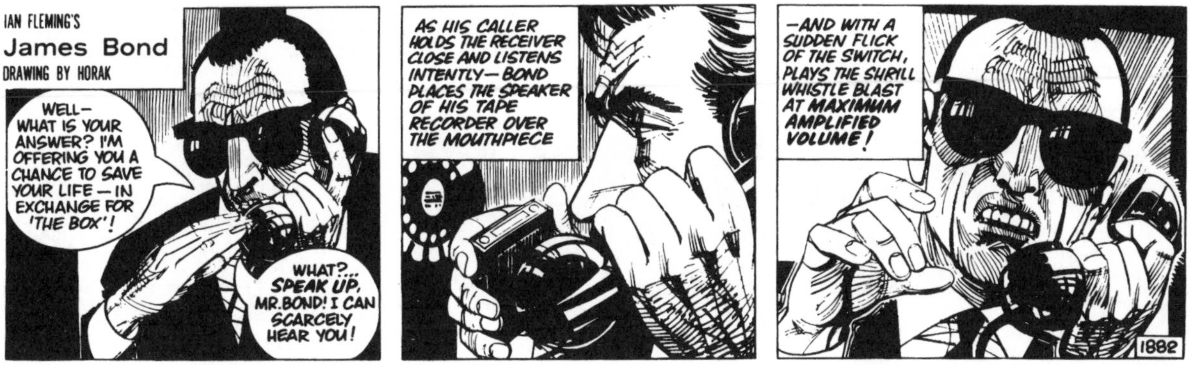
IAN FLEMING'S
James Bond
DRAWING BY HORAK
WELL— WHAT IS YOUR ANSWER? I'M OFFERING YOU A CHANCE TO SAVE YOUR LIFE — IN EXCHANGE FOR 'THE BOX'!
WHAT?... SPEAK UP, MR. BOND! I CAN SCARCELY HEAR YOU!
AS HIS CALLER HOLDS THE RECEIVER CLOSE AND LISTENS INTENTLY— BOND PLACES THE SPEAKER OF HIS TAPE RECORDER OVER THE MOUTHPIECE
—AND WITH A SUDDEN FLICK OF THE SWITCH, PLAYS THE SHRILL WHISTLE BLAST AT MAXIMUM AMPLIFIED VOLUME!
1882

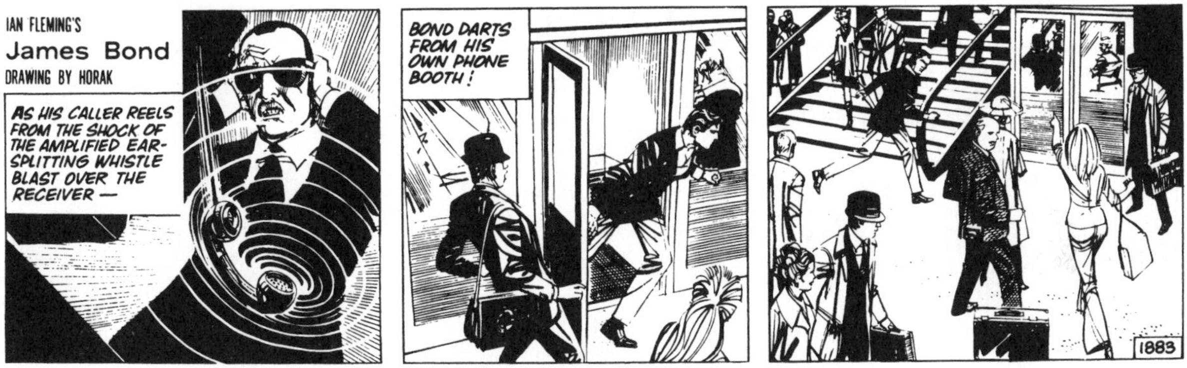
IAN FLEMING'S
James Bond
DRAWING BY HORAK
AS HIS CALLER REELS FROM THE SHOCK OF THE AMPLIFIED EAR-SPLITTING WHISTLE BLAST OVER THE RECEIVER —
BOND DARTS FROM HIS OWN PHONE BOOTH!
1883

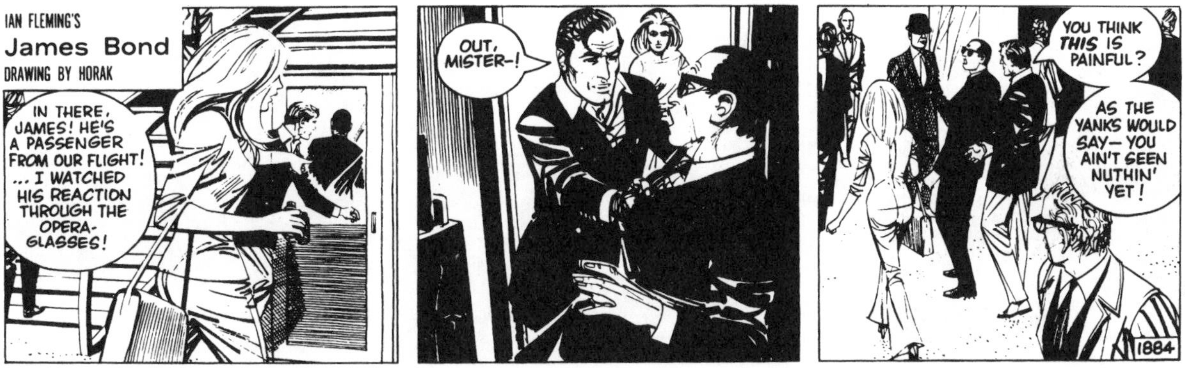
IAN FLEMING'S
James Bond
DRAWING BY HORAK
IN THERE, JAMES! HE'S A PASSENGER FROM OUR FLIGHT! ... I WATCHED HIS REACTION THROUGH THE OPERA-GLASSES!
OUT, MISTER—!
YOU THINK THIS IS PAINFUL?
AS THE YANKS WOULD SAY— YOU AIN'T SEEN NUTHIN' YET!
1884

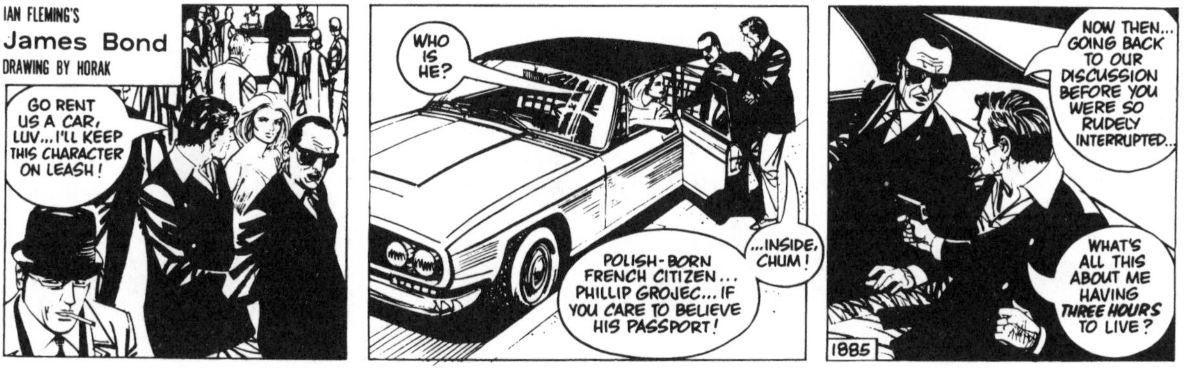
IAN FLEMING'S
James Bond
DRAWING BY HORAK
GO RENT US A CAR, LUV... I'LL KEEP THIS CHARACTER ON LEASH!
WHO IS HE?
POLISH-BORN FRENCH CITIZEN... PHILLIP GROJEC... IF YOU CARE TO BELIEVE HIS PASSPORT!
...INSIDE, CHUM!
NOW THEN... GOING BACK TO OUR DISCUSSION BEFORE YOU WERE SO RUDELY INTERRUPTED...
WHAT'S ALL THIS ABOUT ME HAVING THREE HOURS TO LIVE?
1885

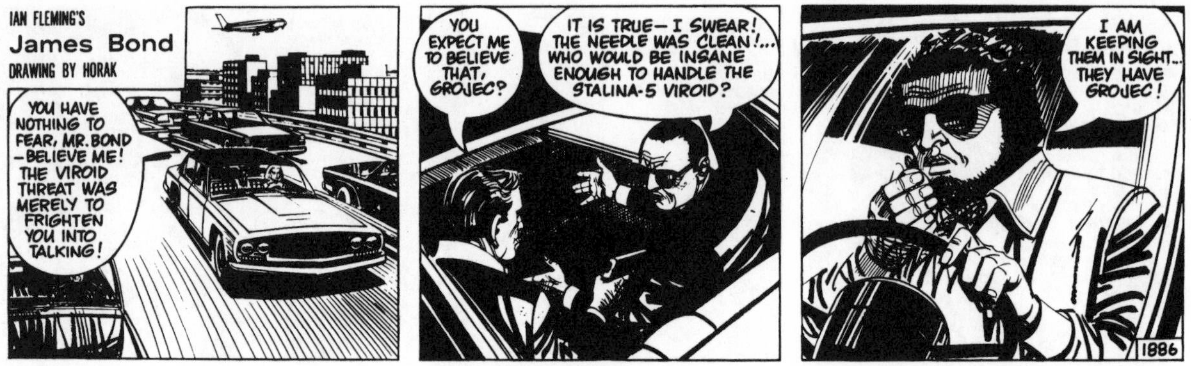
IAN FLEMING'S
James Bond
DRAWING BY HORAK
YOU HAVE NOTHING TO FEAR, MR. BOND —BELIEVE ME! THE VIROID THREAT WAS MERELY TO FRIGHTEN YOU INTO TALKING!
YOU EXPECT ME TO BELIEVE THAT, GROJEC?
IT IS TRUE— I SWEAR! THE NEEDLE WAS CLEAN!... WHO WOULD BE INSANE ENOUGH TO HANDLE THE STALINA-5 VIROID?
I AM KEEPING THEM IN SIGHT... THEY HAVE GROJEC!
1886

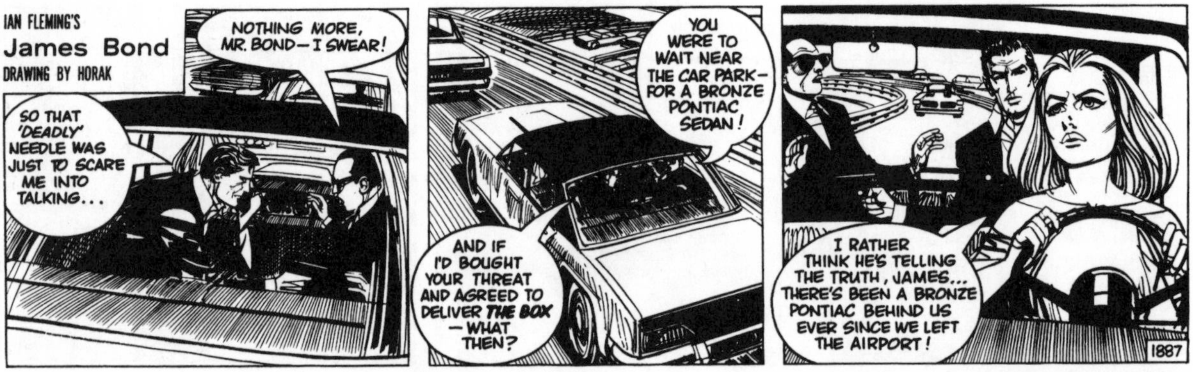
IAN FLEMING'S
James Bond
DRAWING BY HORAK
SO THAT 'DEADLY' NEEDLE WAS JUST TO SCARE ME INTO TALKING...
NOTHING MORE, MR. BOND— I SWEAR!
AND IF I'D BOUGHT YOUR THREAT AND AGREED TO DELIVER THE BOX —WHAT THEN?
YOU WERE TO WAIT NEAR THE CAR PARK- FOR A BRONZE PONTIAC SEDAN!
I RATHER THINK HE'S TELLING THE TRUTH, JAMES... THERE'S BEEN A BRONZE PONTIAC BEHIND US EVER SINCE WE LEFT THE AIRPORT!
1887

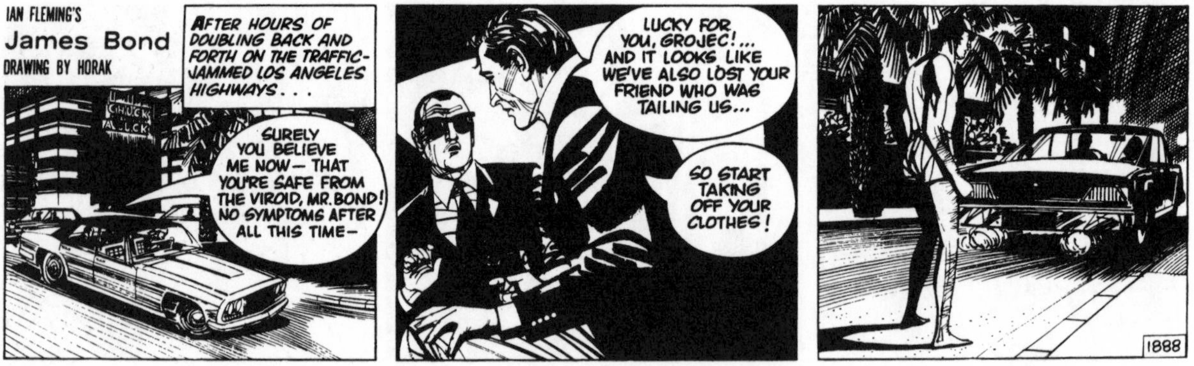
IAN FLEMING'S
James Bond
DRAWING BY HORAK
AFTER HOURS OF DOUBLING BACK AND FORTH ON THE TRAFFIC-JAMMED LOS ANGELES HIGHWAYS...
SURELY YOU BELIEVE ME NOW— THAT YOU'RE SAFE FROM THE VIROID, MR. BOND! NO SYMPTOMS AFTER ALL THIS TIME-
LUCKY FOR YOU, GROJEC!... AND IT LOOKS LIKE WE'VE ALSO LOST YOUR FRIEND WHO WAS TAILING US...
SO START TAKING OFF YOUR CLOTHES!
1888

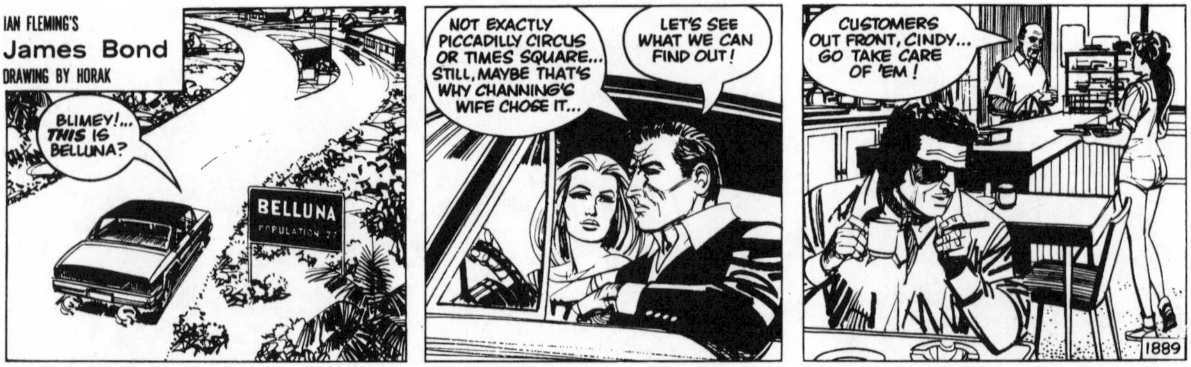
IAN FLEMING'S
James Bond
DRAWING BY HORAK
BLIMEY!... THIS IS BELLUNA?
BELLUNA
NOT EXACTLY PICCADILLY CIRCUS OR TIMES SQUARE... STILL, MAYBE THAT'S WHY CHANNING'S WIFE CHOSE IT...
LET'S SEE WHAT WE CAN FIND OUT!
CUSTOMERS OUT FRONT, CINDY... GO TAKE CARE OF 'EM!
1889

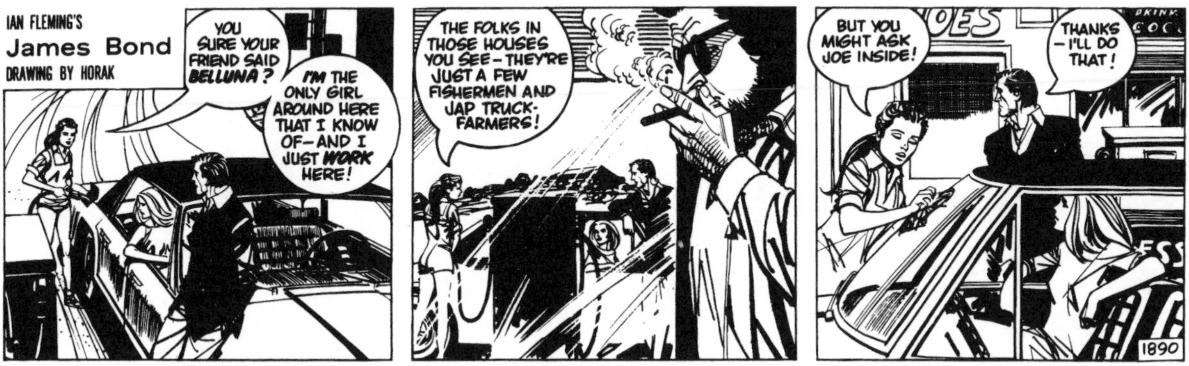
IAN FLEMING'S
James Bond
DRAWING BY HORAK
YOU SURE YOUR FRIEND SAID BELLUNA?
I'M THE ONLY GIRL AROUND HERE THAT I KNOW OF—AND I JUST WORK HERE!
THE FOLKS IN THOSE HOUSES YOU SEE—THEY'RE JUST A FEW FISHERMEN AND JAP TRUCK-FARMERS!
BUT YOU MIGHT ASK JOE INSIDE!
THANKS—I'LL DO THAT!
1890

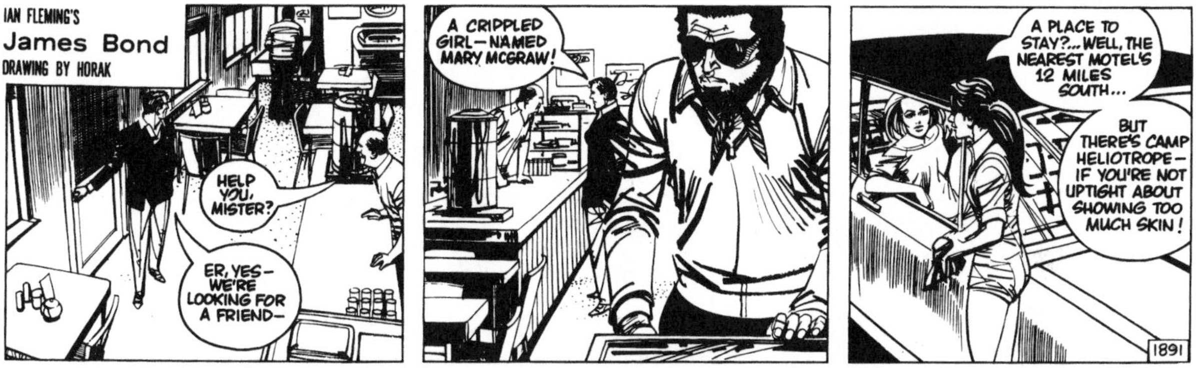
IAN FLEMING'S
James Bond
DRAWING BY HORAK
HELP YOU, MISTER?
ER, YES—WE'RE LOOKING FOR A FRIEND—
A CRIPPLED GIRL—NAMED MARY McGRAW!
A PLACE TO STAY?... WELL, THE NEAREST MOTEL'S 12 MILES SOUTH...
BUT THERE'S CAMP HELIOTROPE—IF YOU'RE NOT UPTIGHT ABOUT SHOWING TOO MUCH SKIN!
1891

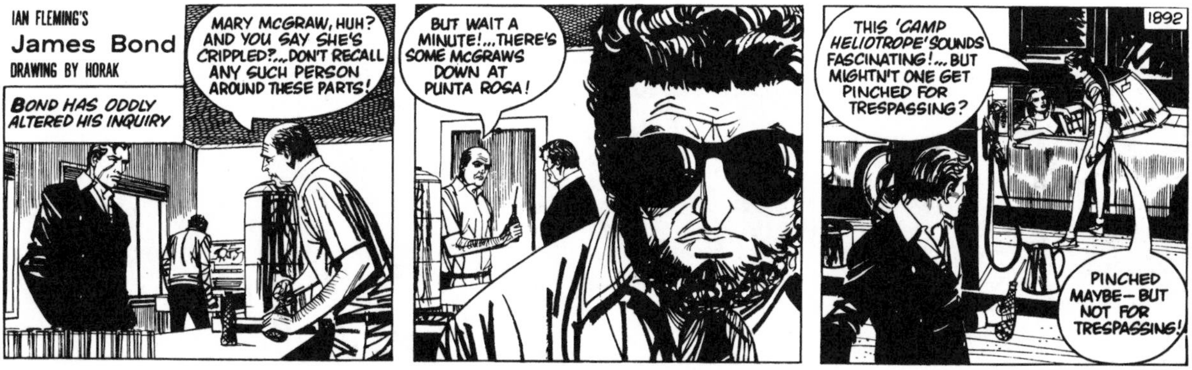
IAN FLEMING'S
James Bond
DRAWING BY HORAK
BOND HAS ODDLY ALTERED HIS INQUIRY
MARY McGRAW, HUH? AND YOU SAY SHE'S CRIPPLED?... DON'T RECALL ANY SUCH PERSON AROUND THESE PARTS!
BUT WAIT A MINUTE!... THERE'S SOME McGRAWS DOWN AT PUNTA ROSA!
1892
THIS 'CAMP HELIOTROPE' SOUNDS FASCINATING!... BUT MIGHTN'T ONE GET PINCHED FOR TRESPASSING?
PINCHED MAYBE—BUT NOT FOR TRESPASSING!

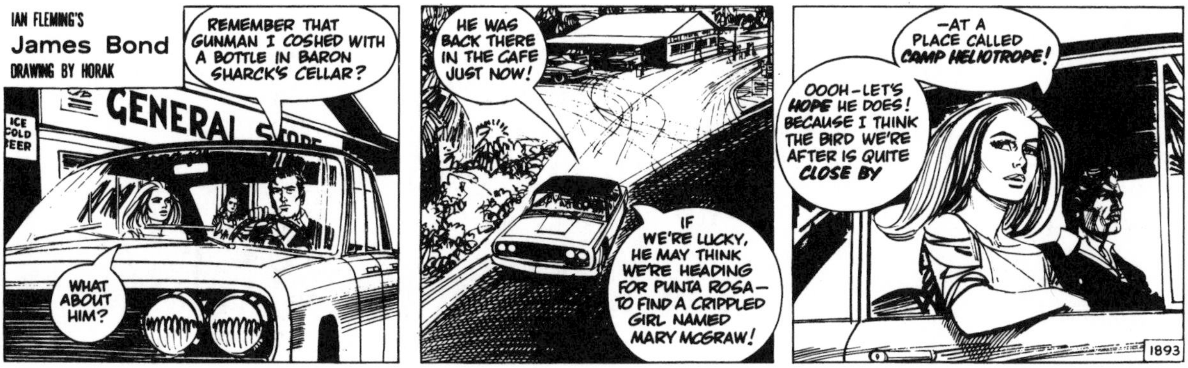
IAN FLEMING'S
James Bond
DRAWING BY HORAK
REMEMBER THAT GUNMAN I COSHED WITH A BOTTLE IN BARON SHARCK'S CELLAR?
GENERAL
WHAT ABOUT HIM?
HE WAS BACK THERE IN THE CAFE JUST NOW!
IF WE'RE LUCKY, HE MAY THINK WE'RE HEADING FOR PUNTA ROSA—TO FIND A CRIPPLED GIRL NAMED MARY McGRAW!
OOOH—LET'S HOPE HE DOES! BECAUSE I THINK THE BIRD WE'RE AFTER IS QUITE CLOSE BY
—AT A PLACE CALLED CAMP HELIOTROPE!
1893

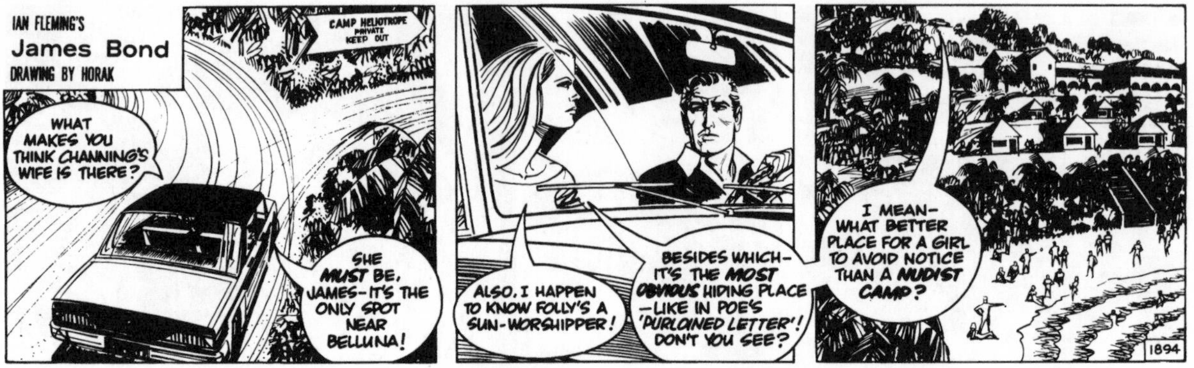
IAN FLEMING'S
James Bond
DRAWING BY HORAK
CAMP HELIOTROPE PRIVATE KEEP OUT
WHAT MAKES YOU THINK CHANNING'S WIFE IS THERE?
SHE MUST BE, JAMES–IT'S THE ONLY SPOT NEAR BELLUNA!
ALSO, I HAPPEN TO KNOW FOLLY'S A SUN-WORSHIPPER!
BESIDES WHICH– IT'S THE MOST OBVIOUS HIDING PLACE –LIKE IN POE'S 'PURLOINED LETTER'! DON'T YOU SEE?
I MEAN– WHAT BETTER PLACE FOR A GIRL TO AVOID NOTICE THAN A NUDIST CAMP?
1894

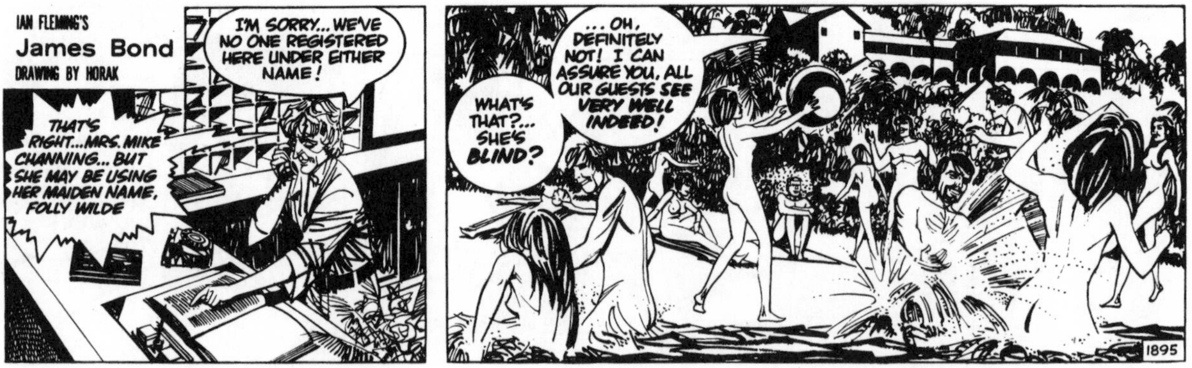
IAN FLEMING'S
James Bond
DRAWING BY HORAK
I'M SORRY... WE'VE NO ONE REGISTERED HERE UNDER EITHER NAME!
THAT'S RIGHT...MRS. MIKE CHANNING... BUT SHE MAY BE USING HER MAIDEN NAME, FOLLY WILDE
WHAT'S THAT?... SHE'S BLIND?
...OH, DEFINITELY NOT! I CAN ASSURE YOU, ALL OUR GUESTS SEE VERY WELL INDEED!
1895

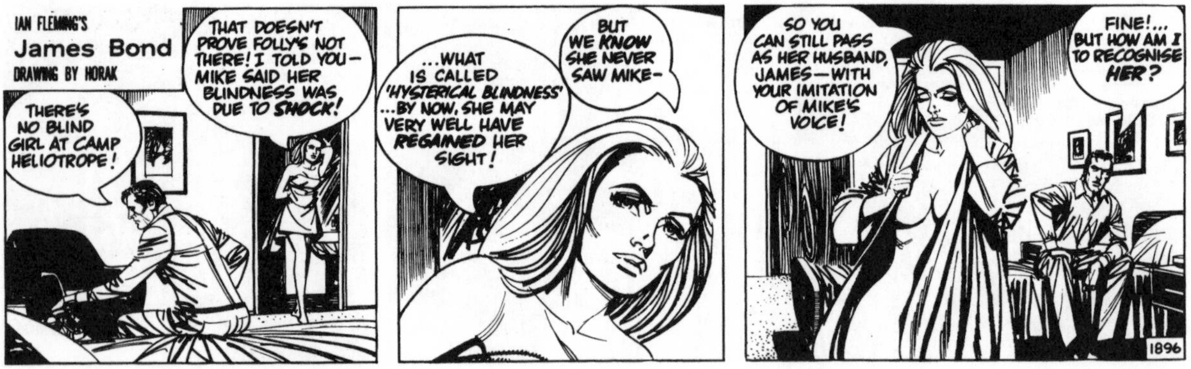
IAN FLEMING'S
James Bond
DRAWING BY HORAK
THERE'S NO BLIND GIRL AT CAMP HELIOTROPE!
THAT DOESN'T PROVE FOLLY'S NOT THERE! I TOLD YOU– MIKE SAID HER BLINDNESS WAS DUE TO SHOCK!
...WHAT IS CALLED 'HYSTERICAL BLINDNESS' ...BY NOW, SHE MAY VERY WELL HAVE REGAINED HER SIGHT!
BUT WE KNOW SHE NEVER SAW MIKE–
SO YOU CAN STILL PASS AS HER HUSBAND, JAMES—WITH YOUR IMITATION OF MIKE'S VOICE!
FINE!... BUT HOW AM I TO RECOGNISE HER?
1896

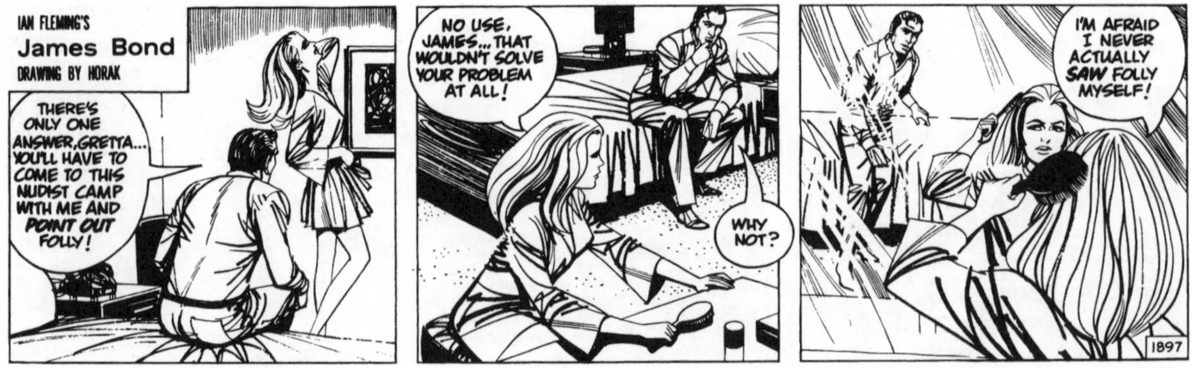
IAN FLEMING'S
James Bond
DRAWING BY HORAK
THERE'S ONLY ONE ANSWER, GRETTA... YOU'LL HAVE TO COME TO THIS NUDIST CAMP WITH ME AND POINT OUT FOLLY!
NO USE, JAMES... THAT WOULDN'T SOLVE YOUR PROBLEM AT ALL!
WHY NOT?
I'M AFRAID I NEVER ACTUALLY SAW FOLLY MYSELF!
1897

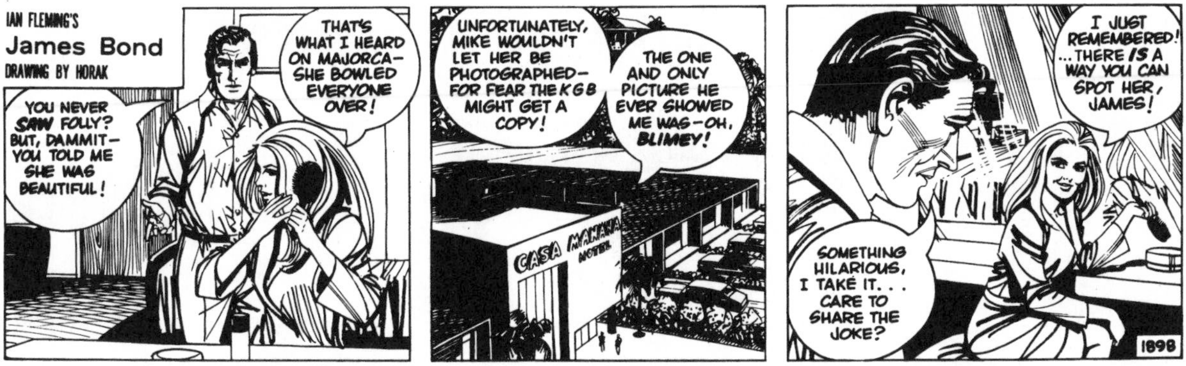
IAN FLEMING'S
James Bond
DRAWING BY HORAK
YOU NEVER SAW FOLLY? BUT, DAMMIT—YOU TOLD ME SHE WAS BEAUTIFUL!
THAT'S WHAT I HEARD ON MAJORCA—SHE BOWLED EVERYONE OVER!
UNFORTUNATELY, MIKE WOULDN'T LET HER BE PHOTOGRAPHED—FOR FEAR THE KGB MIGHT GET A COPY!
THE ONE AND ONLY PICTURE HE EVER SHOWED ME WAS—OH, BLIMEY!
CASA MANANA MOTEL
I JUST REMEMBERED! ...THERE IS A WAY YOU CAN SPOT HER, JAMES!
SOMETHING HILARIOUS, I TAKE IT. . . CARE TO SHARE THE JOKE?
1898

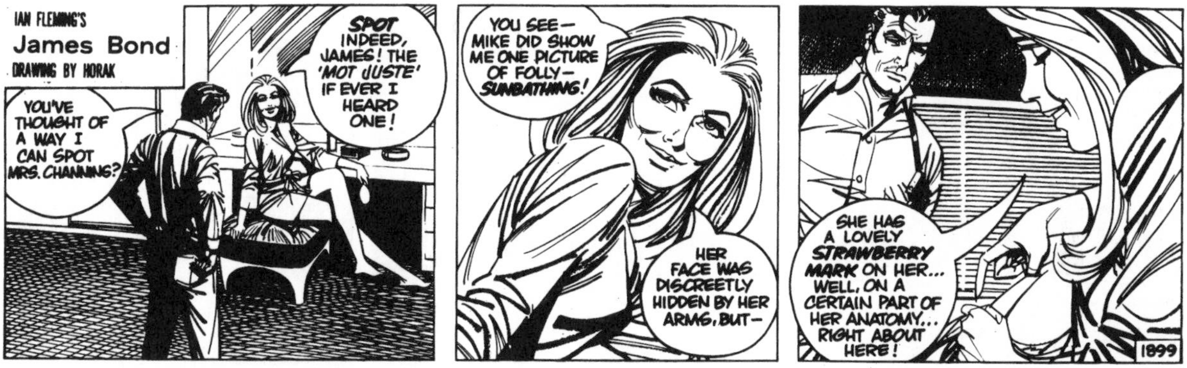
IAN FLEMING'S
James Bond
DRAWING BY HORAK
YOU'VE THOUGHT OF A WAY I CAN SPOT MRS. CHANNING?
SPOT INDEED, JAMES! THE 'MOT JUSTE' IF EVER I HEARD ONE!
YOU SEE—MIKE DID SHOW ME ONE PICTURE OF FOLLY—SUNBATHING!
HER FACE WAS DISCREETLY HIDDEN BY HER ARMS, BUT—
SHE HAS A LOVELY STRAWBERRY MARK ON HER... WELL, ON A CERTAIN PART OF HER ANATOMY... RIGHT ABOUT HERE!
1899

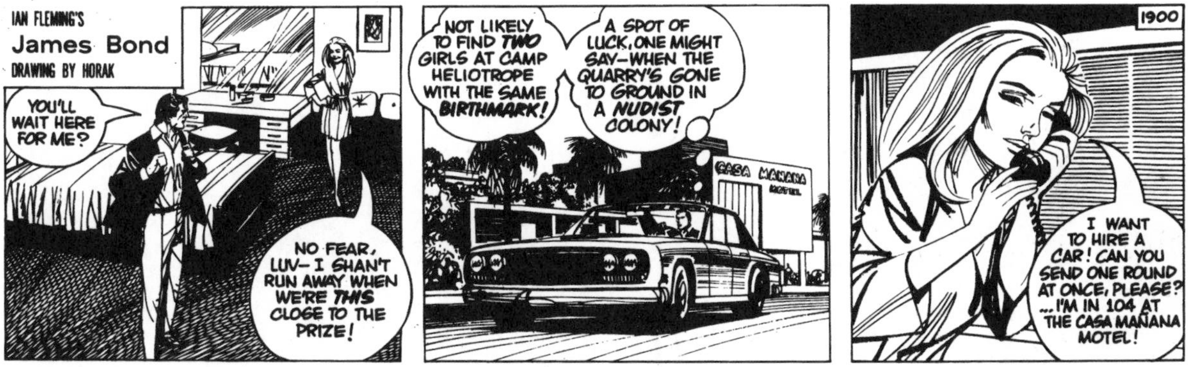
IAN FLEMING'S
James Bond
DRAWING BY HORAK
YOU'LL WAIT HERE FOR ME?
NO FEAR, LUV—I SHAN'T RUN AWAY WHEN WE'RE THIS CLOSE TO THE PRIZE!
NOT LIKELY TO FIND TWO GIRLS AT CAMP HELIOTROPE WITH THE SAME BIRTHMARK!
A SPOT OF LUCK, ONE MIGHT SAY—WHEN THE QUARRY'S GONE TO GROUND IN A NUDIST COLONY!
CASA MANANA MOTEL
1900
I WANT TO HIRE A CAR! CAN YOU SEND ONE ROUND AT ONCE, PLEASE? ...I'M IN 104 AT THE CASA MAÑANA MOTEL!

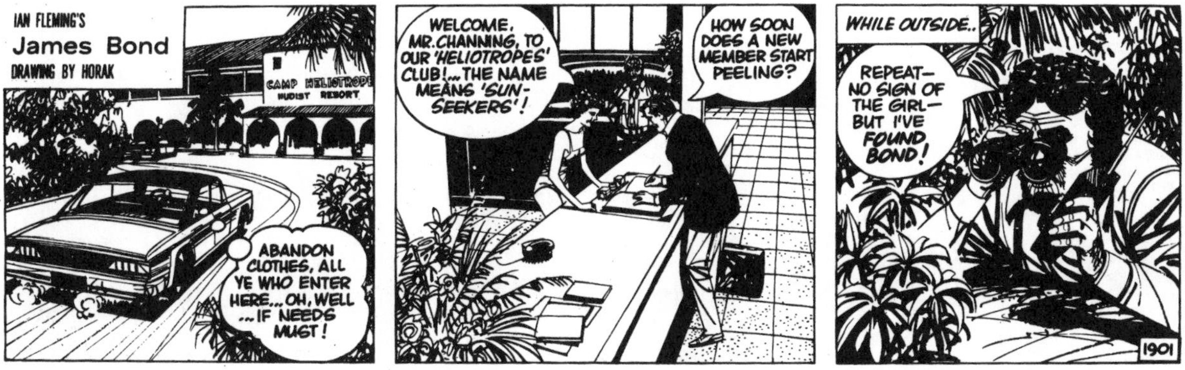
IAN FLEMING'S
James Bond
DRAWING BY HORAK
CAMP HELIOTROPE NUDIST RESORT
ABANDON CLOTHES, ALL YE WHO ENTER HERE... OH, WELL ...IF NEEDS MUST!
WELCOME, MR. CHANNING, TO OUR 'HELIOTROPES' CLUB!... THE NAME MEANS 'SUN-SEEKERS'!
HOW SOON DOES A NEW MEMBER START PEELING?
WHILE OUTSIDE..
REPEAT—NO SIGN OF THE GIRL—BUT I'VE FOUND BOND!
1901

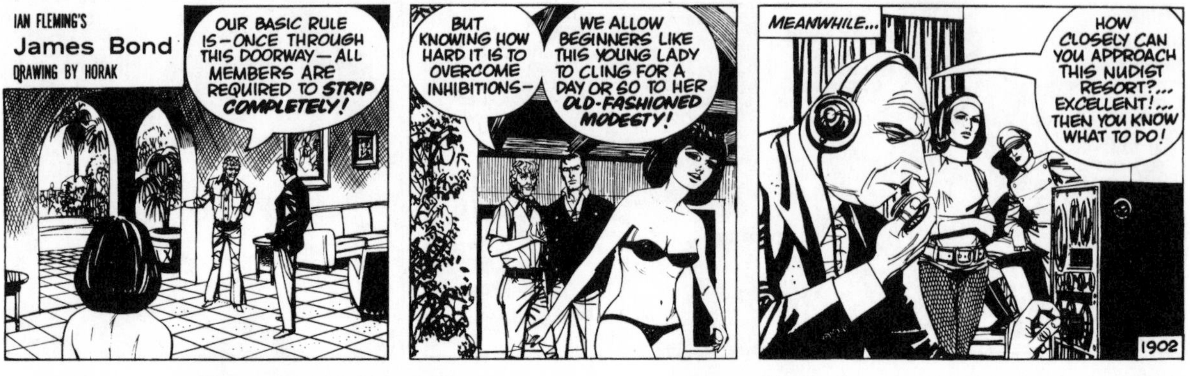
IAN FLEMING'S
James Bond
DRAWING BY HORAK
OUR BASIC RULE IS—ONCE THROUGH THIS DOORWAY—ALL MEMBERS ARE REQUIRED TO STRIP COMPLETELY!
BUT KNOWING HOW HARD IT IS TO OVERCOME INHIBITIONS—
WE ALLOW BEGINNERS LIKE THIS YOUNG LADY TO CLING FOR A DAY OR SO TO HER OLD-FASHIONED MODESTY!
MEANWHILE...
HOW CLOSELY CAN YOU APPROACH THIS NUDIST RESORT?... EXCELLENT!... THEN YOU KNOW WHAT TO DO!
1902

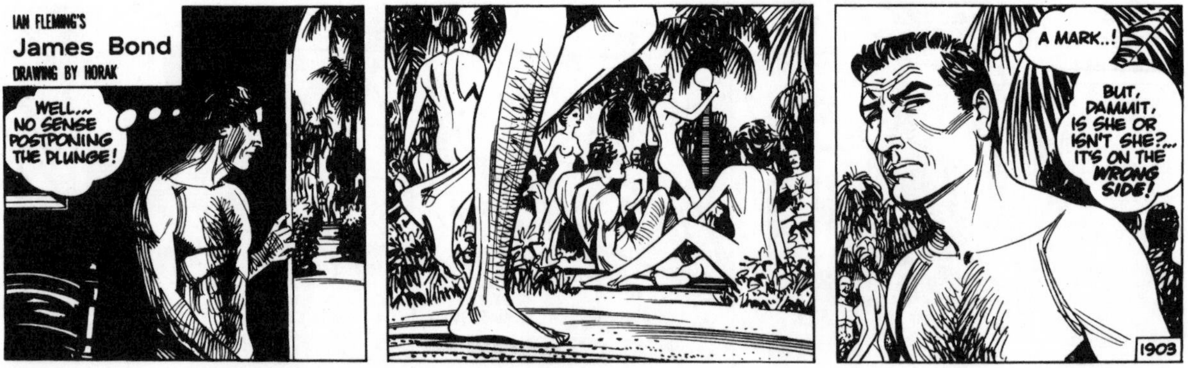
IAN FLEMING'S
James Bond
DRAWING BY HORAK
WELL... NO SENSE POSTPONING THE PLUNGE!
A MARK..!
BUT, DAMMIT, IS SHE OR ISN'T SHE?... IT'S ON THE WRONG SIDE!
1903

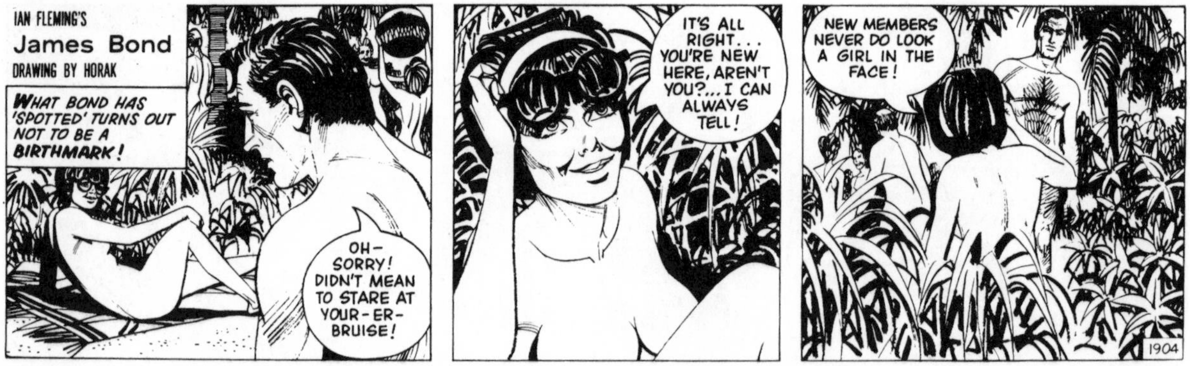
IAN FLEMING'S
James Bond
DRAWING BY HORAK
WHAT BOND HAS 'SPOTTED' TURNS OUT NOT TO BE A BIRTHMARK!
OH—SORRY! DIDN'T MEAN TO STARE AT YOUR-ER-BRUISE!
IT'S ALL RIGHT... YOU'RE NEW HERE, AREN'T YOU?... I CAN ALWAYS TELL!
NEW MEMBERS NEVER DO LOOK A GIRL IN THE FACE!
1904

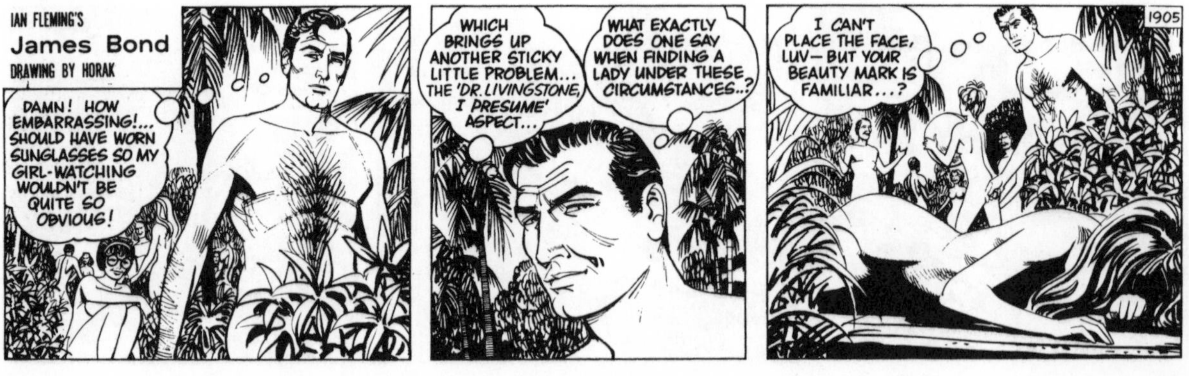
IAN FLEMING'S
James Bond
DRAWING BY HORAK
DAMN! HOW EMBARRASSING!... SHOULD HAVE WORN SUNGLASSES SO MY GIRL-WATCHING WOULDN'T BE QUITE SO OBVIOUS!
WHICH BRINGS UP ANOTHER STICKY LITTLE PROBLEM... THE 'DR. LIVINGSTONE, I PRESUME' ASPECT...
WHAT EXACTLY DOES ONE SAY WHEN FINDING A LADY UNDER THESE CIRCUMSTANCES..?
1905
I CAN'T PLACE THE FACE, LUV—BUT YOUR BEAUTY MARK IS FAMILIAR...?

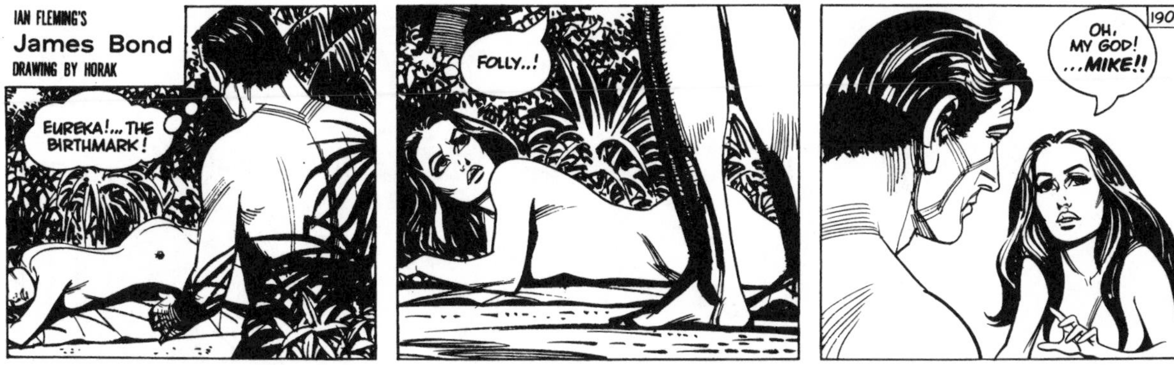
IAN FLEMING'S
James Bond
DRAWING BY HORAK
EUREKA!... THE BIRTHMARK!
FOLLY..!
1906
OH, MY GOD! ...MIKE!!

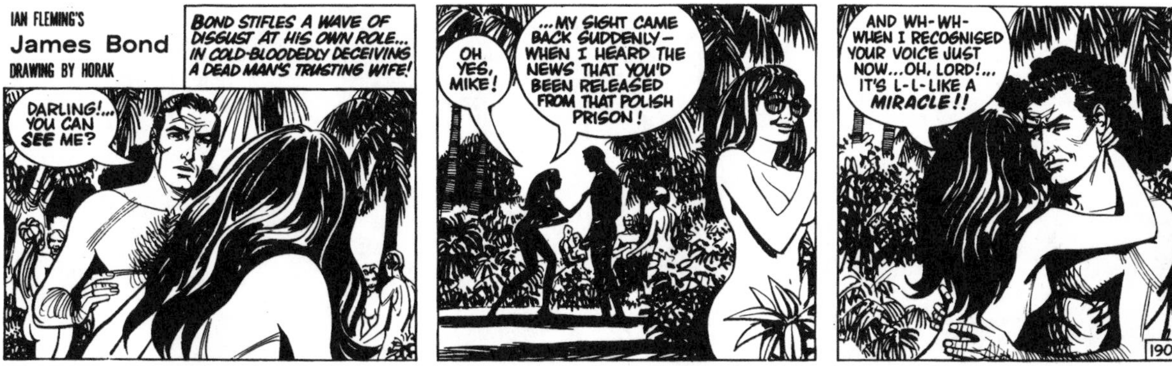
IAN FLEMING'S
James Bond
DRAWING BY HORAK
BOND STIFLES A WAVE OF DISGUST AT HIS OWN ROLE... IN COLD-BLOODEDLY DECEIVING A DEAD MAN'S TRUSTING WIFE!
DARLING!... YOU CAN SEE ME?
OH YES, MIKE!
...MY SIGHT CAME BACK SUDDENLY– WHEN I HEARD THE NEWS THAT YOU'D BEEN RELEASED FROM THAT POLISH PRISON!
AND WH-WH-WHEN I RECOGNISED YOUR VOICE JUST NOW...OH, LORD!... IT'S L-L-LIKE A MIRACLE!!
1907

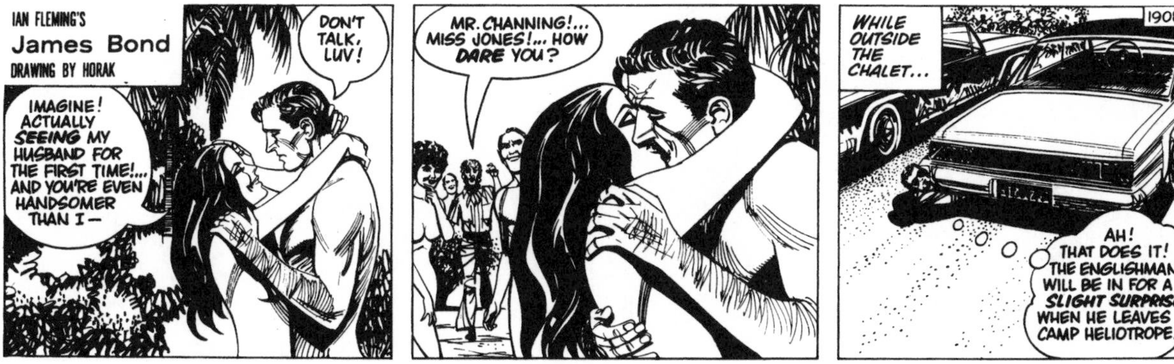
IAN FLEMING'S
James Bond
DRAWING BY HORAK
IMAGINE! ACTUALLY SEEING MY HUSBAND FOR THE FIRST TIME!... AND YOU'RE EVEN HANDSOMER THAN I–
DON'T TALK, LUV!
MR. CHANNING!... MISS JONES!... HOW DARE YOU?
1908
WHILE OUTSIDE THE CHALET...
AH! THAT DOES IT! THE ENGLISHMAN WILL BE IN FOR A SLIGHT SURPRISE WHEN HE LEAVES CAMP HELIOTROPE!

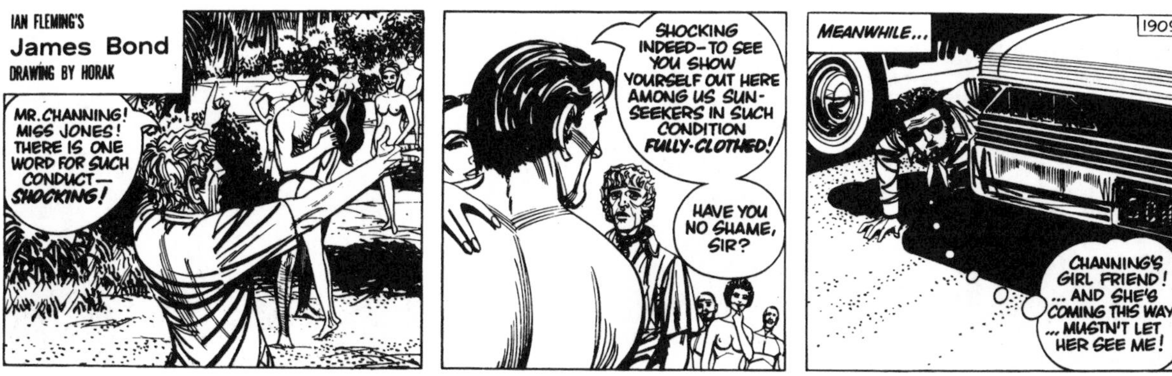
IAN FLEMING'S
James Bond
DRAWING BY HORAK
MR. CHANNING! MISS JONES! THERE IS ONE WORD FOR SUCH CONDUCT— SHOCKING!
SHOCKING INDEED–TO SEE YOU SHOW YOURSELF OUT HERE AMONG US SUN-SEEKERS IN SUCH CONDITION FULLY-CLOTHED!
HAVE YOU NO SHAME, SIR?
1909
MEANWHILE...
CHANNING'S GIRL FRIEND! ...AND SHE'S COMING THIS WAY! ...MUSTN'T LET HER SEE ME!

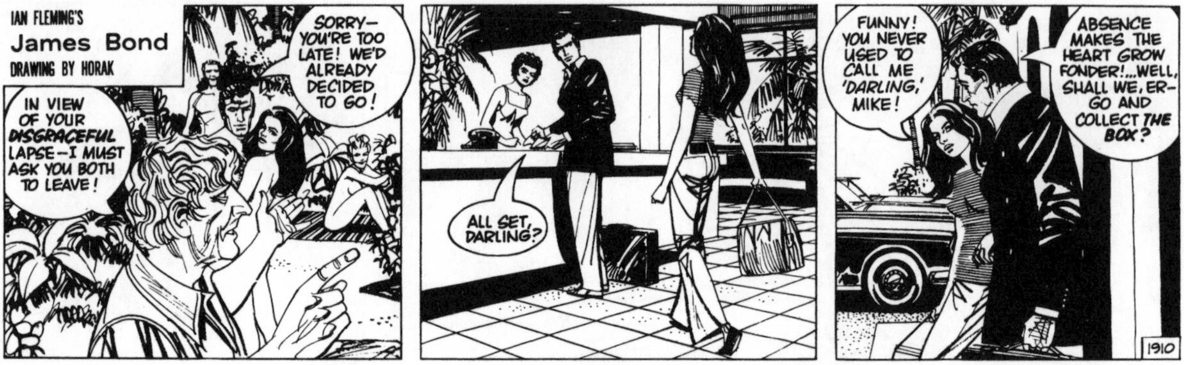
IAN FLEMING'S
James Bond
DRAWING BY HORAK
IN VIEW OF YOUR DISGRACEFUL LAPSE—I MUST ASK YOU BOTH TO LEAVE!
SORRY—YOU'RE TOO LATE! WE'D ALREADY DECIDED TO GO!
ALL SET, DARLING?
FUNNY! YOU NEVER USED TO CALL ME 'DARLING,' MIKE!
ABSENCE MAKES THE HEART GROW FONDER!... WELL, SHALL WE, ER-GO AND COLLECT THE BOX?
1910

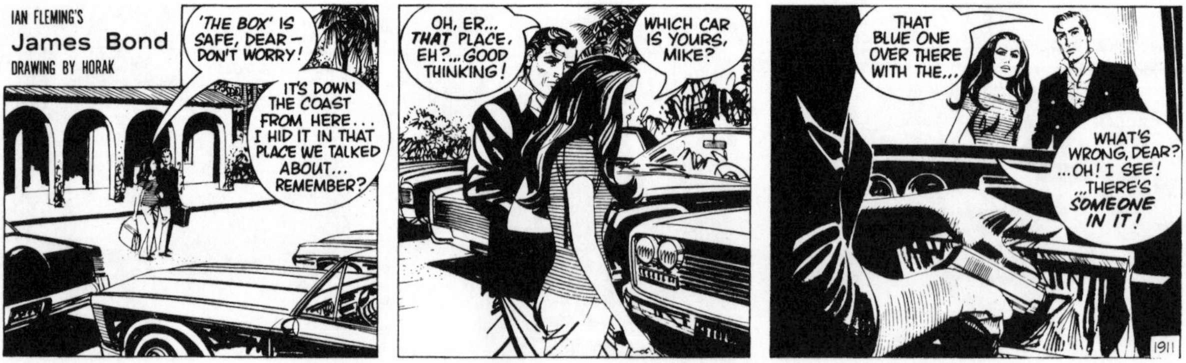
IAN FLEMING'S
James Bond
DRAWING BY HORAK
'THE BOX' IS SAFE, DEAR—DON'T WORRY!
IT'S DOWN THE COAST FROM HERE... I HID IT IN THAT PLACE WE TALKED ABOUT... REMEMBER?
OH, ER... THAT PLACE, EH?... GOOD THINKING!
WHICH CAR IS YOURS, MIKE?
THAT BLUE ONE OVER THERE WITH THE...
WHAT'S WRONG, DEAR? ...OH! I SEE! ...THERE'S SOMEONE IN IT!
1911

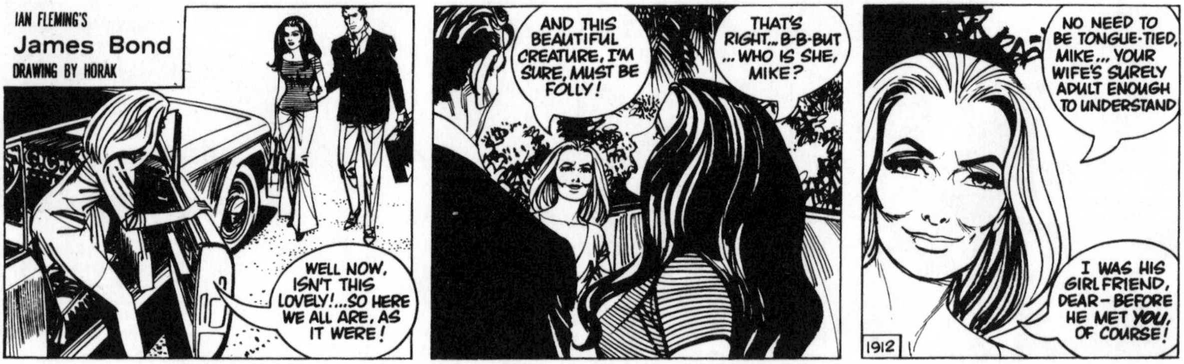
IAN FLEMING'S
James Bond
DRAWING BY HORAK
WELL NOW, ISN'T THIS LOVELY!... SO HERE WE ALL ARE, AS IT WERE!
AND THIS BEAUTIFUL CREATURE, I'M SURE, MUST BE FOLLY!
THAT'S RIGHT... B-B-BUT ... WHO IS SHE, MIKE?
NO NEED TO BE TONGUE-TIED, MIKE... YOUR WIFE'S SURELY ADULT ENOUGH TO UNDERSTAND
I WAS HIS GIRLFRIEND, DEAR—BEFORE HE MET YOU, OF COURSE!
1912

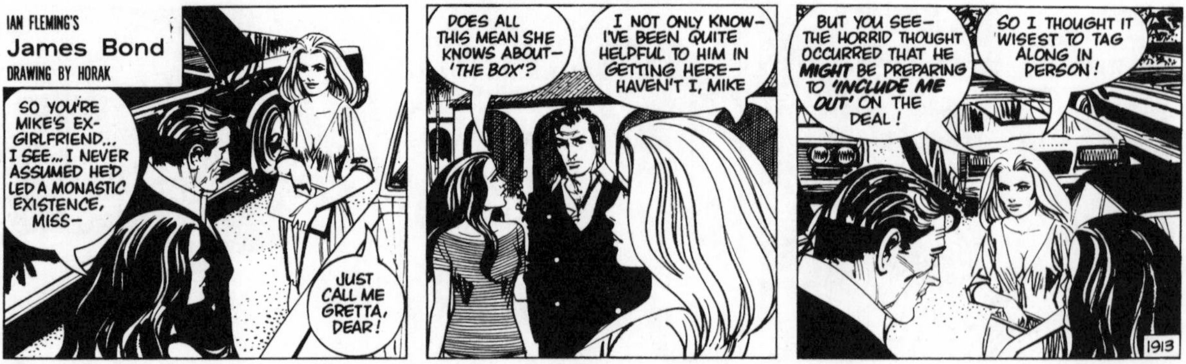
IAN FLEMING'S
James Bond
DRAWING BY HORAK
SO YOU'RE MIKE'S EX-GIRLFRIEND... I SEE... I NEVER ASSUMED HE'D LED A MONASTIC EXISTENCE, MISS—
JUST CALL ME GRETTA, DEAR!
DOES ALL THIS MEAN SHE KNOWS ABOUT—'THE BOX'?
I NOT ONLY KNOW—I'VE BEEN QUITE HELPFUL TO HIM IN GETTING HERE—HAVEN'T I, MIKE
BUT YOU SEE—THE HORRID THOUGHT OCCURRED THAT HE MIGHT BE PREPARING TO 'INCLUDE ME OUT' ON THE DEAL!
SO I THOUGHT IT WISEST TO TAG ALONG IN PERSON!
1913

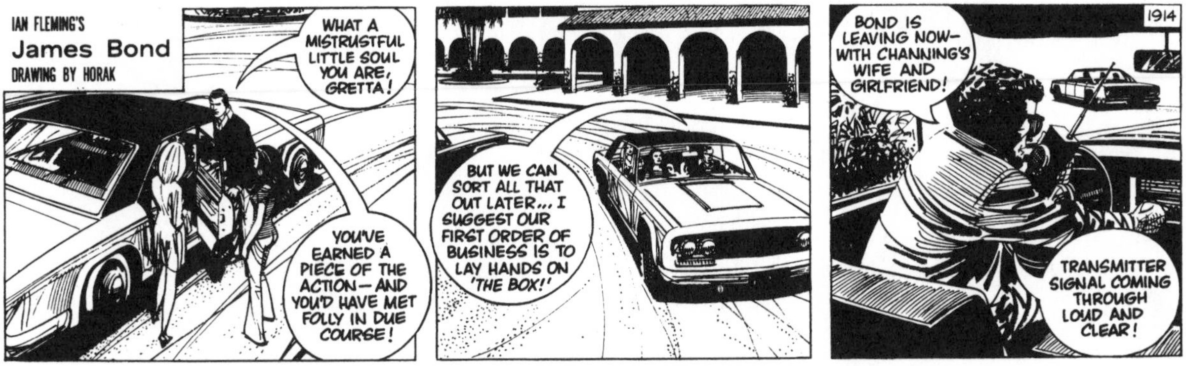
IAN FLEMING'S
James Bond
DRAWING BY HORAK
WHAT A MISTRUSTFUL LITTLE SOUL YOU ARE, GRETTA!
YOU'VE EARNED A PIECE OF THE ACTION—AND YOU'D HAVE MET FOLLY IN DUE COURSE!
BUT WE CAN SORT ALL THAT OUT LATER... I SUGGEST OUR FIRST ORDER OF BUSINESS IS TO LAY HANDS ON 'THE BOX!'
1914
BOND IS LEAVING NOW—WITH CHANNING'S WIFE AND GIRLFRIEND!
TRANSMITTER SIGNAL COMING THROUGH LOUD AND CLEAR!

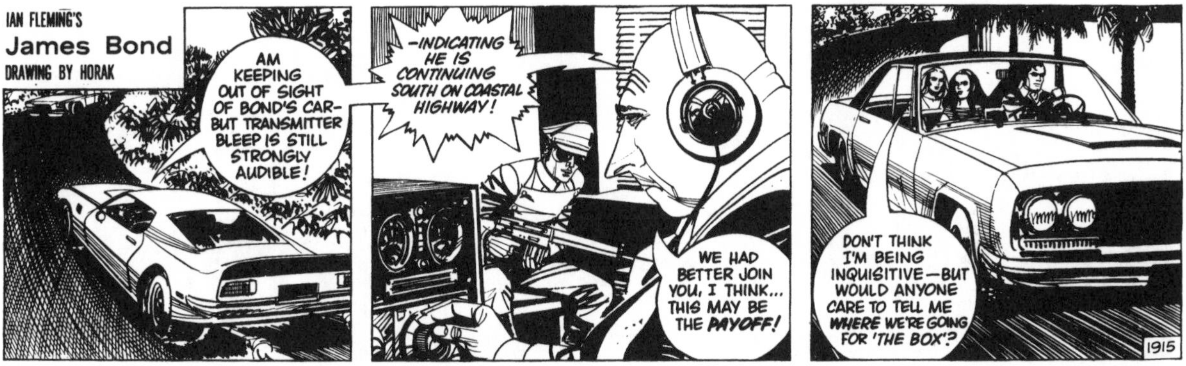
IAN FLEMING'S
James Bond
DRAWING BY HORAK
AM KEEPING OUT OF SIGHT OF BOND'S CAR—BUT TRANSMITTER BLEEP IS STILL STRONGLY AUDIBLE!
—INDICATING HE IS CONTINUING SOUTH ON COASTAL HIGHWAY!
WE HAD BETTER JOIN YOU, I THINK... THIS MAY BE THE PAYOFF!
DON'T THINK I'M BEING INQUISITIVE—BUT WOULD ANYONE CARE TO TELL ME WHERE WE'RE GOING FOR 'THE BOX'?
1915

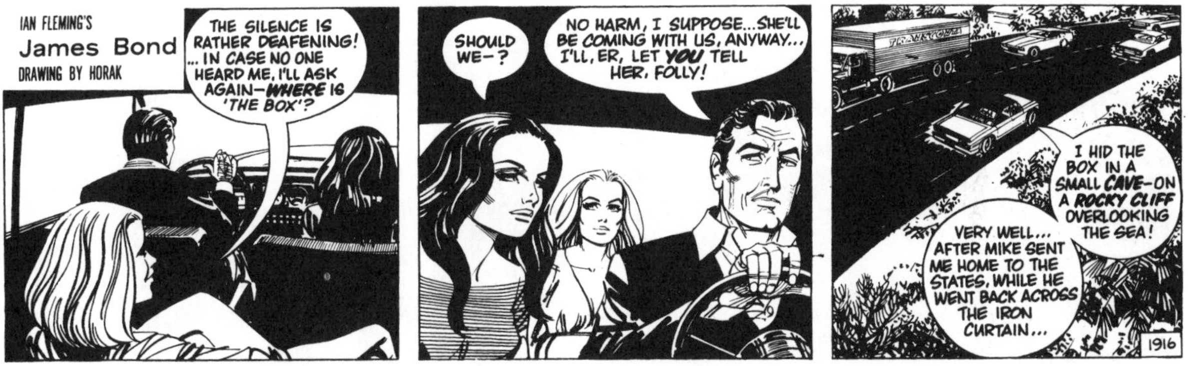
IAN FLEMING'S
James Bond
DRAWING BY HORAK
THE SILENCE IS RATHER DEAFENING! ... IN CASE NO ONE HEARD ME, I'LL ASK AGAIN—WHERE IS 'THE BOX'?
SHOULD WE—?
NO HARM, I SUPPOSE... SHE'LL BE COMING WITH US, ANYWAY... I'LL, ER, LET YOU TELL HER, FOLLY!
VERY WELL... AFTER MIKE SENT ME HOME TO THE STATES, WHILE HE WENT BACK ACROSS THE IRON CURTAIN...
I HID THE BOX IN A SMALL CAVE—ON A ROCKY CLIFF OVERLOOKING THE SEA!
1916

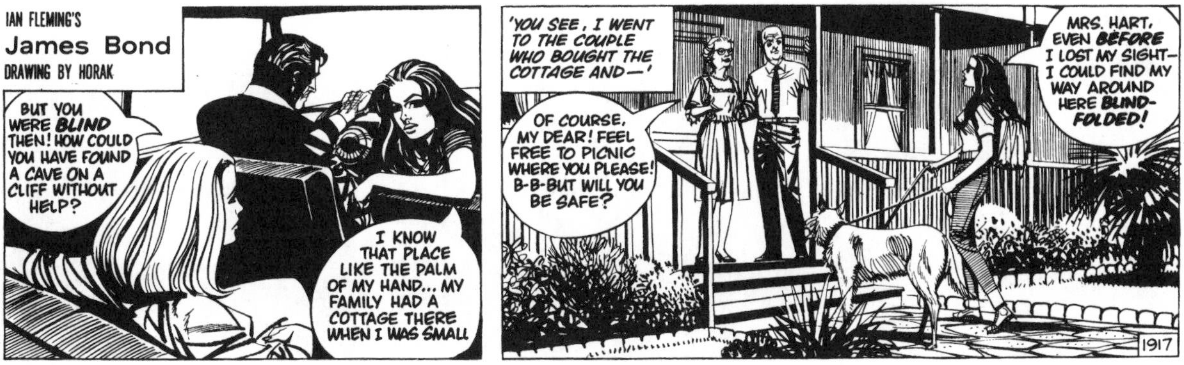
IAN FLEMING'S
James Bond
DRAWING BY HORAK
BUT YOU WERE BLIND THEN! HOW COULD YOU HAVE FOUND A CAVE ON A CLIFF WITHOUT HELP?
I KNOW THAT PLACE LIKE THE PALM OF MY HAND... MY FAMILY HAD A COTTAGE THERE WHEN I WAS SMALL
'YOU SEE, I WENT TO THE COUPLE WHO BOUGHT THE COTTAGE AND—'
MRS. HART, EVEN BEFORE I LOST MY SIGHT—I COULD FIND MY WAY AROUND HERE BLIND-FOLDED!
OF COURSE, MY DEAR! FEEL FREE TO PICNIC WHERE YOU PLEASE! B-B-BUT WILL YOU BE SAFE?
1917

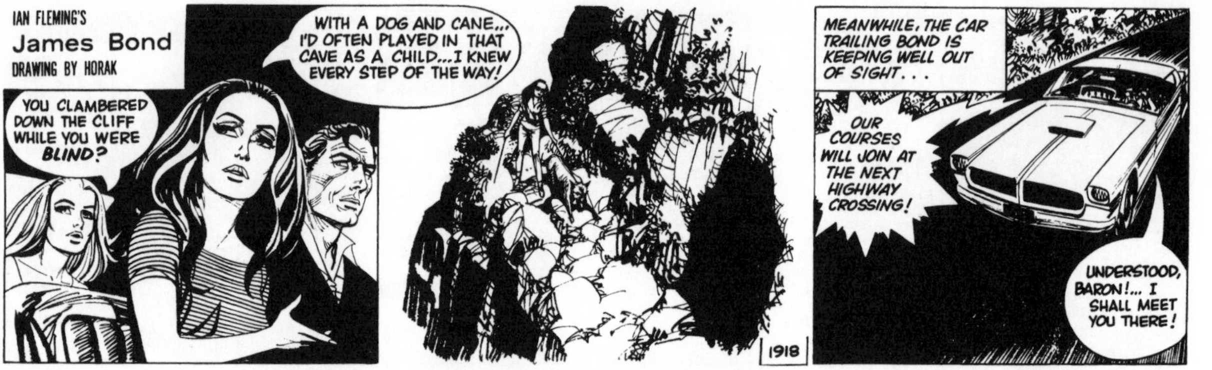
IAN FLEMING'S
James Bond
DRAWING BY HORAK
YOU CLAMBERED DOWN THE CLIFF WHILE YOU WERE *BLIND?*
WITH A DOG AND CANE... I'D OFTEN PLAYED IN THAT CAVE AS A CHILD... I KNEW EVERY STEP OF THE WAY!
1918
MEANWHILE, THE CAR TRAILING BOND IS KEEPING WELL OUT OF SIGHT...
OUR COURSES WILL JOIN AT THE NEXT HIGHWAY CROSSING!
UNDERSTOOD, BARON!... I SHALL MEET YOU THERE!

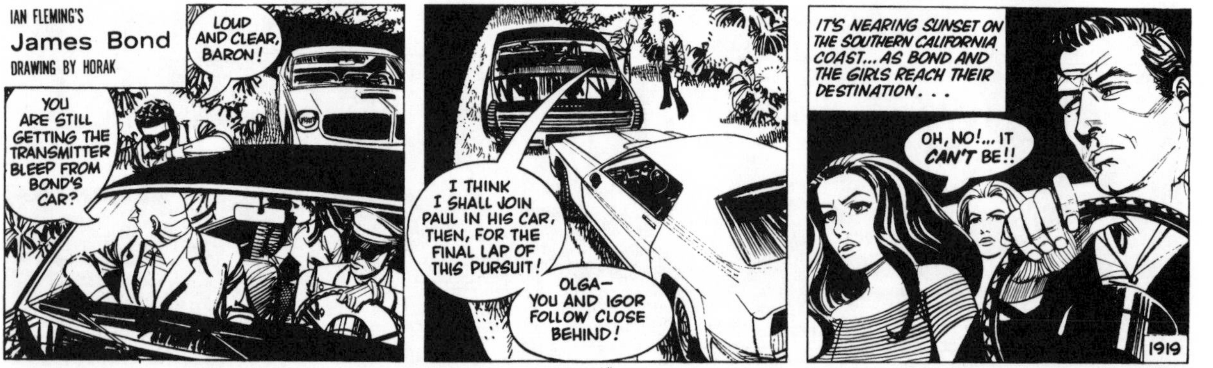
IAN FLEMING'S
James Bond
DRAWING BY HORAK
LOUD AND CLEAR, BARON!
YOU ARE STILL GETTING THE TRANSMITTER BLEEP FROM BOND'S CAR?
I THINK I SHALL JOIN PAUL IN HIS CAR, THEN, FOR THE FINAL LAP OF THIS PURSUIT!
OLGA— YOU AND IGOR FOLLOW CLOSE BEHIND!
IT'S NEARING SUNSET ON THE SOUTHERN CALIFORNIA COAST... AS BOND AND THE GIRLS REACH THEIR DESTINATION...
OH, NO!... IT *CAN'T* BE!!
1919

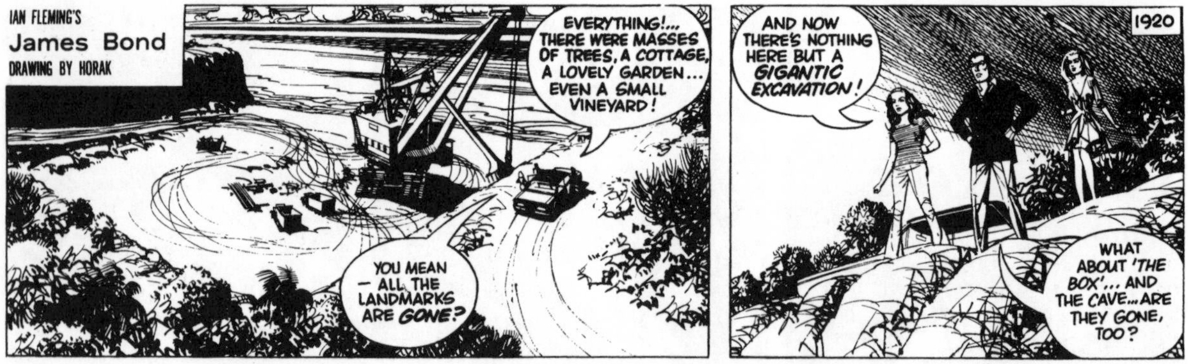
IAN FLEMING'S
James Bond
DRAWING BY HORAK
EVERYTHING!... THERE WERE MASSES OF TREES, A COTTAGE, A LOVELY GARDEN... EVEN A SMALL VINEYARD!
YOU MEAN — ALL THE LANDMARKS ARE *GONE?*
1920
AND NOW THERE'S NOTHING HERE BUT A *GIGANTIC EXCAVATION!*
WHAT ABOUT *'THE BOX'*... AND THE CAVE... ARE THEY GONE, TOO?

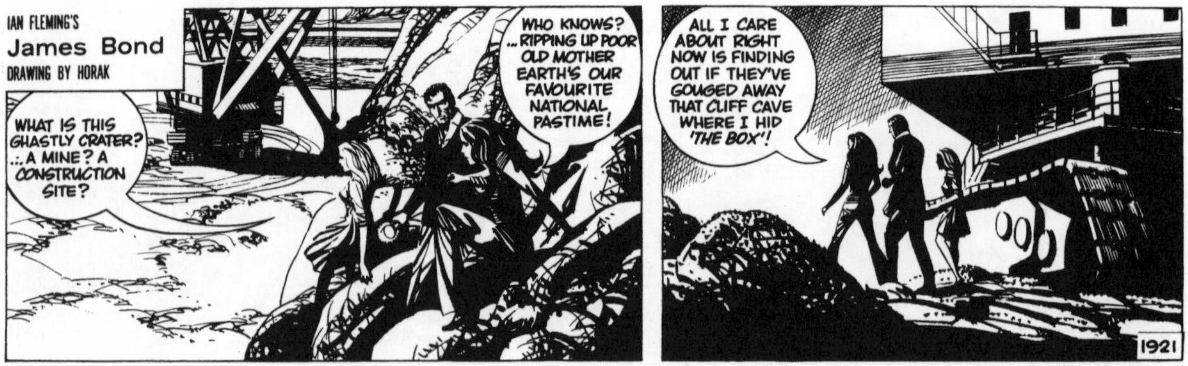
IAN FLEMING'S
James Bond
DRAWING BY HORAK
WHAT IS THIS GHASTLY CRATER? ... A MINE? A CONSTRUCTION SITE?
WHO KNOWS? ... RIPPING UP POOR OLD MOTHER EARTH'S OUR FAVOURITE NATIONAL PASTIME!
ALL I CARE ABOUT RIGHT NOW IS FINDING OUT IF THEY'VE GOUGED AWAY THAT CLIFF CAVE WHERE I HID *'THE BOX'!*
1921

**IAN FLEMING'S**
# James Bond
DRAWING BY HORAK

**Panel 1:** THE CLIFF SITE WHERE FOLLY HID 'THE BOX' HAS BEEN EXCAVATED BY A GIANT POWER SHOVEL!

LET'S HOPE THEY HAVEN'T DUG DEEP ENOUGH TO DESTROY THAT CAVE IN THE CLIFF!

**Panel 2:** GOT YOUR BEARINGS YET?

I...I'M NOT SURE, BUT...

**Panel 3:** YES! THERE'S THE CAVE, MIKE! ...'THE BOX' MUST STILL BE SAFE DOWN THERE!

1922

---

**IAN FLEMING'S**
# James Bond
DRAWING BY HORAK

**Panel 4:** WATCH YOUR STEP!... THERE'S A SHEER DROP BELOW THE CAVE!

DON'T THINK I WASN'T AWARE OF THAT WHEN I CAME DOWN HERE BLIND!

**Panel 5:**

**Panel 6:** IT SHOULD BE OVER THERE, MIKE—BEHIND THAT ROCK!

1923

---

**IAN FLEMING'S**
# James Bond
DRAWING BY HORAK

**Panel 7:** HOORAY! IT'S HERE—KNAPSACK AND ALL!

**Panel 8:** AND HERE'S THE METAL BOX—WELDED SHUT!

I, ER... SUPPOSE THERE'S NO USE ASKING... WHAT'S IN IT?

**Panel 9:** AT THAT MOMENT...

THERE IS BOND'S CAR, BARON!...HE AND THE WOMEN MUST BE DOWN IN THAT EXCAVATION!

1924

---

**IAN FLEMING'S**
# James Bond
DRAWING BY HORAK

**Panel 10:** DON'T LOOK DOWN! AND DON'T FRET ABOUT 'THE BOX'—I HAVE IT IN THE KNAPSACK!

**Panel 11:** MIKE! LOOK!...THERE ARE PEOPLE UP THERE!

IT'S BARON SHARCK AND HIS LOT!

**Panel 12:** GOOD! YOU'VE RECOGNISED ME, I SEE!

SO NOW, MR. BOND—THE TIME HAS COME TO FINISH OUR BUSINESS!

1925

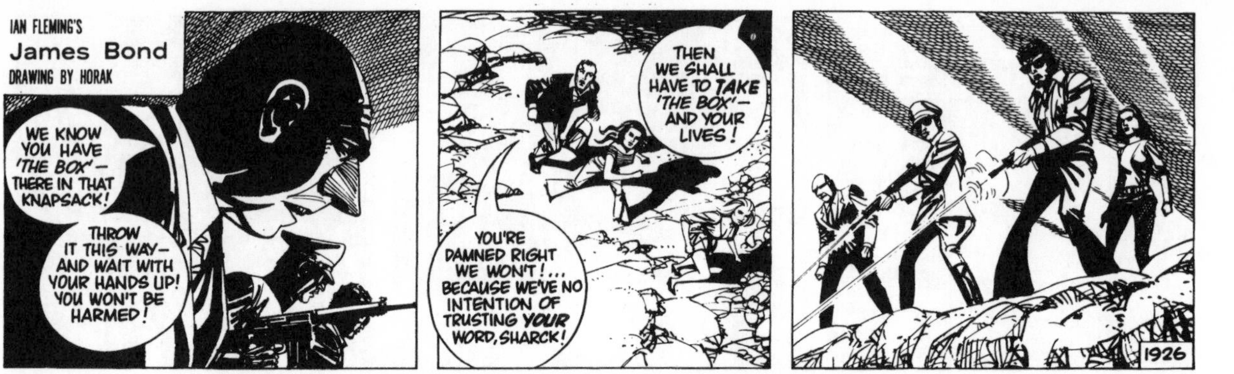
IAN FLEMING'S
James Bond
DRAWING BY HORAK
WE KNOW YOU HAVE 'THE BOX'— THERE IN THAT KNAPSACK!
THROW IT THIS WAY— AND WAIT WITH YOUR HANDS UP! YOU WON'T BE HARMED!
YOU'RE DAMNED RIGHT WE WON'T!... BECAUSE WE'VE NO INTENTION OF TRUSTING YOUR WORD, SHARCK!
THEN WE SHALL HAVE TO TAKE 'THE BOX'— AND YOUR LIVES!
1926

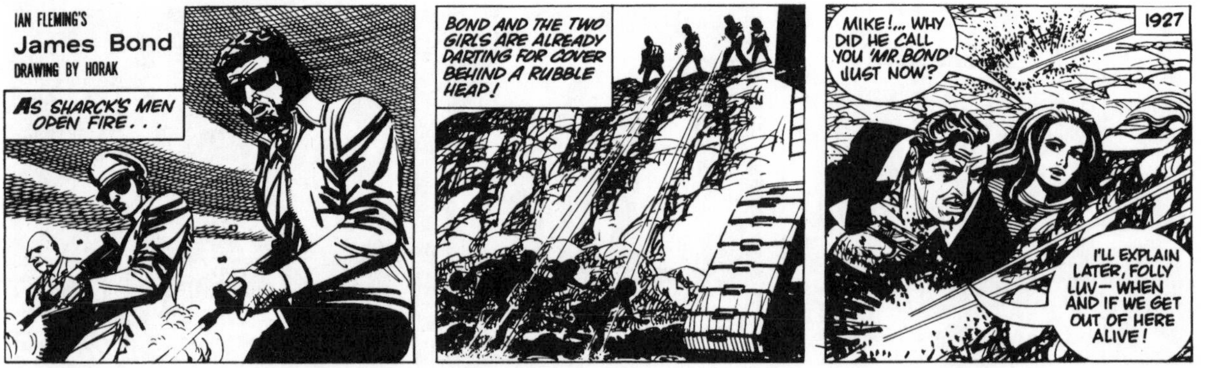
IAN FLEMING'S
James Bond
DRAWING BY HORAK
AS SHARCK'S MEN OPEN FIRE . . .
BOND AND THE TWO GIRLS ARE ALREADY DARTING FOR COVER BEHIND A RUBBLE HEAP!
1927
MIKE!... WHY DID HE CALL YOU 'MR. BOND' JUST NOW?
I'LL EXPLAIN LATER, FOLLY LUV— WHEN AND IF WE GET OUT OF HERE ALIVE!

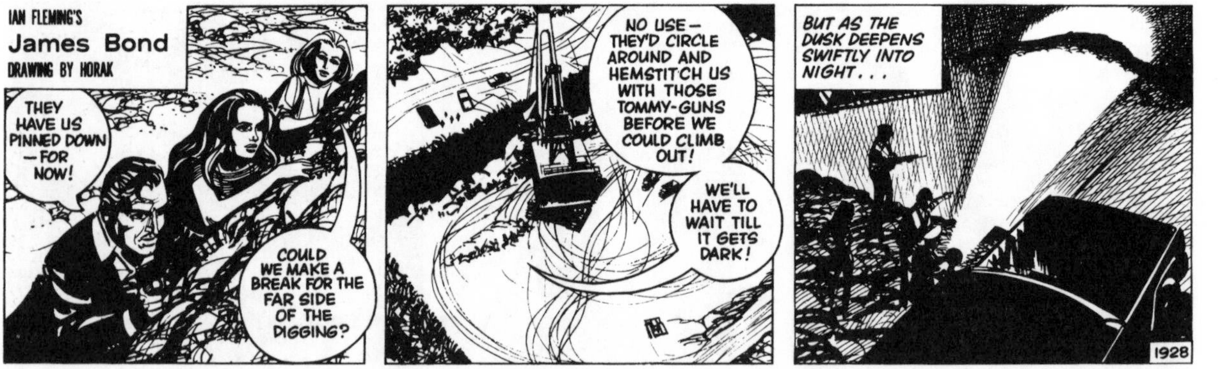
IAN FLEMING'S
James Bond
DRAWING BY HORAK
THEY HAVE US PINNED DOWN —FOR NOW!
COULD WE MAKE A BREAK FOR THE FAR SIDE OF THE DIGGING?
NO USE— THEY'D CIRCLE AROUND AND HEMSTITCH US WITH THOSE TOMMY-GUNS BEFORE WE COULD CLIMB OUT!
WE'LL HAVE TO WAIT TILL IT GETS DARK!
BUT AS THE DUSK DEEPENS SWIFTLY INTO NIGHT . . .
1928

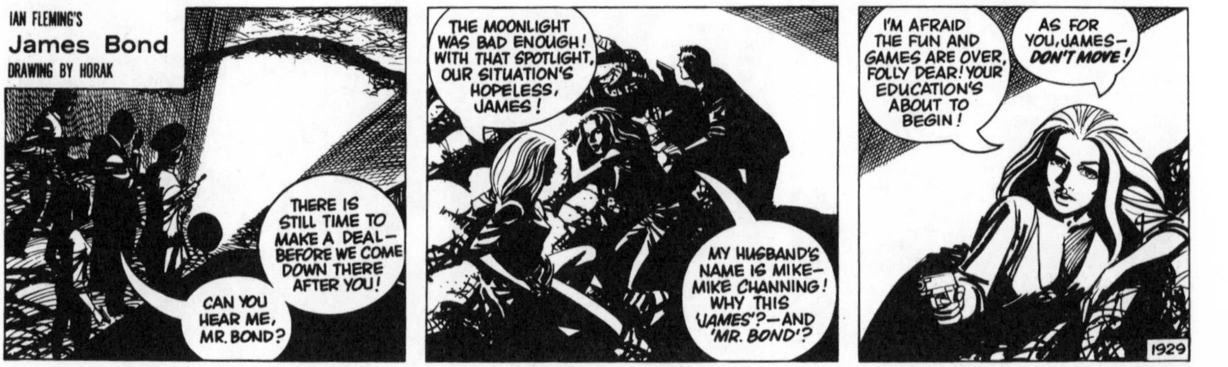
IAN FLEMING'S
James Bond
DRAWING BY HORAK
THERE IS STILL TIME TO MAKE A DEAL— BEFORE WE COME DOWN THERE AFTER YOU!
CAN YOU HEAR ME, MR. BOND?
THE MOONLIGHT WAS BAD ENOUGH! WITH THAT SPOTLIGHT, OUR SITUATION'S HOPELESS, JAMES!
MY HUSBAND'S NAME IS MIKE— MIKE CHANNING! WHY THIS 'JAMES'?—AND 'MR. BOND'?
I'M AFRAID THE FUN AND GAMES ARE OVER, FOLLY DEAR! YOUR EDUCATION'S ABOUT TO BEGIN!
AS FOR YOU, JAMES— DON'T MOVE!
1929

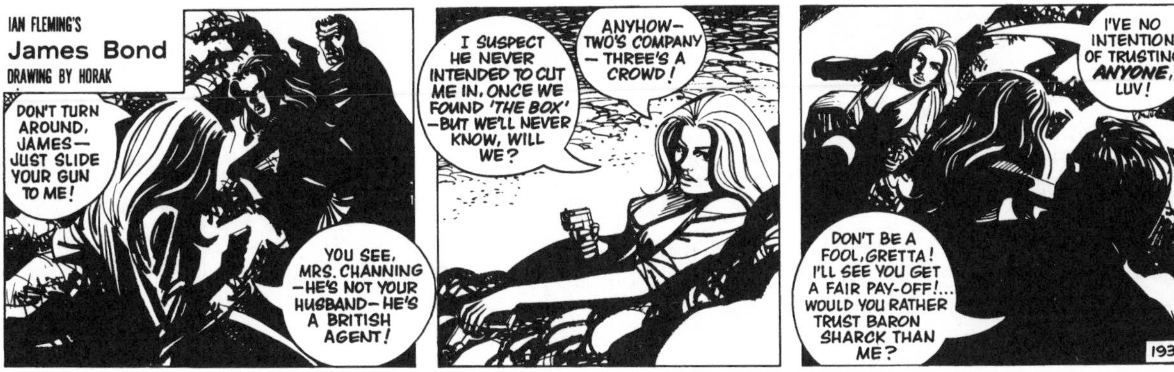
IAN FLEMING'S
James Bond
DRAWING BY HORAK
DON'T TURN AROUND, JAMES— JUST SLIDE YOUR GUN TO ME!
YOU SEE, MRS. CHANNING —HE'S NOT YOUR HUSBAND—HE'S A BRITISH AGENT!
I SUSPECT HE NEVER INTENDED TO CUT ME IN. ONCE WE FOUND 'THE BOX' —BUT WE'LL NEVER KNOW, WILL WE?
ANYHOW— TWO'S COMPANY —THREE'S A CROWD!
I'VE NO INTENTION OF TRUSTING ANYONE, LUV!
DON'T BE A FOOL, GRETTA! I'LL SEE YOU GET A FAIR PAY-OFF!... WOULD YOU RATHER TRUST BARON SHARCK THAN ME?
1930

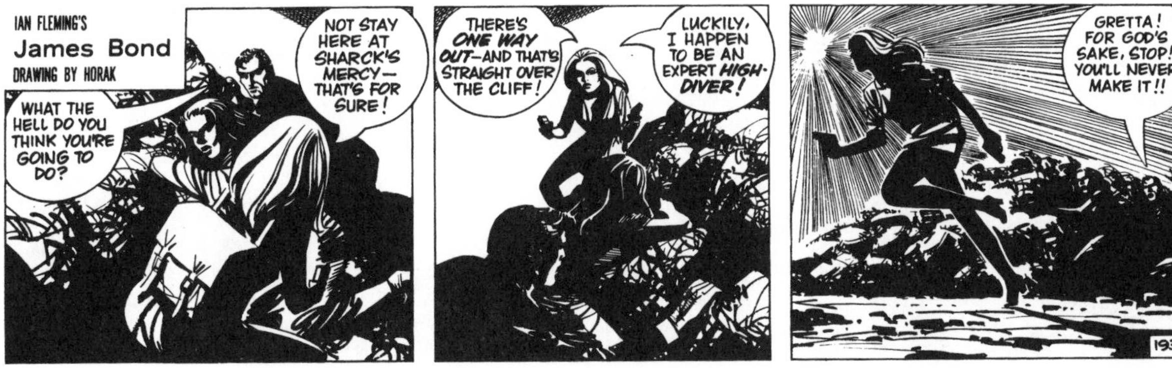
IAN FLEMING'S
James Bond
DRAWING BY HORAK
WHAT THE HELL DO YOU THINK YOU'RE GOING TO DO?
NOT STAY HERE AT SHARCK'S MERCY— THAT'S FOR SURE!
THERE'S ONE WAY OUT—AND THAT'S STRAIGHT OVER THE CLIFF!
LUCKILY, I HAPPEN TO BE AN EXPERT HIGH-DIVER!
GRETTA! FOR GOD'S SAKE, STOP!... YOU'LL NEVER MAKE IT!!
1931

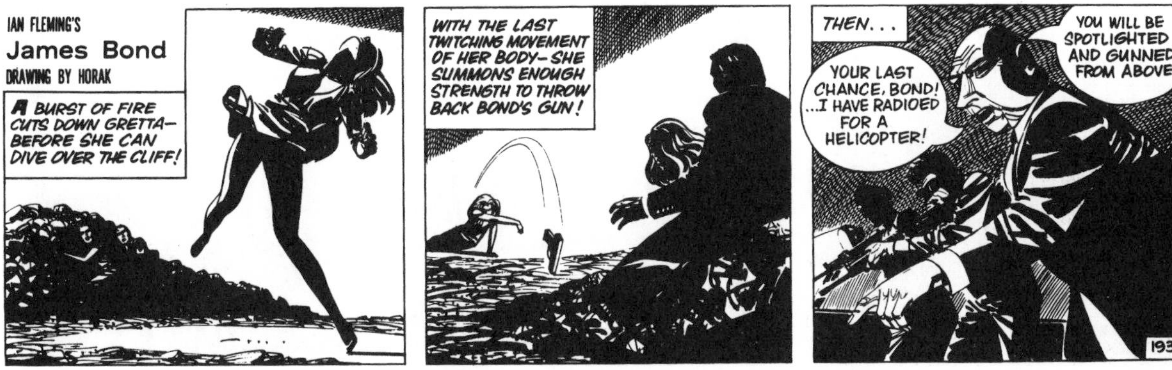
IAN FLEMING'S
James Bond
DRAWING BY HORAK
A BURST OF FIRE CUTS DOWN GRETTA— BEFORE SHE CAN DIVE OVER THE CLIFF!
WITH THE LAST TWITCHING MOVEMENT OF HER BODY—SHE SUMMONS ENOUGH STRENGTH TO THROW BACK BOND'S GUN!
THEN...
YOUR LAST CHANCE, BOND! ...I HAVE RADIOED FOR A HELICOPTER!
YOU WILL BE SPOTLIGHTED AND GUNNED FROM ABOVE!
1932

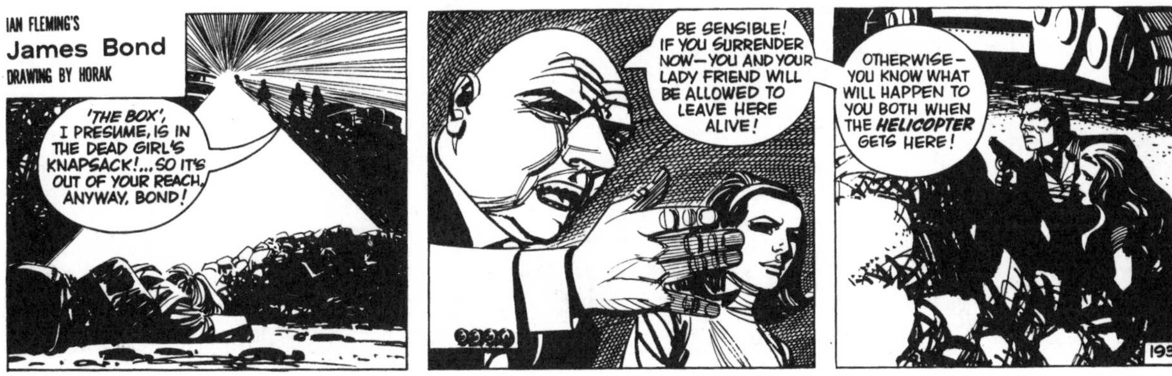
IAN FLEMING'S
James Bond
DRAWING BY HORAK
'THE BOX', I PRESUME, IS IN THE DEAD GIRL'S KNAPSACK!... SO IT'S OUT OF YOUR REACH, ANYWAY, BOND!
BE SENSIBLE! IF YOU SURRENDER NOW—YOU AND YOUR LADY FRIEND WILL BE ALLOWED TO LEAVE HERE ALIVE!
OTHERWISE— YOU KNOW WHAT WILL HAPPEN TO YOU BOTH WHEN THE HELICOPTER GETS HERE!
1933

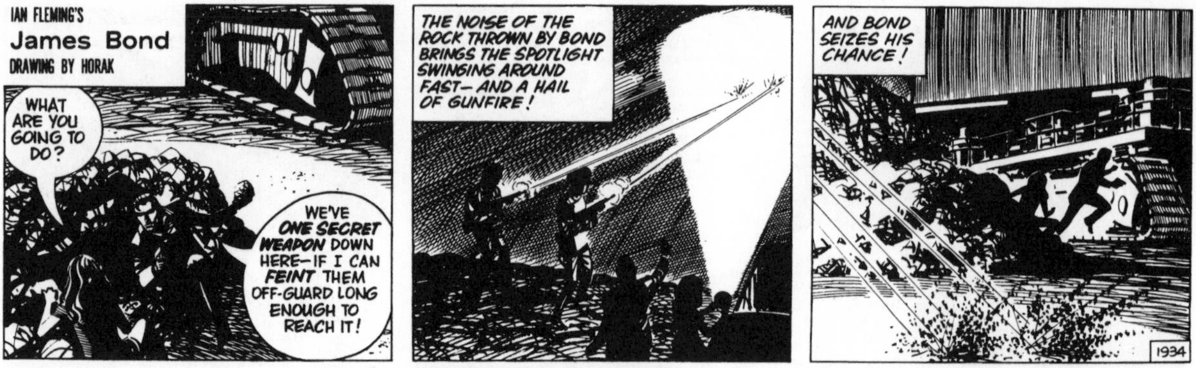
IAN FLEMING'S
James Bond
DRAWING BY HORAK
WHAT ARE YOU GOING TO DO?
WE'VE ONE SECRET WEAPON DOWN HERE— IF I CAN FEINT THEM OFF-GUARD LONG ENOUGH TO REACH IT!
THE NOISE OF THE ROCK THROWN BY BOND BRINGS THE SPOTLIGHT SWINGING AROUND FAST— AND A HAIL OF GUNFIRE!
AND BOND SEIZES HIS CHANCE!
1934

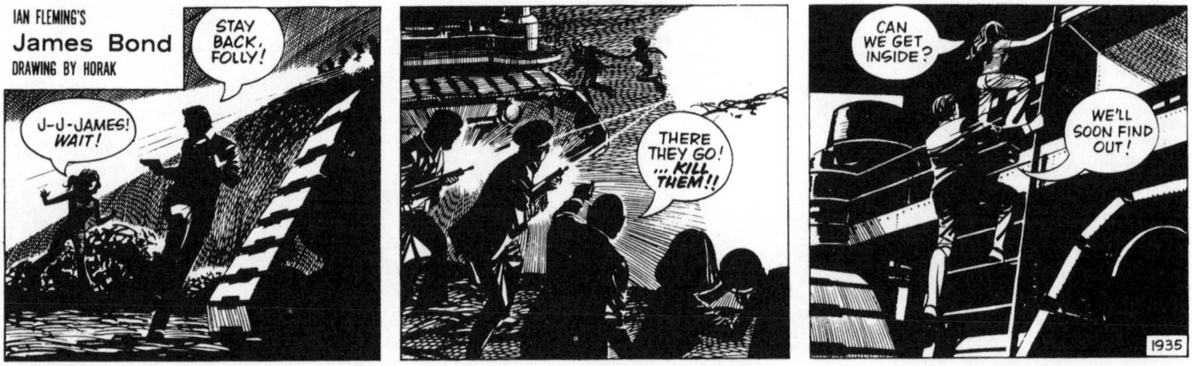
IAN FLEMING'S
James Bond
DRAWING BY HORAK
STAY BACK, FOLLY!
J-J-JAMES! WAIT!
THERE THEY GO! ...KILL THEM!!
CAN WE GET INSIDE?
WE'LL SOON FIND OUT!
1935

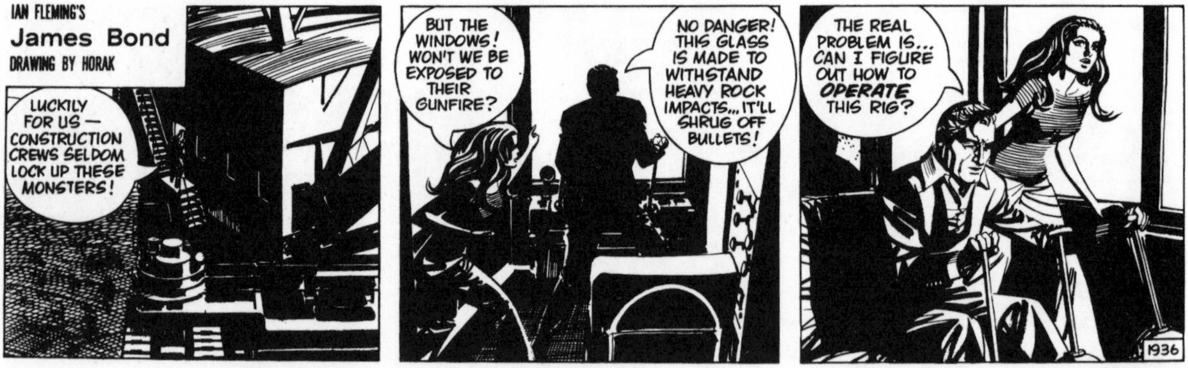
IAN FLEMING'S
James Bond
DRAWING BY HORAK
LUCKILY FOR US — CONSTRUCTION CREWS SELDOM LOCK UP THESE MONSTERS!
BUT THE WINDOWS! WON'T WE BE EXPOSED TO THEIR GUNFIRE?
NO DANGER! THIS GLASS IS MADE TO WITHSTAND HEAVY ROCK IMPACTS... IT'LL SHRUG OFF BULLETS!
THE REAL PROBLEM IS... CAN I FIGURE OUT HOW TO OPERATE THIS RIG?
1936

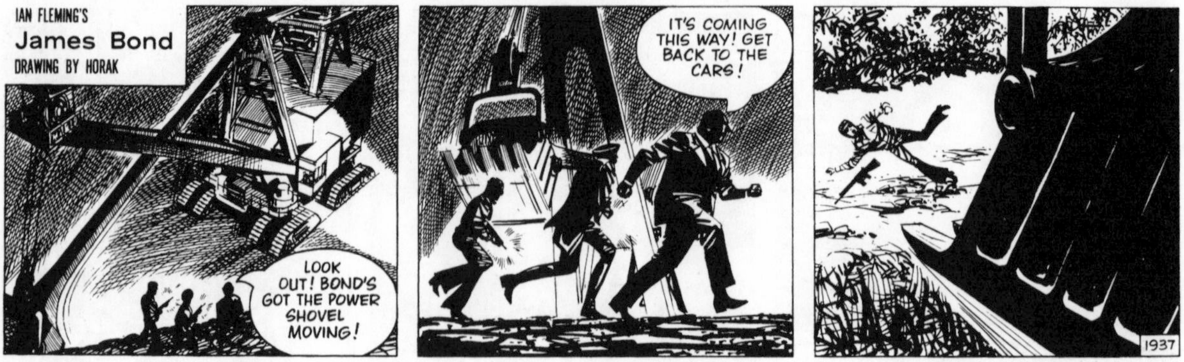
IAN FLEMING'S
James Bond
DRAWING BY HORAK
LOOK OUT! BOND'S GOT THE POWER SHOVEL MOVING!
IT'S COMING THIS WAY! GET BACK TO THE CARS!
1937

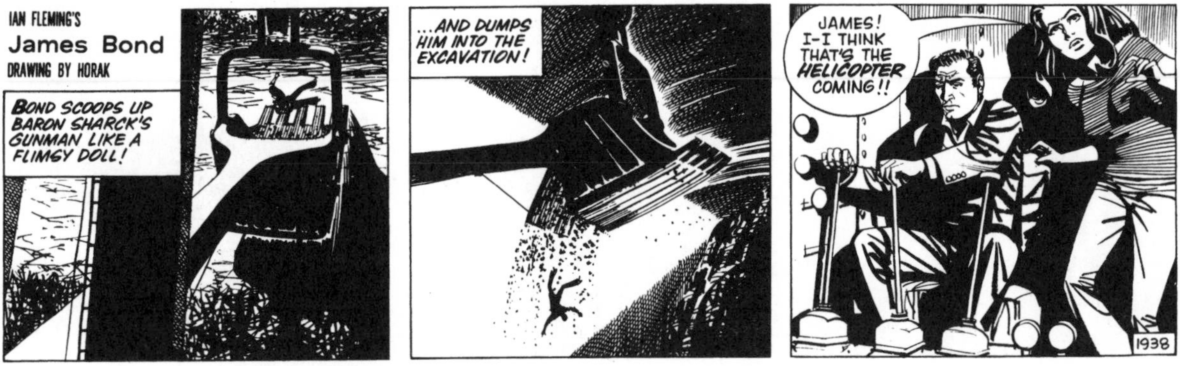
IAN FLEMING'S
James Bond
DRAWING BY HORAK
BOND SCOOPS UP BARON SHARCK'S GUNMAN LIKE A FLIMGY DOLL!
...AND DUMPS HIM INTO THE EXCAVATION!
JAMES! I-I THINK THAT'S THE HELICOPTER COMING!!
1938

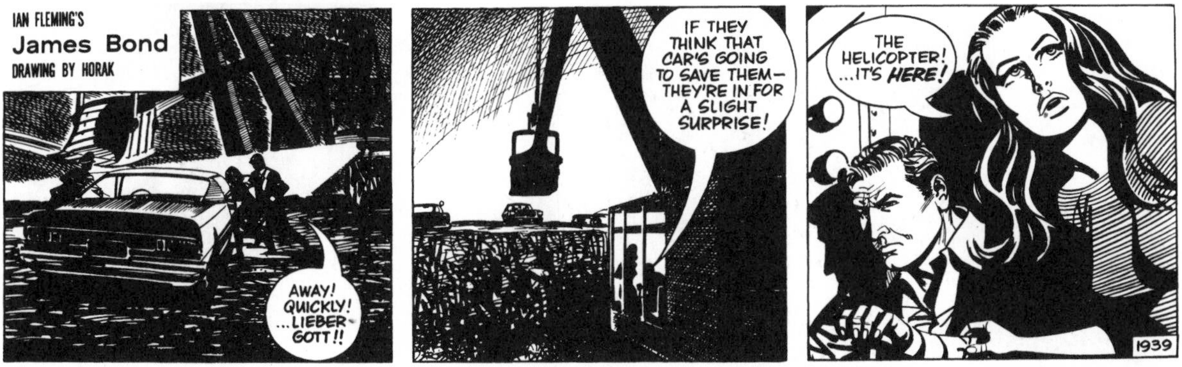
IAN FLEMING'S
James Bond
DRAWING BY HORAK
AWAY! QUICKLY! ...LIEBER GOTT!!
IF THEY THINK THAT CAR'S GOING TO SAVE THEM— THEY'RE IN FOR A SLIGHT SURPRISE!
THE HELICOPTER! ...IT'S HERE!
1939

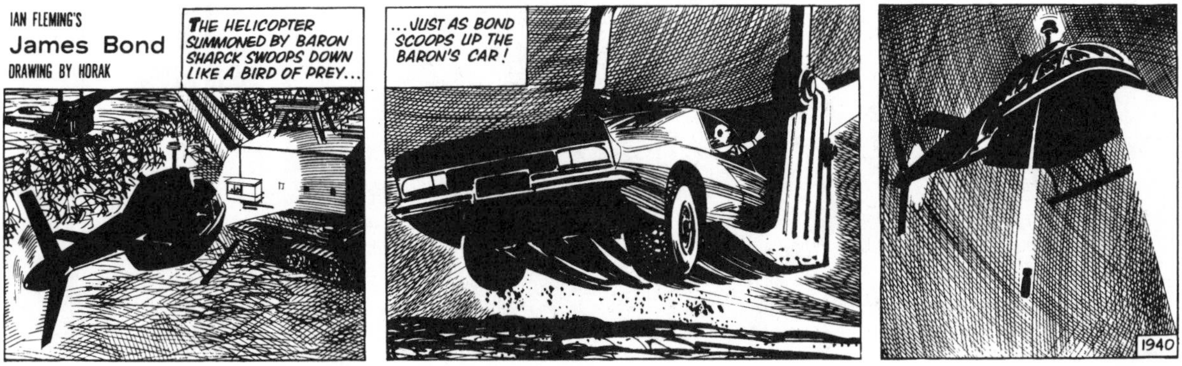
IAN FLEMING'S
James Bond
DRAWING BY HORAK
THE HELICOPTER SUMMONED BY BARON SHARCK SWOOPS DOWN LIKE A BIRD OF PREY...
...JUST AS BOND SCOOPS UP THE BARON'S CAR!
1940

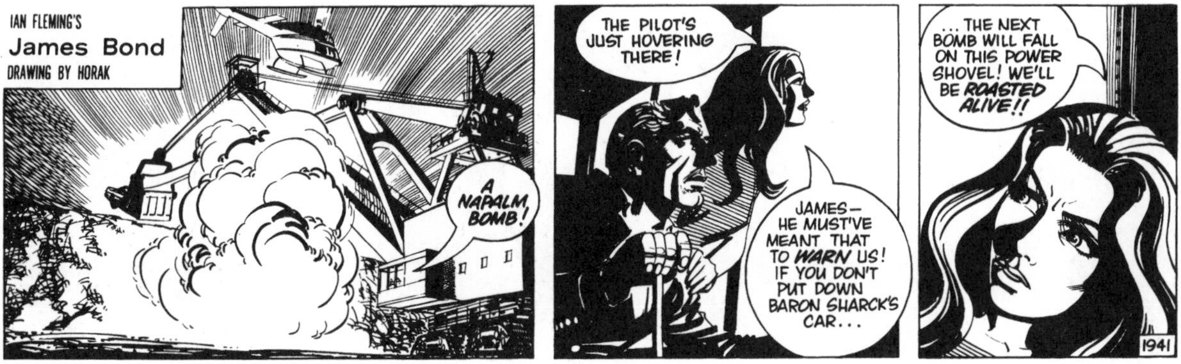
IAN FLEMING'S
James Bond
DRAWING BY HORAK
A NAPALM BOMB!
THE PILOT'S JUST HOVERING THERE!
JAMES— HE MUST'VE MEANT THAT TO WARN US! IF YOU DON'T PUT DOWN BARON SHARCK'S CAR...
... THE NEXT BOMB WILL FALL ON THIS POWER SHOVEL! WE'LL BE ROASTED ALIVE!!
1941

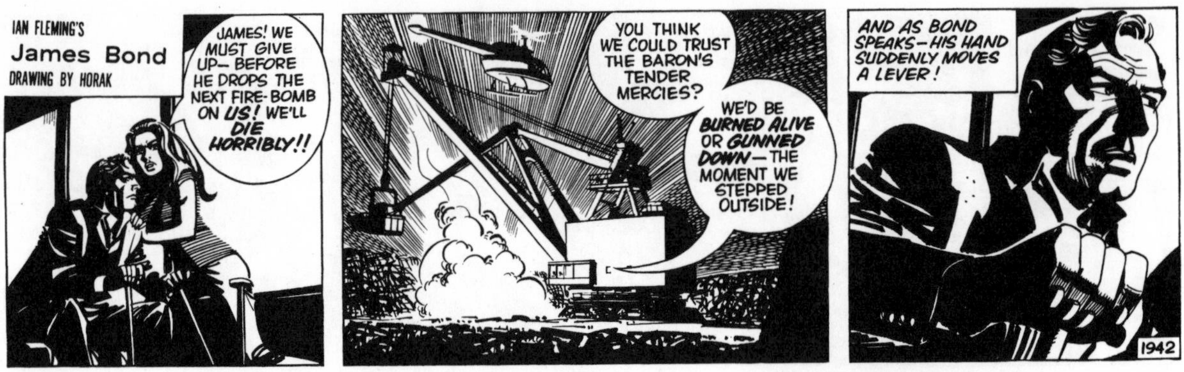
IAN FLEMING'S
James Bond
DRAWING BY HORAK
JAMES! WE MUST GIVE UP– BEFORE HE DROPS THE NEXT FIRE-BOMB ON US! WE'LL DIE HORRIBLY!!
YOU THINK WE COULD TRUST THE BARON'S TENDER MERCIES?
WE'D BE BURNED ALIVE OR GUNNED DOWN– THE MOMENT WE STEPPED OUTSIDE!
AND AS BOND SPEAKS– HIS HAND SUDDENLY MOVES A LEVER!
1942

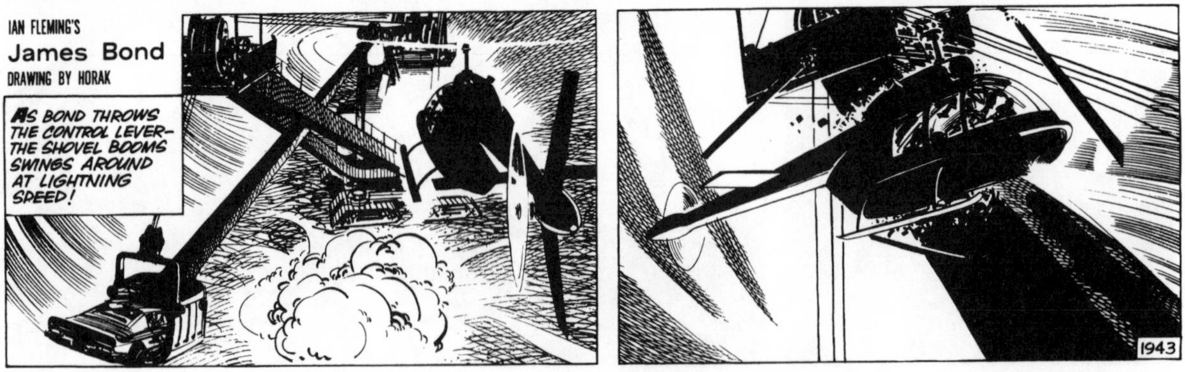
IAN FLEMING'S
James Bond
DRAWING BY HORAK
AS BOND THROWS THE CONTROL LEVER– THE SHOVEL BOOMS SWINGS AROUND AT LIGHTNING SPEED!
1943

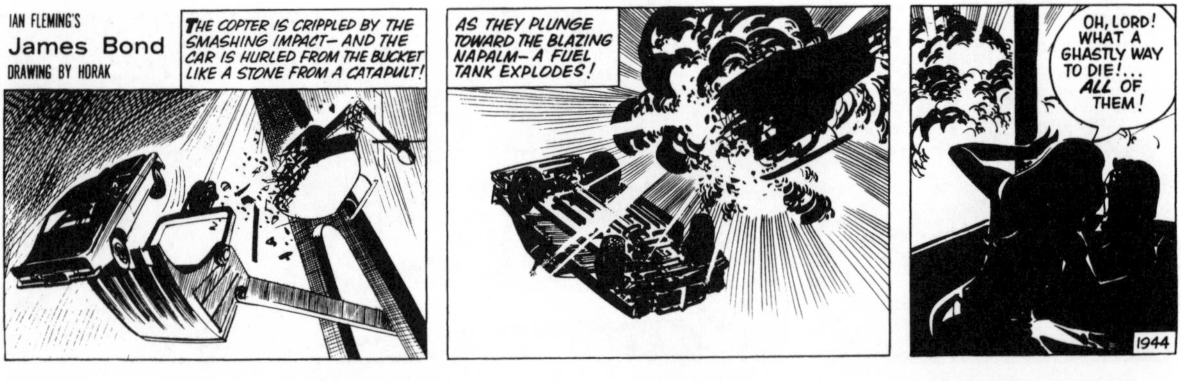
IAN FLEMING'S
James Bond
DRAWING BY HORAK
THE COPTER IS CRIPPLED BY THE SMASHING IMPACT– AND THE CAR IS HURLED FROM THE BUCKET LIKE A STONE FROM A CATAPULT!
AS THEY PLUNGE TOWARD THE BLAZING NAPALM– A FUEL TANK EXPLODES!
OH, LORD! WHAT A GHASTLY WAY TO DIE!... ALL OF THEM!
1944

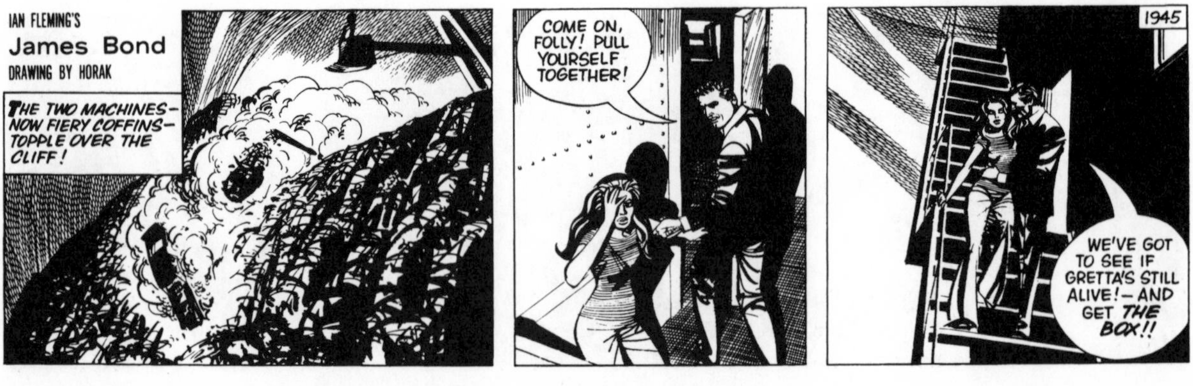
IAN FLEMING'S
James Bond
DRAWING BY HORAK
THE TWO MACHINES– NOW FIERY COFFINS– TOPPLE OVER THE CLIFF!
COME ON, FOLLY! PULL YOURSELF TOGETHER!
1945
WE'VE GOT TO SEE IF GRETTA'S STILL ALIVE!– AND GET THE BOX!!

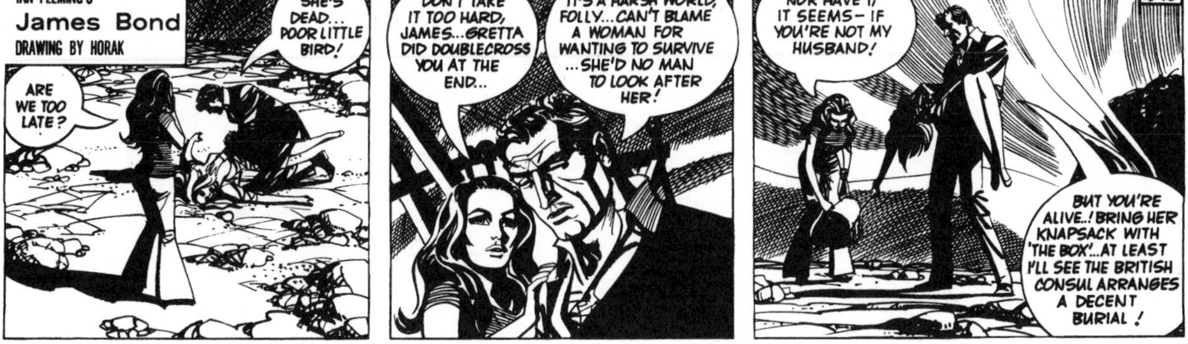
IAN FLEMING'S
James Bond
DRAWING BY HORAK
ARE WE TOO LATE?
SHE'S DEAD... POOR LITTLE BIRD!
DON'T TAKE IT TOO HARD, JAMES...GRETTA DID DOUBLECROSS YOU AT THE END...
IT'S A HARSH WORLD, FOLLY...CAN'T BLAME A WOMAN FOR WANTING TO SURVIVE ...SHE'D NO MAN TO LOOK AFTER HER!
NOR HAVE I, IT SEEMS– IF YOU'RE NOT MY HUSBAND!
BUT YOU'RE ALIVE..! BRING HER KNAPSACK WITH 'THE BOX'...AT LEAST I'LL SEE THE BRITISH CONSUL ARRANGES A DECENT BURIAL!
1946

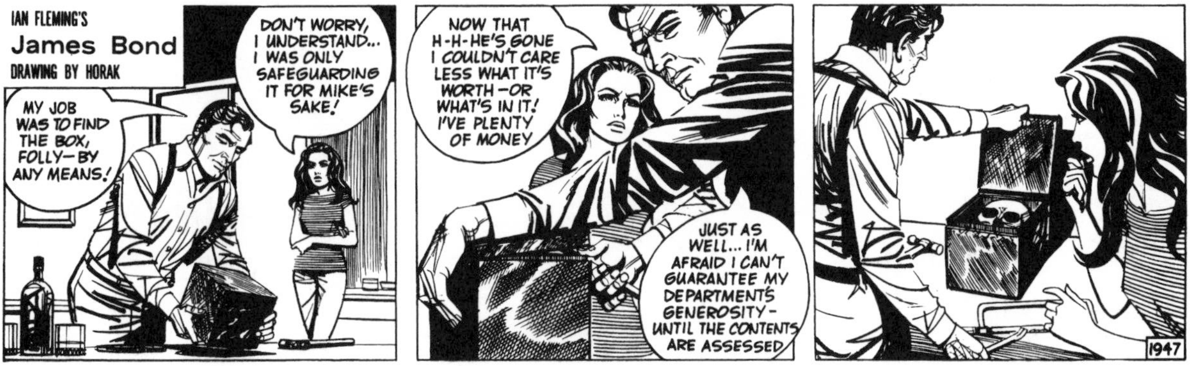
IAN FLEMING'S
James Bond
DRAWING BY HORAK
MY JOB WAS TO FIND THE BOX, FOLLY– BY ANY MEANS!
DON'T WORRY, I UNDERSTAND... I WAS ONLY SAFEGUARDING IT FOR MIKE'S SAKE!
NOW THAT H-H-HE'S GONE I COULDN'T CARE LESS WHAT IT'S WORTH –OR WHAT'S IN IT! I'VE PLENTY OF MONEY
JUST AS WELL... I'M AFRAID I CAN'T GUARANTEE MY DEPARTMENT'S GENEROSITY– UNTIL THE CONTENTS ARE ASSESSED
1947

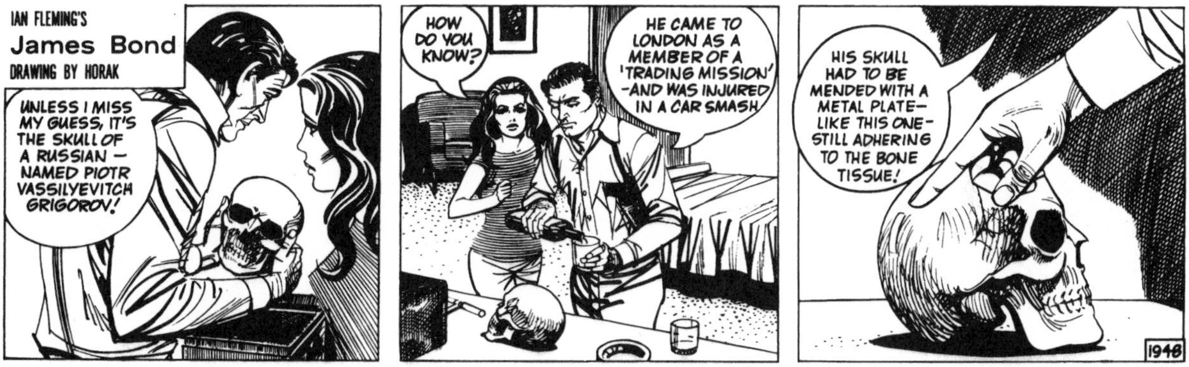
IAN FLEMING'S
James Bond
DRAWING BY HORAK
UNLESS I MISS MY GUESS, IT'S THE SKULL OF A RUSSIAN – NAMED PIOTR VASSILYEVITCH GRIGOROV!
HOW DO YOU KNOW?
HE CAME TO LONDON AS A MEMBER OF A 'TRADING MISSION' -AND WAS INJURED IN A CAR SMASH
HIS SKULL HAD TO BE MENDED WITH A METAL PLATE– LIKE THIS ONE– STILL ADHERING TO THE BONE TISSUE!
1948

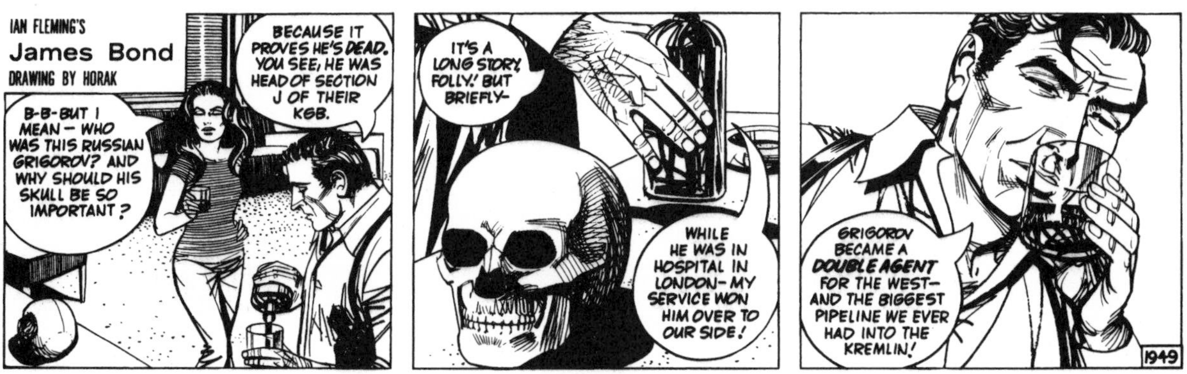
IAN FLEMING'S
James Bond
DRAWING BY HORAK
B-B-BUT I MEAN – WHO WAS THIS RUSSIAN GRIGOROV? AND WHY SHOULD HIS SKULL BE SO IMPORTANT?
BECAUSE IT PROVES HE'S DEAD. YOU SEE, HE WAS HEAD OF SECTION J OF THEIR KGB.
IT'S A LONG STORY, FOLLY! BUT BRIEFLY–
WHILE HE WAS IN HOSPITAL IN LONDON– MY SERVICE WON HIM OVER TO OUR SIDE!
GRIGOROV BECAME A DOUBLE AGENT FOR THE WEST– AND THE BIGGEST PIPELINE WE EVER HAD INTO THE KREMLIN!
1949

IAN FLEMING'S
James Bond
DRAWING BY HORAK
FOR TWO YEARS, OUR ALLIED SERVICES SUSPECTED THAT GRIGOROV MIGHT'VE BEEN RUMBLED—BUT WE COULDN'T BE SURE
AGENTS' LIVES—AND MAJOR POLITICAL MOVES—HAD TO BE STAKED ON THE INFORMATION HE WAS FEEDING US!
—YET WE'D NO CLUE TO WHETHER THE REAL GRIGOROV HAD BEEN REMOVED FROM SECTION J OR EXECUTED
WELL... NOW WE KNOW!
1950

IAN FLEMING'S
James Bond
DRAWING BY HORAK
IT'S GRIGOROV, ALL RIGHT, SIR! THE SKULL-TREPHINING DETAILS CHECK OUT PRECISELY—AND SO DO THE DENTAL X-RAYS
Q.E.D. EH? SO IT APPEARS 007 HAS EARNED HIS TWO WEEKS OF LEAVE IN THE STATES!
THIS SEEMS VERY REAL TO ME, FOLLY!
I KNOW OUR 'MARRIAGE' WAS JUST MAKE-BELIEVE, MIKE, ER JAMES! B-B-BUT I DON'T SUPPOSE YOU'D CARE TO MAKE IT REAL!
1951

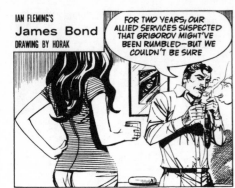

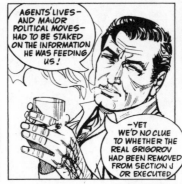

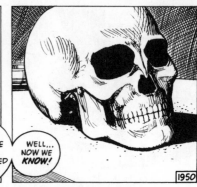

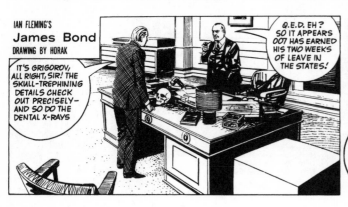

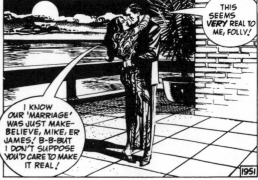

# ISLE OF CONDORS

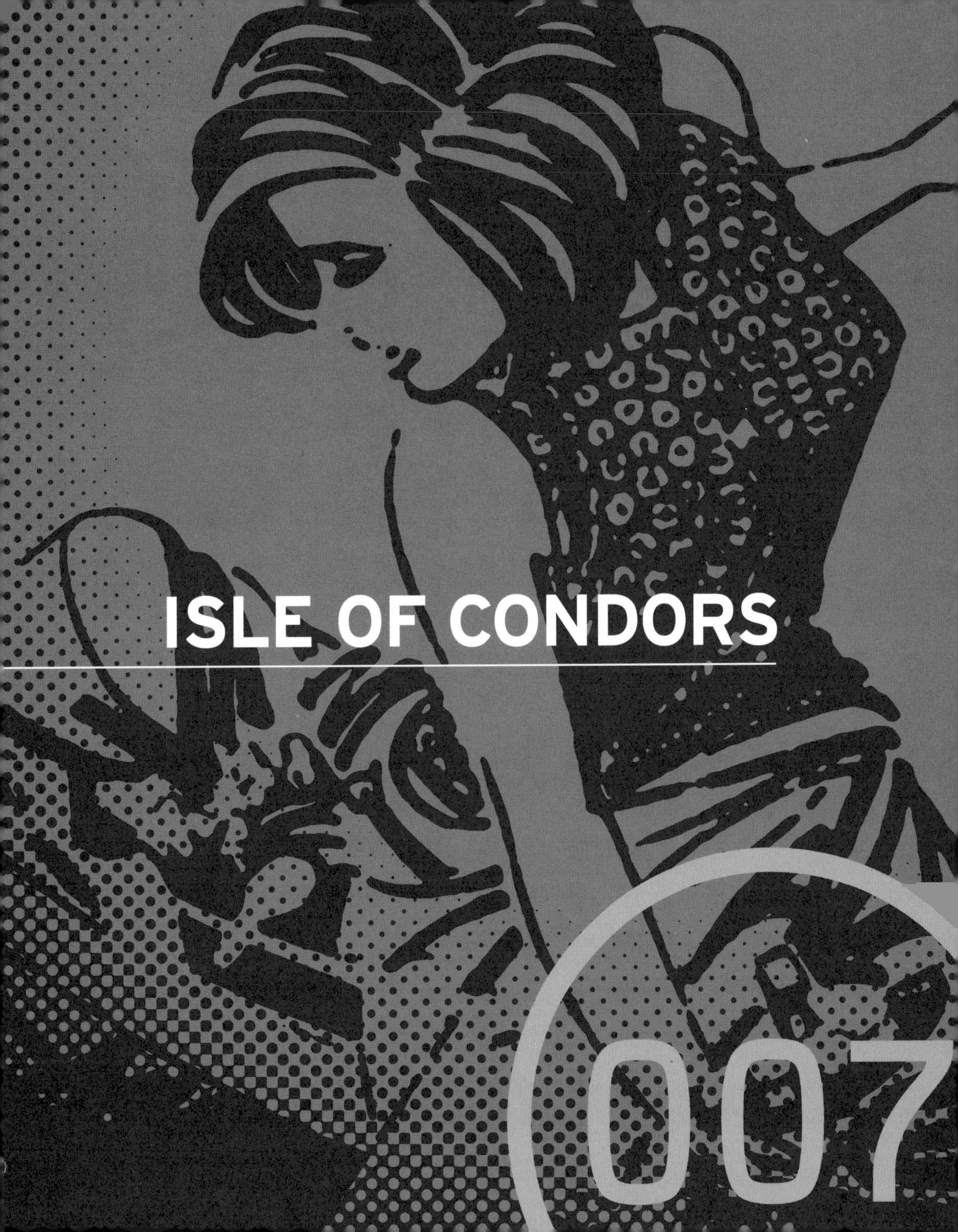
007

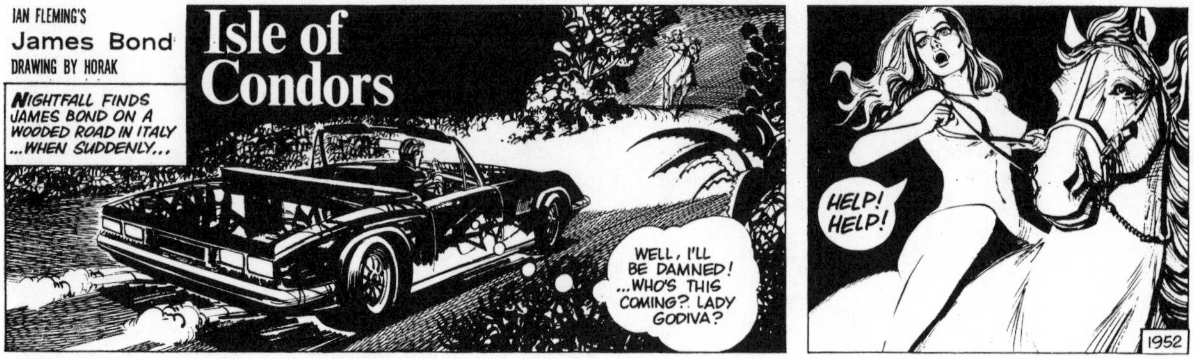
IAN FLEMING'S
James Bond
DRAWING BY HORAK
Isle of Condors
NIGHTFALL FINDS JAMES BOND ON A WOODED ROAD IN ITALY ...WHEN SUDDENLY...
WELL, I'LL BE DAMNED! ...WHO'S THIS COMING?. LADY GODIVA?
HELP! HELP!
1952

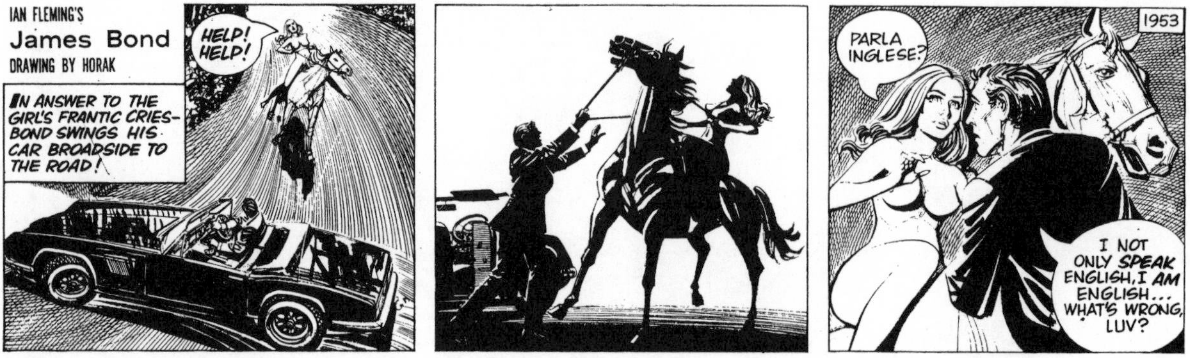
IAN FLEMING'S
James Bond
DRAWING BY HORAK
HELP! HELP!
IN ANSWER TO THE GIRL'S FRANTIC CRIES- BOND SWINGS HIS CAR BROADSIDE TO THE ROAD!
1953
PARLA INGLESE?
I NOT ONLY SPEAK ENGLISH, I AM ENGLISH... WHAT'S WRONG, LUV?

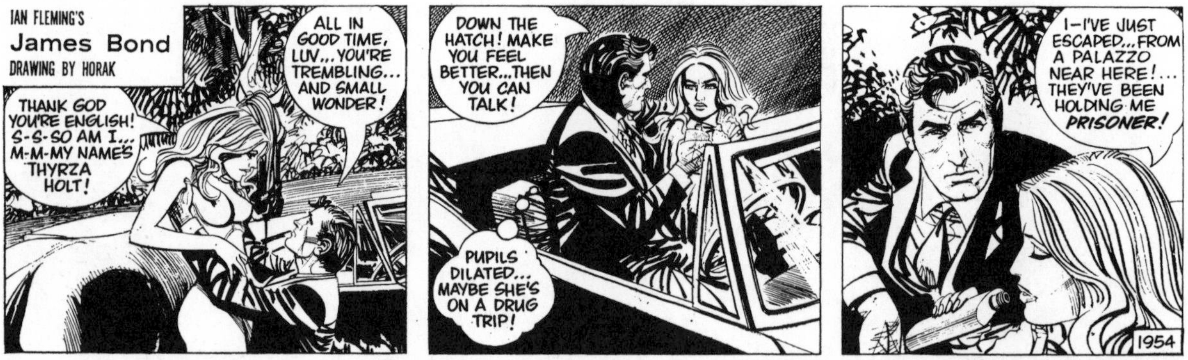
IAN FLEMING'S
James Bond
DRAWING BY HORAK
ALL IN GOOD TIME, LUV... YOU'RE TREMBLING... AND SMALL WONDER!
THANK GOD YOU'RE ENGLISH! S-S-SO AM I... M-M-MY NAME'S THYRZA HOLT!
DOWN THE HATCH! MAKE YOU FEEL BETTER...THEN YOU CAN TALK!
PUPILS DILATED... MAYBE SHE'S ON A DRUG TRIP!
I-I'VE JUST ESCAPED... FROM A PALAZZO NEAR HERE!... THEY'VE BEEN HOLDING ME PRISONER!
1954

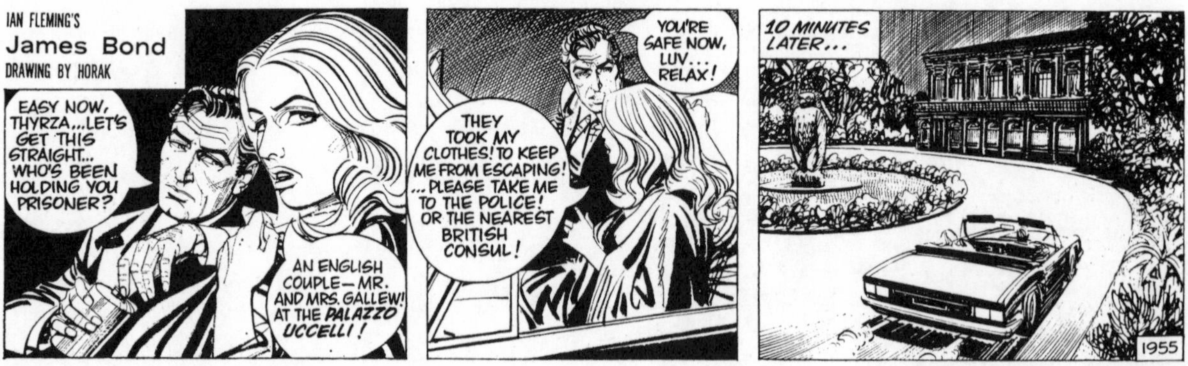
IAN FLEMING'S
James Bond
DRAWING BY HORAK
EASY NOW, THYRZA...LET'S GET THIS STRAIGHT... WHO'S BEEN HOLDING YOU PRISONER?
AN ENGLISH COUPLE—MR. AND MRS. GALLEW! AT THE PALAZZO UCCELLI!
YOU'RE SAFE NOW, LUV... RELAX!
THEY TOOK MY CLOTHES! TO KEEP ME FROM ESCAPING! ...PLEASE TAKE ME TO THE POLICE! OR THE NEAREST BRITISH CONSUL!
10 MINUTES LATER...
1955

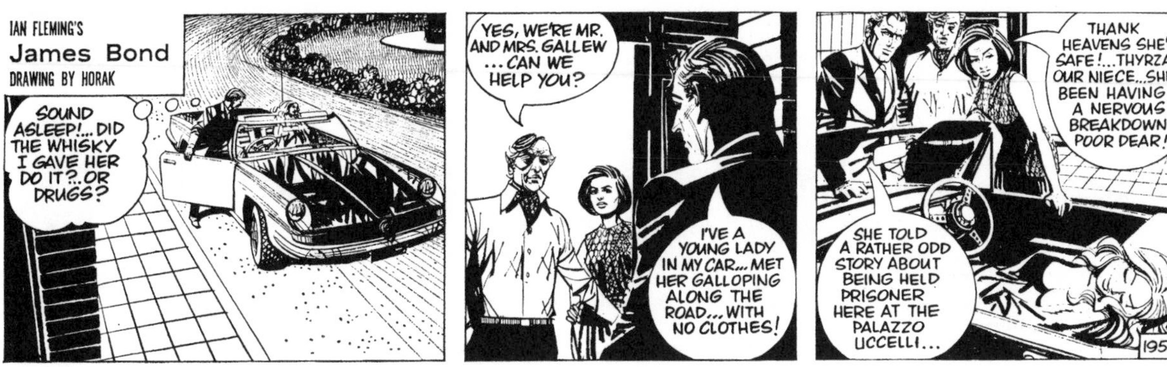
IAN FLEMING'S
James Bond
DRAWING BY HORAK
SOUND ASLEEP!... DID THE WHISKY I GAVE HER DO IT?.. OR DRUGS?
YES, WE'RE MR. AND MRS. GALLEW ... CAN WE HELP YOU?
I'VE A YOUNG LADY IN MY CAR... MET HER GALLOPING ALONG THE ROAD... WITH NO CLOTHES!
THANK HEAVENS SHE'S SAFE!... THYRZA'S OUR NIECE... SHE'S BEEN HAVING A NERVOUS BREAKDOWN, POOR DEAR!
SHE TOLD A RATHER ODD STORY ABOUT BEING HELD PRISONER HERE AT THE PALAZZO UCCELLI...
1956

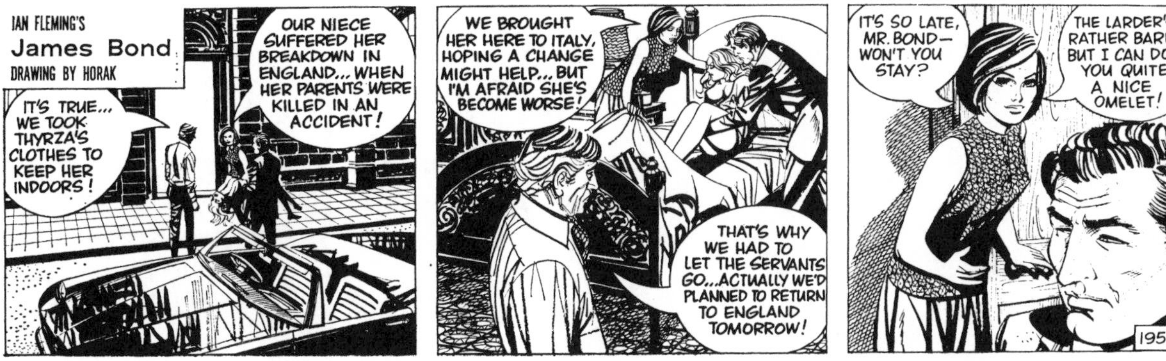
IAN FLEMING'S
James Bond
DRAWING BY HORAK
IT'S TRUE... WE TOOK THYRZA'S CLOTHES TO KEEP HER INDOORS!
OUR NIECE SUFFERED HER BREAKDOWN IN ENGLAND... WHEN HER PARENTS WERE KILLED IN AN ACCIDENT!
WE BROUGHT HER HERE TO ITALY, HOPING A CHANGE MIGHT HELP... BUT I'M AFRAID SHE'S BECOME WORSE!
THAT'S WHY WE HAD TO LET THE SERVANTS GO... ACTUALLY WE'D PLANNED TO RETURN TO ENGLAND TOMORROW!
IT'S SO LATE, MR. BOND— WON'T YOU STAY?
THE LARDER'S RATHER BARE, BUT I CAN DO YOU QUITE A NICE OMELET!
1957

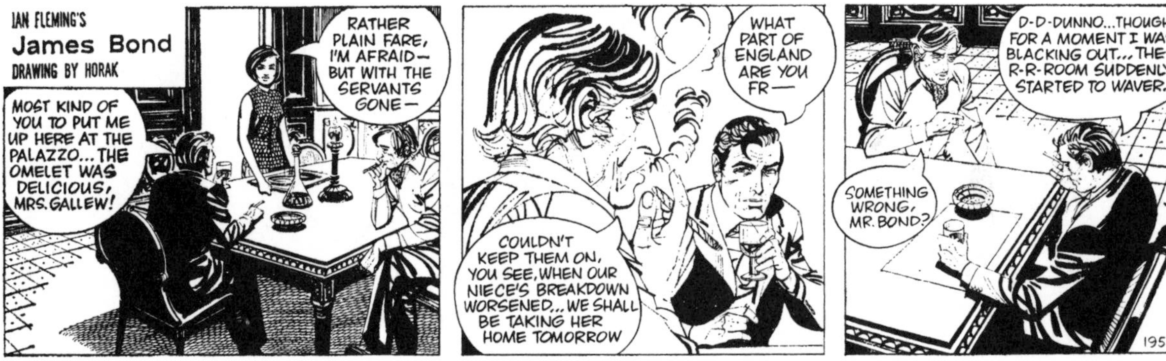
IAN FLEMING'S
James Bond
DRAWING BY HORAK
MOST KIND OF YOU TO PUT ME UP HERE AT THE PALAZZO... THE OMELET WAS DELICIOUS, MRS. GALLEW!
RATHER PLAIN FARE, I'M AFRAID— BUT WITH THE SERVANTS GONE—
COULDN'T KEEP THEM ON, YOU SEE, WHEN OUR NIECE'S BREAKDOWN WORSENED... WE SHALL BE TAKING HER HOME TOMORROW
WHAT PART OF ENGLAND ARE YOU FR—
D-D-DUNNO... THOUGHT FOR A MOMENT I WAS BLACKING OUT... THE R-R-ROOM SUDDENLY STARTED TO WAVER...
SOMETHING WRONG, MR. BOND?
1958

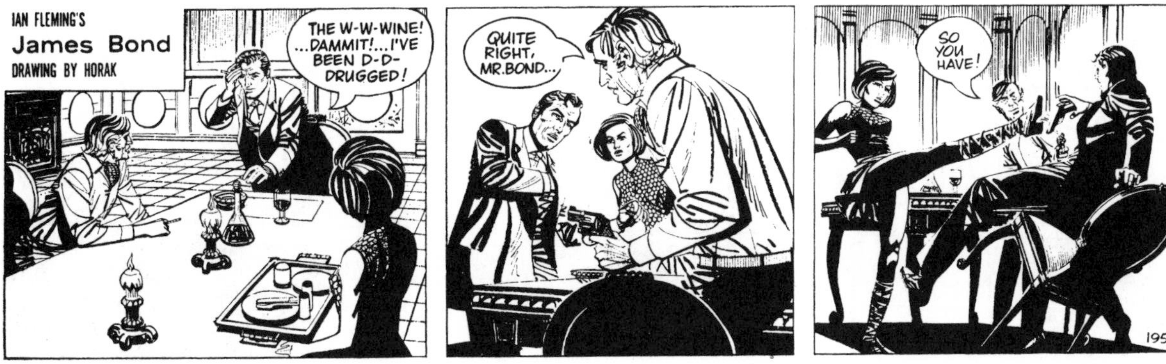
IAN FLEMING'S
James Bond
DRAWING BY HORAK
THE W-W-WINE! ...DAMMIT!... I'VE BEEN D-D-DRUGGED!
QUITE RIGHT, MR. BOND...
SO YOU HAVE!
1959

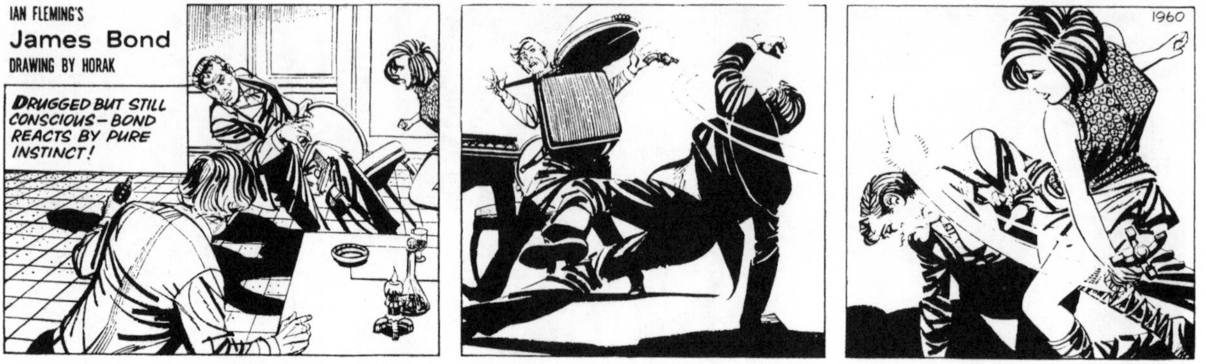
IAN FLEMING'S
James Bond
DRAWING BY HORAK
DRUGGED BUT STILL CONSCIOUS—BOND REACTS BY PURE INSTINCT!
1960

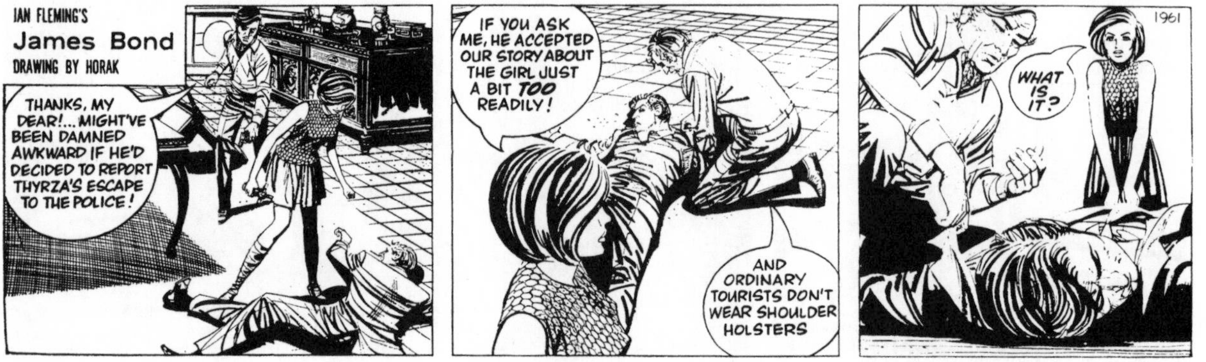
IAN FLEMING'S
James Bond
DRAWING BY HORAK
THANKS, MY DEAR!... MIGHT'VE BEEN DAMNED AWKWARD IF HE'D DECIDED TO REPORT THYRZA'S ESCAPE TO THE POLICE!
IF YOU ASK ME, HE ACCEPTED OUR STORY ABOUT THE GIRL JUST A BIT TOO READILY!
AND ORDINARY TOURISTS DON'T WEAR SHOULDER HOLSTERS
WHAT IS IT?
1961

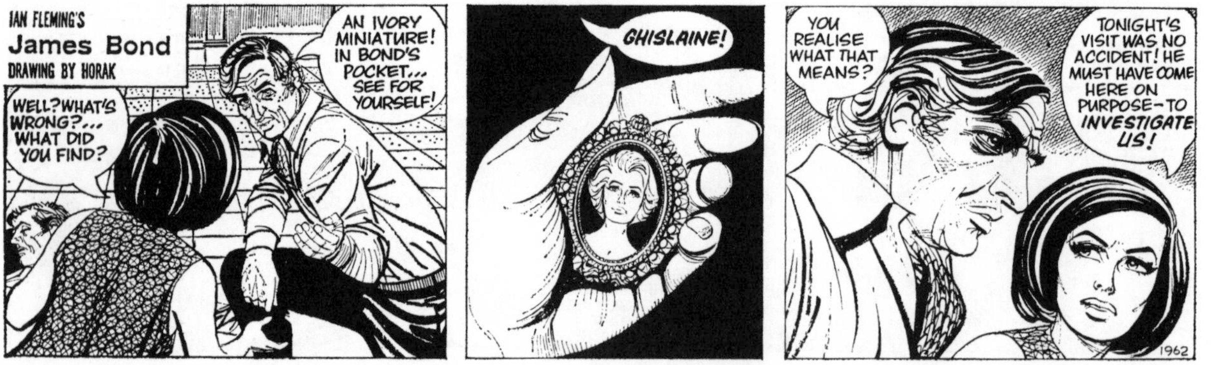
IAN FLEMING'S
James Bond
DRAWING BY HORAK
WELL? WHAT'S WRONG?... WHAT DID YOU FIND?
AN IVORY MINIATURE! IN BOND'S POCKET... SEE FOR YOURSELF!
GHISLAINE!
YOU REALISE WHAT THAT MEANS?
TONIGHT'S VISIT WAS NO ACCIDENT! HE MUST HAVE COME HERE ON PURPOSE—TO INVESTIGATE US!
1962

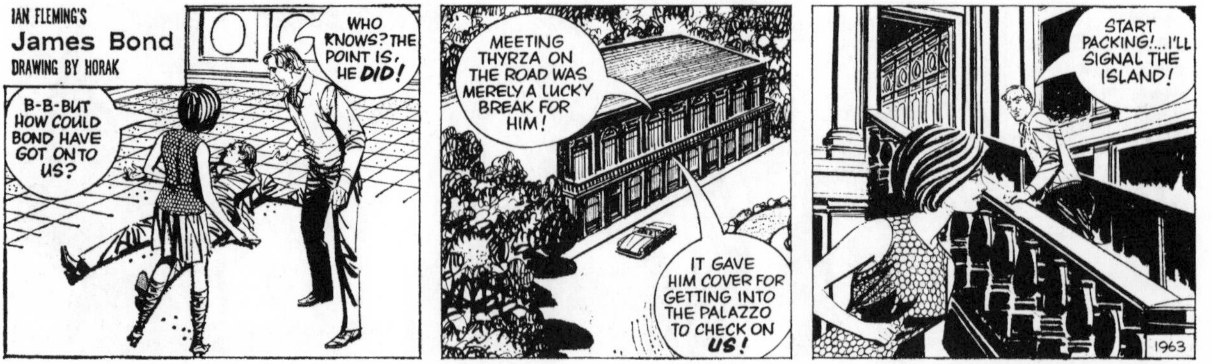
IAN FLEMING'S
James Bond
DRAWING BY HORAK
B-B-BUT HOW COULD BOND HAVE GOT ON TO US?
WHO KNOWS? THE POINT IS, HE DID!
MEETING THYRZA ON THE ROAD WAS MERELY A LUCKY BREAK FOR HIM!
IT GAVE HIM COVER FOR GETTING INTO THE PALAZZO TO CHECK ON US!
START PACKING!... I'LL SIGNAL THE ISLAND!
1963

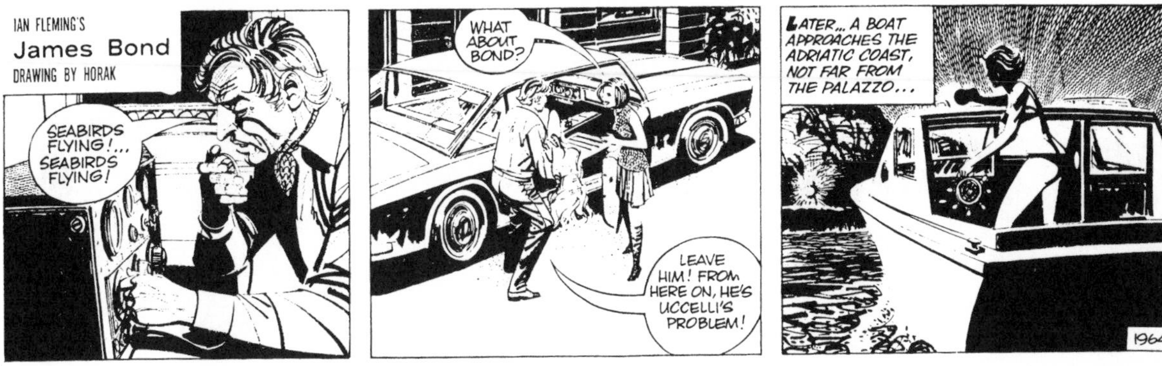
IAN FLEMING'S
James Bond
DRAWING BY HORAK
SEABIRDS FLYING!... SEABIRDS FLYING!
WHAT ABOUT BOND?
LEAVE HIM! FROM HERE ON, HE'S UCCELLI'S PROBLEM!
LATER... A BOAT APPROACHES THE ADRIATIC COAST, NOT FAR FROM THE PALAZZO...
1964

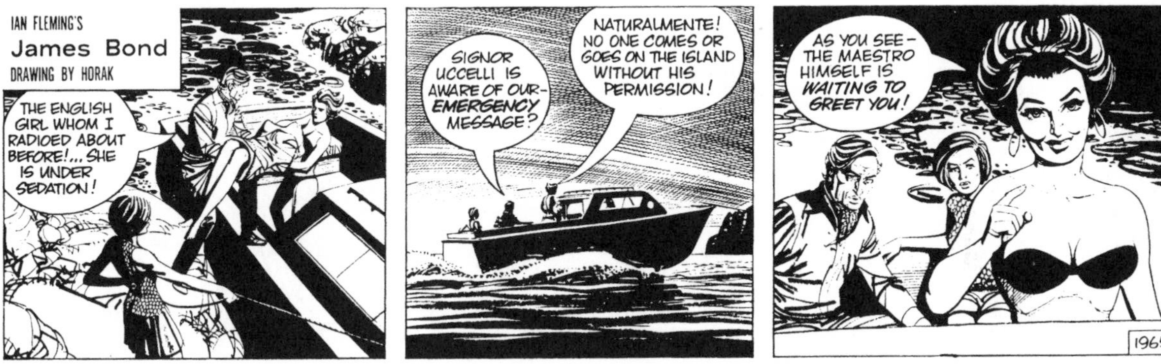
IAN FLEMING'S
James Bond
DRAWING BY HORAK
THE ENGLISH GIRL WHOM I RADIOED ABOUT BEFORE!... SHE IS UNDER SEDATION!
SIGNOR UCCELLI IS AWARE OF OUR EMERGENCY MESSAGE?
NATURALMENTE! NO ONE COMES OR GOES ON THE ISLAND WITHOUT HIS PERMISSION!
AS YOU SEE— THE MAESTRO HIMSELF IS WAITING TO GREET YOU!
1965

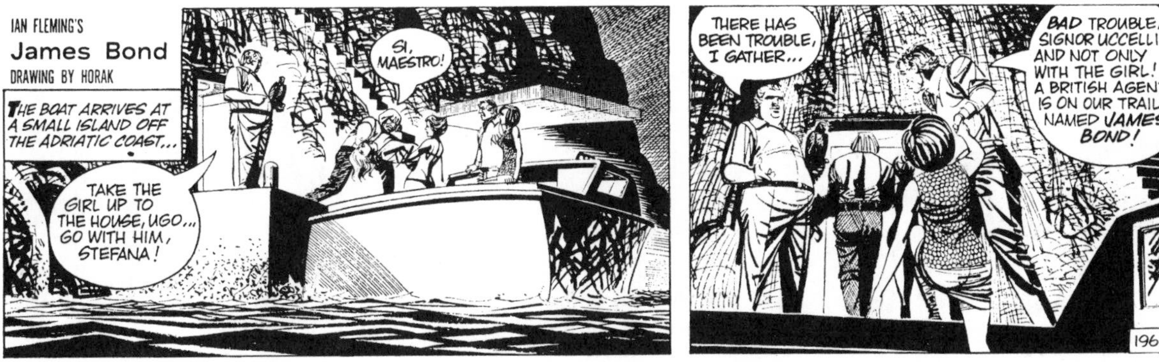
IAN FLEMING'S
James Bond
DRAWING BY HORAK
THE BOAT ARRIVES AT A SMALL ISLAND OFF THE ADRIATIC COAST...
SI, MAESTRO!
TAKE THE GIRL UP TO THE HOUSE, UGO... GO WITH HIM, STEFANA!
THERE HAS BEEN TROUBLE, I GATHER...
BAD TROUBLE, SIGNOR UCCELLI— AND NOT ONLY WITH THE GIRL! A BRITISH AGENT IS ON OUR TRAIL— NAMED JAMES BOND!
1966

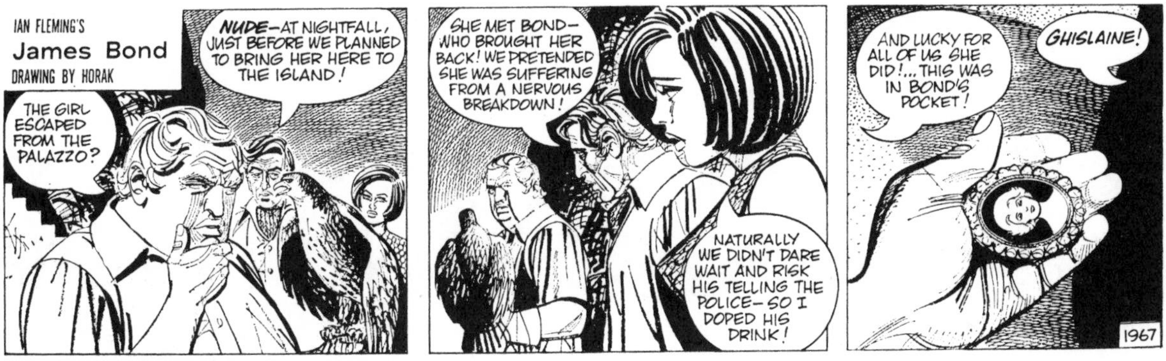
IAN FLEMING'S
James Bond
DRAWING BY HORAK
THE GIRL ESCAPED FROM THE PALAZZO?
NUDE—AT NIGHTFALL, JUST BEFORE WE PLANNED TO BRING HER HERE TO THE ISLAND!
SHE MET BOND— WHO BROUGHT HER BACK! WE PRETENDED SHE WAS SUFFERING FROM A NERVOUS BREAKDOWN!
NATURALLY WE DIDN'T DARE WAIT AND RISK HIS TELLING THE POLICE—SO I DOPED HIS DRINK!
AND LUCKY FOR ALL OF US SHE DID!... THIS WAS IN BOND'S POCKET!
GHISLAINE!
1967

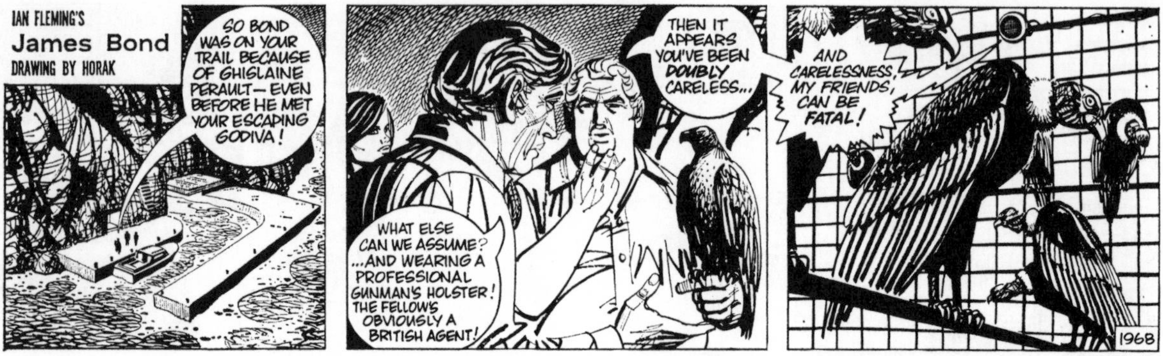
IAN FLEMING'S
James Bond
DRAWING BY HORAK
SO BOND WAS ON YOUR TRAIL BECAUSE OF GHISLAINE PERAULT— EVEN BEFORE HE MET YOUR ESCAPING GODIVA!
WHAT ELSE CAN WE ASSUME? ...AND WEARING A PROFESSIONAL GUNMAN'S HOLSTER! THE FELLOW'S OBVIOUSLY A BRITISH AGENT!
THEN IT APPEARS YOU'VE BEEN DOUBLY CARELESS...
AND CARELESSNESS, MY FRIENDS, CAN BE FATAL!
1968

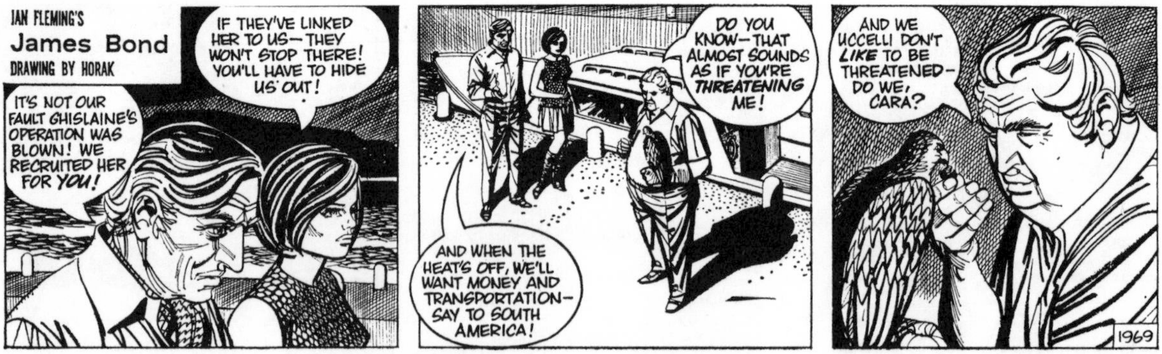
IAN FLEMING'S
James Bond
DRAWING BY HORAK
IT'S NOT OUR FAULT GHISLAINE'S OPERATION WAS BLOWN! WE RECRUITED HER FOR YOU!
IF THEY'VE LINKED HER TO US— THEY WON'T STOP THERE! YOU'LL HAVE TO HIDE US OUT!
AND WHEN THE HEAT'S OFF, WE'LL WANT MONEY AND TRANSPORTATION— SAY TO SOUTH AMERICA!
DO YOU KNOW— THAT ALMOST SOUNDS AS IF YOU'RE THREATENING ME!
AND WE UCCELLI DON'T LIKE TO BE THREATENED— DO WE, CARA?
1969

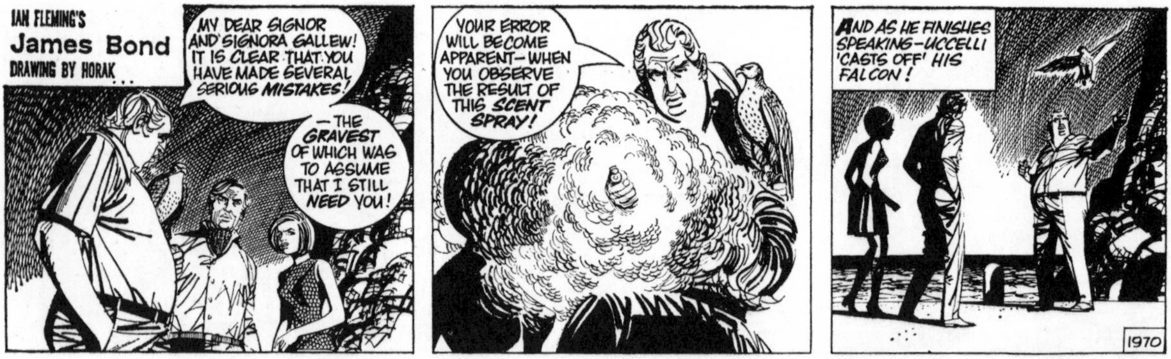
IAN FLEMING'S
James Bond
DRAWING BY HORAK...
MY DEAR SIGNOR AND SIGNORA GALLEW! IT IS CLEAR THAT YOU HAVE MADE SEVERAL SERIOUS MISTAKES!
— THE GRAVEST OF WHICH WAS TO ASSUME THAT I STILL NEED YOU!
YOUR ERROR WILL BECOME APPARENT— WHEN YOU OBSERVE THE RESULT OF THIS SCENT SPRAY!
AND AS HE FINISHES SPEAKING— UCCELLI 'CASTS OFF' HIS FALCON!
1970

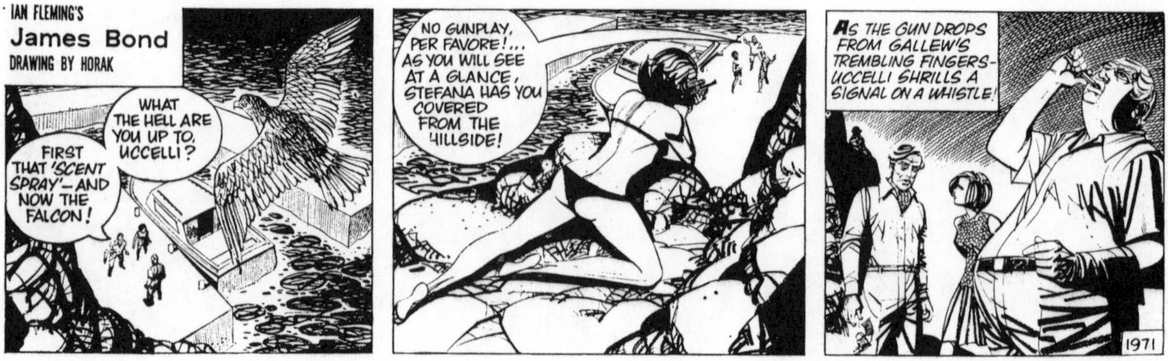
IAN FLEMING'S
James Bond
DRAWING BY HORAK
WHAT THE HELL ARE YOU UP TO, UCCELLI?
FIRST THAT 'SCENT SPRAY'— AND NOW THE FALCON!
NO GUNPLAY, PER FAVORE!... AS YOU WILL SEE AT A GLANCE, STEFANA HAS YOU COVERED FROM THE HILLSIDE!
AS THE GUN DROPS FROM GALLEW'S TREMBLING FINGERS— UCCELLI SHRILLS A SIGNAL ON A WHISTLE!
1971

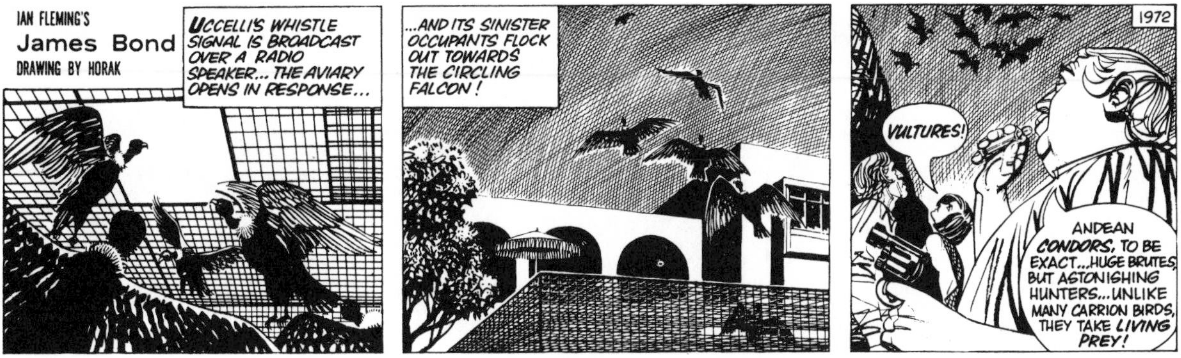
IAN FLEMING'S
James Bond
DRAWING BY HORAK
UCCELLI'S WHISTLE SIGNAL IS BROADCAST OVER A RADIO SPEAKER... THE AVIARY OPENS IN RESPONSE...
...AND ITS SINISTER OCCUPANTS FLOCK OUT TOWARDS THE CIRCLING FALCON!
1972
VULTURES!
ANDEAN CONDORS, TO BE EXACT...HUGE BRUTES, BUT ASTONISHING HUNTERS...UNLIKE MANY CARRION BIRDS, THEY TAKE LIVING PREY!

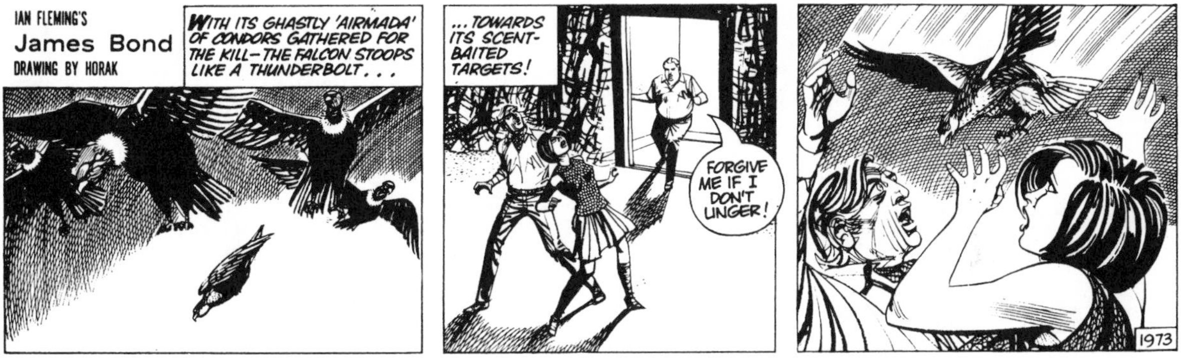
IAN FLEMING'S
James Bond
DRAWING BY HORAK
WITH ITS GHASTLY 'AIRMADA' OF CONDORS GATHERED FOR THE KILL–THE FALCON STOOPS LIKE A THUNDERBOLT . . .
...TOWARDS ITS SCENT-BAITED TARGETS!
FORGIVE ME IF I DON'T LINGER!
1973

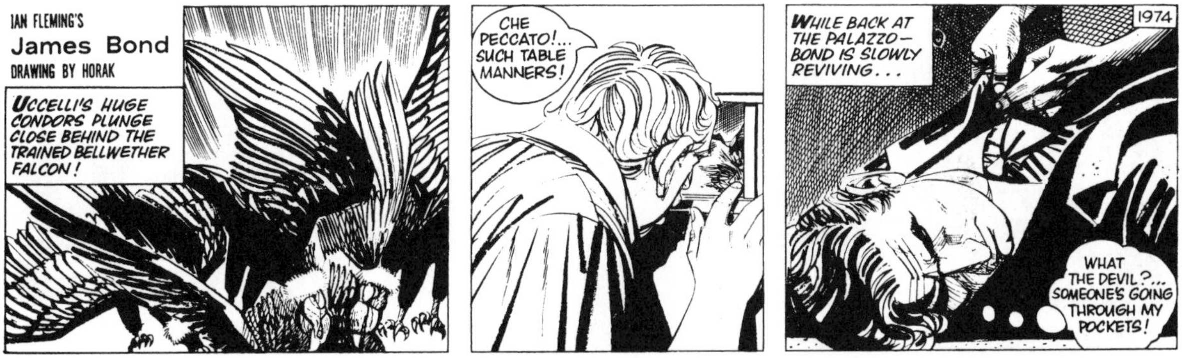
IAN FLEMING'S
James Bond
DRAWING BY HORAK
UCCELLI'S HUGE CONDORS PLUNGE CLOSE BEHIND THE TRAINED BELLWETHER FALCON!
CHE PECCATO!... SUCH TABLE MANNERS!
1974
WHILE BACK AT THE PALAZZO– BOND IS SLOWLY REVIVING . . .
WHAT THE DEVIL?... SOMEONE'S GOING THROUGH MY POCKETS!

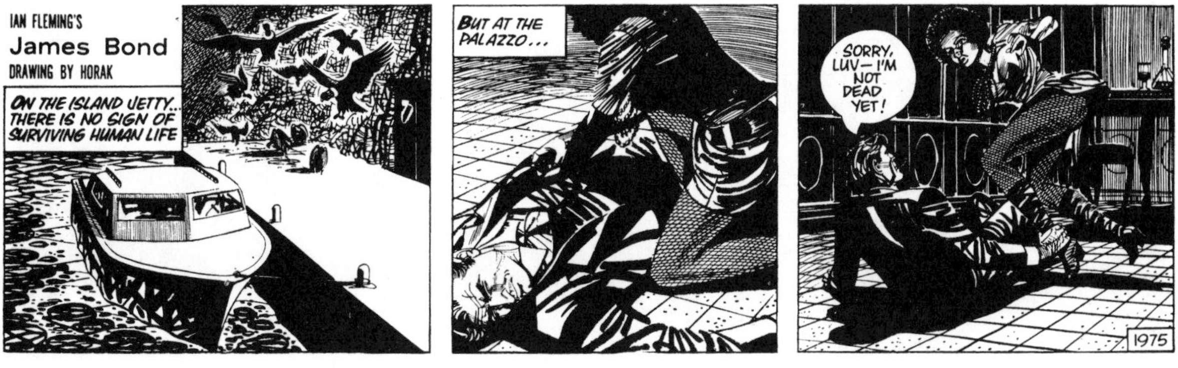
IAN FLEMING'S
James Bond
DRAWING BY HORAK
ON THE ISLAND JETTY... THERE IS NO SIGN OF SURVIVING HUMAN LIFE
BUT AT THE PALAZZO...
SORRY, LUV– I'M NOT DEAD YET!
1975

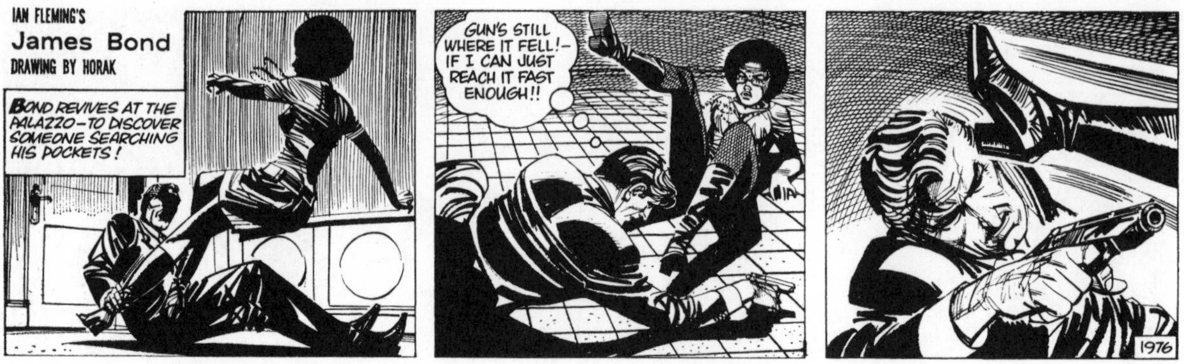
IAN FLEMING'S
James Bond
DRAWING BY HORAK
BOND REVIVES AT THE PALAZZO—TO DISCOVER SOMEONE SEARCHING HIS POCKETS!
GUN'S STILL WHERE IT FELL!—IF I CAN JUST REACH IT FAST ENOUGH!!
1976

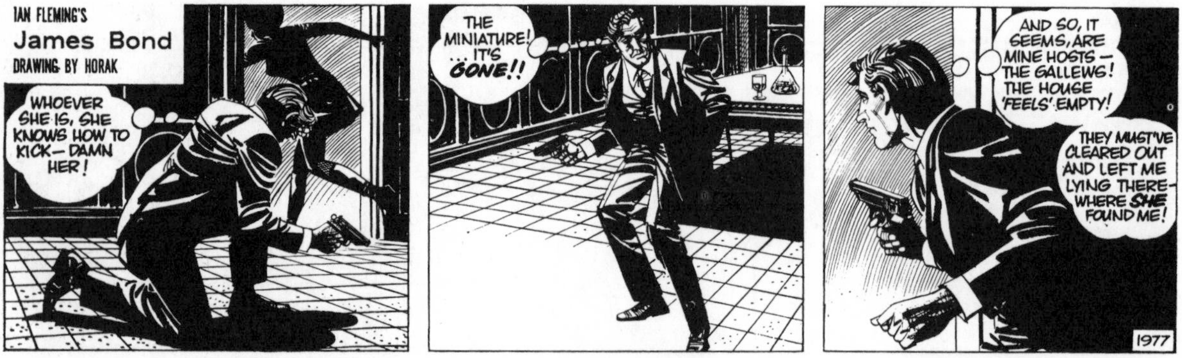
IAN FLEMING'S
James Bond
DRAWING BY HORAK
WHOEVER SHE IS, SHE KNOWS HOW TO KICK—DAMN HER!
THE MINIATURE! ... IT'S GONE!!
AND SO, IT SEEMS, ARE MINE HOSTS—THE GALLEWS! THE HOUSE 'FEELS' EMPTY!
THEY MUST'VE CLEARED OUT AND LEFT ME LYING THERE—WHERE SHE FOUND ME!
1977

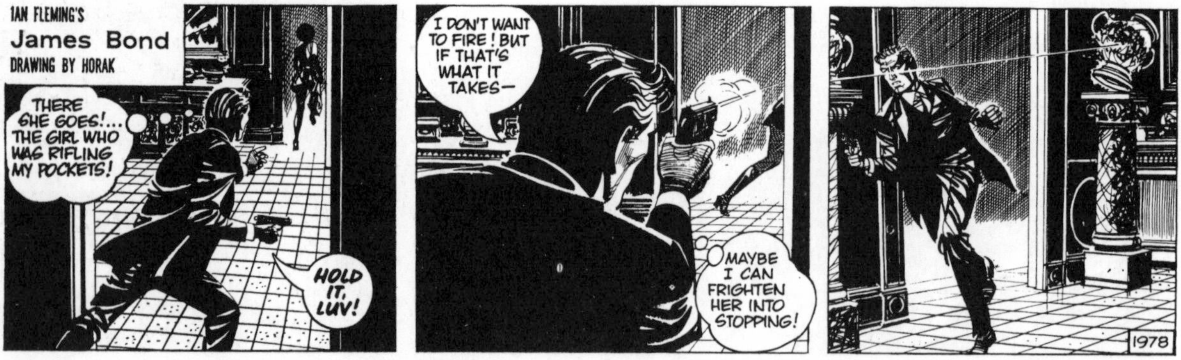
IAN FLEMING'S
James Bond
DRAWING BY HORAK
THERE SHE GOES!... THE GIRL WHO WAS RIFLING MY POCKETS!
HOLD IT, LUV!
I DON'T WANT TO FIRE! BUT IF THAT'S WHAT IT TAKES—
MAYBE I CAN FRIGHTEN HER INTO STOPPING!
1978

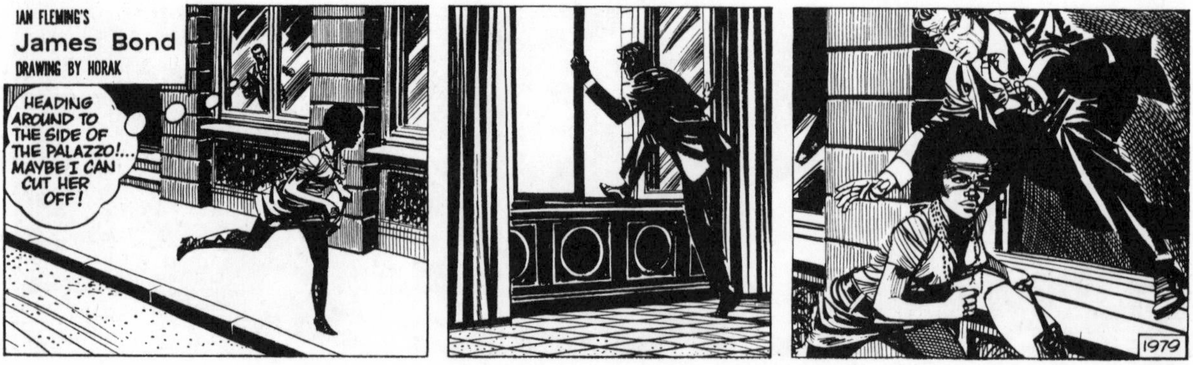
IAN FLEMING'S
James Bond
DRAWING BY HORAK
HEADING AROUND TO THE SIDE OF THE PALAZZO!... MAYBE I CAN CUT HER OFF!
1979

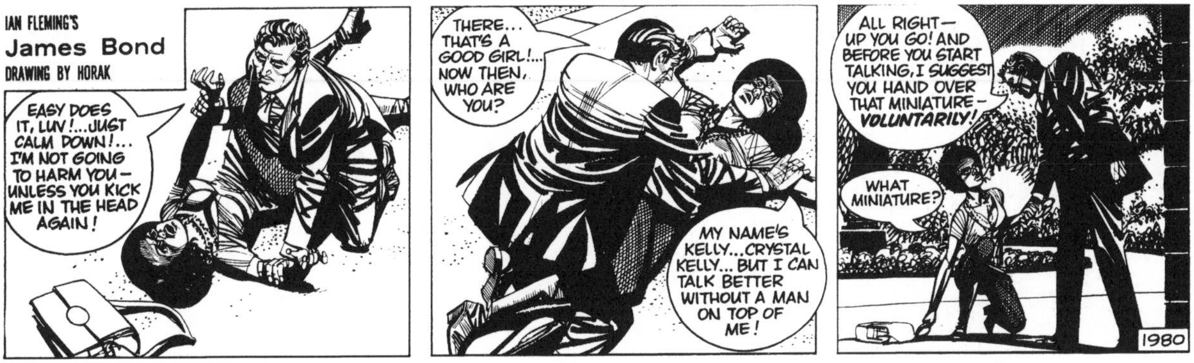
IAN FLEMING'S
James Bond
DRAWING BY HORAK
EASY DOES IT, LUV!... JUST CALM DOWN!... I'M NOT GOING TO HARM YOU — UNLESS YOU KICK ME IN THE HEAD AGAIN!
THERE... THAT'S A GOOD GIRL!... NOW THEN, WHO ARE YOU?
MY NAME'S KELLY... CRYSTAL KELLY... BUT I CAN TALK BETTER WITHOUT A MAN ON TOP OF ME!
ALL RIGHT — UP YOU GO! AND BEFORE YOU START TALKING, I SUGGEST YOU HAND OVER THAT MINIATURE — VOLUNTARILY!
WHAT MINIATURE?
1980

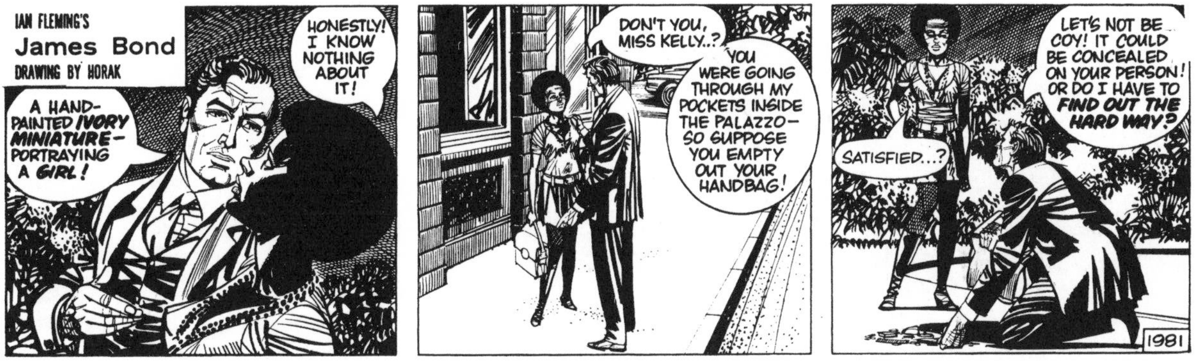
IAN FLEMING'S
James Bond
DRAWING BY HORAK
A HAND-PAINTED IVORY MINIATURE — PORTRAYING A GIRL!
HONESTLY! I KNOW NOTHING ABOUT IT!
DON'T YOU, MISS KELLY..?
YOU WERE GOING THROUGH MY POCKETS INSIDE THE PALAZZO — SO SUPPOSE YOU EMPTY OUT YOUR HANDBAG!
SATISFIED...?
LET'S NOT BE COY! IT COULD BE CONCEALED ON YOUR PERSON! OR DO I HAVE TO FIND OUT THE HARD WAY?
1981

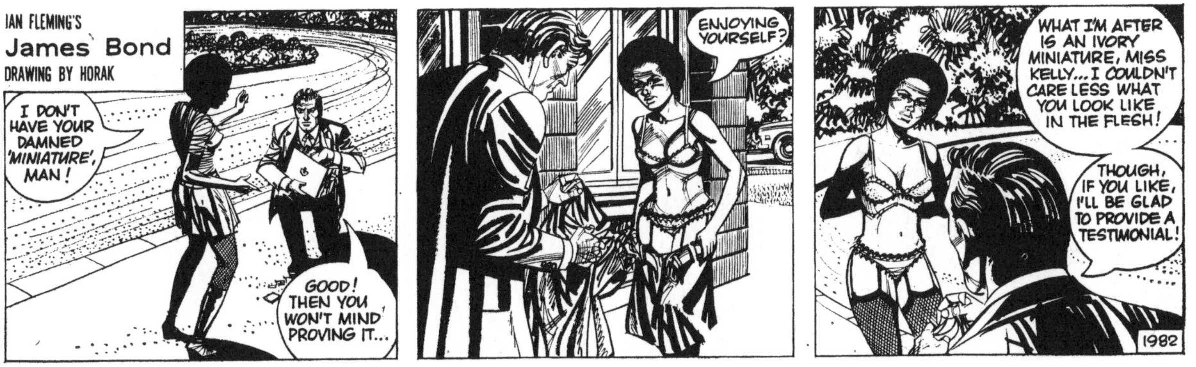
IAN FLEMING'S
James Bond
DRAWING BY HORAK
I DON'T HAVE YOUR DAMNED 'MINIATURE', MAN!
GOOD! THEN YOU WON'T MIND PROVING IT...
ENJOYING YOURSELF?
WHAT I'M AFTER IS AN IVORY MINIATURE, MISS KELLY... I COULDN'T CARE LESS WHAT YOU LOOK LIKE IN THE FLESH!
THOUGH, IF YOU LIKE, I'LL BE GLAD TO PROVIDE A TESTIMONIAL!
1982

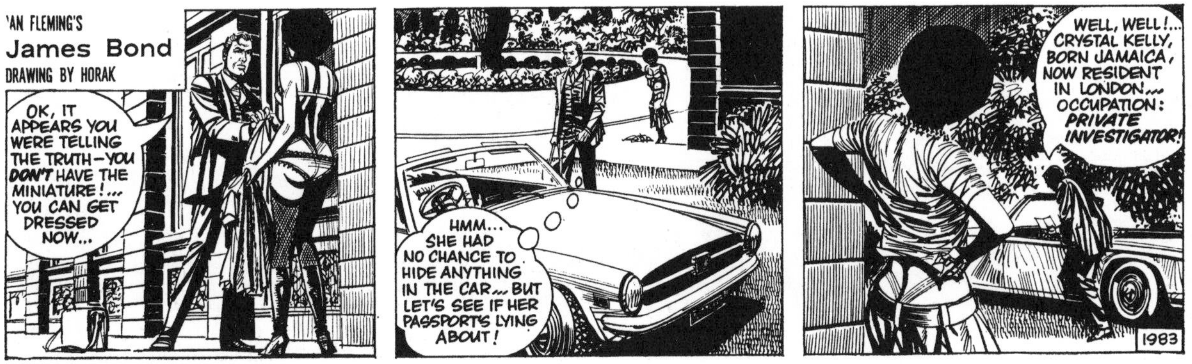
IAN FLEMING'S
James Bond
DRAWING BY HORAK
OK, IT APPEARS YOU WERE TELLING THE TRUTH — YOU DON'T HAVE THE MINIATURE!... YOU CAN GET DRESSED NOW...
HMM... SHE HAD NO CHANCE TO HIDE ANYTHING IN THE CAR... BUT LET'S SEE IF HER PASSPORT'S LYING ABOUT!
WELL, WELL!... CRYSTAL KELLY, BORN JAMAICA, NOW RESIDENT IN LONDON!... OCCUPATION: PRIVATE INVESTIGATOR!
1983

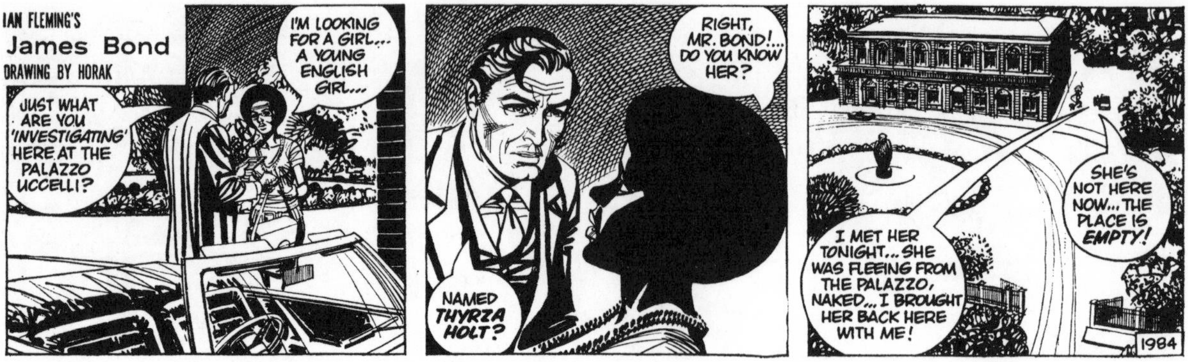
IAN FLEMING'S
James Bond
DRAWING BY HORAK
JUST WHAT ARE YOU 'INVESTIGATING' HERE AT THE PALAZZO UCCELLI?
I'M LOOKING FOR A GIRL... A YOUNG ENGLISH GIRL...
RIGHT, MR. BOND!... DO YOU KNOW HER?
NAMED THYRZA HOLT?
SHE'S NOT HERE NOW... THE PLACE IS EMPTY!
I MET HER TONIGHT... SHE WAS FLEEING FROM THE PALAZZO, NAKED... I BROUGHT HER BACK HERE WITH ME!
1984

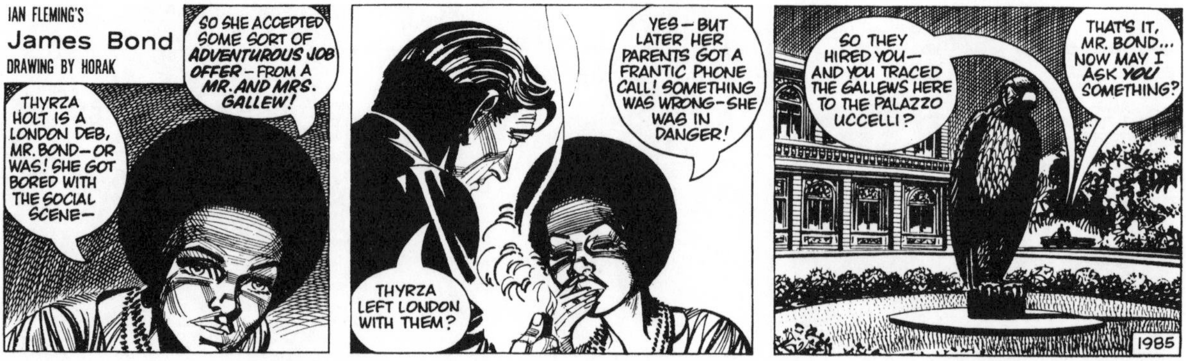
IAN FLEMING'S
James Bond
DRAWING BY HORAK
THYRZA HOLT IS A LONDON DEB, MR. BOND—OR WAS! SHE GOT BORED WITH THE SOCIAL SCENE—
SO SHE ACCEPTED SOME SORT OF ADVENTUROUS JOB OFFER—FROM A MR. AND MRS. GALLEW!
THYRZA LEFT LONDON WITH THEM?
YES—BUT LATER HER PARENTS GOT A FRANTIC PHONE CALL! SOMETHING WAS WRONG—SHE WAS IN DANGER!
SO THEY HIRED YOU—AND YOU TRACED THE GALLEWS HERE TO THE PALAZZO UCCELLI?
THAT'S IT, MR. BOND... NOW MAY I ASK YOU SOMETHING?
1985

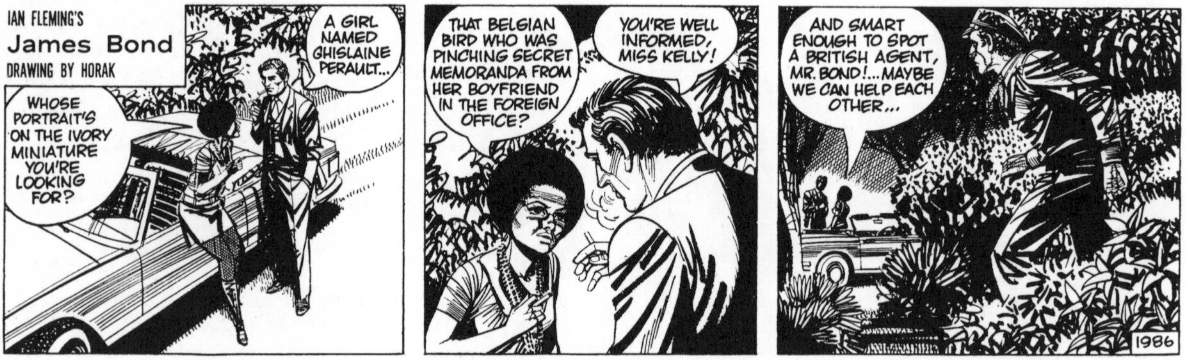
IAN FLEMING'S
James Bond
DRAWING BY HORAK
WHOSE PORTRAIT'S ON THE IVORY MINIATURE YOU'RE LOOKING FOR?
A GIRL NAMED GHISLAINE PERAULT...
THAT BELGIAN BIRD WHO WAS PINCHING SECRET MEMORANDA FROM HER BOYFRIEND IN THE FOREIGN OFFICE?
YOU'RE WELL INFORMED, MISS KELLY!
AND SMART ENOUGH TO SPOT A BRITISH AGENT, MR. BOND!... MAYBE WE CAN HELP EACH OTHER...
1986

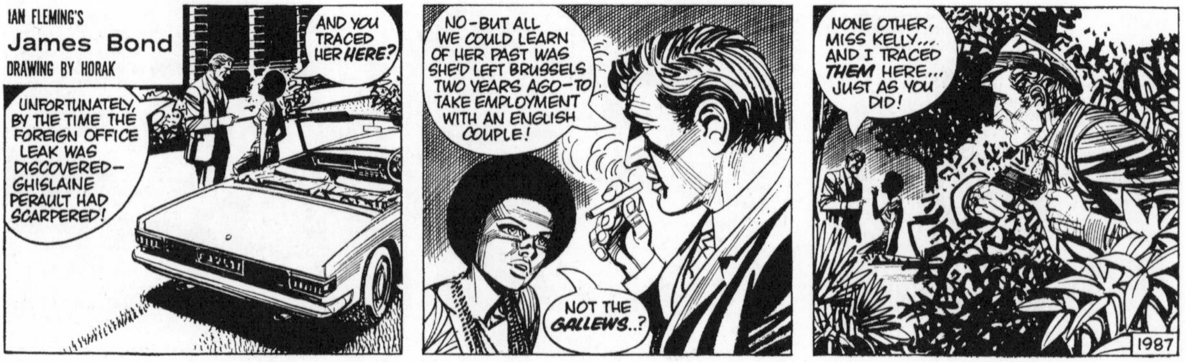
IAN FLEMING'S
James Bond
DRAWING BY HORAK
AND YOU TRACED HER HERE?
UNFORTUNATELY, BY THE TIME THE FOREIGN OFFICE LEAK WAS DISCOVERED—GHISLAINE PERAULT HAD SCARPERED!
NO—BUT ALL WE COULD LEARN OF HER PAST WAS SHE'D LEFT BRUSSELS TWO YEARS AGO—TO TAKE EMPLOYMENT WITH AN ENGLISH COUPLE!
NOT THE GALLEWS..?
NONE OTHER, MISS KELLY... AND I TRACED THEM HERE... JUST AS YOU DID!
1987

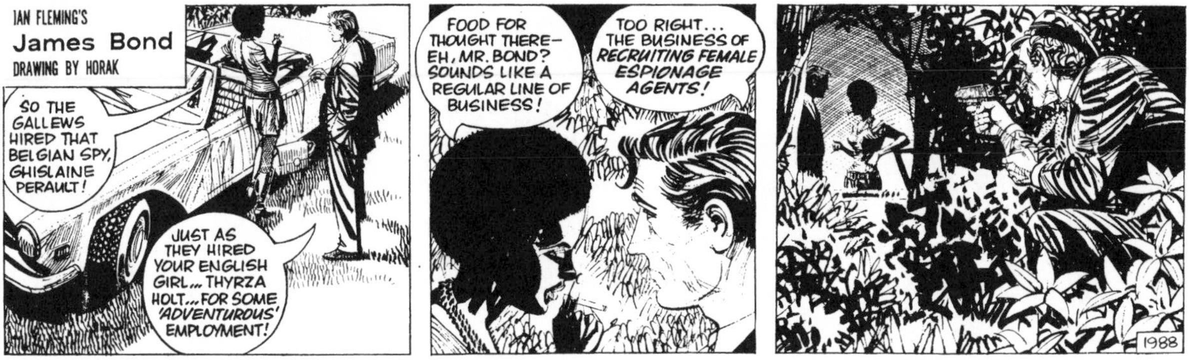
IAN FLEMING'S
James Bond
DRAWING BY HORAK
SO THE GALLEWS HIRED THAT BELGIAN SPY, GHISLAINE PERAULT!
JUST AS THEY HIRED YOUR ENGLISH GIRL... THYRZA HOLT... FOR SOME 'ADVENTUROUS' EMPLOYMENT!
FOOD FOR THOUGHT THERE— EH, MR. BOND? SOUNDS LIKE A REGULAR LINE OF BUSINESS!
TOO RIGHT... THE BUSINESS OF RECRUITING FEMALE ESPIONAGE AGENTS!
1988

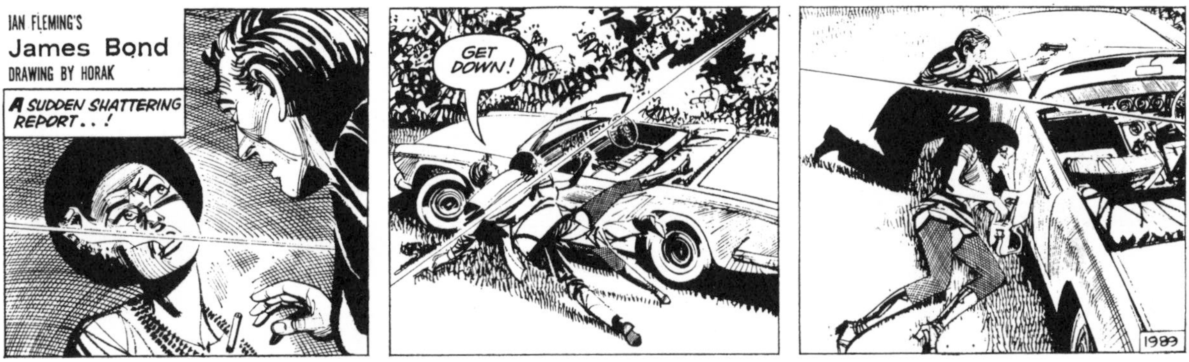
IAN FLEMING'S
James Bond
DRAWING BY HORAK
A SUDDEN SHATTERING REPORT..!
GET DOWN!
1989

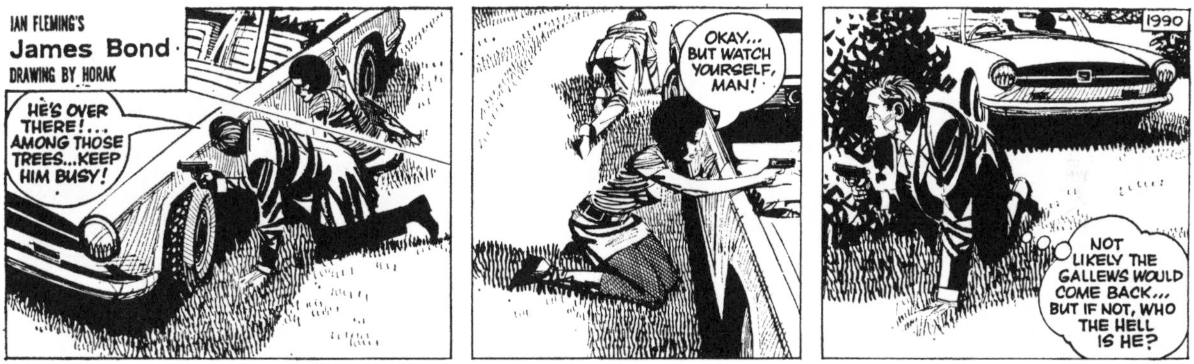
IAN FLEMING'S
James Bond
DRAWING BY HORAK
HE'S OVER THERE!... AMONG THOSE TREES... KEEP HIM BUSY!
OKAY... BUT WATCH YOURSELF, MAN!
1990
NOT LIKELY THE GALLEWS WOULD COME BACK... BUT IF NOT, WHO THE HELL IS HE?

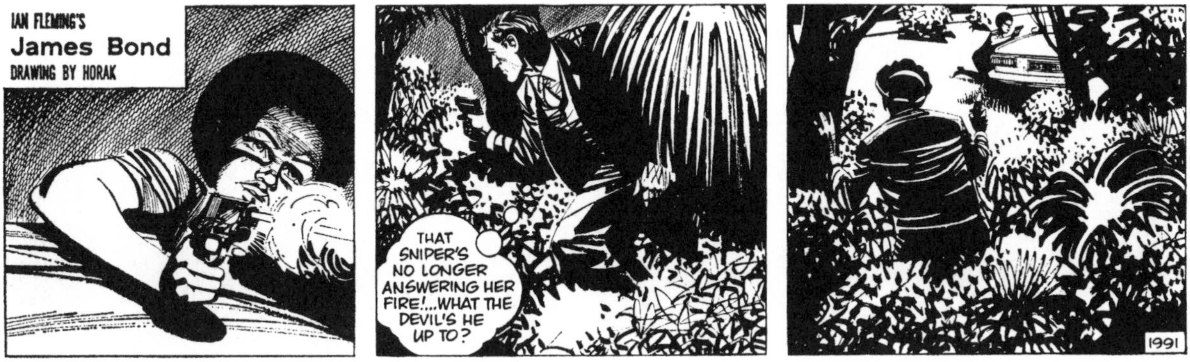
IAN FLEMING'S
James Bond
DRAWING BY HORAK
THAT SNIPER'S NO LONGER ANSWERING HER FIRE!... WHAT THE DEVIL'S HE UP TO?
1991

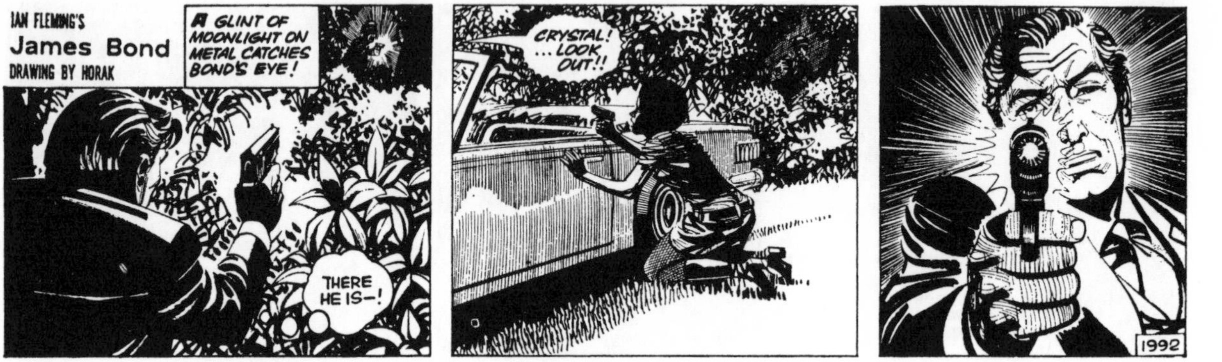

IAN FLEMING'S
James Bond
DRAWING BY HORAK
A GLINT OF MOONLIGHT ON METAL CATCHES BOND'S EYE!
THERE HE IS—!
CRYSTAL! ...LOOK OUT!!
1992


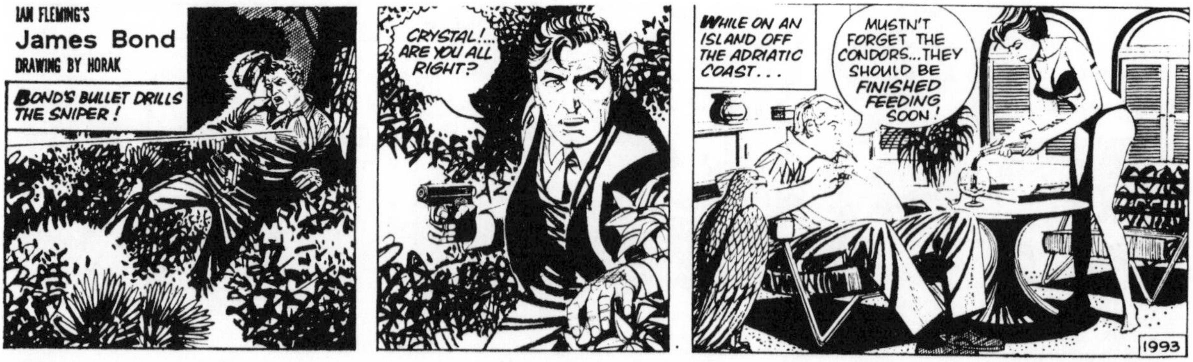

IAN FLEMING'S
James Bond
DRAWING BY HORAK
BOND'S BULLET DRILLS THE SNIPER!
CRYSTAL!... ARE YOU ALL RIGHT?
WHILE ON AN ISLAND OFF THE ADRIATIC COAST...
MUSTN'T FORGET THE CONDORS...THEY SHOULD BE FINISHED FEEDING SOON!
1993


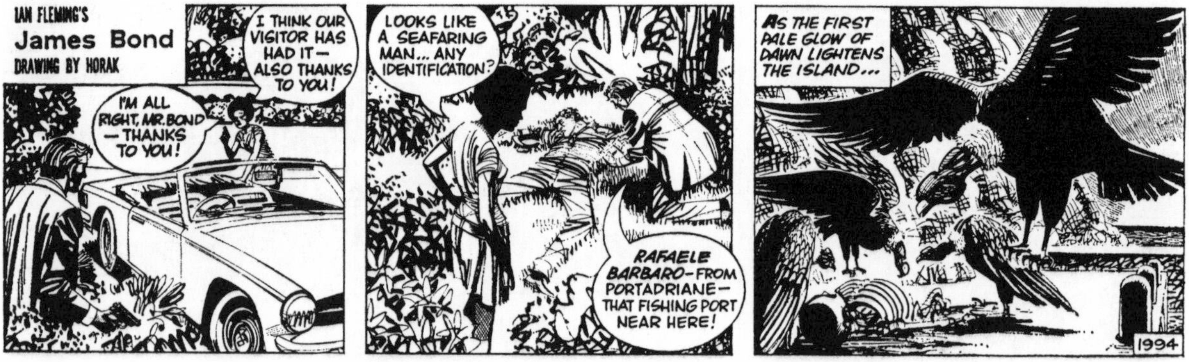

IAN FLEMING'S
James Bond
DRAWING BY HORAK
I'M ALL RIGHT, MR. BOND —THANKS TO YOU!
I THINK OUR VISITOR HAS HAD IT— ALSO THANKS TO YOU!
LOOKS LIKE A SEAFARING MAN... ANY IDENTIFICATION?
RAFAELE BARBARO—FROM PORTADRIANE— THAT FISHING PORT NEAR HERE!
AS THE FIRST PALE GLOW OF DAWN LIGHTENS THE ISLAND...
1994


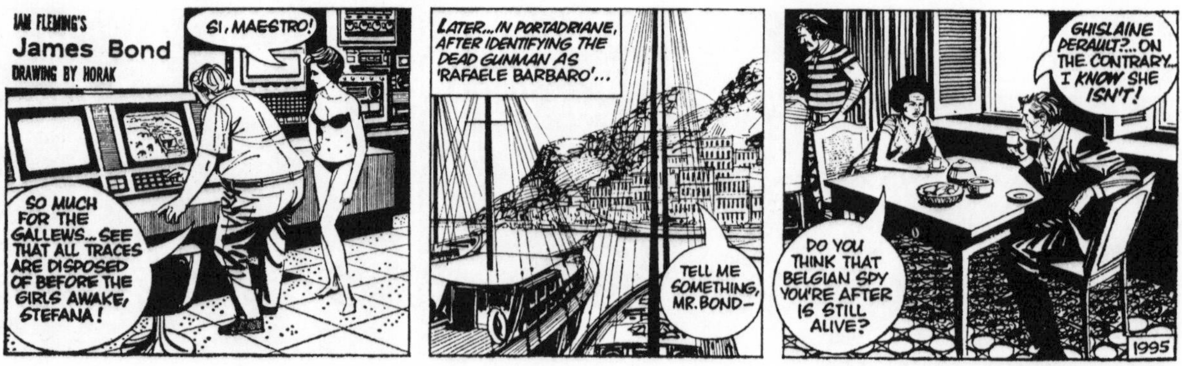

IAN FLEMING'S
James Bond
DRAWING BY HORAK
SO MUCH FOR THE GALLEWS... SEE THAT ALL TRACES ARE DISPOSED OF BEFORE THE GIRLS AWAKE, STEFANA!
SI, MAESTRO!
LATER... IN PORTADRIANE, AFTER IDENTIFYING THE DEAD GUNMAN AS 'RAFAELE BARBARO'...
TELL ME SOMETHING, MR. BOND—
DO YOU THINK THAT BELGIAN SPY YOU'RE AFTER IS STILL ALIVE?
GHISLAINE PERAULT?... ON THE CONTRARY... I KNOW SHE ISN'T!
1995

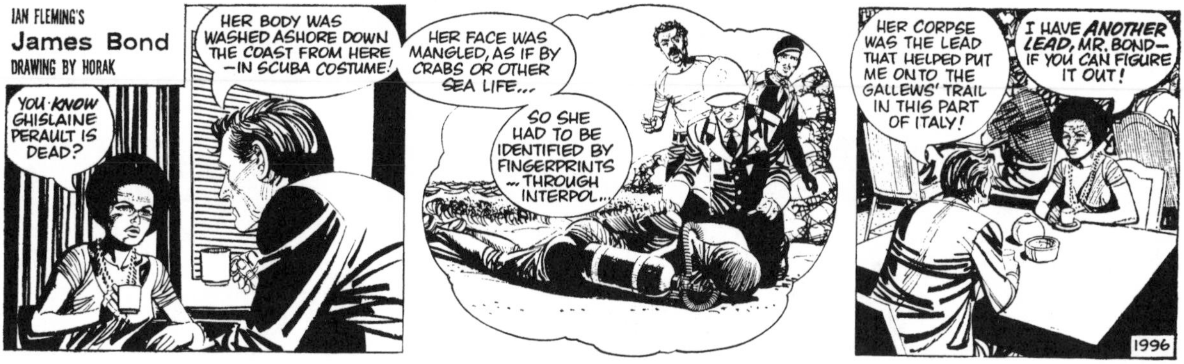
IAN FLEMING'S
James Bond
DRAWING BY HORAK
YOU KNOW GHISLAINE PERAULT IS DEAD?
HER BODY WAS WASHED ASHORE DOWN THE COAST FROM HERE —IN SCUBA COSTUME!
HER FACE WAS MANGLED, AS IF BY CRABS OR OTHER SEA LIFE...
SO SHE HAD TO BE IDENTIFIED BY FINGERPRINTS —THROUGH INTERPOL...
HER CORPSE WAS THE LEAD THAT HELPED PUT ME ONTO THE GALLEWS' TRAIL IN THIS PART OF ITALY!
I HAVE ANOTHER LEAD, MR. BOND— IF YOU CAN FIGURE IT OUT!
1996

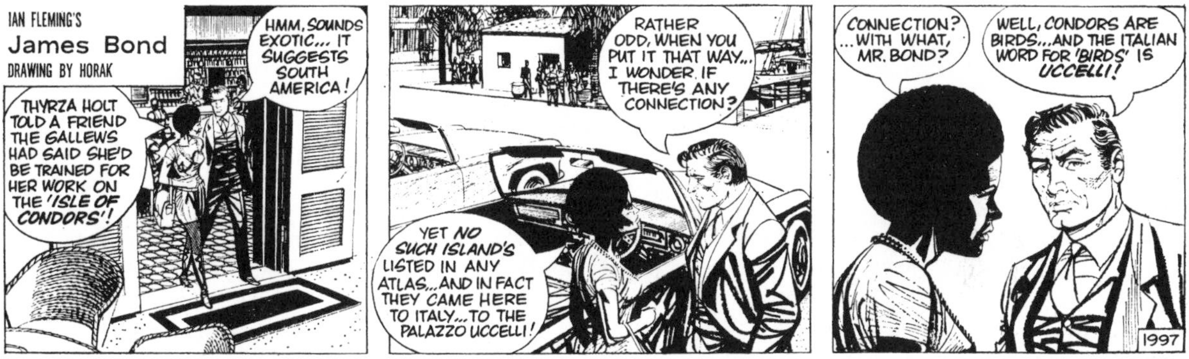
IAN FLEMING'S
James Bond
DRAWING BY HORAK
THYRZA HOLT TOLD A FRIEND THE GALLEWS HAD SAID SHE'D BE TRAINED FOR HER WORK ON THE 'ISLE OF CONDORS'!
HMM, SOUNDS EXOTIC... IT SUGGESTS SOUTH AMERICA!
YET NO SUCH ISLAND'S LISTED IN ANY ATLAS... AND IN FACT THEY CAME HERE TO ITALY... TO THE PALAZZO UCCELLI!
RATHER ODD, WHEN YOU PUT IT THAT WAY... I WONDER IF THERE'S ANY CONNECTION?
CONNECTION? ...WITH WHAT, MR. BOND?
WELL, CONDORS ARE BIRDS... AND THE ITALIAN WORD FOR 'BIRDS' IS UCCELLI!
1997

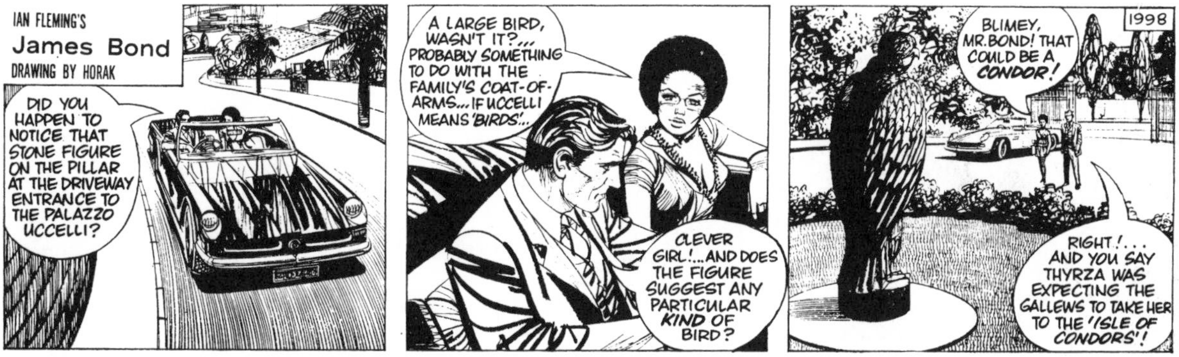
IAN FLEMING'S
James Bond
DRAWING BY HORAK
DID YOU HAPPEN TO NOTICE THAT STONE FIGURE ON THE PILLAR AT THE DRIVEWAY ENTRANCE TO THE PALAZZO UCCELLI?
A LARGE BIRD, WASN'T IT?... PROBABLY SOMETHING TO DO WITH THE FAMILY'S COAT-OF-ARMS... IF UCCELLI MEANS 'BIRDS'...
CLEVER GIRL!... AND DOES THE FIGURE SUGGEST ANY PARTICULAR KIND OF BIRD?
1998
BLIMEY, MR. BOND! THAT COULD BE A CONDOR!
RIGHT!... AND YOU SAY THYRZA WAS EXPECTING THE GALLEWS TO TAKE HER TO THE 'ISLE OF CONDORS'!

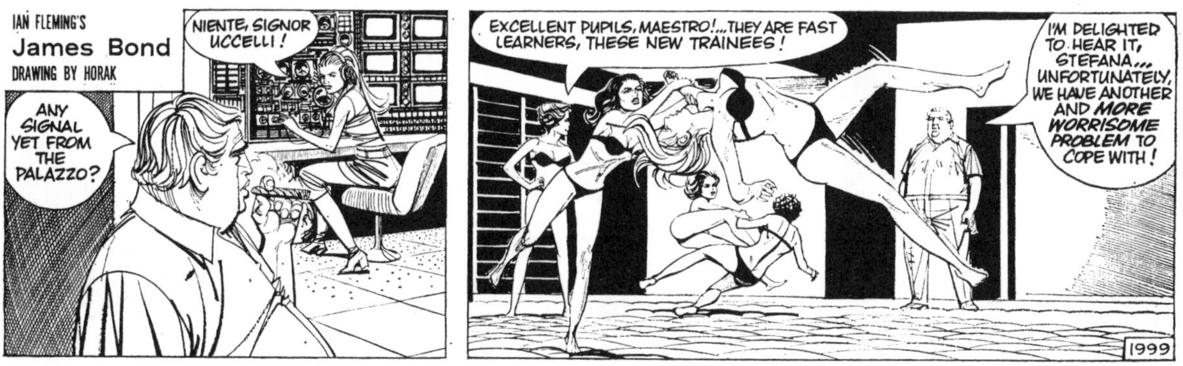
IAN FLEMING'S
James Bond
DRAWING BY HORAK
ANY SIGNAL YET FROM THE PALAZZO?
NIENTE, SIGNOR UCCELLI!
EXCELLENT PUPILS, MAESTRO!... THEY ARE FAST LEARNERS, THESE NEW TRAINEES!
I'M DELIGHTED TO HEAR IT, STEFANA... UNFORTUNATELY, WE HAVE ANOTHER AND MORE WORRISOME PROBLEM TO COPE WITH!
1999

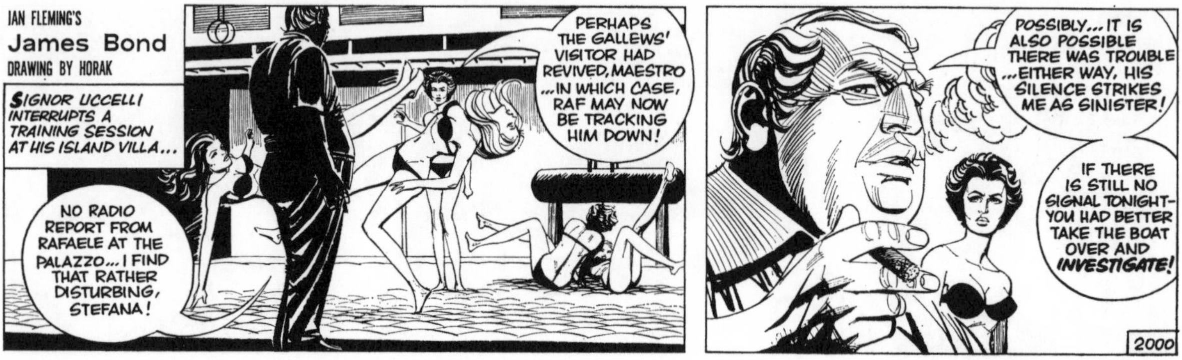
IAN FLEMING'S
James Bond
DRAWING BY HORAK
SIGNOR UCCELLI INTERRUPTS A TRAINING SESSION AT HIS ISLAND VILLA...
NO RADIO REPORT FROM RAFAELE AT THE PALAZZO... I FIND THAT RATHER DISTURBING, STEFANA!
PERHAPS THE GALLEWS' VISITOR HAD REVIVED, MAESTRO ...IN WHICH CASE, RAF MAY NOW BE TRACKING HIM DOWN!
POSSIBLY... IT IS ALSO POSSIBLE THERE WAS TROUBLE ...EITHER WAY, HIS SILENCE STRIKES ME AS SINISTER!
IF THERE IS STILL NO SIGNAL TONIGHT-YOU HAD BETTER TAKE THE BOAT OVER AND INVESTIGATE!
2000

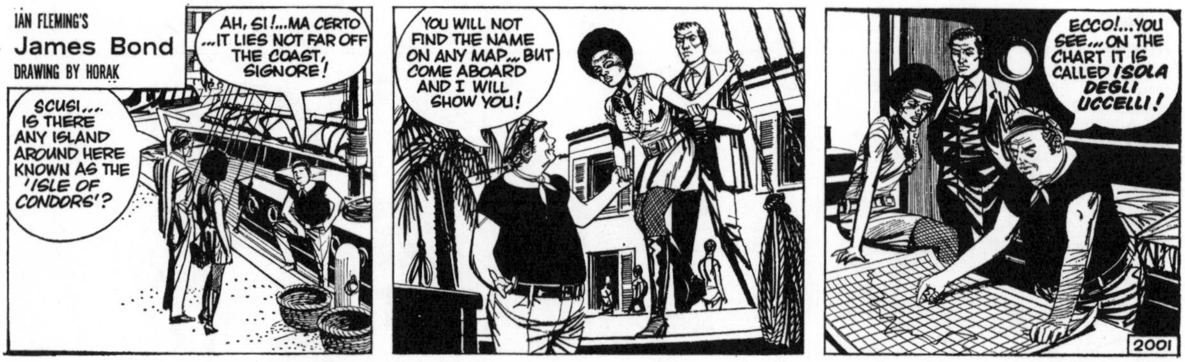
IAN FLEMING'S
James Bond
DRAWING BY HORAK
SCUSI... IS THERE ANY ISLAND AROUND HERE KNOWN AS THE 'ISLE OF CONDORS'?
AH, SI!...MA CERTO ...IT LIES NOT FAR OFF THE COAST, SIGNORE!
YOU WILL NOT FIND THE NAME ON ANY MAP... BUT COME ABOARD AND I WILL SHOW YOU!
ECCO!...YOU SEE... ON THE CHART IT IS CALLED ISOLA DEGLI UCCELLI!
2001

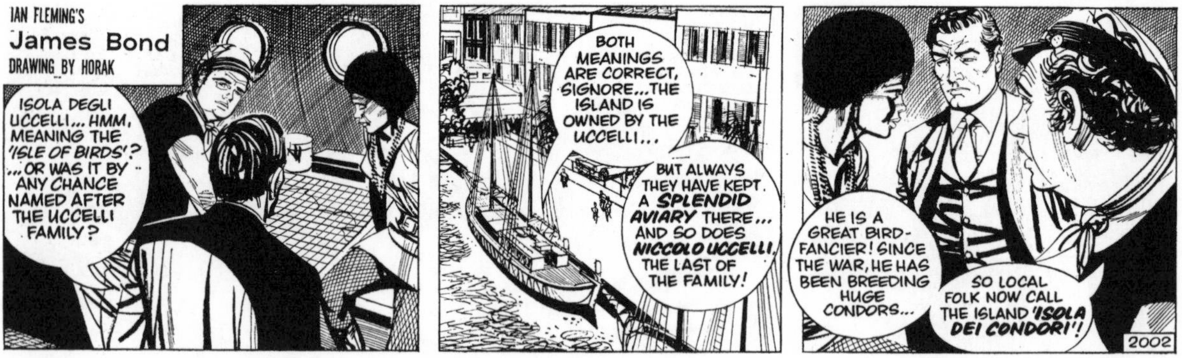
IAN FLEMING'S
James Bond
DRAWING BY HORAK
ISOLA DEGLI UCCELLI... HMM, MEANING THE 'ISLE OF BIRDS'? ...OR WAS IT BY ANY CHANCE NAMED AFTER THE UCCELLI FAMILY?
BOTH MEANINGS ARE CORRECT, SIGNORE... THE ISLAND IS OWNED BY THE UCCELLI...
BUT ALWAYS THEY HAVE KEPT A SPLENDID AVIARY THERE... AND SO DOES NICCOLO UCCELLI, THE LAST OF THE FAMILY!
HE IS A GREAT BIRD-FANCIER! SINCE THE WAR, HE HAS BEEN BREEDING HUGE CONDORS...
SO LOCAL FOLK NOW CALL THE ISLAND 'ISOLA DEI CONDORI'!
2002

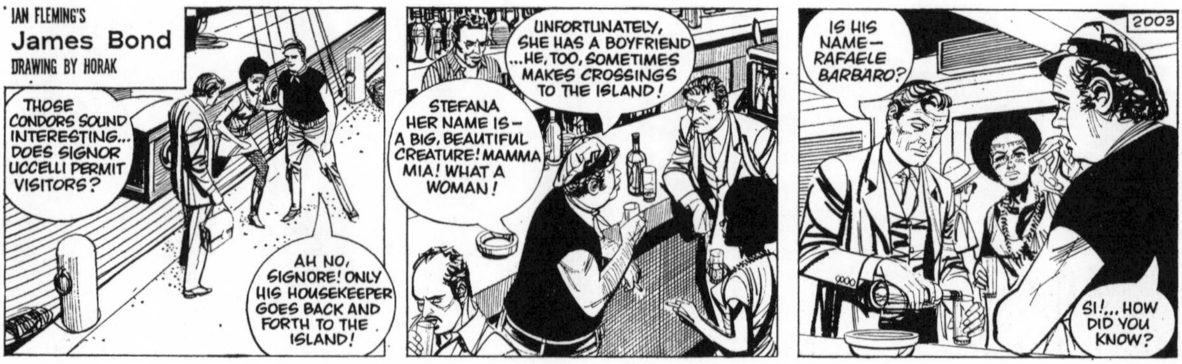
IAN FLEMING'S
James Bond
DRAWING BY HORAK
THOSE CONDORS SOUND INTERESTING... DOES SIGNOR UCCELLI PERMIT VISITORS?
AH NO, SIGNORE! ONLY HIS HOUSEKEEPER GOES BACK AND FORTH TO THE ISLAND!
STEFANA HER NAME IS-A BIG, BEAUTIFUL CREATURE! MAMMA MIA! WHAT A WOMAN!
UNFORTUNATELY, SHE HAS A BOYFRIEND ...HE, TOO, SOMETIMES MAKES CROSSINGS TO THE ISLAND!
2003
IS HIS NAME-RAFAELE BARBARO?
SI!... HOW DID YOU KNOW?

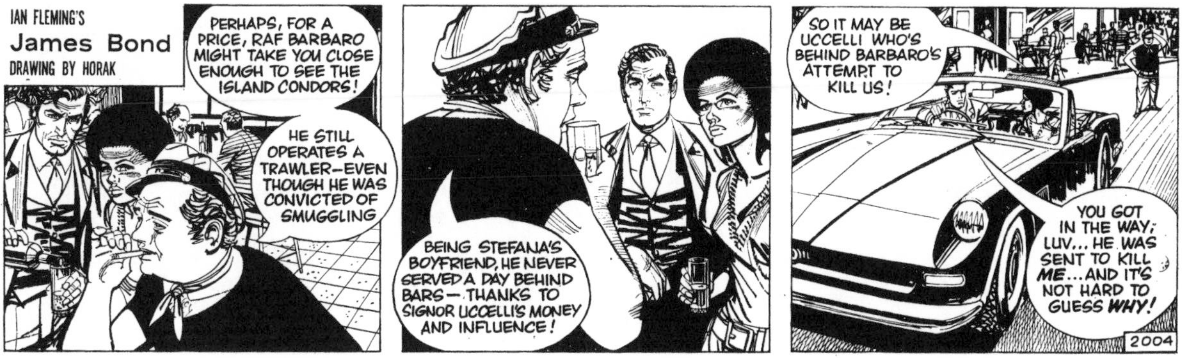
IAN FLEMING'S
James Bond
DRAWING BY HORAK
PERHAPS, FOR A PRICE, RAF BARBARO MIGHT TAKE YOU CLOSE ENOUGH TO SEE THE ISLAND CONDORS!
HE STILL OPERATES A TRAWLER—EVEN THOUGH HE WAS CONVICTED OF SMUGGLING
BEING STEFANA'S BOYFRIEND, HE NEVER SERVED A DAY BEHIND BARS— THANKS TO SIGNOR UCCELLI'S MONEY AND INFLUENCE!
SO IT MAY BE UCCELLI WHO'S BEHIND BARBARO'S ATTEMPT TO KILL US!
YOU GOT IN THE WAY, LUV... HE WAS SENT TO KILL **ME**... AND IT'S NOT HARD TO GUESS **WHY**!
2004

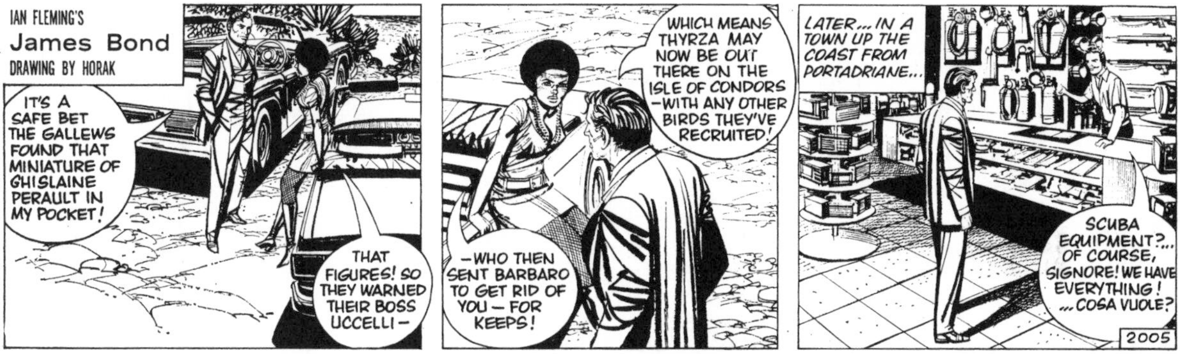
IAN FLEMING'S
James Bond
DRAWING BY HORAK
IT'S A SAFE BET THE GALLEWS FOUND THAT MINIATURE OF GHISLAINE PERAULT IN MY POCKET!
THAT FIGURES! SO THEY WARNED THEIR BOSS UCCELLI—
WHICH MEANS THYRZA MAY NOW BE OUT THERE ON THE ISLE OF CONDORS —WITH ANY OTHER BIRDS THEY'VE RECRUITED!
—WHO THEN SENT BARBARO TO GET RID OF YOU— FOR KEEPS!
LATER... IN A TOWN UP THE COAST FROM PORTADRIANE...
SCUBA EQUIPMENT?... OF COURSE, SIGNORE! WE HAVE EVERYTHING! ... COSA VUOLE?
2005

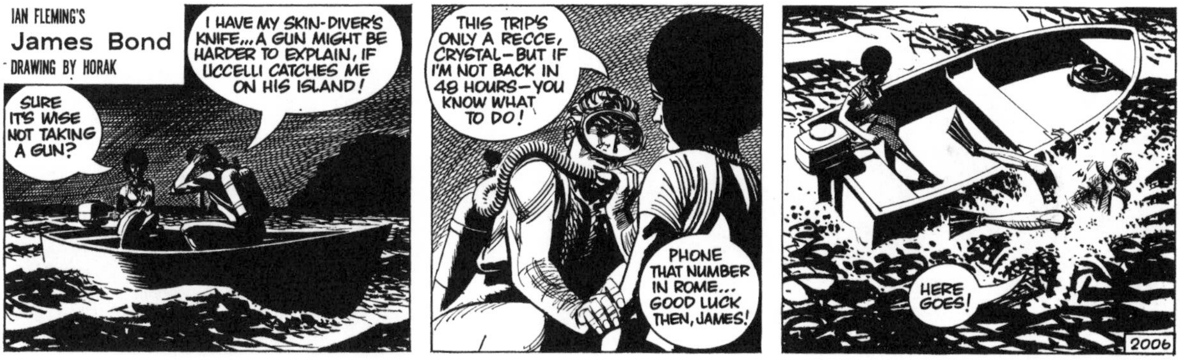
IAN FLEMING'S
James Bond
DRAWING BY HORAK
SURE IT'S WISE NOT TAKING A GUN?
I HAVE MY SKIN-DIVER'S KNIFE... A GUN MIGHT BE HARDER TO EXPLAIN, IF UCCELLI CATCHES ME ON HIS ISLAND!
THIS TRIP'S ONLY A RECCE, CRYSTAL— BUT IF I'M NOT BACK IN 48 HOURS— YOU KNOW WHAT TO DO!
PHONE THAT NUMBER IN ROME... GOOD LUCK THEN, JAMES!
HERE GOES!
2006

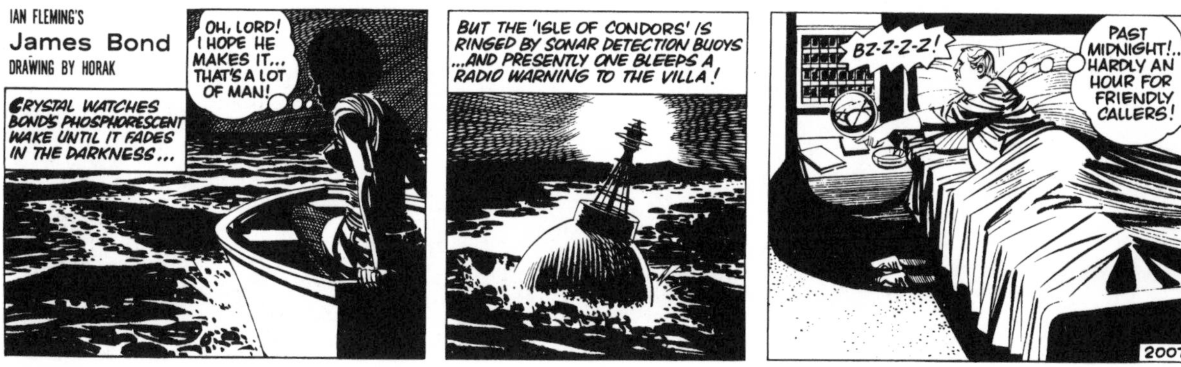
IAN FLEMING'S
James Bond
DRAWING BY HORAK
CRYSTAL WATCHES BOND'S PHOSPHORESCENT WAKE UNTIL IT FADES IN THE DARKNESS...
OH, LORD! I HOPE HE MAKES IT... THAT'S A LOT OF MAN!
BUT THE 'ISLE OF CONDORS' IS RINGED BY SONAR DETECTION BUOYS ...AND PRESENTLY ONE BLEEPS A RADIO WARNING TO THE VILLA!
BZ-Z-Z-Z!
PAST MIDNIGHT!... HARDLY AN HOUR FOR FRIENDLY CALLERS!
2007

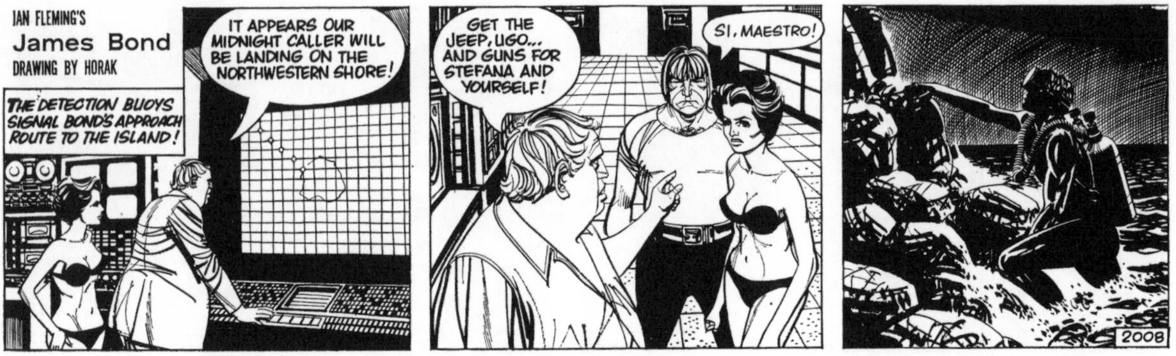
IAN FLEMING'S
James Bond
DRAWING BY HORAK
THE DETECTION BUOYS SIGNAL BOND'S APPROACH ROUTE TO THE ISLAND!
IT APPEARS OUR MIDNIGHT CALLER WILL BE LANDING ON THE NORTHWESTERN SHORE!
GET THE JEEP, UGO... AND GUNS FOR STEFANA AND YOURSELF!
SI, MAESTRO!
2008

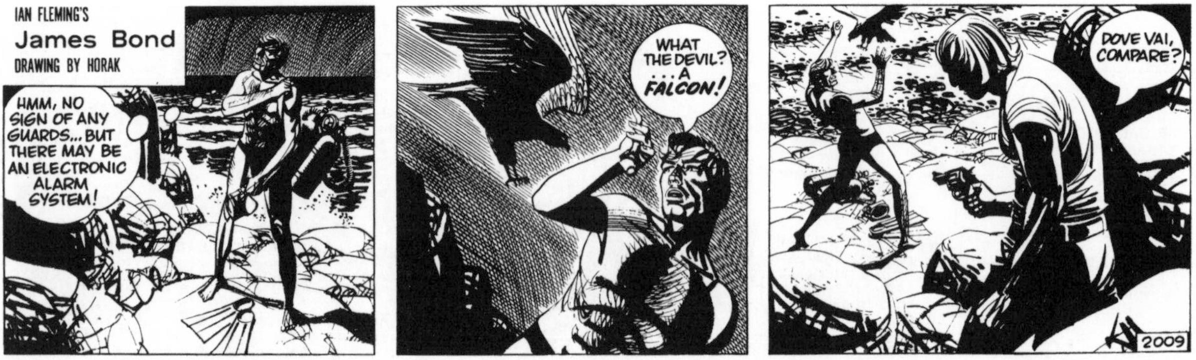
IAN FLEMING'S
James Bond
DRAWING BY HORAK
HMM, NO SIGN OF ANY GUARDS... BUT THERE MAY BE AN ELECTRONIC ALARM SYSTEM!
WHAT THE DEVIL? ... A FALCON!
DOVE VAI, COMPARE?
2009

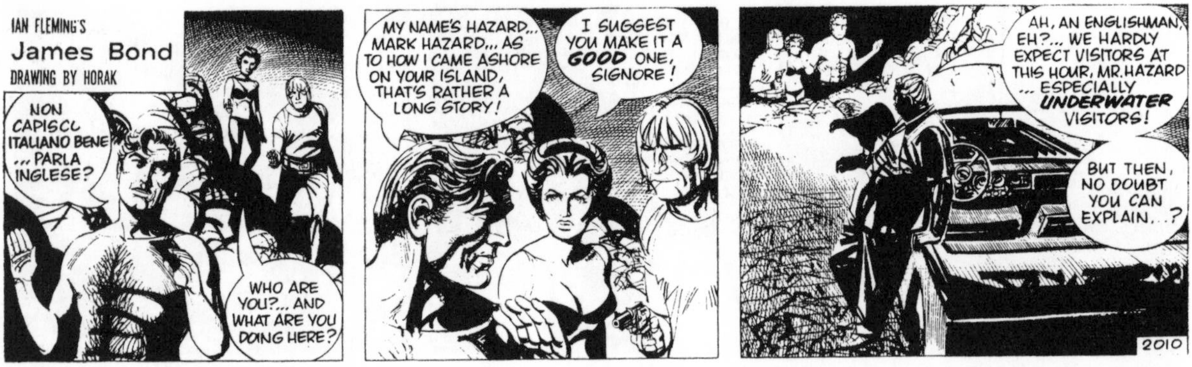
IAN FLEMING'S
James Bond
DRAWING BY HORAK
NON CAPISCO ITALIANO BENE ... PARLA INGLESE?
WHO ARE YOU?... AND WHAT ARE YOU DOING HERE?
MY NAME'S HAZARD... MARK HAZARD... AS TO HOW I CAME ASHORE ON YOUR ISLAND, THAT'S RATHER A LONG STORY!
I SUGGEST YOU MAKE IT A GOOD ONE, SIGNORE!
AH, AN ENGLISHMAN, EH?... WE HARDLY EXPECT VISITORS AT THIS HOUR, MR. HAZARD ... ESPECIALLY UNDERWATER VISITORS!
BUT THEN, NO DOUBT YOU CAN EXPLAIN...?
2010

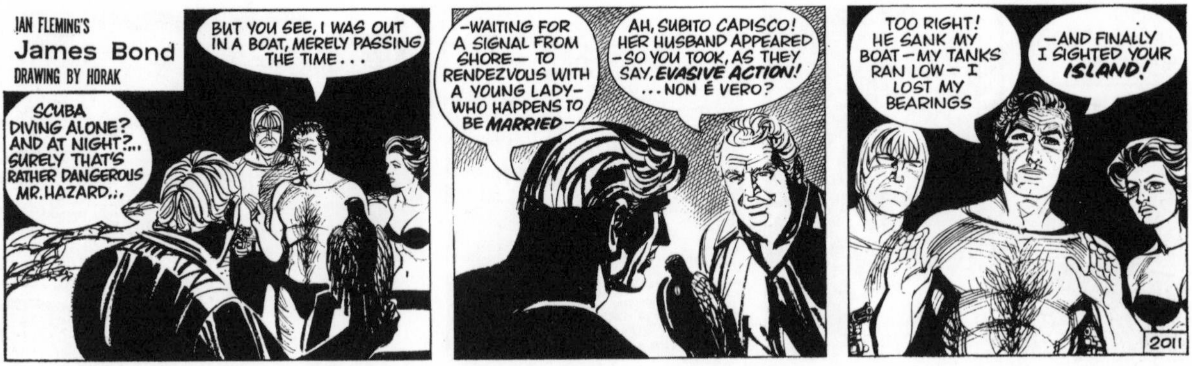
IAN FLEMING'S
James Bond
DRAWING BY HORAK
SCUBA DIVING ALONE? AND AT NIGHT?... SURELY THAT'S RATHER DANGEROUS MR. HAZARD...
BUT YOU SEE, I WAS OUT IN A BOAT, MERELY PASSING THE TIME...
-WAITING FOR A SIGNAL FROM SHORE- TO RENDEZVOUS WITH A YOUNG LADY- WHO HAPPENS TO BE MARRIED-
AH, SUBITO CAPISCO! HER HUSBAND APPEARED -SO YOU TOOK, AS THEY SAY, EVASIVE ACTION! ... NON É VERO?
TOO RIGHT! HE SANK MY BOAT-MY TANKS RAN LOW- I LOST MY BEARINGS
-AND FINALLY I SIGHTED YOUR ISLAND!
2011

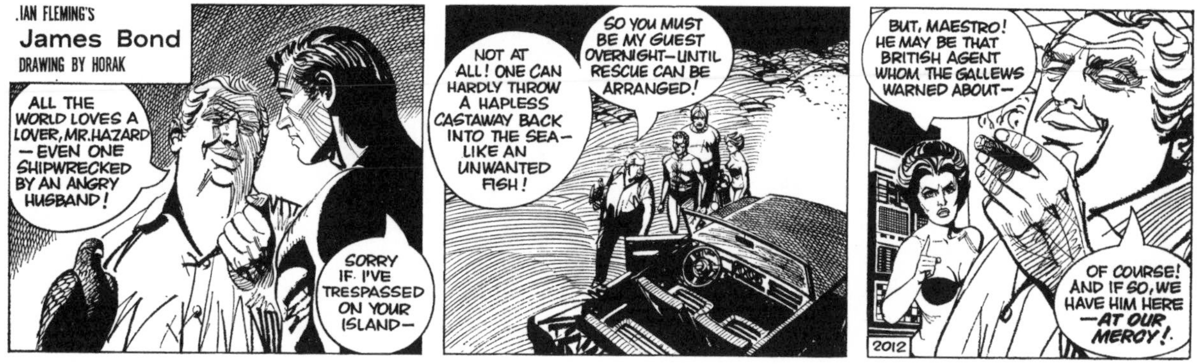
IAN FLEMING'S
James Bond
DRAWING BY HORAK
ALL THE WORLD LOVES A LOVER, MR. HAZARD —EVEN ONE SHIPWRECKED BY AN ANGRY HUSBAND!
SORRY IF I'VE TRESPASSED ON YOUR ISLAND—
NOT AT ALL! ONE CAN HARDLY THROW A HAPLESS CASTAWAY BACK INTO THE SEA—LIKE AN UNWANTED FISH!
SO YOU MUST BE MY GUEST OVERNIGHT—UNTIL RESCUE CAN BE ARRANGED!
BUT, MAESTRO! HE MAY BE THAT BRITISH AGENT WHOM THE GALLEWS WARNED ABOUT—
OF COURSE! AND IF SO, WE HAVE HIM HERE —AT OUR MERCY!
2012

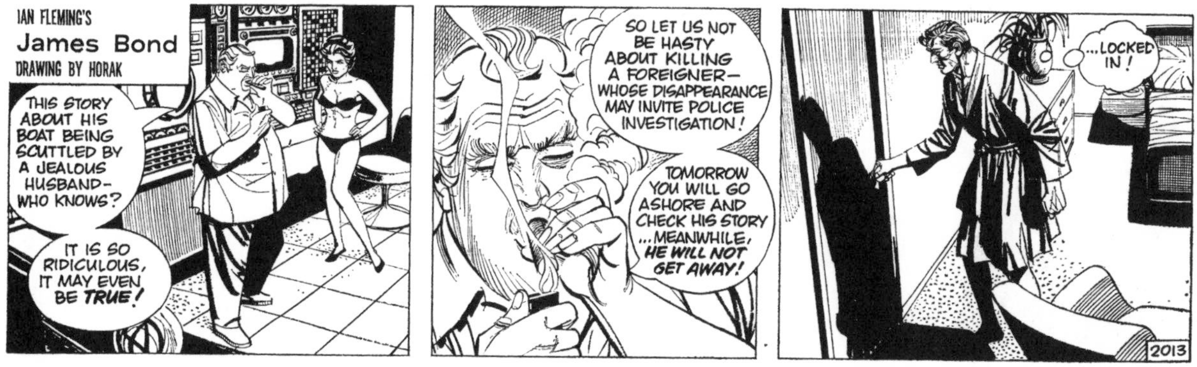
IAN FLEMING'S
James Bond
DRAWING BY HORAK
THIS STORY ABOUT HIS BOAT BEING SCUTTLED BY A JEALOUS HUSBAND— WHO KNOWS?
IT IS SO RIDICULOUS, IT MAY EVEN BE TRUE!
SO LET US NOT BE HASTY ABOUT KILLING A FOREIGNER— WHOSE DISAPPEARANCE MAY INVITE POLICE INVESTIGATION!
TOMORROW YOU WILL GO ASHORE AND CHECK HIS STORY ...MEANWHILE, HE WILL NOT GET AWAY!
...LOCKED IN!
2013

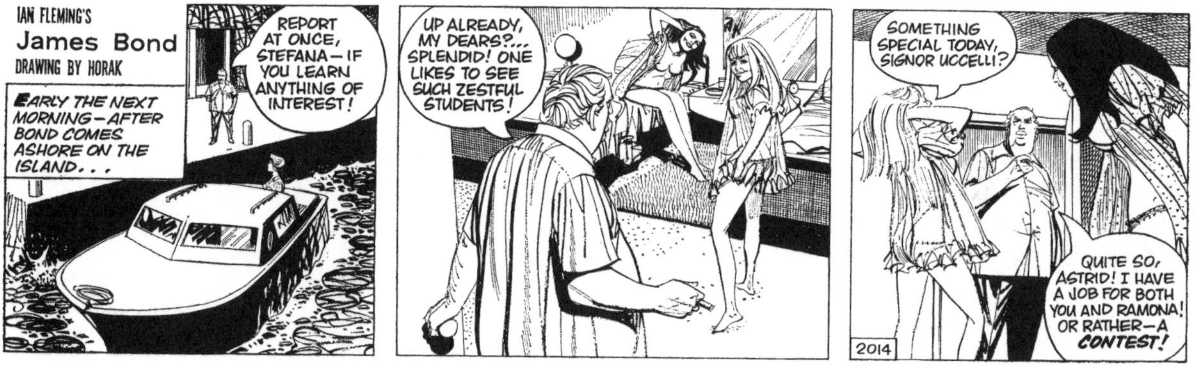
IAN FLEMING'S
James Bond
DRAWING BY HORAK
EARLY THE NEXT MORNING—AFTER BOND COMES ASHORE ON THE ISLAND...
REPORT AT ONCE, STEFANA—IF YOU LEARN ANYTHING OF INTEREST!
UP ALREADY, MY DEARS?... SPLENDID! ONE LIKES TO SEE SUCH ZESTFUL STUDENTS!
SOMETHING SPECIAL TODAY, SIGNOR UCCELLI?
QUITE SO, ASTRID! I HAVE A JOB FOR BOTH YOU AND RAMONA! OR RATHER—A CONTEST!
2014

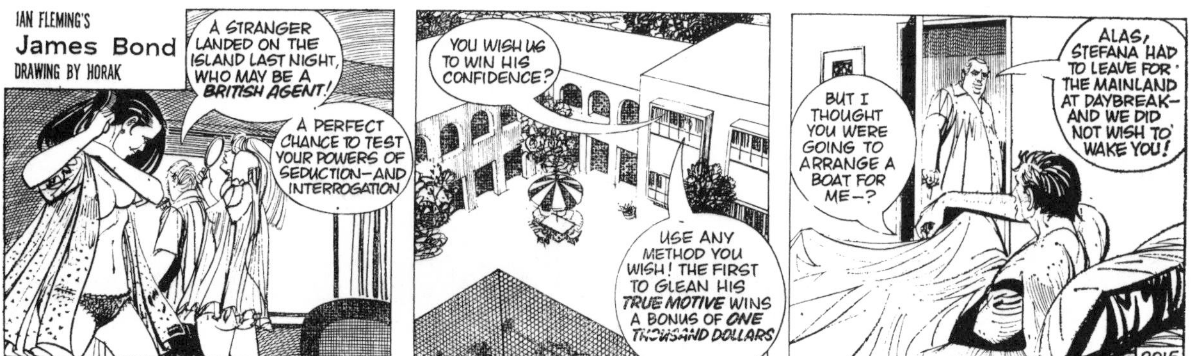
IAN FLEMING'S
James Bond
DRAWING BY HORAK
A STRANGER LANDED ON THE ISLAND LAST NIGHT, WHO MAY BE A BRITISH AGENT!
A PERFECT CHANCE TO TEST YOUR POWERS OF SEDUCTION—AND INTERROGATION
YOU WISH US TO WIN HIS CONFIDENCE?
USE ANY METHOD YOU WISH! THE FIRST TO GLEAN HIS TRUE MOTIVE WINS A BONUS OF ONE THOUSAND DOLLARS
BUT I THOUGHT YOU WERE GOING TO ARRANGE A BOAT FOR ME—?
ALAS, STEFANA HAD TO LEAVE FOR THE MAINLAND AT DAYBREAK— AND WE DID NOT WISH TO WAKE YOU!
2015

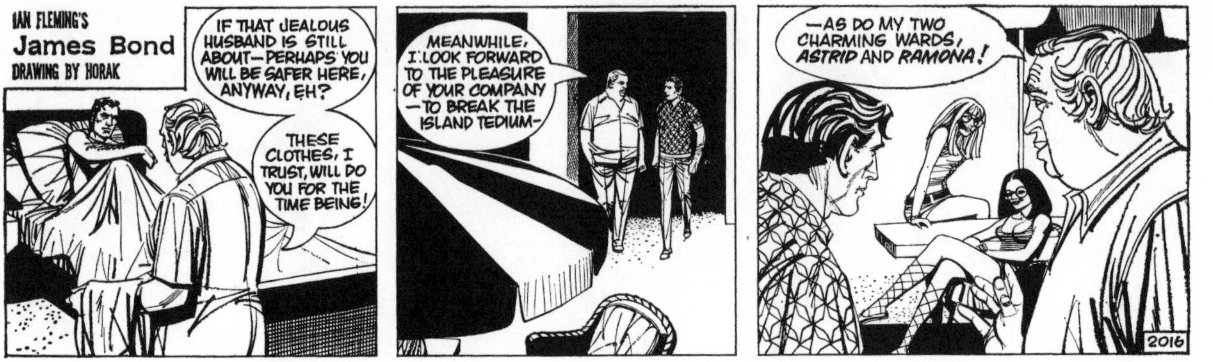
IAN FLEMING'S
James Bond
DRAWING BY HORAK
IF THAT JEALOUS HUSBAND IS STILL ABOUT—PERHAPS YOU WILL BE SAFER HERE, ANYWAY, EH?
THESE CLOTHES, I TRUST, WILL DO YOU FOR THE TIME BEING!
MEANWHILE, I LOOK FORWARD TO THE PLEASURE OF YOUR COMPANY —TO BREAK THE ISLAND TEDIUM—
—AS DO MY TWO CHARMING WARDS, ASTRID AND RAMONA!
2016

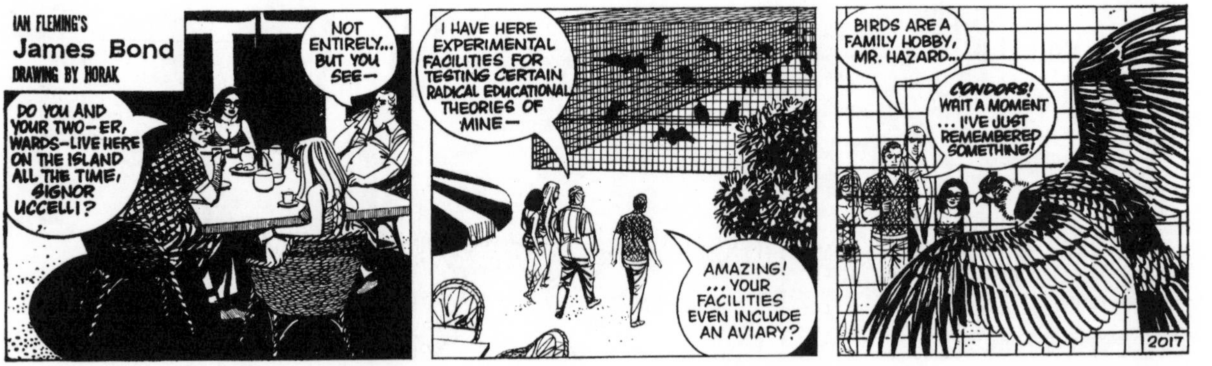
IAN FLEMING'S
James Bond
DRAWING BY HORAK
DO YOU AND YOUR TWO—ER, WARDS—LIVE HERE ON THE ISLAND ALL THE TIME, SIGNOR UCCELLI?
NOT ENTIRELY... BUT YOU SEE—
I HAVE HERE EXPERIMENTAL FACILITIES FOR TESTING CERTAIN RADICAL EDUCATIONAL THEORIES OF MINE—
AMAZING! ... YOUR FACILITIES EVEN INCLUDE AN AVIARY?
BIRDS ARE A FAMILY HOBBY, MR. HAZARD...
CONDORS! WAIT A MOMENT ... I'VE JUST REMEMBERED SOMETHING!
2017

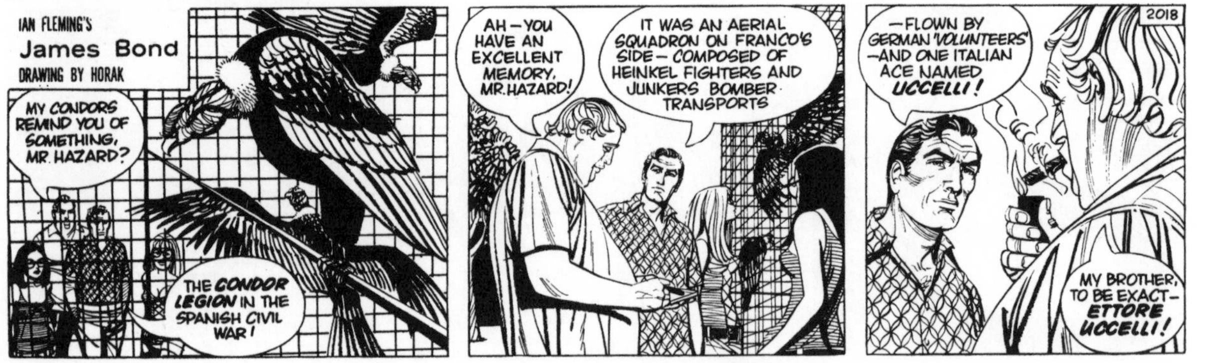
IAN FLEMING'S
James Bond
DRAWING BY HORAK
MY CONDORS REMIND YOU OF SOMETHING, MR. HAZARD?
THE CONDOR LEGION IN THE SPANISH CIVIL WAR!
AH—YOU HAVE AN EXCELLENT MEMORY, MR. HAZARD!
IT WAS AN AERIAL SQUADRON ON FRANCO'S SIDE—COMPOSED OF HEINKEL FIGHTERS AND JUNKERS BOMBER TRANSPORTS
—FLOWN BY GERMAN 'VOLUNTEERS' —AND ONE ITALIAN ACE NAMED UCCELLI!
MY BROTHER, TO BE EXACT— ETTORE UCCELLI!
2018

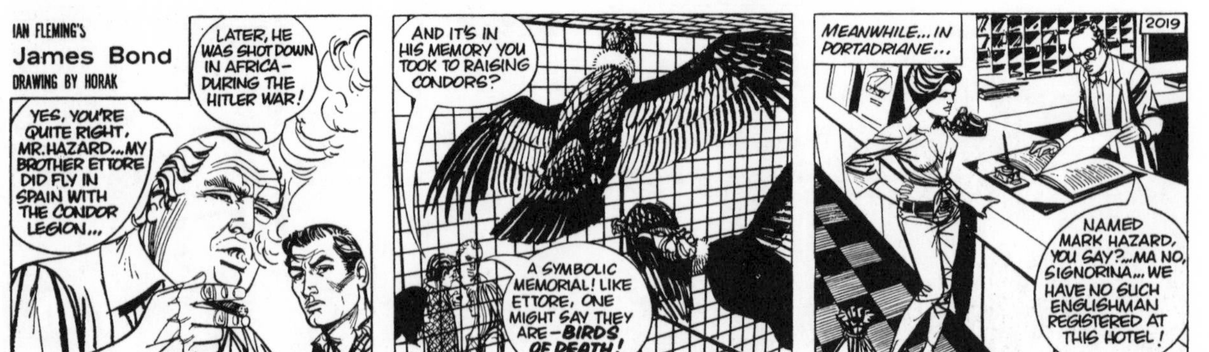
IAN FLEMING'S
James Bond
DRAWING BY HORAK
YES, YOU'RE QUITE RIGHT, MR. HAZARD... MY BROTHER ETTORE DID FLY IN SPAIN WITH THE CONDOR LEGION...
LATER, HE WAS SHOT DOWN IN AFRICA—DURING THE HITLER WAR!
AND IT'S IN HIS MEMORY YOU TOOK TO RAISING CONDORS?
A SYMBOLIC MEMORIAL! LIKE ETTORE, ONE MIGHT SAY THEY ARE—BIRDS OF DEATH!
MEANWHILE... IN PORTADRIANE...
NAMED MARK HAZARD, YOU SAY?...MA NO, SIGNORINA... WE HAVE NO SUCH ENGLISHMAN REGISTERED AT THIS HOTEL!
2019

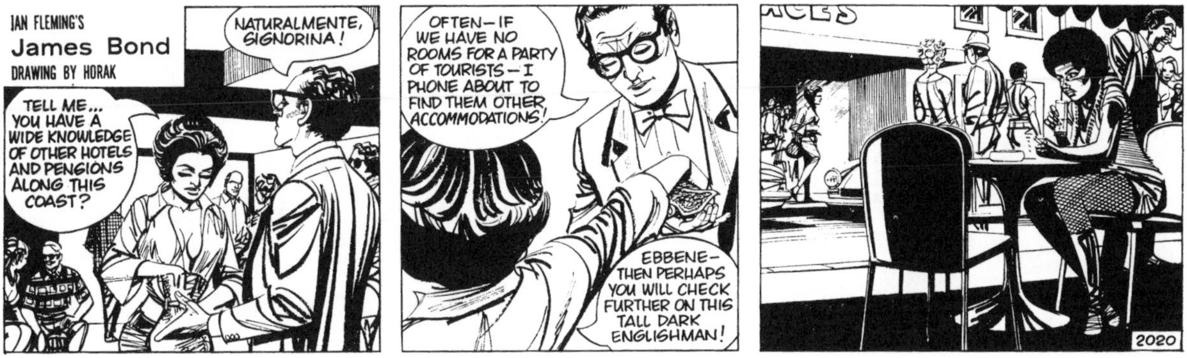
IAN FLEMING'S
James Bond
DRAWING BY HORAK
TELL ME... YOU HAVE A WIDE KNOWLEDGE OF OTHER HOTELS AND PENSIONS ALONG THIS COAST?
NATURALMENTE, SIGNORINA!
OFTEN—IF WE HAVE NO ROOMS FOR A PARTY OF TOURISTS—I PHONE ABOUT TO FIND THEM OTHER ACCOMMODATIONS!
EBBENE—THEN PERHAPS YOU WILL CHECK FURTHER ON THIS TALL DARK ENGLISHMAN!
2020

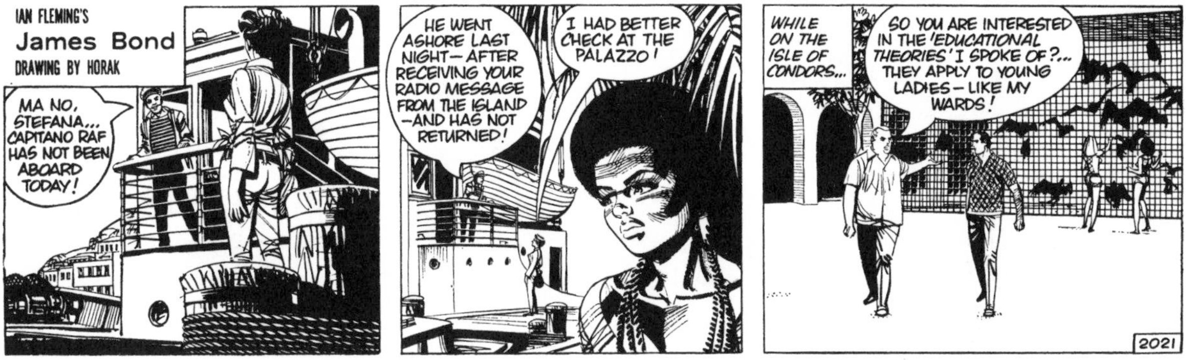
IAN FLEMING'S
James Bond
DRAWING BY HORAK
MA NO, STEFANA... CAPITANO RAF HAS NOT BEEN ABOARD TODAY!
HE WENT ASHORE LAST NIGHT—AFTER RECEIVING YOUR RADIO MESSAGE FROM THE ISLAND—AND HAS NOT RETURNED!
I HAD BETTER CHECK AT THE PALAZZO!
WHILE ON THE ISLE OF CONDORS...
SO YOU ARE INTERESTED IN THE 'EDUCATIONAL THEORIES' I SPOKE OF?... THEY APPLY TO YOUNG LADIES—LIKE MY WARDS!
2021

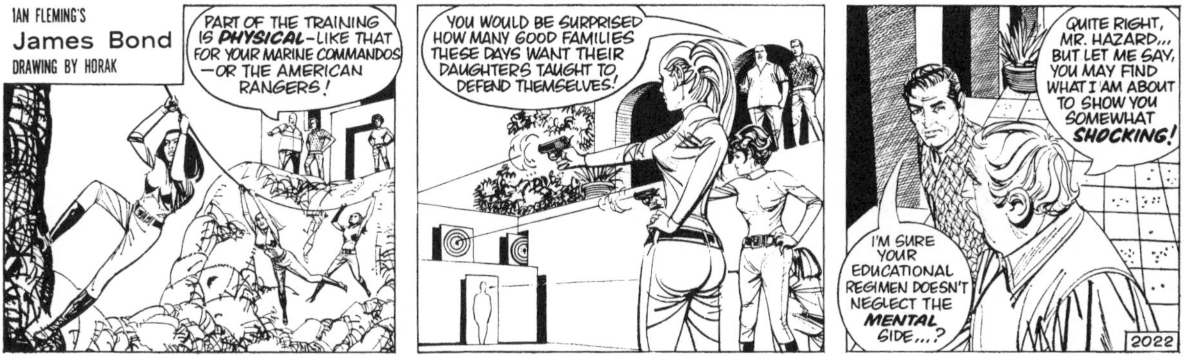
IAN FLEMING'S
James Bond
DRAWING BY HORAK
PART OF THE TRAINING IS PHYSICAL—LIKE THAT FOR YOUR MARINE COMMANDOS—OR THE AMERICAN RANGERS!
YOU WOULD BE SURPRISED HOW MANY GOOD FAMILIES THESE DAYS WANT THEIR DAUGHTERS TAUGHT TO DEFEND THEMSELVES!
I'M SURE YOUR EDUCATIONAL REGIMEN DOESN'T NEGLECT THE MENTAL SIDE...?
QUITE RIGHT, MR. HAZARD... BUT LET ME SAY, YOU MAY FIND WHAT I AM ABOUT TO SHOW YOU SOMEWHAT SHOCKING!
2022

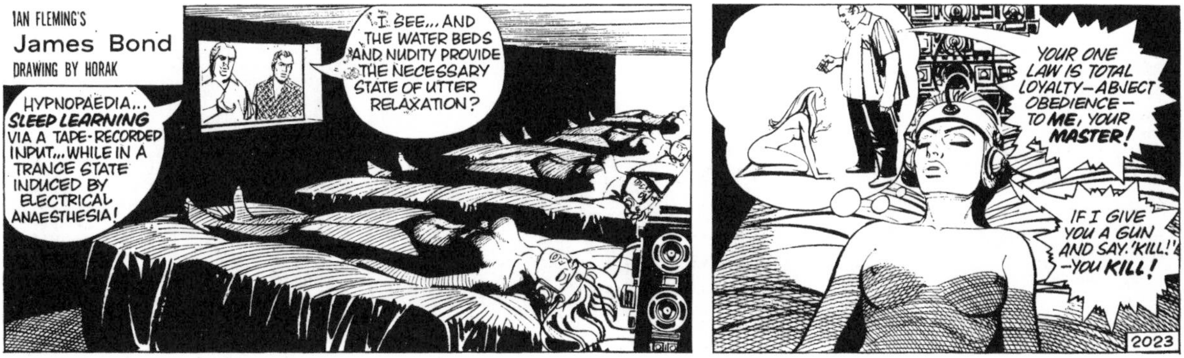
IAN FLEMING'S
James Bond
DRAWING BY HORAK
HYPNOPAEDIA... SLEEP LEARNING VIA A TAPE-RECORDED INPUT... WHILE IN A TRANCE STATE INDUCED BY ELECTRICAL ANAESTHESIA!
I SEE... AND THE WATER BEDS AND NUDITY PROVIDE THE NECESSARY STATE OF UTTER RELAXATION?
YOUR ONE LAW IS TOTAL LOYALTY—ABJECT OBEDIENCE—TO ME, YOUR MASTER!
IF I GIVE YOU A GUN AND SAY 'KILL!'—YOU KILL!
2023

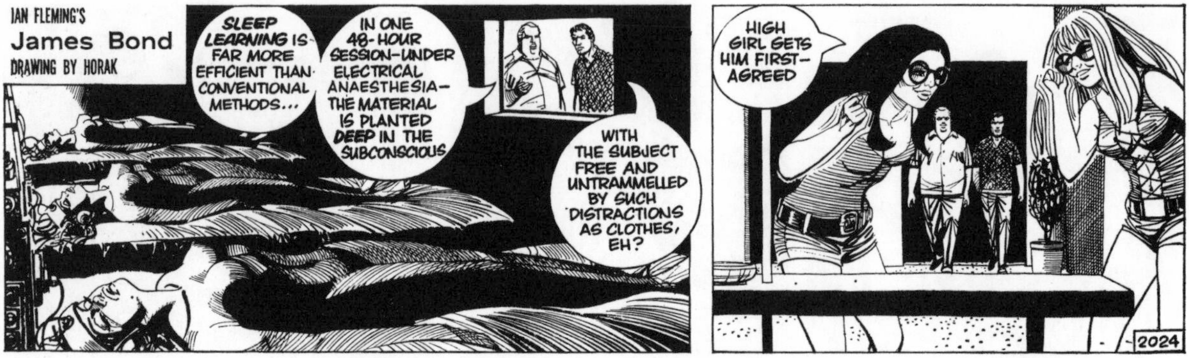
IAN FLEMING'S
James Bond
DRAWING BY HORAK
SLEEP LEARNING IS FAR MORE EFFICIENT THAN CONVENTIONAL METHODS...
IN ONE 48-HOUR SESSION-UNDER ELECTRICAL ANAESTHESIA-THE MATERIAL IS PLANTED DEEP IN THE SUBCONSCIOUS
WITH THE SUBJECT FREE AND UNTRAMMELLED BY SUCH DISTRACTIONS AS CLOTHES, EH?
HIGH GIRL GETS HIM FIRST-AGREED
2024

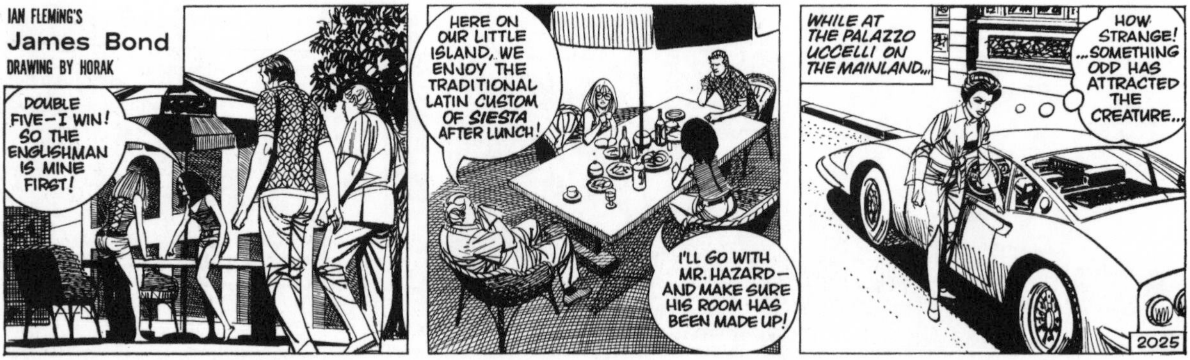
IAN FLEMING'S
James Bond
DRAWING BY HORAK
DOUBLE FIVE-I WIN! SO THE ENGLISHMAN IS MINE FIRST!
HERE ON OUR LITTLE ISLAND, WE ENJOY THE TRADITIONAL LATIN CUSTOM OF SIESTA AFTER LUNCH!
I'LL GO WITH MR. HAZARD-AND MAKE SURE HIS ROOM HAS BEEN MADE UP!
WHILE AT THE PALAZZO UCCELLI ON THE MAINLAND...
HOW STRANGE! ...SOMETHING ODD HAS ATTRACTED THE CREATURE...
2025

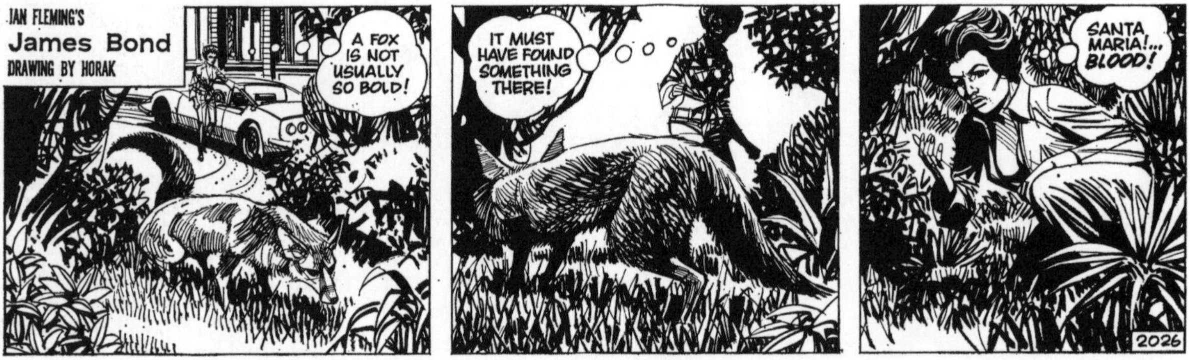
IAN FLEMING'S
James Bond
DRAWING BY HORAK
A FOX IS NOT USUALLY SO BOLD!
IT MUST HAVE FOUND SOMETHING THERE!
SANTA MARIA!... BLOOD!
2026

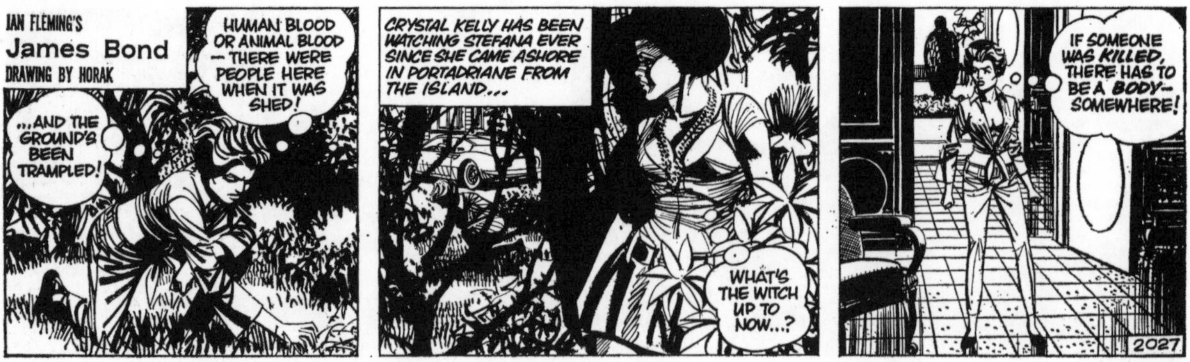
IAN FLEMING'S
James Bond
DRAWING BY HORAK
HUMAN BLOOD OR ANIMAL BLOOD -THERE WERE PEOPLE HERE WHEN IT WAS SHED!
...AND THE GROUND'S BEEN TRAMPLED!
CRYSTAL KELLY HAS BEEN WATCHING STEFANA EVER SINCE SHE CAME ASHORE IN PORTADRIANE FROM THE ISLAND...
WHAT'S THE WITCH UP TO NOW...?
IF SOMEONE WAS KILLED, THERE HAS TO BE A BODY-SOMEWHERE!
2027

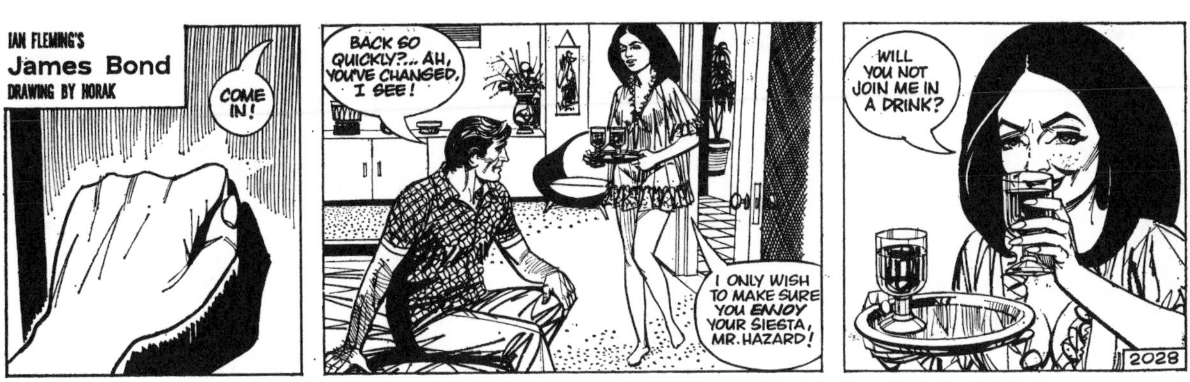
IAN FLEMING'S
James Bond
DRAWING BY HORAK
COME IN!
BACK SO QUICKLY?... AH, YOU'VE CHANGED, I SEE!
I ONLY WISH TO MAKE SURE YOU ENJOY YOUR SIESTA, MR. HAZARD!
WILL YOU NOT JOIN ME IN A DRINK?
2028

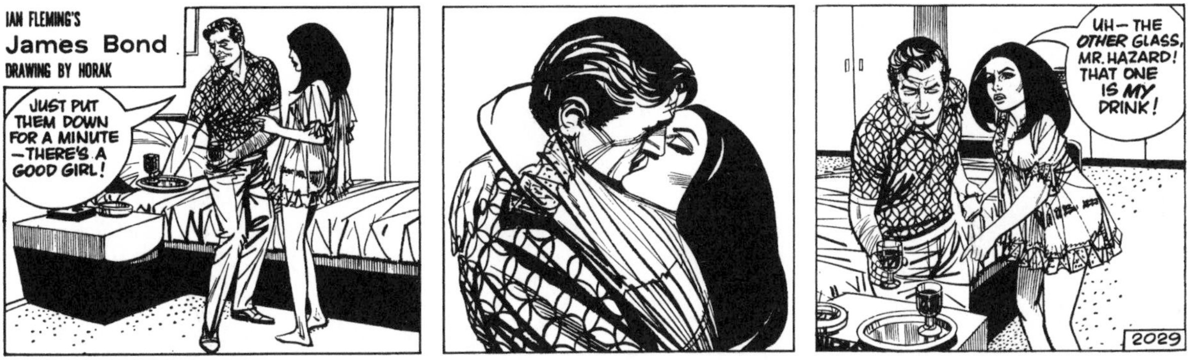
IAN FLEMING'S
James Bond
DRAWING BY HORAK
JUST PUT THEM DOWN FOR A MINUTE —THERE'S A GOOD GIRL!
UH— THE OTHER GLASS, MR. HAZARD! THAT ONE IS MY DRINK!
2029

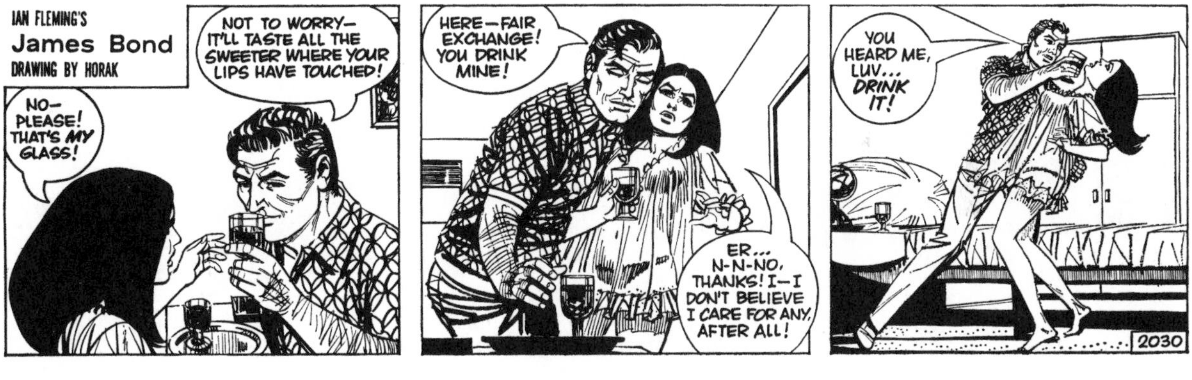
IAN FLEMING'S
James Bond
DRAWING BY HORAK
NOT TO WORRY— IT'LL TASTE ALL THE SWEETER WHERE YOUR LIPS HAVE TOUCHED!
NO— PLEASE! THAT'S MY GLASS!
HERE—FAIR EXCHANGE! YOU DRINK MINE!
ER... N-N-NO, THANKS! I—I DON'T BELIEVE I CARE FOR ANY, AFTER ALL!
YOU HEARD ME, LUV... DRINK IT!
2030

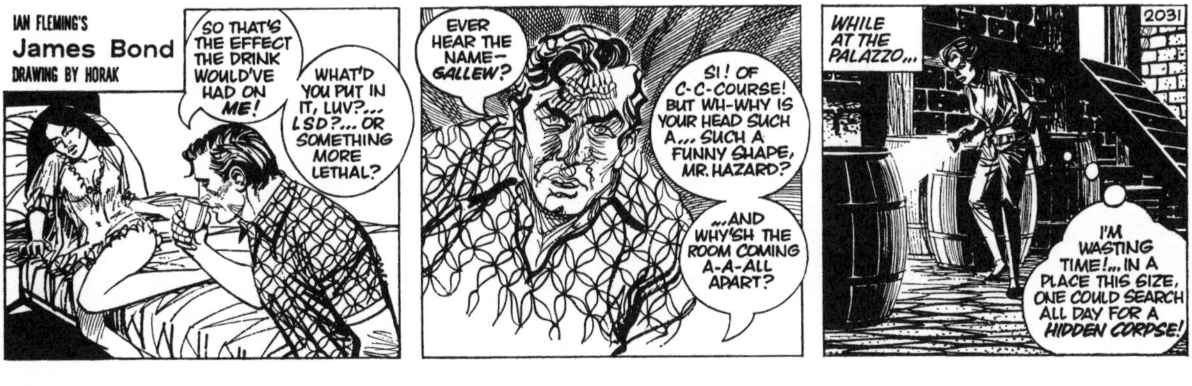
IAN FLEMING'S
James Bond
DRAWING BY HORAK
SO THAT'S THE EFFECT THE DRINK WOULD'VE HAD ON ME!
WHAT'D YOU PUT IN IT, LUV?... LSD?... OR SOMETHING MORE LETHAL?
EVER HEAR THE NAME— GALLEW?
SI! OF C-C-COURSE! BUT WH-WHY IS YOUR HEAD SUCH A... SUCH A FUNNY SHAPE, MR. HAZARD?
...AND WHY'SH THE ROOM COMING A-A-ALL APART?
WHILE AT THE PALAZZO...
2031
I'M WASTING TIME!... IN A PLACE THIS SIZE, ONE COULD SEARCH ALL DAY FOR A HIDDEN CORPSE!

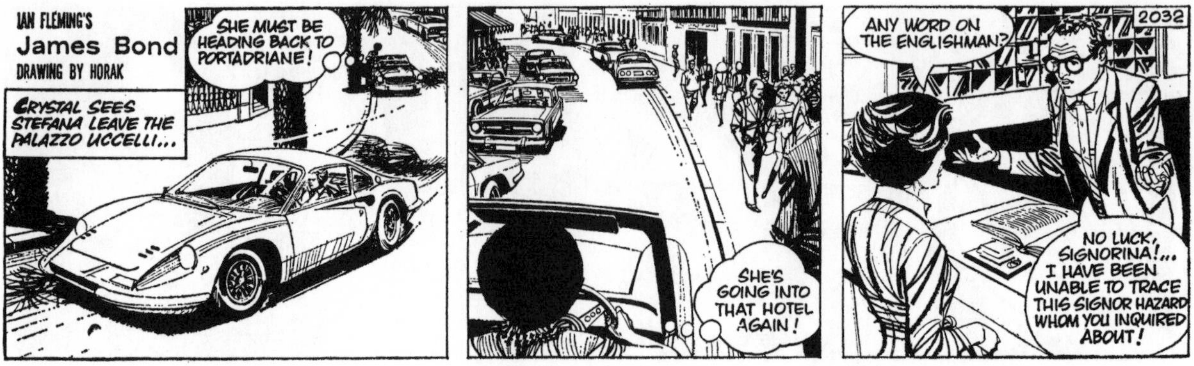
IAN FLEMING'S
James Bond
DRAWING BY HORAK
CRYSTAL SEES STEFANA LEAVE THE PALAZZO UCCELLI...
SHE MUST BE HEADING BACK TO PORTADRIANE!
SHE'S GOING INTO THAT HOTEL AGAIN!
2032
ANY WORD ON THE ENGLISHMAN?
NO LUCK, SIGNORINA!... I HAVE BEEN UNABLE TO TRACE THIS SIGNOR HAZARD WHOM YOU INQUIRED ABOUT!

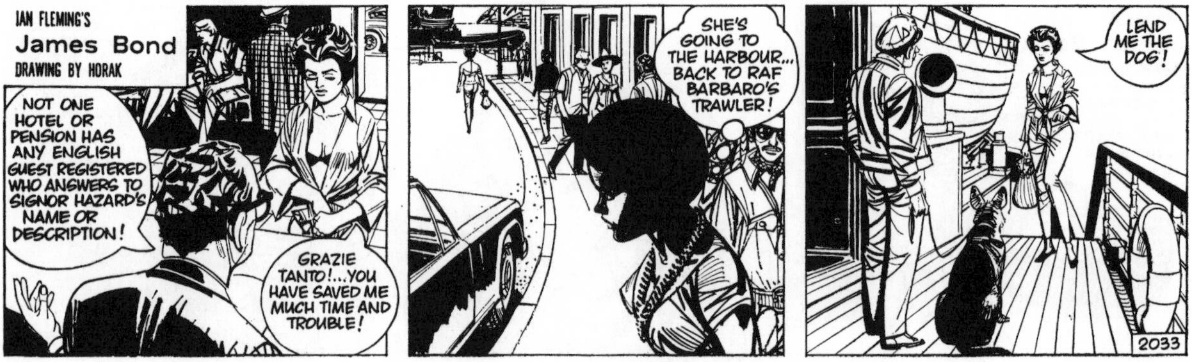
IAN FLEMING'S
James Bond
DRAWING BY HORAK
NOT ONE HOTEL OR PENSION HAS ANY ENGLISH GUEST REGISTERED WHO ANSWERS TO SIGNOR HAZARD'S NAME OR DESCRIPTION!
GRAZIE TANTO!...YOU HAVE SAVED ME MUCH TIME AND TROUBLE!
SHE'S GOING TO THE HARBOUR... BACK TO RAF BARBARO'S TRAWLER!
LEND ME THE DOG!
2033

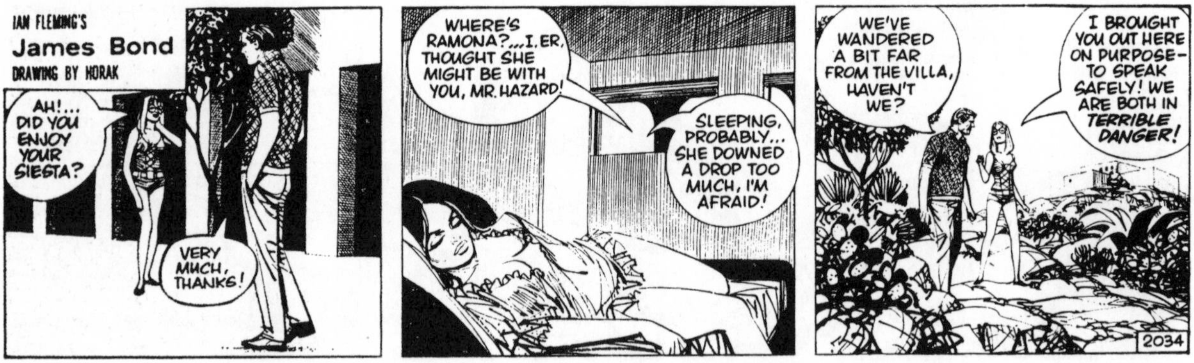
IAN FLEMING'S
James Bond
DRAWING BY HORAK
AH!... DID YOU ENJOY YOUR SIESTA?
VERY MUCH, THANKS!
WHERE'S RAMONA?... I, ER, THOUGHT SHE MIGHT BE WITH YOU, MR. HAZARD!
SLEEPING, PROBABLY... SHE DOWNED A DROP TOO MUCH, I'M AFRAID!
WE'VE WANDERED A BIT FAR FROM THE VILLA, HAVEN'T WE?
I BROUGHT YOU OUT HERE ON PURPOSE- TO SPEAK SAFELY! WE ARE BOTH IN TERRIBLE DANGER!
2034

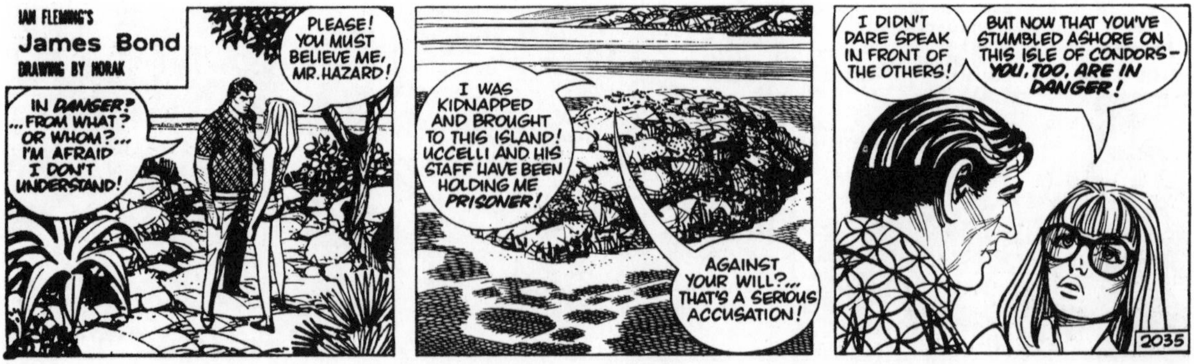
IAN FLEMING'S
James Bond
DRAWING BY HORAK
IN DANGER? ...FROM WHAT? OR WHOM?... I'M AFRAID I DON'T UNDERSTAND!
PLEASE! YOU MUST BELIEVE ME, MR. HAZARD!
I WAS KIDNAPPED AND BROUGHT TO THIS ISLAND! UCCELLI AND HIS STAFF HAVE BEEN HOLDING ME PRISONER!
AGAINST YOUR WILL?... THAT'S A SERIOUS ACCUSATION!
I DIDN'T DARE SPEAK IN FRONT OF THE OTHERS!
BUT NOW THAT YOU'VE STUMBLED ASHORE ON THIS ISLE OF CONDORS- YOU, TOO, ARE IN DANGER!
2035

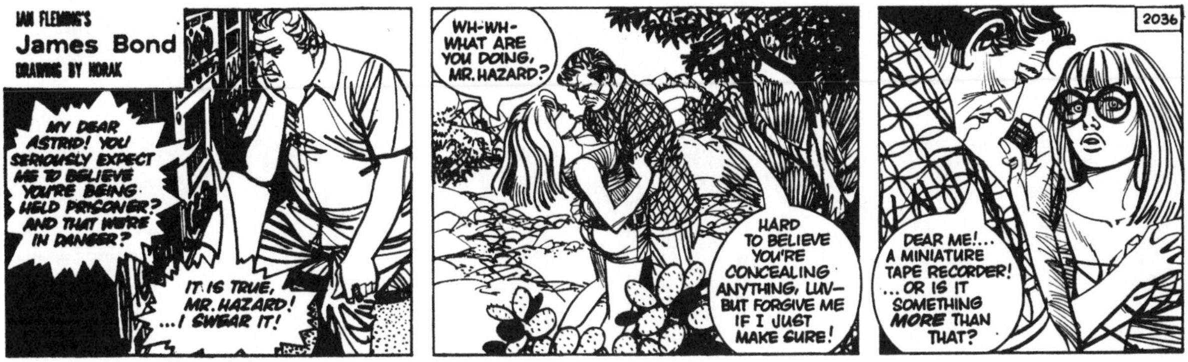
IAN FLEMING'S
James Bond
DRAWING BY HORAK
MY DEAR ASTRID! YOU SERIOUSLY EXPECT ME TO BELIEVE YOU'RE BEING HELD PRISONER? AND THAT WE'RE IN DANGER?
IT IS TRUE, MR. HAZARD! ...I SWEAR IT!
WH-WH-WHAT ARE YOU DOING, MR. HAZARD?
HARD TO BELIEVE YOU'RE CONCEALING ANYTHING, LUV-BUT FORGIVE ME IF I JUST MAKE SURE!
2036
DEAR ME!... A MINIATURE TAPE RECORDER! ...OR IS IT SOMETHING MORE THAN THAT?

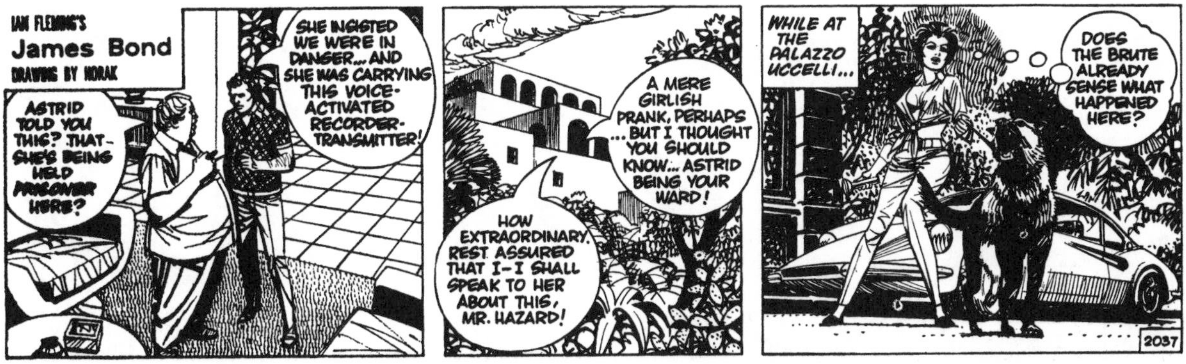
IAN FLEMING'S
James Bond
DRAWING BY HORAK
ASTRID TOLD YOU THIS? THAT SHE'S BEING HELD PRISONER HERE?
SHE INSISTED WE WERE IN DANGER... AND SHE WAS CARRYING THIS VOICE-ACTIVATED RECORDER-TRANSMITTER!
A MERE GIRLISH PRANK, PERHAPS ...BUT I THOUGHT YOU SHOULD KNOW... ASTRID BEING YOUR WARD!
HOW EXTRAORDINARY. REST ASSURED THAT I-I SHALL SPEAK TO HER ABOUT THIS, MR. HAZARD!
WHILE AT THE PALAZZO UCCELLI...
DOES THE BRUTE ALREADY SENSE WHAT HAPPENED HERE?
2037

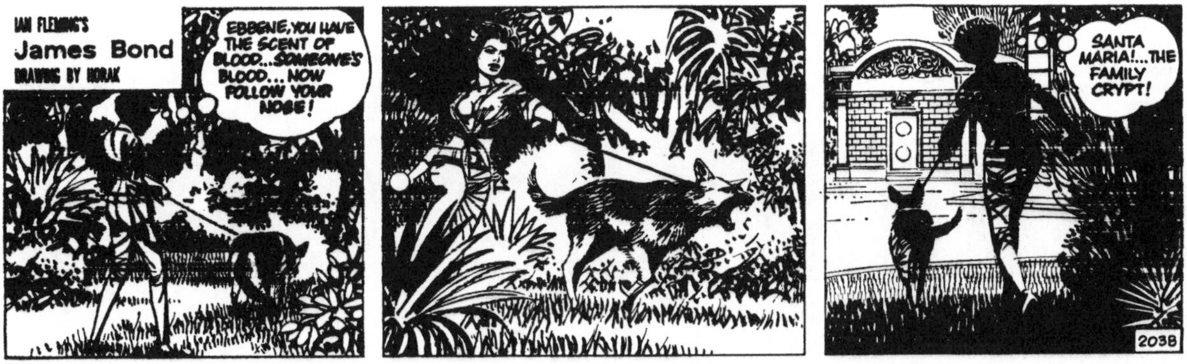
IAN FLEMING'S
James Bond
DRAWING BY HORAK
EBBENE, YOU HAVE THE SCENT OF BLOOD... SOMEONE'S BLOOD... NOW FOLLOW YOUR NOSE!
SANTA MARIA!... THE FAMILY CRYPT!
2038

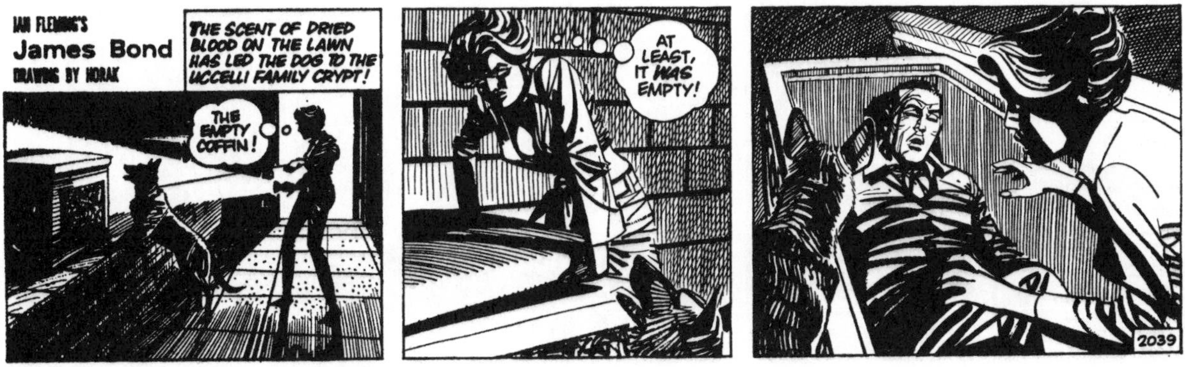
IAN FLEMING'S
James Bond
DRAWING BY HORAK
THE SCENT OF DRIED BLOOD ON THE LAWN HAS LED THE DOG TO THE UCCELLI FAMILY CRYPT!
THE EMPTY COFFIN!
AT LEAST, IT WAS EMPTY!
2039

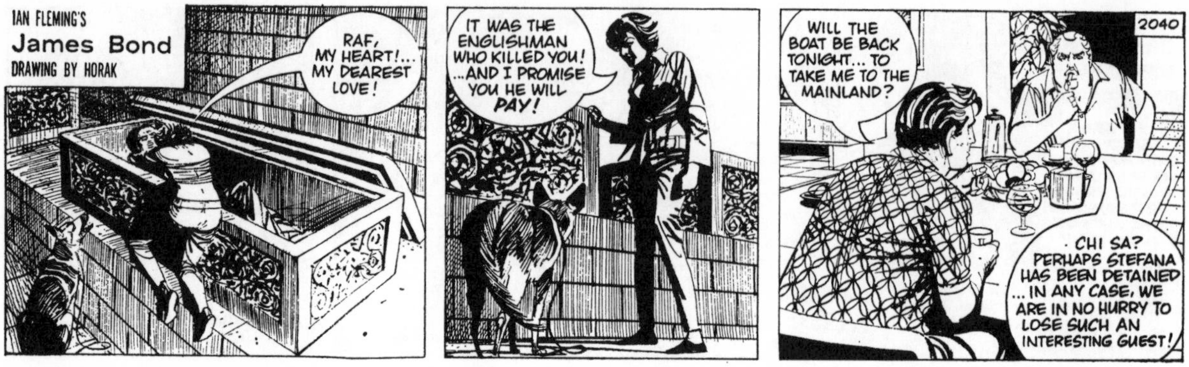
IAN FLEMING'S
James Bond
DRAWING BY HORAK
RAF, MY HEART!... MY DEAREST LOVE!
IT WAS THE ENGLISHMAN WHO KILLED YOU! ...AND I PROMISE YOU HE WILL PAY!
2040
WILL THE BOAT BE BACK TONIGHT... TO TAKE ME TO THE MAINLAND?
CHI SA? PERHAPS STEFANA HAS BEEN DETAINED ... IN ANY CASE, WE ARE IN NO HURRY TO LOSE SUCH AN INTERESTING GUEST!

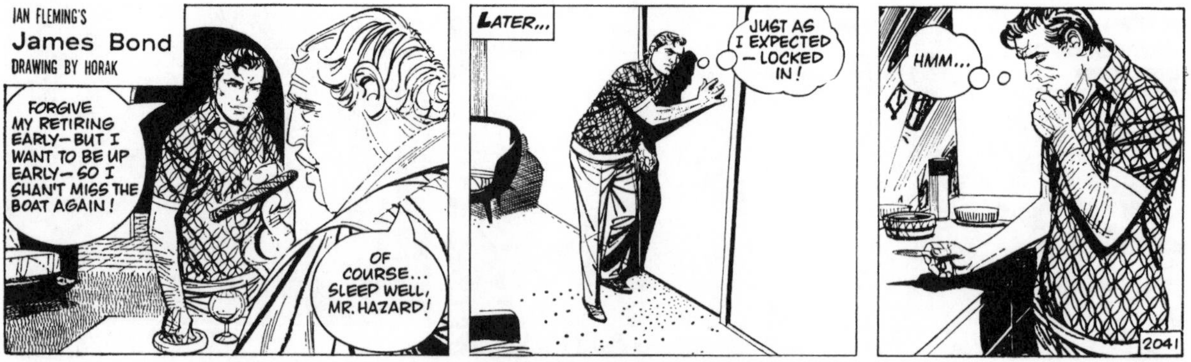
IAN FLEMING'S
James Bond
DRAWING BY HORAK
FORGIVE MY RETIRING EARLY–BUT I WANT TO BE UP EARLY–SO I SHAN'T MISS THE BOAT AGAIN!
OF COURSE... SLEEP WELL, MR. HAZARD!
LATER...
JUST AS I EXPECTED –LOCKED IN!
HMM...
2041

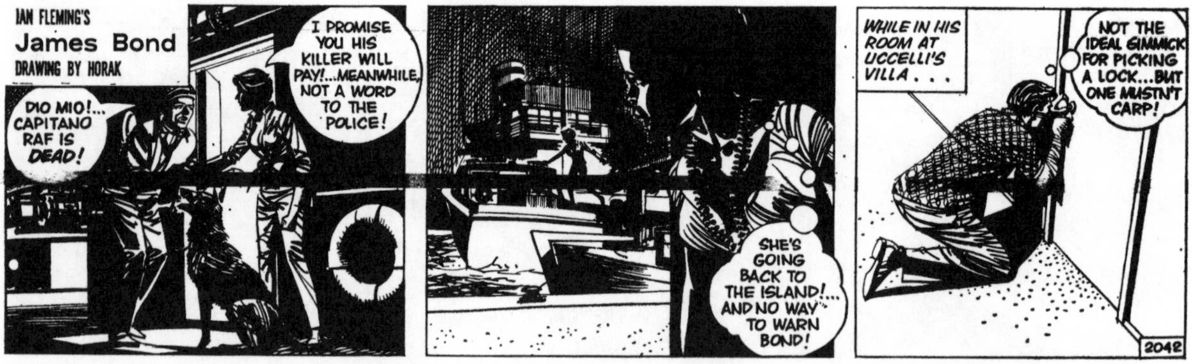
IAN FLEMING'S
James Bond
DRAWING BY HORAK
DIO MIO!... CAPITANO RAF IS DEAD!
I PROMISE YOU HIS KILLER WILL PAY!...MEANWHILE, NOT A WORD TO THE POLICE!
SHE'S GOING BACK TO THE ISLAND!... AND NO WAY TO WARN BOND!
WHILE IN HIS ROOM AT UCCELLI'S VILLA . . .
NOT THE IDEAL GIMMICK FOR PICKING A LOCK...BUT ONE MUSTN'T CARP!
2042

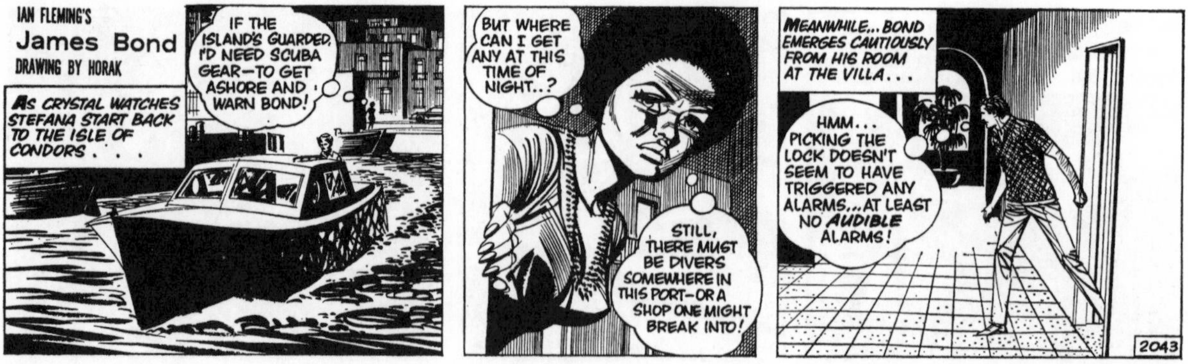
IAN FLEMING'S
James Bond
DRAWING BY HORAK
AS CRYSTAL WATCHES STEFANA START BACK TO THE ISLE OF CONDORS . . .
IF THE ISLAND'S GUARDED, I'D NEED SCUBA GEAR–TO GET ASHORE AND WARN BOND!
BUT WHERE CAN I GET ANY AT THIS TIME OF NIGHT..?
STILL, THERE MUST BE DIVERS SOMEWHERE IN THIS PORT–OR A SHOP ONE MIGHT BREAK INTO!
MEANWHILE... BOND EMERGES CAUTIOUSLY FROM HIS ROOM AT THE VILLA . . .
HMM... PICKING THE LOCK DOESN'T SEEM TO HAVE TRIGGERED ANY ALARMS...AT LEAST NO AUDIBLE ALARMS!
2043

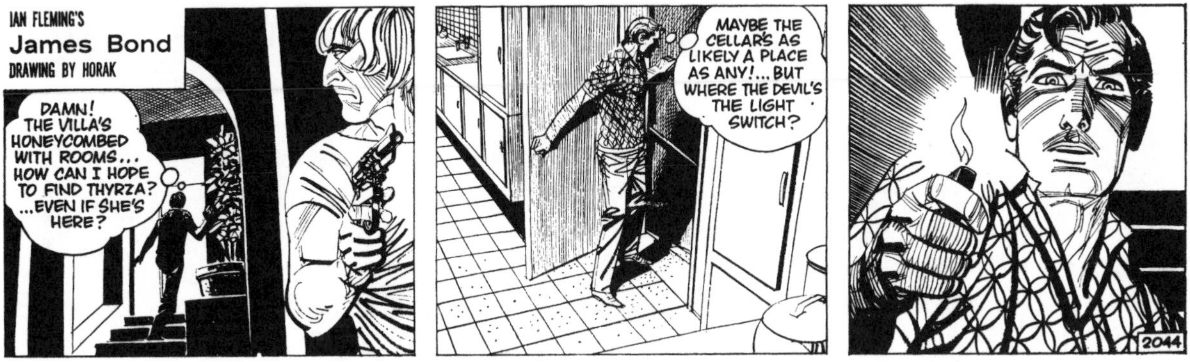
IAN FLEMING'S
James Bond
DRAWING BY HORAK
DAMN! THE VILLA'S HONEYCOMBED WITH ROOMS... HOW CAN I HOPE TO FIND THYRZA? ...EVEN IF SHE'S HERE?
MAYBE THE CELLAR'S AS LIKELY A PLACE AS ANY!... BUT WHERE THE DEVIL'S THE LIGHT SWITCH?
2044

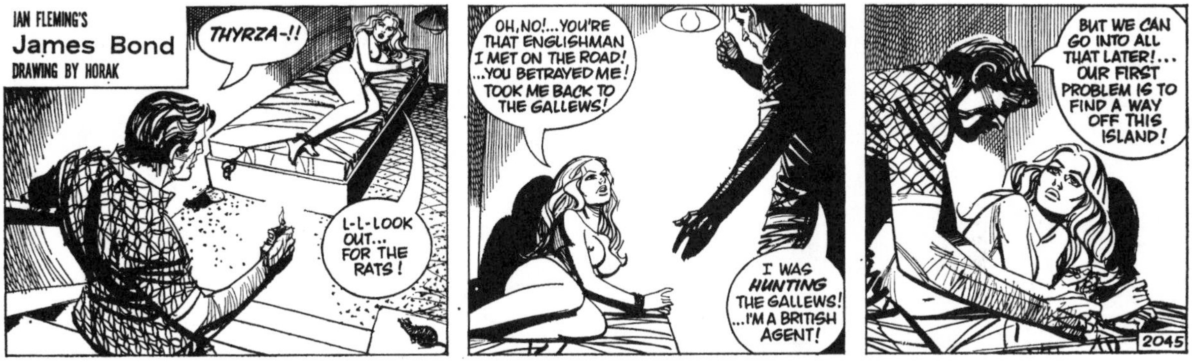
IAN FLEMING'S
James Bond
DRAWING BY HORAK
THYRZA-!!
L-L-LOOK OUT... FOR THE RATS!
OH, NO!... YOU'RE THAT ENGLISHMAN I MET ON THE ROAD! ...YOU BETRAYED ME! TOOK ME BACK TO THE GALLEWS!
I WAS HUNTING THE GALLEWS! ...I'M A BRITISH AGENT!
BUT WE CAN GO INTO ALL THAT LATER!... OUR FIRST PROBLEM IS TO FIND A WAY OFF THIS ISLAND!
2045

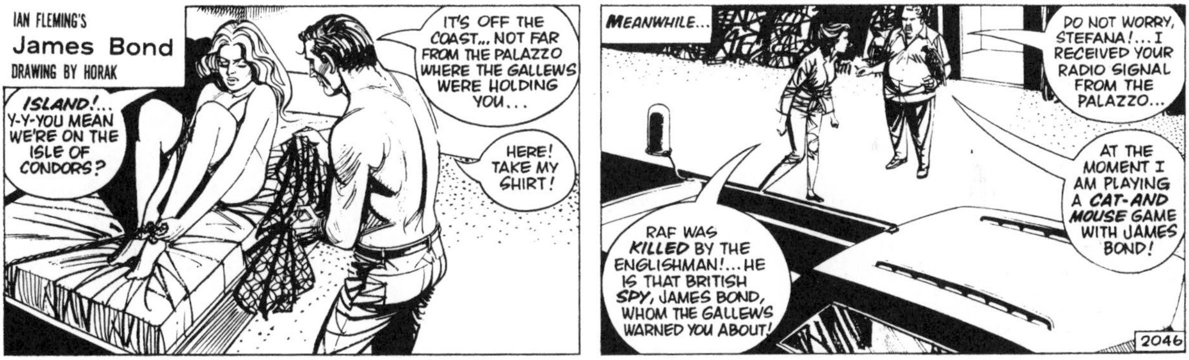
IAN FLEMING'S
James Bond
DRAWING BY HORAK
ISLAND!... Y-Y-YOU MEAN WE'RE ON THE ISLE OF CONDORS?
IT'S OFF THE COAST... NOT FAR FROM THE PALAZZO WHERE THE GALLEWS WERE HOLDING YOU...
HERE! TAKE MY SHIRT!
MEANWHILE...
RAF WAS KILLED BY THE ENGLISHMAN!... HE IS THAT BRITISH SPY, JAMES BOND, WHOM THE GALLEWS WARNED YOU ABOUT!
DO NOT WORRY, STEFANA!... I RECEIVED YOUR RADIO SIGNAL FROM THE PALAZZO...
AT THE MOMENT I AM PLAYING A CAT-AND MOUSE GAME WITH JAMES BOND!
2046

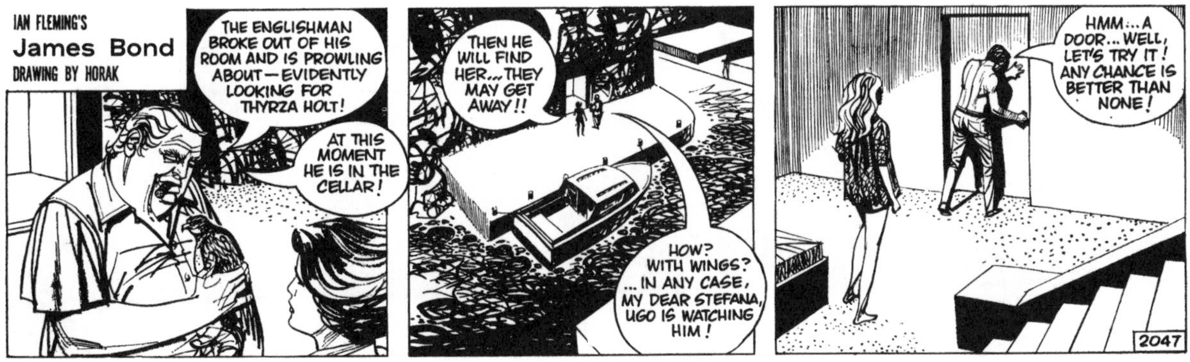
IAN FLEMING'S
James Bond
DRAWING BY HORAK
THE ENGLISHMAN BROKE OUT OF HIS ROOM AND IS PROWLING ABOUT—EVIDENTLY LOOKING FOR THYRZA HOLT!
AT THIS MOMENT HE IS IN THE CELLAR!
THEN HE WILL FIND HER... THEY MAY GET AWAY!!
HOW? WITH WINGS? ...IN ANY CASE, MY DEAR STEFANA, UGO IS WATCHING HIM!
HMM... A DOOR... WELL, LET'S TRY IT! ANY CHANCE IS BETTER THAN NONE!
2047

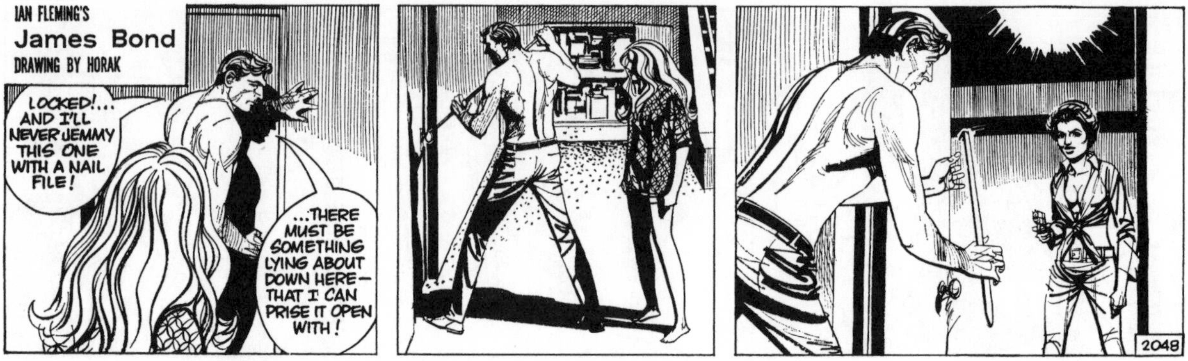
IAN FLEMING'S
James Bond
DRAWING BY HORAK
LOCKED!... AND I'LL NEVER JEMMY THIS ONE WITH A NAIL FILE!
...THERE MUST BE SOMETHING LYING ABOUT DOWN HERE—THAT I CAN PRISE IT OPEN WITH!
2048

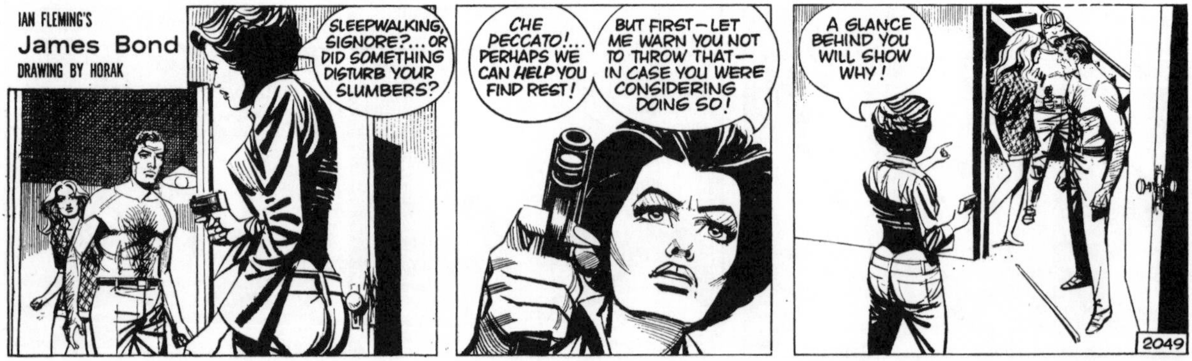
IAN FLEMING'S
James Bond
DRAWING BY HORAK
SLEEPWALKING, SIGNORE?...OR DID SOMETHING DISTURB YOUR SLUMBERS?
CHE PECCATO!... PERHAPS WE CAN HELP YOU FIND REST!
BUT FIRST—LET ME WARN YOU NOT TO THROW THAT—IN CASE YOU WERE CONSIDERING DOING SO!
A GLANCE BEHIND YOU WILL SHOW WHY!
2049

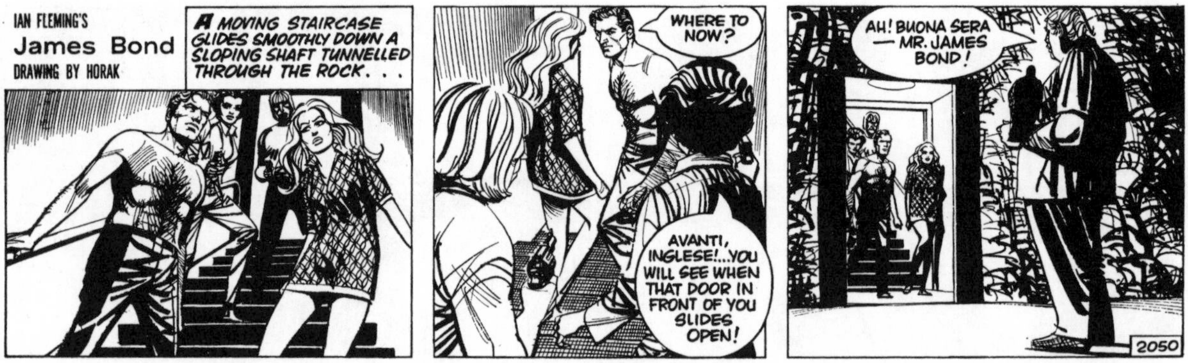
IAN FLEMING'S
James Bond
DRAWING BY HORAK
A MOVING STAIRCASE GLIDES SMOOTHLY DOWN A SLOPING SHAFT TUNNELLED THROUGH THE ROCK. . .
WHERE TO NOW?
AVANTI, INGLESE!...YOU WILL SEE WHEN THAT DOOR IN FRONT OF YOU SLIDES OPEN!
AH! BUONA SERA —MR. JAMES BOND!
2050

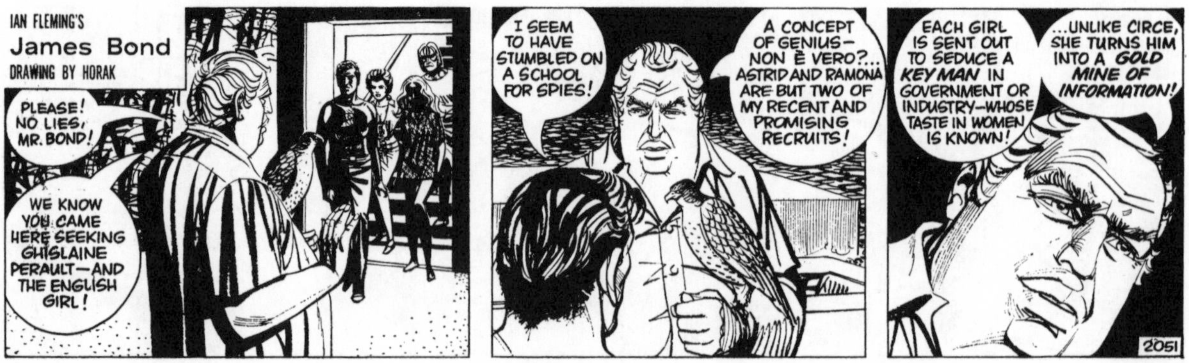
IAN FLEMING'S
James Bond
DRAWING BY HORAK
PLEASE! NO LIES, MR. BOND!
WE KNOW YOU CAME HERE SEEKING GHISLAINE PERAULT—AND THE ENGLISH GIRL!
I SEEM TO HAVE STUMBLED ON A SCHOOL FOR SPIES!
A CONCEPT OF GENIUS—NON È VERO?... ASTRID AND RAMONA ARE BUT TWO OF MY RECENT AND PROMISING RECRUITS!
EACH GIRL IS SENT OUT TO SEDUCE A KEY MAN IN GOVERNMENT OR INDUSTRY—WHOSE TASTE IN WOMEN IS KNOWN!
...UNLIKE CIRCE, SHE TURNS HIM INTO A GOLD MINE OF INFORMATION!
2051

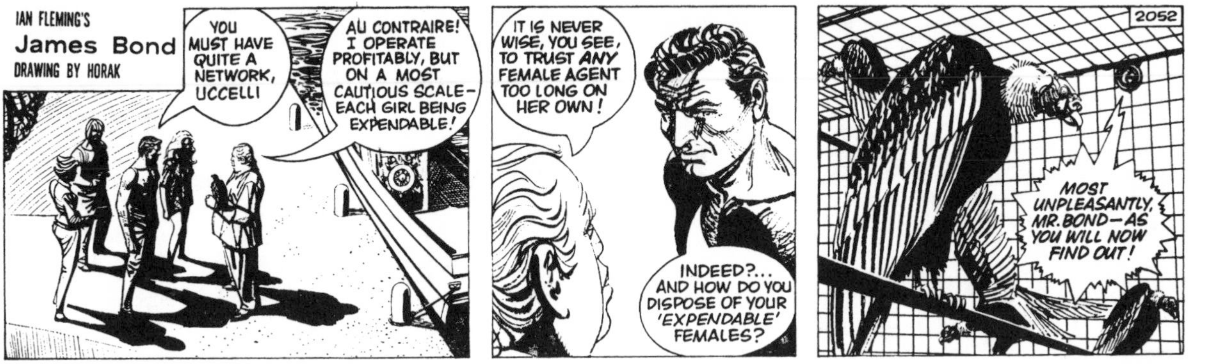
IAN FLEMING'S
James Bond
DRAWING BY HORAK
YOU MUST HAVE QUITE A NETWORK, UCCELLI
AU CONTRAIRE! I OPERATE PROFITABLY, BUT ON A MOST CAUTIOUS SCALE— EACH GIRL BEING EXPENDABLE!
IT IS NEVER WISE, YOU SEE, TO TRUST ANY FEMALE AGENT TOO LONG ON HER OWN!
INDEED?... AND HOW DO YOU DISPOSE OF YOUR 'EXPENDABLE' FEMALES?
2052
MOST UNPLEASANTLY, MR. BOND—AS YOU WILL NOW FIND OUT!

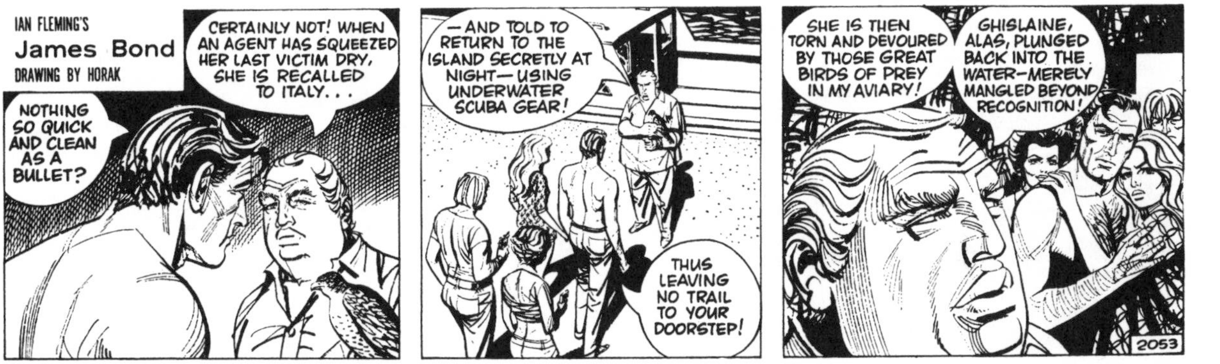
IAN FLEMING'S
James Bond
DRAWING BY HORAK
NOTHING SO QUICK AND CLEAN AS A BULLET?
CERTAINLY NOT! WHEN AN AGENT HAS SQUEEZED HER LAST VICTIM DRY, SHE IS RECALLED TO ITALY...
—AND TOLD TO RETURN TO THE ISLAND SECRETLY AT NIGHT—USING UNDERWATER SCUBA GEAR!
THUS LEAVING NO TRAIL TO YOUR DOORSTEP!
SHE IS THEN TORN AND DEVOURED BY THOSE GREAT BIRDS OF PREY IN MY AVIARY!
GHISLAINE, ALAS, PLUNGED BACK INTO THE WATER—MERELY MANGLED BEYOND RECOGNITION!
2053

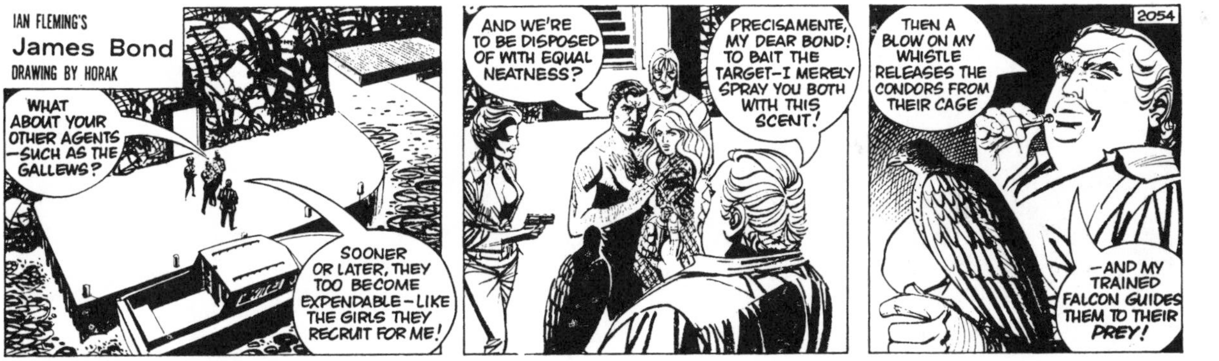
IAN FLEMING'S
James Bond
DRAWING BY HORAK
WHAT ABOUT YOUR OTHER AGENTS —SUCH AS THE GALLEWS?
SOONER OR LATER, THEY TOO BECOME EXPENDABLE—LIKE THE GIRLS THEY RECRUIT FOR ME!
AND WE'RE TO BE DISPOSED OF WITH EQUAL NEATNESS?
PRECISAMENTE, MY DEAR BOND! TO BAIT THE TARGET—I MERELY SPRAY YOU BOTH WITH THIS SCENT!
2054
THEN A BLOW ON MY WHISTLE RELEASES THE CONDORS FROM THEIR CAGE
—AND MY TRAINED FALCON GUIDES THEM TO THEIR PREY!

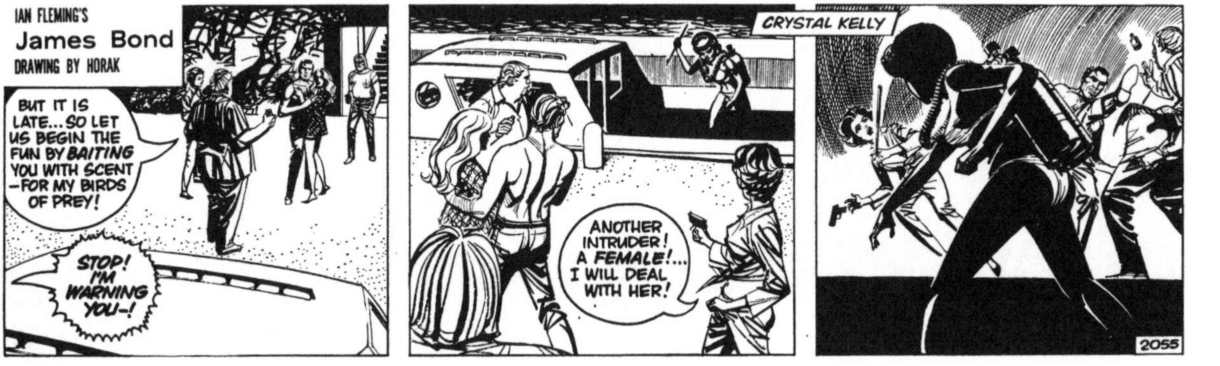
IAN FLEMING'S
James Bond
DRAWING BY HORAK
BUT IT IS LATE... SO LET US BEGIN THE FUN BY BAITING YOU WITH SCENT —FOR MY BIRDS OF PREY!
STOP! I'M WARNING YOU—!
CRYSTAL KELLY
ANOTHER INTRUDER! A FEMALE!... I WILL DEAL WITH HER!
2055

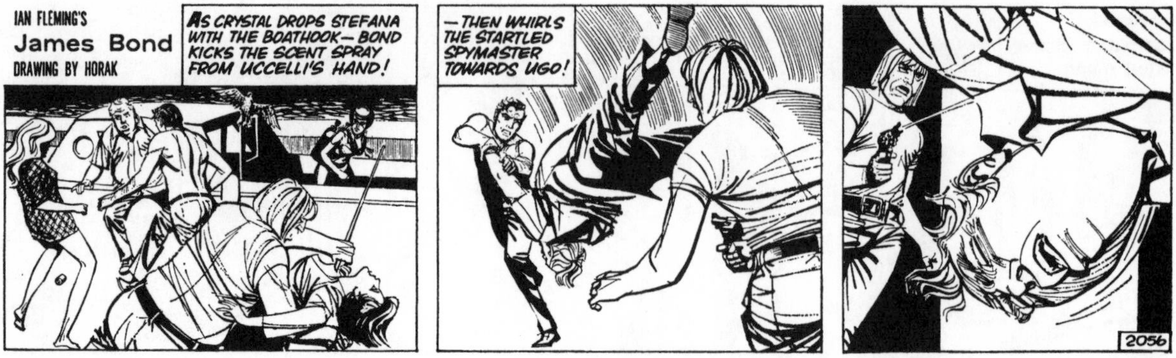
IAN FLEMING'S
James Bond
DRAWING BY HORAK
AS CRYSTAL DROPS STEFANA WITH THE BOATHOOK—BOND KICKS THE SCENT SPRAY FROM UCCELLI'S HAND!
—THEN WHIRLS THE STARTLED SPYMASTER TOWARDS UGO!
2056

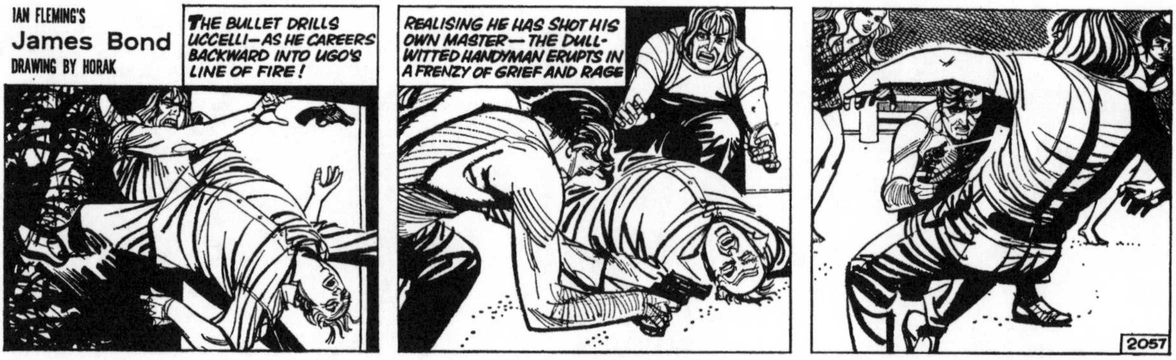
IAN FLEMING'S
James Bond
DRAWING BY HORAK
THE BULLET DRILLS UCCELLI—AS HE CAREERS BACKWARD INTO UGO'S LINE OF FIRE!
REALISING HE HAS SHOT HIS OWN MASTER—THE DULL-WITTED HANDYMAN ERUPTS IN A FRENZY OF GRIEF AND RAGE
2057

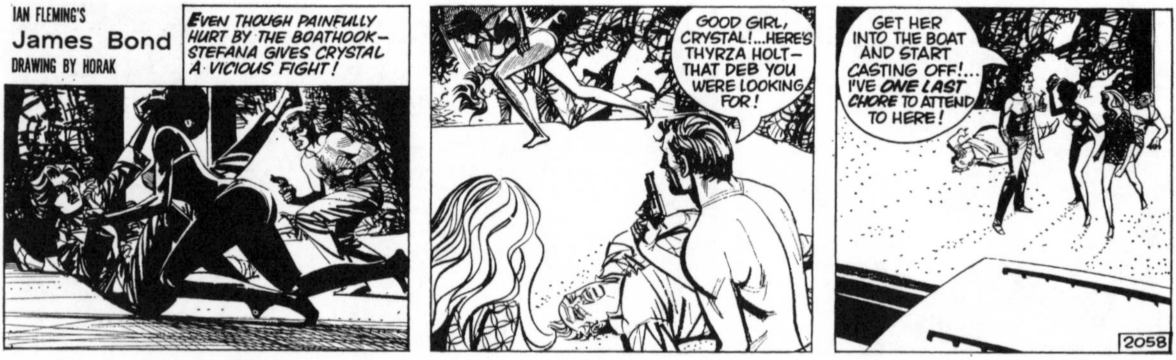
IAN FLEMING'S
James Bond
DRAWING BY HORAK
EVEN THOUGH PAINFULLY HURT BY THE BOATHOOK—STEFANA GIVES CRYSTAL A VICIOUS FIGHT!
GOOD GIRL, CRYSTAL!...HERE'S THYRZA HOLT—THAT DEB YOU WERE LOOKING FOR!
GET HER INTO THE BOAT AND START CASTING OFF!... I'VE ONE LAST CHORE TO ATTEND TO HERE!
2058

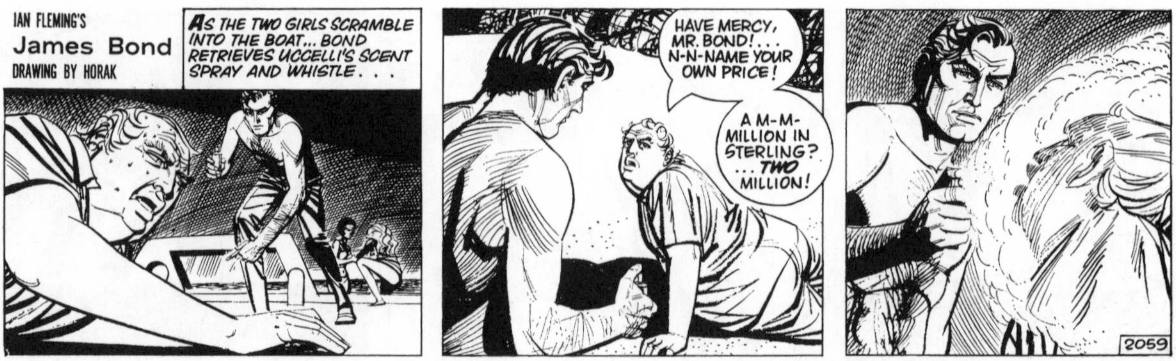
IAN FLEMING'S
James Bond
DRAWING BY HORAK
AS THE TWO GIRLS SCRAMBLE INTO THE BOAT... BOND RETRIEVES UCCELLI'S SCENT SPRAY AND WHISTLE . . .
HAVE MERCY, MR. BOND!... N-N-NAME YOUR OWN PRICE!
A M-M-MILLION IN STERLING? ... TWO MILLION!
2059

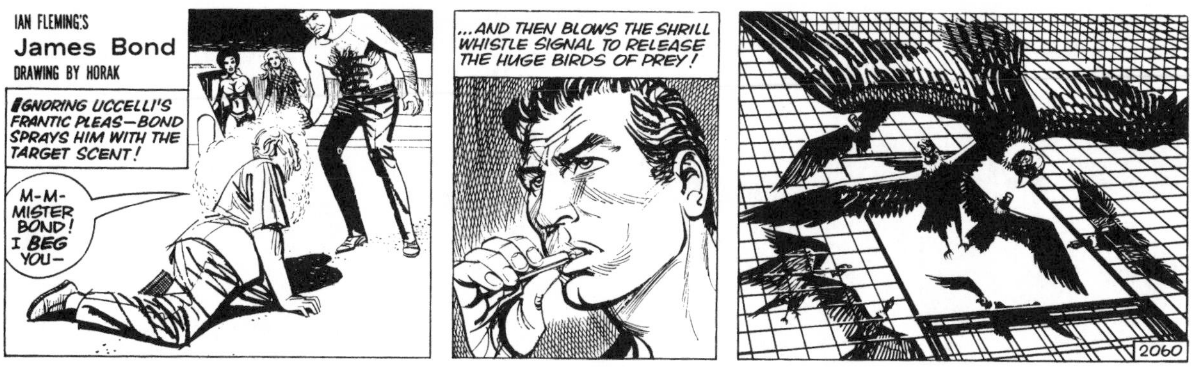
IAN FLEMING'S
James Bond
DRAWING BY HORAK
IGNORING UCCELLI'S FRANTIC PLEAS—BOND SPRAYS HIM WITH THE TARGET SCENT!
M-M-MISTER BOND! I BEG YOU—
...AND THEN BLOWS THE SHRILL WHISTLE SIGNAL TO RELEASE THE HUGE BIRDS OF PREY!
2060

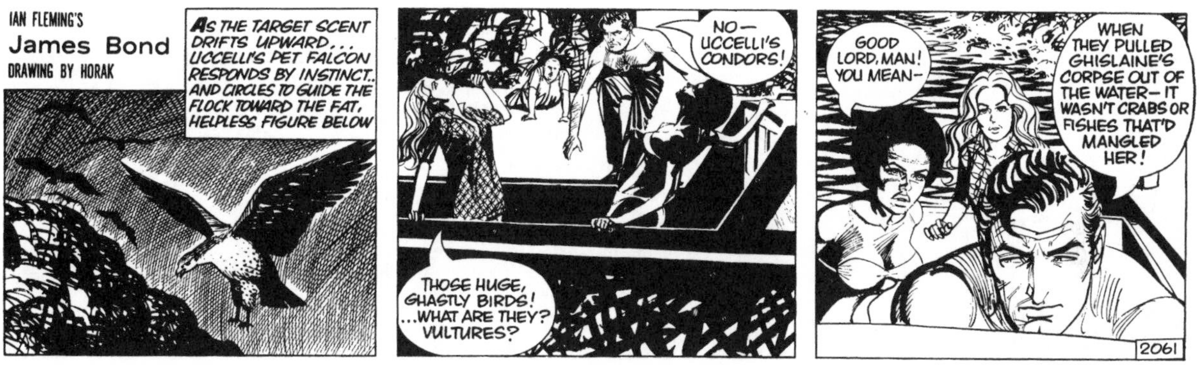
IAN FLEMING'S
James Bond
DRAWING BY HORAK
AS THE TARGET SCENT DRIFTS UPWARD... UCCELLI'S PET FALCON RESPONDS BY INSTINCT... AND CIRCLES TO GUIDE THE FLOCK TOWARD THE FAT, HELPLESS FIGURE BELOW
NO—UCCELLI'S CONDORS!
THOSE HUGE, GHASTLY BIRDS! ...WHAT ARE THEY? VULTURES?
GOOD LORD, MAN! YOU MEAN—
WHEN THEY PULLED GHISLAINE'S CORPSE OUT OF THE WATER—IT WASN'T CRABS OR FISHES THAT'D MANGLED HER!
2061

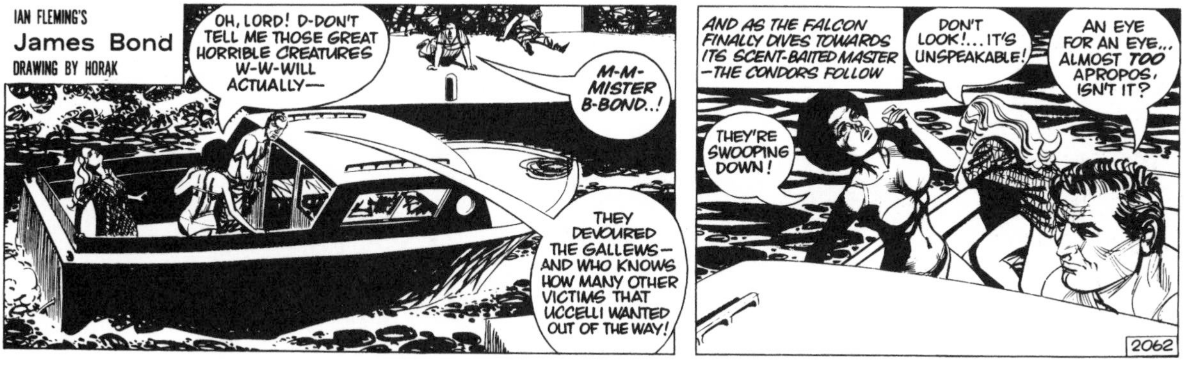
IAN FLEMING'S
James Bond
DRAWING BY HORAK
OH, LORD! D-DON'T TELL ME THOSE GREAT HORRIBLE CREATURES W-W-WILL ACTUALLY—
M-M-MISTER B-BOND..!
THEY DEVOURED THE GALLEWS—AND WHO KNOWS HOW MANY OTHER VICTIMS THAT UCCELLI WANTED OUT OF THE WAY!
AND AS THE FALCON FINALLY DIVES TOWARDS ITS SCENT-BAITED MASTER —THE CONDORS FOLLOW
THEY'RE SWOOPING DOWN!
DON'T LOOK!...IT'S UNSPEAKABLE!
AN EYE FOR AN EYE... ALMOST TOO APROPOS, ISN'T IT?
2062

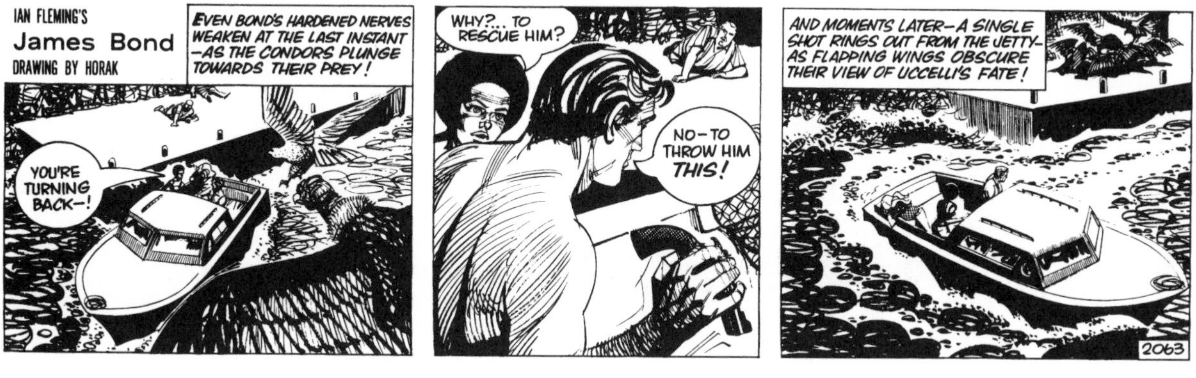
IAN FLEMING'S
James Bond
DRAWING BY HORAK
EVEN BOND'S HARDENED NERVES WEAKEN AT THE LAST INSTANT —AS THE CONDORS PLUNGE TOWARDS THEIR PREY!
YOU'RE TURNING BACK—!
WHY?... TO RESCUE HIM?
NO—TO THROW HIM THIS!
AND MOMENTS LATER—A SINGLE SHOT RINGS OUT FROM THE JETTY—AS FLAPPING WINGS OBSCURE THEIR VIEW OF UCCELLI'S FATE!
2063

IAN FLEMING'S
James Bond
DRAWING BY HORAK
NO ONE'S STIRRING YET– FORTUNATELY! WE'LL GET OUR CARS AND ROLL– BEFORE THE PORT WAKES UP!
WHAT ABOUT ALL THOSE OTHER GIRLS, STILL ON CONDOR ISLAND?
WE'D BEST LEAVE THAT SMALL DETAIL TO NATO INTELLIGENCE!
RATHER A TERSE SIGNAL ...AND WHAT'S THIS LAST BIT, ABOUT UCCELLI?
JAMES DIDN'T EXPLAIN... I ASKED HIM TO REPEAT, BUT THAT WAS THE END OF MESSAGE–"STRICTLY FOR THE BIRDS"!
2064

IAN FLEMING'S
James Bond
DRAWING BY HORAK
THYRZA IS DELIVERED SAFELY TO HER PARENTS IN LONDON . . .
MY DEAR MISS KELLY! WHATEVER YOUR FEE– WE CAN NEVER ADEQUATELY EXPRESS OUR GRATITUDE!
WE'LL MEET AGAIN, I HOPE...
ME TOO, JAMES– ESPECIALLY IF YOU MISLAY ANY MORE IVORY MINIATURES!
TWO GIRLS! DEAR ME– AND THYRZA HOLT'S A BLUE-BLOODED LONDON DEB... WHAT ABOUT THE OTHER?
CRYSTAL KELLY– BLACK IRISH!
2065
END OF STORY

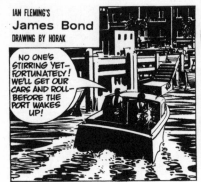

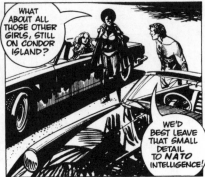

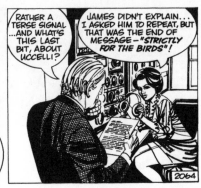

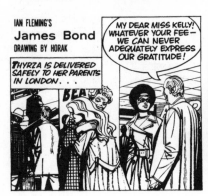

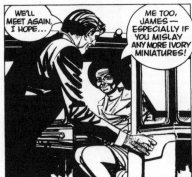

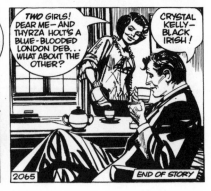

# THE LEAGUE OF VAMPIRES

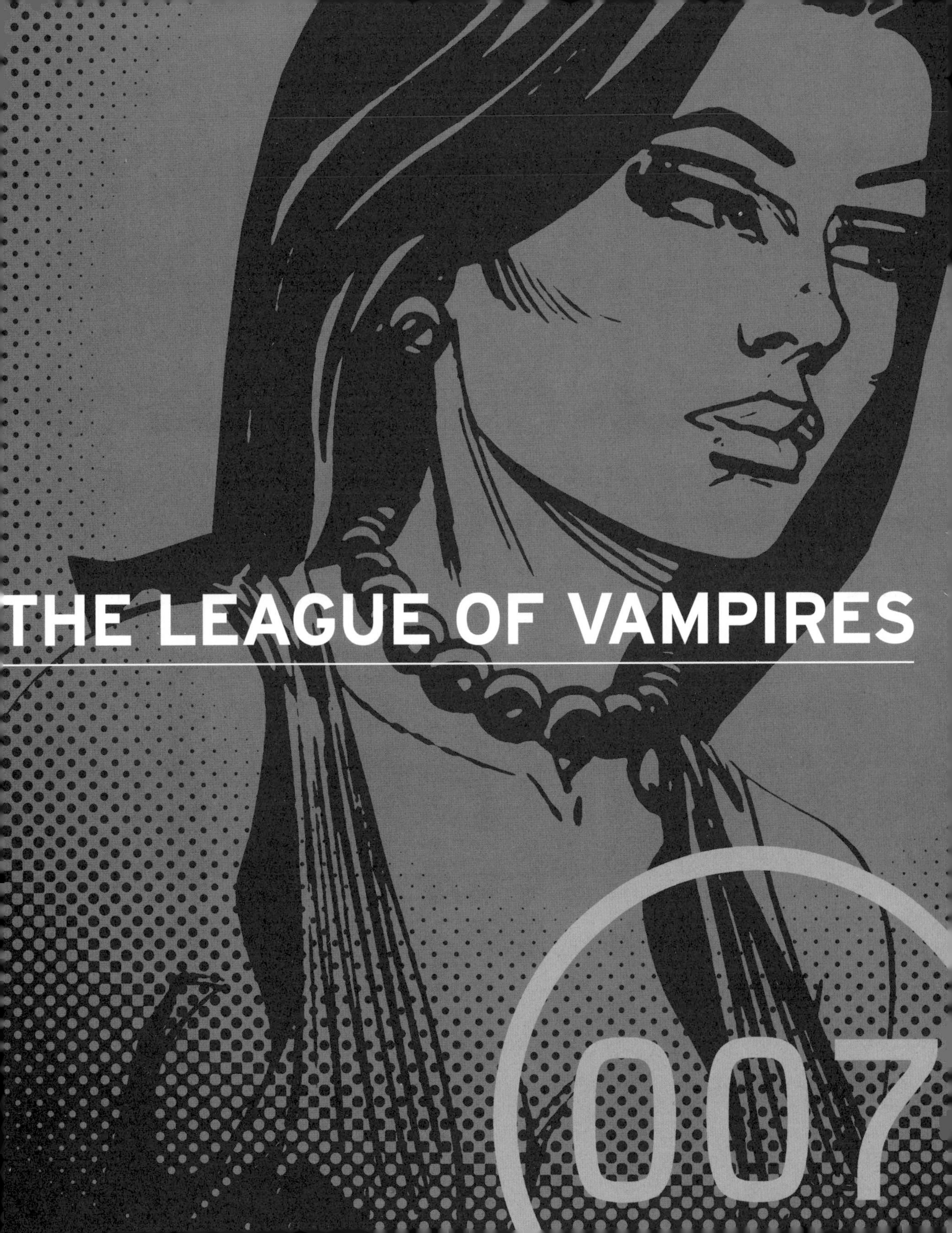

007

# The LEAGUE of VAMPIRES

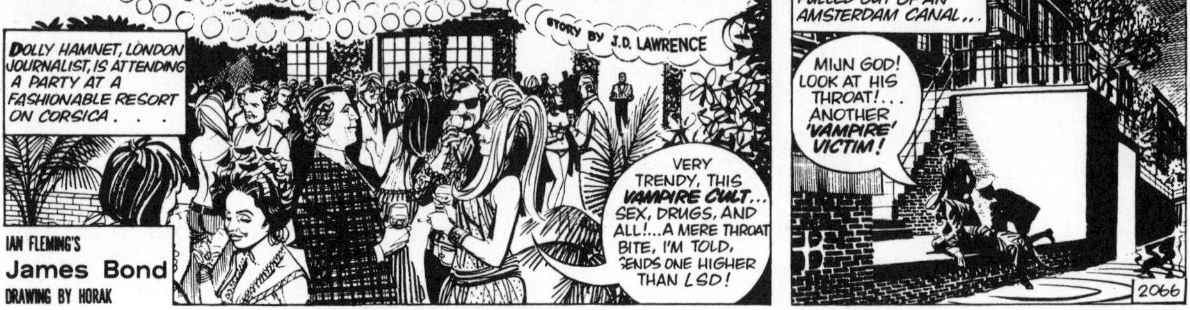

STORY BY J.D. LAWRENCE
DOLLY HAMNET, LONDON JOURNALIST, IS ATTENDING A PARTY AT A FASHIONABLE RESORT ON CORSICA . . .
IAN FLEMING'S James Bond DRAWING BY HORAK
VERY TRENDY, THIS VAMPIRE CULT... SEX, DRUGS, AND ALL!...A MERE THROAT BITE, I'M TOLD, SENDS ONE HIGHER THAN LSD!
AT THAT MOMENT... A CORPSE IS BEING PULLED OUT OF AN AMSTERDAM CANAL...
MIJN GOD! LOOK AT HIS THROAT!... ANOTHER 'VAMPIRE' VICTIM!
2066


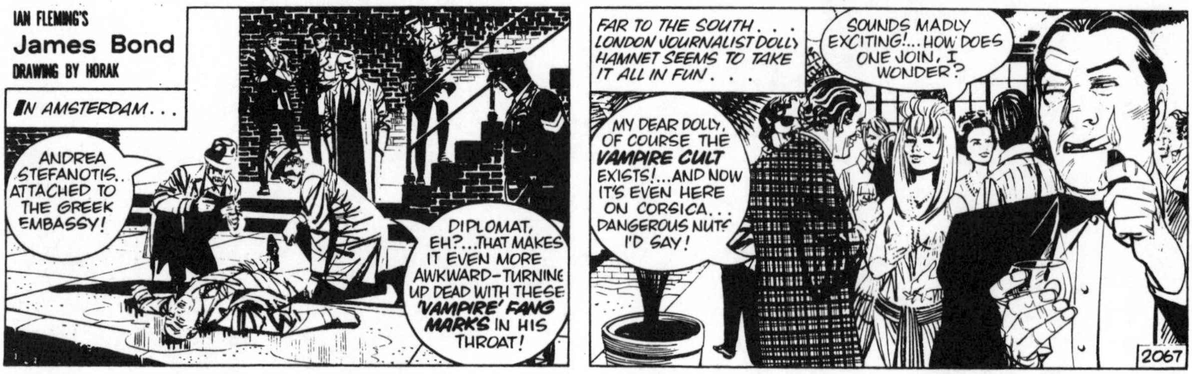

IAN FLEMING'S James Bond DRAWING BY HORAK
IN AMSTERDAM . . .
ANDREA STEFANOTIS.. ATTACHED TO THE GREEK EMBASSY!
DIPLOMAT, EH?...THAT MAKES IT EVEN MORE AWKWARD-TURNING UP DEAD WITH THESE 'VAMPIRE' FANG MARKS IN HIS THROAT!
FAR TO THE SOUTH . . . LONDON JOURNALIST DOLLY HAMNET SEEMS TO TAKE IT ALL IN FUN . . .
SOUNDS MADLY EXCITING!...HOW DOES ONE JOIN, I WONDER?
MY DEAR DOLLY, OF COURSE THE VAMPIRE CULT EXISTS!...AND NOW IT'S EVEN HERE ON CORSICA... DANGEROUS NUTS I'D SAY!
2067


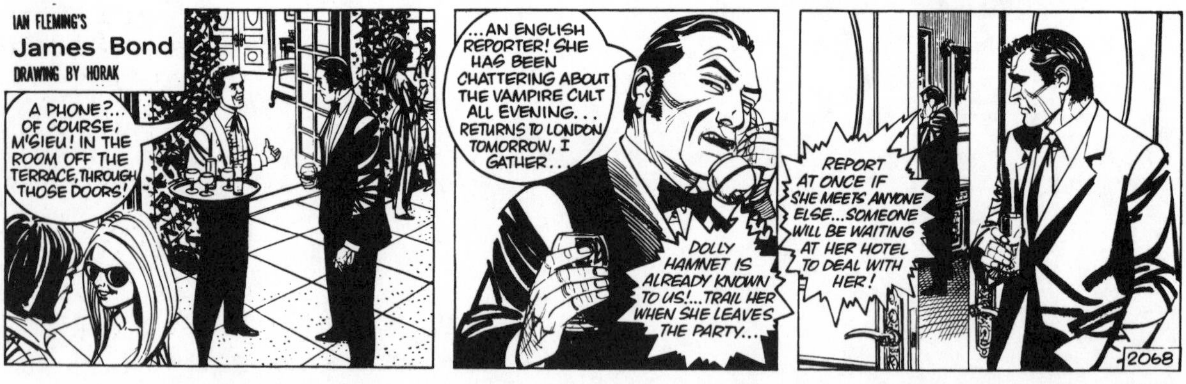

IAN FLEMING'S James Bond DRAWING BY HORAK
A PHONE?... OF COURSE, M'SIEU! IN THE ROOM OFF THE TERRACE, THROUGH THOSE DOORS!
...AN ENGLISH REPORTER! SHE HAS BEEN CHATTERING ABOUT THE VAMPIRE CULT ALL EVENING... RETURNS TO LONDON TOMORROW, I GATHER...
DOLLY HAMNET IS ALREADY KNOWN TO US!...TRAIL HER WHEN SHE LEAVES THE PARTY...
REPORT AT ONCE IF SHE MEETS ANYONE ELSE...SOMEONE WILL BE WAITING AT HER HOTEL TO DEAL WITH HER!
2068


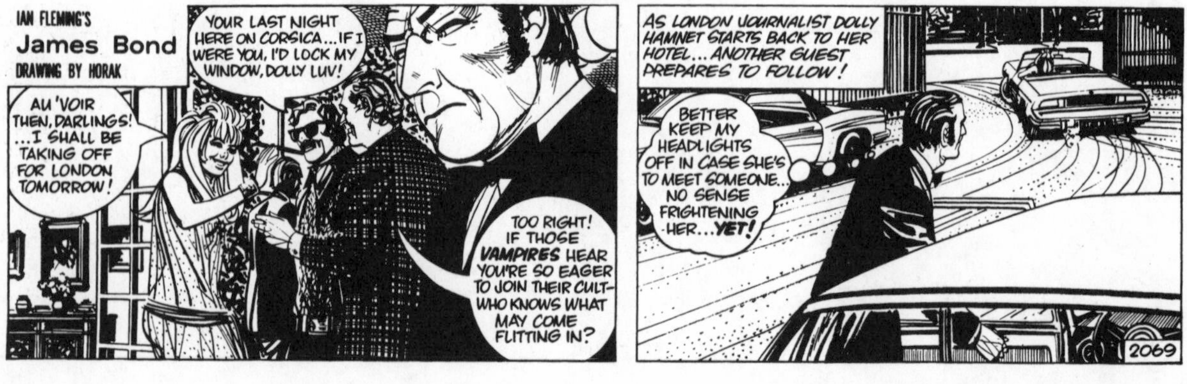

IAN FLEMING'S James Bond DRAWING BY HORAK
AU 'VOIR THEN, DARLINGS! ...I SHALL BE TAKING OFF FOR LONDON TOMORROW!
YOUR LAST NIGHT HERE ON CORSICA...IF I WERE YOU, I'D LOCK MY WINDOW, DOLLY LUV!
TOO RIGHT! IF THOSE VAMPIRES HEAR YOU'RE SO EAGER TO JOIN THEIR CULT-WHO KNOWS WHAT MAY COME FLITTING IN?
AS LONDON JOURNALIST DOLLY HAMNET STARTS BACK TO HER HOTEL... ANOTHER GUEST PREPARES TO FOLLOW!
BETTER KEEP MY HEADLIGHTS OFF IN CASE SHE'S TO MEET SOMEONE... NO SENSE FRIGHTENING HER...YET!
2069

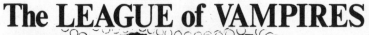

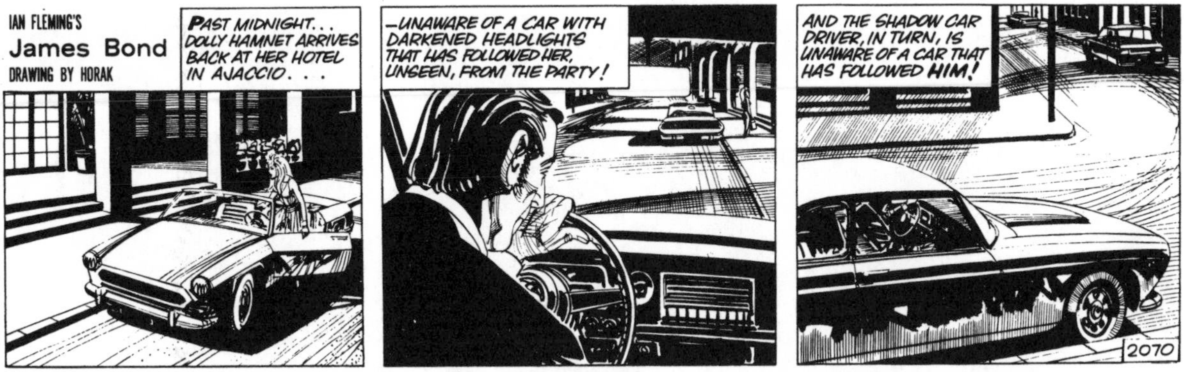
IAN FLEMING'S
James Bond
DRAWING BY HORAK
PAST MIDNIGHT... DOLLY HAMNET ARRIVES BACK AT HER HOTEL IN AJACCIO...
—UNAWARE OF A CAR WITH DARKENED HEADLIGHTS THAT HAS FOLLOWED HER, UNSEEN, FROM THE PARTY!
AND THE SHADOW CAR DRIVER, IN TURN, IS UNAWARE OF A CAR THAT HAS FOLLOWED HIM!
2070

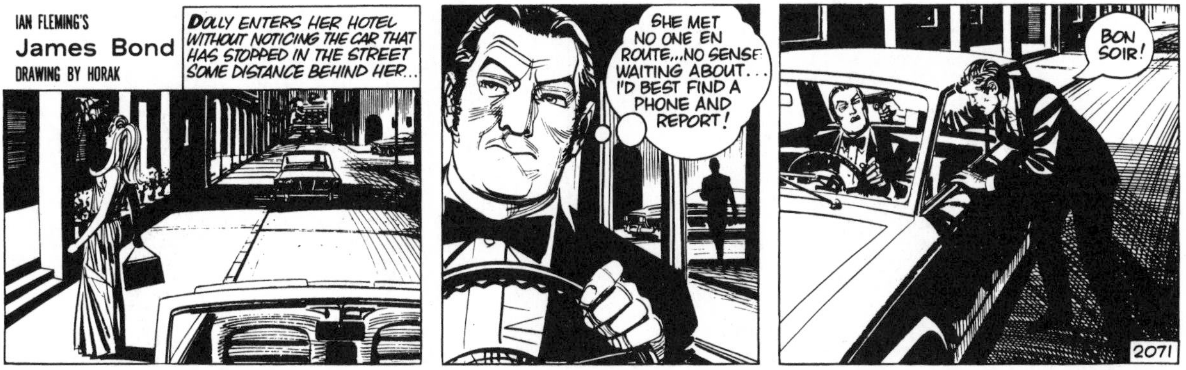
IAN FLEMING'S
James Bond
DRAWING BY HORAK
DOLLY ENTERS HER HOTEL WITHOUT NOTICING THE CAR THAT HAS STOPPED IN THE STREET SOME DISTANCE BEHIND HER...
SHE MET NO ONE EN ROUTE,..NO SENSE WAITING ABOUT... I'D BEST FIND A PHONE AND REPORT!
BON SOIR!
2071

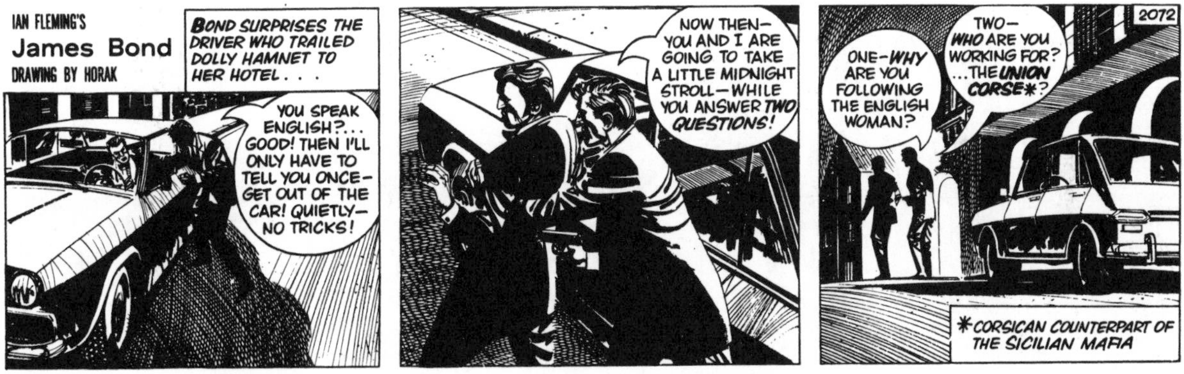
IAN FLEMING'S
James Bond
DRAWING BY HORAK
BOND SURPRISES THE DRIVER WHO TRAILED DOLLY HAMNET TO HER HOTEL...
YOU SPEAK ENGLISH?... GOOD! THEN I'LL ONLY HAVE TO TELL YOU ONCE-GET OUT OF THE CAR! QUIETLY-NO TRICKS!
NOW THEN-YOU AND I ARE GOING TO TAKE A LITTLE MIDNIGHT STROLL-WHILE YOU ANSWER TWO QUESTIONS!
2072
ONE-WHY ARE YOU FOLLOWING THE ENGLISH WOMAN?
TWO-WHO ARE YOU WORKING FOR? ...THE UNION CORSE*?
*CORSICAN COUNTERPART OF THE SICILIAN MAFIA

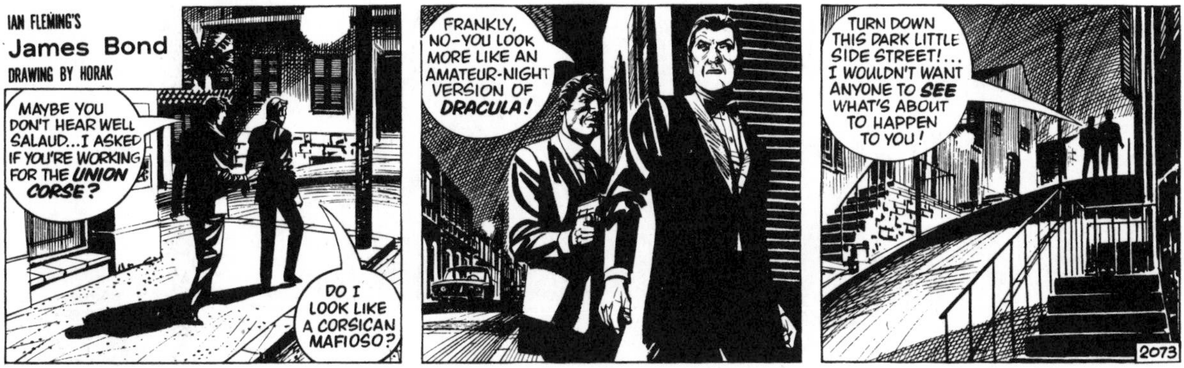
IAN FLEMING'S
James Bond
DRAWING BY HORAK
MAYBE YOU DON'T HEAR WELL SALAUD...I ASKED IF YOU'RE WORKING FOR THE UNION CORSE?
DO I LOOK LIKE A CORSICAN MAFIOSO?
FRANKLY, NO-YOU LOOK MORE LIKE AN AMATEUR-NIGHT VERSION OF DRACULA!
TURN DOWN THIS DARK LITTLE SIDE STREET!... I WOULDN'T WANT ANYONE TO SEE WHAT'S ABOUT TO HAPPEN TO YOU!
2073

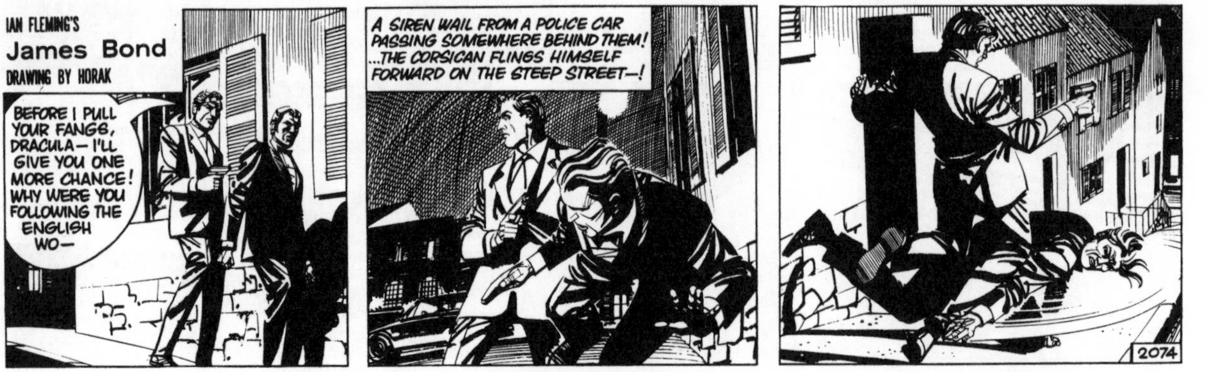
IAN FLEMING'S
James Bond
DRAWING BY HORAK
BEFORE I PULL YOUR FANGS, DRACULA—I'LL GIVE YOU ONE MORE CHANCE! WHY WERE YOU FOLLOWING THE ENGLISH WO—
A SIREN WAIL FROM A POLICE CAR PASSING SOMEWHERE BEHIND THEM! ...THE CORSICAN FLINGS HIMSELF FORWARD ON THE STEEP STREET—!
2074

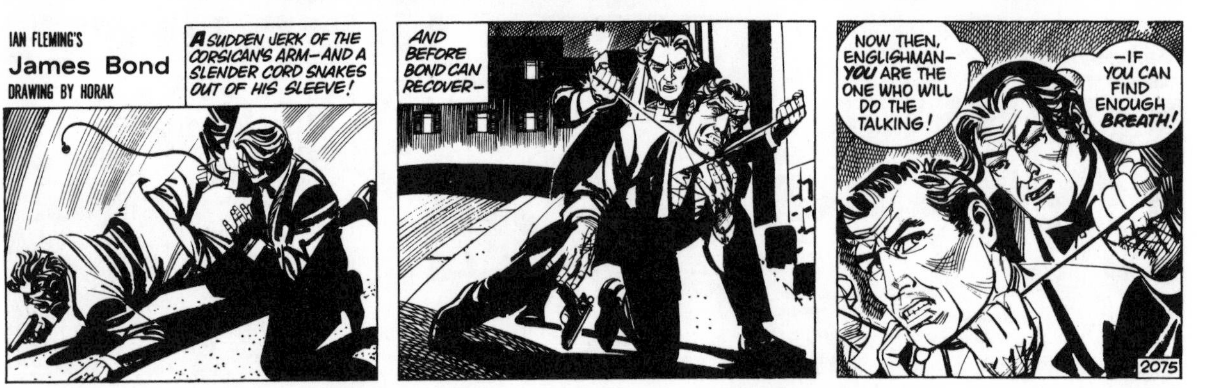
IAN FLEMING'S
James Bond
DRAWING BY HORAK
A SUDDEN JERK OF THE CORSICAN'S ARM—AND A SLENDER CORD SNAKES OUT OF HIS SLEEVE!
AND BEFORE BOND CAN RECOVER—
NOW THEN, ENGLISHMAN—YOU ARE THE ONE WHO WILL DO THE TALKING!
—IF YOU CAN FIND ENOUGH BREATH!
2075

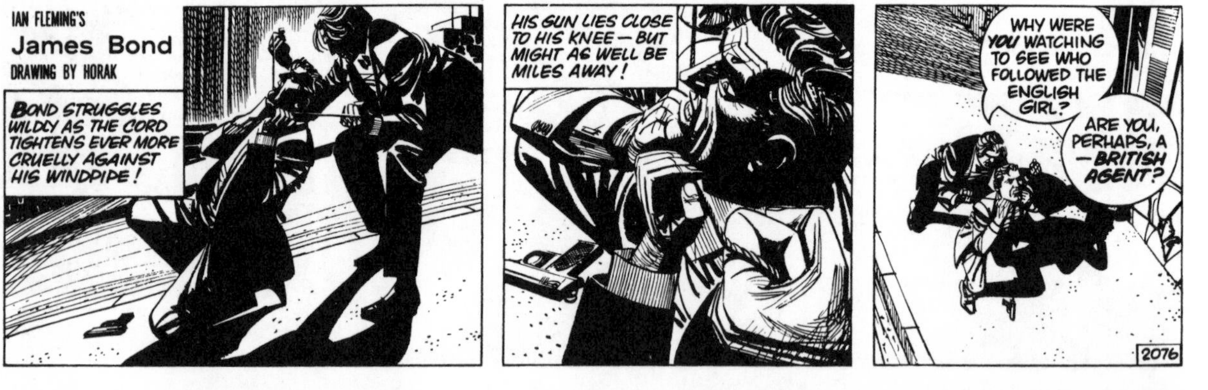
IAN FLEMING'S
James Bond
DRAWING BY HORAK
BOND STRUGGLES WILDLY AS THE CORD TIGHTENS EVER MORE CRUELLY AGAINST HIS WINDPIPE!
HIS GUN LIES CLOSE TO HIS KNEE—BUT MIGHT AS WELL BE MILES AWAY!
WHY WERE YOU WATCHING TO SEE WHO FOLLOWED THE ENGLISH GIRL?
ARE YOU, PERHAPS, A—BRITISH AGENT?
2076

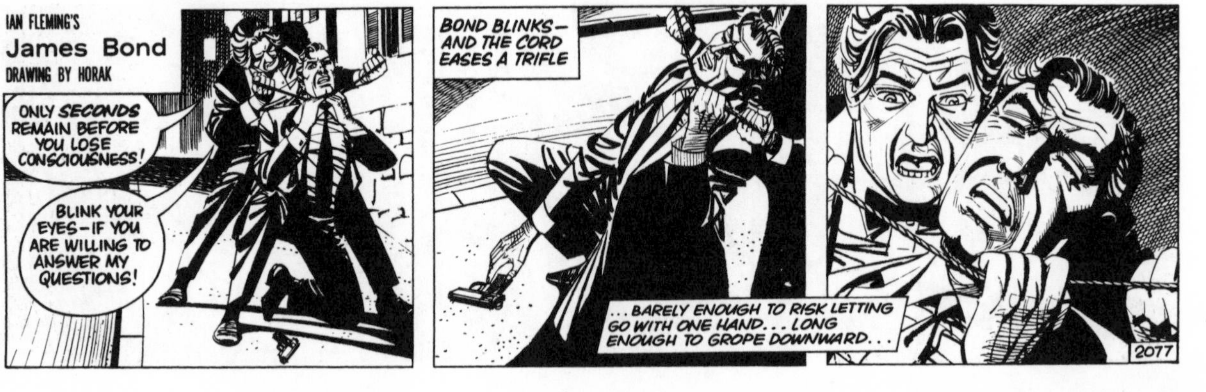
IAN FLEMING'S
James Bond
DRAWING BY HORAK
ONLY SECONDS REMAIN BEFORE YOU LOSE CONSCIOUSNESS!
BLINK YOUR EYES—IF YOU ARE WILLING TO ANSWER MY QUESTIONS!
BOND BLINKS—AND THE CORD EASES A TRIFLE
...BARELY ENOUGH TO RISK LETTING GO WITH ONE HAND... LONG ENOUGH TO GROPE DOWNWARD...
2077

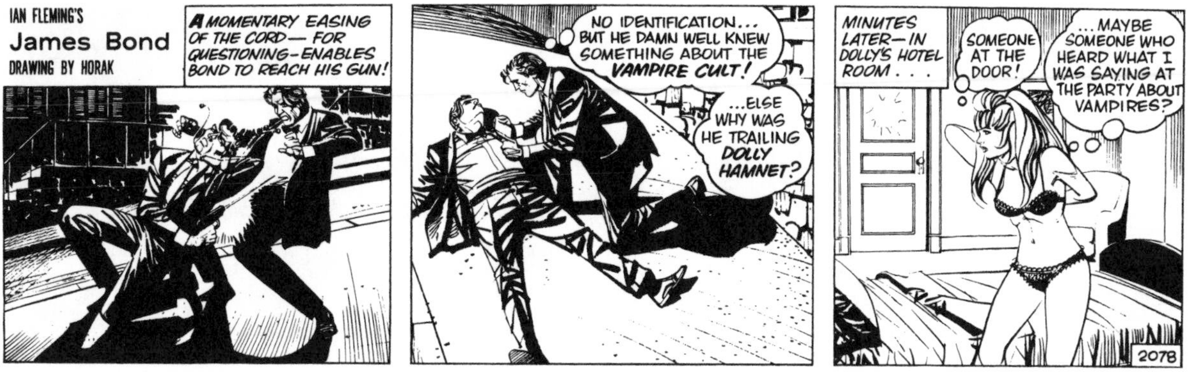
IAN FLEMING'S
James Bond
DRAWING BY HORAK
A MOMENTARY EASING OF THE CORD— FOR QUESTIONING—ENABLES BOND TO REACH HIS GUN!
NO IDENTIFICATION... BUT HE DAMN WELL KNEW SOMETHING ABOUT THE VAMPIRE CULT!
...ELSE WHY WAS HE TRAILING DOLLY HAMNET?
MINUTES LATER—IN DOLLY'S HOTEL ROOM...
SOMEONE AT THE DOOR!
... MAYBE SOMEONE WHO HEARD WHAT I WAS SAYING AT THE PARTY ABOUT VAMPIRES?
2078

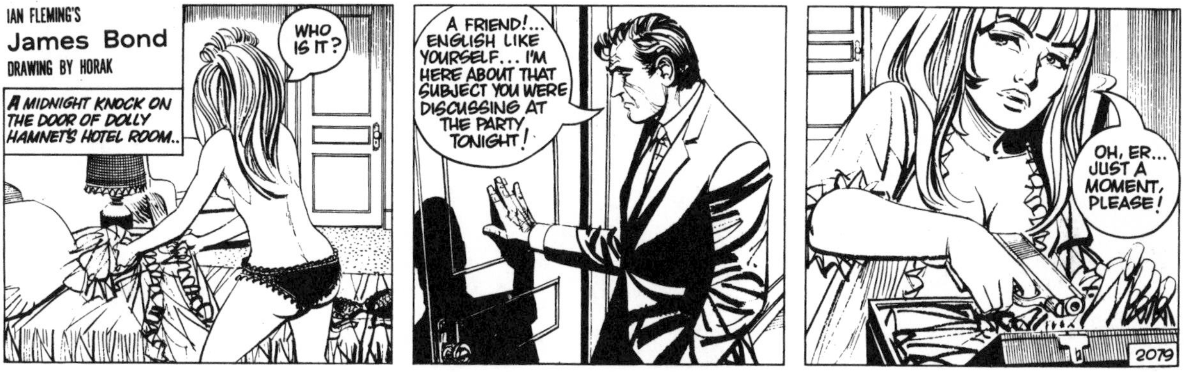
IAN FLEMING'S
James Bond
DRAWING BY HORAK
A MIDNIGHT KNOCK ON THE DOOR OF DOLLY HAMNET'S HOTEL ROOM..
WHO IS IT?
A FRIEND!... ENGLISH LIKE YOURSELF... I'M HERE ABOUT THAT SUBJECT YOU WERE DISCUSSING AT THE PARTY TONIGHT!
OH, ER... JUST A MOMENT, PLEASE!
2079

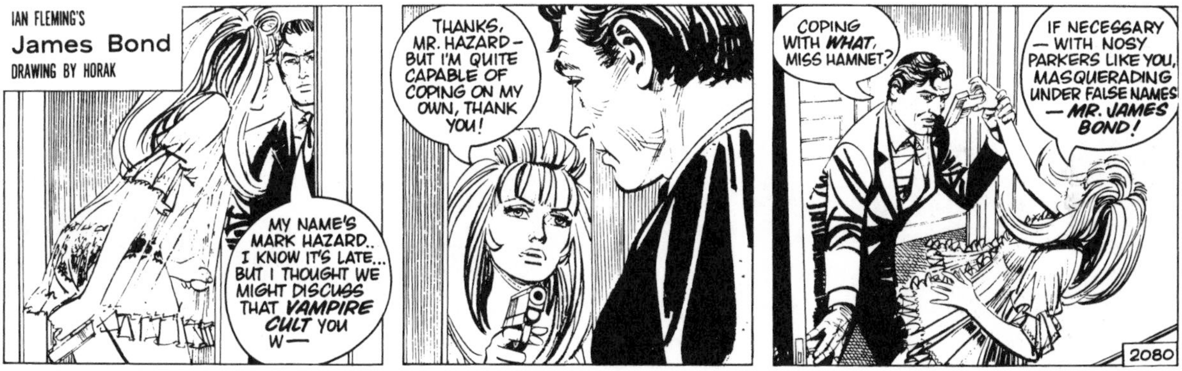
IAN FLEMING'S
James Bond
DRAWING BY HORAK
MY NAME'S MARK HAZARD.. I KNOW IT'S LATE... BUT I THOUGHT WE MIGHT DISCUSS THAT VAMPIRE CULT YOU W—
THANKS, MR. HAZARD—BUT I'M QUITE CAPABLE OF COPING ON MY OWN, THANK YOU!
COPING WITH WHAT, MISS HAMNET?
IF NECESSARY —WITH NOSY PARKERS LIKE YOU, MASQUERADING UNDER FALSE NAMES —MR. JAMES BOND!
2080

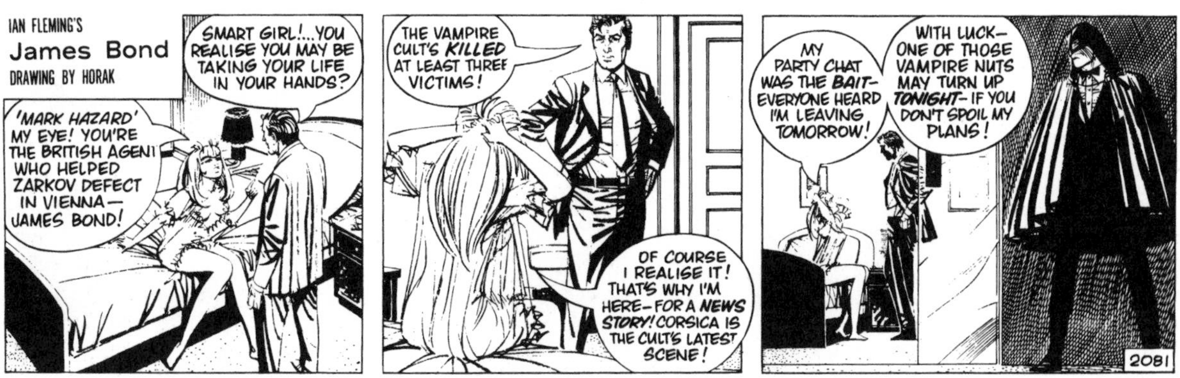
IAN FLEMING'S
James Bond
DRAWING BY HORAK
'MARK HAZARD' MY EYE! YOU'RE THE BRITISH AGENT WHO HELPED ZARKOV DEFECT IN VIENNA— JAMES BOND!
SMART GIRL!...YOU REALISE YOU MAY BE TAKING YOUR LIFE IN YOUR HANDS?
THE VAMPIRE CULT'S KILLED AT LEAST THREE VICTIMS!
OF COURSE I REALISE IT! THAT'S WHY I'M HERE—FOR A NEWS STORY! CORSICA IS THE CULT'S LATEST SCENE!
MY PARTY CHAT WAS THE BAIT— EVERYONE HEARD I'M LEAVING TOMORROW!
WITH LUCK— ONE OF THOSE VAMPIRE NUTS MAY TURN UP TONIGHT—IF YOU DON'T SPOIL MY PLANS!
2081

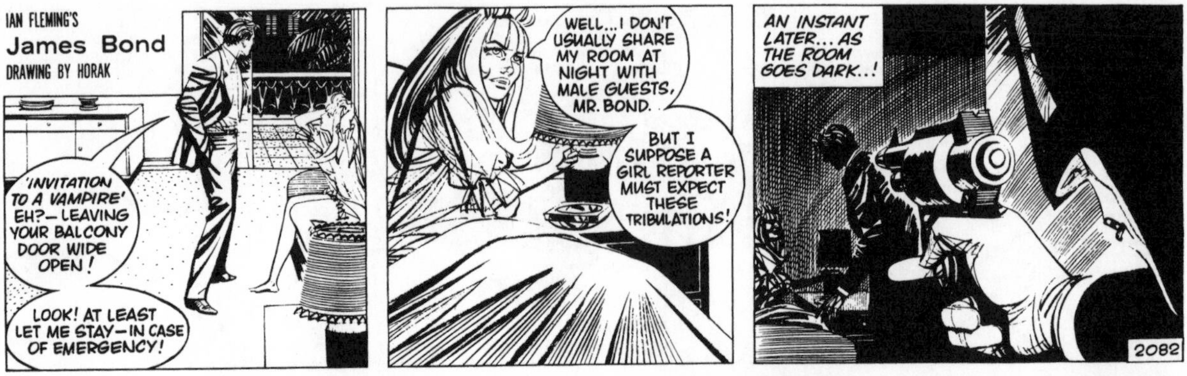
IAN FLEMING'S
James Bond
DRAWING BY HORAK
'INVITATION TO A VAMPIRE' EH?— LEAVING YOUR BALCONY DOOR WIDE OPEN!
LOOK! AT LEAST LET ME STAY—IN CASE OF EMERGENCY!
WELL... I DON'T USUALLY SHARE MY ROOM AT NIGHT WITH MALE GUESTS, MR. BOND..
BUT I SUPPOSE A GIRL REPORTER MUST EXPECT THESE TRIBULATIONS!
AN INSTANT LATER... AS THE ROOM GOES DARK..!
2082

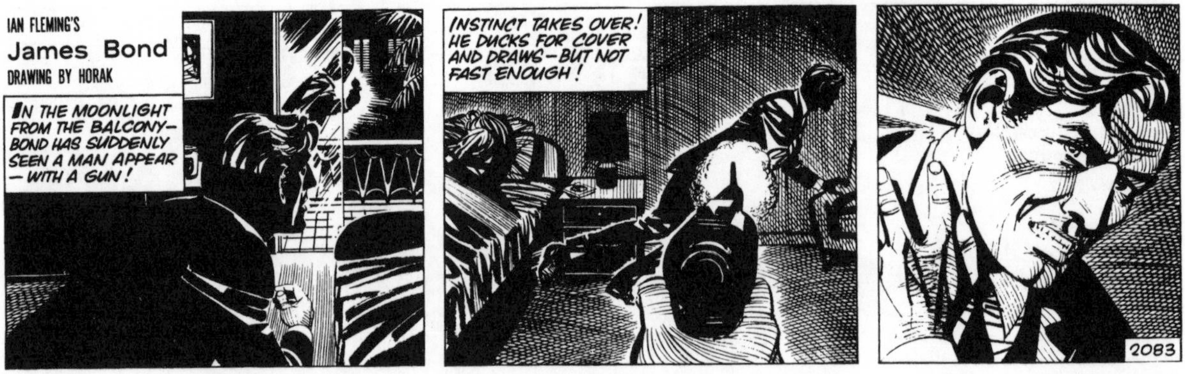
IAN FLEMING'S
James Bond
DRAWING BY HORAK
IN THE MOONLIGHT FROM THE BALCONY-BOND HAS SUDDENLY SEEN A MAN APPEAR —WITH A GUN!
INSTINCT TAKES OVER! HE DUCKS FOR COVER AND DRAWS—BUT NOT FAST ENOUGH!
2083

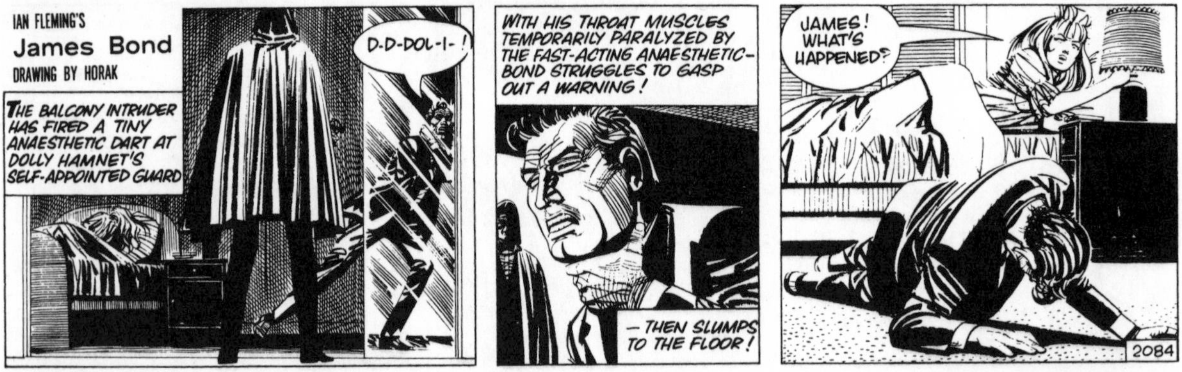
IAN FLEMING'S
James Bond
DRAWING BY HORAK
THE BALCONY INTRUDER HAS FIRED A TINY ANAESTHETIC DART AT DOLLY HAMNET'S SELF-APPOINTED GUARD
D-D-DOL-I-!
WITH HIS THROAT MUSCLES TEMPORARILY PARALYZED BY THE FAST-ACTING ANAESTHETIC-BOND STRUGGLES TO GASP OUT A WARNING!
—THEN SLUMPS TO THE FLOOR!
JAMES! WHAT'S HAPPENED?
2084

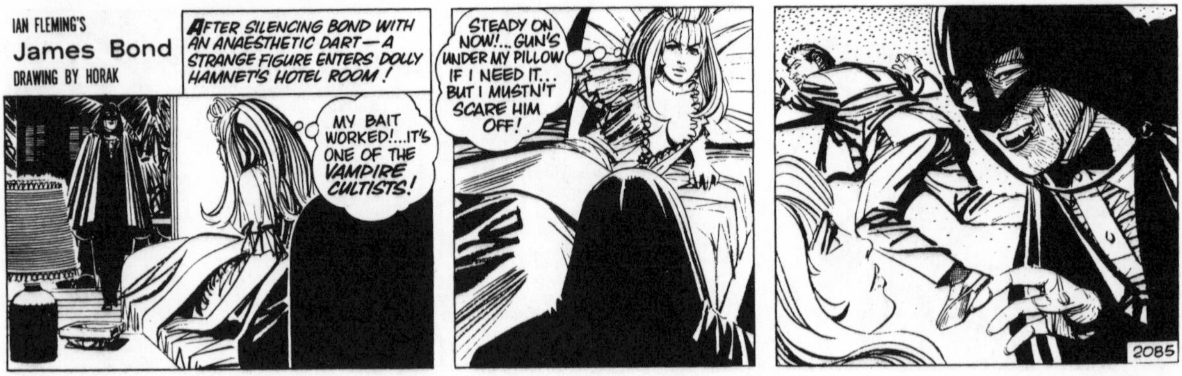
IAN FLEMING'S
James Bond
DRAWING BY HORAK
AFTER SILENCING BOND WITH AN ANAESTHETIC DART—A STRANGE FIGURE ENTERS DOLLY HAMNET'S HOTEL ROOM!
MY BAIT WORKED!... IT'S ONE OF THE VAMPIRE CULTISTS!
STEADY ON NOW!... GUN'S UNDER MY PILLOW IF I NEED IT... BUT I MUSTN'T SCARE HIM OFF!
2085

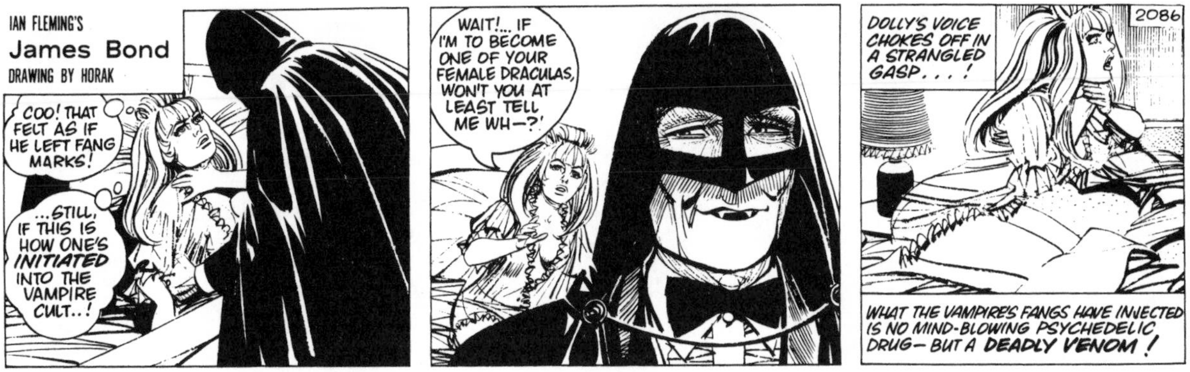
IAN FLEMING'S
James Bond
DRAWING BY HORAK
COO! THAT FELT AS IF HE LEFT FANG MARKS!
...STILL, IF THIS IS HOW ONE'S INITIATED INTO THE VAMPIRE CULT..!
WAIT!... IF I'M TO BECOME ONE OF YOUR FEMALE DRACULAS, WON'T YOU AT LEAST TELL ME WH—?'
2086
DOLLY'S VOICE CHOKES OFF IN A STRANGLED GASP. . . !
WHAT THE VAMPIRE'S FANGS HAVE INJECTED IS NO MIND-BLOWING PSYCHEDELIC DRUG— BUT A DEADLY VENOM!

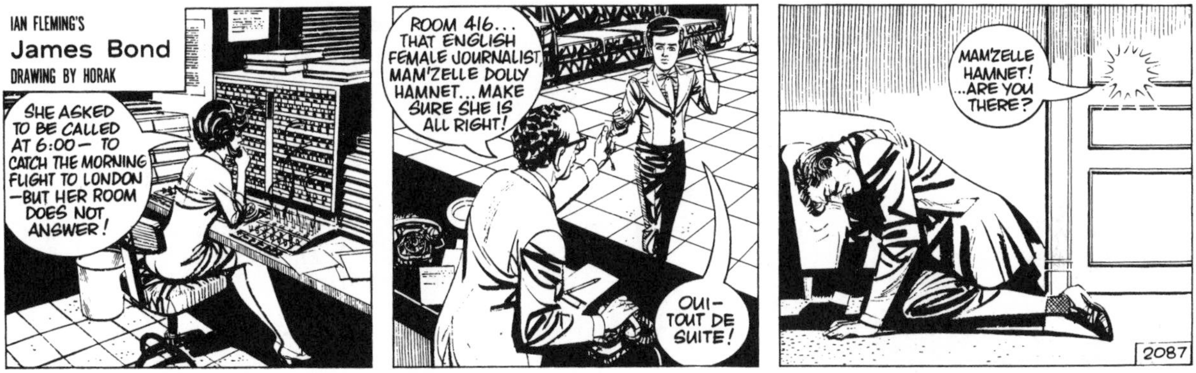
IAN FLEMING'S
James Bond
DRAWING BY HORAK
SHE ASKED TO BE CALLED AT 6:00— TO CATCH THE MORNING FLIGHT TO LONDON —BUT HER ROOM DOES NOT ANSWER!
ROOM 416... THAT ENGLISH FEMALE JOURNALIST, MAM'ZELLE DOLLY HAMNET... MAKE SURE SHE IS ALL RIGHT!
OUI- TOUT DE SUITE!
MAM'ZELLE HAMNET! ...ARE YOU THERE?
2087

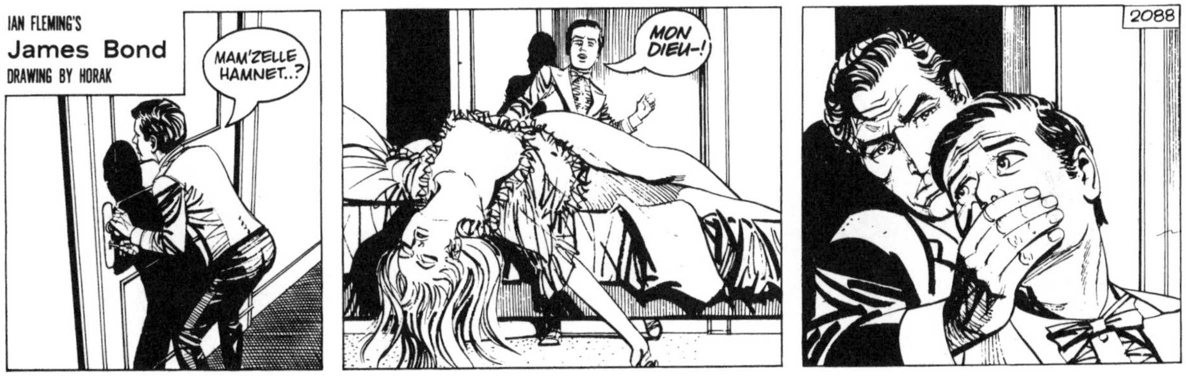
IAN FLEMING'S
James Bond
DRAWING BY HORAK
MAM'ZELLE HAMNET..?
MON DIEU-!
2088

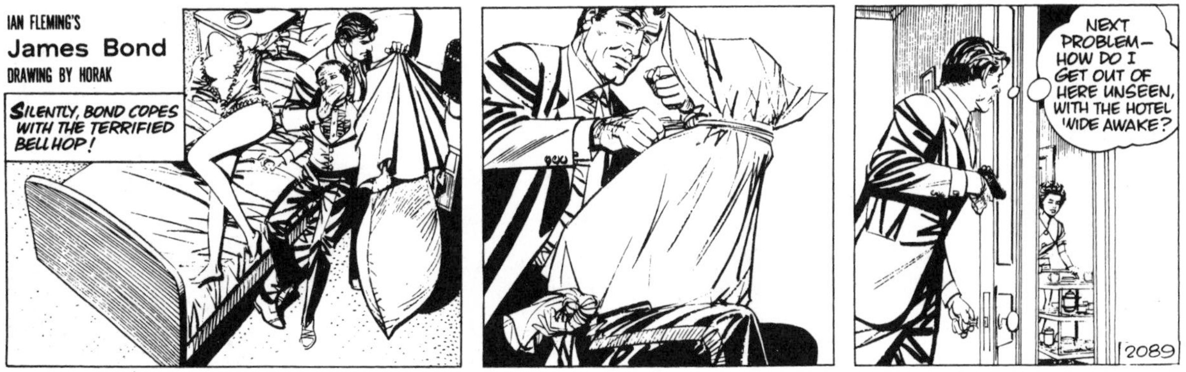
IAN FLEMING'S
James Bond
DRAWING BY HORAK
SILENTLY, BOND COPES WITH THE TERRIFIED BELLHOP!
NEXT PROBLEM— HOW DO I GET OUT OF HERE UNSEEN, WITH THE HOTEL WIDE AWAKE?
2089

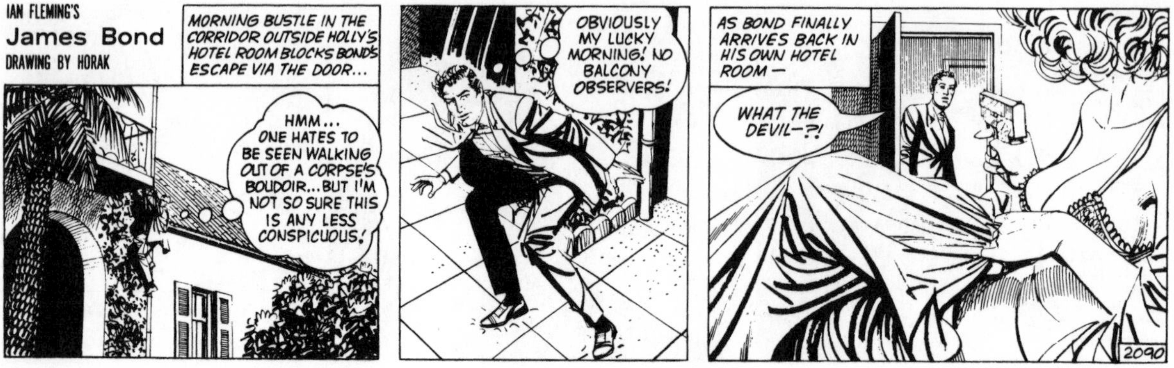
IAN FLEMING'S
James Bond
DRAWING BY HORAK
MORNING BUSTLE IN THE CORRIDOR OUTSIDE HOLLY'S HOTEL ROOM BLOCKS BOND'S ESCAPE VIA THE DOOR...
HMM... ONE HATES TO BE SEEN WALKING OUT OF A CORPSE'S BOUDOIR... BUT I'M NOT SO SURE THIS IS ANY LESS CONSPICUOUS!
OBVIOUSLY MY LUCKY MORNING! NO BALCONY OBSERVERS!
AS BOND FINALLY ARRIVES BACK IN HIS OWN HOTEL ROOM —
WHAT THE DEVIL—?!
2090

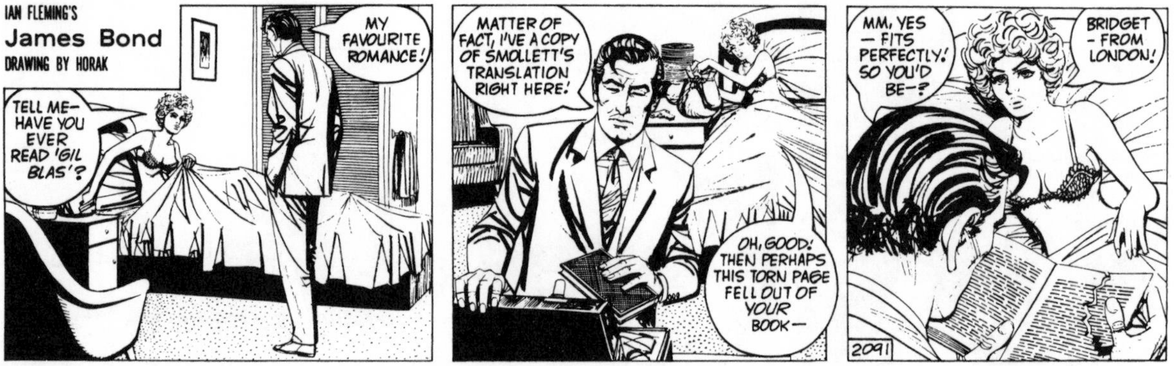
IAN FLEMING'S
James Bond
DRAWING BY HORAK
TELL ME— HAVE YOU EVER READ 'GIL BLAS'?
MY FAVOURITE ROMANCE!
MATTER OF FACT, I'VE A COPY OF SMOLLETT'S TRANSLATION RIGHT HERE!
OH, GOOD! THEN PERHAPS THIS TORN PAGE FELL OUT OF YOUR BOOK—
MM, YES — FITS PERFECTLY! SO YOU'D BE—?
BRIDGET — FROM LONDON!
2091

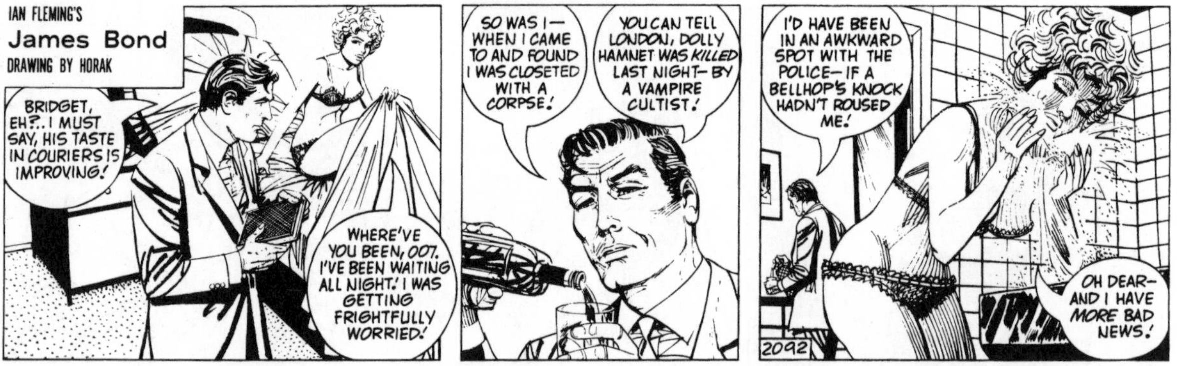
IAN FLEMING'S
James Bond
DRAWING BY HORAK
BRIDGET, EH?.. I MUST SAY, HIS TASTE IN COURIERS IS IMPROVING!
WHERE'VE YOU BEEN, 007. I'VE BEEN WAITING ALL NIGHT! I WAS GETTING FRIGHTFULLY WORRIED!
SO WAS I— WHEN I CAME TO AND FOUND I WAS CLOSETED WITH A CORPSE!
YOU CAN TELL LONDON, DOLLY HAMNET WAS KILLED LAST NIGHT— BY A VAMPIRE CULTIST!
I'D HAVE BEEN IN AN AWKWARD SPOT WITH THE POLICE— IF A BELLHOP'S KNOCK HADN'T ROUSED ME!
OH DEAR— AND I HAVE MORE BAD NEWS!
2092

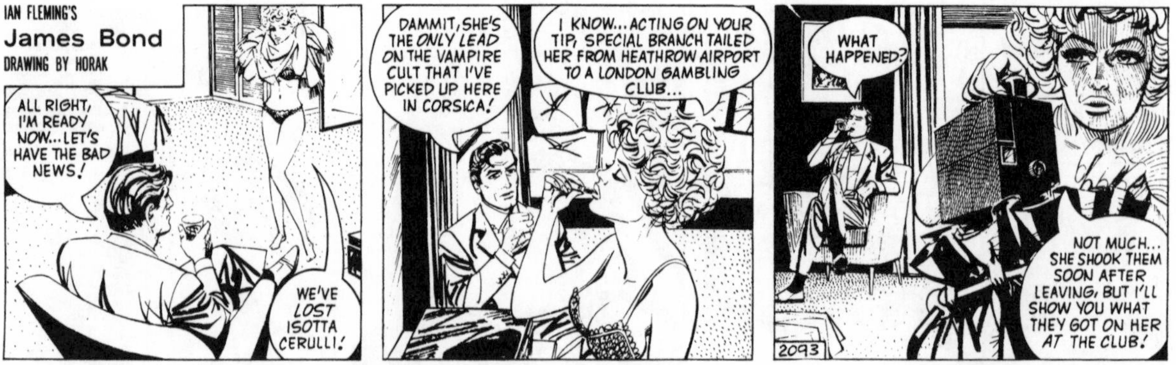
IAN FLEMING'S
James Bond
DRAWING BY HORAK
ALL RIGHT, I'M READY NOW... LET'S HAVE THE BAD NEWS!
WE'VE LOST ISOTTA CERULLI!
DAMMIT, SHE'S THE ONLY LEAD ON THE VAMPIRE CULT THAT I'VE PICKED UP HERE IN CORSICA!
I KNOW... ACTING ON YOUR TIP, SPECIAL BRANCH TAILED HER FROM HEATHROW AIRPORT TO A LONDON GAMBLING CLUB...
WHAT HAPPENED?
NOT MUCH... SHE SHOOK THEM SOON AFTER LEAVING, BUT I'LL SHOW YOU WHAT THEY GOT ON HER AT THE CLUB!
2093

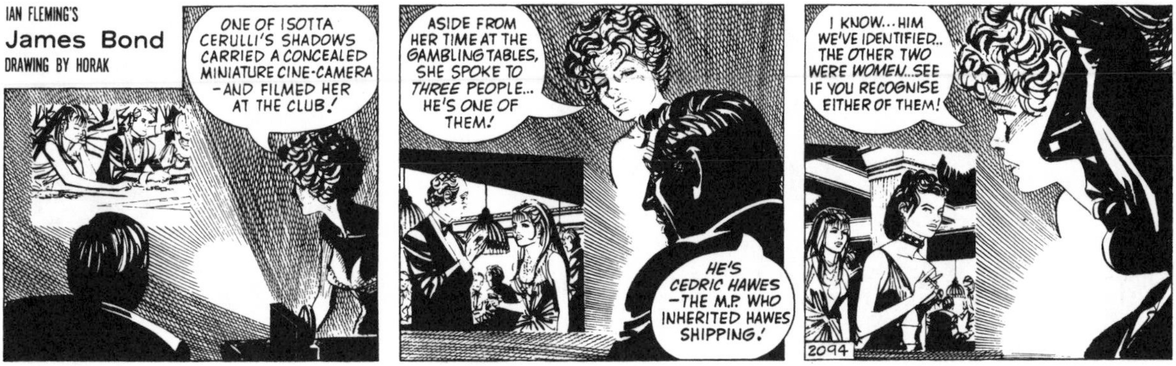
IAN FLEMING'S
James Bond
DRAWING BY HORAK
ONE OF ISOTTA CERULLI'S SHADOWS CARRIED A CONCEALED MINIATURE CINE-CAMERA –AND FILMED HER AT THE CLUB!
ASIDE FROM HER TIME AT THE GAMBLING TABLES, SHE SPOKE TO THREE PEOPLE... HE'S ONE OF THEM!
HE'S CEDRIC HAWES –THE M.P. WHO INHERITED HAWES SHIPPING!
I KNOW... HIM WE'VE IDENTIFIED.. THE OTHER TWO WERE WOMEN...SEE IF YOU RECOGNISE EITHER OF THEM!
2094

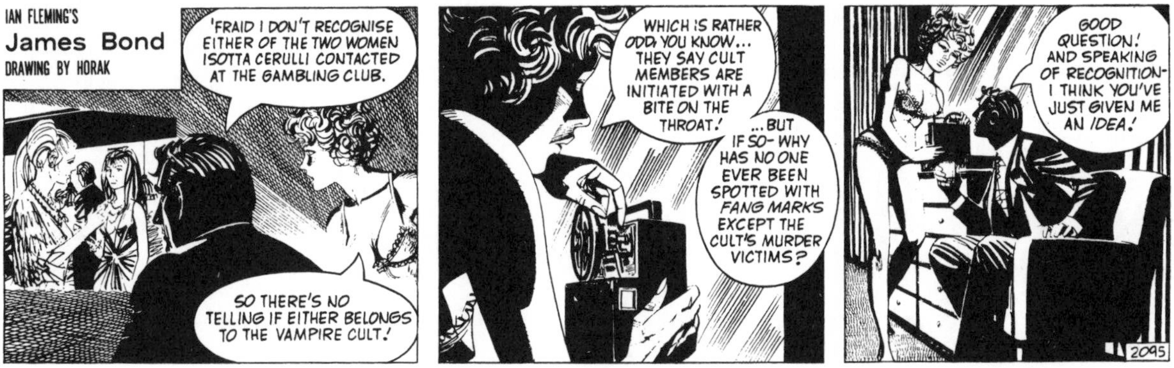
IAN FLEMING'S
James Bond
DRAWING BY HORAK
'FRAID I DON'T RECOGNISE EITHER OF THE TWO WOMEN ISOTTA CERULLI CONTACTED AT THE GAMBLING CLUB.
SO THERE'S NO TELLING IF EITHER BELONGS TO THE VAMPIRE CULT!
WHICH IS RATHER ODD, YOU KNOW... THEY SAY CULT MEMBERS ARE INITIATED WITH A BITE ON THE THROAT!
...BUT IF SO– WHY HAS NO ONE EVER BEEN SPOTTED WITH FANG MARKS EXCEPT THE CULT'S MURDER VICTIMS?
GOOD QUESTION! AND SPEAKING OF RECOGNITION– I THINK YOU'VE JUST GIVEN ME AN IDEA!
2095

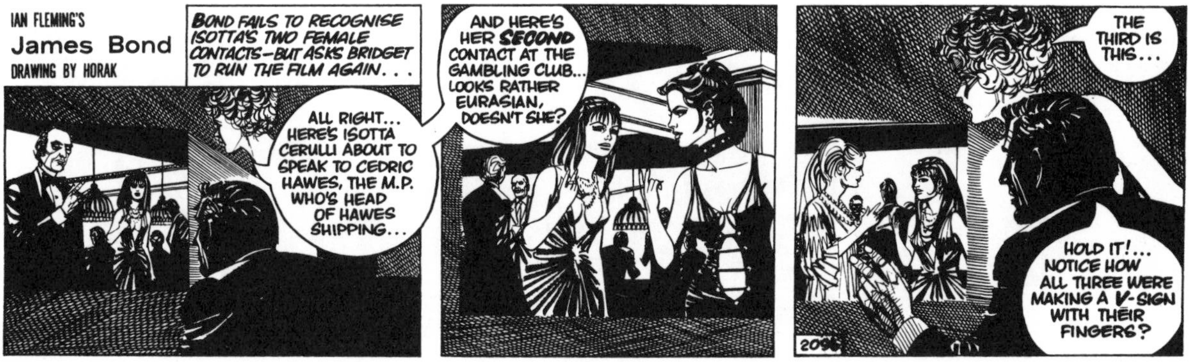
IAN FLEMING'S
James Bond
DRAWING BY HORAK
BOND FAILS TO RECOGNISE ISOTTA'S TWO FEMALE CONTACTS–BUT ASKS BRIDGET TO RUN THE FILM AGAIN . . .
ALL RIGHT... HERE'S ISOTTA CERULLI ABOUT TO SPEAK TO CEDRIC HAWES, THE M.P. WHO'S HEAD OF HAWES SHIPPING...
AND HERE'S HER SECOND CONTACT AT THE GAMBLING CLUB... LOOKS RATHER EURASIAN, DOESN'T SHE?
THE THIRD IS THIS...
HOLD IT!... NOTICE HOW ALL THREE WERE MAKING A V-SIGN WITH THEIR FINGERS?
2096

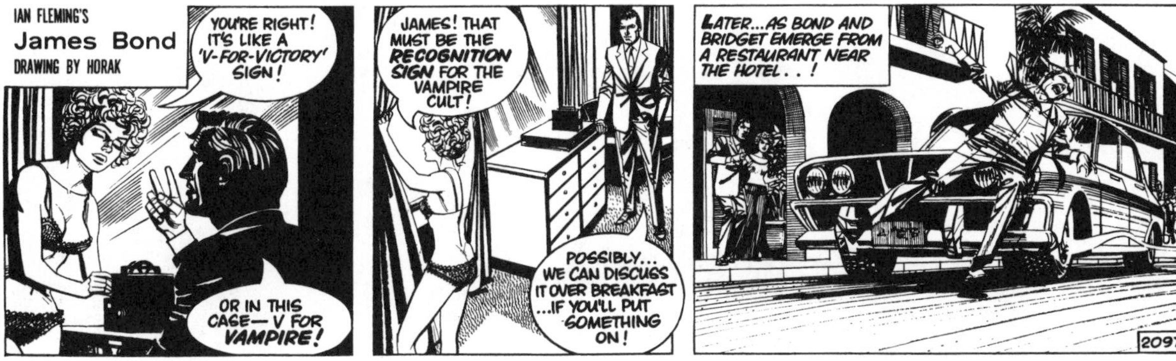
IAN FLEMING'S
James Bond
DRAWING BY HORAK
YOU'RE RIGHT! IT'S LIKE A 'V-FOR-VICTORY' SIGN!
OR IN THIS CASE– V FOR VAMPIRE!
JAMES! THAT MUST BE THE RECOGNITION SIGN FOR THE VAMPIRE CULT!
POSSIBLY... WE CAN DISCUSS IT OVER BREAKFAST ...IF YOU'LL PUT SOMETHING ON!
LATER...AS BOND AND BRIDGET EMERGE FROM A RESTAURANT NEAR THE HOTEL . . !
2097

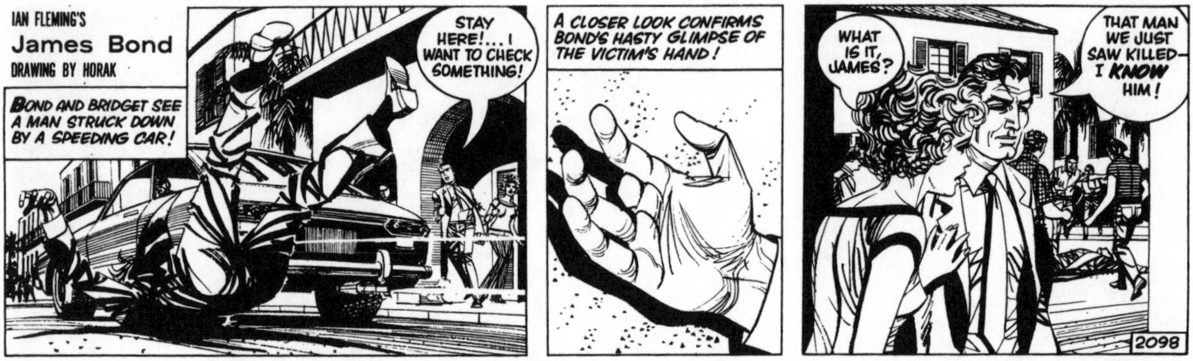
IAN FLEMING'S
James Bond
DRAWING BY HORAK
BOND AND BRIDGET SEE A MAN STRUCK DOWN BY A SPEEDING CAR!
STAY HERE!... I WANT TO CHECK SOMETHING!
A CLOSER LOOK CONFIRMS BOND'S HASTY GLIMPSE OF THE VICTIM'S HAND!
WHAT IS IT, JAMES?
THAT MAN WE JUST SAW KILLED— I KNOW HIM!
2098

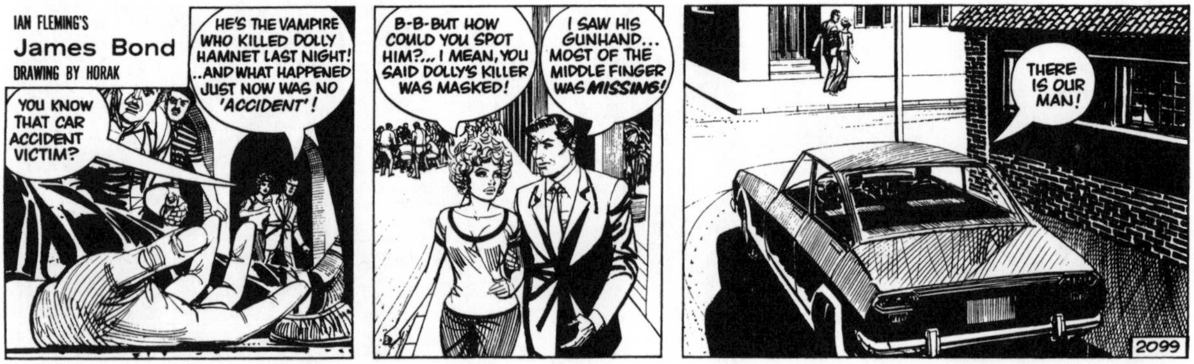
IAN FLEMING'S
James Bond
DRAWING BY HORAK
YOU KNOW THAT CAR ACCIDENT VICTIM?
HE'S THE VAMPIRE WHO KILLED DOLLY HAMNET LAST NIGHT! ..AND WHAT HAPPENED JUST NOW WAS NO 'ACCIDENT'!
B-B-BUT HOW COULD YOU SPOT HIM?... I MEAN, YOU SAID DOLLY'S KILLER WAS MASKED!
I SAW HIS GUNHAND... MOST OF THE MIDDLE FINGER WAS MISSING!
THERE IS OUR MAN!
2099

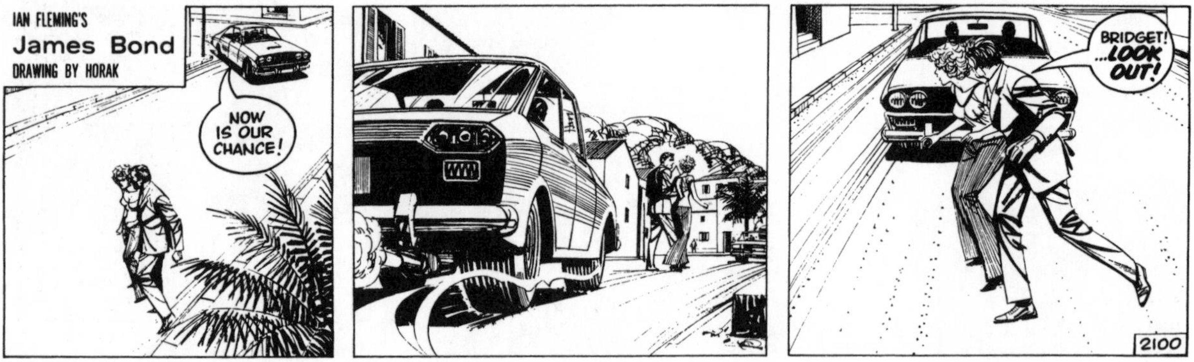
IAN FLEMING'S
James Bond
DRAWING BY HORAK
NOW IS OUR CHANCE!
BRIDGET! ...LOOK OUT!
2100

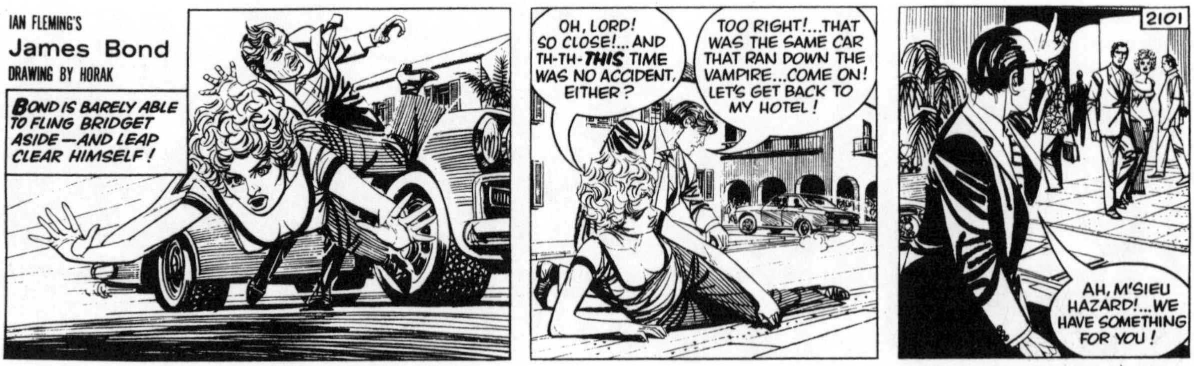
IAN FLEMING'S
James Bond
DRAWING BY HORAK
BOND IS BARELY ABLE TO FLING BRIDGET ASIDE—AND LEAP CLEAR HIMSELF!
OH, LORD! SO CLOSE!... AND TH-TH-THIS TIME WAS NO ACCIDENT, EITHER?
TOO RIGHT!... THAT WAS THE SAME CAR THAT RAN DOWN THE VAMPIRE... COME ON! LET'S GET BACK TO MY HOTEL!
2101
AH, M'SIEU HAZARD!... WE HAVE SOMETHING FOR YOU!

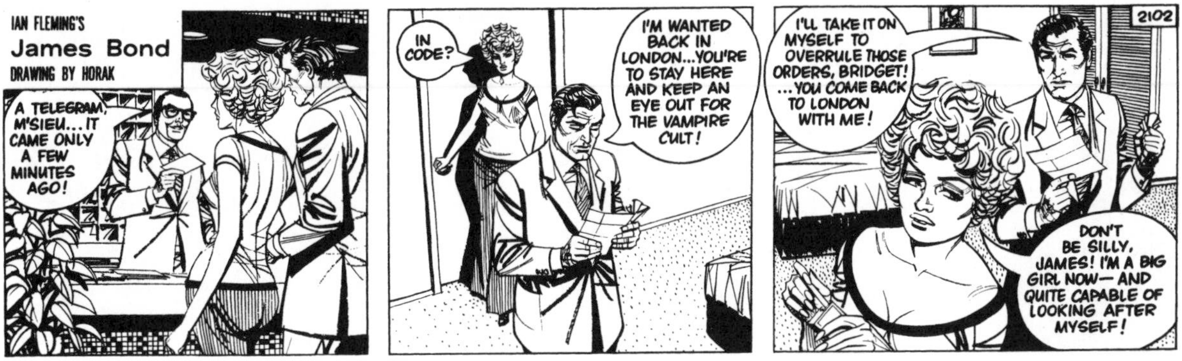
IAN FLEMING'S
James Bond
DRAWING BY HORAK
A TELEGRAM, M'SIEU... IT CAME ONLY A FEW MINUTES AGO!
IN CODE?
I'M WANTED BACK IN LONDON... YOU'RE TO STAY HERE AND KEEP AN EYE OUT FOR THE VAMPIRE CULT!
2102
I'LL TAKE IT ON MYSELF TO OVERRULE THOSE ORDERS, BRIDGET! ... YOU COME BACK TO LONDON WITH ME!
DON'T BE SILLY, JAMES! I'M A BIG GIRL NOW— AND QUITE CAPABLE OF LOOKING AFTER MYSELF!

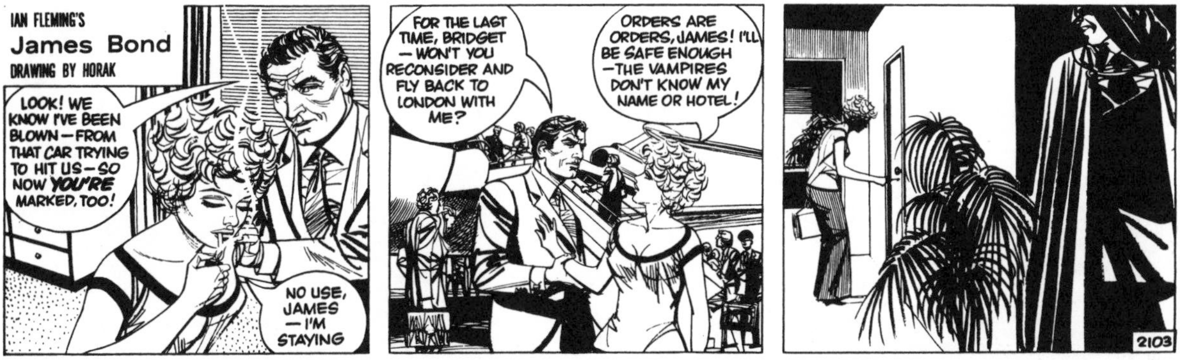
IAN FLEMING'S
James Bond
DRAWING BY HORAK
LOOK! WE KNOW I'VE BEEN BLOWN—FROM THAT CAR TRYING TO HIT US—SO NOW YOU'RE MARKED, TOO!
NO USE, JAMES —I'M STAYING
FOR THE LAST TIME, BRIDGET —WON'T YOU RECONSIDER AND FLY BACK TO LONDON WITH ME?
ORDERS ARE ORDERS, JAMES! I'LL BE SAFE ENOUGH —THE VAMPIRES DON'T KNOW MY NAME OR HOTEL!
2103

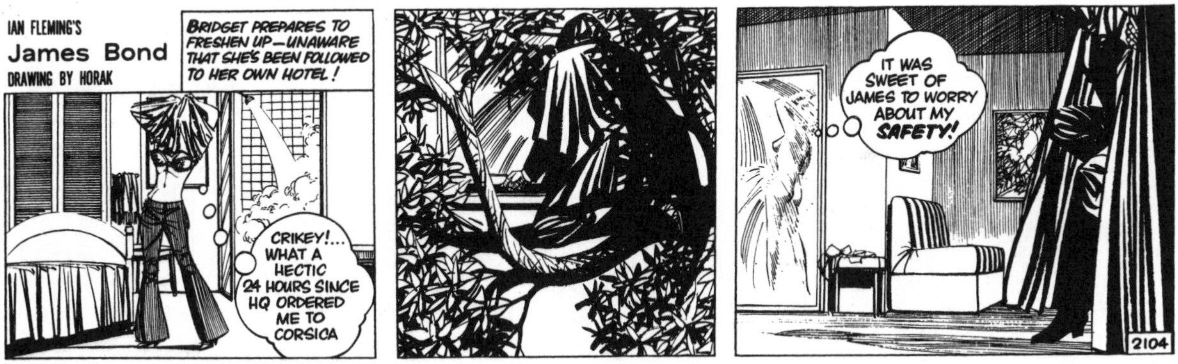
IAN FLEMING'S
James Bond
DRAWING BY HORAK
BRIDGET PREPARES TO FRESHEN UP—UNAWARE THAT SHE'S BEEN FOLLOWED TO HER OWN HOTEL!
CRIKEY!... WHAT A HECTIC 24 HOURS SINCE HQ ORDERED ME TO CORSICA
IT WAS SWEET OF JAMES TO WORRY ABOUT MY SAFETY!
2104

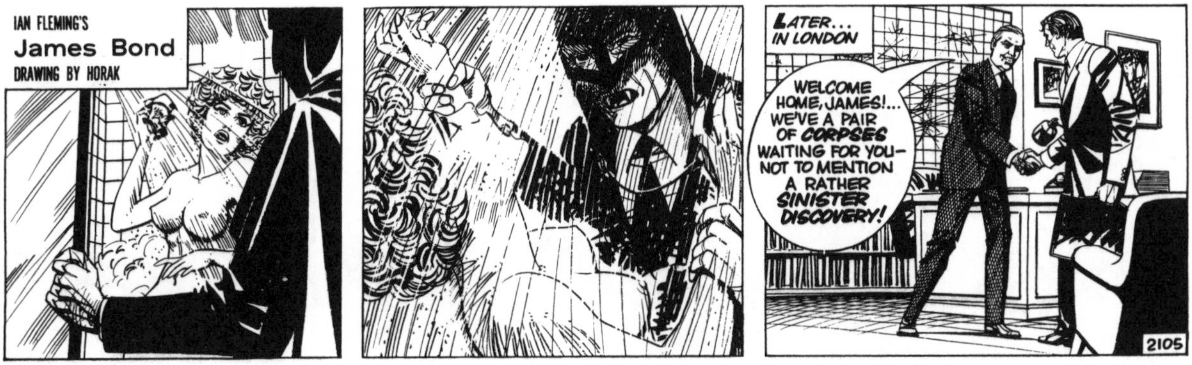
IAN FLEMING'S
James Bond
DRAWING BY HORAK
LATER... IN LONDON
WELCOME HOME, JAMES!... WE'VE A PAIR OF CORPSES WAITING FOR YOU- NOT TO MENTION A RATHER SINISTER DISCOVERY!
2105

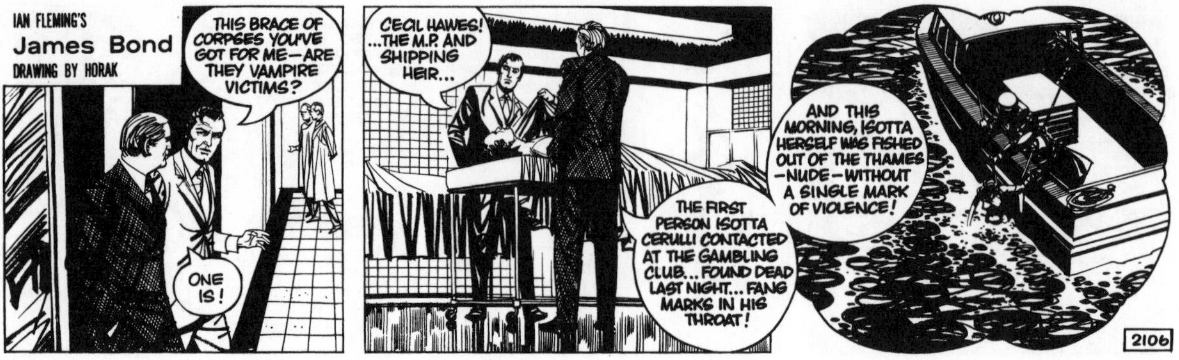

IAN FLEMING'S
James Bond
DRAWING BY HORAK
THIS BRACE OF CORPSES YOU'VE GOT FOR ME—ARE THEY VAMPIRE VICTIMS?
ONE IS!
CECIL HAWES! ...THE M.P. AND SHIPPING HEIR...
THE FIRST PERSON ISOTTA CERULLI CONTACTED AT THE GAMBLING CLUB... FOUND DEAD LAST NIGHT... FANG MARKS IN HIS THROAT!
AND THIS MORNING, ISOTTA HERSELF WAS FISHED OUT OF THE THAMES —NUDE—WITHOUT A SINGLE MARK OF VIOLENCE!
2106


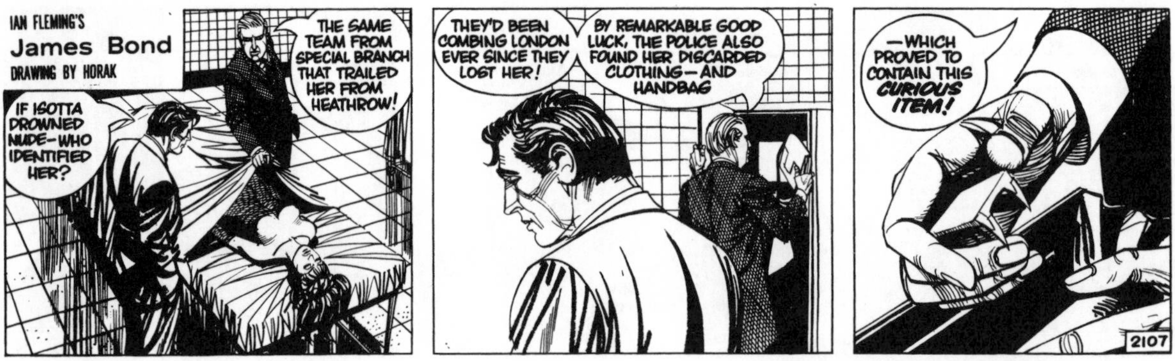

IAN FLEMING'S
James Bond
DRAWING BY HORAK
IF ISOTTA DROWNED NUDE—WHO IDENTIFIED HER?
THE SAME TEAM FROM SPECIAL BRANCH THAT TRAILED HER FROM HEATHROW!
THEY'D BEEN COMBING LONDON EVER SINCE THEY LOST HER!
BY REMARKABLE GOOD LUCK, THE POLICE ALSO FOUND HER DISCARDED CLOTHING—AND HANDBAG
—WHICH PROVED TO CONTAIN THIS CURIOUS ITEM!
2107


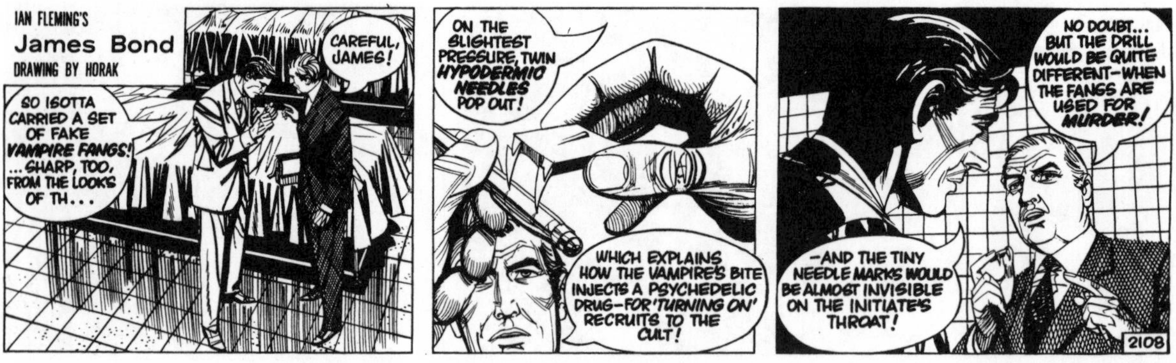

IAN FLEMING'S
James Bond
DRAWING BY HORAK
SO ISOTTA CARRIED A SET OF FAKE VAMPIRE FANGS! ...SHARP, TOO, FROM THE LOOKS OF TH...
CAREFUL, JAMES!
ON THE SLIGHTEST PRESSURE, TWIN HYPODERMIC NEEDLES POP OUT!
WHICH EXPLAINS HOW THE VAMPIRE'S BITE INJECTS A PSYCHEDELIC DRUG—FOR 'TURNING ON' RECRUITS TO THE CULT!
NO DOUBT... BUT THE DRILL WOULD BE QUITE DIFFERENT—WHEN THE FANGS ARE USED FOR MURDER!
—AND THE TINY NEEDLE MARKS WOULD BE ALMOST INVISIBLE ON THE INITIATE'S THROAT!
2108


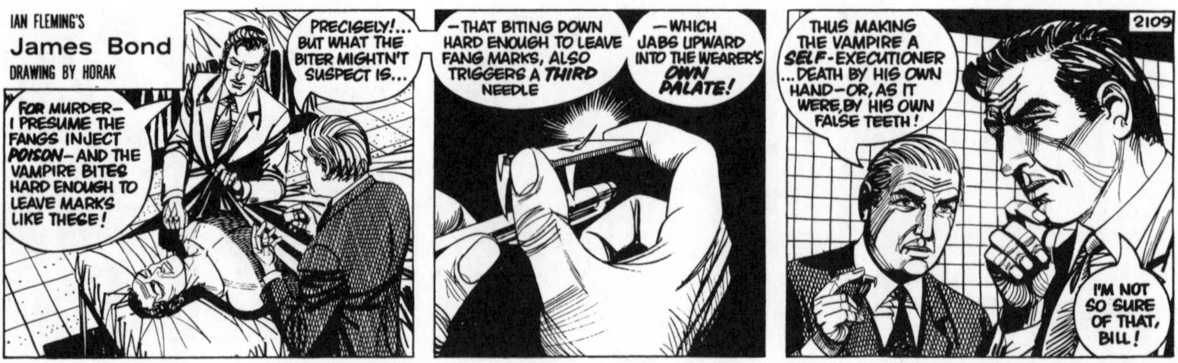

IAN FLEMING'S
James Bond
DRAWING BY HORAK
FOR MURDER—I PRESUME THE FANGS INJECT POISON—AND THE VAMPIRE BITES HARD ENOUGH TO LEAVE MARKS LIKE THESE!
PRECISELY!... BUT WHAT THE BITER MIGHTN'T SUSPECT IS...
—THAT BITING DOWN HARD ENOUGH TO LEAVE FANG MARKS, ALSO TRIGGERS A THIRD NEEDLE
—WHICH JABS UPWARD INTO THE WEARER'S OWN PALATE!
THUS MAKING THE VAMPIRE A SELF-EXECUTIONER ...DEATH BY HIS OWN HAND—OR, AS IT WERE, BY HIS OWN FALSE TEETH!
I'M NOT SO SURE OF THAT, BILL!
2109

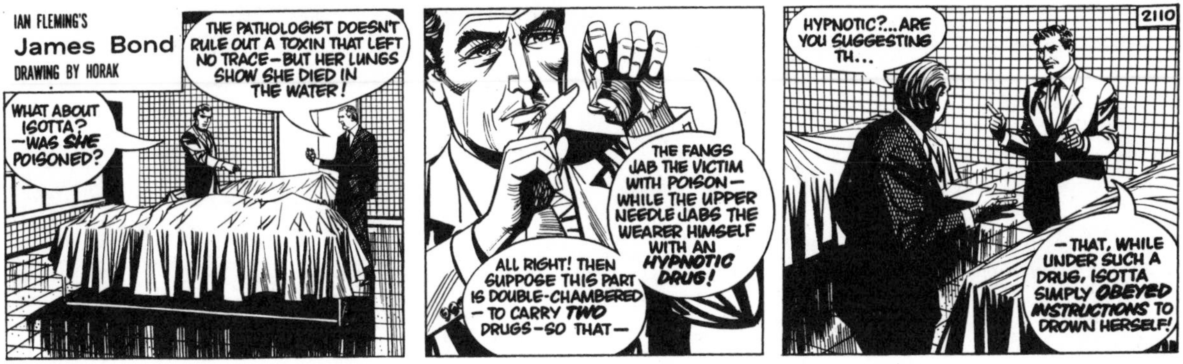
IAN FLEMING'S
James Bond
DRAWING BY HORAK
THE PATHOLOGIST DOESN'T RULE OUT A TOXIN THAT LEFT NO TRACE—BUT HER LUNGS SHOW SHE DIED IN THE WATER!
WHAT ABOUT ISOTTA? —WAS SHE POISONED?
ALL RIGHT! THEN SUPPOSE THIS PART IS DOUBLE-CHAMBERED —TO CARRY TWO DRUGS—SO THAT—
THE FANGS JAB THE VICTIM WITH POISON—WHILE THE UPPER NEEDLE JABS THE WEARER HIMSELF WITH AN HYPNOTIC DRUG!
2110
HYPNOTIC?...ARE YOU SUGGESTING TH...
—THAT, WHILE UNDER SUCH A DRUG, ISOTTA SIMPLY OBEYED INSTRUCTIONS TO DROWN HERSELF!

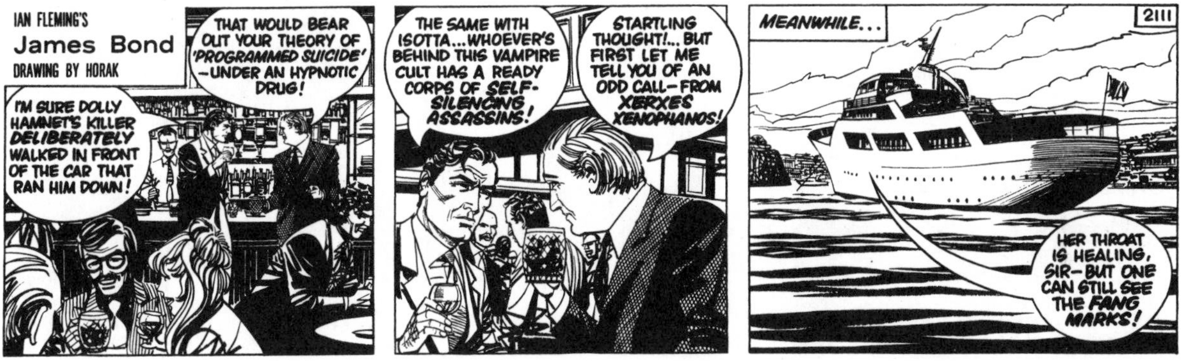
IAN FLEMING'S
James Bond
DRAWING BY HORAK
I'M SURE DOLLY HAMNET'S KILLER DELIBERATELY WALKED IN FRONT OF THE CAR THAT RAN HIM DOWN!
THAT WOULD BEAR OUT YOUR THEORY OF 'PROGRAMMED SUICIDE' —UNDER AN HYPNOTIC DRUG!
THE SAME WITH ISOTTA...WHOEVER'S BEHIND THIS VAMPIRE CULT HAS A READY CORPS OF SELF-SILENCING ASSASSINS!
STARTLING THOUGHT!... BUT FIRST LET ME TELL YOU OF AN ODD CALL—FROM XERXES XENOPHANOS!
MEANWHILE...
2111
HER THROAT IS HEALING, SIR—BUT ONE CAN STILL SEE THE FANG MARKS!

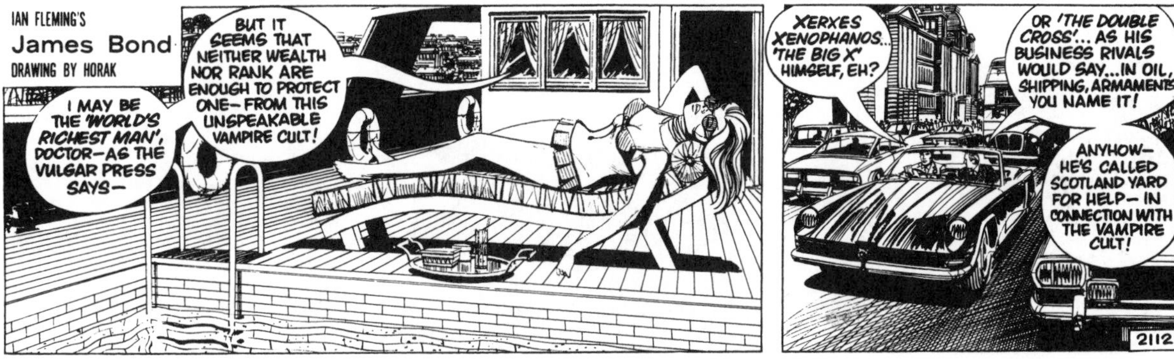
IAN FLEMING'S
James Bond
DRAWING BY HORAK
I MAY BE THE 'WORLD'S RICHEST MAN', DOCTOR—AS THE VULGAR PRESS SAYS—
BUT IT SEEMS THAT NEITHER WEALTH NOR RANK ARE ENOUGH TO PROTECT ONE—FROM THIS UNSPEAKABLE VAMPIRE CULT!
XERXES XENOPHANOS... 'THE BIG X' HIMSELF, EH?
OR 'THE DOUBLE CROSS'!... AS HIS BUSINESS RIVALS WOULD SAY...IN OIL, SHIPPING, ARMAMENTS, YOU NAME IT!
ANYHOW—HE'S CALLED SCOTLAND YARD FOR HELP—IN CONNECTION WITH THE VAMPIRE CULT!
2112

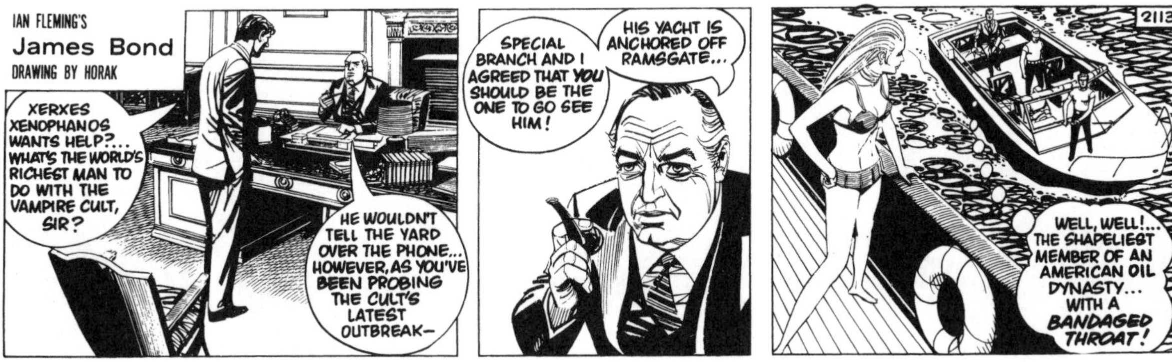
IAN FLEMING'S
James Bond
DRAWING BY HORAK
XERXES XENOPHANOS WANTS HELP?... WHAT'S THE WORLD'S RICHEST MAN TO DO WITH THE VAMPIRE CULT, SIR?
HE WOULDN'T TELL THE YARD OVER THE PHONE... HOWEVER, AS YOU'VE BEEN PROBING THE CULT'S LATEST OUTBREAK—
SPECIAL BRANCH AND I AGREED THAT YOU SHOULD BE THE ONE TO GO SEE HIM!
HIS YACHT IS ANCHORED OFF RAMSGATE...
2113
WELL, WELL!... THE SHAPELIEST MEMBER OF AN AMERICAN OIL DYNASTY... WITH A BANDAGED THROAT!

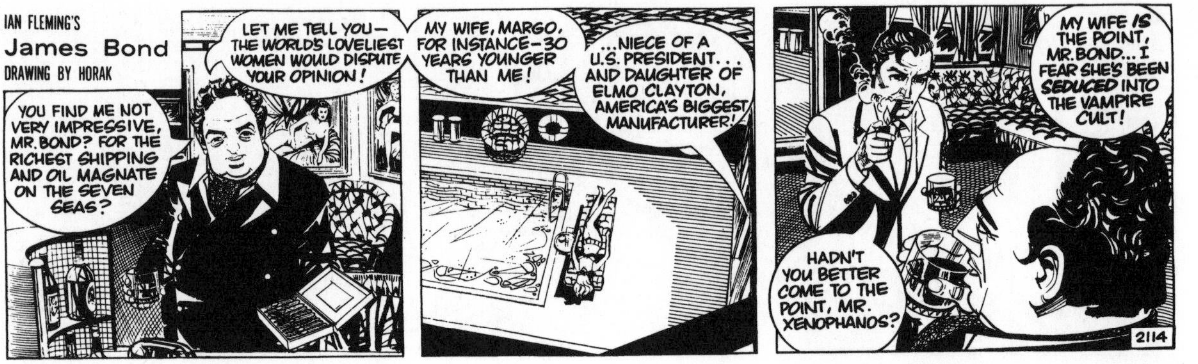
IAN FLEMING'S
James Bond
DRAWING BY HORAK
YOU FIND ME NOT VERY IMPRESSIVE, MR. BOND? FOR THE RICHEST SHIPPING AND OIL MAGNATE ON THE SEVEN SEAS?
LET ME TELL YOU— THE WORLD'S LOVELIEST WOMEN WOULD DISPUTE YOUR OPINION!
MY WIFE, MARGO, FOR INSTANCE—30 YEARS YOUNGER THAN ME!
...NIECE OF A U.S. PRESIDENT... AND DAUGHTER OF ELMO CLAYTON, AMERICA'S BIGGEST MANUFACTURER!
HADN'T YOU BETTER COME TO THE POINT, MR. XENOPHANOS?
MY WIFE IS THE POINT, MR. BOND... I FEAR SHE'S BEEN SEDUCED INTO THE VAMPIRE CULT!
2114

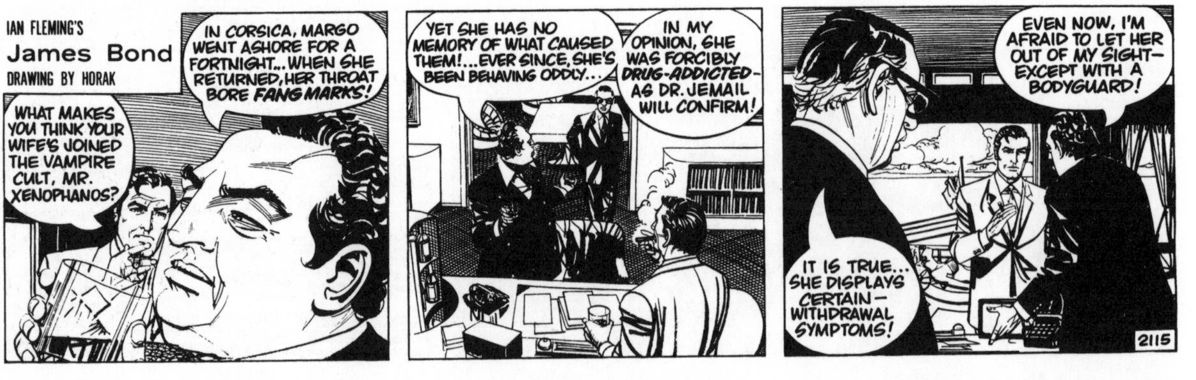
IAN FLEMING'S
James Bond
DRAWING BY HORAK
WHAT MAKES YOU THINK YOUR WIFE'S JOINED THE VAMPIRE CULT, MR. XENOPHANOS?
IN CORSICA, MARGO WENT ASHORE FOR A FORTNIGHT... WHEN SHE RETURNED, HER THROAT BORE FANG MARKS!
YET SHE HAS NO MEMORY OF WHAT CAUSED THEM!... EVER SINCE, SHE'S BEEN BEHAVING ODDLY...
IN MY OPINION, SHE WAS FORCIBLY DRUG-ADDICTED— AS DR. JEMAIL WILL CONFIRM!
IT IS TRUE... SHE DISPLAYS CERTAIN— WITHDRAWAL SYMPTOMS!
EVEN NOW, I'M AFRAID TO LET HER OUT OF MY SIGHT— EXCEPT WITH A BODYGUARD!
2115

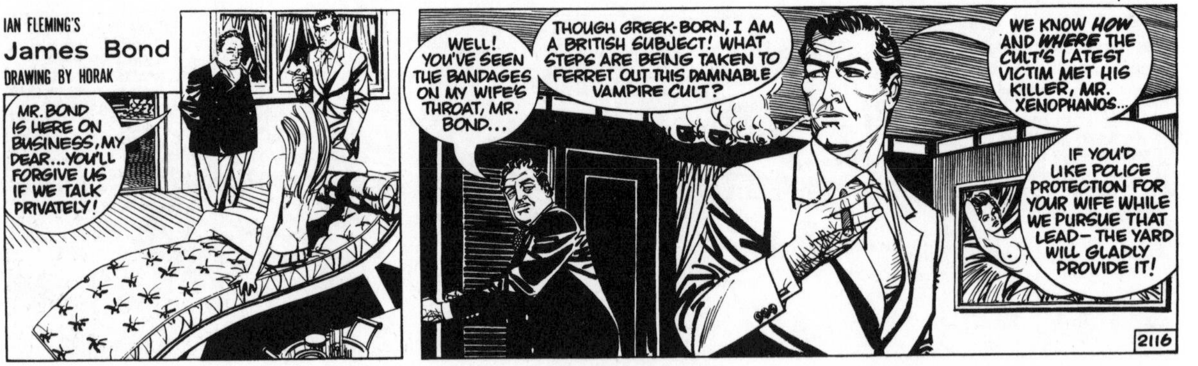
IAN FLEMING'S
James Bond
DRAWING BY HORAK
MR. BOND IS HERE ON BUSINESS, MY DEAR... YOU'LL FORGIVE US IF WE TALK PRIVATELY!
WELL! YOU'VE SEEN THE BANDAGES ON MY WIFE'S THROAT, MR. BOND...
THOUGH GREEK-BORN, I AM A BRITISH SUBJECT! WHAT STEPS ARE BEING TAKEN TO FERRET OUT THIS DAMNABLE VAMPIRE CULT?
WE KNOW HOW AND WHERE THE CULT'S LATEST VICTIM MET HIS KILLER, MR. XENOPHANOS...
IF YOU'D LIKE POLICE PROTECTION FOR YOUR WIFE WHILE WE PURSUE THAT LEAD— THE YARD WILL GLADLY PROVIDE IT!
2116

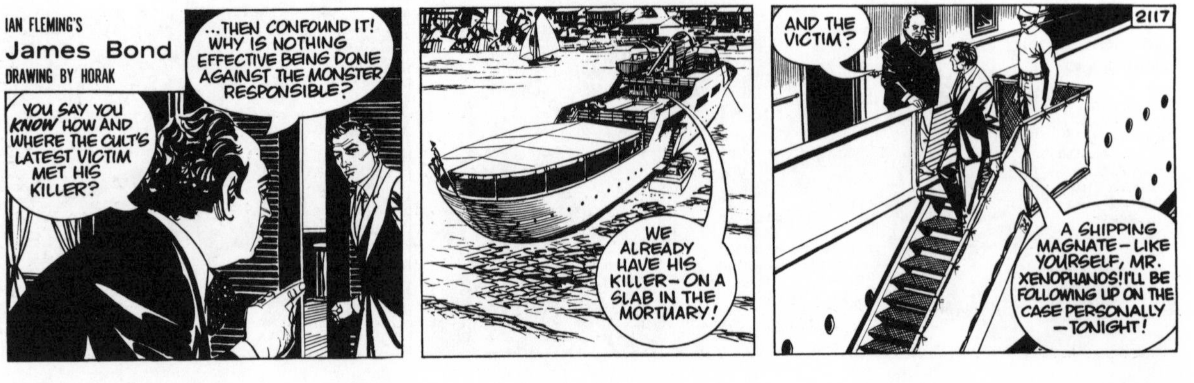
IAN FLEMING'S
James Bond
DRAWING BY HORAK
YOU SAY YOU KNOW HOW AND WHERE THE CULT'S LATEST VICTIM MET HIS KILLER?
...THEN CONFOUND IT! WHY IS NOTHING EFFECTIVE BEING DONE AGAINST THE MONSTER RESPONSIBLE?
WE ALREADY HAVE HIS KILLER— ON A SLAB IN THE MORTUARY!
2117
AND THE VICTIM?
A SHIPPING MAGNATE— LIKE YOURSELF, MR. XENOPHANOS! I'LL BE FOLLOWING UP ON THE CASE PERSONALLY —TONIGHT!

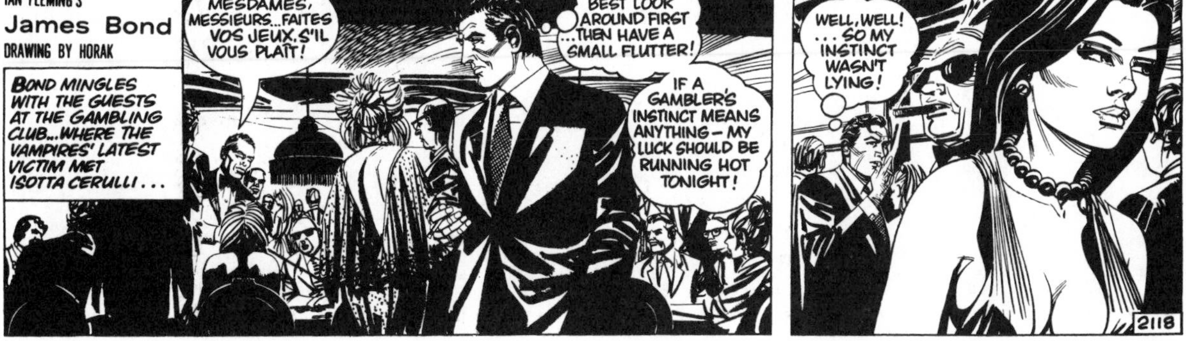
IAN FLEMING'S
James Bond
DRAWING BY HORAK
BOND MINGLES WITH THE GUESTS AT THE GAMBLING CLUB...WHERE THE VAMPIRES' LATEST VICTIM MET ISOTTA CERULLI . . .
MESDAMES, MESSIEURS...FAITES VOS JEUX, S'IL VOUS PLAÎT!
BEST LOOK AROUND FIRST ...THEN HAVE A SMALL FLUTTER!
IF A GAMBLER'S INSTINCT MEANS ANYTHING – MY LUCK SHOULD BE RUNNING HOT TONIGHT!
WELL, WELL! . . . SO MY INSTINCT WASN'T LYING!
2118

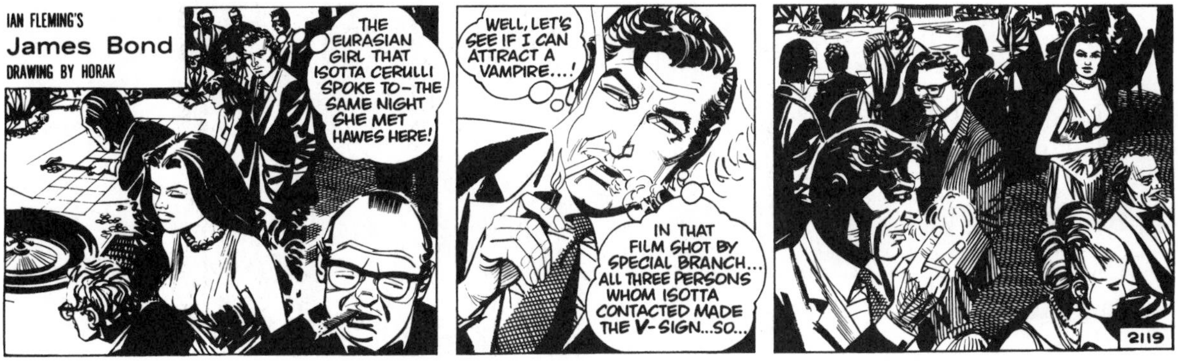
IAN FLEMING'S
James Bond
DRAWING BY HORAK
THE EURASIAN GIRL THAT ISOTTA CERULLI SPOKE TO – THE SAME NIGHT SHE MET HAWES HERE!
WELL, LET'S SEE IF I CAN ATTRACT A VAMPIRE...!
IN THAT FILM SHOT BY SPECIAL BRANCH... ALL THREE PERSONS WHOM ISOTTA CONTACTED MADE THE V-SIGN...SO...
2119

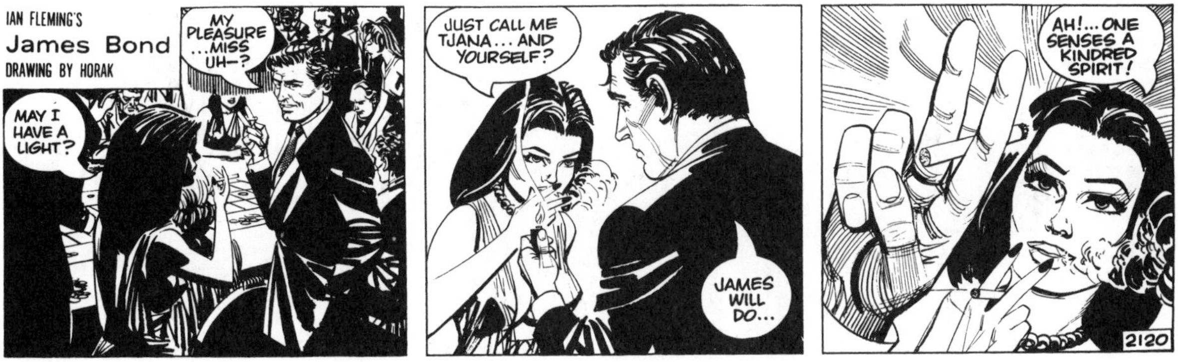
IAN FLEMING'S
James Bond
DRAWING BY HORAK
MAY I HAVE A LIGHT?
MY PLEASURE ...MISS UH–?
JUST CALL ME TJANA . . . AND YOURSELF?
JAMES WILL DO . . .
AH! . . . ONE SENSES A KINDRED SPIRIT!
2120

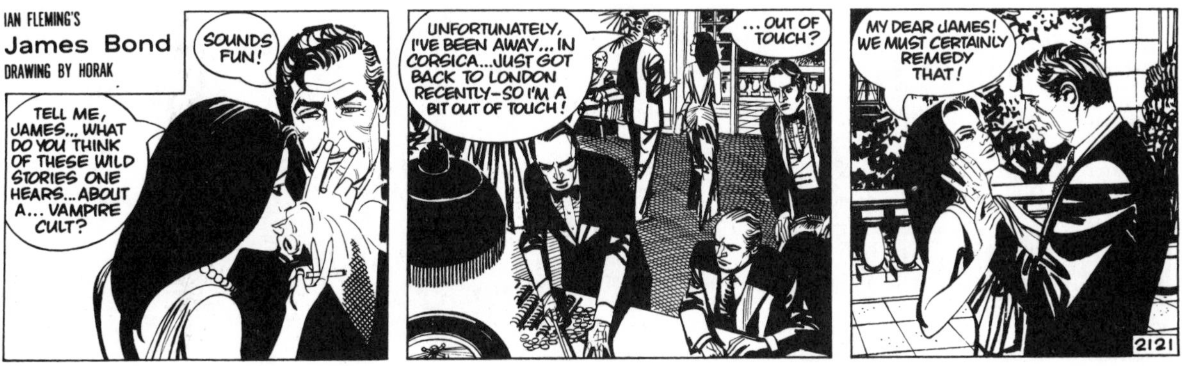
IAN FLEMING'S
James Bond
DRAWING BY HORAK
TELL ME, JAMES... WHAT DO YOU THINK OF THESE WILD STORIES ONE HEARS...ABOUT A... VAMPIRE CULT?
SOUNDS FUN!
UNFORTUNATELY, I'VE BEEN AWAY... IN CORSICA...JUST GOT BACK TO LONDON RECENTLY–SO I'M A BIT OUT OF TOUCH!
...OUT OF TOUCH?
MY DEAR JAMES! WE MUST CERTAINLY REMEDY THAT!
2121

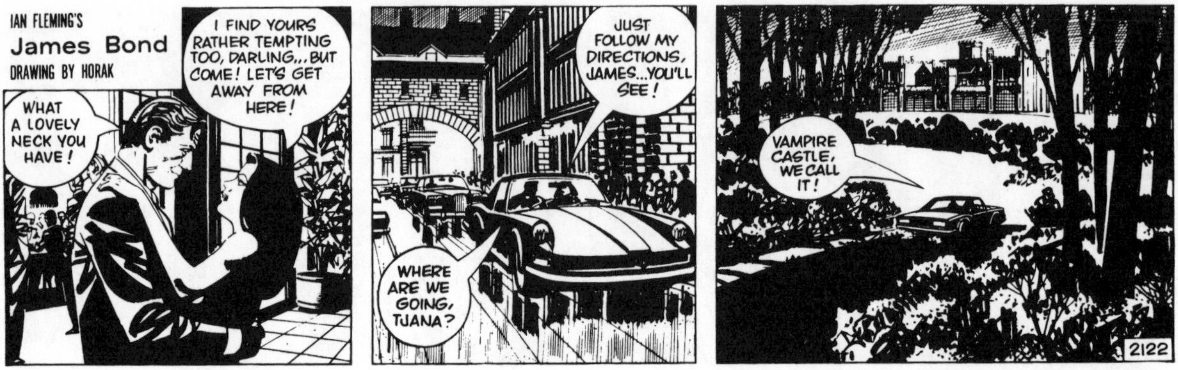
IAN FLEMING'S
James Bond
DRAWING BY HORAK
WHAT A LOVELY NECK YOU HAVE!
I FIND YOURS RATHER TEMPTING TOO, DARLING,,, BUT COME! LET'S GET AWAY FROM HERE!
WHERE ARE WE GOING, TJANA?
JUST FOLLOW MY DIRECTIONS, JAMES...YOU'LL SEE!
VAMPIRE CASTLE, WE CALL IT!
2122

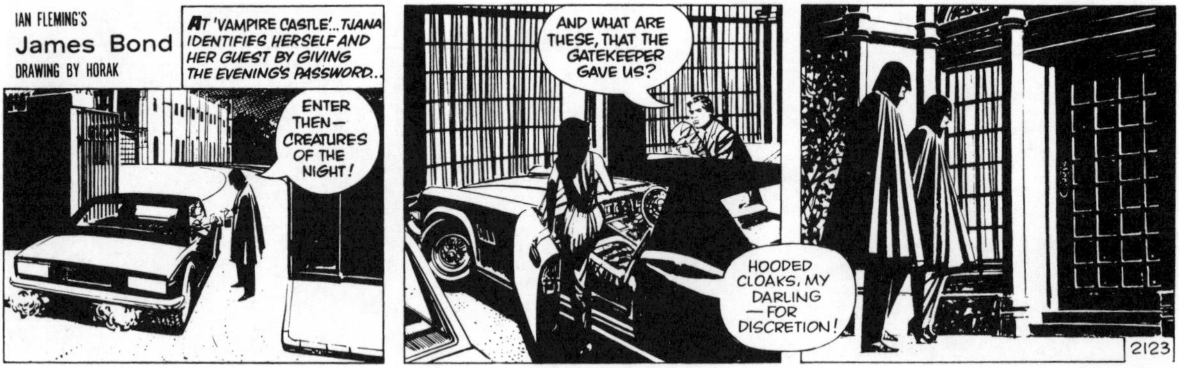
IAN FLEMING'S
James Bond
DRAWING BY HORAK
AT 'VAMPIRE CASTLE'... TJANA IDENTIFIES HERSELF AND HER GUEST BY GIVING THE EVENING'S PASSWORD...
ENTER THEN— CREATURES OF THE NIGHT!
AND WHAT ARE THESE, THAT THE GATEKEEPER GAVE US?
HOODED CLOAKS, MY DARLING —FOR DISCRETION!
2123

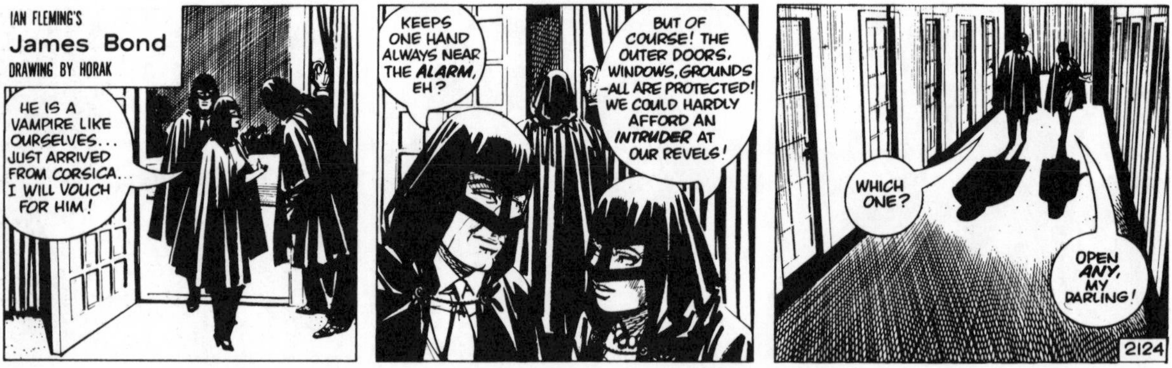
IAN FLEMING'S
James Bond
DRAWING BY HORAK
HE IS A VAMPIRE LIKE OURSELVES... JUST ARRIVED FROM CORSICA... I WILL VOUCH FOR HIM!
KEEPS ONE HAND ALWAYS NEAR THE ALARM, EH?
BUT OF COURSE! THE OUTER DOORS, WINDOWS, GROUNDS -ALL ARE PROTECTED! WE COULD HARDLY AFFORD AN INTRUDER AT OUR REVELS!
WHICH ONE?
OPEN ANY, MY DARLING!
2124

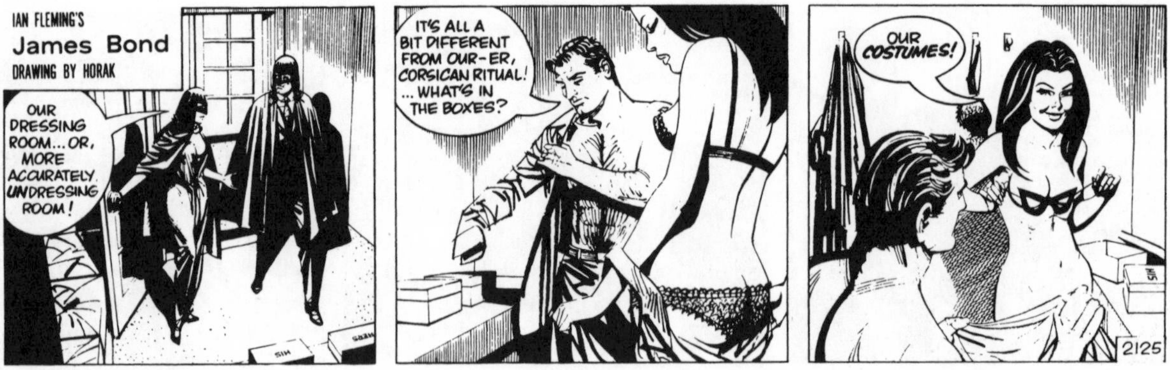
IAN FLEMING'S
James Bond
DRAWING BY HORAK
OUR DRESSING ROOM... OR, MORE ACCURATELY UNDRESSING ROOM!
IT'S ALL A BIT DIFFERENT FROM OUR-ER, CORSICAN RITUAL! ...WHAT'S IN THE BOXES?
OUR COSTUMES!
2125

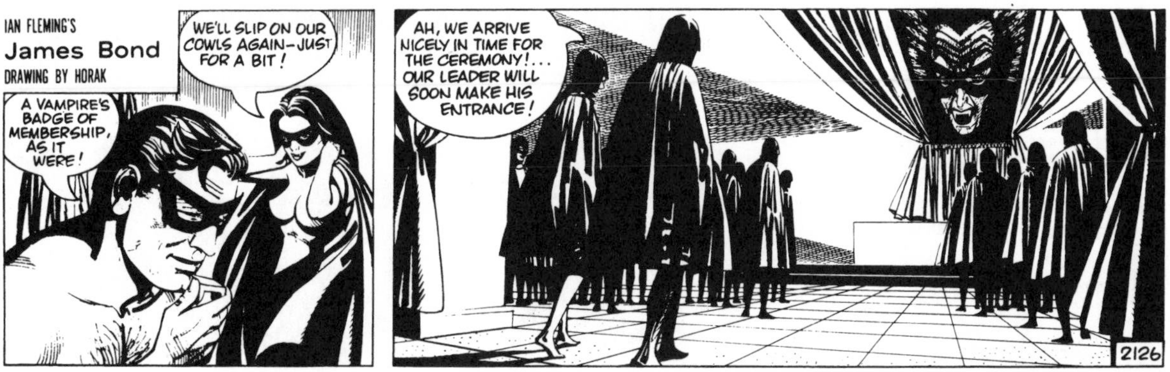
IAN FLEMING'S
James Bond
DRAWING BY HORAK
WE'LL SLIP ON OUR COWLS AGAIN—JUST FOR A BIT!
A VAMPIRE'S BADGE OF MEMBERSHIP, AS IT WERE!
AH, WE ARRIVE NICELY IN TIME FOR THE CEREMONY!... OUR LEADER WILL SOON MAKE HIS ENTRANCE!
2126

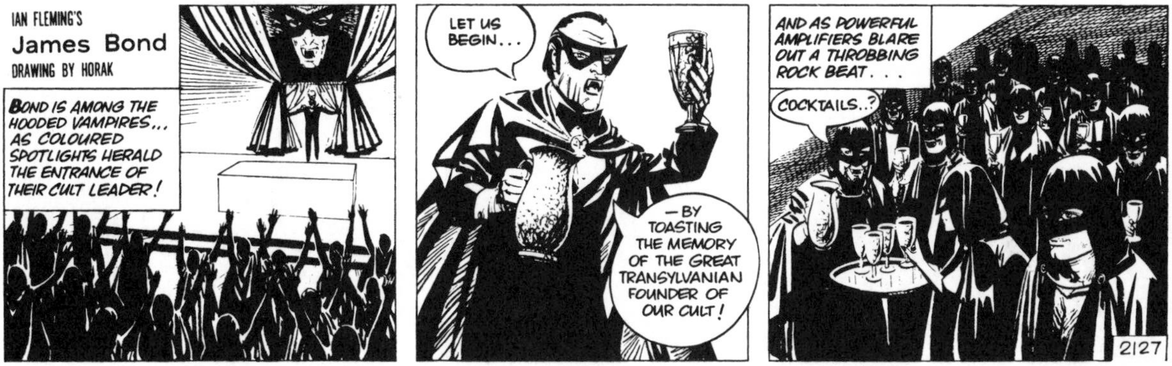
IAN FLEMING'S
James Bond
DRAWING BY HORAK
BOND IS AMONG THE HOODED VAMPIRES... AS COLOURED SPOTLIGHTS HERALD THE ENTRANCE OF THEIR CULT LEADER!
LET US BEGIN...
—BY TOASTING THE MEMORY OF THE GREAT TRANSYLVANIAN FOUNDER OF OUR CULT!
AND AS POWERFUL AMPLIFIERS BLARE OUT A THROBBING ROCK BEAT...
COCKTAILS..?
2127

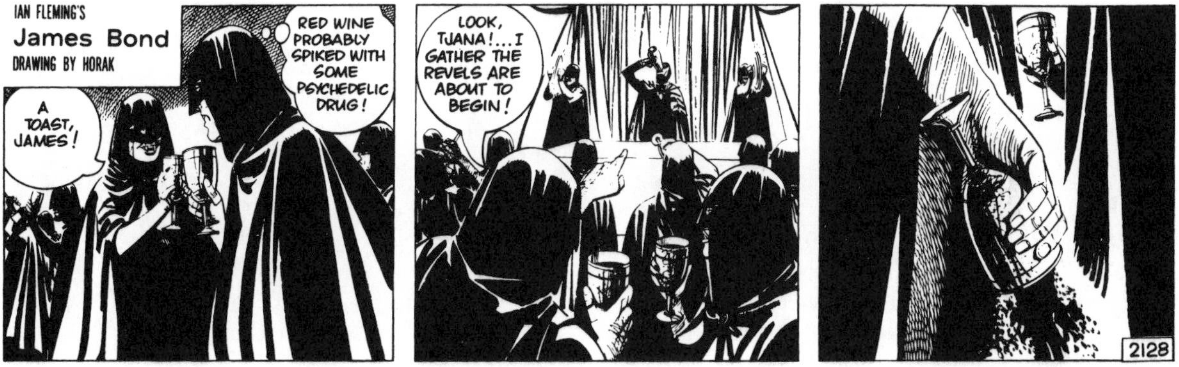
IAN FLEMING'S
James Bond
DRAWING BY HORAK
A TOAST, JAMES!
RED WINE PROBABLY SPIKED WITH SOME PSYCHEDELIC DRUG!
LOOK, TJANA!... I GATHER THE REVELS ARE ABOUT TO BEGIN!
2128

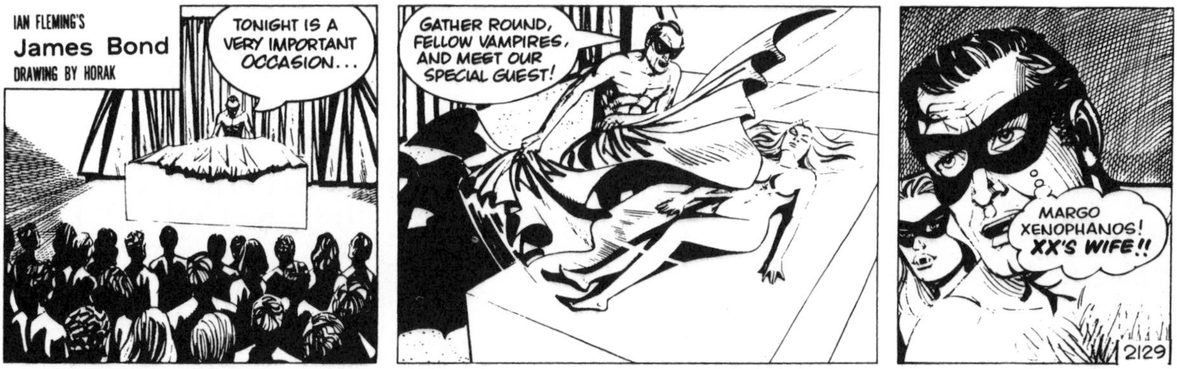
IAN FLEMING'S
James Bond
DRAWING BY HORAK
TONIGHT IS A VERY IMPORTANT OCCASION...
GATHER ROUND, FELLOW VAMPIRES, AND MEET OUR SPECIAL GUEST!
MARGO XENOPHANOS! XX'S WIFE!!
2129

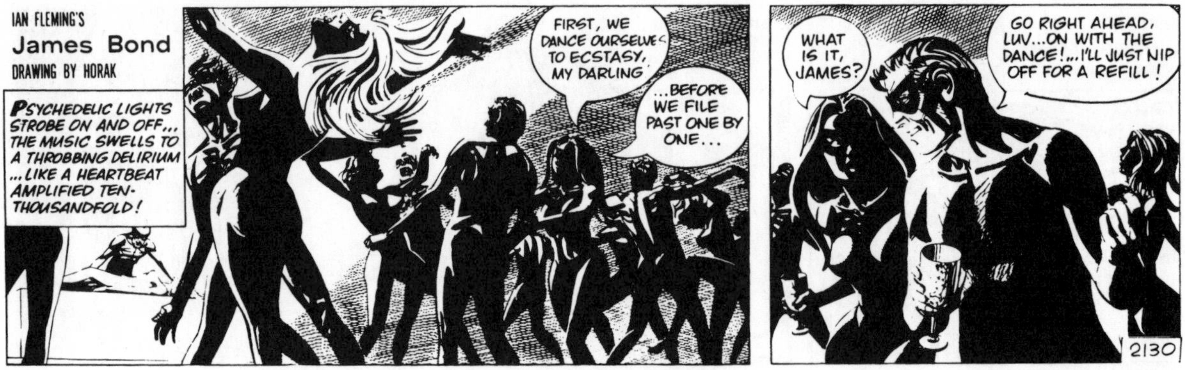
IAN FLEMING'S
James Bond
DRAWING BY HORAK
PSYCHEDELIC LIGHTS STROBE ON AND OFF... THE MUSIC SWELLS TO A THROBBING DELIRIUM ...LIKE A HEARTBEAT AMPLIFIED TEN-THOUSANDFOLD!
FIRST, WE DANCE OURSELVES TO ECSTASY, MY DARLING
...BEFORE WE FILE PAST ONE BY ONE...
WHAT IS IT, JAMES?
GO RIGHT AHEAD, LUV...ON WITH THE DANCE!...I'LL JUST NIP OFF FOR A REFILL!
2130

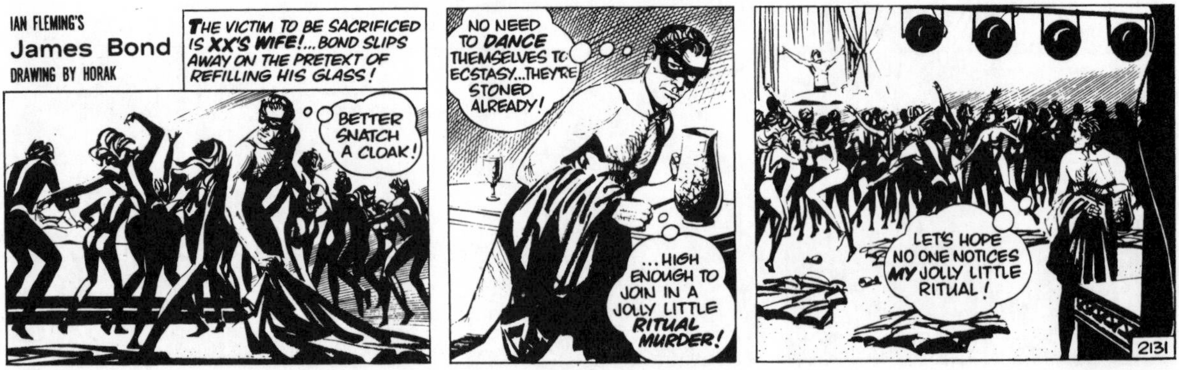
IAN FLEMING'S
James Bond
DRAWING BY HORAK
THE VICTIM TO BE SACRIFICED IS XX'S WIFE!...BOND SLIPS AWAY ON THE PRETEXT OF REFILLING HIS GLASS!
BETTER SNATCH A CLOAK!
NO NEED TO DANCE THEMSELVES TO ECSTASY...THEY'RE STONED ALREADY!
...HIGH ENOUGH TO JOIN IN A JOLLY LITTLE RITUAL MURDER!
LET'S HOPE NO ONE NOTICES MY JOLLY LITTLE RITUAL!
2131

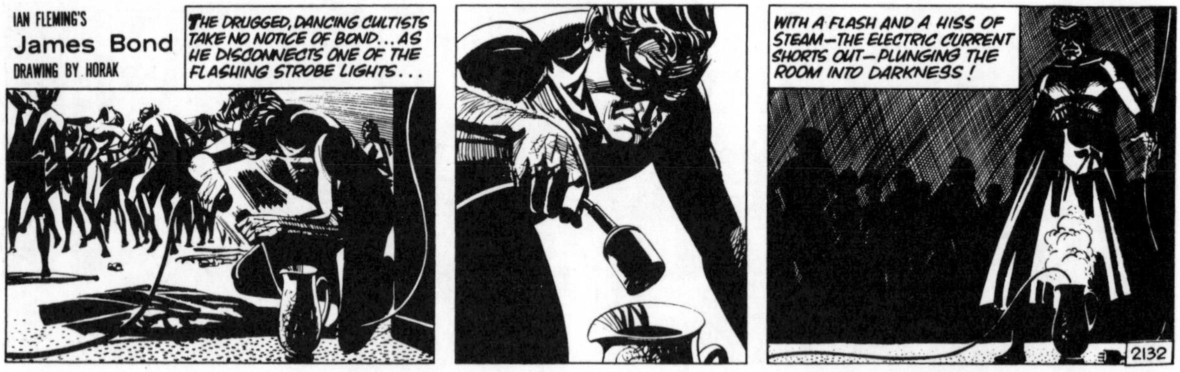
IAN FLEMING'S
James Bond
DRAWING BY HORAK
THE DRUGGED, DANCING CULTISTS TAKE NO NOTICE OF BOND...AS HE DISCONNECTS ONE OF THE FLASHING STROBE LIGHTS...
WITH A FLASH AND A HISS OF STEAM—THE ELECTRIC CURRENT SHORTS OUT—PLUNGING THE ROOM INTO DARKNESS!
2132

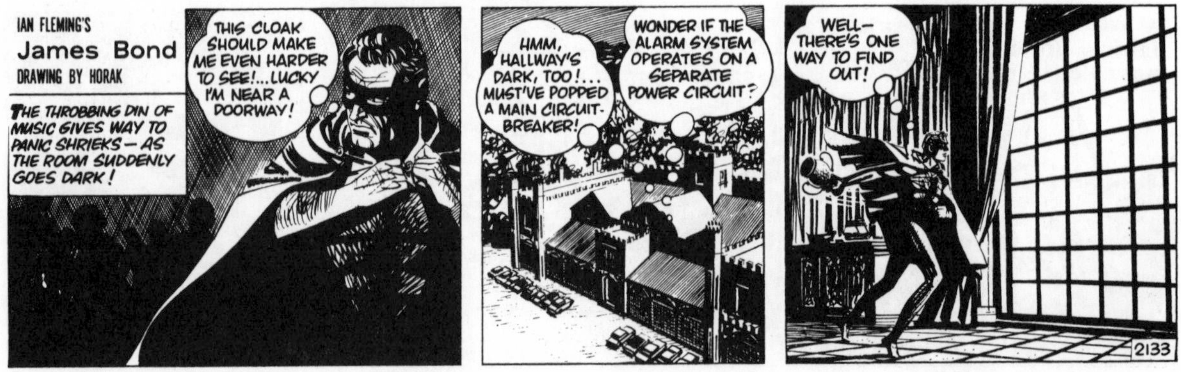
IAN FLEMING'S
James Bond
DRAWING BY HORAK
THE THROBBING DIN OF MUSIC GIVES WAY TO PANIC SHRIEKS—AS THE ROOM SUDDENLY GOES DARK!
THIS CLOAK SHOULD MAKE ME EVEN HARDER TO SEE!...LUCKY I'M NEAR A DOORWAY!
HMM, HALLWAY'S DARK, TOO!... MUST'VE POPPED A MAIN CIRCUIT-BREAKER!
WONDER IF THE ALARM SYSTEM OPERATES ON A SEPARATE POWER CIRCUIT?
WELL—THERE'S ONE WAY TO FIND OUT!
2133

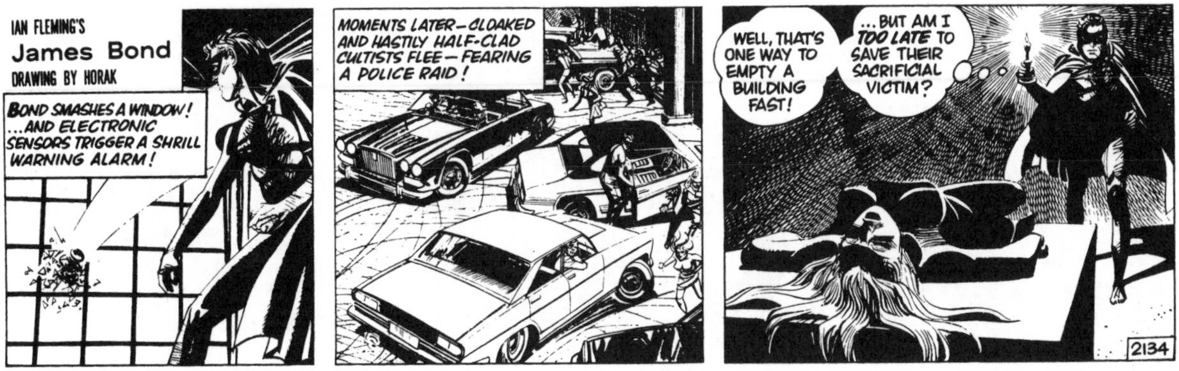
IAN FLEMING'S
James Bond
DRAWING BY HORAK
BOND SMASHES A WINDOW! ...AND ELECTRONIC SENSORS TRIGGER A SHRILL WARNING ALARM!
MOMENTS LATER—CLOAKED AND HASTILY HALF-CLAD CULTISTS FLEE—FEARING A POLICE RAID!
WELL, THAT'S ONE WAY TO EMPTY A BUILDING FAST!
...BUT AM I TOO LATE TO SAVE THEIR SACRIFICIAL VICTIM?
2134

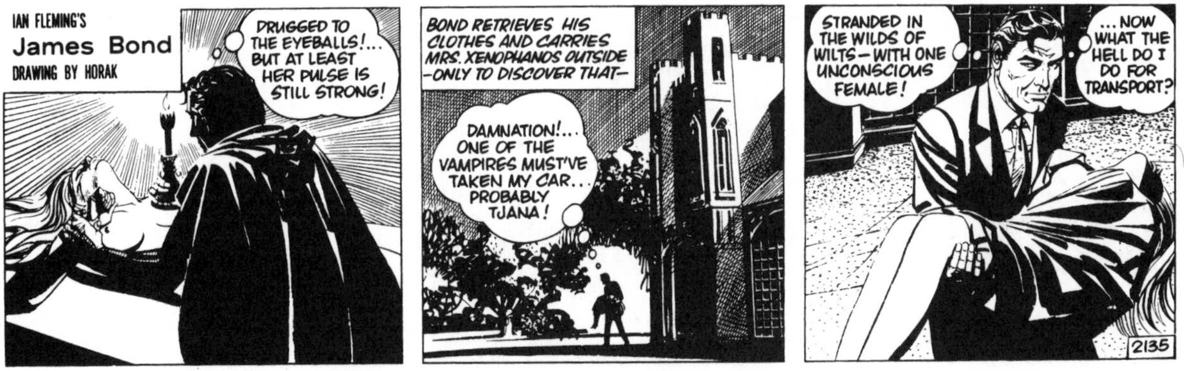
IAN FLEMING'S
James Bond
DRAWING BY HORAK
DRUGGED TO THE EYEBALLS!... BUT AT LEAST HER PULSE IS STILL STRONG!
BOND RETRIEVES HIS CLOTHES AND CARRIES MRS. XENOPHANOS OUTSIDE —ONLY TO DISCOVER THAT—
DAMNATION!... ONE OF THE VAMPIRES MUST'VE TAKEN MY CAR... PROBABLY TJANA!
STRANDED IN THE WILDS OF WILTS—WITH ONE UNCONSCIOUS FEMALE!
...NOW WHAT THE HELL DO I DO FOR TRANSPORT?
2135

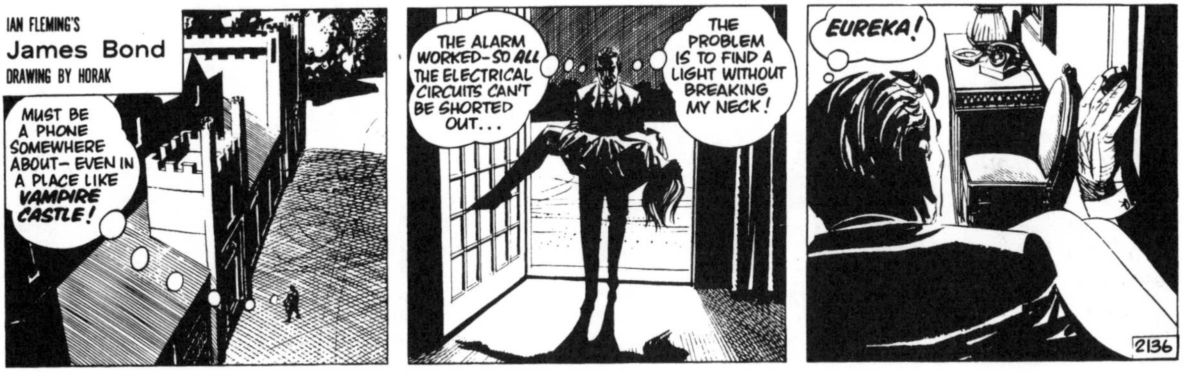
IAN FLEMING'S
James Bond
DRAWING BY HORAK
MUST BE A PHONE SOMEWHERE ABOUT—EVEN IN A PLACE LIKE VAMPIRE CASTLE!
THE ALARM WORKED—SO ALL THE ELECTRICAL CIRCUITS CAN'T BE SHORTED OUT...
THE PROBLEM IS TO FIND A LIGHT WITHOUT BREAKING MY NECK!
EUREKA!
2136

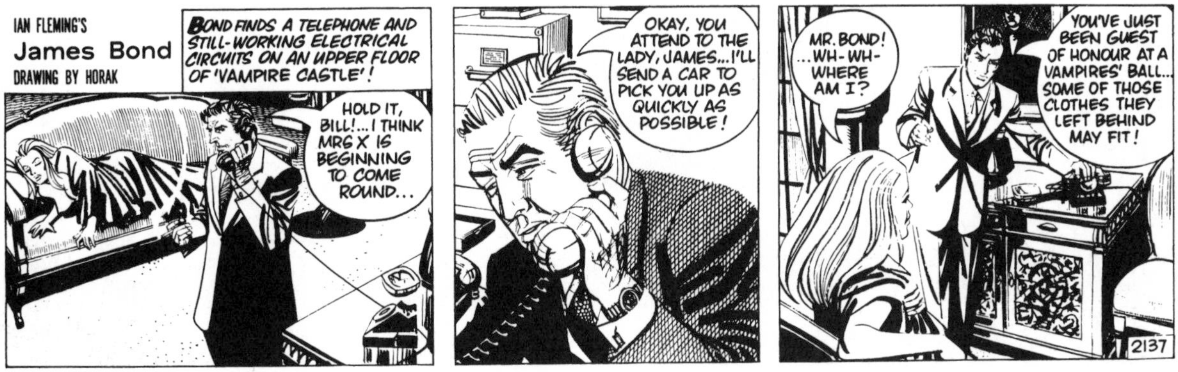
IAN FLEMING'S
James Bond
DRAWING BY HORAK
BOND FINDS A TELEPHONE AND STILL-WORKING ELECTRICAL CIRCUITS ON AN UPPER FLOOR OF 'VAMPIRE CASTLE'!
HOLD IT, BILL!...I THINK MRS X IS BEGINNING TO COME ROUND...
OKAY, YOU ATTEND TO THE LADY, JAMES...I'LL SEND A CAR TO PICK YOU UP AS QUICKLY AS POSSIBLE!
MR. BOND! ...WH-WH-WHERE AM I?
YOU'VE JUST BEEN GUEST OF HONOUR AT A VAMPIRES' BALL... SOME OF THOSE CLOTHES THEY LEFT BEHIND MAY FIT!
2137

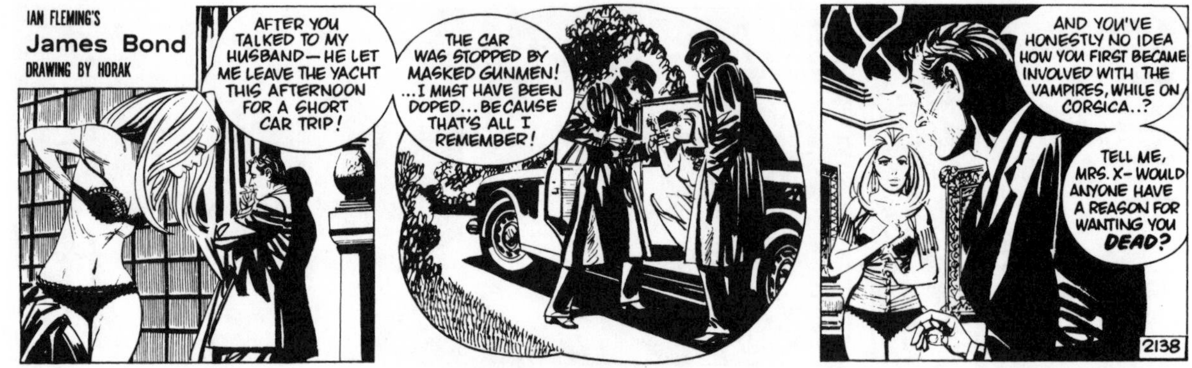

IAN FLEMING'S
James Bond
DRAWING BY HORAK
AFTER YOU TALKED TO MY HUSBAND—HE LET ME LEAVE THE YACHT THIS AFTERNOON FOR A SHORT CAR TRIP!
THE CAR WAS STOPPED BY MASKED GUNMEN! ...I MUST HAVE BEEN DOPED... BECAUSE THAT'S ALL I REMEMBER!
AND YOU'VE HONESTLY NO IDEA HOW YOU FIRST BECAME INVOLVED WITH THE VAMPIRES, WHILE ON CORSICA..?
TELL ME, MRS. X—WOULD ANYONE HAVE A REASON FOR WANTING YOU DEAD?
2138


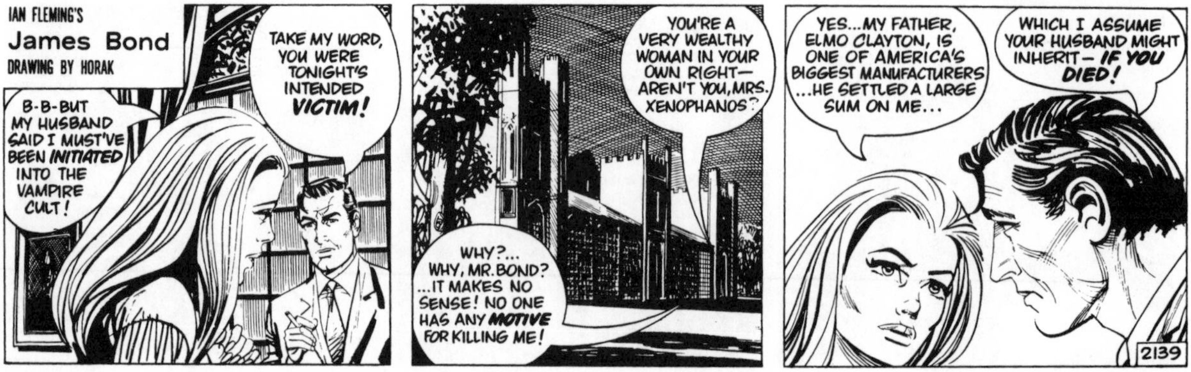

IAN FLEMING'S
James Bond
DRAWING BY HORAK
B-B-BUT MY HUSBAND SAID I MUST'VE BEEN INITIATED INTO THE VAMPIRE CULT!
TAKE MY WORD, YOU WERE TONIGHT'S INTENDED VICTIM!
YOU'RE A VERY WEALTHY WOMAN IN YOUR OWN RIGHT—AREN'T YOU, MRS. XENOPHANOS?
WHY?... WHY, MR. BOND? ...IT MAKES NO SENSE! NO ONE HAS ANY MOTIVE FOR KILLING ME!
YES...MY FATHER, ELMO CLAYTON, IS ONE OF AMERICA'S BIGGEST MANUFACTURERS ...HE SETTLED A LARGE SUM ON ME...
WHICH I ASSUME YOUR HUSBAND MIGHT INHERIT—IF YOU DIED!
2139


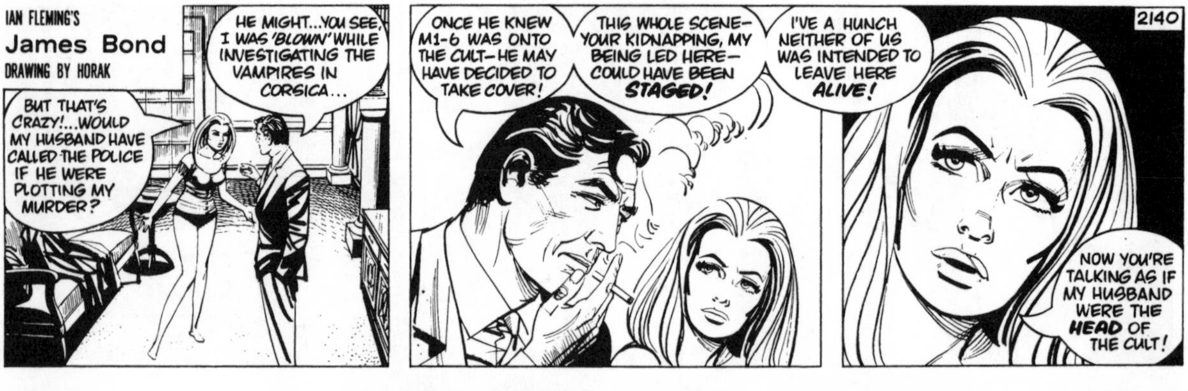

IAN FLEMING'S
James Bond
DRAWING BY HORAK
BUT THAT'S CRAZY!...WOULD MY HUSBAND HAVE CALLED THE POLICE IF HE WERE PLOTTING MY MURDER?
HE MIGHT...YOU SEE, I WAS 'BLOWN' WHILE INVESTIGATING THE VAMPIRES IN CORSICA...
ONCE HE KNEW M1-6 WAS ONTO THE CULT—HE MAY HAVE DECIDED TO TAKE COVER!
THIS WHOLE SCENE—YOUR KIDNAPPING, MY BEING LED HERE—COULD HAVE BEEN STAGED!
I'VE A HUNCH NEITHER OF US WAS INTENDED TO LEAVE HERE ALIVE!
2140
NOW YOU'RE TALKING AS IF MY HUSBAND WERE THE HEAD OF THE CULT!


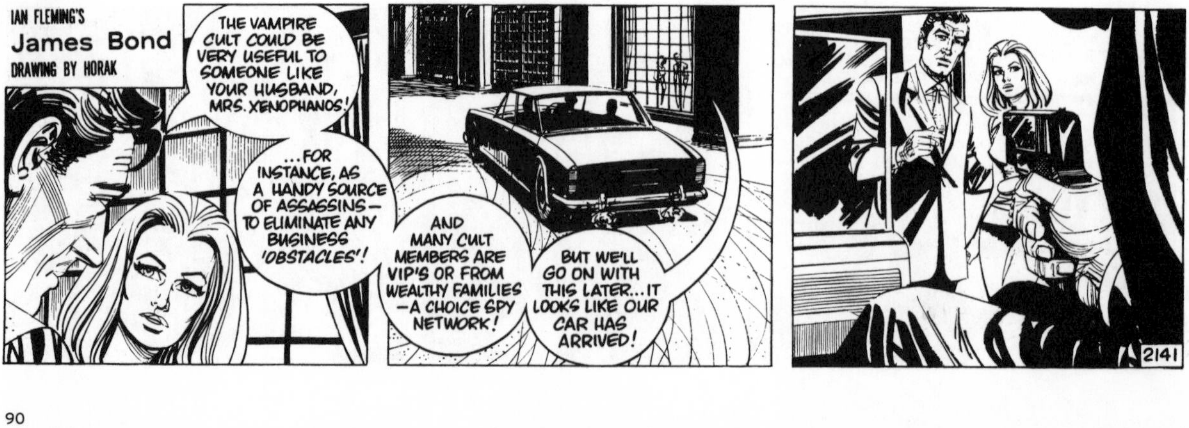

IAN FLEMING'S
James Bond
DRAWING BY HORAK
THE VAMPIRE CULT COULD BE VERY USEFUL TO SOMEONE LIKE YOUR HUSBAND, MRS. XENOPHANOS!
...FOR INSTANCE, AS A HANDY SOURCE OF ASSASSINS—TO ELIMINATE ANY BUSINESS 'OBSTACLES'!
AND MANY CULT MEMBERS ARE VIP'S OR FROM WEALTHY FAMILIES—A CHOICE SPY NETWORK!
BUT WE'LL GO ON WITH THIS LATER...IT LOOKS LIKE OUR CAR HAS ARRIVED!
2141

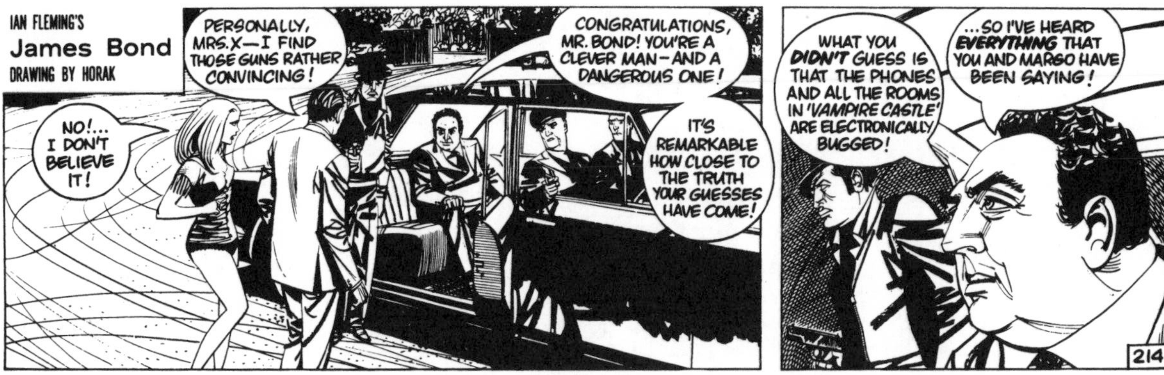
IAN FLEMING'S
James Bond
DRAWING BY HORAK
PERSONALLY, MRS. X—I FIND THOSE GUNS RATHER CONVINCING!
NO!... I DON'T BELIEVE IT!
CONGRATULATIONS, MR. BOND! YOU'RE A CLEVER MAN—AND A DANGEROUS ONE!
IT'S REMARKABLE HOW CLOSE TO THE TRUTH YOUR GUESSES HAVE COME!
WHAT YOU DIDN'T GUESS IS THAT THE PHONES AND ALL THE ROOMS IN 'VAMPIRE CASTLE' ARE ELECTRONICALLY BUGGED!
...SO I'VE HEARD EVERYTHING THAT YOU AND MARGO HAVE BEEN SAYING!
2142

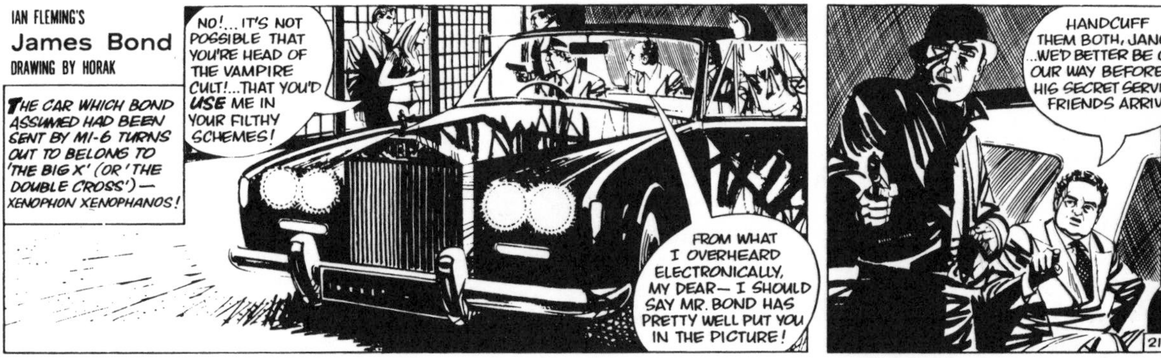
IAN FLEMING'S
James Bond
DRAWING BY HORAK
THE CAR WHICH BOND ASSUMED HAD BEEN SENT BY MI-6 TURNS OUT TO BELONG TO 'THE BIG X' (OR 'THE DOUBLE CROSS')—XENOPHON XENOPHANOS!
NO!... IT'S NOT POSSIBLE THAT YOU'RE HEAD OF THE VAMPIRE CULT!... THAT YOU'D USE ME IN YOUR FILTHY SCHEMES!
FROM WHAT I OVERHEARD ELECTRONICALLY, MY DEAR—I SHOULD SAY MR. BOND HAS PRETTY WELL PUT YOU IN THE PICTURE!
HANDCUFF THEM BOTH, JANOS ...WE'D BETTER BE ON OUR WAY BEFORE HIS SECRET SERVICE FRIENDS ARRIVE!
2143

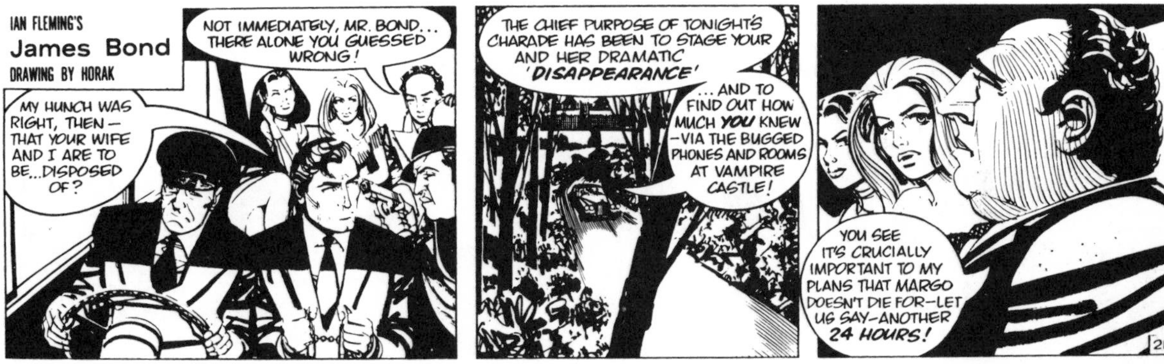
IAN FLEMING'S
James Bond
DRAWING BY HORAK
MY HUNCH WAS RIGHT, THEN—THAT YOUR WIFE AND I ARE TO BE...DISPOSED OF?
NOT IMMEDIATELY, MR. BOND... THERE ALONE YOU GUESSED WRONG!
THE CHIEF PURPOSE OF TONIGHT'S CHARADE HAS BEEN TO STAGE YOUR AND HER DRAMATIC 'DISAPPEARANCE'
...AND TO FIND OUT HOW MUCH YOU KNEW—VIA THE BUGGED PHONES AND ROOMS AT VAMPIRE CASTLE!
YOU SEE IT'S CRUCIALLY IMPORTANT TO MY PLANS THAT MARGO DOESN'T DIE FOR—LET US SAY—ANOTHER 24 HOURS!
2144

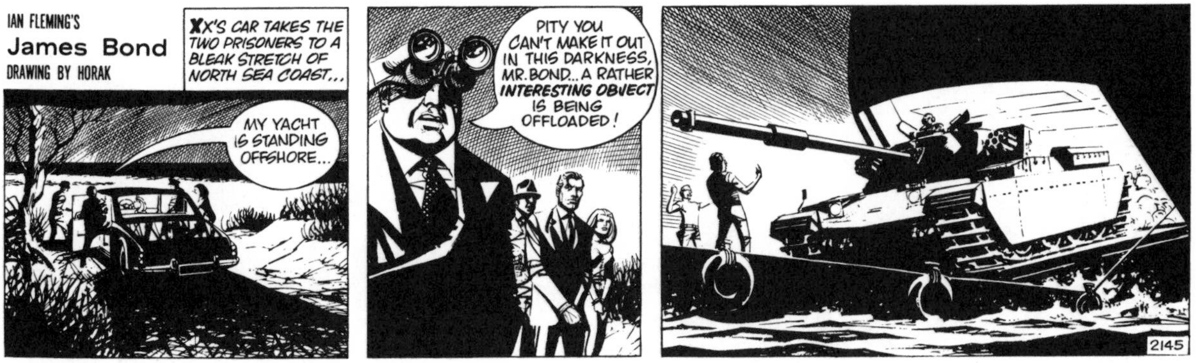
IAN FLEMING'S
James Bond
DRAWING BY HORAK
X'S CAR TAKES THE TWO PRISONERS TO A BLEAK STRETCH OF NORTH SEA COAST...
MY YACHT IS STANDING OFFSHORE...
PITY YOU CAN'T MAKE IT OUT IN THIS DARKNESS, MR. BOND... A RATHER INTERESTING OBJECT IS BEING OFFLOADED!
2145

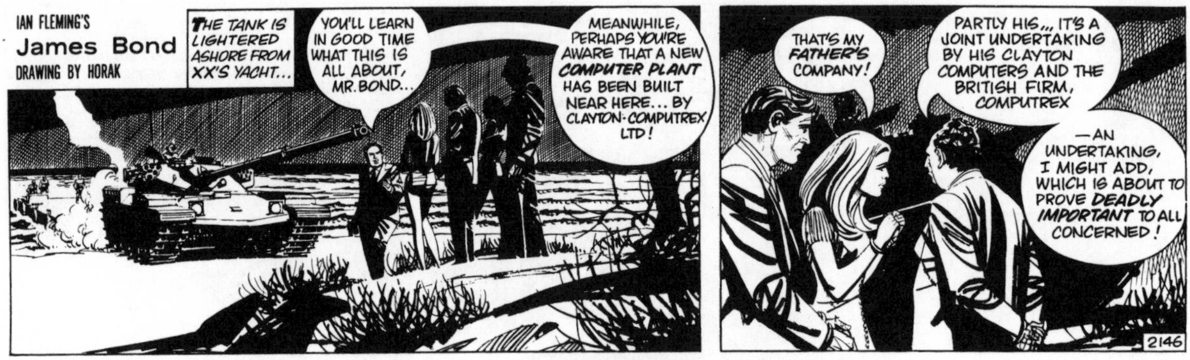

IAN FLEMING'S
James Bond
DRAWING BY HORAK
THE TANK IS LIGHTERED ASHORE FROM XX'S YACHT...
YOU'LL LEARN IN GOOD TIME WHAT THIS IS ALL ABOUT, MR. BOND...
MEANWHILE, PERHAPS YOU'RE AWARE THAT A NEW COMPUTER PLANT HAS BEEN BUILT NEAR HERE... BY CLAYTON-COMPUTREX LTD!
THAT'S MY FATHER'S COMPANY!
PARTLY HIS... IT'S A JOINT UNDERTAKING BY HIS CLAYTON COMPUTERS AND THE BRITISH FIRM, COMPUTREX
—AN UNDERTAKING, I MIGHT ADD, WHICH IS ABOUT TO PROVE DEADLY IMPORTANT TO ALL CONCERNED!
2146


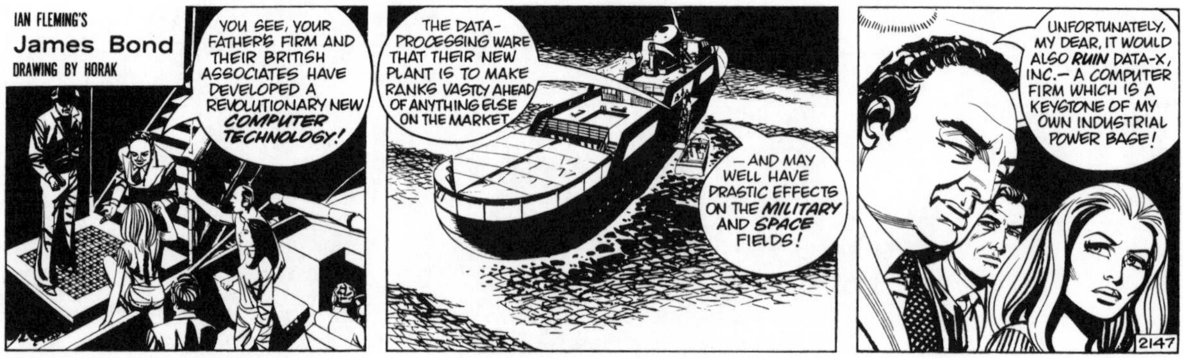

IAN FLEMING'S
James Bond
DRAWING BY HORAK
YOU SEE, YOUR FATHER'S FIRM AND THEIR BRITISH ASSOCIATES HAVE DEVELOPED A REVOLUTIONARY NEW COMPUTER TECHNOLOGY!
THE DATA-PROCESSING WARE THAT THEIR NEW PLANT IS TO MAKE RANKS VASTLY AHEAD OF ANYTHING ELSE ON THE MARKET
—AND MAY WELL HAVE DRASTIC EFFECTS ON THE MILITARY AND SPACE FIELDS!
UNFORTUNATELY, MY DEAR, IT WOULD ALSO RUIN DATA-X, INC.—A COMPUTER FIRM WHICH IS A KEYSTONE OF MY OWN INDUSTRIAL POWER BASE!
2147


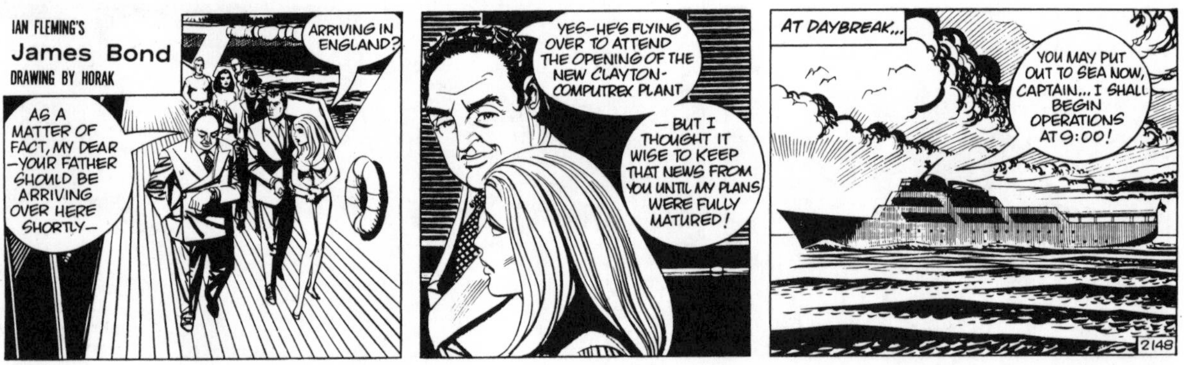

IAN FLEMING'S
James Bond
DRAWING BY HORAK
AS A MATTER OF FACT, MY DEAR —YOUR FATHER SHOULD BE ARRIVING OVER HERE SHORTLY—
ARRIVING IN ENGLAND?
YES—HE'S FLYING OVER TO ATTEND THE OPENING OF THE NEW CLAYTON-COMPUTREX PLANT
—BUT I THOUGHT IT WISE TO KEEP THAT NEWS FROM YOU UNTIL MY PLANS WERE FULLY MATURED!
AT DAYBREAK...
YOU MAY PUT OUT TO SEA NOW, CAPTAIN... I SHALL BEGIN OPERATIONS AT 9:00!
2148


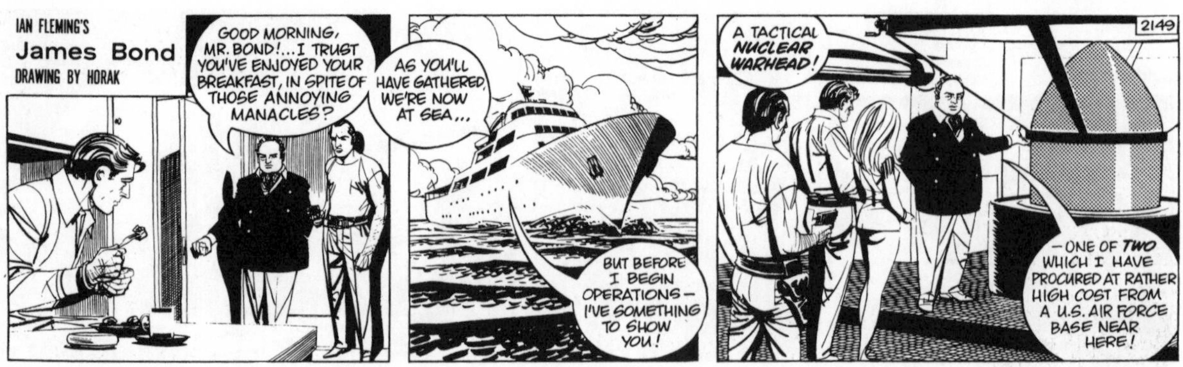

IAN FLEMING'S
James Bond
DRAWING BY HORAK
GOOD MORNING, MR. BOND!... I TRUST YOU'VE ENJOYED YOUR BREAKFAST, IN SPITE OF THOSE ANNOYING MANACLES?
AS YOU'LL HAVE GATHERED, WE'RE NOW AT SEA...
BUT BEFORE I BEGIN OPERATIONS—I'VE SOMETHING TO SHOW YOU!
2149
A TACTICAL NUCLEAR WARHEAD!
—ONE OF TWO WHICH I HAVE PROCURED AT RATHER HIGH COST FROM A U.S. AIR FORCE BASE NEAR HERE!

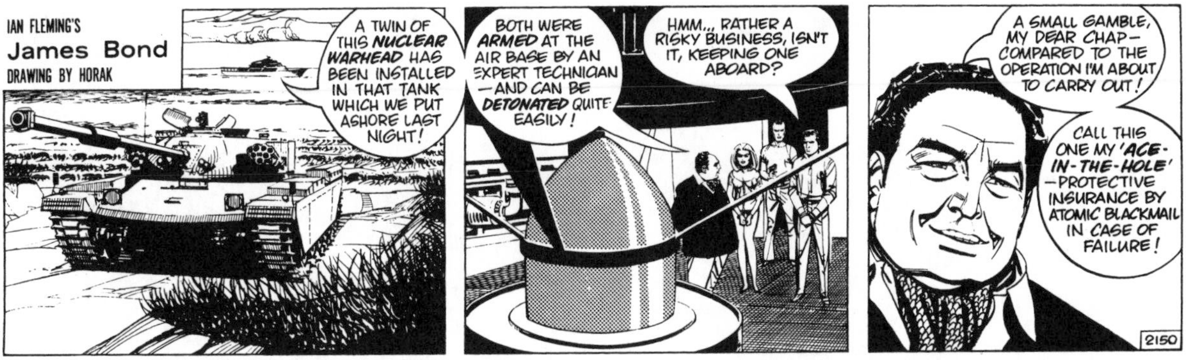
IAN FLEMING'S
James Bond
DRAWING BY HORAK
A TWIN OF THIS NUCLEAR WARHEAD HAS BEEN INSTALLED IN THAT TANK WHICH WE PUT ASHORE LAST NIGHT!
BOTH WERE ARMED AT THE AIR BASE BY AN EXPERT TECHNICIAN —AND CAN BE DETONATED QUITE EASILY!
HMM... RATHER A RISKY BUSINESS, ISN'T IT, KEEPING ONE ABOARD?
A SMALL GAMBLE, MY DEAR CHAP— COMPARED TO THE OPERATION I'M ABOUT TO CARRY OUT!
CALL THIS ONE MY 'ACE-IN-THE-HOLE' —PROTECTIVE INSURANCE BY ATOMIC BLACKMAIL IN CASE OF FAILURE!
2150

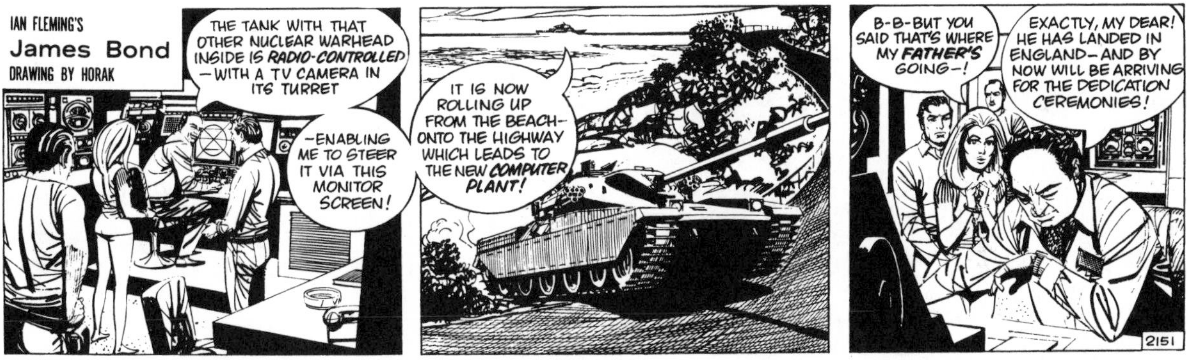
IAN FLEMING'S
James Bond
DRAWING BY HORAK
THE TANK WITH THAT OTHER NUCLEAR WARHEAD INSIDE IS RADIO-CONTROLLED —WITH A TV CAMERA IN ITS TURRET
—ENABLING ME TO STEER IT VIA THIS MONITOR SCREEN!
IT IS NOW ROLLING UP FROM THE BEACH— ONTO THE HIGHWAY WHICH LEADS TO THE NEW COMPUTER PLANT!
B-B-BUT YOU SAID THAT'S WHERE MY FATHER'S GOING—!
EXACTLY, MY DEAR! HE HAS LANDED IN ENGLAND—AND BY NOW WILL BE ARRIVING FOR THE DEDICATION CEREMONIES!
2151

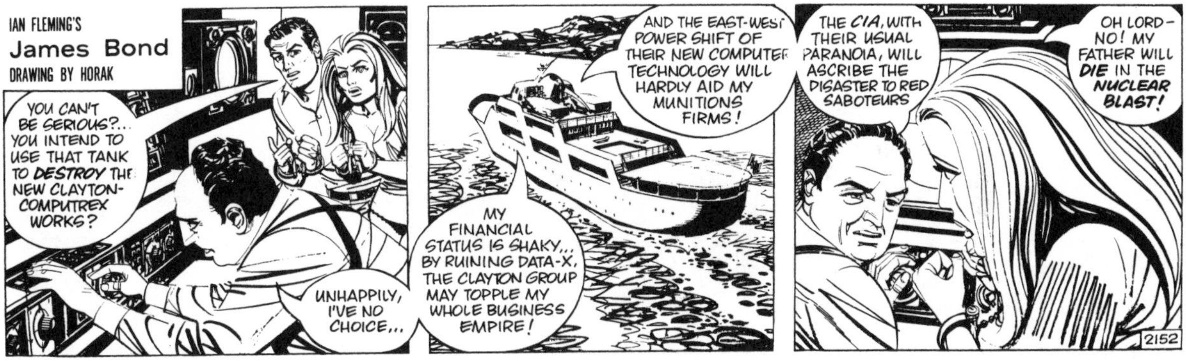
IAN FLEMING'S
James Bond
DRAWING BY HORAK
YOU CAN'T BE SERIOUS?... YOU INTEND TO USE THAT TANK TO DESTROY THE NEW CLAYTON-COMPUTREX WORKS?
UNHAPPILY, I'VE NO CHOICE...
AND THE EAST-WEST POWER SHIFT OF THEIR NEW COMPUTER TECHNOLOGY WILL HARDLY AID MY MUNITIONS FIRMS!
MY FINANCIAL STATUS IS SHAKY... BY RUINING DATA-X, THE CLAYTON GROUP MAY TOPPLE MY WHOLE BUSINESS EMPIRE!
THE CIA, WITH THEIR USUAL PARANOIA, WILL ASCRIBE THE DISASTER TO RED SABOTEURS
OH LORD— NO! MY FATHER WILL DIE IN THE NUCLEAR BLAST!
2152

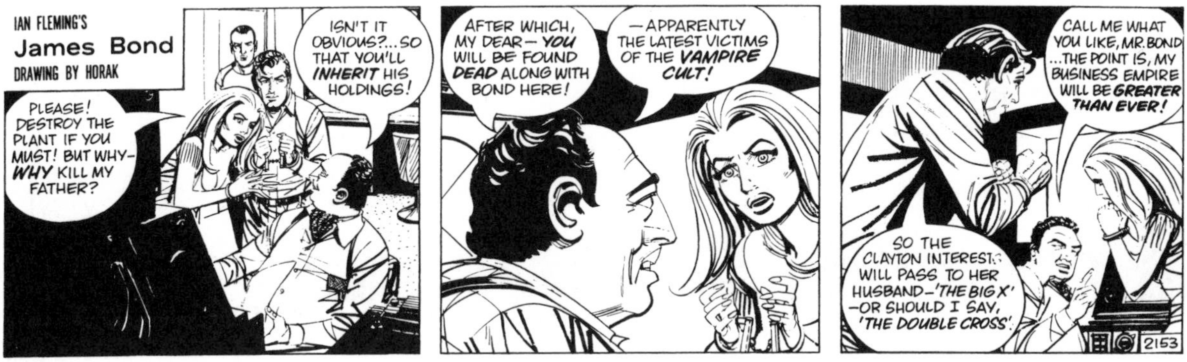
IAN FLEMING'S
James Bond
DRAWING BY HORAK
PLEASE! DESTROY THE PLANT IF YOU MUST! BUT WHY— WHY KILL MY FATHER?
ISN'T IT OBVIOUS?... SO THAT YOU'LL INHERIT HIS HOLDINGS!
AFTER WHICH, MY DEAR— YOU WILL BE FOUND DEAD ALONG WITH BOND HERE!
—APPARENTLY THE LATEST VICTIMS OF THE VAMPIRE CULT!
CALL ME WHAT YOU LIKE, MR. BOND ...THE POINT IS, MY BUSINESS EMPIRE WILL BE GREATER THAN EVER!
SO THE CLAYTON INTERESTS WILL PASS TO HER HUSBAND—'THE BIG X' —OR SHOULD I SAY, 'THE DOUBLE CROSS'.
2153

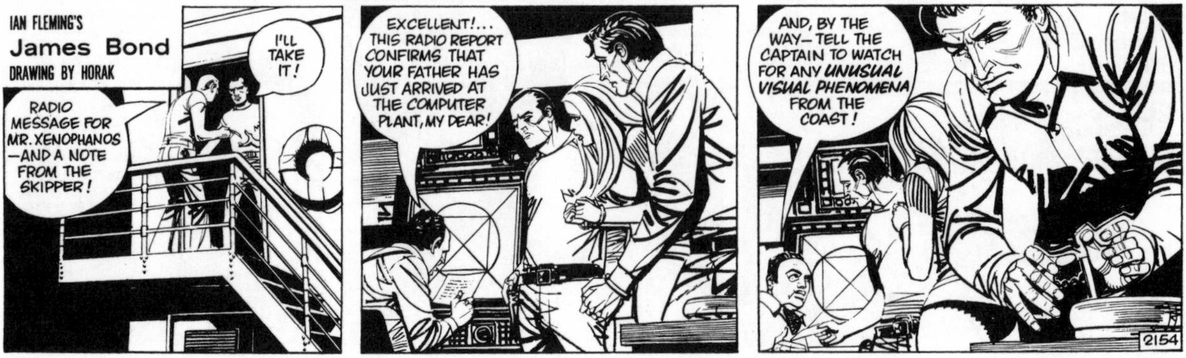
IAN FLEMING'S
James Bond
DRAWING BY HORAK
I'LL TAKE IT!
RADIO MESSAGE FOR MR. XENOPHANOS —AND A NOTE FROM THE SKIPPER!
EXCELLENT!... THIS RADIO REPORT CONFIRMS THAT YOUR FATHER HAS JUST ARRIVED AT THE COMPUTER PLANT, MY DEAR!
AND, BY THE WAY— TELL THE CAPTAIN TO WATCH FOR ANY UNUSUAL VISUAL PHENOMENA FROM THE COAST!
2154

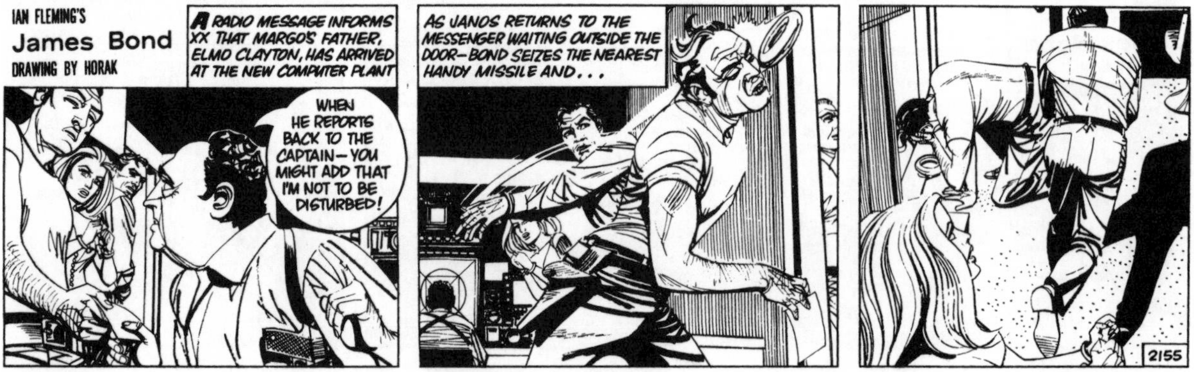
IAN FLEMING'S
James Bond
DRAWING BY HORAK
A RADIO MESSAGE INFORMS XX THAT MARGO'S FATHER, ELMO CLAYTON, HAS ARRIVED AT THE NEW COMPUTER PLANT
WHEN HE REPORTS BACK TO THE CAPTAIN— YOU MIGHT ADD THAT I'M NOT TO BE DISTURBED!
AS JANOS RETURNS TO THE MESSENGER WAITING OUTSIDE THE DOOR— BOND SEIZES THE NEAREST HANDY MISSILE AND...
2155

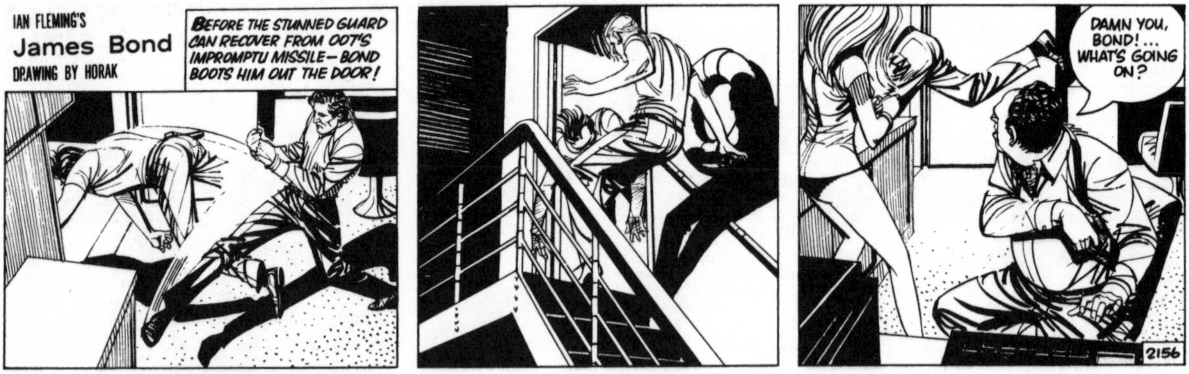
IAN FLEMING'S
James Bond
DRAWING BY HORAK
BEFORE THE STUNNED GUARD CAN RECOVER FROM 007'S IMPROMPTU MISSILE— BOND BOOTS HIM OUT THE DOOR!
DAMN YOU, BOND!... WHAT'S GOING ON?
2156

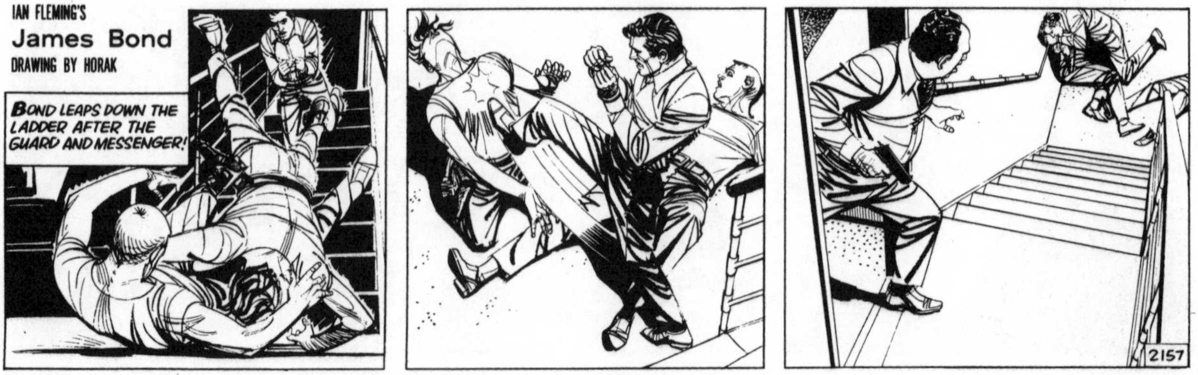
IAN FLEMING'S
James Bond
DRAWING BY HORAK
BOND LEAPS DOWN THE LADDER AFTER THE GUARD AND MESSENGER!
2157

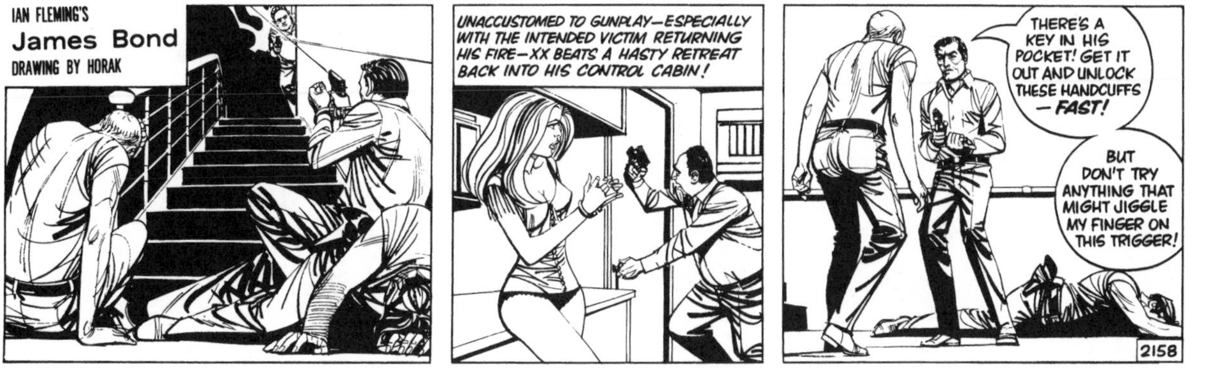
IAN FLEMING'S
James Bond
DRAWING BY HORAK
UNACCUSTOMED TO GUNPLAY—ESPECIALLY WITH THE INTENDED VICTIM RETURNING HIS FIRE—XX BEATS A HASTY RETREAT BACK INTO HIS CONTROL CABIN!
THERE'S A KEY IN HIS POCKET! GET IT OUT AND UNLOCK THESE HANDCUFFS —FAST!
BUT DON'T TRY ANYTHING THAT MIGHT JIGGLE MY FINGER ON THIS TRIGGER!
2158

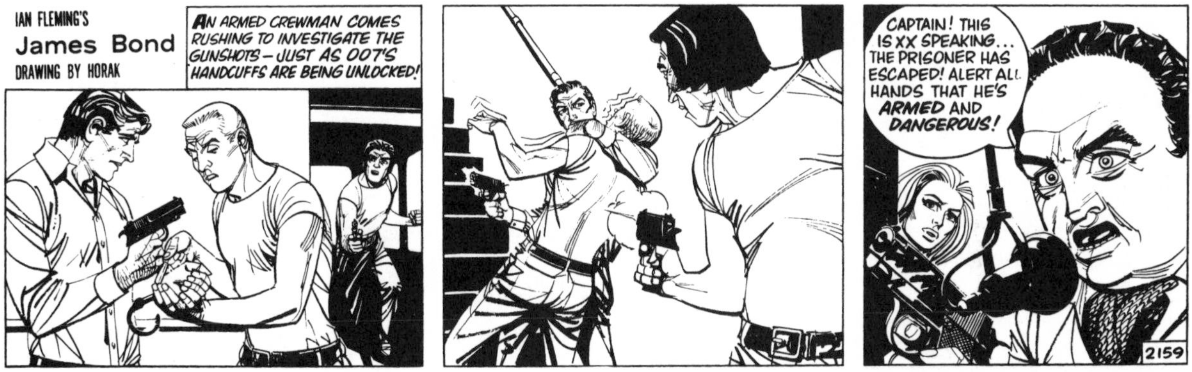
IAN FLEMING'S
James Bond
DRAWING BY HORAK
AN ARMED CREWMAN COMES RUSHING TO INVESTIGATE THE GUNSHOTS—JUST AS 007'S HANDCUFFS ARE BEING UNLOCKED!
CAPTAIN! THIS IS XX SPEAKING... THE PRISONER HAS ESCAPED! ALERT ALL HANDS THAT HE'S ARMED AND DANGEROUS!
2159

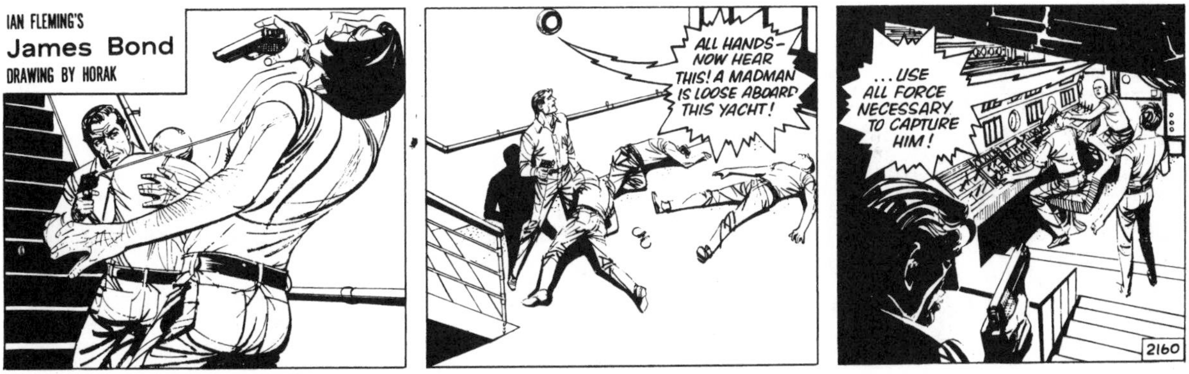
IAN FLEMING'S
James Bond
DRAWING BY HORAK
ALL HANDS—NOW HEAR THIS! A MADMAN IS LOOSE ABOARD THIS YACHT!
...USE ALL FORCE NECESSARY TO CAPTURE HIM!
2160

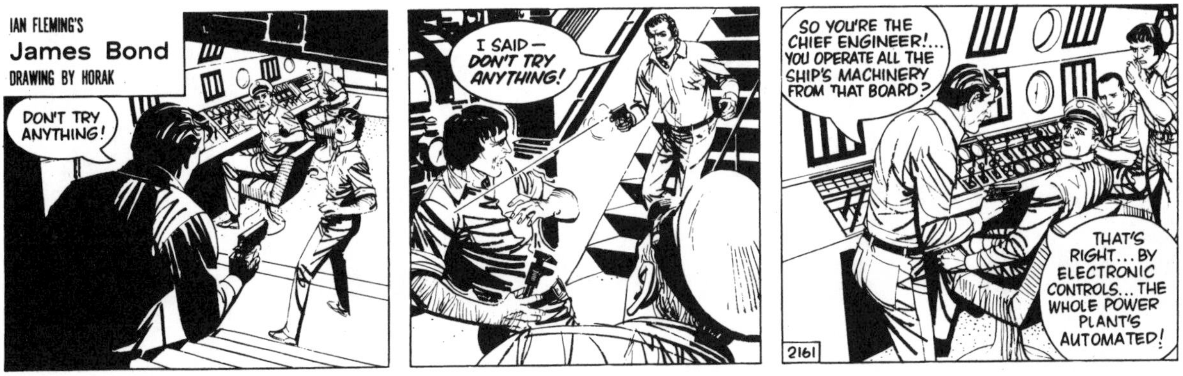
IAN FLEMING'S
James Bond
DRAWING BY HORAK
DON'T TRY ANYTHING!
I SAID—DON'T TRY ANYTHING!
SO YOU'RE THE CHIEF ENGINEER!... YOU OPERATE ALL THE SHIP'S MACHINERY FROM THAT BOARD?
THAT'S RIGHT... BY ELECTRONIC CONTROLS... THE WHOLE POWER PLANT'S AUTOMATED!
2161

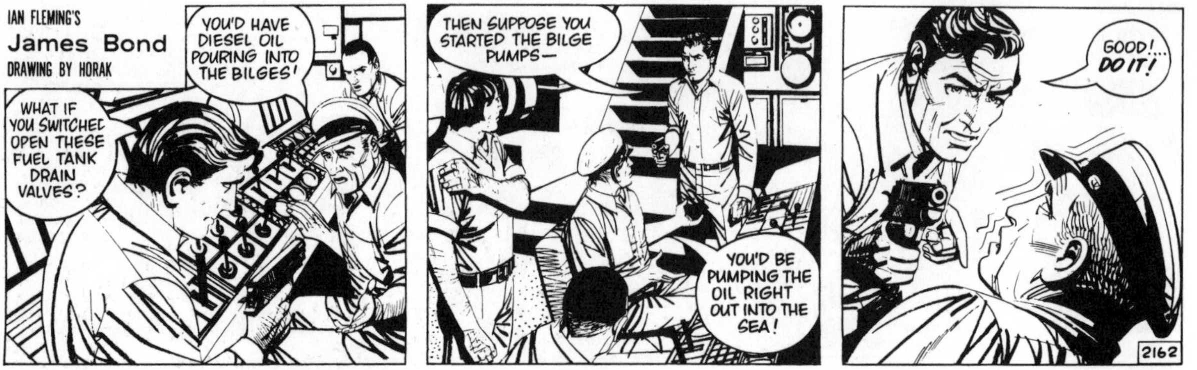
IAN FLEMING'S
James Bond
DRAWING BY HORAK
YOU'D HAVE DIESEL OIL POURING INTO THE BILGES!
WHAT IF YOU SWITCHED OPEN THESE FUEL TANK DRAIN VALVES?
THEN SUPPOSE YOU STARTED THE BILGE PUMPS—
YOU'D BE PUMPING THE OIL RIGHT OUT INTO THE SEA!
GOOD!... DO IT!
2162

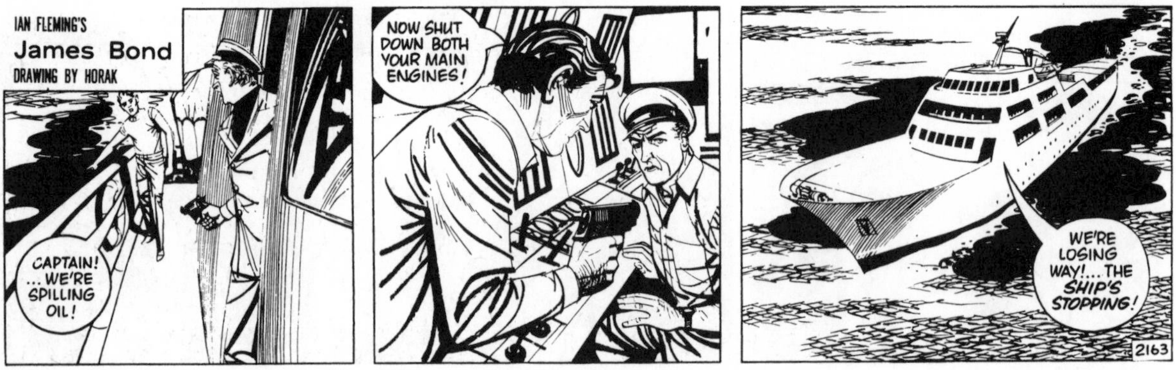
IAN FLEMING'S
James Bond
DRAWING BY HORAK
CAPTAIN! ...WE'RE SPILLING OIL!
NOW SHUT DOWN BOTH YOUR MAIN ENGINES!
WE'RE LOSING WAY!... THE SHIP'S STOPPING!
2163

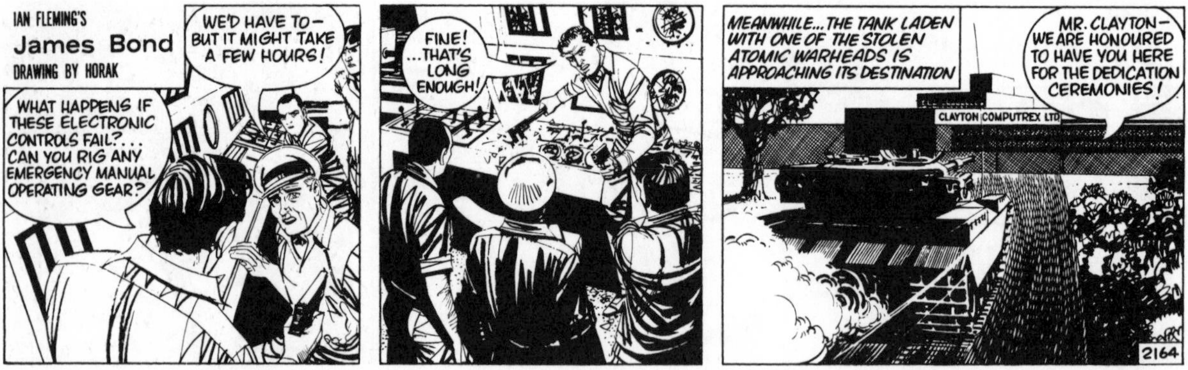
IAN FLEMING'S
James Bond
DRAWING BY HORAK
WE'D HAVE TO— BUT IT MIGHT TAKE A FEW HOURS!
WHAT HAPPENS IF THESE ELECTRONIC CONTROLS FAIL?... CAN YOU RIG ANY EMERGENCY MANUAL OPERATING GEAR?
FINE! ...THAT'S LONG ENOUGH!
MEANWHILE... THE TANK LADEN WITH ONE OF THE STOLEN ATOMIC WARHEADS IS APPROACHING ITS DESTINATION
MR. CLAYTON— WE ARE HONOURED TO HAVE YOU HERE FOR THE DEDICATION CEREMONIES!
CLAYTON COMPUTREX LTD
2164

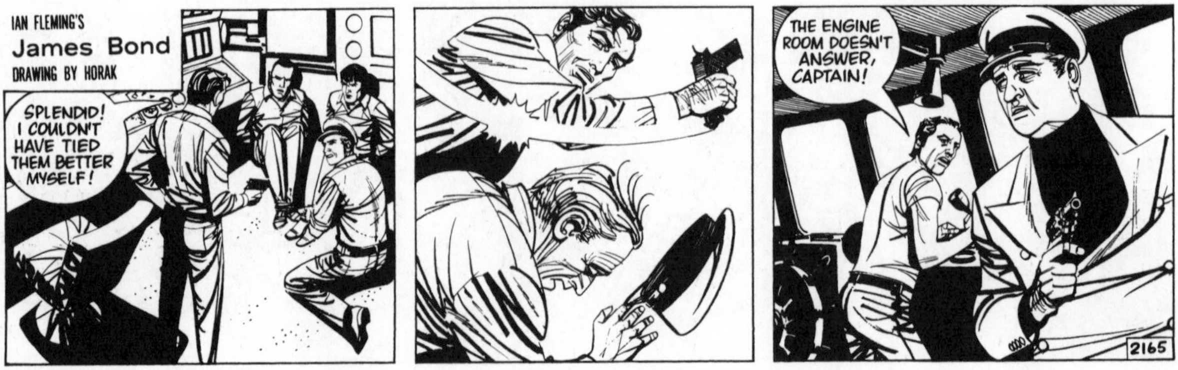
IAN FLEMING'S
James Bond
DRAWING BY HORAK
SPLENDID! I COULDN'T HAVE TIED THEM BETTER MYSELF!
THE ENGINE ROOM DOESN'T ANSWER, CAPTAIN!
2165

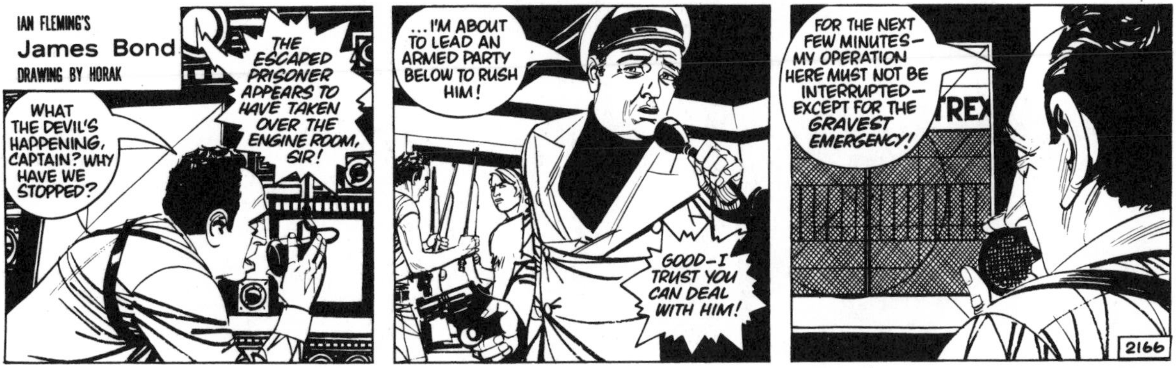
IAN FLEMING'S
James Bond
DRAWING BY HORAK
WHAT THE DEVIL'S HAPPENING, CAPTAIN? WHY HAVE WE STOPPED?
THE ESCAPED PRISONER APPEARS TO HAVE TAKEN OVER THE ENGINE ROOM, SIR!
...I'M ABOUT TO LEAD AN ARMED PARTY BELOW TO RUSH HIM!
GOOD—I TRUST YOU CAN DEAL WITH HIM!
FOR THE NEXT FEW MINUTES—MY OPERATION HERE MUST NOT BE INTERRUPTED—EXCEPT FOR THE GRAVEST EMERGENCY!
TREX
2166

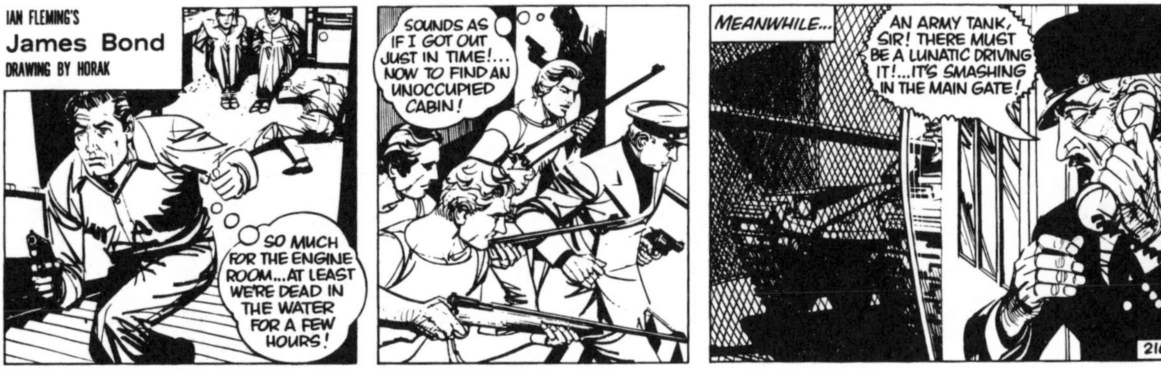
IAN FLEMING'S
James Bond
DRAWING BY HORAK
SO MUCH FOR THE ENGINE ROOM...AT LEAST WE'RE DEAD IN THE WATER FOR A FEW HOURS!
SOUNDS AS IF I GOT OUT JUST IN TIME!... NOW TO FIND AN UNOCCUPIED CABIN!
MEANWHILE...
AN ARMY TANK, SIR! THERE MUST BE A LUNATIC DRIVING IT!...IT'S SMASHING IN THE MAIN GATE!
2167

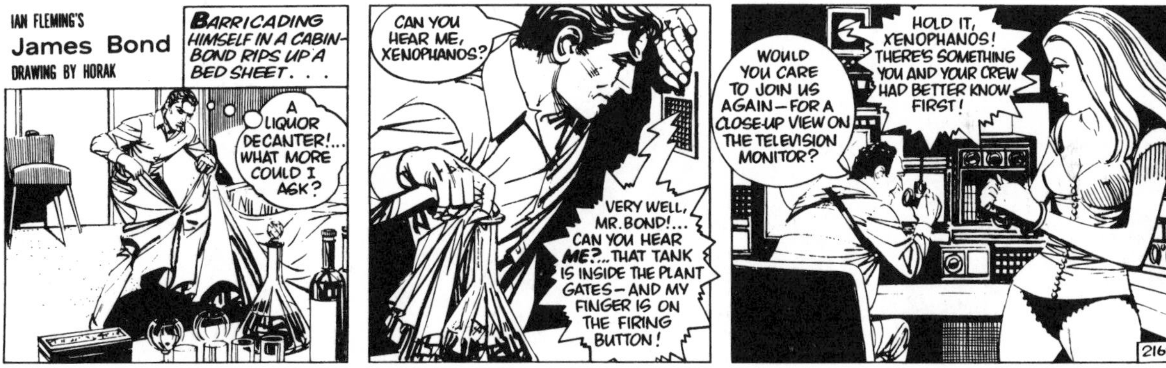
IAN FLEMING'S
James Bond
DRAWING BY HORAK
BARRICADING HIMSELF IN A CABIN-BOND RIPS UP A BED SHEET...
A LIQUOR DECANTER!... WHAT MORE COULD I ASK?
CAN YOU HEAR ME, XENOPHANOS?
VERY WELL, MR. BOND!... CAN YOU HEAR ME?...THAT TANK IS INSIDE THE PLANT GATES—AND MY FINGER IS ON THE FIRING BUTTON!
WOULD YOU CARE TO JOIN US AGAIN—FOR A CLOSE-UP VIEW ON THE TELEVISION MONITOR?
HOLD IT, XENOPHANOS! THERE'S SOMETHING YOU AND YOUR CREW HAD BETTER KNOW FIRST!
2168

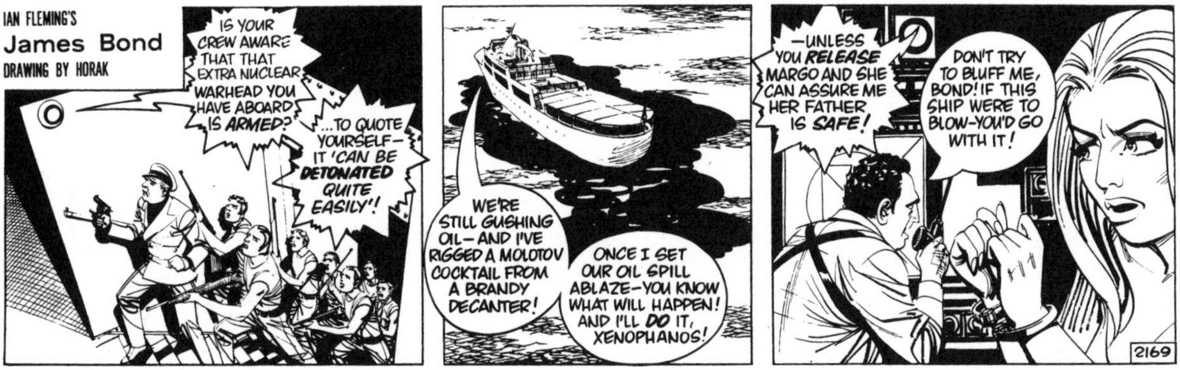
IAN FLEMING'S
James Bond
DRAWING BY HORAK
IS YOUR CREW AWARE THAT THAT EXTRA NUCLEAR WARHEAD YOU HAVE ABOARD IS ARMED?
...TO QUOTE YOURSELF—IT 'CAN BE DETONATED QUITE EASILY'!
WE'RE STILL GUSHING OIL—AND I'VE RIGGED A MOLOTOV COCKTAIL FROM A BRANDY DECANTER!
ONCE I SET OUR OIL SPILL ABLAZE—YOU KNOW WHAT WILL HAPPEN! AND I'LL DO IT, XENOPHANOS!
—UNLESS YOU RELEASE MARGO AND SHE CAN ASSURE ME HER FATHER IS SAFE!
DON'T TRY TO BLUFF ME, BOND! IF THIS SHIP WERE TO BLOW—YOU'D GO WITH IT!
2169

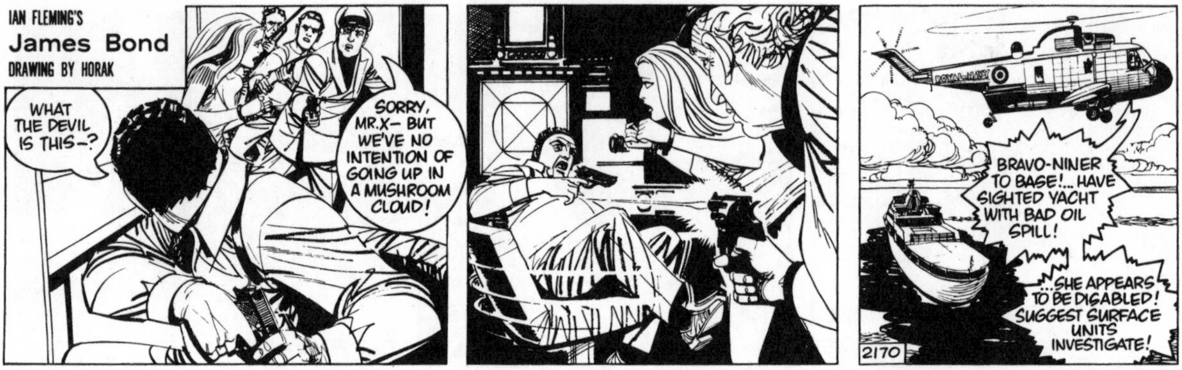
IAN FLEMING'S
James Bond
DRAWING BY HORAK
WHAT THE DEVIL IS THIS–?
SORRY, MR.X– BUT WE'VE NO INTENTION OF GOING UP IN A MUSHROOM CLOUD!
ROYAL NAVY
BRAVO-NINER TO BASE!... HAVE SIGHTED YACHT WITH BAD OIL SPILL!
...SHE APPEARS TO BE DISABLED! SUGGEST SURFACE UNITS INVESTIGATE!
2170

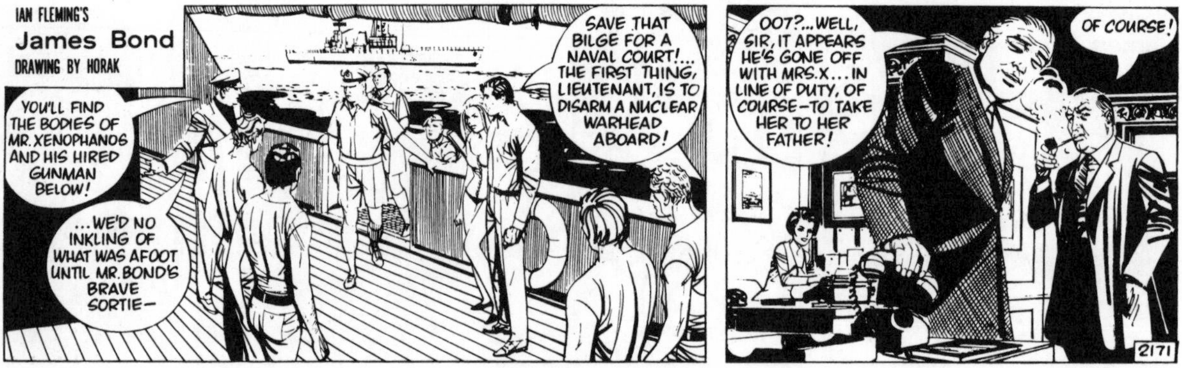
IAN FLEMING'S
James Bond
DRAWING BY HORAK
YOU'LL FIND THE BODIES OF MR. XENOPHANOS AND HIS HIRED GUNMAN BELOW!
...WE'D NO INKLING OF WHAT WAS AFOOT UNTIL MR. BOND'S BRAVE SORTIE–
SAVE THAT BILGE FOR A NAVAL COURT!... THE FIRST THING, LIEUTENANT, IS TO DISARM A NUCLEAR WARHEAD ABOARD!
007?...WELL, SIR, IT APPEARS HE'S GONE OFF WITH MRS.X... IN LINE OF DUTY, OF COURSE–TO TAKE HER TO HER FATHER!
OF COURSE!
2171

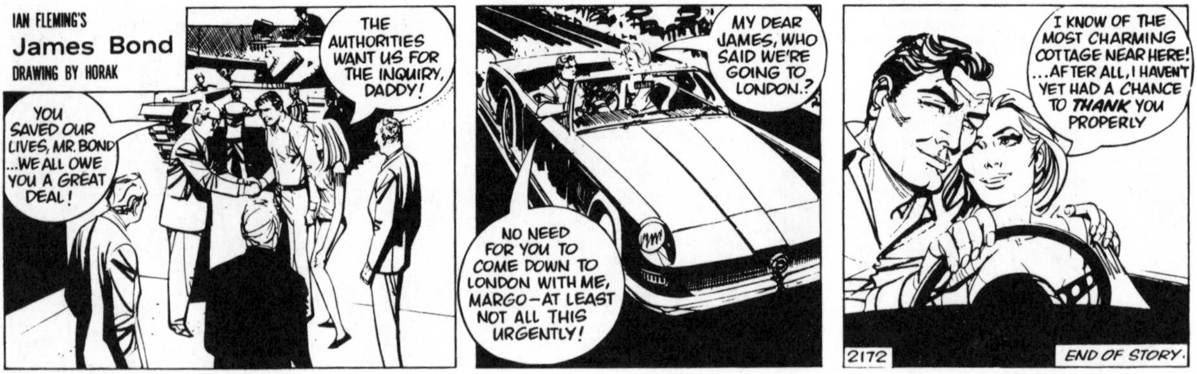
IAN FLEMING'S
James Bond
DRAWING BY HORAK
YOU SAVED OUR LIVES, MR. BOND ...WE ALL OWE YOU A GREAT DEAL!
THE AUTHORITIES WANT US FOR THE INQUIRY, DADDY!
MY DEAR JAMES, WHO SAID WE'RE GOING TO LONDON.?
NO NEED FOR YOU TO COME DOWN TO LONDON WITH ME, MARGO–AT LEAST NOT ALL THIS URGENTLY!
I KNOW OF THE MOST CHARMING COTTAGE NEAR HERE! ...AFTER ALL, I HAVEN'T YET HAD A CHANCE TO THANK YOU PROPERLY
2172
END OF STORY.

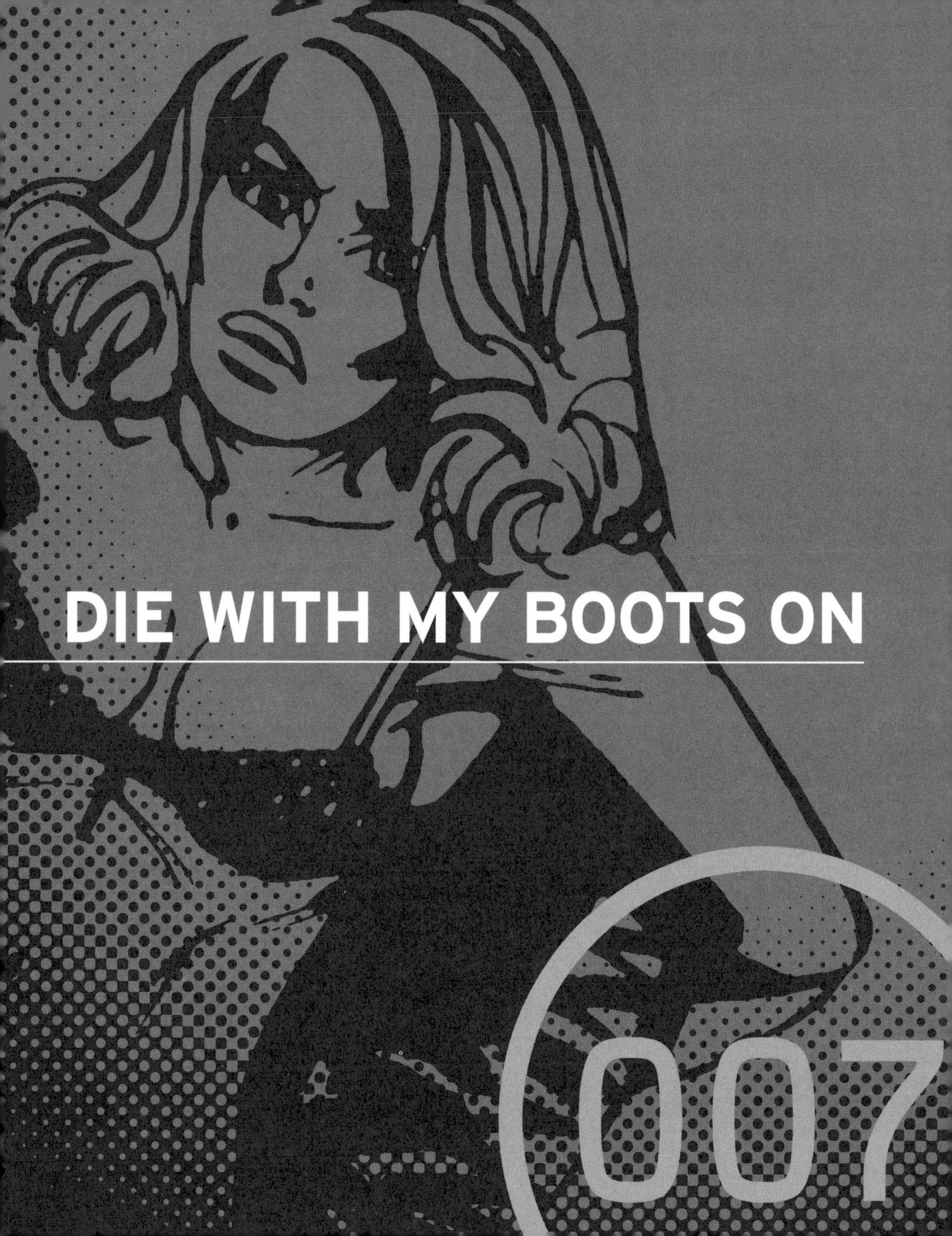

# DIE WITH MY BOOTS ON

007

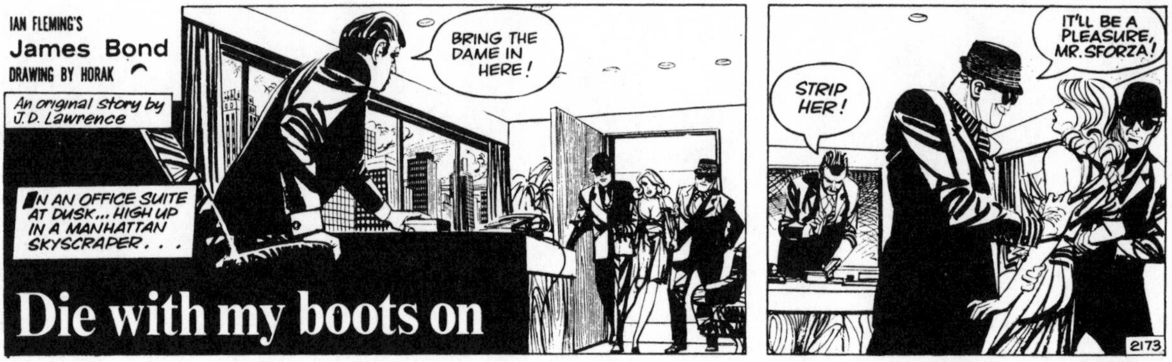
IAN FLEMING'S
James Bond
DRAWING BY HORAK
An original story by J.D. Lawrence
IN AN OFFICE SUITE AT DUSK... HIGH UP IN A MANHATTAN SKYSCRAPER...
BRING THE DAME IN HERE!
Die with my boots on
STRIP HER!
IT'LL BE A PLEASURE, MR. SFORZA!
2173

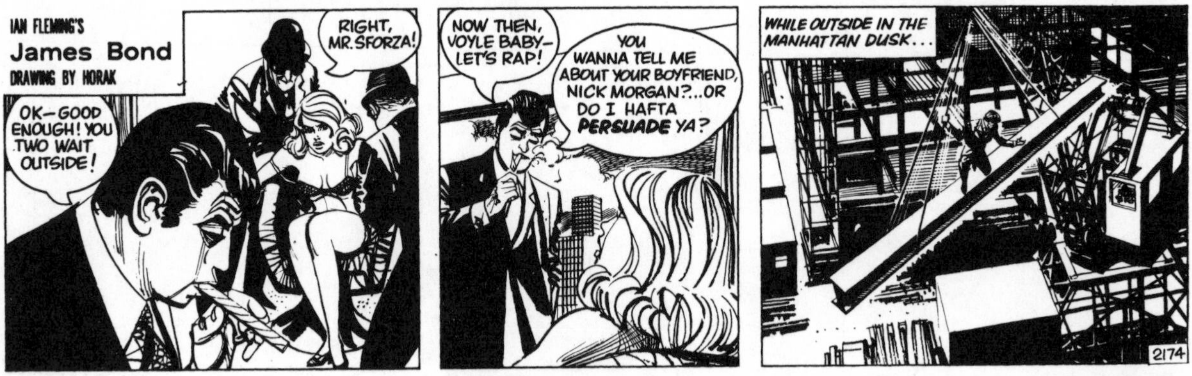
IAN FLEMING'S
James Bond
DRAWING BY HORAK
RIGHT, MR. SFORZA!
OK—GOOD ENOUGH! YOU TWO WAIT OUTSIDE!
NOW THEN, VOYLE BABY—LET'S RAP!
YOU WANNA TELL ME ABOUT YOUR BOYFRIEND, NICK MORGAN?...OR DO I HAFTA PERSUADE YA?
WHILE OUTSIDE IN THE MANHATTAN DUSK...
2174

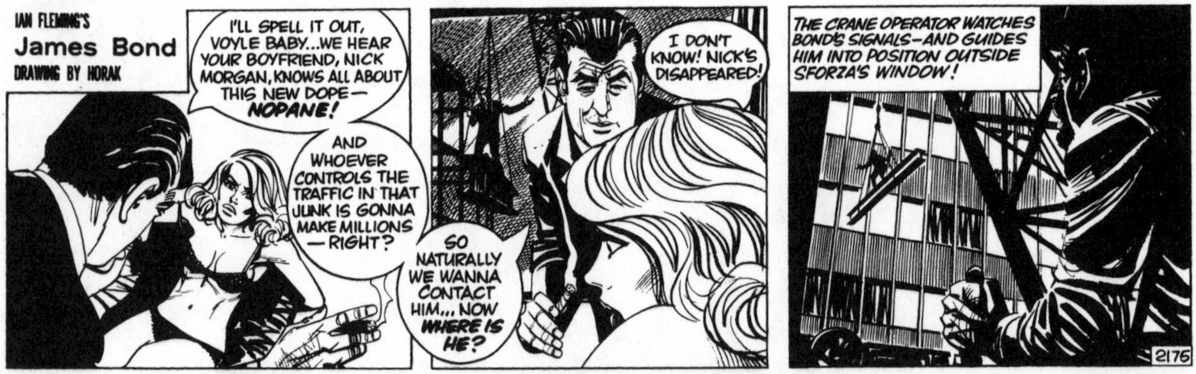
IAN FLEMING'S
James Bond
DRAWING BY HORAK
I'LL SPELL IT OUT, VOYLE BABY...WE HEAR YOUR BOYFRIEND, NICK MORGAN, KNOWS ALL ABOUT THIS NEW DOPE—NOPANE!
AND WHOEVER CONTROLS THE TRAFFIC IN THAT JUNK IS GONNA MAKE MILLIONS —RIGHT?
SO NATURALLY WE WANNA CONTACT HIM... NOW WHERE IS HE?
I DON'T KNOW! NICK'S DISAPPEARED!
THE CRANE OPERATOR WATCHES BOND'S SIGNALS—AND GUIDES HIM INTO POSITION OUTSIDE SFORZA'S WINDOW!
2175

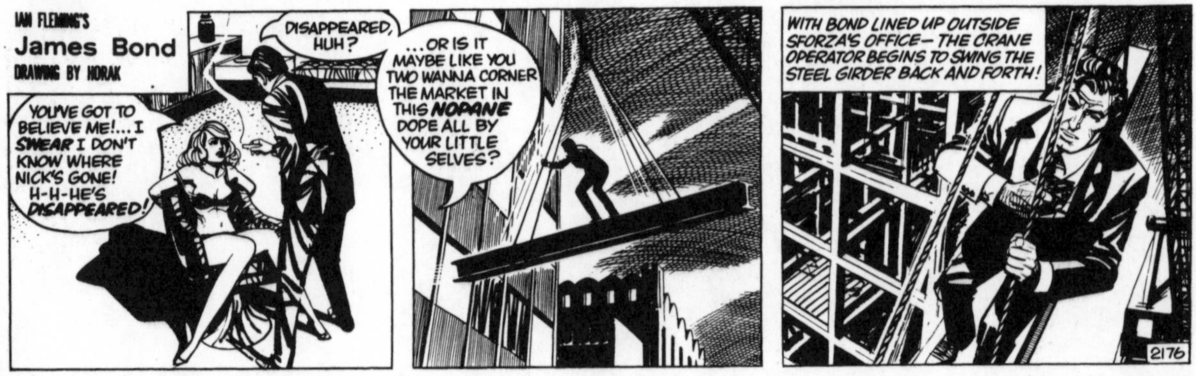
IAN FLEMING'S
James Bond
DRAWING BY HORAK
DISAPPEARED, HUH?
YOU'VE GOT TO BELIEVE ME!... I SWEAR I DON'T KNOW WHERE NICK'S GONE! H-H-HE'S DISAPPEARED!
...OR IS IT MAYBE LIKE YOU TWO WANNA CORNER THE MARKET IN THIS NOPANE DOPE ALL BY YOUR LITTLE SELVES?
WITH BOND LINED UP OUTSIDE SFORZA'S OFFICE—THE CRANE OPERATOR BEGINS TO SWING THE STEEL GIRDER BACK AND FORTH!
2176

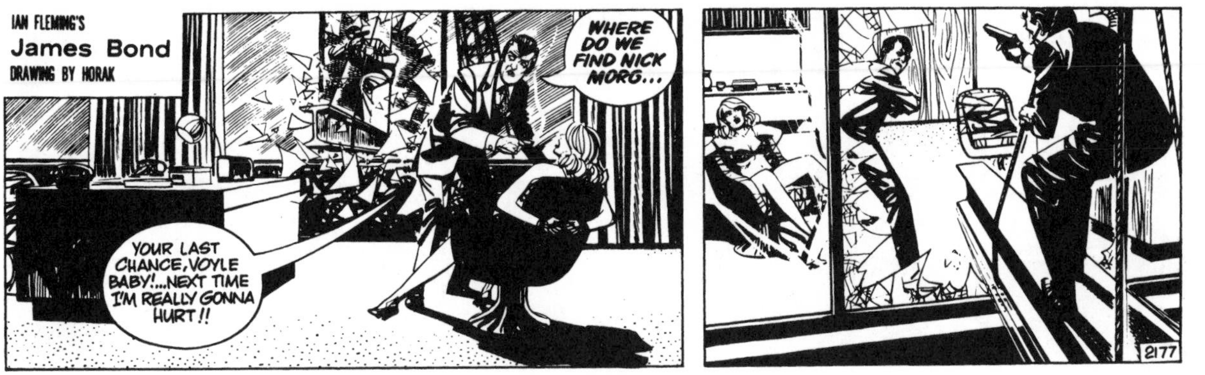
IAN FLEMING'S
James Bond
DRAWING BY HORAK
YOUR LAST CHANCE, VOYLE BABY!...NEXT TIME I'M REALLY GONNA HURT!!
WHERE DO WE FIND NICK MORG...
2177

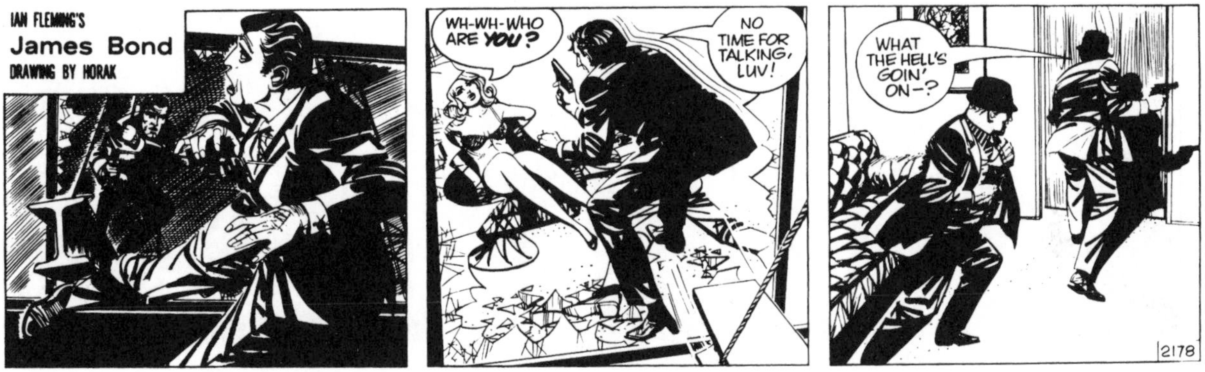
IAN FLEMING'S
James Bond
DRAWING BY HORAK
WH-WH-WHO ARE YOU?
NO TIME FOR TALKING, LUV!
WHAT THE HELL'S GOIN' ON—?
2178

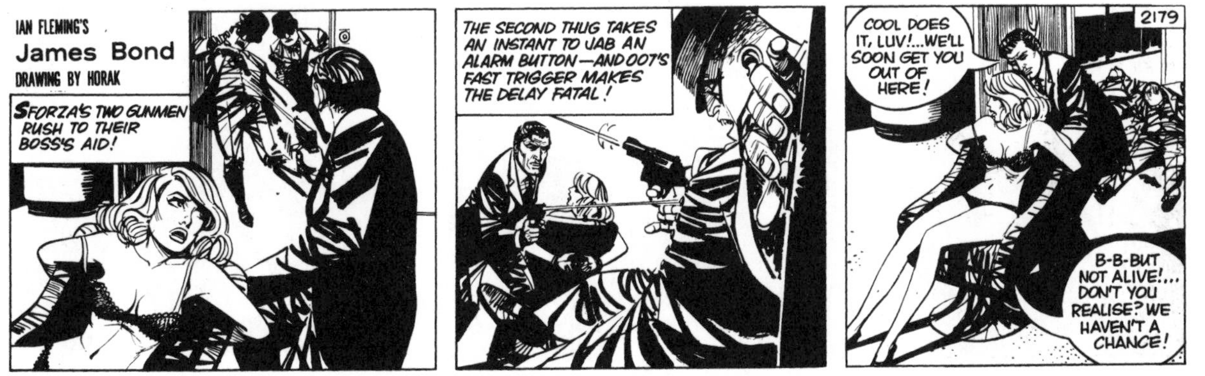
IAN FLEMING'S
James Bond
DRAWING BY HORAK
SFORZA'S TWO GUNMEN RUSH TO THEIR BOSS'S AID!
THE SECOND THUG TAKES AN INSTANT TO JAB AN ALARM BUTTON—AND 007'S FAST TRIGGER MAKES THE DELAY FATAL!
2179
COOL DOES IT, LUV!...WE'LL SOON GET YOU OUT OF HERE!
B-B-BUT NOT ALIVE!... DON'T YOU REALISE? WE HAVEN'T A CHANCE!

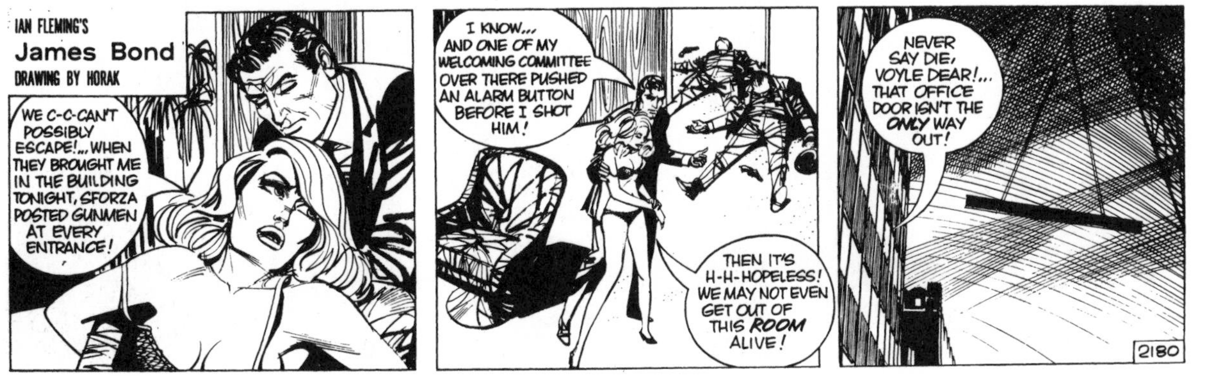
IAN FLEMING'S
James Bond
DRAWING BY HORAK
WE C-C-CAN'T POSSIBLY ESCAPE!... WHEN THEY BROUGHT ME IN THE BUILDING TONIGHT, SFORZA POSTED GUNMEN AT EVERY ENTRANCE!
I KNOW... AND ONE OF MY WELCOMING COMMITTEE OVER THERE PUSHED AN ALARM BUTTON BEFORE I SHOT HIM!
THEN IT'S H-H-HOPELESS! WE MAY NOT EVEN GET OUT OF THIS ROOM ALIVE!
NEVER SAY DIE, VOYLE DEAR!... THAT OFFICE DOOR ISN'T THE ONLY WAY OUT!
2180

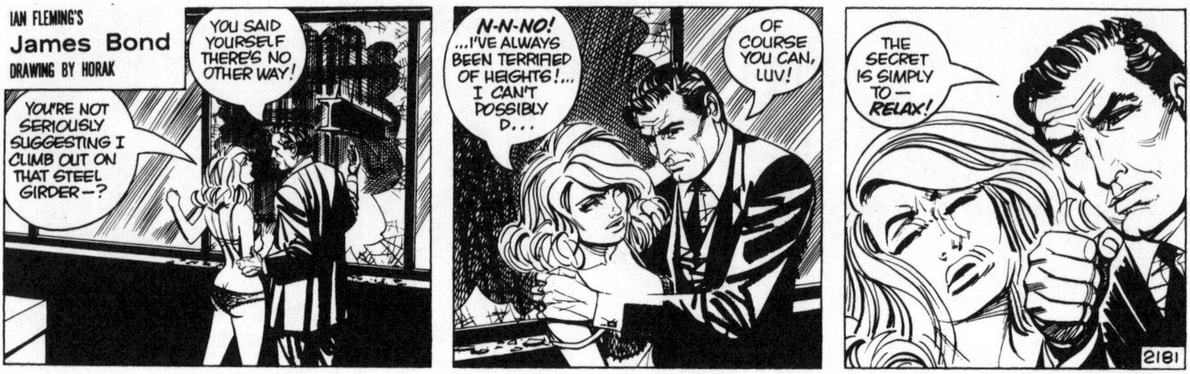
IAN FLEMING'S
James Bond
DRAWING BY HORAK
YOU'RE NOT SERIOUSLY SUGGESTING I CLIMB OUT ON THAT STEEL GIRDER—?
YOU SAID YOURSELF THERE'S NO OTHER WAY!
N-N-NO! ...I'VE ALWAYS BEEN TERRIFIED OF HEIGHTS!... I CAN'T POSSIBLY D...
OF COURSE YOU CAN, LUV!
THE SECRET IS SIMPLY TO— RELAX!
2181

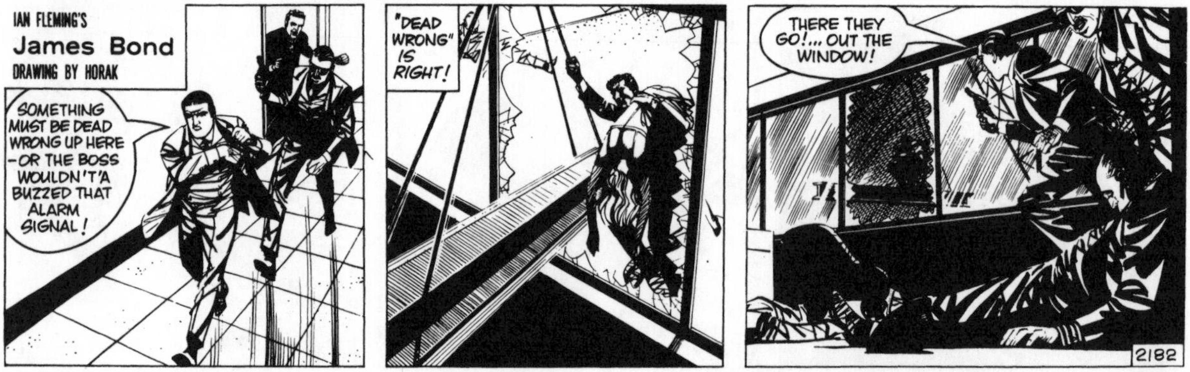
IAN FLEMING'S
James Bond
DRAWING BY HORAK
SOMETHING MUST BE DEAD WRONG UP HERE —OR THE BOSS WOULDN'T'A BUZZED THAT ALARM SIGNAL!
"DEAD WRONG" IS RIGHT!
THERE THEY GO!... OUT THE WINDOW!
2182

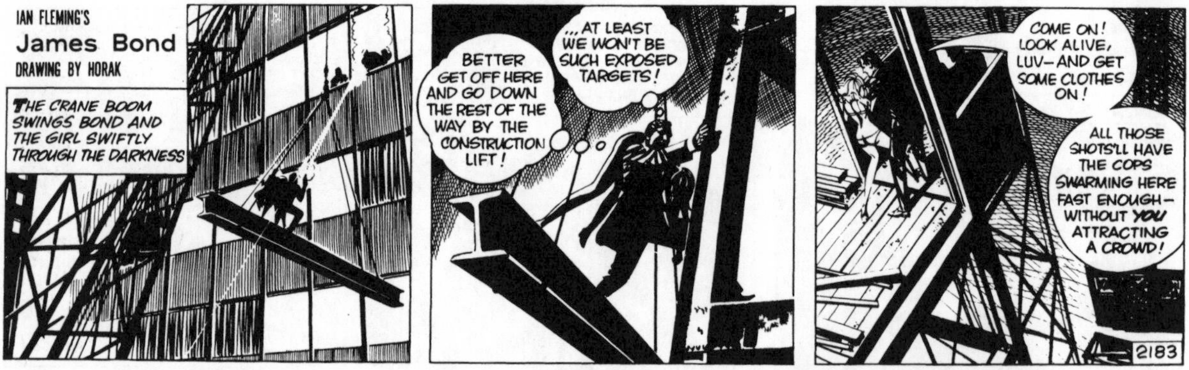
IAN FLEMING'S
James Bond
DRAWING BY HORAK
THE CRANE BOOM SWINGS BOND AND THE GIRL SWIFTLY THROUGH THE DARKNESS
BETTER GET OFF HERE AND GO DOWN THE REST OF THE WAY BY THE CONSTRUCTION LIFT!
...AT LEAST WE WON'T BE SUCH EXPOSED TARGETS!
COME ON! LOOK ALIVE, LUV—AND GET SOME CLOTHES ON!
ALL THOSE SHOTS'LL HAVE THE COPS SWARMING HERE FAST ENOUGH— WITHOUT YOU ATTRACTING A CROWD!
2183

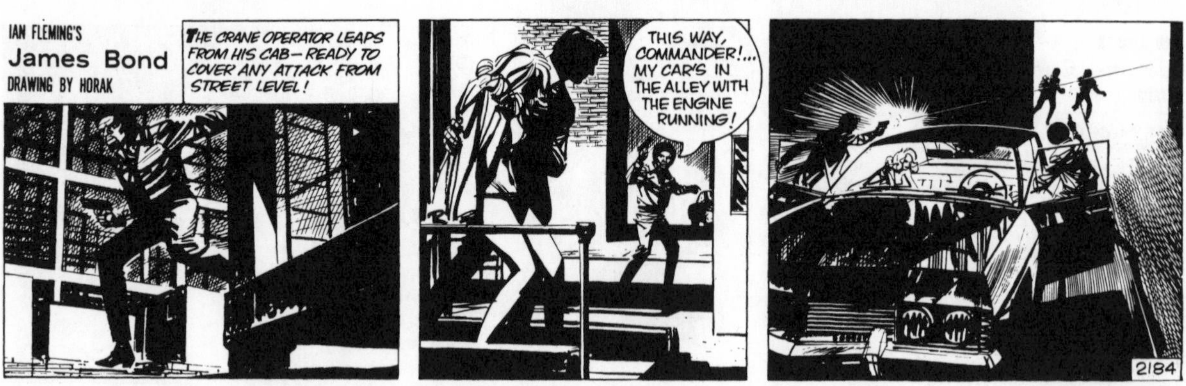
IAN FLEMING'S
James Bond
DRAWING BY HORAK
THE CRANE OPERATOR LEAPS FROM HIS CAB—READY TO COVER ANY ATTACK FROM STREET LEVEL!
THIS WAY, COMMANDER!... MY CAR'S IN THE ALLEY WITH THE ENGINE RUNNING!
2184

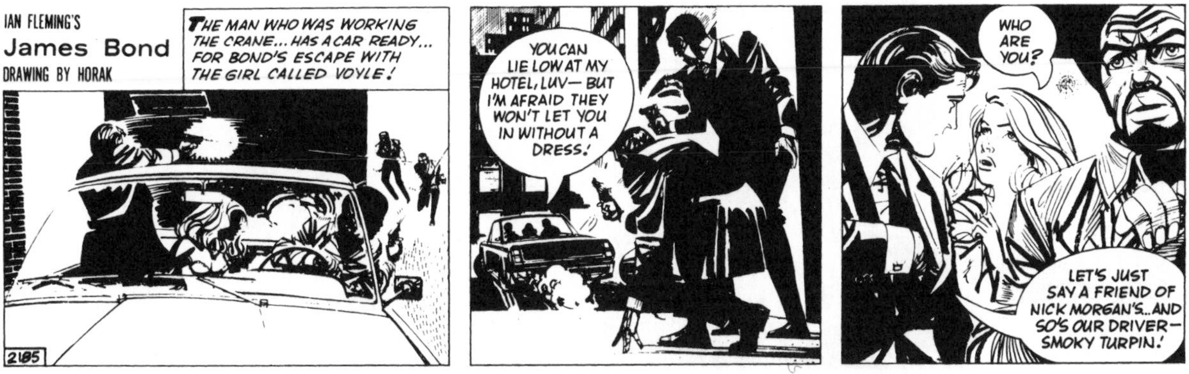
IAN FLEMING'S
James Bond
DRAWING BY HORAK
THE MAN WHO WAS WORKING THE CRANE... HAS A CAR READY... FOR BOND'S ESCAPE WITH THE GIRL CALLED VOYLE!
2185
YOU CAN LIE LOW AT MY HOTEL, LUV— BUT I'M AFRAID THEY WON'T LET YOU IN WITHOUT A DRESS!
WHO ARE YOU?
LET'S JUST SAY A FRIEND OF NICK MORGAN'S... AND SO'S OUR DRIVER— SMOKY TURPIN!

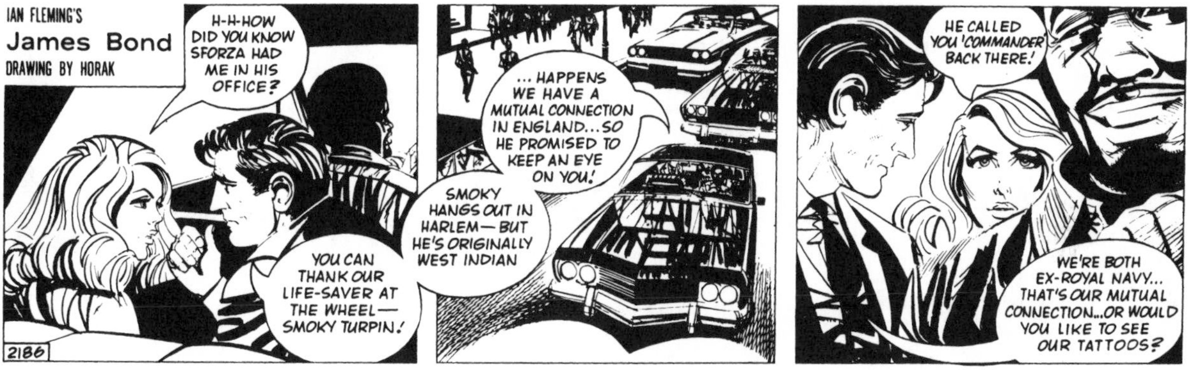
IAN FLEMING'S
James Bond
DRAWING BY HORAK
H-H-HOW DID YOU KNOW SFORZA HAD ME IN HIS OFFICE?
YOU CAN THANK OUR LIFE-SAVER AT THE WHEEL— SMOKY TURPIN!
2186
... HAPPENS WE HAVE A MUTUAL CONNECTION IN ENGLAND... SO HE PROMISED TO KEEP AN EYE ON YOU!
SMOKY HANGS OUT IN HARLEM— BUT HE'S ORIGINALLY WEST INDIAN
HE CALLED YOU 'COMMANDER' BACK THERE!
WE'RE BOTH EX-ROYAL NAVY... THAT'S OUR MUTUAL CONNECTION... OR WOULD YOU LIKE TO SEE OUR TATTOOS?

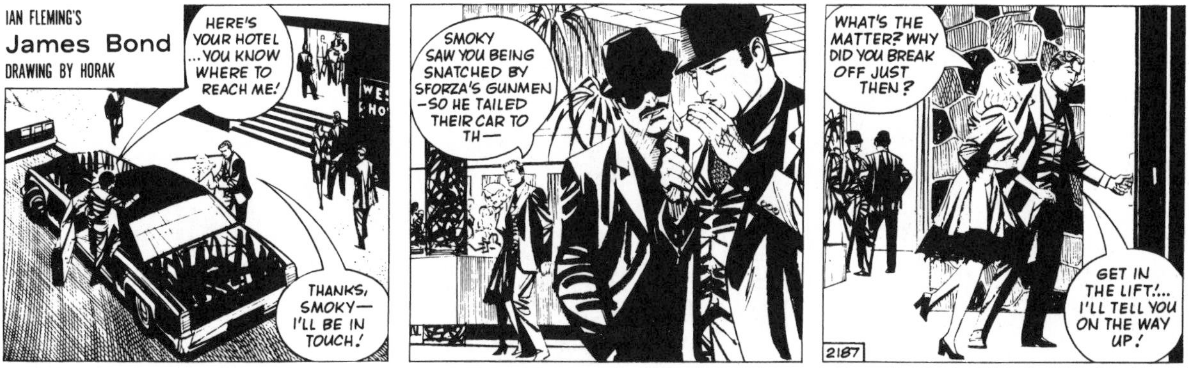
IAN FLEMING'S
James Bond
DRAWING BY HORAK
HERE'S YOUR HOTEL ...YOU KNOW WHERE TO REACH ME!
THANKS, SMOKY— I'LL BE IN TOUCH!
SMOKY SAW YOU BEING SNATCHED BY SFORZA'S GUNMEN —SO HE TAILED THEIR CAR TO TH—
WHAT'S THE MATTER? WHY DID YOU BREAK OFF JUST THEN?
GET IN THE LIFT!... I'LL TELL YOU ON THE WAY UP!
2187

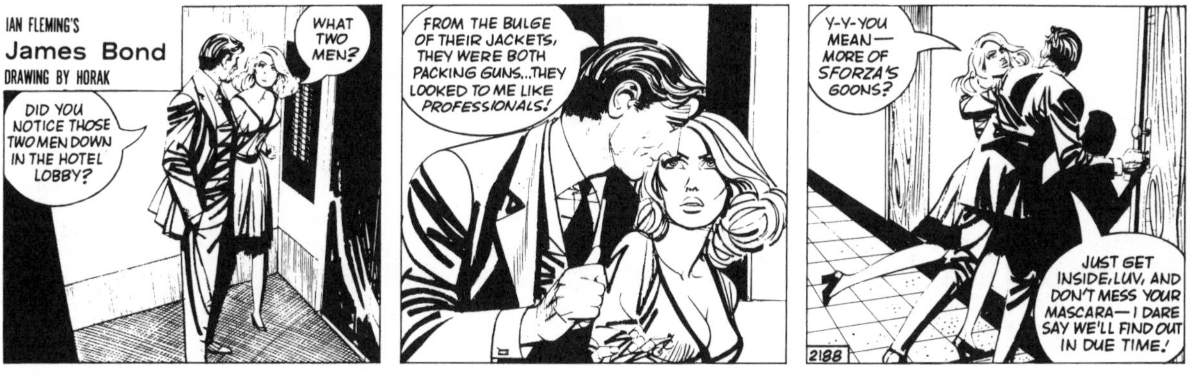
IAN FLEMING'S
James Bond
DRAWING BY HORAK
DID YOU NOTICE THOSE TWO MEN DOWN IN THE HOTEL LOBBY?
WHAT TWO MEN?
FROM THE BULGE OF THEIR JACKETS, THEY WERE BOTH PACKING GUNS... THEY LOOKED TO ME LIKE PROFESSIONALS!
Y-Y-YOU MEAN— MORE OF SFORZA'S GOONS?
JUST GET INSIDE, LUV, AND DON'T MESS YOUR MASCARA— I DARE SAY WE'LL FIND OUT IN DUE TIME!
2188

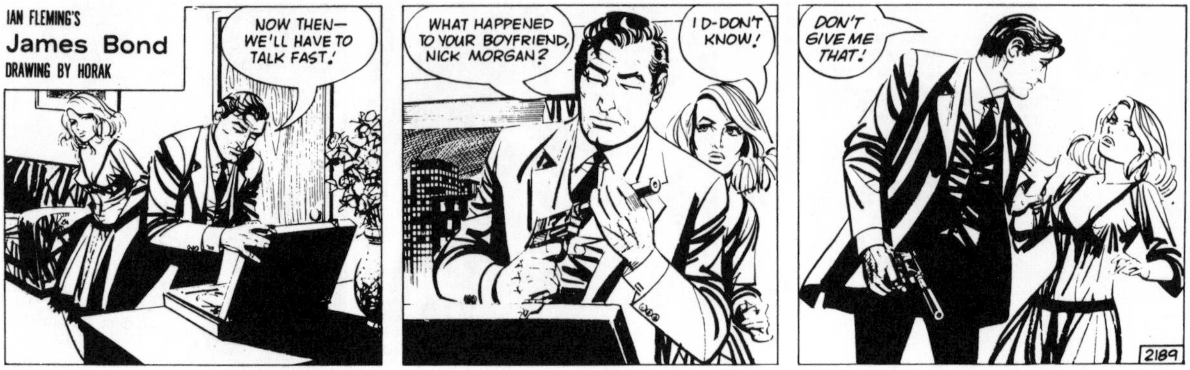
IAN FLEMING'S
James Bond
DRAWING BY HORAK
NOW THEN— WE'LL HAVE TO TALK FAST!
WHAT HAPPENED TO YOUR BOYFRIEND, NICK MORGAN?
I D-DON'T KNOW!
DON'T GIVE ME THAT!
2189

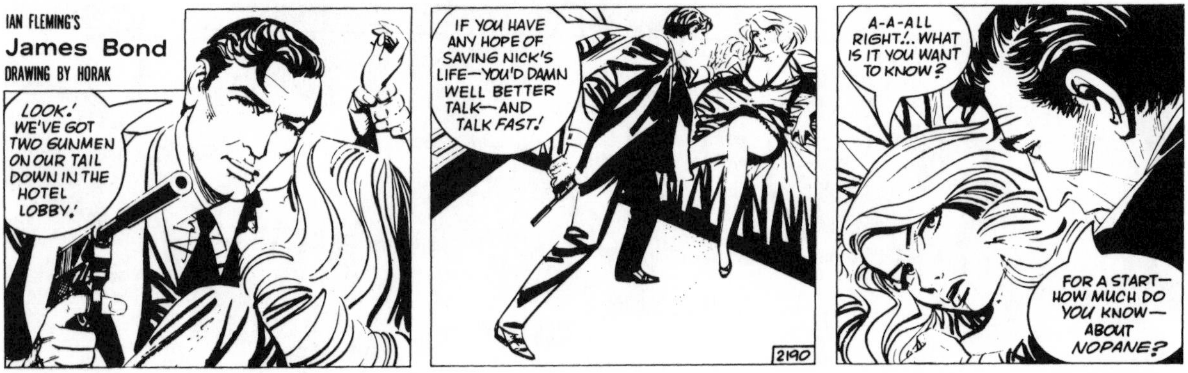
IAN FLEMING'S
James Bond
DRAWING BY HORAK
LOOK! WE'VE GOT TWO GUNMEN ON OUR TAIL DOWN IN THE HOTEL LOBBY!
IF YOU HAVE ANY HOPE OF SAVING NICK'S LIFE—YOU'D DAMN WELL BETTER TALK—AND TALK FAST!
2190
A-A-ALL RIGHT!.. WHAT IS IT YOU WANT TO KNOW?
FOR A START— HOW MUCH DO YOU KNOW— ABOUT NOPANE?

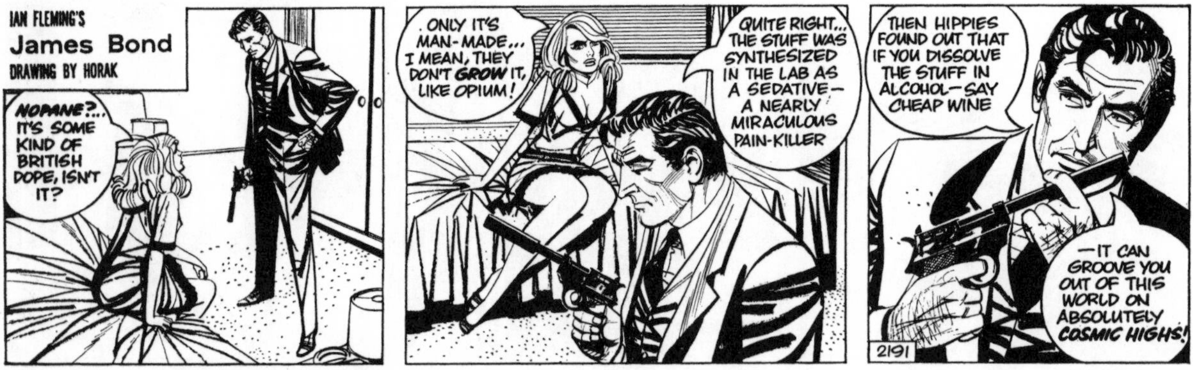
IAN FLEMING'S
James Bond
DRAWING BY HORAK
NOPANE?... IT'S SOME KIND OF BRITISH DOPE, ISN'T IT?
ONLY IT'S MAN-MADE... I MEAN, THEY DON'T GROW IT, LIKE OPIUM!
QUITE RIGHT... THE STUFF WAS SYNTHESIZED IN THE LAB AS A SEDATIVE— A NEARLY MIRACULOUS PAIN-KILLER
THEN HIPPIES FOUND OUT THAT IF YOU DISSOLVE THE STUFF IN ALCOHOL—SAY CHEAP WINE
—IT CAN GROOVE YOU OUT OF THIS WORLD ON ABSOLUTELY COSMIC HIGHS!
2191

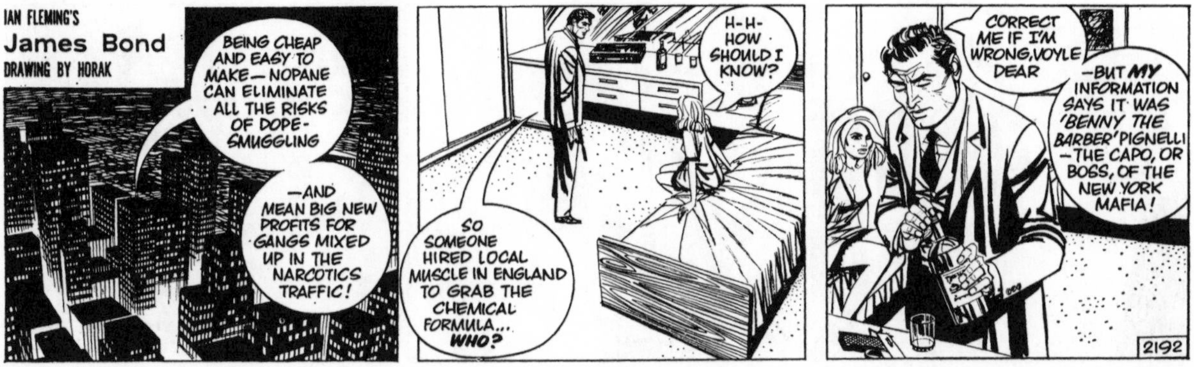
IAN FLEMING'S
James Bond
DRAWING BY HORAK
BEING CHEAP AND EASY TO MAKE—NOPANE CAN ELIMINATE ALL THE RISKS OF DOPE-SMUGGLING
—AND MEAN BIG NEW PROFITS FOR GANGS MIXED UP IN THE NARCOTICS TRAFFIC!
H-H-HOW SHOULD I KNOW?
SO SOMEONE HIRED LOCAL MUSCLE IN ENGLAND TO GRAB THE CHEMICAL FORMULA... WHO?
CORRECT ME IF I'M WRONG, VOYLE DEAR
—BUT MY INFORMATION SAYS IT WAS 'BENNY THE BARBER' PIGNELLI —THE CAPO, OR BOSS, OF THE NEW YORK MAFIA!
2192

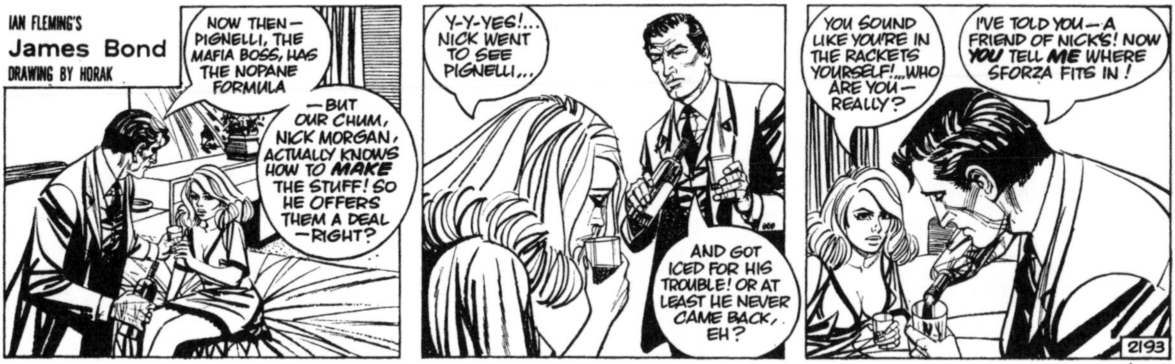
IAN FLEMING'S
James Bond
DRAWING BY HORAK
NOW THEN—PIGNELLI, THE MAFIA BOSS, HAS THE NOPANE FORMULA
—BUT OUR CHUM, NICK MORGAN, ACTUALLY KNOWS HOW TO MAKE THE STUFF! SO HE OFFERS THEM A DEAL —RIGHT?
Y-Y-YES!... NICK WENT TO SEE PIGNELLI...
AND GOT ICED FOR HIS TROUBLE! OR AT LEAST HE NEVER CAME BACK, EH?
YOU SOUND LIKE YOU'RE IN THE RACKETS YOURSELF!...WHO ARE YOU—REALLY?
I'VE TOLD YOU—A FRIEND OF NICK'S! NOW YOU TELL ME WHERE SFORZA FITS IN!
2193

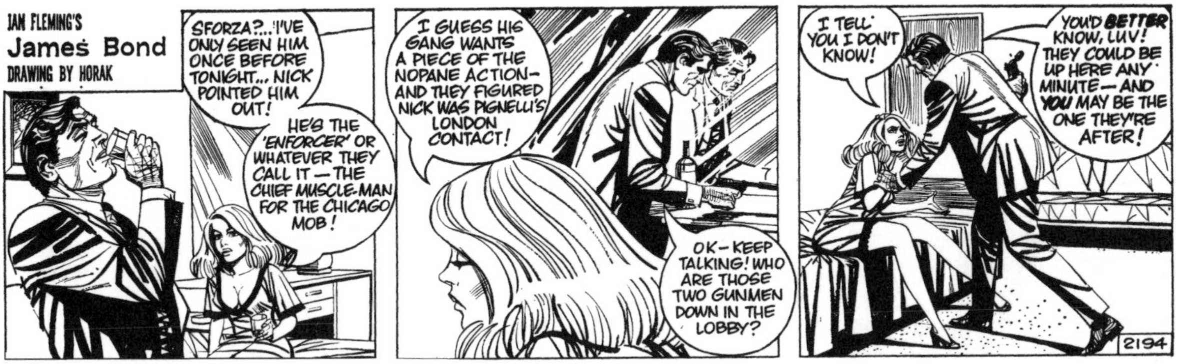
IAN FLEMING'S
James Bond
DRAWING BY HORAK
SFORZA?...I'VE ONLY SEEN HIM ONCE BEFORE TONIGHT... NICK POINTED HIM OUT!
HE'S THE 'ENFORCER' OR WHATEVER THEY CALL IT — THE CHIEF MUSCLE-MAN FOR THE CHICAGO MOB!
I GUESS HIS GANG WANTS A PIECE OF THE NOPANE ACTION-AND THEY FIGURED NICK WAS PIGNELLI'S LONDON CONTACT!
OK—KEEP TALKING! WHO ARE THOSE TWO GUNMEN DOWN IN THE LOBBY?
I TELL YOU I DON'T KNOW!
YOU'D BETTER KNOW, LUV! THEY COULD BE UP HERE ANY MINUTE—AND YOU MAY BE THE ONE THEY'RE AFTER!
2194

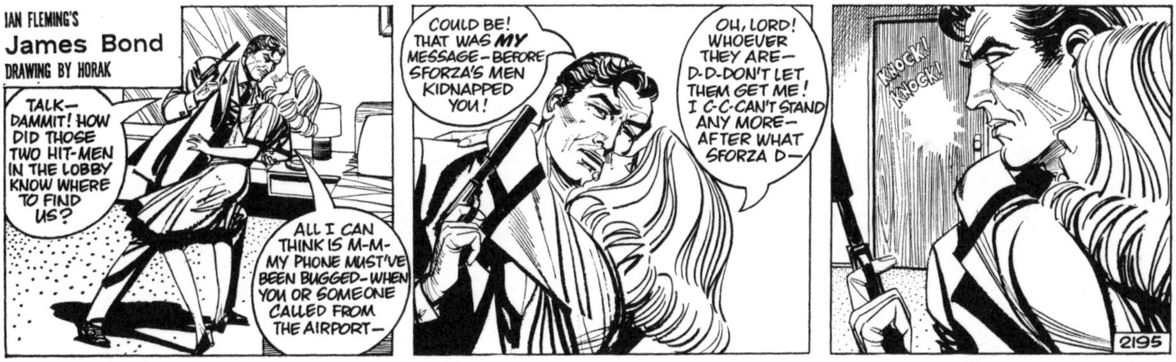
IAN FLEMING'S
James Bond
DRAWING BY HORAK
TALK—DAMMIT! HOW DID THOSE TWO HIT-MEN IN THE LOBBY KNOW WHERE TO FIND US?
ALL I CAN THINK IS M-M-MY PHONE MUST'VE BEEN BUGGED-WHEN YOU OR SOMEONE CALLED FROM THE AIRPORT—
COULD BE! THAT WAS MY MESSAGE—BEFORE SFORZA'S MEN KIDNAPPED YOU!
OH, LORD! WHOEVER THEY ARE—D-D-DON'T LET THEM GET ME! I C-C-CAN'T STAND ANY MORE—AFTER WHAT SFORZA D—
KNOCK! KNOCK!
2195

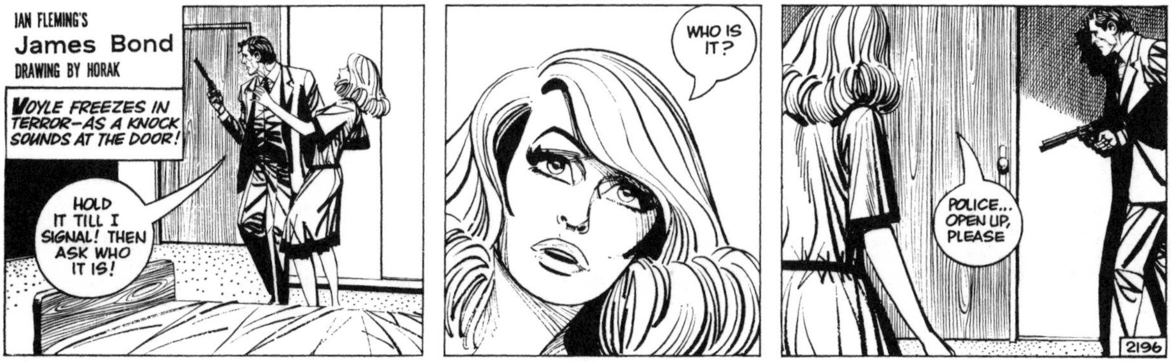
IAN FLEMING'S
James Bond
DRAWING BY HORAK
VOYLE FREEZES IN TERROR—AS A KNOCK SOUNDS AT THE DOOR!
HOLD IT TILL I SIGNAL! THEN ASK WHO IT IS!
WHO IS IT?
POLICE... OPEN UP, PLEASE
2196

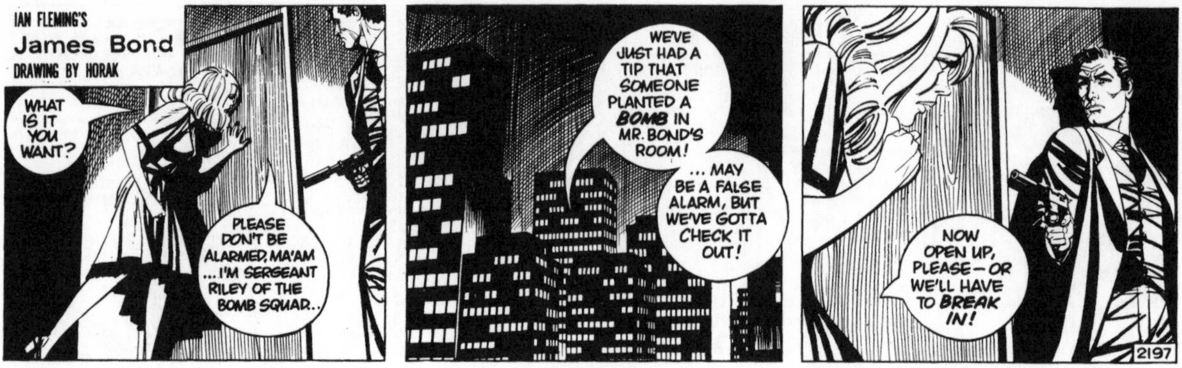
IAN FLEMING'S
James Bond
DRAWING BY HORAK
WHAT IS IT YOU WANT?
PLEASE DON'T BE ALARMED, MA'AM ...I'M SERGEANT RILEY OF THE BOMB SQUAD...
WE'VE JUST HAD A TIP THAT SOMEONE PLANTED A BOMB IN MR. BOND'S ROOM!
... MAY BE A FALSE ALARM, BUT WE'VE GOTTA CHECK IT OUT!
NOW OPEN UP, PLEASE—OR WE'LL HAVE TO BREAK IN!
2197

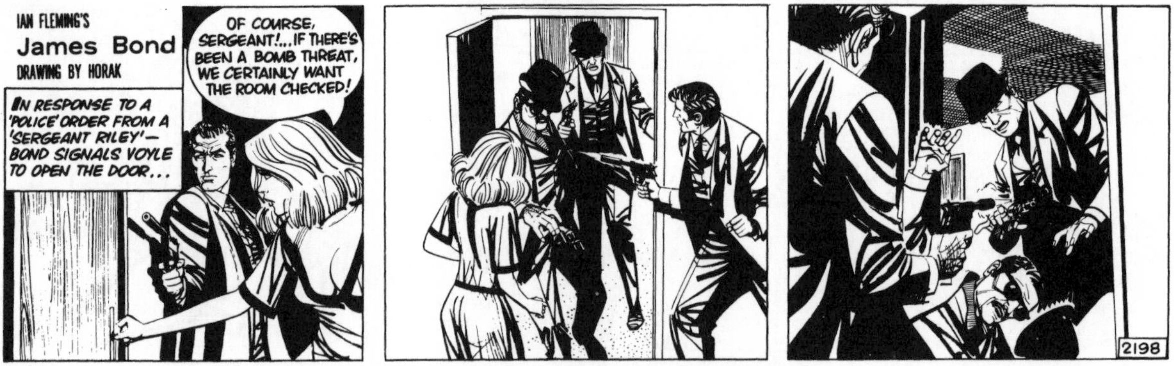
IAN FLEMING'S
James Bond
DRAWING BY HORAK
IN RESPONSE TO A 'POLICE' ORDER FROM A 'SERGEANT RILEY'—BOND SIGNALS VOYLE TO OPEN THE DOOR...
OF COURSE, SERGEANT!... IF THERE'S BEEN A BOMB THREAT, WE CERTAINLY WANT THE ROOM CHECKED!
2198

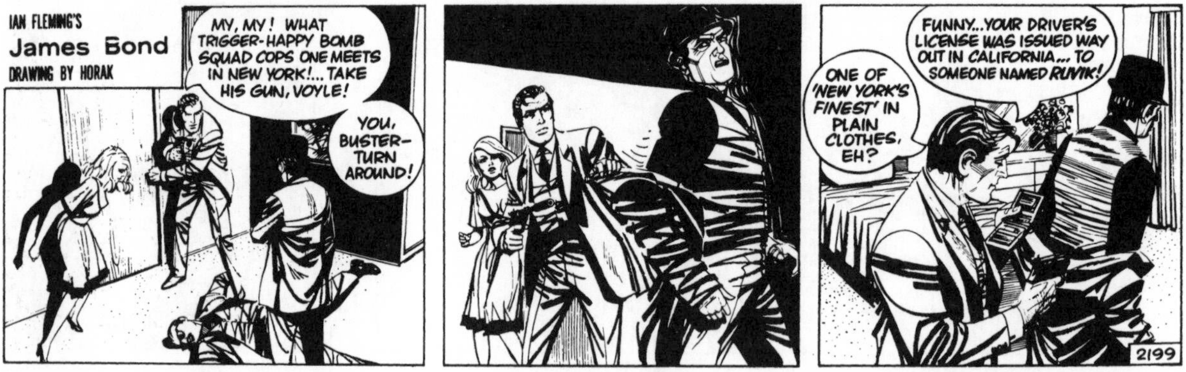
IAN FLEMING'S
James Bond
DRAWING BY HORAK
MY, MY! WHAT TRIGGER-HAPPY BOMB SQUAD COPS ONE MEETS IN NEW YORK!... TAKE HIS GUN, VOYLE!
YOU, BUSTER—TURN AROUND!
ONE OF 'NEW YORK'S FINEST' IN PLAIN CLOTHES, EH?
FUNNY... YOUR DRIVER'S LICENSE WAS ISSUED WAY OUT IN CALIFORNIA... TO SOMEONE NAMED RUVIK!
2199

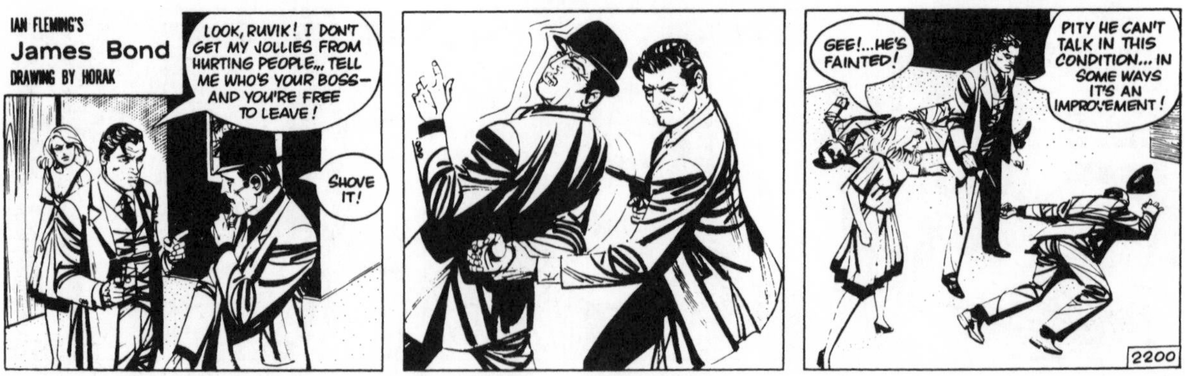
IAN FLEMING'S
James Bond
DRAWING BY HORAK
LOOK, RUVIK! I DON'T GET MY JOLLIES FROM HURTING PEOPLE... TELL ME WHO'S YOUR BOSS—AND YOU'RE FREE TO LEAVE!
SHOVE IT!
GEE!... HE'S FAINTED!
PITY HE CAN'T TALK IN THIS CONDITION... IN SOME WAYS IT'S AN IMPROVEMENT!
2200

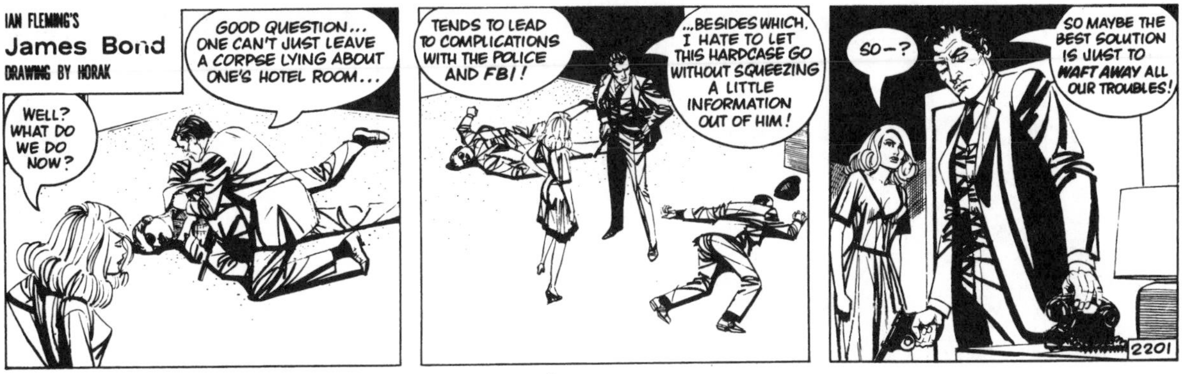
IAN FLEMING'S
James Bond
DRAWING BY HORAK
WELL? WHAT DO WE DO NOW?
GOOD QUESTION... ONE CAN'T JUST LEAVE A CORPSE LYING ABOUT ONE'S HOTEL ROOM...
TENDS TO LEAD TO COMPLICATIONS WITH THE POLICE AND FBI!
...BESIDES WHICH, I HATE TO LET THIS HARDCASE GO WITHOUT SQUEEZING A LITTLE INFORMATION OUT OF HIM!
SO—?
SO MAYBE THE BEST SOLUTION IS JUST TO WAFT AWAY ALL OUR TROUBLES!
2201

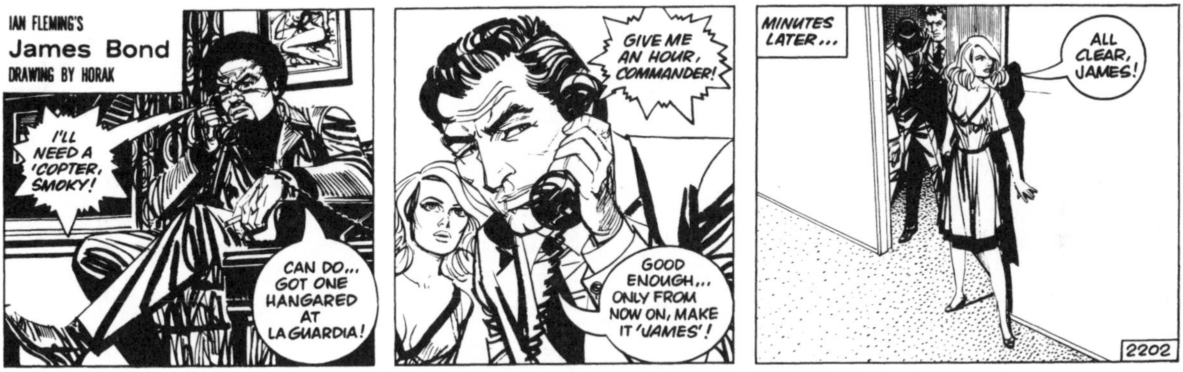
IAN FLEMING'S
James Bond
DRAWING BY HORAK
I'LL NEED A 'COPTER, SMOKY!
CAN DO... GOT ONE HANGARED AT LA GUARDIA!
GIVE ME AN HOUR, COMMANDER!
GOOD ENOUGH... ONLY FROM NOW ON, MAKE IT 'JAMES'!
MINUTES LATER...
ALL CLEAR, JAMES!
2202

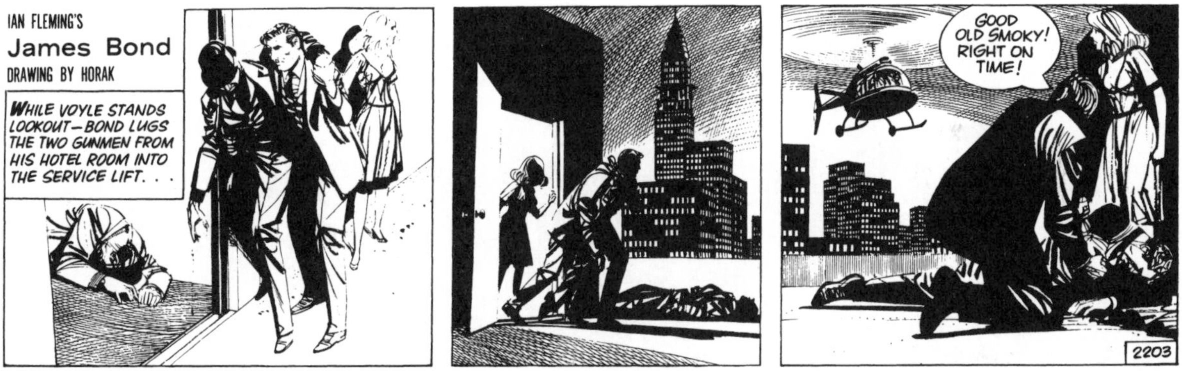
IAN FLEMING'S
James Bond
DRAWING BY HORAK
WHILE VOYLE STANDS LOOKOUT—BOND LUGS THE TWO GUNMEN FROM HIS HOTEL ROOM INTO THE SERVICE LIFT...
GOOD OLD SMOKY! RIGHT ON TIME!
2203

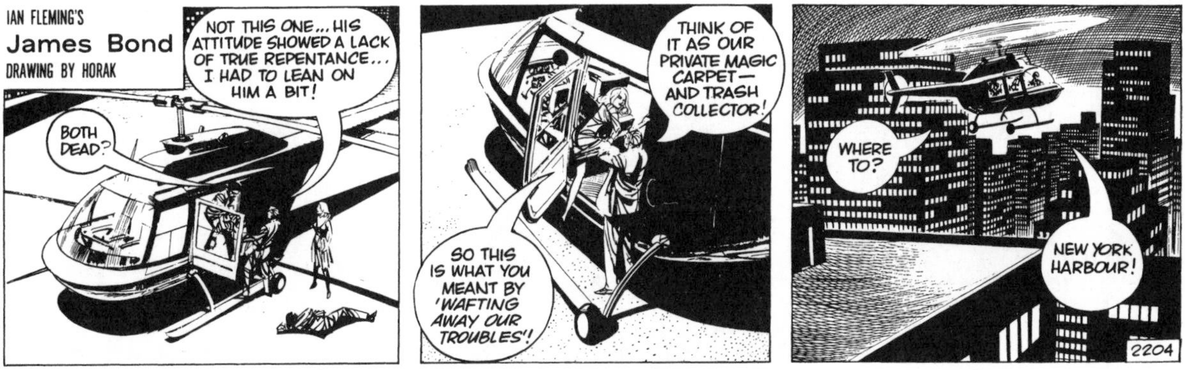
IAN FLEMING'S
James Bond
DRAWING BY HORAK
BOTH DEAD?
NOT THIS ONE... HIS ATTITUDE SHOWED A LACK OF TRUE REPENTANCE... I HAD TO LEAN ON HIM A BIT!
SO THIS IS WHAT YOU MEANT BY 'WAFTING AWAY OUR TROUBLES'!
THINK OF IT AS OUR PRIVATE MAGIC CARPET—AND TRASH COLLECTOR!
WHERE TO?
NEW YORK HARBOUR!
2204

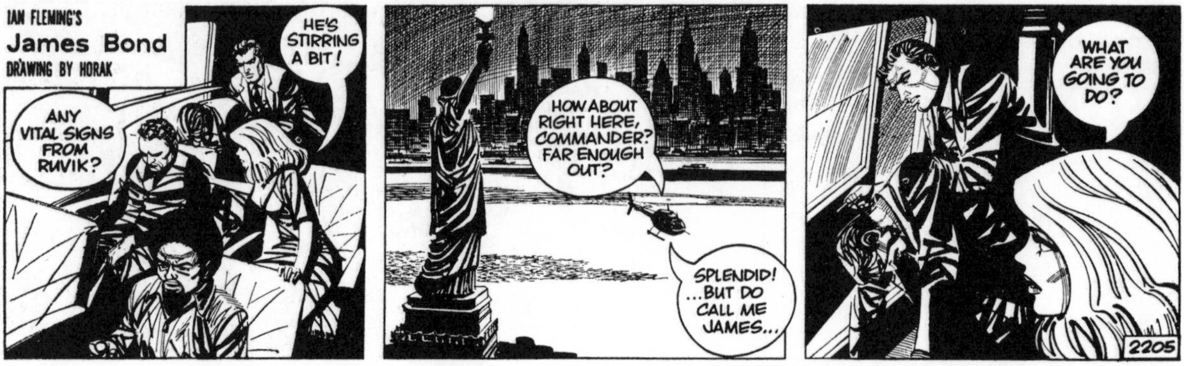
IAN FLEMING'S
James Bond
DRAWING BY HORAK
HE'S STIRRING A BIT!
ANY VITAL SIGNS FROM RUVIK?
HOW ABOUT RIGHT HERE, COMMANDER? FAR ENOUGH OUT?
SPLENDID! ...BUT DO CALL ME JAMES...
WHAT ARE YOU GOING TO DO?
2205

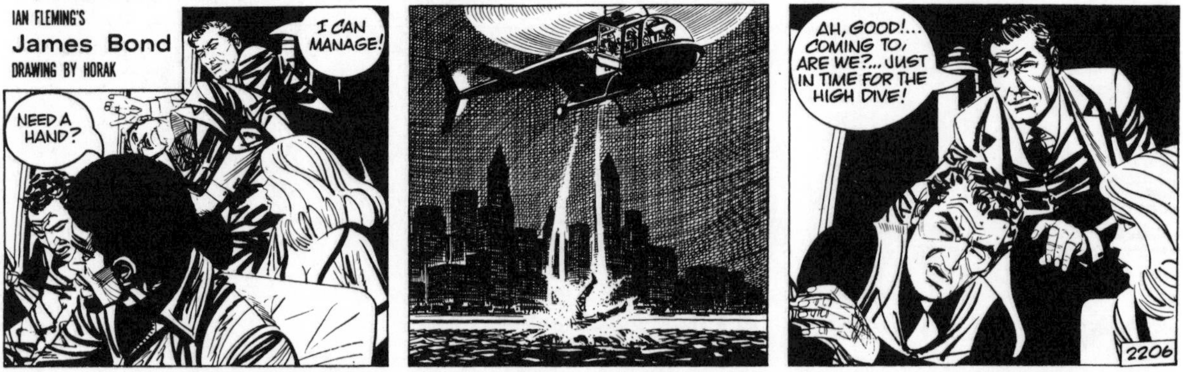
IAN FLEMING'S
James Bond
DRAWING BY HORAK
I CAN MANAGE!
NEED A HAND?
AH, GOOD!... COMING TO, ARE WE?... JUST IN TIME FOR THE HIGH DIVE!
2206

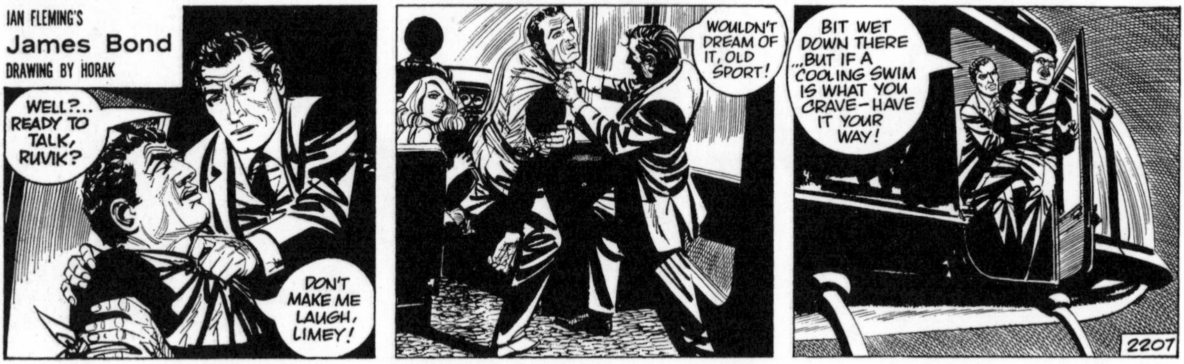
IAN FLEMING'S
James Bond
DRAWING BY HORAK
WELL?... READY TO TALK, RUVIK?
DON'T MAKE ME LAUGH, LIMEY!
WOULDN'T DREAM OF IT, OLD SPORT!
BIT WET DOWN THERE ...BUT IF A COOLING SWIM IS WHAT YOU CRAVE—HAVE IT YOUR WAY!
2207

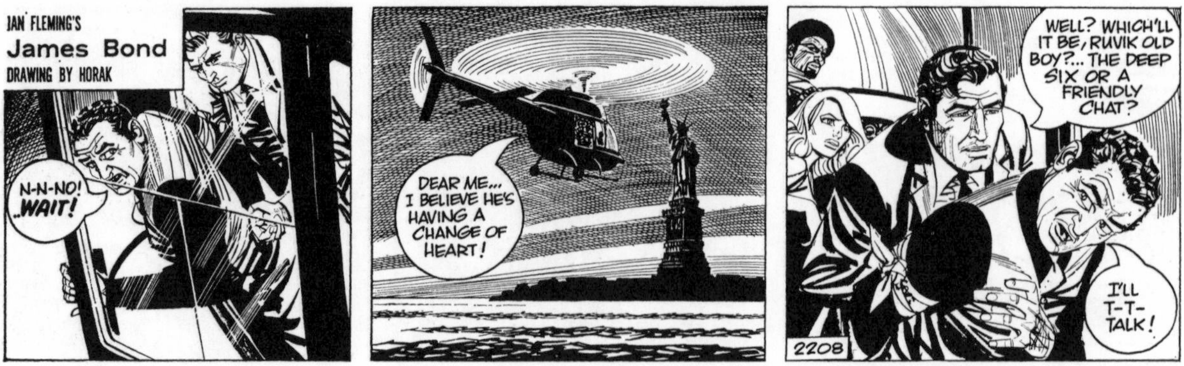
IAN FLEMING'S
James Bond
DRAWING BY HORAK
N-N-NO! ..WAIT!
DEAR ME... I BELIEVE HE'S HAVING A CHANGE OF HEART!
2208
WELL? WHICH'LL IT BE, RUVIK OLD BOY?... THE DEEP SIX OR A FRIENDLY CHAT?
I'LL T-T-TALK!

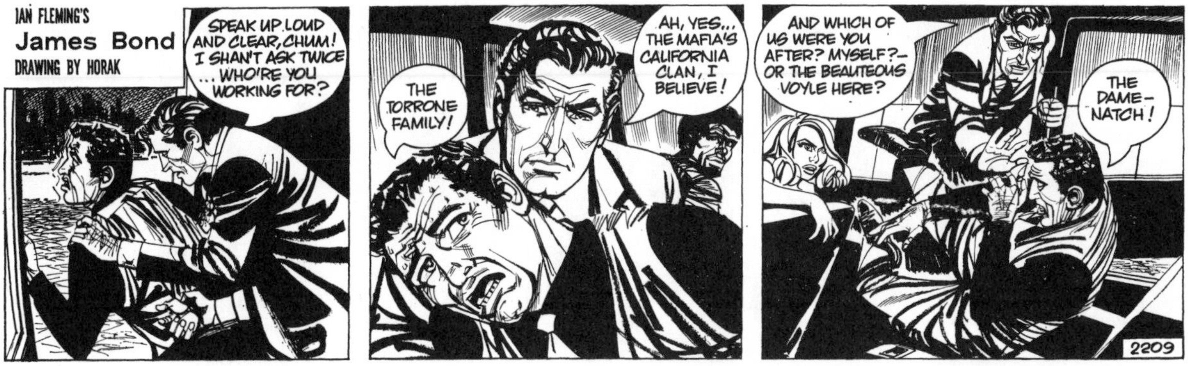
IAN FLEMING'S
James Bond
DRAWING BY HORAK
SPEAK UP LOUD AND CLEAR, CHUM! I SHAN'T ASK TWICE ... WHO'RE YOU WORKING FOR?
THE TORRONE FAMILY!
AH, YES... THE MAFIA'S CALIFORNIA CLAN, I BELIEVE!
AND WHICH OF US WERE YOU AFTER? MYSELF?— OR THE BEAUTEOUS VOYLE HERE?
THE DAME— NATCH!
2209

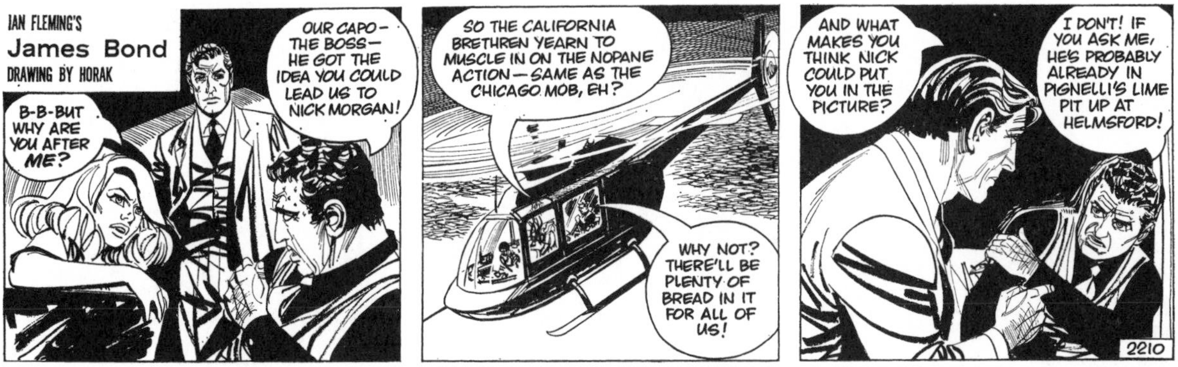
IAN FLEMING'S
James Bond
DRAWING BY HORAK
B-B-BUT WHY ARE YOU AFTER ME?
OUR CAPO— THE BOSS— HE GOT THE IDEA YOU COULD LEAD US TO NICK MORGAN!
SO THE CALIFORNIA BRETHREN YEARN TO MUSCLE IN ON THE NOPANE ACTION— SAME AS THE CHICAGO MOB, EH?
WHY NOT? THERE'LL BE PLENTY OF BREAD IN IT FOR ALL OF US!
AND WHAT MAKES YOU THINK NICK COULD PUT YOU IN THE PICTURE?
I DON'T! IF YOU ASK ME, HE'S PROBABLY ALREADY IN PIGNELLI'S LIME PIT UP AT HELMSFORD!
2210

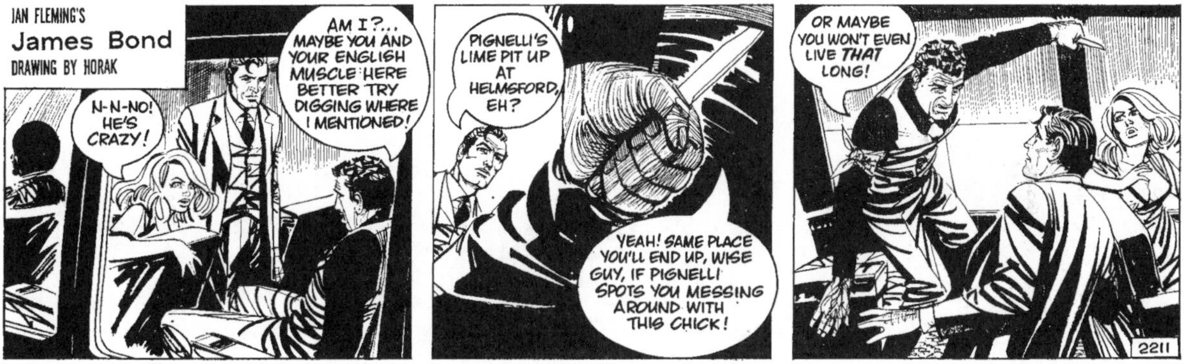
IAN FLEMING'S
James Bond
DRAWING BY HORAK
N-N-NO! HE'S CRAZY!
AM I?... MAYBE YOU AND YOUR ENGLISH MUSCLE HERE BETTER TRY DIGGING WHERE I MENTIONED!
PIGNELLI'S LIME PIT UP AT HELMSFORD, EH?
YEAH! SAME PLACE YOU'LL END UP, WISE GUY, IF PIGNELLI SPOTS YOU MESSING AROUND WITH THIS CHICK!
OR MAYBE YOU WON'T EVEN LIVE THAT LONG!
2211

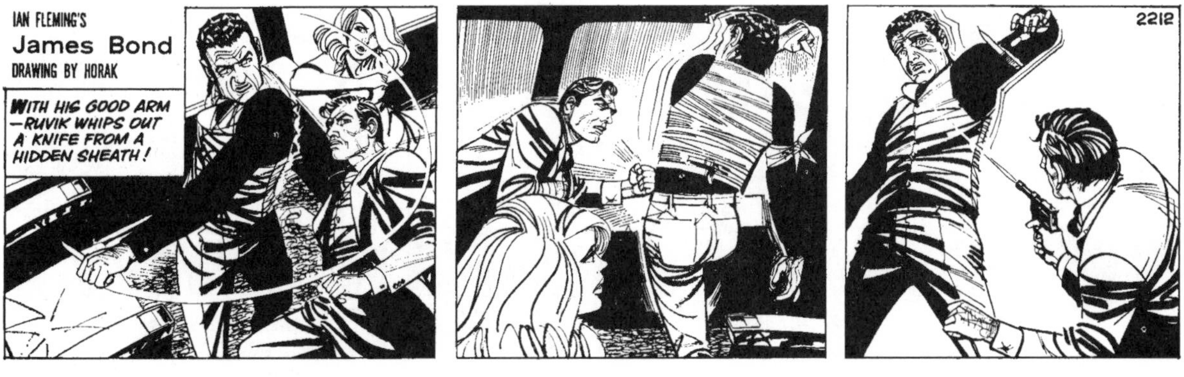
IAN FLEMING'S
James Bond
DRAWING BY HORAK
WITH HIS GOOD ARM —RUVIK WHIPS OUT A KNIFE FROM A HIDDEN SHEATH!
2212

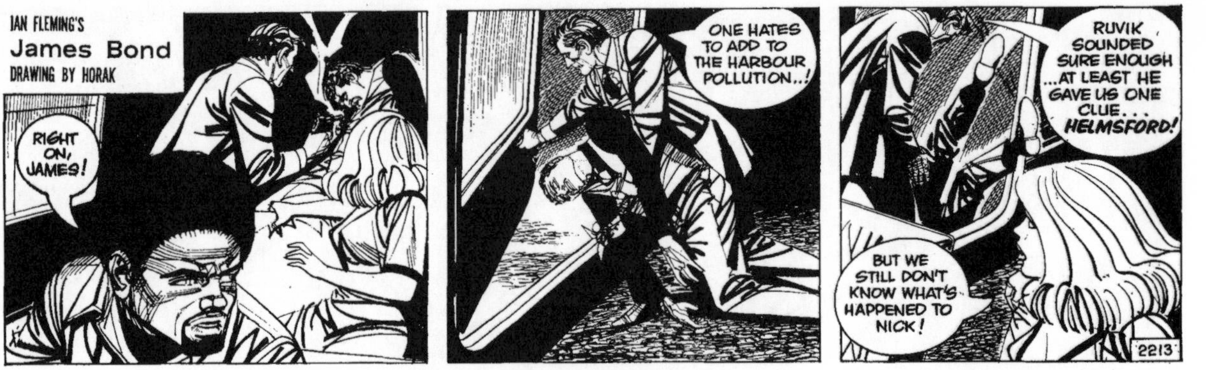
IAN FLEMING'S
James Bond
DRAWING BY HORAK
RIGHT ON, JAMES!
ONE HATES TO ADD TO THE HARBOUR POLLUTION..!
RUVIK SOUNDED SURE ENOUGH ...AT LEAST HE GAVE US ONE CLUE... HELMSFORD!
BUT WE STILL DON'T KNOW WHAT'S HAPPENED TO NICK!
2213

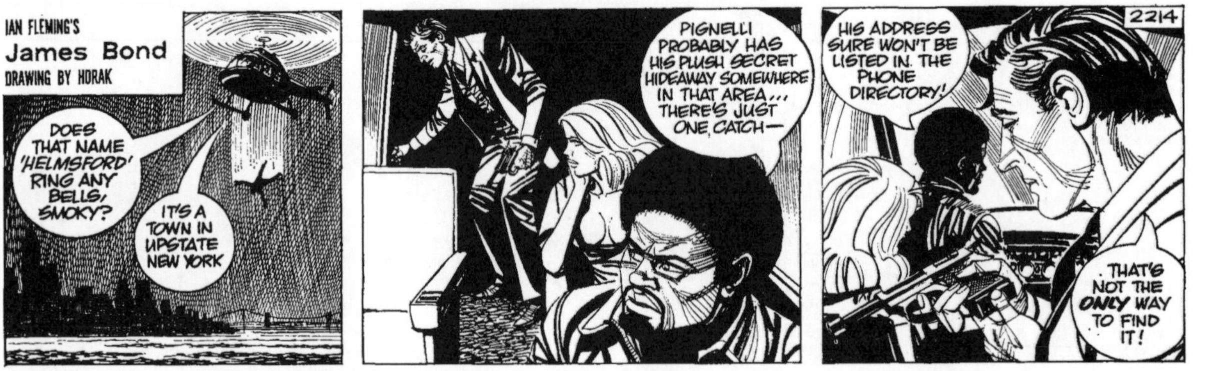
IAN FLEMING'S
James Bond
DRAWING BY HORAK
DOES THAT NAME 'HELMSFORD' RING ANY BELLS, SMOKY?
IT'S A TOWN IN UPSTATE NEW YORK
PIGNELLI PROBABLY HAS HIS PLUSH SECRET HIDEAWAY SOMEWHERE IN THAT AREA... THERE'S JUST ONE CATCH—
2214
HIS ADDRESS SURE WON'T BE LISTED IN THE PHONE DIRECTORY!
...THAT'S NOT THE ONLY WAY TO FIND IT!

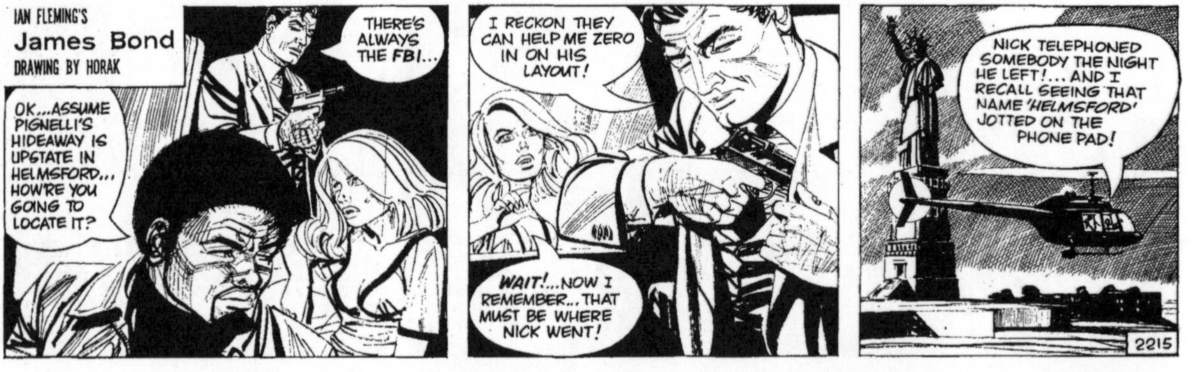
IAN FLEMING'S
James Bond
DRAWING BY HORAK
THERE'S ALWAYS THE FBI...
OK...ASSUME PIGNELLI'S HIDEAWAY IS UPSTATE IN HELMSFORD... HOW'RE YOU GOING TO LOCATE IT?
I RECKON THEY CAN HELP ME ZERO IN ON HIS LAYOUT!
WAIT!...NOW I REMEMBER... THAT MUST BE WHERE NICK WENT!
NICK TELEPHONED SOMEBODY THE NIGHT HE LEFT!... AND I RECALL SEEING THAT NAME 'HELMSFORD' JOTTED ON THE PHONE PAD!
2215

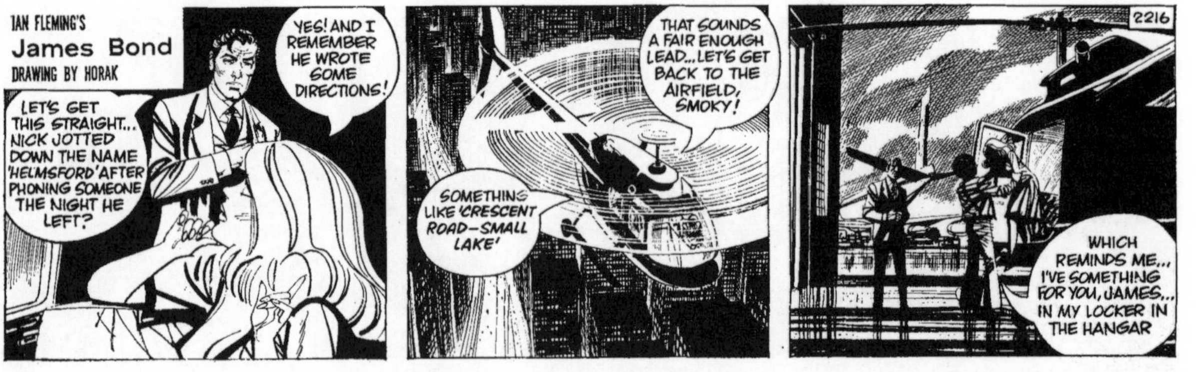
IAN FLEMING'S
James Bond
DRAWING BY HORAK
YES! AND I REMEMBER HE WROTE SOME DIRECTIONS!
LET'S GET THIS STRAIGHT... NICK JOTTED DOWN THE NAME 'HELMSFORD' AFTER PHONING SOMEONE THE NIGHT HE LEFT?
THAT SOUNDS A FAIR ENOUGH LEAD... LET'S GET BACK TO THE AIRFIELD, SMOKY!
SOMETHING LIKE 'CRESCENT ROAD—SMALL LAKE'
2216
WHICH REMINDS ME... I'VE SOMETHING FOR YOU, JAMES... IN MY LOCKER IN THE HANGAR

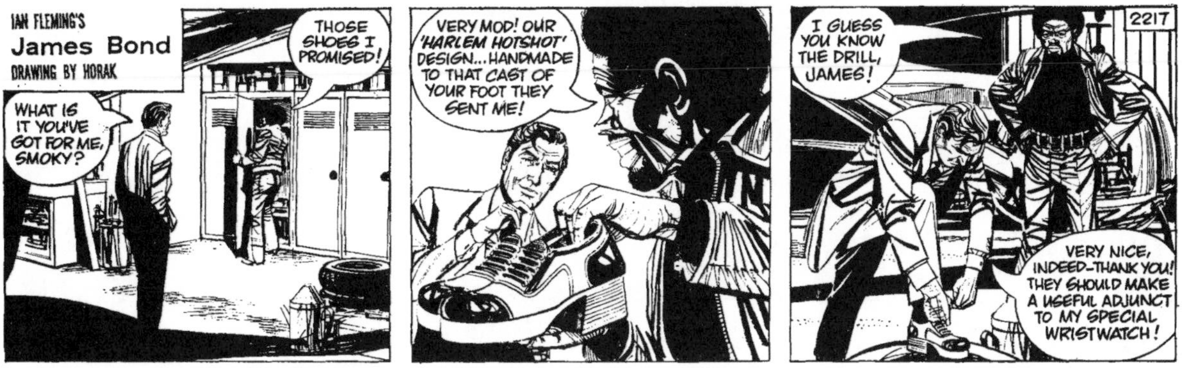
IAN FLEMING'S
James Bond
DRAWING BY HORAK
WHAT IS IT YOU'VE GOT FOR ME, SMOKY?
THOSE SHOES I PROMISED!
VERY MOD! OUR 'HARLEM HOTSHOT' DESIGN... HANDMADE TO THAT CAST OF YOUR FOOT THEY SENT ME!
2217
I GUESS YOU KNOW THE DRILL, JAMES!
VERY NICE, INDEED–THANK YOU! THEY SHOULD MAKE A USEFUL ADJUNCT TO MY SPECIAL WRISTWATCH!

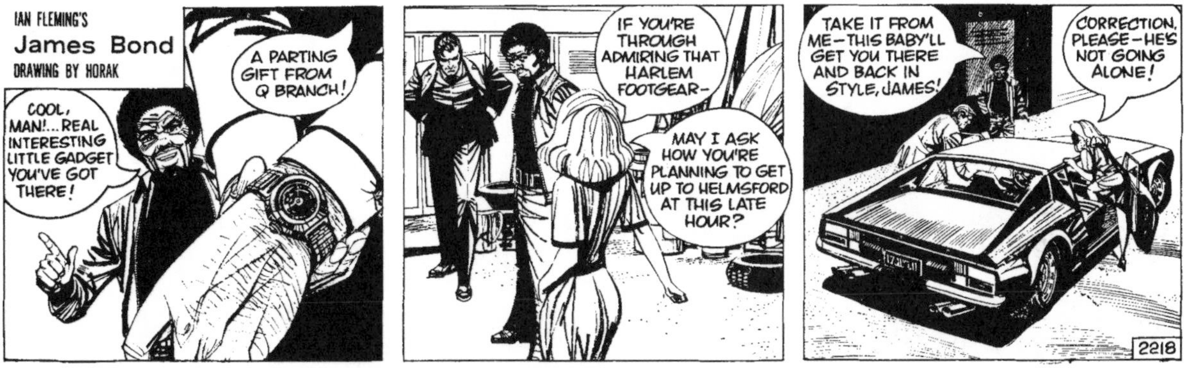
IAN FLEMING'S
James Bond
DRAWING BY HORAK
A PARTING GIFT FROM Q BRANCH!
COOL, MAN!... REAL INTERESTING LITTLE GADGET YOU'VE GOT THERE!
IF YOU'RE THROUGH ADMIRING THAT HARLEM FOOTGEAR–
MAY I ASK HOW YOU'RE PLANNING TO GET UP TO HELMSFORD AT THIS LATE HOUR?
TAKE IT FROM ME–THIS BABY'LL GET YOU THERE AND BACK IN STYLE, JAMES!
CORRECTION, PLEASE–HE'S NOT GOING ALONE!
2218

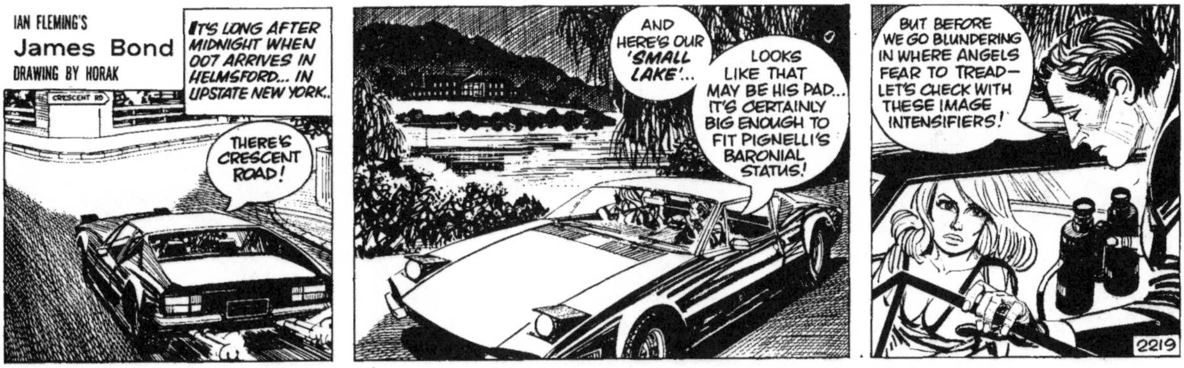
IAN FLEMING'S
James Bond
DRAWING BY HORAK
IT'S LONG AFTER MIDNIGHT WHEN 007 ARRIVES IN HELMSFORD... IN UPSTATE NEW YORK..
CRESCENT RD
THERE'S CRESCENT ROAD!
AND HERE'S OUR 'SMALL LAKE'...
LOOKS LIKE THAT MAY BE HIS PAD... IT'S CERTAINLY BIG ENOUGH TO FIT PIGNELLI'S BARONIAL STATUS!
BUT BEFORE WE GO BLUNDERING IN WHERE ANGELS FEAR TO TREAD–LET'S CHECK WITH THESE IMAGE INTENSIFIERS!
2219

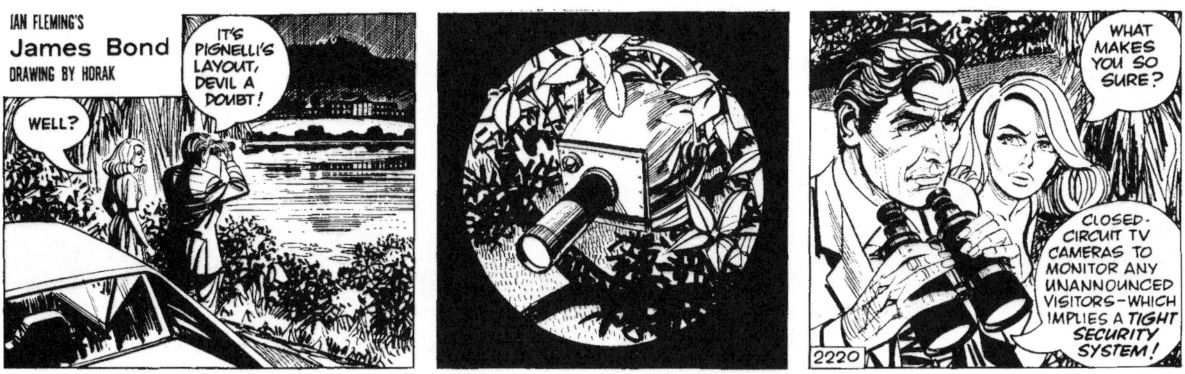
IAN FLEMING'S
James Bond
DRAWING BY HORAK
WELL?
IT'S PIGNELLI'S LAYOUT, DEVIL A DOUBT!
WHAT MAKES YOU SO SURE?
CLOSED-CIRCUIT TV CAMERAS TO MONITOR ANY UNANNOUNCED VISITORS–WHICH IMPLIES A TIGHT SECURITY SYSTEM!
2220

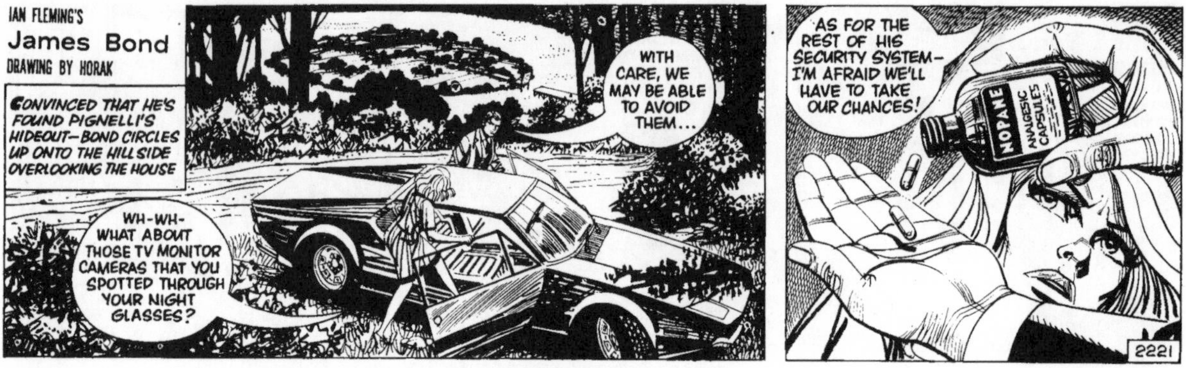
IAN FLEMING'S
James Bond
DRAWING BY HORAK
CONVINCED THAT HE'S FOUND PIGNELLI'S HIDEOUT—BOND CIRCLES UP ONTO THE HILL SIDE OVERLOOKING THE HOUSE
WH-WH- WHAT ABOUT THOSE TV MONITOR CAMERAS THAT YOU SPOTTED THROUGH YOUR NIGHT GLASSES?
WITH CARE, WE MAY BE ABLE TO AVOID THEM...
AS FOR THE REST OF HIS SECURITY SYSTEM—I'M AFRAID WE'LL HAVE TO TAKE OUR CHANCES!
NOPANE
ANALGESIC CAPSULES
2221

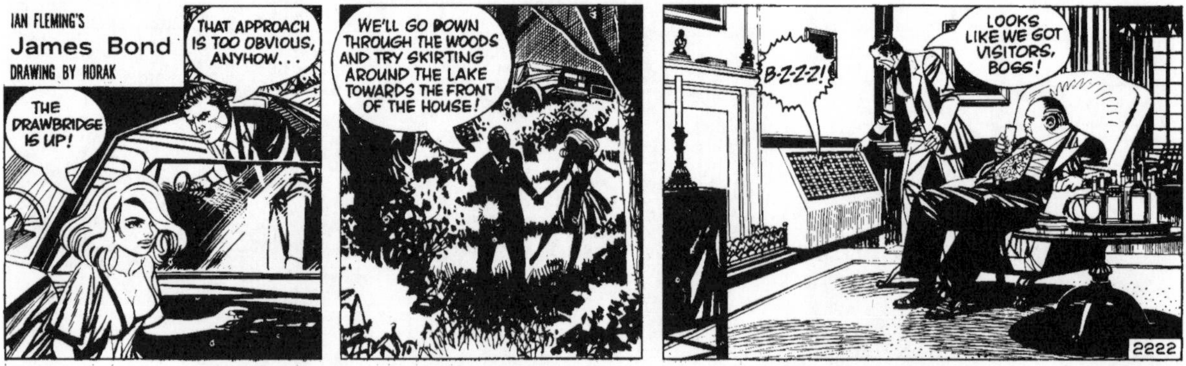
IAN FLEMING'S
James Bond
DRAWING BY HORAK
THE DRAWBRIDGE IS UP!
THAT APPROACH IS TOO OBVIOUS, ANYHOW...
WE'LL GO DOWN THROUGH THE WOODS AND TRY SKIRTING AROUND THE LAKE TOWARDS THE FRONT OF THE HOUSE!
B-Z-Z-Z!
LOOKS LIKE WE GOT VISITORS, BOSS!
2222

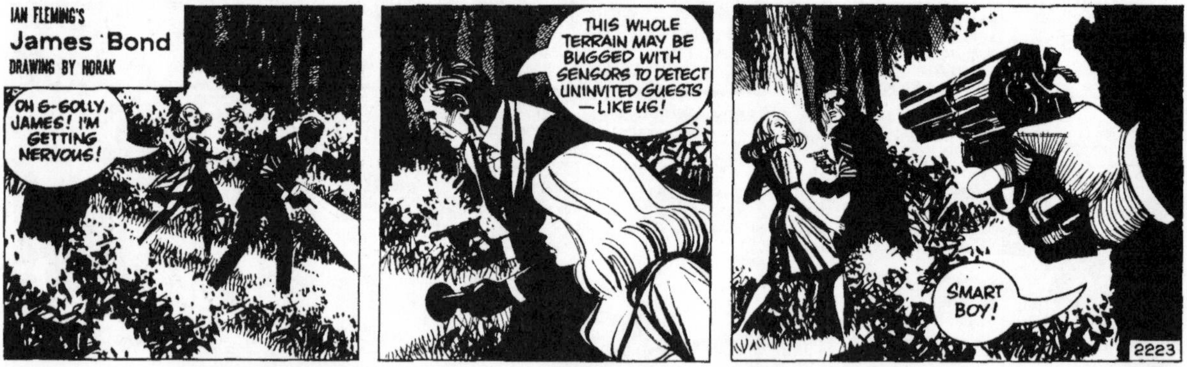
IAN FLEMING'S
James Bond
DRAWING BY HORAK
OH G-GOLLY, JAMES! I'M GETTING NERVOUS!
THIS WHOLE TERRAIN MAY BE BUGGED WITH SENSORS TO DETECT UNINVITED GUESTS —LIKE US!
SMART BOY!
2223

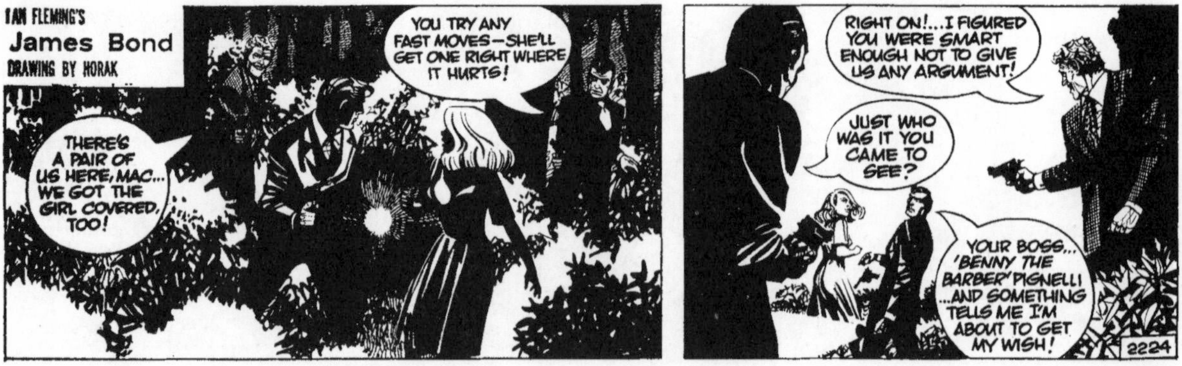
IAN FLEMING'S
James Bond
DRAWING BY HORAK
THERE'S A PAIR OF US HERE, MAC... WE GOT THE GIRL COVERED, TOO!
YOU TRY ANY FAST MOVES—SHE'LL GET ONE RIGHT WHERE IT HURTS!
RIGHT ON!...I FIGURED YOU WERE SMART ENOUGH NOT TO GIVE US ANY ARGUMENT!
JUST WHO WAS IT YOU CAME TO SEE?
YOUR BOSS... 'BENNY THE BARBER' PIGNELLI ...AND SOMETHING TELLS ME I'M ABOUT TO GET MY WISH!
2224

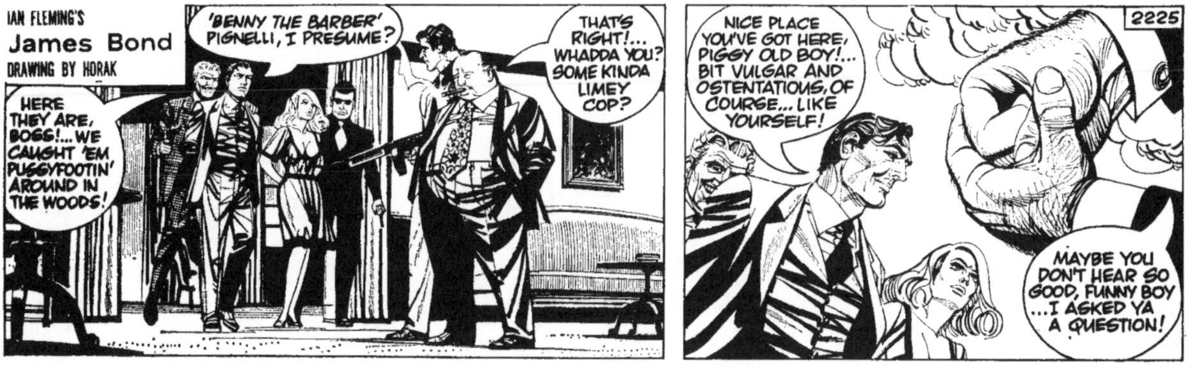
IAN FLEMING'S
James Bond
DRAWING BY HORAK
HERE THEY ARE, BOSS!... WE CAUGHT 'EM PUSSYFOOTIN' AROUND IN THE WOODS!
'BENNY THE BARBER' PIGNELLI, I PRESUME?
THAT'S RIGHT!... WHADDA YOU? SOME KINDA LIMEY COP?
2225
NICE PLACE YOU'VE GOT HERE, PIGGY OLD BOY!... BIT VULGAR AND OSTENTATIOUS, OF COURSE... LIKE YOURSELF!
MAYBE YOU DON'T HEAR SO GOOD, FUNNY BOY ...I ASKED YA A QUESTION!

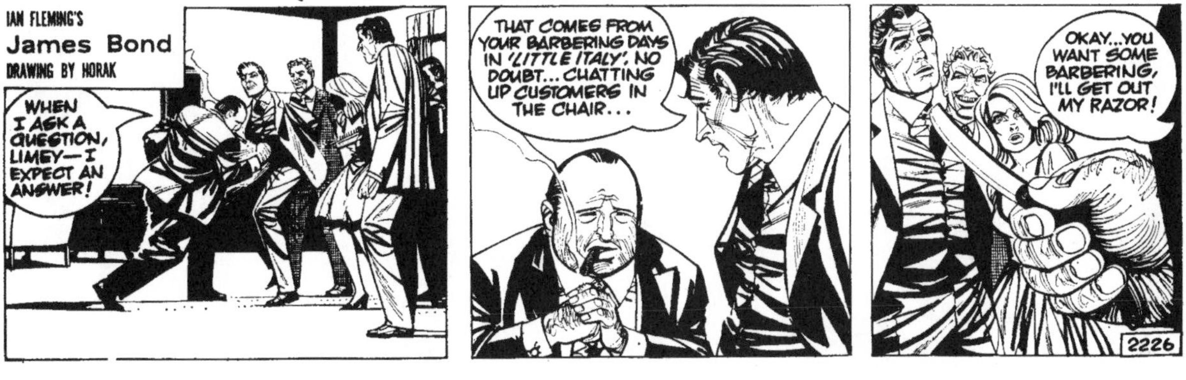
IAN FLEMING'S
James Bond
DRAWING BY HORAK
WHEN I ASK A QUESTION, LIMEY—I EXPECT AN ANSWER!
THAT COMES FROM YOUR BARBERING DAYS IN 'LITTLE ITALY', NO DOUBT... CHATTING UP CUSTOMERS IN THE CHAIR...
OKAY... YOU WANT SOME BARBERING, I'LL GET OUT MY RAZOR!
2226

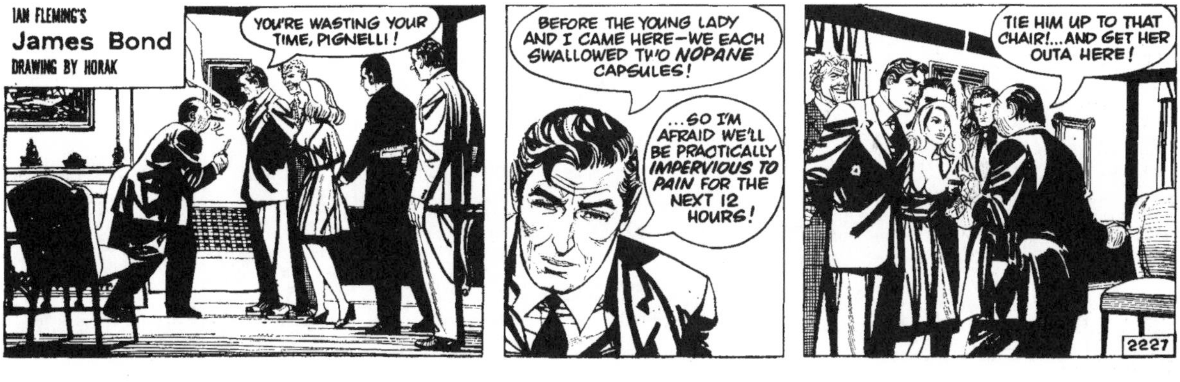
IAN FLEMING'S
James Bond
DRAWING BY HORAK
YOU'RE WASTING YOUR TIME, PIGNELLI!
BEFORE THE YOUNG LADY AND I CAME HERE—WE EACH SWALLOWED TWO NOPANE CAPSULES!
...SO I'M AFRAID WE'LL BE PRACTICALLY IMPERVIOUS TO PAIN FOR THE NEXT 12 HOURS!
TIE HIM UP TO THAT CHAIR!... AND GET HER OUTA HERE!
2227

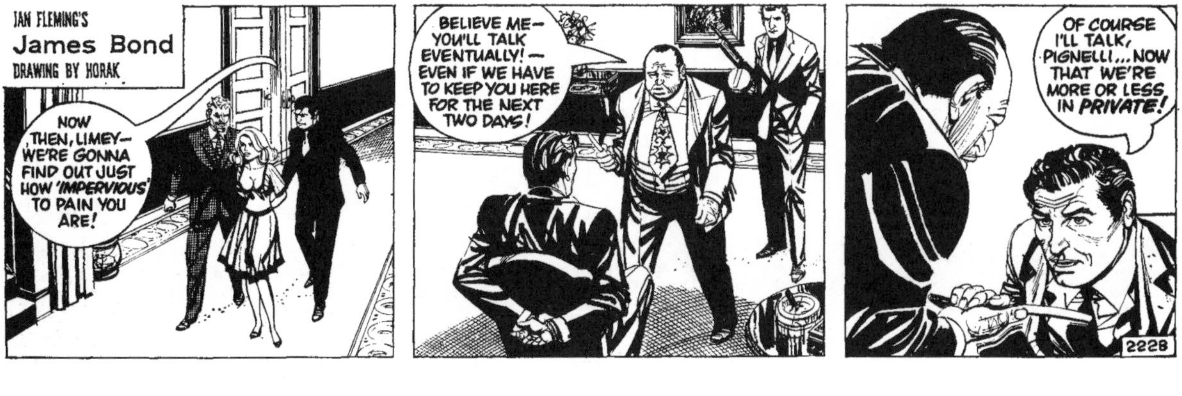
IAN FLEMING'S
James Bond
DRAWING BY HORAK
NOW THEN, LIMEY—WE'RE GONNA FIND OUT JUST HOW 'IMPERVIOUS' TO PAIN YOU ARE!
BELIEVE ME—YOU'LL TALK EVENTUALLY!—EVEN IF WE HAVE TO KEEP YOU HERE FOR THE NEXT TWO DAYS!
OF COURSE I'LL TALK, PIGNELLI... NOW THAT WE'RE MORE OR LESS IN PRIVATE!
2228

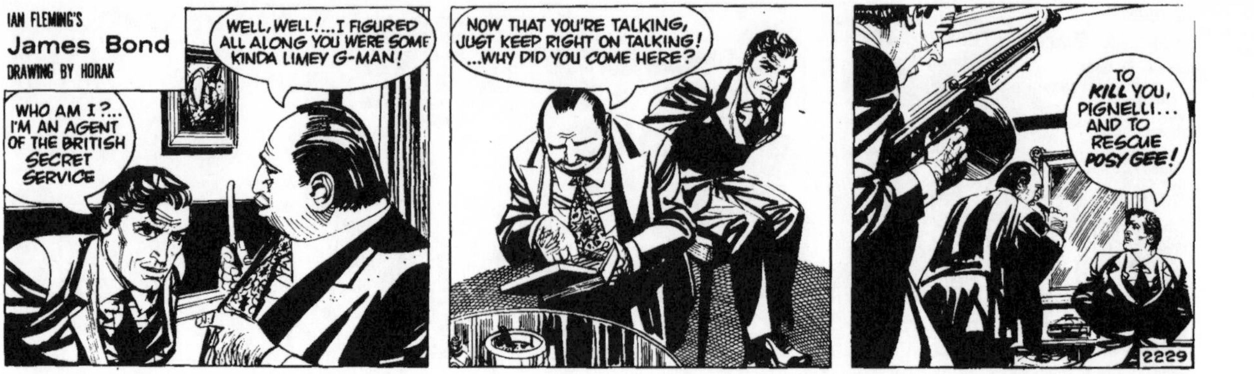
IAN FLEMING'S
James Bond
DRAWING BY HORAK
WELL, WELL!...I FIGURED ALL ALONG YOU WERE SOME KINDA LIMEY G-MAN!
WHO AM I?... I'M AN AGENT OF THE BRITISH SECRET SERVICE
NOW THAT YOU'RE TALKING, JUST KEEP RIGHT ON TALKING! ...WHY DID YOU COME HERE?
TO KILL YOU, PIGNELLI... AND TO RESCUE POSY GEE!
2229

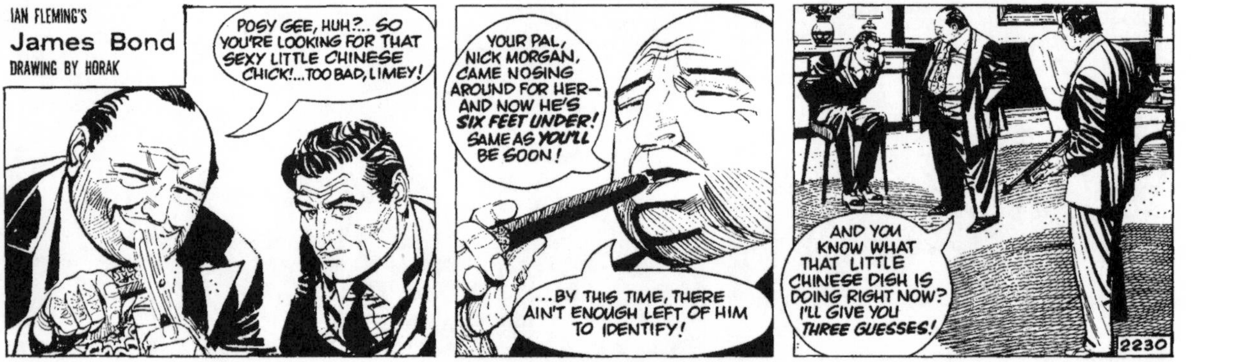
IAN FLEMING'S
James Bond
DRAWING BY HORAK
POSY GEE, HUH?.. SO YOU'RE LOOKING FOR THAT SEXY LITTLE CHINESE CHICK!...TOO BAD, LIMEY!
YOUR PAL, NICK MORGAN, CAME NOSING AROUND FOR HER- AND NOW HE'S SIX FEET UNDER! SAME AS YOU'LL BE SOON!
...BY THIS TIME, THERE AIN'T ENOUGH LEFT OF HIM TO IDENTIFY!
AND YOU KNOW WHAT THAT LITTLE CHINESE DISH IS DOING RIGHT NOW? I'LL GIVE YOU THREE GUESSES!
2230

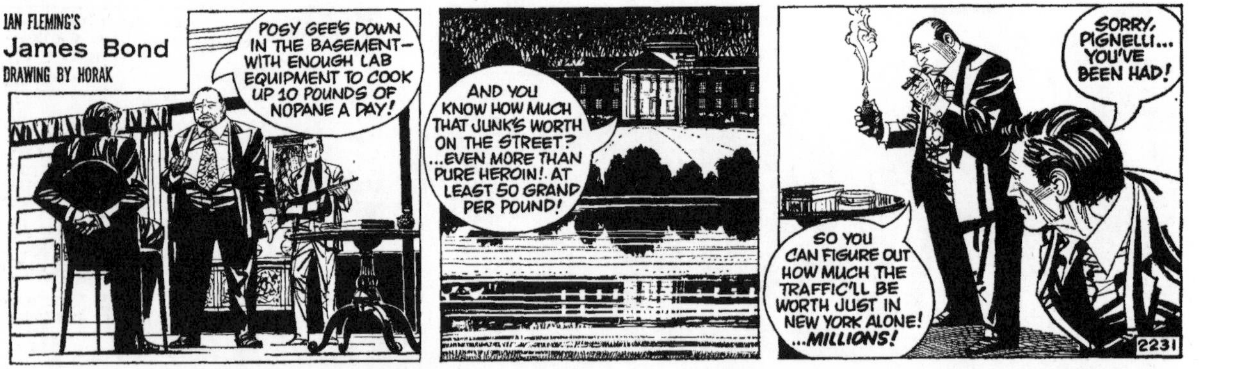
IAN FLEMING'S
James Bond
DRAWING BY HORAK
POSY GEE'S DOWN IN THE BASEMENT- WITH ENOUGH LAB EQUIPMENT TO COOK UP 10 POUNDS OF NOPANE A DAY!
AND YOU KNOW HOW MUCH THAT JUNK'S WORTH ON THE STREET? ...EVEN MORE THAN PURE HEROIN! AT LEAST 50 GRAND PER POUND!
SO YOU CAN FIGURE OUT HOW MUCH THE TRAFFIC'LL BE WORTH JUST IN NEW YORK ALONE! ...MILLIONS!
SORRY, PIGNELLI... YOU'VE BEEN HAD!
2231

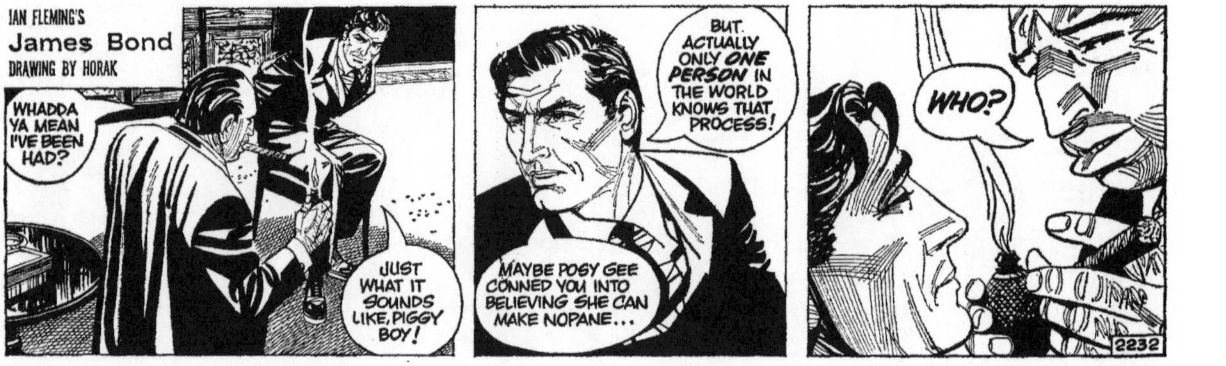
IAN FLEMING'S
James Bond
DRAWING BY HORAK
WHADDA YA MEAN I'VE BEEN HAD?
JUST WHAT IT SOUNDS LIKE, PIGGY BOY!
BUT. ACTUALLY ONLY ONE PERSON IN THE WORLD KNOWS THAT PROCESS!
MAYBE POSY GEE CONNED YOU INTO BELIEVING SHE CAN MAKE NOPANE...
WHO?
2232

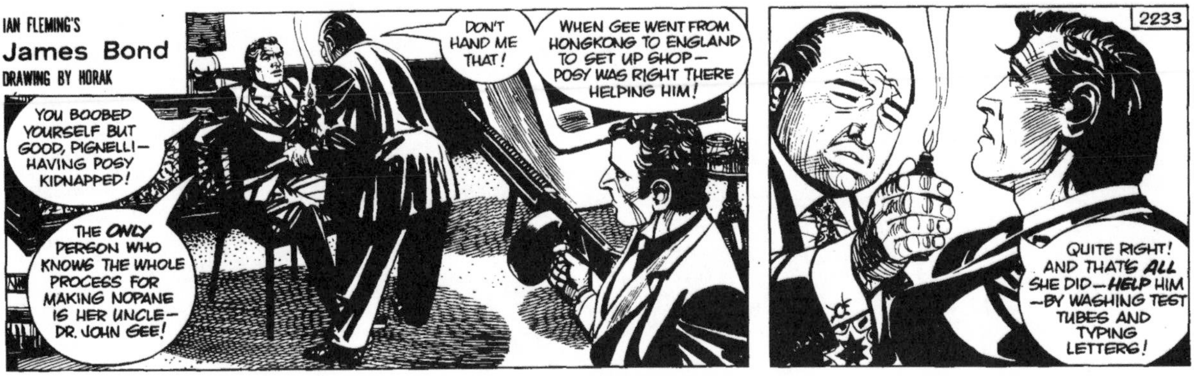
IAN FLEMING'S
James Bond
DRAWING BY HORAK
YOU BOOBED YOURSELF BUT GOOD, PIGNELLI— HAVING POSY KIDNAPPED!
THE ONLY PERSON WHO KNOWS THE WHOLE PROCESS FOR MAKING NOPANE IS HER UNCLE— DR. JOHN GEE!
DON'T HAND ME THAT!
WHEN GEE WENT FROM HONGKONG TO ENGLAND TO SET UP SHOP— POSY WAS RIGHT THERE HELPING HIM!
2233
QUITE RIGHT! AND THAT'S ALL SHE DID—HELP HIM —BY WASHING TEST TUBES AND TYPING LETTERS!

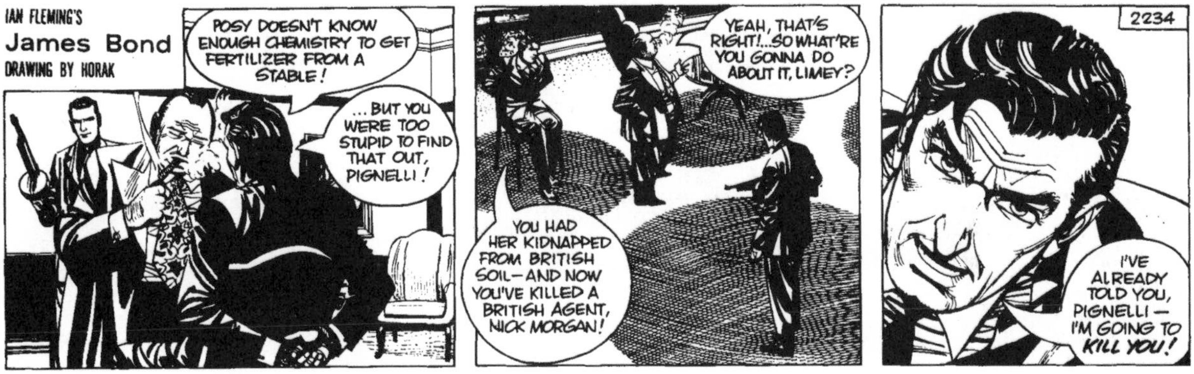
IAN FLEMING'S
James Bond
DRAWING BY HORAK
POSY DOESN'T KNOW ENOUGH CHEMISTRY TO GET FERTILIZER FROM A STABLE!
... BUT YOU WERE TOO STUPID TO FIND THAT OUT, PIGNELLI!
YEAH, THAT'S RIGHT!...SO WHAT'RE YOU GONNA DO ABOUT IT, LIMEY?
YOU HAD HER KIDNAPPED FROM BRITISH SOIL—AND NOW YOU'VE KILLED A BRITISH AGENT, NICK MORGAN!
2234
I'VE ALREADY TOLD YOU, PIGNELLI— I'M GOING TO KILL YOU!

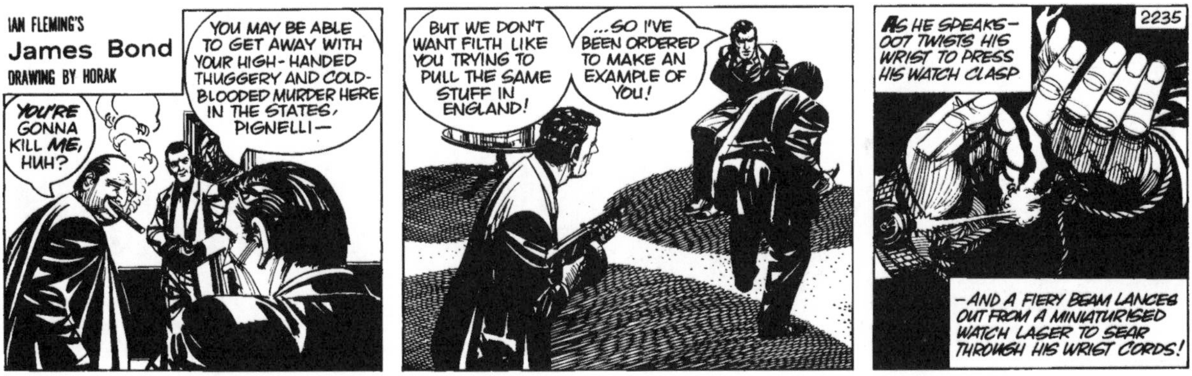
IAN FLEMING'S
James Bond
DRAWING BY HORAK
YOU'RE GONNA KILL ME, HUH?
YOU MAY BE ABLE TO GET AWAY WITH YOUR HIGH-HANDED THUGGERY AND COLD-BLOODED MURDER HERE IN THE STATES, PIGNELLI—
BUT WE DON'T WANT FILTH LIKE YOU TRYING TO PULL THE SAME STUFF IN ENGLAND!
...SO I'VE BEEN ORDERED TO MAKE AN EXAMPLE OF YOU!
AS HE SPEAKS— 007 TWISTS HIS WRIST TO PRESS HIS WATCH CLASP
2235
—AND A FIERY BEAM LANCES OUT FROM A MINIATURISED WATCH LASER TO SEAR THROUGH HIS WRIST CORDS!

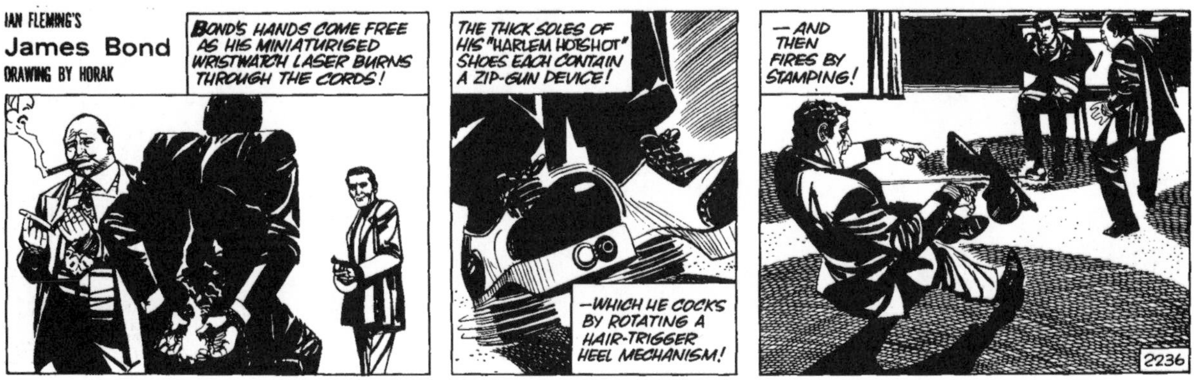
IAN FLEMING'S
James Bond
DRAWING BY HORAK
BOND'S HANDS COME FREE AS HIS MINIATURISED WRISTWATCH LASER BURNS THROUGH THE CORDS!
THE THICK SOLES OF HIS "HARLEM HOTSHOT" SHOES EACH CONTAIN A ZIP-GUN DEVICE!
—WHICH HE COCKS BY ROTATING A HAIR-TRIGGER HEEL MECHANISM!
—AND THEN FIRES BY STAMPING!
2236

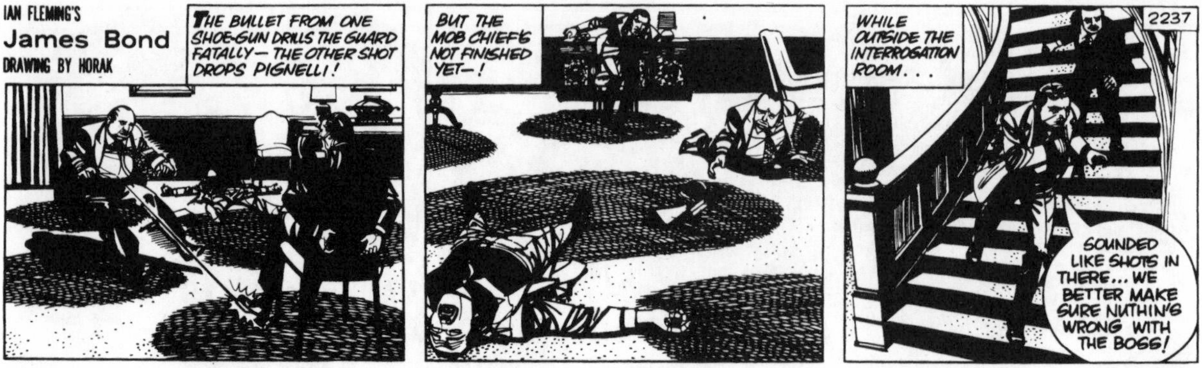
IAN FLEMING'S
James Bond
DRAWING BY HORAK
THE BULLET FROM ONE SHOE-GUN DRILLS THE GUARD FATALLY — THE OTHER SHOT DROPS PIGNELLI!
BUT THE MOB CHIEF'S NOT FINISHED YET—!
WHILE OUTSIDE THE INTERROGATION ROOM...
2237
SOUNDED LIKE SHOTS IN THERE... WE BETTER MAKE SURE NUTHIN'S WRONG WITH THE BOSS!

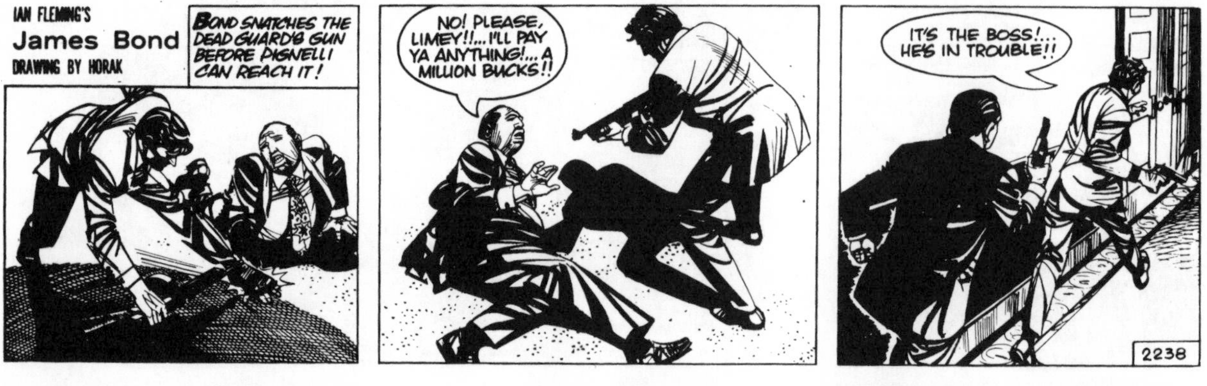
IAN FLEMING'S
James Bond
DRAWING BY HORAK
BOND SNATCHES THE DEAD GUARD'S GUN BEFORE PIGNELLI CAN REACH IT!
NO! PLEASE, LIMEY!!... I'LL PAY YA ANYTHING!... A MILLION BUCKS!!
IT'S THE BOSS!... HE'S IN TROUBLE!!
2238

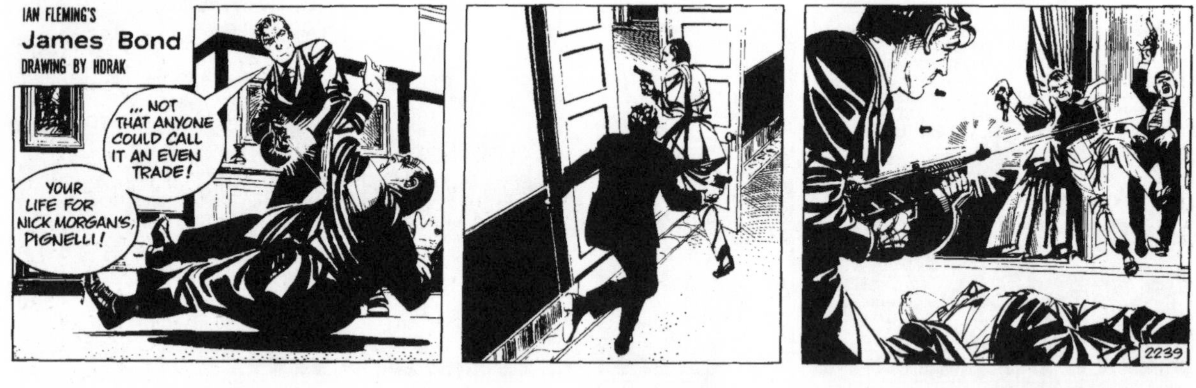
IAN FLEMING'S
James Bond
DRAWING BY HORAK
YOUR LIFE FOR NICK MORGAN'S, PIGNELLI!
... NOT THAT ANYONE COULD CALL IT AN EVEN TRADE!
2239

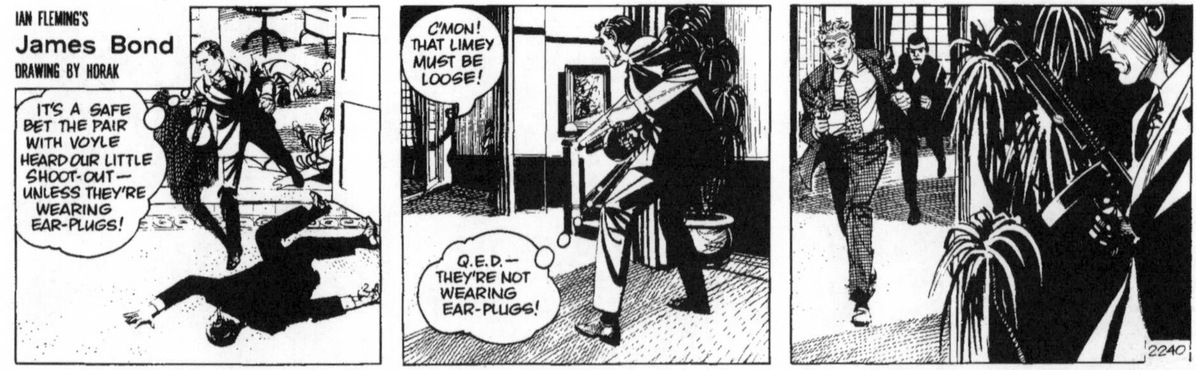
IAN FLEMING'S
James Bond
DRAWING BY HORAK
IT'S A SAFE BET THE PAIR WITH VOYLE HEARD OUR LITTLE SHOOT-OUT — UNLESS THEY'RE WEARING EAR-PLUGS!
C'MON! THAT LIMEY MUST BE LOOSE!
Q.E.D.— THEY'RE NOT WEARING EAR-PLUGS!
2240

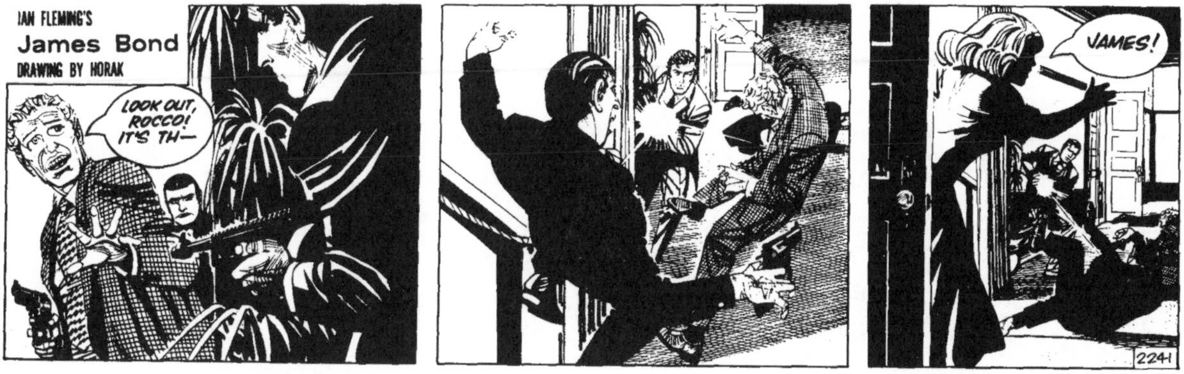
IAN FLEMING'S
James Bond
DRAWING BY HORAK
LOOK OUT, ROCCO! IT'S TH—
JAMES!
2241

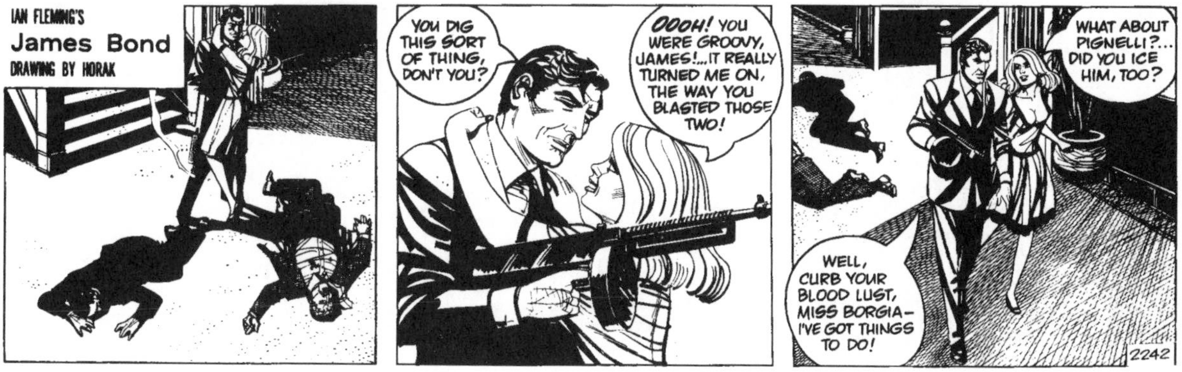
IAN FLEMING'S
James Bond
DRAWING BY HORAK
YOU DIG THIS SORT OF THING, DON'T YOU?
OOOH! YOU WERE GROOVY, JAMES!... IT REALLY TURNED ME ON, THE WAY YOU BLASTED THOSE TWO!
WHAT ABOUT PIGNELLI?... DID YOU ICE HIM, TOO?
WELL, CURB YOUR BLOOD LUST, MISS BORGIA— I'VE GOT THINGS TO DO!
2242

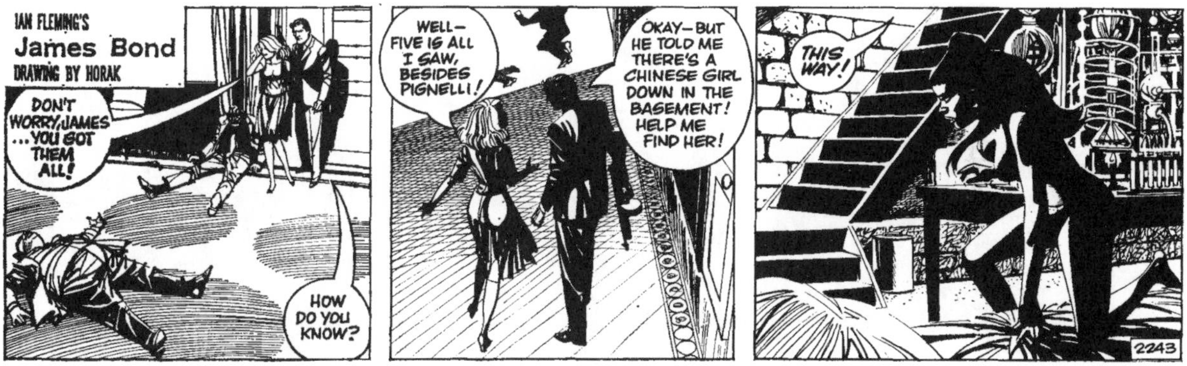
IAN FLEMING'S
James Bond
DRAWING BY HORAK
DON'T WORRY, JAMES ... YOU GOT THEM ALL!
HOW DO YOU KNOW?
WELL— FIVE IS ALL I SAW, BESIDES PIGNELLI!
OKAY—BUT HE TOLD ME THERE'S A CHINESE GIRL DOWN IN THE BASEMENT! HELP ME FIND HER!
THIS WAY!
2243

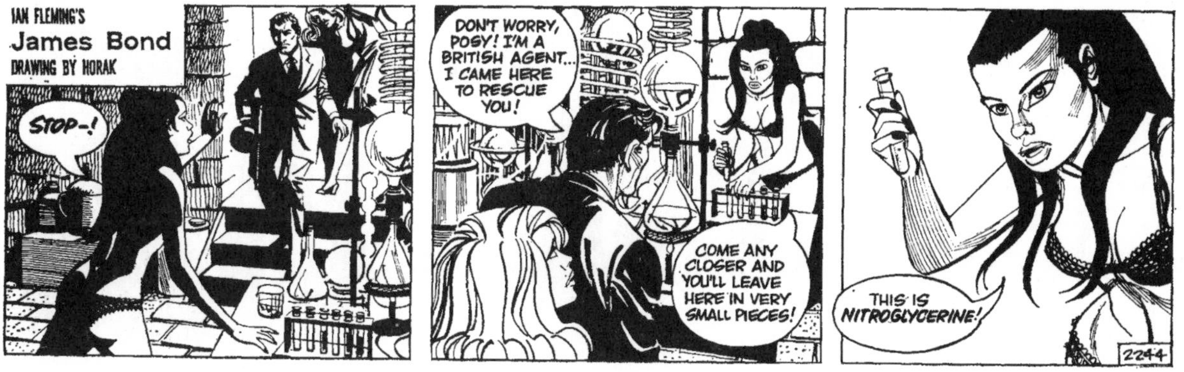
IAN FLEMING'S
James Bond
DRAWING BY HORAK
STOP—!
DON'T WORRY, POSY! I'M A BRITISH AGENT... I CAME HERE TO RESCUE YOU!
COME ANY CLOSER AND YOU'LL LEAVE HERE IN VERY SMALL PIECES!
THIS IS NITROGLYCERINE!
2244

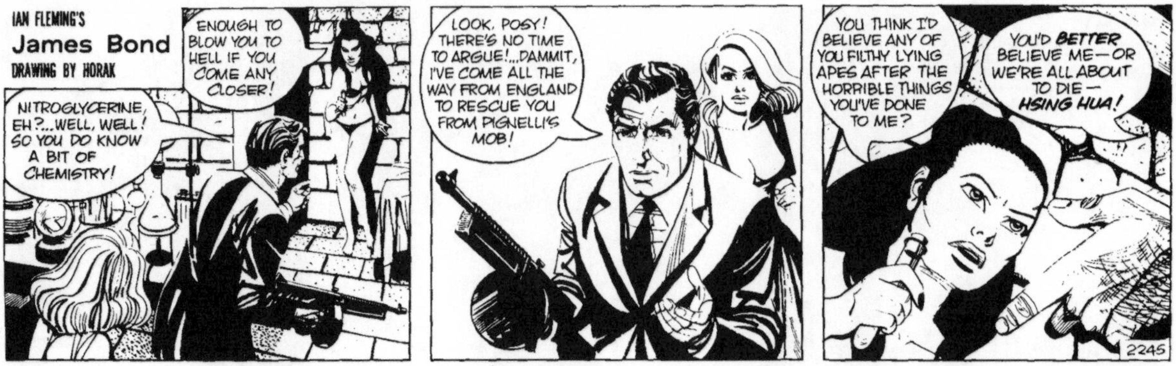
IAN FLEMING'S
James Bond
DRAWING BY HORAK
NITROGLYCERINE, EH?...WELL, WELL! SO YOU DO KNOW A BIT OF CHEMISTRY!
ENOUGH TO BLOW YOU TO HELL IF YOU COME ANY CLOSER!
LOOK, POSY! THERE'S NO TIME TO ARGUE!...DAMMIT, I'VE COME ALL THE WAY FROM ENGLAND TO RESCUE YOU FROM PIGNELLI'S MOB!
YOU THINK I'D BELIEVE ANY OF YOU FILTHY LYING APES AFTER THE HORRIBLE THINGS YOU'VE DONE TO ME?
YOU'D BETTER BELIEVE ME—OR WE'RE ALL ABOUT TO DIE—HSING HUA!
2245

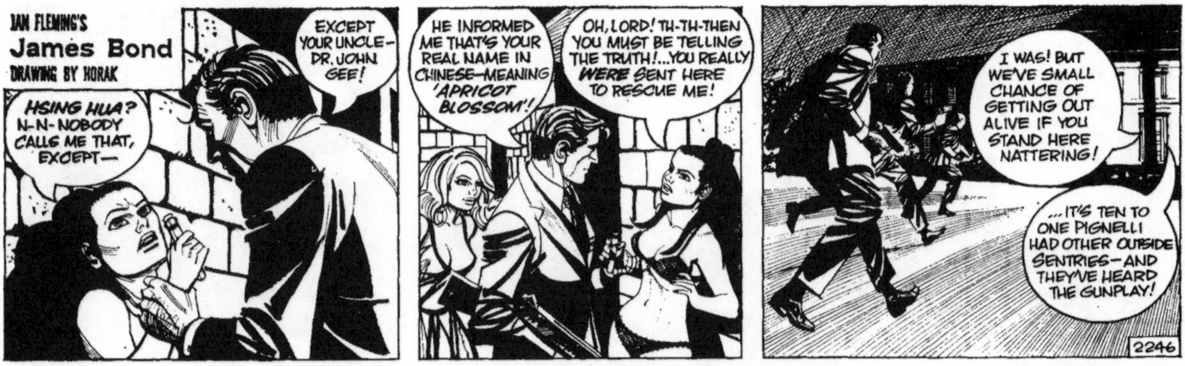
IAN FLEMING'S
James Bond
DRAWING BY HORAK
HSING HUA? N-N-NOBODY CALLS ME THAT, EXCEPT—
EXCEPT YOUR UNCLE-DR. JOHN GEE!
HE INFORMED ME THAT'S YOUR REAL NAME IN CHINESE—MEANING 'APRICOT BLOSSOM'!
OH, LORD! TH-TH-THEN YOU MUST BE TELLING THE TRUTH!...YOU REALLY WERE SENT HERE TO RESCUE ME!
I WAS! BUT WE'VE SMALL CHANCE OF GETTING OUT ALIVE IF YOU STAND HERE NATTERING!
...IT'S TEN TO ONE PIGNELLI HAD OTHER OUTSIDE SENTRIES—AND THEY'VE HEARD THE GUNPLAY!
2246

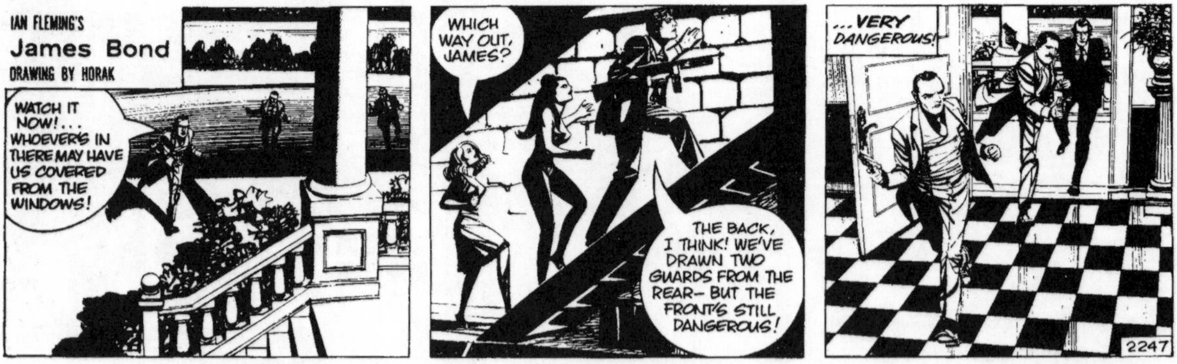
IAN FLEMING'S
James Bond
DRAWING BY HORAK
WATCH IT NOW!... WHOEVER'S IN THERE MAY HAVE US COVERED FROM THE WINDOWS!
WHICH WAY OUT, JAMES?
THE BACK, I THINK! WE'VE DRAWN TWO GUARDS FROM THE REAR—BUT THE FRONT'S STILL DANGEROUS!
...VERY DANGEROUS!
2247

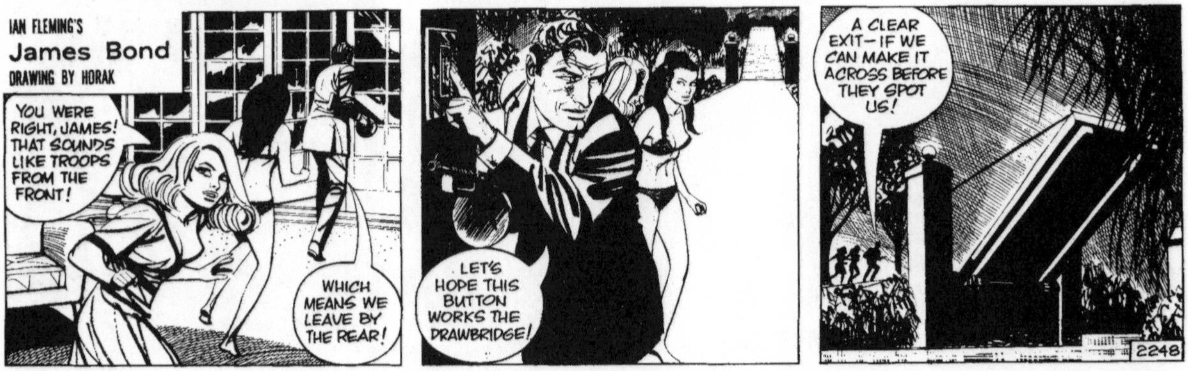
IAN FLEMING'S
James Bond
DRAWING BY HORAK
YOU WERE RIGHT, JAMES! THAT SOUNDS LIKE TROOPS FROM THE FRONT!
WHICH MEANS WE LEAVE BY THE REAR!
LET'S HOPE THIS BUTTON WORKS THE DRAWBRIDGE!
A CLEAR EXIT—IF WE CAN MAKE IT ACROSS BEFORE THEY SPOT US!
2248

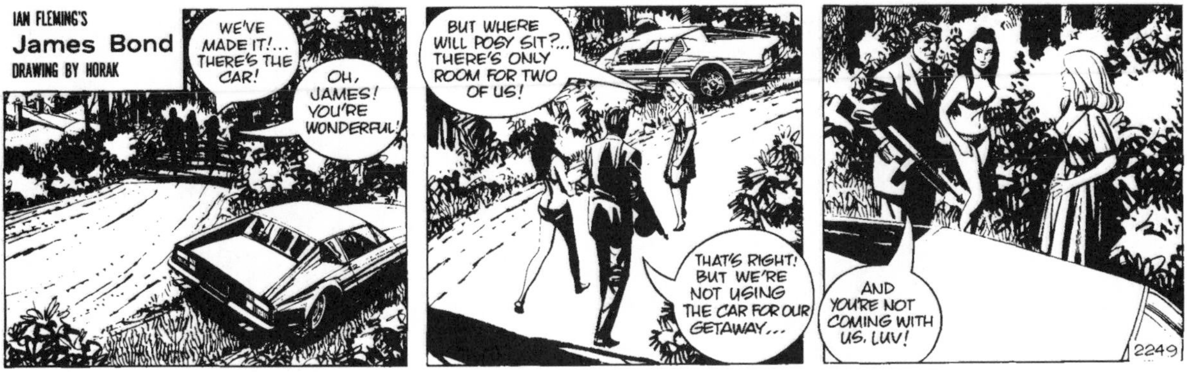
IAN FLEMING'S
James Bond
DRAWING BY HORAK
WE'VE MADE IT!... THERE'S THE CAR!
OH, JAMES! YOU'RE WONDERFUL!
BUT WHERE WILL POSY SIT?... THERE'S ONLY ROOM FOR TWO OF US!
THAT'S RIGHT! BUT WE'RE NOT USING THE CAR FOR OUR GETAWAY...
AND YOU'RE NOT COMING WITH US, LUV!
2249

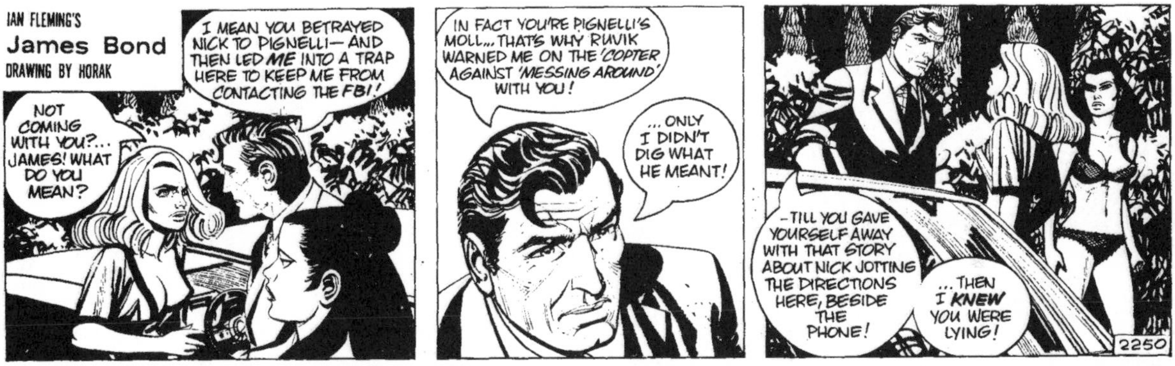
IAN FLEMING'S
James Bond
DRAWING BY HORAK
NOT COMING WITH YOU?... JAMES! WHAT DO YOU MEAN?
I MEAN YOU BETRAYED NICK TO PIGNELLI—AND THEN LED ME INTO A TRAP HERE TO KEEP ME FROM CONTACTING THE FBI!
IN FACT YOU'RE PIGNELLI'S MOLL... THAT'S WHY RUVIK WARNED ME ON THE 'COPTER AGAINST 'MESSING AROUND' WITH YOU!
...ONLY I DIDN'T DIG WHAT HE MEANT!
—TILL YOU GAVE YOURSELF AWAY WITH THAT STORY ABOUT NICK JOTTING THE DIRECTIONS HERE, BESIDE THE PHONE!
...THEN I KNEW YOU WERE LYING!
2250

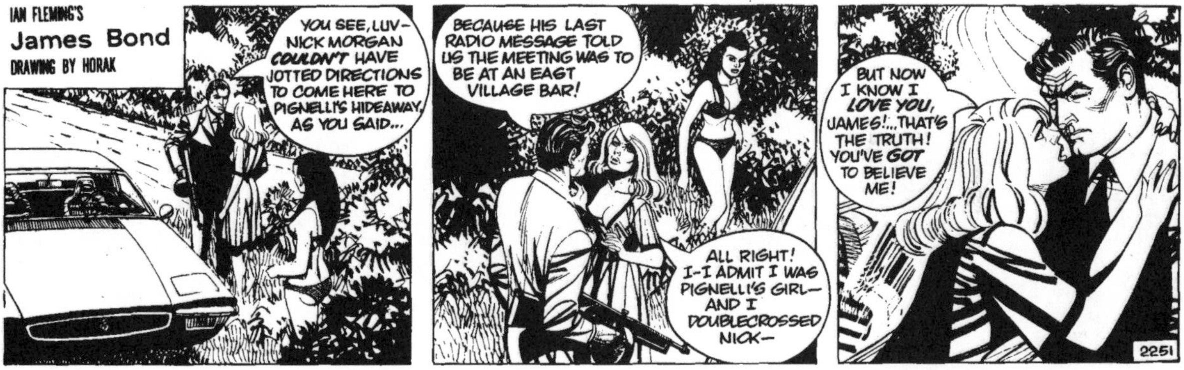
IAN FLEMING'S
James Bond
DRAWING BY HORAK
YOU SEE, LUV—NICK MORGAN COULDN'T HAVE JOTTED DIRECTIONS TO COME HERE TO PIGNELLI'S HIDEAWAY, AS YOU SAID...
BECAUSE HIS LAST RADIO MESSAGE TOLD US THE MEETING WAS TO BE AT AN EAST VILLAGE BAR!
ALL RIGHT! I-I ADMIT I WAS PIGNELLI'S GIRL—AND I DOUBLECROSSED NICK—
BUT NOW I KNOW I LOVE YOU, JAMES!... THAT'S THE TRUTH! YOU'VE GOT TO BELIEVE ME!
2251

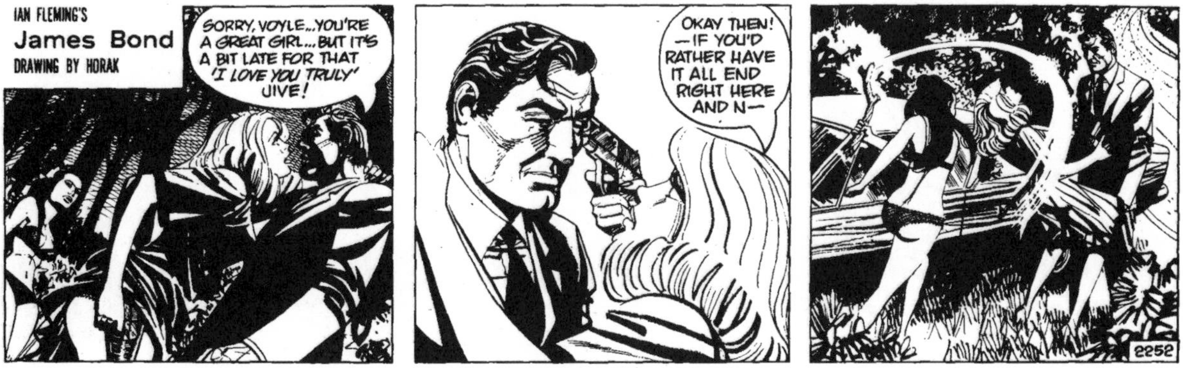
IAN FLEMING'S
James Bond
DRAWING BY HORAK
SORRY, VOYLE... YOU'RE A GREAT GIRL... BUT IT'S A BIT LATE FOR THAT 'I LOVE YOU TRULY' JIVE!
OKAY THEN! —IF YOU'D RATHER HAVE IT ALL END RIGHT HERE AND N—
2252

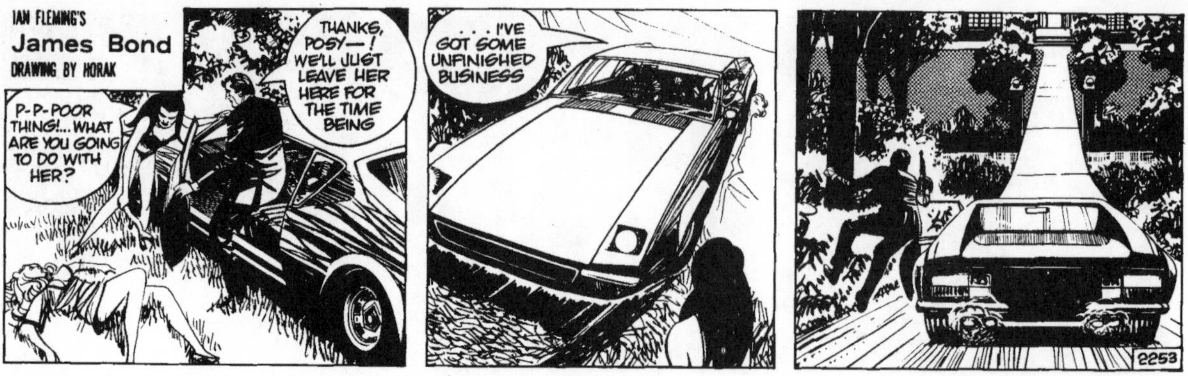
IAN FLEMING'S
James Bond
DRAWING BY HORAK
P-P-POOR THING!... WHAT ARE YOU GOING TO DO WITH HER?
THANKS, POSY—! WE'LL JUST LEAVE HER HERE FOR THE TIME BEING
. . . I'VE GOT SOME UNFINISHED BUSINESS
2253

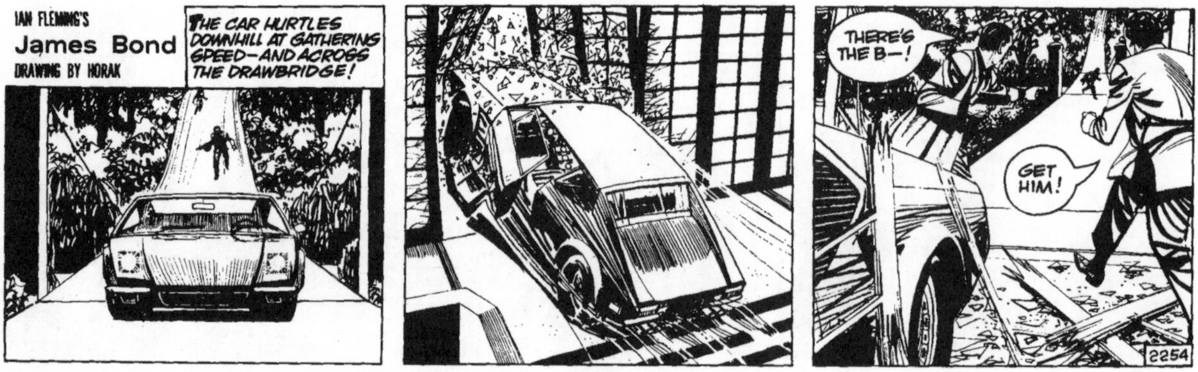
IAN FLEMING'S
James Bond
DRAWING BY HORAK
THE CAR HURTLES DOWNHILL AT GATHERING SPEED—AND ACROSS THE DRAWBRIDGE!
THERE'S THE B—!
GET HIM!
2254

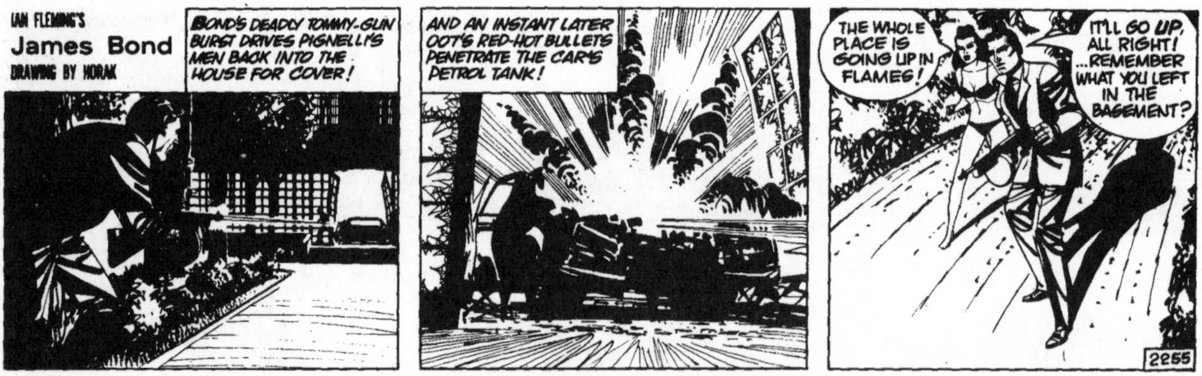
IAN FLEMING'S
James Bond
DRAWING BY HORAK
BOND'S DEADLY TOMMY-GUN BURST DRIVES PIGNELLI'S MEN BACK INTO THE HOUSE FOR COVER!
AND AN INSTANT LATER OOT'S RED-HOT BULLETS PENETRATE THE CAR'S PETROL TANK!
THE WHOLE PLACE IS GOING UP IN FLAMES!
IT'LL GO UP, ALL RIGHT! ...REMEMBER WHAT YOU LEFT IN THE BASEMENT?
2255

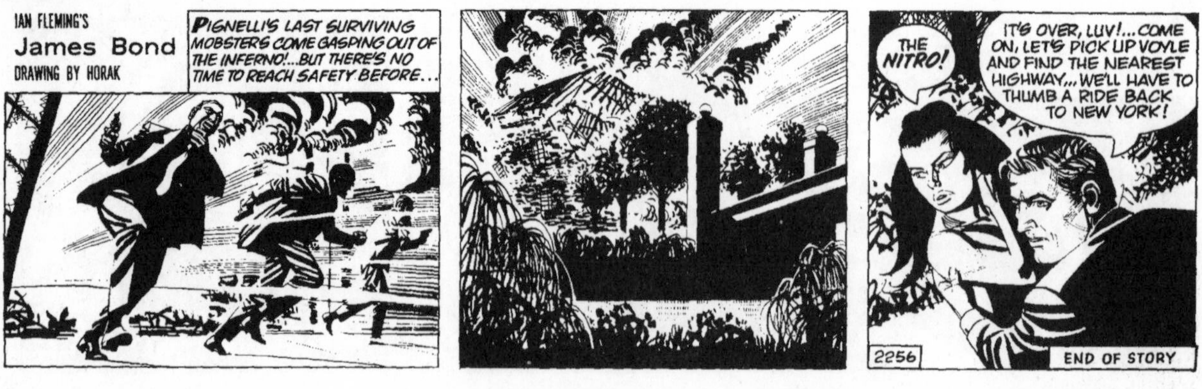
IAN FLEMING'S
James Bond
DRAWING BY HORAK
PIGNELLI'S LAST SURVIVING MOBSTERS COME GASPING OUT OF THE INFERNO!...BUT THERE'S NO TIME TO REACH SAFETY BEFORE...
THE NITRO!
IT'S OVER, LUV!...COME ON, LET'S PICK UP VOYLE AND FIND THE NEAREST HIGHWAY... WE'LL HAVE TO THUMB A RIDE BACK TO NEW YORK!
2256
END OF STORY

# THE GIRL MACHINE

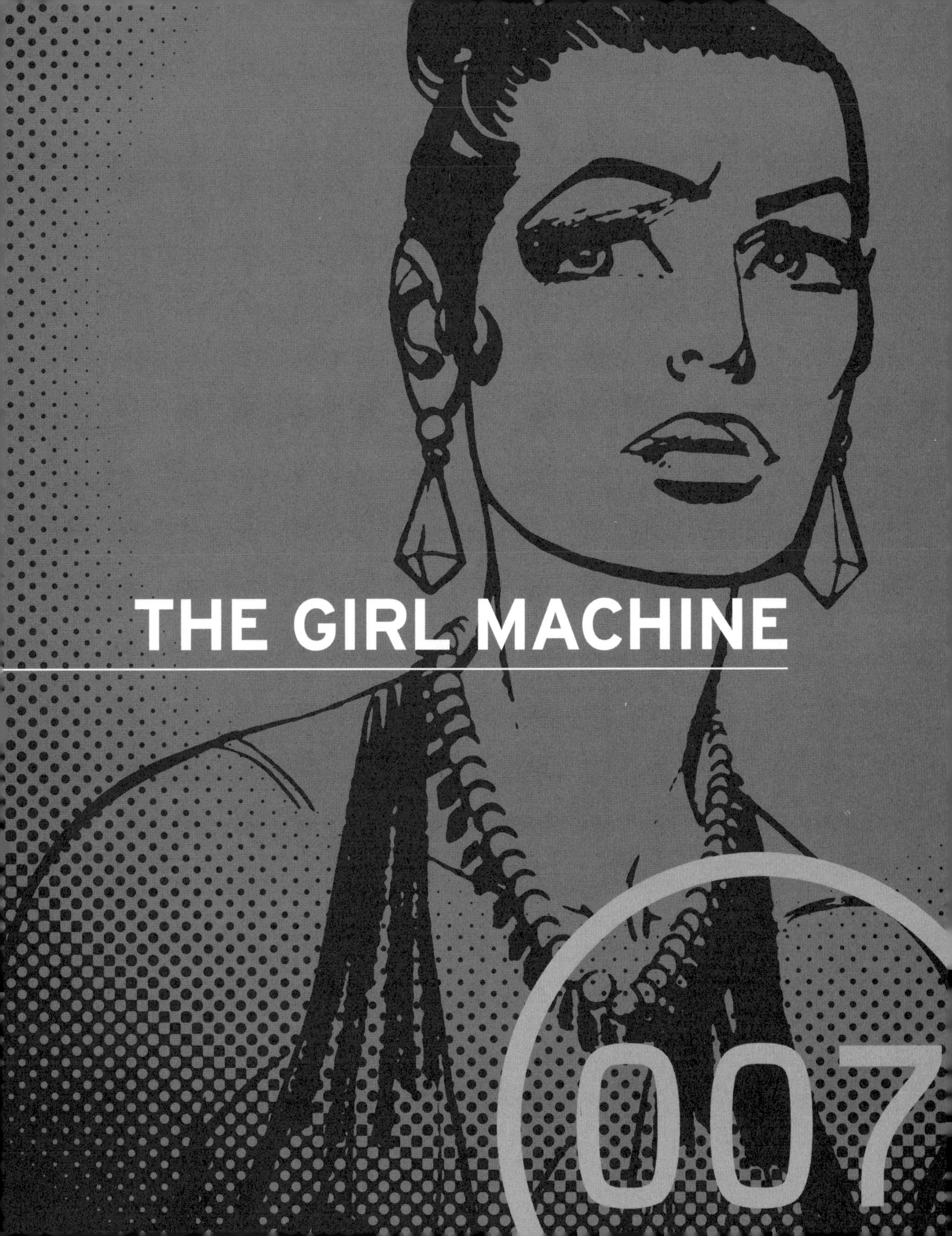
007

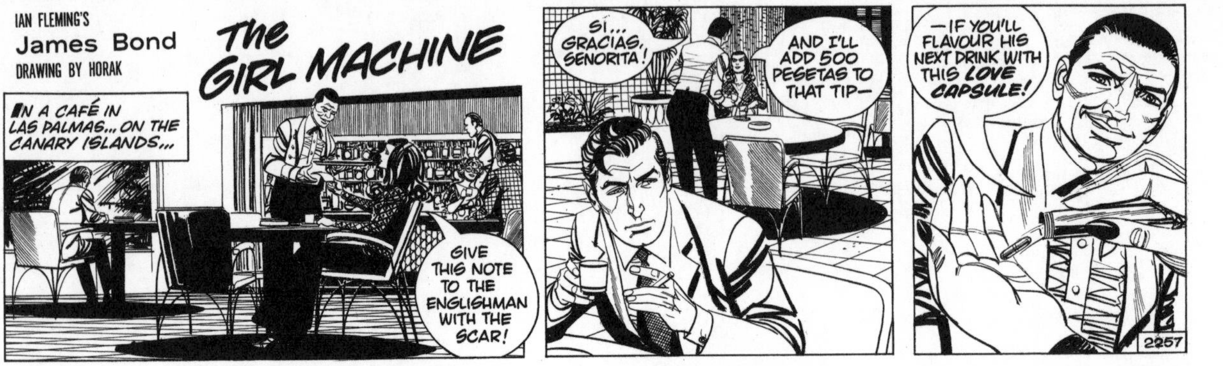
IAN FLEMING'S
James Bond
DRAWING BY HORAK
The GIRL MACHINE
IN A CAFÉ IN LAS PALMAS... ON THE CANARY ISLANDS...
GIVE THIS NOTE TO THE ENGLISHMAN WITH THE SCAR!
SÍ... GRACIAS, SENORITA!
AND I'LL ADD 500 PESETAS TO THAT TIP—
—IF YOU'LL FLAVOUR HIS NEXT DRINK WITH THIS LOVE CAPSULE!
2257

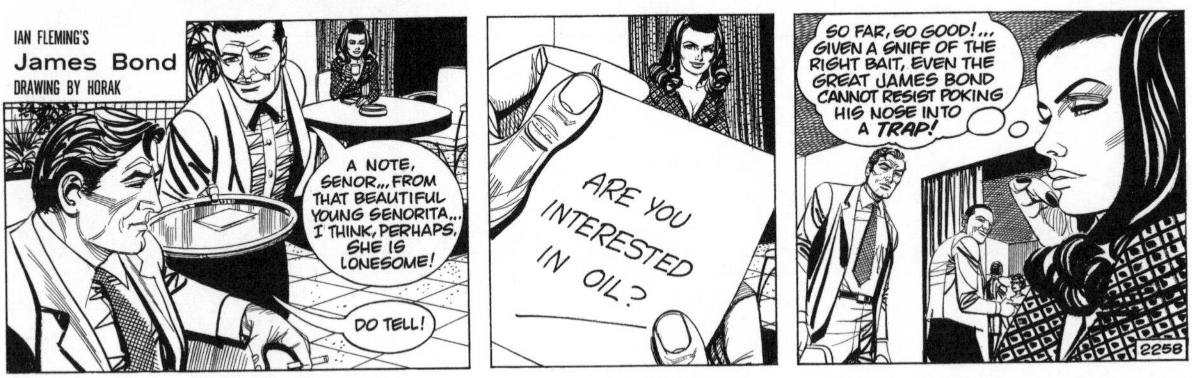
IAN FLEMING'S
James Bond
DRAWING BY HORAK
A NOTE, SENOR... FROM THAT BEAUTIFUL YOUNG SENORITA... I THINK, PERHAPS, SHE IS LONESOME!
DO TELL!
ARE YOU INTERESTED IN OIL?
SO FAR, SO GOOD!... GIVEN A SNIFF OF THE RIGHT BAIT, EVEN THE GREAT JAMES BOND CANNOT RESIST POKING HIS NOSE INTO A TRAP!
2258

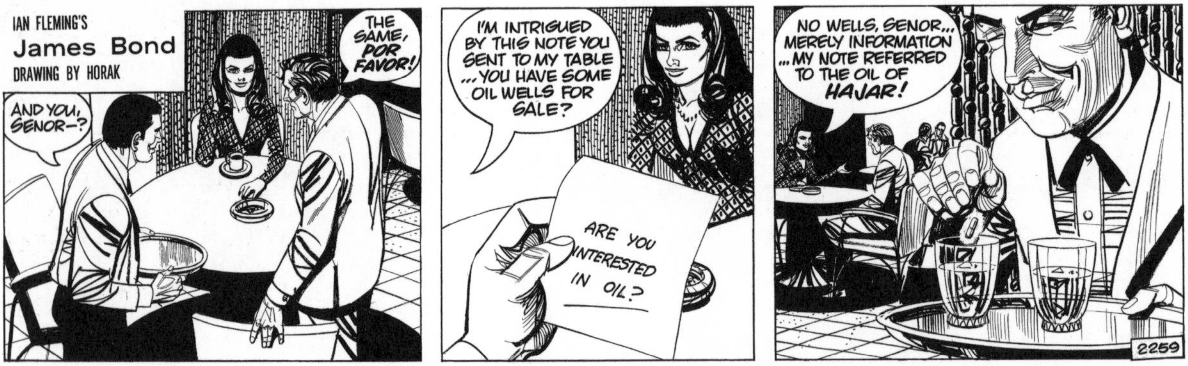
IAN FLEMING'S
James Bond
DRAWING BY HORAK
AND YOU, SENOR—?
THE SAME, POR FAVOR!
I'M INTRIGUED BY THIS NOTE YOU SENT TO MY TABLE ...YOU HAVE SOME OIL WELLS FOR SALE?
ARE YOU INTERESTED IN OIL?
NO WELLS, SENOR... MERELY INFORMATION ...MY NOTE REFERRED TO THE OIL OF HAJAR!
2259

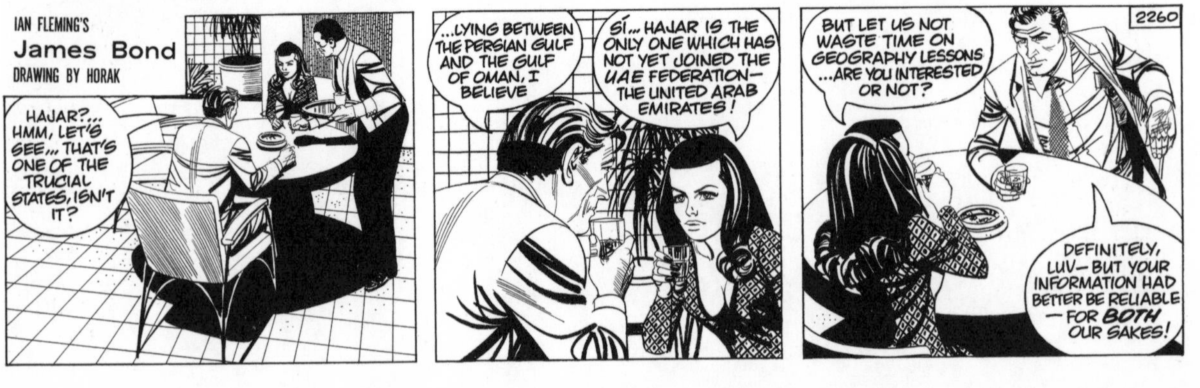
IAN FLEMING'S
James Bond
DRAWING BY HORAK
HAJAR?... HMM, LET'S SEE... THAT'S ONE OF THE TRUCIAL STATES, ISN'T IT?
...LYING BETWEEN THE PERSIAN GULF AND THE GULF OF OMAN, I BELIEVE
SÍ... HAJAR IS THE ONLY ONE WHICH HAS NOT YET JOINED THE UAE FEDERATION— THE UNITED ARAB EMIRATES!
2260
BUT LET US NOT WASTE TIME ON GEOGRAPHY LESSONS ...ARE YOU INTERESTED OR NOT?
DEFINITELY, LUV— BUT YOUR INFORMATION HAD BETTER BE RELIABLE —FOR BOTH OUR SAKES!

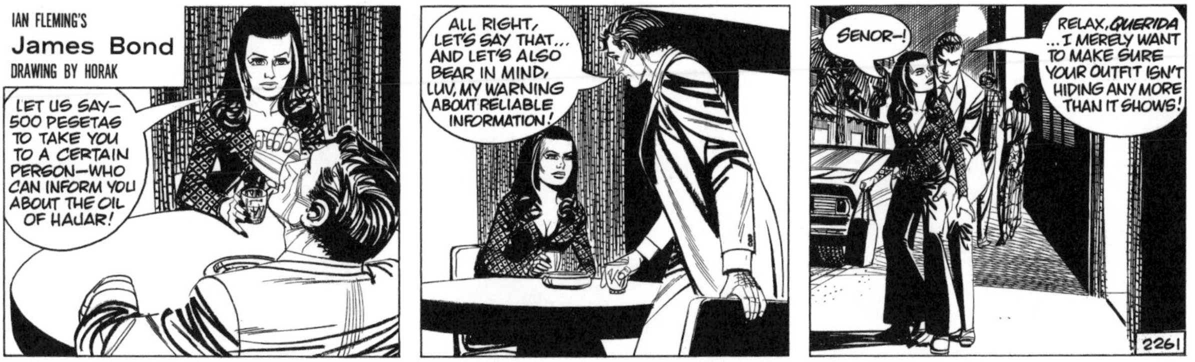
IAN FLEMING'S
James Bond
DRAWING BY HORAK
LET US SAY—500 PESETAS TO TAKE YOU TO A CERTAIN PERSON—WHO CAN INFORM YOU ABOUT THE OIL OF HAJAR!
ALL RIGHT, LET'S SAY THAT... AND LET'S ALSO BEAR IN MIND, LUV, MY WARNING ABOUT RELIABLE INFORMATION!
SENOR—!
RELAX, QUERIDA ...I MERELY WANT TO MAKE SURE YOUR OUTFIT ISN'T HIDING ANY MORE THAN IT SHOWS!
2261

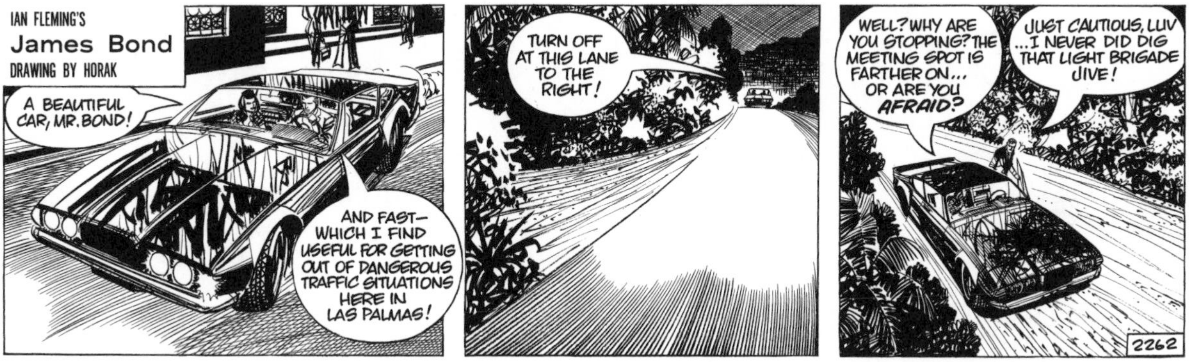
IAN FLEMING'S
James Bond
DRAWING BY HORAK
A BEAUTIFUL CAR, MR. BOND!
AND FAST—WHICH I FIND USEFUL FOR GETTING OUT OF DANGEROUS TRAFFIC SITUATIONS HERE IN LAS PALMAS!
TURN OFF AT THIS LANE TO THE RIGHT!
WELL? WHY ARE YOU STOPPING? THE MEETING SPOT IS FARTHER ON... OR ARE YOU AFRAID?
JUST CAUTIOUS, LUV ...I NEVER DID DIG THAT LIGHT BRIGADE JIVE!
2262

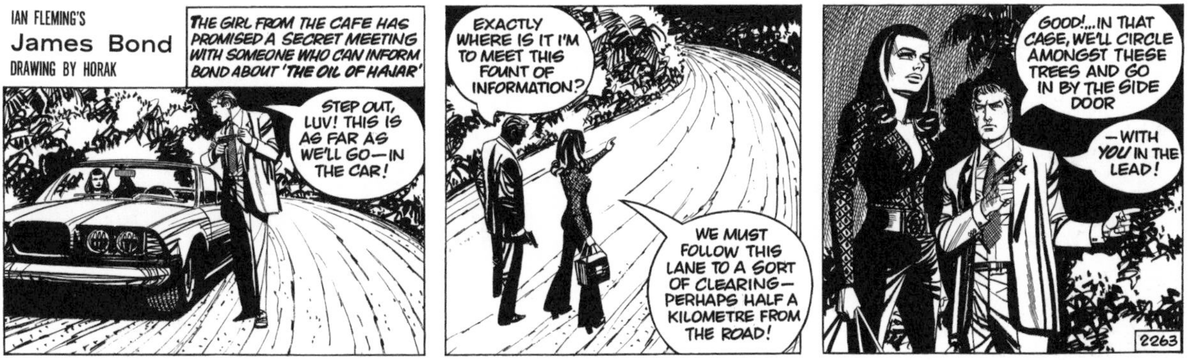
IAN FLEMING'S
James Bond
DRAWING BY HORAK
THE GIRL FROM THE CAFE HAS PROMISED A SECRET MEETING WITH SOMEONE WHO CAN INFORM BOND ABOUT 'THE OIL OF HAJAR'
STEP OUT, LUV! THIS IS AS FAR AS WE'LL GO—IN THE CAR!
EXACTLY WHERE IS IT I'M TO MEET THIS FOUNT OF INFORMATION?
WE MUST FOLLOW THIS LANE TO A SORT OF CLEARING—PERHAPS HALF A KILOMETRE FROM THE ROAD!
GOOD!...IN THAT CASE, WE'LL CIRCLE AMONGST THESE TREES AND GO IN BY THE SIDE DOOR
—WITH YOU IN THE LEAD!
2263

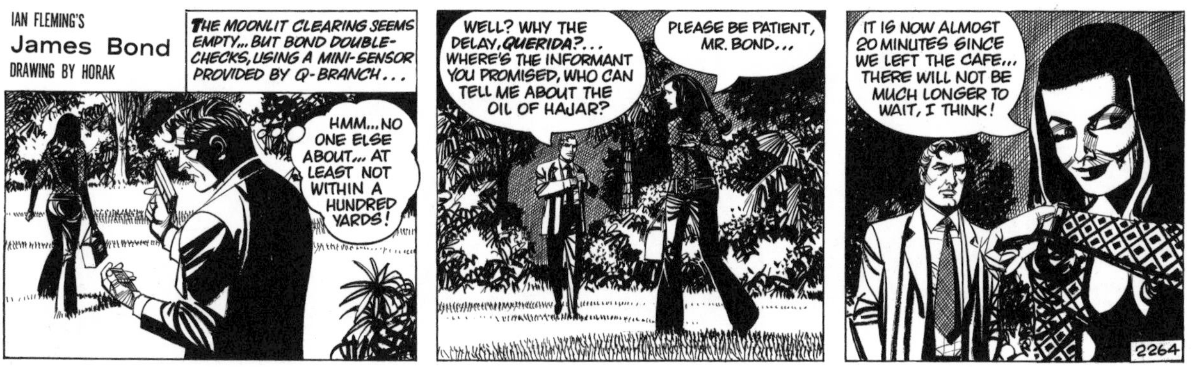
IAN FLEMING'S
James Bond
DRAWING BY HORAK
THE MOONLIT CLEARING SEEMS EMPTY... BUT BOND DOUBLE-CHECKS, USING A MINI-SENSOR PROVIDED BY Q-BRANCH...
HMM... NO ONE ELSE ABOUT... AT LEAST NOT WITHIN A HUNDRED YARDS!
WELL? WHY THE DELAY, QUERIDA?... WHERE'S THE INFORMANT YOU PROMISED, WHO CAN TELL ME ABOUT THE OIL OF HAJAR?
PLEASE BE PATIENT, MR. BOND...
IT IS NOW ALMOST 20 MINUTES SINCE WE LEFT THE CAFE... THERE WILL NOT BE MUCH LONGER TO WAIT, I THINK!
2264

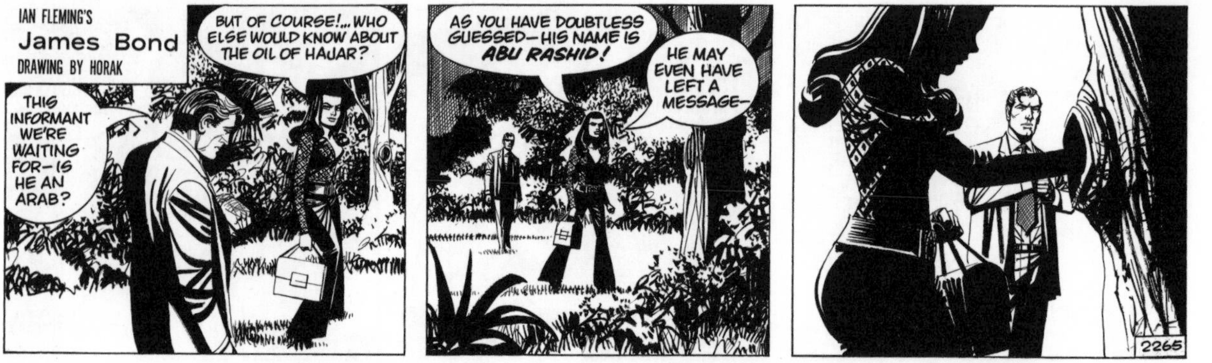
IAN FLEMING'S
James Bond
DRAWING BY HORAK
THIS INFORMANT WE'RE WAITING FOR—IS HE AN ARAB?
BUT OF COURSE!... WHO ELSE WOULD KNOW ABOUT THE OIL OF HAJAR?
AS YOU HAVE DOUBTLESS GUESSED—HIS NAME IS **ABU RASHID!**
HE MAY EVEN HAVE LEFT A MESSAGE—
2265

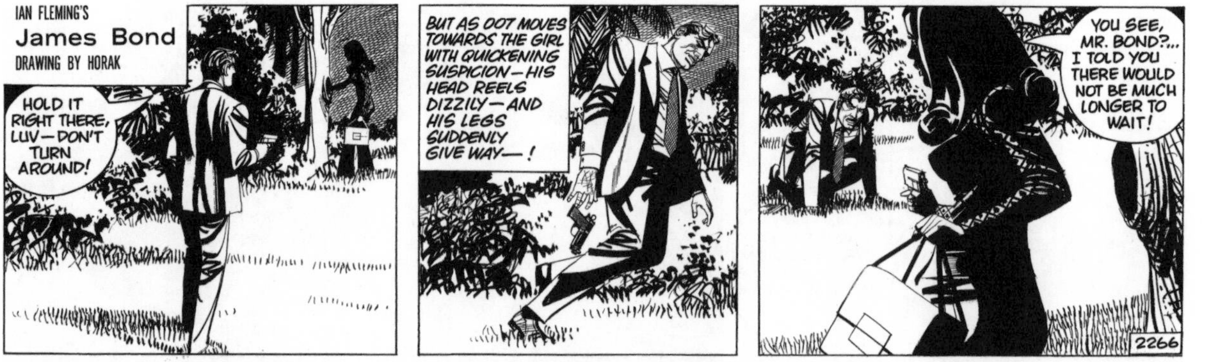
IAN FLEMING'S
James Bond
DRAWING BY HORAK
HOLD IT RIGHT THERE, LUV—DON'T TURN AROUND!
BUT AS 007 MOVES TOWARDS THE GIRL WITH QUICKENING SUSPICION—HIS HEAD REELS DIZZILY—AND HIS LEGS SUDDENLY GIVE WAY—!
YOU SEE, MR. BOND?... I TOLD YOU THERE WOULD NOT BE MUCH LONGER TO WAIT!
2266

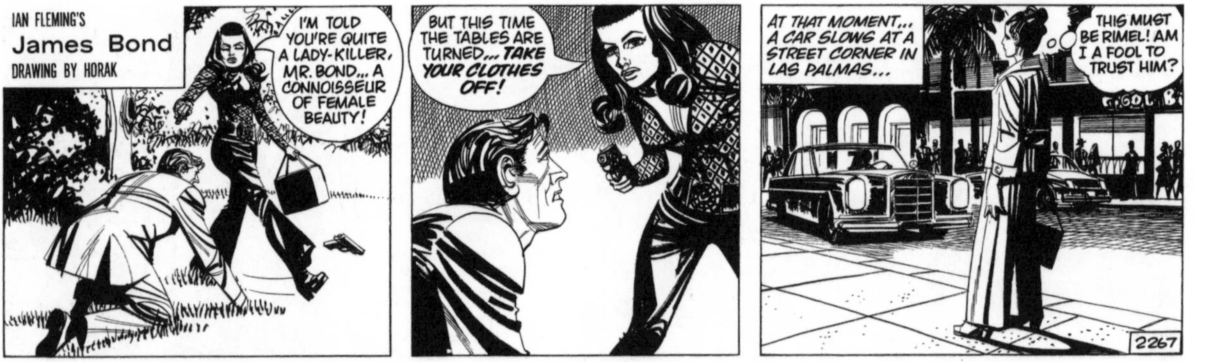
IAN FLEMING'S
James Bond
DRAWING BY HORAK
I'M TOLD YOU'RE QUITE A LADY-KILLER, MR. BOND... A CONNOISSEUR OF FEMALE BEAUTY!
BUT THIS TIME THE TABLES ARE TURNED... **TAKE YOUR CLOTHES OFF!**
AT THAT MOMENT... A CAR SLOWS AT A STREET CORNER IN LAS PALMAS...
THIS MUST BE RIMEL! AM I A FOOL TO TRUST HIM?
2267

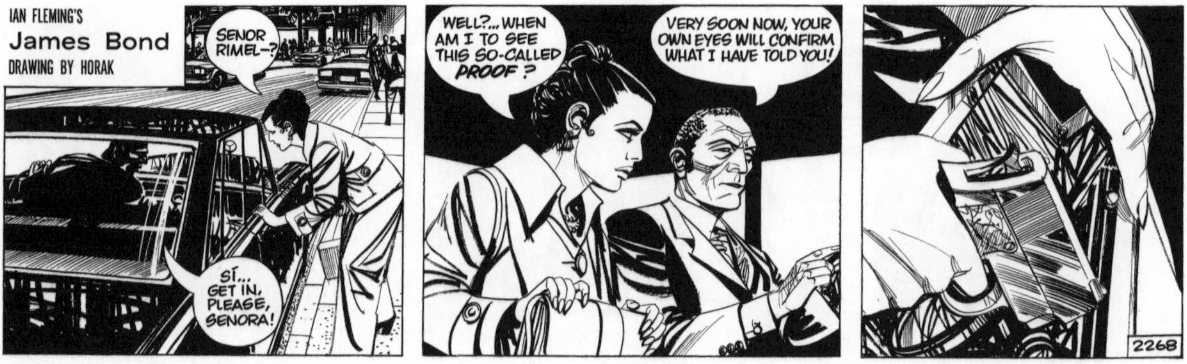
IAN FLEMING'S
James Bond
DRAWING BY HORAK
SENOR RIMEL—?
SÍ... GET IN, PLEASE, SENORA!
WELL?... WHEN AM I TO SEE THIS SO-CALLED **PROOF**?
VERY SOON NOW, YOUR OWN EYES WILL CONFIRM WHAT I HAVE TOLD YOU!
2268

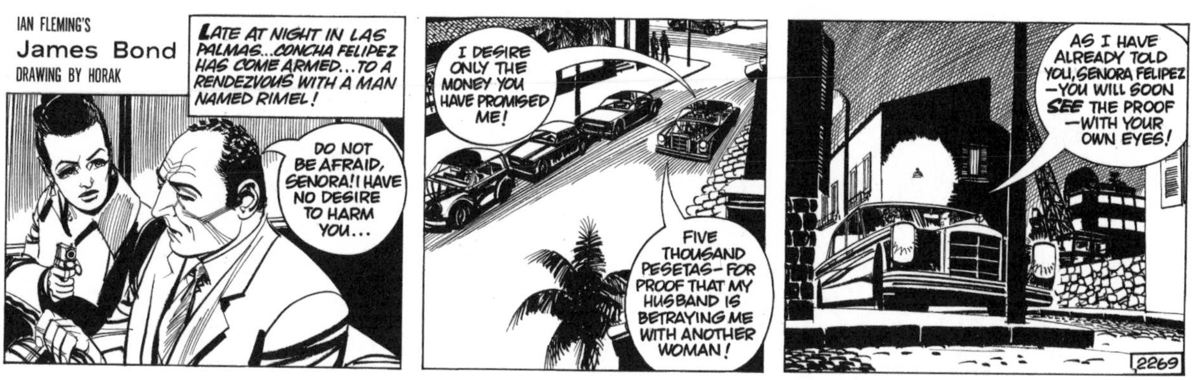
IAN FLEMING'S
James Bond
DRAWING BY HORAK
LATE AT NIGHT IN LAS PALMAS...CONCHA FELIPEZ HAS COME ARMED...TO A RENDEZVOUS WITH A MAN NAMED RIMEL!
DO NOT BE AFRAID, SENORA! I HAVE NO DESIRE TO HARM YOU...
I DESIRE ONLY THE MONEY YOU HAVE PROMISED ME!
FIVE THOUSAND PESETAS- FOR PROOF THAT MY HUSBAND IS BETRAYING ME WITH ANOTHER WOMAN!
AS I HAVE ALREADY TOLD YOU, SENORA FELIPEZ —YOU WILL SOON SEE THE PROOF —WITH YOUR OWN EYES!
2269

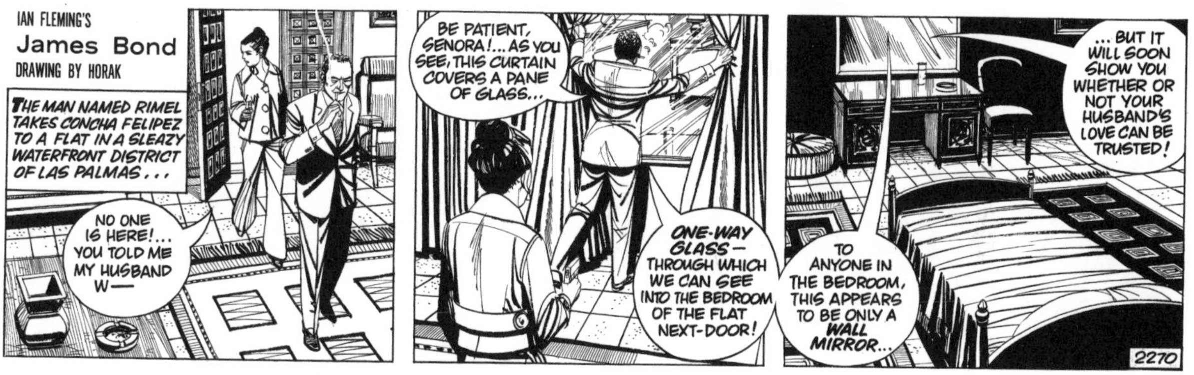
IAN FLEMING'S
James Bond
DRAWING BY HORAK
THE MAN NAMED RIMEL TAKES CONCHA FELIPEZ TO A FLAT IN A SLEAZY WATERFRONT DISTRICT OF LAS PALMAS...
NO ONE IS HERE!... YOU TOLD ME MY HUSBAND W—
BE PATIENT, SENORA!... AS YOU SEE, THIS CURTAIN COVERS A PANE OF GLASS...
ONE-WAY GLASS— THROUGH WHICH WE CAN SEE INTO THE BEDROOM OF THE FLAT NEXT-DOOR!
TO ANYONE IN THE BEDROOM, THIS APPEARS TO BE ONLY A WALL MIRROR...
...BUT IT WILL SOON SHOW YOU WHETHER OR NOT YOUR HUSBAND'S LOVE CAN BE TRUSTED!
2270

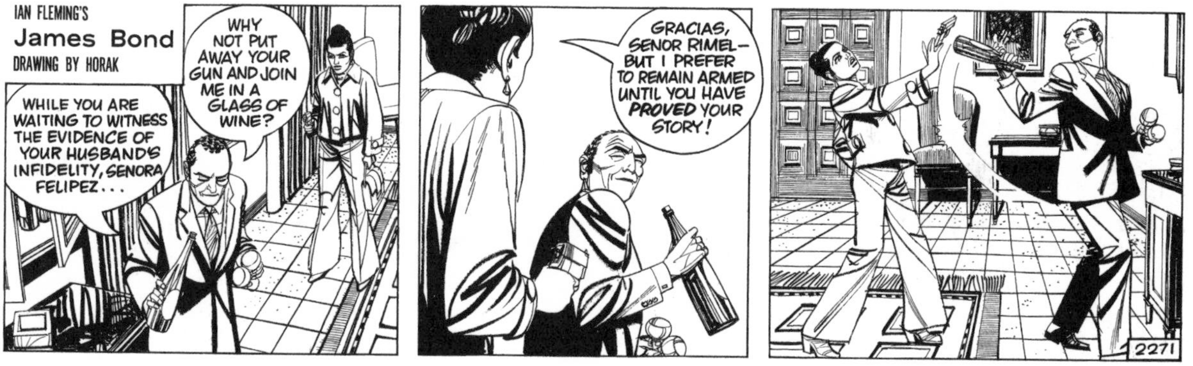
IAN FLEMING'S
James Bond
DRAWING BY HORAK
WHILE YOU ARE WAITING TO WITNESS THE EVIDENCE OF YOUR HUSBAND'S INFIDELITY, SENORA FELIPEZ...
WHY NOT PUT AWAY YOUR GUN AND JOIN ME IN A GLASS OF WINE?
GRACIAS, SENOR RIMEL- BUT I PREFER TO REMAIN ARMED UNTIL YOU HAVE PROVED YOUR STORY!
2271

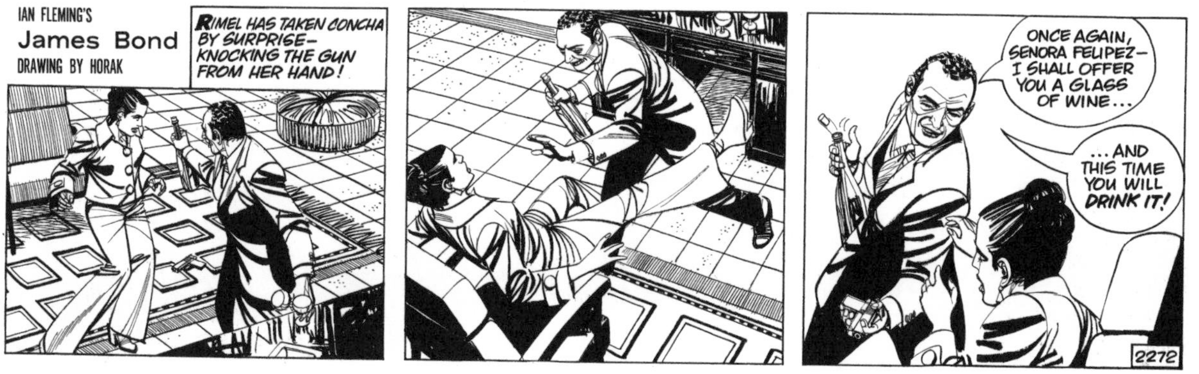
IAN FLEMING'S
James Bond
DRAWING BY HORAK
RIMEL HAS TAKEN CONCHA BY SURPRISE- KNOCKING THE GUN FROM HER HAND!
ONCE AGAIN, SENORA FELIPEZ— I SHALL OFFER YOU A GLASS OF WINE...
...AND THIS TIME YOU WILL DRINK IT!
2272

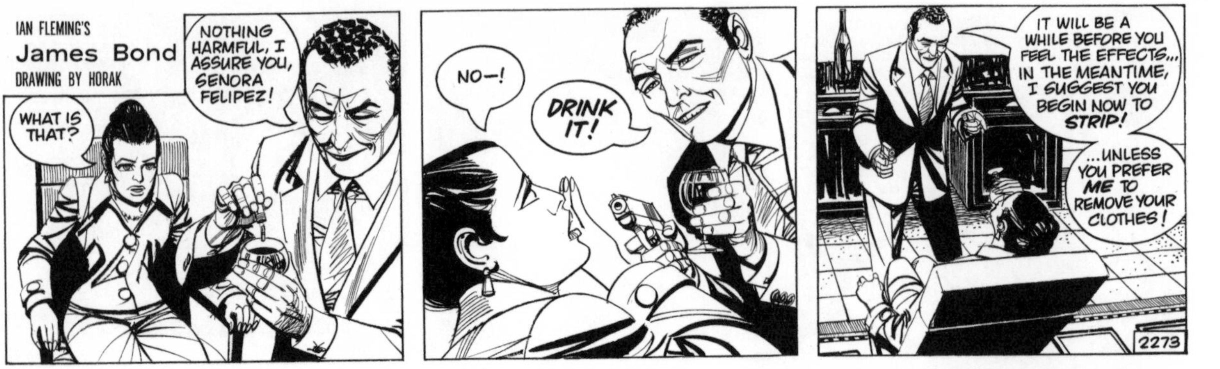
IAN FLEMING'S
James Bond
DRAWING BY HORAK
NOTHING HARMFUL, I ASSURE YOU, SENORA FELIPEZ!
WHAT IS THAT?
NO—!
DRINK IT!
IT WILL BE A WHILE BEFORE YOU FEEL THE EFFECTS... IN THE MEANTIME, I SUGGEST YOU BEGIN NOW TO STRIP!
...UNLESS YOU PREFER ME TO REMOVE YOUR CLOTHES!
2273

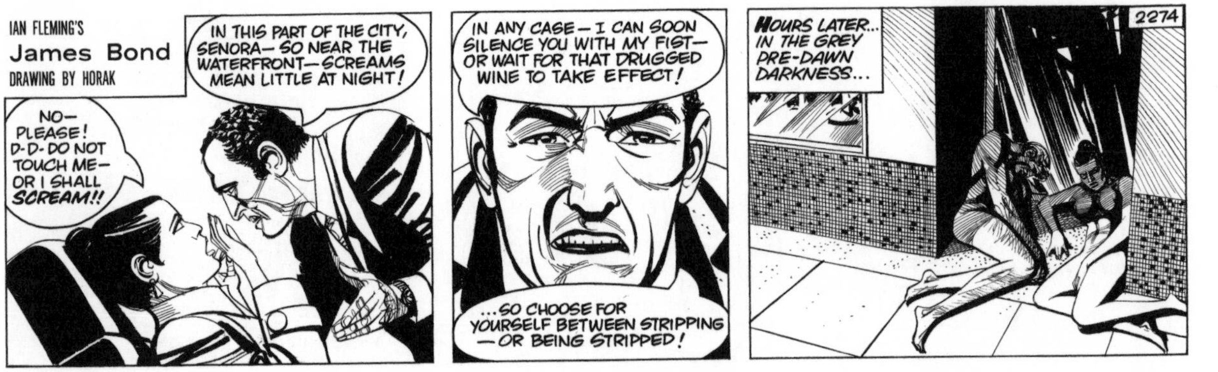
IAN FLEMING'S
James Bond
DRAWING BY HORAK
IN THIS PART OF THE CITY, SENORA— SO NEAR THE WATERFRONT—SCREAMS MEAN LITTLE AT NIGHT!
NO— PLEASE! D-D-DO NOT TOUCH ME— OR I SHALL SCREAM!!
IN ANY CASE—I CAN SOON SILENCE YOU WITH MY FIST— OR WAIT FOR THAT DRUGGED WINE TO TAKE EFFECT!
...SO CHOOSE FOR YOURSELF BETWEEN STRIPPING —OR BEING STRIPPED!
HOURS LATER... IN THE GREY PRE-DAWN DARKNESS...
2274

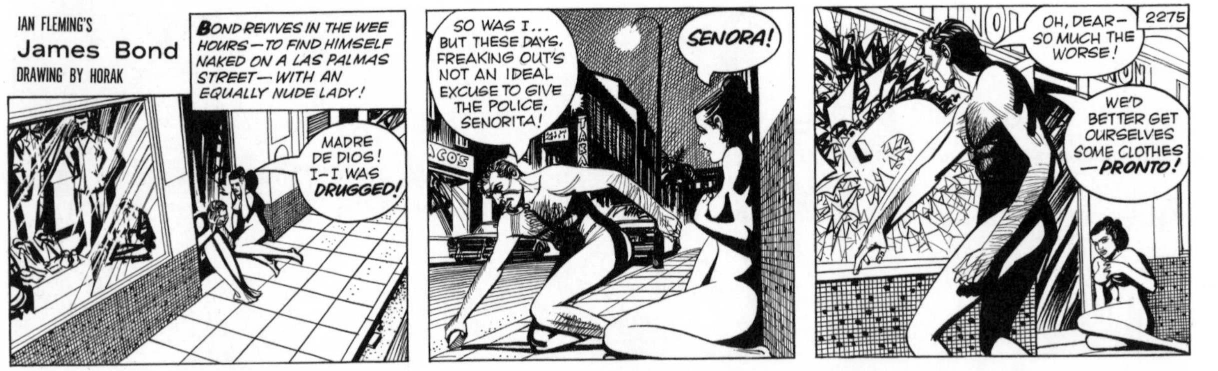
IAN FLEMING'S
James Bond
DRAWING BY HORAK
BOND REVIVES IN THE WEE HOURS—TO FIND HIMSELF NAKED ON A LAS PALMAS STREET—WITH AN EQUALLY NUDE LADY!
MADRE DE DIOS! I-I WAS DRUGGED!
SO WAS I... BUT THESE DAYS, FREAKING OUT'S NOT AN IDEAL EXCUSE TO GIVE THE POLICE, SENORITA!
SENORA!
OH, DEAR— SO MUCH THE WORSE!
WE'D BETTER GET OURSELVES SOME CLOTHES —PRONTO!
2275

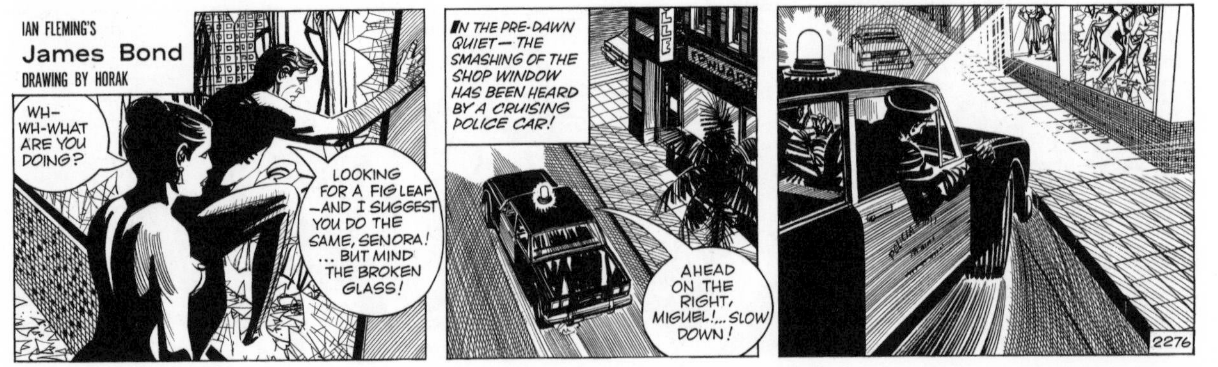
IAN FLEMING'S
James Bond
DRAWING BY HORAK
WH— WH-WHAT ARE YOU DOING?
LOOKING FOR A FIG LEAF —AND I SUGGEST YOU DO THE SAME, SENORA! ... BUT MIND THE BROKEN GLASS!
IN THE PRE-DAWN QUIET—THE SMASHING OF THE SHOP WINDOW HAS BEEN HEARD BY A CRUISING POLICE CAR!
AHEAD ON THE RIGHT, MIGUEL!... SLOW DOWN!
2276

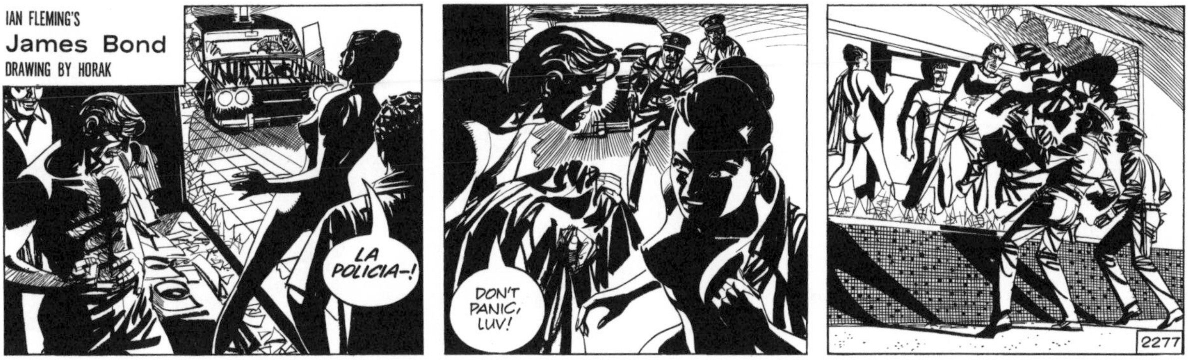
IAN FLEMING'S
James Bond
DRAWING BY HORAK
LA POLICIA–!
DON'T PANIC, LUV!
2277

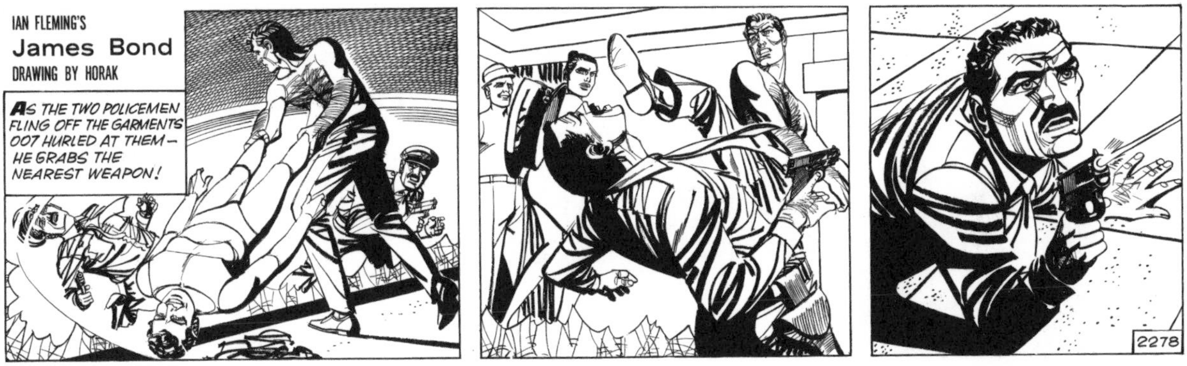
IAN FLEMING'S
James Bond
DRAWING BY HORAK
AS THE TWO POLICEMEN FLING OFF THE GARMENTS 007 HURLED AT THEM – HE GRABS THE NEAREST WEAPON!
2278

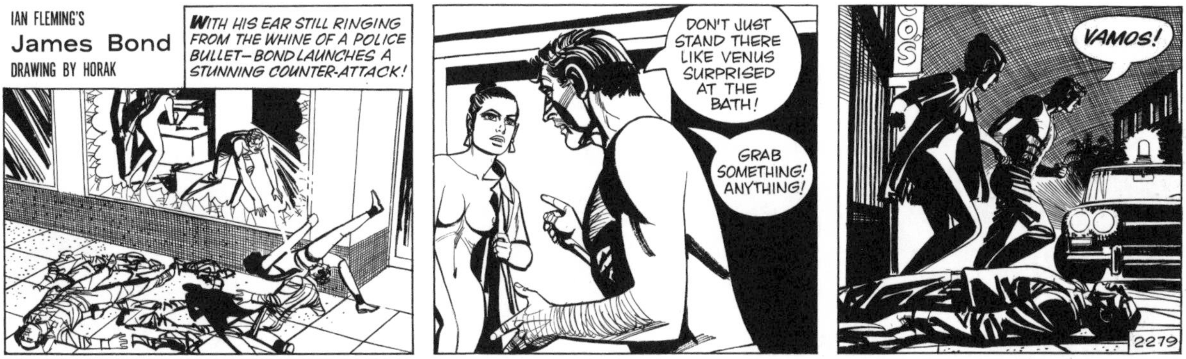
IAN FLEMING'S
James Bond
DRAWING BY HORAK
WITH HIS EAR STILL RINGING FROM THE WHINE OF A POLICE BULLET – BOND LAUNCHES A STUNNING COUNTER-ATTACK!
DON'T JUST STAND THERE LIKE VENUS SURPRISED AT THE BATH!
GRAB SOMETHING! ANYTHING!
VAMOS!
2279

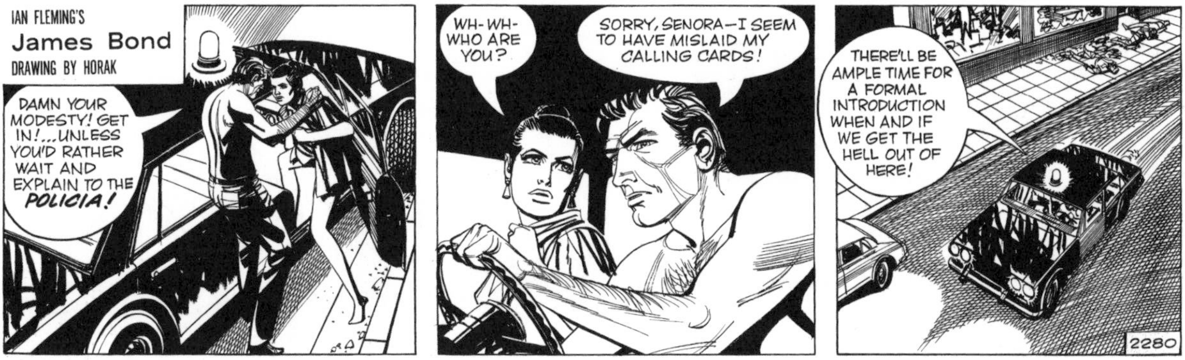
IAN FLEMING'S
James Bond
DRAWING BY HORAK
DAMN YOUR MODESTY! GET IN!...UNLESS YOU'D RATHER WAIT AND EXPLAIN TO THE POLICIA!
WH-WH-WHO ARE YOU?
SORRY, SENORA—I SEEM TO HAVE MISLAID MY CALLING CARDS!
THERE'LL BE AMPLE TIME FOR A FORMAL INTRODUCTION WHEN AND IF WE GET THE HELL OUT OF HERE!
2280

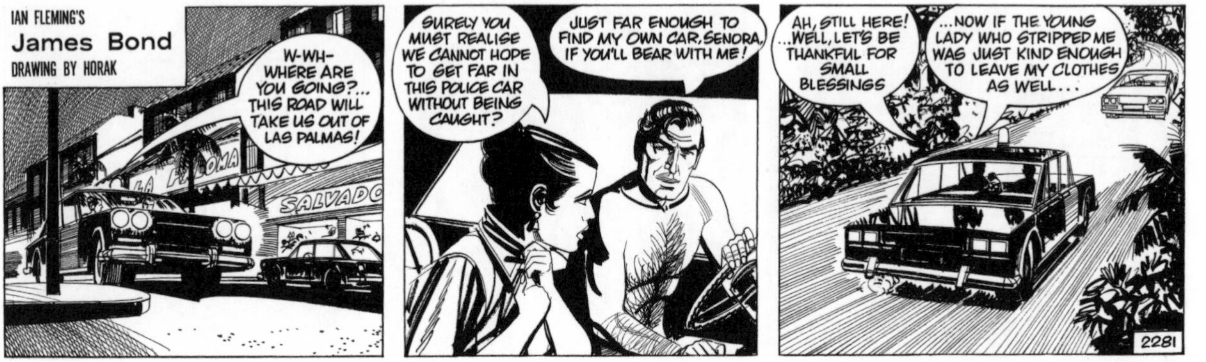
IAN FLEMING'S
James Bond
DRAWING BY HORAK
W-WH- WHERE ARE YOU GOING?... THIS ROAD WILL TAKE US OUT OF LAS PALMAS!
SALVADO
SURELY YOU MUST REALISE WE CANNOT HOPE TO GET FAR IN THIS POLICE CAR WITHOUT BEING CAUGHT?
JUST FAR ENOUGH TO FIND MY OWN CAR, SENORA, IF YOU'LL BEAR WITH ME!
AH, STILL HERE! ...WELL, LET'S BE THANKFUL FOR SMALL BLESSINGS
...NOW IF THE YOUNG LADY WHO STRIPPED ME WAS JUST KIND ENOUGH TO LEAVE MY CLOTHES AS WELL...
2281

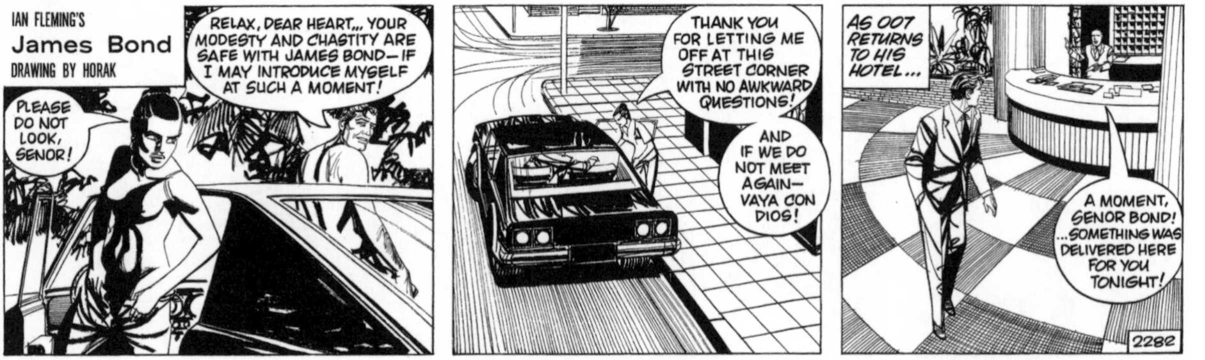
IAN FLEMING'S
James Bond
DRAWING BY HORAK
RELAX, DEAR HEART,.. YOUR MODESTY AND CHASTITY ARE SAFE WITH JAMES BOND—IF I MAY INTRODUCE MYSELF AT SUCH A MOMENT!
PLEASE DO NOT LOOK, SENOR!
THANK YOU FOR LETTING ME OFF AT THIS STREET CORNER WITH NO AWKWARD QUESTIONS!
AND IF WE DO NOT MEET AGAIN- VAYA CON DIOS!
AS 007 RETURNS TO HIS HOTEL...
A MOMENT, SENOR BOND! ...SOMETHING WAS DELIVERED HERE FOR YOU TONIGHT!
2282

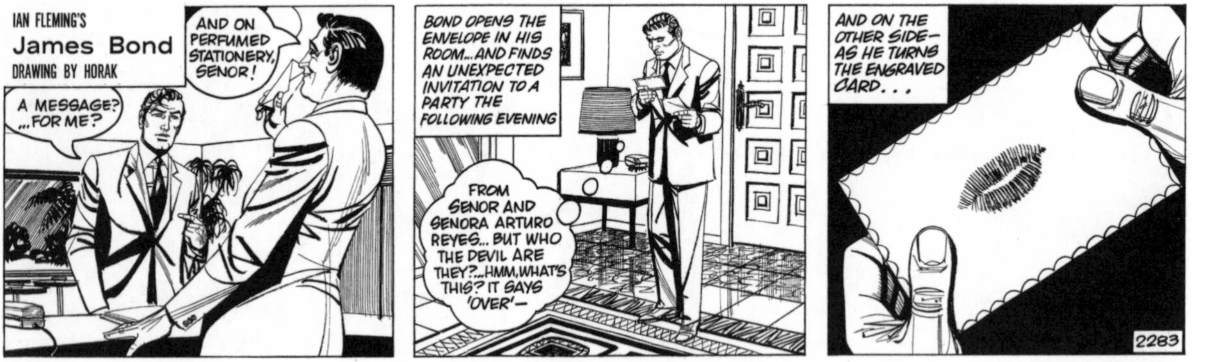
IAN FLEMING'S
James Bond
DRAWING BY HORAK
A MESSAGE? ...FOR ME?
AND ON PERFUMED STATIONERY, SENOR!
BOND OPENS THE ENVELOPE IN HIS ROOM...AND FINDS AN UNEXPECTED INVITATION TO A PARTY THE FOLLOWING EVENING
FROM SENOR AND SENORA ARTURO REYES... BUT WHO THE DEVIL ARE THEY?...HMM, WHAT'S THIS? IT SAYS 'OVER'—
AND ON THE OTHER SIDE— AS HE TURNS THE ENGRAVED CARD...
2283

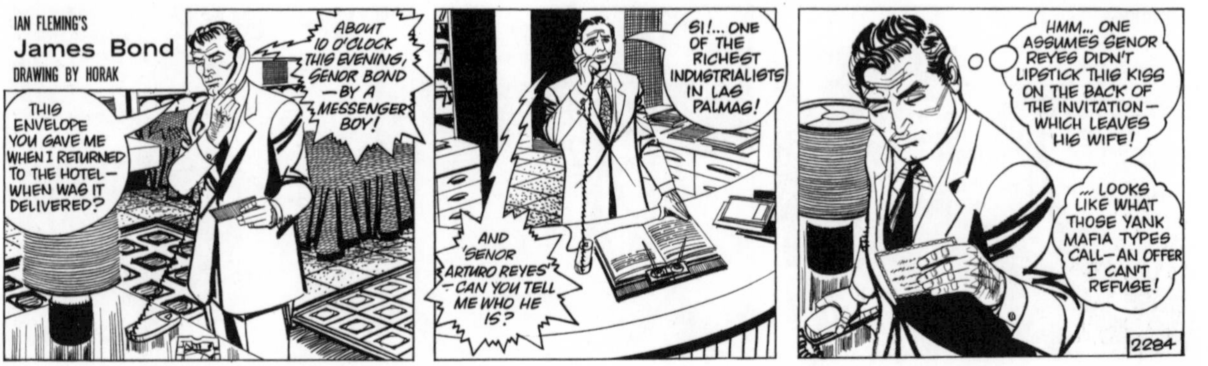
IAN FLEMING'S
James Bond
DRAWING BY HORAK
THIS ENVELOPE YOU GAVE ME WHEN I RETURNED TO THE HOTEL— WHEN WAS IT DELIVERED?
ABOUT 10 O'CLOCK THIS EVENING, SENOR BOND —BY A MESSENGER BOY!
AND 'SENOR ARTURO REYES' —CAN YOU TELL ME WHO HE IS?
SI!... ONE OF THE RICHEST INDUSTRIALISTS IN LAS PALMAS!
HMM... ONE ASSUMES SENOR REYES DIDN'T LIPSTICK THIS KISS ON THE BACK OF THE INVITATION— WHICH LEAVES HIS WIFE!
...LOOKS LIKE WHAT THOSE YANK MAFIA TYPES CALL—AN OFFER I CAN'T REFUSE!
2284

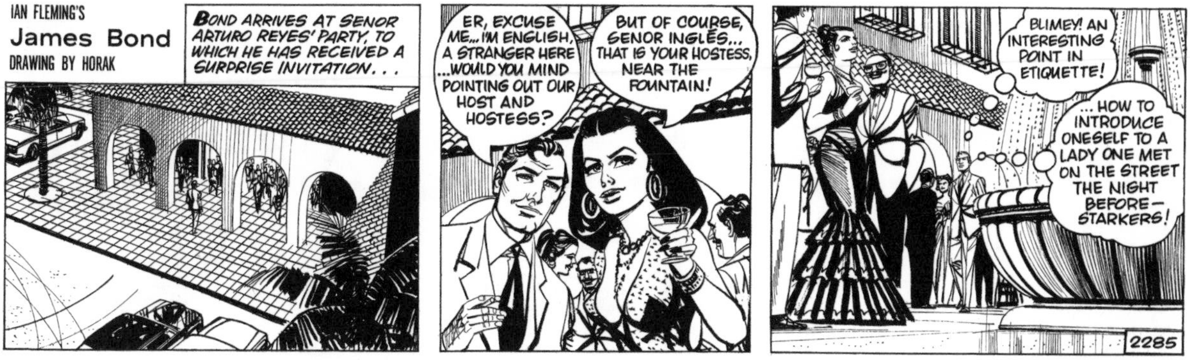
IAN FLEMING'S
James Bond
DRAWING BY HORAK
BOND ARRIVES AT SENOR ARTURO REYES' PARTY, TO WHICH HE HAS RECEIVED A SURPRISE INVITATION . . .
ER, EXCUSE ME... I'M ENGLISH, A STRANGER HERE ...WOULD YOU MIND POINTING OUT OUR HOST AND HOSTESS?
BUT OF COURSE, SENOR INGLÉS... THAT IS YOUR HOSTESS, NEAR THE FOUNTAIN!
BLIMEY! AN INTERESTING POINT IN ETIQUETTE!
...HOW TO INTRODUCE ONESELF TO A LADY ONE MET ON THE STREET THE NIGHT BEFORE— STARKERS!
2285

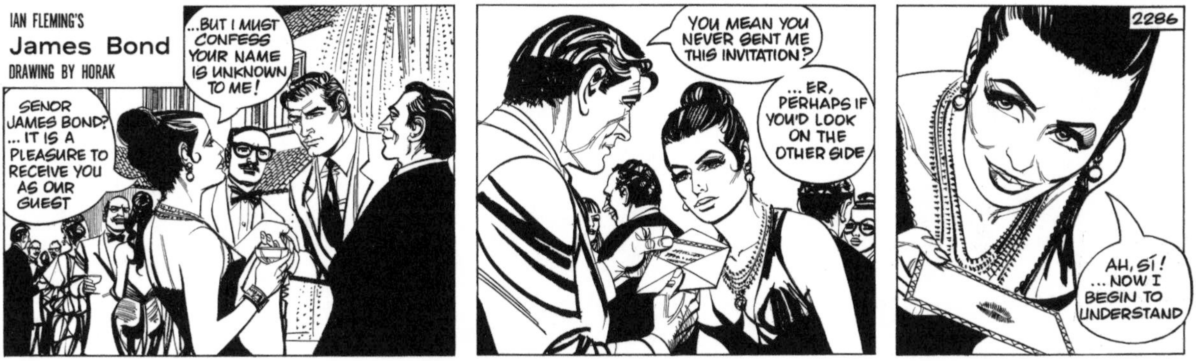
IAN FLEMING'S
James Bond
DRAWING BY HORAK
SENOR JAMES BOND? ... IT IS A PLEASURE TO RECEIVE YOU AS OUR GUEST
...BUT I MUST CONFESS YOUR NAME IS UNKNOWN TO ME!
YOU MEAN YOU NEVER SENT ME THIS INVITATION?
... ER, PERHAPS IF YOU'D LOOK ON THE OTHER SIDE
2286
AH, SÍ! ... NOW I BEGIN TO UNDERSTAND

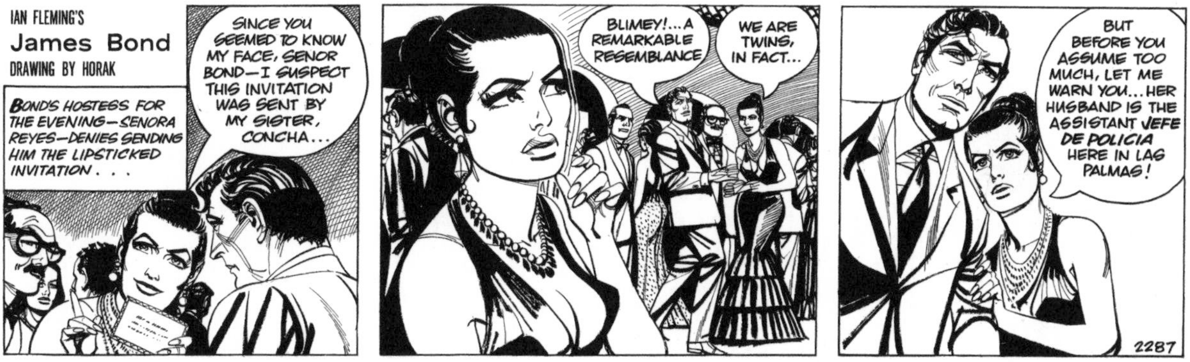
IAN FLEMING'S
James Bond
DRAWING BY HORAK
BOND'S HOSTESS FOR THE EVENING—SENORA REYES—DENIES SENDING HIM THE LIPSTICKED INVITATION . . .
SINCE YOU SEEMED TO KNOW MY FACE, SENOR BOND—I SUSPECT THIS INVITATION WAS SENT BY MY SISTER, CONCHA...
BLIMEY!... A REMARKABLE RESEMBLANCE
WE ARE TWINS, IN FACT...
BUT BEFORE YOU ASSUME TOO MUCH, LET ME WARN YOU... HER HUSBAND IS THE ASSISTANT JEFE DE POLICIA HERE IN LAS PALMAS!
2287

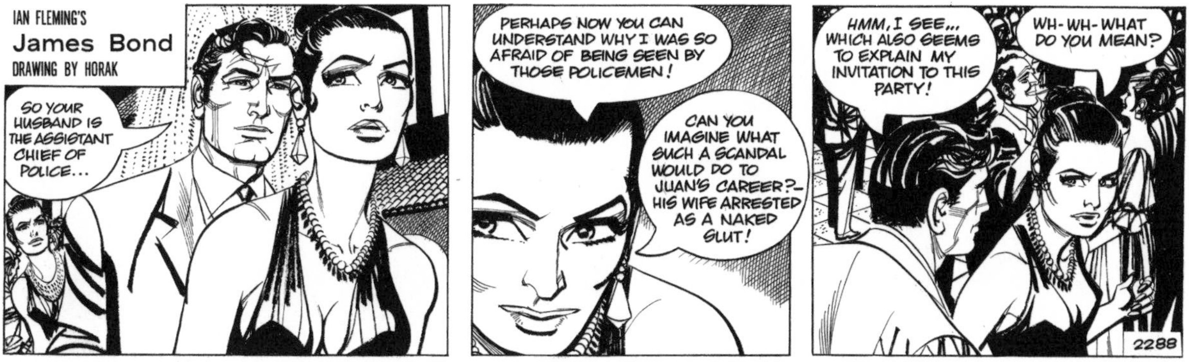
IAN FLEMING'S
James Bond
DRAWING BY HORAK
SO YOUR HUSBAND IS THE ASSISTANT CHIEF OF POLICE...
PERHAPS NOW YOU CAN UNDERSTAND WHY I WAS SO AFRAID OF BEING SEEN BY THOSE POLICEMEN!
CAN YOU IMAGINE WHAT SUCH A SCANDAL WOULD DO TO JUAN'S CAREER?— HIS WIFE ARRESTED AS A NAKED SLUT!
HMM, I SEE... WHICH ALSO SEEMS TO EXPLAIN MY INVITATION TO THIS PARTY!
WH-WH-WHAT DO YOU MEAN?
2288

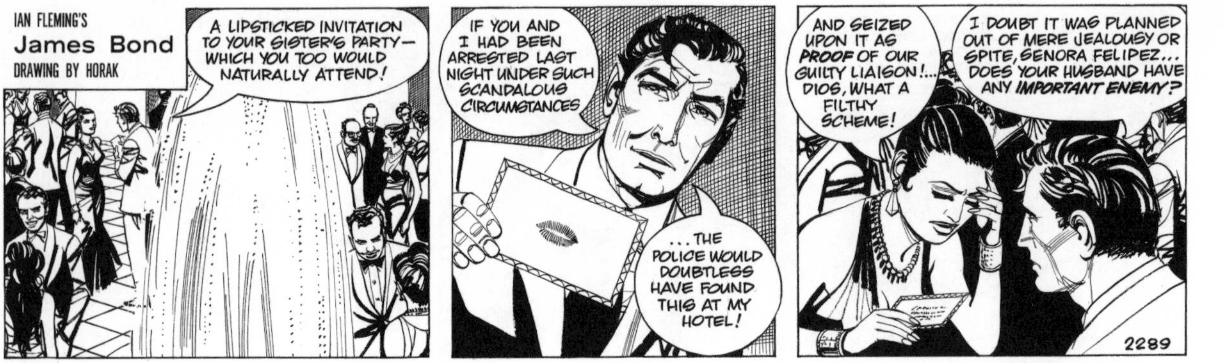
IAN FLEMING'S
James Bond
DRAWING BY HORAK
A LIPSTICKED INVITATION TO YOUR SISTER'S PARTY—WHICH YOU TOO WOULD NATURALLY ATTEND!
IF YOU AND I HAD BEEN ARRESTED LAST NIGHT UNDER SUCH SCANDALOUS CIRCUMSTANCES
...THE POLICE WOULD DOUBTLESS HAVE FOUND THIS AT MY HOTEL!
AND SEIZED UPON IT AS PROOF OF OUR GUILTY LIAISON!... DIOS, WHAT A FILTHY SCHEME!
I DOUBT IT WAS PLANNED OUT OF MERE JEALOUSY OR SPITE, SENORA FELIPEZ... DOES YOUR HUSBAND HAVE ANY IMPORTANT ENEMY?
2289

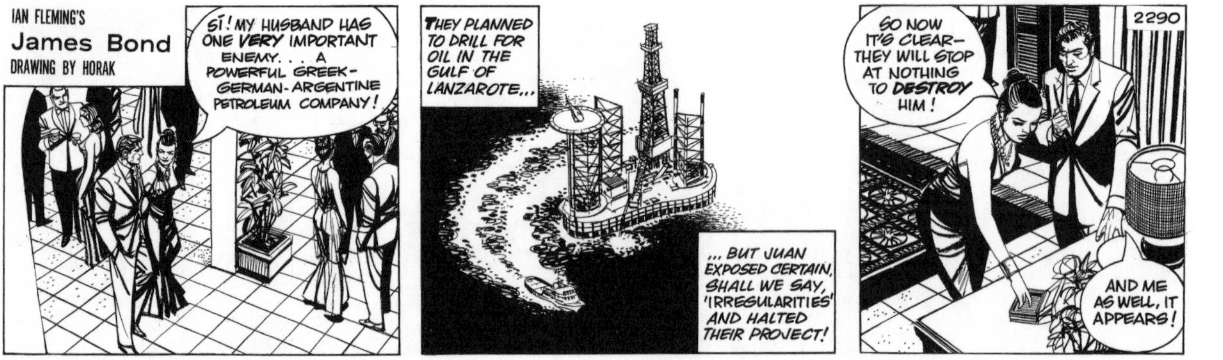
IAN FLEMING'S
James Bond
DRAWING BY HORAK
SÍ! MY HUSBAND HAS ONE VERY IMPORTANT ENEMY... A POWERFUL GREEK-GERMAN-ARGENTINE PETROLEUM COMPANY!
THEY PLANNED TO DRILL FOR OIL IN THE GULF OF LANZAROTE...
...BUT JUAN EXPOSED CERTAIN, SHALL WE SAY, 'IRREGULARITIES' AND HALTED THEIR PROJECT!
2290
SO NOW IT'S CLEAR—THEY WILL STOP AT NOTHING TO DESTROY HIM!
AND ME AS WELL, IT APPEARS!

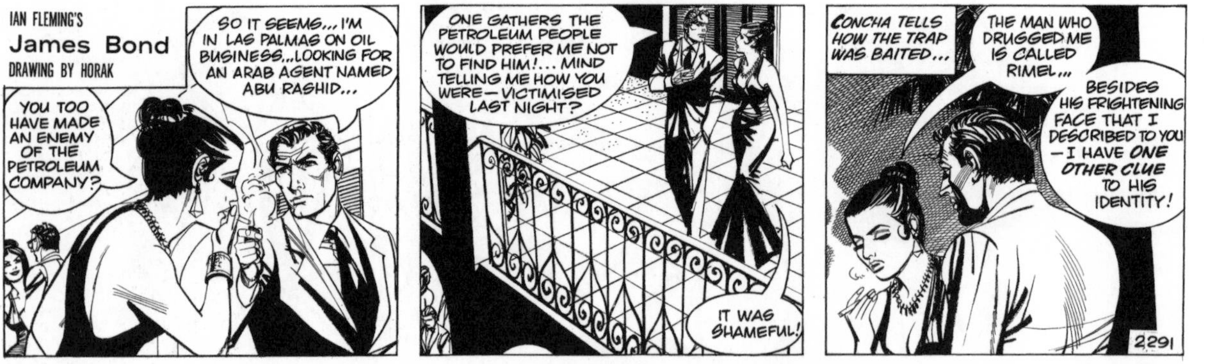
IAN FLEMING'S
James Bond
DRAWING BY HORAK
YOU TOO HAVE MADE AN ENEMY OF THE PETROLEUM COMPANY?
SO IT SEEMS... I'M IN LAS PALMAS ON OIL BUSINESS... LOOKING FOR AN ARAB AGENT NAMED ABU RASHID...
ONE GATHERS THE PETROLEUM PEOPLE WOULD PREFER ME NOT TO FIND HIM!... MIND TELLING ME HOW YOU WERE—VICTIMISED LAST NIGHT?
IT WAS SHAMEFUL!
CONCHA TELLS HOW THE TRAP WAS BAITED...
THE MAN WHO DRUGGED ME IS CALLED RIMEL...
BESIDES HIS FRIGHTENING FACE THAT I DESCRIBED TO YOU—I HAVE ONE OTHER CLUE TO HIS IDENTITY!
2291

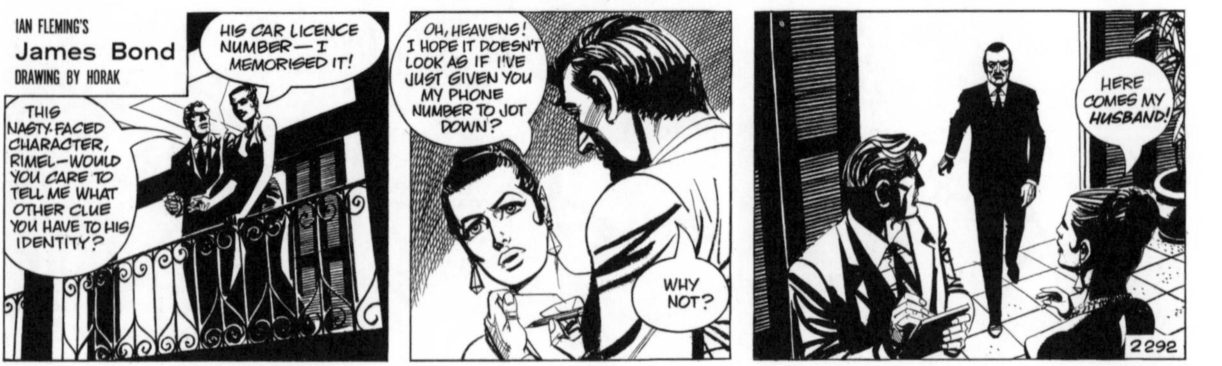
IAN FLEMING'S
James Bond
DRAWING BY HORAK
THIS NASTY-FACED CHARACTER, RIMEL—WOULD YOU CARE TO TELL ME WHAT OTHER CLUE YOU HAVE TO HIS IDENTITY?
HIS CAR LICENCE NUMBER—I MEMORISED IT!
OH, HEAVENS! I HOPE IT DOESN'T LOOK AS IF I'VE JUST GIVEN YOU MY PHONE NUMBER TO JOT DOWN?
WHY NOT?
HERE COMES MY HUSBAND!
2292

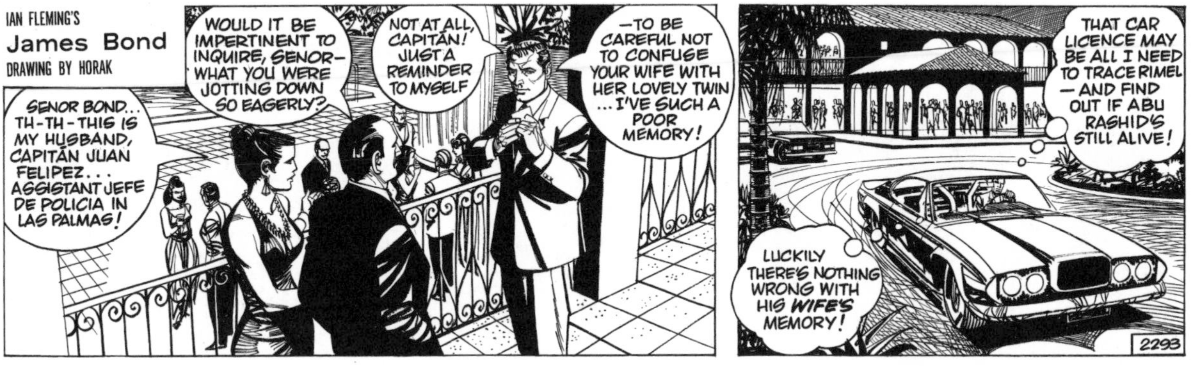
IAN FLEMING'S
James Bond
DRAWING BY HORAK
SENOR BOND... TH-TH-THIS IS MY HUSBAND, CAPITÁN JUAN FELIPEZ... ASSISTANT JEFE DE POLICIA IN LAS PALMAS!
WOULD IT BE IMPERTINENT TO INQUIRE, SENOR—WHAT YOU WERE JOTTING DOWN SO EAGERLY?
NOT AT ALL, CAPITÁN! JUST A REMINDER TO MYSELF
—TO BE CAREFUL NOT TO CONFUSE YOUR WIFE WITH HER LOVELY TWIN ...I'VE SUCH A POOR MEMORY!
THAT CAR LICENCE MAY BE ALL I NEED TO TRACE RIMEL —AND FIND OUT IF ABU RASHID'S STILL ALIVE!
LUCKILY THERE'S NOTHING WRONG WITH HIS WIFE'S MEMORY!
2293

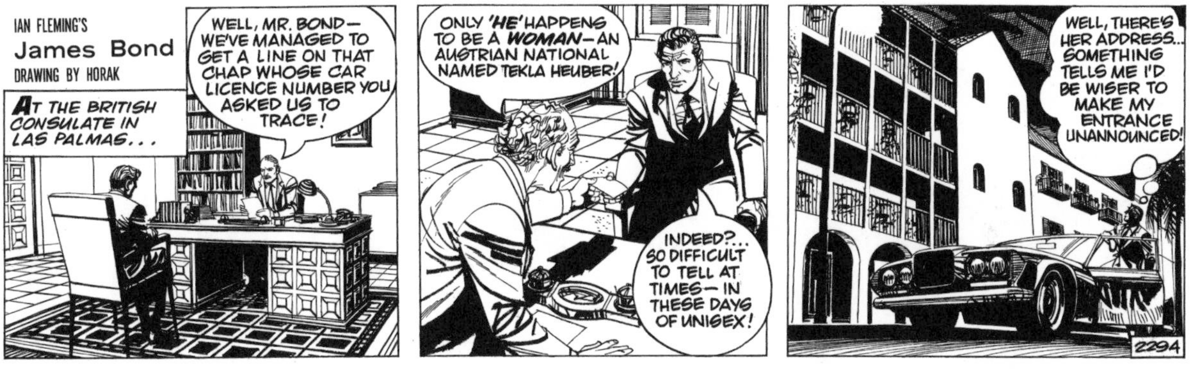
IAN FLEMING'S
James Bond
DRAWING BY HORAK
AT THE BRITISH CONSULATE IN LAS PALMAS...
WELL, MR. BOND—WE'VE MANAGED TO GET A LINE ON THAT CHAP WHOSE CAR LICENCE NUMBER YOU ASKED US TO TRACE!
ONLY 'HE' HAPPENS TO BE A WOMAN—AN AUSTRIAN NATIONAL NAMED TEKLA HEUBER!
INDEED?... SO DIFFICULT TO TELL AT TIMES—IN THESE DAYS OF UNISEX!
WELL, THERE'S HER ADDRESS... SOMETHING TELLS ME I'D BE WISER TO MAKE MY ENTRANCE UNANNOUNCED!
2294

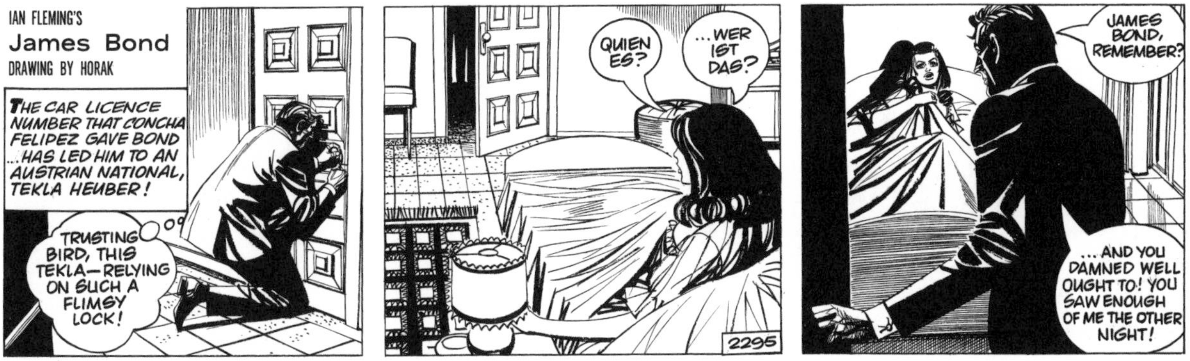
IAN FLEMING'S
James Bond
DRAWING BY HORAK
THE CAR LICENCE NUMBER THAT CONCHA FELIPEZ GAVE BOND ...HAS LED HIM TO AN AUSTRIAN NATIONAL, TEKLA HEUBER!
TRUSTING BIRD, THIS TEKLA—RELYING ON SUCH A FLIMSY LOCK!
QUIEN ES?
...WER IST DAS?
2295
JAMES BOND, REMEMBER?
...AND YOU DAMNED WELL OUGHT TO! YOU SAW ENOUGH OF ME THE OTHER NIGHT!

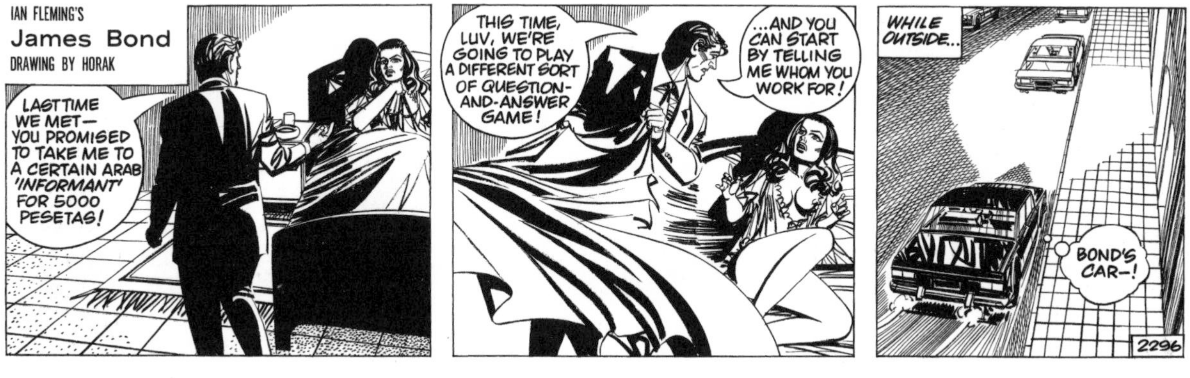
IAN FLEMING'S
James Bond
DRAWING BY HORAK
LAST TIME WE MET—YOU PROMISED TO TAKE ME TO A CERTAIN ARAB 'INFORMANT' FOR 5000 PESETAS!
THIS TIME, LUV, WE'RE GOING TO PLAY A DIFFERENT SORT OF QUESTION-AND-ANSWER GAME!
...AND YOU CAN START BY TELLING ME WHOM YOU WORK FOR!
WHILE OUTSIDE...
BOND'S CAR—!
2296

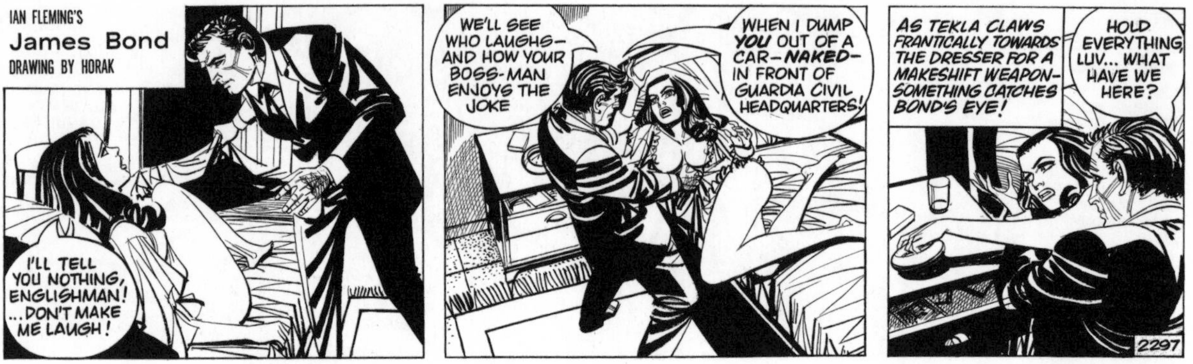
IAN FLEMING'S
James Bond
DRAWING BY HORAK
I'LL TELL YOU NOTHING, ENGLISHMAN! ...DON'T MAKE ME LAUGH!
WE'LL SEE WHO LAUGHS— AND HOW YOUR BOSS-MAN ENJOYS THE JOKE
WHEN I DUMP YOU OUT OF A CAR—NAKED— IN FRONT OF GUARDIA CIVIL HEADQUARTERS!
AS TEKLA CLAWS FRANTICALLY TOWARDS THE DRESSER FOR A MAKESHIFT WEAPON— SOMETHING CATCHES BOND'S EYE!
HOLD EVERYTHING, LUV... WHAT HAVE WE HERE?
2297

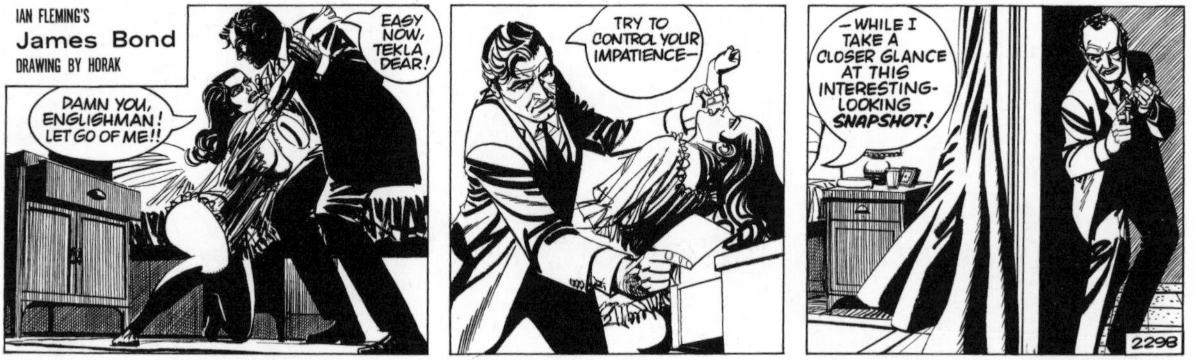
IAN FLEMING'S
James Bond
DRAWING BY HORAK
EASY NOW, TEKLA DEAR!
DAMN YOU, ENGLISHMAN! LET GO OF ME!!
TRY TO CONTROL YOUR IMPATIENCE—
—WHILE I TAKE A CLOSER GLANCE AT THIS INTERESTING-LOOKING SNAPSHOT!
2298

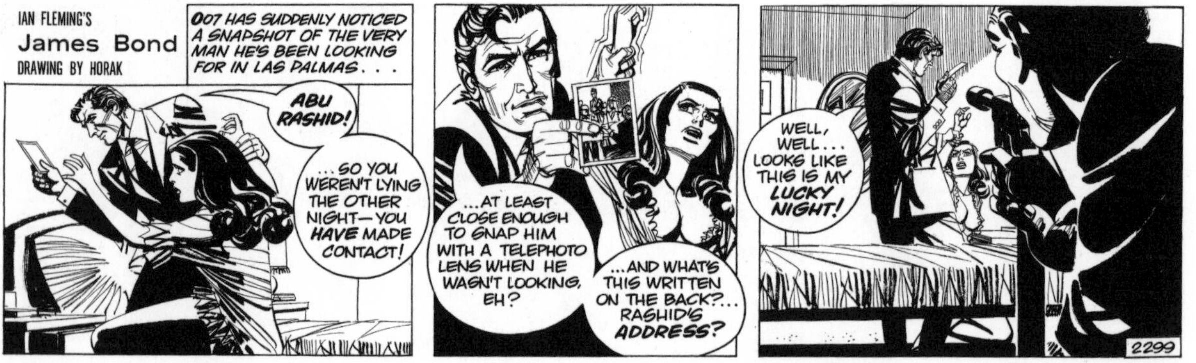
IAN FLEMING'S
James Bond
DRAWING BY HORAK
007 HAS SUDDENLY NOTICED A SNAPSHOT OF THE VERY MAN HE'S BEEN LOOKING FOR IN LAS PALMAS . . .
ABU RASHID!
. . . SO YOU WEREN'T LYING THE OTHER NIGHT—YOU HAVE MADE CONTACT!
...AT LEAST CLOSE ENOUGH TO SNAP HIM WITH A TELEPHOTO LENS WHEN HE WASN'T LOOKING, EH?
...AND WHAT'S THIS WRITTEN ON THE BACK?... RASHID'S ADDRESS?
WELL, WELL... LOOKS LIKE THIS IS MY LUCKY NIGHT!
2299

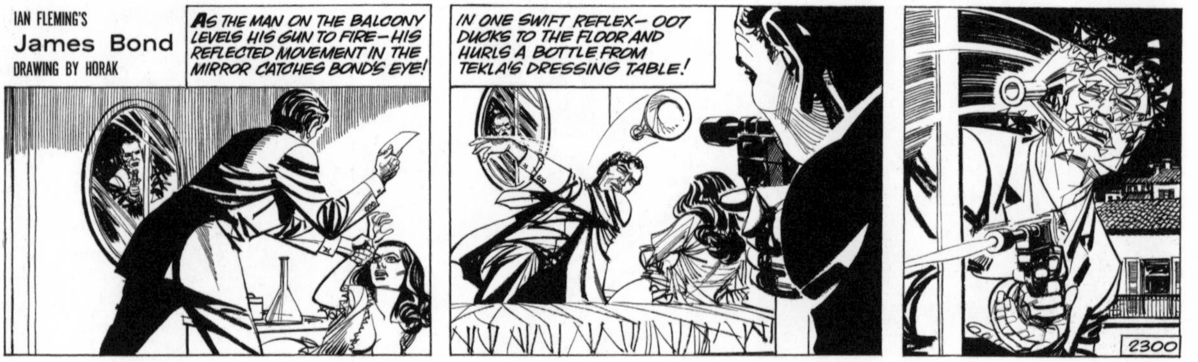
IAN FLEMING'S
James Bond
DRAWING BY HORAK
AS THE MAN ON THE BALCONY LEVELS HIS GUN TO FIRE—HIS REFLECTED MOVEMENT IN THE MIRROR CATCHES BOND'S EYE!
IN ONE SWIFT REFLEX— 007 DUCKS TO THE FLOOR AND HURLS A BOTTLE FROM TEKLA'S DRESSING TABLE!
2300

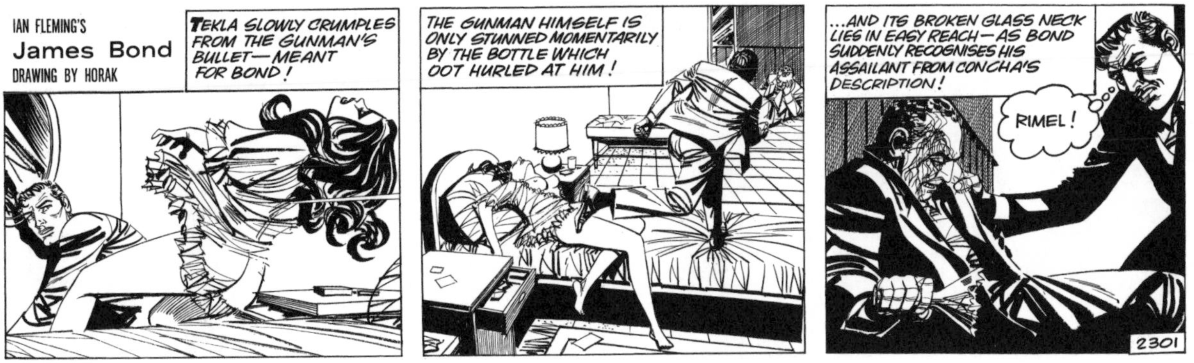
IAN FLEMING'S
James Bond
DRAWING BY HORAK
TEKLA SLOWLY CRUMPLES FROM THE GUNMAN'S BULLET—MEANT FOR BOND!
THE GUNMAN HIMSELF IS ONLY STUNNED MOMENTARILY BY THE BOTTLE WHICH 007 HURLED AT HIM!
...AND ITS BROKEN GLASS NECK LIES IN EASY REACH—AS BOND SUDDENLY RECOGNISES HIS ASSAILANT FROM CONCHA'S DESCRIPTION!
RIMEL!
2301

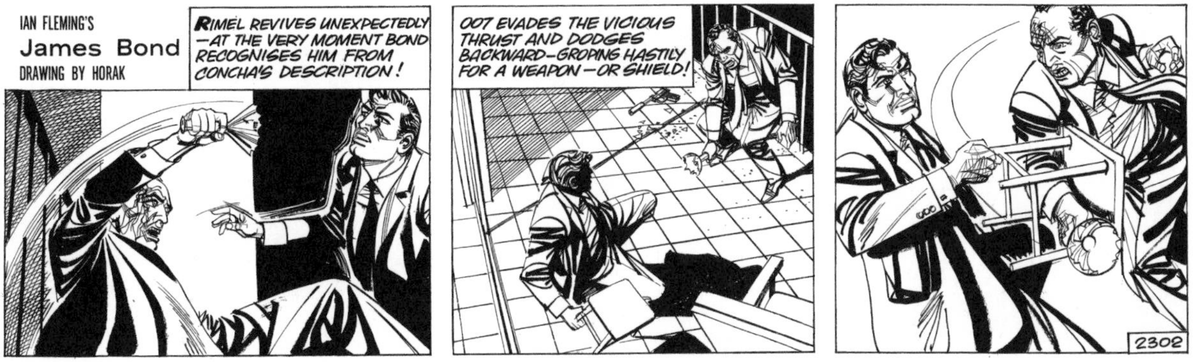
IAN FLEMING'S
James Bond
DRAWING BY HORAK
RIMEL REVIVES UNEXPECTEDLY—AT THE VERY MOMENT BOND RECOGNISES HIM FROM CONCHA'S DESCRIPTION!
007 EVADES THE VICIOUS THRUST AND DODGES BACKWARD—GROPING HASTILY FOR A WEAPON—OR SHIELD!
2302

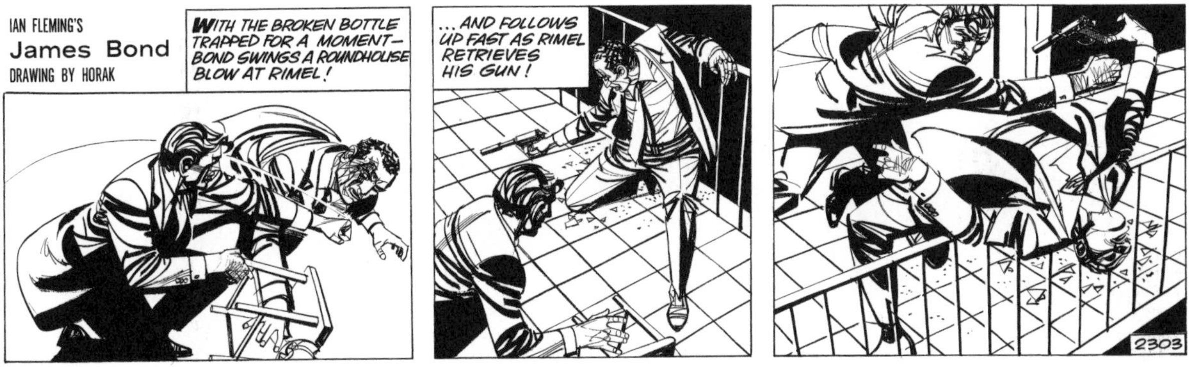
IAN FLEMING'S
James Bond
DRAWING BY HORAK
WITH THE BROKEN BOTTLE TRAPPED FOR A MOMENT—BOND SWINGS A ROUNDHOUSE BLOW AT RIMEL!
...AND FOLLOWS UP FAST AS RIMEL RETRIEVES HIS GUN!
2303

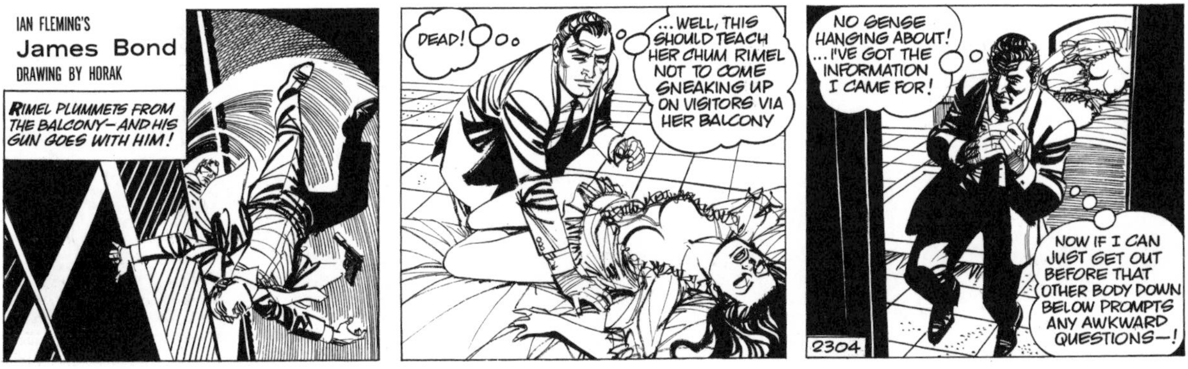
IAN FLEMING'S
James Bond
DRAWING BY HORAK
RIMEL PLUMMETS FROM THE BALCONY—AND HIS GUN GOES WITH HIM!
DEAD!
...WELL, THIS SHOULD TEACH HER CHUM RIMEL NOT TO COME SNEAKING UP ON VISITORS VIA HER BALCONY
2304
NO SENSE HANGING ABOUT! ...I'VE GOT THE INFORMATION I CAME FOR!
NOW IF I CAN JUST GET OUT BEFORE THAT OTHER BODY DOWN BELOW PROMPTS ANY AWKWARD QUESTIONS—!

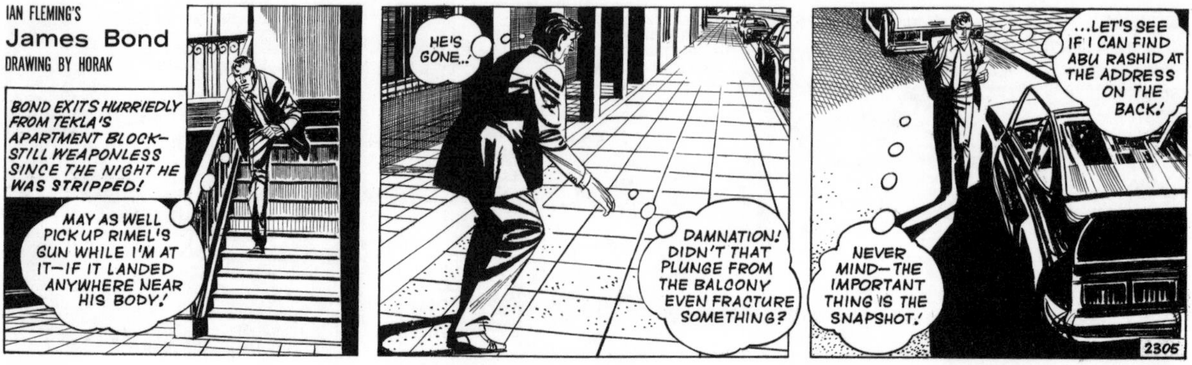
IAN FLEMING'S
James Bond
DRAWING BY HORAK
BOND EXITS HURRIEDLY FROM TEKLA'S APARTMENT BLOCK-STILL WEAPONLESS SINCE THE NIGHT HE WAS STRIPPED!
MAY AS WELL PICK UP RIMEL'S GUN WHILE I'M AT IT—IF IT LANDED ANYWHERE NEAR HIS BODY!
HE'S GONE..!
DAMNATION! DIDN'T THAT PLUNGE FROM THE BALCONY EVEN FRACTURE SOMETHING?
NEVER MIND—THE IMPORTANT THING IS THE SNAPSHOT!
...LET'S SEE IF I CAN FIND ABU RASHID AT THE ADDRESS ON THE BACK!
2305

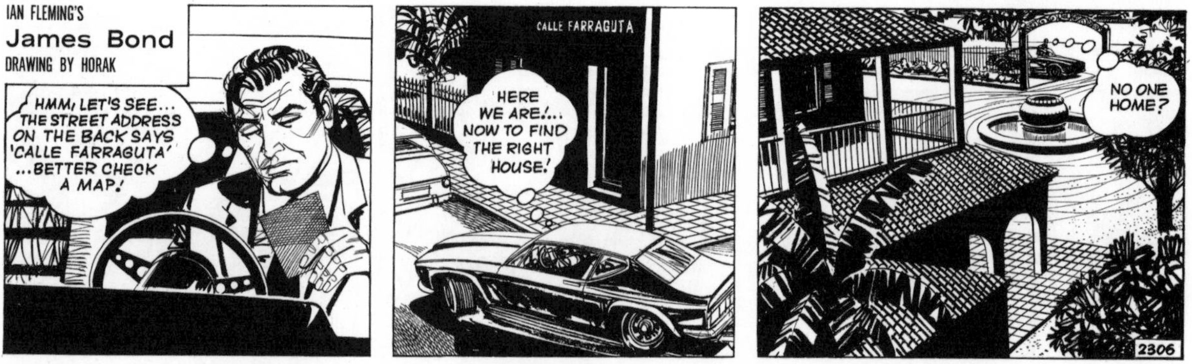
IAN FLEMING'S
James Bond
DRAWING BY HORAK
HMM, LET'S SEE... THE STREET ADDRESS ON THE BACK SAYS 'CALLE FARRAGUTA' ...BETTER CHECK A MAP!
CALLE FARRAGUTA
HERE WE ARE!... NOW TO FIND THE RIGHT HOUSE!
NO ONE HOME?
2306

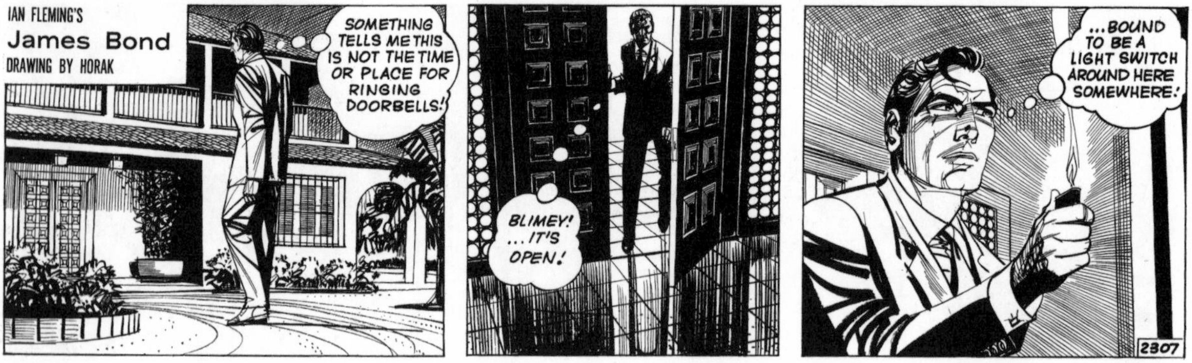
IAN FLEMING'S
James Bond
DRAWING BY HORAK
SOMETHING TELLS ME THIS IS NOT THE TIME OR PLACE FOR RINGING DOORBELLS!
BLIMEY! ...IT'S OPEN!
...BOUND TO BE A LIGHT SWITCH AROUND HERE SOMEWHERE!
2307

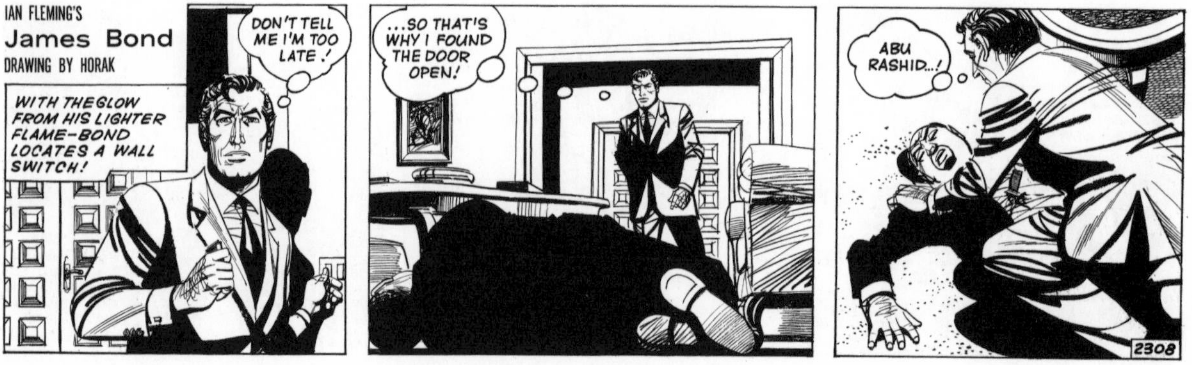
IAN FLEMING'S
James Bond
DRAWING BY HORAK
WITH THE GLOW FROM HIS LIGHTER FLAME-BOND LOCATES A WALL SWITCH!
DON'T TELL ME I'M TOO LATE!
...SO THAT'S WHY I FOUND THE DOOR OPEN!
ABU RASHID...!
2308

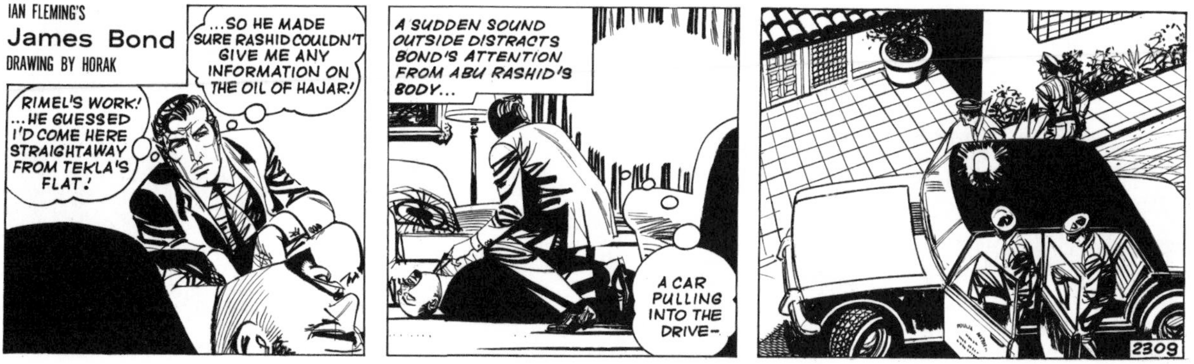
IAN FLEMING'S
James Bond
DRAWING BY HORAK
...SO HE MADE SURE RASHID COULDN'T GIVE ME ANY INFORMATION ON THE OIL OF HAJAR!
RIMEL'S WORK! ...HE GUESSED I'D COME HERE STRAIGHTAWAY FROM TEKLA'S FLAT!
A SUDDEN SOUND OUTSIDE DISTRACTS BOND'S ATTENTION FROM ABU RASHID'S BODY...
A CAR PULLING INTO THE DRIVE-
2309

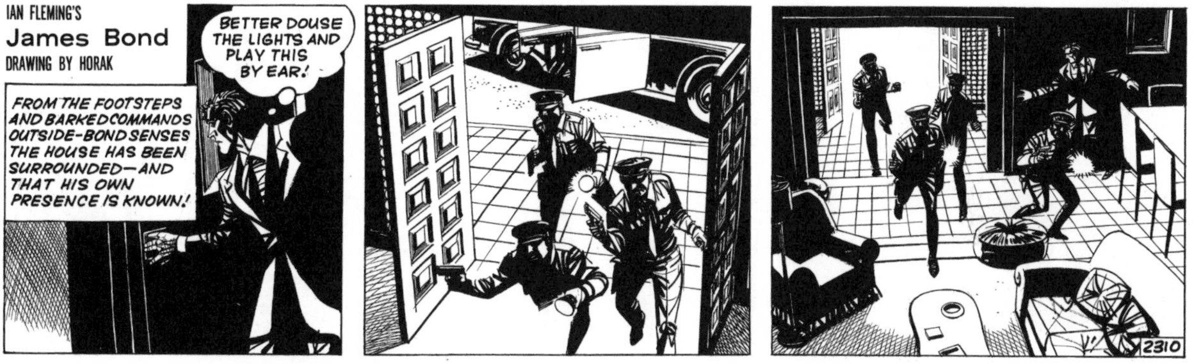
IAN FLEMING'S
James Bond
DRAWING BY HORAK
BETTER DOUSE THE LIGHTS AND PLAY THIS BY EAR!
FROM THE FOOTSTEPS AND BARKED COMMANDS OUTSIDE-BOND SENSES THE HOUSE HAS BEEN SURROUNDED—AND THAT HIS OWN PRESENCE IS KNOWN!
2310

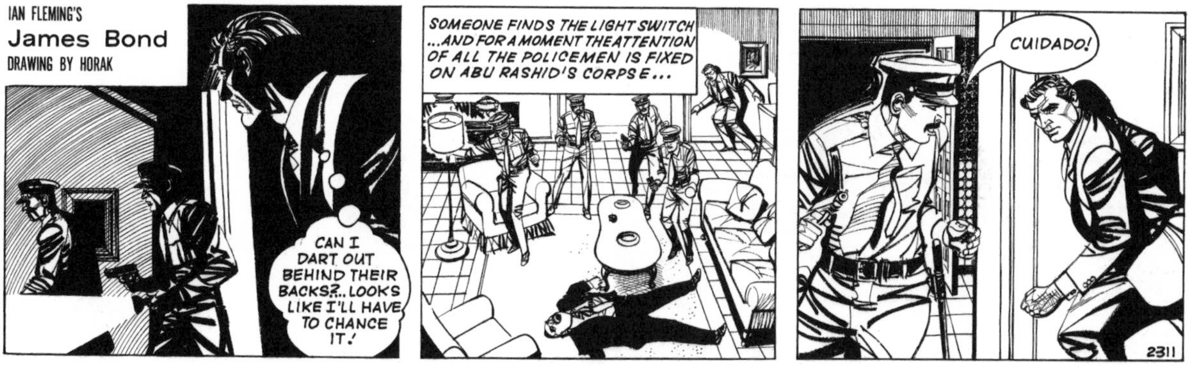
IAN FLEMING'S
James Bond
DRAWING BY HORAK
CAN I DART OUT BEHIND THEIR BACKS?..LOOKS LIKE I'LL HAVE TO CHANCE IT!
SOMEONE FINDS THE LIGHT SWITCH ...AND FOR A MOMENT THE ATTENTION OF ALL THE POLICEMEN IS FIXED ON ABU RASHID'S CORPSE...
CUIDADO!
2311

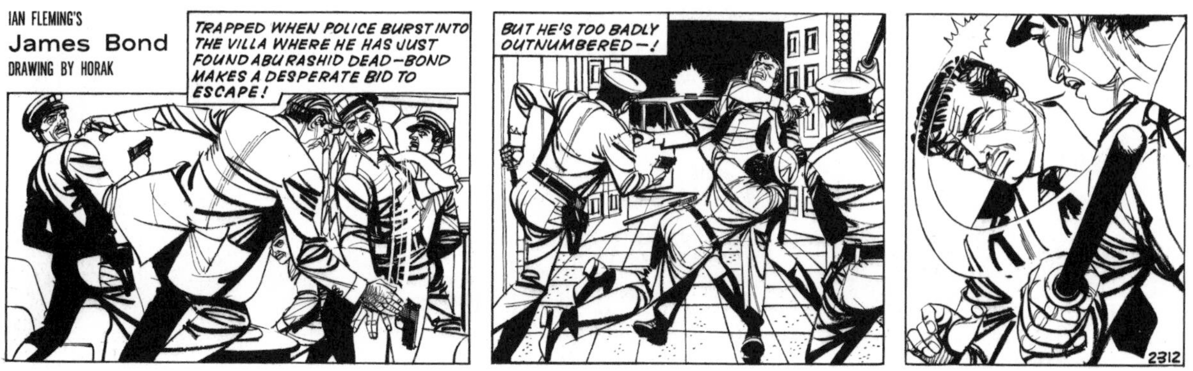
IAN FLEMING'S
James Bond
DRAWING BY HORAK
TRAPPED WHEN POLICE BURST INTO THE VILLA WHERE HE HAS JUST FOUND ABU RASHID DEAD—BOND MAKES A DESPERATE BID TO ESCAPE!
BUT HE'S TOO BADLY OUTNUMBERED—!
2312

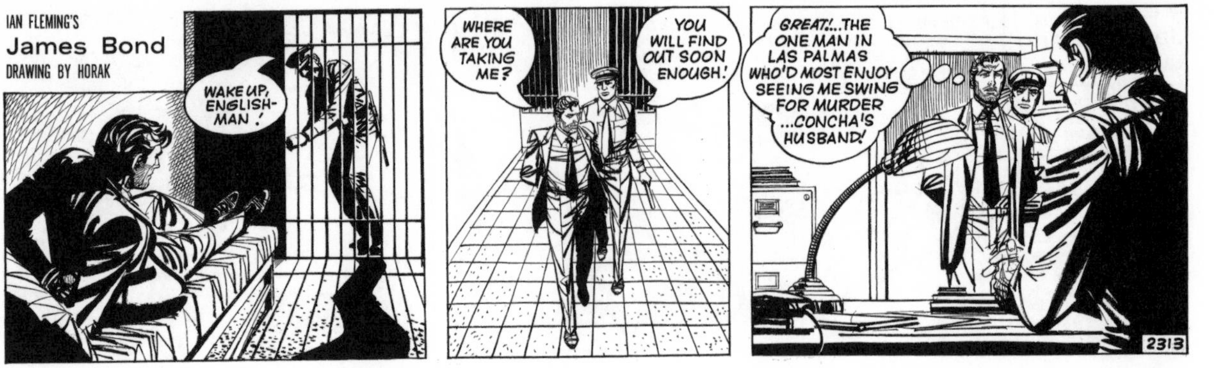
IAN FLEMING'S
James Bond
DRAWING BY HORAK
WAKE UP, ENGLISH-MAN!
WHERE ARE YOU TAKING ME?
YOU WILL FIND OUT SOON ENOUGH!
GREAT!...THE ONE MAN IN LAS PALMAS WHO'D MOST ENJOY SEEING ME SWING FOR MURDER ...CONCHA'S HUSBAND!
2313

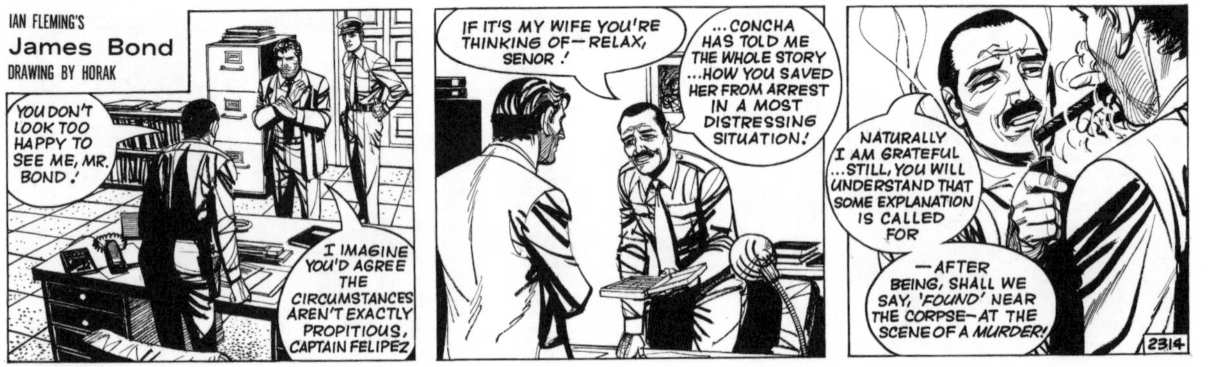
IAN FLEMING'S
James Bond
DRAWING BY HORAK
YOU DON'T LOOK TOO HAPPY TO SEE ME, MR. BOND!
I IMAGINE YOU'D AGREE THE CIRCUMSTANCES AREN'T EXACTLY PROPITIOUS, CAPTAIN FELIPEZ
IF IT'S MY WIFE YOU'RE THINKING OF—RELAX, SENOR!
...CONCHA HAS TOLD ME THE WHOLE STORY ...HOW YOU SAVED HER FROM ARREST IN A MOST DISTRESSING SITUATION!
NATURALLY I AM GRATEFUL ...STILL, YOU WILL UNDERSTAND THAT SOME EXPLANATION IS CALLED FOR
—AFTER BEING, SHALL WE SAY, 'FOUND' NEAR THE CORPSE—AT THE SCENE OF A MURDER!
2314

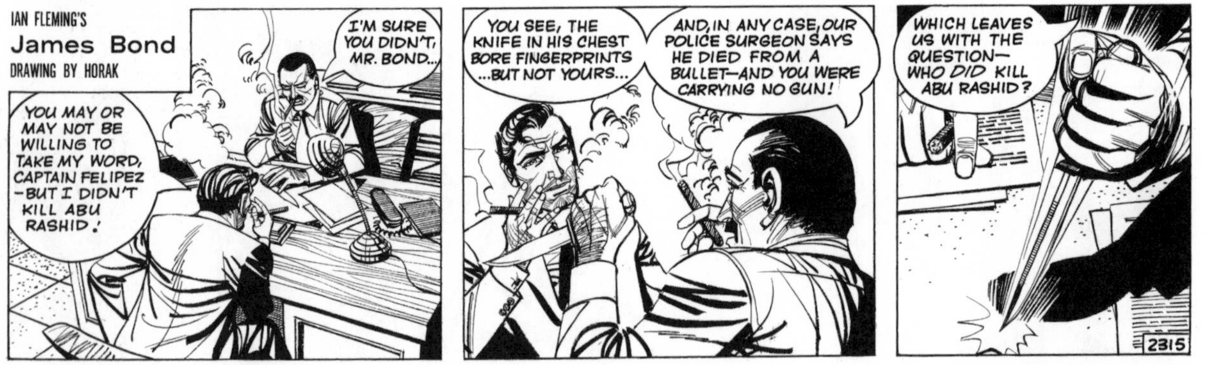
IAN FLEMING'S
James Bond
DRAWING BY HORAK
YOU MAY OR MAY NOT BE WILLING TO TAKE MY WORD, CAPTAIN FELIPEZ —BUT I DIDN'T KILL ABU RASHID!
I'M SURE YOU DIDN'T, MR. BOND...
YOU SEE, THE KNIFE IN HIS CHEST BORE FINGERPRINTS ...BUT NOT YOURS...
AND, IN ANY CASE, OUR POLICE SURGEON SAYS HE DIED FROM A BULLET—AND YOU WERE CARRYING NO GUN!
WHICH LEAVES US WITH THE QUESTION— WHO DID KILL ABU RASHID?
2315

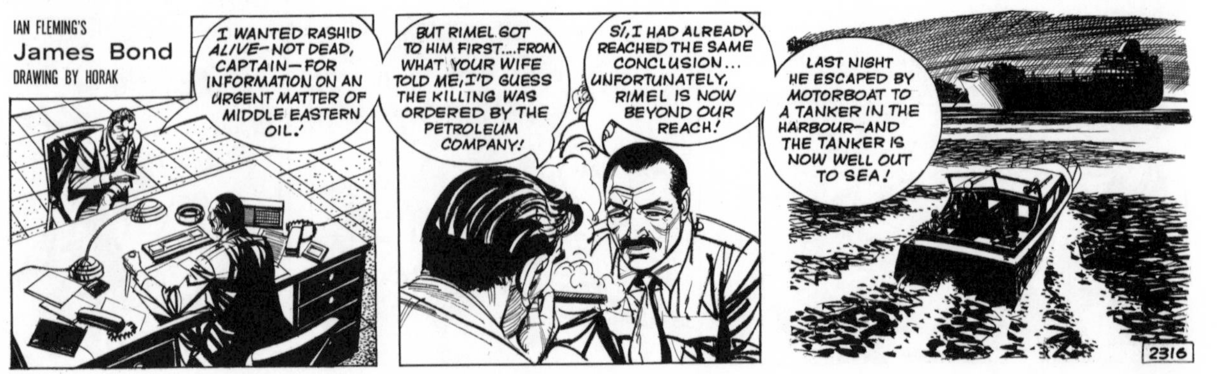
IAN FLEMING'S
James Bond
DRAWING BY HORAK
I WANTED RASHID ALIVE—NOT DEAD, CAPTAIN—FOR INFORMATION ON AN URGENT MATTER OF MIDDLE EASTERN OIL!
BUT RIMEL GOT TO HIM FIRST....FROM WHAT YOUR WIFE TOLD ME, I'D GUESS THE KILLING WAS ORDERED BY THE PETROLEUM COMPANY!
SÍ, I HAD ALREADY REACHED THE SAME CONCLUSION... UNFORTUNATELY, RIMEL IS NOW BEYOND OUR REACH!
LAST NIGHT HE ESCAPED BY MOTORBOAT TO A TANKER IN THE HARBOUR—AND THE TANKER IS NOW WELL OUT TO SEA!
2316

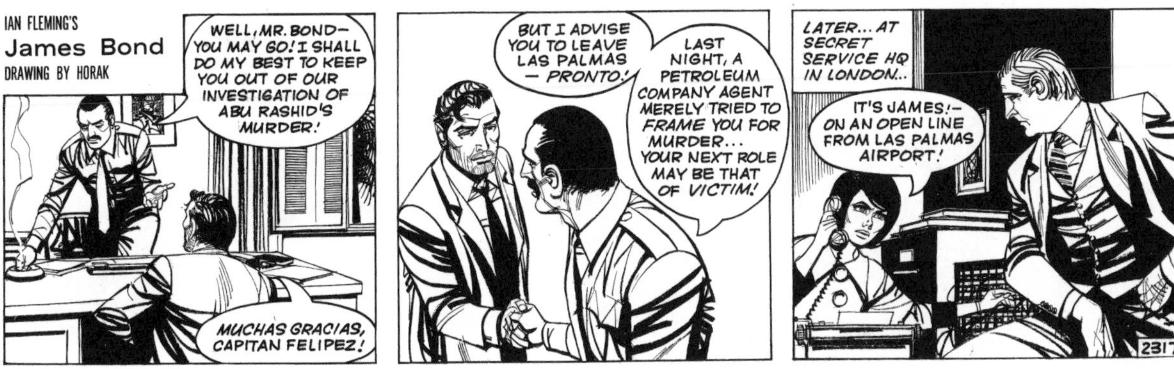
IAN FLEMING'S
James Bond
DRAWING BY HORAK
WELL, MR. BOND— YOU MAY GO! I SHALL DO MY BEST TO KEEP YOU OUT OF OUR INVESTIGATION OF ABU RASHID'S MURDER!
MUCHAS GRACIAS, CAPITAN FELIPEZ!
BUT I ADVISE YOU TO LEAVE LAS PALMAS — PRONTO!
LAST NIGHT, A PETROLEUM COMPANY AGENT MERELY TRIED TO FRAME YOU FOR MURDER... YOUR NEXT ROLE MAY BE THAT OF VICTIM!
LATER... AT SECRET SERVICE HQ IN LONDON...
IT'S JAMES!— ON AN OPEN LINE FROM LAS PALMAS AIRPORT!
2317

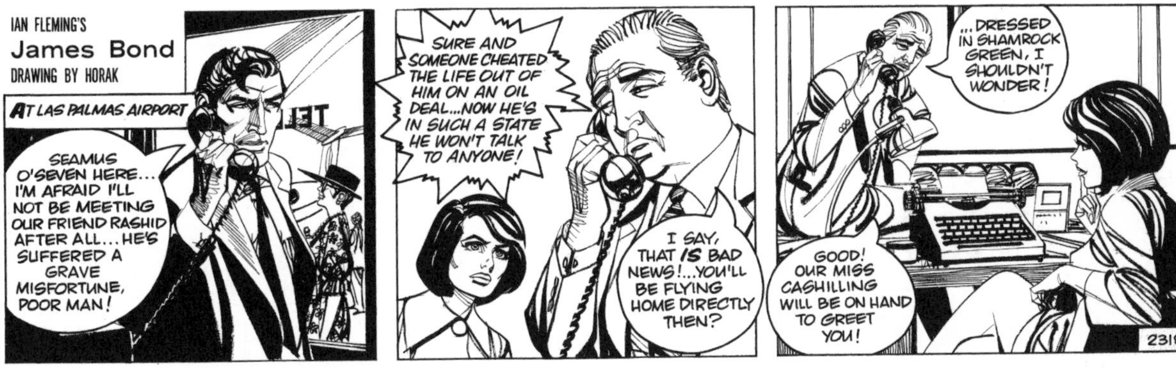
IAN FLEMING'S
James Bond
DRAWING BY HORAK
AT LAS PALMAS AIRPORT
SEAMUS O'SEVEN HERE... I'M AFRAID I'LL NOT BE MEETING OUR FRIEND RASHID AFTER ALL... HE'S SUFFERED A GRAVE MISFORTUNE, POOR MAN!
SURE AND SOMEONE CHEATED THE LIFE OUT OF HIM ON AN OIL DEAL... NOW HE'S IN SUCH A STATE HE WON'T TALK TO ANYONE!
I SAY, THAT IS BAD NEWS!... YOU'LL BE FLYING HOME DIRECTLY THEN?
...DRESSED IN SHAMROCK GREEN, I SHOULDN'T WONDER!
GOOD! OUR MISS CASHILLING WILL BE ON HAND TO GREET YOU!
2318

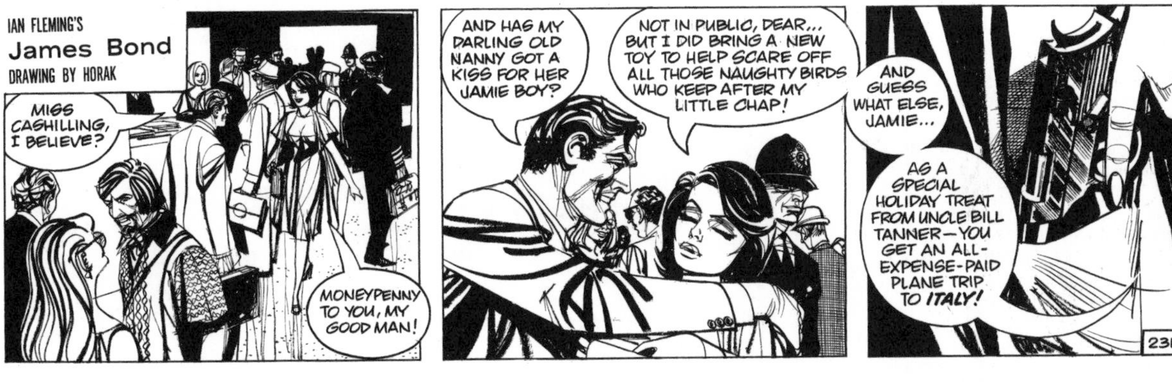
IAN FLEMING'S
James Bond
DRAWING BY HORAK
MISS CASHILLING, I BELIEVE?
MONEYPENNY TO YOU, MY GOOD MAN!
AND HAS MY DARLING OLD NANNY GOT A KISS FOR HER JAMIE BOY?
NOT IN PUBLIC, DEAR... BUT I DID BRING A NEW TOY TO HELP SCARE OFF ALL THOSE NAUGHTY BIRDS WHO KEEP AFTER MY LITTLE CHAP!
AND GUESS WHAT ELSE, JAMIE...
AS A SPECIAL HOLIDAY TREAT FROM UNCLE BILL TANNER—YOU GET AN ALL-EXPENSE-PAID PLANE TRIP TO ITALY!
2319

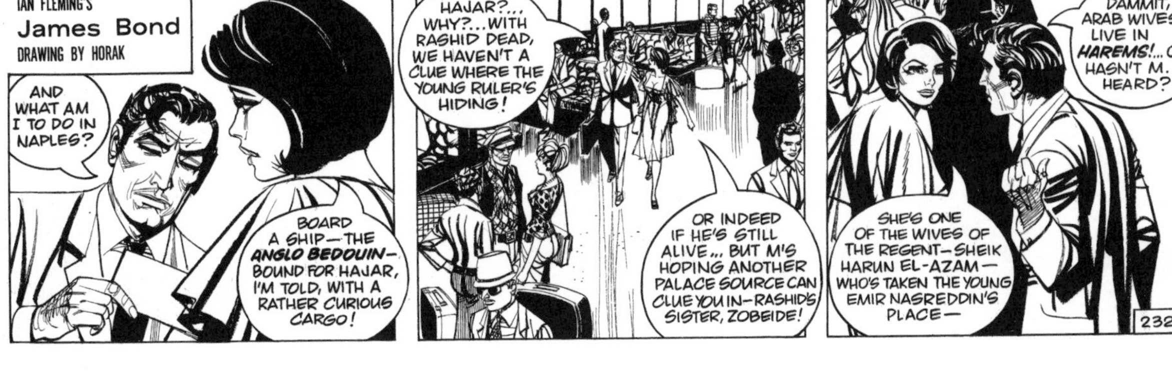
IAN FLEMING'S
James Bond
DRAWING BY HORAK
AND WHAT AM I TO DO IN NAPLES?
BOARD A SHIP—THE ANGLO BEDOUIN— BOUND FOR HAJAR, I'M TOLD, WITH A RATHER CURIOUS CARGO!
HAJAR?... WHY?... WITH RASHID DEAD, WE HAVEN'T A CLUE WHERE THE YOUNG RULER'S HIDING!
OR INDEED IF HE'S STILL ALIVE... BUT M'S HOPING ANOTHER PALACE SOURCE CAN CLUE YOU IN—RASHID'S SISTER, ZOBEIDE!
DAMMIT, ARAB WIVES LIVE IN HAREMS!... OR HASN'T M. HEARD?
SHE'S ONE OF THE WIVES OF THE REGENT—SHEIK HARUN EL-AZAM— WHO'S TAKEN THE YOUNG EMIR NASREDDIN'S PLACE—
2320

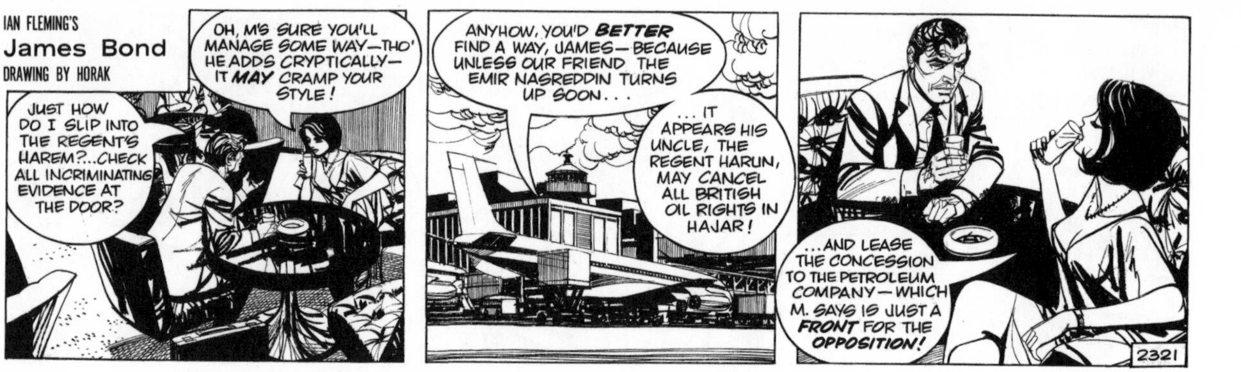
IAN FLEMING'S
James Bond
DRAWING BY HORAK
JUST HOW DO I SLIP INTO THE REGENT'S HAREM?...CHECK ALL INCRIMINATING EVIDENCE AT THE DOOR?
OH, M'S SURE YOU'LL MANAGE SOME WAY—THO' HE ADDS CRYPTICALLY—IT MAY CRAMP YOUR STYLE!
ANYHOW, YOU'D BETTER FIND A WAY, JAMES—BECAUSE UNLESS OUR FRIEND THE EMIR NASREDDIN TURNS UP SOON . . .
. . . IT APPEARS HIS UNCLE, THE REGENT HARUN, MAY CANCEL ALL BRITISH OIL RIGHTS IN HAJAR!
. . . AND LEASE THE CONCESSION TO THE PETROLEUM COMPANY—WHICH M. SAYS IS JUST A FRONT FOR THE OPPOSITION!
2321

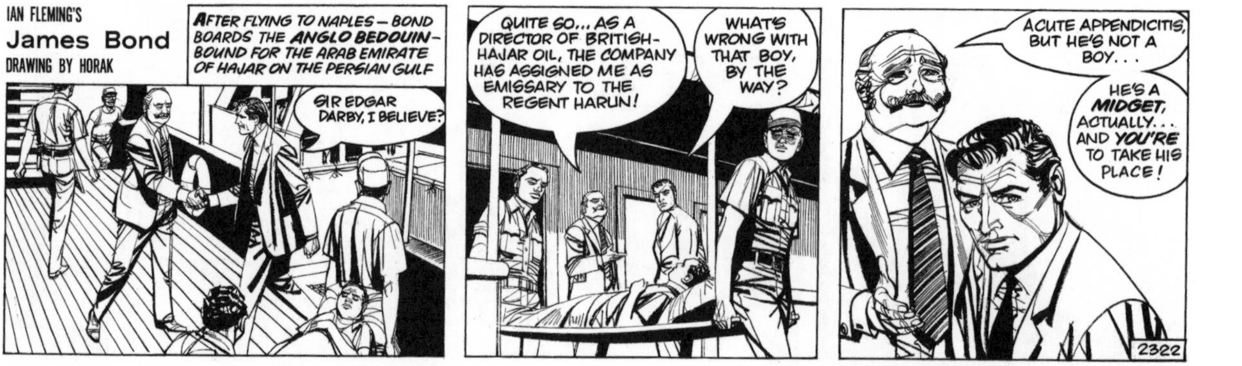
IAN FLEMING'S
James Bond
DRAWING BY HORAK
AFTER FLYING TO NAPLES—BOND BOARDS THE ANGLO BEDOUIN—BOUND FOR THE ARAB EMIRATE OF HAJAR ON THE PERSIAN GULF
SIR EDGAR DARBY, I BELIEVE?
QUITE SO... AS A DIRECTOR OF BRITISH-HAJAR OIL, THE COMPANY HAS ASSIGNED ME AS EMISSARY TO THE REGENT HARUN!
WHAT'S WRONG WITH THAT BOY, BY THE WAY?
ACUTE APPENDICITIS, BUT HE'S NOT A BOY . . .
HE'S A MIDGET, ACTUALLY . . . AND YOU'RE TO TAKE HIS PLACE!
2322

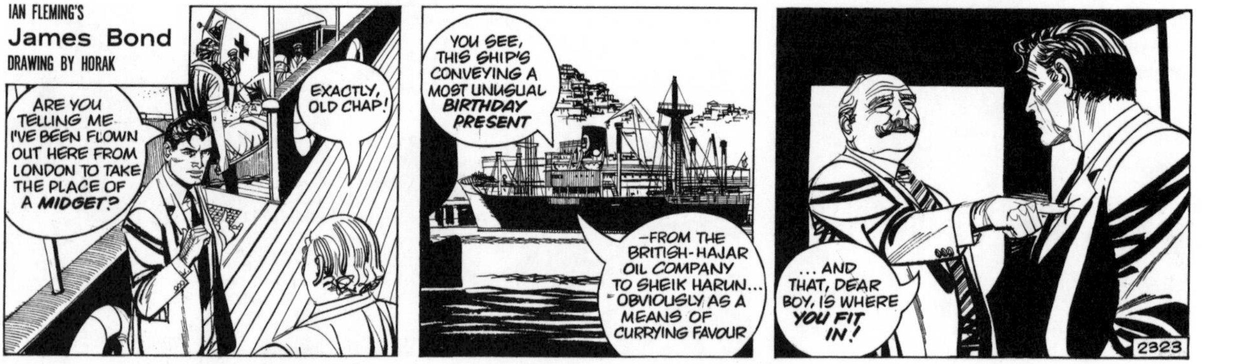
IAN FLEMING'S
James Bond
DRAWING BY HORAK
ARE YOU TELLING ME I'VE BEEN FLOWN OUT HERE FROM LONDON TO TAKE THE PLACE OF A MIDGET?
EXACTLY, OLD CHAP!
YOU SEE, THIS SHIP'S CONVEYING A MOST UNUSUAL BIRTHDAY PRESENT
—FROM THE BRITISH-HAJAR OIL COMPANY TO SHEIK HARUN... OBVIOUSLY AS A MEANS OF CURRYING FAVOUR
. . . AND THAT, DEAR BOY, IS WHERE YOU FIT IN!
2323

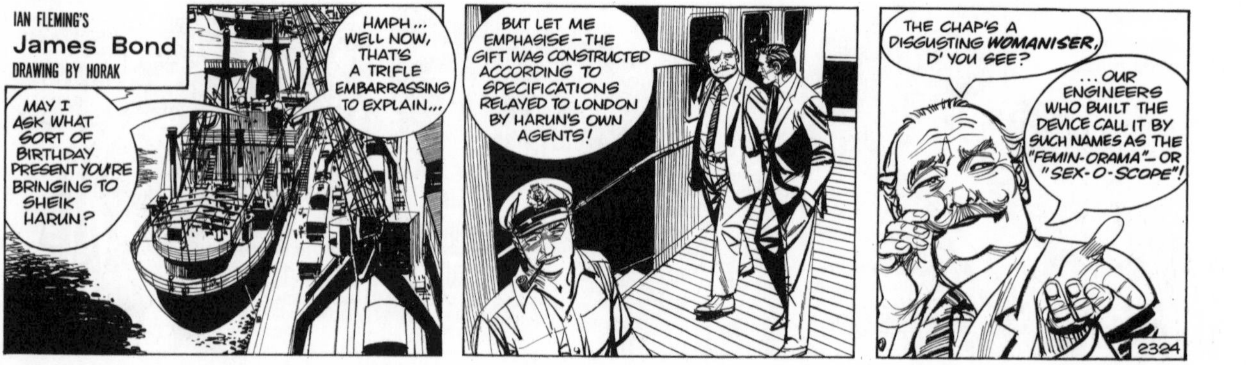
IAN FLEMING'S
James Bond
DRAWING BY HORAK
MAY I ASK WHAT SORT OF BIRTHDAY PRESENT YOU'RE BRINGING TO SHEIK HARUN?
HMPH... WELL NOW, THAT'S A TRIFLE EMBARRASSING TO EXPLAIN...
BUT LET ME EMPHASISE—THE GIFT WAS CONSTRUCTED ACCORDING TO SPECIFICATIONS RELAYED TO LONDON BY HARUN'S OWN AGENTS!
THE CHAP'S A DISGUSTING WOMANISER, D' YOU SEE?
. . . OUR ENGINEERS WHO BUILT THE DEVICE CALL IT BY SUCH NAMES AS THE "FEMIN-ORAMA"—OR "SEX-O-SCOPE"!
2324

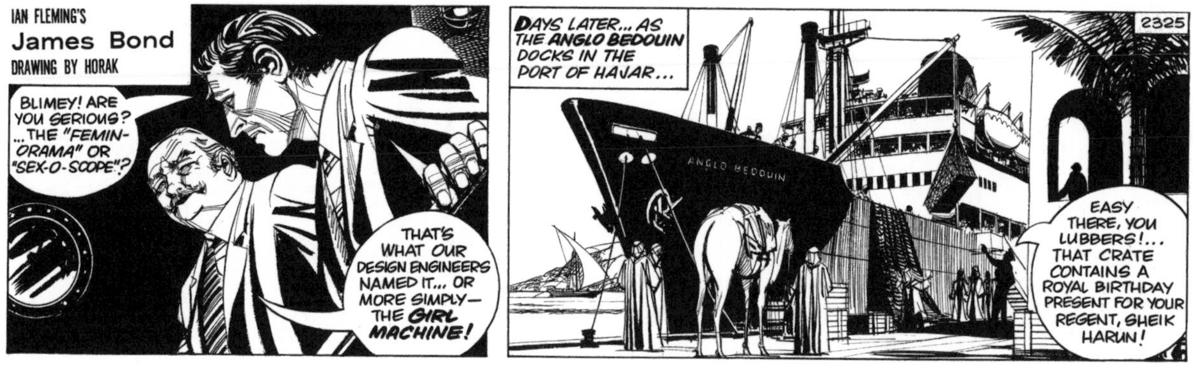
IAN FLEMING'S
James Bond
DRAWING BY HORAK
BLIMEY! ARE YOU SERIOUS? ...THE "FEMIN-ORAMA" OR "SEX-O-SCOPE"?
THAT'S WHAT OUR DESIGN ENGINEERS NAMED IT... OR MORE SIMPLY— THE GIRL MACHINE!
DAYS LATER... AS THE ANGLO BEDOUIN DOCKS IN THE PORT OF HAJAR...
2325
ANGLO BEDOUIN
EASY THERE, YOU LUBBERS!... THAT CRATE CONTAINS A ROYAL BIRTHDAY PRESENT FOR YOUR REGENT, SHEIK HARUN!

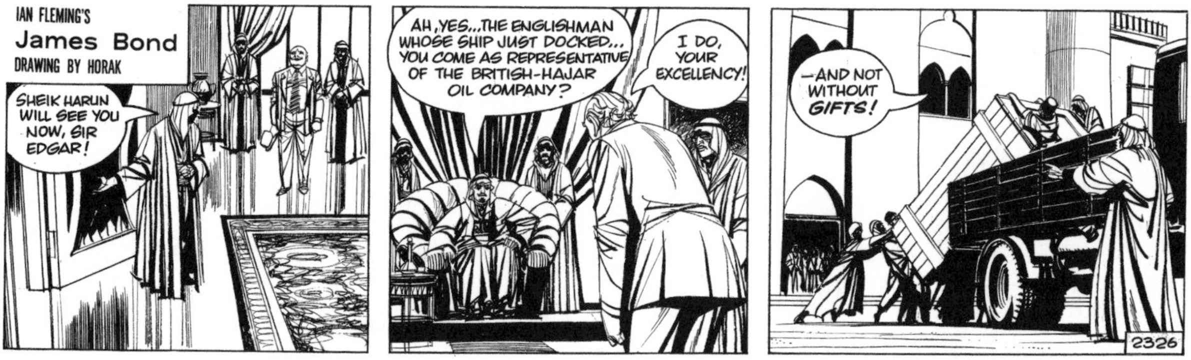
IAN FLEMING'S
James Bond
DRAWING BY HORAK
SHEIK HARUN WILL SEE YOU NOW, SIR EDGAR!
AH, YES... THE ENGLISHMAN WHOSE SHIP JUST DOCKED... YOU COME AS REPRESENTATIVE OF THE BRITISH-HAJAR OIL COMPANY?
I DO, YOUR EXCELLENCY!
—AND NOT WITHOUT GIFTS!
2326

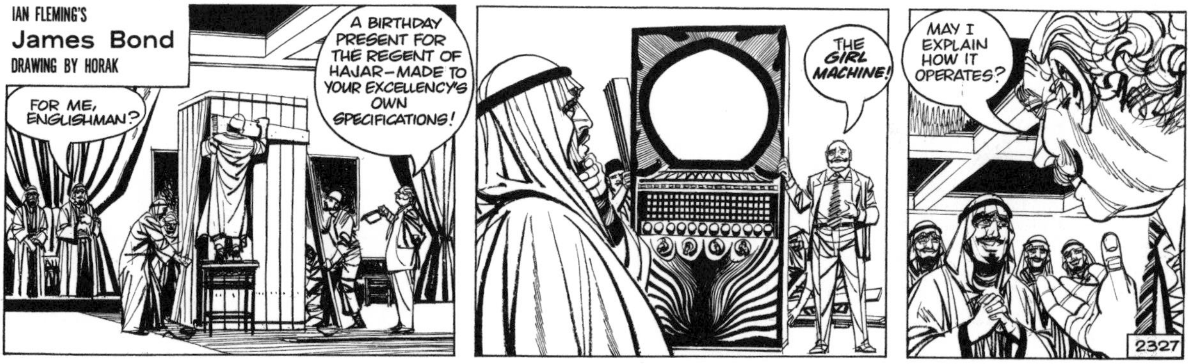
IAN FLEMING'S
James Bond
DRAWING BY HORAK
FOR ME, ENGLISHMAN?
A BIRTHDAY PRESENT FOR THE REGENT OF HAJAR—MADE TO YOUR EXCELLENCY'S OWN SPECIFICATIONS!
THE GIRL MACHINE!
MAY I EXPLAIN HOW IT OPERATES?
2327

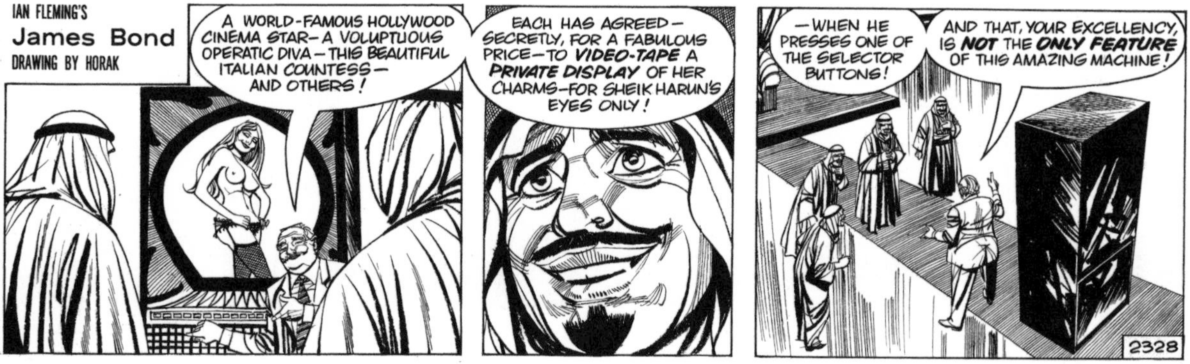
IAN FLEMING'S
James Bond
DRAWING BY HORAK
A WORLD-FAMOUS HOLLYWOOD CINEMA STAR—A VOLUPTUOUS OPERATIC DIVA—THIS BEAUTIFUL ITALIAN COUNTESS— AND OTHERS!
EACH HAS AGREED— SECRETLY, FOR A FABULOUS PRICE—TO VIDEO-TAPE A PRIVATE DISPLAY OF HER CHARMS—FOR SHEIK HARUN'S EYES ONLY!
—WHEN HE PRESSES ONE OF THE SELECTOR BUTTONS!
AND THAT, YOUR EXCELLENCY, IS NOT THE ONLY FEATURE OF THIS AMAZING MACHINE!
2328

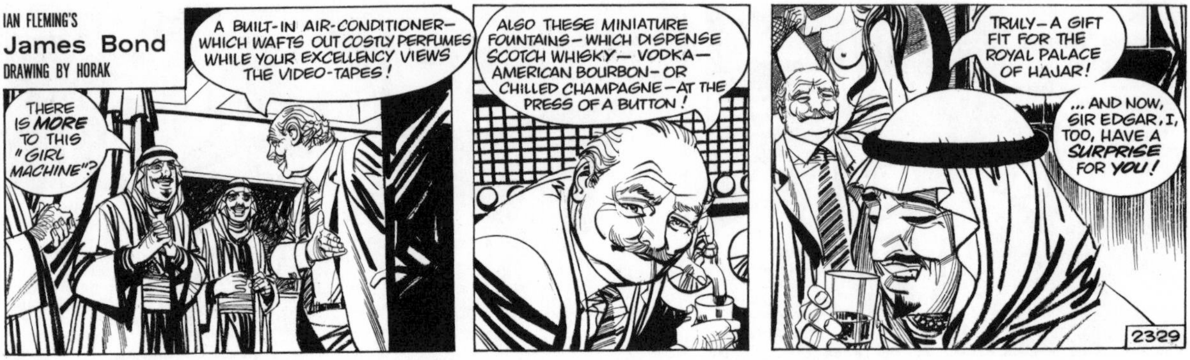
IAN FLEMING'S
James Bond
DRAWING BY HORAK
THERE IS MORE TO THIS "GIRL MACHINE"?
A BUILT-IN AIR-CONDITIONER—WHICH WAFTS OUT COSTLY PERFUMES WHILE YOUR EXCELLENCY VIEWS THE VIDEO-TAPES!
ALSO THESE MINIATURE FOUNTAINS—WHICH DISPENSE SCOTCH WHISKY—VODKA—AMERICAN BOURBON—OR CHILLED CHAMPAGNE—AT THE PRESS OF A BUTTON!
TRULY—A GIFT FIT FOR THE ROYAL PALACE OF HAJAR!
... AND NOW, SIR EDGAR, I, TOO, HAVE A SURPRISE FOR YOU!
2329

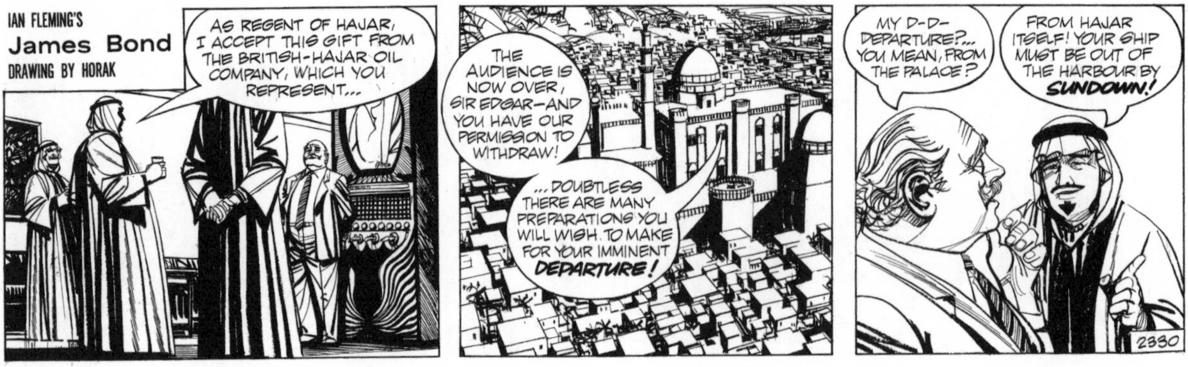
IAN FLEMING'S
James Bond
DRAWING BY HORAK
AS REGENT OF HAJAR, I ACCEPT THIS GIFT FROM THE BRITISH-HAJAR OIL COMPANY, WHICH YOU REPRESENT...
THE AUDIENCE IS NOW OVER, SIR EDGAR—AND YOU HAVE OUR PERMISSION TO WITHDRAW!
... DOUBTLESS THERE ARE MANY PREPARATIONS YOU WILL WISH TO MAKE FOR YOUR IMMINENT DEPARTURE!
MY D-D-DEPARTURE?... YOU MEAN, FROM THE PALACE?
FROM HAJAR ITSELF! YOUR SHIP MUST BE OUT OF THE HARBOUR BY SUNDOWN!
2330

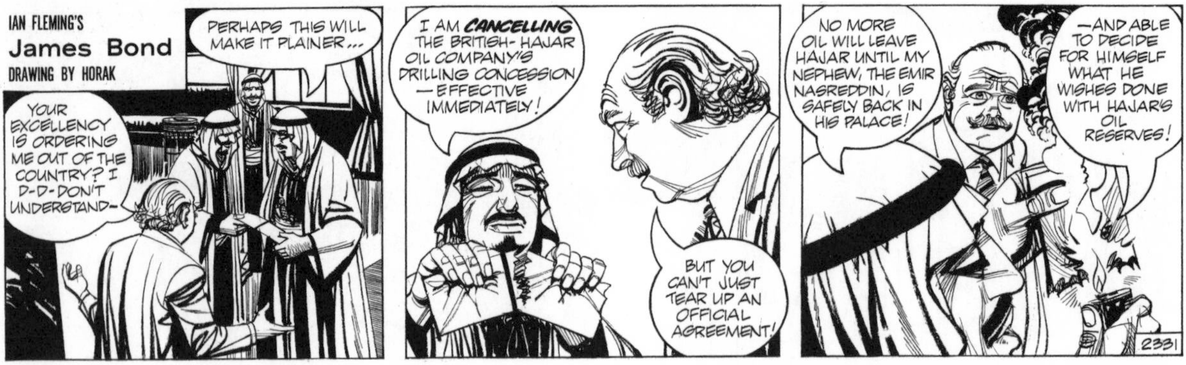
IAN FLEMING'S
James Bond
DRAWING BY HORAK
PERHAPS THIS WILL MAKE IT PLAINER...
YOUR EXCELLENCY IS ORDERING ME OUT OF THE COUNTRY? I D-D-DON'T UNDERSTAND—
I AM CANCELLING THE BRITISH-HAJAR OIL COMPANY'S DRILLING CONCESSION—EFFECTIVE IMMEDIATELY!
BUT YOU CAN'T JUST TEAR UP AN OFFICIAL AGREEMENT!
NO MORE OIL WILL LEAVE HAJAR UNTIL MY NEPHEW, THE EMIR NASREDDIN, IS SAFELY BACK IN HIS PALACE!
—AND ABLE TO DECIDE FOR HIMSELF WHAT HE WISHES DONE WITH HAJAR'S OIL RESERVES!
2331

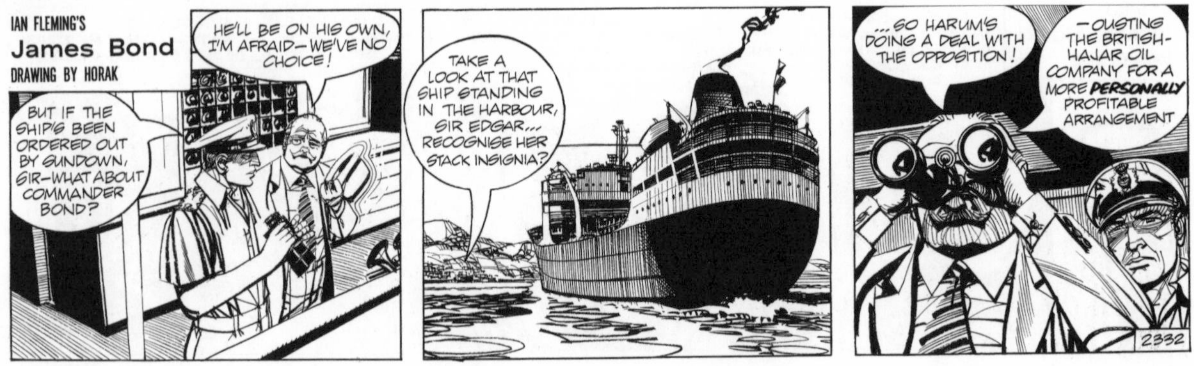
IAN FLEMING'S
James Bond
DRAWING BY HORAK
BUT IF THE SHIP'S BEEN ORDERED OUT BY SUNDOWN, SIR—WHAT ABOUT COMMANDER BOND?
HE'LL BE ON HIS OWN, I'M AFRAID—WE'VE NO CHOICE!
TAKE A LOOK AT THAT SHIP STANDING IN THE HARBOUR, SIR EDGAR... RECOGNISE HER STACK INSIGNIA?
... SO HARUM'S DOING A DEAL WITH THE OPPOSITION!
—OUSTING THE BRITISH-HAJAR OIL COMPANY FOR A MORE PERSONALLY PROFITABLE ARRANGEMENT
2332

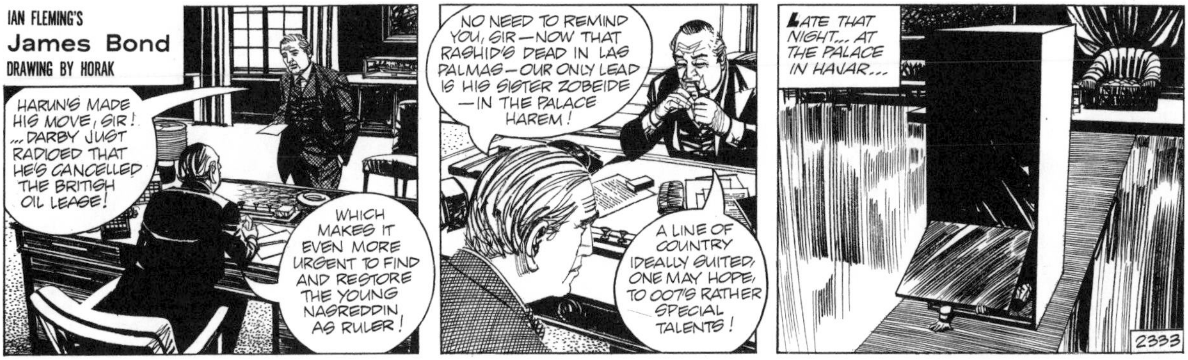
IAN FLEMING'S
James Bond
DRAWING BY HORAK
HARUN'S MADE HIS MOVE, SIR! ... DARBY JUST RADIOED THAT HE'S CANCELLED THE BRITISH OIL LEASE!
WHICH MAKES IT EVEN MORE URGENT TO FIND AND RESTORE THE YOUNG NASREDDIN AS RULER!
NO NEED TO REMIND YOU, SIR — NOW THAT RASHID'S DEAD IN LAS PALMAS — OUR ONLY LEAD IS HIS SISTER ZOBEIDE — IN THE PALACE HAREM!
A LINE OF COUNTRY IDEALLY SUITED, ONE MAY HOPE, TO 007'S RATHER SPECIAL TALENTS!
LATE THAT NIGHT... AT THE PALACE IN HAVAR...
2333

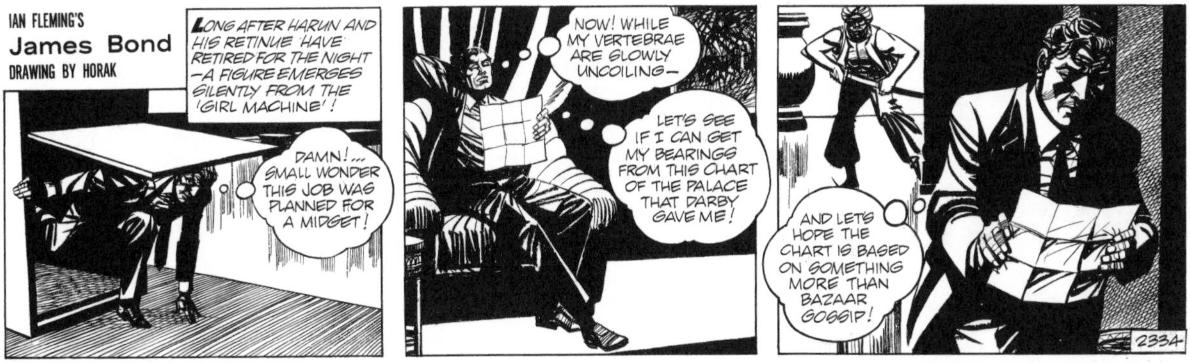
IAN FLEMING'S
James Bond
DRAWING BY HORAK
LONG AFTER HARUN AND HIS RETINUE HAVE RETIRED FOR THE NIGHT — A FIGURE EMERGES SILENTLY FROM THE 'GIRL MACHINE'!
DAMN!... SMALL WONDER THIS JOB WAS PLANNED FOR A MIDGET!
NOW! WHILE MY VERTEBRAE ARE SLOWLY UNCOILING —
LET'S SEE IF I CAN GET MY BEARINGS FROM THIS CHART OF THE PALACE THAT DARBY GAVE ME!
AND LET'S HOPE THE CHART IS BASED ON SOMETHING MORE THAN BAZAAR GOSSIP!
2334

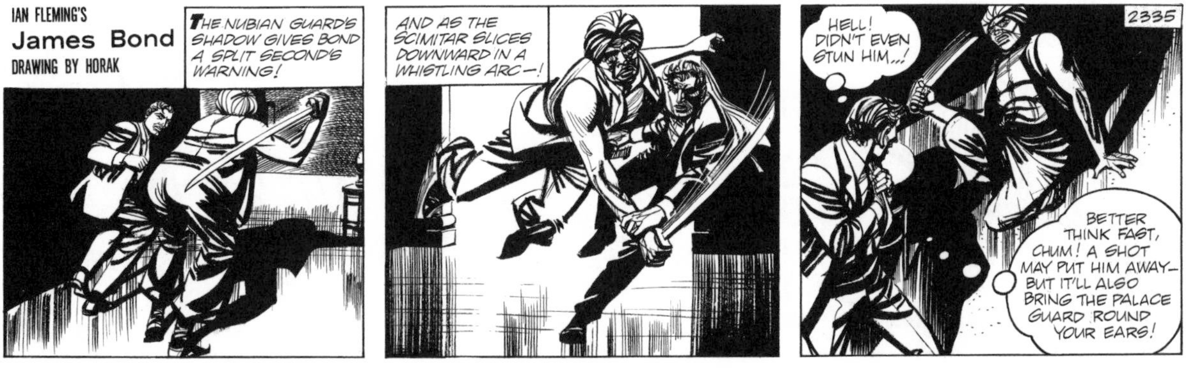
IAN FLEMING'S
James Bond
DRAWING BY HORAK
THE NUBIAN GUARD'S SHADOW GIVES BOND A SPLIT SECOND'S WARNING!
AND AS THE SCIMITAR SLICES DOWNWARD IN A WHISTLING ARC —!
HELL! DIDN'T EVEN STUN HIM...!
BETTER THINK FAST, CHUM! A SHOT MAY PUT HIM AWAY — BUT IT'LL ALSO BRING THE PALACE GUARD ROUND YOUR EARS!
2335

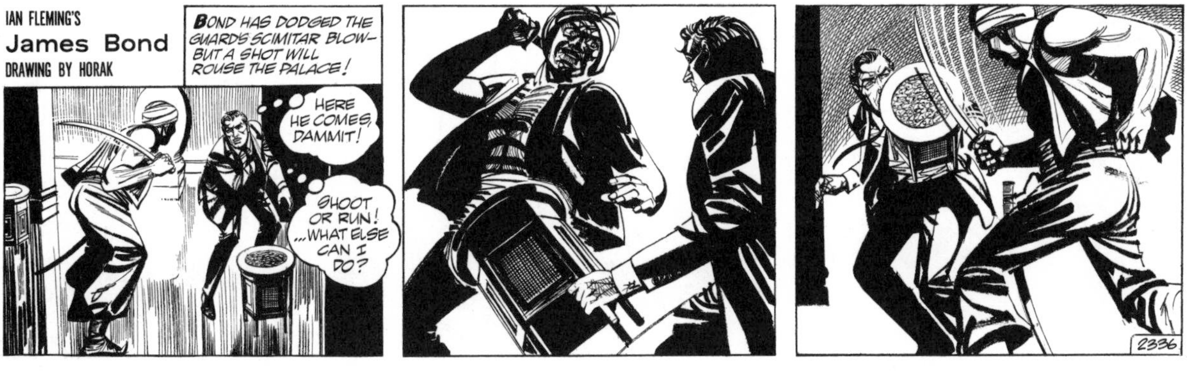
IAN FLEMING'S
James Bond
DRAWING BY HORAK
BOND HAS DODGED THE GUARD'S SCIMITAR BLOW — BUT A SHOT WILL ROUSE THE PALACE!
HERE HE COMES, DAMMIT!
SHOOT OR RUN! ...WHAT ELSE CAN I DO?
2336

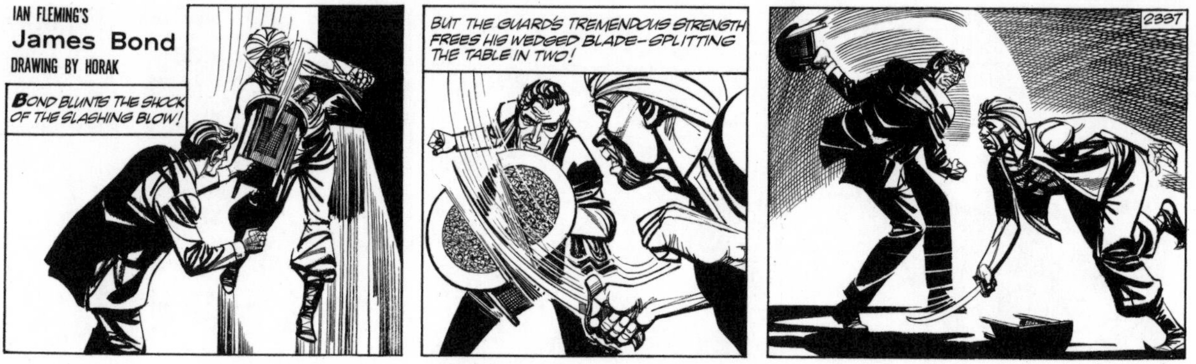
IAN FLEMING'S
James Bond
DRAWING BY HORAK
BOND BLUNTS THE SHOCK OF THE SLASHING BLOW!
BUT THE GUARD'S TREMENDOUS STRENGTH FREES HIS WEDGED BLADE—SPLITTING THE TABLE IN TWO!
2337

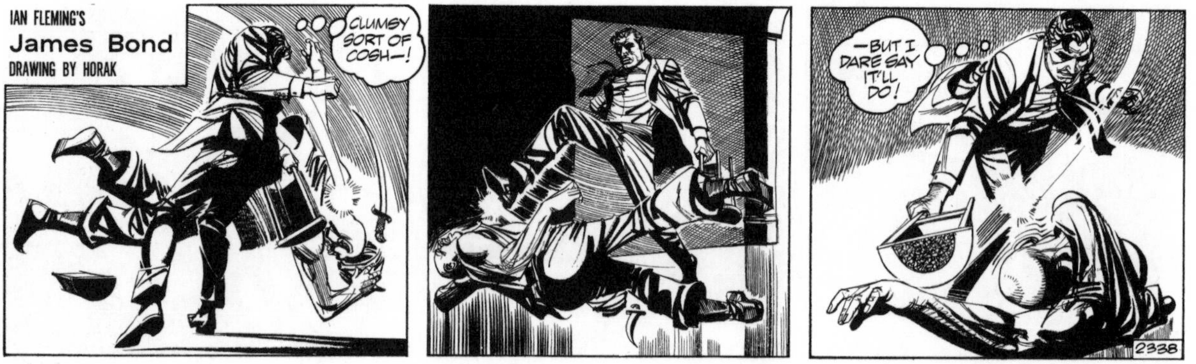
IAN FLEMING'S
James Bond
DRAWING BY HORAK
CLUMSY SORT OF COSH—!
—BUT I DARE SAY IT'LL DO!
2338

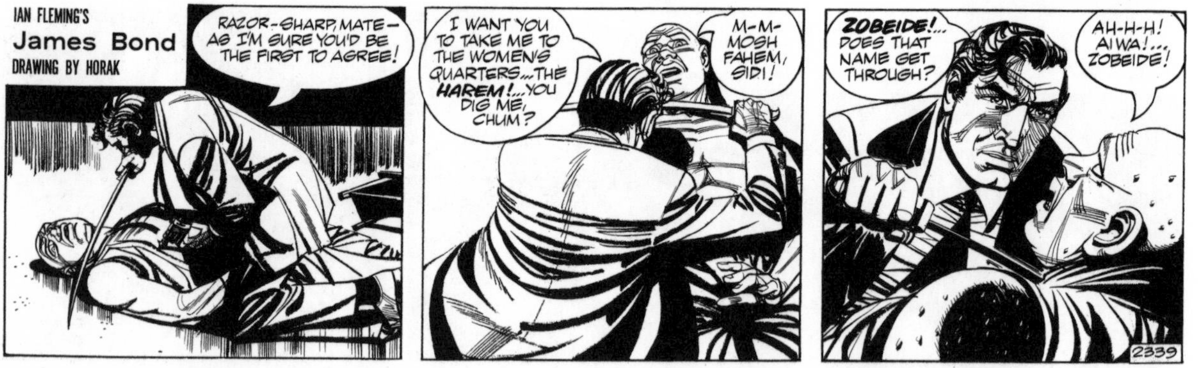
IAN FLEMING'S
James Bond
DRAWING BY HORAK
RAZOR-SHARP, MATE—AS I'M SURE YOU'D BE THE FIRST TO AGREE!
I WANT YOU TO TAKE ME TO THE WOMEN'S QUARTERS... THE HAREM!... YOU DIG ME, CHUM?
M-M-MOSH FAHEM, SIDI!
ZOBEIDE!... DOES THAT NAME GET THROUGH?
AH-H-H! AIWA!... ZOBEIDE!
2339

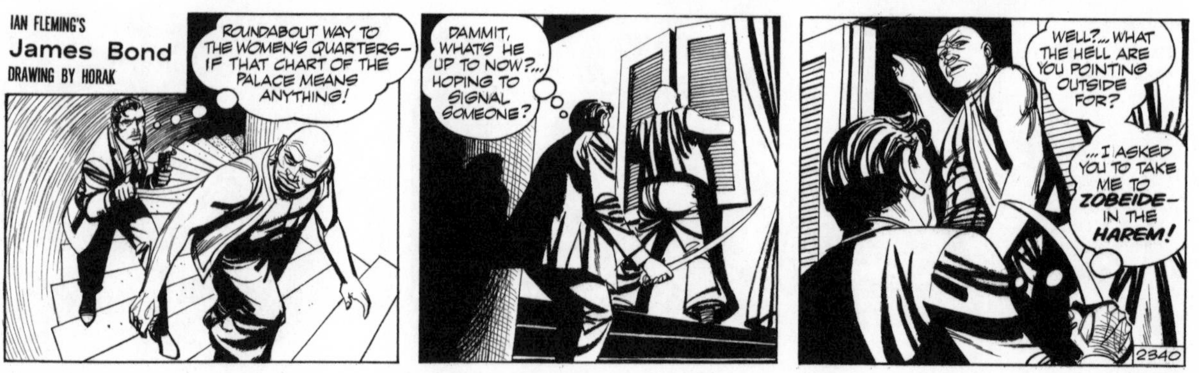
IAN FLEMING'S
James Bond
DRAWING BY HORAK
ROUNDABOUT WAY TO THE WOMEN'S QUARTERS—IF THAT CHART OF THE PALACE MEANS ANYTHING!
DAMMIT, WHAT'S HE UP TO NOW?... HOPING TO SIGNAL SOMEONE?
WELL?... WHAT THE HELL ARE YOU POINTING OUTSIDE FOR?
...I ASKED YOU TO TAKE ME TO ZOBEIDE—IN THE HAREM!
2340

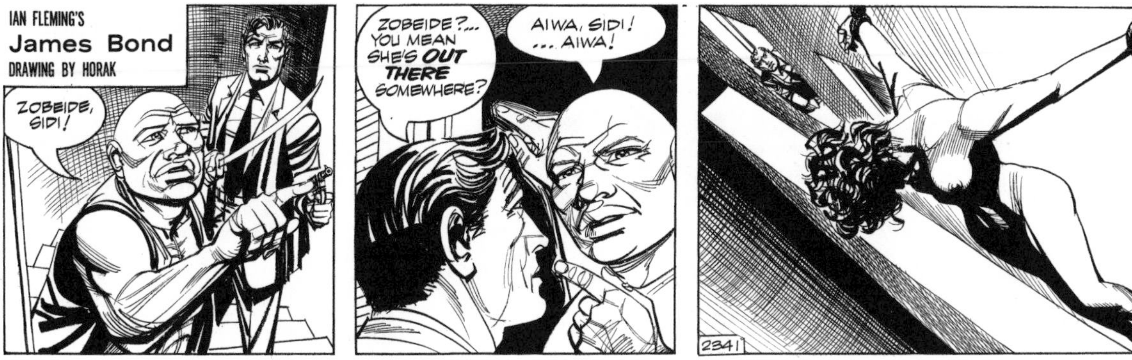
IAN FLEMING'S
James Bond
DRAWING BY HORAK
ZOBEIDE, SIDI!
ZOBEIDE?... YOU MEAN SHE'S OUT THERE SOMEWHERE?
AIWA, SIDI! ... AIWA!
2341

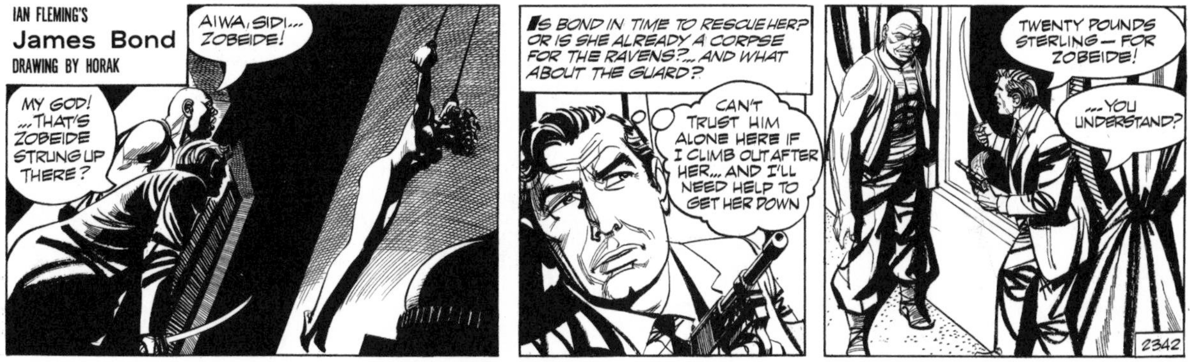
IAN FLEMING'S
James Bond
DRAWING BY HORAK
AIWA, SIDI... ZOBEIDE!
MY GOD! ...THAT'S ZOBEIDE STRUNG UP THERE?
IS BOND IN TIME TO RESCUE HER? OR IS SHE ALREADY A CORPSE FOR THE RAVENS?... AND WHAT ABOUT THE GUARD?
CAN'T TRUST HIM ALONE HERE IF I CLIMB OUT AFTER HER... AND I'LL NEED HELP TO GET HER DOWN
TWENTY POUNDS STERLING — FOR ZOBEIDE!
...YOU UNDERSTAND?
2342

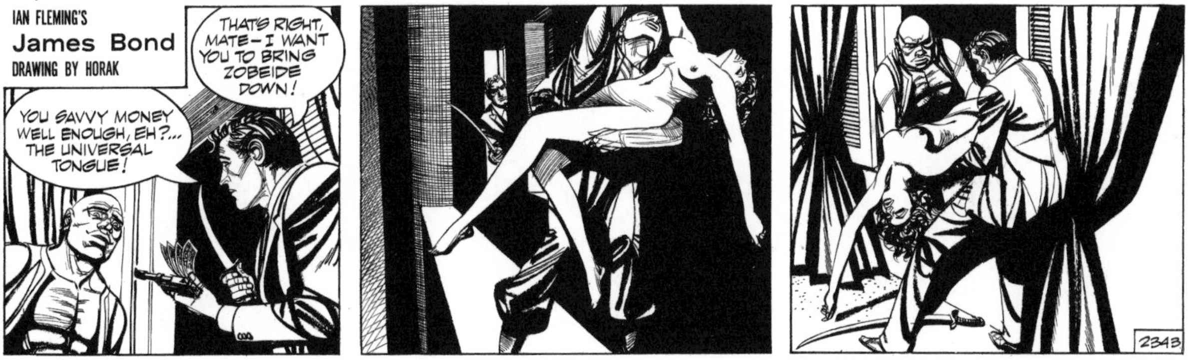
IAN FLEMING'S
James Bond
DRAWING BY HORAK
THAT'S RIGHT, MATE — I WANT YOU TO BRING ZOBEIDE DOWN!
YOU SAVVY MONEY WELL ENOUGH, EH?... THE UNIVERSAL TONGUE!
2343

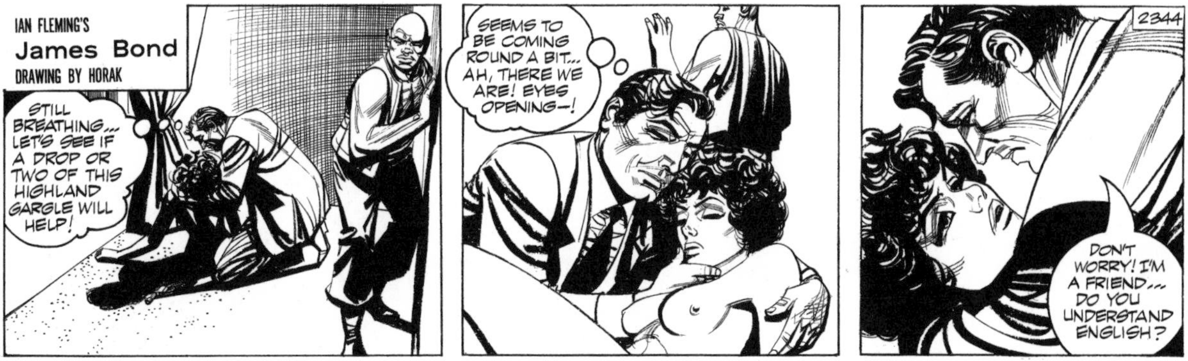
IAN FLEMING'S
James Bond
DRAWING BY HORAK
STILL BREATHING... LET'S SEE IF A DROP OR TWO OF THIS HIGHLAND GARGLE WILL HELP!
SEEMS TO BE COMING ROUND A BIT... AH, THERE WE ARE! EYES OPENING —!
2344
DON'T WORRY! I'M A FRIEND... DO YOU UNDERSTAND ENGLISH?

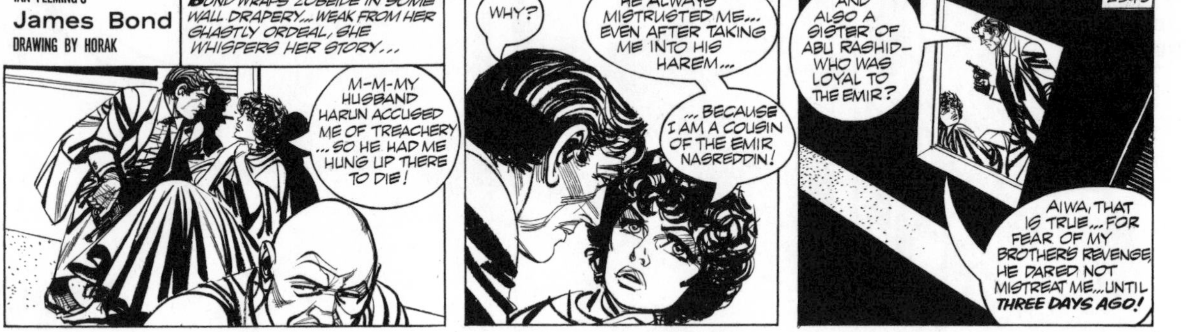
IAN FLEMING'S
James Bond
DRAWING BY HORAK
BOND WRAPS ZOBEIDE IN SOME WALL DRAPERY... WEAK FROM HER GHASTLY ORDEAL, SHE WHISPERS HER STORY...
M-M-MY HUSBAND HARUN ACCUSED ME OF TREACHERY ...SO HE HAD ME HUNG UP THERE TO DIE!
WHY?
HE ALWAYS MISTRUSTED ME... EVEN AFTER TAKING ME INTO HIS HAREM...
...BECAUSE I AM A COUSIN OF THE EMIR NASREDDIN!
2345
AND ALSO A SISTER OF ABU RASHID- WHO WAS LOYAL TO THE EMIR?
AIWA, THAT IS TRUE... FOR FEAR OF MY BROTHER'S REVENGE HE DARED NOT MISTREAT ME... UNTIL THREE DAYS AGO!

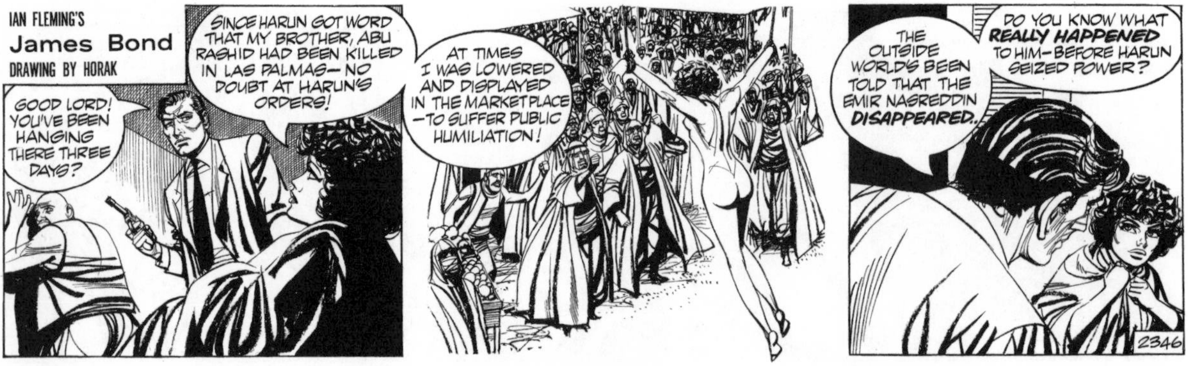
IAN FLEMING'S
James Bond
DRAWING BY HORAK
GOOD LORD! YOU'VE BEEN HANGING THERE THREE DAYS?
SINCE HARUN GOT WORD THAT MY BROTHER, ABU RASHID HAD BEEN KILLED IN LAS PALMAS—NO DOUBT AT HARUN'S ORDERS!
AT TIMES I WAS LOWERED AND DISPLAYED IN THE MARKET PLACE—TO SUFFER PUBLIC HUMILIATION!
THE OUTSIDE WORLD'S BEEN TOLD THAT THE EMIR NASREDDIN DISAPPEARED...
DO YOU KNOW WHAT REALLY HAPPENED TO HIM—BEFORE HARUN SEIZED POWER?
2346

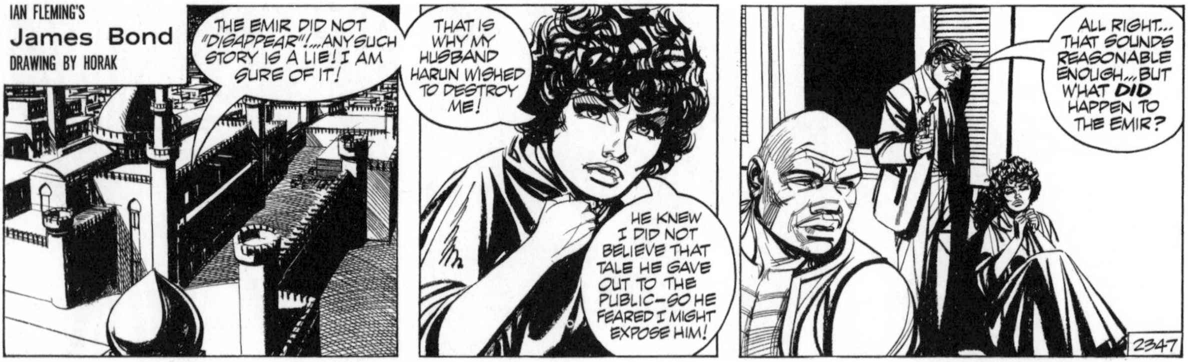
IAN FLEMING'S
James Bond
DRAWING BY HORAK
THE EMIR DID NOT "DISAPPEAR"!... ANY SUCH STORY IS A LIE! I AM SURE OF IT!
THAT IS WHY MY HUSBAND HARUN WISHED TO DESTROY ME!
HE KNEW I DID NOT BELIEVE THAT TALE HE GAVE OUT TO THE PUBLIC—SO HE FEARED I MIGHT EXPOSE HIM!
ALL RIGHT... THAT SOUNDS REASONABLE ENOUGH... BUT WHAT DID HAPPEN TO THE EMIR?
2347

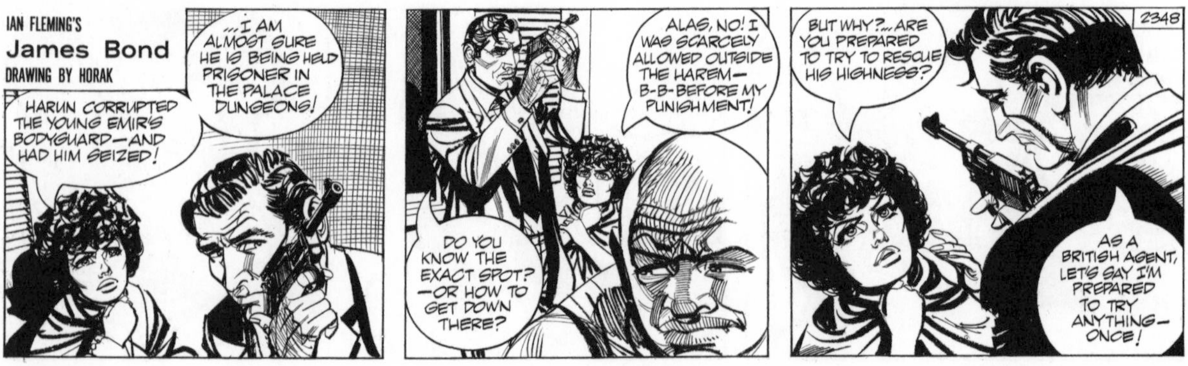
IAN FLEMING'S
James Bond
DRAWING BY HORAK
HARUN CORRUPTED THE YOUNG EMIR'S BODYGUARD—AND HAD HIM SEIZED!
...I AM ALMOST SURE HE IS BEING HELD PRISONER IN THE PALACE DUNGEONS!
DO YOU KNOW THE EXACT SPOT?—OR HOW TO GET DOWN THERE?
ALAS, NO! I WAS SCARCELY ALLOWED OUTSIDE THE HAREM—B-B-BEFORE MY PUNISHMENT!
2348
BUT WHY?... ARE YOU PREPARED TO TRY TO RESCUE HIS HIGHNESS?
AS A BRITISH AGENT, LET'S SAY I'M PREPARED TO TRY ANYTHING—ONCE!

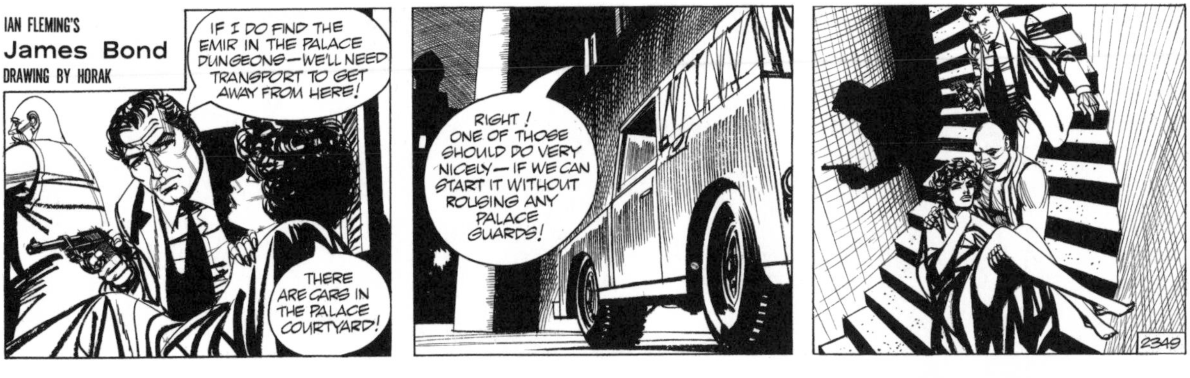
IAN FLEMING'S
James Bond
DRAWING BY HORAK
IF I DO FIND THE EMIR IN THE PALACE DUNGEONS—WE'LL NEED TRANSPORT TO GET AWAY FROM HERE!
THERE ARE CARS IN THE PALACE COURTYARD!
RIGHT! ONE OF THOSE SHOULD DO VERY NICELY—IF WE CAN START IT WITHOUT ROUSING ANY PALACE GUARDS!
2349

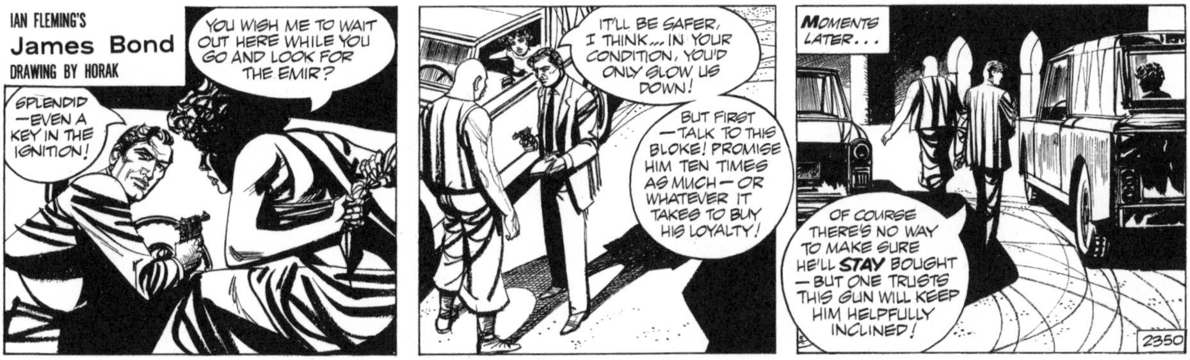
IAN FLEMING'S
James Bond
DRAWING BY HORAK
YOU WISH ME TO WAIT OUT HERE WHILE YOU GO AND LOOK FOR THE EMIR?
SPLENDID—EVEN A KEY IN THE IGNITION!
IT'LL BE SAFER, I THINK... IN YOUR CONDITION, YOU'D ONLY SLOW US DOWN!
BUT FIRST—TALK TO THIS BLOKE! PROMISE HIM TEN TIMES AS MUCH—OR WHATEVER IT TAKES TO BUY HIS LOYALTY!
MOMENTS LATER...
OF COURSE THERE'S NO WAY TO MAKE SURE HE'LL STAY BOUGHT—BUT ONE TRUSTS THIS GUN WILL KEEP HIM HELPFULLY INCLINED!
2350

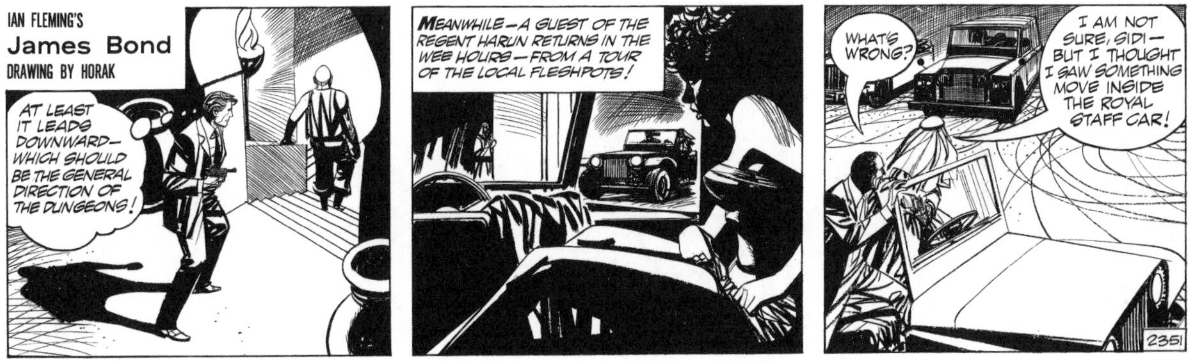
IAN FLEMING'S
James Bond
DRAWING BY HORAK
AT LEAST IT LEADS DOWNWARD—WHICH SHOULD BE THE GENERAL DIRECTION OF THE DUNGEONS!
MEANWHILE—A GUEST OF THE REGENT HARUN RETURNS IN THE WEE HOURS—FROM A TOUR OF THE LOCAL FLESHPOTS!
WHAT'S WRONG?
I AM NOT SURE, SIDI—BUT I THOUGHT I SAW SOMETHING MOVE INSIDE THE ROYAL STAFF CAR!
2351

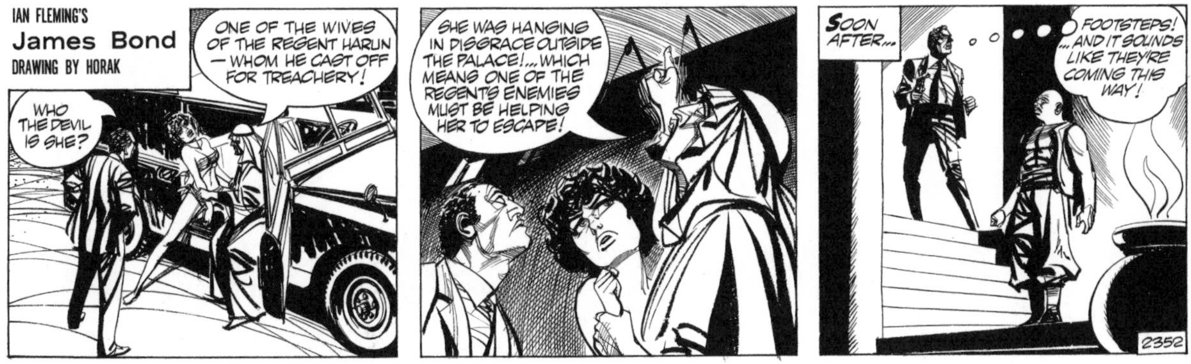
IAN FLEMING'S
James Bond
DRAWING BY HORAK
WHO THE DEVIL IS SHE?
ONE OF THE WIVES OF THE REGENT HARUN—WHOM HE CAST OFF FOR TREACHERY!
SHE WAS HANGING IN DISGRACE OUTSIDE THE PALACE!... WHICH MEANS ONE OF THE REGENT'S ENEMIES MUST BE HELPING HER TO ESCAPE!
SOON AFTER...
FOOTSTEPS! ...AND IT SOUNDS LIKE THEY'RE COMING THIS WAY!
2352

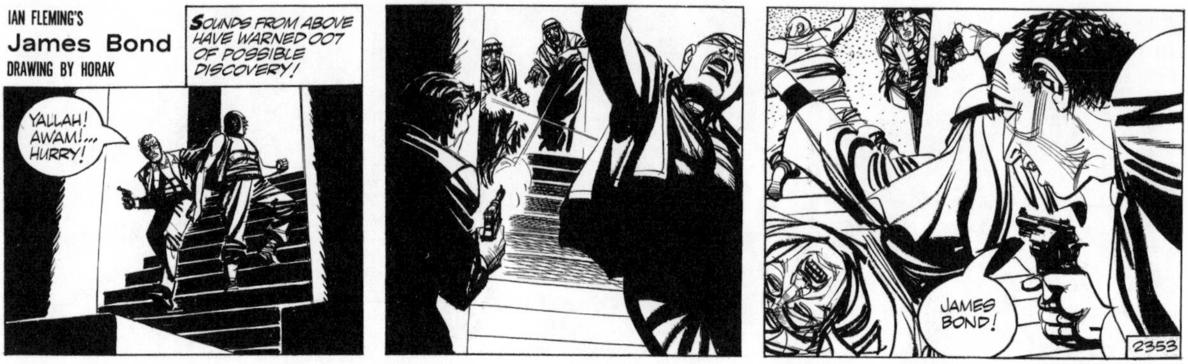
IAN FLEMING'S
James Bond
DRAWING BY HORAK
SOUNDS FROM ABOVE HAVE WARNED 007 OF POSSIBLE DISCOVERY!
YALLAH! AWAM!... HURRY!
JAMES BOND!
2353

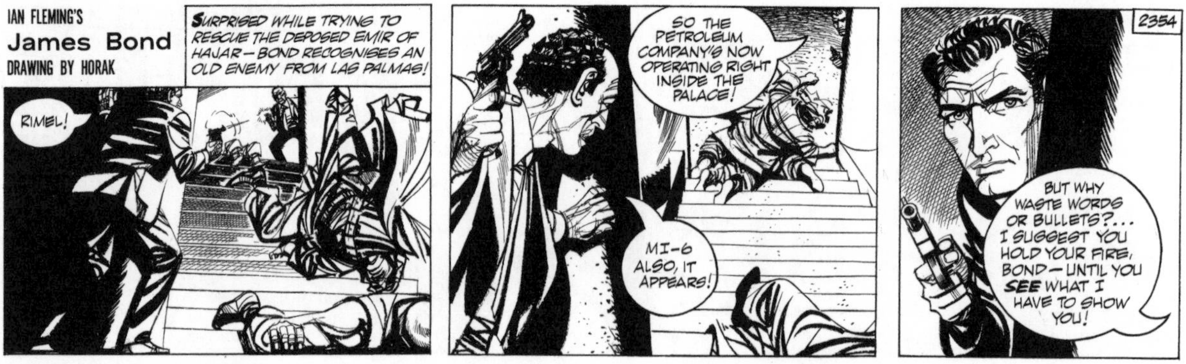
IAN FLEMING'S
James Bond
DRAWING BY HORAK
SURPRISED WHILE TRYING TO RESCUE THE DEPOSED EMIR OF HAJAR—BOND RECOGNISES AN OLD ENEMY FROM LAS PALMAS!
RIMEL!
SO THE PETROLEUM COMPANY'S NOW OPERATING RIGHT INSIDE THE PALACE!
MI-6 ALSO, IT APPEARS!
2354
BUT WHY WASTE WORDS OR BULLETS?... I SUGGEST YOU HOLD YOUR FIRE, BOND—UNTIL YOU SEE WHAT I HAVE TO SHOW YOU!

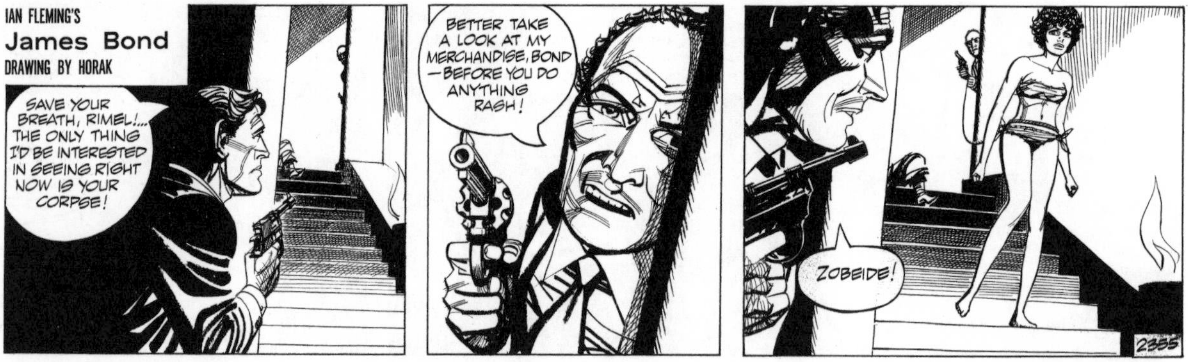
IAN FLEMING'S
James Bond
DRAWING BY HORAK
SAVE YOUR BREATH, RIMEL!... THE ONLY THING I'D BE INTERESTED IN SEEING RIGHT NOW IS YOUR CORPSE!
BETTER TAKE A LOOK AT MY MERCHANDISE, BOND —BEFORE YOU DO ANYTHING RASH!
ZOBEIDE!
2355

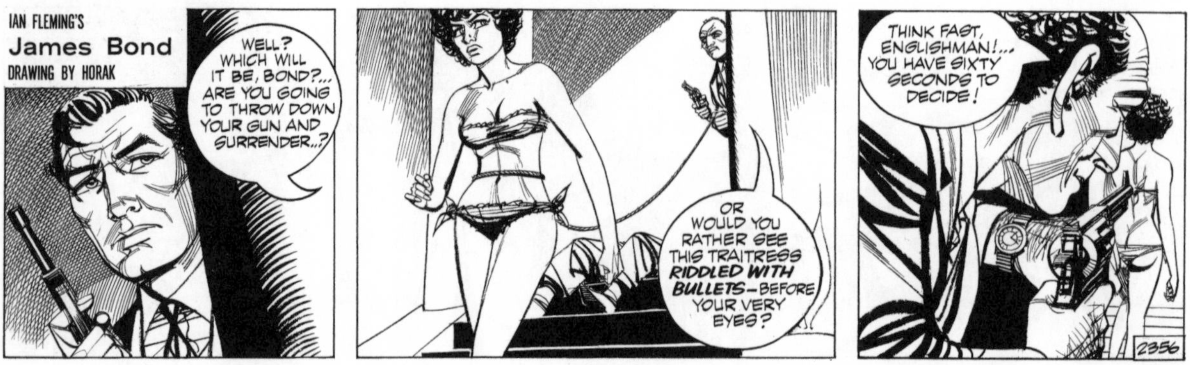
IAN FLEMING'S
James Bond
DRAWING BY HORAK
WELL? WHICH WILL IT BE, BOND?... ARE YOU GOING TO THROW DOWN YOUR GUN AND SURRENDER...?
OR WOULD YOU RATHER SEE THIS TRAITRESS RIDDLED WITH BULLETS—BEFORE YOUR VERY EYES?
THINK FAST, ENGLISHMAN!... YOU HAVE SIXTY SECONDS TO DECIDE!
2356

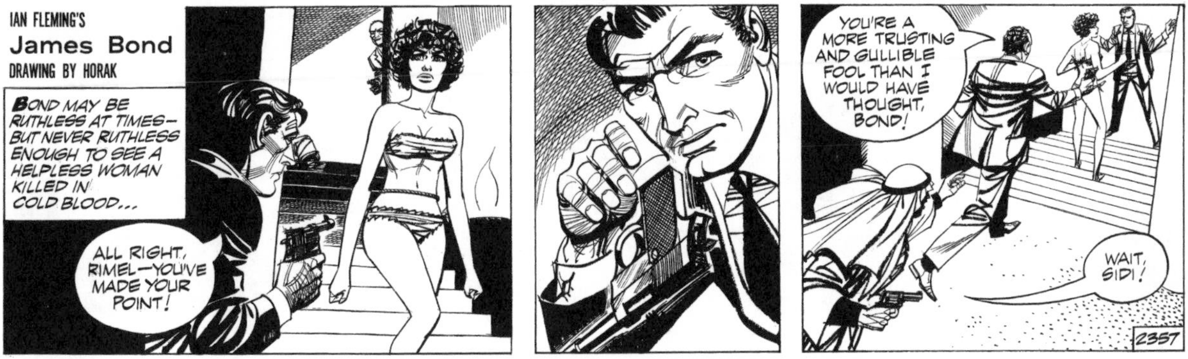
IAN FLEMING'S
James Bond
DRAWING BY HORAK
BOND MAY BE RUTHLESS AT TIMES—BUT NEVER RUTHLESS ENOUGH TO SEE A HELPLESS WOMAN KILLED IN COLD BLOOD...
ALL RIGHT, RIMEL—YOU'VE MADE YOUR POINT!
YOU'RE A MORE TRUSTING AND GULLIBLE FOOL THAN I WOULD HAVE THOUGHT, BOND!
WAIT, SIDI!
2357

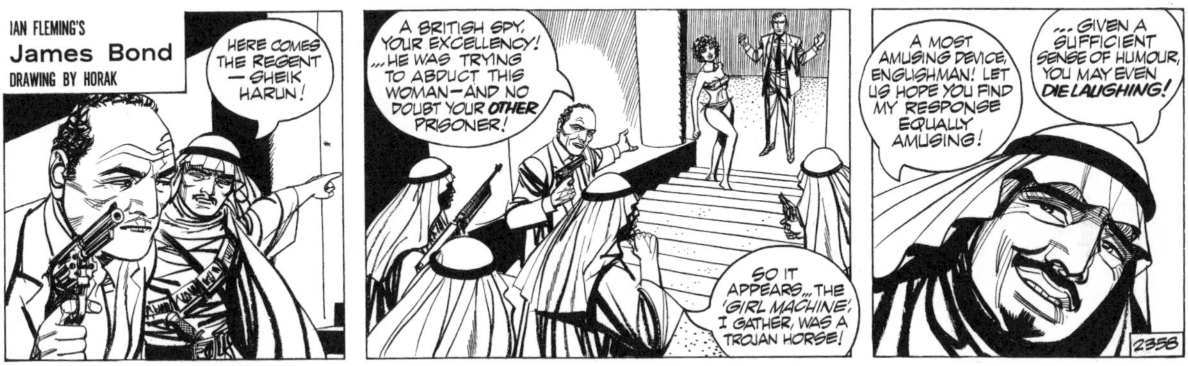
IAN FLEMING'S
James Bond
DRAWING BY HORAK
HERE COMES THE REGENT —SHEIK HARUN!
A BRITISH SPY, YOUR EXCELLENCY! ...HE WAS TRYING TO ABDUCT THIS WOMAN—AND NO DOUBT YOUR OTHER PRISONER!
SO IT APPEARS... THE 'GIRL MACHINE', I GATHER, WAS A TROJAN HORSE!
A MOST AMUSING DEVICE, ENGLISHMAN! LET US HOPE YOU FIND MY RESPONSE EQUALLY AMUSING!
...GIVEN A SUFFICIENT SENSE OF HUMOUR, YOU MAY EVEN DIE LAUGHING!
2358

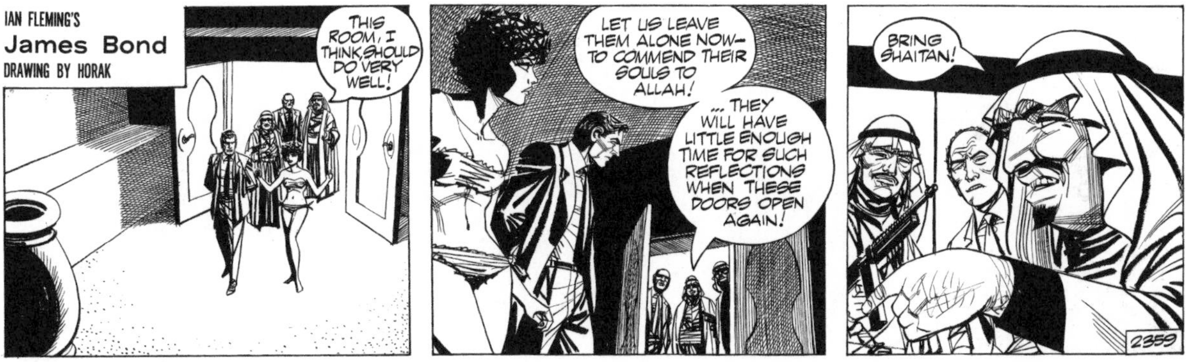
IAN FLEMING'S
James Bond
DRAWING BY HORAK
THIS ROOM, I THINK, SHOULD DO VERY WELL!
LET US LEAVE THEM ALONE NOW—TO COMMEND THEIR SOULS TO ALLAH!
...THEY WILL HAVE LITTLE ENOUGH TIME FOR SUCH REFLECTIONS WHEN THESE DOORS OPEN AGAIN!
BRING SHAITAN!
2359

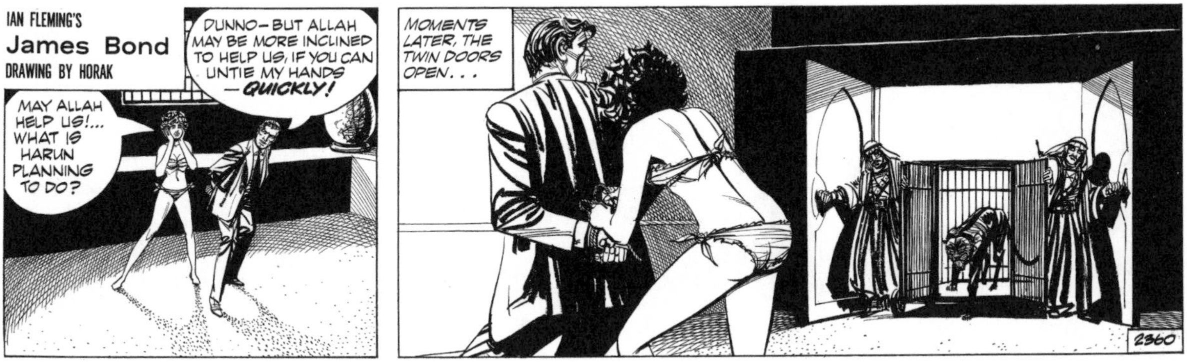
IAN FLEMING'S
James Bond
DRAWING BY HORAK
MAY ALLAH HELP US!... WHAT IS HARUN PLANNING TO DO?
DUNNO—BUT ALLAH MAY BE MORE INCLINED TO HELP US, IF YOU CAN UNTIE MY HANDS—QUICKLY!
MOMENTS LATER, THE TWIN DOORS OPEN...
2360

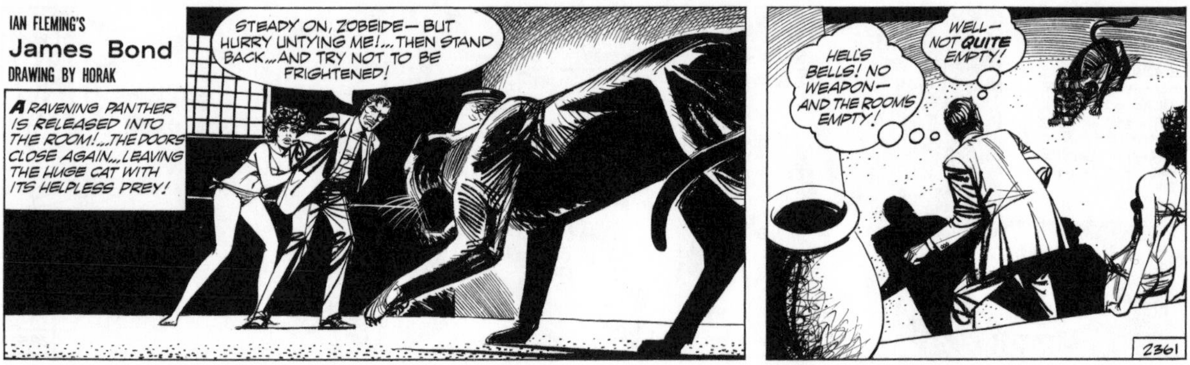
IAN FLEMING'S
James Bond
DRAWING BY HORAK
A RAVENING PANTHER IS RELEASED INTO THE ROOM!...THE DOORS CLOSE AGAIN...LEAVING THE HUGE CAT WITH ITS HELPLESS PREY!
STEADY ON, ZOBEIDE— BUT HURRY UNTYING ME!...THEN STAND BACK...AND TRY NOT TO BE FRIGHTENED!
HELL'S BELLS! NO WEAPON— AND THE ROOM'S EMPTY!
WELL— NOT QUITE EMPTY!
2361

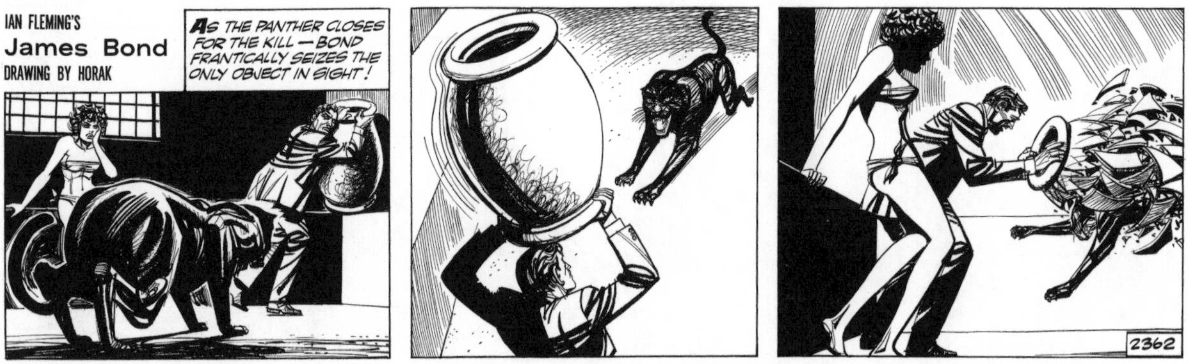
IAN FLEMING'S
James Bond
DRAWING BY HORAK
AS THE PANTHER CLOSES FOR THE KILL —BOND FRANTICALLY SEIZES THE ONLY OBJECT IN SIGHT!
2362

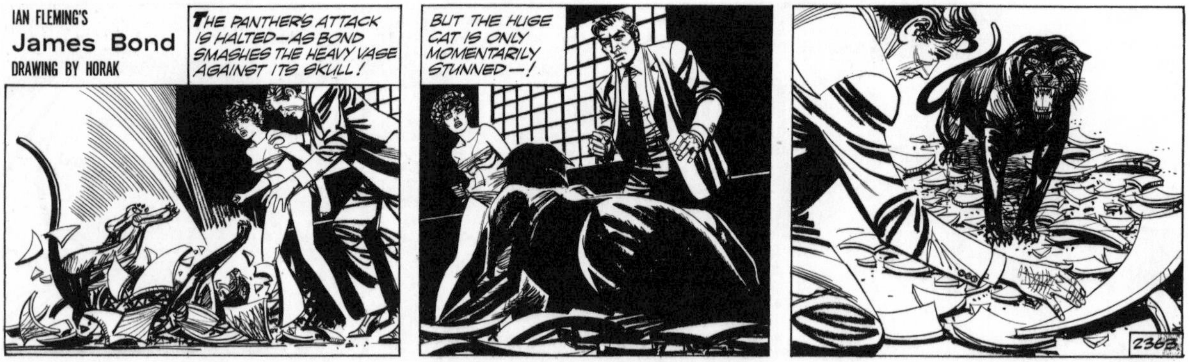
IAN FLEMING'S
James Bond
DRAWING BY HORAK
THE PANTHER'S ATTACK IS HALTED—AS BOND SMASHES THE HEAVY VASE AGAINST ITS SKULL!
BUT THE HUGE CAT IS ONLY MOMENTARILY STUNNED—!
2363

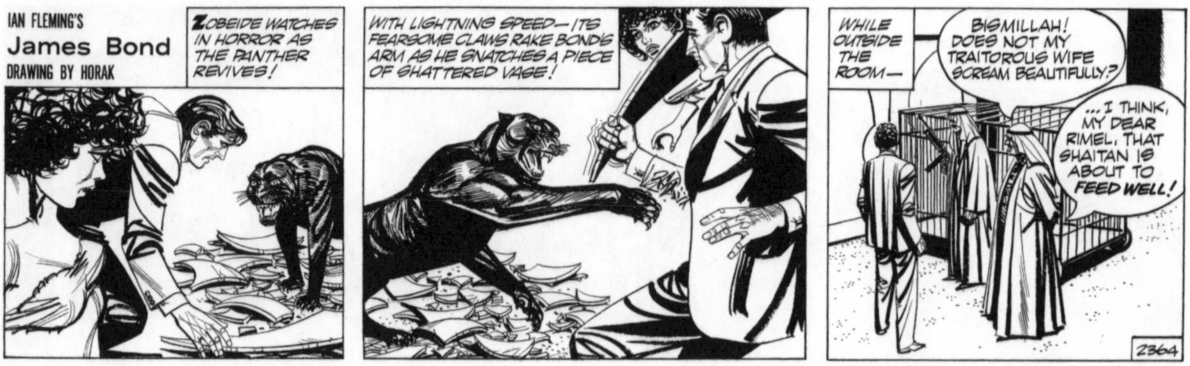
IAN FLEMING'S
James Bond
DRAWING BY HORAK
ZOBEIDE WATCHES IN HORROR AS THE PANTHER REVIVES!
WITH LIGHTNING SPEED—ITS FEARSOME CLAWS RAKE BOND'S ARM AS HE SNATCHES A PIECE OF SHATTERED VASE!
WHILE OUTSIDE THE ROOM—
BISMILLAH! DOES NOT MY TRAITOROUS WIFE SCREAM BEAUTIFULLY?
...I THINK, MY DEAR RIMEL, THAT SHAITAN IS ABOUT TO FEED WELL!
2364

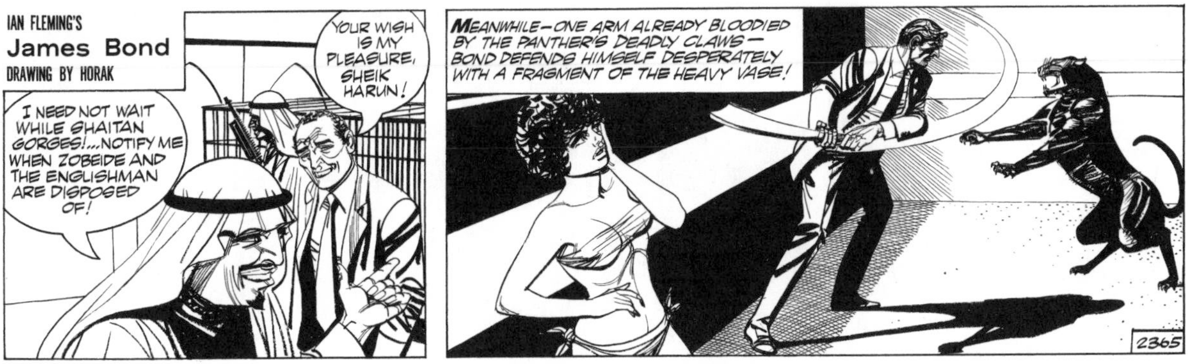
IAN FLEMING'S
James Bond
DRAWING BY HORAK
YOUR WISH IS MY PLEASURE, SHEIK HARUN!
I NEED NOT WAIT WHILE SHAITAN GORGES!...NOTIFY ME WHEN ZOBEIDE AND THE ENGLISHMAN ARE DISPOSED OF!
MEANWHILE—ONE ARM ALREADY BLOODIED BY THE PANTHER'S DEADLY CLAWS—BOND DEFENDS HIMSELF DESPERATELY WITH A FRAGMENT OF THE HEAVY VASE!
2365

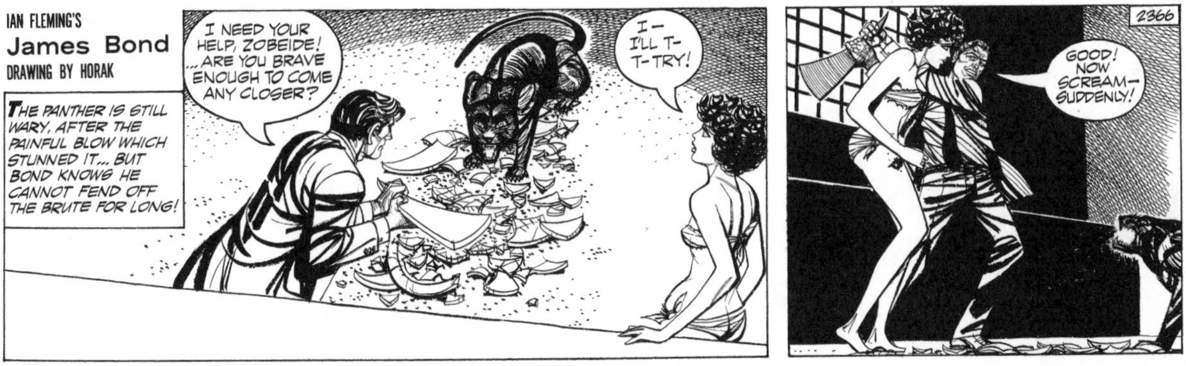
IAN FLEMING'S
James Bond
DRAWING BY HORAK
THE PANTHER IS STILL WARY, AFTER THE PAINFUL BLOW WHICH STUNNED IT... BUT BOND KNOWS HE CANNOT FEND OFF THE BRUTE FOR LONG!
I NEED YOUR HELP, ZOBEIDE! ...ARE YOU BRAVE ENOUGH TO COME ANY CLOSER?
I— I'LL T-T-TRY!
2366
GOOD! NOW SCREAM— SUDDENLY!

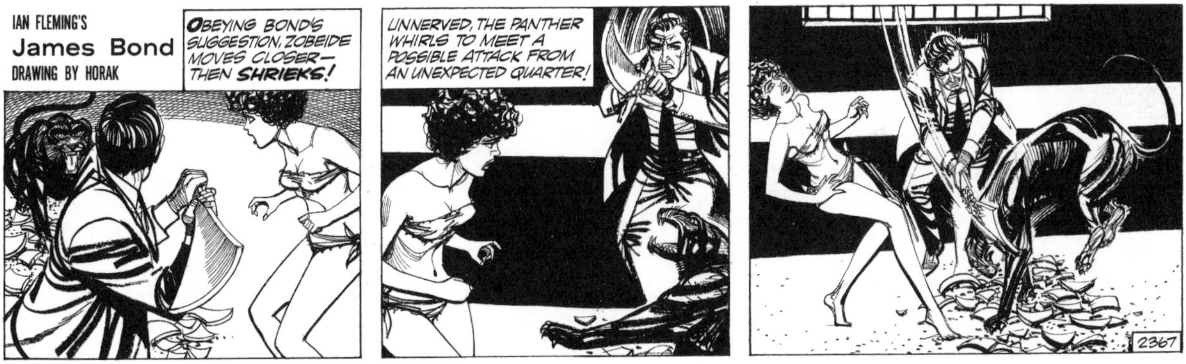
IAN FLEMING'S
James Bond
DRAWING BY HORAK
OBEYING BOND'S SUGGESTION, ZOBEIDE MOVES CLOSER— THEN SHRIEKS!
UNNERVED, THE PANTHER WHIRLS TO MEET A POSSIBLE ATTACK FROM AN UNEXPECTED QUARTER!
2367

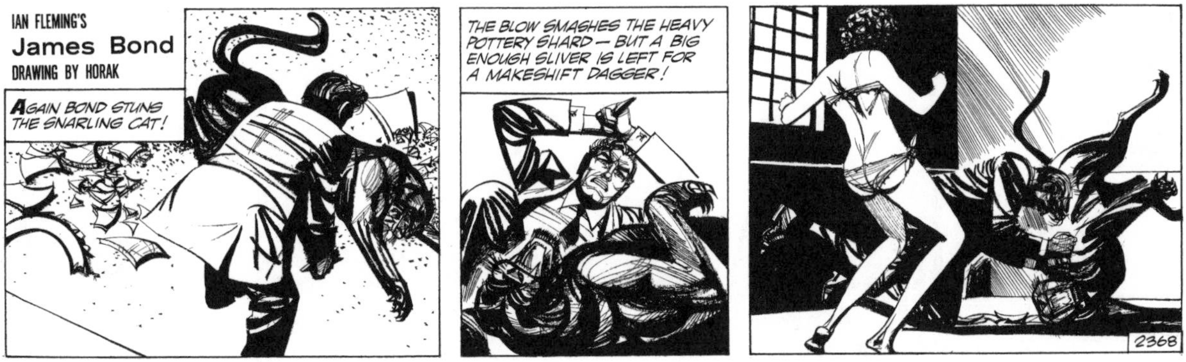
IAN FLEMING'S
James Bond
DRAWING BY HORAK
AGAIN BOND STUNS THE SNARLING CAT!
THE BLOW SMASHES THE HEAVY POTTERY SHARD—BUT A BIG ENOUGH SLIVER IS LEFT FOR A MAKESHIFT DAGGER!
2368

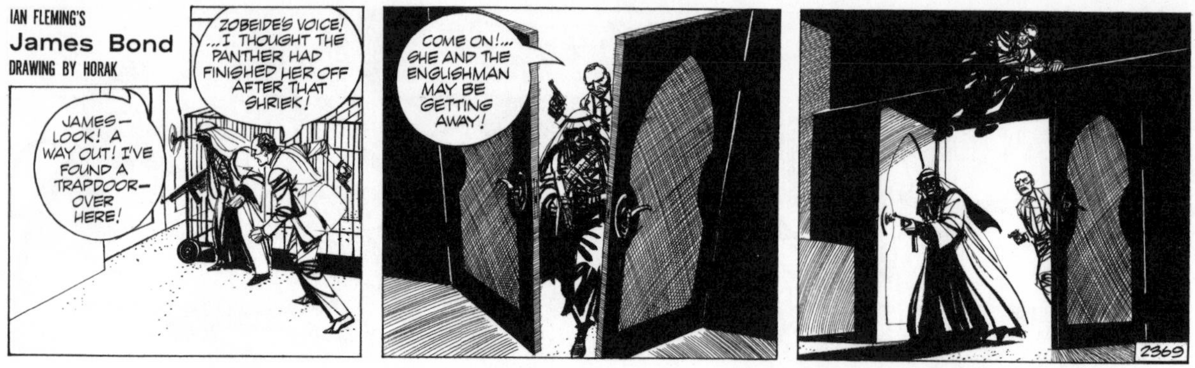
IAN FLEMING'S
James Bond
DRAWING BY HORAK
ZOBEIDE'S VOICE! ...I THOUGHT THE PANTHER HAD FINISHED HER OFF AFTER THAT SHRIEK!
JAMES— LOOK! A WAY OUT! I'VE FOUND A TRAPDOOR— OVER HERE!
COME ON!... SHE AND THE ENGLISHMAN MAY BE GETTING AWAY!
2369

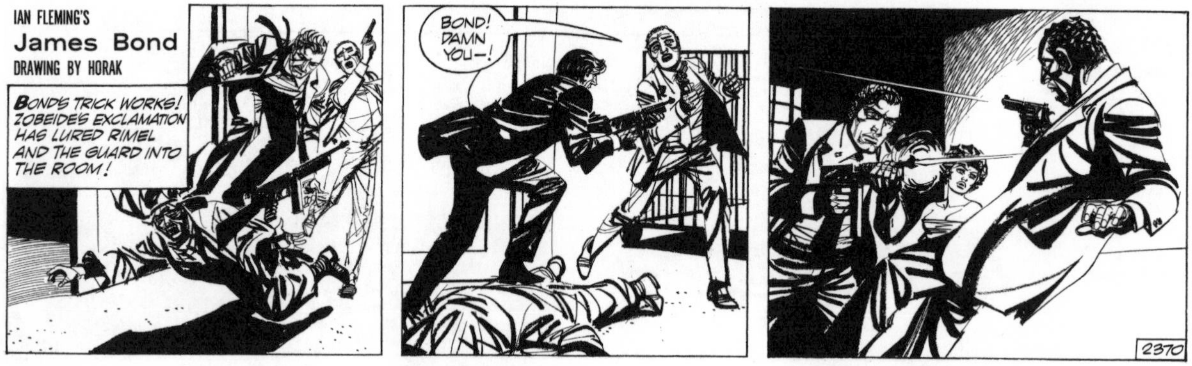
IAN FLEMING'S
James Bond
DRAWING BY HORAK
BOND'S TRICK WORKS! ZOBEIDE'S EXCLAMATION HAS LURED RIMEL AND THE GUARD INTO THE ROOM!
BOND! DAMN YOU—!
2370

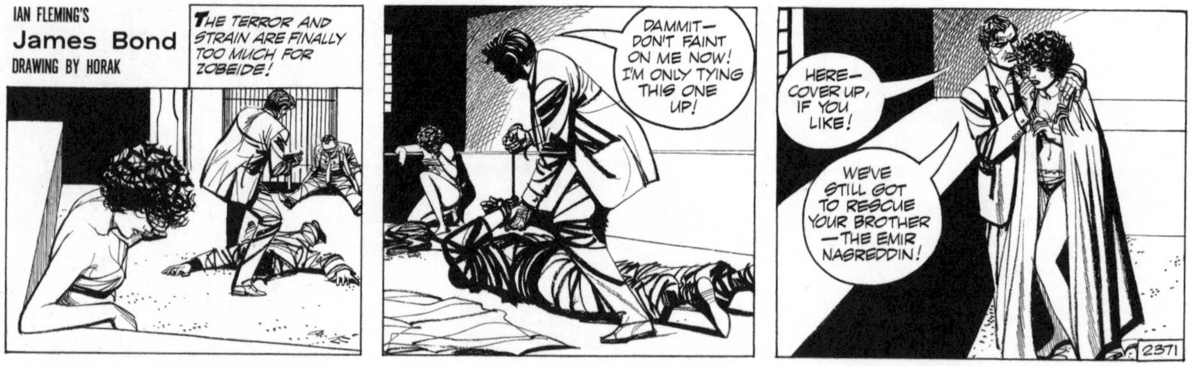
IAN FLEMING'S
James Bond
DRAWING BY HORAK
THE TERROR AND STRAIN ARE FINALLY TOO MUCH FOR ZOBEIDE!
DAMMIT— DON'T FAINT ON ME NOW! I'M ONLY TYING THIS ONE UP!
HERE— COVER UP, IF YOU LIKE!
WE'VE STILL GOT TO RESCUE YOUR BROTHER —THE EMIR NASREDDIN!
2371

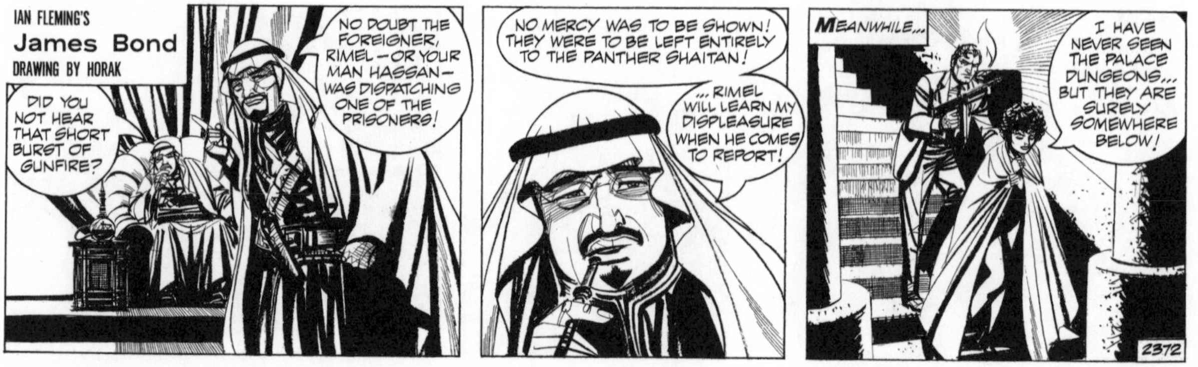
IAN FLEMING'S
James Bond
DRAWING BY HORAK
DID YOU NOT HEAR THAT SHORT BURST OF GUNFIRE?
NO DOUBT THE FOREIGNER, RIMEL—OR YOUR MAN HASSAN— WAS DISPATCHING ONE OF THE PRISONERS!
NO MERCY WAS TO BE SHOWN! THEY WERE TO BE LEFT ENTIRELY TO THE PANTHER SHAITAN!
...RIMEL WILL LEARN MY DISPLEASURE WHEN HE COMES TO REPORT!
MEANWHILE...
I HAVE NEVER SEEN THE PALACE DUNGEONS... BUT THEY ARE SURELY SOMEWHERE BELOW!
2372

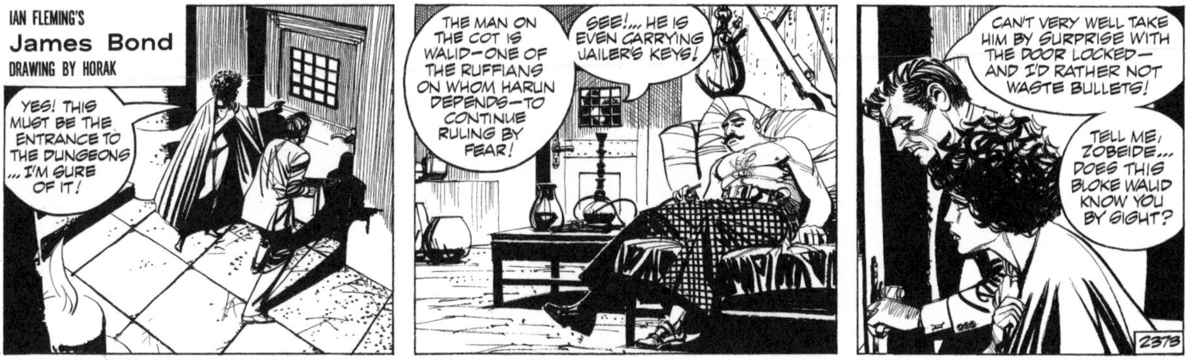
IAN FLEMING'S
James Bond
DRAWING BY HORAK
YES! THIS MUST BE THE ENTRANCE TO THE DUNGEONS ... I'M SURE OF IT!
THE MAN ON THE COT IS WALID—ONE OF THE RUFFIANS ON WHOM HARUN DEPENDS—TO CONTINUE RULING BY FEAR!
SEE!... HE IS EVEN CARRYING JAILER'S KEYS!
CAN'T VERY WELL TAKE HIM BY SURPRISE WITH THE DOOR LOCKED—AND I'D RATHER NOT WASTE BULLETS!
TELL ME, ZOBEIDE... DOES THIS BLOKE WALID KNOW YOU BY SIGHT?
2373

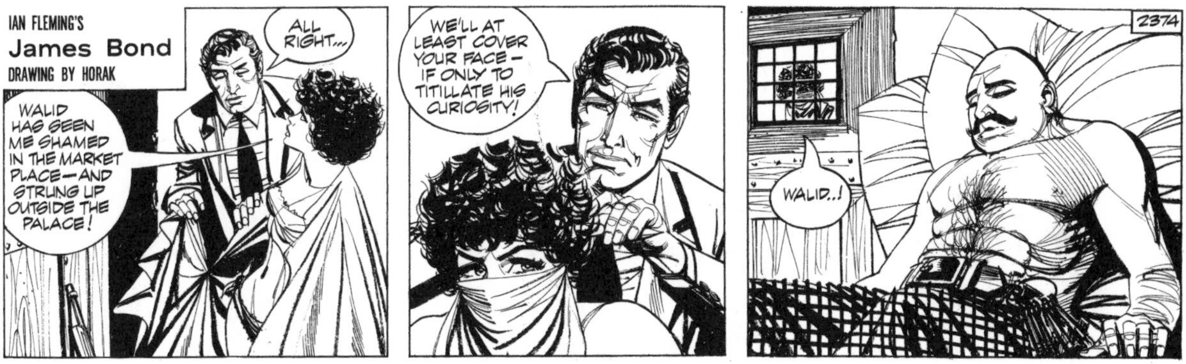
IAN FLEMING'S
James Bond
DRAWING BY HORAK
ALL RIGHT...
WALID HAS SEEN ME SHAMED IN THE MARKET PLACE—AND STRUNG UP OUTSIDE THE PALACE!
WE'LL AT LEAST COVER YOUR FACE—IF ONLY TO TITILLATE HIS CURIOSITY!
2374
WALID..!

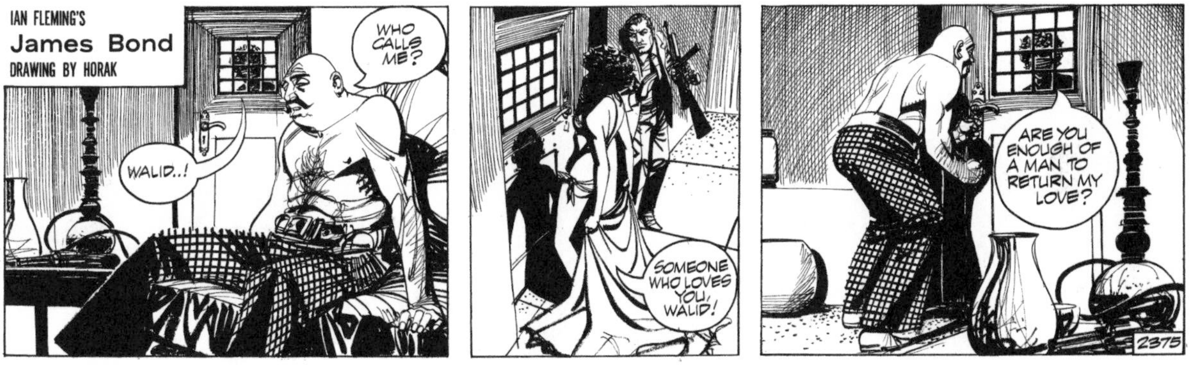
IAN FLEMING'S
James Bond
DRAWING BY HORAK
WHO CALLS ME?
WALID..!
SOMEONE WHO LOVES YOU, WALID!
ARE YOU ENOUGH OF A MAN TO RETURN MY LOVE?
2375

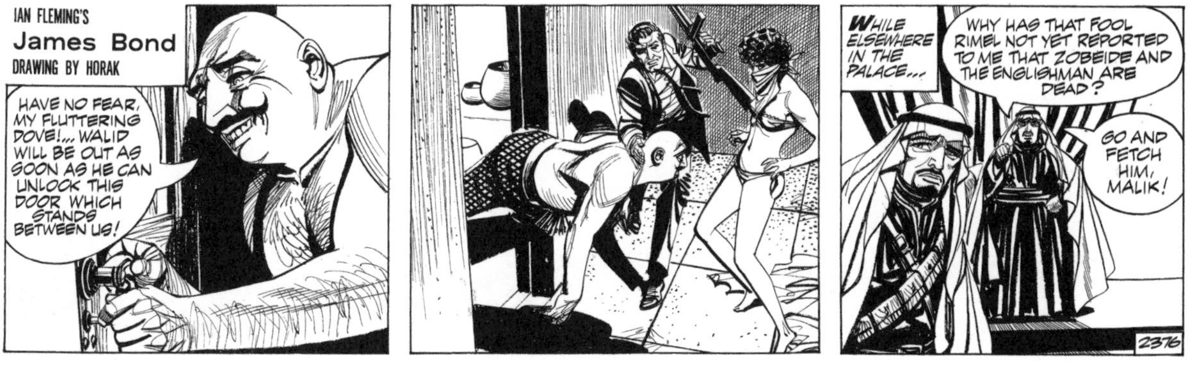
IAN FLEMING'S
James Bond
DRAWING BY HORAK
HAVE NO FEAR, MY FLUTTERING DOVE!... WALID WILL BE OUT AS SOON AS HE CAN UNLOCK THIS DOOR WHICH STANDS BETWEEN US!
WHILE ELSEWHERE IN THE PALACE...
WHY HAS THAT FOOL RIMEL NOT YET REPORTED TO ME THAT ZOBEIDE AND THE ENGLISHMAN ARE DEAD?
GO AND FETCH HIM, MALIK!
2376

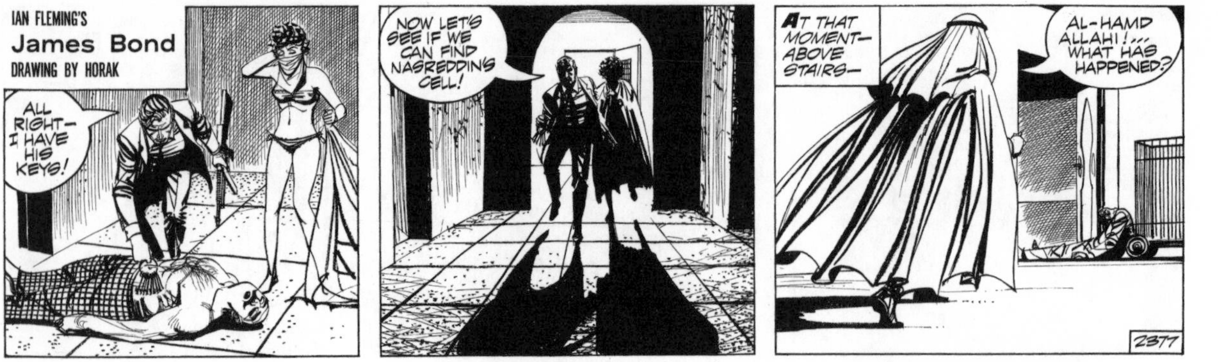
IAN FLEMING'S
James Bond
DRAWING BY HORAK
ALL RIGHT—I HAVE HIS KEYS!
NOW LET'S SEE IF WE CAN FIND NASREDDIN'S CELL!
AT THAT MOMENT—ABOVE STAIRS—
AL-HAMD ALLAH!... WHAT HAS HAPPENED?
2377

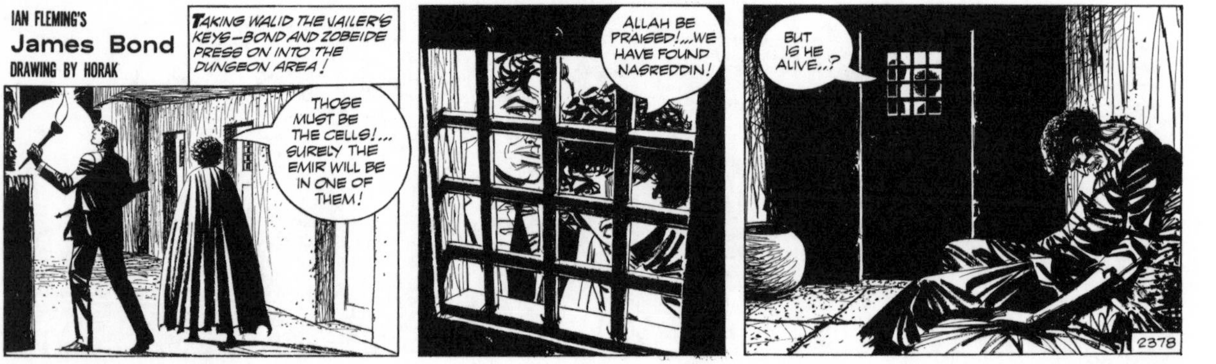
IAN FLEMING'S
James Bond
DRAWING BY HORAK
TAKING WALID THE JAILER'S KEYS—BOND AND ZOBEIDE PRESS ON INTO THE DUNGEON AREA!
THOSE MUST BE THE CELLS!... SURELY THE EMIR WILL BE IN ONE OF THEM!
ALLAH BE PRAISED!...WE HAVE FOUND NASREDDIN!
BUT IS HE ALIVE..?
2378

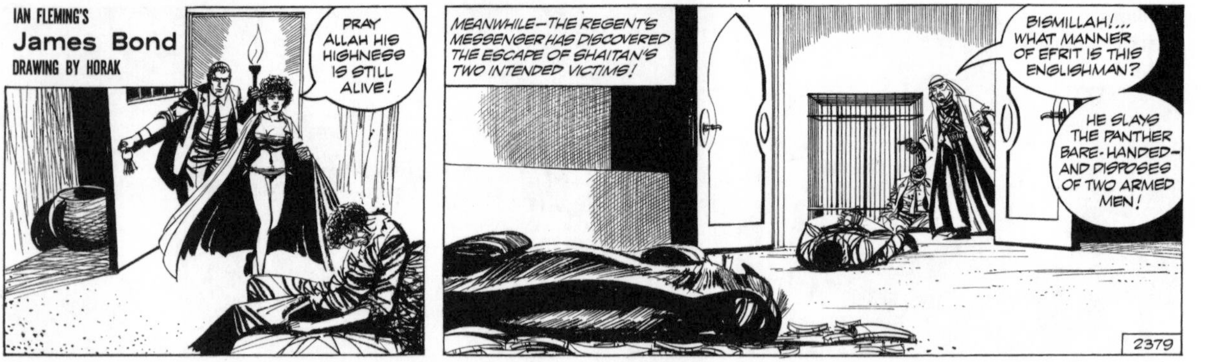
IAN FLEMING'S
James Bond
DRAWING BY HORAK
PRAY ALLAH HIS HIGHNESS IS STILL ALIVE!
MEANWHILE—THE REGENT'S MESSENGER HAS DISCOVERED THE ESCAPE OF SHAITAN'S TWO INTENDED VICTIMS!
BISMILLAH!... WHAT MANNER OF EFRIT IS THIS ENGLISHMAN?
HE SLAYS THE PANTHER BARE-HANDED—AND DISPOSES OF TWO ARMED MEN!
2379

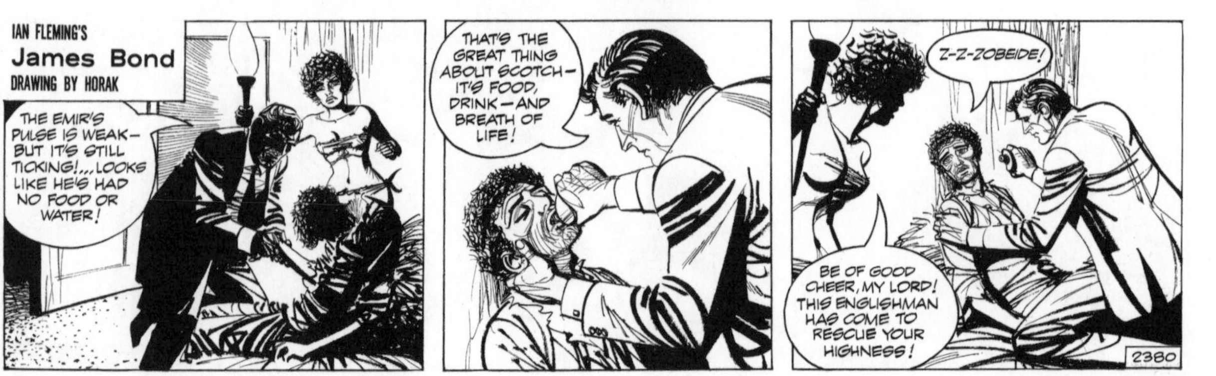
IAN FLEMING'S
James Bond
DRAWING BY HORAK
THE EMIR'S PULSE IS WEAK—BUT IT'S STILL TICKING!... LOOKS LIKE HE'S HAD NO FOOD OR WATER!
THAT'S THE GREAT THING ABOUT SCOTCH—IT'S FOOD, DRINK—AND BREATH OF LIFE!
Z-Z-ZOBEIDE!
BE OF GOOD CHEER, MY LORD! THIS ENGLISHMAN HAS COME TO RESCUE YOUR HIGHNESS!
2380

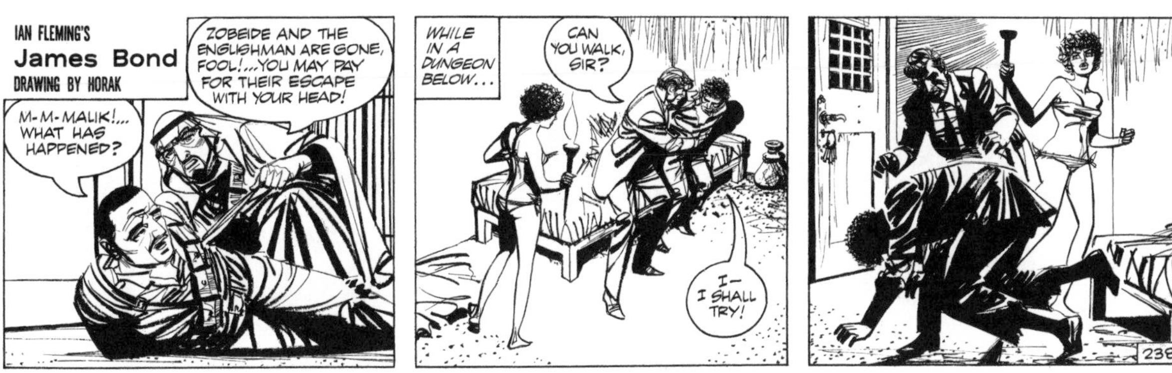
IAN FLEMING'S
James Bond
DRAWING BY HORAK
ZOBEIDE AND THE ENGLISHMAN ARE GONE, FOOL!... YOU MAY PAY FOR THEIR ESCAPE WITH YOUR HEAD!
M-M-MALIK!... WHAT HAS HAPPENED?
WHILE IN A DUNGEON BELOW...
CAN YOU WALK, SIR?
I- I SHALL TRY!
2381

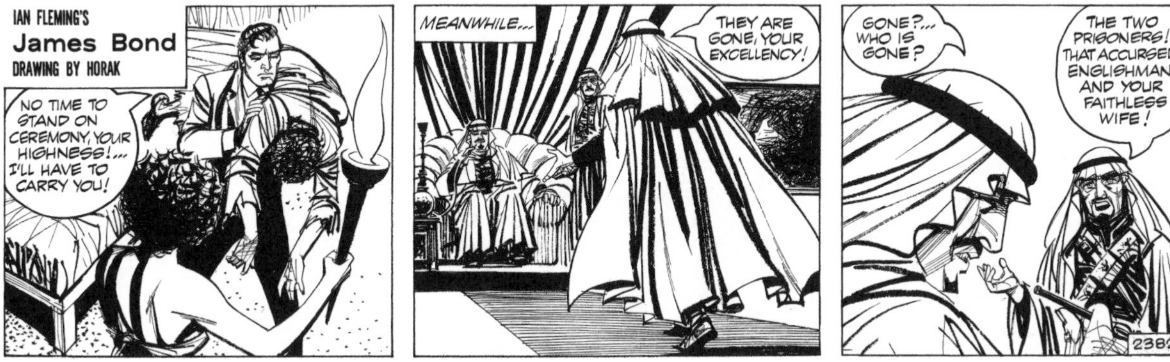
IAN FLEMING'S
James Bond
DRAWING BY HORAK
NO TIME TO STAND ON CEREMONY, YOUR HIGHNESS!... I'LL HAVE TO CARRY YOU!
MEANWHILE...
THEY ARE GONE, YOUR EXCELLENCY!
GONE?... WHO IS GONE?
THE TWO PRISONERS! THAT ACCURSED ENGLISHMAN AND YOUR FAITHLESS WIFE!
2382

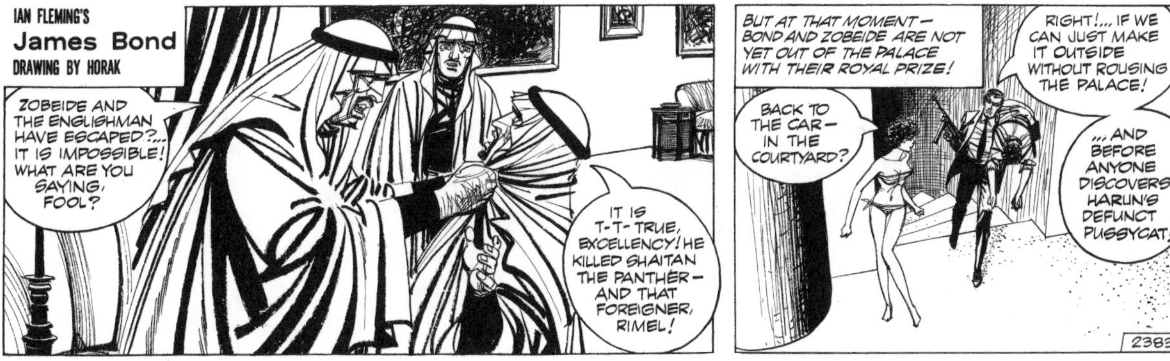
IAN FLEMING'S
James Bond
DRAWING BY HORAK
ZOBEIDE AND THE ENGLISHMAN HAVE ESCAPED?... IT IS IMPOSSIBLE! WHAT ARE YOU SAYING, FOOL?
IT IS T-T-TRUE, EXCELLENCY! HE KILLED SHAITAN THE PANTHER— AND THAT FOREIGNER, RIMEL!
BUT AT THAT MOMENT— BOND AND ZOBEIDE ARE NOT YET OUT OF THE PALACE WITH THEIR ROYAL PRIZE!
BACK TO THE CAR— IN THE COURTYARD?
RIGHT!... IF WE CAN JUST MAKE IT OUTSIDE WITHOUT ROUSING THE PALACE!
...AND BEFORE ANYONE DISCOVERS HARUN'S DEFUNCT PUSSYCAT!
2383

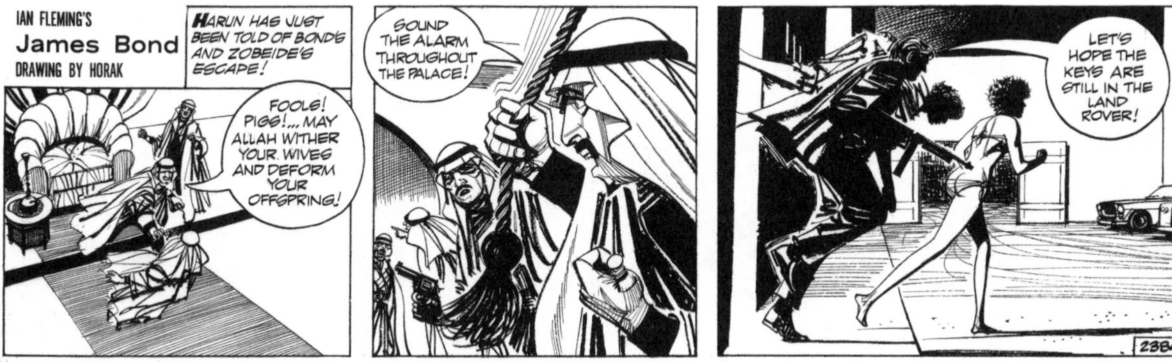
IAN FLEMING'S
James Bond
DRAWING BY HORAK
HARUN HAS JUST BEEN TOLD OF BOND'S AND ZOBEIDE'S ESCAPE!
FOOLS! PIGS!... MAY ALLAH WITHER YOUR WIVES AND DEFORM YOUR OFFSPRING!
SOUND THE ALARM THROUGHOUT THE PALACE!
LET'S HOPE THE KEYS ARE STILL IN THE LAND ROVER!
2384

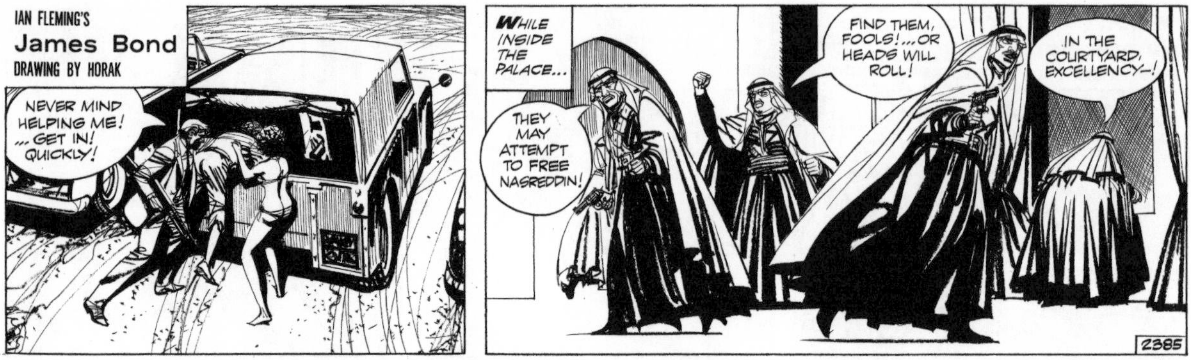
IAN FLEMING'S
James Bond
DRAWING BY HORAK
NEVER MIND HELPING ME! ... GET IN! QUICKLY!
WHILE INSIDE THE PALACE...
THEY MAY ATTEMPT TO FREE NASREDDIN!
FIND THEM, FOOLS! ... OR HEADS WILL ROLL!
... IN THE COURTYARD, EXCELLENCY--!
2385

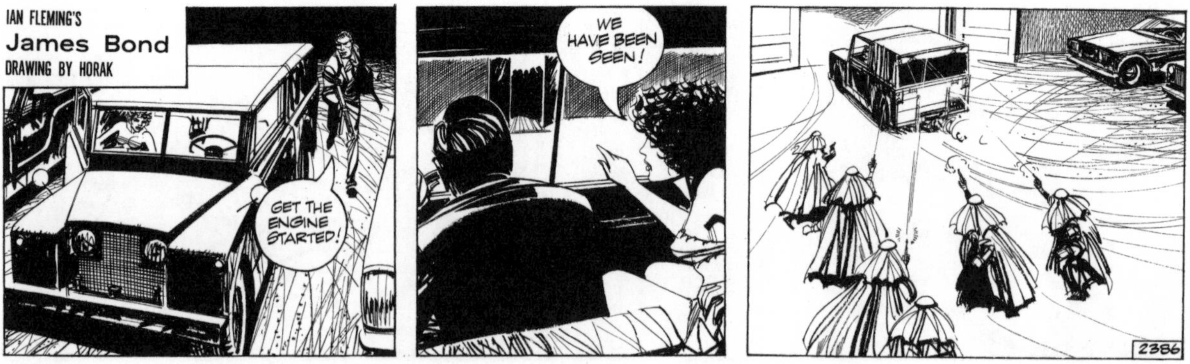
IAN FLEMING'S
James Bond
DRAWING BY HORAK
GET THE ENGINE STARTED!
WE HAVE BEEN SEEN!
2386

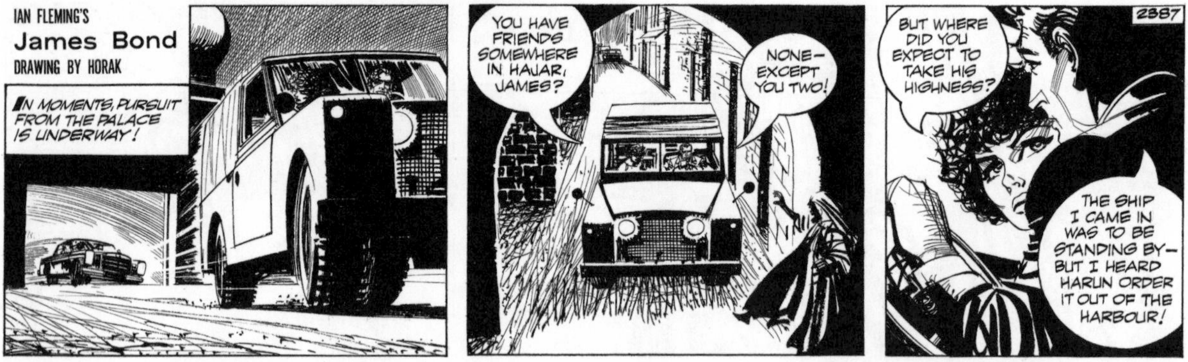
IAN FLEMING'S
James Bond
DRAWING BY HORAK
IN MOMENTS, PURSUIT FROM THE PALACE IS UNDERWAY!
YOU HAVE FRIENDS SOMEWHERE IN HAJAR, JAMES?
NONE-- EXCEPT YOU TWO!
2387
BUT WHERE DID YOU EXPECT TO TAKE HIS HIGHNESS?
THE SHIP I CAME IN WAS TO BE STANDING BY-- BUT I HEARD HARUN ORDER IT OUT OF THE HARBOUR!

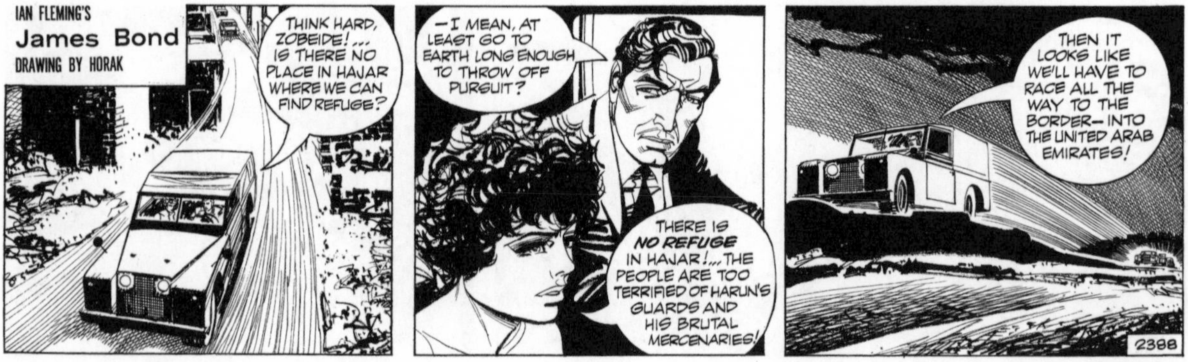
IAN FLEMING'S
James Bond
DRAWING BY HORAK
THINK HARD, ZOBEIDE! ... IS THERE NO PLACE IN HAJAR WHERE WE CAN FIND REFUGE?
--I MEAN, AT LEAST GO TO EARTH LONG ENOUGH TO THROW OFF PURSUIT?
THERE IS NO REFUGE IN HAJAR! ... THE PEOPLE ARE TOO TERRIFIED OF HARUN'S GUARDS AND HIS BRUTAL MERCENARIES!
THEN IT LOOKS LIKE WE'LL HAVE TO RACE ALL THE WAY TO THE BORDER-- INTO THE UNITED ARAB EMIRATES!
2388

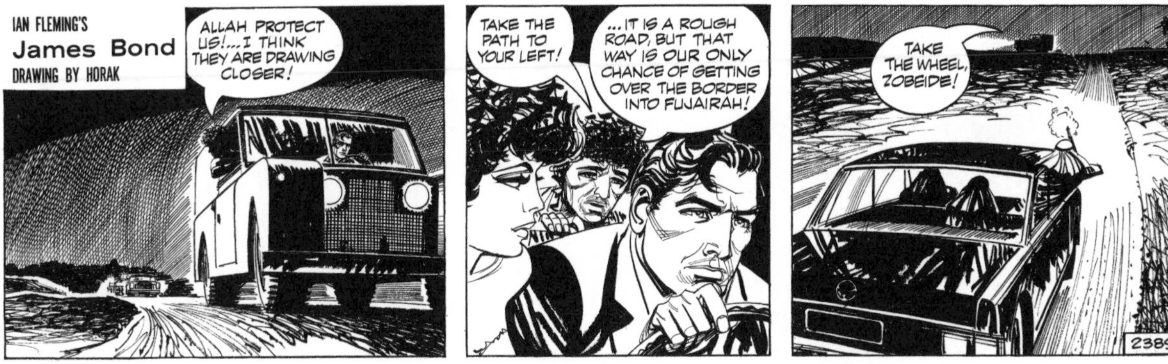
IAN FLEMING'S
James Bond
DRAWING BY HORAK
ALLAH PROTECT US!... I THINK THEY ARE DRAWING CLOSER!
TAKE THE PATH TO YOUR LEFT!
...IT IS A ROUGH ROAD, BUT THAT WAY IS OUR ONLY CHANCE OF GETTING OVER THE BORDER INTO FUJAIRAH!
TAKE THE WHEEL, ZOBEIDE!
2389

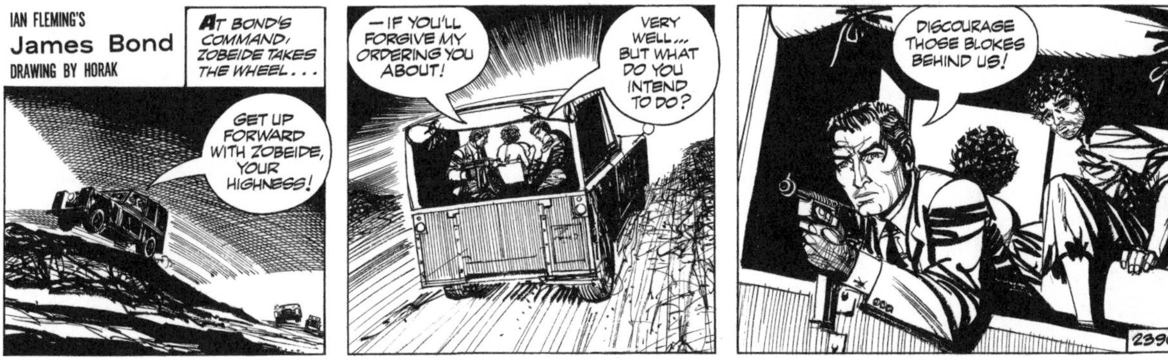
IAN FLEMING'S
James Bond
DRAWING BY HORAK
AT BOND'S COMMAND, ZOBEIDE TAKES THE WHEEL...
GET UP FORWARD WITH ZOBEIDE, YOUR HIGHNESS!
—IF YOU'LL FORGIVE MY ORDERING YOU ABOUT!
VERY WELL... BUT WHAT DO YOU INTEND TO DO?
DISCOURAGE THOSE BLOKES BEHIND US!
2390

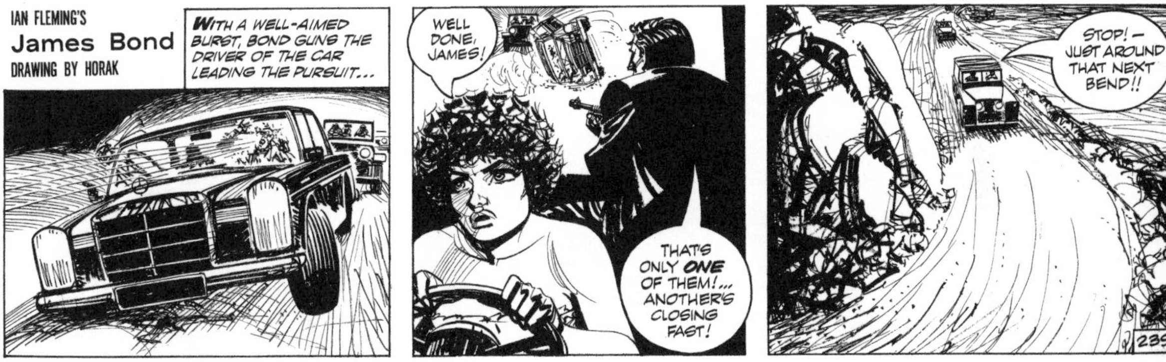
IAN FLEMING'S
James Bond
DRAWING BY HORAK
WITH A WELL-AIMED BURST, BOND GUNS THE DRIVER OF THE CAR LEADING THE PURSUIT...
WELL DONE, JAMES!
THAT'S ONLY ONE OF THEM!... ANOTHER'S CLOSING FAST!
STOP! — JUST AROUND THAT NEXT BEND!!
2391

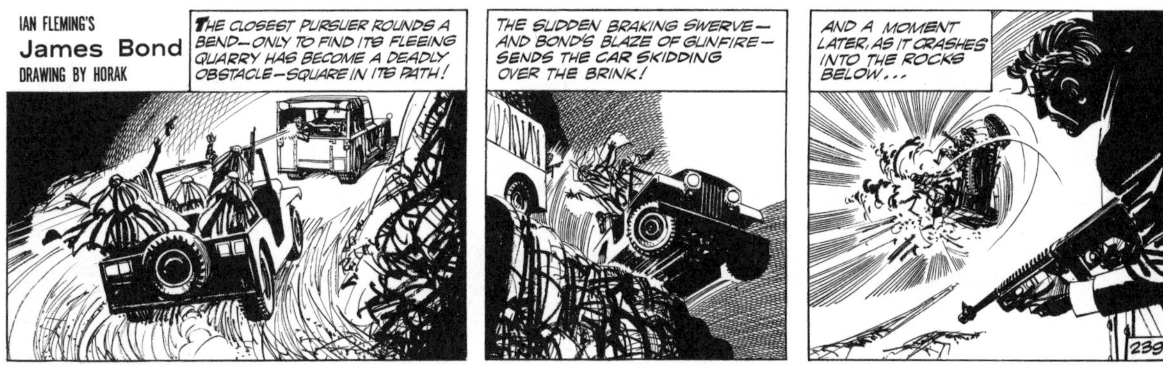
IAN FLEMING'S
James Bond
DRAWING BY HORAK
THE CLOSEST PURSUER ROUNDS A BEND—ONLY TO FIND ITS FLEEING QUARRY HAS BECOME A DEADLY OBSTACLE—SQUARE IN ITS PATH!
THE SUDDEN BRAKING SWERVE— AND BOND'S BLAZE OF GUNFIRE— SENDS THE CAR SKIDDING OVER THE BRINK!
AND A MOMENT LATER, AS IT CRASHES INTO THE ROCKS BELOW...
2392

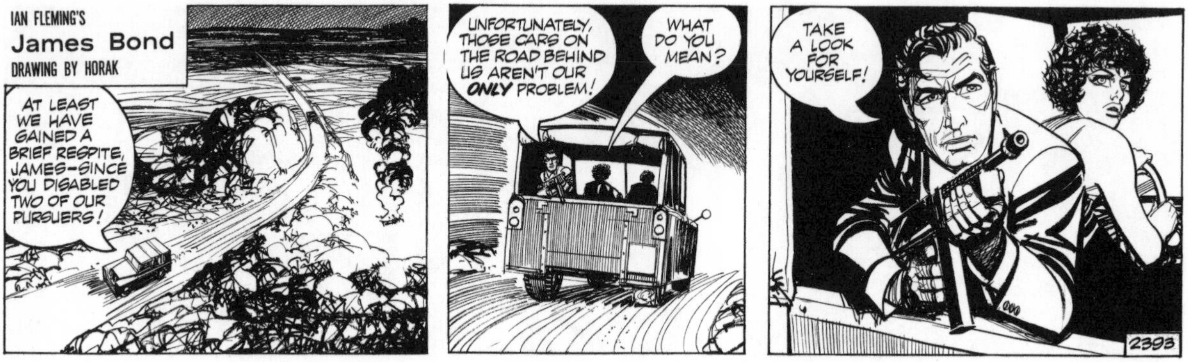
IAN FLEMING'S
James Bond
DRAWING BY HORAK
AT LEAST WE HAVE GAINED A BRIEF RESPITE, JAMES—SINCE YOU DISABLED TWO OF OUR PURSUERS!
UNFORTUNATELY, THOSE CARS ON THE ROAD BEHIND US AREN'T OUR ONLY PROBLEM!
WHAT DO YOU MEAN?
TAKE A LOOK FOR YOURSELF!
2393

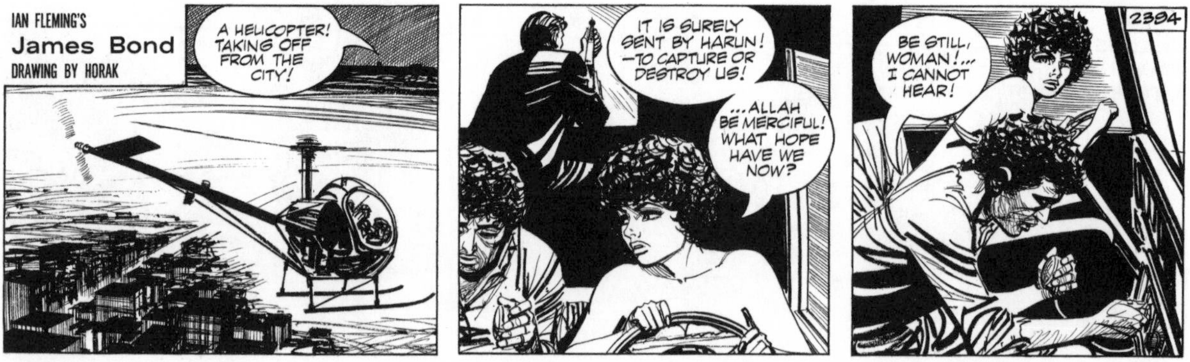
IAN FLEMING'S
James Bond
DRAWING BY HORAK
A HELICOPTER! TAKING OFF FROM THE CITY!
IT IS SURELY SENT BY HARUN! —TO CAPTURE OR DESTROY US!
...ALLAH BE MERCIFUL! WHAT HOPE HAVE WE NOW?
2394
BE STILL, WOMAN!... I CANNOT HEAR!

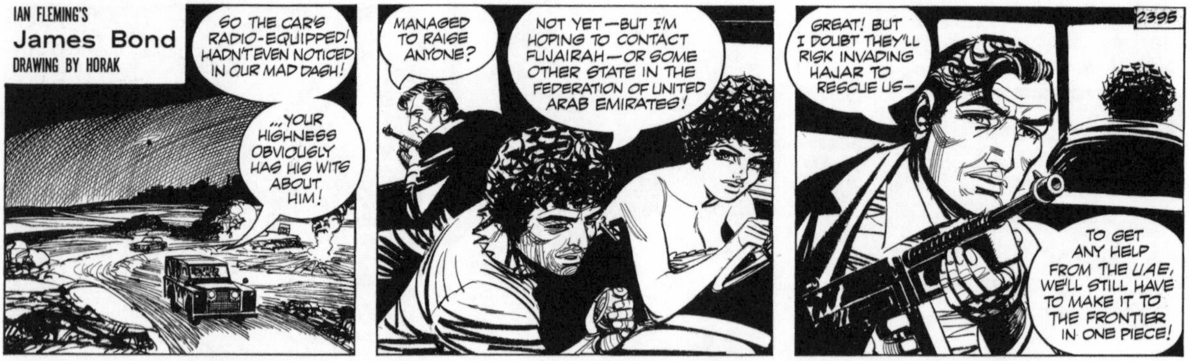
IAN FLEMING'S
James Bond
DRAWING BY HORAK
SO THE CAR'S RADIO-EQUIPPED! HADN'T EVEN NOTICED IN OUR MAD DASH!
...YOUR HIGHNESS OBVIOUSLY HAS HIS WITS ABOUT HIM!
MANAGED TO RAISE ANYONE?
NOT YET—BUT I'M HOPING TO CONTACT FUJAIRAH—OR SOME OTHER STATE IN THE FEDERATION OF UNITED ARAB EMIRATES!
2395
GREAT! BUT I DOUBT THEY'LL RISK INVADING HAJAR TO RESCUE US—
TO GET ANY HELP FROM THE UAE, WE'LL STILL HAVE TO MAKE IT TO THE FRONTIER IN ONE PIECE!

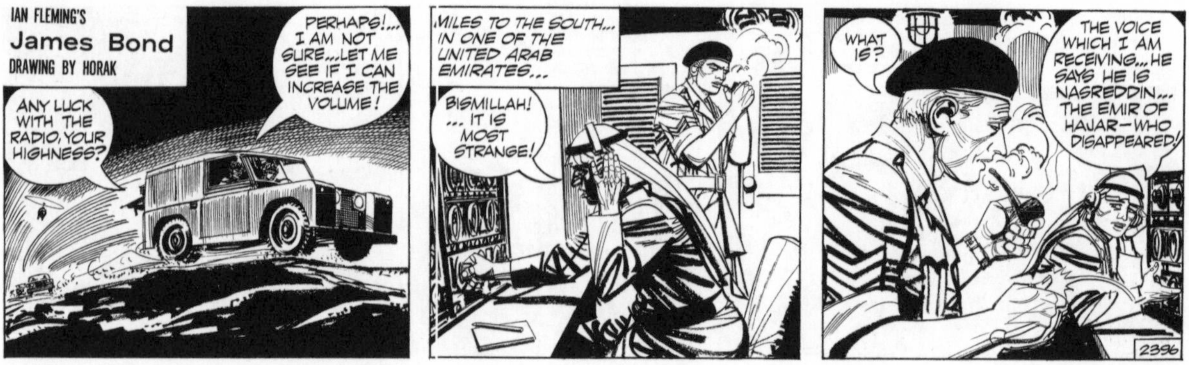
IAN FLEMING'S
James Bond
DRAWING BY HORAK
ANY LUCK WITH THE RADIO, YOUR HIGHNESS?
PERHAPS!... I AM NOT SURE... LET ME SEE IF I CAN INCREASE THE VOLUME!
MILES TO THE SOUTH... IN ONE OF THE UNITED ARAB EMIRATES...
BISMILLAH! ... IT IS MOST STRANGE!
WHAT IS?
THE VOICE WHICH I AM RECEIVING... HE SAYS HE IS NASREDDIN... THE EMIR OF HAJAR—WHO DISAPPEARED!
2396

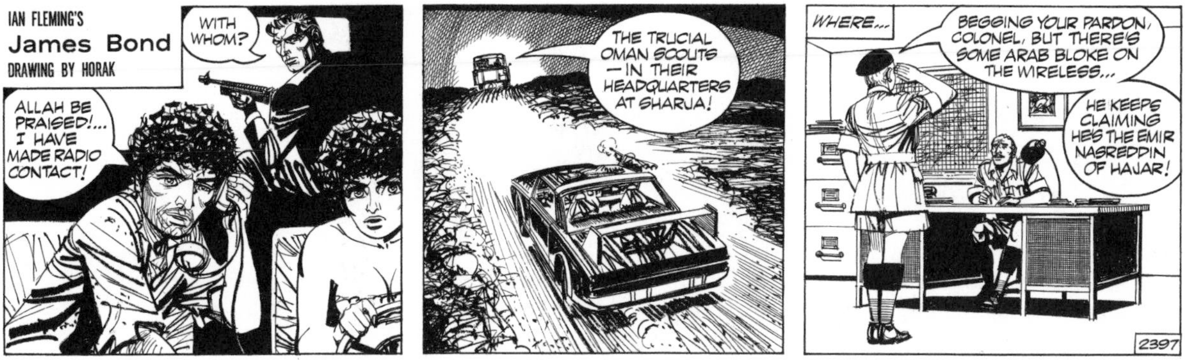
IAN FLEMING'S
James Bond
DRAWING BY HORAK
WITH WHOM?
ALLAH BE PRAISED!... I HAVE MADE RADIO CONTACT!
THE TRUCIAL OMAN SCOUTS—IN THEIR HEADQUARTERS AT SHARJA!
WHERE...
BEGGING YOUR PARDON, COLONEL, BUT THERE'S SOME ARAB BLOKE ON THE WIRELESS...
HE KEEPS CLAIMING HE'S THE EMIR NASREDDIN OF HAJAR!
2397

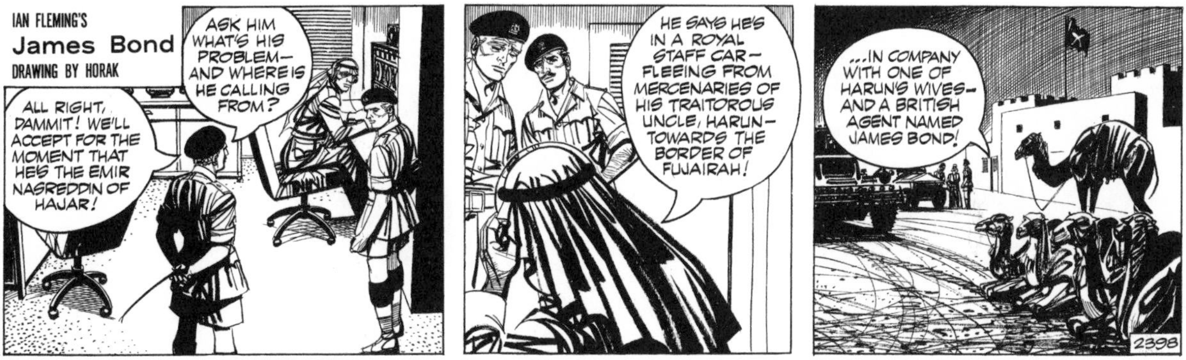
IAN FLEMING'S
James Bond
DRAWING BY HORAK
ASK HIM WHAT'S HIS PROBLEM— AND WHERE IS HE CALLING FROM?
ALL RIGHT, DAMMIT! WE'LL ACCEPT FOR THE MOMENT THAT HE'S THE EMIR NASREDDIN OF HAJAR!
HE SAYS HE'S IN A ROYAL STAFF CAR—FLEEING FROM MERCENARIES OF HIS TRAITOROUS UNCLE, HARUN—TOWARDS THE BORDER OF FUJAIRAH!
...IN COMPANY WITH ONE OF HARUN'S WIVES—AND A BRITISH AGENT NAMED JAMES BOND!
2398

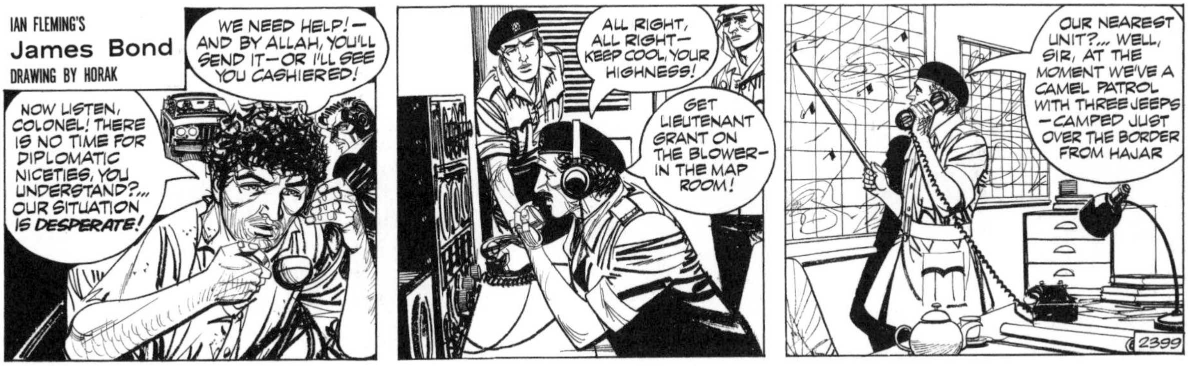
IAN FLEMING'S
James Bond
DRAWING BY HORAK
WE NEED HELP!—AND BY ALLAH, YOU'LL SEND IT—OR I'LL SEE YOU CASHIERED!
NOW LISTEN, COLONEL! THERE IS NO TIME FOR DIPLOMATIC NICETIES, YOU UNDERSTAND?... OUR SITUATION IS DESPERATE!
ALL RIGHT, ALL RIGHT—KEEP COOL, YOUR HIGHNESS!
GET LIEUTENANT GRANT ON THE BLOWER—IN THE MAP ROOM!
OUR NEAREST UNIT?... WELL, SIR, AT THE MOMENT WE'VE A CAMEL PATROL WITH THREE JEEPS—CAMPED JUST OVER THE BORDER FROM HAJAR
2399

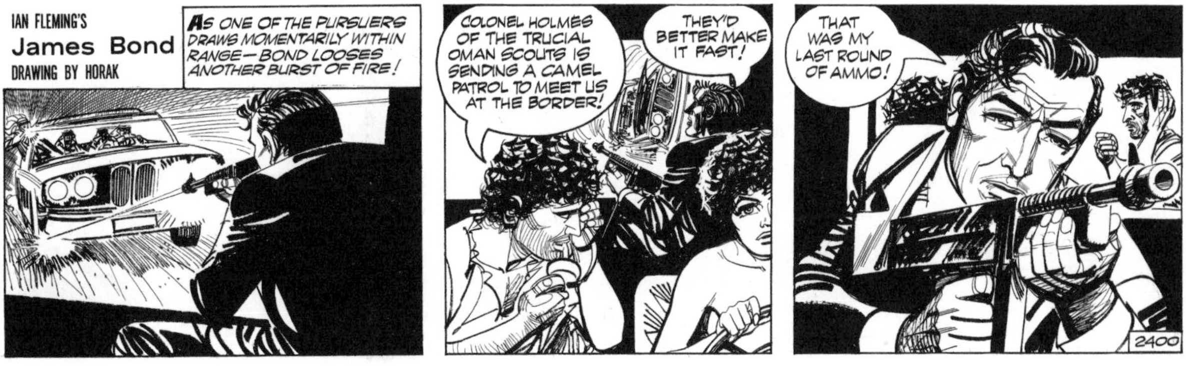
IAN FLEMING'S
James Bond
DRAWING BY HORAK
AS ONE OF THE PURSUERS DRAWS MOMENTARILY WITHIN RANGE—BOND LOOSES ANOTHER BURST OF FIRE!
COLONEL HOLMES OF THE TRUCIAL OMAN SCOUTS IS SENDING A CAMEL PATROL TO MEET US AT THE BORDER!
THEY'D BETTER MAKE IT FAST!
THAT WAS MY LAST ROUND OF AMMO!
2400

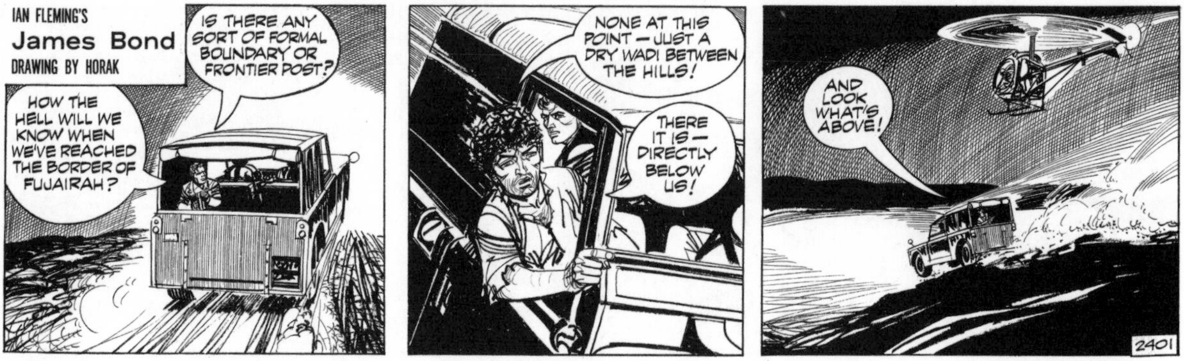
IAN FLEMING'S
James Bond
DRAWING BY HORAK
HOW THE HELL WILL WE KNOW WHEN WE'VE REACHED THE BORDER OF FUJAIRAH?
IS THERE ANY SORT OF FORMAL BOUNDARY OR FRONTIER POST?
NONE AT THIS POINT — JUST A DRY WADI BETWEEN THE HILLS!
THERE IT IS — DIRECTLY BELOW US!
AND LOOK WHAT'S ABOVE!
2401

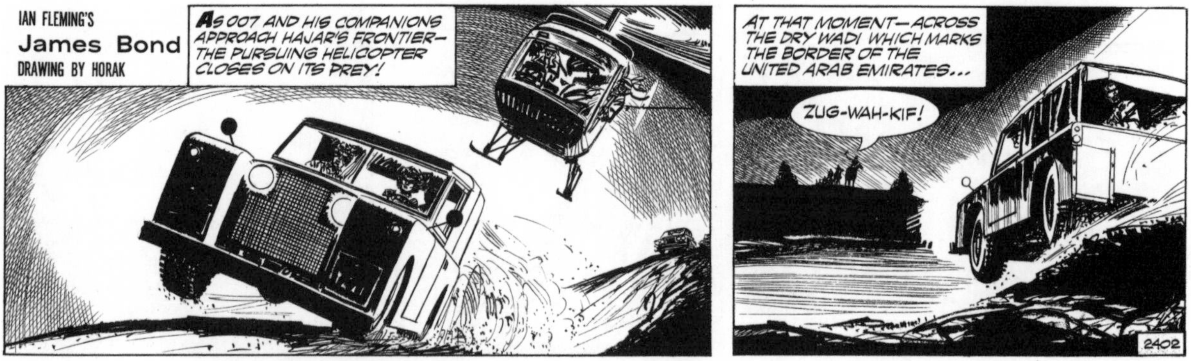
IAN FLEMING'S
James Bond
DRAWING BY HORAK
AS 007 AND HIS COMPANIONS APPROACH HAJAR'S FRONTIER — THE PURSUING HELICOPTER CLOSES ON ITS PREY!
AT THAT MOMENT — ACROSS THE DRY WADI WHICH MARKS THE BORDER OF THE UNITED ARAB EMIRATES...
ZUG-WAH-KIF!
2402

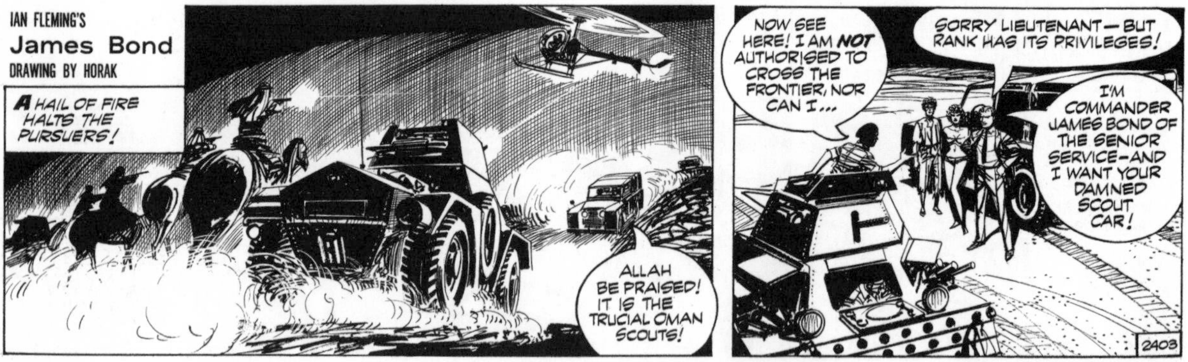
IAN FLEMING'S
James Bond
DRAWING BY HORAK
A HAIL OF FIRE HALTS THE PURSUERS!
ALLAH BE PRAISED! IT IS THE TRUCIAL OMAN SCOUTS!
NOW SEE HERE! I AM NOT AUTHORISED TO CROSS THE FRONTIER, NOR CAN I...
SORRY LIEUTENANT — BUT RANK HAS ITS PRIVILEGES!
I'M COMMANDER JAMES BOND OF THE SENIOR SERVICE — AND I WANT YOUR DAMNED SCOUT CAR!
2403

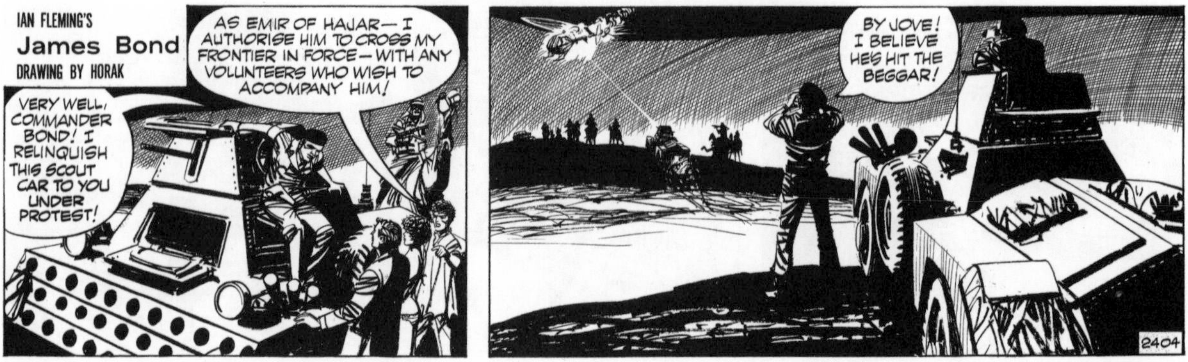
IAN FLEMING'S
James Bond
DRAWING BY HORAK
VERY WELL, COMMANDER BOND! I RELINQUISH THIS SCOUT CAR TO YOU UNDER PROTEST!
AS EMIR OF HAJAR — I AUTHORISE HIM TO CROSS MY FRONTIER IN FORCE — WITH ANY VOLUNTEERS WHO WISH TO ACCOMPANY HIM!
BY JOVE! I BELIEVE HE'S HIT THE BEGGAR!
2404

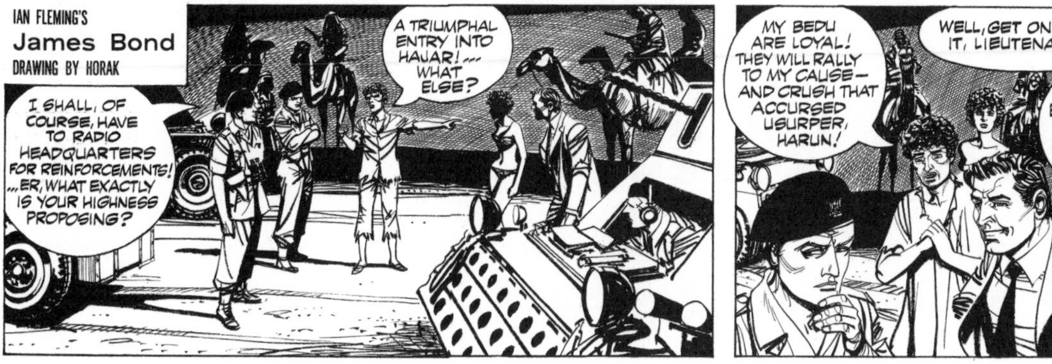
IAN FLEMING'S
James Bond
DRAWING BY HORAK
I SHALL, OF COURSE, HAVE TO RADIO HEADQUARTERS FOR REINFORCEMENTS! ...ER, WHAT EXACTLY IS YOUR HIGHNESS PROPOSING?
A TRIUMPHAL ENTRY INTO HAJAR! ... WHAT ELSE?
MY BEDU ARE LOYAL! THEY WILL RALLY TO MY CAUSE— AND CRUSH THAT ACCURSED USURPER, HARUN!
WELL, GET ON WITH IT, LIEUTENANT!
... I KNOW YOU AND I ARE BOTH INFIDELS— BUT MUST YOU ACT LIKE SUCH AN UNBELIEVING FOOL?
2405

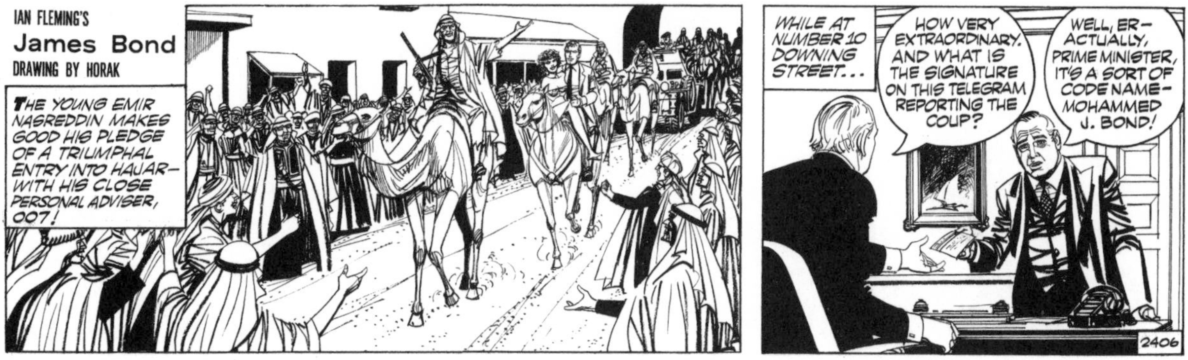
IAN FLEMING'S
James Bond
DRAWING BY HORAK
THE YOUNG EMIR NASREDDIN MAKES GOOD HIS PLEDGE OF A TRIUMPHAL ENTRY INTO HAJAR— WITH HIS CLOSE PERSONAL ADVISER, 007!
WHILE AT NUMBER 10 DOWNING STREET...
HOW VERY EXTRAORDINARY. AND WHAT IS THE SIGNATURE ON THIS TELEGRAM REPORTING THE COUP?
WELL, ER— ACTUALLY, PRIME MINISTER, IT'S A SORT OF CODE NAME— MOHAMMED J. BOND!
2406

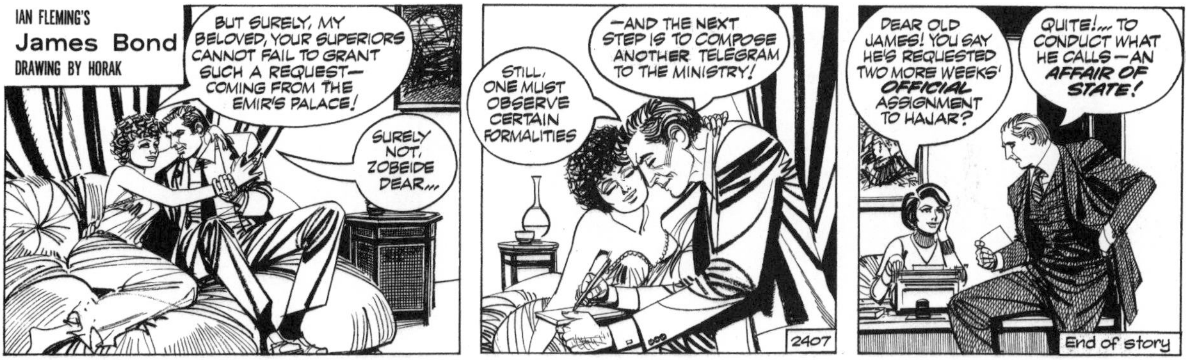
IAN FLEMING'S
James Bond
DRAWING BY HORAK
BUT SURELY, MY BELOVED, YOUR SUPERIORS CANNOT FAIL TO GRANT SUCH A REQUEST— COMING FROM THE EMIR'S PALACE!
SURELY NOT, ZOBEIDE DEAR...
STILL, ONE MUST OBSERVE CERTAIN FORMALITIES
—AND THE NEXT STEP IS TO COMPOSE ANOTHER TELEGRAM TO THE MINISTRY!
2407
DEAR OLD JAMES! YOU SAY HE'S REQUESTED TWO MORE WEEKS' OFFICIAL ASSIGNMENT TO HAJAR?
QUITE!... TO CONDUCT WHAT HE CALLS—AN AFFAIR OF STATE!
End of story

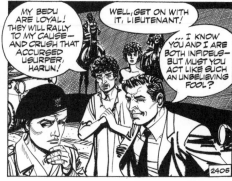

# BEWARE OF BUTTERFLIES

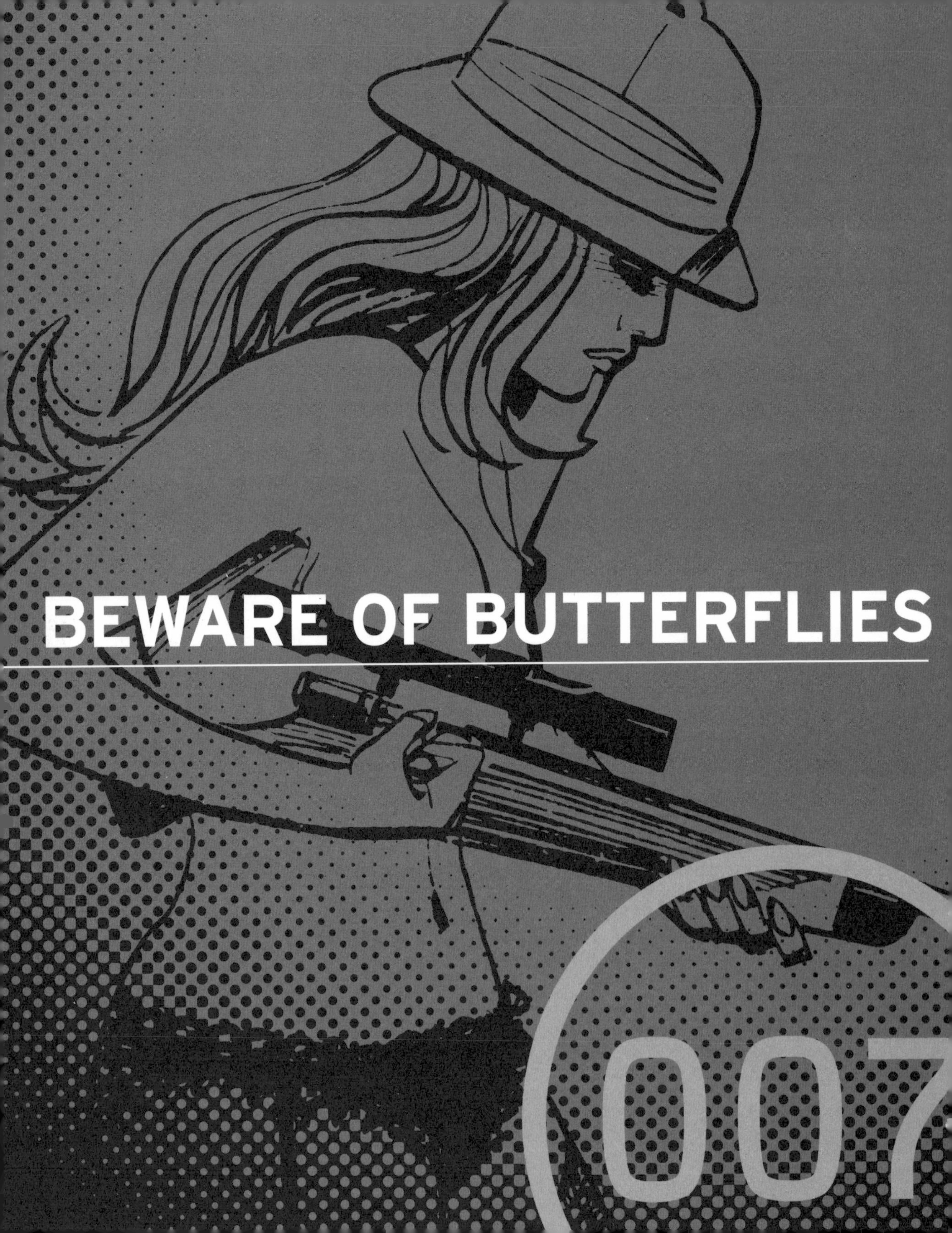
007

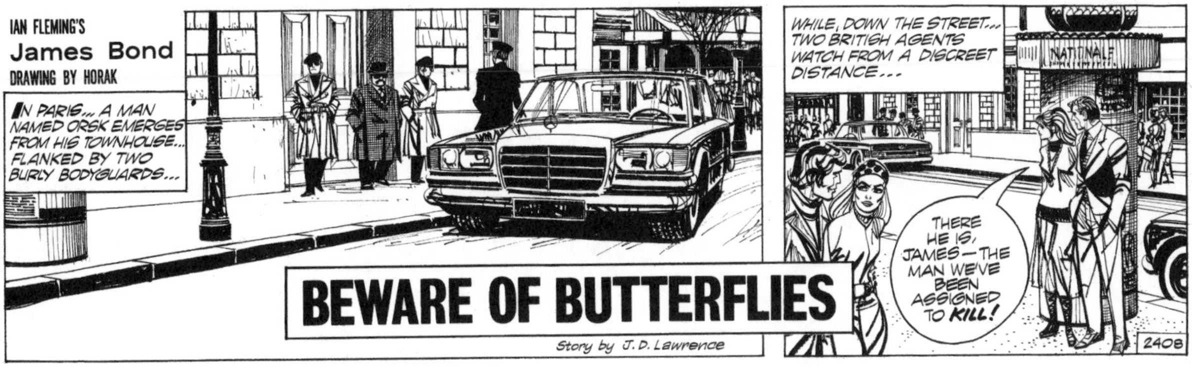
IAN FLEMING'S
James Bond
DRAWING BY HORAK
IN PARIS... A MAN NAMED ORSK EMERGES FROM HIS TOWNHOUSE... FLANKED BY TWO BURLY BODYGUARDS...
WHILE, DOWN THE STREET... TWO BRITISH AGENTS WATCH FROM A DISCREET DISTANCE...
NATIONALE
THERE HE IS, JAMES—THE MAN WE'VE BEEN ASSIGNED TO KILL!
BEWARE OF BUTTERFLIES
Story by J. D. Lawrence
2408

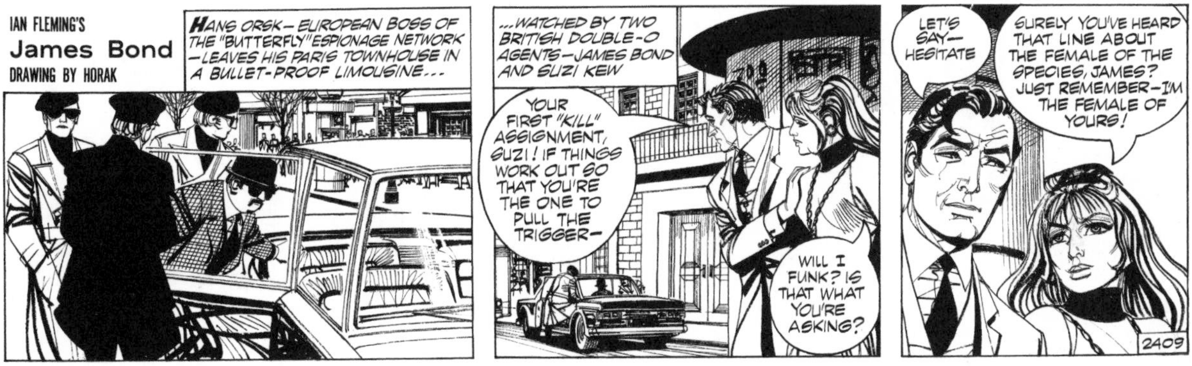
IAN FLEMING'S
James Bond
DRAWING BY HORAK
HANS ORSK—EUROPEAN BOSS OF THE "BUTTERFLY" ESPIONAGE NETWORK—LEAVES HIS PARIS TOWNHOUSE IN A BULLET-PROOF LIMOUSINE...
...WATCHED BY TWO BRITISH DOUBLE-O AGENTS—JAMES BOND AND SUZI KEW
YOUR FIRST "KILL" ASSIGNMENT, SUZI! IF THINGS WORK OUT SO THAT YOU'RE THE ONE TO PULL THE TRIGGER—
WILL I FUNK? IS THAT WHAT YOU'RE ASKING?
LET'S SAY—HESITATE
SURELY YOU'VE HEARD THAT LINE ABOUT THE FEMALE OF THE SPECIES, JAMES? JUST REMEMBER—I'M THE FEMALE OF YOURS!
2409

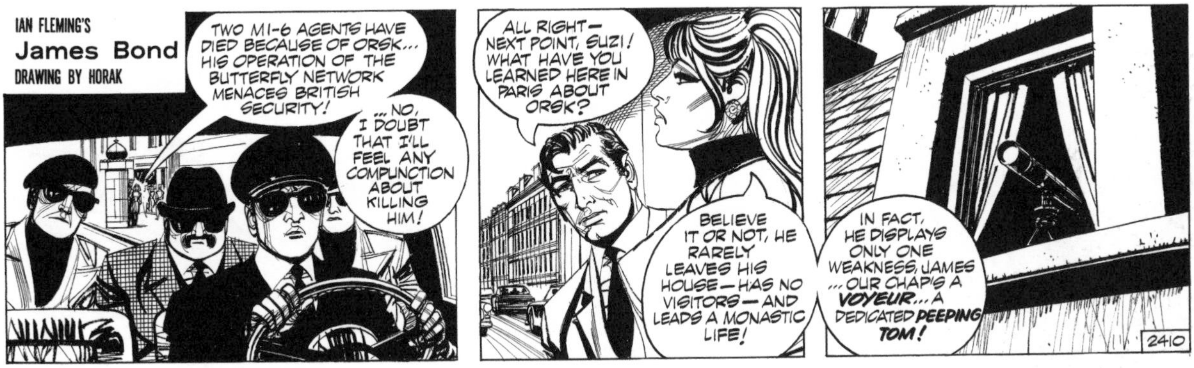
IAN FLEMING'S
James Bond
DRAWING BY HORAK
TWO MI-6 AGENTS HAVE DIED BECAUSE OF ORSK... HIS OPERATION OF THE BUTTERFLY NETWORK MENACES BRITISH SECURITY!
...NO, I DOUBT THAT I'LL FEEL ANY COMPUNCTION ABOUT KILLING HIM!
ALL RIGHT—NEXT POINT, SUZI! WHAT HAVE YOU LEARNED HERE IN PARIS ABOUT ORSK?
BELIEVE IT OR NOT, HE RARELY LEAVES HIS HOUSE—HAS NO VISITORS—AND LEADS A MONASTIC LIFE!
IN FACT, HE DISPLAYS ONLY ONE WEAKNESS, JAMES ...OUR CHAP'S A VOYEUR... A DEDICATED PEEPING TOM!
2410

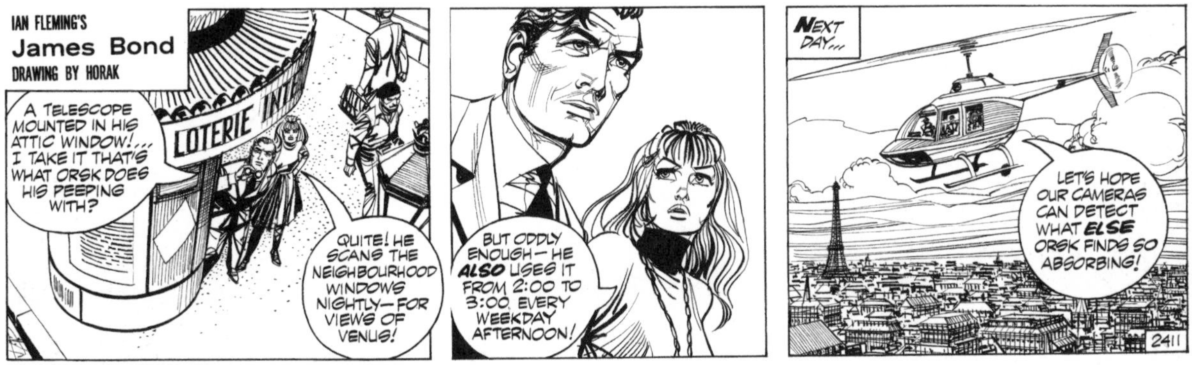
IAN FLEMING'S
James Bond
DRAWING BY HORAK
A TELESCOPE MOUNTED IN HIS ATTIC WINDOW!... I TAKE IT THAT'S WHAT ORSK DOES HIS PEEPING WITH?
LOTERIE
QUITE! HE SCANS THE NEIGHBOURHOOD WINDOWS NIGHTLY—FOR VIEWS OF VENUS!
BUT ODDLY ENOUGH—HE ALSO USES IT FROM 2:00 TO 3:00, EVERY WEEKDAY AFTERNOON!
NEXT DAY...
LET'S HOPE OUR CAMERAS CAN DETECT WHAT ELSE ORSK FINDS SO ABSORBING!
2411

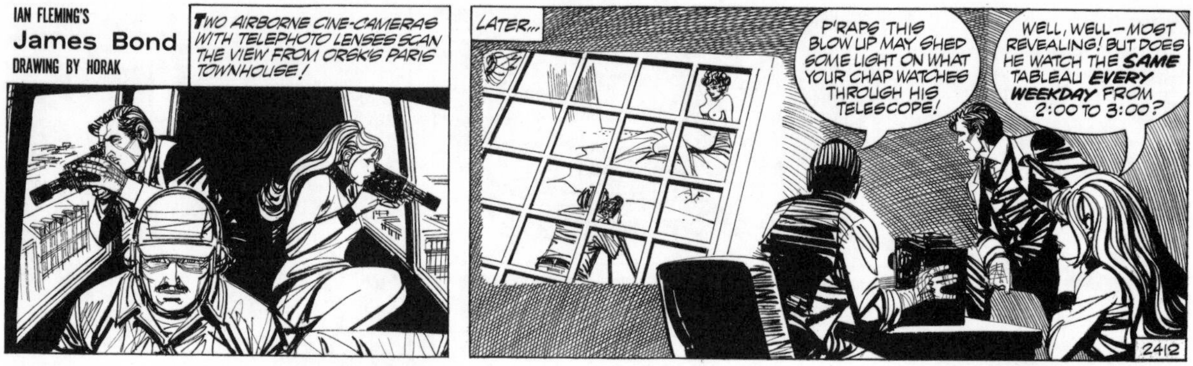
IAN FLEMING'S
James Bond
DRAWING BY HORAK
TWO AIRBORNE CINE-CAMERAS WITH TELEPHOTO LENSES SCAN THE VIEW FROM ORSK'S PARIS TOWNHOUSE!
LATER...
P'RAPS THIS BLOW UP MAY SHED SOME LIGHT ON WHAT YOUR CHAP WATCHES THROUGH HIS TELESCOPE!
WELL, WELL—MOST REVEALING! BUT DOES HE WATCH THE SAME TABLEAU EVERY WEEKDAY FROM 2:00 TO 3:00?
2412

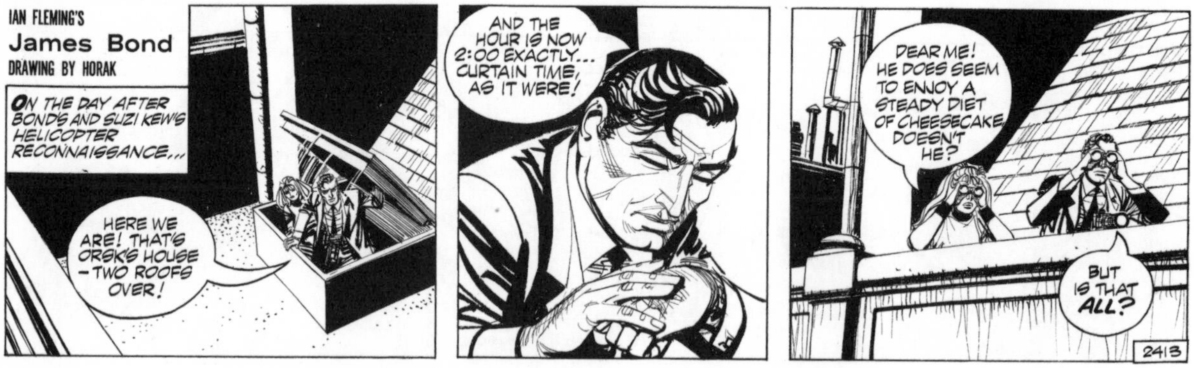
IAN FLEMING'S
James Bond
DRAWING BY HORAK
ON THE DAY AFTER BOND'S AND SUZI KEW'S HELICOPTER RECONNAISSANCE...
HERE WE ARE! THAT'S ORSK'S HOUSE —TWO ROOFS OVER!
AND THE HOUR IS NOW 2:00 EXACTLY... CURTAIN TIME, AS IT WERE!
DEAR ME! HE DOES SEEM TO ENJOY A STEADY DIET OF CHEESECAKE DOESN'T HE?
BUT IS THAT ALL?
2413

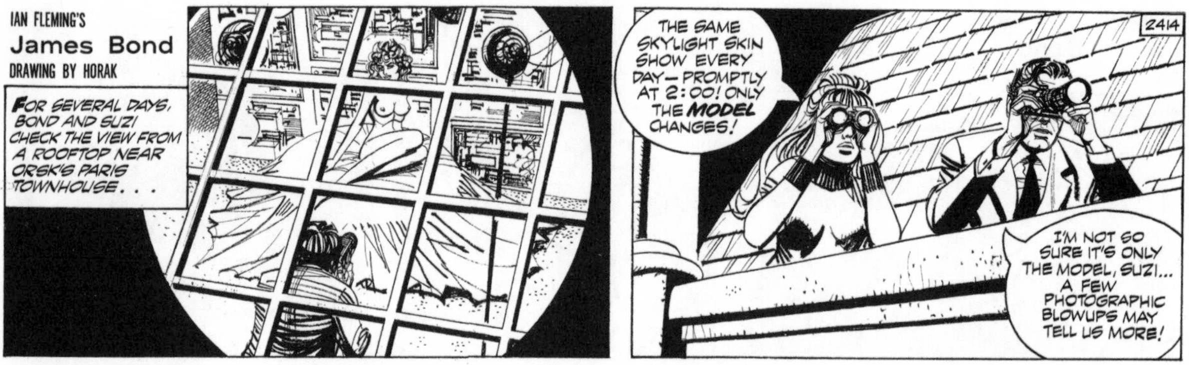
IAN FLEMING'S
James Bond
DRAWING BY HORAK
FOR SEVERAL DAYS, BOND AND SUZI CHECK THE VIEW FROM A ROOFTOP NEAR ORSK'S PARIS TOWNHOUSE...
THE SAME SKYLIGHT SKIN SHOW EVERY DAY—PROMPTLY AT 2:00! ONLY THE MODEL CHANGES!
I'M NOT SO SURE IT'S ONLY THE MODEL, SUZI... A FEW PHOTOGRAPHIC BLOWUPS MAY TELL US MORE!
2414

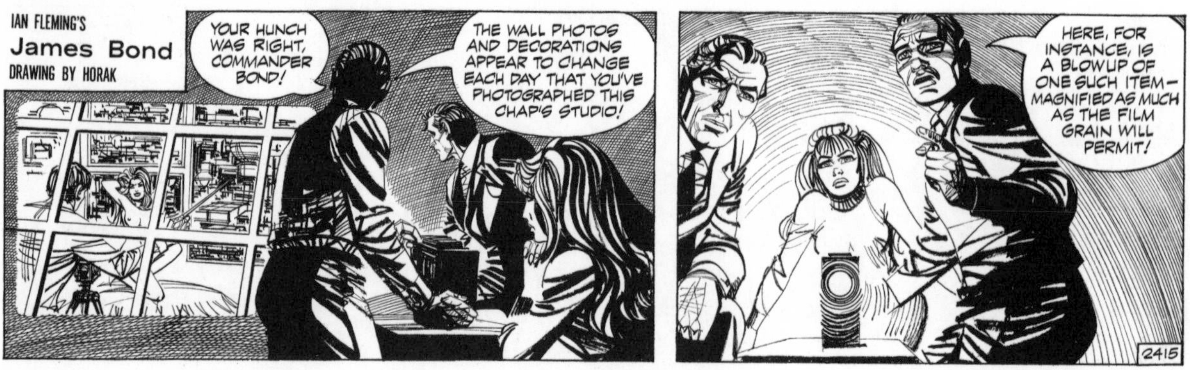
IAN FLEMING'S
James Bond
DRAWING BY HORAK
YOUR HUNCH WAS RIGHT, COMMANDER BOND!
THE WALL PHOTOS AND DECORATIONS APPEAR TO CHANGE EACH DAY THAT YOU'VE PHOTOGRAPHED THIS CHAP'S STUDIO!
HERE, FOR INSTANCE, IS A BLOWUP OF ONE SUCH ITEM—MAGNIFIED AS MUCH AS THE FILM GRAIN WILL PERMIT!
2415

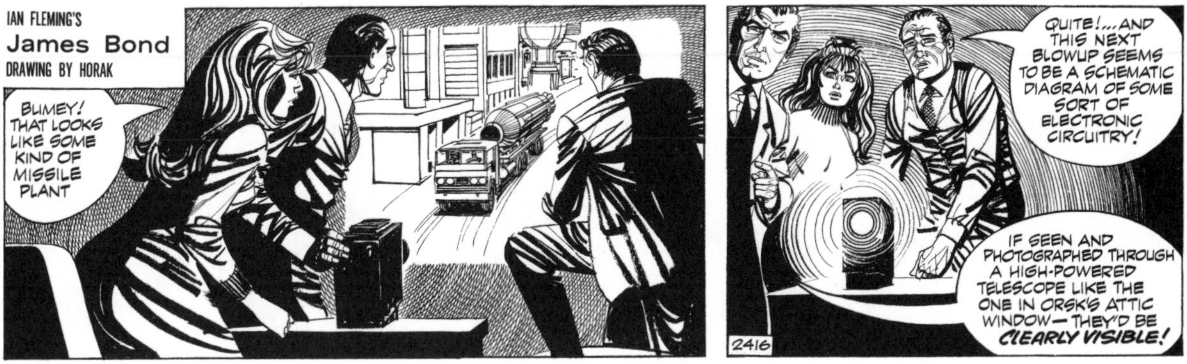
IAN FLEMING'S
James Bond
DRAWING BY HORAK
BLIMEY! THAT LOOKS LIKE SOME KIND OF MISSILE PLANT
QUITE!... AND THIS NEXT BLOWUP SEEMS TO BE A SCHEMATIC DIAGRAM OF SOME SORT OF ELECTRONIC CIRCUITRY!
IF SEEN AND PHOTOGRAPHED THROUGH A HIGH-POWERED TELESCOPE LIKE THE ONE IN ORSK'S ATTIC WINDOW— THEY'D BE CLEARLY VISIBLE!
2416

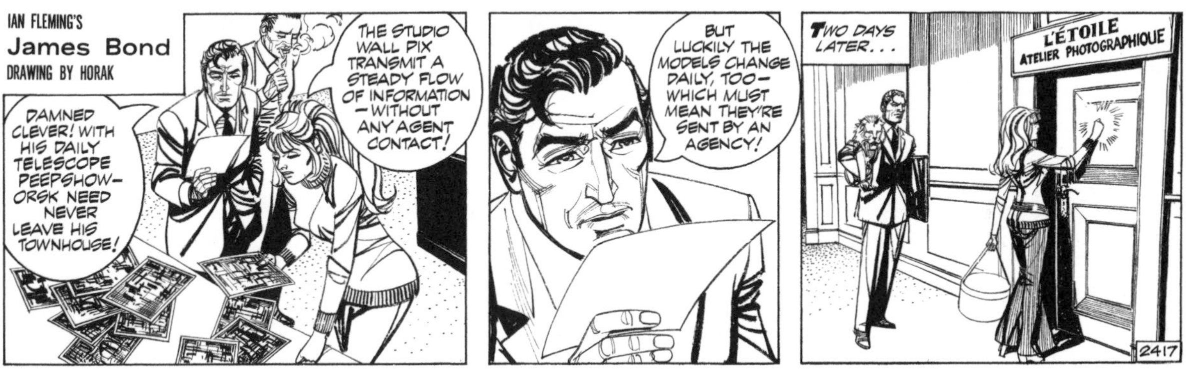
IAN FLEMING'S
James Bond
DRAWING BY HORAK
DAMNED CLEVER! WITH HIS DAILY TELESCOPE PEEPSHOW— ORSK NEED NEVER LEAVE HIS TOWNHOUSE!
THE STUDIO WALL PIX TRANSMIT A STEADY FLOW OF INFORMATION —WITHOUT ANY AGENT CONTACT!
BUT LUCKILY THE MODELS CHANGE DAILY, TOO— WHICH MUST MEAN THEY'RE SENT BY AN AGENCY!
TWO DAYS LATER...
L'ÉTOILE
ATELIER PHOTOGRAPHIQUE
2417

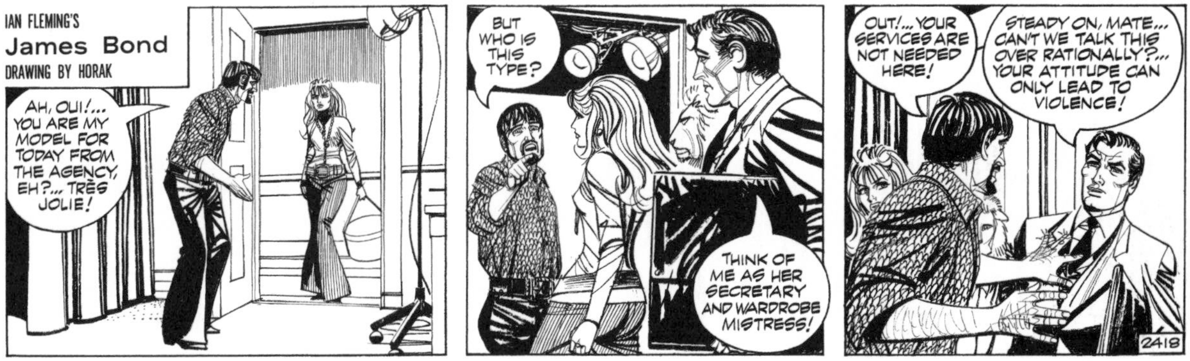
IAN FLEMING'S
James Bond
DRAWING BY HORAK
AH, OUI!... YOU ARE MY MODEL FOR TODAY FROM THE AGENCY, EH?... TRÈS JOLIE!
BUT WHO IS THIS TYPE?
THINK OF ME AS HER SECRETARY AND WARDROBE MISTRESS!
OUT!... YOUR SERVICES ARE NOT NEEDED HERE!
STEADY ON, MATE... CAN'T WE TALK THIS OVER RATIONALLY?... YOUR ATTITUDE CAN ONLY LEAD TO VIOLENCE!
2418

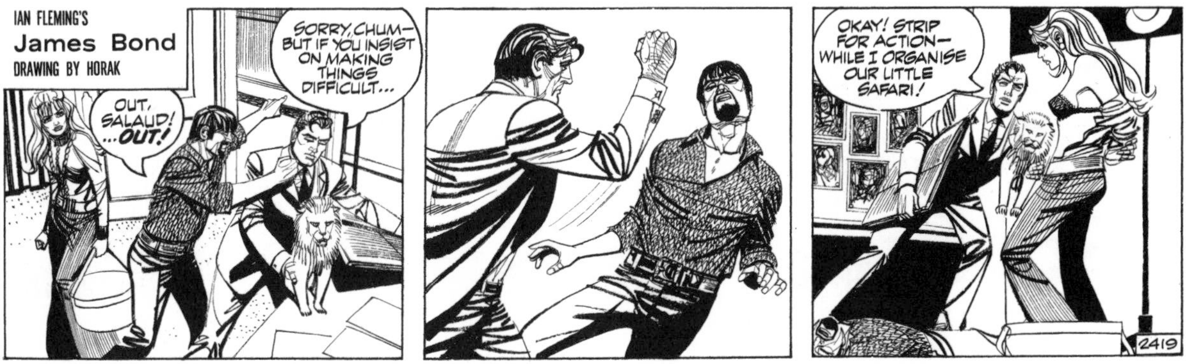
IAN FLEMING'S
James Bond
DRAWING BY HORAK
OUT, SALAUD! ...OUT!
SORRY, CHUM— BUT IF YOU INSIST ON MAKING THINGS DIFFICULT...
OKAY! STRIP FOR ACTION— WHILE I ORGANISE OUR LITTLE SAFARI!
2419

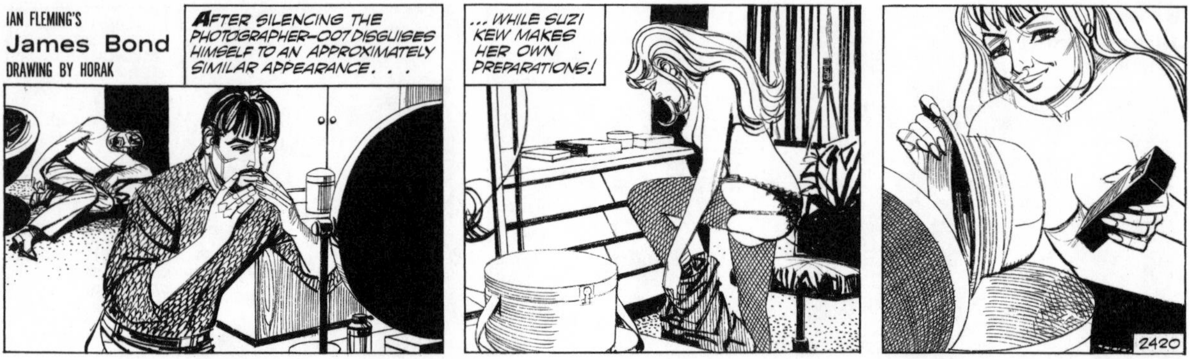
IAN FLEMING'S
James Bond
DRAWING BY HORAK
AFTER SILENCING THE PHOTOGRAPHER—007 DISGUISES HIMSELF TO AN APPROXIMATELY SIMILAR APPEARANCE . . .
... WHILE SUZI KEW MAKES HER OWN PREPARATIONS!
2420

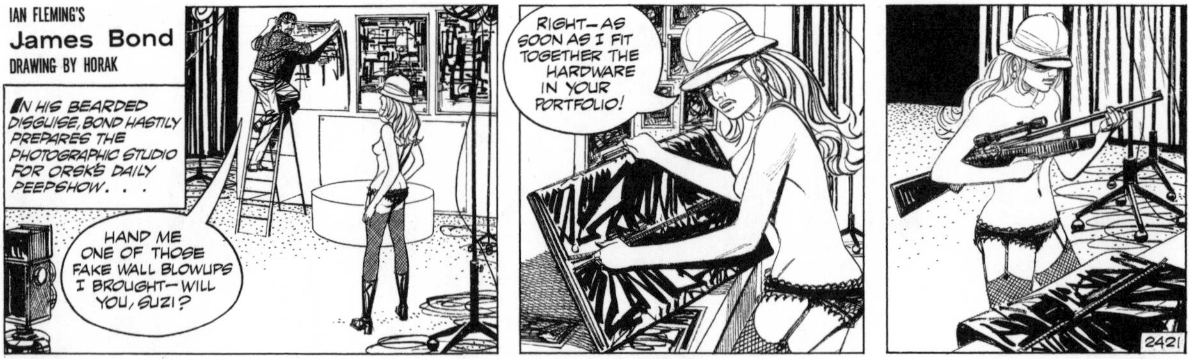
IAN FLEMING'S
James Bond
DRAWING BY HORAK
IN HIS BEARDED DISGUISE, BOND HASTILY PREPARES THE PHOTOGRAPHIC STUDIO FOR ORSK'S DAILY PEEPSHOW . . .
HAND ME ONE OF THOSE FAKE WALL BLOWUPS I BROUGHT—WILL YOU, SUZI?
RIGHT—AS SOON AS I FIT TOGETHER THE HARDWARE IN YOUR PORTFOLIO!
2421

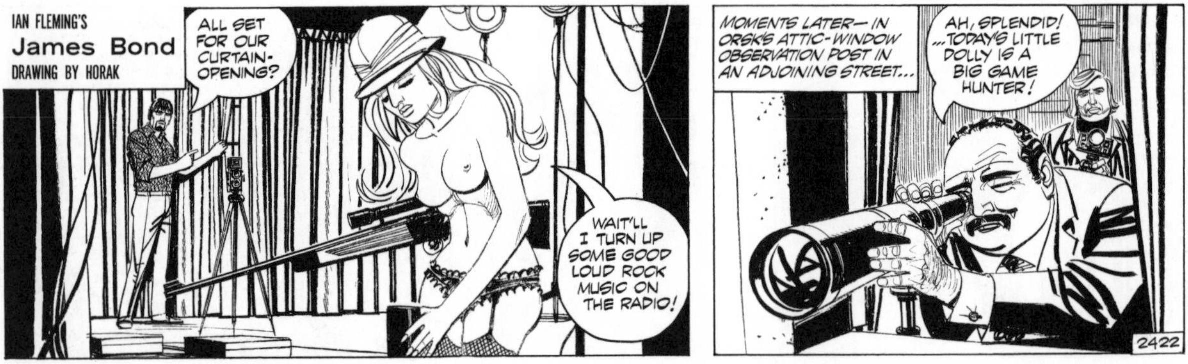
IAN FLEMING'S
James Bond
DRAWING BY HORAK
ALL SET FOR OUR CURTAIN-OPENING?
WAIT'LL I TURN UP SOME GOOD LOUD ROCK MUSIC ON THE RADIO!
MOMENTS LATER—IN ORSK'S ATTIC-WINDOW OBSERVATION POST IN AN ADJOINING STREET...
AH, SPLENDID! ...TODAY'S LITTLE DOLLY IS A BIG GAME HUNTER!
2422

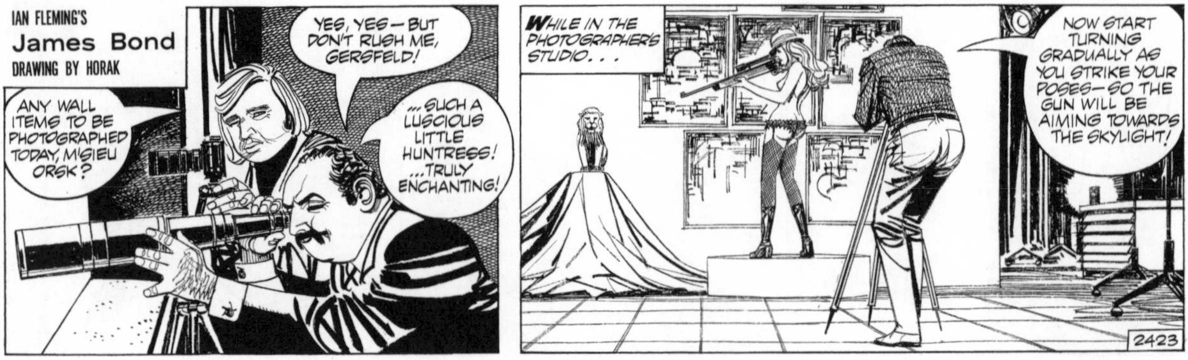
IAN FLEMING'S
James Bond
DRAWING BY HORAK
ANY WALL ITEMS TO BE PHOTOGRAPHED TODAY, M'SIEU ORSK?
YES, YES—BUT DON'T RUSH ME, GERSFELD!
...SUCH A LUSCIOUS LITTLE HUNTRESS! ...TRULY ENCHANTING!
WHILE IN THE PHOTOGRAPHER'S STUDIO . . .
NOW START TURNING GRADUALLY AS YOU STRIKE YOUR POSES—SO THE GUN WILL BE AIMING TOWARDS THE SKYLIGHT!
2423

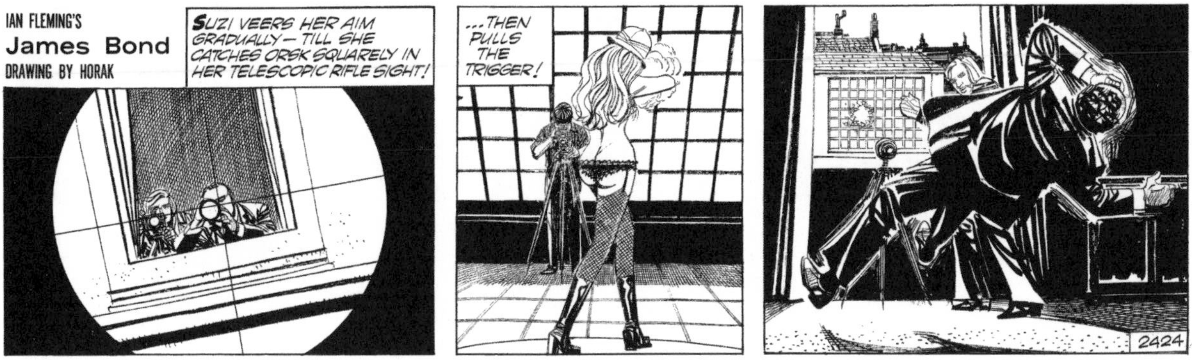
IAN FLEMING'S
James Bond
DRAWING BY HORAK
SUZI VEERS HER AIM GRADUALLY—TILL SHE CATCHES ORSK SQUARELY IN HER TELESCOPIC RIFLE SIGHT!
...THEN PULLS THE TRIGGER!
2424

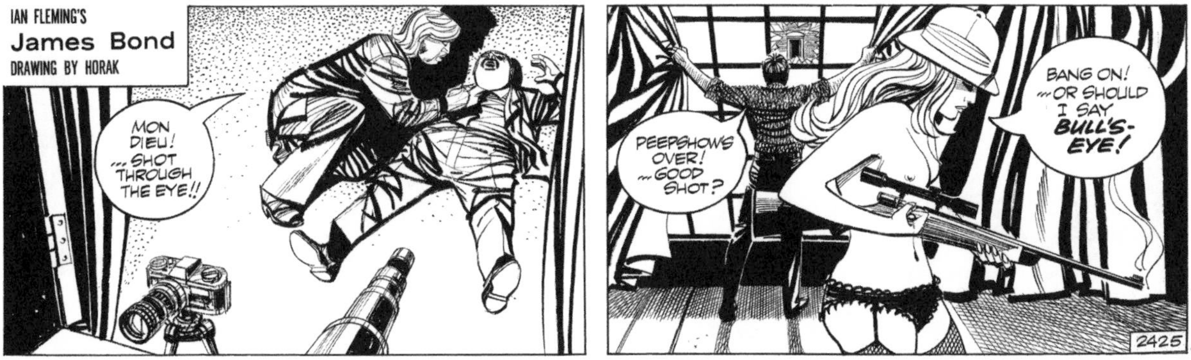
IAN FLEMING'S
James Bond
DRAWING BY HORAK
MON DIEU! ...SHOT THROUGH THE EYE!!
PEEPSHOW'S OVER! ...GOOD SHOT?
BANG ON! ...OR SHOULD I SAY BULL'S-EYE!
2425

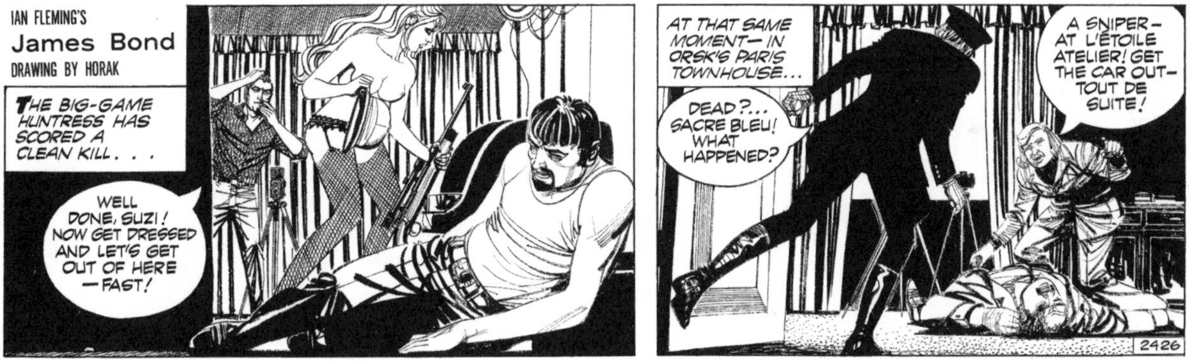
IAN FLEMING'S
James Bond
DRAWING BY HORAK
THE BIG-GAME HUNTRESS HAS SCORED A CLEAN KILL . . .
WELL DONE, SUZI! NOW GET DRESSED AND LET'S GET OUT OF HERE —FAST!
AT THAT SAME MOMENT— IN ORSK'S PARIS TOWNHOUSE...
DEAD?... SACRE BLEU! WHAT HAPPENED?
A SNIPER— AT L'ETOILE ATELIER! GET THE CAR OUT— TOUT DE SUITE!
2426

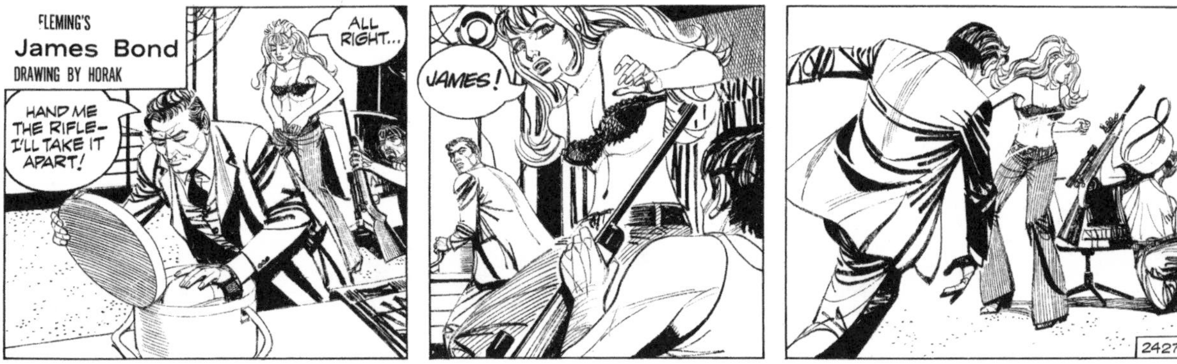
FLEMING'S
James Bond
DRAWING BY HORAK
ALL RIGHT...
HAND ME THE RIFLE— I'LL TAKE IT APART!
JAMES!
2427

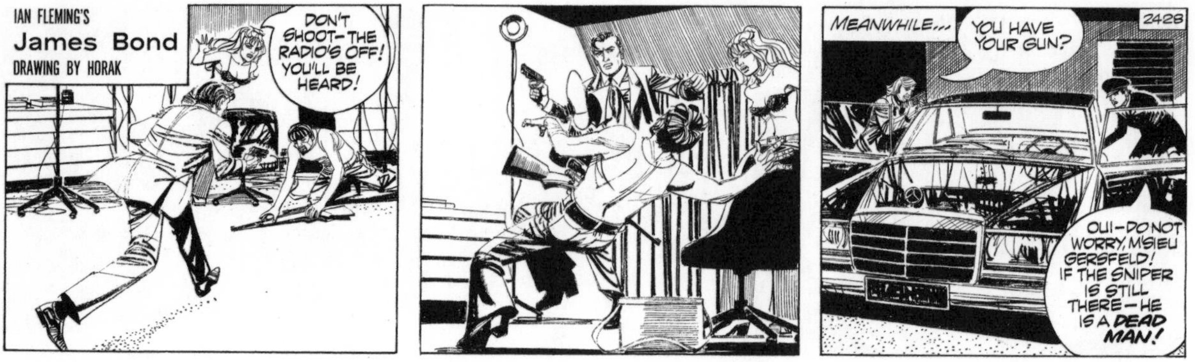
IAN FLEMING'S
James Bond
DRAWING BY HORAK
DON'T SHOOT—THE RADIO'S OFF! YOU'LL BE HEARD!
MEANWHILE...
YOU HAVE YOUR GUN?
2428
OUI—DO NOT WORRY, M'SIEU GERSFELD! IF THE SNIPER IS STILL THERE—HE IS A DEAD MAN!

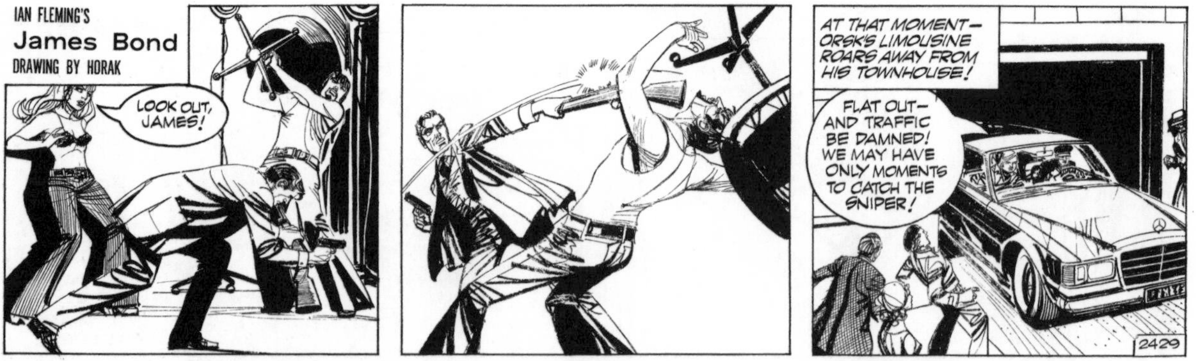
IAN FLEMING'S
James Bond
DRAWING BY HORAK
LOOK OUT, JAMES!
AT THAT MOMENT—ORSK'S LIMOUSINE ROARS AWAY FROM HIS TOWNHOUSE!
FLAT OUT—AND TRAFFIC BE DAMNED! WE MAY HAVE ONLY MOMENTS TO CATCH THE SNIPER!
2429

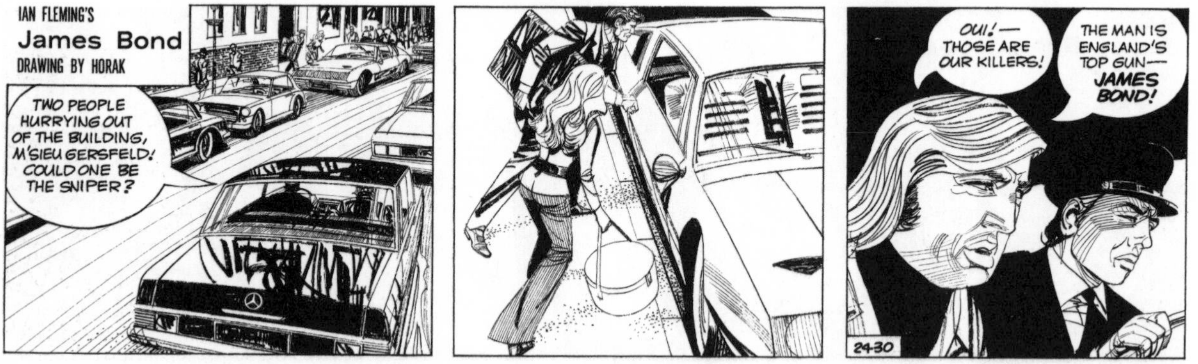
IAN FLEMING'S
James Bond
DRAWING BY HORAK
TWO PEOPLE HURRYING OUT OF THE BUILDING, M'SIEU GERSFELD! COULD ONE BE THE SNIPER?
OUI!—THOSE ARE OUR KILLERS!
THE MAN IS ENGLAND'S TOP GUN—JAMES BOND!
2430

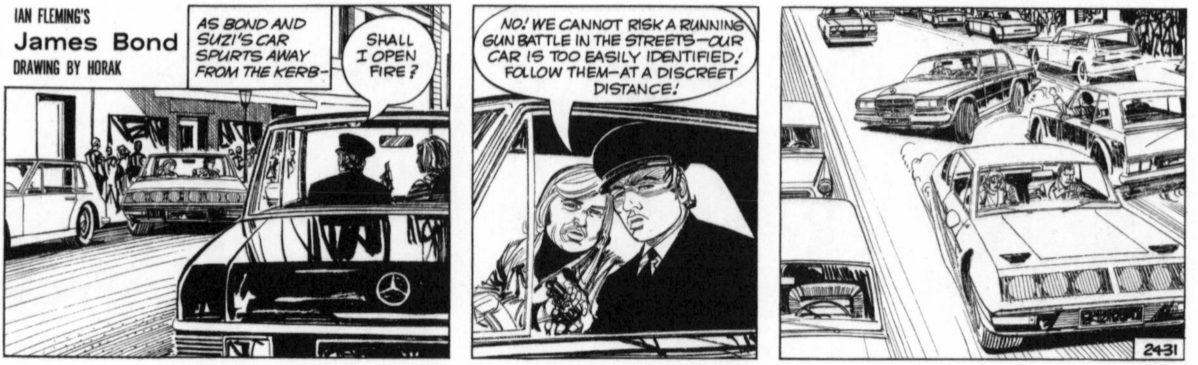
IAN FLEMING'S
James Bond
DRAWING BY HORAK
AS BOND AND SUZI'S CAR SPURTS AWAY FROM THE KERB—
SHALL I OPEN FIRE?
NO! WE CANNOT RISK A RUNNING GUN BATTLE IN THE STREETS—OUR CAR IS TOO EASILY IDENTIFIED! FOLLOW THEM—AT A DISCREET DISTANCE!
2431

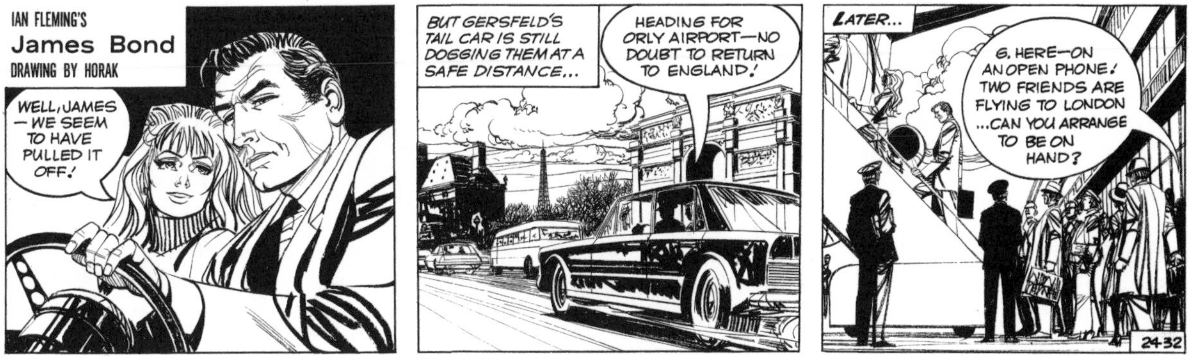
IAN FLEMING'S
James Bond
DRAWING BY HORAK
WELL, JAMES — WE SEEM TO HAVE PULLED IT OFF!
BUT GERSFELD'S TAIL CAR IS STILL DOGGING THEM AT A SAFE DISTANCE...
HEADING FOR ORLY AIRPORT—NO DOUBT TO RETURN TO ENGLAND!
LATER...
G. HERE—ON AN OPEN PHONE! TWO FRIENDS ARE FLYING TO LONDON ...CAN YOU ARRANGE TO BE ON HAND?
24·32

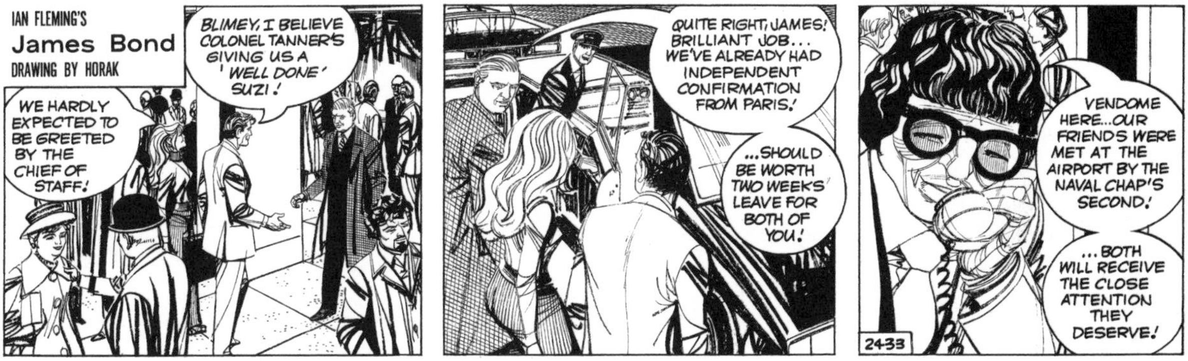
IAN FLEMING'S
James Bond
DRAWING BY HORAK
WE HARDLY EXPECTED TO BE GREETED BY THE CHIEF OF STAFF!
BLIMEY, I BELIEVE COLONEL TANNER'S GIVING US A 'WELL DONE' SUZI!
QUITE RIGHT, JAMES! BRILLIANT JOB... WE'VE ALREADY HAD INDEPENDENT CONFIRMATION FROM PARIS!
...SHOULD BE WORTH TWO WEEKS' LEAVE FOR BOTH OF YOU!
VENDOME HERE...OUR FRIENDS WERE MET AT THE AIRPORT BY THE NAVAL CHAP'S SECOND!
...BOTH WILL RECEIVE THE CLOSE ATTENTION THEY DESERVE!
24·33

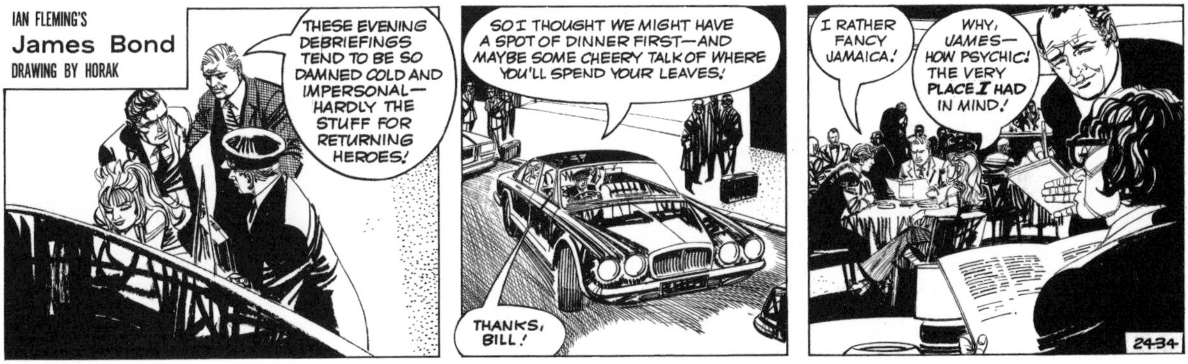
IAN FLEMING'S
James Bond
DRAWING BY HORAK
THESE EVENING DEBRIEFINGS TEND TO BE SO DAMNED COLD AND IMPERSONAL—HARDLY THE STUFF FOR RETURNING HEROES!
SO I THOUGHT WE MIGHT HAVE A SPOT OF DINNER FIRST—AND MAYBE SOME CHEERY TALK OF WHERE YOU'LL SPEND YOUR LEAVES!
THANKS, BILL!
I RATHER FANCY JAMAICA!
WHY, JAMES—HOW PSYCHIC! THE VERY PLACE I HAD IN MIND!
24·34

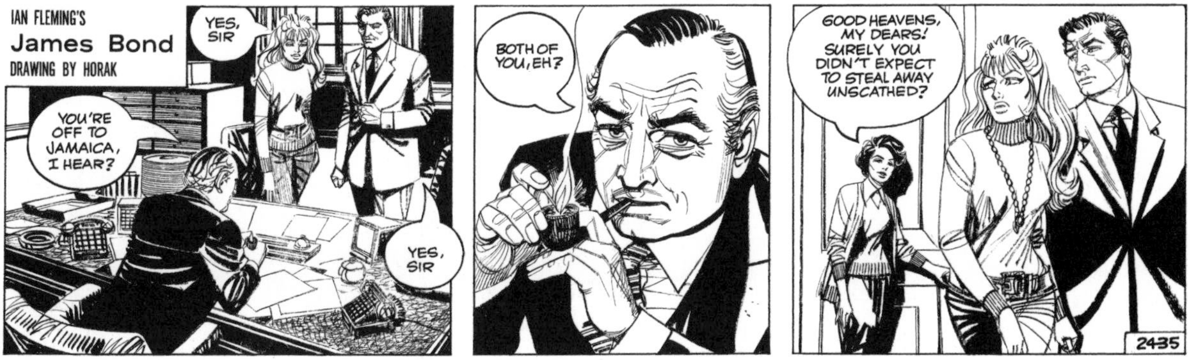
IAN FLEMING'S
James Bond
DRAWING BY HORAK
YOU'RE OFF TO JAMAICA, I HEAR?
YES, SIR
YES, SIR
BOTH OF YOU, EH?
GOOD HEAVENS, MY DEARS! SURELY YOU DIDN'T EXPECT TO STEAL AWAY UNSCATHED?
24·35

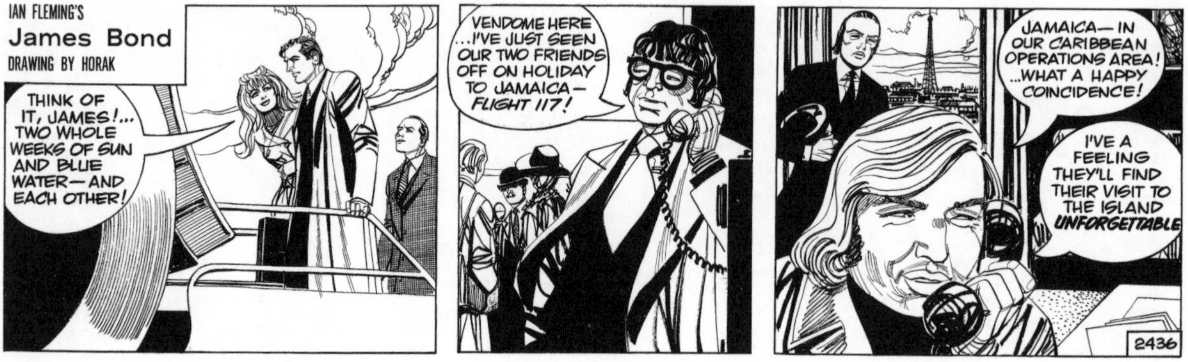
IAN FLEMING'S
James Bond
DRAWING BY HORAK
THINK OF IT, JAMES!... TWO WHOLE WEEKS OF SUN AND BLUE WATER—AND EACH OTHER!
VENDOME HERE ...I'VE JUST SEEN OUR TWO FRIENDS OFF ON HOLIDAY TO JAMAICA—FLIGHT 117!
JAMAICA—IN OUR CARIBBEAN OPERATIONS AREA! ...WHAT A HAPPY COINCIDENCE!
I'VE A FEELING THEY'LL FIND THEIR VISIT TO THE ISLAND UNFORGETTABLE
2436

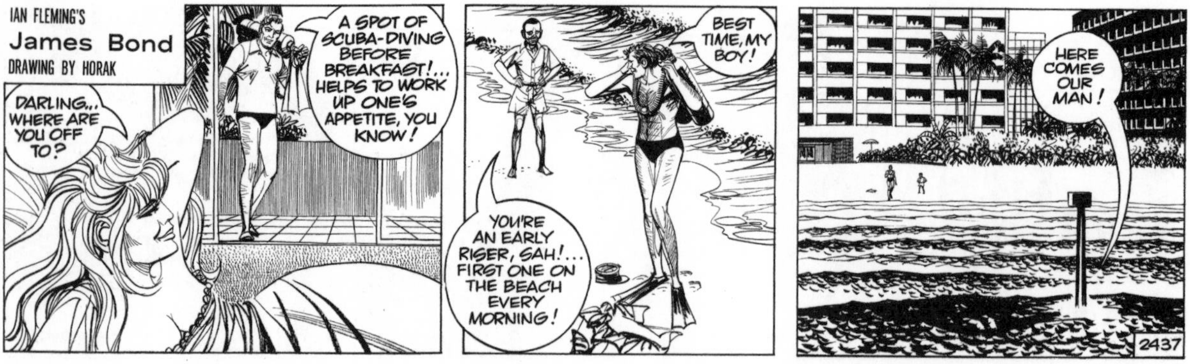
IAN FLEMING'S
James Bond
DRAWING BY HORAK
DARLING... WHERE ARE YOU OFF TO?
A SPOT OF SCUBA-DIVING BEFORE BREAKFAST!... HELPS TO WORK UP ONE'S APPETITE, YOU KNOW!
YOU'RE AN EARLY RISER, SAH!... FIRST ONE ON THE BEACH EVERY MORNING!
BEST TIME, MY BOY!
HERE COMES OUR MAN!
2437

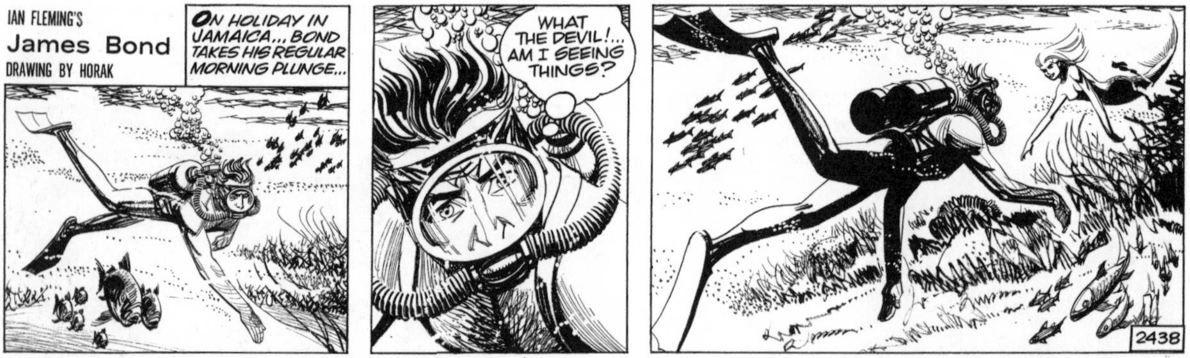
IAN FLEMING'S
James Bond
DRAWING BY HORAK
ON HOLIDAY IN JAMAICA... BOND TAKES HIS REGULAR MORNING PLUNGE...
WHAT THE DEVIL!... AM I SEEING THINGS?
2438

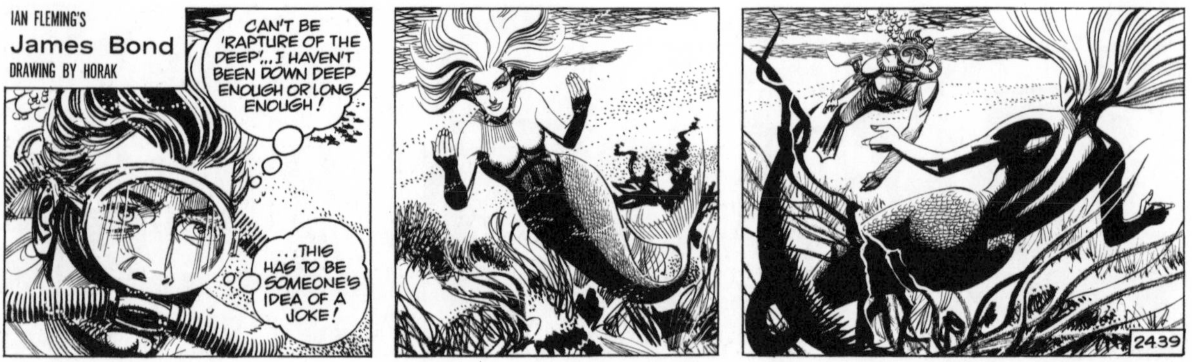
IAN FLEMING'S
James Bond
DRAWING BY HORAK
CAN'T BE 'RAPTURE OF THE DEEP'!...I HAVEN'T BEEN DOWN DEEP ENOUGH OR LONG ENOUGH!
...THIS HAS TO BE SOMEONE'S IDEA OF A JOKE!
2439

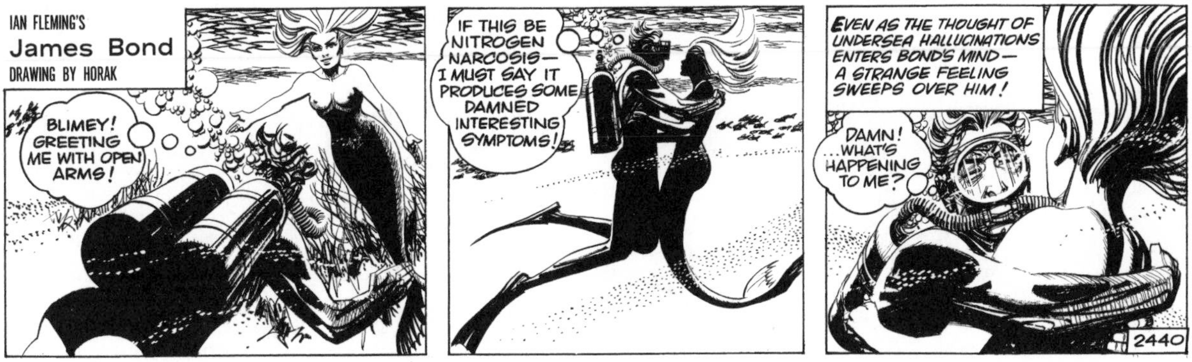
IAN FLEMING'S
James Bond
DRAWING BY HORAK
BLIMEY! GREETING ME WITH OPEN ARMS!
IF THIS BE NITROGEN NARCOSIS— I MUST SAY IT PRODUCES SOME DAMNED INTERESTING SYMPTOMS!
EVEN AS THE THOUGHT OF UNDERSEA HALLUCINATIONS ENTERS BOND'S MIND— A STRANGE FEELING SWEEPS OVER HIM!
DAMN! ...WHAT'S HAPPENING TO ME?
2440

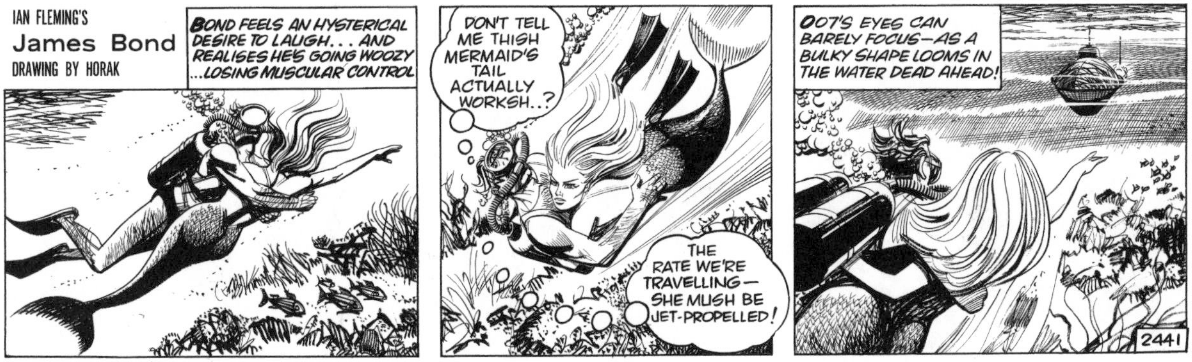
IAN FLEMING'S
James Bond
DRAWING BY HORAK
BOND FEELS AN HYSTERICAL DESIRE TO LAUGH... AND REALISES HE'S GOING WOOZY ...LOSING MUSCULAR CONTROL
DON'T TELL ME THISH MERMAID'S TAIL ACTUALLY WORKSH..?
THE RATE WE'RE TRAVELLING— SHE MUSH BE JET-PROPELLED!
007'S EYES CAN BARELY FOCUS—AS A BULKY SHAPE LOOMS IN THE WATER DEAD AHEAD!
2441

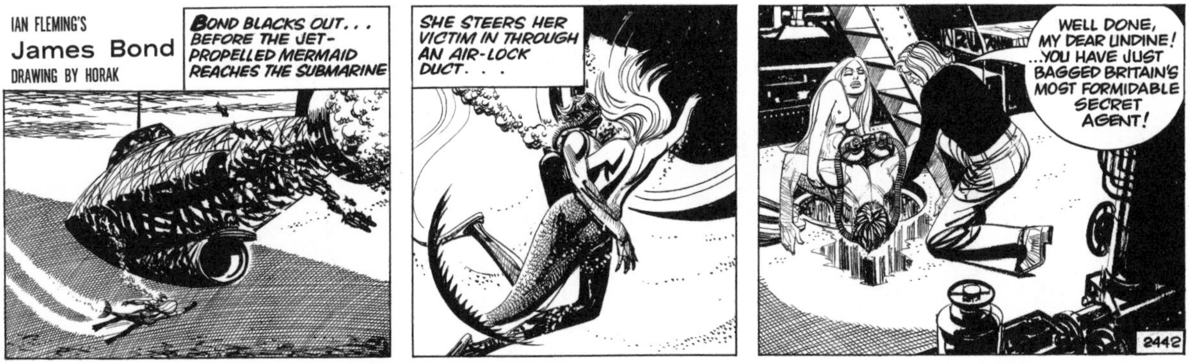
IAN FLEMING'S
James Bond
DRAWING BY HORAK
BOND BLACKS OUT... BEFORE THE JET-PROPELLED MERMAID REACHES THE SUBMARINE
SHE STEERS HER VICTIM IN THROUGH AN AIR-LOCK DUCT...
WELL DONE, MY DEAR UNDINE! ...YOU HAVE JUST BAGGED BRITAIN'S MOST FORMIDABLE SECRET AGENT!
2442

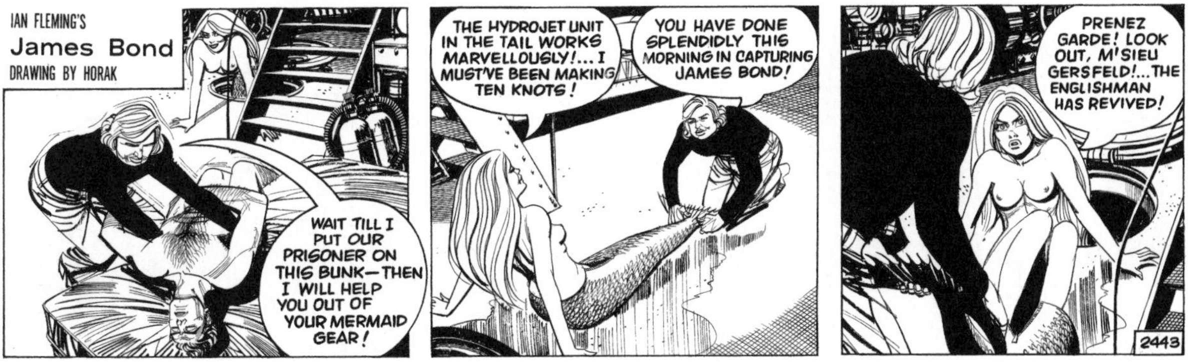
IAN FLEMING'S
James Bond
DRAWING BY HORAK
WAIT TILL I PUT OUR PRISONER ON THIS BUNK—THEN I WILL HELP YOU OUT OF YOUR MERMAID GEAR!
THE HYDROJET UNIT IN THE TAIL WORKS MARVELLOUSLY!... I MUST'VE BEEN MAKING TEN KNOTS!
YOU HAVE DONE SPLENDIDLY THIS MORNING IN CAPTURING JAMES BOND!
PRENEZ GARDE! LOOK OUT, M'SIEU GERSFELD!... THE ENGLISHMAN HAS REVIVED!
2443

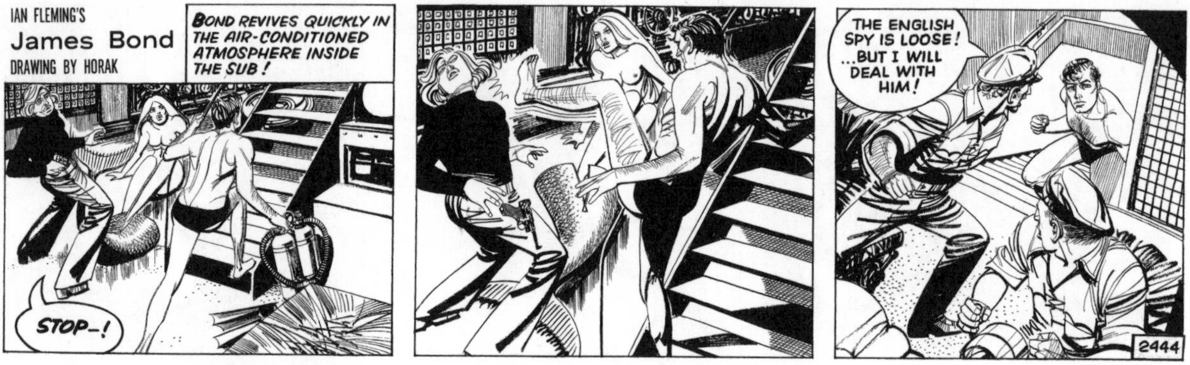
IAN FLEMING'S
James Bond
DRAWING BY HORAK
BOND REVIVES QUICKLY IN THE AIR-CONDITIONED ATMOSPHERE INSIDE THE SUB!
STOP-!
THE ENGLISH SPY IS LOOSE! ...BUT I WILL DEAL WITH HIM!
2444

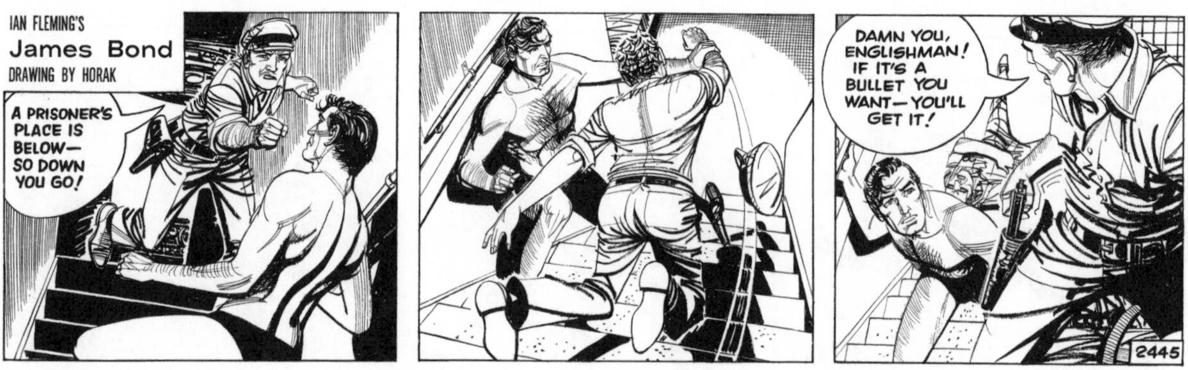
IAN FLEMING'S
James Bond
DRAWING BY HORAK
A PRISONER'S PLACE IS BELOW— SO DOWN YOU GO!
DAMN YOU, ENGLISHMAN! IF IT'S A BULLET YOU WANT—YOU'LL GET IT!
2445

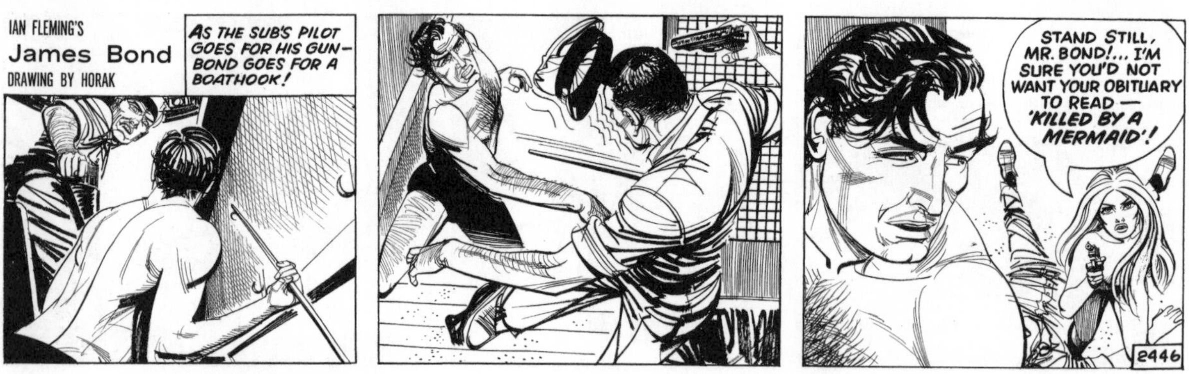
IAN FLEMING'S
James Bond
DRAWING BY HORAK
AS THE SUB'S PILOT GOES FOR HIS GUN-BOND GOES FOR A BOATHOOK!
STAND STILL, MR. BOND!... I'M SURE YOU'D NOT WANT YOUR OBITUARY TO READ — 'KILLED BY A MERMAID'!
2446

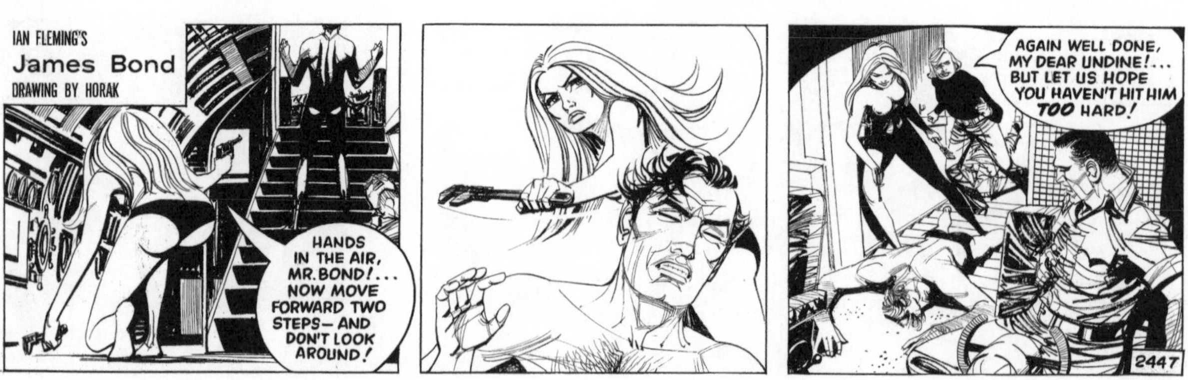
IAN FLEMING'S
James Bond
DRAWING BY HORAK
HANDS IN THE AIR, MR. BOND!... NOW MOVE FORWARD TWO STEPS— AND DON'T LOOK AROUND!
AGAIN WELL DONE, MY DEAR UNDINE!... BUT LET US HOPE YOU HAVEN'T HIT HIM TOO HARD!
2447

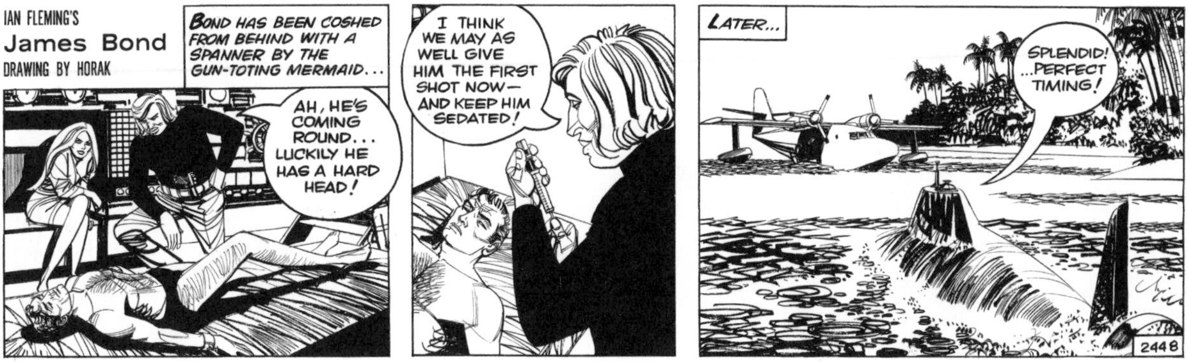
IAN FLEMING'S
James Bond
DRAWING BY HORAK
BOND HAS BEEN COSHED FROM BEHIND WITH A SPANNER BY THE GUN-TOTING MERMAID...
AH, HE'S COMING ROUND... LUCKILY HE HAS A HARD HEAD!
I THINK WE MAY AS WELL GIVE HIM THE FIRST SHOT NOW— AND KEEP HIM SEDATED!
LATER...
SPLENDID! ...PERFECT TIMING!
2448

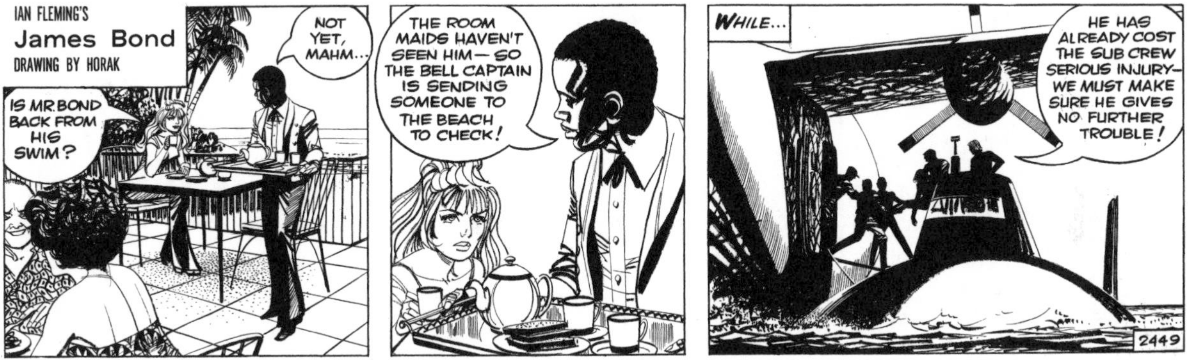
IAN FLEMING'S
James Bond
DRAWING BY HORAK
IS MR. BOND BACK FROM HIS SWIM?
NOT YET, MAHM...
THE ROOM MAIDS HAVEN'T SEEN HIM— SO THE BELL CAPTAIN IS SENDING SOMEONE TO THE BEACH TO CHECK!
WHILE...
HE HAS ALREADY COST THE SUB CREW SERIOUS INJURY— WE MUST MAKE SURE HE GIVES NO FURTHER TROUBLE!
2449

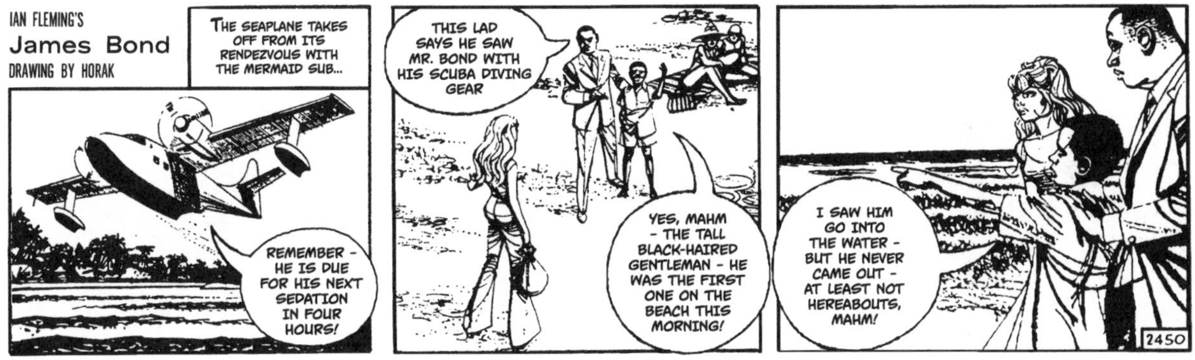
IAN FLEMING'S
James Bond
DRAWING BY HORAK
THE SEAPLANE TAKES OFF FROM ITS RENDEZVOUS WITH THE MERMAID SUB...
REMEMBER - HE IS DUE FOR HIS NEXT SEDATION IN FOUR HOURS!
THIS LAD SAYS HE SAW MR. BOND WITH HIS SCUBA DIVING GEAR
YES, MAHM - THE TALL BLACK-HAIRED GENTLEMAN - HE WAS THE FIRST ONE ON THE BEACH THIS MORNING!
I SAW HIM GO INTO THE WATER - BUT HE NEVER CAME OUT - AT LEAST NOT HEREABOUTS, MAHM!
2450

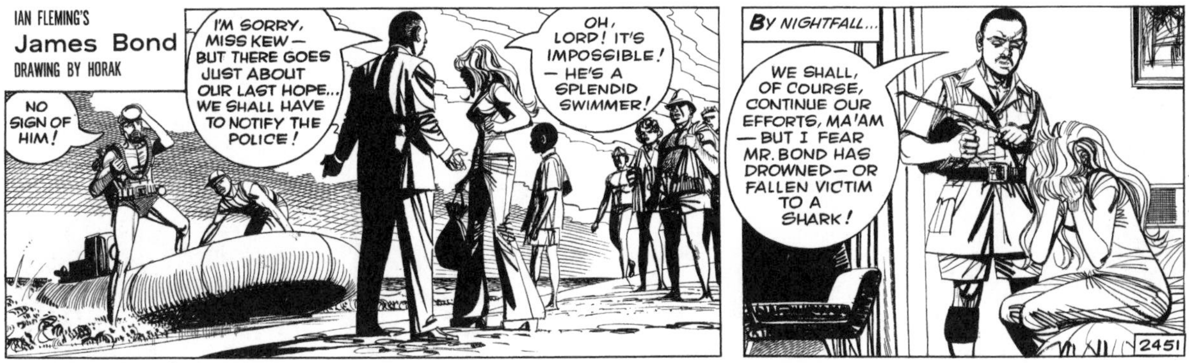
IAN FLEMING'S
James Bond
DRAWING BY HORAK
NO SIGN OF HIM!
I'M SORRY, MISS KEW— BUT THERE GOES JUST ABOUT OUR LAST HOPE... WE SHALL HAVE TO NOTIFY THE POLICE!
OH, LORD! IT'S IMPOSSIBLE! — HE'S A SPLENDID SWIMMER!
BY NIGHTFALL...
WE SHALL, OF COURSE, CONTINUE OUR EFFORTS, MA'AM — BUT I FEAR MR. BOND HAS DROWNED— OR FALLEN VICTIM TO A SHARK!
2451

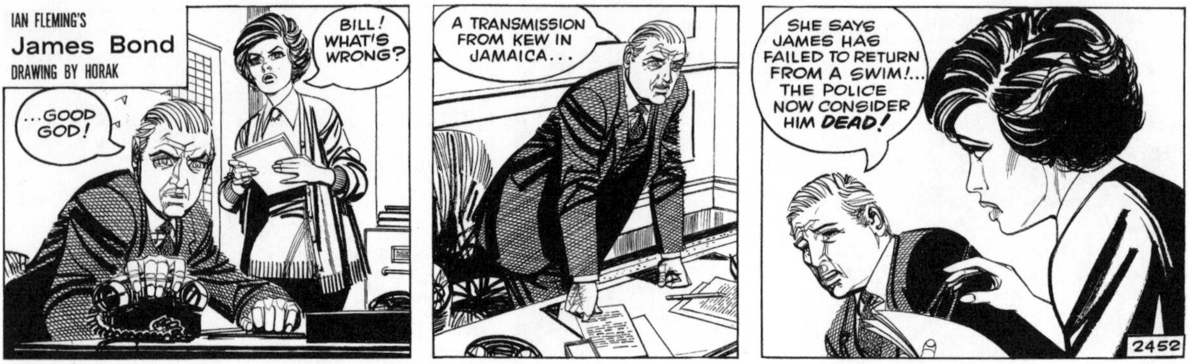
IAN FLEMING'S
James Bond
DRAWING BY HORAK
BILL! WHAT'S WRONG?
...GOOD GOD!
A TRANSMISSION FROM KEW IN JAMAICA...
SHE SAYS JAMES HAS FAILED TO RETURN FROM A SWIM!... THE POLICE NOW CONSIDER HIM DEAD!
2452

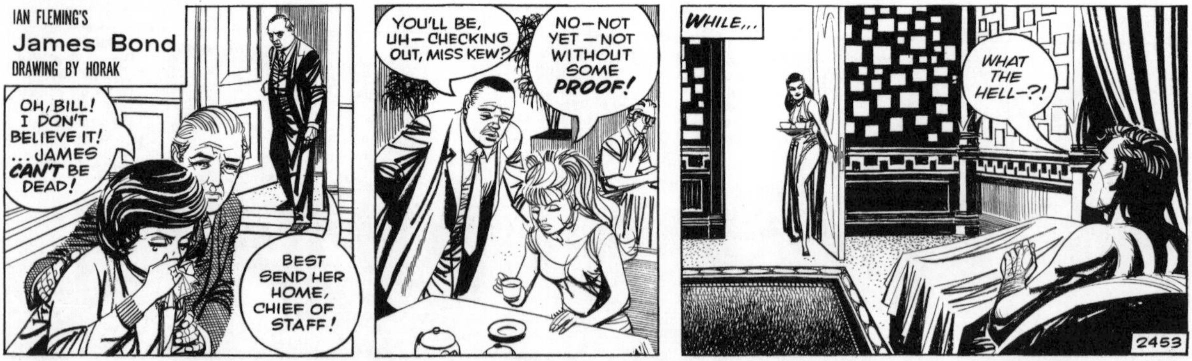
IAN FLEMING'S
James Bond
DRAWING BY HORAK
OH, BILL! I DON'T BELIEVE IT! ...JAMES CAN'T BE DEAD!
BEST SEND HER HOME, CHIEF OF STAFF!
YOU'LL BE, UH—CHECKING OUT, MISS KEW?
NO—NOT YET—NOT WITHOUT SOME PROOF!
WHILE,..
WHAT THE HELL—?!
2453

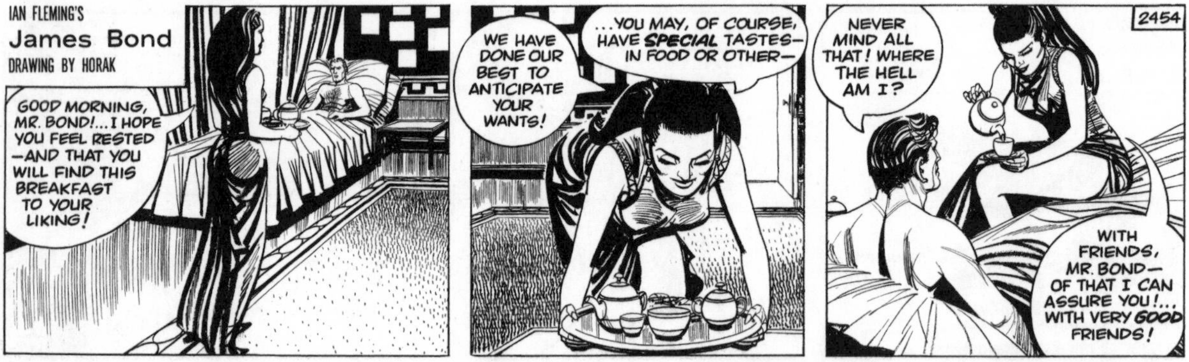
IAN FLEMING'S
James Bond
DRAWING BY HORAK
GOOD MORNING, MR. BOND!...I HOPE YOU FEEL RESTED —AND THAT YOU WILL FIND THIS BREAKFAST TO YOUR LIKING!
WE HAVE DONE OUR BEST TO ANTICIPATE YOUR WANTS!
...YOU MAY, OF COURSE, HAVE SPECIAL TASTES— IN FOOD OR OTHER—
NEVER MIND ALL THAT! WHERE THE HELL AM I?
WITH FRIENDS, MR. BOND— OF THAT I CAN ASSURE YOU!... WITH VERY GOOD FRIENDS!
2454

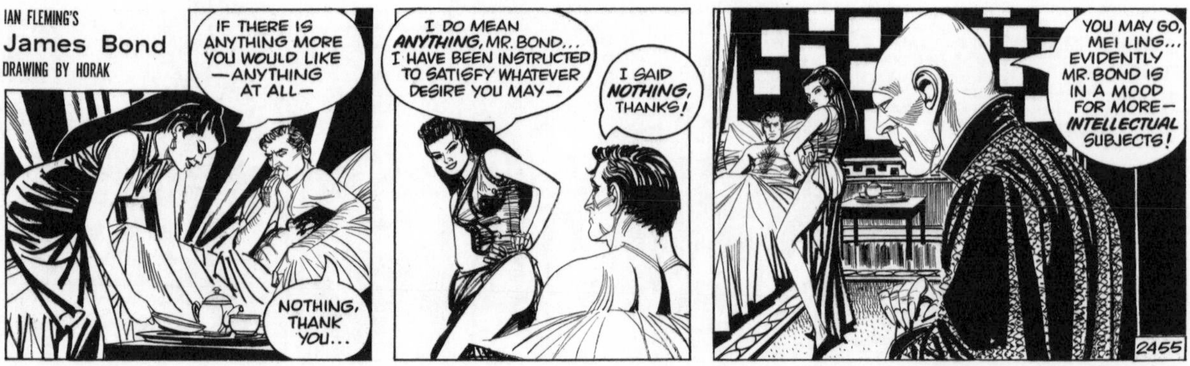
IAN FLEMING'S
James Bond
DRAWING BY HORAK
IF THERE IS ANYTHING MORE YOU WOULD LIKE —ANYTHING AT ALL—
NOTHING, THANK YOU...
I DO MEAN ANYTHING, MR. BOND... I HAVE BEEN INSTRUCTED TO SATISFY WHATEVER DESIRE YOU MAY—
I SAID NOTHING, THANKS!
YOU MAY GO, MEI LING... EVIDENTLY MR. BOND IS IN A MOOD FOR MORE— INTELLECTUAL SUBJECTS!
2455

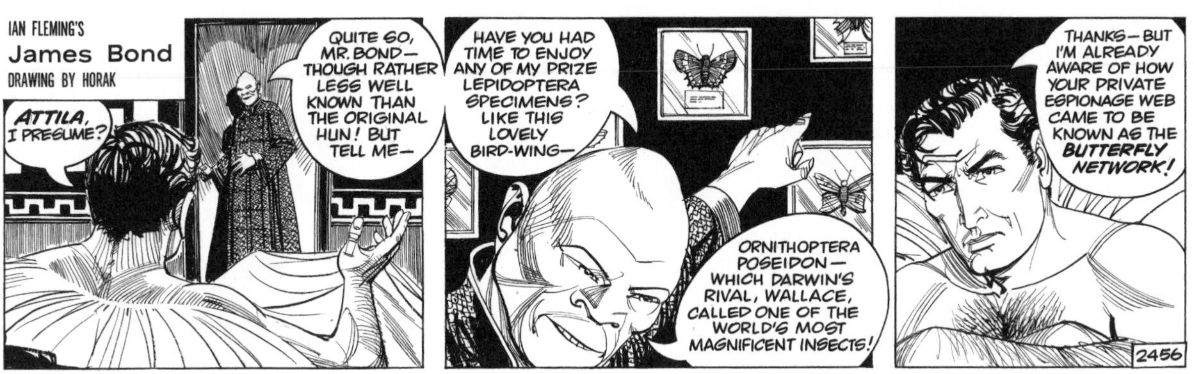
IAN FLEMING'S
James Bond
DRAWING BY HORAK
ATTILA, I PRESUME?
QUITE SO, MR. BOND—THOUGH RATHER LESS WELL KNOWN THAN THE ORIGINAL HUN! BUT TELL ME—
HAVE YOU HAD TIME TO ENJOY ANY OF MY PRIZE LEPIDOPTERA SPECIMENS? LIKE THIS LOVELY BIRD-WING—
ORNITHOPTERA POSEIDON—WHICH DARWIN'S RIVAL, WALLACE, CALLED ONE OF THE WORLD'S MOST MAGNIFICENT INSECTS!
THANKS—BUT I'M ALREADY AWARE OF HOW YOUR PRIVATE ESPIONAGE WEB CAME TO BE KNOWN AS THE BUTTERFLY NETWORK!
2456

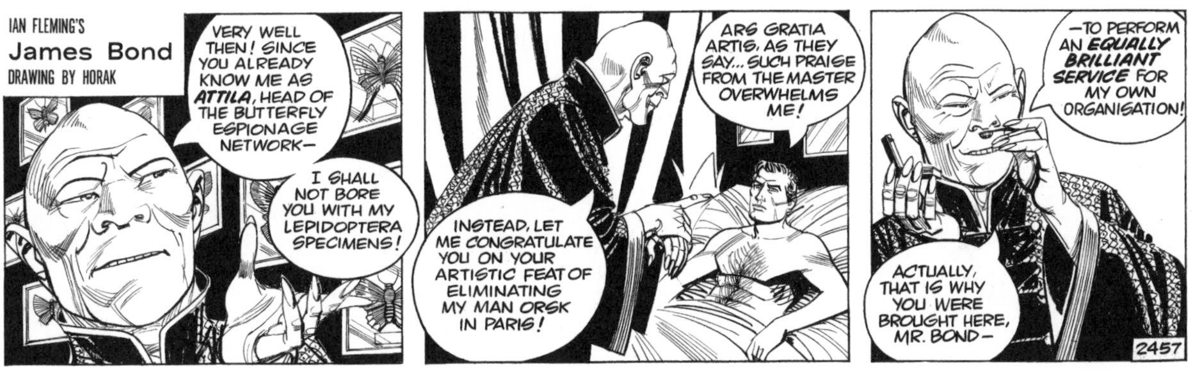
IAN FLEMING'S
James Bond
DRAWING BY HORAK
VERY WELL THEN! SINCE YOU ALREADY KNOW ME AS ATTILA, HEAD OF THE BUTTERFLY ESPIONAGE NETWORK—
I SHALL NOT BORE YOU WITH MY LEPIDOPTERA SPECIMENS!
INSTEAD, LET ME CONGRATULATE YOU ON YOUR ARTISTIC FEAT OF ELIMINATING MY MAN ORSK IN PARIS!
ARS GRATIA ARTIS, AS THEY SAY... SUCH PRAISE FROM THE MASTER OVERWHELMS ME!
—TO PERFORM AN EQUALLY BRILLIANT SERVICE FOR MY OWN ORGANISATION!
ACTUALLY, THAT IS WHY YOU WERE BROUGHT HERE, MR. BOND—
2457

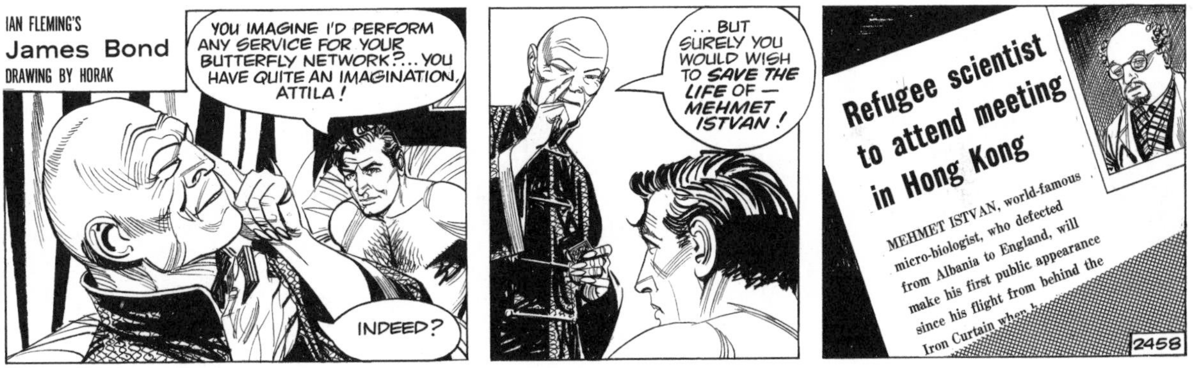
IAN FLEMING'S
James Bond
DRAWING BY HORAK
YOU IMAGINE I'D PERFORM ANY SERVICE FOR YOUR BUTTERFLY NETWORK?... YOU HAVE QUITE AN IMAGINATION, ATTILA!
INDEED?
... BUT SURELY YOU WOULD WISH TO SAVE THE LIFE OF—MEHMET ISTVAN!
Refugee scientist to attend meeting in Hong Kong
MEHMET ISTVAN, world-famous micro-biologist, who defected from Albania to England, will make his first public appearance since his flight from behind the Iron Curtain when
2458

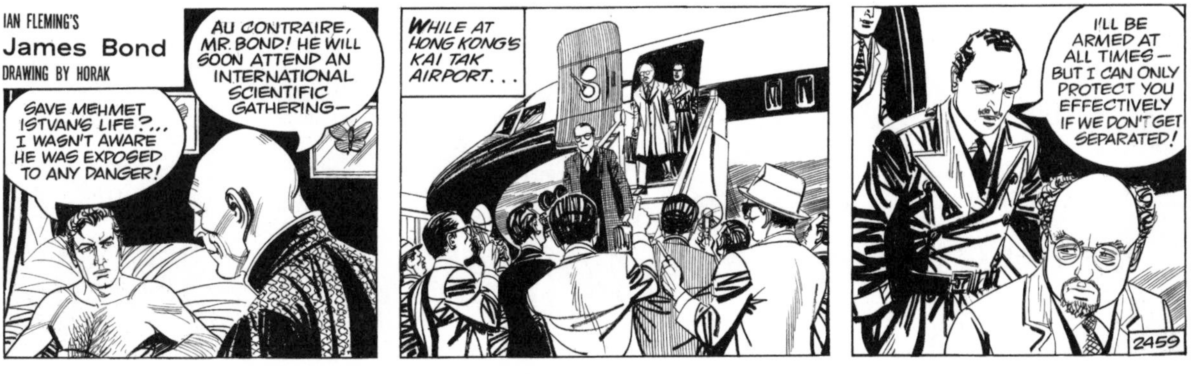
IAN FLEMING'S
James Bond
DRAWING BY HORAK
SAVE MEHMET ISTVAN'S LIFE?... I WASN'T AWARE HE WAS EXPOSED TO ANY DANGER!
AU CONTRAIRE, MR. BOND! HE WILL SOON ATTEND AN INTERNATIONAL SCIENTIFIC GATHERING—
WHILE AT HONG KONG'S KAI TAK AIRPORT...
I'LL BE ARMED AT ALL TIMES—BUT I CAN ONLY PROTECT YOU EFFECTIVELY IF WE DON'T GET SEPARATED!
2459

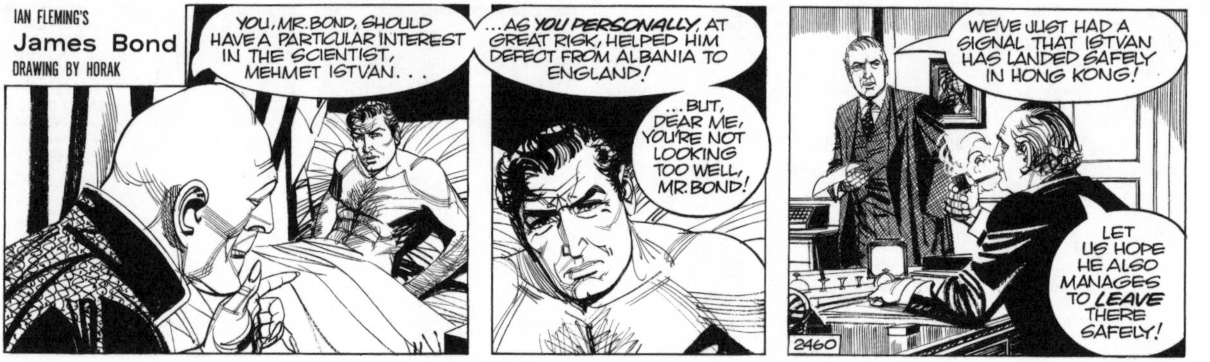
IAN FLEMING'S
James Bond
DRAWING BY HORAK
YOU, MR. BOND, SHOULD HAVE A PARTICULAR INTEREST IN THE SCIENTIST, MEHMET ISTVAN. . .
. . . AS YOU PERSONALLY, AT GREAT RISK, HELPED HIM DEFECT FROM ALBANIA TO ENGLAND!
. . . BUT, DEAR ME, YOU'RE NOT LOOKING TOO WELL, MR. BOND!
WE'VE JUST HAD A SIGNAL THAT ISTVAN HAS LANDED SAFELY IN HONG KONG!
LET US HOPE HE ALSO MANAGES TO LEAVE THERE SAFELY!
2460

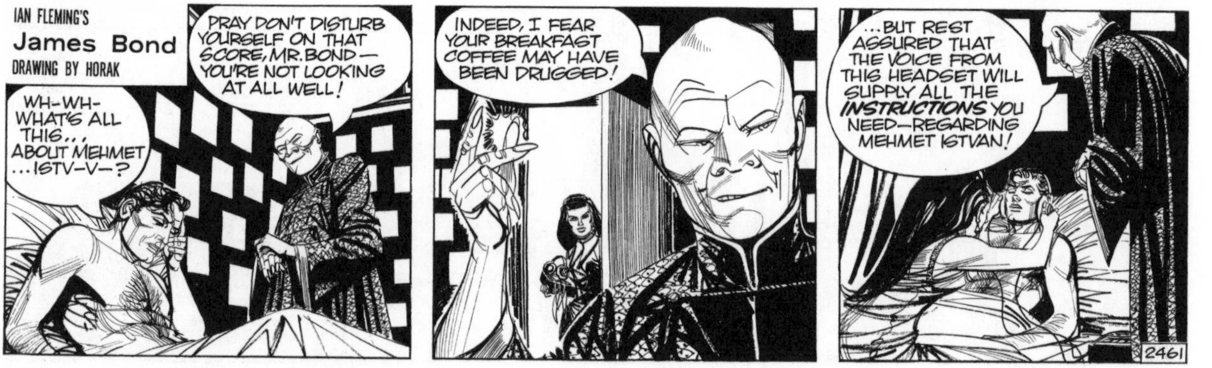
IAN FLEMING'S
James Bond
DRAWING BY HORAK
WH-WH-WHAT'S ALL THIS. . . ABOUT MEHMET . . . ISTV-V-?
PRAY DON'T DISTURB YOURSELF ON THAT SCORE, MR. BOND— YOU'RE NOT LOOKING AT ALL WELL!
INDEED, I FEAR YOUR BREAKFAST COFFEE MAY HAVE BEEN DRUGGED!
. . . BUT REST ASSURED THAT THE VOICE FROM THIS HEADSET WILL SUPPLY ALL THE INSTRUCTIONS YOU NEED—REGARDING MEHMET ISTVAN!
2461

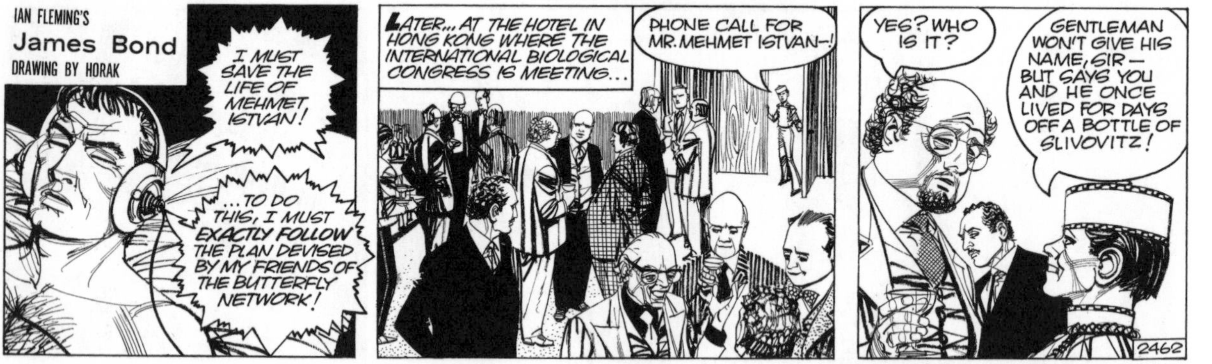
IAN FLEMING'S
James Bond
DRAWING BY HORAK
I MUST SAVE THE LIFE OF MEHMET ISTVAN!
. . . TO DO THIS, I MUST EXACTLY FOLLOW THE PLAN DEVISED BY MY FRIENDS OF THE BUTTERFLY NETWORK!
LATER. . . AT THE HOTEL IN HONG KONG WHERE THE INTERNATIONAL BIOLOGICAL CONGRESS IS MEETING. . .
PHONE CALL FOR MR. MEHMET ISTVAN-!
YES? WHO IS IT?
GENTLEMAN WON'T GIVE HIS NAME, SIR— BUT SAYS YOU AND HE ONCE LIVED FOR DAYS OFF A BOTTLE OF SLIVOVITZ!
2462

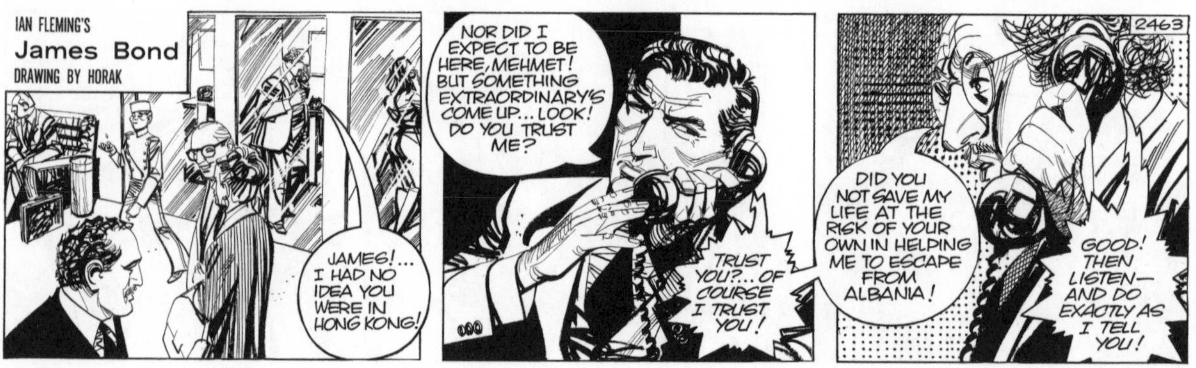
IAN FLEMING'S
James Bond
DRAWING BY HORAK
JAMES! . . . I HAD NO IDEA YOU WERE IN HONG KONG!
NOR DID I EXPECT TO BE HERE, MEHMET! BUT SOMETHING EXTRAORDINARY'S COME UP. . . LOOK! DO YOU TRUST ME?
TRUST YOU?. . . OF COURSE I TRUST YOU!
2463
DID YOU NOT SAVE MY LIFE AT THE RISK OF YOUR OWN IN HELPING ME TO ESCAPE FROM ALBANIA!
GOOD! THEN LISTEN— AND DO EXACTLY AS I TELL YOU!

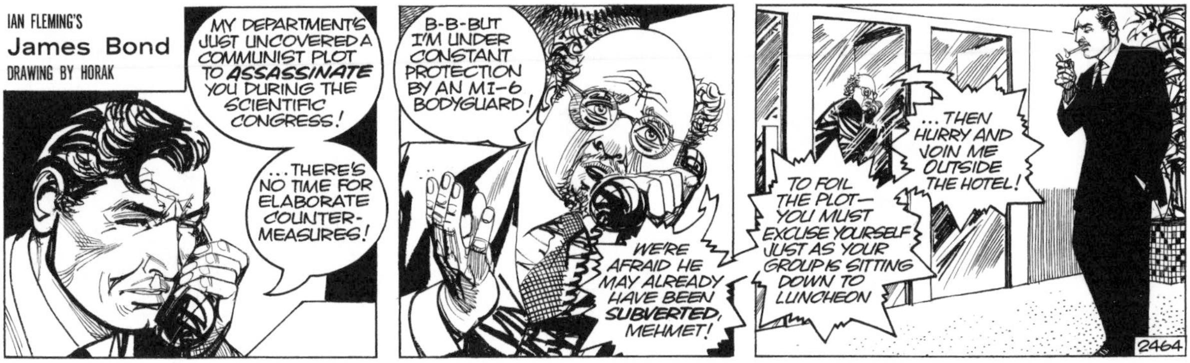
IAN FLEMING'S
James Bond
DRAWING BY HORAK
MY DEPARTMENT'S JUST UNCOVERED A COMMUNIST PLOT TO ASSASSINATE YOU DURING THE SCIENTIFIC CONGRESS!
...THERE'S NO TIME FOR ELABORATE COUNTER-MEASURES!
B-B-BUT I'M UNDER CONSTANT PROTECTION BY AN MI-6 BODYGUARD!
WE'RE AFRAID HE MAY ALREADY HAVE BEEN SUBVERTED, MEHMET!
TO FOIL THE PLOT—YOU MUST EXCUSE YOURSELF JUST AS YOUR GROUP IS SITTING DOWN TO LUNCHEON
...THEN HURRY AND JOIN ME OUTSIDE THE HOTEL!
2464

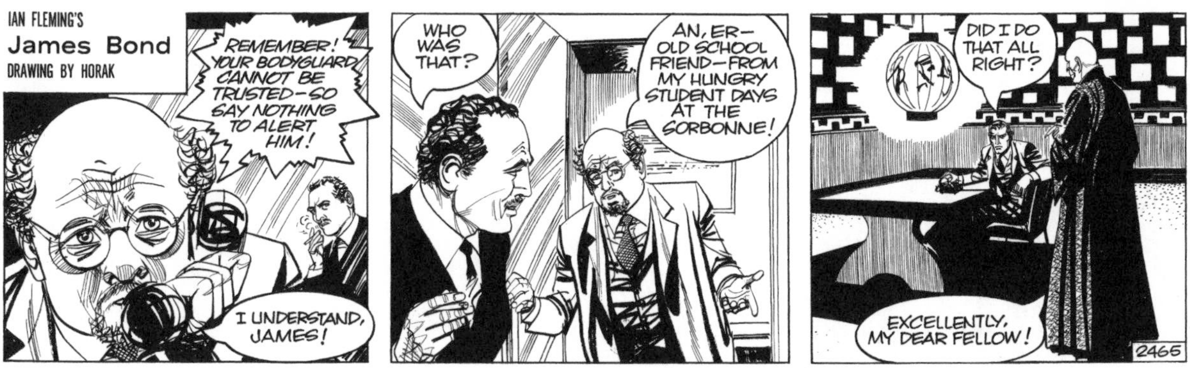
IAN FLEMING'S
James Bond
DRAWING BY HORAK
REMEMBER! YOUR BODYGUARD CANNOT BE TRUSTED—SO SAY NOTHING TO ALERT HIM!
I UNDERSTAND, JAMES!
WHO WAS THAT?
AN, ER—OLD SCHOOL FRIEND—FROM MY HUNGRY STUDENT DAYS AT THE SORBONNE!
DID I DO THAT ALL RIGHT?
EXCELLENTLY, MY DEAR FELLOW!
2465

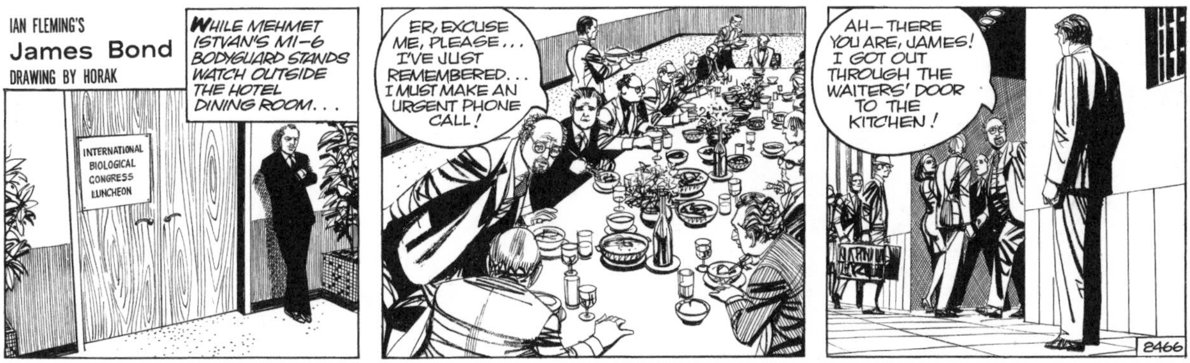
IAN FLEMING'S
James Bond
DRAWING BY HORAK
WHILE MEHMET ISTVAN'S MI-6 BODYGUARD STANDS WATCH OUTSIDE THE HOTEL DINING ROOM...
INTERNATIONAL BIOLOGICAL CONGRESS LUNCHEON
ER, EXCUSE ME, PLEASE... I'VE JUST REMEMBERED... I MUST MAKE AN URGENT PHONE CALL!
AH—THERE YOU ARE, JAMES! I GOT OUT THROUGH THE WAITERS' DOOR TO THE KITCHEN!
2466

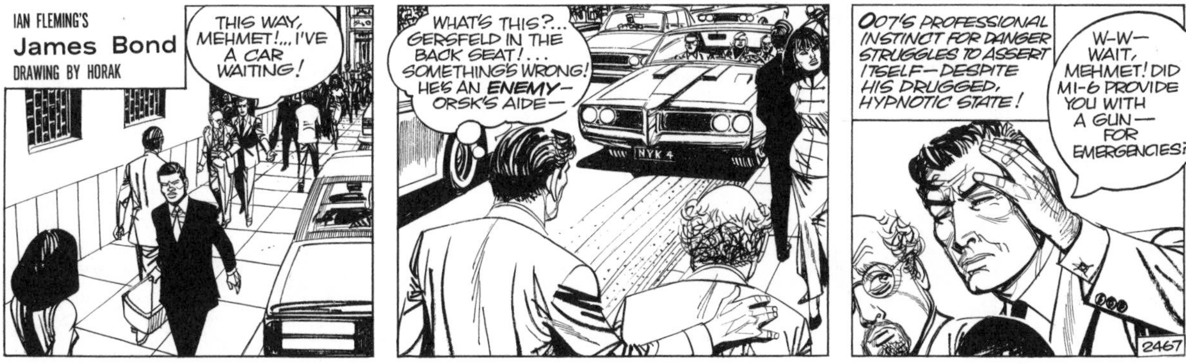
IAN FLEMING'S
James Bond
DRAWING BY HORAK
THIS WAY, MEHMET!... I'VE A CAR WAITING!
WHAT'S THIS?... GERSFELD IN THE BACK SEAT!... SOMETHING'S WRONG! HE'S AN ENEMY—ORSK'S AIDE—
NYK 4
007'S PROFESSIONAL INSTINCT FOR DANGER STRUGGLES TO ASSERT ITSELF—DESPITE HIS DRUGGED, HYPNOTIC STATE!
W-W-WAIT, MEHMET! DID MI-6 PROVIDE YOU WITH A GUN—FOR EMERGENCIES?
2467

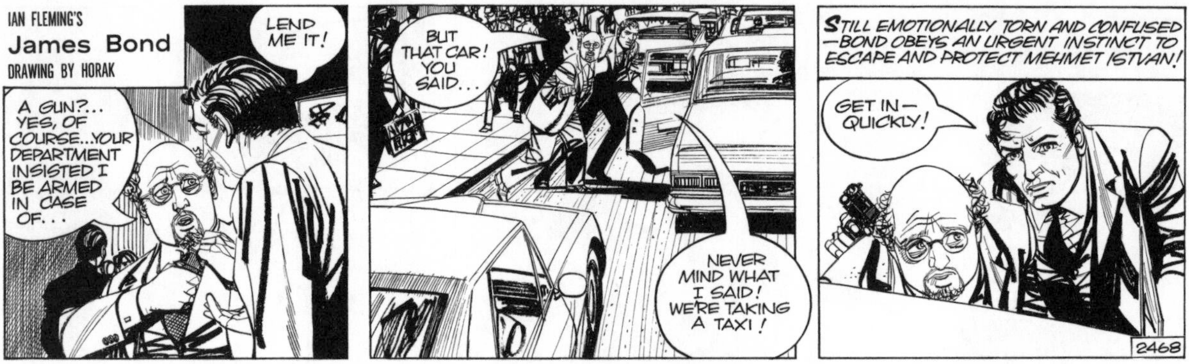
IAN FLEMING'S
James Bond
DRAWING BY HORAK
LEND ME IT!
A GUN?... YES, OF COURSE...YOUR DEPARTMENT INSISTED I BE ARMED IN CASE OF...
BUT THAT CAR! YOU SAID...
NEVER MIND WHAT I SAID! WE'RE TAKING A TAXI!
STILL EMOTIONALLY TORN AND CONFUSED—BOND OBEYS AN URGENT INSTINCT TO ESCAPE AND PROTECT MEHMET ISTVAN!
GET IN—QUICKLY!
2468

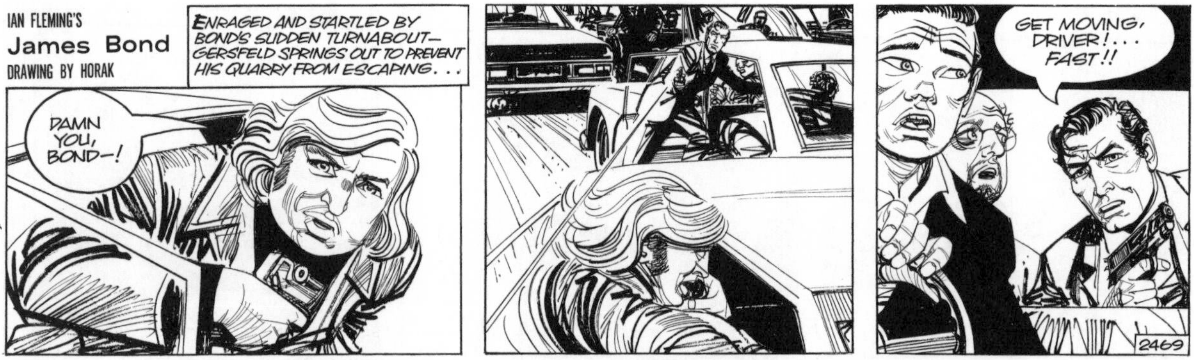
IAN FLEMING'S
James Bond
DRAWING BY HORAK
ENRAGED AND STARTLED BY BOND'S SUDDEN TURNABOUT—GERSFELD SPRINGS OUT TO PREVENT HIS QUARRY FROM ESCAPING...
DAMN YOU, BOND—!
GET MOVING, DRIVER!... FAST!!
2469

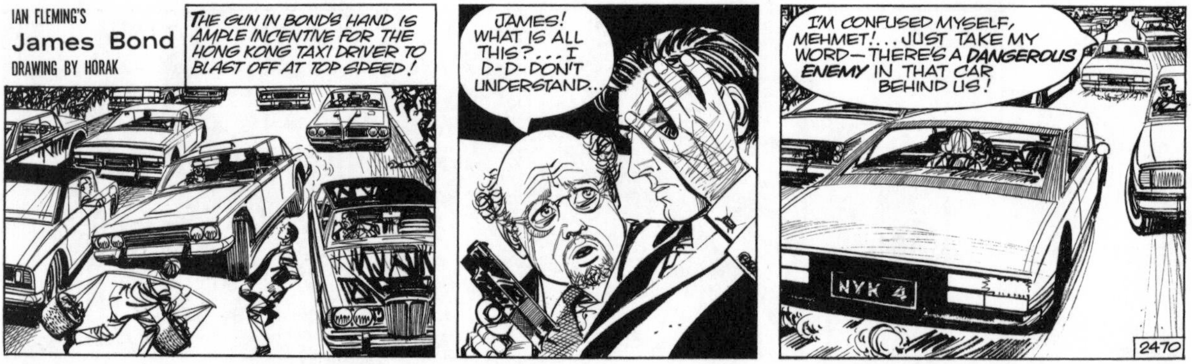
IAN FLEMING'S
James Bond
DRAWING BY HORAK
THE GUN IN BOND'S HAND IS AMPLE INCENTIVE FOR THE HONG KONG TAXI DRIVER TO BLAST OFF AT TOP SPEED!
JAMES! WHAT IS ALL THIS?... I D-D-DON'T UNDERSTAND...
I'M CONFUSED MYSELF, MEHMET!... JUST TAKE MY WORD—THERE'S A DANGEROUS ENEMY IN THAT CAR BEHIND US!
NYK 4
2470

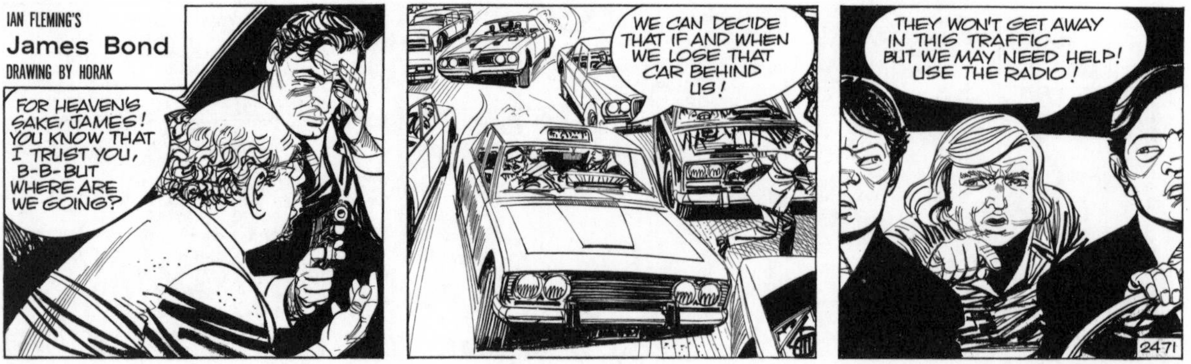
IAN FLEMING'S
James Bond
DRAWING BY HORAK
FOR HEAVEN'S SAKE, JAMES! YOU KNOW THAT I TRUST YOU, B-B-BUT WHERE ARE WE GOING?
WE CAN DECIDE THAT IF AND WHEN WE LOSE THAT CAR BEHIND US!
THEY WON'T GET AWAY IN THIS TRAFFIC—BUT WE MAY NEED HELP! USE THE RADIO!
2471

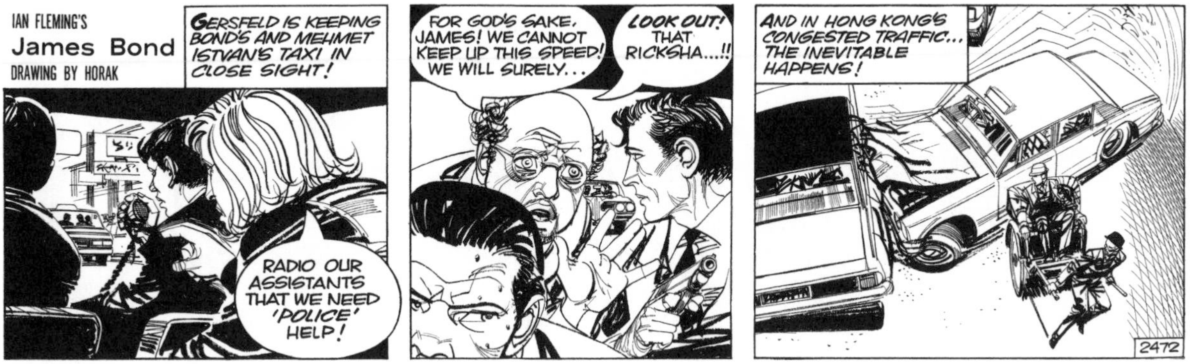
IAN FLEMING'S
James Bond
DRAWING BY HORAK
GERSFELD IS KEEPING BOND'S AND MEHMET ISTVAN'S TAXI IN CLOSE SIGHT!
RADIO OUR ASSISTANTS THAT WE NEED 'POLICE' HELP!
FOR GOD'S SAKE, JAMES! WE CANNOT KEEP UP THIS SPEED! WE WILL SURELY...
LOOK OUT! THAT RICKSHA...!!
AND IN HONG KONG'S CONGESTED TRAFFIC... THE INEVITABLE HAPPENS!
2472

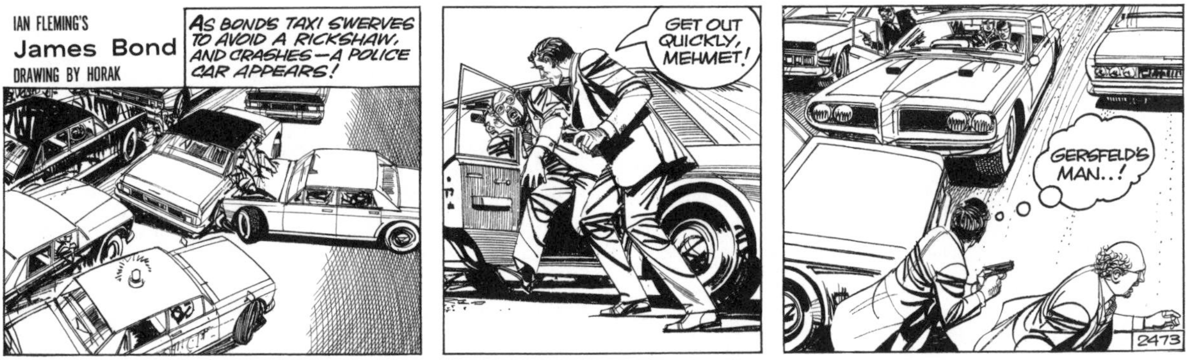
IAN FLEMING'S
James Bond
DRAWING BY HORAK
AS BOND'S TAXI SWERVES TO AVOID A RICKSHAW, AND CRASHES—A POLICE CAR APPEARS!
GET OUT QUICKLY, MEHMET!
GERSFELD'S MAN..!
2473

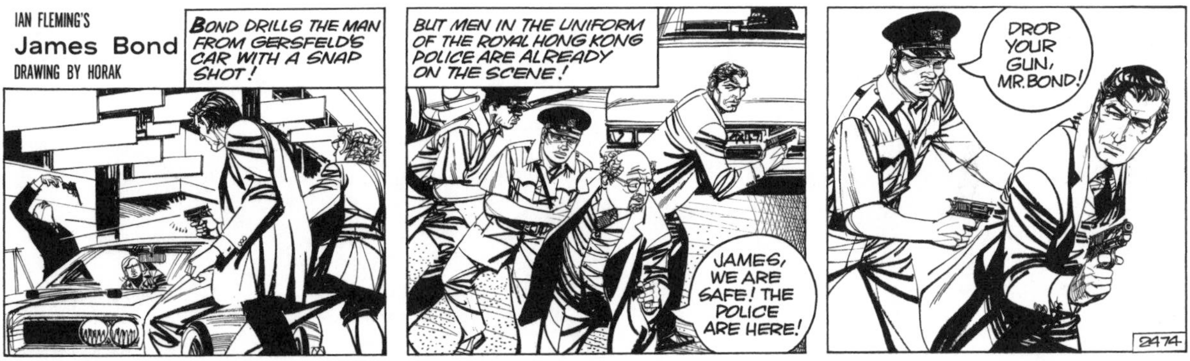
IAN FLEMING'S
James Bond
DRAWING BY HORAK
BOND DRILLS THE MAN FROM GERSFELD'S CAR WITH A SNAP SHOT!
BUT MEN IN THE UNIFORM OF THE ROYAL HONG KONG POLICE ARE ALREADY ON THE SCENE!
JAMES, WE ARE SAFE! THE POLICE ARE HERE!
DROP YOUR GUN, MR. BOND!
2474

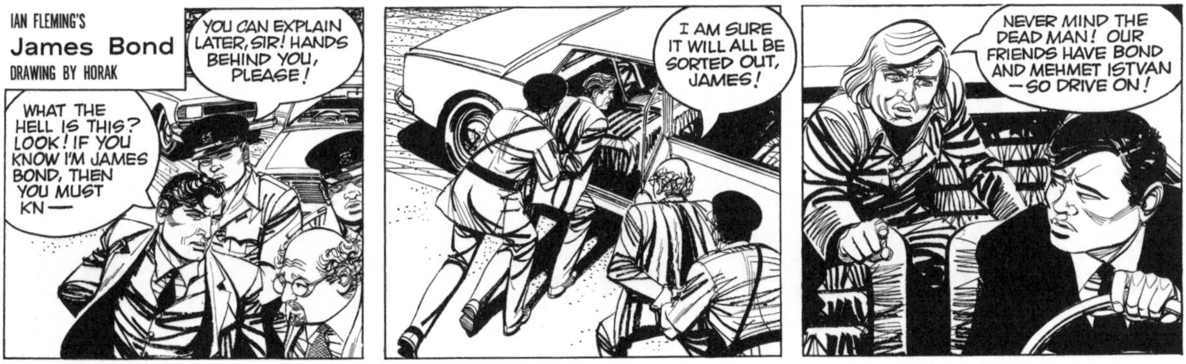
IAN FLEMING'S
James Bond
DRAWING BY HORAK
YOU CAN EXPLAIN LATER, SIR! HANDS BEHIND YOU, PLEASE!
WHAT THE HELL IS THIS? LOOK! IF YOU KNOW I'M JAMES BOND, THEN YOU MUST KN—
I AM SURE IT WILL ALL BE SORTED OUT, JAMES!
NEVER MIND THE DEAD MAN! OUR FRIENDS HAVE BOND AND MEHMET ISTVAN —SO DRIVE ON!

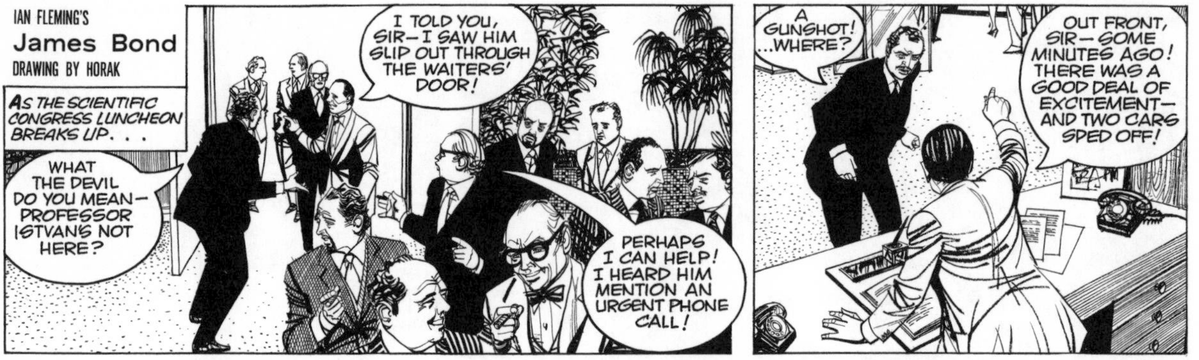
IAN FLEMING'S
James Bond
DRAWING BY HORAK
AS THE SCIENTIFIC CONGRESS LUNCHEON BREAKS UP. . .
WHAT THE DEVIL DO YOU MEAN—PROFESSOR ISTVAN'S NOT HERE?
I TOLD YOU, SIR—I SAW HIM SLIP OUT THROUGH THE WAITERS' DOOR!
PERHAPS I CAN HELP! I HEARD HIM MENTION AN URGENT PHONE CALL!
A GUNSHOT! ...WHERE?
OUT FRONT, SIR—SOME MINUTES AGO! THERE WAS A GOOD DEAL OF EXCITEMENT—AND TWO CARS SPED OFF!

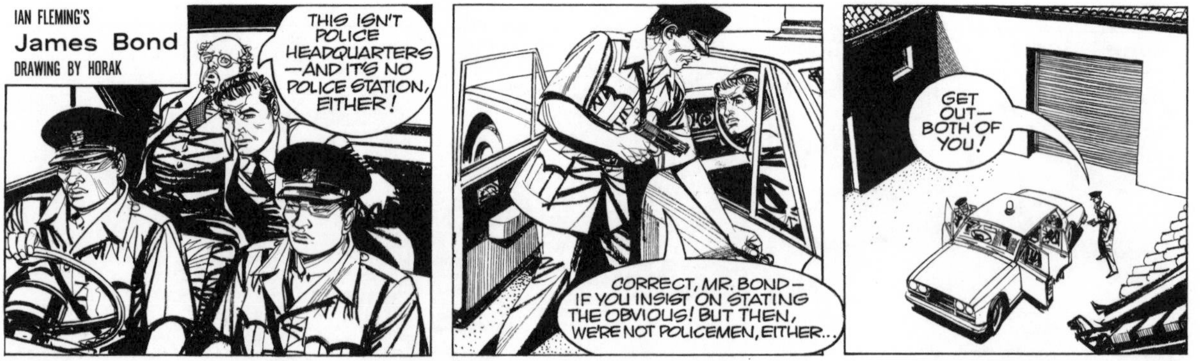
IAN FLEMING'S
James Bond
DRAWING BY HORAK
THIS ISN'T POLICE HEADQUARTERS—AND IT'S NO POLICE STATION, EITHER!
CORRECT, MR. BOND—IF YOU INSIST ON STATING THE OBVIOUS! BUT THEN, WE'RE NOT POLICEMEN, EITHER...
GET OUT—BOTH OF YOU!

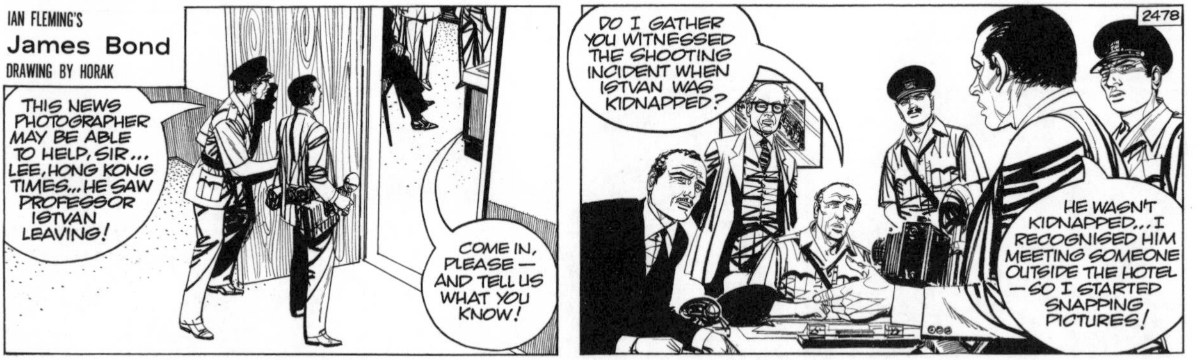
IAN FLEMING'S
James Bond
DRAWING BY HORAK
THIS NEWS PHOTOGRAPHER MAY BE ABLE TO HELP, SIR... LEE, HONG KONG TIMES... HE SAW PROFESSOR ISTVAN LEAVING!
COME IN, PLEASE—AND TELL US WHAT YOU KNOW!
2478
DO I GATHER YOU WITNESSED THE SHOOTING INCIDENT WHEN ISTVAN WAS KIDNAPPED?
HE WASN'T KIDNAPPED... I RECOGNISED HIM MEETING SOMEONE OUTSIDE THE HOTEL—SO I STARTED SNAPPING PICTURES!

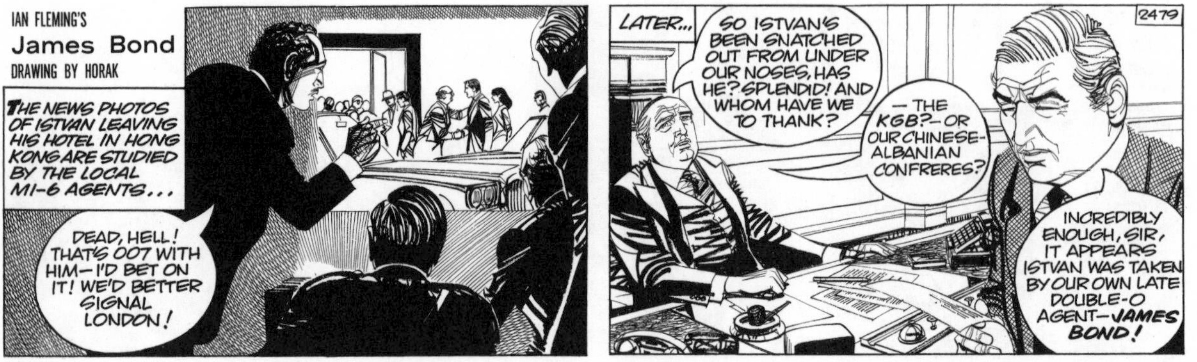
IAN FLEMING'S
James Bond
DRAWING BY HORAK
THE NEWS PHOTOS OF ISTVAN LEAVING HIS HOTEL IN HONG KONG ARE STUDIED BY THE LOCAL MI-6 AGENTS...
DEAD, HELL! THAT'S 007 WITH HIM—I'D BET ON IT! WE'D BETTER SIGNAL LONDON!
2479
LATER...
SO ISTVAN'S BEEN SNATCHED OUT FROM UNDER OUR NOSES, HAS HE? SPLENDID! AND WHOM HAVE WE TO THANK?
—THE KGB?—OR OUR CHINESE-ALBANIAN CONFRERES?
INCREDIBLY ENOUGH, SIR, IT APPEARS ISTVAN WAS TAKEN BY OUR OWN LATE DOUBLE-O AGENT—JAMES BOND!

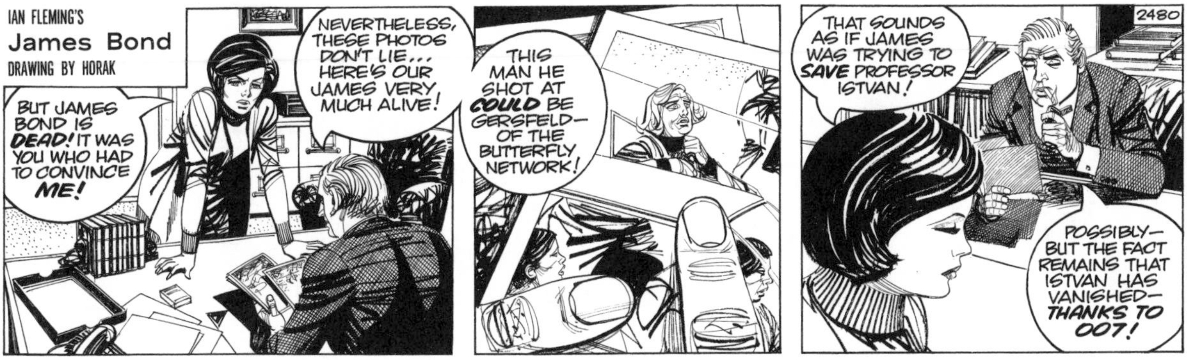
IAN FLEMING'S
James Bond
DRAWING BY HORAK
BUT JAMES BOND IS DEAD! IT WAS YOU WHO HAD TO CONVINCE ME!
NEVERTHELESS, THESE PHOTOS DON'T LIE... HERE'S OUR JAMES VERY MUCH ALIVE!
THIS MAN HE SHOT AT COULD BE GERSFELD— OF THE BUTTERFLY NETWORK!
2480
THAT SOUNDS AS IF JAMES WAS TRYING TO SAVE PROFESSOR ISTVAN!
POSSIBLY— BUT THE FACT REMAINS THAT ISTVAN HAS VANISHED— THANKS TO 007!

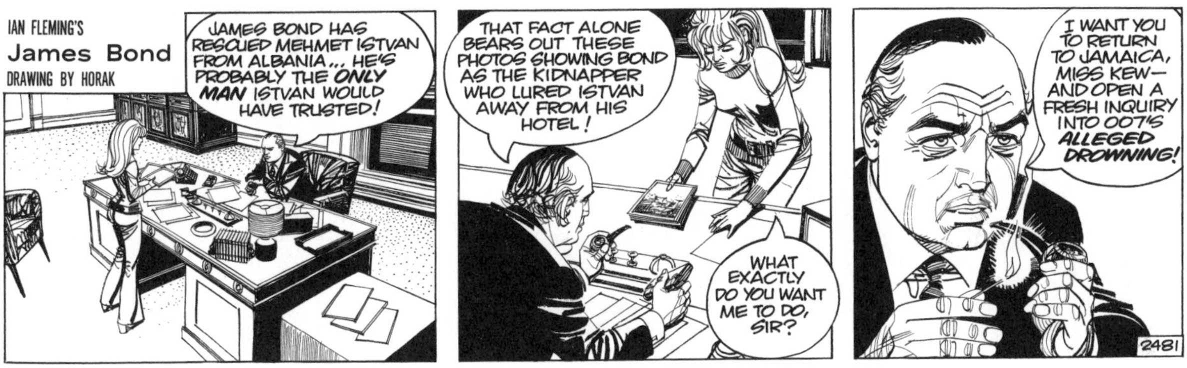
IAN FLEMING'S
James Bond
DRAWING BY HORAK
JAMES BOND HAS RESCUED MEHMET ISTVAN FROM ALBANIA... HE'S PROBABLY THE ONLY MAN ISTVAN WOULD HAVE TRUSTED!
THAT FACT ALONE BEARS OUT THESE PHOTOS SHOWING BOND AS THE KIDNAPPER WHO LURED ISTVAN AWAY FROM HIS HOTEL!
WHAT EXACTLY DO YOU WANT ME TO DO, SIR?
I WANT YOU TO RETURN TO JAMAICA, MISS KEW— AND OPEN A FRESH INQUIRY INTO 007'S ALLEGED DROWNING!
2481

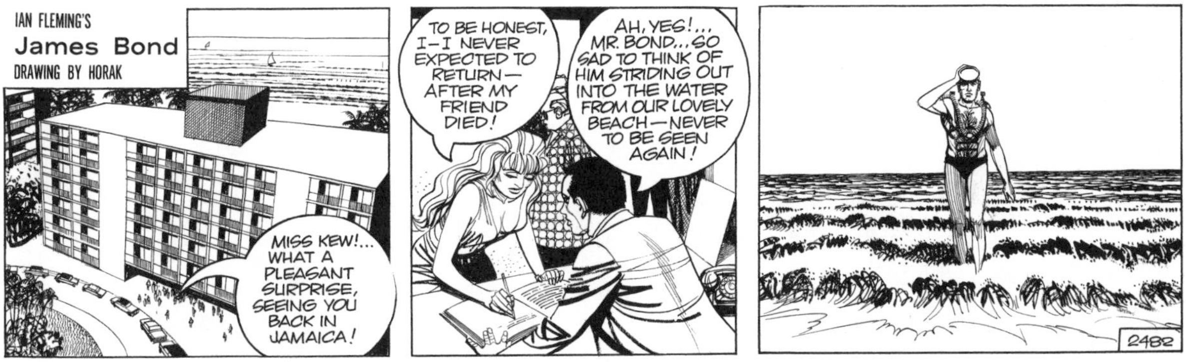
IAN FLEMING'S
James Bond
DRAWING BY HORAK
MISS KEW!... WHAT A PLEASANT SURPRISE, SEEING YOU BACK IN JAMAICA!
TO BE HONEST, I-I NEVER EXPECTED TO RETURN— AFTER MY FRIEND DIED!
AH, YES!... MR. BOND... SO SAD TO THINK OF HIM STRIDING OUT INTO THE WATER FROM OUR LOVELY BEACH—NEVER TO BE SEEN AGAIN!
2482

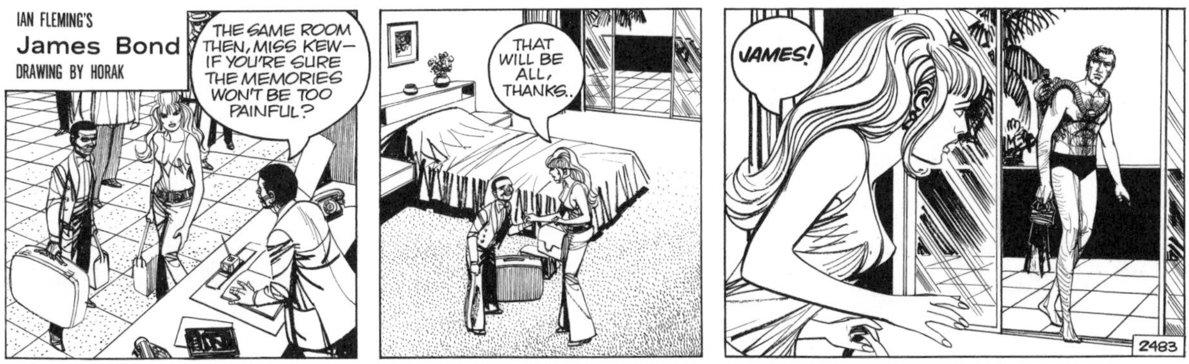
IAN FLEMING'S
James Bond
DRAWING BY HORAK
THE SAME ROOM THEN, MISS KEW— IF YOU'RE SURE THE MEMORIES WON'T BE TOO PAINFUL?
THAT WILL BE ALL, THANKS..
JAMES!
2483

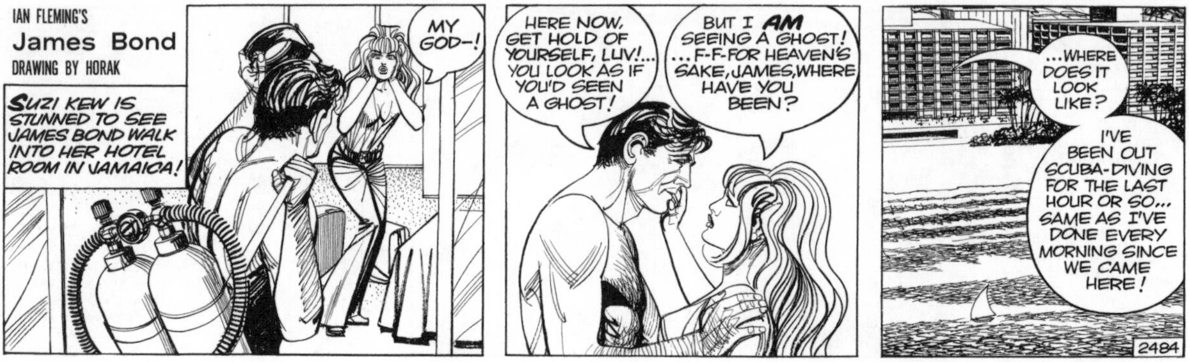
IAN FLEMING'S
James Bond
DRAWING BY HORAK
SUZI KEW IS STUNNED TO SEE JAMES BOND WALK INTO HER HOTEL ROOM IN JAMAICA!
MY GOD—!
HERE NOW, GET HOLD OF YOURSELF, LUV!... YOU LOOK AS IF YOU'D SEEN A GHOST!
BUT I AM SEEING A GHOST! ...F-F-FOR HEAVEN'S SAKE, JAMES, WHERE HAVE YOU BEEN?
...WHERE DOES IT LOOK LIKE?
I'VE BEEN OUT SCUBA-DIVING FOR THE LAST HOUR OR SO... SAME AS I'VE DONE EVERY MORNING SINCE WE CAME HERE!
2484

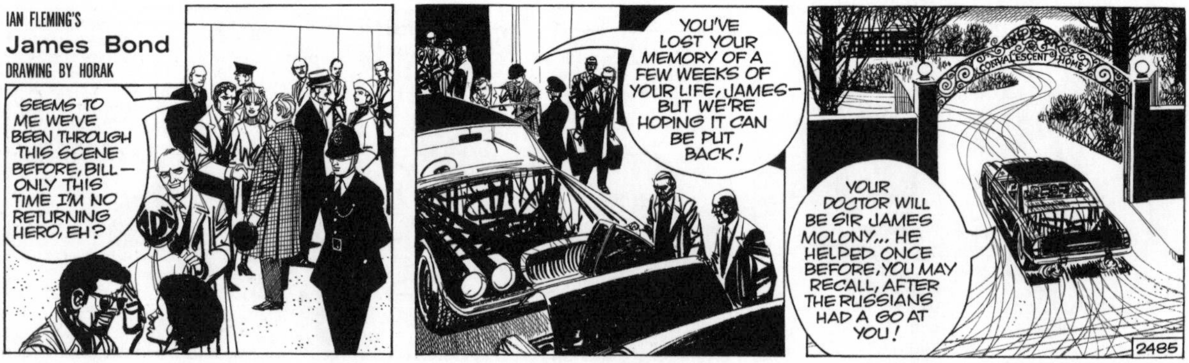
IAN FLEMING'S
James Bond
DRAWING BY HORAK
SEEMS TO ME WE'VE BEEN THROUGH THIS SCENE BEFORE, BILL— ONLY THIS TIME I'M NO RETURNING HERO, EH?
YOU'VE LOST YOUR MEMORY OF A FEW WEEKS OF YOUR LIFE, JAMES— BUT WE'RE HOPING IT CAN BE PUT BACK!
CONVALESCENT HOME
YOUR DOCTOR WILL BE SIR JAMES MOLONY... HE HELPED ONCE BEFORE, YOU MAY RECALL, AFTER THE RUSSIANS HAD A GO AT YOU!
2485

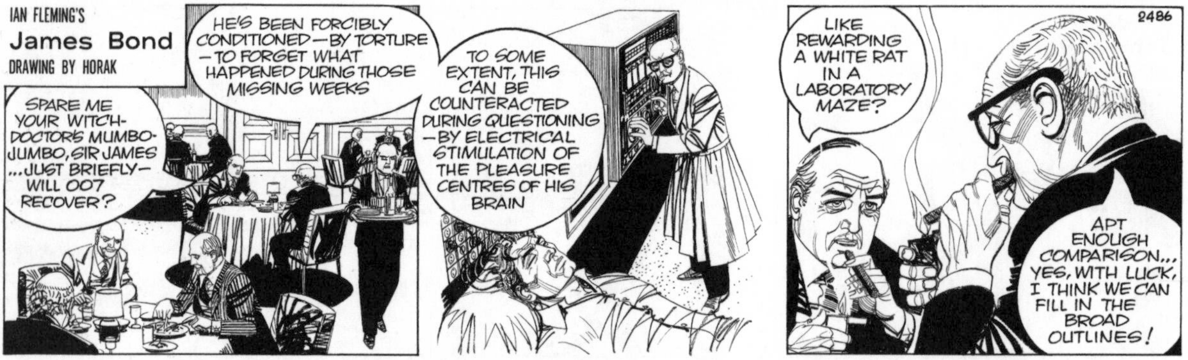
IAN FLEMING'S
James Bond
DRAWING BY HORAK
SPARE ME YOUR WITCH-DOCTOR'S MUMBO-JUMBO, SIR JAMES ...JUST BRIEFLY— WILL 007 RECOVER?
HE'S BEEN FORCIBLY CONDITIONED—BY TORTURE —TO FORGET WHAT HAPPENED DURING THOSE MISSING WEEKS
TO SOME EXTENT, THIS CAN BE COUNTERACTED DURING QUESTIONING —BY ELECTRICAL STIMULATION OF THE PLEASURE CENTRES OF HIS BRAIN
2486
LIKE REWARDING A WHITE RAT IN A LABORATORY MAZE?
APT ENOUGH COMPARISON... YES, WITH LUCK, I THINK WE CAN FILL IN THE BROAD OUTLINES!

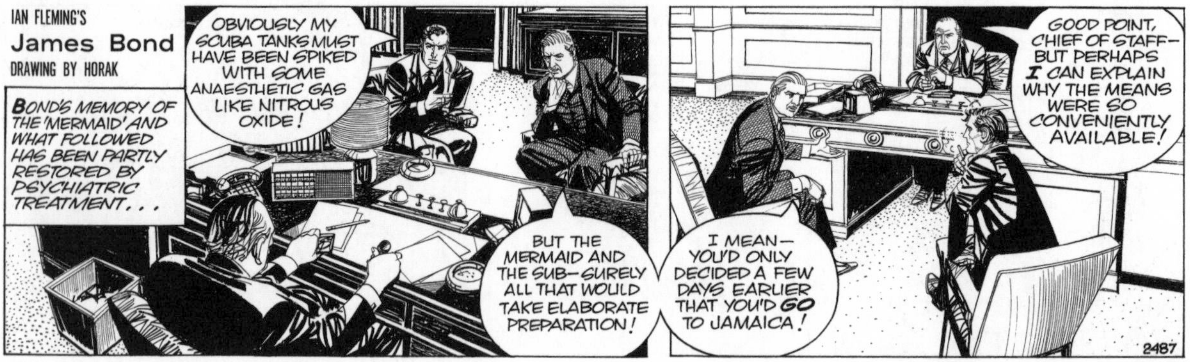
IAN FLEMING'S
James Bond
DRAWING BY HORAK
BOND'S MEMORY OF THE 'MERMAID' AND WHAT FOLLOWED HAS BEEN PARTLY RESTORED BY PSYCHIATRIC TREATMENT...
OBVIOUSLY MY SCUBA TANKS MUST HAVE BEEN SPIKED WITH SOME ANAESTHETIC GAS LIKE NITROUS OXIDE!
BUT THE MERMAID AND THE SUB—SURELY ALL THAT WOULD TAKE ELABORATE PREPARATION!
I MEAN— YOU'D ONLY DECIDED A FEW DAYS EARLIER THAT YOU'D GO TO JAMAICA!
GOOD POINT, CHIEF OF STAFF— BUT PERHAPS I CAN EXPLAIN WHY THE MEANS WERE SO CONVENIENTLY AVAILABLE!
2487

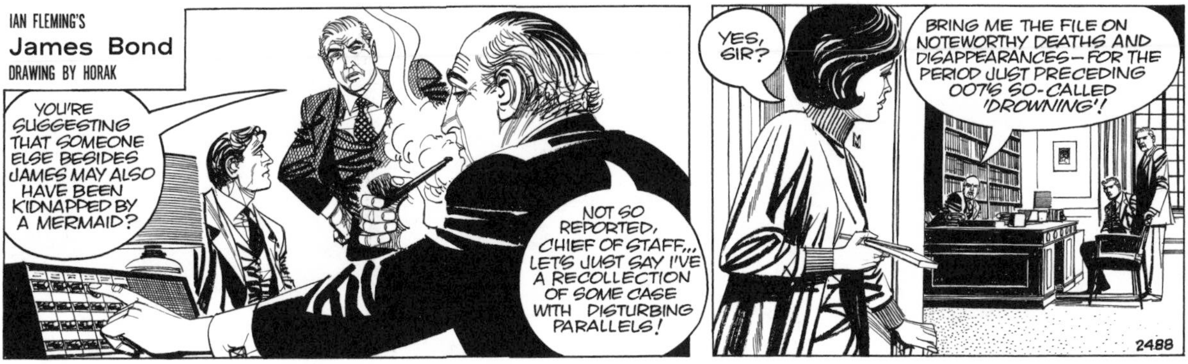
IAN FLEMING'S
James Bond
DRAWING BY HORAK
YOU'RE SUGGESTING THAT SOMEONE ELSE BESIDES JAMES MAY ALSO HAVE BEEN KIDNAPPED BY A MERMAID?
NOT SO REPORTED, CHIEF OF STAFF... LET'S JUST SAY I'VE A RECOLLECTION OF SOME CASE WITH DISTURBING PARALLELS!
YES, SIR?
BRING ME THE FILE ON NOTEWORTHY DEATHS AND DISAPPEARANCES—FOR THE PERIOD JUST PRECEDING 007'S SO-CALLED 'DROWNING'!
2488

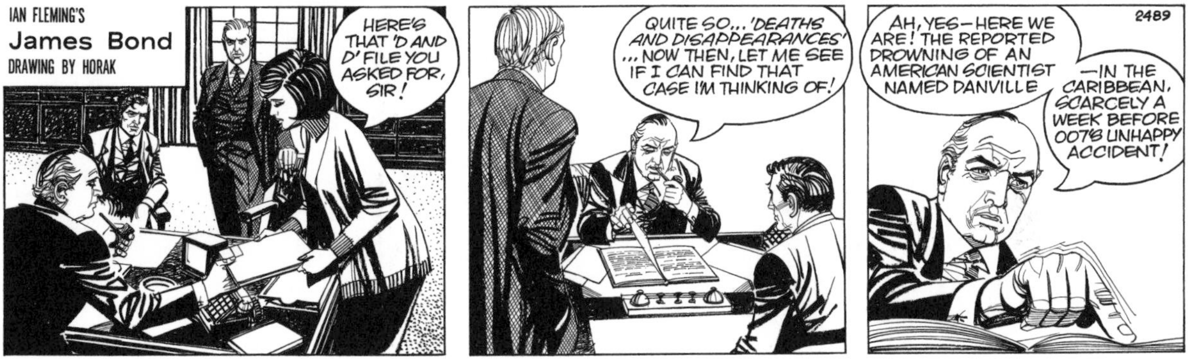
IAN FLEMING'S
James Bond
DRAWING BY HORAK
HERE'S THAT 'D AND D' FILE YOU ASKED FOR, SIR!
QUITE SO... 'DEATHS AND DISAPPEARANCES' ... NOW THEN, LET ME SEE IF I CAN FIND THAT CASE I'M THINKING OF!
2489
AH, YES—HERE WE ARE! THE REPORTED DROWNING OF AN AMERICAN SCIENTIST NAMED DANVILLE
—IN THE CARIBBEAN, SCARCELY A WEEK BEFORE 007'S UNHAPPY ACCIDENT!

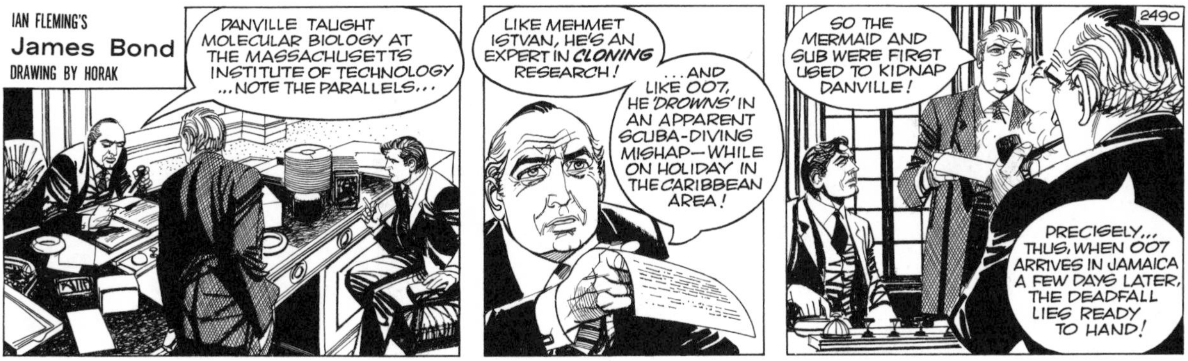
IAN FLEMING'S
James Bond
DRAWING BY HORAK
DANVILLE TAUGHT MOLECULAR BIOLOGY AT THE MASSACHUSETTS INSTITUTE OF TECHNOLOGY ...NOTE THE PARALLELS...
LIKE MEHMET ISTVAN, HE'S AN EXPERT IN CLONING RESEARCH!
...AND LIKE 007, HE 'DROWNS' IN AN APPARENT SCUBA-DIVING MISHAP—WHILE ON HOLIDAY IN THE CARIBBEAN AREA!
2490
SO THE MERMAID AND SUB WERE FIRST USED TO KIDNAP DANVILLE!
PRECISELY... THUS, WHEN 007 ARRIVES IN JAMAICA A FEW DAYS LATER, THE DEADFALL LIES READY TO HAND!

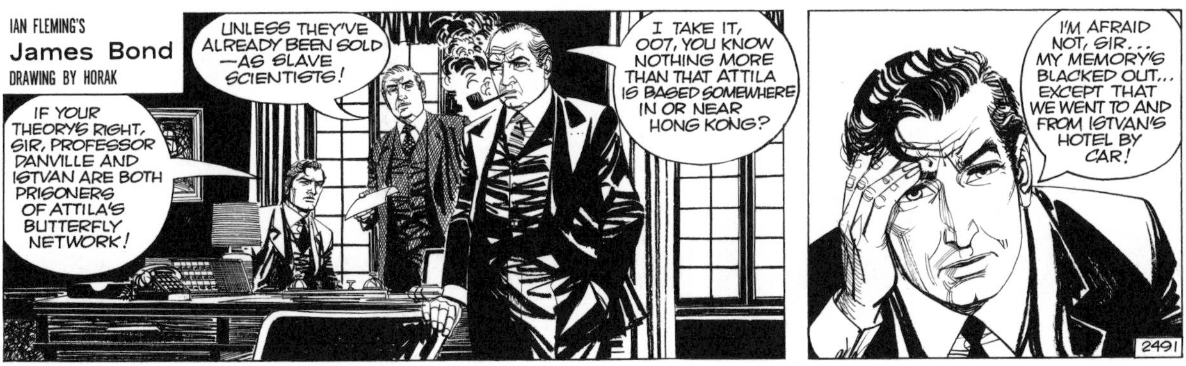
IAN FLEMING'S
James Bond
DRAWING BY HORAK
IF YOUR THEORY'S RIGHT, SIR, PROFESSOR DANVILLE AND ISTVAN ARE BOTH PRISONERS OF ATTILA'S BUTTERFLY NETWORK!
UNLESS THEY'VE ALREADY BEEN SOLD —AS SLAVE SCIENTISTS!
I TAKE IT, 007, YOU KNOW NOTHING MORE THAN THAT ATTILA IS BASED SOMEWHERE IN OR NEAR HONG KONG?
I'M AFRAID NOT, SIR... MY MEMORY'S BLACKED OUT... EXCEPT THAT WE WENT TO AND FROM ISTVAN'S HOTEL BY CAR!
2491

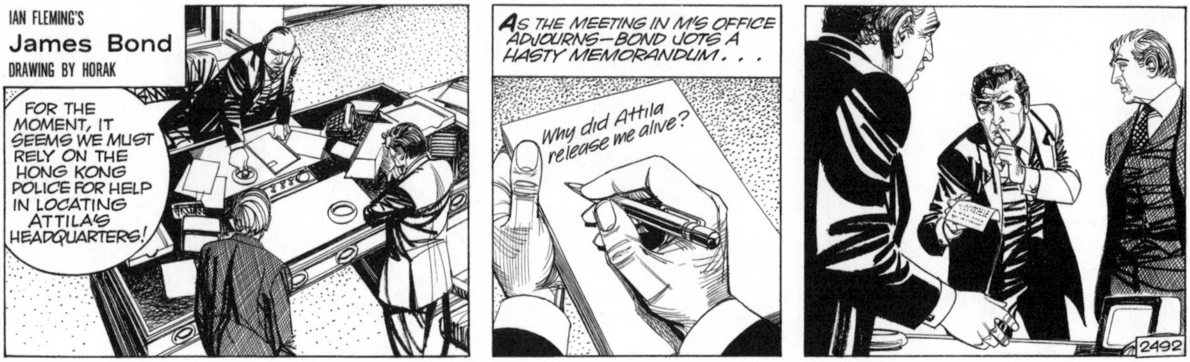
IAN FLEMING'S
James Bond
DRAWING BY HORAK
FOR THE MOMENT, IT SEEMS WE MUST RELY ON THE HONG KONG POLICE FOR HELP IN LOCATING ATTILA'S HEADQUARTERS!
AS THE MEETING IN M'S OFFICE ADJOURNS—BOND JOTS A HASTY MEMORANDUM . . .
Why did Attila release me alive?
2492

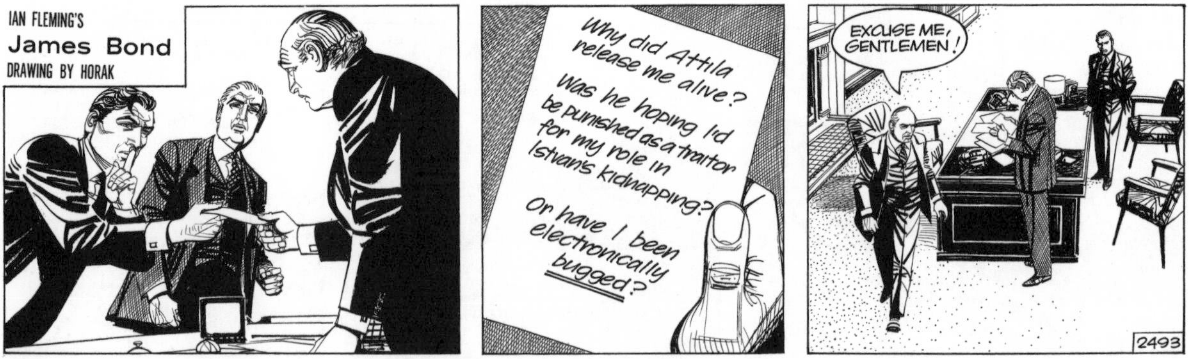
IAN FLEMING'S
James Bond
DRAWING BY HORAK
Why did Attila release me alive?
Was he hoping I'd be punished as a traitor for my role in Istvan's kidnapping?
Or have I been electronically bugged?
EXCUSE ME, GENTLEMEN!
2493

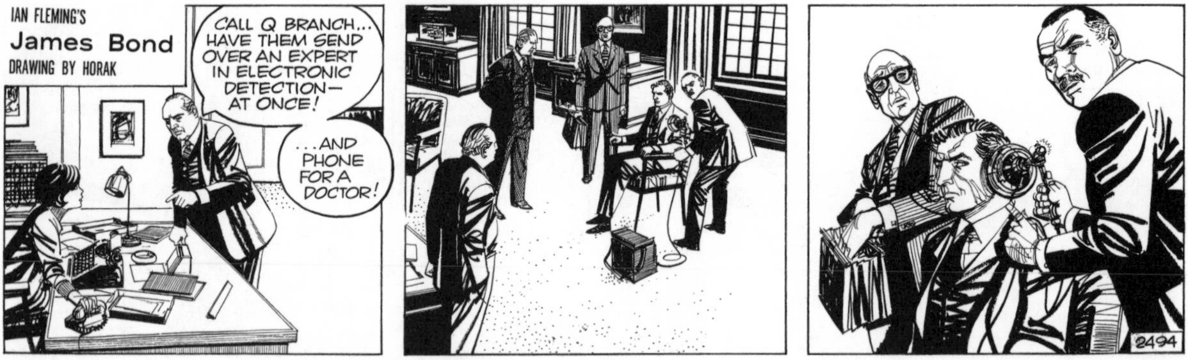
IAN FLEMING'S
James Bond
DRAWING BY HORAK
CALL Q BRANCH... HAVE THEM SEND OVER AN EXPERT IN ELECTRONIC DETECTION—AT ONCE!
...AND PHONE FOR A DOCTOR!
2494

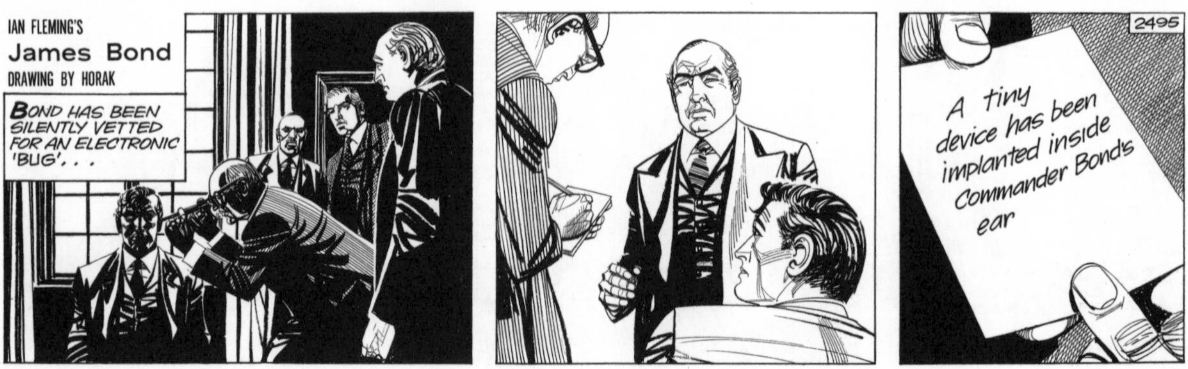
IAN FLEMING'S
James Bond
DRAWING BY HORAK
BOND HAS BEEN SILENTLY VETTED FOR AN ELECTRONIC 'BUG'. . .
2495
A tiny device has been implanted inside Commander Bond's ear

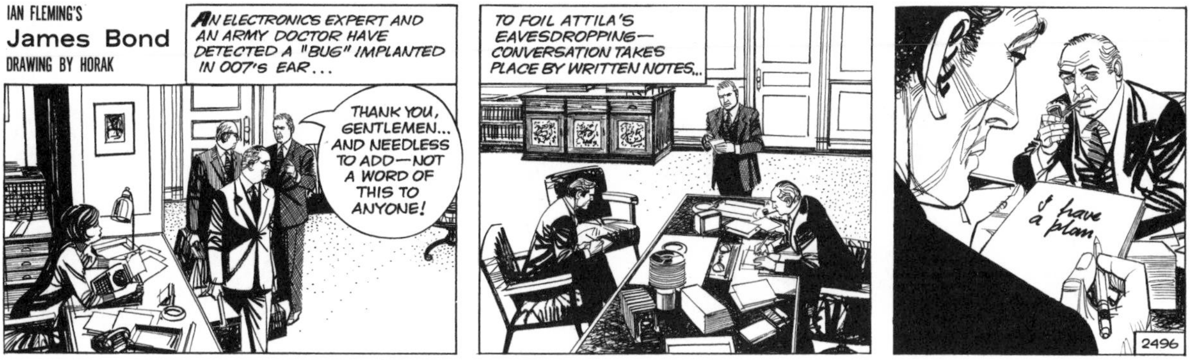
IAN FLEMING'S
James Bond
DRAWING BY HORAK
AN ELECTRONICS EXPERT AND AN ARMY DOCTOR HAVE DETECTED A "BUG" IMPLANTED IN 007'S EAR...
THANK YOU, GENTLEMEN... AND NEEDLESS TO ADD—NOT A WORD OF THIS TO ANYONE!
TO FOIL ATTILA'S EAVESDROPPING—CONVERSATION TAKES PLACE BY WRITTEN NOTES...
I have a plan
2496

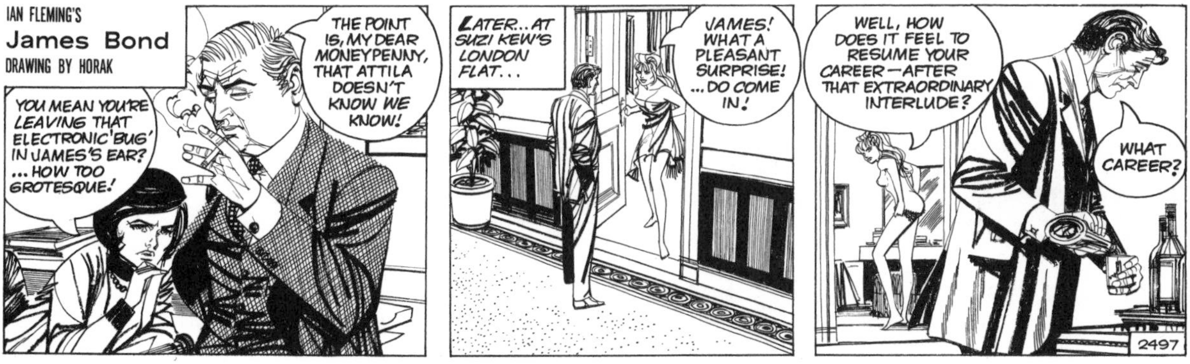
IAN FLEMING'S
James Bond
DRAWING BY HORAK
YOU MEAN YOU'RE LEAVING THAT ELECTRONIC 'BUG' IN JAMES'S EAR? ...HOW TOO GROTESQUE!
THE POINT IS, MY DEAR MONEYPENNY, THAT ATTILA DOESN'T KNOW WE KNOW!
LATER... AT SUZI KEW'S LONDON FLAT...
JAMES! WHAT A PLEASANT SURPRISE! ...DO COME IN!
WELL, HOW DOES IT FEEL TO RESUME YOUR CAREER—AFTER THAT EXTRAORDINARY INTERLUDE?
WHAT CAREER?
2497

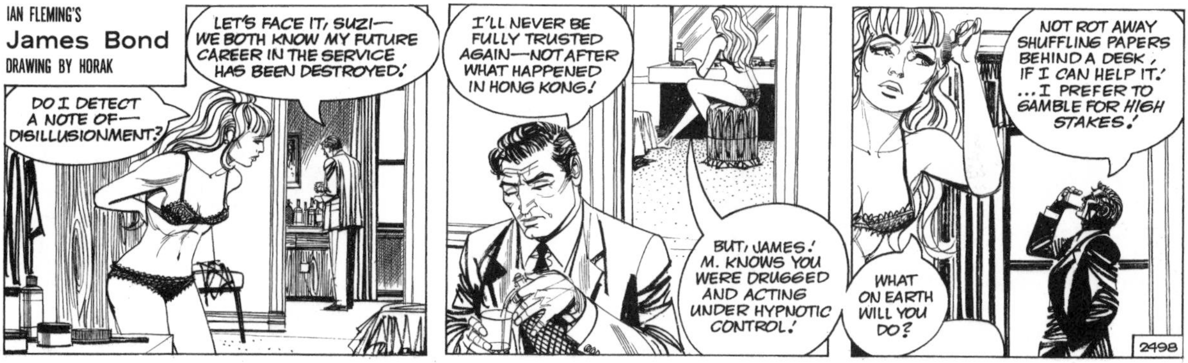
IAN FLEMING'S
James Bond
DRAWING BY HORAK
DO I DETECT A NOTE OF—DISILLUSIONMENT?
LET'S FACE IT, SUZI—WE BOTH KNOW MY FUTURE CAREER IN THE SERVICE HAS BEEN DESTROYED!
I'LL NEVER BE FULLY TRUSTED AGAIN—NOT AFTER WHAT HAPPENED IN HONG KONG!
BUT, JAMES! M. KNOWS YOU WERE DRUGGED AND ACTING UNDER HYPNOTIC CONTROL!
WHAT ON EARTH WILL YOU DO?
NOT ROT AWAY SHUFFLING PAPERS BEHIND A DESK, IF I CAN HELP IT! ...I PREFER TO GAMBLE FOR HIGH STAKES!
2498

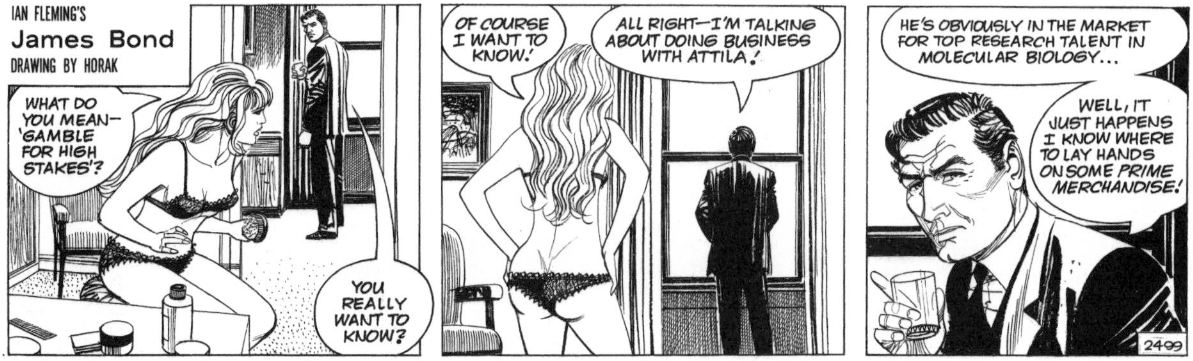
IAN FLEMING'S
James Bond
DRAWING BY HORAK
WHAT DO YOU MEAN—'GAMBLE FOR HIGH STAKES'?
YOU REALLY WANT TO KNOW?
OF COURSE I WANT TO KNOW!
ALL RIGHT—I'M TALKING ABOUT DOING BUSINESS WITH ATTILA!
HE'S OBVIOUSLY IN THE MARKET FOR TOP RESEARCH TALENT IN MOLECULAR BIOLOGY...
WELL, IT JUST HAPPENS I KNOW WHERE TO LAY HANDS ON SOME PRIME MERCHANDISE!
2499

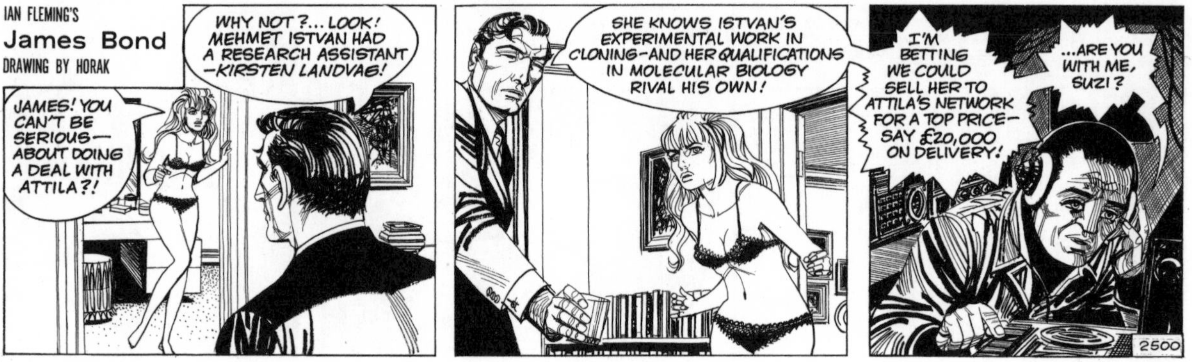
IAN FLEMING'S
James Bond
DRAWING BY HORAK
JAMES! YOU CAN'T BE SERIOUS— ABOUT DOING A DEAL WITH ATTILA?!
WHY NOT?... LOOK! MEHMET ISTVAN HAD A RESEARCH ASSISTANT —KIRSTEN LANDVAG!
SHE KNOWS ISTVAN'S EXPERIMENTAL WORK IN CLONING—AND HER QUALIFICATIONS IN MOLECULAR BIOLOGY RIVAL HIS OWN!
I'M BETTING WE COULD SELL HER TO ATTILA'S NETWORK FOR A TOP PRICE— SAY £20,000 ON DELIVERY!
...ARE YOU WITH ME, SUZI?
2500

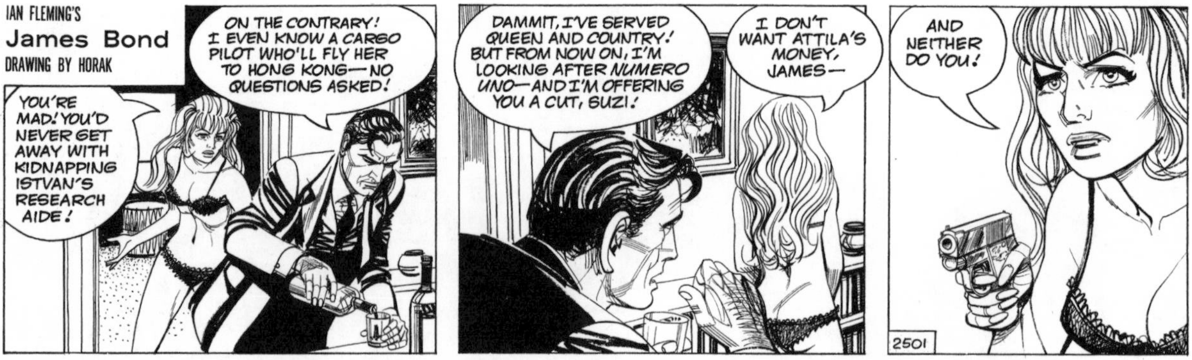
IAN FLEMING'S
James Bond
DRAWING BY HORAK
YOU'RE MAD! YOU'D NEVER GET AWAY WITH KIDNAPPING ISTVAN'S RESEARCH AIDE!
ON THE CONTRARY! I EVEN KNOW A CARGO PILOT WHO'LL FLY HER TO HONG KONG—NO QUESTIONS ASKED!
DAMMIT, I'VE SERVED QUEEN AND COUNTRY! BUT FROM NOW ON, I'M LOOKING AFTER NUMERO UNO—AND I'M OFFERING YOU A CUT, SUZI!
I DON'T WANT ATTILA'S MONEY, JAMES—
2501
AND NEITHER DO YOU!

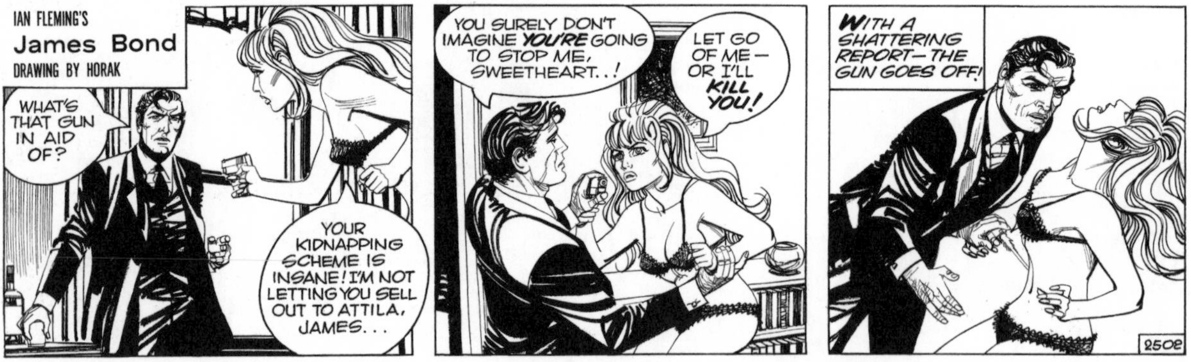
IAN FLEMING'S
James Bond
DRAWING BY HORAK
WHAT'S THAT GUN IN AID OF?
YOUR KIDNAPPING SCHEME IS INSANE! I'M NOT LETTING YOU SELL OUT TO ATTILA, JAMES...
YOU SURELY DON'T IMAGINE YOU'RE GOING TO STOP ME, SWEETHEART..!
LET GO OF ME— OR I'LL KILL YOU!
WITH A SHATTERING REPORT—THE GUN GOES OFF!
2502

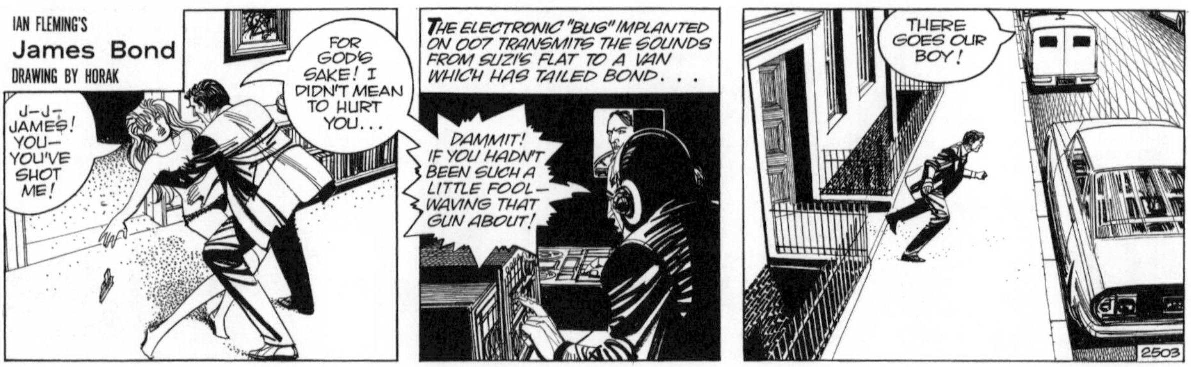
IAN FLEMING'S
James Bond
DRAWING BY HORAK
J-J-JAMES! YOU— YOU'VE SHOT ME!
FOR GOD'S SAKE! I DIDN'T MEAN TO HURT YOU...
THE ELECTRONIC "BUG" IMPLANTED ON 007 TRANSMITS THE SOUNDS FROM SUZI'S FLAT TO A VAN WHICH HAS TAILED BOND...
DAMMIT! IF YOU HADN'T BEEN SUCH A LITTLE FOOL— WAVING THAT GUN ABOUT!
THERE GOES OUR BOY!
2503

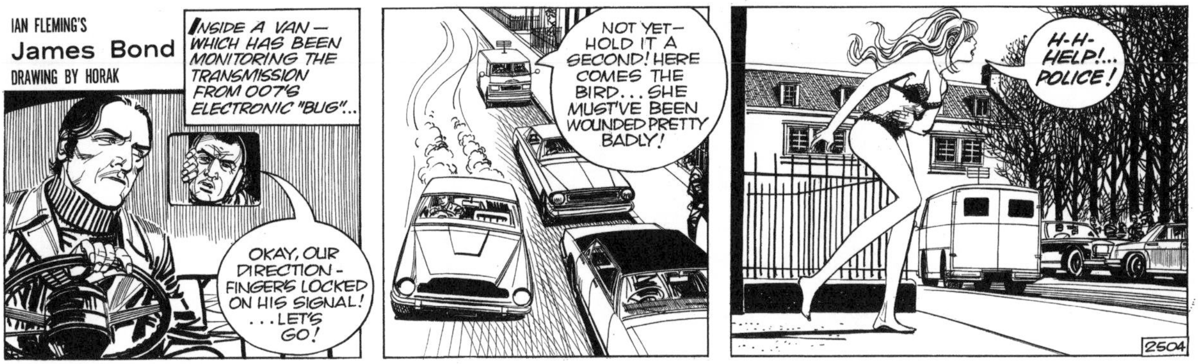
IAN FLEMING'S
James Bond
DRAWING BY HORAK
INSIDE A VAN — WHICH HAS BEEN MONITORING THE TRANSMISSION FROM 007'S ELECTRONIC "BUG"...
OKAY, OUR DIRECTION-FINGER'S LOCKED ON HIS SIGNAL! . . . LET'S GO!
NOT YET— HOLD IT A SECOND! HERE COMES THE BIRD... SHE MUST'VE BEEN WOUNDED PRETTY BADLY!
H-H-HELP!... POLICE!
2504

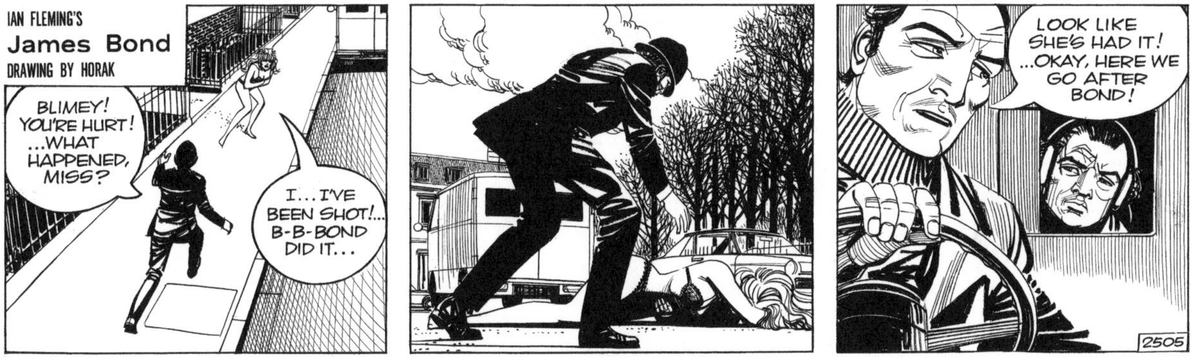
IAN FLEMING'S
James Bond
DRAWING BY HORAK
BLIMEY! YOU'RE HURT! ...WHAT HAPPENED, MISS?
I... I'VE BEEN SHOT!... B-B-BOND DID IT...
LOOK LIKE SHE'S HAD IT! ...OKAY, HERE WE GO AFTER BOND!
2505

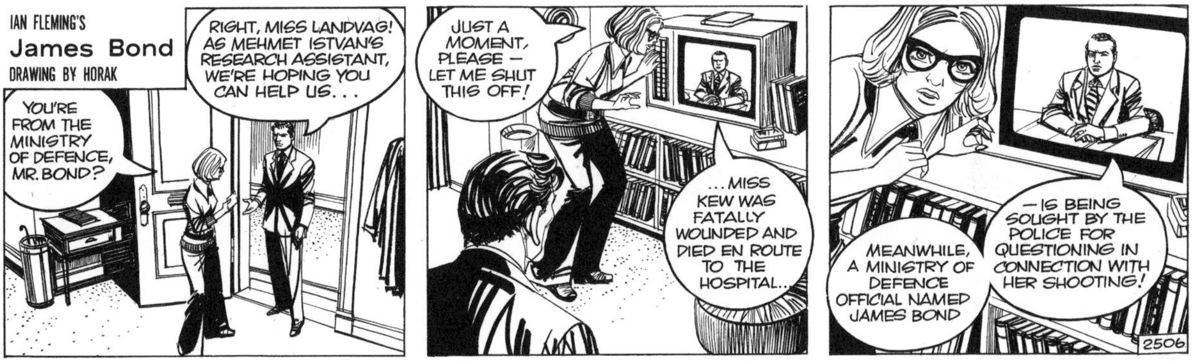
IAN FLEMING'S
James Bond
DRAWING BY HORAK
YOU'RE FROM THE MINISTRY OF DEFENCE, MR. BOND?
RIGHT, MISS LANDVAG! AS MEHMET ISTVAN'S RESEARCH ASSISTANT, WE'RE HOPING YOU CAN HELP US...
JUST A MOMENT, PLEASE — LET ME SHUT THIS OFF!
...MISS KEW WAS FATALLY WOUNDED AND DIED EN ROUTE TO THE HOSPITAL...
MEANWHILE, A MINISTRY OF DEFENCE OFFICIAL NAMED JAMES BOND
—IS BEING SOUGHT BY THE POLICE FOR QUESTIONING IN CONNECTION WITH HER SHOOTING!
2506

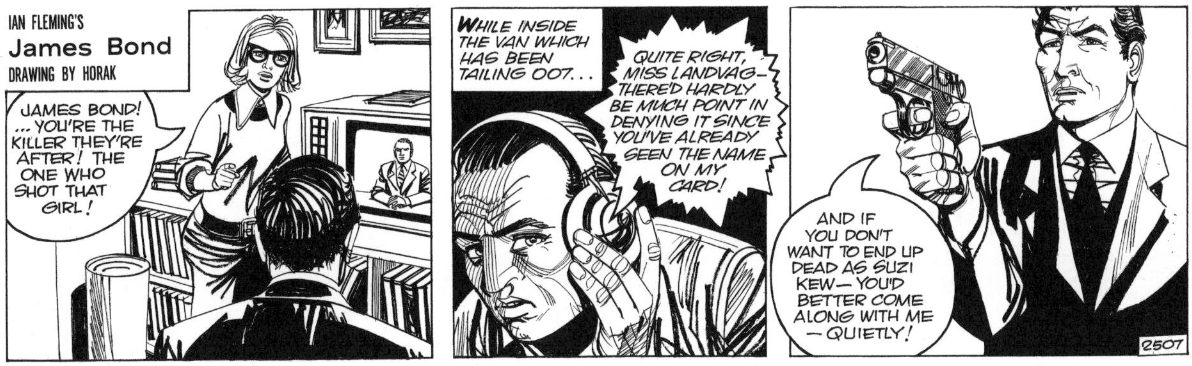
IAN FLEMING'S
James Bond
DRAWING BY HORAK
JAMES BOND! ...YOU'RE THE KILLER THEY'RE AFTER! THE ONE WHO SHOT THAT GIRL!
WHILE INSIDE THE VAN WHICH HAS BEEN TAILING 007...
QUITE RIGHT, MISS LANDVAG— THERE'D HARDLY BE MUCH POINT IN DENYING IT SINCE YOU'VE ALREADY SEEN THE NAME ON MY CARD!
AND IF YOU DON'T WANT TO END UP DEAD AS SUZI KEW— YOU'D BETTER COME ALONG WITH ME — QUIETLY!
2507

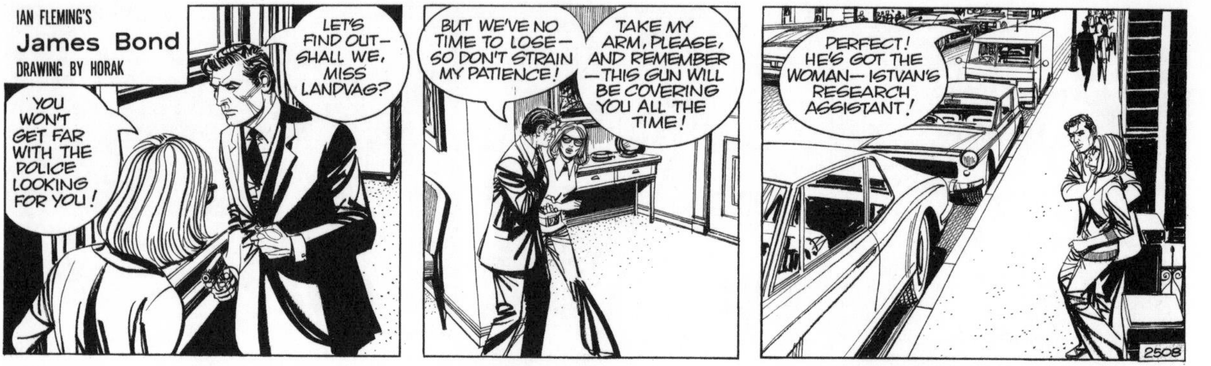
IAN FLEMING'S
James Bond
DRAWING BY HORAK
LET'S FIND OUT— SHALL WE, MISS LANDVAG?
YOU WON'T GET FAR WITH THE POLICE LOOKING FOR YOU!
BUT WE'VE NO TIME TO LOSE— SO DON'T STRAIN MY PATIENCE!
TAKE MY ARM, PLEASE, AND REMEMBER —THIS GUN WILL BE COVERING YOU ALL THE TIME!
PERFECT! HE'S GOT THE WOMAN— ISTVAN'S RESEARCH ASSISTANT!
2508

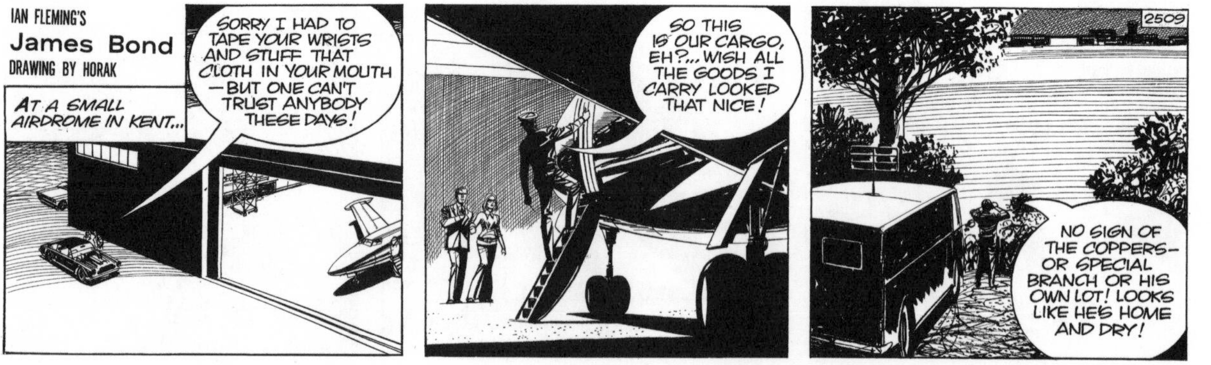
IAN FLEMING'S
James Bond
DRAWING BY HORAK
AT A SMALL AIRDROME IN KENT...
SORRY I HAD TO TAPE YOUR WRISTS AND STUFF THAT CLOTH IN YOUR MOUTH —BUT ONE CAN'T TRUST ANYBODY THESE DAYS!
SO THIS IS OUR CARGO, EH?... WISH ALL THE GOODS I CARRY LOOKED THAT NICE!
2509
NO SIGN OF THE COPPERS— OR SPECIAL BRANCH OR HIS OWN LOT! LOOKS LIKE HE'S HOME AND DRY!

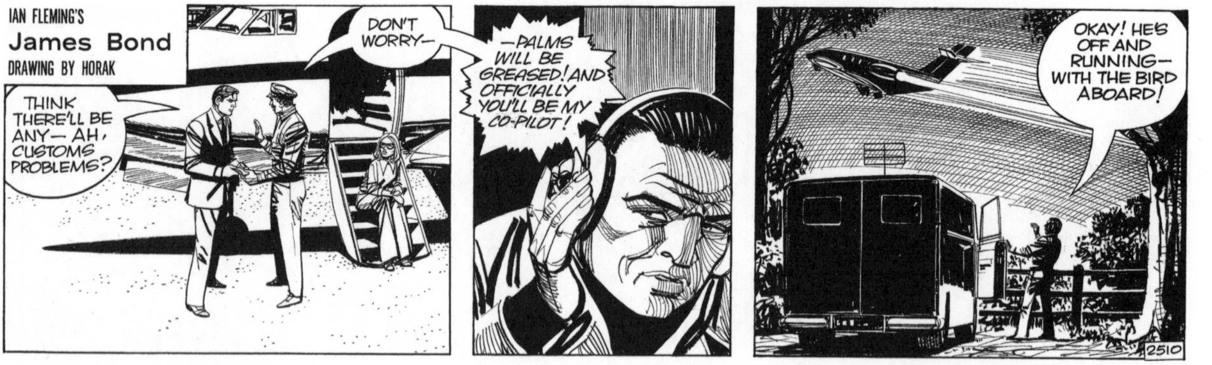
IAN FLEMING'S
James Bond
DRAWING BY HORAK
THINK THERE'LL BE ANY— AH, CUSTOMS PROBLEMS?
DON'T WORRY—
—PALMS WILL BE GREASED! AND OFFICIALLY YOU'LL BE MY CO-PILOT!
OKAY! HE'S OFF AND RUNNING— WITH THE BIRD ABOARD!
2510

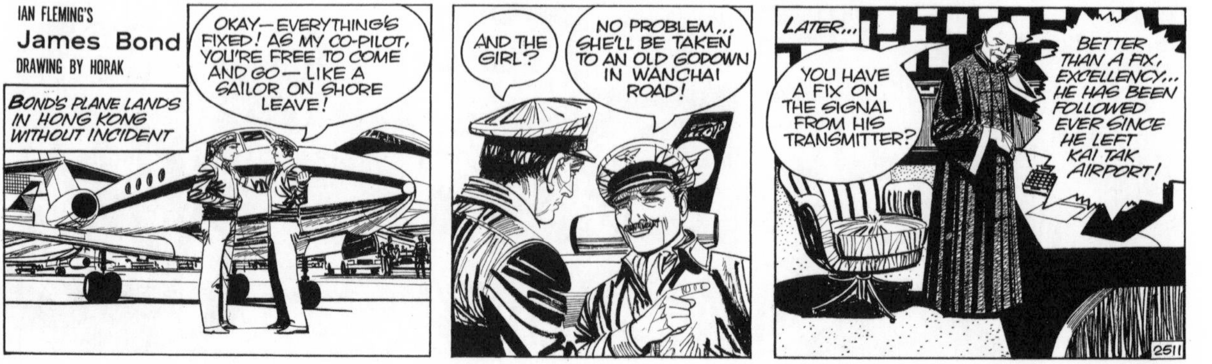
IAN FLEMING'S
James Bond
DRAWING BY HORAK
BOND'S PLANE LANDS IN HONG KONG WITHOUT INCIDENT
OKAY— EVERYTHING'S FIXED! AS MY CO-PILOT, YOU'RE FREE TO COME AND GO— LIKE A SAILOR ON SHORE LEAVE!
AND THE GIRL?
NO PROBLEM... SHE'LL BE TAKEN TO AN OLD GODOWN IN WANCHAI ROAD!
LATER...
YOU HAVE A FIX ON THE SIGNAL FROM HIS TRANSMITTER?
BETTER THAN A FIX, EXCELLENCY... HE HAS BEEN FOLLOWED EVER SINCE HE LEFT KAI TAK AIRPORT!
2511

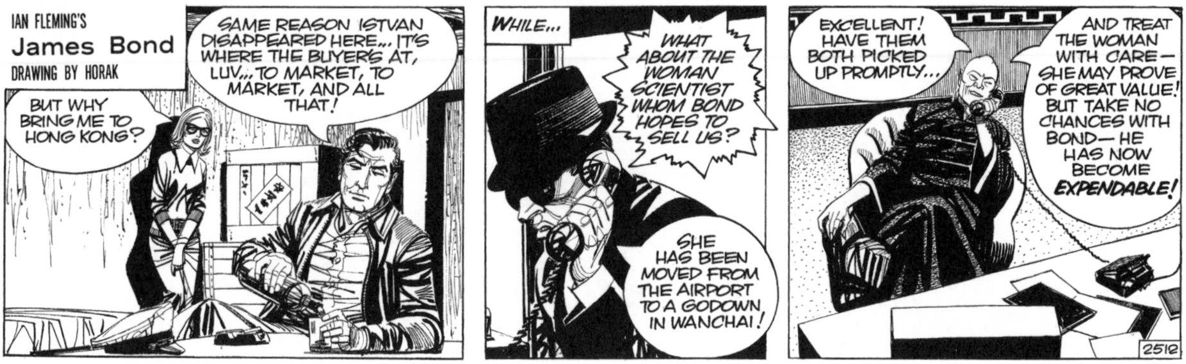
IAN FLEMING'S
James Bond
DRAWING BY HORAK
BUT WHY BRING ME TO HONG KONG?
SAME REASON ISTVAN DISAPPEARED HERE... IT'S WHERE THE BUYER'S AT, LUV... TO MARKET, TO MARKET, AND ALL THAT!
WHILE...
WHAT ABOUT THE WOMAN SCIENTIST WHOM BOND HOPES TO SELL US?
SHE HAS BEEN MOVED FROM THE AIRPORT TO A GODOWN IN WANCHAI!
EXCELLENT! HAVE THEM BOTH PICKED UP PROMPTLY...
AND TREAT THE WOMAN WITH CARE–SHE MAY PROVE OF GREAT VALUE! BUT TAKE NO CHANCES WITH BOND–HE HAS NOW BECOME *EXPENDABLE!*
2512

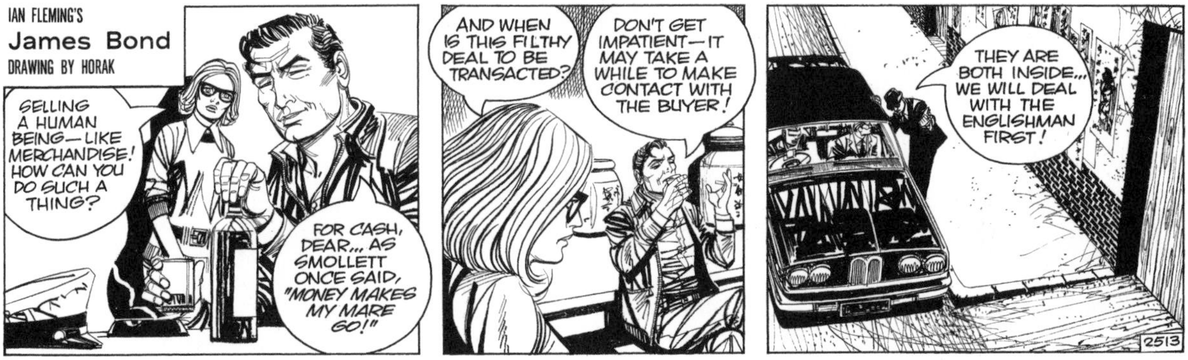
IAN FLEMING'S
James Bond
DRAWING BY HORAK
SELLING A HUMAN BEING–LIKE MERCHANDISE! HOW CAN YOU DO SUCH A THING?
FOR CASH, DEAR... AS SMOLLETT ONCE SAID, "MONEY MAKES MY MARE GO!"
AND WHEN IS THIS FILTHY DEAL TO BE TRANSACTED?
DON'T GET IMPATIENT–IT MAY TAKE A WHILE TO MAKE CONTACT WITH THE BUYER!
THEY ARE BOTH INSIDE... WE WILL DEAL WITH THE ENGLISHMAN FIRST!
2513

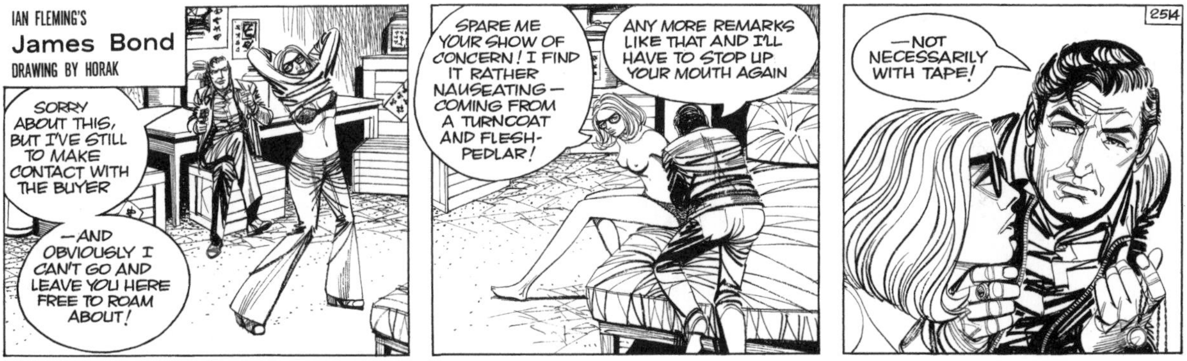
IAN FLEMING'S
James Bond
DRAWING BY HORAK
SORRY ABOUT THIS, BUT I'VE STILL TO MAKE CONTACT WITH THE BUYER
–AND OBVIOUSLY I CAN'T GO AND LEAVE YOU HERE FREE TO ROAM ABOUT!
SPARE ME YOUR SHOW OF CONCERN! I FIND IT RATHER NAUSEATING–COMING FROM A TURNCOAT AND FLESH-PEDLAR!
ANY MORE REMARKS LIKE THAT AND I'LL HAVE TO STOP UP YOUR MOUTH AGAIN
–NOT NECESSARILY WITH TAPE!
2514

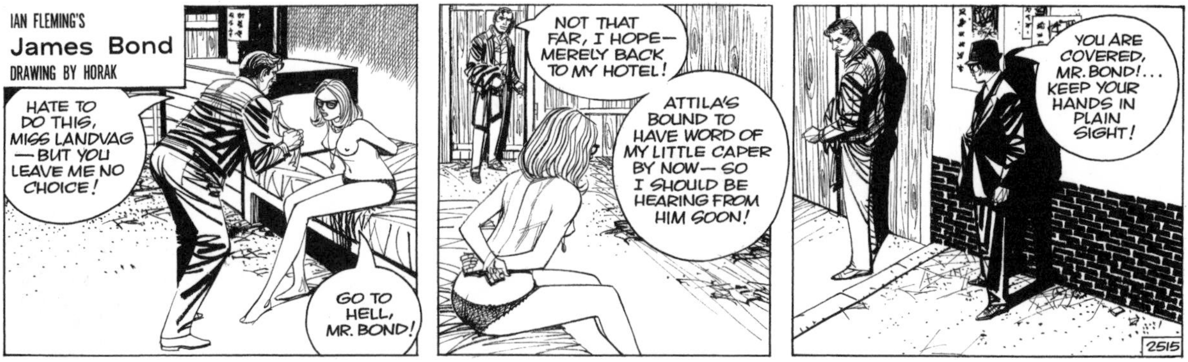
IAN FLEMING'S
James Bond
DRAWING BY HORAK
HATE TO DO THIS, MISS LANDVAG–BUT YOU LEAVE ME NO CHOICE!
GO TO HELL, MR. BOND!
NOT THAT FAR, I HOPE–MERELY BACK TO MY HOTEL!
ATTILA'S BOUND TO HAVE WORD OF MY LITTLE CAPER BY NOW–SO I SHOULD BE HEARING FROM HIM SOON!
YOU ARE COVERED, MR. BOND!... KEEP YOUR HANDS IN PLAIN SIGHT!
2515

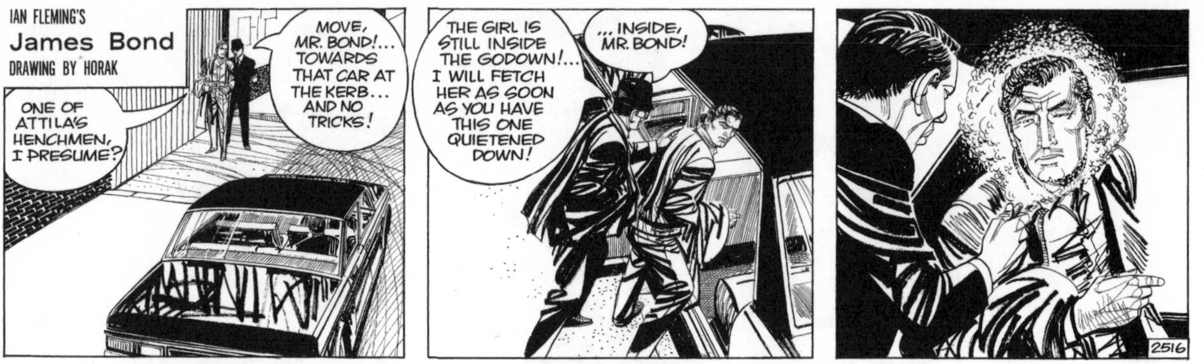
IAN FLEMING'S
James Bond
DRAWING BY HORAK
ONE OF ATTILA'S HENCHMEN, I PRESUME?
MOVE, MR. BOND!... TOWARDS THAT CAR AT THE KERB... AND NO TRICKS!
THE GIRL IS STILL INSIDE THE GODOWN!... I WILL FETCH HER AS SOON AS YOU HAVE THIS ONE QUIETENED DOWN!
... INSIDE, MR. BOND!
2516

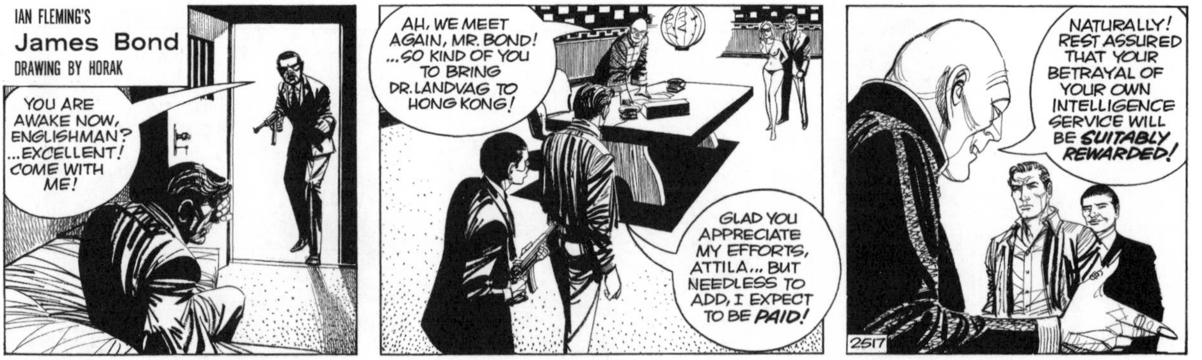
IAN FLEMING'S
James Bond
DRAWING BY HORAK
YOU ARE AWAKE NOW, ENGLISHMAN? ...EXCELLENT! COME WITH ME!
AH, WE MEET AGAIN, MR. BOND! ...SO KIND OF YOU TO BRING DR. LANDVAG TO HONG KONG!
GLAD YOU APPRECIATE MY EFFORTS, ATTILA... BUT NEEDLESS TO ADD, I EXPECT TO BE PAID!
2517
NATURALLY! REST ASSURED THAT YOUR BETRAYAL OF YOUR OWN INTELLIGENCE SERVICE WILL BE SUITABLY REWARDED!

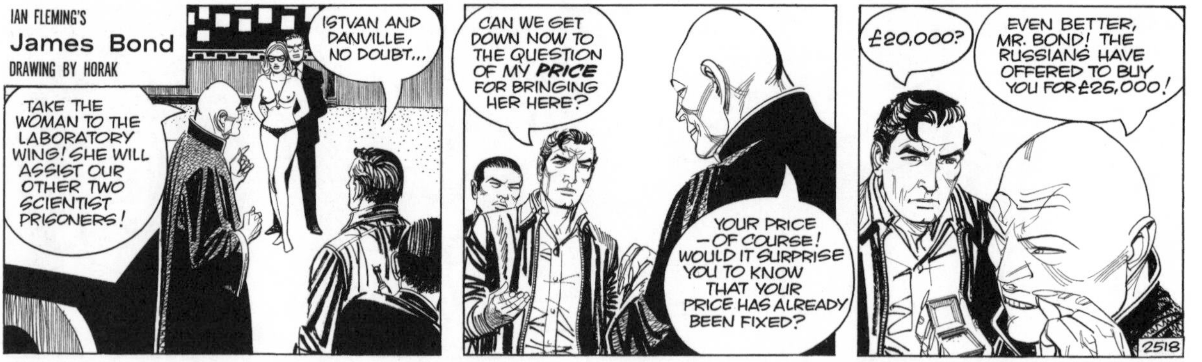
IAN FLEMING'S
James Bond
DRAWING BY HORAK
TAKE THE WOMAN TO THE LABORATORY WING! SHE WILL ASSIST OUR OTHER TWO SCIENTIST PRISONERS!
ISTVAN AND DANVILLE, NO DOUBT...
CAN WE GET DOWN NOW TO THE QUESTION OF MY PRICE FOR BRINGING HER HERE?
YOUR PRICE —OF COURSE! WOULD IT SURPRISE YOU TO KNOW THAT YOUR PRICE HAS ALREADY BEEN FIXED?
£20,000?
EVEN BETTER, MR. BOND! THE RUSSIANS HAVE OFFERED TO BUY YOU FOR £25,000!
2518

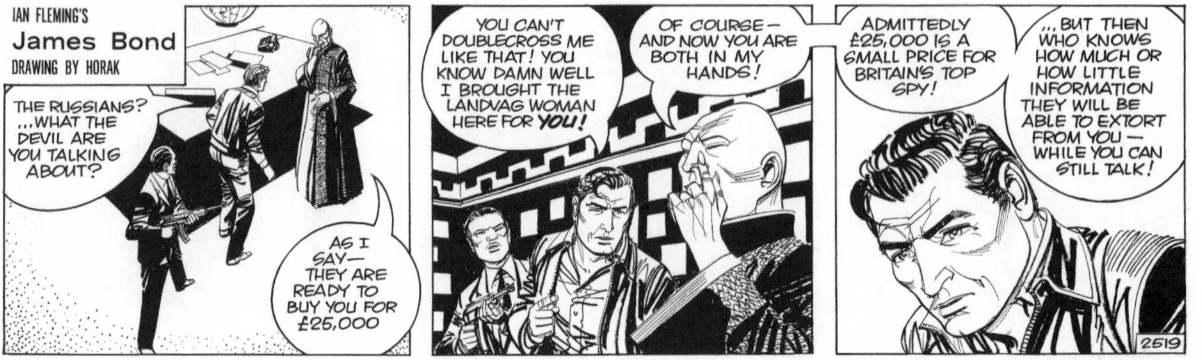
IAN FLEMING'S
James Bond
DRAWING BY HORAK
THE RUSSIANS? ...WHAT THE DEVIL ARE YOU TALKING ABOUT?
AS I SAY— THEY ARE READY TO BUY YOU FOR £25,000
YOU CAN'T DOUBLECROSS ME LIKE THAT! YOU KNOW DAMN WELL I BROUGHT THE LANDVAG WOMAN HERE FOR YOU!
OF COURSE — AND NOW YOU ARE BOTH IN MY HANDS!
ADMITTEDLY £25,000 IS A SMALL PRICE FOR BRITAIN'S TOP SPY!
... BUT THEN WHO KNOWS HOW MUCH OR HOW LITTLE INFORMATION THEY WILL BE ABLE TO EXTORT FROM YOU — WHILE YOU CAN STILL TALK!
2519

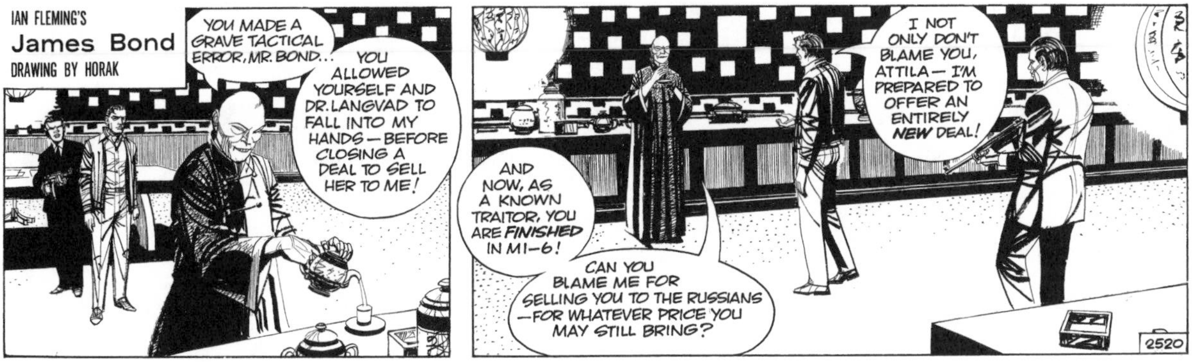
IAN FLEMING'S
James Bond
DRAWING BY HORAK
YOU MADE A GRAVE TACTICAL ERROR, MR. BOND...
YOU ALLOWED YOURSELF AND DR. LANGVAD TO FALL INTO MY HANDS — BEFORE CLOSING A DEAL TO SELL HER TO ME!
AND NOW, AS A KNOWN TRAITOR, YOU ARE FINISHED IN MI-6!
CAN YOU BLAME ME FOR SELLING YOU TO THE RUSSIANS — FOR WHATEVER PRICE YOU MAY STILL BRING?
I NOT ONLY DON'T BLAME YOU, ATTILA — I'M PREPARED TO OFFER AN ENTIRELY NEW DEAL!
2520

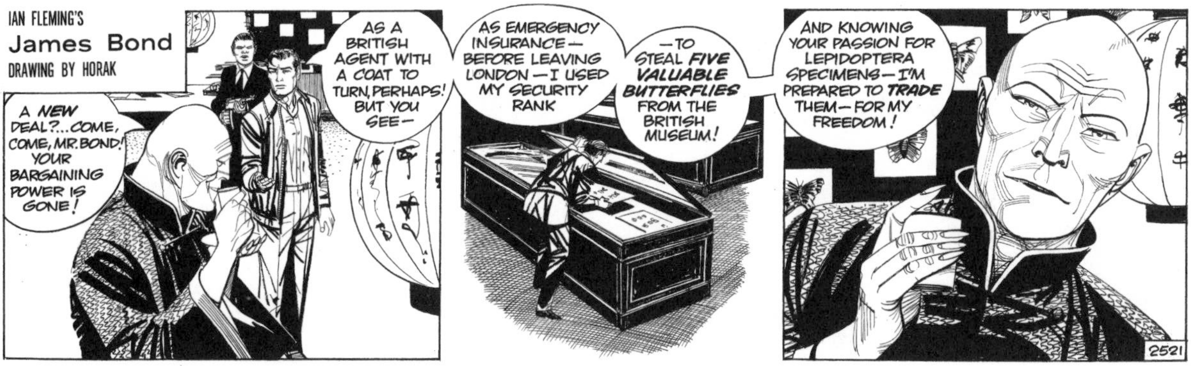
IAN FLEMING'S
James Bond
DRAWING BY HORAK
A NEW DEAL?...COME, COME, MR. BOND! YOUR BARGAINING POWER IS GONE!
AS A BRITISH AGENT WITH A COAT TO TURN, PERHAPS! BUT YOU SEE—
AS EMERGENCY INSURANCE — BEFORE LEAVING LONDON — I USED MY SECURITY RANK
—TO STEAL FIVE VALUABLE BUTTERFLIES FROM THE BRITISH MUSEUM!
AND KNOWING YOUR PASSION FOR LEPIDOPTERA SPECIMENS — I'M PREPARED TO TRADE THEM — FOR MY FREEDOM!
2521

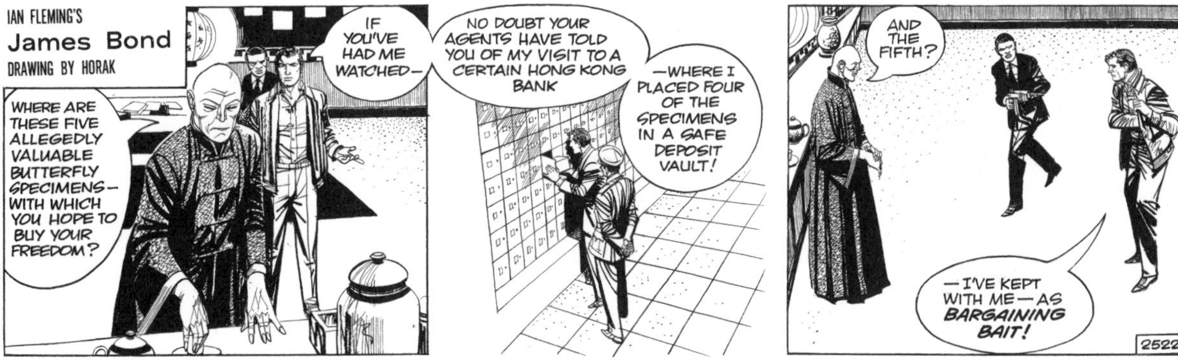
IAN FLEMING'S
James Bond
DRAWING BY HORAK
WHERE ARE THESE FIVE ALLEGEDLY VALUABLE BUTTERFLY SPECIMENS — WITH WHICH YOU HOPE TO BUY YOUR FREEDOM?
IF YOU'VE HAD ME WATCHED—
NO DOUBT YOUR AGENTS HAVE TOLD YOU OF MY VISIT TO A CERTAIN HONG KONG BANK
—WHERE I PLACED FOUR OF THE SPECIMENS IN A SAFE DEPOSIT VAULT!
AND THE FIFTH?
—I'VE KEPT WITH ME — AS BARGAINING BAIT!
2522

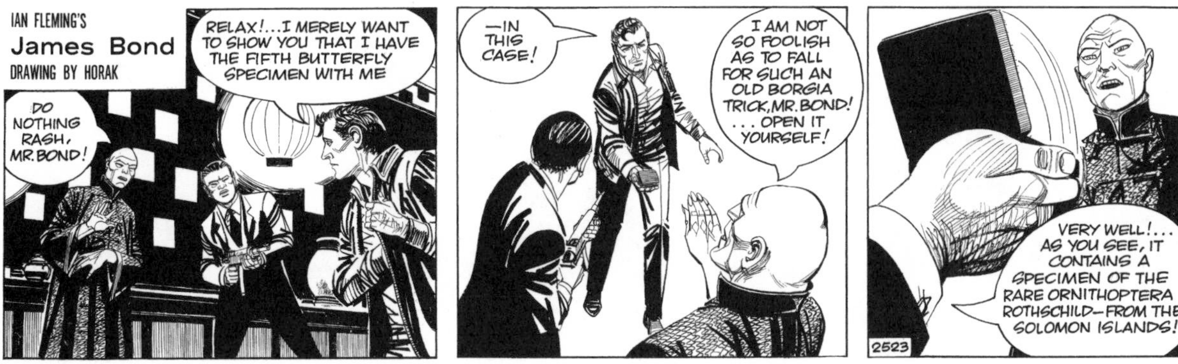
IAN FLEMING'S
James Bond
DRAWING BY HORAK
DO NOTHING RASH, MR. BOND!
RELAX!...I MERELY WANT TO SHOW YOU THAT I HAVE THE FIFTH BUTTERFLY SPECIMEN WITH ME
—IN THIS CASE!
I AM NOT SO FOOLISH AS TO FALL FOR SUCH AN OLD BORGIA TRICK, MR. BOND! ... OPEN IT YOURSELF!
VERY WELL!... AS YOU SEE, IT CONTAINS A SPECIMEN OF THE RARE ORNITHOPTERA ROTHSCHILD — FROM THE SOLOMON ISLANDS!
2523

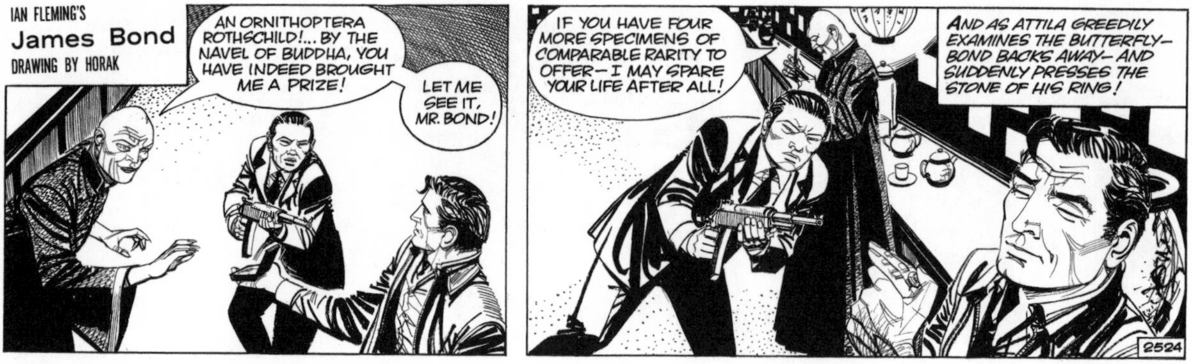
IAN FLEMING'S
James Bond
DRAWING BY HORAK
AN ORNITHOPTERA ROTHSCHILD!... BY THE NAVEL OF BUDDHA, YOU HAVE INDEED BROUGHT ME A PRIZE!
LET ME SEE IT, MR. BOND!
IF YOU HAVE FOUR MORE SPECIMENS OF COMPARABLE RARITY TO OFFER—I MAY SPARE YOUR LIFE AFTER ALL!
AND AS ATTILA GREEDILY EXAMINES THE BUTTERFLY—BOND BACKS AWAY—AND SUDDENLY PRESSES THE STONE OF HIS RING!
2524

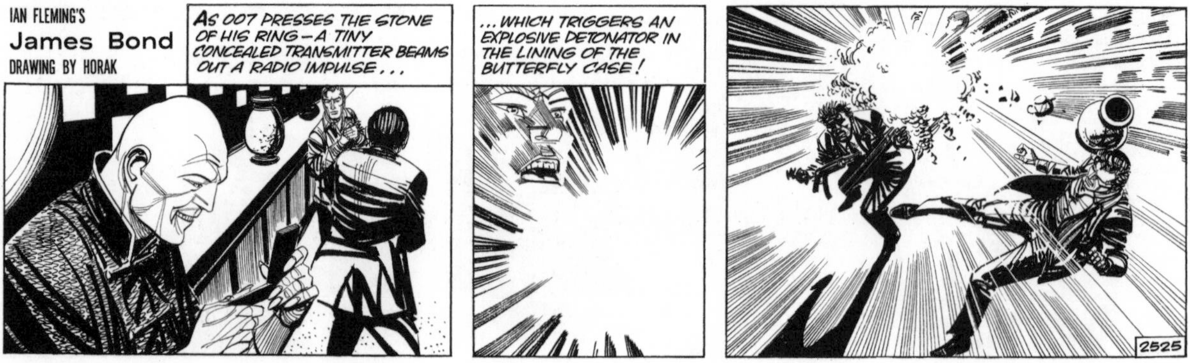
IAN FLEMING'S
James Bond
DRAWING BY HORAK
AS 007 PRESSES THE STONE OF HIS RING—A TINY CONCEALED TRANSMITTER BEAMS OUT A RADIO IMPULSE...
...WHICH TRIGGERS AN EXPLOSIVE DETONATOR IN THE LINING OF THE BUTTERFLY CASE!
2525

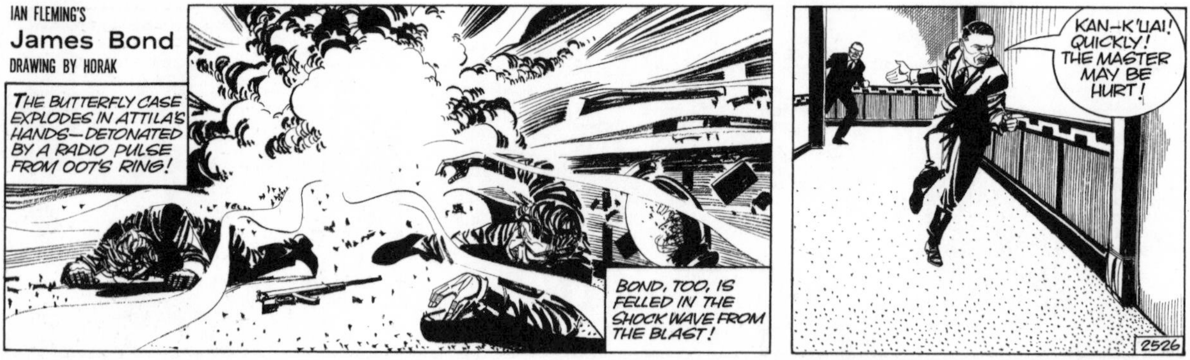
IAN FLEMING'S
James Bond
DRAWING BY HORAK
THE BUTTERFLY CASE EXPLODES IN ATTILA'S HANDS—DETONATED BY A RADIO PULSE FROM 007'S RING!
BOND, TOO, IS FELLED IN THE SHOCK WAVE FROM THE BLAST!
KAN-K'UAI! QUICKLY! THE MASTER MAY BE HURT!
2526

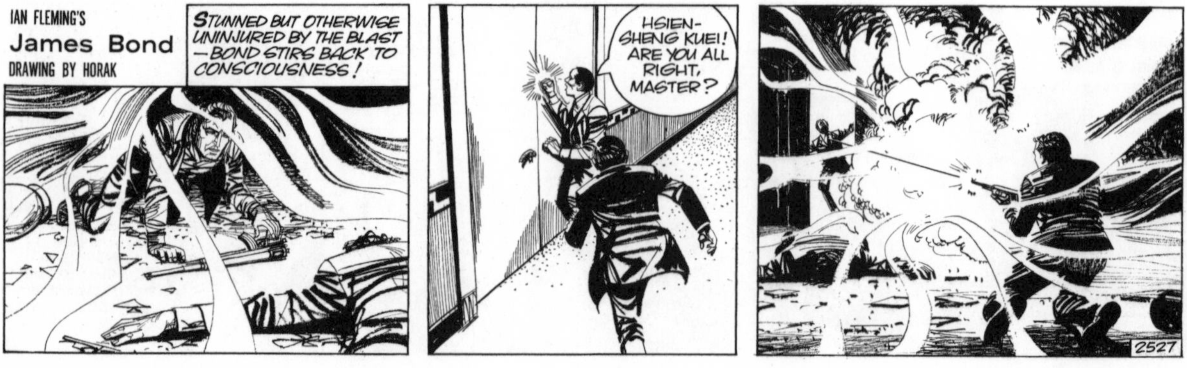
IAN FLEMING'S
James Bond
DRAWING BY HORAK
STUNNED BUT OTHERWISE UNINJURED BY THE BLAST—BOND STIRS BACK TO CONSCIOUSNESS!
HSIEN-SHENG KUEI! ARE YOU ALL RIGHT, MASTER?
2527

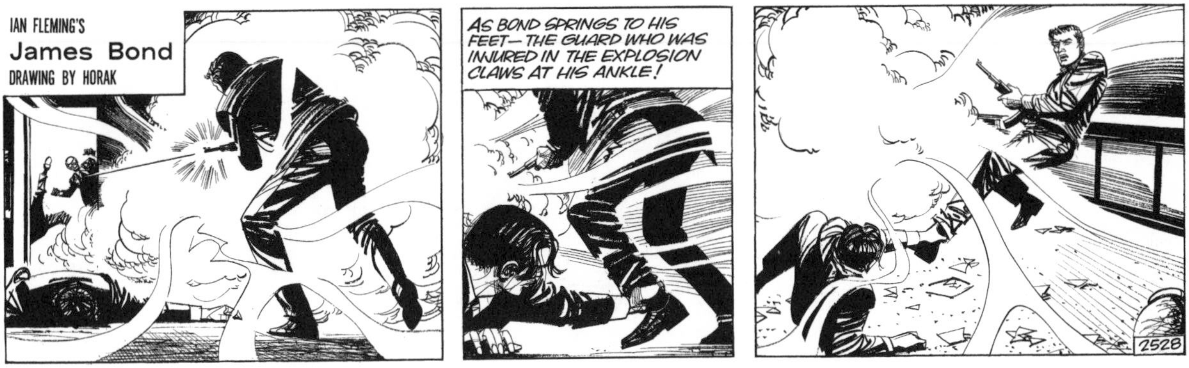
IAN FLEMING'S
James Bond
DRAWING BY HORAK
AS BOND SPRINGS TO HIS FEET— THE GUARD WHO WAS INJURED IN THE EXPLOSION CLAWS AT HIS ANKLE!
2528

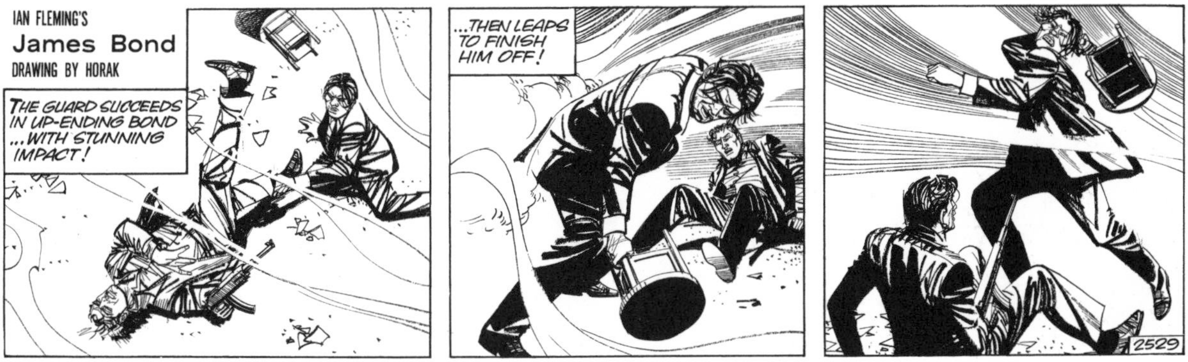
IAN FLEMING'S
James Bond
DRAWING BY HORAK
THE GUARD SUCCEEDS IN UP-ENDING BOND ...WITH STUNNING IMPACT!
...THEN LEAPS TO FINISH HIM OFF!
2529

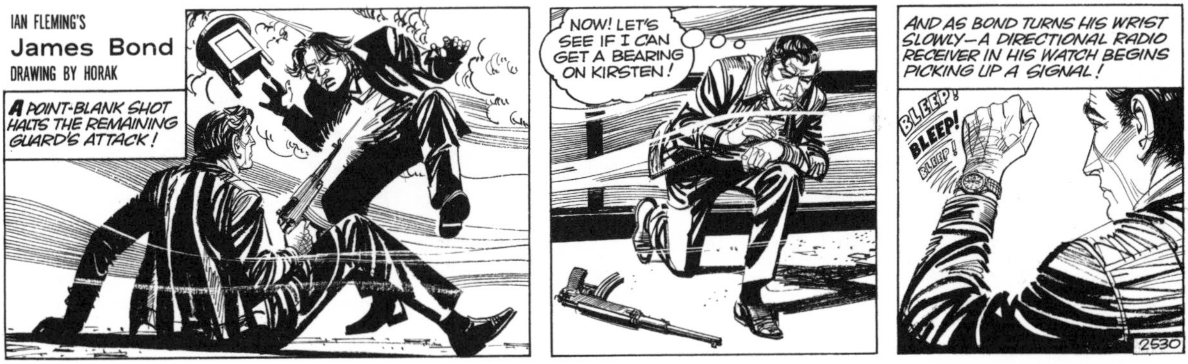
IAN FLEMING'S
James Bond
DRAWING BY HORAK
A POINT-BLANK SHOT HALTS THE REMAINING GUARD'S ATTACK!
NOW! LET'S SEE IF I CAN GET A BEARING ON KIRSTEN!
AND AS BOND TURNS HIS WRIST SLOWLY—A DIRECTIONAL RADIO RECEIVER IN HIS WATCH BEGINS PICKING UP A SIGNAL!
BLEEP!
BLEEP!
BLEEP!
2530

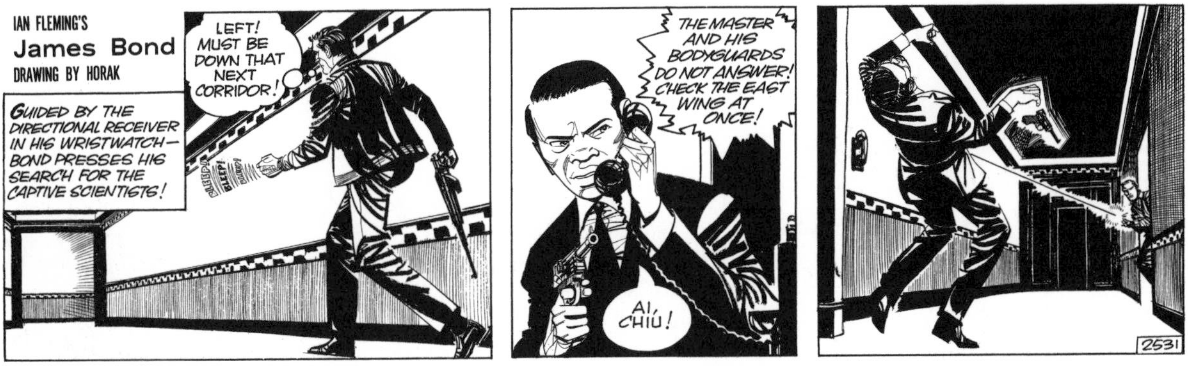
IAN FLEMING'S
James Bond
DRAWING BY HORAK
GUIDED BY THE DIRECTIONAL RECEIVER IN HIS WRISTWATCH— BOND PRESSES HIS SEARCH FOR THE CAPTIVE SCIENTISTS!
LEFT! MUST BE DOWN THAT NEXT CORRIDOR!
THE MASTER AND HIS BODYGUARDS DO NOT ANSWER! CHECK THE EAST WING AT ONCE!
AI, CHIU!
2531

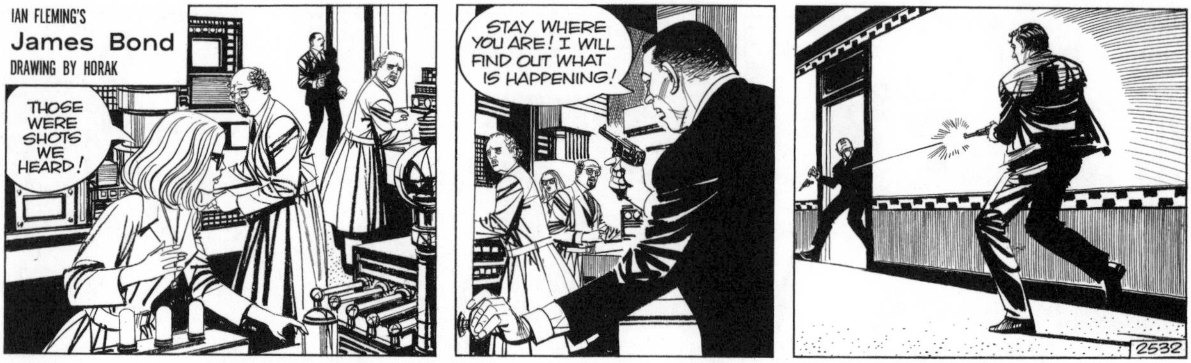
IAN FLEMING'S
James Bond
DRAWING BY HORAK
THOSE WERE SHOTS WE HEARD!
STAY WHERE YOU ARE! I WILL FIND OUT WHAT IS HAPPENING!
2532

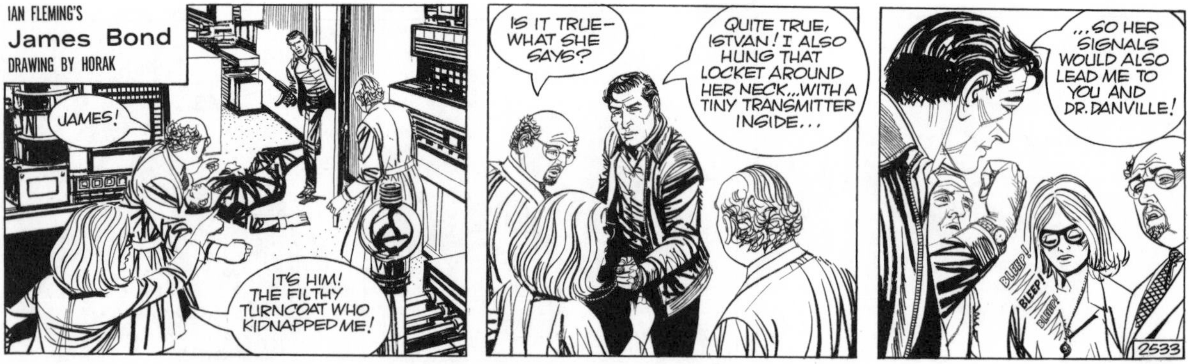
IAN FLEMING'S
James Bond
DRAWING BY HORAK
JAMES!
IT'S HIM! THE FILTHY TURNCOAT WHO KIDNAPPED ME!
IS IT TRUE- WHAT SHE SAYS?
QUITE TRUE, ISTVAN! I ALSO HUNG THAT LOCKET AROUND HER NECK...WITH A TINY TRANSMITTER INSIDE...
...SO HER SIGNALS WOULD ALSO LEAD ME TO YOU AND DR. DANVILLE!
BLEEP! BLEEP!
2533

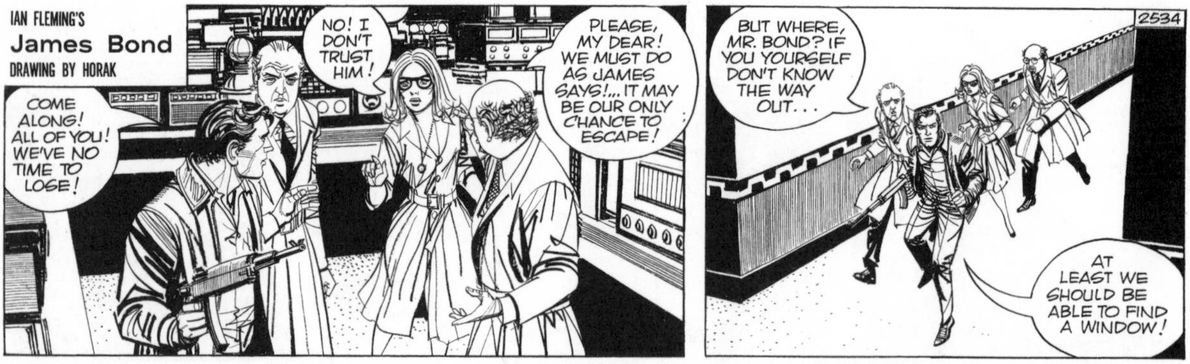
IAN FLEMING'S
James Bond
DRAWING BY HORAK
COME ALONG! ALL OF YOU! WE'VE NO TIME TO LOSE!
NO! I DON'T TRUST HIM!
PLEASE, MY DEAR! WE MUST DO AS JAMES SAYS!... IT MAY BE OUR ONLY CHANCE TO ESCAPE!
BUT WHERE, MR. BOND? IF YOU YOURSELF DON'T KNOW THE WAY OUT...
AT LEAST WE SHOULD BE ABLE TO FIND A WINDOW!
2534

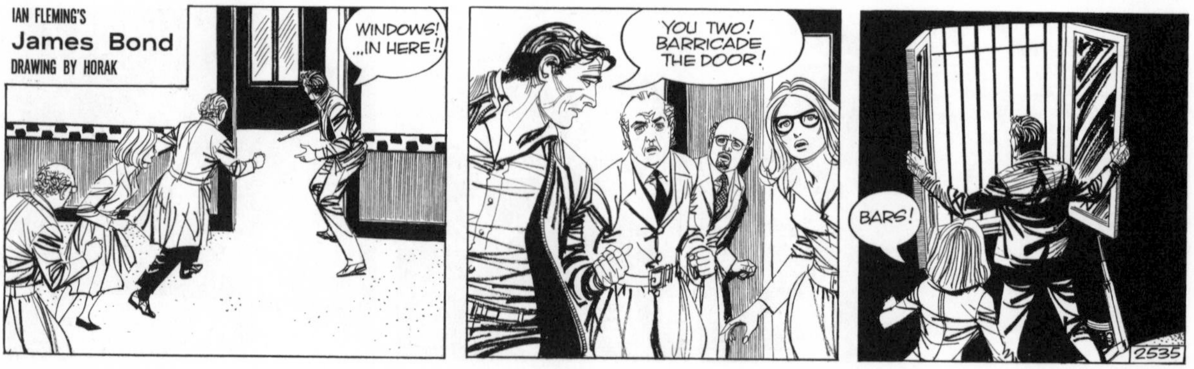
IAN FLEMING'S
James Bond
DRAWING BY HORAK
WINDOWS! ...IN HERE!!
YOU TWO! BARRICADE THE DOOR!
BARS!
2535

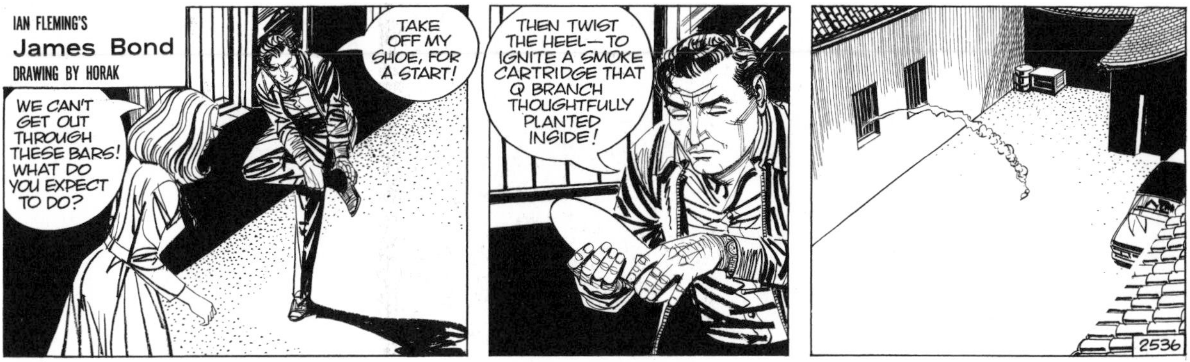
IAN FLEMING'S
James Bond
DRAWING BY HORAK
WE CAN'T GET OUT THROUGH THESE BARS! WHAT DO YOU EXPECT TO DO?
TAKE OFF MY SHOE, FOR A START!
THEN TWIST THE HEEL—TO IGNITE A SMOKE CARTRIDGE THAT Q BRANCH THOUGHTFULLY PLANTED INSIDE!
2536

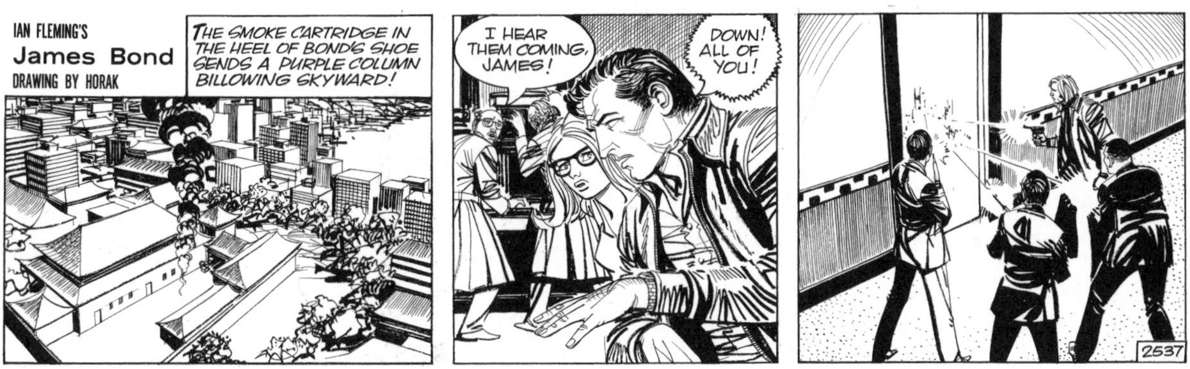
IAN FLEMING'S
James Bond
DRAWING BY HORAK
THE SMOKE CARTRIDGE IN THE HEEL OF BOND'S SHOE SENDS A PURPLE COLUMN BILLOWING SKYWARD!
I HEAR THEM COMING, JAMES!
DOWN! ALL OF YOU!
2537

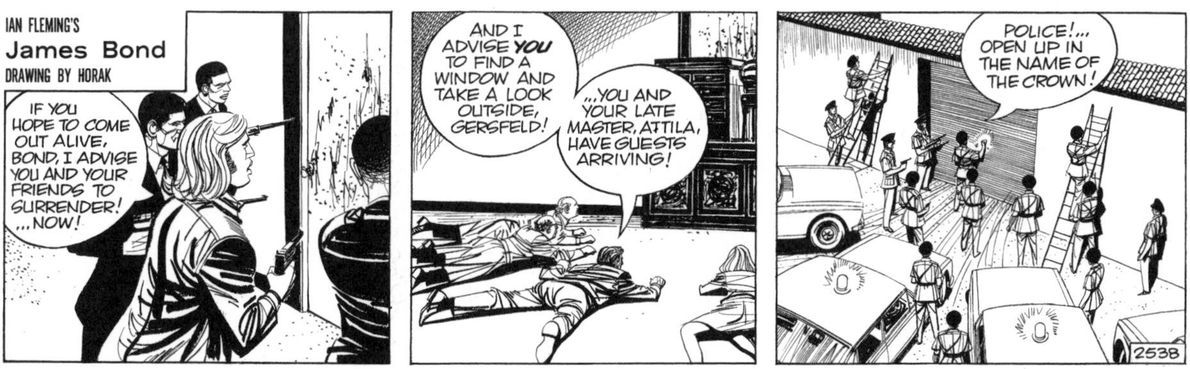
IAN FLEMING'S
James Bond
DRAWING BY HORAK
IF YOU HOPE TO COME OUT ALIVE, BOND, I ADVISE YOU AND YOUR FRIENDS TO SURRENDER! ...NOW!
AND I ADVISE YOU TO FIND A WINDOW AND TAKE A LOOK OUTSIDE, GERSFELD!
...YOU AND YOUR LATE MASTER, ATTILA, HAVE GUESTS ARRIVING!
POLICE!... OPEN UP IN THE NAME OF THE CROWN!
2538

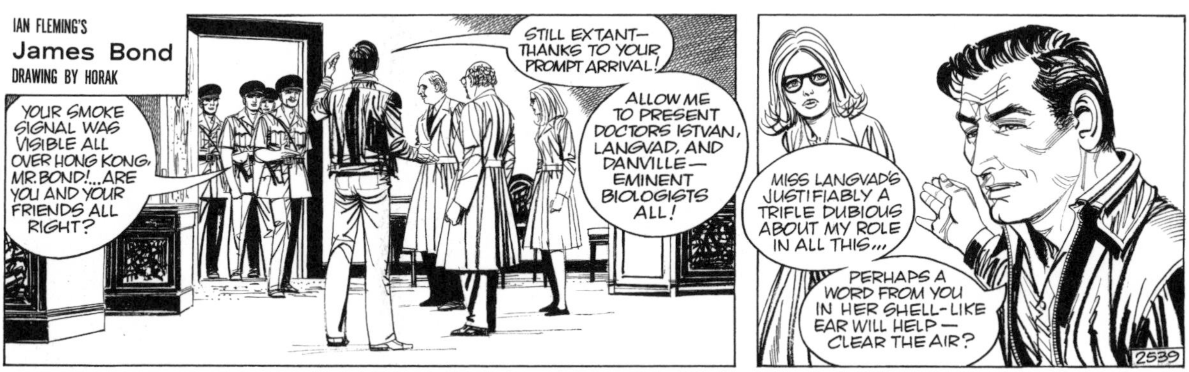
IAN FLEMING'S
James Bond
DRAWING BY HORAK
YOUR SMOKE SIGNAL WAS VISIBLE ALL OVER HONG KONG, MR. BOND!... ARE YOU AND YOUR FRIENDS ALL RIGHT?
STILL EXTANT—THANKS TO YOUR PROMPT ARRIVAL!
ALLOW ME TO PRESENT DOCTORS ISTVAN, LANGVAD, AND DANVILLE—EMINENT BIOLOGISTS ALL!
MISS LANGVAD'S JUSTIFIABLY A TRIFLE DUBIOUS ABOUT MY ROLE IN ALL THIS...,
PERHAPS A WORD FROM YOU IN HER SHELL-LIKE EAR WILL HELP—CLEAR THE AIR?
2539

IAN FLEMING'S
James Bond
DRAWING BY HORAK
THEN YOU— YOU NEVER REALLY SHOT THAT GIRL, SUZI KEW, BACK IN LONDON?
ONLY WITH A BLANK... IT WAS ALL PART OF OUR ACT!
YOU SEE, MISS LANGVAD— LITERALLY AND ELECTRONICALLY— I HAD A BUG IN MY EAR!
I'VE MISJUDGED YOU, MR. BOND
DO YOU THINK I CAN EVER CORRECT YOUR INITIAL FALSE IMPRESSION —KIRSTEN?
I'M SURE YOU'LL FIND A WAY— ON CLOSER ACQUAINTANCE, JAMES!
2540

IAN FLEMING'S
James Bond
DRAWING BY HORAK
WELL THEN, KIRSTEN LUV—IF THE WAY TO TRUER UNDERSTANDING IS A CLOSER ACQUAINTANCE
THE SOONER OURS STARTS RIPENING, THE BETTER WE'LL—
OH, OH!
JAMES! WHAT'S WRONG?
SHHH— REMEMBER THAT BUG! I'D BETTER PLUG UP MY EAR!
2541
AFTER ALL— WE WOULDN'T WANT ANYONE LISTENING IN—BEFORE I'VE BEEN SURGICALLY CORRECTED!
End of Story

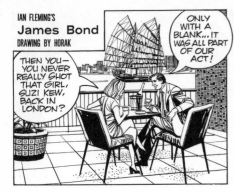

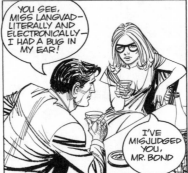

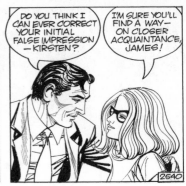

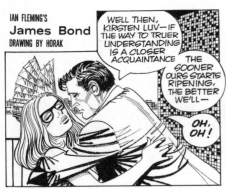

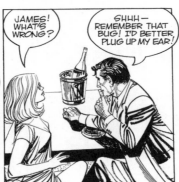

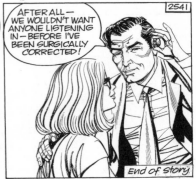

# THE NEVSKY NUDE

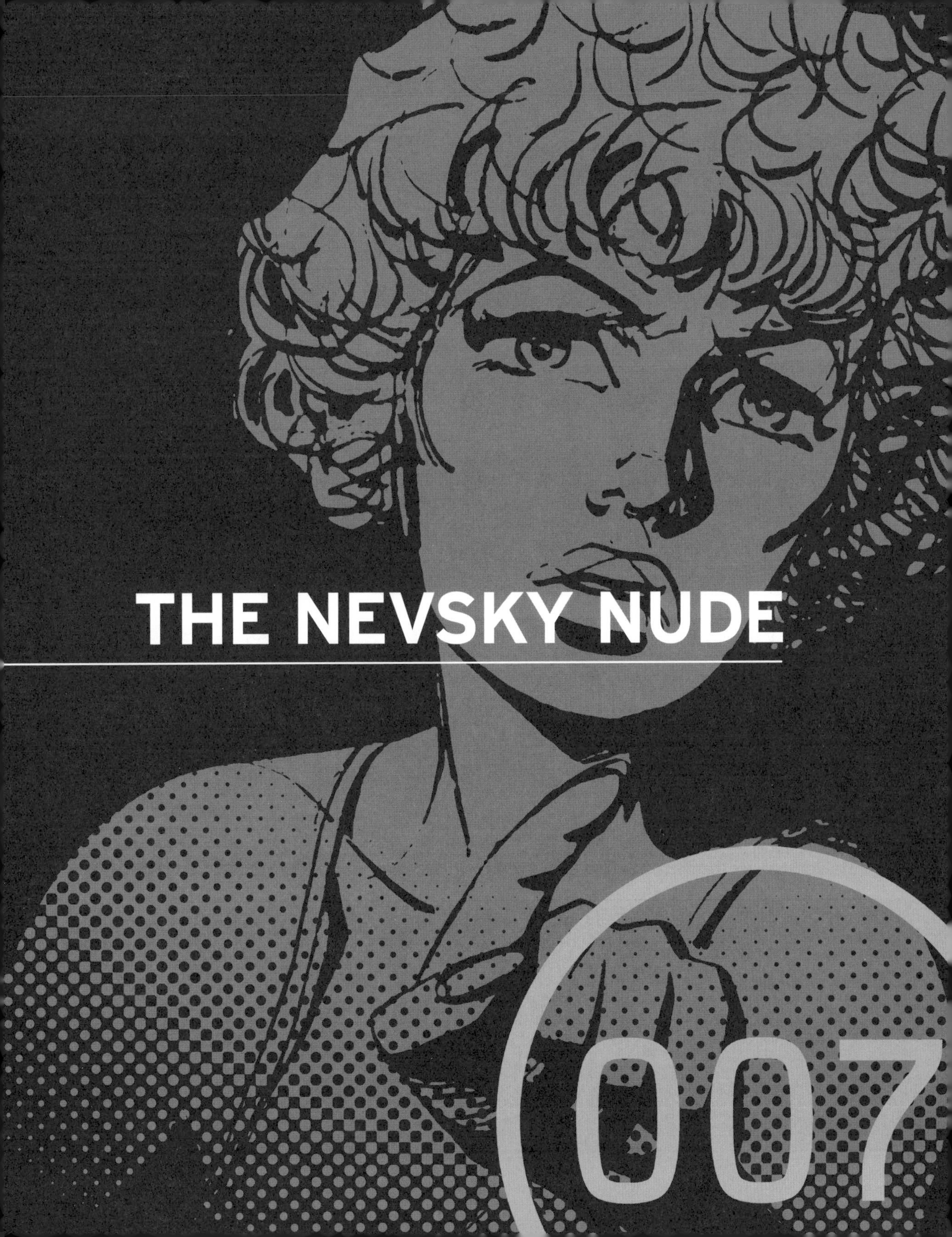

007

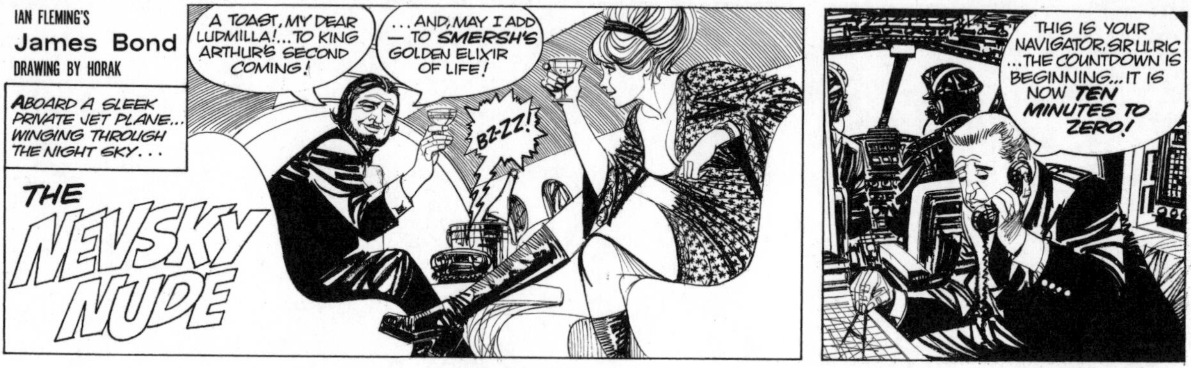
IAN FLEMING'S
James Bond
DRAWING BY HORAK
ABOARD A SLEEK PRIVATE JET PLANE... WINGING THROUGH THE NIGHT SKY...
THE NEVSKY NUDE
A TOAST, MY DEAR LUDMILLA!... TO KING ARTHUR'S SECOND COMING!
... AND, MAY I ADD — TO SMERSH'S GOLDEN ELIXIR OF LIFE!
BZ-ZZ!
THIS IS YOUR NAVIGATOR, SIR ULRIC ... THE COUNTDOWN IS BEGINNING... IT IS NOW TEN MINUTES TO ZERO!

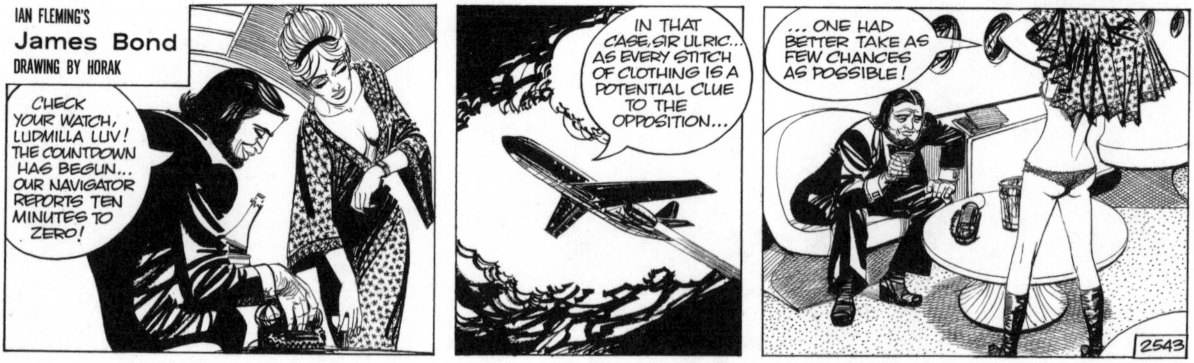
IAN FLEMING'S
James Bond
DRAWING BY HORAK
CHECK YOUR WATCH, LUDMILLA LUV! THE COUNTDOWN HAS BEGUN... OUR NAVIGATOR REPORTS TEN MINUTES TO ZERO!
IN THAT CASE, SIR ULRIC... AS EVERY STITCH OF CLOTHING IS A POTENTIAL CLUE TO THE OPPOSITION...
... ONE HAD BETTER TAKE AS FEW CHANCES AS POSSIBLE!
2543

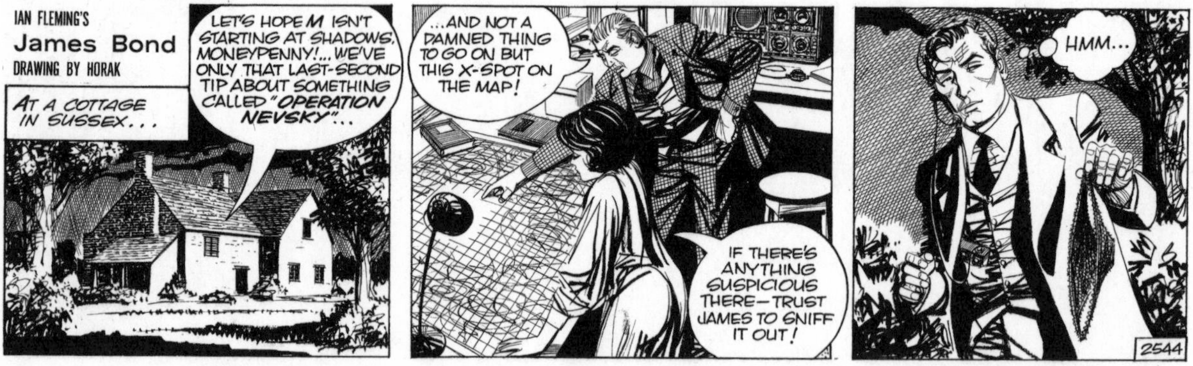
IAN FLEMING'S
James Bond
DRAWING BY HORAK
AT A COTTAGE IN SUSSEX...
LET'S HOPE M ISN'T STARTING AT SHADOWS, MONEYPENNY!... WE'VE ONLY THAT LAST-SECOND TIP ABOUT SOMETHING CALLED "OPERATION NEVSKY"...
...AND NOT A DAMNED THING TO GO ON BUT THIS X-SPOT ON THE MAP!
IF THERE'S ANYTHING SUSPICIOUS THERE—TRUST JAMES TO SNIFF IT OUT!
HMM...
2544

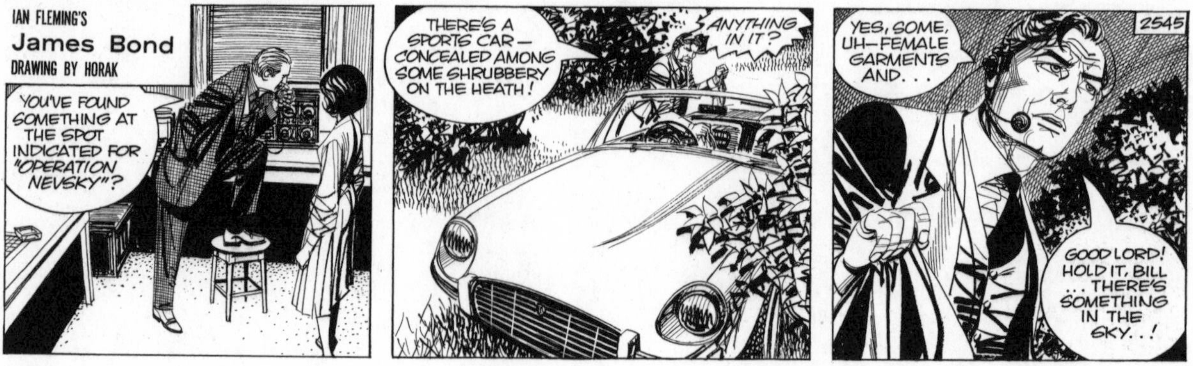
IAN FLEMING'S
James Bond
DRAWING BY HORAK
YOU'VE FOUND SOMETHING AT THE SPOT INDICATED FOR "OPERATION NEVSKY"?
THERE'S A SPORTS CAR — CONCEALED AMONG SOME SHRUBBERY ON THE HEATH!
ANYTHING IN IT?
2545
YES, SOME, UH—FEMALE GARMENTS AND...
GOOD LORD! HOLD IT, BILL ... THERE'S SOMETHING IN THE SKY..!

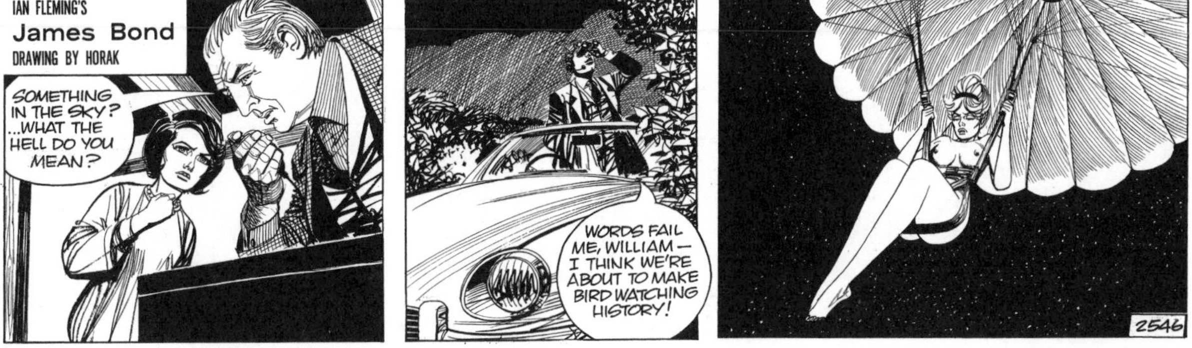
IAN FLEMING'S
James Bond
DRAWING BY HORAK
SOMETHING IN THE SKY? ...WHAT THE HELL DO YOU MEAN?
WORDS FAIL ME, WILLIAM — I THINK WE'RE ABOUT TO MAKE BIRD WATCHING HISTORY!
2546

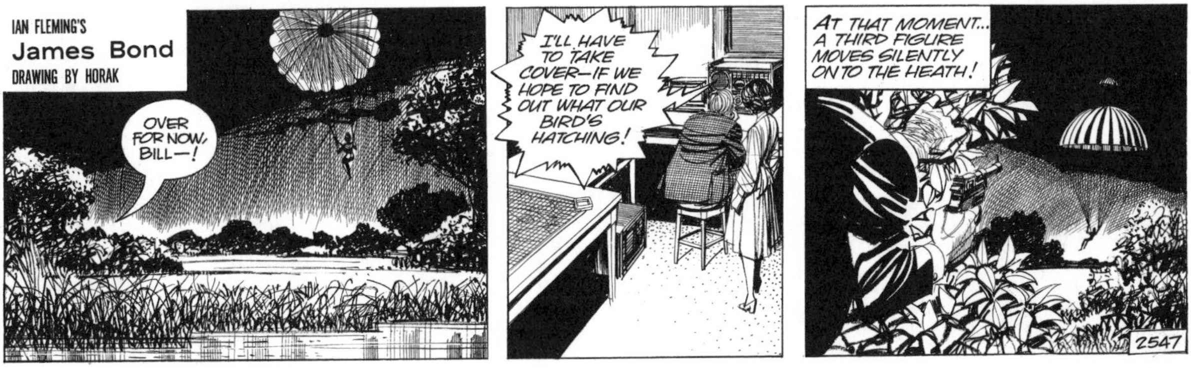
IAN FLEMING'S
James Bond
DRAWING BY HORAK
OVER FOR NOW, BILL—!
I'LL HAVE TO TAKE COVER—IF WE HOPE TO FIND OUT WHAT OUR BIRD'S HATCHING!
AT THAT MOMENT... A THIRD FIGURE MOVES SILENTLY ON TO THE HEATH!
2547

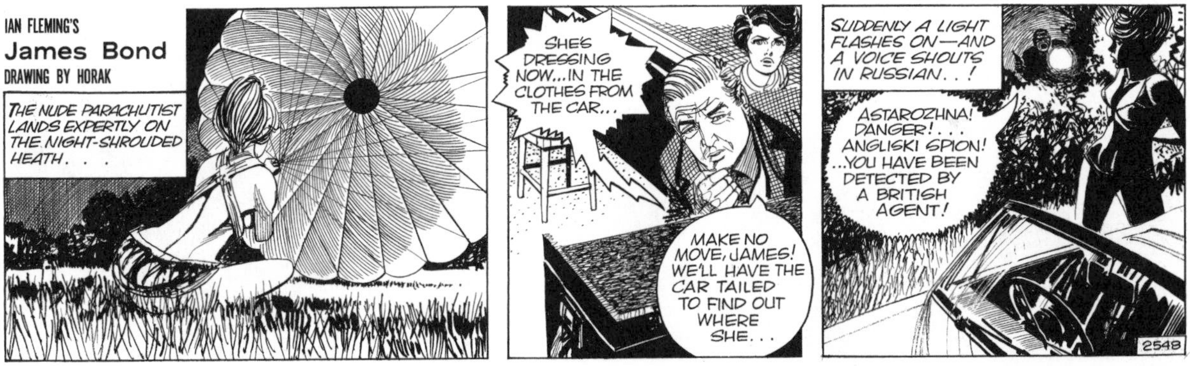
IAN FLEMING'S
James Bond
DRAWING BY HORAK
THE NUDE PARACHUTIST LANDS EXPERTLY ON THE NIGHT-SHROUDED HEATH . . .
SHE'S DRESSING NOW... IN THE CLOTHES FROM THE CAR...
MAKE NO MOVE, JAMES! WE'LL HAVE THE CAR TAILED TO FIND OUT WHERE SHE...
SUDDENLY A LIGHT FLASHES ON — AND A VOICE SHOUTS IN RUSSIAN. . !
ASTAROZHNA! DANGER!... ANGLISKI SPION! ...YOU HAVE BEEN DETECTED BY A BRITISH AGENT!
2548

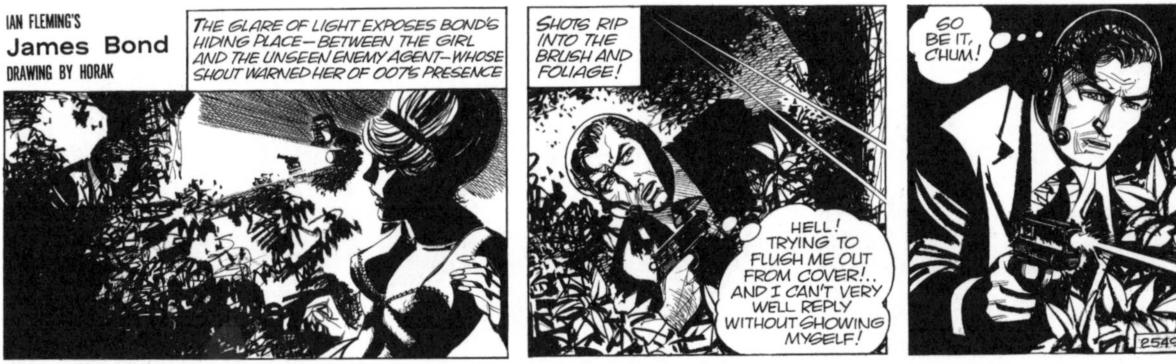
IAN FLEMING'S
James Bond
DRAWING BY HORAK
THE GLARE OF LIGHT EXPOSES BOND'S HIDING PLACE—BETWEEN THE GIRL AND THE UNSEEN ENEMY AGENT—WHOSE SHOUT WARNED HER OF 007'S PRESENCE
SHOTS RIP INTO THE BRUSH AND FOLIAGE!
HELL! TRYING TO FLUSH ME OUT FROM COVER!.. AND I CAN'T VERY WELL REPLY WITHOUT SHOWING MYSELF!
SO BE IT, CHUM!
2549

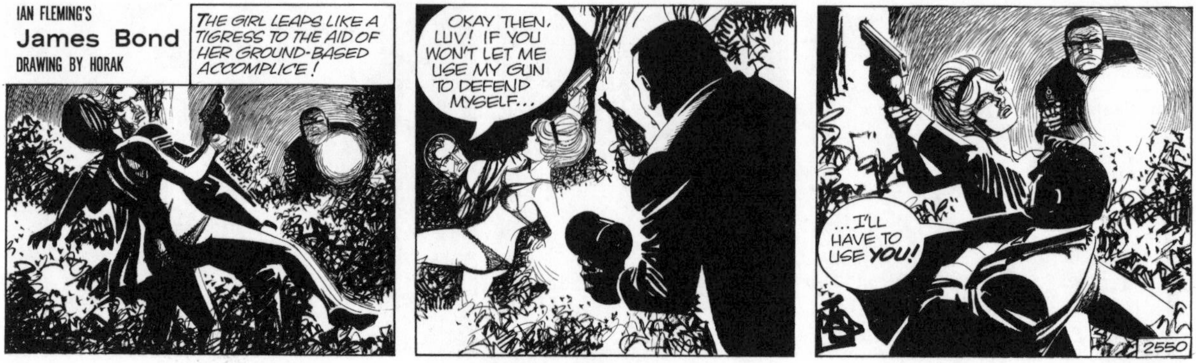
IAN FLEMING'S
James Bond
DRAWING BY HORAK
THE GIRL LEAPS LIKE A TIGRESS TO THE AID OF HER GROUND-BASED ACCOMPLICE!
OKAY THEN, LUV! IF YOU WON'T LET ME USE MY GUN TO DEFEND MYSELF...
...I'LL HAVE TO USE YOU!
2550

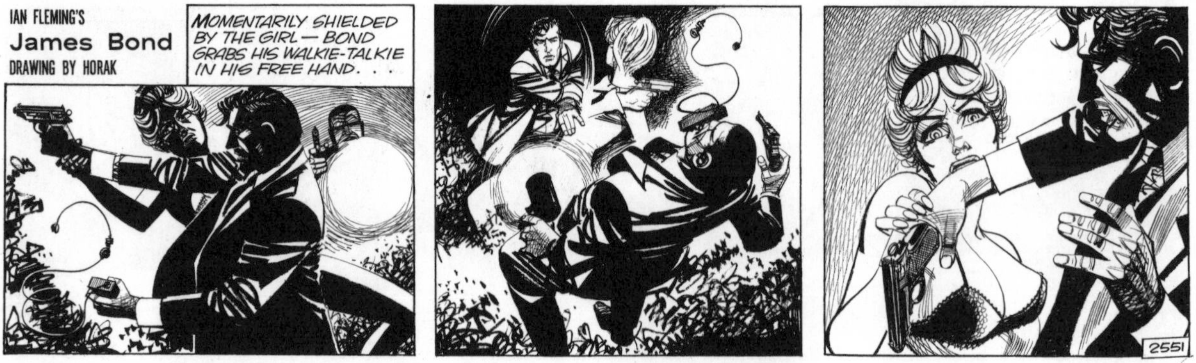
IAN FLEMING'S
James Bond
DRAWING BY HORAK
MOMENTARILY SHIELDED BY THE GIRL — BOND GRABS HIS WALKIE-TALKIE IN HIS FREE HAND...
2551

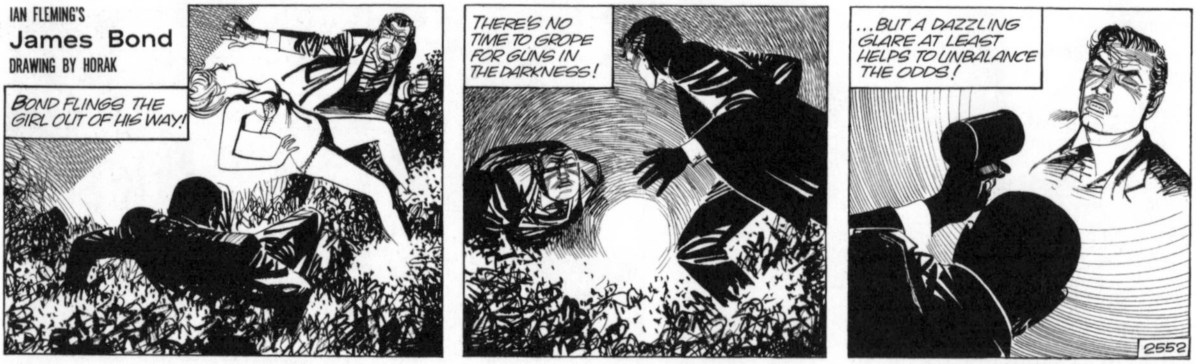
IAN FLEMING'S
James Bond
DRAWING BY HORAK
BOND FLINGS THE GIRL OUT OF HIS WAY!
THERE'S NO TIME TO GROPE FOR GUNS IN THE DARKNESS!
...BUT A DAZZLING GLARE AT LEAST HELPS TO UNBALANCE THE ODDS!
2552

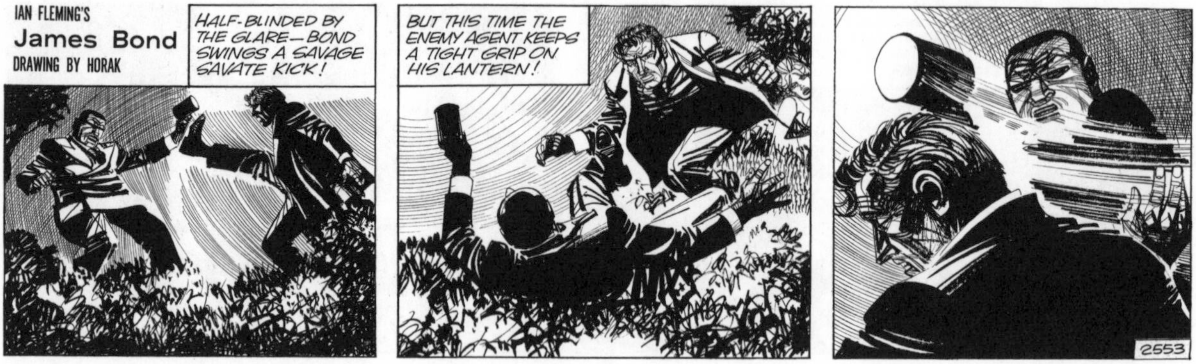
IAN FLEMING'S
James Bond
DRAWING BY HORAK
HALF-BLINDED BY THE GLARE — BOND SWINGS A SAVAGE SAVATE KICK!
BUT THIS TIME THE ENEMY AGENT KEEPS A TIGHT GRIP ON HIS LANTERN!
2553

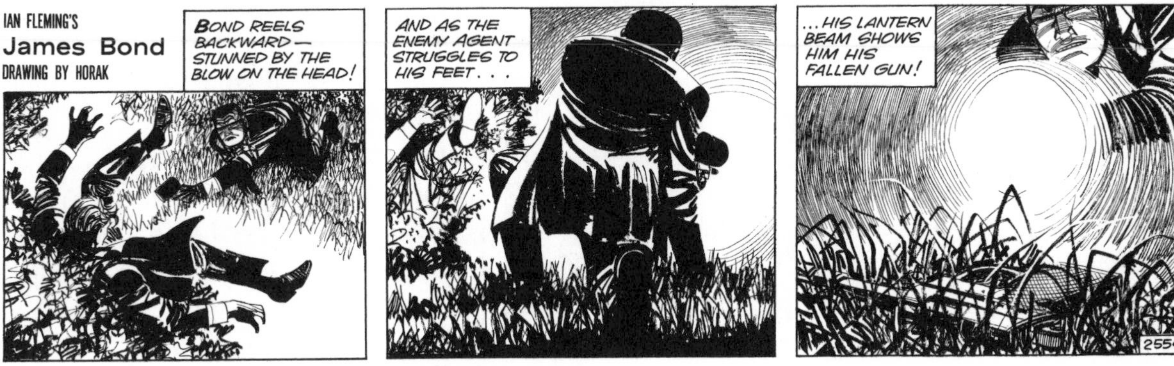
IAN FLEMING'S
James Bond
DRAWING BY HORAK
BOND REELS BACKWARD— STUNNED BY THE BLOW ON THE HEAD!
AND AS THE ENEMY AGENT STRUGGLES TO HIS FEET . . .
...HIS LANTERN BEAM SHOWS HIM HIS FALLEN GUN!
2554

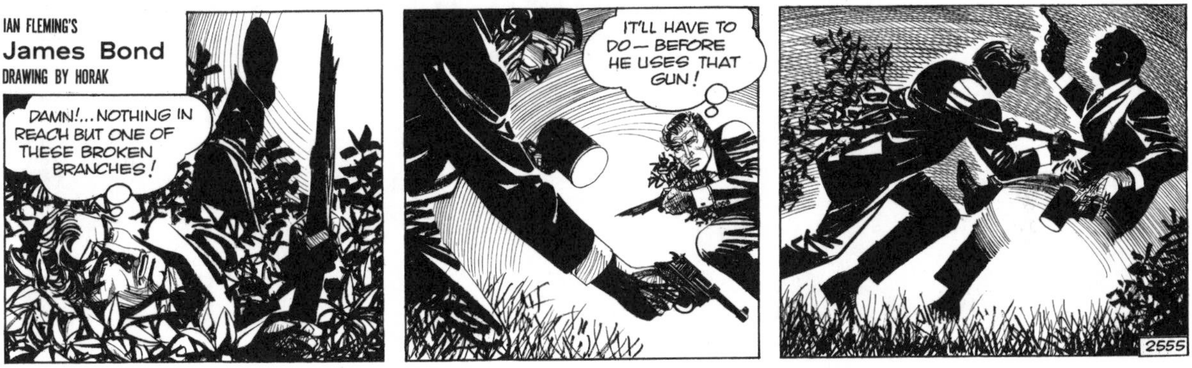
IAN FLEMING'S
James Bond
DRAWING BY HORAK
DAMN!... NOTHING IN REACH BUT ONE OF THESE BROKEN BRANCHES!
IT'LL HAVE TO DO— BEFORE HE USES THAT GUN!
2555

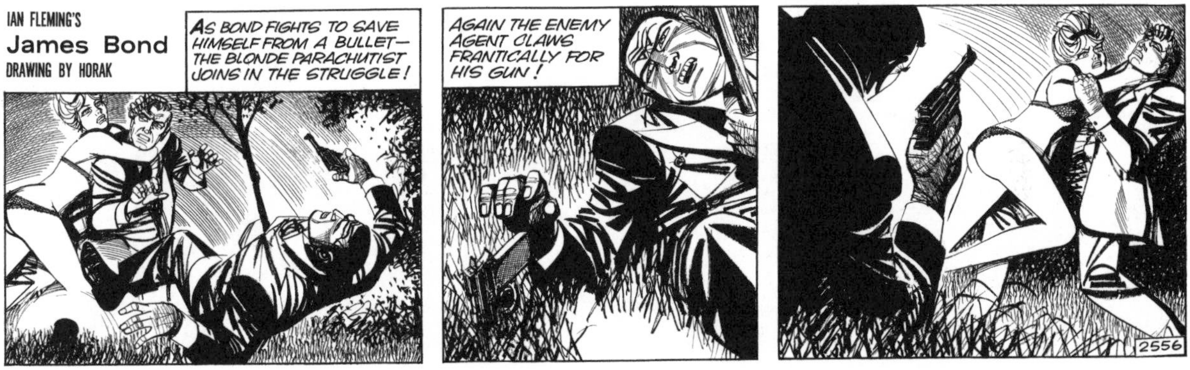
IAN FLEMING'S
James Bond
DRAWING BY HORAK
AS BOND FIGHTS TO SAVE HIMSELF FROM A BULLET— THE BLONDE PARACHUTIST JOINS IN THE STRUGGLE!
AGAIN THE ENEMY AGENT CLAWS FRANTICALLY FOR HIS GUN!
2556

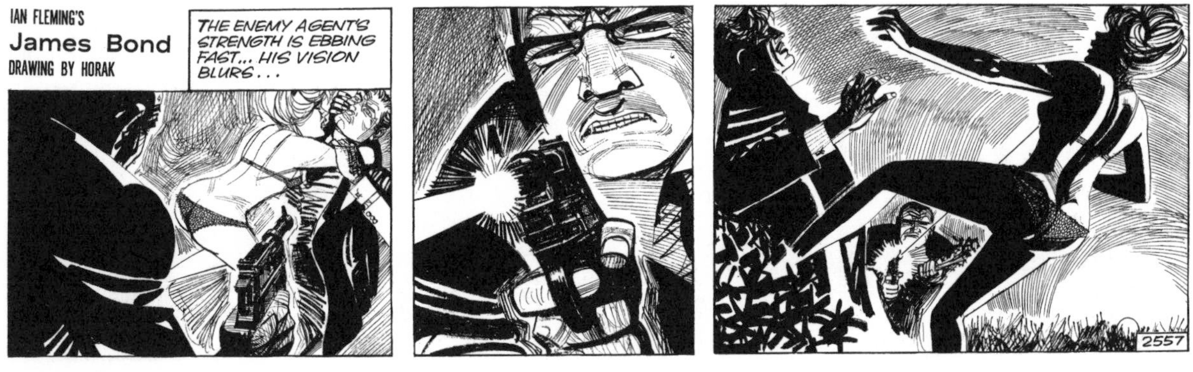
IAN FLEMING'S
James Bond
DRAWING BY HORAK
THE ENEMY AGENT'S STRENGTH IS EBBING FAST... HIS VISION BLURS...
2557

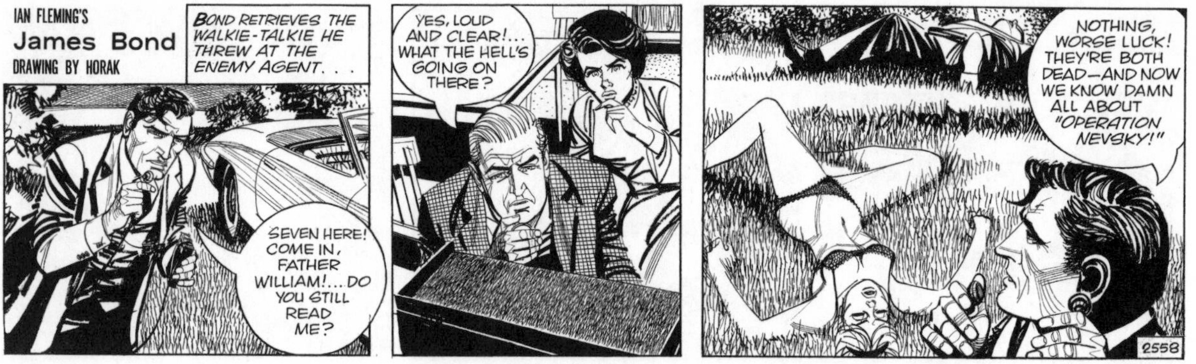
IAN FLEMING'S
James Bond
DRAWING BY HORAK
BOND RETRIEVES THE WALKIE-TALKIE HE THREW AT THE ENEMY AGENT. . .
SEVEN HERE! COME IN, FATHER WILLIAM!... DO YOU STILL READ ME?
YES, LOUD AND CLEAR!... WHAT THE HELL'S GOING ON THERE?
NOTHING, WORSE LUCK! THEY'RE BOTH DEAD—AND NOW WE KNOW DAMN ALL ABOUT "OPERATION NEVSKY!"
2558

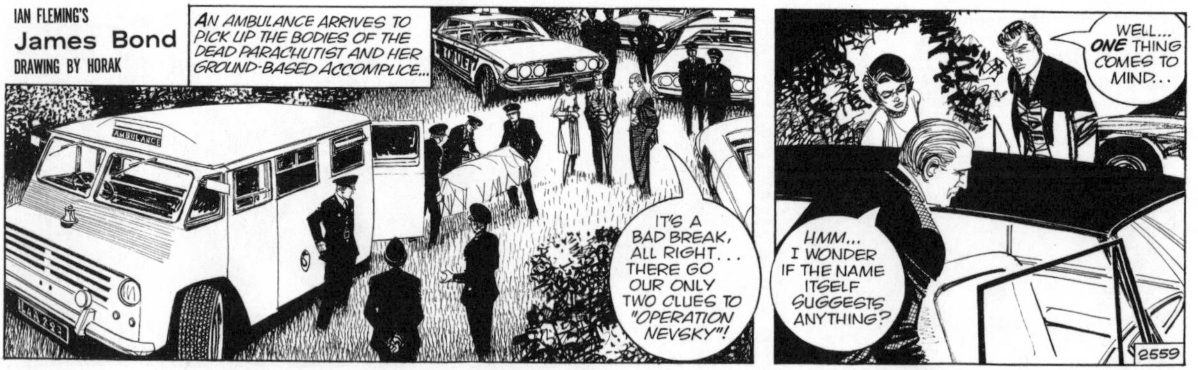
IAN FLEMING'S
James Bond
DRAWING BY HORAK
AN AMBULANCE ARRIVES TO PICK UP THE BODIES OF THE DEAD PARACHUTIST AND HER GROUND-BASED ACCOMPLICE...
AMBULANCE
IT'S A BAD BREAK, ALL RIGHT. . . THERE GO OUR ONLY TWO CLUES TO "OPERATION NEVSKY"!
HMM... I WONDER IF THE NAME ITSELF SUGGESTS ANYTHING?
WELL... ONE THING COMES TO MIND...
2559

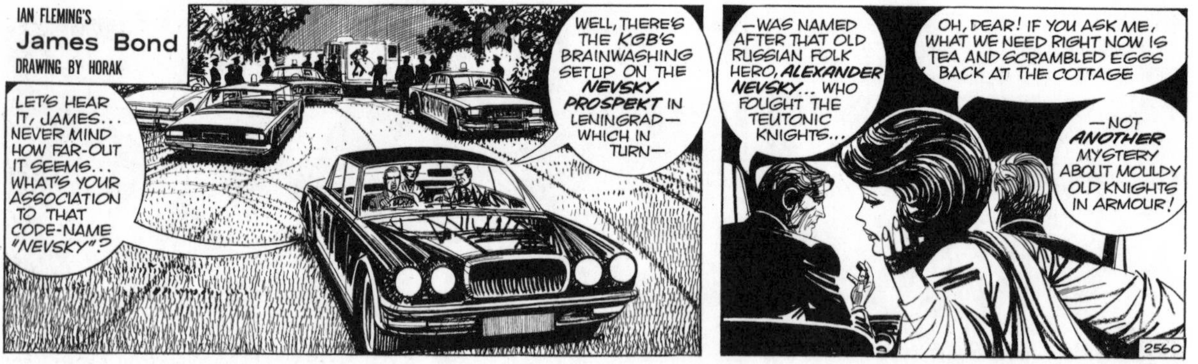
IAN FLEMING'S
James Bond
DRAWING BY HORAK
LET'S HEAR IT, JAMES... NEVER MIND HOW FAR-OUT IT SEEMS... WHAT'S YOUR ASSOCIATION TO THAT CODE-NAME "NEVSKY"?
WELL, THERE'S THE KGB'S BRAINWASHING SETUP ON THE NEVSKY PROSPEKT IN LENINGRAD—WHICH IN TURN—
—WAS NAMED AFTER THAT OLD RUSSIAN FOLK HERO, ALEXANDER NEVSKY... WHO FOUGHT THE TEUTONIC KNIGHTS...
OH, DEAR! IF YOU ASK ME, WHAT WE NEED RIGHT NOW IS TEA AND SCRAMBLED EGGS BACK AT THE COTTAGE
—NOT ANOTHER MYSTERY ABOUT MOULDY OLD KNIGHTS IN ARMOUR!
2560

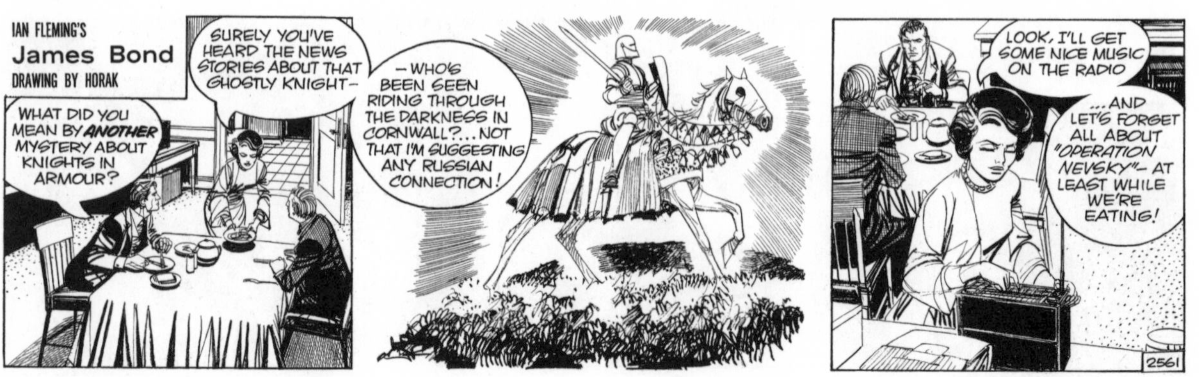
IAN FLEMING'S
James Bond
DRAWING BY HORAK
WHAT DID YOU MEAN BY ANOTHER MYSTERY ABOUT KNIGHTS IN ARMOUR?
SURELY YOU'VE HEARD THE NEWS STORIES ABOUT THAT GHOSTLY KNIGHT-
—WHO'S BEEN SEEN RIDING THROUGH THE DARKNESS IN CORNWALL?... NOT THAT I'M SUGGESTING ANY RUSSIAN CONNECTION!
LOOK, I'LL GET SOME NICE MUSIC ON THE RADIO
...AND LET'S FORGET ALL ABOUT "OPERATION NEVSKY"—AT LEAST WHILE WE'RE EATING!
2561

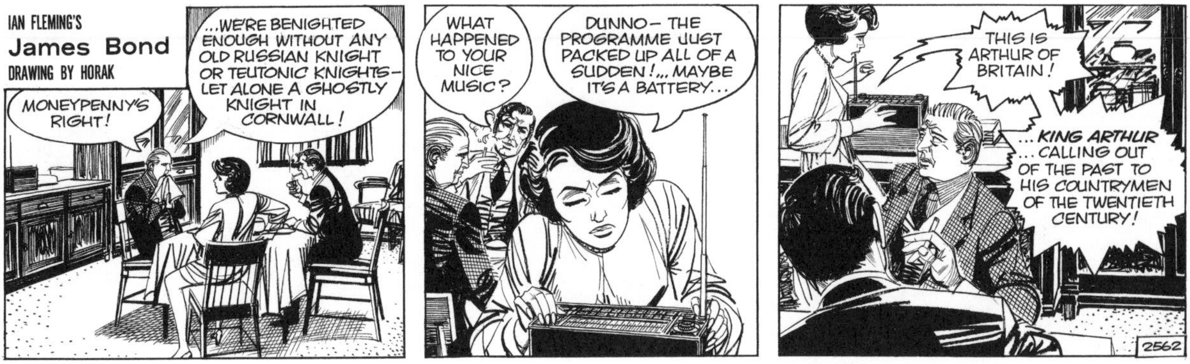
IAN FLEMING'S
James Bond
DRAWING BY HORAK
MONEYPENNY'S RIGHT!
...WE'RE BENIGHTED ENOUGH WITHOUT ANY OLD RUSSIAN KNIGHT OR TEUTONIC KNIGHTS– LET ALONE A GHOSTLY KNIGHT IN CORNWALL!
WHAT HAPPENED TO YOUR NICE MUSIC?
DUNNO– THE PROGRAMME JUST PACKED UP ALL OF A SUDDEN!... MAYBE IT'S A BATTERY...
THIS IS ARTHUR OF BRITAIN!
...**KING ARTHUR** ...CALLING OUT OF THE PAST TO HIS COUNTRYMEN OF THE TWENTIETH CENTURY!
2562

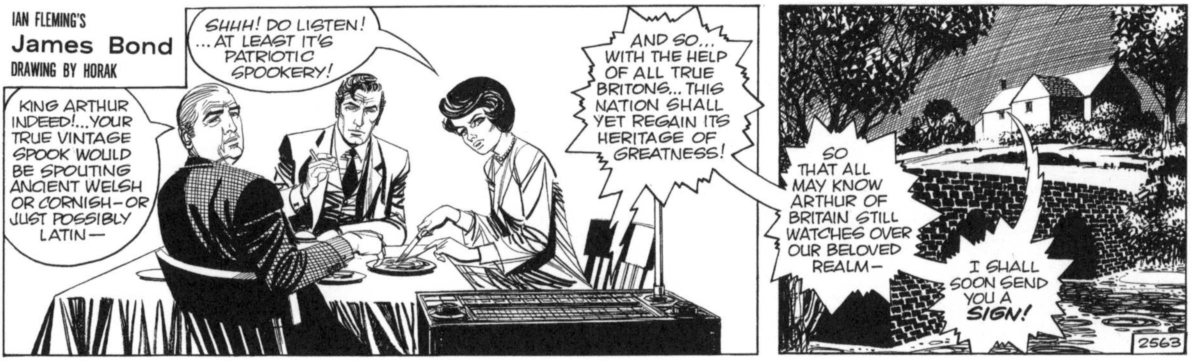
IAN FLEMING'S
James Bond
DRAWING BY HORAK
KING ARTHUR INDEED!... YOUR TRUE VINTAGE SPOOK WOULD BE SPOUTING ANCIENT WELSH OR CORNISH–OR JUST POSSIBLY LATIN–
SHHH! DO LISTEN! ...AT LEAST IT'S PATRIOTIC SPOOKERY!
AND SO... WITH THE HELP OF ALL TRUE BRITONS... THIS NATION SHALL YET REGAIN ITS HERITAGE OF GREATNESS!
SO THAT ALL MAY KNOW ARTHUR OF BRITAIN STILL WATCHES OVER OUR BELOVED REALM–
I SHALL SOON SEND YOU A **SIGN!**
2563

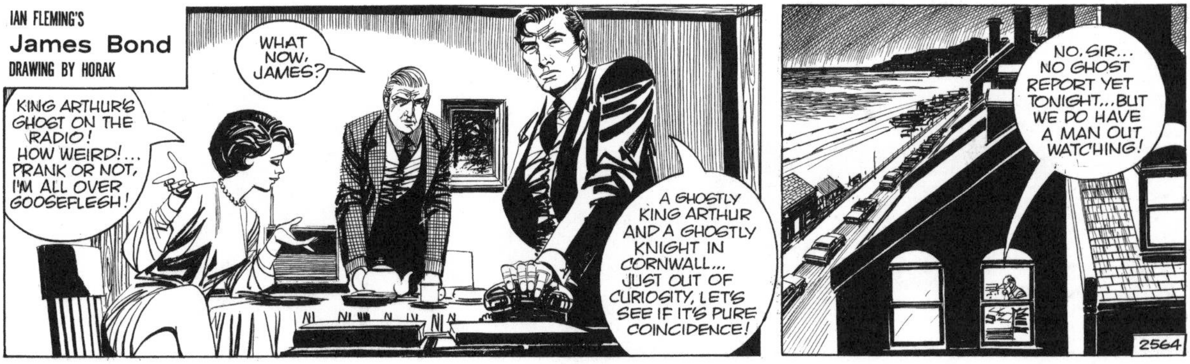
IAN FLEMING'S
James Bond
DRAWING BY HORAK
KING ARTHUR'S GHOST ON THE RADIO! HOW WEIRD!... PRANK OR NOT, I'M ALL OVER GOOSEFLESH!
WHAT NOW, JAMES?
A GHOSTLY KING ARTHUR AND A GHOSTLY KNIGHT IN CORNWALL... JUST OUT OF CURIOSITY, LET'S SEE IF IT'S PURE COINCIDENCE!
NO, SIR... NO GHOST REPORT YET TONIGHT... BUT WE DO HAVE A MAN OUT WATCHING!
2564

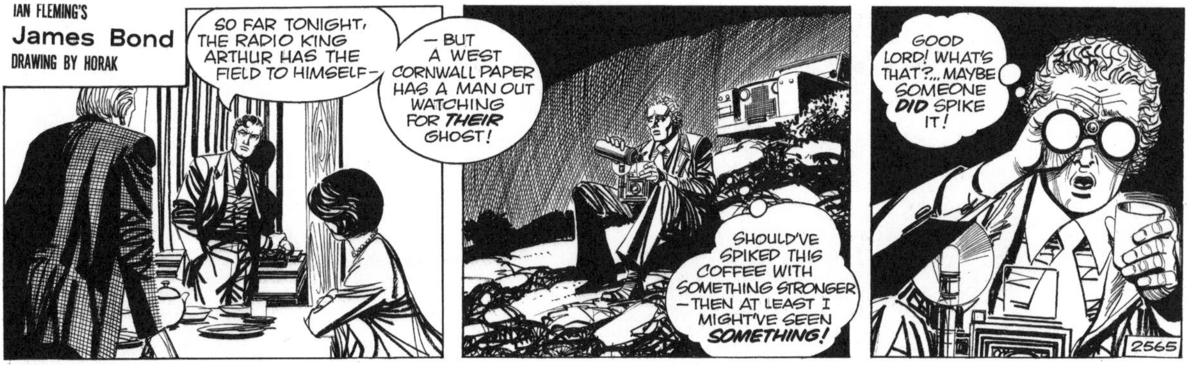
IAN FLEMING'S
James Bond
DRAWING BY HORAK
SO FAR TONIGHT, THE RADIO KING ARTHUR HAS THE FIELD TO HIMSELF–
–BUT A WEST CORNWALL PAPER HAS A MAN OUT WATCHING FOR **THEIR** GHOST!
SHOULD'VE SPIKED THIS COFFEE WITH SOMETHING STRONGER –THEN AT LEAST I MIGHT'VE SEEN **SOMETHING!**
GOOD LORD! WHAT'S THAT?... MAYBE SOMEONE **DID** SPIKE IT!
2565

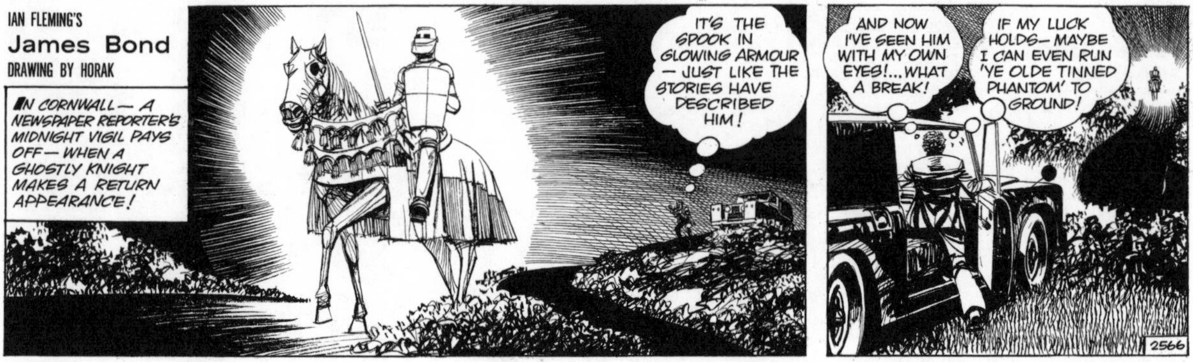
IAN FLEMING'S
James Bond
DRAWING BY HORAK
IN CORNWALL— A NEWSPAPER REPORTER'S MIDNIGHT VIGIL PAYS OFF—WHEN A GHOSTLY KNIGHT MAKES A RETURN APPEARANCE!
IT'S THE SPOOK IN GLOWING ARMOUR — JUST LIKE THE STORIES HAVE DESCRIBED HIM!
AND NOW I'VE SEEN HIM WITH MY OWN EYES!...WHAT A BREAK!
IF MY LUCK HOLDS— MAYBE I CAN EVEN RUN 'YE OLDE TINNED PHANTOM' TO GROUND!
2566

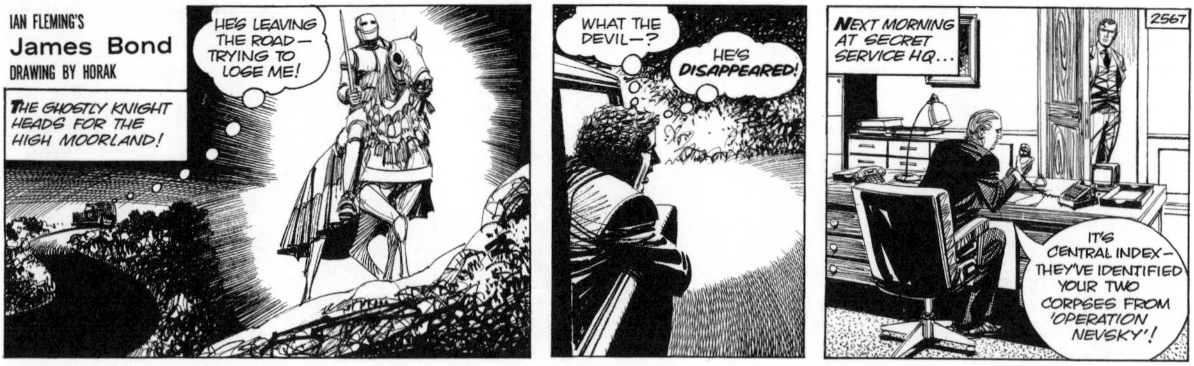
IAN FLEMING'S
James Bond
DRAWING BY HORAK
THE GHOSTLY KNIGHT HEADS FOR THE HIGH MOORLAND!
HE'S LEAVING THE ROAD— TRYING TO LOSE ME!
WHAT THE DEVIL—?
HE'S DISAPPEARED!
NEXT MORNING AT SECRET SERVICE HQ...
2567
IT'S CENTRAL INDEX— THEY'VE IDENTIFIED YOUR TWO CORPSES FROM 'OPERATION NEVSKY'!

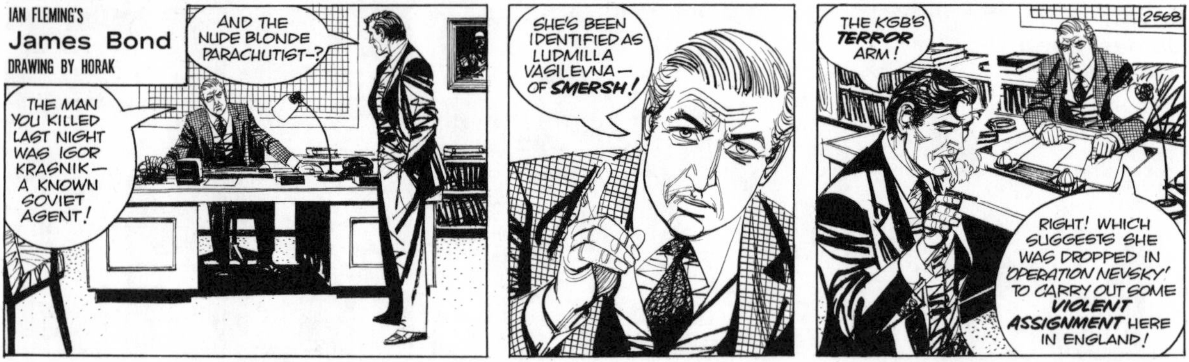
IAN FLEMING'S
James Bond
DRAWING BY HORAK
AND THE NUDE BLONDE PARACHUTIST—?
THE MAN YOU KILLED LAST NIGHT WAS IGOR KRASNIK— A KNOWN SOVIET AGENT!
SHE'S BEEN IDENTIFIED AS LUDMILLA VASILEVNA— OF SMERSH!
2568
THE KGB'S TERROR ARM!
RIGHT! WHICH SUGGESTS SHE WAS DROPPED IN 'OPERATION NEVSKY' TO CARRY OUT SOME VIOLENT ASSIGNMENT HERE IN ENGLAND!

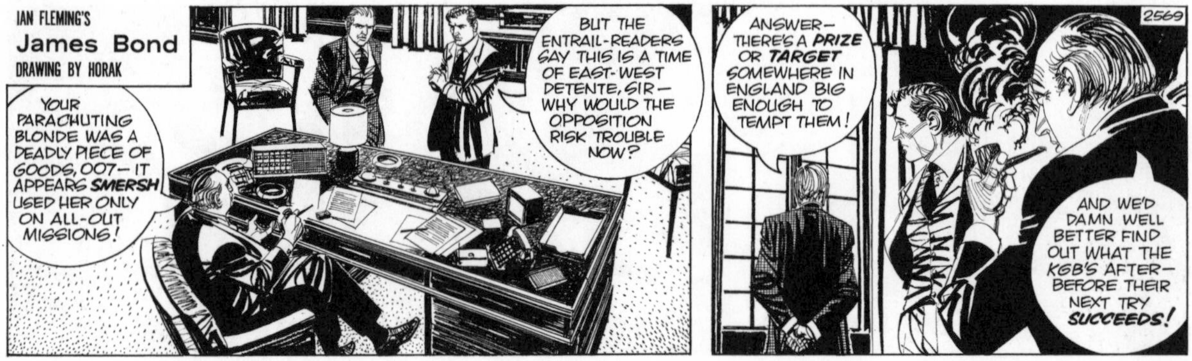
IAN FLEMING'S
James Bond
DRAWING BY HORAK
YOUR PARACHUTING BLONDE WAS A DEADLY PIECE OF GOODS, 007— IT APPEARS SMERSH USED HER ONLY ON ALL-OUT MISSIONS!
BUT THE ENTRAIL-READERS SAY THIS IS A TIME OF EAST-WEST DETENTE, SIR— WHY WOULD THE OPPOSITION RISK TROUBLE NOW?
2569
ANSWER— THERE'S A PRIZE OR TARGET SOMEWHERE IN ENGLAND BIG ENOUGH TO TEMPT THEM!
AND WE'D DAMN WELL BETTER FIND OUT WHAT THE KGB'S AFTER— BEFORE THEIR NEXT TRY SUCCEEDS!

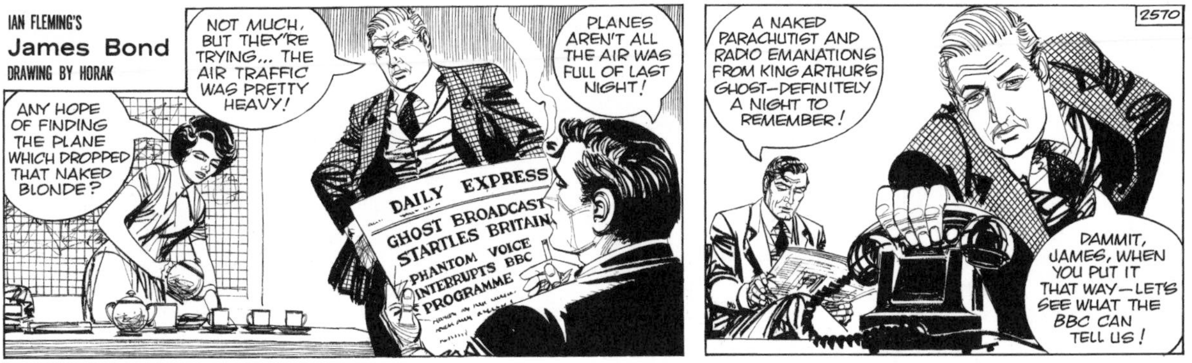
IAN FLEMING'S
James Bond
DRAWING BY HORAK
ANY HOPE OF FINDING THE PLANE WHICH DROPPED THAT NAKED BLONDE?
NOT MUCH, BUT THEY'RE TRYING... THE AIR TRAFFIC WAS PRETTY HEAVY!
PLANES AREN'T ALL THE AIR WAS FULL OF LAST NIGHT!
DAILY EXPRESS
GHOST BROADCAST STARTLES BRITAIN
PHANTOM VOICE INTERRUPTS BBC PROGRAMME
2570
A NAKED PARACHUTIST AND RADIO EMANATIONS FROM KING ARTHUR'S GHOST—DEFINITELY A NIGHT TO REMEMBER!
DAMMIT, JAMES, WHEN YOU PUT IT THAT WAY—LET'S SEE WHAT THE BBC CAN TELL US!

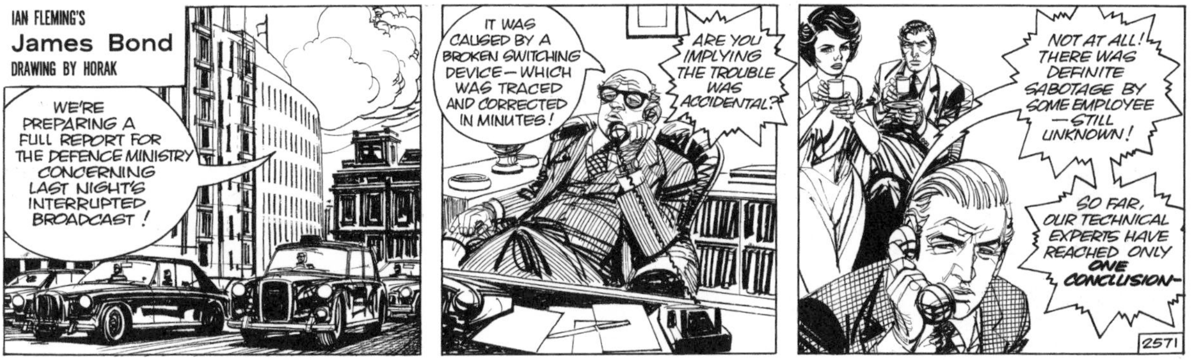
IAN FLEMING'S
James Bond
DRAWING BY HORAK
WE'RE PREPARING A FULL REPORT FOR THE DEFENCE MINISTRY CONCERNING LAST NIGHT'S INTERRUPTED BROADCAST!
IT WAS CAUSED BY A BROKEN SWITCHING DEVICE—WHICH WAS TRACED AND CORRECTED IN MINUTES!
ARE YOU IMPLYING THE TROUBLE WAS ACCIDENTAL?
NOT AT ALL! THERE WAS DEFINITE SABOTAGE BY SOME EMPLOYEE —STILL UNKNOWN!
SO FAR, OUR TECHNICAL EXPERTS HAVE REACHED ONLY ONE CONCLUSION—
2571

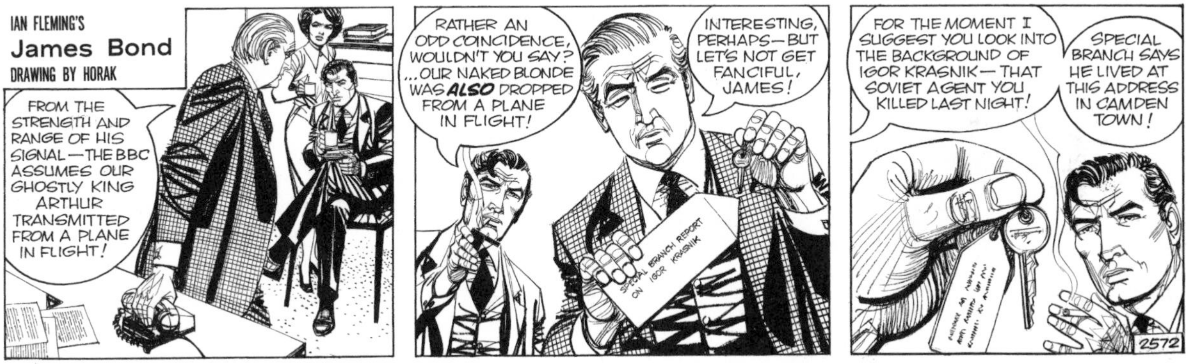
IAN FLEMING'S
James Bond
DRAWING BY HORAK
FROM THE STRENGTH AND RANGE OF HIS SIGNAL—THE BBC ASSUMES OUR GHOSTLY KING ARTHUR TRANSMITTED FROM A PLANE IN FLIGHT!
RATHER AN ODD COINCIDENCE, WOULDN'T YOU SAY? ...OUR NAKED BLONDE WAS ALSO DROPPED FROM A PLANE IN FLIGHT!
INTERESTING, PERHAPS—BUT LET'S NOT GET FANCIFUL, JAMES!
SPECIAL BRANCH REPORT ON IGOR KRASNIK
FOR THE MOMENT I SUGGEST YOU LOOK INTO THE BACKGROUND OF IGOR KRASNIK—THAT SOVIET AGENT YOU KILLED LAST NIGHT!
SPECIAL BRANCH SAYS HE LIVED AT THIS ADDRESS IN CAMDEN TOWN!
2572

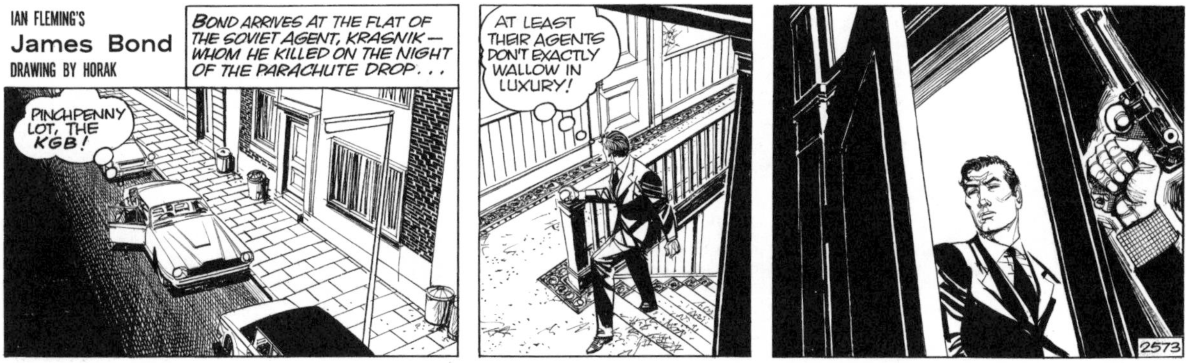
IAN FLEMING'S
James Bond
DRAWING BY HORAK
BOND ARRIVES AT THE FLAT OF THE SOVIET AGENT, KRASNIK—WHOM HE KILLED ON THE NIGHT OF THE PARACHUTE DROP...
PINCHPENNY LOT, THE KGB!
AT LEAST THEIR AGENTS DON'T EXACTLY WALLOW IN LUXURY!
2573

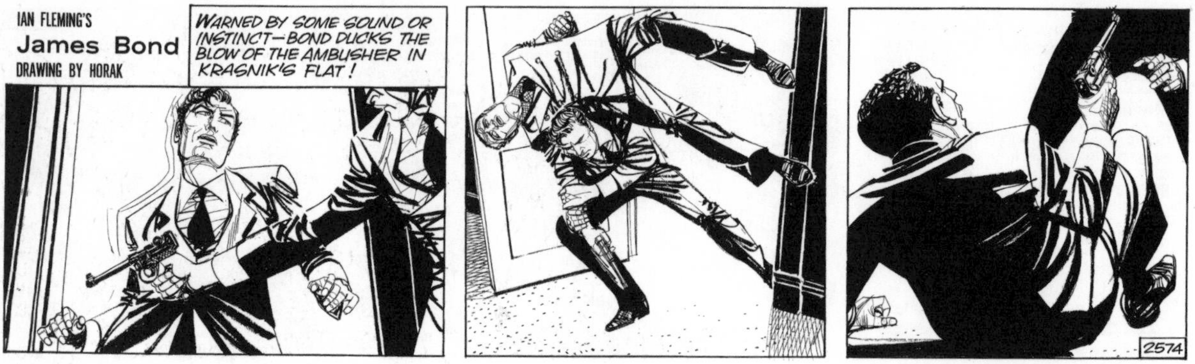
IAN FLEMING'S
James Bond
DRAWING BY HORAK
WARNED BY SOME SOUND OR INSTINCT—BOND DUCKS THE BLOW OF THE AMBUSHER IN KRASNIK'S FLAT!
2574

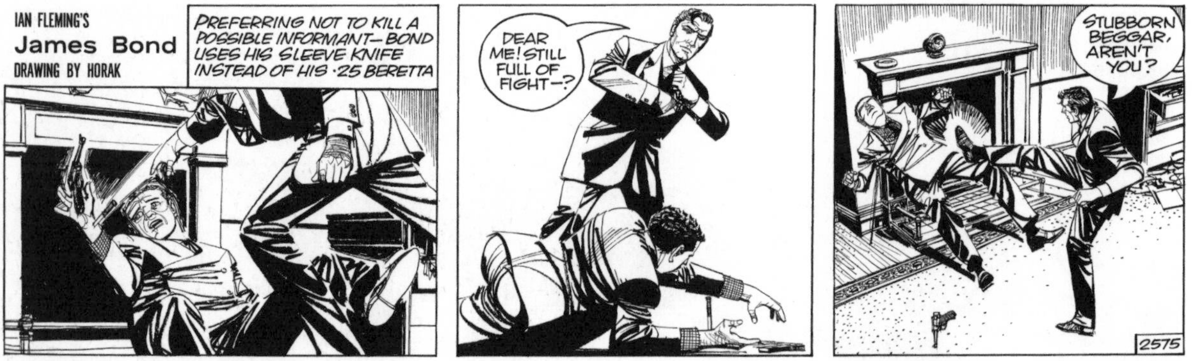
IAN FLEMING'S
James Bond
DRAWING BY HORAK
PREFERRING NOT TO KILL A POSSIBLE INFORMANT—BOND USES HIS SLEEVE KNIFE INSTEAD OF HIS ·25 BERETTA
DEAR ME! STILL FULL OF FIGHT—?
STUBBORN BEGGAR, AREN'T YOU?
2575

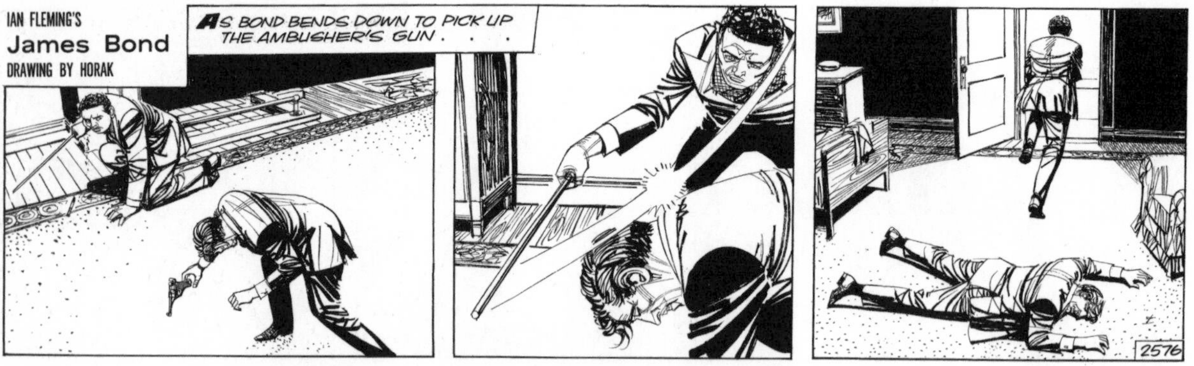
IAN FLEMING'S
James Bond
DRAWING BY HORAK
AS BOND BENDS DOWN TO PICK UP THE AMBUSHER'S GUN . . . .
2576

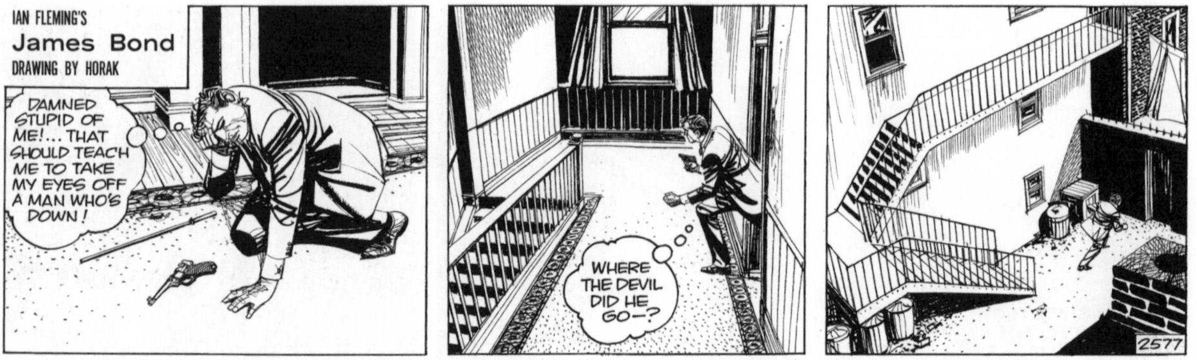
IAN FLEMING'S
James Bond
DRAWING BY HORAK
DAMNED STUPID OF ME!... THAT SHOULD TEACH ME TO TAKE MY EYES OFF A MAN WHO'S DOWN!
WHERE THE DEVIL DID HE GO—?
2577

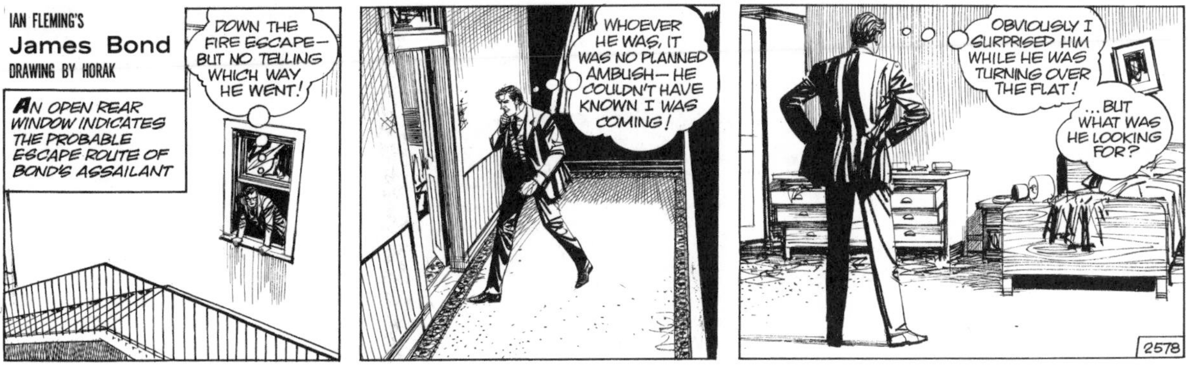
IAN FLEMING'S
James Bond
DRAWING BY HORAK
AN OPEN REAR WINDOW INDICATES THE PROBABLE ESCAPE ROUTE OF BOND'S ASSAILANT
DOWN THE FIRE ESCAPE— BUT NO TELLING WHICH WAY HE WENT!
WHOEVER HE WAS, IT WAS NO PLANNED AMBUSH—HE COULDN'T HAVE KNOWN I WAS COMING!
OBVIOUSLY I SURPRISED HIM WHILE HE WAS TURNING OVER THE FLAT!
...BUT WHAT WAS HE LOOKING FOR?
2578

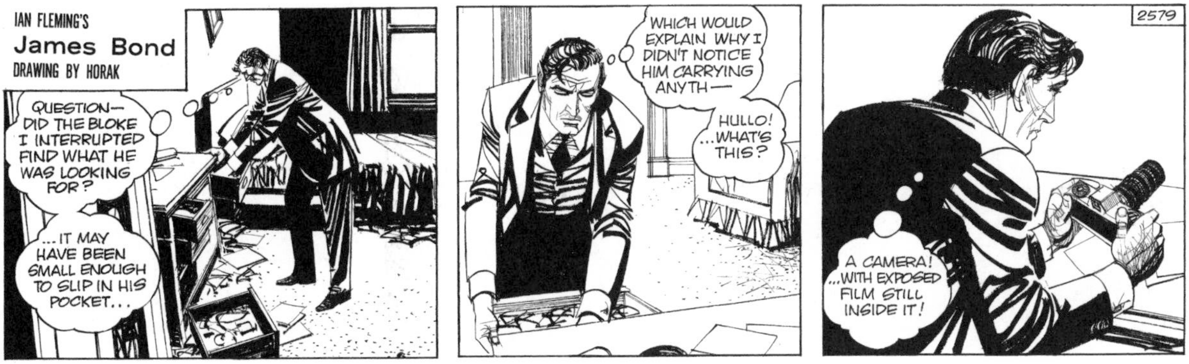
IAN FLEMING'S
James Bond
DRAWING BY HORAK
QUESTION— DID THE BLOKE I INTERRUPTED FIND WHAT HE WAS LOOKING FOR?
...IT MAY HAVE BEEN SMALL ENOUGH TO SLIP IN HIS POCKET...
WHICH WOULD EXPLAIN WHY I DIDN'T NOTICE HIM CARRYING ANYTH—
HULLO! ...WHAT'S THIS?
2579
A CAMERA! ...WITH EXPOSED FILM STILL INSIDE IT!

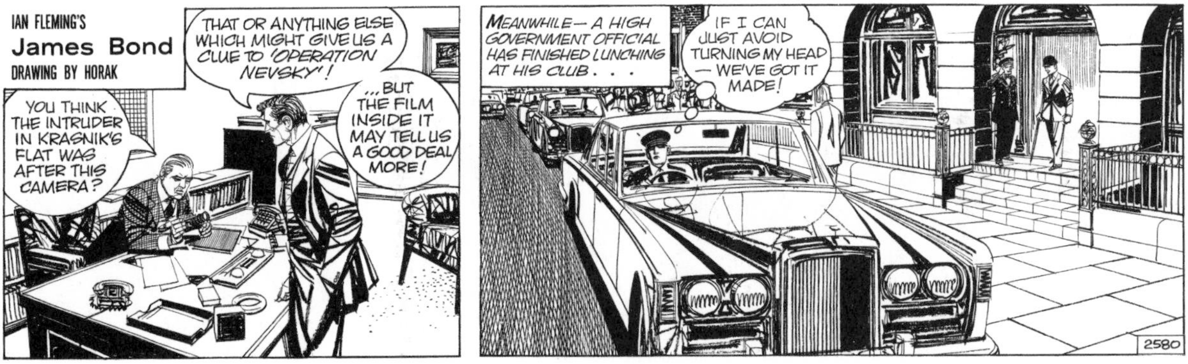
IAN FLEMING'S
James Bond
DRAWING BY HORAK
YOU THINK THE INTRUDER IN KRASNIK'S FLAT WAS AFTER THIS CAMERA?
THAT OR ANYTHING ELSE WHICH MIGHT GIVE US A CLUE TO 'OPERATION NEVSKY'!
...BUT THE FILM INSIDE IT MAY TELL US A GOOD DEAL MORE!
MEANWHILE— A HIGH GOVERNMENT OFFICIAL HAS FINISHED LUNCHING AT HIS CLUB . . .
IF I CAN JUST AVOID TURNING MY HEAD — WE'VE GOT IT MADE!
2580

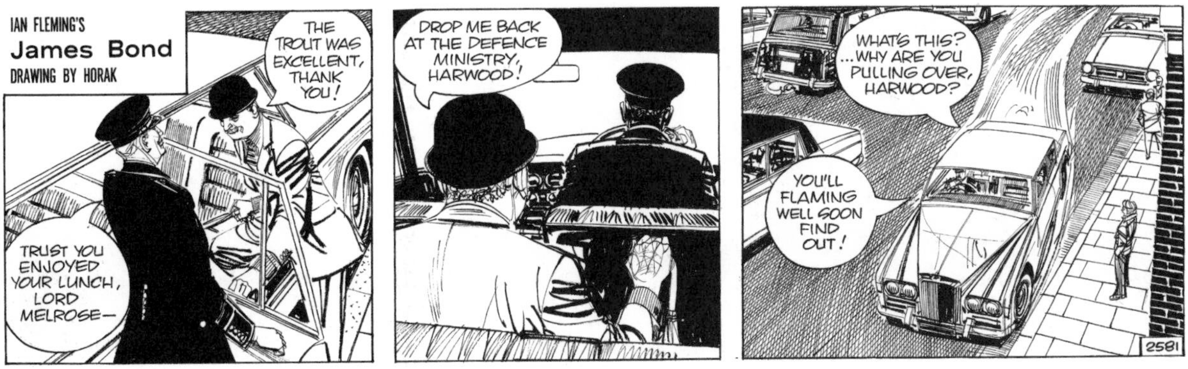
IAN FLEMING'S
James Bond
DRAWING BY HORAK
TRUST YOU ENJOYED YOUR LUNCH, LORD MELROSE—
THE TROUT WAS EXCELLENT, THANK YOU!
DROP ME BACK AT THE DEFENCE MINISTRY, HARWOOD!
WHAT'S THIS? ...WHY ARE YOU PULLING OVER, HARWOOD?
YOU'LL FLAMING WELL SOON FIND OUT!
2581

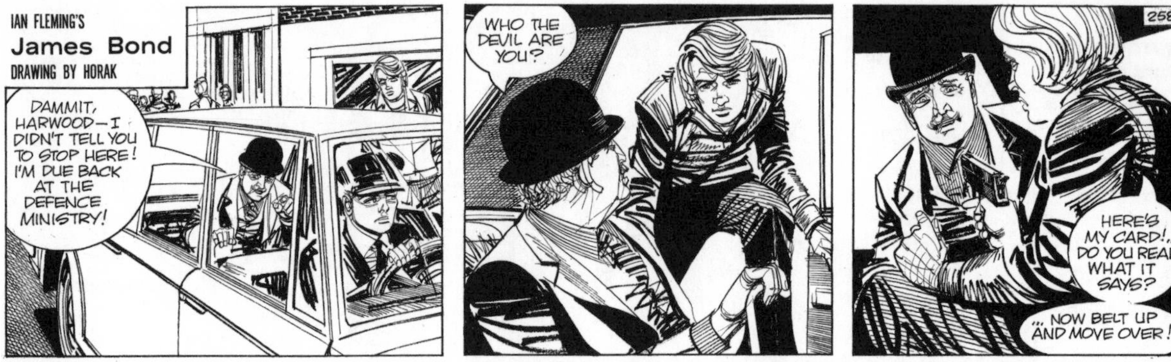
IAN FLEMING'S
James Bond
DRAWING BY HORAK
DAMMIT, HARWOOD—I DIDN'T TELL YOU TO STOP HERE! I'M DUE BACK AT THE DEFENCE MINISTRY!
WHO THE DEVIL ARE YOU?
2582
HERE'S MY CARD!... DO YOU READ WHAT IT SAYS?
... NOW BELT UP AND MOVE OVER!

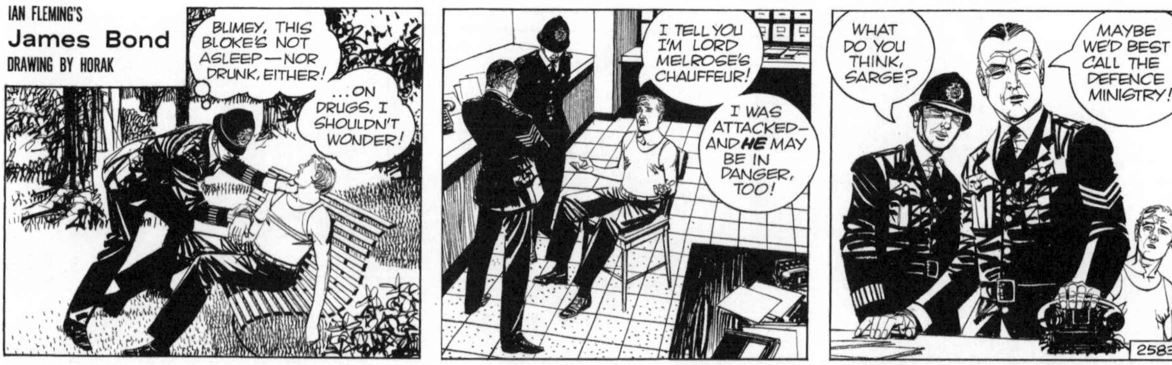
IAN FLEMING'S
James Bond
DRAWING BY HORAK
BLIMEY, THIS BLOKE'S NOT ASLEEP—NOR DRUNK, EITHER!
...ON DRUGS, I SHOULDN'T WONDER!
I TELL YOU I'M LORD MELROSE'S CHAUFFEUR!
I WAS ATTACKED—AND HE MAY BE IN DANGER, TOO!
WHAT DO YOU THINK, SARGE?
MAYBE WE'D BEST CALL THE DEFENCE MINISTRY!
2583

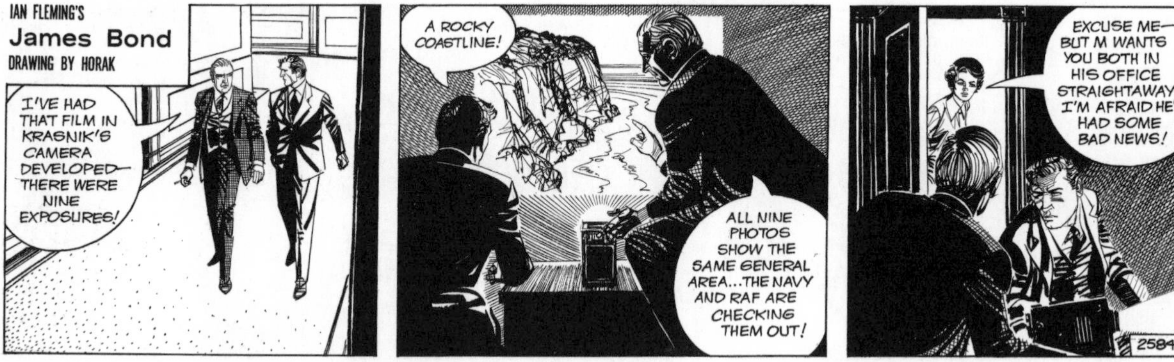
IAN FLEMING'S
James Bond
DRAWING BY HORAK
I'VE HAD THAT FILM IN KRASNIK'S CAMERA DEVELOPED—THERE WERE NINE EXPOSURES!
A ROCKY COASTLINE!
ALL NINE PHOTOS SHOW THE SAME GENERAL AREA... THE NAVY AND RAF ARE CHECKING THEM OUT!
EXCUSE ME—BUT M WANTS YOU BOTH IN HIS OFFICE STRAIGHTAWAY! I'M AFRAID HE'S HAD SOME BAD NEWS!
2584

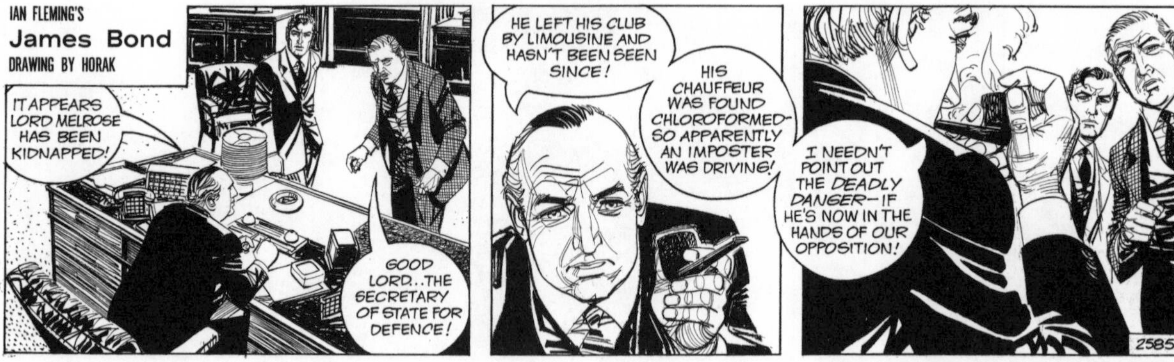
IAN FLEMING'S
James Bond
DRAWING BY HORAK
IT APPEARS LORD MELROSE HAS BEEN KIDNAPPED!
GOOD LORD... THE SECRETARY OF STATE FOR DEFENCE!
HE LEFT HIS CLUB BY LIMOUSINE AND HASN'T BEEN SEEN SINCE!
HIS CHAUFFEUR WAS FOUND CHLOROFORMED—SO APPARENTLY AN IMPOSTER WAS DRIVING!
I NEEDN'T POINT OUT THE DEADLY DANGER—IF HE'S NOW IN THE HANDS OF OUR OPPOSITION!
2585

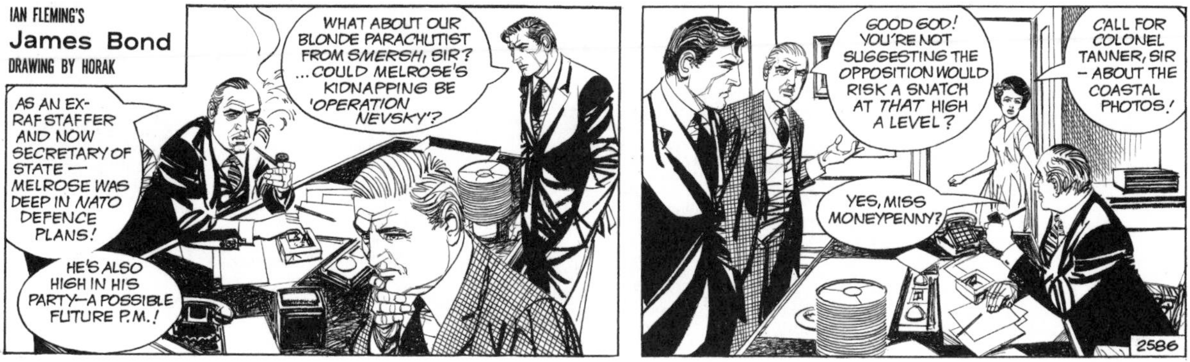
IAN FLEMING'S
James Bond
DRAWING BY HORAK
AS AN EX-RAF STAFFER AND NOW SECRETARY OF STATE — MELROSE WAS DEEP IN NATO DEFENCE PLANS!
WHAT ABOUT OUR BLONDE PARACHUTIST FROM SMERSH, SIR? ...COULD MELROSE'S KIDNAPPING BE 'OPERATION NEVSKY'?
HE'S ALSO HIGH IN HIS PARTY—A POSSIBLE FUTURE P.M.!
GOOD GOD! YOU'RE NOT SUGGESTING THE OPPOSITION WOULD RISK A SNATCH AT THAT HIGH A LEVEL?
CALL FOR COLONEL TANNER, SIR — ABOUT THE COASTAL PHOTOS!
YES, MISS MONEYPENNY?
2586

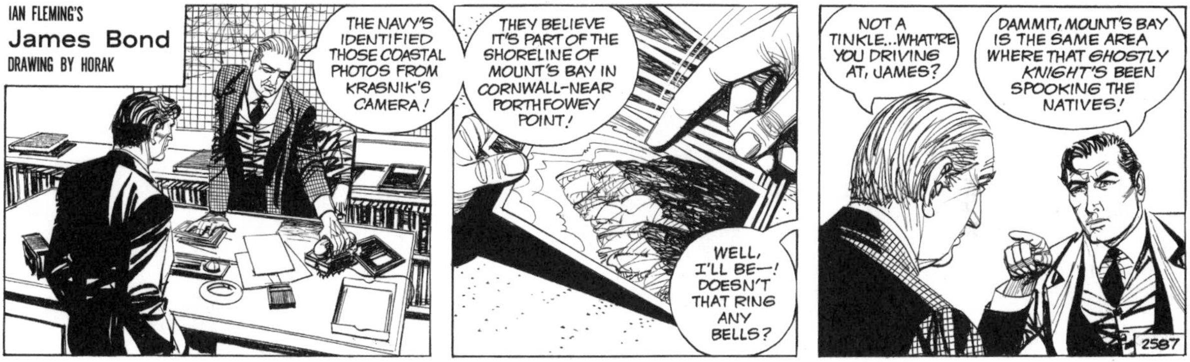
IAN FLEMING'S
James Bond
DRAWING BY HORAK
THE NAVY'S IDENTIFIED THOSE COASTAL PHOTOS FROM KRASNIK'S CAMERA!
THEY BELIEVE IT'S PART OF THE SHORELINE OF MOUNT'S BAY IN CORNWALL-NEAR PORTHFOWEY POINT!
WELL, I'LL BE—! DOESN'T THAT RING ANY BELLS?
NOT A TINKLE...WHAT'RE YOU DRIVING AT, JAMES?
DAMMIT, MOUNT'S BAY IS THE SAME AREA WHERE THAT GHOSTLY KNIGHT'S BEEN SPOOKING THE NATIVES!
2587

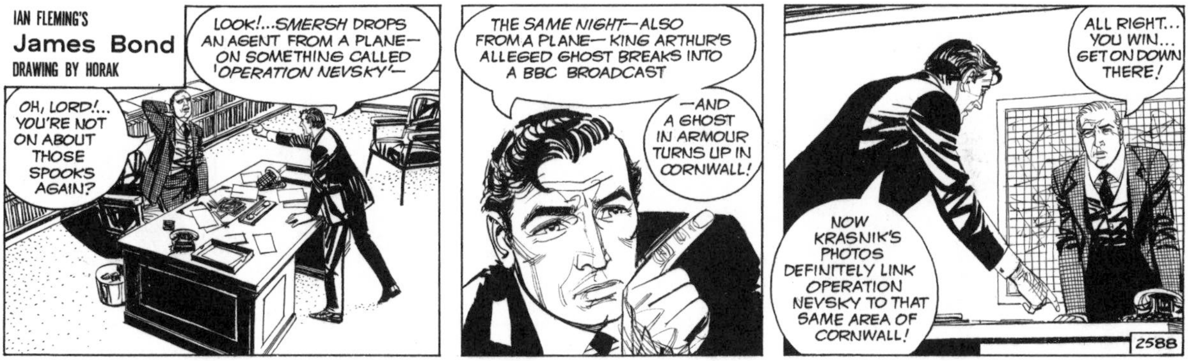
IAN FLEMING'S
James Bond
DRAWING BY HORAK
LOOK!...SMERSH DROPS AN AGENT FROM A PLANE— ON SOMETHING CALLED 'OPERATION NEVSKY'—
OH, LORD!... YOU'RE NOT ON ABOUT THOSE SPOOKS AGAIN?
THE SAME NIGHT—ALSO FROM A PLANE— KING ARTHUR'S ALLEGED GHOST BREAKS INTO A BBC BROADCAST
—AND A GHOST IN ARMOUR TURNS UP IN CORNWALL!
NOW KRASNIK'S PHOTOS DEFINITELY LINK OPERATION NEVSKY TO THAT SAME AREA OF CORNWALL!
ALL RIGHT... YOU WIN... GET ON DOWN THERE!
2588

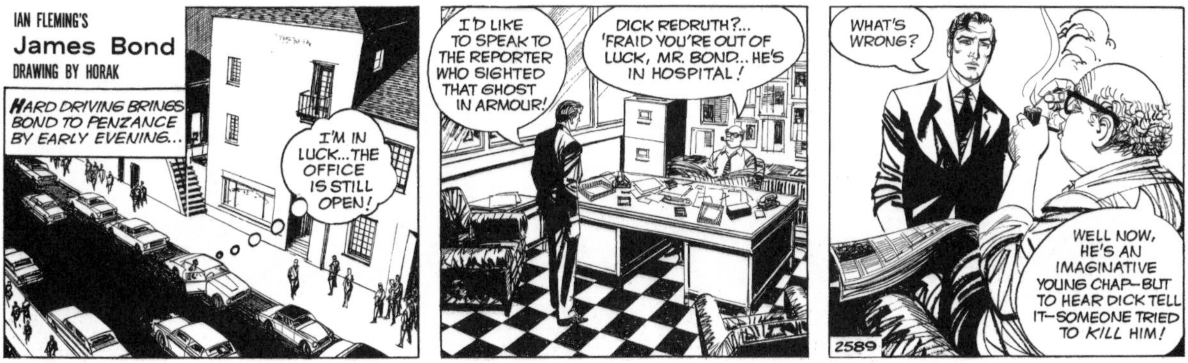
IAN FLEMING'S
James Bond
DRAWING BY HORAK
HARD DRIVING BRINGS BOND TO PENZANCE BY EARLY EVENING...
I'M IN LUCK...THE OFFICE IS STILL OPEN!
I'D LIKE TO SPEAK TO THE REPORTER WHO SIGHTED THAT GHOST IN ARMOUR!
DICK REDRUTH?... 'FRAID YOU'RE OUT OF LUCK, MR. BOND...HE'S IN HOSPITAL!
2589
WHAT'S WRONG?
WELL NOW, HE'S AN IMAGINATIVE YOUNG CHAP—BUT TO HEAR DICK TELL IT—SOMEONE TRIED TO KILL HIM!

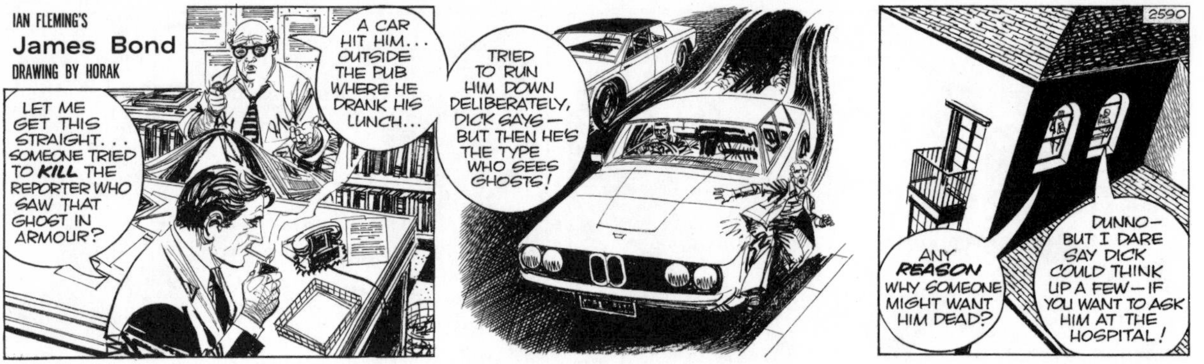
IAN FLEMING'S
James Bond
DRAWING BY HORAK
LET ME GET THIS STRAIGHT. . . SOMEONE TRIED TO KILL THE REPORTER WHO SAW THAT GHOST IN ARMOUR?
A CAR HIT HIM... OUTSIDE THE PUB WHERE HE DRANK HIS LUNCH...
TRIED TO RUN HIM DOWN DELIBERATELY, DICK SAYS— BUT THEN HE'S THE TYPE WHO SEES GHOSTS!
2590
ANY REASON WHY SOMEONE MIGHT WANT HIM DEAD?
DUNNO— BUT I DARE SAY DICK COULD THINK UP A FEW—IF YOU WANT TO ASK HIM AT THE HOSPITAL!

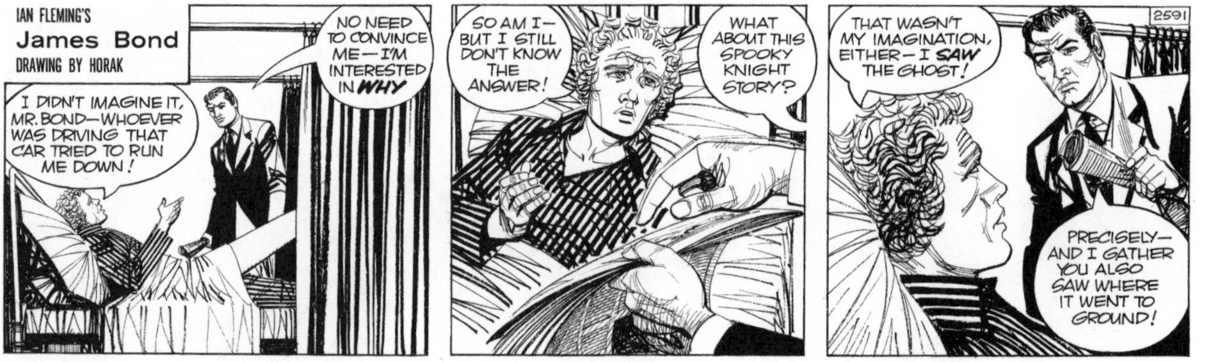
IAN FLEMING'S
James Bond
DRAWING BY HORAK
I DIDN'T IMAGINE IT, MR. BOND—WHOEVER WAS DRIVING THAT CAR TRIED TO RUN ME DOWN!
NO NEED TO CONVINCE ME—I'M INTERESTED IN WHY
SO AM I— BUT I STILL DON'T KNOW THE ANSWER!
WHAT ABOUT THIS SPOOKY KNIGHT STORY?
2591
THAT WASN'T MY IMAGINATION, EITHER—I SAW THE GHOST!
PRECISELY— AND I GATHER YOU ALSO SAW WHERE IT WENT TO GROUND!

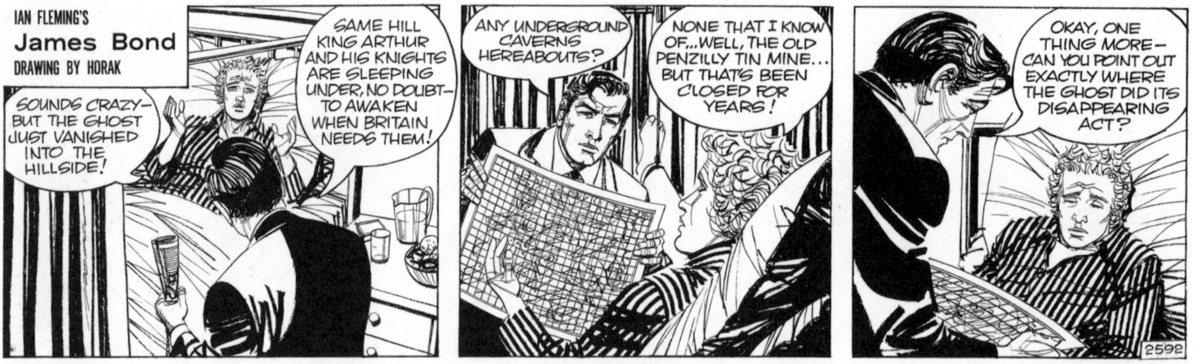
IAN FLEMING'S
James Bond
DRAWING BY HORAK
SOUNDS CRAZY— BUT THE GHOST JUST VANISHED INTO THE HILLSIDE!
SAME HILL KING ARTHUR AND HIS KNIGHTS ARE SLEEPING UNDER, NO DOUBT— TO AWAKEN WHEN BRITAIN NEEDS THEM!
ANY UNDERGROUND CAVERNS HEREABOUTS?
NONE THAT I KNOW OF... WELL, THE OLD PENZILLY TIN MINE... BUT THAT'S BEEN CLOSED FOR YEARS!
OKAY, ONE THING MORE— CAN YOU POINT OUT EXACTLY WHERE THE GHOST DID ITS DISAPPEARING ACT?
2592

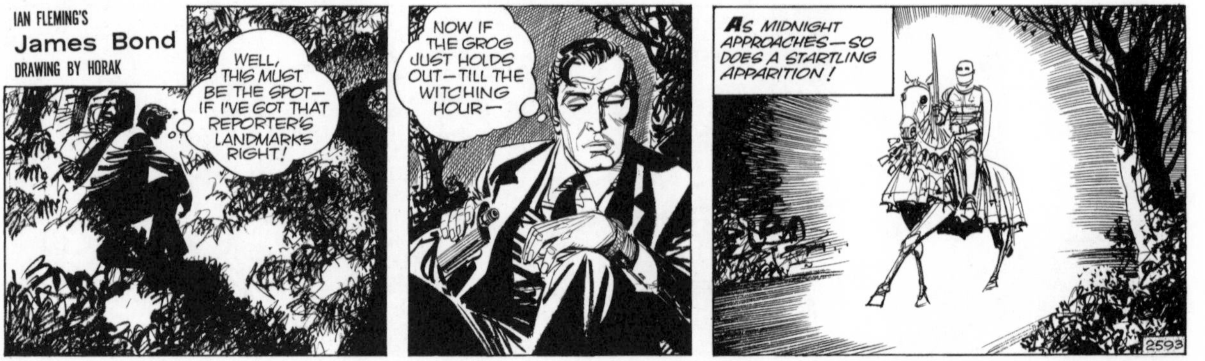
IAN FLEMING'S
James Bond
DRAWING BY HORAK
WELL, THIS MUST BE THE SPOT— IF I'VE GOT THAT REPORTER'S LANDMARKS RIGHT!
NOW IF THE GROG JUST HOLDS OUT—TILL THE WITCHING HOUR—
AS MIDNIGHT APPROACHES—SO DOES A STARTLING APPARITION!
2593

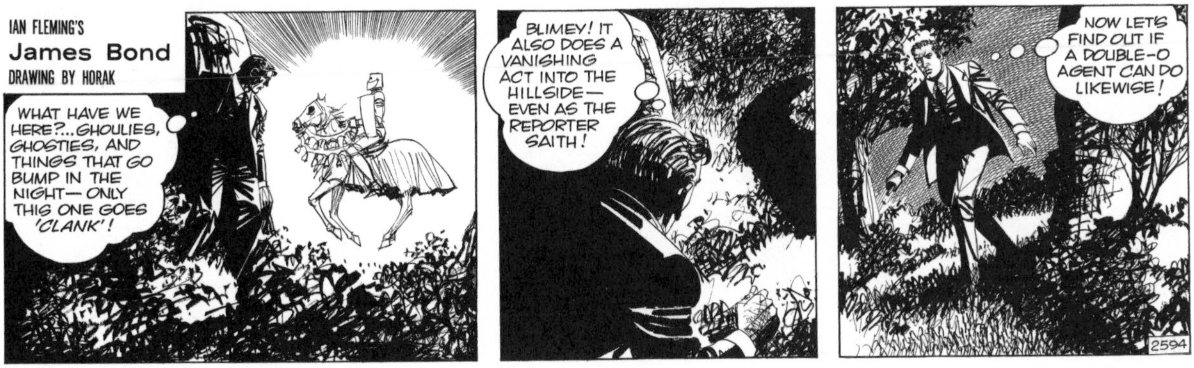
IAN FLEMING'S
James Bond
DRAWING BY HORAK
WHAT HAVE WE HERE?.. GHOULIES, GHOSTIES, AND THINGS THAT GO BUMP IN THE NIGHT—ONLY THIS ONE GOES 'CLANK'!
BLIMEY! IT ALSO DOES A VANISHING ACT INTO THE HILLSIDE—EVEN AS THE REPORTER SAITH!
NOW LET'S FIND OUT IF A DOUBLE-O AGENT CAN DO LIKEWISE!
2594

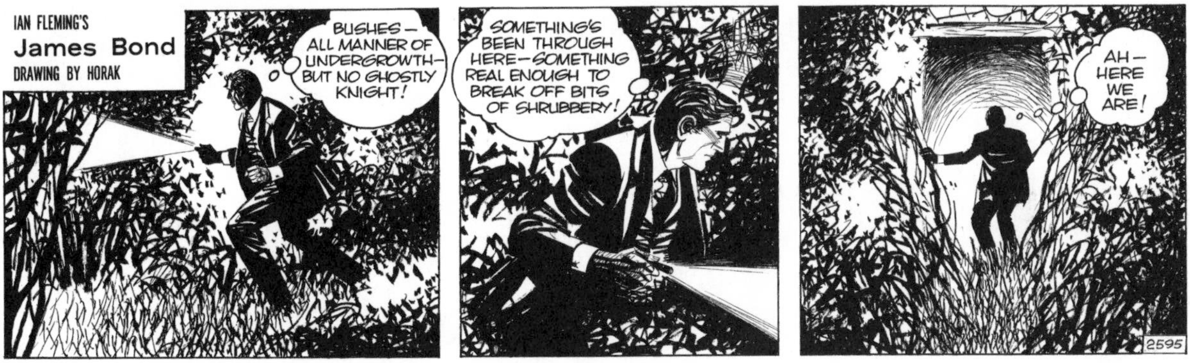
IAN FLEMING'S
James Bond
DRAWING BY HORAK
BUSHES—ALL MANNER OF UNDERGROWTH—BUT NO GHOSTLY KNIGHT!
SOMETHING'S BEEN THROUGH HERE—SOMETHING REAL ENOUGH TO BREAK OFF BITS OF SHRUBBERY!
AH—HERE WE ARE!
2595

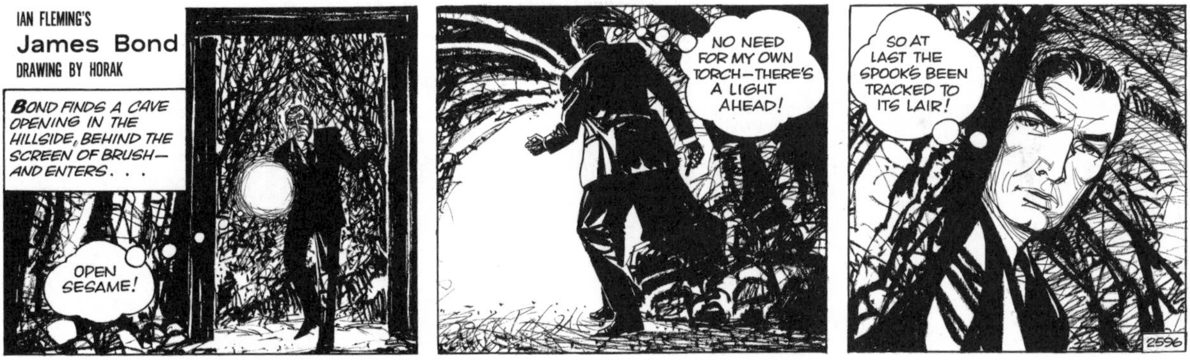
IAN FLEMING'S
James Bond
DRAWING BY HORAK
BOND FINDS A CAVE OPENING IN THE HILLSIDE, BEHIND THE SCREEN OF BRUSH—AND ENTERS . . .
OPEN SESAME!
NO NEED FOR MY OWN TORCH—THERE'S A LIGHT AHEAD!
SO AT LAST THE SPOOK'S BEEN TRACKED TO ITS LAIR!
2596

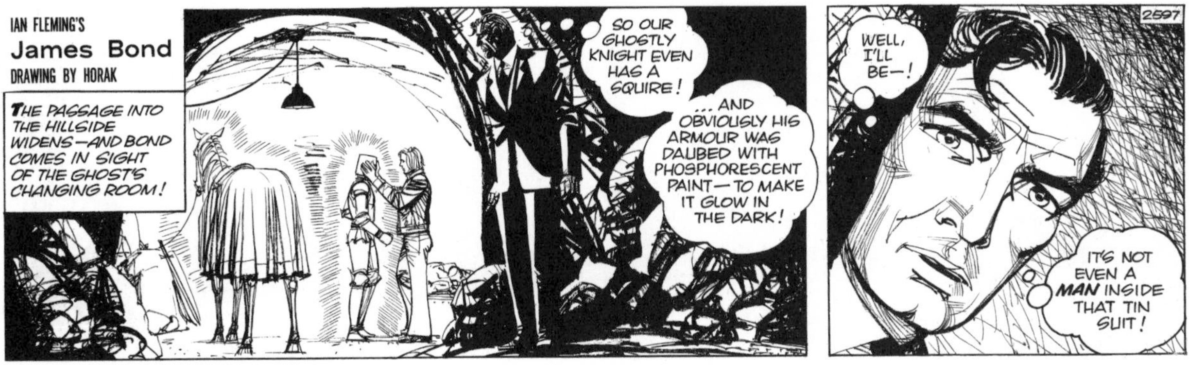
IAN FLEMING'S
James Bond
DRAWING BY HORAK
THE PASSAGE INTO THE HILLSIDE WIDENS—AND BOND COMES IN SIGHT OF THE GHOST'S CHANGING ROOM!
SO OUR GHOSTLY KNIGHT EVEN HAS A SQUIRE!
. . . AND OBVIOUSLY HIS ARMOUR WAS DAUBED WITH PHOSPHORESCENT PAINT—TO MAKE IT GLOW IN THE DARK!
2597
WELL, I'LL BE—!
IT'S NOT EVEN A MAN INSIDE THAT TIN SUIT!

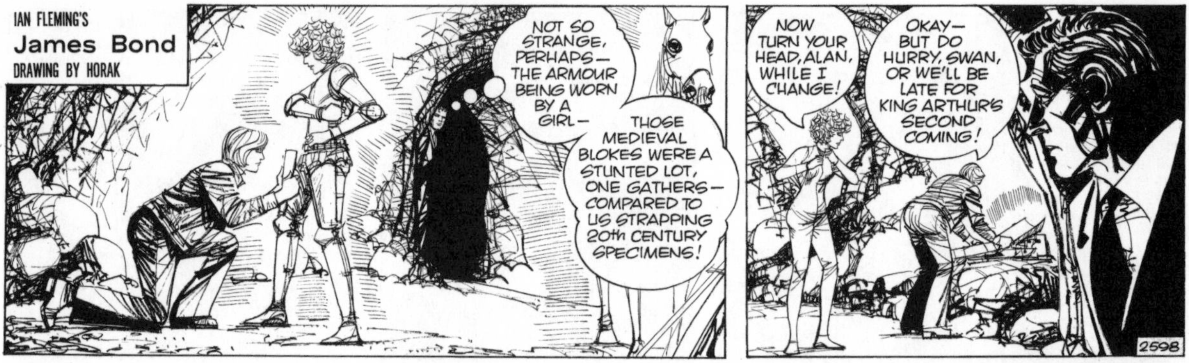
IAN FLEMING'S
James Bond
DRAWING BY HORAK
NOT SO STRANGE, PERHAPS — THE ARMOUR BEING WORN BY A GIRL—
THOSE MEDIEVAL BLOKES WERE A STUNTED LOT, ONE GATHERS — COMPARED TO US STRAPPING 20th CENTURY SPECIMENS!
NOW TURN YOUR HEAD, ALAN, WHILE I CHANGE!
OKAY— BUT DO HURRY, SWAN, OR WE'LL BE LATE FOR KING ARTHUR'S SECOND COMING!
2598

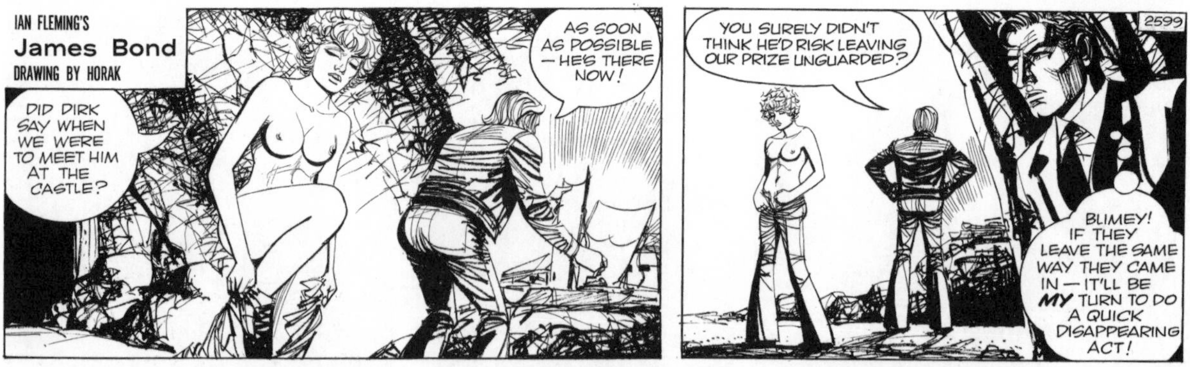
IAN FLEMING'S
James Bond
DRAWING BY HORAK
DID DIRK SAY WHEN WE WERE TO MEET HIM AT THE CASTLE?
AS SOON AS POSSIBLE — HE'S THERE NOW!
2599
YOU SURELY DIDN'T THINK HE'D RISK LEAVING OUR PRIZE UNGUARDED?
BLIMEY! IF THEY LEAVE THE SAME WAY THEY CAME IN — IT'LL BE MY TURN TO DO A QUICK DISAPPEARING ACT!

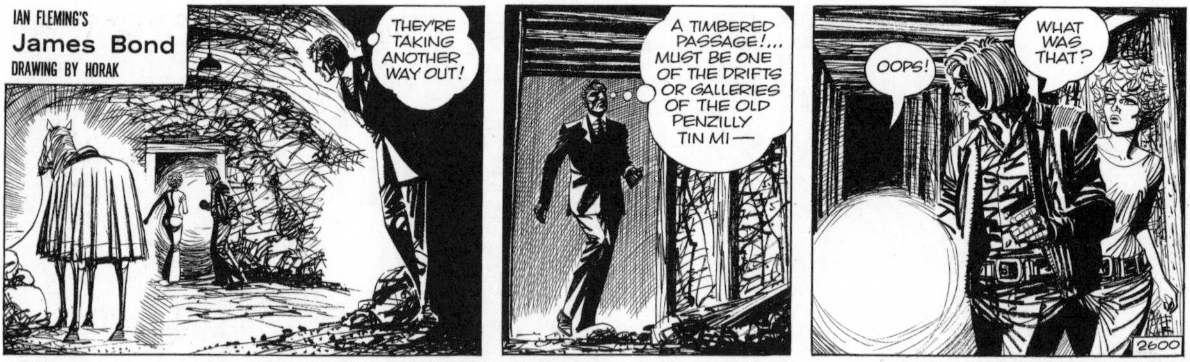
IAN FLEMING'S
James Bond
DRAWING BY HORAK
THEY'RE TAKING ANOTHER WAY OUT!
A TIMBERED PASSAGE!... MUST BE ONE OF THE DRIFTS OR GALLERIES OF THE OLD PENZILLY TIN MI —
OOPS!
WHAT WAS THAT?
2600

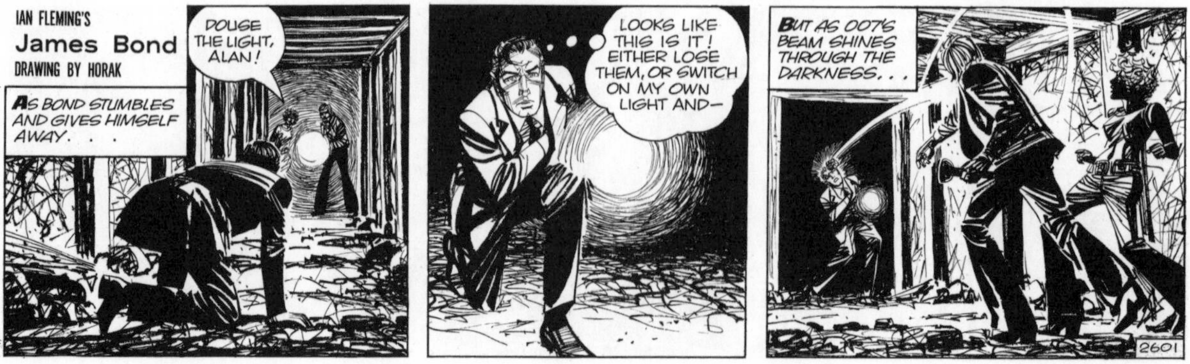
IAN FLEMING'S
James Bond
DRAWING BY HORAK
AS BOND STUMBLES AND GIVES HIMSELF AWAY. . .
DOUSE THE LIGHT, ALAN!
LOOKS LIKE THIS IS IT! EITHER LOSE THEM, OR SWITCH ON MY OWN LIGHT AND—
BUT AS 007'S BEAM SHINES THROUGH THE DARKNESS. . .
2601

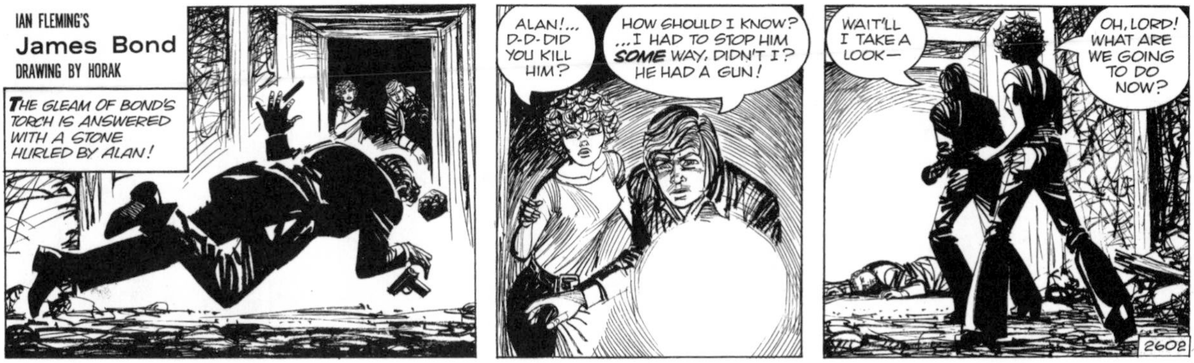
IAN FLEMING'S
James Bond
DRAWING BY HORAK
THE GLEAM OF BOND'S TORCH IS ANSWERED WITH A STONE HURLED BY ALAN!
ALAN!... D-D-DID YOU KILL HIM?
HOW SHOULD I KNOW? ...I HAD TO STOP HIM SOME WAY, DIDN'T I? HE HAD A GUN!
WAIT'LL I TAKE A LOOK—
OH, LORD! WHAT ARE WE GOING TO DO NOW?
2602

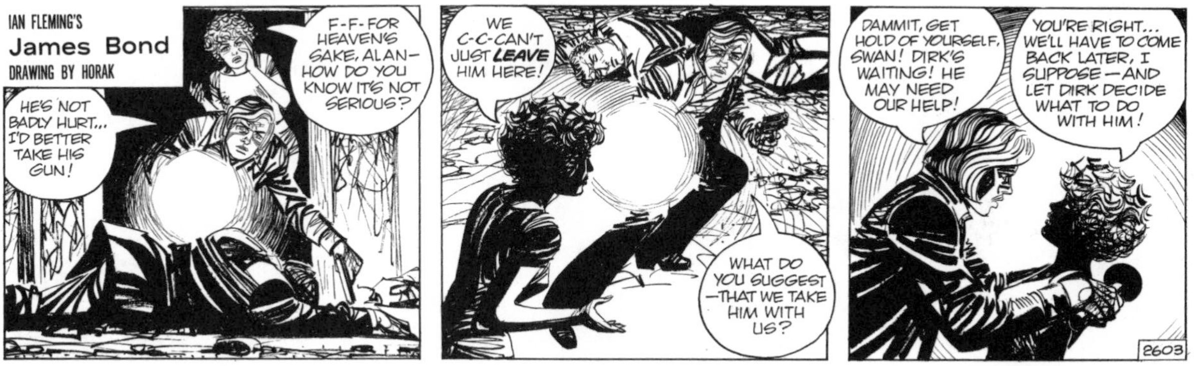
IAN FLEMING'S
James Bond
DRAWING BY HORAK
HE'S NOT BADLY HURT... I'D BETTER TAKE HIS GUN!
F-F-FOR HEAVEN'S SAKE, ALAN— HOW DO YOU KNOW IT'S NOT SERIOUS?
WE C-C-CAN'T JUST LEAVE HIM HERE!
WHAT DO YOU SUGGEST —THAT WE TAKE HIM WITH US?
DAMMIT, GET HOLD OF YOURSELF, SWAN! DIRK'S WAITING! HE MAY NEED OUR HELP!
YOU'RE RIGHT... WE'LL HAVE TO COME BACK LATER, I SUPPOSE —AND LET DIRK DECIDE WHAT TO DO WITH HIM!
2603

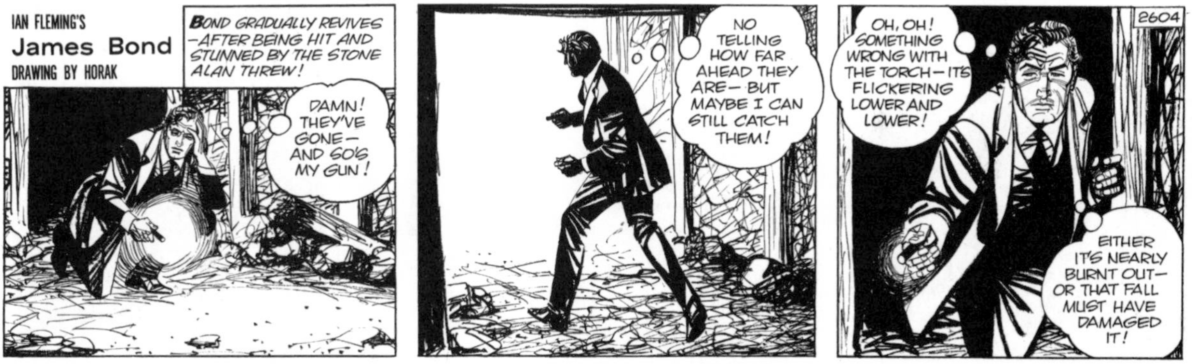
IAN FLEMING'S
James Bond
DRAWING BY HORAK
BOND GRADUALLY REVIVES —AFTER BEING HIT AND STUNNED BY THE STONE ALAN THREW!
DAMN! THEY'VE GONE— AND SO'S MY GUN!
NO TELLING HOW FAR AHEAD THEY ARE— BUT MAYBE I CAN STILL CATCH THEM!
2604
OH, OH! SOMETHING WRONG WITH THE TORCH— IT'S FLICKERING LOWER AND LOWER!
EITHER IT'S NEARLY BURNT OUT— OR THAT FALL MUST HAVE DAMAGED IT!

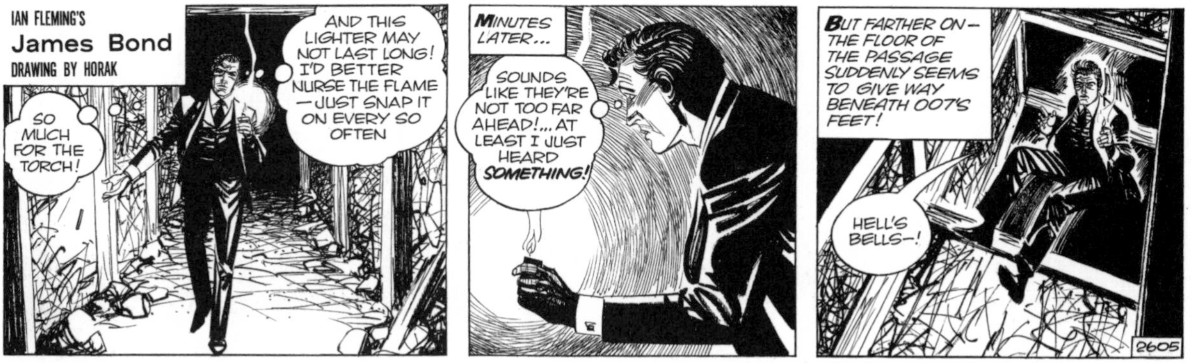
IAN FLEMING'S
James Bond
DRAWING BY HORAK
SO MUCH FOR THE TORCH!
AND THIS LIGHTER MAY NOT LAST LONG! I'D BETTER NURSE THE FLAME —JUST SNAP IT ON EVERY SO OFTEN
MINUTES LATER...
SOUNDS LIKE THEY'RE NOT TOO FAR AHEAD!... AT LEAST I JUST HEARD SOMETHING!
BUT FARTHER ON— THE FLOOR OF THE PASSAGE SUDDENLY SEEMS TO GIVE WAY BENEATH 007'S FEET!
HELL'S BELLS—!
2605

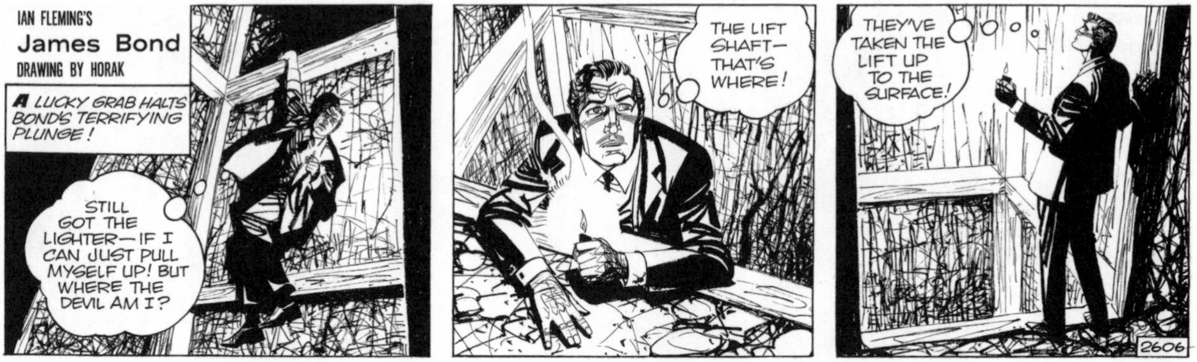
IAN FLEMING'S
James Bond
DRAWING BY HORAK
A LUCKY GRAB HALTS BOND'S TERRIFYING PLUNGE!
STILL GOT THE LIGHTER—IF I CAN JUST PULL MYSELF UP! BUT WHERE THE DEVIL AM I?
THE LIFT SHAFT—THAT'S WHERE!
THEY'VE TAKEN THE LIFT UP TO THE SURFACE!
2606

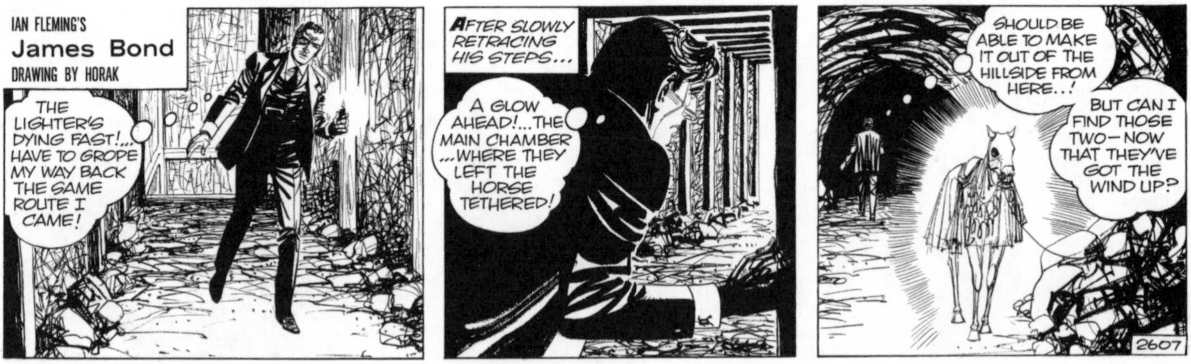
IAN FLEMING'S
James Bond
DRAWING BY HORAK
THE LIGHTER'S DYING FAST!... HAVE TO GROPE MY WAY BACK THE SAME ROUTE I CAME!
AFTER SLOWLY RETRACING HIS STEPS...
A GLOW AHEAD!...THE MAIN CHAMBER ...WHERE THEY LEFT THE HORSE TETHERED!
SHOULD BE ABLE TO MAKE IT OUT OF THE HILLSIDE FROM HERE...!
BUT CAN I FIND THOSE TWO—NOW THAT THEY'VE GOT THE WIND UP?
2607

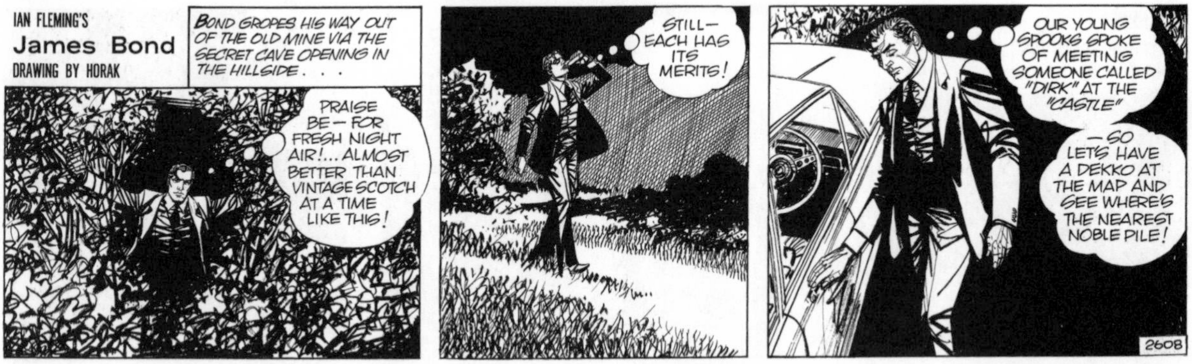
IAN FLEMING'S
James Bond
DRAWING BY HORAK
BOND GROPES HIS WAY OUT OF THE OLD MINE VIA THE SECRET CAVE OPENING IN THE HILLSIDE . . .
PRAISE BE—FOR FRESH NIGHT AIR!... ALMOST BETTER THAN VINTAGE SCOTCH AT A TIME LIKE THIS!
STILL—EACH HAS ITS MERITS!
OUR YOUNG SPOOKS SPOKE OF MEETING SOMEONE CALLED "DIRK" AT THE "CASTLE"
—SO LET'S HAVE A DEKKO AT THE MAP AND SEE WHERE'S THE NEAREST NOBLE PILE!
2608

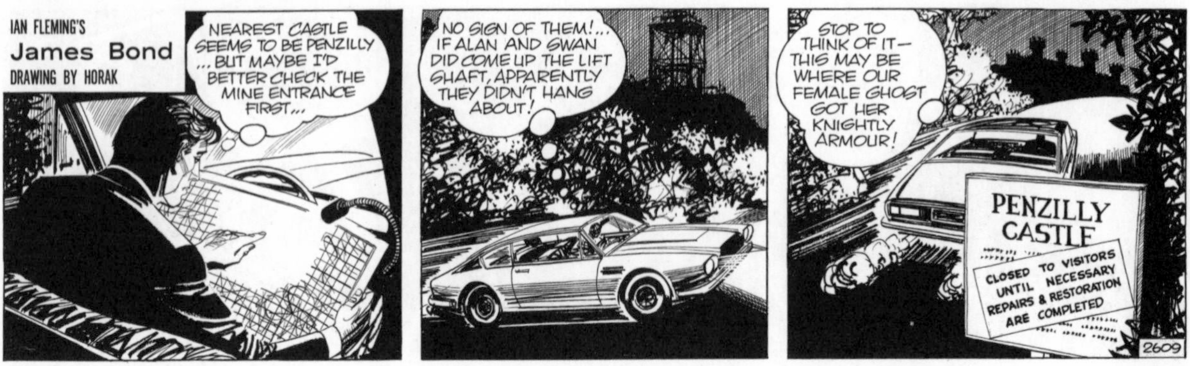
IAN FLEMING'S
James Bond
DRAWING BY HORAK
NEAREST CASTLE SEEMS TO BE PENZILLY ...BUT MAYBE I'D BETTER CHECK THE MINE ENTRANCE FIRST...
NO SIGN OF THEM!... IF ALAN AND SWAN DID COME UP THE LIFT SHAFT, APPARENTLY THEY DIDN'T HANG ABOUT!
STOP TO THINK OF IT—THIS MAY BE WHERE OUR FEMALE GHOST GOT HER KNIGHTLY ARMOUR!
PENZILLY CASTLE
CLOSED TO VISITORS UNTIL NECESSARY REPAIRS & RESTORATION ARE COMPLETED
2609

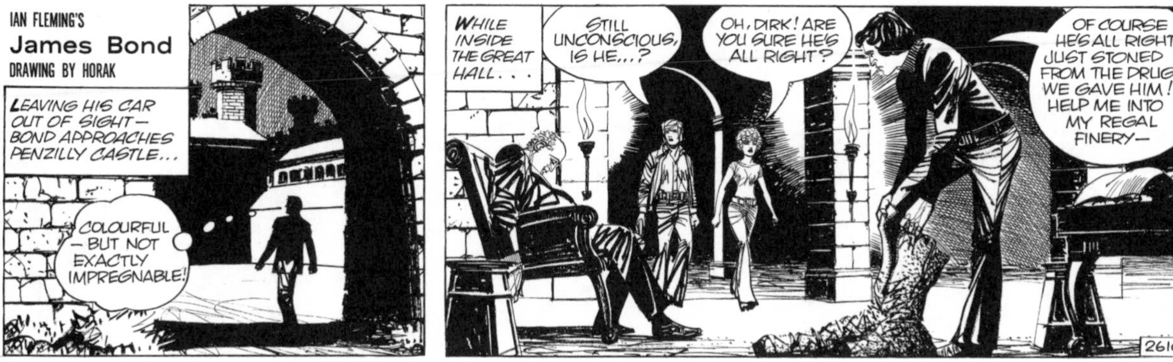
IAN FLEMING'S
James Bond
DRAWING BY HORAK
LEAVING HIS CAR OUT OF SIGHT— BOND APPROACHES PENZILLY CASTLE...
COLOURFUL — BUT NOT EXACTLY IMPREGNABLE!
WHILE INSIDE THE GREAT HALL...
STILL UNCONSCIOUS, IS HE...?
OH, DIRK! ARE YOU SURE HE'S ALL RIGHT?
OF COURSE HE'S ALL RIGHT— JUST STONED FROM THE DRUG WE GAVE HIM! HELP ME INTO MY REGAL FINERY—
2610

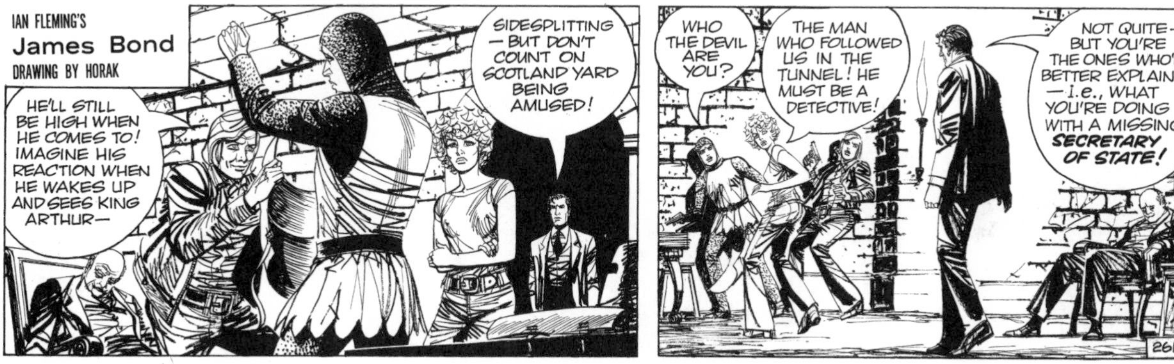
IAN FLEMING'S
James Bond
DRAWING BY HORAK
HE'LL STILL BE HIGH WHEN HE COMES TO! IMAGINE HIS REACTION WHEN HE WAKES UP AND SEES KING ARTHUR—
SIDESPLITTING — BUT DON'T COUNT ON SCOTLAND YARD BEING AMUSED!
WHO THE DEVIL ARE YOU?
THE MAN WHO FOLLOWED US IN THE TUNNEL! HE MUST BE A DETECTIVE!
NOT QUITE— BUT YOU'RE THE ONES WHO'D BETTER EXPLAIN — I.E., WHAT YOU'RE DOING WITH A MISSING SECRETARY OF STATE!
2611

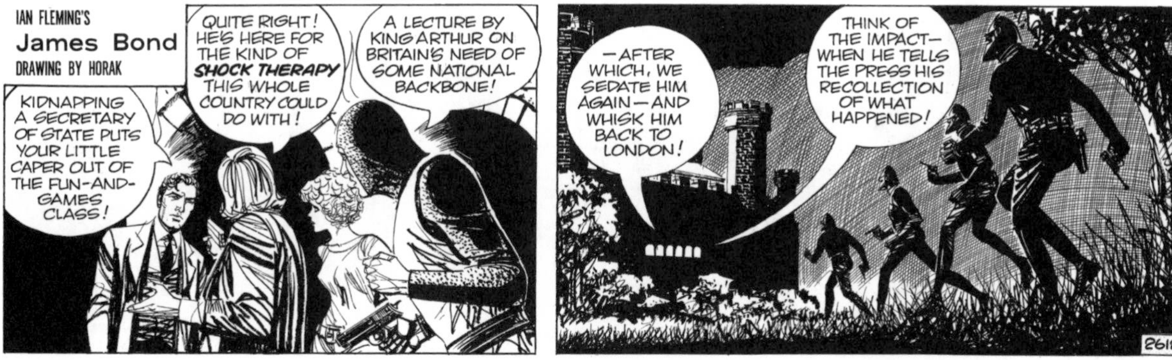
IAN FLEMING'S
James Bond
DRAWING BY HORAK
KIDNAPPING A SECRETARY OF STATE PUTS YOUR LITTLE CAPER OUT OF THE FUN-AND-GAMES CLASS!
QUITE RIGHT! HE'S HERE FOR THE KIND OF SHOCK THERAPY THIS WHOLE COUNTRY COULD DO WITH!
A LECTURE BY KING ARTHUR ON BRITAIN'S NEED OF SOME NATIONAL BACKBONE!
—AFTER WHICH, WE SEDATE HIM AGAIN—AND WHISK HIM BACK TO LONDON!
THINK OF THE IMPACT— WHEN HE TELLS THE PRESS HIS RECOLLECTION OF WHAT HAPPENED!
2612

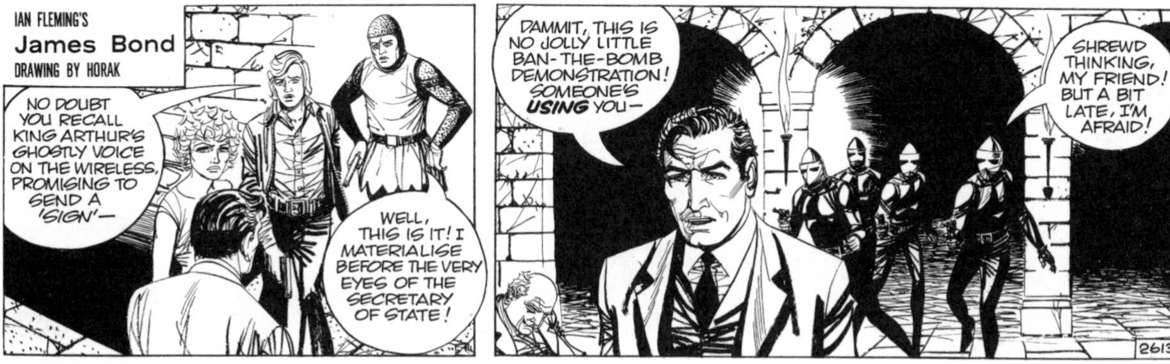
IAN FLEMING'S
James Bond
DRAWING BY HORAK
NO DOUBT YOU RECALL KING ARTHUR'S GHOSTLY VOICE ON THE WIRELESS, PROMISING TO SEND A 'SIGN'—
WELL, THIS IS IT! I MATERIALISE BEFORE THE VERY EYES OF THE SECRETARY OF STATE!
DAMMIT, THIS IS NO JOLLY LITTLE BAN-THE-BOMB DEMONSTRATION! SOMEONE'S USING YOU—
SHREWD THINKING, MY FRIEND! BUT A BIT LATE, I'M AFRAID!
2613

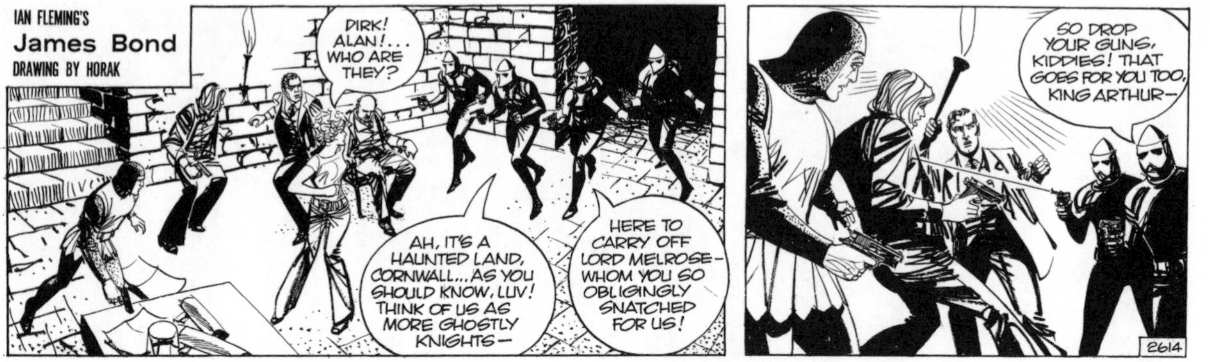
IAN FLEMING'S
James Bond
DRAWING BY HORAK
DIRK! ALAN!... WHO ARE THEY?
AH, IT'S A HAUNTED LAND, CORNWALL... AS YOU SHOULD KNOW, LUV! THINK OF US AS MORE GHOSTLY KNIGHTS—
HERE TO CARRY OFF LORD MELROSE—WHOM YOU SO OBLIGINGLY SNATCHED FOR US!
SO DROP YOUR GUNS, KIDDIES! THAT GOES FOR YOU TOO, KING ARTHUR—
2614

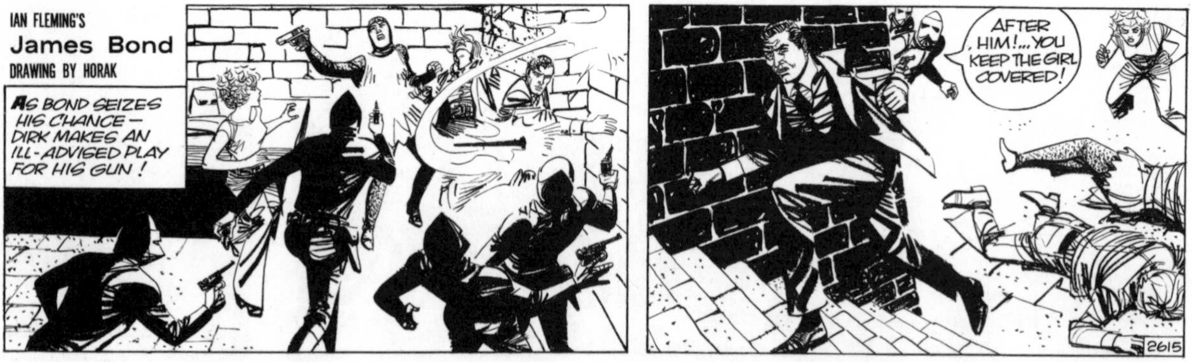
IAN FLEMING'S
James Bond
DRAWING BY HORAK
AS BOND SEIZES HIS CHANCE—DIRK MAKES AN ILL-ADVISED PLAY FOR HIS GUN!
AFTER HIM!... YOU KEEP THE GIRL COVERED!
2615

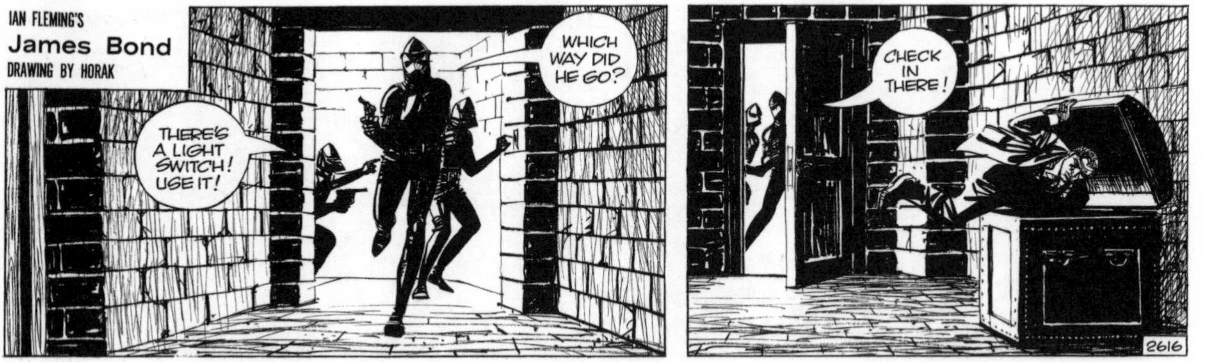
IAN FLEMING'S
James Bond
DRAWING BY HORAK
WHICH WAY DID HE GO?
THERE'S A LIGHT SWITCH! USE IT!
CHECK IN THERE!
2616

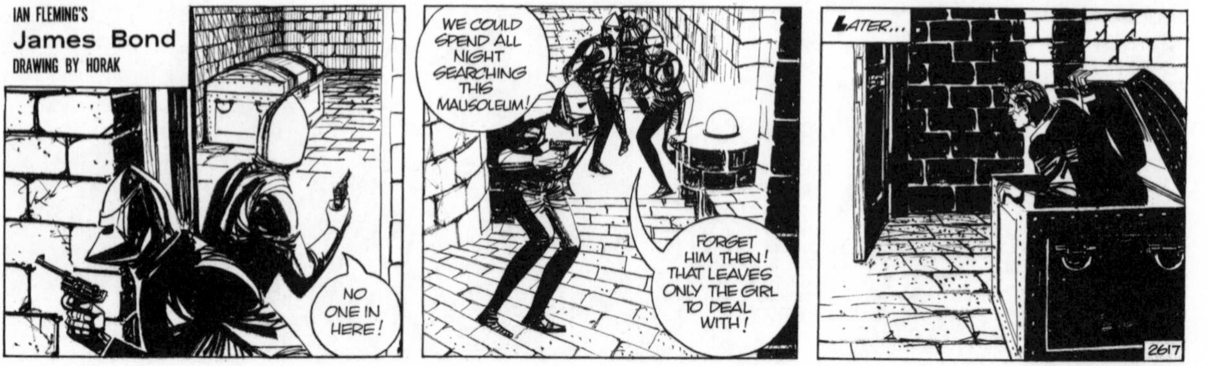
IAN FLEMING'S
James Bond
DRAWING BY HORAK
NO ONE IN HERE!
WE COULD SPEND ALL NIGHT SEARCHING THIS MAUSOLEUM!
FORGET HIM THEN! THAT LEAVES ONLY THE GIRL TO DEAL WITH!
LATER...
2617

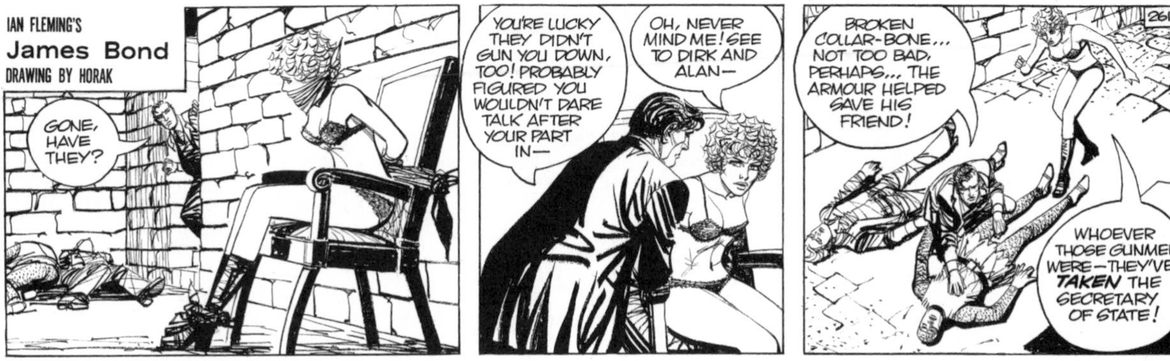
IAN FLEMING'S
James Bond
DRAWING BY HORAK
GONE, HAVE THEY?
YOU'RE LUCKY THEY DIDN'T GUN YOU DOWN, TOO! PROBABLY FIGURED YOU WOULDN'T DARE TALK AFTER YOUR PART IN—
OH, NEVER MIND ME! SEE TO DIRK AND ALAN—
2618
BROKEN COLLAR-BONE,... NOT TOO BAD, PERHAPS,... THE ARMOUR HELPED SAVE HIS FRIEND!
WHOEVER THOSE GUNMEN WERE—THEY'VE TAKEN THE SECRETARY OF STATE!

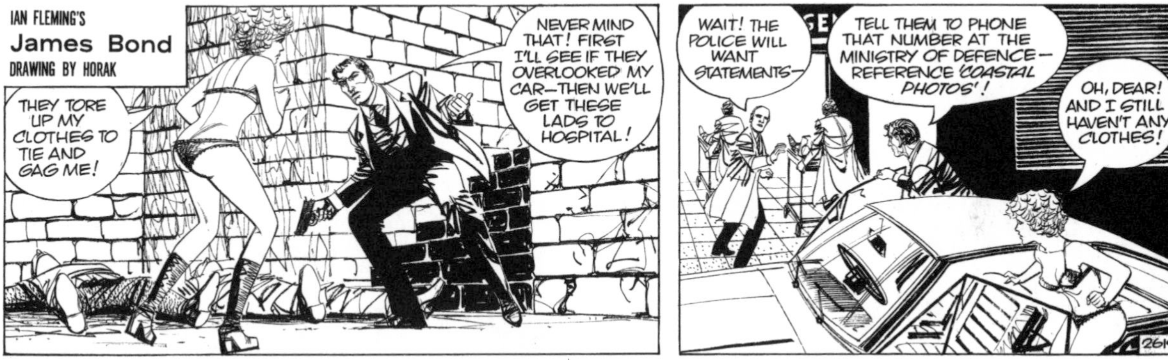
IAN FLEMING'S
James Bond
DRAWING BY HORAK
THEY TORE UP MY CLOTHES TO TIE AND GAG ME!
NEVER MIND THAT! FIRST I'LL SEE IF THEY OVERLOOKED MY CAR—THEN WE'LL GET THESE LADS TO HOSPITAL!
WAIT! THE POLICE WILL WANT STATEMENTS—
TELL THEM TO PHONE THAT NUMBER AT THE MINISTRY OF DEFENCE—REFERENCE 'COASTAL PHOTOS'!
OH, DEAR! AND I STILL HAVEN'T ANY CLOTHES!
2619

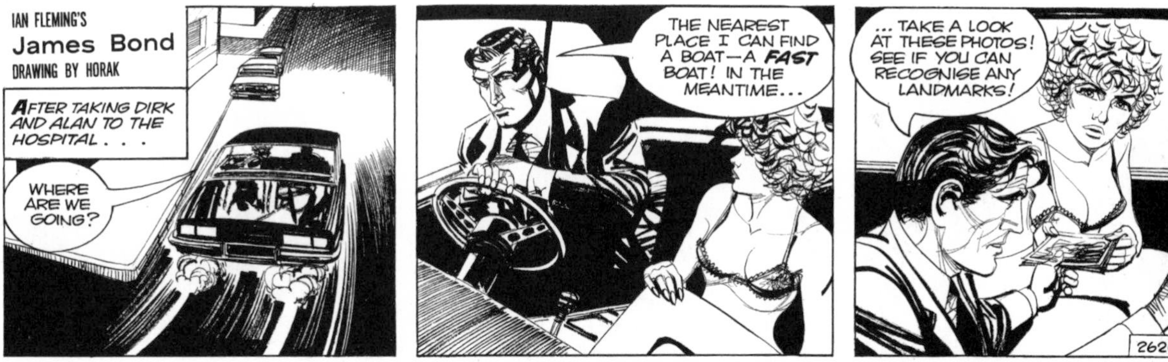
IAN FLEMING'S
James Bond
DRAWING BY HORAK
AFTER TAKING DIRK AND ALAN TO THE HOSPITAL . . .
WHERE ARE WE GOING?
THE NEAREST PLACE I CAN FIND A BOAT—A FAST BOAT! IN THE MEANTIME...
... TAKE A LOOK AT THESE PHOTOS! SEE IF YOU CAN RECOGNISE ANY LANDMARKS!
2620

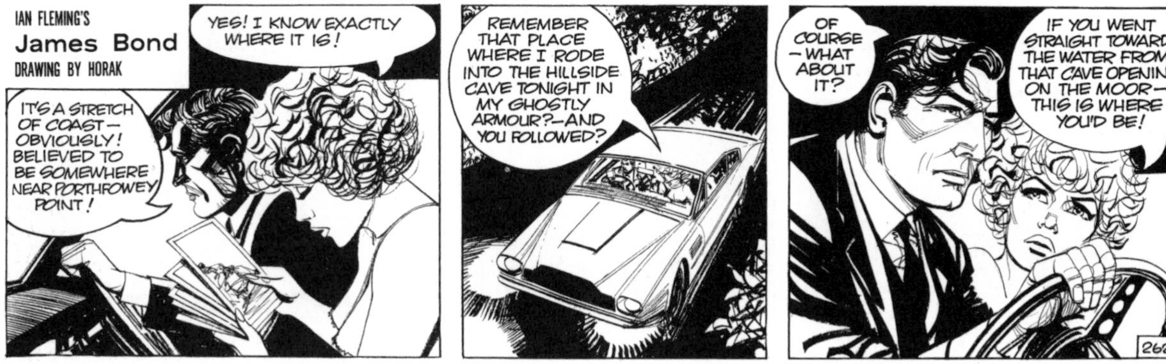
IAN FLEMING'S
James Bond
DRAWING BY HORAK
YES! I KNOW EXACTLY WHERE IT IS!
IT'S A STRETCH OF COAST—OBVIOUSLY! BELIEVED TO BE SOMEWHERE NEAR PORTHFOWEY POINT!
REMEMBER THAT PLACE WHERE I RODE INTO THE HILLSIDE CAVE TONIGHT IN MY GHOSTLY ARMOUR?—AND YOU FOLLOWED?
OF COURSE—WHAT ABOUT IT?
IF YOU WENT STRAIGHT TOWARDS THE WATER FROM THAT CAVE OPENING ON THE MOOR—THIS IS WHERE YOU'D BE!
2621

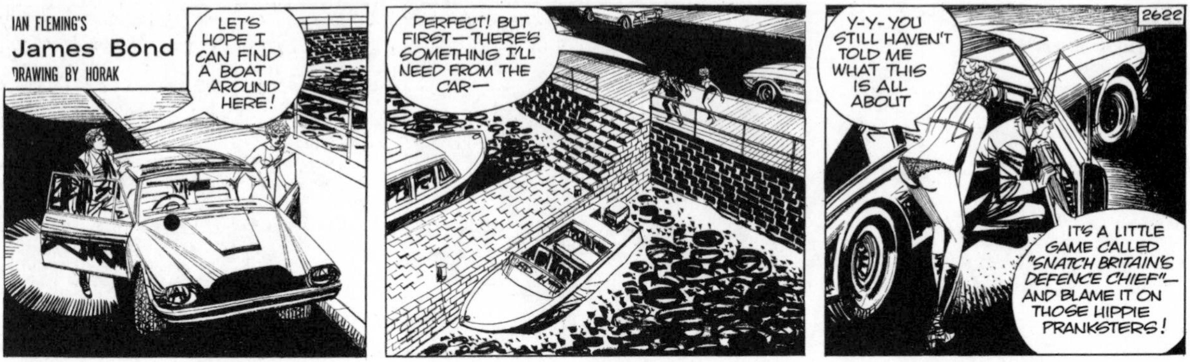
IAN FLEMING'S
James Bond
DRAWING BY HORAK
LET'S HOPE I CAN FIND A BOAT AROUND HERE!
PERFECT! BUT FIRST—THERE'S SOMETHING I'LL NEED FROM THE CAR—
2622
Y-Y-YOU STILL HAVEN'T TOLD ME WHAT THIS IS ALL ABOUT
IT'S A LITTLE GAME CALLED "SNATCH BRITAIN'S DEFENCE CHIEF"—AND BLAME IT ON THOSE HIPPIE PRANKSTERS!

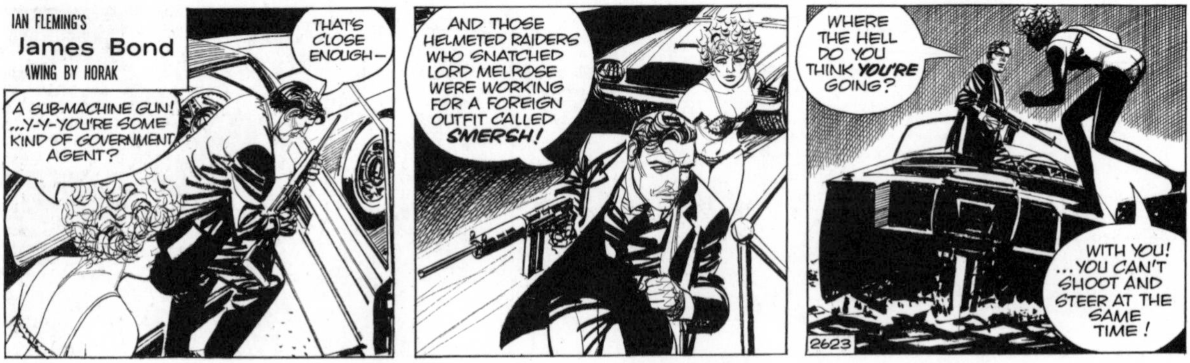
IAN FLEMING'S
James Bond
AWING BY HORAK
THAT'S CLOSE ENOUGH—
A SUB-MACHINE GUN! ...Y-Y-YOU'RE SOME KIND OF GOVERNMENT AGENT?
AND THOSE HELMETED RAIDERS WHO SNATCHED LORD MELROSE WERE WORKING FOR A FOREIGN OUTFIT CALLED SMERSH!
WHERE THE HELL DO YOU THINK YOU'RE GOING?
WITH YOU! ...YOU CAN'T SHOOT AND STEER AT THE SAME TIME!
2623

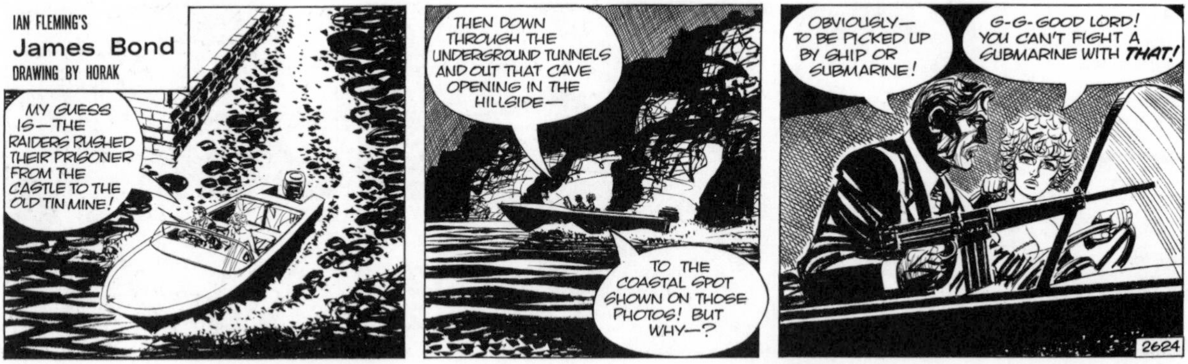
IAN FLEMING'S
James Bond
DRAWING BY HORAK
MY GUESS IS—THE RAIDERS RUSHED THEIR PRISONER FROM THE CASTLE TO THE OLD TIN MINE!
THEN DOWN THROUGH THE UNDERGROUND TUNNELS AND OUT THAT CAVE OPENING IN THE HILLSIDE—
TO THE COASTAL SPOT SHOWN ON THOSE PHOTOS! BUT WHY—?
OBVIOUSLY—TO BE PICKED UP BY SHIP OR SUBMARINE!
G-G-GOOD LORD! YOU CAN'T FIGHT A SUBMARINE WITH THAT!
2624

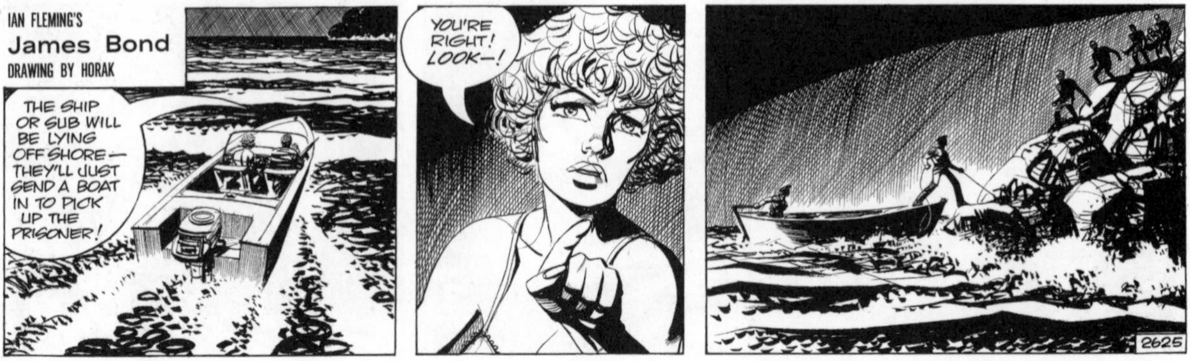
IAN FLEMING'S
James Bond
DRAWING BY HORAK
THE SHIP OR SUB WILL BE LYING OFF SHORE—THEY'LL JUST SEND A BOAT IN TO PICK UP THE PRISONER!
YOU'RE RIGHT! LOOK—!
2625

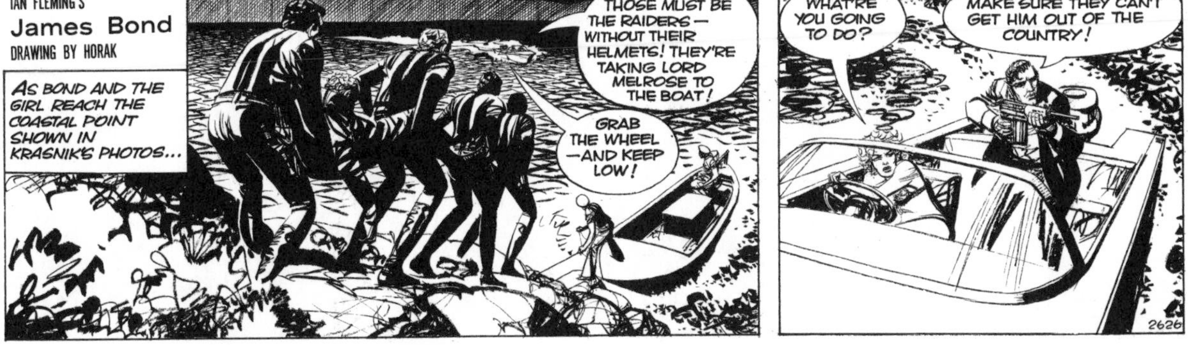
IAN FLEMING'S
James Bond
DRAWING BY HORAK
AS BOND AND THE GIRL REACH THE COASTAL POINT SHOWN IN KRASNIK'S PHOTOS...
THOSE MUST BE THE RAIDERS — WITHOUT THEIR HELMETS! THEY'RE TAKING LORD MELROSE TO THE BOAT!
GRAB THE WHEEL —AND KEEP LOW!
WHAT'RE YOU GOING TO DO?
MAKE SURE THEY CAN'T GET HIM OUT OF THE COUNTRY!
2626

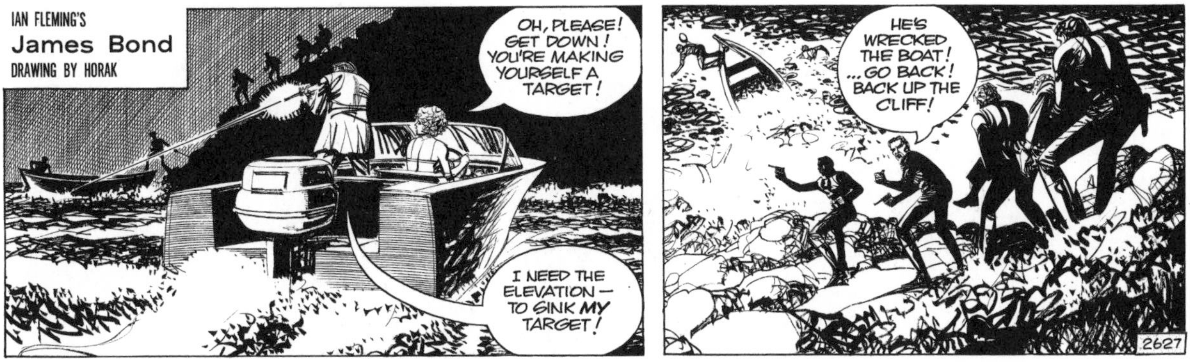
IAN FLEMING'S
James Bond
DRAWING BY HORAK
OH, PLEASE! GET DOWN! YOU'RE MAKING YOURSELF A TARGET!
I NEED THE ELEVATION — TO SINK MY TARGET!
HE'S WRECKED THE BOAT! ...GO BACK! BACK UP THE CLIFF!
2627

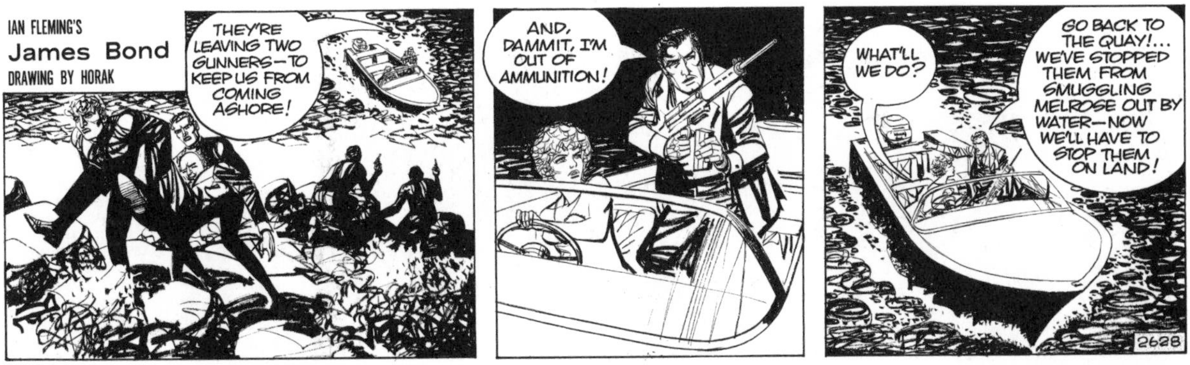
IAN FLEMING'S
James Bond
DRAWING BY HORAK
THEY'RE LEAVING TWO GUNNERS—TO KEEP US FROM COMING ASHORE!
AND, DAMMIT, I'M OUT OF AMMUNITION!
WHAT'LL WE DO?
GO BACK TO THE QUAY!... WE'VE STOPPED THEM FROM SMUGGLING MELROSE OUT BY WATER—NOW WE'LL HAVE TO STOP THEM ON LAND!
2628

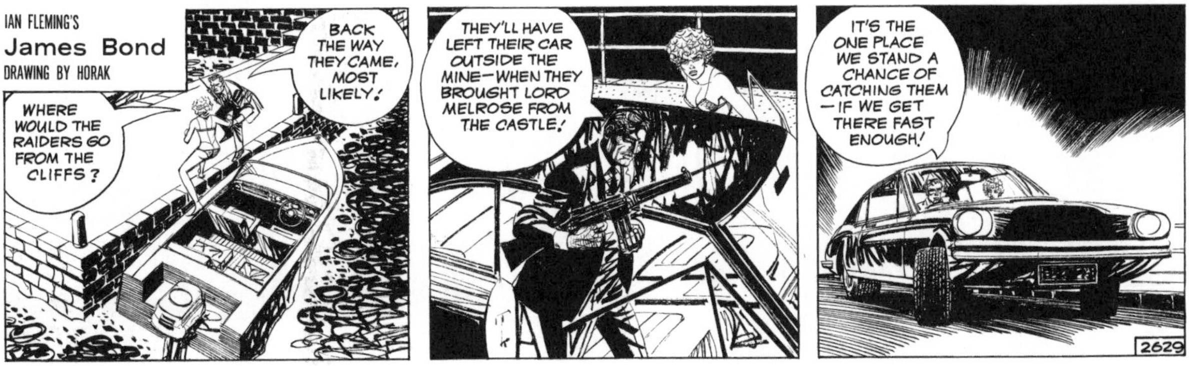
IAN FLEMING'S
James Bond
DRAWING BY HORAK
WHERE WOULD THE RAIDERS GO FROM THE CLIFFS?
BACK THE WAY THEY CAME, MOST LIKELY!
THEY'LL HAVE LEFT THEIR CAR OUTSIDE THE MINE—WHEN THEY BROUGHT LORD MELROSE FROM THE CASTLE!
IT'S THE ONE PLACE WE STAND A CHANCE OF CATCHING THEM —IF WE GET THERE FAST ENOUGH!
2629

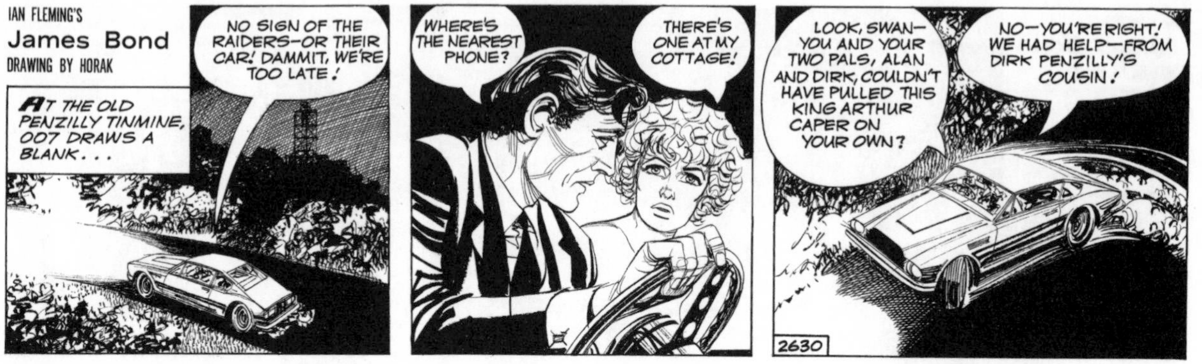

IAN FLEMING'S
James Bond
DRAWING BY HORAK
AT THE OLD PENZILLY TINMINE, 007 DRAWS A BLANK...
NO SIGN OF THE RAIDERS—OR THEIR CAR! DAMMIT, WE'RE TOO LATE!
WHERE'S THE NEAREST PHONE?
THERE'S ONE AT MY COTTAGE!
LOOK, SWAN— YOU AND YOUR TWO PALS, ALAN AND DIRK, COULDN'T HAVE PULLED THIS KING ARTHUR CAPER ON YOUR OWN?
NO—YOU'RE RIGHT! WE HAD HELP—FROM DIRK PENZILLY'S COUSIN!
2630


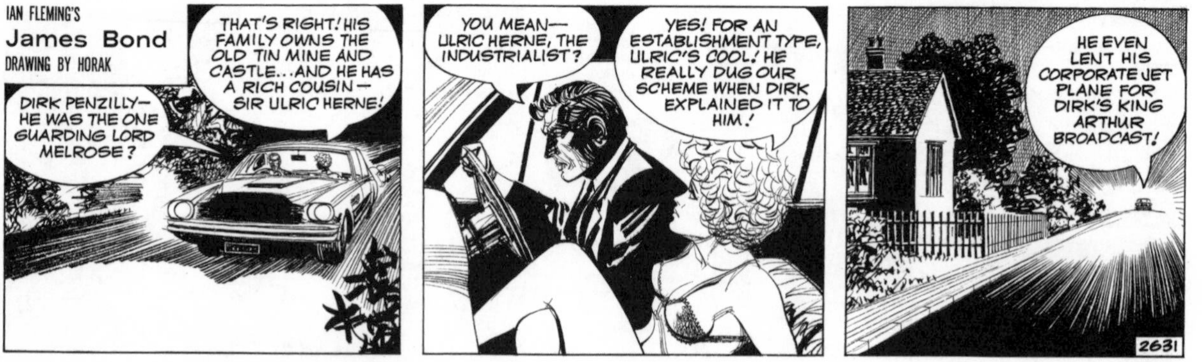

IAN FLEMING'S
James Bond
DRAWING BY HORAK
DIRK PENZILLY— HE WAS THE ONE GUARDING LORD MELROSE?
THAT'S RIGHT! HIS FAMILY OWNS THE OLD TIN MINE AND CASTLE... AND HE HAS A RICH COUSIN— SIR ULRIC HERNE!
YOU MEAN— ULRIC HERNE, THE INDUSTRIALIST?
YES! FOR AN ESTABLISHMENT TYPE, ULRIC'S COOL! HE REALLY DUG OUR SCHEME WHEN DIRK EXPLAINED IT TO HIM!
HE EVEN LENT HIS CORPORATE JET PLANE FOR DIRK'S KING ARTHUR BROADCAST!
2631


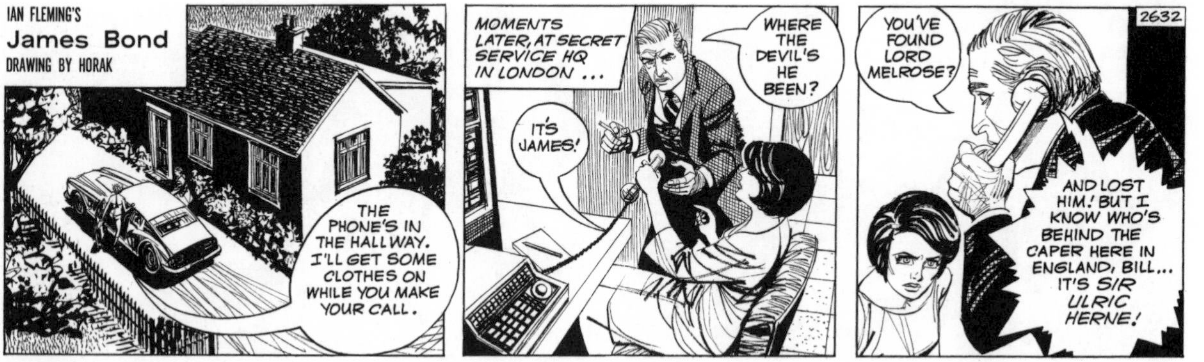

IAN FLEMING'S
James Bond
DRAWING BY HORAK
THE PHONE'S IN THE HALLWAY. I'LL GET SOME CLOTHES ON WHILE YOU MAKE YOUR CALL.
MOMENTS LATER, AT SECRET SERVICE HQ IN LONDON...
IT'S JAMES!
WHERE THE DEVIL'S HE BEEN?
2632
YOU'VE FOUND LORD MELROSE?
AND LOST HIM! BUT I KNOW WHO'S BEHIND THE CAPER HERE IN ENGLAND, BILL... IT'S SIR ULRIC HERNE!


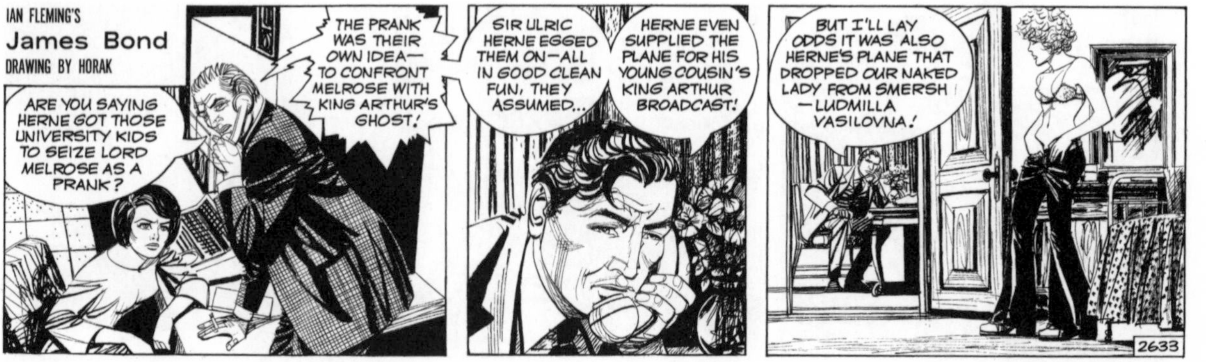

IAN FLEMING'S
James Bond
DRAWING BY HORAK
ARE YOU SAYING HERNE GOT THOSE UNIVERSITY KIDS TO SEIZE LORD MELROSE AS A PRANK?
THE PRANK WAS THEIR OWN IDEA— TO CONFRONT MELROSE WITH KING ARTHUR'S GHOST!
SIR ULRIC HERNE EGGED THEM ON—ALL IN GOOD CLEAN FUN, THEY ASSUMED...
HERNE EVEN SUPPLIED THE PLANE FOR HIS YOUNG COUSIN'S KING ARTHUR BROADCAST!
BUT I'LL LAY ODDS IT WAS ALSO HERNE'S PLANE THAT DROPPED OUR NAKED LADY FROM SMERSH —LUDMILLA VASILOVNA!
2633

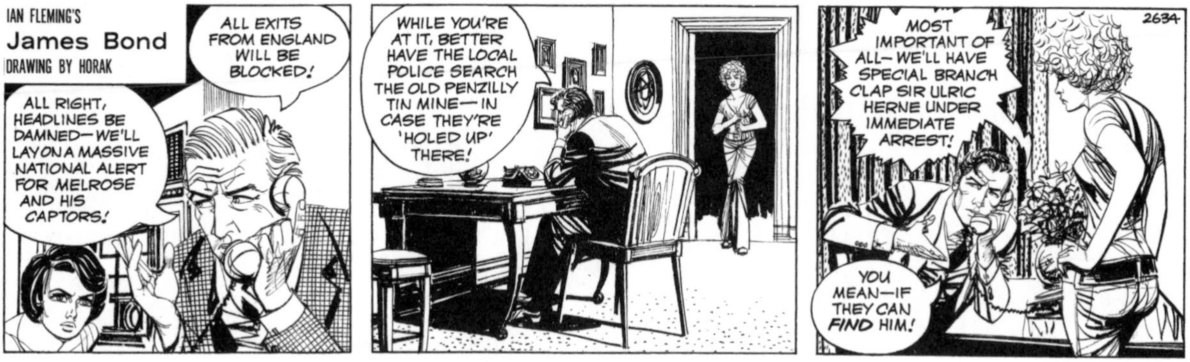
IAN FLEMING'S
James Bond
DRAWING BY HORAK
ALL EXITS FROM ENGLAND WILL BE BLOCKED!
ALL RIGHT, HEADLINES BE DAMNED—WE'LL LAY ON A MASSIVE NATIONAL ALERT FOR MELROSE AND HIS CAPTORS!
WHILE YOU'RE AT IT, BETTER HAVE THE LOCAL POLICE SEARCH THE OLD PENZILLY TIN MINE—IN CASE THEY'RE 'HOLED UP' THERE!
2634
MOST IMPORTANT OF ALL—WE'LL HAVE SPECIAL BRANCH CLAP SIR ULRIC HERNE UNDER IMMEDIATE ARREST!
YOU MEAN—IF THEY CAN FIND HIM!

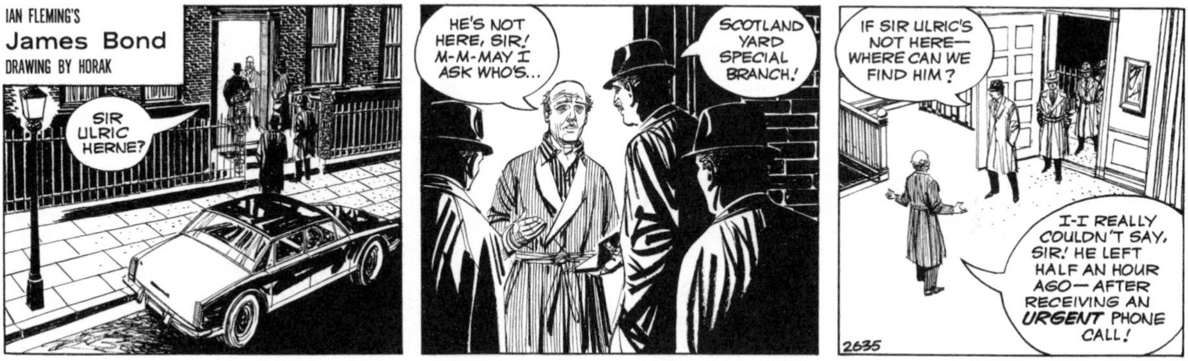
IAN FLEMING'S
James Bond
DRAWING BY HORAK
SIR ULRIC HERNE?
HE'S NOT HERE, SIR! M-M-MAY I ASK WHO'S...
SCOTLAND YARD SPECIAL BRANCH!
IF SIR ULRIC'S NOT HERE—WHERE CAN WE FIND HIM?
I-I REALLY COULDN'T SAY, SIR! HE LEFT HALF AN HOUR AGO—AFTER RECEIVING AN URGENT PHONE CALL!
2635

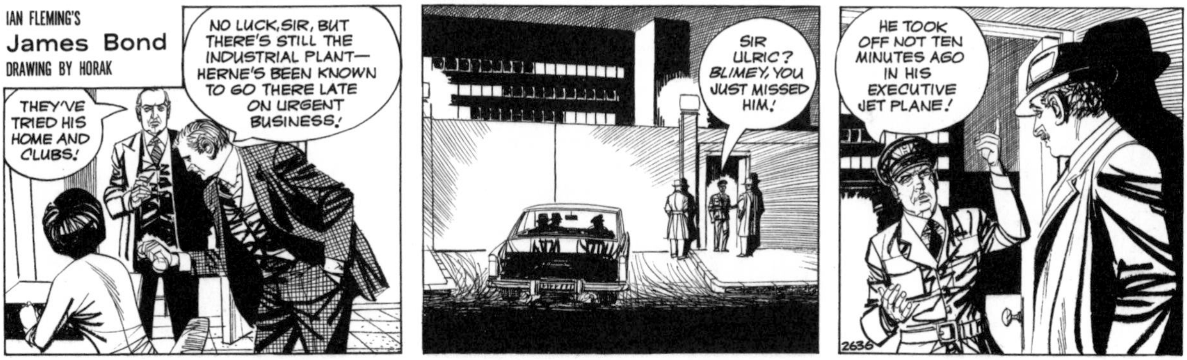
IAN FLEMING'S
James Bond
DRAWING BY HORAK
THEY'VE TRIED HIS HOME AND CLUBS!
NO LUCK, SIR, BUT THERE'S STILL THE INDUSTRIAL PLANT—HERNE'S BEEN KNOWN TO GO THERE LATE ON URGENT BUSINESS!
SIR ULRIC? BLIMEY, YOU JUST MISSED HIM!
HE TOOK OFF NOT TEN MINUTES AGO IN HIS EXECUTIVE JET PLANE!
2636

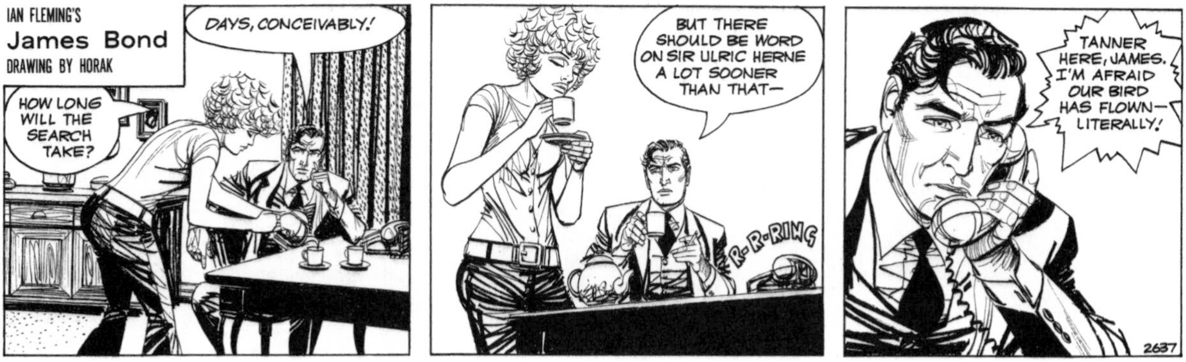
IAN FLEMING'S
James Bond
DRAWING BY HORAK
HOW LONG WILL THE SEARCH TAKE?
DAYS, CONCEIVABLY!
BUT THERE SHOULD BE WORD ON SIR ULRIC HERNE A LOT SOONER THAN THAT—
R-R-RING
TANNER HERE, JAMES. I'M AFRAID OUR BIRD HAS FLOWN—LITERALLY!
2637

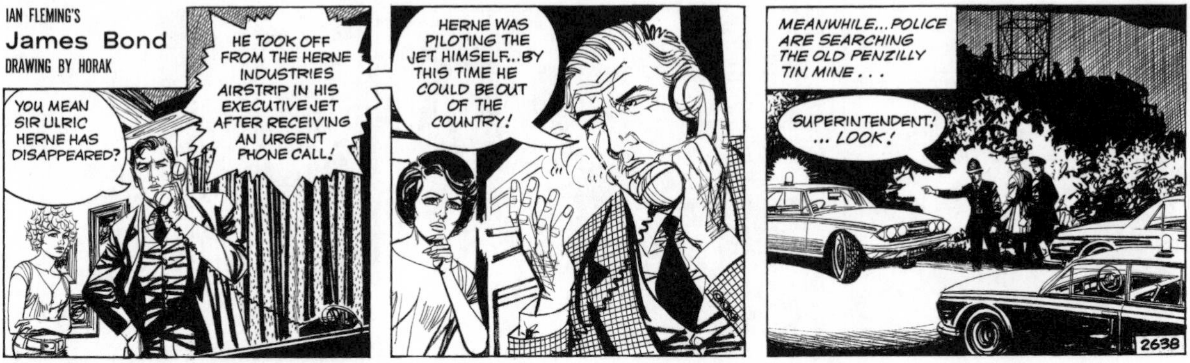
IAN FLEMING'S
James Bond
DRAWING BY HORAK
YOU MEAN SIR ULRIC HERNE HAS DISAPPEARED?
HE TOOK OFF FROM THE HERNE INDUSTRIES AIRSTRIP IN HIS EXECUTIVE JET AFTER RECEIVING AN URGENT PHONE CALL!
HERNE WAS PILOTING THE JET HIMSELF... BY THIS TIME HE COULD BE OUT OF THE COUNTRY!
MEANWHILE... POLICE ARE SEARCHING THE OLD PENZILLY TIN MINE . . .
SUPERINTENDENT! ... LOOK!
2638

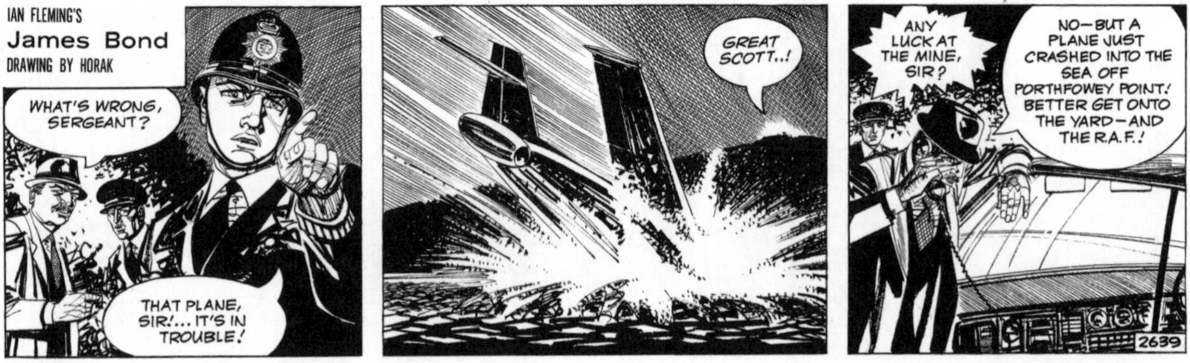
IAN FLEMING'S
James Bond
DRAWING BY HORAK
WHAT'S WRONG, SERGEANT?
THAT PLANE, SIR!... IT'S IN TROUBLE!
GREAT SCOTT..!
ANY LUCK AT THE MINE, SIR?
NO—BUT A PLANE JUST CRASHED INTO THE SEA OFF PORTHFOWEY POINT! BETTER GET ONTO THE YARD—AND THE R.A.F.!
2639

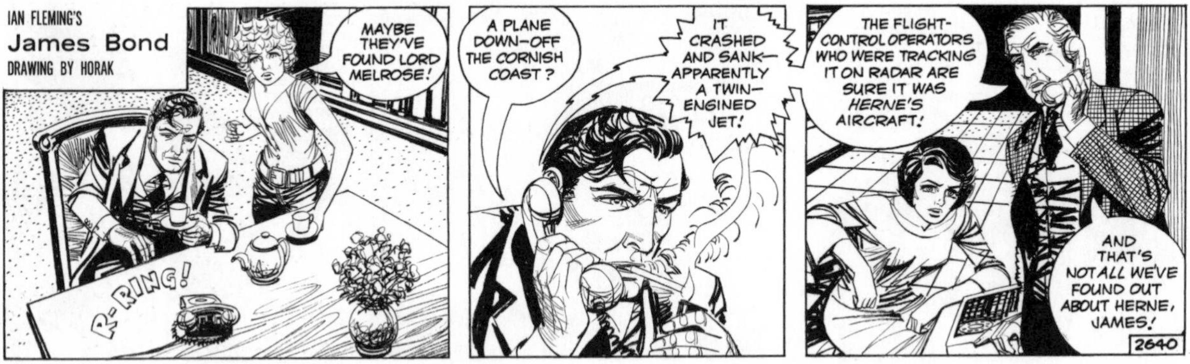
IAN FLEMING'S
James Bond
DRAWING BY HORAK
MAYBE THEY'VE FOUND LORD MELROSE!
R-RING!
A PLANE DOWN—OFF THE CORNISH COAST?
IT CRASHED AND SANK—APPARENTLY A TWIN-ENGINED JET!
THE FLIGHT-CONTROL OPERATORS WHO WERE TRACKING IT ON RADAR ARE SURE IT WAS HERNE'S AIRCRAFT!
AND THAT'S NOT ALL WE'VE FOUND OUT ABOUT HERNE, JAMES!
2640

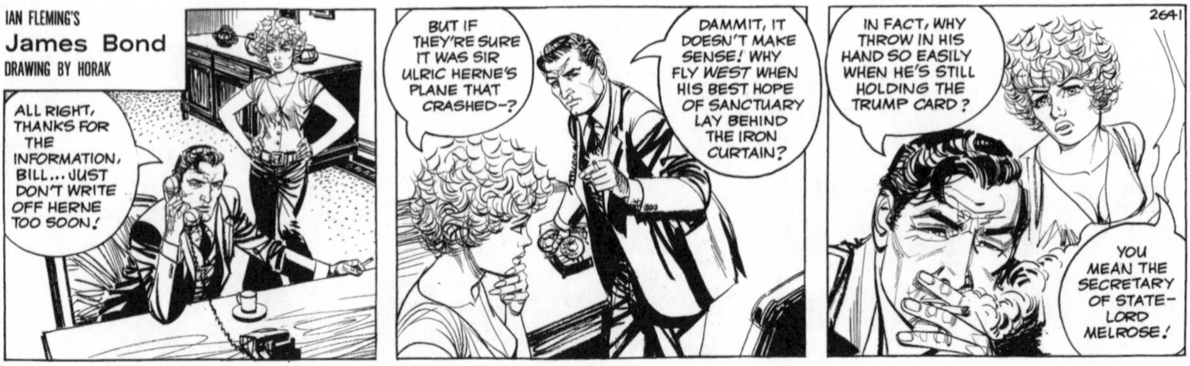
IAN FLEMING'S
James Bond
DRAWING BY HORAK
ALL RIGHT, THANKS FOR THE INFORMATION, BILL... JUST DON'T WRITE OFF HERNE TOO SOON!
BUT IF THEY'RE SURE IT WAS SIR ULRIC HERNE'S PLANE THAT CRASHED—?
DAMMIT, IT DOESN'T MAKE SENSE! WHY FLY WEST WHEN HIS BEST HOPE OF SANCTUARY LAY BEHIND THE IRON CURTAIN?
2641
IN FACT, WHY THROW IN HIS HAND SO EASILY WHEN HE'S STILL HOLDING THE TRUMP CARD?
YOU MEAN THE SECRETARY OF STATE—LORD MELROSE!

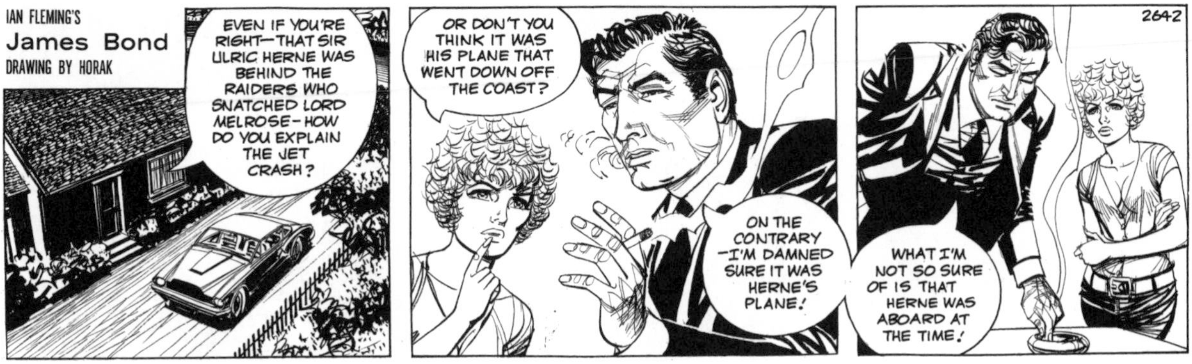
IAN FLEMING'S
James Bond
DRAWING BY HORAK
EVEN IF YOU'RE RIGHT—THAT SIR ULRIC HERNE WAS BEHIND THE RAIDERS WHO SNATCHED LORD MELROSE—HOW DO YOU EXPLAIN THE JET CRASH?
OR DON'T YOU THINK IT WAS HIS PLANE THAT WENT DOWN OFF THE COAST?
ON THE CONTRARY—I'M DAMNED SURE IT WAS HERNE'S PLANE!
2642
WHAT I'M NOT SO SURE OF IS THAT HERNE WAS ABOARD AT THE TIME!

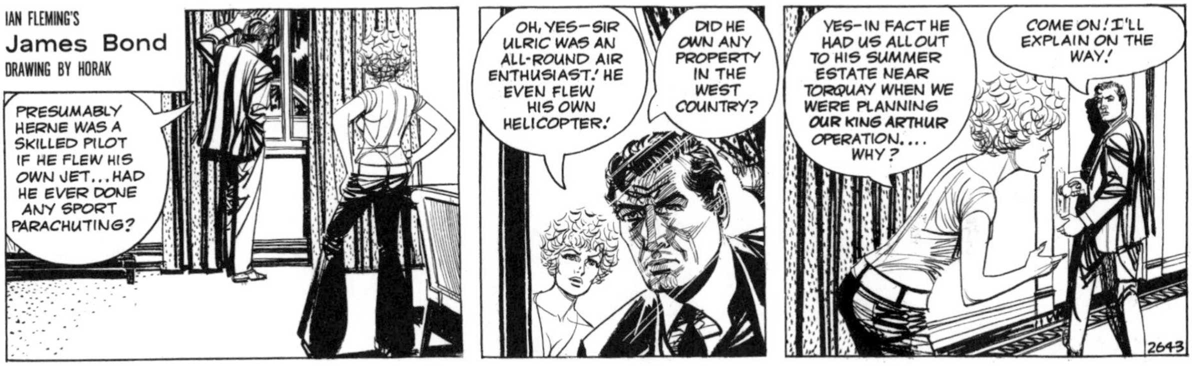
IAN FLEMING'S
James Bond
DRAWING BY HORAK
PRESUMABLY HERNE WAS A SKILLED PILOT IF HE FLEW HIS OWN JET...HAD HE EVER DONE ANY SPORT PARACHUTING?
OH, YES—SIR ULRIC WAS AN ALL-ROUND AIR ENTHUSIAST! HE EVEN FLEW HIS OWN HELICOPTER!
DID HE OWN ANY PROPERTY IN THE WEST COUNTRY?
YES—IN FACT HE HAD US ALL OUT TO HIS SUMMER ESTATE NEAR TORQUAY WHEN WE WERE PLANNING OUR KING ARTHUR OPERATION.... WHY?
COME ON! I'LL EXPLAIN ON THE WAY!
2643

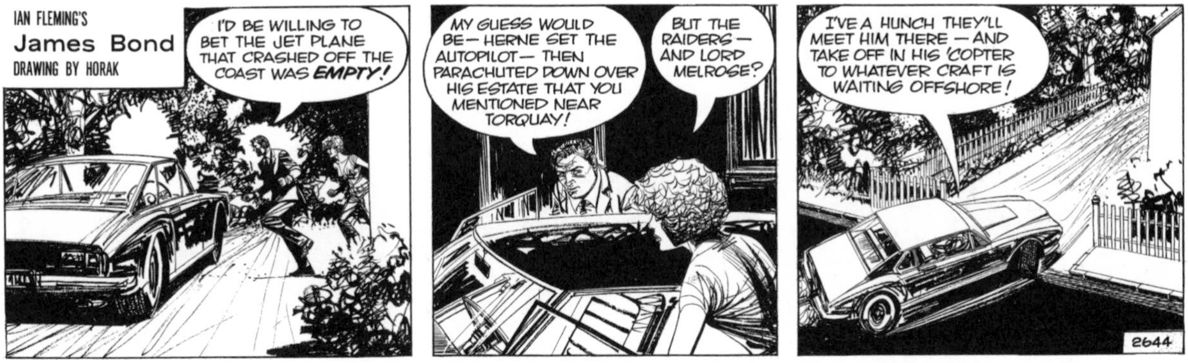
IAN FLEMING'S
James Bond
DRAWING BY HORAK
I'D BE WILLING TO BET THE JET PLANE THAT CRASHED OFF THE COAST WAS EMPTY!
MY GUESS WOULD BE—HERNE SET THE AUTOPILOT—THEN PARACHUTED DOWN OVER HIS ESTATE THAT YOU MENTIONED NEAR TORQUAY!
BUT THE RAIDERS—AND LORD MELROSE?
I'VE A HUNCH THEY'LL MEET HIM THERE—AND TAKE OFF IN HIS 'COPTER TO WHATEVER CRAFT IS WAITING OFFSHORE!
2644

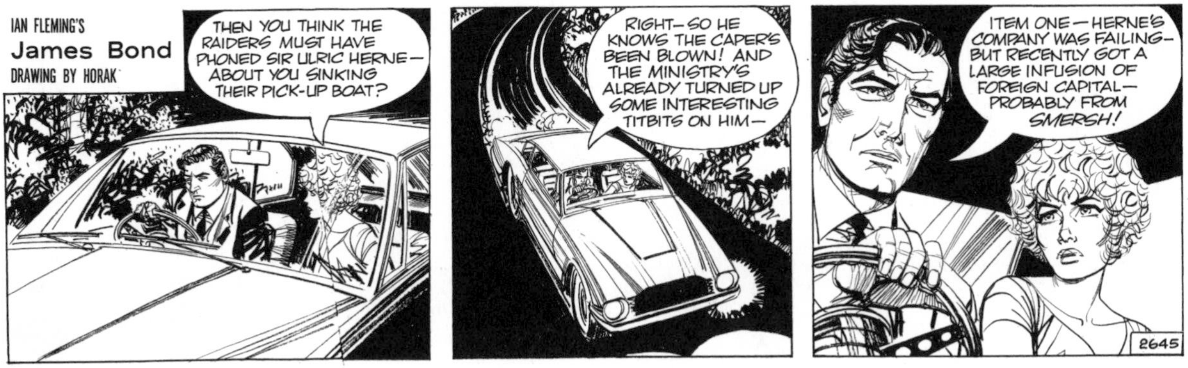
IAN FLEMING'S
James Bond
DRAWING BY HORAK
THEN YOU THINK THE RAIDERS MUST HAVE PHONED SIR ULRIC HERNE—ABOUT YOU SINKING THEIR PICK-UP BOAT?
RIGHT—SO HE KNOWS THE CAPER'S BEEN BLOWN! AND THE MINISTRY'S ALREADY TURNED UP SOME INTERESTING TITBITS ON HIM—
ITEM ONE—HERNE'S COMPANY WAS FAILING—BUT RECENTLY GOT A LARGE INFUSION OF FOREIGN CAPITAL—PROBABLY FROM SMERSH!
2645

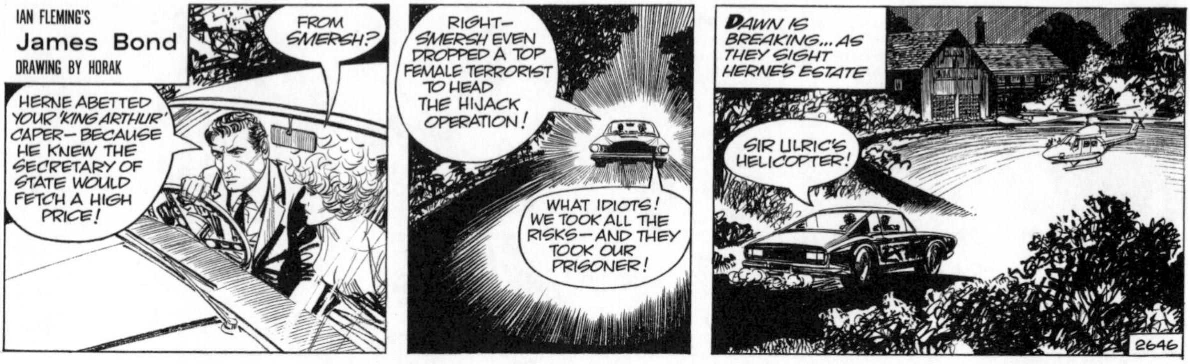
IAN FLEMING'S
James Bond
DRAWING BY HORAK
FROM SMERSH?
HERNE ABETTED YOUR 'KING ARTHUR' CAPER—BECAUSE HE KNEW THE SECRETARY OF STATE WOULD FETCH A HIGH PRICE!
RIGHT— SMERSH EVEN DROPPED A TOP FEMALE TERRORIST TO HEAD THE HIJACK OPERATION!
WHAT IDIOTS! WE TOOK ALL THE RISKS—AND THEY TOOK OUR PRISONER!
DAWN IS BREAKING... AS THEY SIGHT HERNE'S ESTATE
SIR ULRIC'S HELICOPTER!
2646

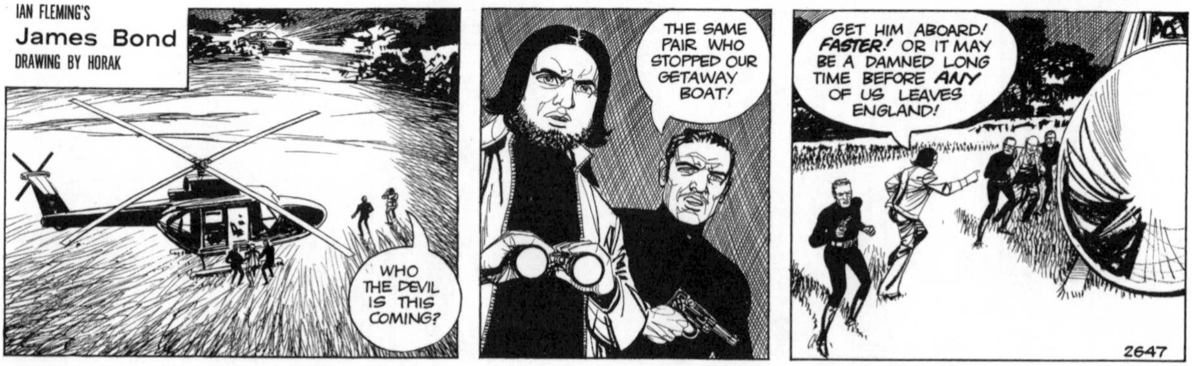
IAN FLEMING'S
James Bond
DRAWING BY HORAK
WHO THE DEVIL IS THIS COMING?
THE SAME PAIR WHO STOPPED OUR GETAWAY BOAT!
GET HIM ABOARD! FASTER! OR IT MAY BE A DAMNED LONG TIME BEFORE ANY OF US LEAVES ENGLAND!
2647

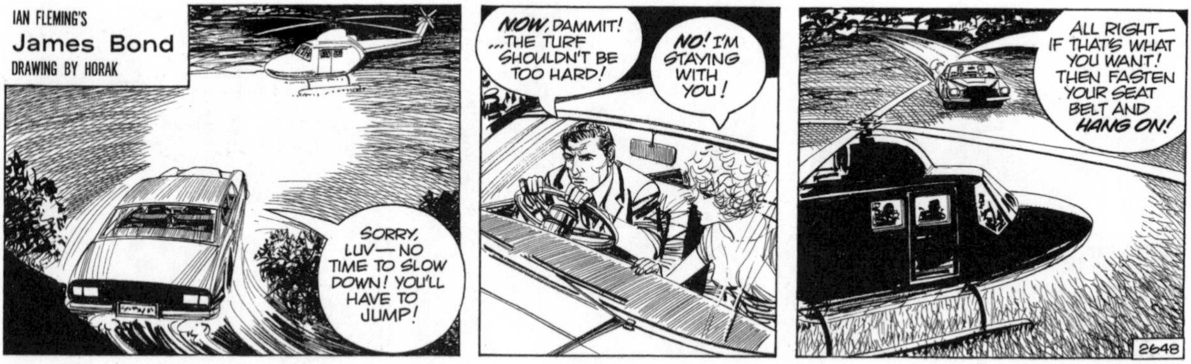
IAN FLEMING'S
James Bond
DRAWING BY HORAK
SORRY, LUV—NO TIME TO SLOW DOWN! YOU'LL HAVE TO JUMP!
NOW, DAMMIT! ...THE TURF SHOULDN'T BE TOO HARD!
NO! I'M STAYING WITH YOU!
ALL RIGHT— IF THAT'S WHAT YOU WANT! THEN FASTEN YOUR SEAT BELT AND HANG ON!
2648

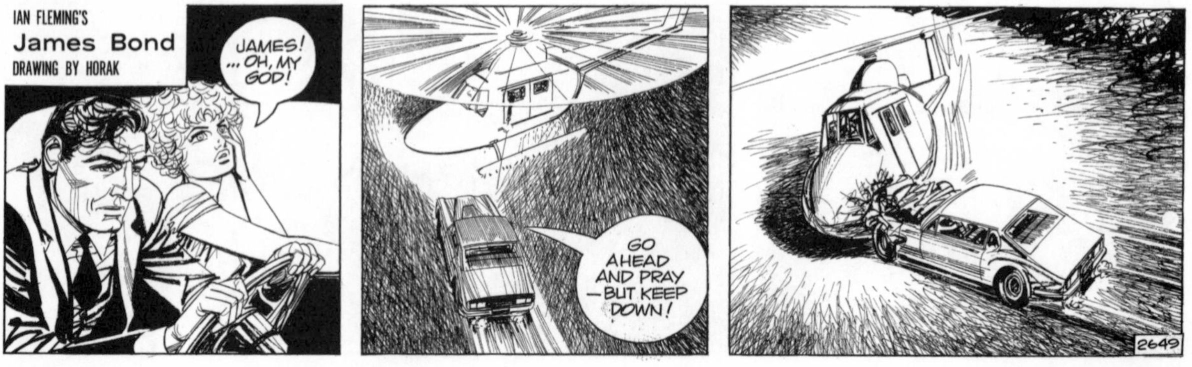
IAN FLEMING'S
James Bond
DRAWING BY HORAK
JAMES! ...OH, MY GOD!
GO AHEAD AND PRAY —BUT KEEP DOWN!
2649

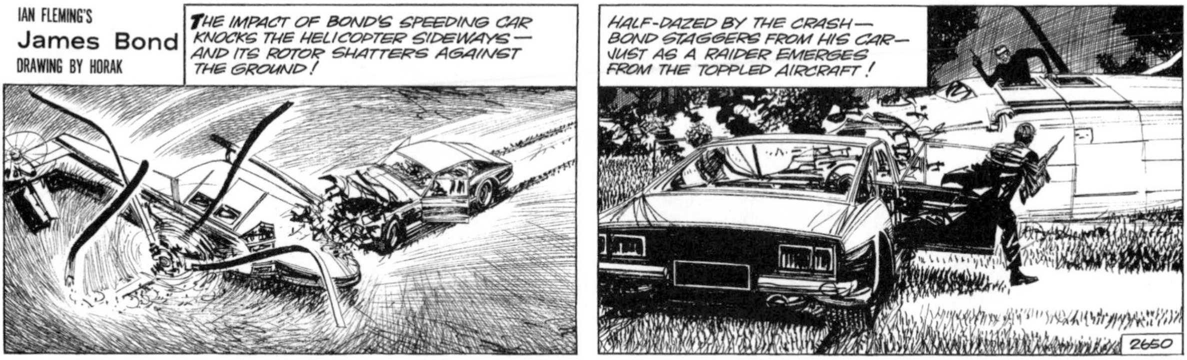
IAN FLEMING'S
James Bond
DRAWING BY HORAK
THE IMPACT OF BOND'S SPEEDING CAR KNOCKS THE HELICOPTER SIDEWAYS— AND ITS ROTOR SHATTERS AGAINST THE GROUND!
HALF-DAZED BY THE CRASH— BOND STAGGERS FROM HIS CAR— JUST AS A RAIDER EMERGES FROM THE TOPPLED AIRCRAFT!
2650

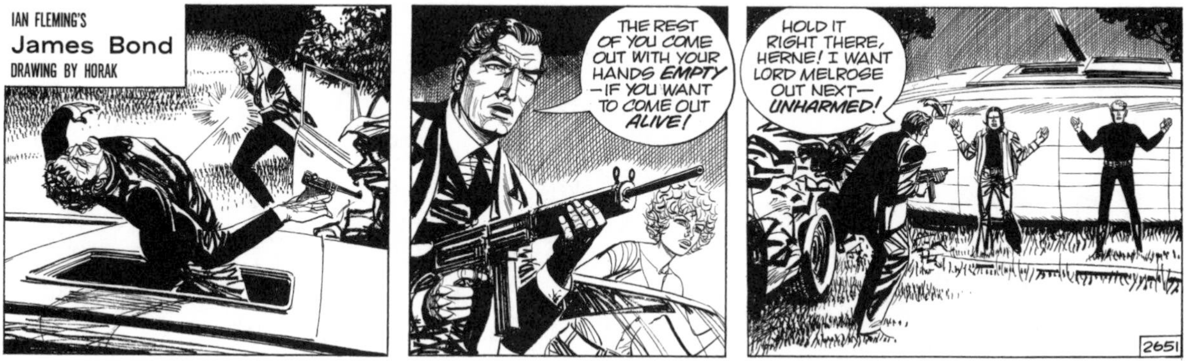
IAN FLEMING'S
James Bond
DRAWING BY HORAK
THE REST OF YOU COME OUT WITH YOUR HANDS EMPTY —IF YOU WANT TO COME OUT ALIVE!
HOLD IT RIGHT THERE, HERNE! I WANT LORD MELROSE OUT NEXT— UNHARMED!
2651

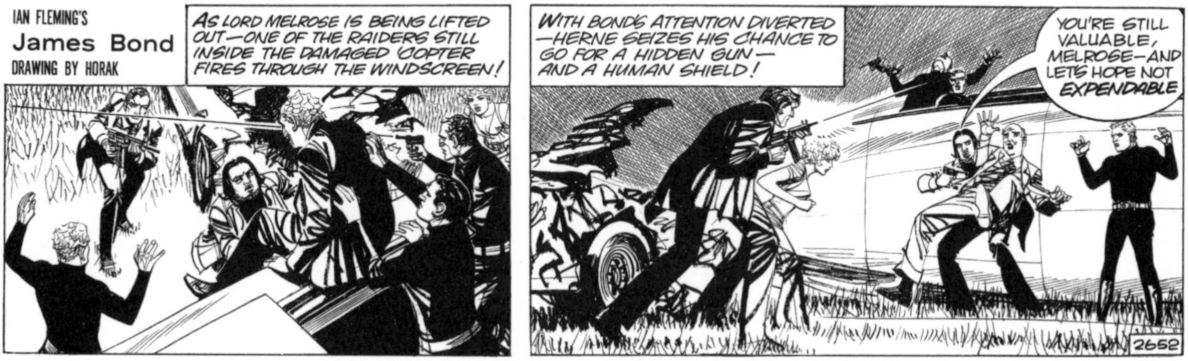
IAN FLEMING'S
James Bond
DRAWING BY HORAK
AS LORD MELROSE IS BEING LIFTED OUT—ONE OF THE RAIDERS STILL INSIDE THE DAMAGED 'COPTER FIRES THROUGH THE WINDSCREEN!
WITH BOND'S ATTENTION DIVERTED —HERNE SEIZES HIS CHANCE TO GO FOR A HIDDEN GUN— AND A HUMAN SHIELD!
YOU'RE STILL VALUABLE, MELROSE—AND LET'S HOPE NOT EXPENDABLE
2652

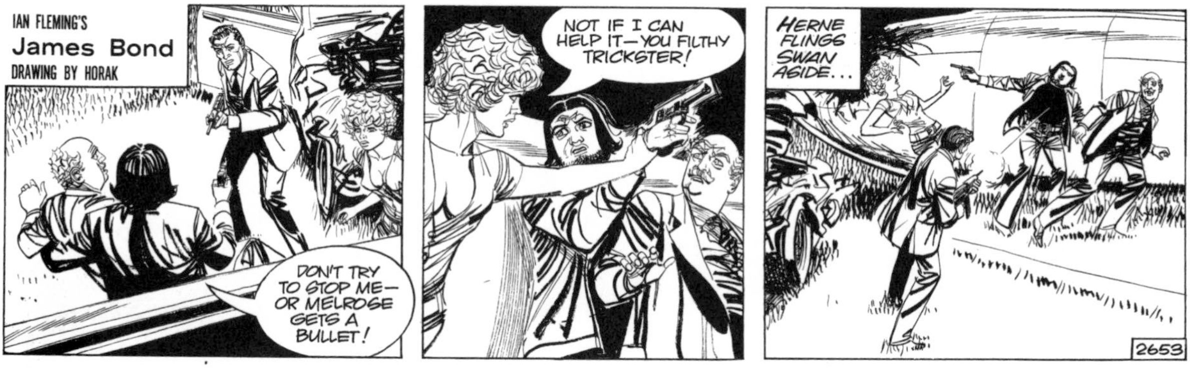
IAN FLEMING'S
James Bond
DRAWING BY HORAK
DON'T TRY TO STOP ME— OR MELROSE GETS A BULLET!
NOT IF I CAN HELP IT—YOU FILTHY TRICKSTER!
HERNE FLINGS SWAN ASIDE...
2653

IAN FLEMING'S
James Bond
DRAWING BY HORAK
LORD MELROSE! ARE YOU ALL RIGHT?
QUITE— THANKS TO COMMANDER BOND AND THIS YOUNG LADY!
OH, JAMES! WHAT WILL HAPPEN WHEN HE LEARNS I WAS INVOLVED IN THE 'KING ARTHUR' PLOT?
YOUR PERFORMANCE JUST NOW SHOULD CLEAR THE SLATE!
BUT I SUGGEST WE HAVE A HEART-TO-HEART TALK— TO EXPLORE YOUR DEFENCES—AND THE MOST DESIRABLE COURSE OF ACTION!
2654

IAN FLEMING'S
James Bond
DRAWING BY HORAK
BETTER HAVE A WORD WITH JAMES!
HE'S ASKING A WEEK'S LEAVE — TO RECRUIT AND INDOCTRINATE THAT GIRL, SWAN— AS A LIKELY TRAINEE FOR INTELLIGENCE WORK!
SHE SHOWS REMARKABLE APTITUDE!
INDEED?... I SHOULD HAVE THOUGHT HER A RATHER IMMATURE TYPE—OF LIMITED INTERESTS—WHAT WITH HER PENCHANT FOR KNIGHTS IN ARMOUR!
AU CONTRAIRE, MONEYPENNY—I FIND HER DELIGHTFULLY WELL-ROUNDED!
End of story
2655

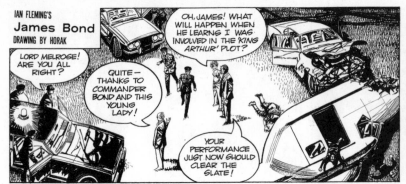

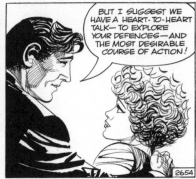

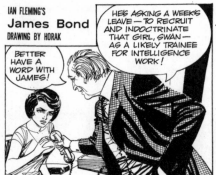

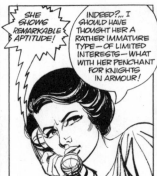

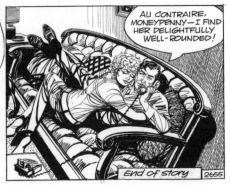

# THE PHOENIX PROJECT

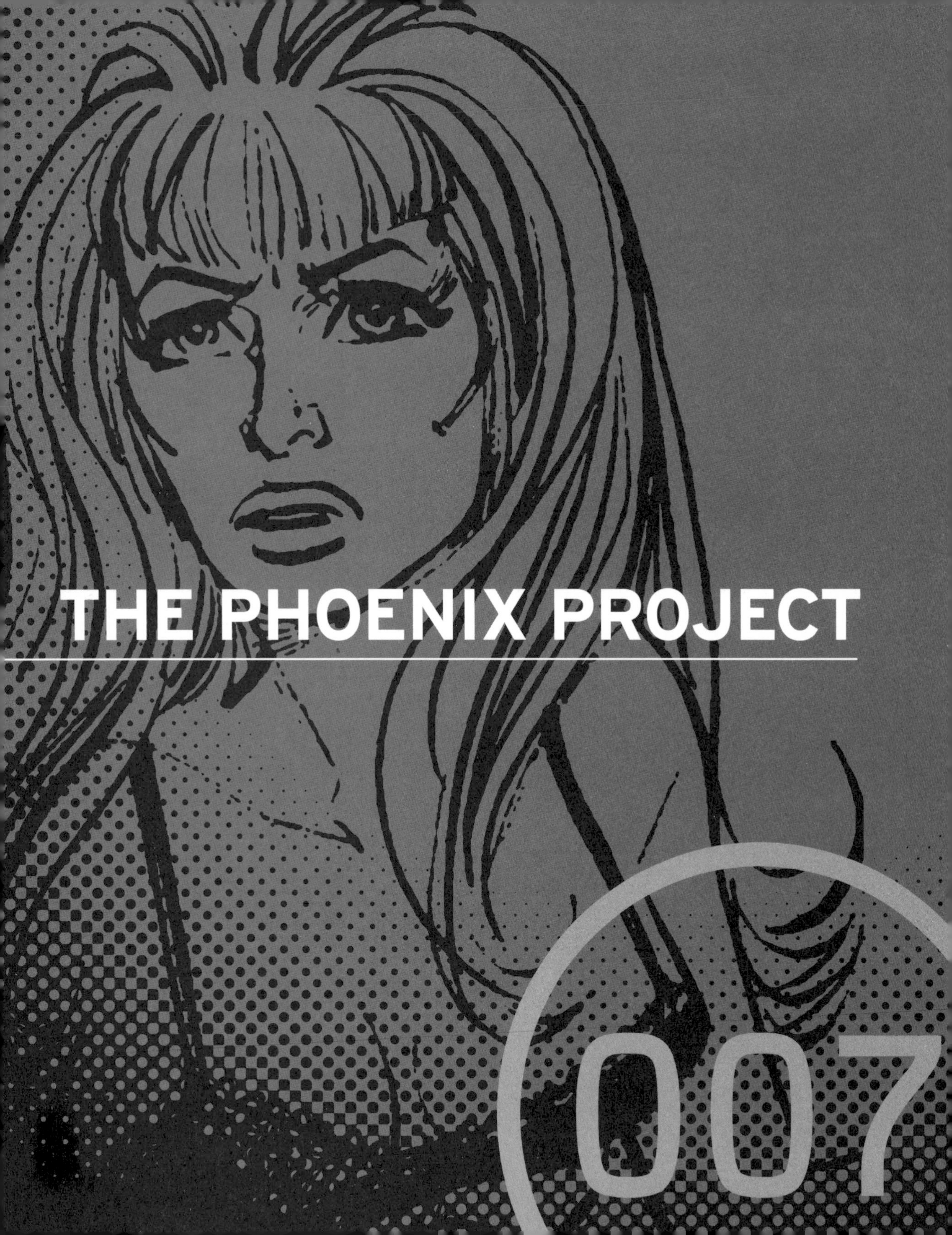
007

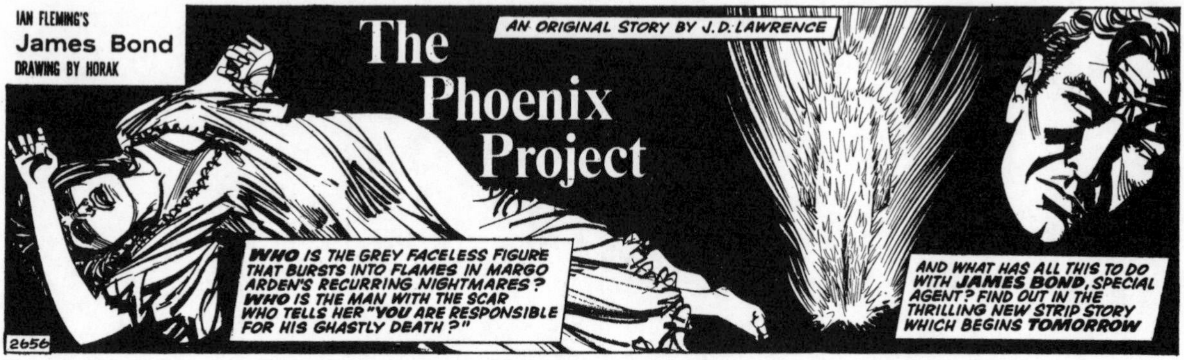
IAN FLEMING'S
James Bond
DRAWING BY HORAK
AN ORIGINAL STORY BY J.D. LAWRENCE
The Phoenix Project
WHO IS THE GREY FACELESS FIGURE THAT BURSTS INTO FLAMES IN MARGO ARDEN'S RECURRING NIGHTMARES? WHO IS THE MAN WITH THE SCAR WHO TELLS HER "YOU ARE RESPONSIBLE FOR HIS GHASTLY DEATH?"
AND WHAT HAS ALL THIS TO DO WITH JAMES BOND, SPECIAL AGENT? FIND OUT IN THE THRILLING NEW STRIP STORY WHICH BEGINS TOMORROW
2656

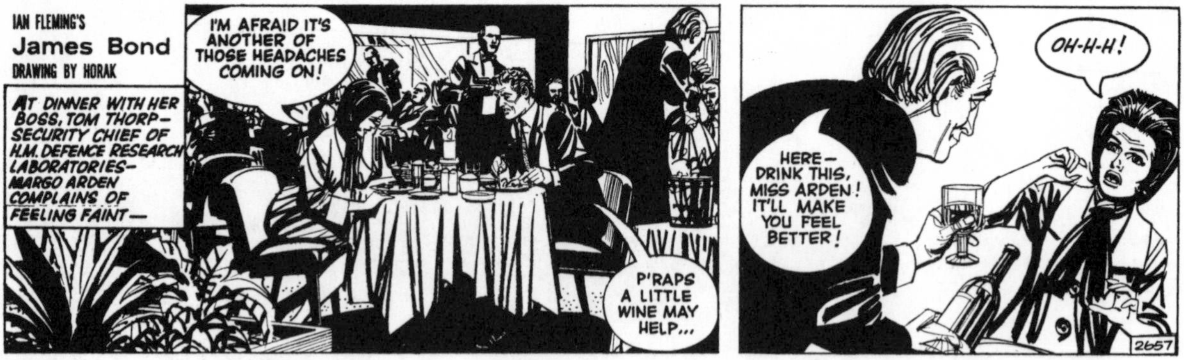
IAN FLEMING'S
James Bond
DRAWING BY HORAK
AT DINNER WITH HER BOSS, TOM THORP— SECURITY CHIEF OF H.M. DEFENCE RESEARCH LABORATORIES— MARGO ARDEN COMPLAINS OF FEELING FAINT—
I'M AFRAID IT'S ANOTHER OF THOSE HEADACHES COMING ON!
P'RAPS A LITTLE WINE MAY HELP...
OH-H-H!
HERE— DRINK THIS, MISS ARDEN! IT'LL MAKE YOU FEEL BETTER!
2657

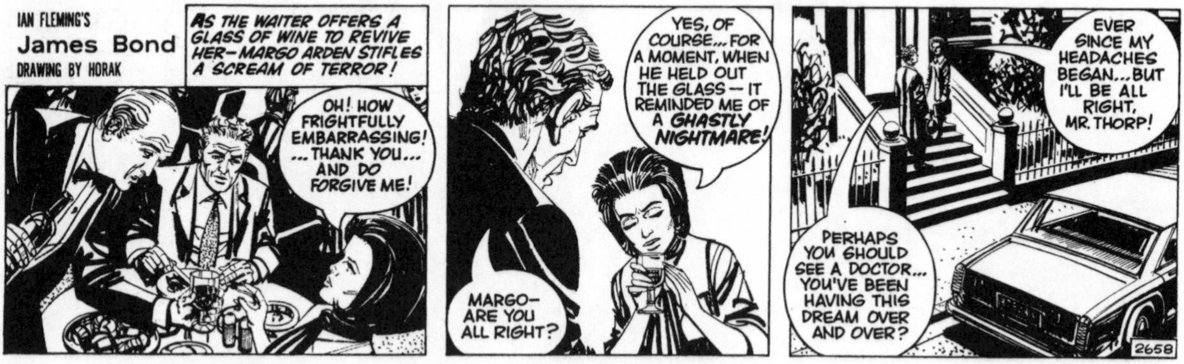
IAN FLEMING'S
James Bond
DRAWING BY HORAK
AS THE WAITER OFFERS A GLASS OF WINE TO REVIVE HER— MARGO ARDEN STIFLES A SCREAM OF TERROR!
OH! HOW FRIGHTFULLY EMBARRASSING! ...THANK YOU... AND DO FORGIVE ME!
MARGO— ARE YOU ALL RIGHT?
YES, OF COURSE... FOR A MOMENT, WHEN HE HELD OUT THE GLASS — IT REMINDED ME OF A GHASTLY NIGHTMARE!
PERHAPS YOU SHOULD SEE A DOCTOR... YOU'VE BEEN HAVING THIS DREAM OVER AND OVER?
EVER SINCE MY HEADACHES BEGAN... BUT I'LL BE ALL RIGHT, MR. THORP!
2658

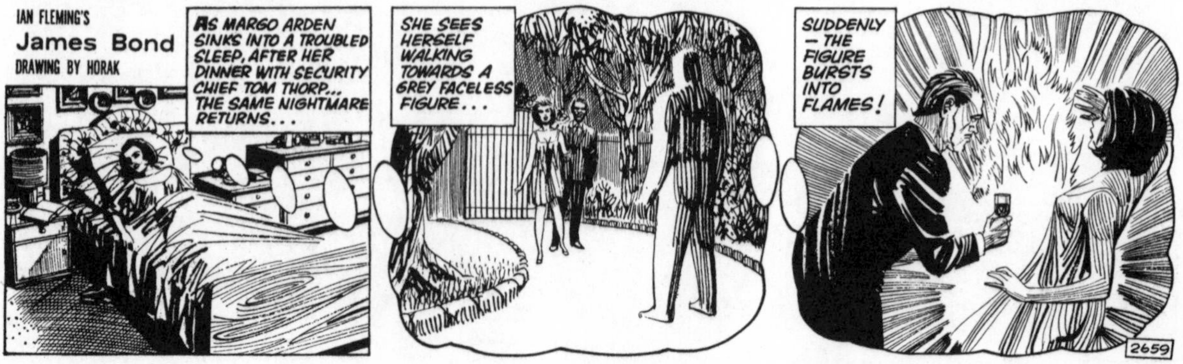
IAN FLEMING'S
James Bond
DRAWING BY HORAK
AS MARGO ARDEN SINKS INTO A TROUBLED SLEEP, AFTER HER DINNER WITH SECURITY CHIEF TOM THORP... THE SAME NIGHTMARE RETURNS...
SHE SEES HERSELF WALKING TOWARDS A GREY FACELESS FIGURE...
SUDDENLY — THE FIGURE BURSTS INTO FLAMES!
2659

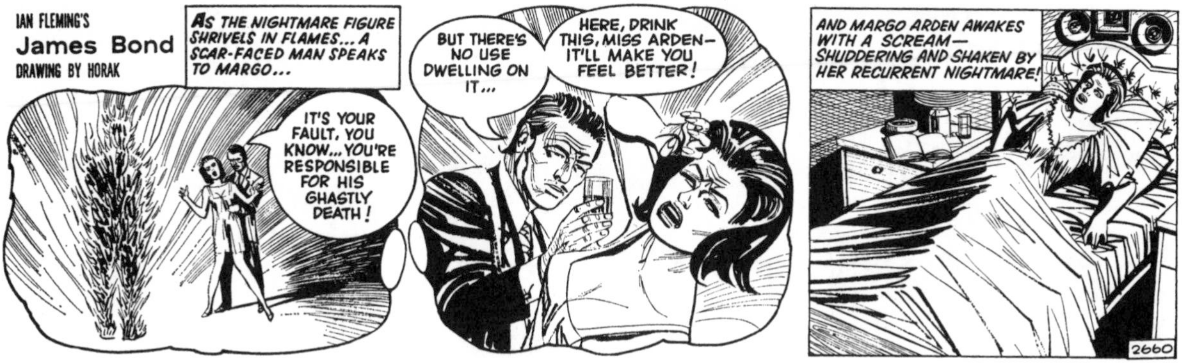
IAN FLEMING'S
James Bond
DRAWING BY HORAK
AS THE NIGHTMARE FIGURE SHRIVELS IN FLAMES... A SCAR-FACED MAN SPEAKS TO MARGO...
IT'S YOUR FAULT, YOU KNOW... YOU'RE RESPONSIBLE FOR HIS GHASTLY DEATH!
HERE, DRINK THIS, MISS ARDEN—IT'LL MAKE YOU FEEL BETTER!
BUT THERE'S NO USE DWELLING ON IT...
AND MARGO ARDEN AWAKES WITH A SCREAM—SHUDDERING AND SHAKEN BY HER RECURRENT NIGHTMARE!
2660

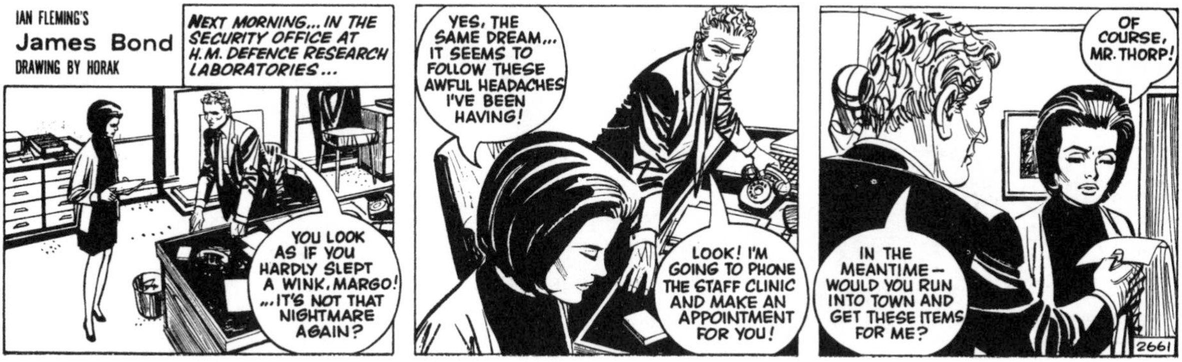
IAN FLEMING'S
James Bond
DRAWING BY HORAK
NEXT MORNING... IN THE SECURITY OFFICE AT H.M. DEFENCE RESEARCH LABORATORIES...
YOU LOOK AS IF YOU HARDLY SLEPT A WINK, MARGO! ...IT'S NOT THAT NIGHTMARE AGAIN?
YES, THE SAME DREAM... IT SEEMS TO FOLLOW THESE AWFUL HEADACHES I'VE BEEN HAVING!
LOOK! I'M GOING TO PHONE THE STAFF CLINIC AND MAKE AN APPOINTMENT FOR YOU!
IN THE MEANTIME—WOULD YOU RUN INTO TOWN AND GET THESE ITEMS FOR ME?
OF COURSE, MR. THORP!
2661

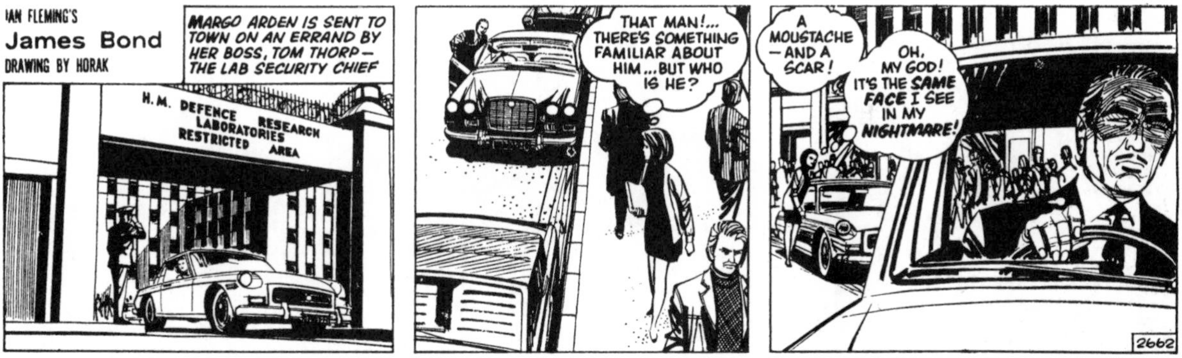
IAN FLEMING'S
James Bond
DRAWING BY HORAK
MARGO ARDEN IS SENT TO TOWN ON AN ERRAND BY HER BOSS, TOM THORP—THE LAB SECURITY CHIEF
H. M. DEFENCE RESEARCH LABORATORIES RESTRICTED AREA
THAT MAN!... THERE'S SOMETHING FAMILIAR ABOUT HIM... BUT WHO IS HE?
A MOUSTACHE—AND A SCAR!
OH, MY GOD! IT'S THE SAME FACE I SEE IN MY NIGHTMARE!
2662

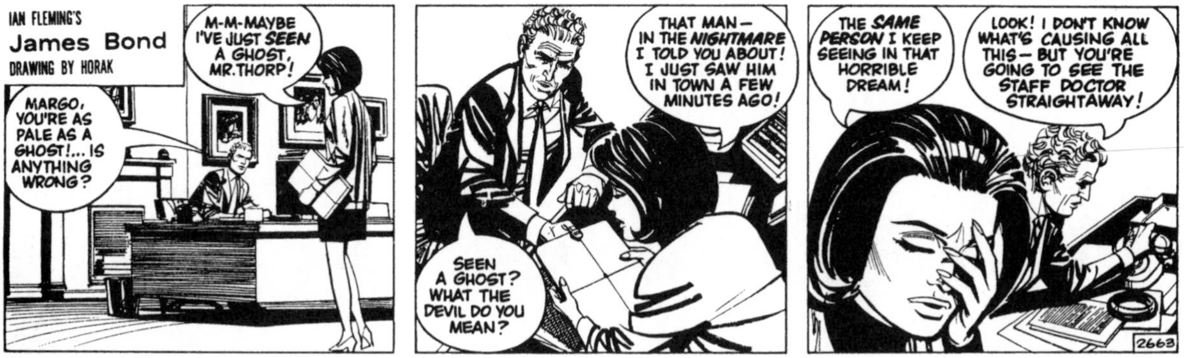
IAN FLEMING'S
James Bond
DRAWING BY HORAK
MARGO, YOU'RE AS PALE AS A GHOST!... IS ANYTHING WRONG?
M-M-MAYBE I'VE JUST SEEN A GHOST, MR. THORP!
SEEN A GHOST? WHAT THE DEVIL DO YOU MEAN?
THAT MAN—IN THE NIGHTMARE I TOLD YOU ABOUT! I JUST SAW HIM IN TOWN A FEW MINUTES AGO!
THE SAME PERSON I KEEP SEEING IN THAT HORRIBLE DREAM!
LOOK! I DON'T KNOW WHAT'S CAUSING ALL THIS—BUT YOU'RE GOING TO SEE THE STAFF DOCTOR STRAIGHTAWAY!
2663

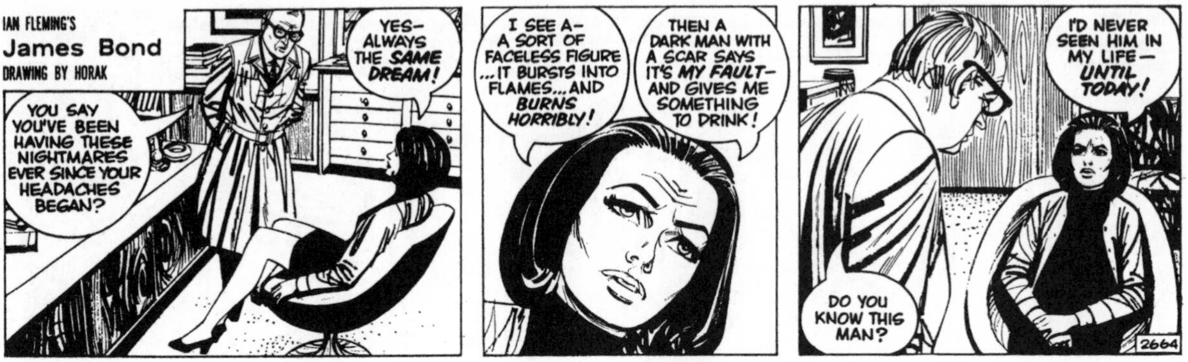
IAN FLEMING'S
James Bond
DRAWING BY HORAK
YOU SAY YOU'VE BEEN HAVING THESE NIGHTMARES EVER SINCE YOUR HEADACHES BEGAN?
YES— ALWAYS THE SAME DREAM!
I SEE A— A SORT OF FACELESS FIGURE ...IT BURSTS INTO FLAMES... AND BURNS HORRIBLY!
THEN A DARK MAN WITH A SCAR SAYS IT'S MY FAULT— AND GIVES ME SOMETHING TO DRINK!
DO YOU KNOW THIS MAN?
I'D NEVER SEEN HIM IN MY LIFE— UNTIL TODAY!
2664

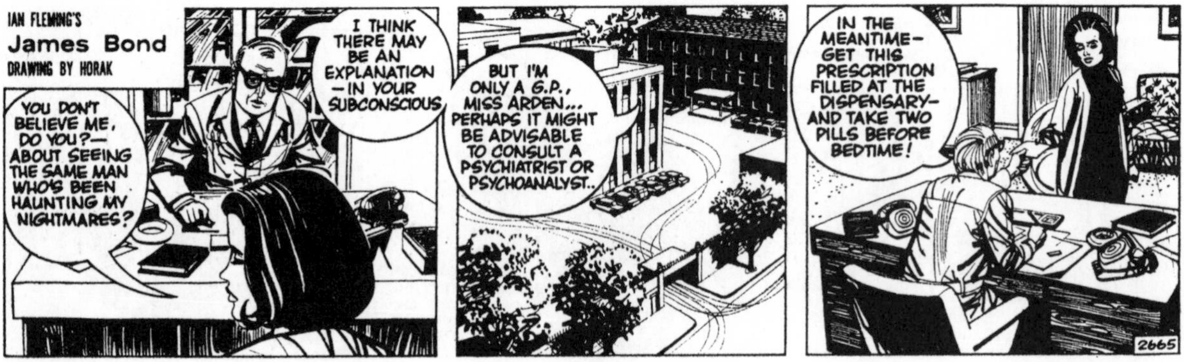
IAN FLEMING'S
James Bond
DRAWING BY HORAK
YOU DON'T BELIEVE ME, DO YOU?— ABOUT SEEING THE SAME MAN WHO'S BEEN HAUNTING MY NIGHTMARES?
I THINK THERE MAY BE AN EXPLANATION —IN YOUR SUBCONSCIOUS
BUT I'M ONLY A G.P., MISS ARDEN... PERHAPS IT MIGHT BE ADVISABLE TO CONSULT A PSYCHIATRIST OR PSYCHOANALYST..
IN THE MEANTIME— GET THIS PRESCRIPTION FILLED AT THE DISPENSARY— AND TAKE TWO PILLS BEFORE BEDTIME!
2665

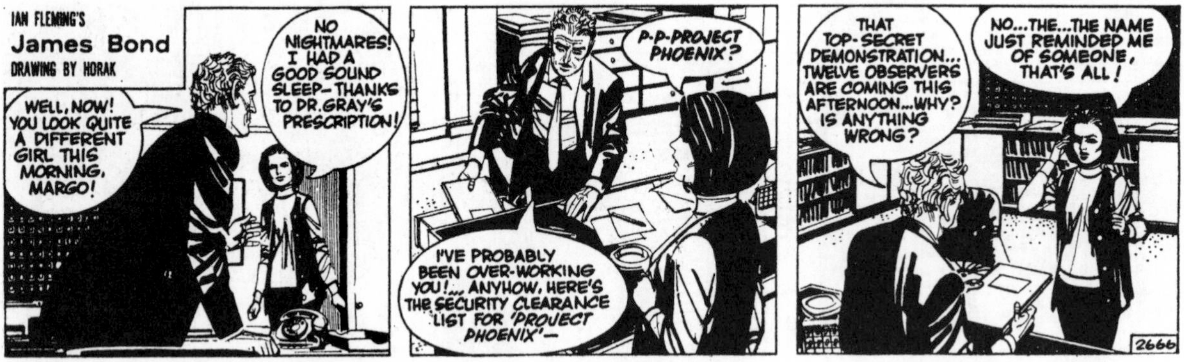
IAN FLEMING'S
James Bond
DRAWING BY HORAK
WELL, NOW! YOU LOOK QUITE A DIFFERENT GIRL THIS MORNING, MARGO!
NO NIGHTMARES! I HAD A GOOD SOUND SLEEP— THANKS TO DR. GRAY'S PRESCRIPTION!
I'VE PROBABLY BEEN OVER-WORKING YOU!... ANYHOW, HERE'S THE SECURITY CLEARANCE LIST FOR 'PROJECT PHOENIX'—
P-P-PROJECT PHOENIX?
THAT TOP-SECRET DEMONSTRATION... TWELVE OBSERVERS ARE COMING THIS AFTERNOON...WHY? IS ANYTHING WRONG?
NO...THE...THE NAME JUST REMINDED ME OF SOMEONE, THAT'S ALL!
2666

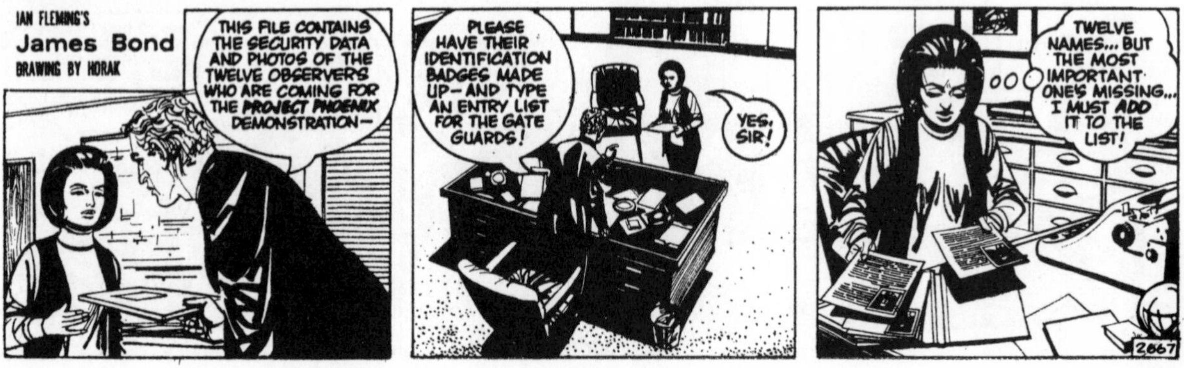
IAN FLEMING'S
James Bond
DRAWING BY HORAK
THIS FILE CONTAINS THE SECURITY DATA AND PHOTOS OF THE TWELVE OBSERVERS WHO ARE COMING FOR THE PROJECT PHOENIX DEMONSTRATION—
PLEASE HAVE THEIR IDENTIFICATION BADGES MADE UP— AND TYPE AN ENTRY LIST FOR THE GATE GUARDS!
YES, SIR!
TWELVE NAMES... BUT THE MOST IMPORTANT ONE'S MISSING... I MUST ADD IT TO THE LIST!
2667

IAN FLEMING'S
**James Bond**
DRAWING BY HORAK

AS MARSO TYPES THE LIST OF OBSERVERS COMING TO WITNESS THE TOP-SECRET 'PROJECT PHOENIX' DEMONSTRATION...

...SHE ADDS ANOTHER NAME TO THE SECURITY CLEARANCE LIST!

George Ness--chief physicist, Naval Weapons Dept., Ministry of Defen...

IAN FLEMING'S
**James Bond**
DRAWING BY HORAK

AFTER TYPING AN EXTRA NAME ON THE 'PROJECT PHOENIX' LIST—MARSO TAKES A PHOTO FROM HER DESK DRAWER...

...AND ADDS IT TO THE PICTURES OF THE OBSERVERS WHO HAVE RECEIVED OFFICIAL SECURITY CLEARANCE!

GEORGE NESS
NAVAL WEAPONS DEPT.
MINISTRY OF DEFENCE

2669

WILL YOU HAVE THEIR IDENTIFICATION BADGES MADE UP BY 12·00, PLEASE? ...THEY'LL BE ARRIVING THIS AFTERNOON

RIGHT, MISS ARDEN!

IAN FLEMING'S
**James Bond**
DRAWING BY HORAK

THE OBSERVERS ARRIVE TO WITNESS THE 'PROJECT PHOENIX' DEMONSTRATION

H.M. DEFENCE
H.M. LABORATORY
RESTRICTED

GEORGE NESS — NAVAL WEAPONS DEPARTMENT, MINISTRY OF DEFENCE!

RIGHT, MR. NESS! YOU'RE NUMBER 13 ON THE LIST... HOPE THAT'S NOT BAD LUCK, SIR!...HERE'S YOUR IDENTIFICATION BADGE!

2670

WHAT *IS* 'PROJECT PHOENIX', MR. THORP?

IT'S TOP SECRET, BUT WE'RE ABOUT TO SEE SOMETHING QUITE UNUSUAL — IF IT WORKS AS THE INVENTOR CLAIMS!

IAN FLEMING'S
**James Bond**
DRAWING BY HORAK

DR. HENDRIX BAAR IS A DUTCH SCIENTIST... HE'S OFFERING OUR GOVERNMENT AN INVENTION CALLED THE *PHOENIX SUIT*...

...TO PROTECT A SOLDIER FROM NAPALM, RADIATION, BULLETS OR EXPLOSIVES!

THIS 'ARMOUR', GENTLEMEN, IS MADE OF BONDED BORON FILAMENTS—ACTUALLY STRONGER THAN STEEL!

...YET LIGHT ENOUGH TO BE WORN IN COMPLETE COMFORT— BECAUSE ITS REAL STRENGTH DERIVES FROM WHAT I CALL THE 'PHOENIX EFFECT'!

2671

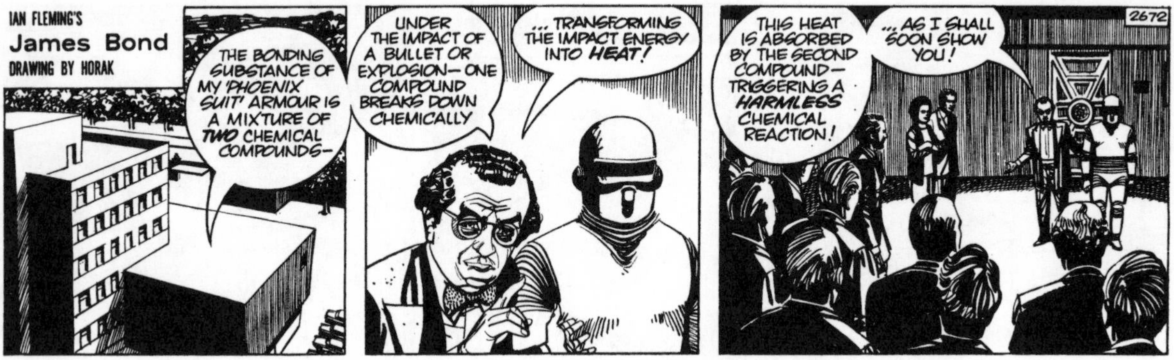
IAN FLEMING'S
James Bond
DRAWING BY HORAK
THE BONDING SUBSTANCE OF MY 'PHOENIX SUIT' ARMOUR IS A MIXTURE OF TWO CHEMICAL COMPOUNDS—
UNDER THE IMPACT OF A BULLET OR EXPLOSION—ONE COMPOUND BREAKS DOWN CHEMICALLY
... TRANSFORMING THE IMPACT ENERGY INTO HEAT!
2672
THIS HEAT IS ABSORBED BY THE SECOND COMPOUND—TRIGGERING A HARMLESS CHEMICAL REACTION!
... AS I SHALL SOON SHOW YOU!

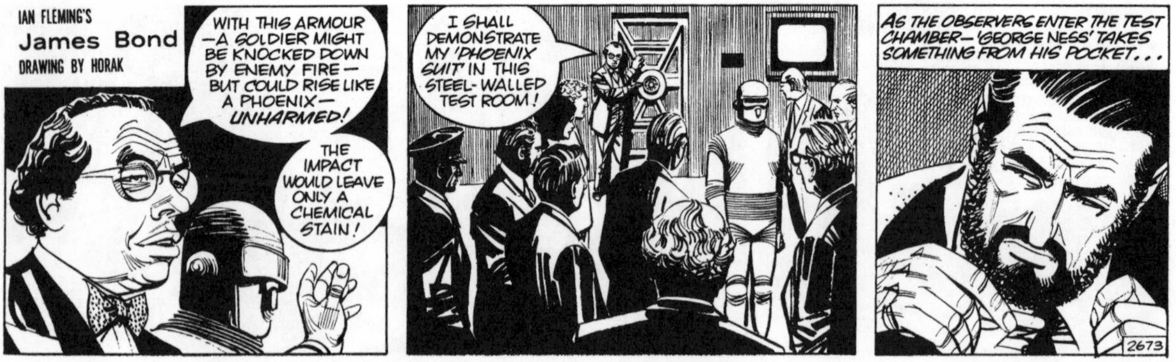
IAN FLEMING'S
James Bond
DRAWING BY HORAK
WITH THIS ARMOUR—A SOLDIER MIGHT BE KNOCKED DOWN BY ENEMY FIRE—BUT COULD RISE LIKE A PHOENIX—UNHARMED!
THE IMPACT WOULD LEAVE ONLY A CHEMICAL STAIN!
I SHALL DEMONSTRATE MY 'PHOENIX SUIT' IN THIS STEEL-WALLED TEST ROOM!
AS THE OBSERVERS ENTER THE TEST CHAMBER—'GEORGE NESS' TAKES SOMETHING FROM HIS POCKET...
2673

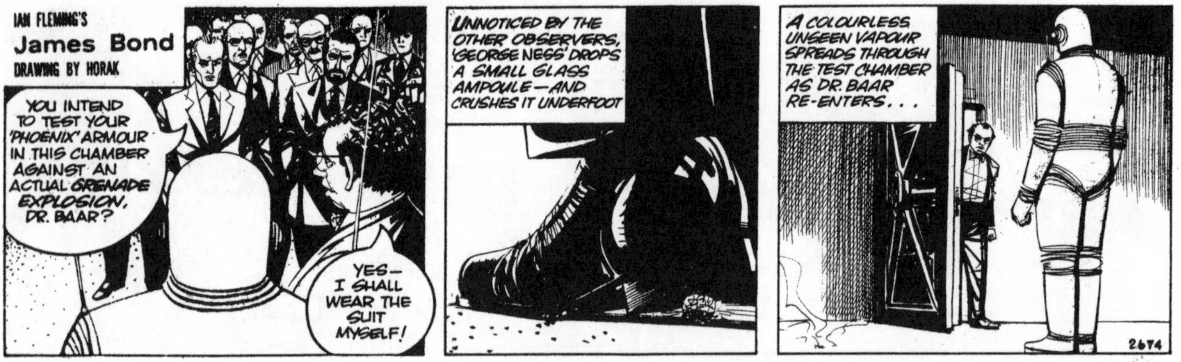
IAN FLEMING'S
James Bond
DRAWING BY HORAK
YOU INTEND TO TEST YOUR 'PHOENIX' ARMOUR IN THIS CHAMBER AGAINST AN ACTUAL GRENADE EXPLOSION, DR. BAAR?
YES—I SHALL WEAR THE SUIT MYSELF!
UNNOTICED BY THE OTHER OBSERVERS, 'GEORGE NESS' DROPS A SMALL GLASS AMPOULE—AND CRUSHES IT UNDERFOOT
A COLOURLESS UNSEEN VAPOUR SPREADS THROUGH THE TEST CHAMBER AS DR. BAAR RE-ENTERS...
2674

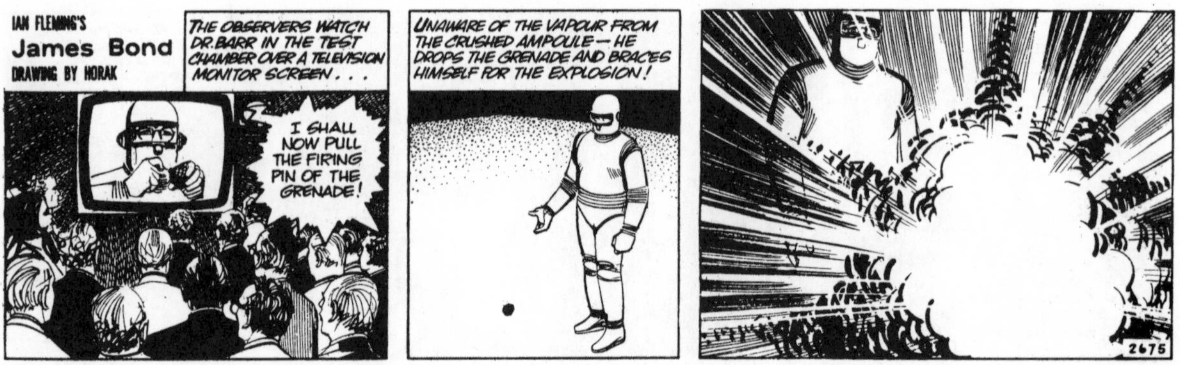
IAN FLEMING'S
James Bond
DRAWING BY HORAK
THE OBSERVERS WATCH DR. BARR IN THE TEST CHAMBER OVER A TELEVISION MONITOR SCREEN...
I SHALL NOW PULL THE FIRING PIN OF THE GRENADE!
UNAWARE OF THE VAPOUR FROM THE CRUSHED AMPOULE—HE DROPS THE GRENADE AND BRACES HIMSELF FOR THE EXPLOSION!
2675

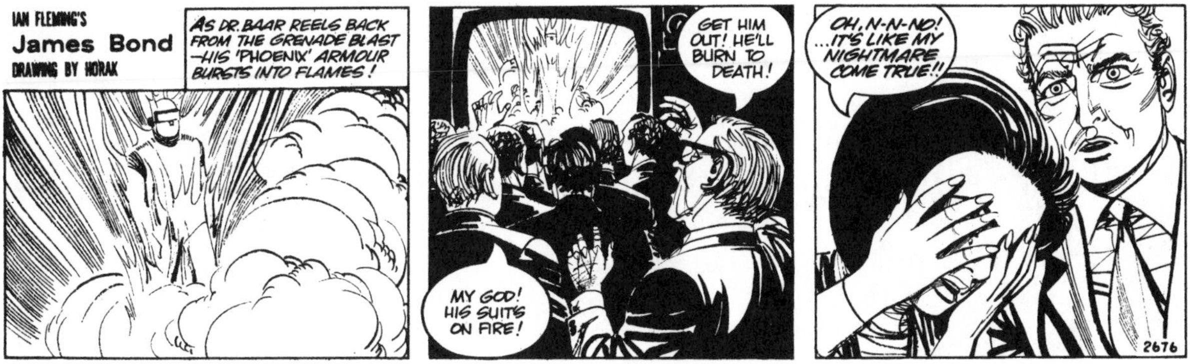
IAN FLEMING'S
James Bond
DRAWING BY HORAK
AS DR. BAAR REELS BACK FROM THE GRENADE BLAST —HIS 'PHOENIX' ARMOUR BURSTS INTO FLAMES!
GET HIM OUT! HE'LL BURN TO DEATH!
MY GOD! HIS SUIT'S ON FIRE!
OH, N-N-NO! ...IT'S LIKE MY NIGHTMARE COME TRUE!!
2676

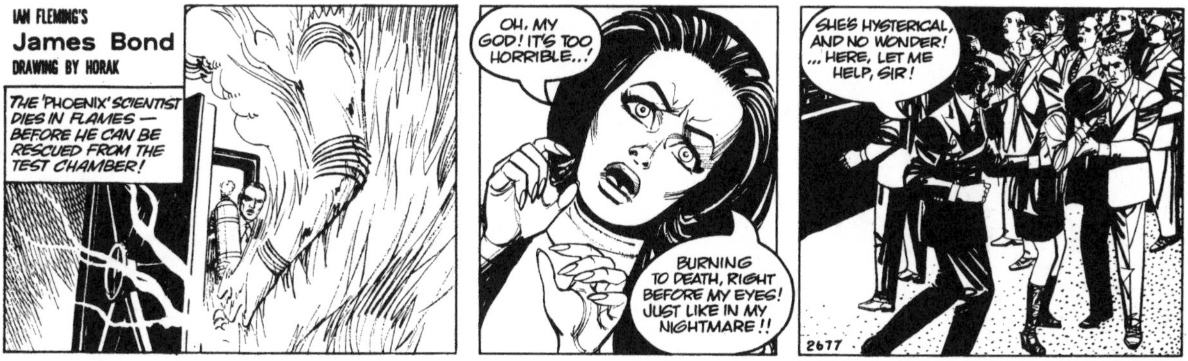
IAN FLEMING'S
James Bond
DRAWING BY HORAK
THE 'PHOENIX' SCIENTIST DIES IN FLAMES — BEFORE HE CAN BE RESCUED FROM THE TEST CHAMBER!
OH, MY GOD! IT'S TOO HORRIBLE...!
BURNING TO DEATH, RIGHT BEFORE MY EYES! JUST LIKE IN MY NIGHTMARE!!
SHE'S HYSTERICAL, AND NO WONDER! ... HERE, LET ME HELP, SIR!
2677

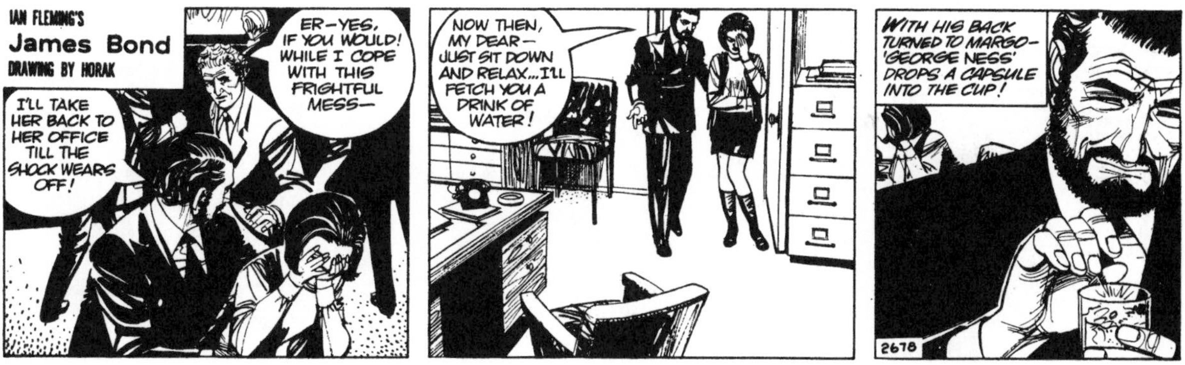
IAN FLEMING'S
James Bond
DRAWING BY HORAK
I'LL TAKE HER BACK TO HER OFFICE TILL THE SHOCK WEARS OFF!
ER—YES, IF YOU WOULD! WHILE I COPE WITH THIS FRIGHTFUL MESS—
NOW THEN, MY DEAR— JUST SIT DOWN AND RELAX... I'LL FETCH YOU A DRINK OF WATER!
WITH HIS BACK TURNED TO MARGO— 'GEORGE NESS' DROPS A CAPSULE INTO THE CUP!
2678

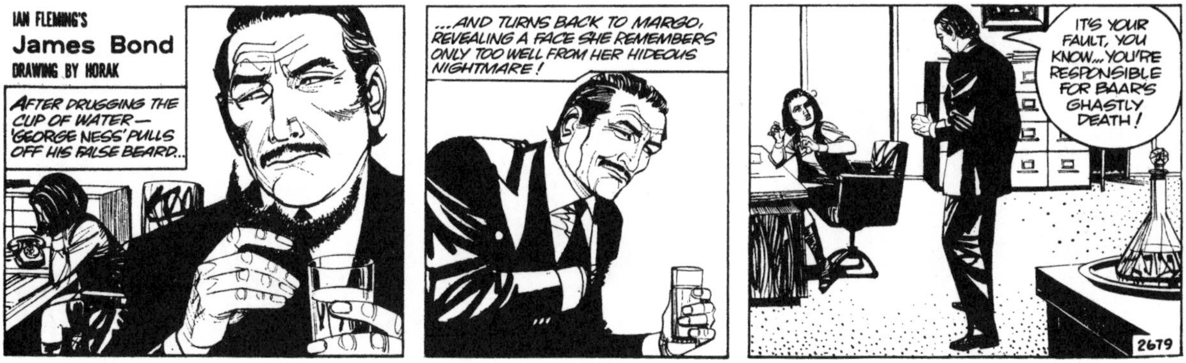
IAN FLEMING'S
James Bond
DRAWING BY HORAK
AFTER DRUGGING THE CUP OF WATER— 'GEORGE NESS' PULLS OFF HIS FALSE BEARD...
...AND TURNS BACK TO MARGO, REVEALING A FACE SHE REMEMBERS ONLY TOO WELL FROM HER HIDEOUS NIGHTMARE!
IT'S YOUR FAULT, YOU KNOW... YOU'RE RESPONSIBLE FOR BAAR'S GHASTLY DEATH!
2679

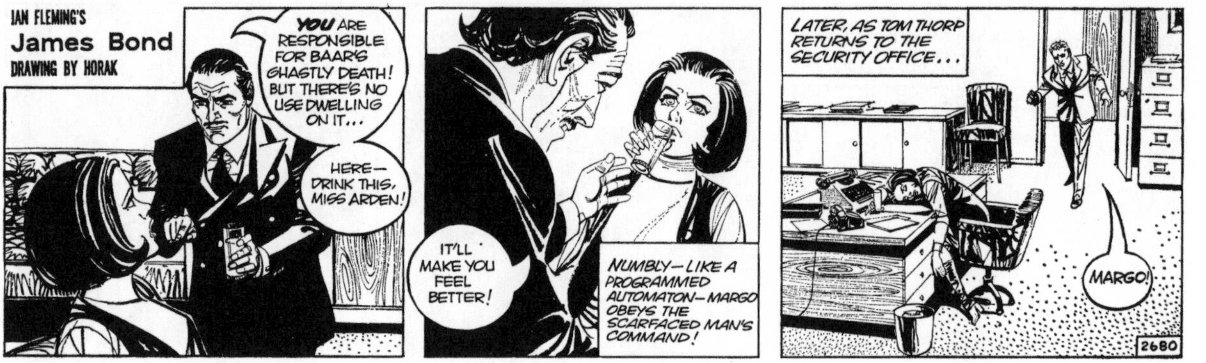
IAN FLEMING'S
James Bond
DRAWING BY HORAK
YOU ARE RESPONSIBLE FOR BAAR'S GHASTLY DEATH! BUT THERE'S NO USE DWELLING ON IT...
HERE— DRINK THIS, MISS ARDEN!
IT'LL MAKE YOU FEEL BETTER!
NUMBLY—LIKE A PROGRAMMED AUTOMATON—MARGO OBEYS THE SCARFACED MAN'S COMMAND!
LATER, AS TOM THORP RETURNS TO THE SECURITY OFFICE...
MARGO!
2680

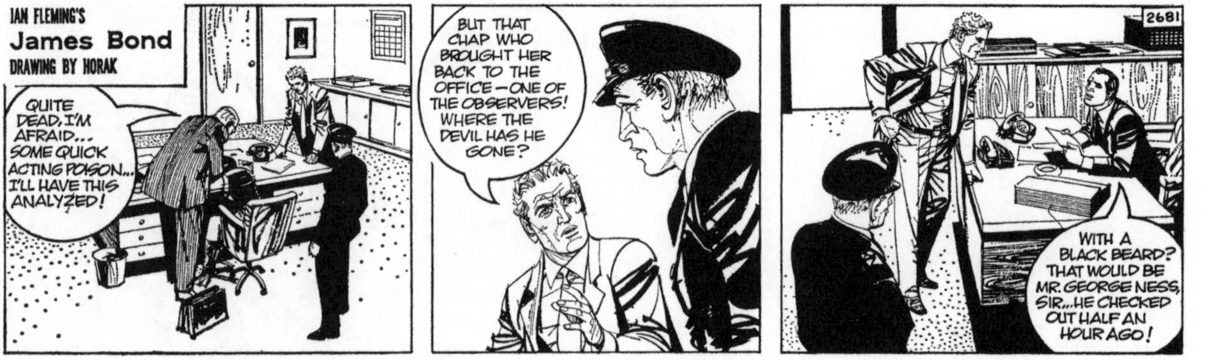
IAN FLEMING'S
James Bond
DRAWING BY HORAK
QUITE DEAD, I'M AFRAID... SOME QUICK ACTING POISON... I'LL HAVE THIS ANALYZED!
BUT THAT CHAP WHO BROUGHT HER BACK TO THE OFFICE—ONE OF THE OBSERVERS! WHERE THE DEVIL HAS HE GONE?
2681
WITH A BLACK BEARD? THAT WOULD BE MR. GEORGE NESS, SIR... HE CHECKED OUT HALF AN HOUR AGO!

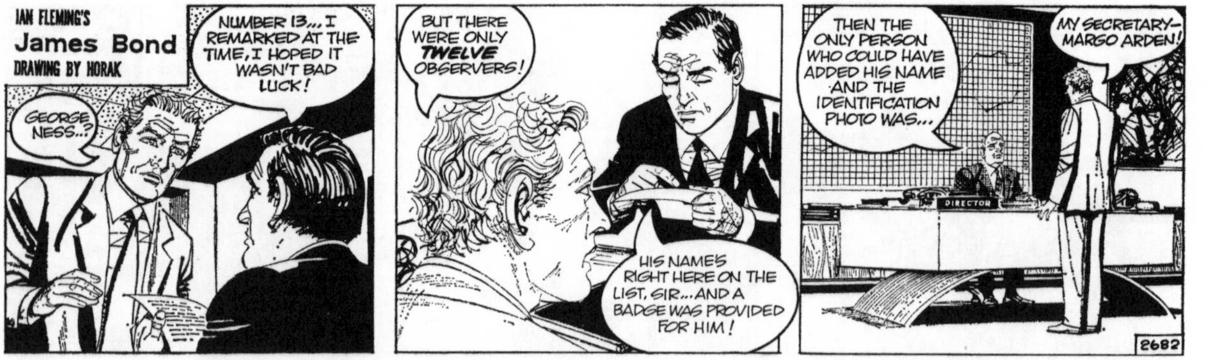
IAN FLEMING'S
James Bond
DRAWING BY HORAK
GEORGE NESS...?
NUMBER 13... I REMARKED AT THE TIME, I HOPED IT WASN'T BAD LUCK!
BUT THERE WERE ONLY TWELVE OBSERVERS!
HIS NAME'S RIGHT HERE ON THE LIST, SIR... AND A BADGE WAS PROVIDED FOR HIM!
THEN THE ONLY PERSON WHO COULD HAVE ADDED HIS NAME AND THE IDENTIFICATION PHOTO WAS...
MY SECRETARY— MARGO ARDEN!
DIRECTOR
2682

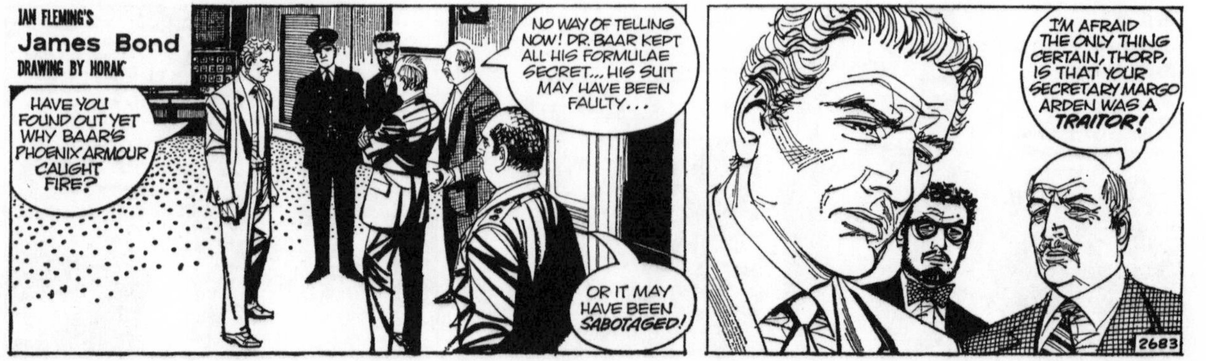
IAN FLEMING'S
James Bond
DRAWING BY HORAK
HAVE YOU FOUND OUT YET WHY BAAR'S PHOENIX ARMOUR CAUGHT FIRE?
NO WAY OF TELLING NOW! DR. BAAR KEPT ALL HIS FORMULAE SECRET... HIS SUIT MAY HAVE BEEN FAULTY...
OR IT MAY HAVE BEEN SABOTAGED!
I'M AFRAID THE ONLY THING CERTAIN, THORP, IS THAT YOUR SECRETARY MARGO ARDEN WAS A TRAITOR!
2683

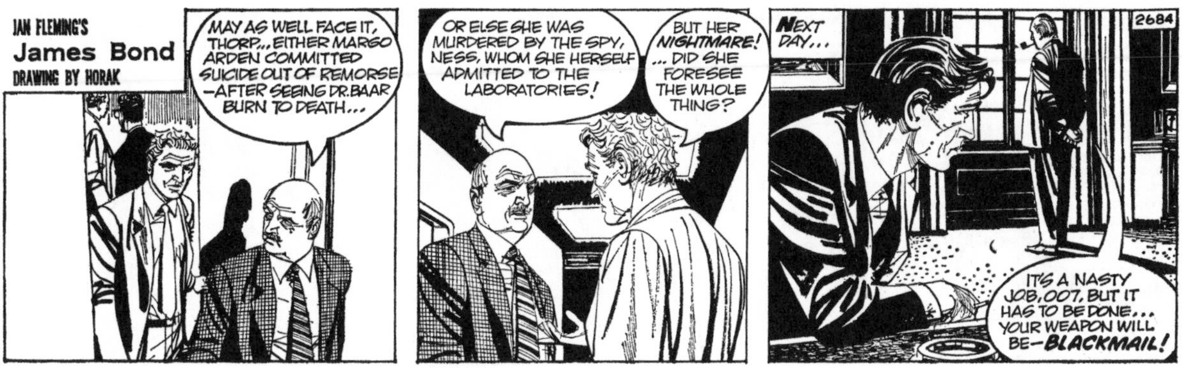
IAN FLEMING'S
James Bond
DRAWING BY HORAK
MAY AS WELL FACE IT, THORP... EITHER MARGO ARDEN COMMITTED SUICIDE OUT OF REMORSE —AFTER SEEING DR. BAAR BURN TO DEATH...
OR ELSE SHE WAS MURDERED BY THE SPY, NESS, WHOM SHE HERSELF ADMITTED TO THE LABORATORIES!
BUT HER NIGHTMARE! ... DID SHE FORESEE THE WHOLE THING?
2684
NEXT DAY...
IT'S A NASTY JOB, 007, BUT IT HAS TO BE DONE... YOUR WEAPON WILL BE—BLACKMAIL!

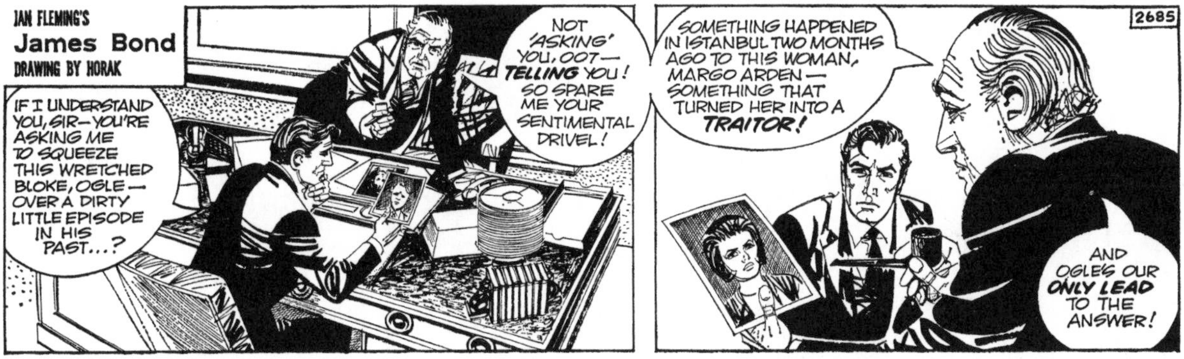
IAN FLEMING'S
James Bond
DRAWING BY HORAK
IF I UNDERSTAND YOU, SIR—YOU'RE ASKING ME TO SQUEEZE THIS WRETCHED BLOKE, OGLE — OVER A DIRTY LITTLE EPISODE IN HIS PAST...?
NOT 'ASKING' YOU, 007— TELLING YOU! SO SPARE ME YOUR SENTIMENTAL DRIVEL!
2685
SOMETHING HAPPENED IN ISTANBUL TWO MONTHS AGO TO THIS WOMAN, MARGO ARDEN — SOMETHING THAT TURNED HER INTO A TRAITOR!
AND OGLE'S OUR ONLY LEAD TO THE ANSWER!

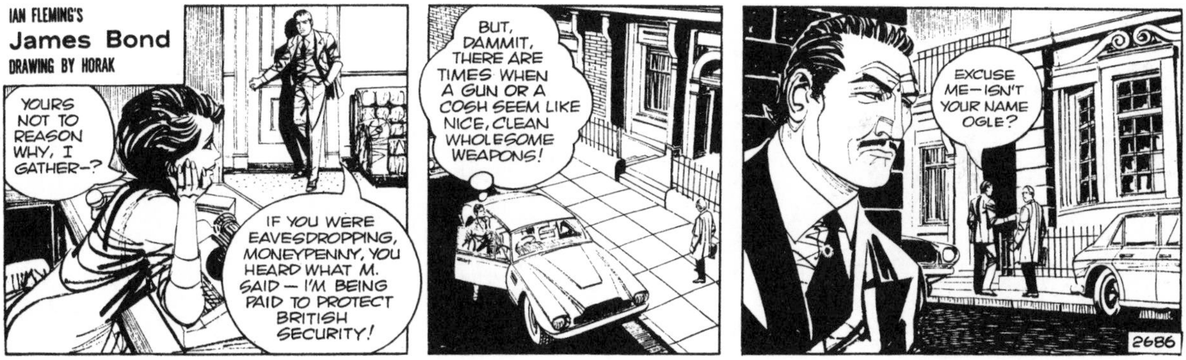
IAN FLEMING'S
James Bond
DRAWING BY HORAK
YOURS NOT TO REASON WHY, I GATHER—?
IF YOU WERE EAVESDROPPING, MONEYPENNY, YOU HEARD WHAT M. SAID — I'M BEING PAID TO PROTECT BRITISH SECURITY!
BUT, DAMMIT, THERE ARE TIMES WHEN A GUN OR A COSH SEEM LIKE NICE, CLEAN WHOLESOME WEAPONS!
EXCUSE ME—ISN'T YOUR NAME OGLE?
2686

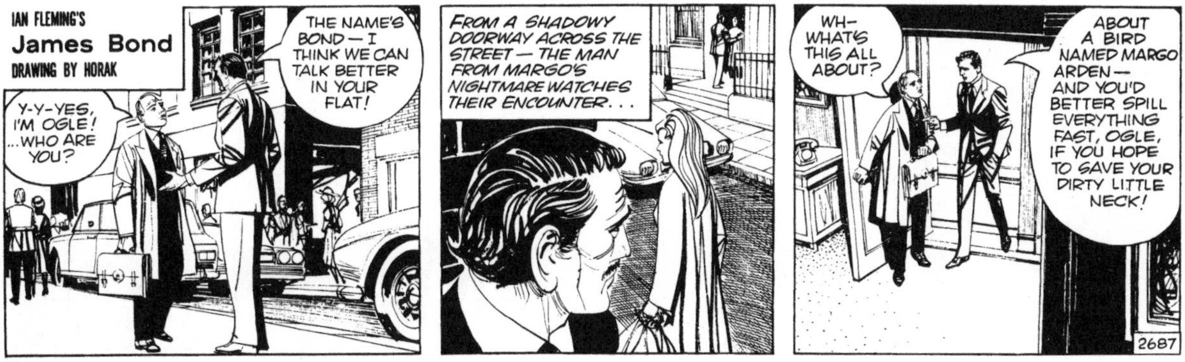
IAN FLEMING'S
James Bond
DRAWING BY HORAK
Y-Y-YES, I'M OGLE! ...WHO ARE YOU?
THE NAME'S BOND — I THINK WE CAN TALK BETTER IN YOUR FLAT!
FROM A SHADOWY DOORWAY ACROSS THE STREET — THE MAN FROM MARGO'S NIGHTMARE WATCHES THEIR ENCOUNTER...
WH— WHAT'S THIS ALL ABOUT?
ABOUT A BIRD NAMED MARGO ARDEN— AND YOU'D BETTER SPILL EVERYTHING FAST, OGLE, IF YOU HOPE TO SAVE YOUR DIRTY LITTLE NECK!
2687

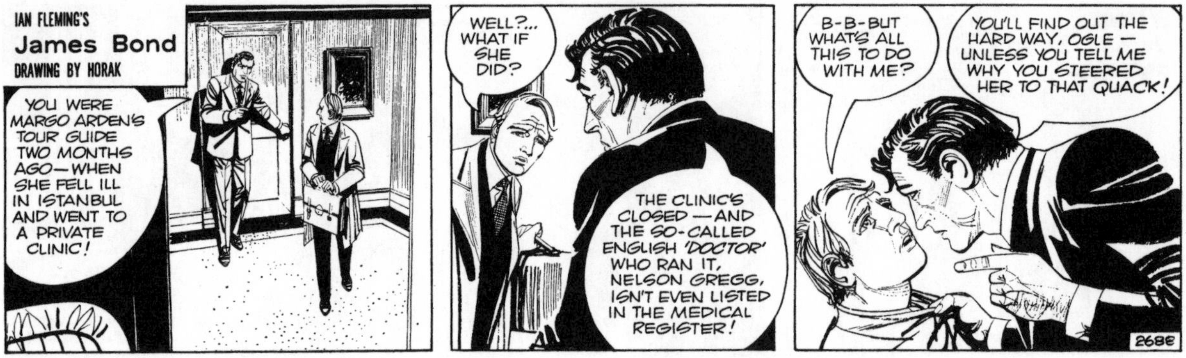
IAN FLEMING'S
James Bond
DRAWING BY HORAK
YOU WERE MARGO ARDEN'S TOUR GUIDE TWO MONTHS AGO—WHEN SHE FELL ILL IN ISTANBUL AND WENT TO A PRIVATE CLINIC!
WELL?... WHAT IF SHE DID?
THE CLINIC'S CLOSED—AND THE SO-CALLED ENGLISH 'DOCTOR' WHO RAN IT, NELSON GREGG, ISN'T EVEN LISTED IN THE MEDICAL REGISTER!
B-B-BUT WHAT'S ALL THIS TO DO WITH ME?
YOU'LL FIND OUT THE HARD WAY, OGLE—UNLESS YOU TELL ME WHY YOU STEERED HER TO THAT QUACK!
2688

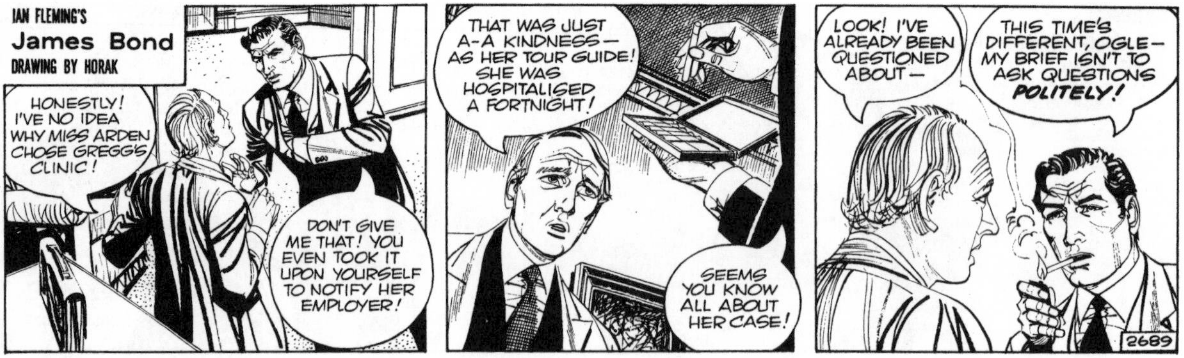
IAN FLEMING'S
James Bond
DRAWING BY HORAK
HONESTLY! I'VE NO IDEA WHY MISS ARDEN CHOSE GREGG'S CLINIC!
DON'T GIVE ME THAT! YOU EVEN TOOK IT UPON YOURSELF TO NOTIFY HER EMPLOYER!
THAT WAS JUST A-A KINDNESS—AS HER TOUR GUIDE! SHE WAS HOSPITALISED A FORTNIGHT!
SEEMS YOU KNOW ALL ABOUT HER CASE!
LOOK! I'VE ALREADY BEEN QUESTIONED ABOUT—
THIS TIME'S DIFFERENT, OGLE—MY BRIEF ISN'T TO ASK QUESTIONS POLITELY!
2689

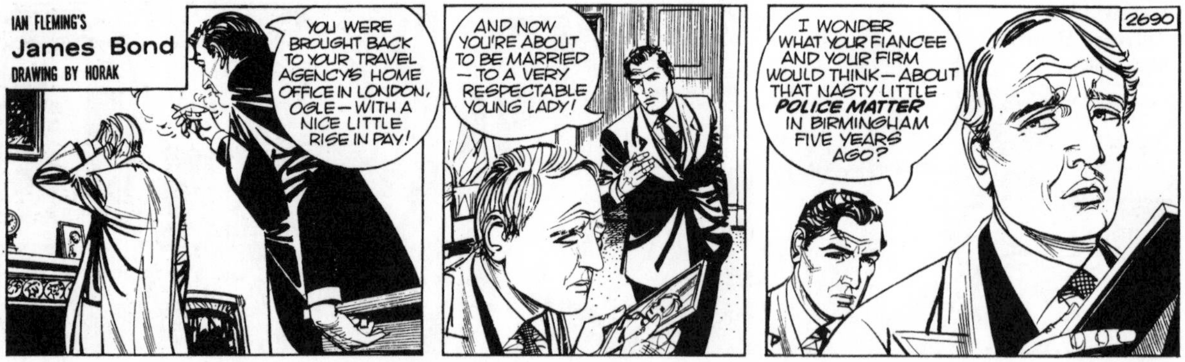
IAN FLEMING'S
James Bond
DRAWING BY HORAK
YOU WERE BROUGHT BACK TO YOUR TRAVEL AGENCY'S HOME OFFICE IN LONDON, OGLE—WITH A NICE LITTLE RISE IN PAY!
AND NOW YOU'RE ABOUT TO BE MARRIED—TO A VERY RESPECTABLE YOUNG LADY!
I WONDER WHAT YOUR FIANCEE AND YOUR FIRM WOULD THINK—ABOUT THAT NASTY LITTLE POLICE MATTER IN BIRMINGHAM FIVE YEARS AGO?
2690

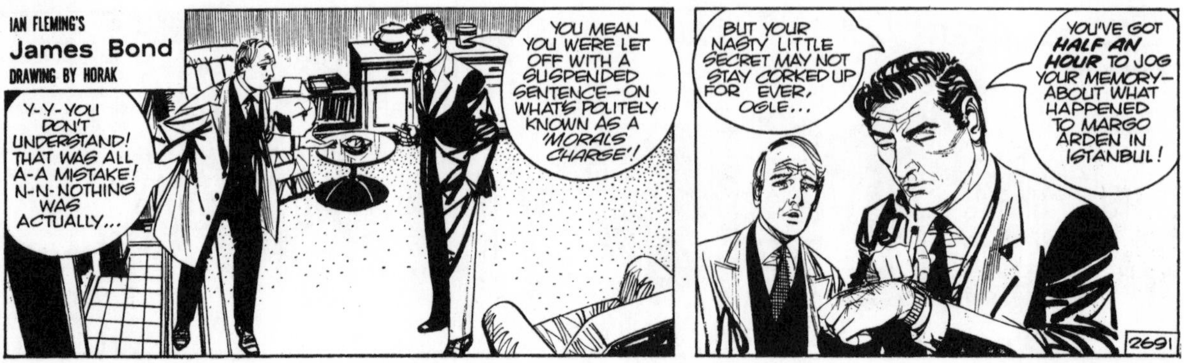
IAN FLEMING'S
James Bond
DRAWING BY HORAK
Y-Y-YOU DON'T UNDERSTAND! THAT WAS ALL A-A MISTAKE! N-N-NOTHING WAS ACTUALLY...
YOU MEAN YOU WERE LET OFF WITH A SUSPENDED SENTENCE—ON WHAT'S POLITELY KNOWN AS A 'MORALS' CHARGE'!
BUT YOUR NASTY LITTLE SECRET MAY NOT STAY CORKED UP FOR EVER, OGLE...
YOU'VE GOT HALF AN HOUR TO JOG YOUR MEMORY—ABOUT WHAT HAPPENED TO MARGO ARDEN IN ISTANBUL!
2691

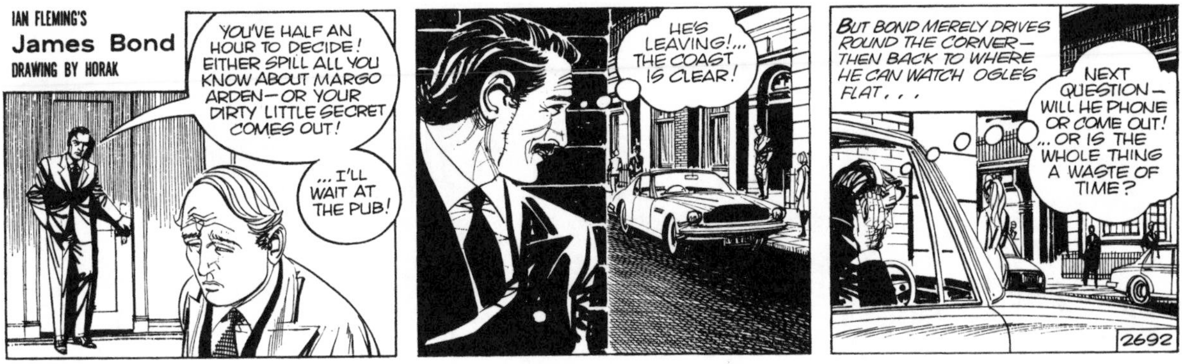
IAN FLEMING'S
James Bond
DRAWING BY HORAK
YOU'VE HALF AN HOUR TO DECIDE! EITHER SPILL ALL YOU KNOW ABOUT MARGO ARDEN—OR YOUR DIRTY LITTLE SECRET COMES OUT!
... I'LL WAIT AT THE PUB!
HE'S LEAVING!... THE COAST IS CLEAR!
BUT BOND MERELY DRIVES ROUND THE CORNER—THEN BACK TO WHERE HE CAN WATCH OGLE'S FLAT . . .
NEXT QUESTION—WILL HE PHONE OR COME OUT! ... OR IS THE WHOLE THING A WASTE OF TIME?
2692

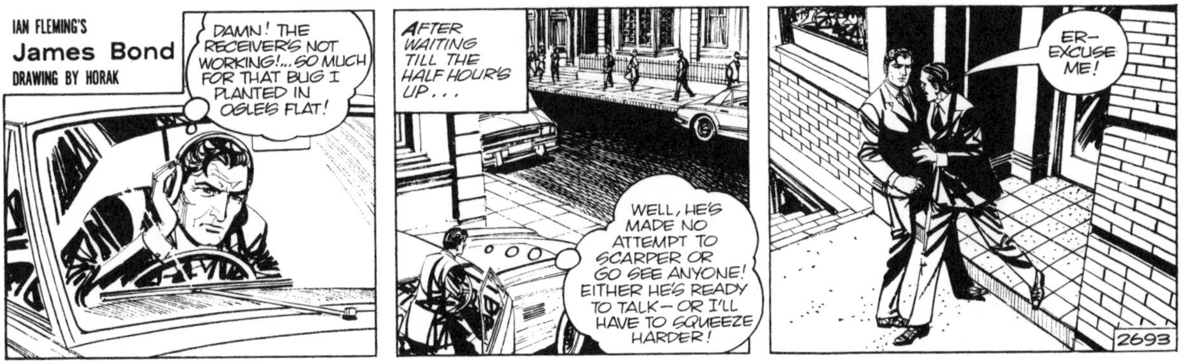
IAN FLEMING'S
James Bond
DRAWING BY HORAK
DAMN! THE RECEIVER'S NOT WORKING!... SO MUCH FOR THAT BUG I PLANTED IN OGLE'S FLAT!
AFTER WAITING TILL THE HALF HOUR'S UP . . .
WELL, HE'S MADE NO ATTEMPT TO SCARPER OR GO SEE ANYONE! EITHER HE'S READY TO TALK—OR I'LL HAVE TO SQUEEZE HARDER!
ER—EXCUSE ME!
2693

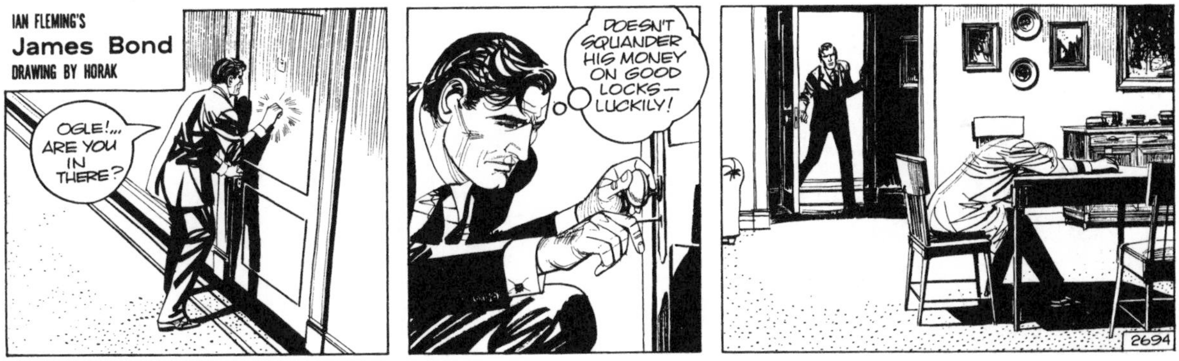
IAN FLEMING'S
James Bond
DRAWING BY HORAK
OGLE!... ARE YOU IN THERE?
DOESN'T SQUANDER HIS MONEY ON GOOD LOCKS—LUCKILY!
2694

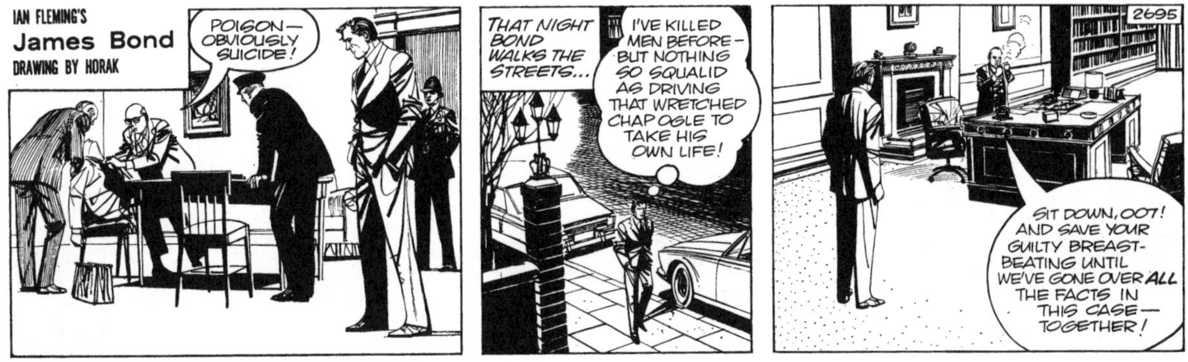
IAN FLEMING'S
James Bond
DRAWING BY HORAK
POISON—OBVIOUSLY SUICIDE!
THAT NIGHT BOND WALKS THE STREETS...
I'VE KILLED MEN BEFORE—BUT NOTHING SO SQUALID AS DRIVING THAT WRETCHED CHAP OGLE TO TAKE HIS OWN LIFE!
2695
SIT DOWN, 007! AND SAVE YOUR GUILTY BREAST-BEATING UNTIL WE'VE GONE OVER ALL THE FACTS IN THIS CASE—TOGETHER!

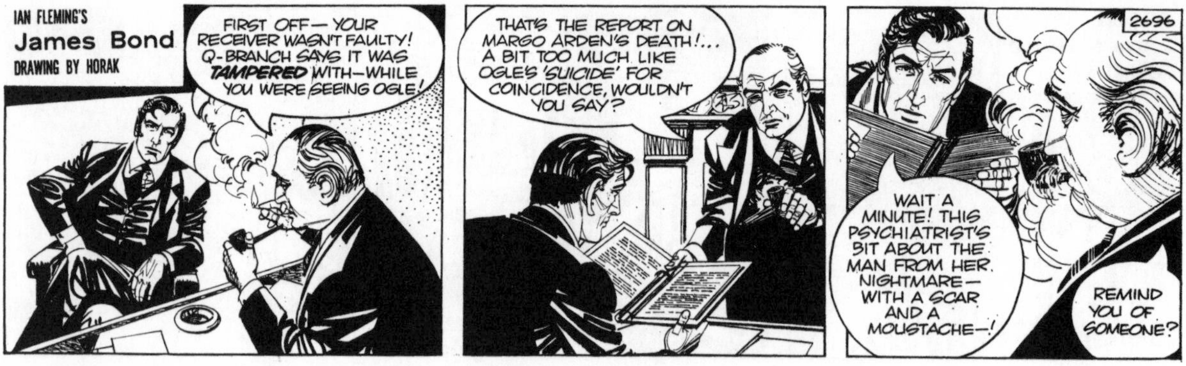
IAN FLEMING'S
James Bond
DRAWING BY HORAK
FIRST OFF—YOUR RECEIVER WASN'T FAULTY! Q-BRANCH SAYS IT WAS TAMPERED WITH—WHILE YOU WERE SEEING OGLE!
THAT'S THE REPORT ON MARGO ARDEN'S DEATH!... A BIT TOO MUCH LIKE OGLE'S 'SUICIDE' FOR COINCIDENCE, WOULDN'T YOU SAY?
2696
WAIT A MINUTE! THIS PSYCHIATRIST'S BIT ABOUT THE MAN FROM HER NIGHTMARE—WITH A SCAR AND A MOUSTACHE—!
REMIND YOU OF SOMEONE?

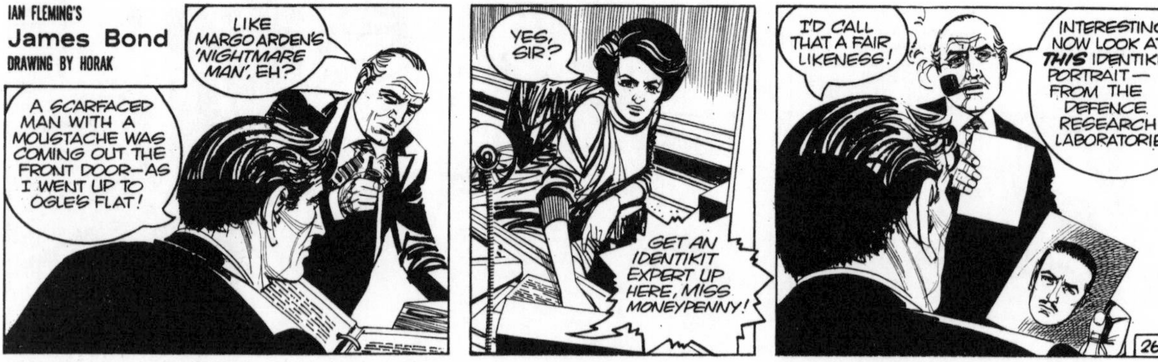
IAN FLEMING'S
James Bond
DRAWING BY HORAK
A SCARFACED MAN WITH A MOUSTACHE WAS COMING OUT THE FRONT DOOR—AS I WENT UP TO OGLE'S FLAT!
LIKE MARGO ARDEN'S 'NIGHTMARE MAN', EH?
YES, SIR?
GET AN IDENTIKIT EXPERT UP HERE, MISS MONEYPENNY!
I'D CALL THAT A FAIR LIKENESS!
INTERESTING! NOW LOOK AT THIS IDENTIKIT PORTRAIT—FROM THE DEFENCE RESEARCH LABORATORIES!
2697

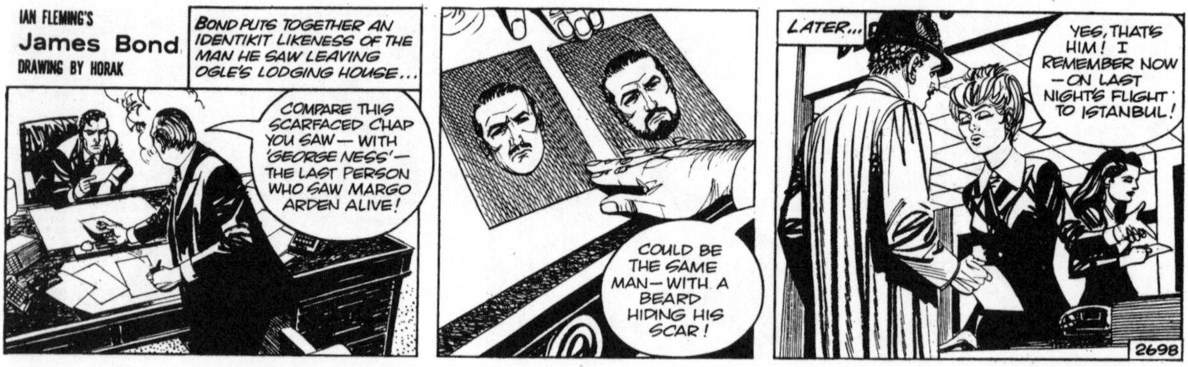
IAN FLEMING'S
James Bond
DRAWING BY HORAK
BOND PUTS TOGETHER AN IDENTIKIT LIKENESS OF THE MAN HE SAW LEAVING OGLE'S LODGING HOUSE...
COMPARE THIS SCARFACED CHAP YOU SAW—WITH 'GEORGE NESS'—THE LAST PERSON WHO SAW MARGO ARDEN ALIVE!
COULD BE THE SAME MAN—WITH A BEARD HIDING HIS SCAR!
LATER...
YES, THAT'S HIM! I REMEMBER NOW—ON LAST NIGHT'S FLIGHT TO ISTANBUL!
2698

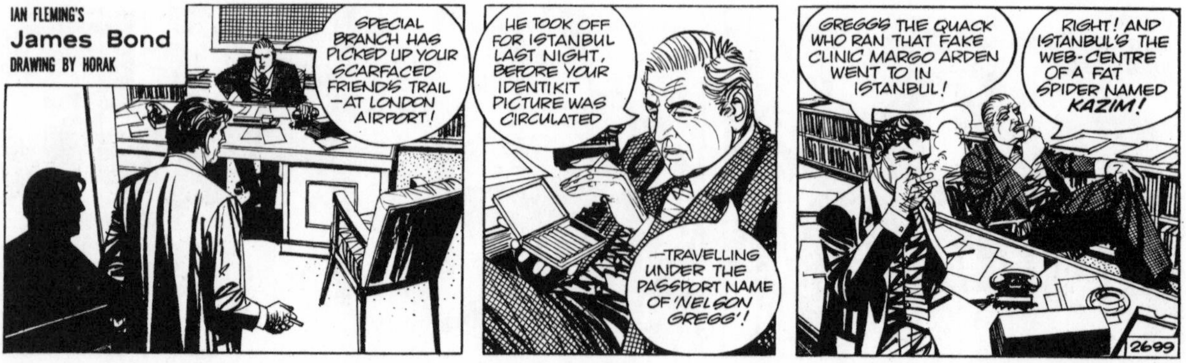
IAN FLEMING'S
James Bond
DRAWING BY HORAK
SPECIAL BRANCH HAS PICKED UP YOUR SCARFACED FRIEND'S TRAIL—AT LONDON AIRPORT!
HE TOOK OFF FOR ISTANBUL LAST NIGHT, BEFORE YOUR IDENTIKIT PICTURE WAS CIRCULATED
—TRAVELLING UNDER THE PASSPORT NAME OF 'NELSON GREGG'!
GREGG'S THE QUACK WHO RAN THAT FAKE CLINIC MARGO ARDEN WENT TO IN ISTANBUL!
RIGHT! AND ISTANBUL'S THE WEB-CENTRE OF A FAT SPIDER NAMED KAZIM!
2699

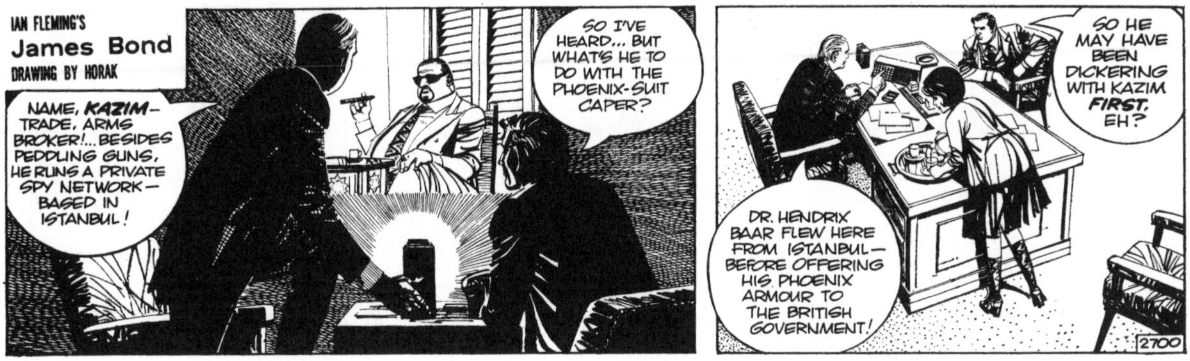
IAN FLEMING'S
James Bond
DRAWING BY HORAK
NAME, KAZIM-TRADE, ARMS BROKER!... BESIDES PEDDLING GUNS, HE RUNS A PRIVATE SPY NETWORK—BASED IN ISTANBUL!
SO I'VE HEARD... BUT WHAT'S HE TO DO WITH THE PHOENIX-SUIT CAPER?
DR. HENDRIX BAAR FLEW HERE FROM ISTANBUL—BEFORE OFFERING HIS PHOENIX ARMOUR TO THE BRITISH GOVERNMENT!
SO HE MAY HAVE BEEN DICKERING WITH KAZIM FIRST, EH?
2700

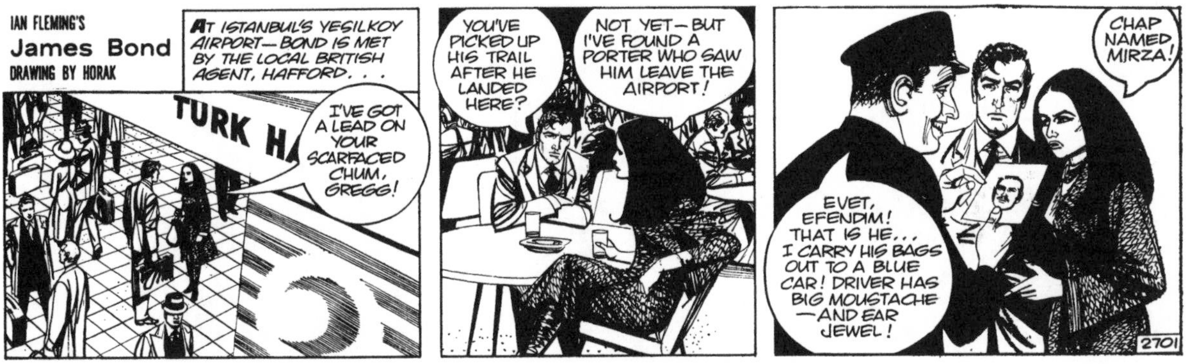
IAN FLEMING'S
James Bond
DRAWING BY HORAK
AT ISTANBUL'S YESILKOY AIRPORT—BOND IS MET BY THE LOCAL BRITISH AGENT, HAFFORD . . .
TURK HA
I'VE GOT A LEAD ON YOUR SCARFACED CHUM, GREGG!
YOU'VE PICKED UP HIS TRAIL AFTER HE LANDED HERE?
NOT YET—BUT I'VE FOUND A PORTER WHO SAW HIM LEAVE THE AIRPORT!
CHAP NAMED MIRZA!
EVET, EFENDIM! THAT IS HE... I CARRY HIS BAGS OUT TO A BLUE CAR! DRIVER HAS BIG MOUSTACHE—AND EAR JEWEL!
2701

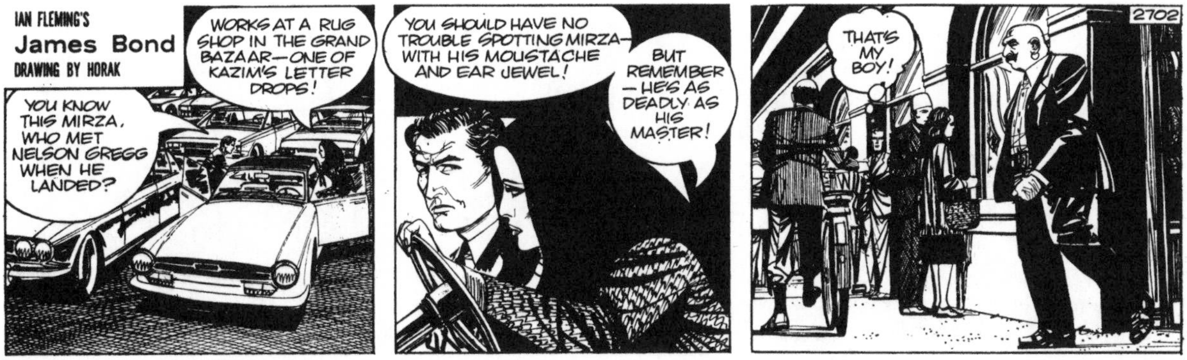
IAN FLEMING'S
James Bond
DRAWING BY HORAK
YOU KNOW THIS MIRZA, WHO MET NELSON GREGG WHEN HE LANDED?
WORKS AT A RUG SHOP IN THE GRAND BAZAAR—ONE OF KAZIM'S LETTER DROPS!
YOU SHOULD HAVE NO TROUBLE SPOTTING MIRZA—WITH HIS MOUSTACHE AND EAR JEWEL!
BUT REMEMBER—HE'S AS DEADLY AS HIS MASTER!
2702
THAT'S MY BOY!

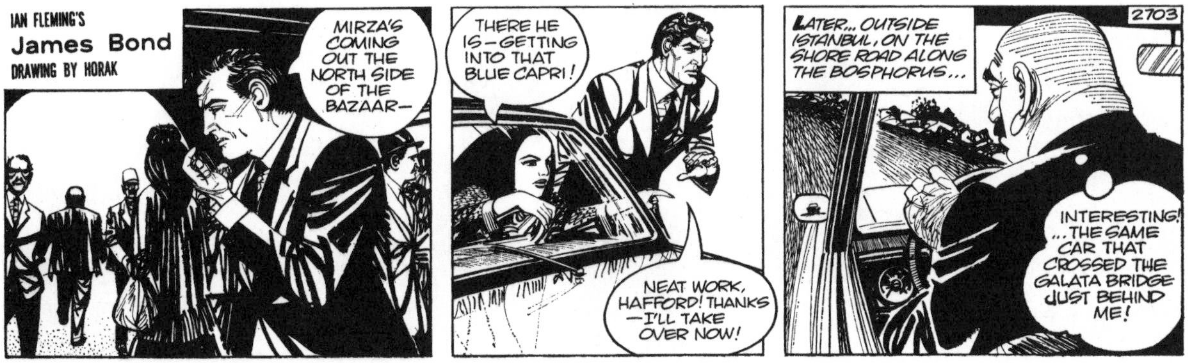
IAN FLEMING'S
James Bond
DRAWING BY HORAK
MIRZA'S COMING OUT THE NORTH SIDE OF THE BAZAAR—
THERE HE IS—GETTING INTO THAT BLUE CAPRI!
NEAT WORK, HAFFORD! THANKS—I'LL TAKE OVER NOW!
LATER... OUTSIDE ISTANBUL, ON THE SHORE ROAD ALONG THE BOSPHORUS...
2703
INTERESTING! ...THE SAME CAR THAT CROSSED THE GALATA BRIDGE JUST BEHIND ME!

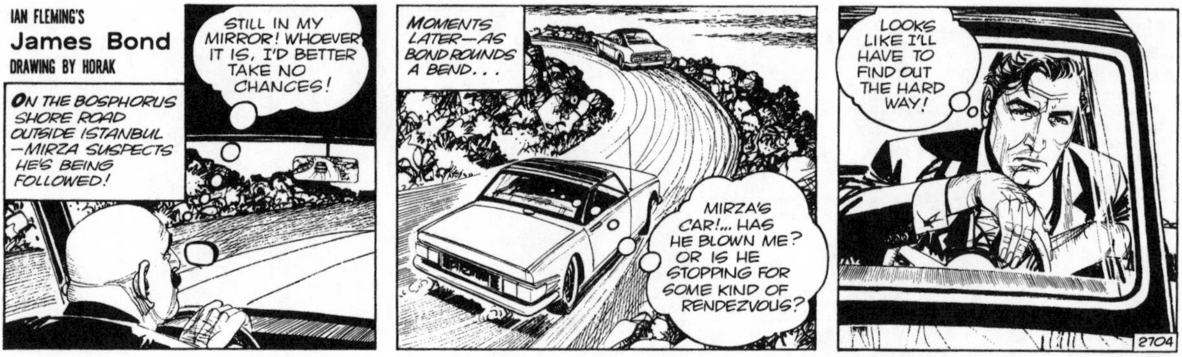
IAN FLEMING'S
James Bond
DRAWING BY HORAK
ON THE BOSPHORUS SHORE ROAD OUTSIDE ISTANBUL —MIRZA SUSPECTS HE'S BEING FOLLOWED!
STILL IN MY MIRROR! WHOEVER IT IS, I'D BETTER TAKE NO CHANCES!
MOMENTS LATER—AS BOND ROUNDS A BEND...
MIRZA'S CAR!... HAS HE BLOWN ME? OR IS HE STOPPING FOR SOME KIND OF RENDEZVOUS?
LOOKS LIKE I'LL HAVE TO FIND OUT THE HARD WAY!
2704

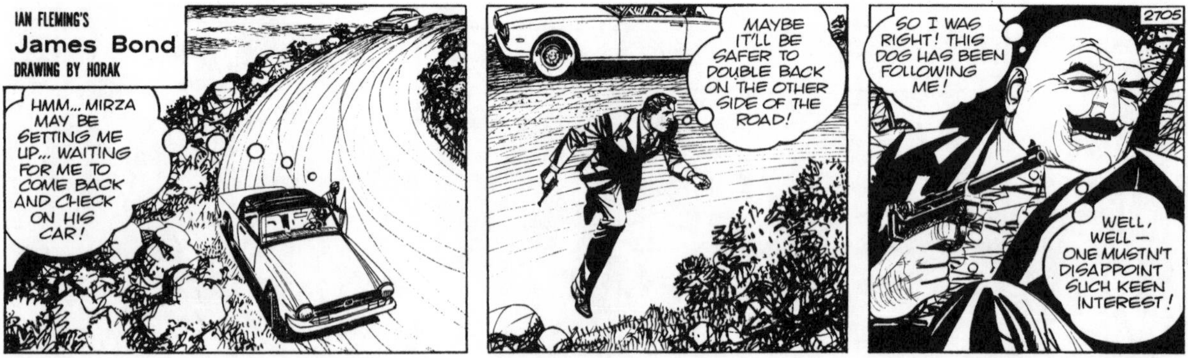
IAN FLEMING'S
James Bond
DRAWING BY HORAK
HMM... MIRZA MAY BE SETTING ME UP... WAITING FOR ME TO COME BACK AND CHECK ON HIS CAR!
MAYBE IT'LL BE SAFER TO DOUBLE BACK ON THE OTHER SIDE OF THE ROAD!
2705
SO I WAS RIGHT! THIS DOG HAS BEEN FOLLOWING ME!
WELL, WELL — ONE MUSTN'T DISAPPOINT SUCH KEEN INTEREST!

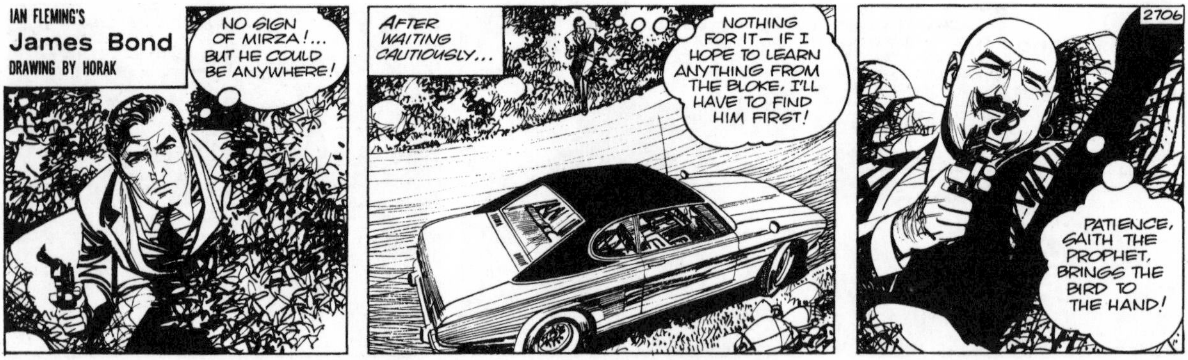
IAN FLEMING'S
James Bond
DRAWING BY HORAK
NO SIGN OF MIRZA!... BUT HE COULD BE ANYWHERE!
AFTER WAITING CAUTIOUSLY...
NOTHING FOR IT— IF I HOPE TO LEARN ANYTHING FROM THE BLOKE, I'LL HAVE TO FIND HIM FIRST!
2706
PATIENCE, SAITH THE PROPHET, BRINGS THE BIRD TO THE HAND!

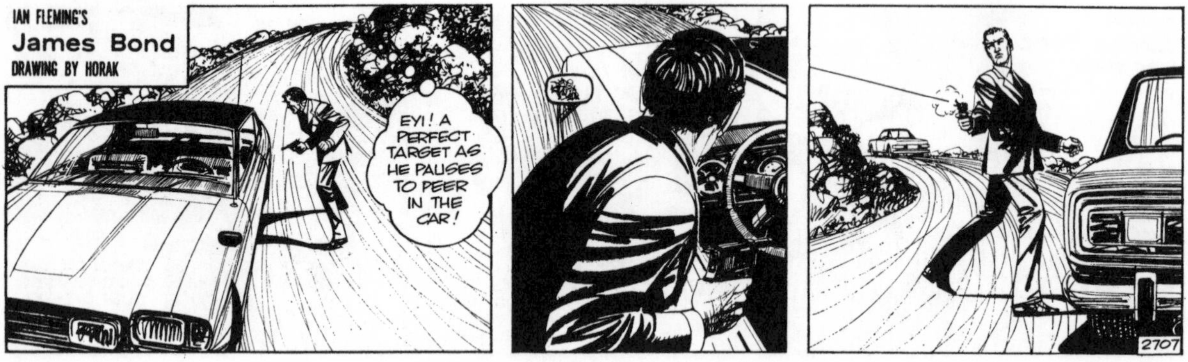
IAN FLEMING'S
James Bond
DRAWING BY HORAK
EYI! A PERFECT TARGET AS HE PAUSES TO PEER IN THE CAR!
2707

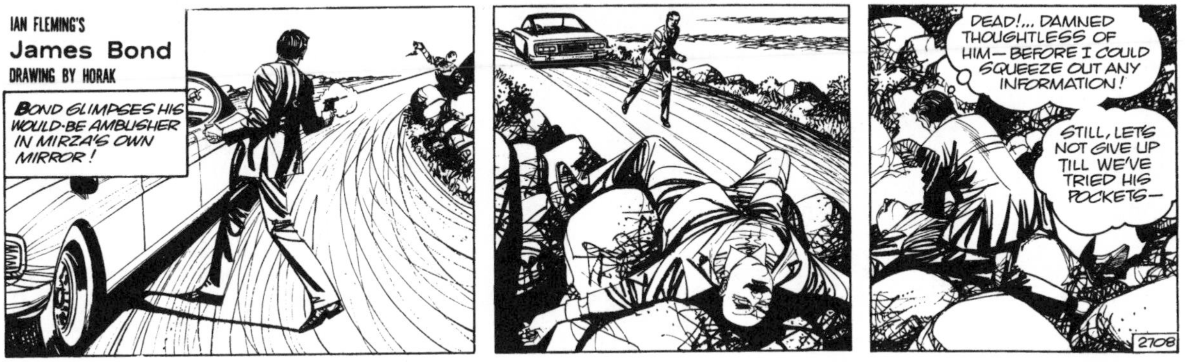
IAN FLEMING'S
James Bond
DRAWING BY HORAK
BOND GLIMPSES HIS WOULD-BE AMBUSHER IN MIRZA'S OWN MIRROR!
DEAD!... DAMNED THOUGHTLESS OF HIM—BEFORE I COULD SQUEEZE OUT ANY INFORMATION!
STILL, LET'S NOT GIVE UP TILL WE'VE TRIED HIS POCKETS—
2708

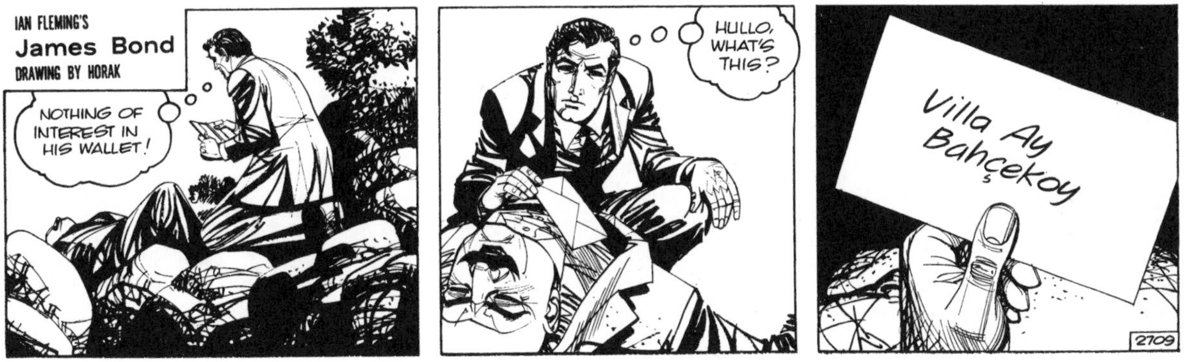
IAN FLEMING'S
James Bond
DRAWING BY HORAK
NOTHING OF INTEREST IN HIS WALLET!
HULLO, WHAT'S THIS?
Villa Ay Bahçekoy
2709

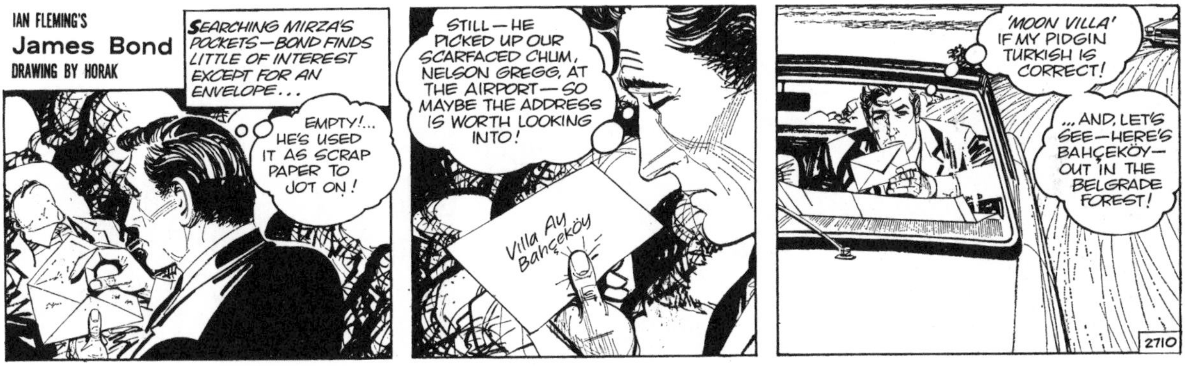
IAN FLEMING'S
James Bond
DRAWING BY HORAK
SEARCHING MIRZA'S POCKETS—BOND FINDS LITTLE OF INTEREST EXCEPT FOR AN ENVELOPE...
EMPTY!... HE'S USED IT AS SCRAP PAPER TO JOT ON!
STILL—HE PICKED UP OUR SCARFACED CHUM, NELSON GREGG, AT THE AIRPORT—SO MAYBE THE ADDRESS IS WORTH LOOKING INTO!
Villa Ay Bahçeköy
'MOON VILLA' IF MY PIDGIN TURKISH IS CORRECT!
...AND, LET'S SEE—HERE'S BAHÇEKÖY—OUT IN THE BELGRADE FOREST!
2710

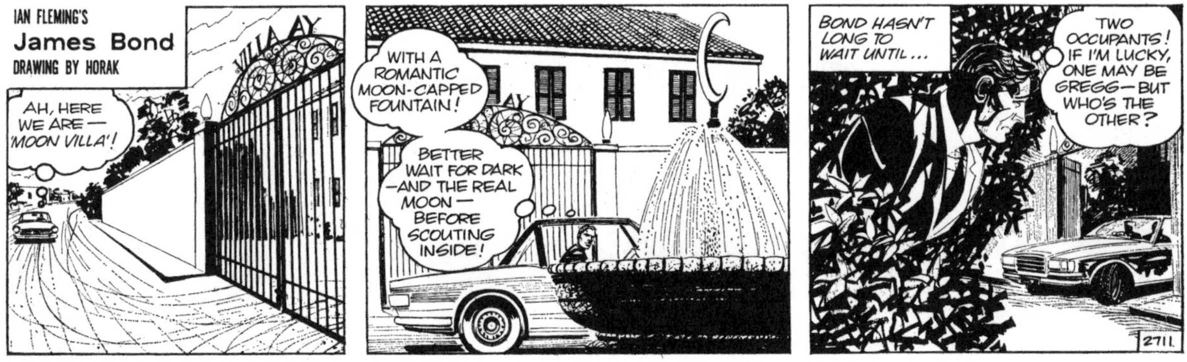
IAN FLEMING'S
James Bond
DRAWING BY HORAK
AH, HERE WE ARE—'MOON VILLA'!
WITH A ROMANTIC MOON-CAPPED FOUNTAIN!
BETTER WAIT FOR DARK—AND THE REAL MOON—BEFORE SCOUTING INSIDE!
BOND HASN'T LONG TO WAIT UNTIL...
TWO OCCUPANTS! IF I'M LUCKY, ONE MAY BE GREGG—BUT WHO'S THE OTHER?
2711

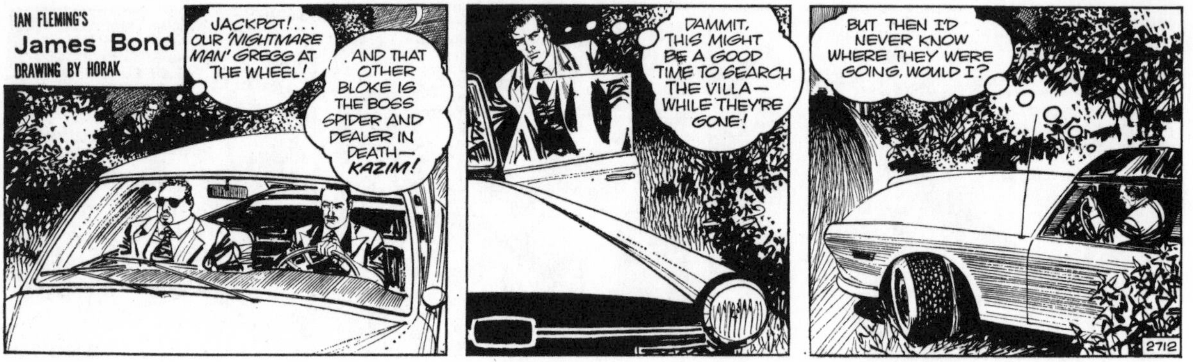
IAN FLEMING'S
James Bond
DRAWING BY HORAK
JACKPOT!... OUR 'NIGHTMARE MAN' GREGG AT THE WHEEL!
. AND THAT OTHER BLOKE IS THE BOSS SPIDER AND DEALER IN DEATH— KAZIM!
DAMMIT, THIS MIGHT BE A GOOD TIME TO SEARCH THE VILLA— WHILE THEY'RE GONE!
BUT THEN I'D NEVER KNOW WHERE THEY WERE GOING, WOULD I?
2712

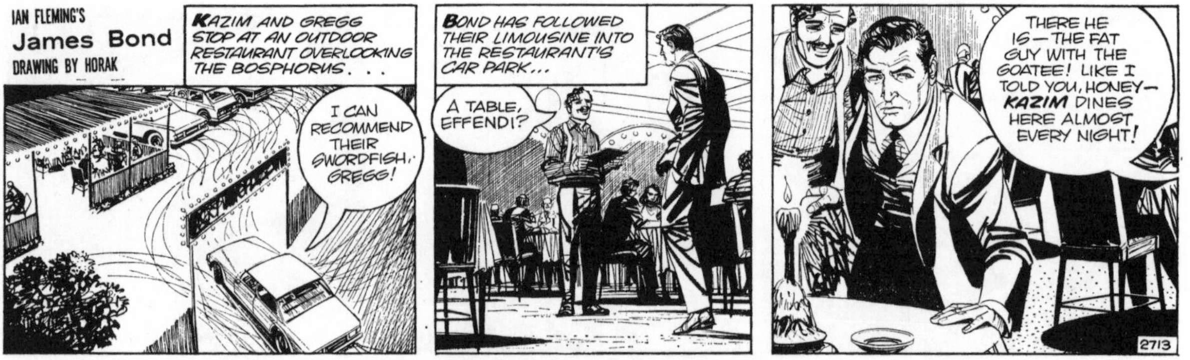
IAN FLEMING'S
James Bond
DRAWING BY HORAK
KAZIM AND GREGG STOP AT AN OUTDOOR RESTAURANT OVERLOOKING THE BOSPHORUS . . .
I CAN RECOMMEND THEIR SWORDFISH, GREGG!
BOND HAS FOLLOWED THEIR LIMOUSINE INTO THE RESTAURANT'S CAR PARK...
A TABLE, EFFENDI?
THERE HE IS—THE FAT GUY WITH THE GOATEE! LIKE I TOLD YOU, HONEY— KAZIM DINES HERE ALMOST EVERY NIGHT!
2713

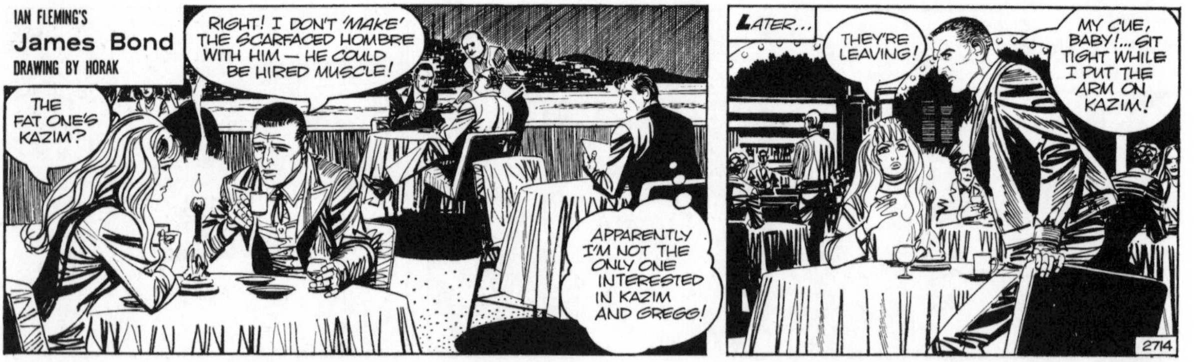
IAN FLEMING'S
James Bond
DRAWING BY HORAK
THE FAT ONE'S KAZIM?
RIGHT! I DON'T 'MAKE' THE SCARFACED HOMBRE WITH HIM — HE COULD BE HIRED MUSCLE!
APPARENTLY I'M NOT THE ONLY ONE INTERESTED IN KAZIM AND GREGG!
LATER...
THEY'RE LEAVING!
MY CUE, BABY!... SIT TIGHT WHILE I PUT THE ARM ON KAZIM!
2714

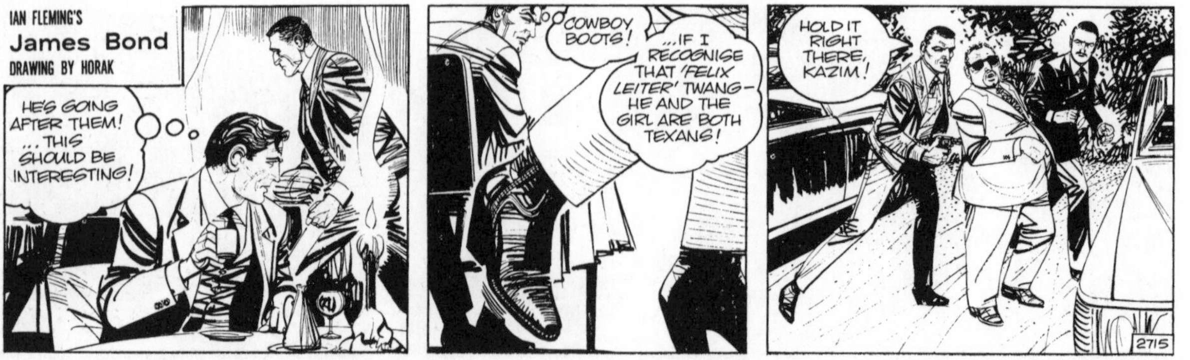
IAN FLEMING'S
James Bond
DRAWING BY HORAK
HE'S GOING AFTER THEM! ... THIS SHOULD BE INTERESTING!
COWBOY BOOTS!
...IF I RECOGNISE THAT 'FELIX LEITER' TWANG— HE AND THE GIRL ARE BOTH TEXANS!
HOLD IT RIGHT THERE, KAZIM!
2715

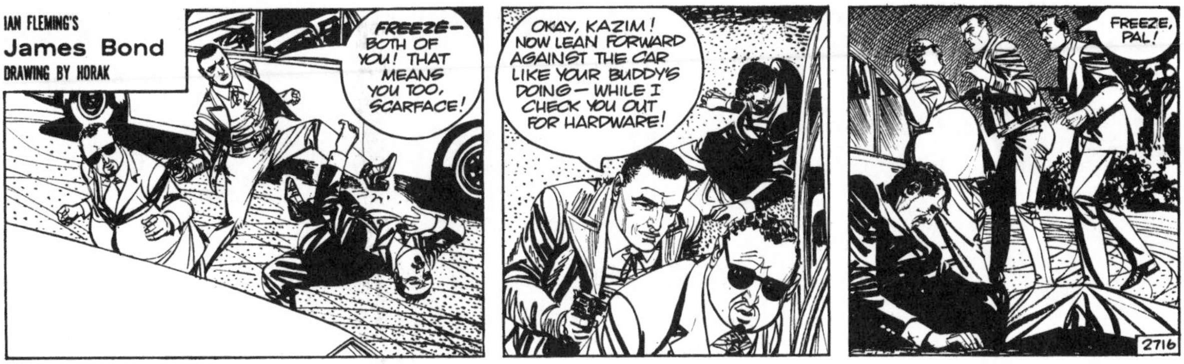
IAN FLEMING'S
James Bond
DRAWING BY HORAK
FREEZE— BOTH OF YOU! THAT MEANS YOU TOO, SCARFACE!
OKAY, KAZIM! NOW LEAN FORWARD AGAINST THE CAR LIKE YOUR BUDDY'S DOING— WHILE I CHECK YOU OUT FOR HARDWARE!
FREEZE, PAL!
2716

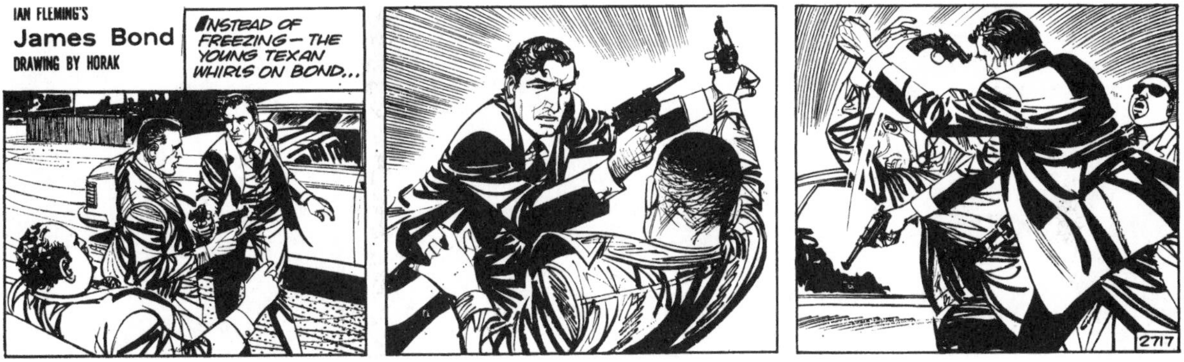
IAN FLEMING'S
James Bond
DRAWING BY HORAK
INSTEAD OF FREEZING— THE YOUNG TEXAN WHIRLS ON BOND...
2717

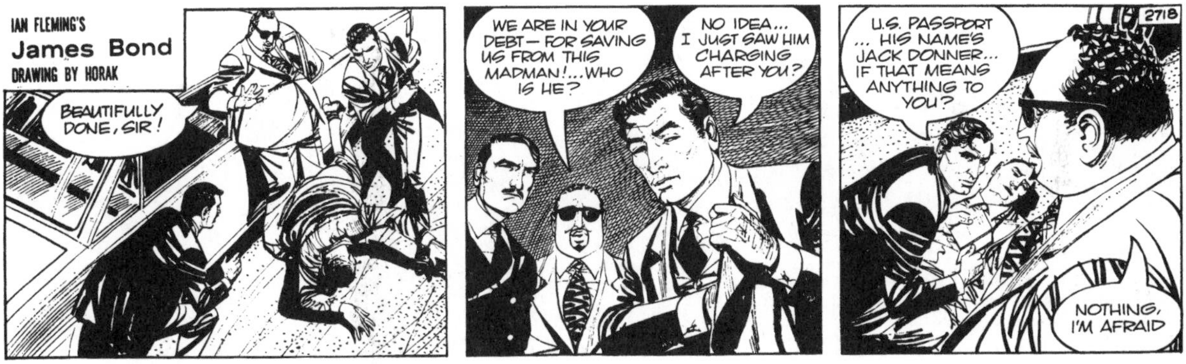
IAN FLEMING'S
James Bond
DRAWING BY HORAK
BEAUTIFULLY DONE, SIR!
WE ARE IN YOUR DEBT— FOR SAVING US FROM THIS MADMAN!... WHO IS HE?
NO IDEA... I JUST SAW HIM CHARGING AFTER YOU?
U.S. PASSPORT ... HIS NAME'S JACK DONNER... IF THAT MEANS ANYTHING TO YOU?
NOTHING, I'M AFRAID
2718

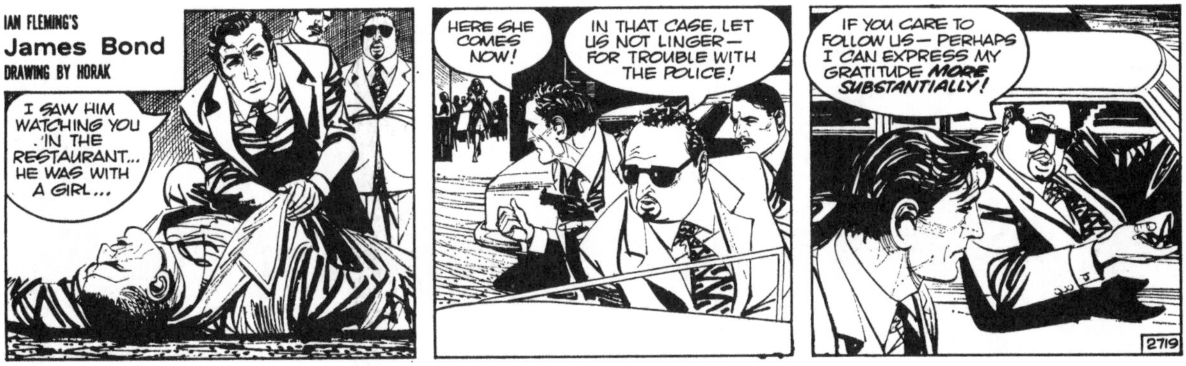
IAN FLEMING'S
James Bond
DRAWING BY HORAK
I SAW HIM WATCHING YOU IN THE RESTAURANT... HE WAS WITH A GIRL...
HERE SHE COMES NOW!
IN THAT CASE, LET US NOT LINGER— FOR TROUBLE WITH THE POLICE!
IF YOU CARE TO FOLLOW US— PERHAPS I CAN EXPRESS MY GRATITUDE MORE SUBSTANTIALLY!
2719

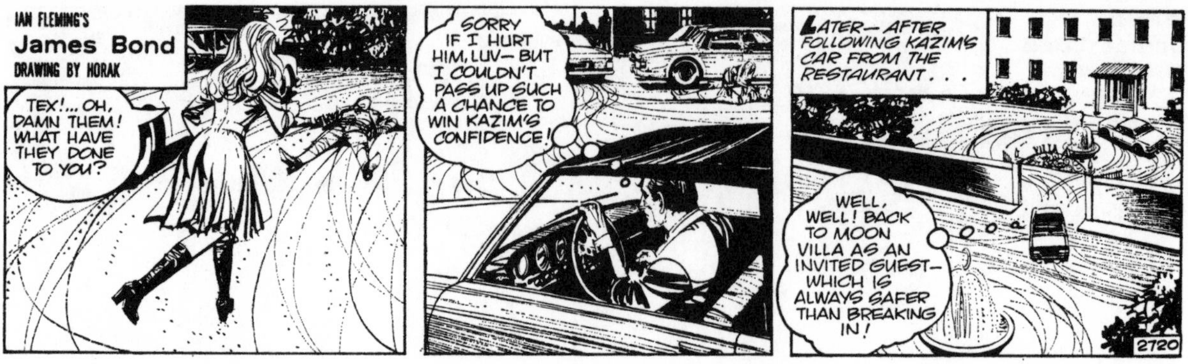
IAN FLEMING'S
James Bond
DRAWING BY HORAK
TEX!... OH, DAMN THEM! WHAT HAVE THEY DONE TO YOU?
SORRY IF I HURT HIM, LUV– BUT I COULDN'T PASS UP SUCH A CHANCE TO WIN KAZIM'S CONFIDENCE!
LATER– AFTER FOLLOWING KAZIM'S CAR FROM THE RESTAURANT . . .
WELL, WELL! BACK TO MOON VILLA AS AN INVITED GUEST– WHICH IS ALWAYS SAFER THAN BREAKING IN!
2720

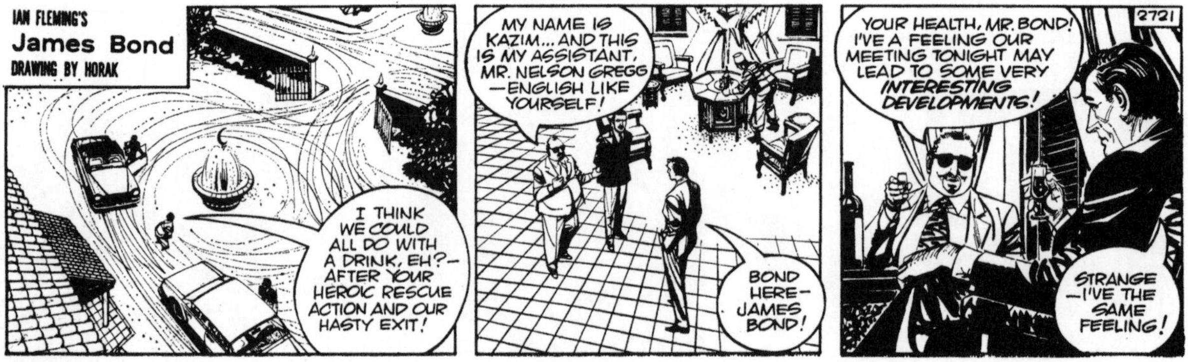
IAN FLEMING'S
James Bond
DRAWING BY HORAK
I THINK WE COULD ALL DO WITH A DRINK, EH?– AFTER YOUR HEROIC RESCUE ACTION AND OUR HASTY EXIT!
MY NAME IS KAZIM... AND THIS IS MY ASSISTANT, MR. NELSON GREGG —ENGLISH LIKE YOURSELF!
BOND HERE– JAMES BOND!
2721
YOUR HEALTH, MR. BOND! I'VE A FEELING OUR MEETING TONIGHT MAY LEAD TO SOME VERY INTERESTING DEVELOPMENTS!
STRANGE —I'VE THE SAME FEELING!

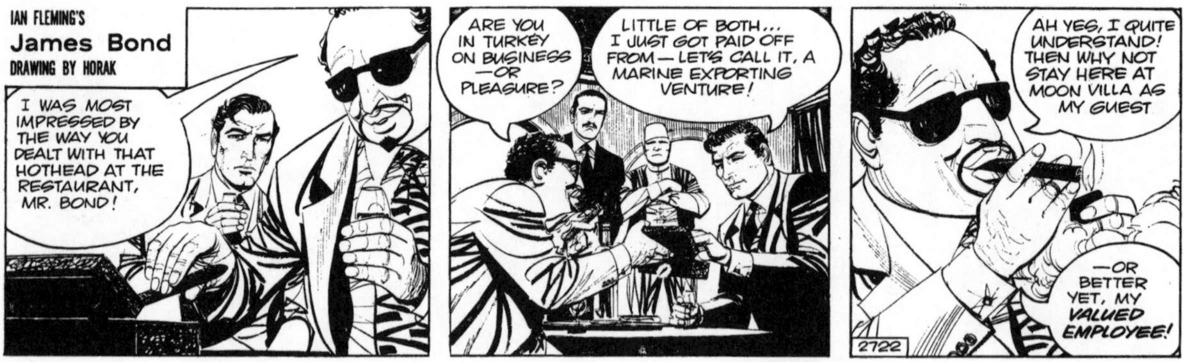
IAN FLEMING'S
James Bond
DRAWING BY HORAK
I WAS MOST IMPRESSED BY THE WAY YOU DEALT WITH THAT HOTHEAD AT THE RESTAURANT, MR. BOND!
ARE YOU IN TURKEY ON BUSINESS —OR PLEASURE?
LITTLE OF BOTH... I JUST GOT PAID OFF FROM — LET'S CALL IT, A MARINE EXPORTING VENTURE!
AH YES, I QUITE UNDERSTAND! THEN WHY NOT STAY HERE AT MOON VILLA AS MY GUEST
—OR BETTER YET, MY VALUED EMPLOYEE!
2722

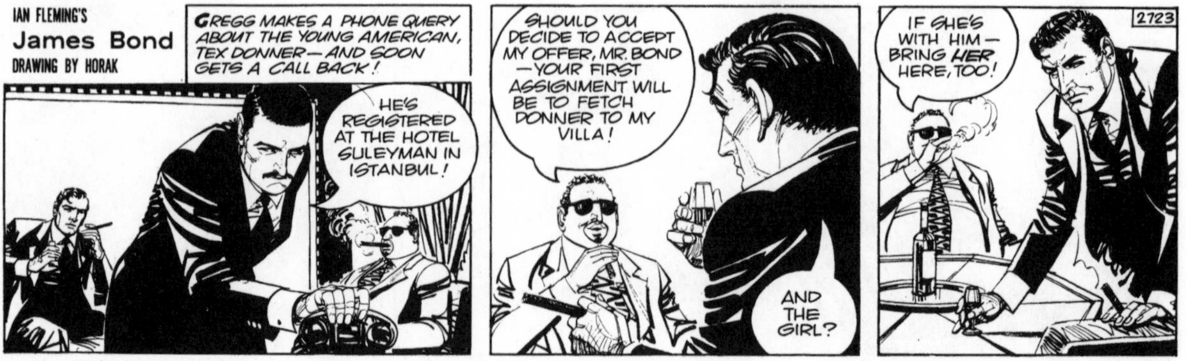
IAN FLEMING'S
James Bond
DRAWING BY HORAK
GREGG MAKES A PHONE QUERY ABOUT THE YOUNG AMERICAN, TEX DONNER— AND SOON GETS A CALL BACK!
HE'S REGISTERED AT THE HOTEL SULEYMAN IN ISTANBUL!
SHOULD YOU DECIDE TO ACCEPT MY OFFER, MR. BOND —YOUR FIRST ASSIGNMENT WILL BE TO FETCH DONNER TO MY VILLA!
AND THE GIRL?
2723
IF SHE'S WITH HIM– BRING HER HERE, TOO!

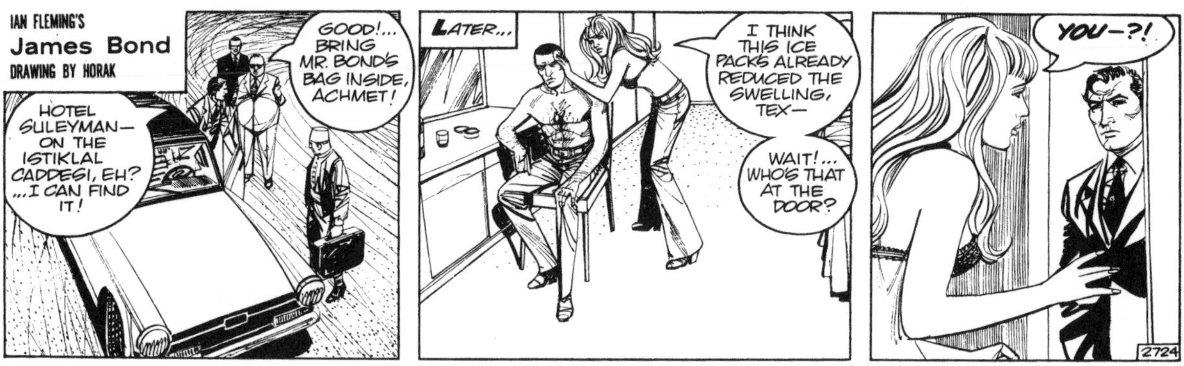
IAN FLEMING'S
James Bond
DRAWING BY HORAK
HOTEL SULEYMAN— ON THE ISTIKLAL CADDESI, EH? ...I CAN FIND IT!
GOOD!... BRING MR. BOND'S BAG INSIDE, ACHMET!
LATER...
I THINK THIS ICE PACK'S ALREADY REDUCED THE SWELLING, TEX—
WAIT!... WHO'S THAT AT THE DOOR?
YOU—?!
2724

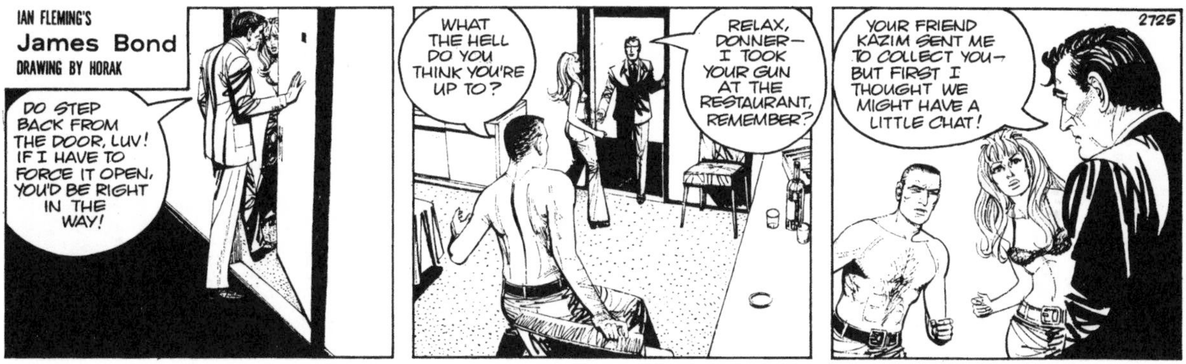
IAN FLEMING'S
James Bond
DRAWING BY HORAK
DO STEP BACK FROM THE DOOR, LUV! IF I HAVE TO FORCE IT OPEN, YOU'D BE RIGHT IN THE WAY!
WHAT THE HELL DO YOU THINK YOU'RE UP TO?
RELAX, DONNER— I TOOK YOUR GUN AT THE RESTAURANT, REMEMBER?
2725
YOUR FRIEND KAZIM SENT ME TO COLLECT YOU— BUT FIRST I THOUGHT WE MIGHT HAVE A LITTLE CHAT!

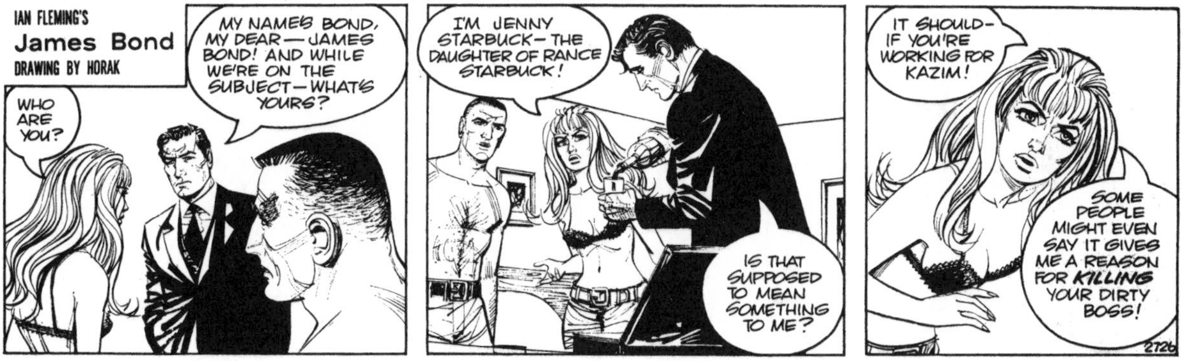
IAN FLEMING'S
James Bond
DRAWING BY HORAK
WHO ARE YOU?
MY NAME'S BOND, MY DEAR — JAMES BOND! AND WHILE WE'RE ON THE SUBJECT—WHAT'S YOURS?
I'M JENNY STARBUCK— THE DAUGHTER OF RANCE STARBUCK!
IS THAT SUPPOSED TO MEAN SOMETHING TO ME?
IT SHOULD— IF YOU'RE WORKING FOR KAZIM!
SOME PEOPLE MIGHT EVEN SAY IT GIVES ME A REASON FOR KILLING YOUR DIRTY BOSS!
2726

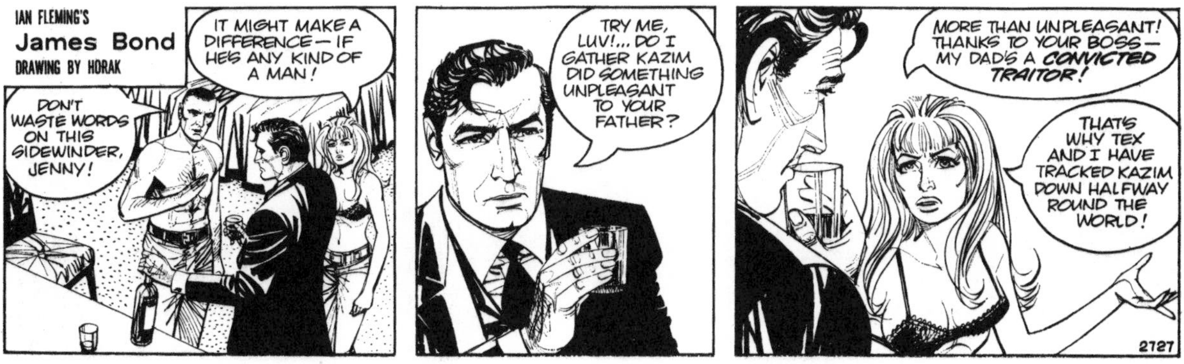
IAN FLEMING'S
James Bond
DRAWING BY HORAK
DON'T WASTE WORDS ON THIS SIDEWINDER, JENNY!
IT MIGHT MAKE A DIFFERENCE — IF HE'S ANY KIND OF A MAN!
TRY ME, LUV!... DO I GATHER KAZIM DID SOMETHING UNPLEASANT TO YOUR FATHER?
MORE THAN UNPLEASANT! THANKS TO YOUR BOSS— MY DAD'S A CONVICTED TRAITOR!
THAT'S WHY TEX AND I HAVE TRACKED KAZIM DOWN HALFWAY ROUND THE WORLD!
2727

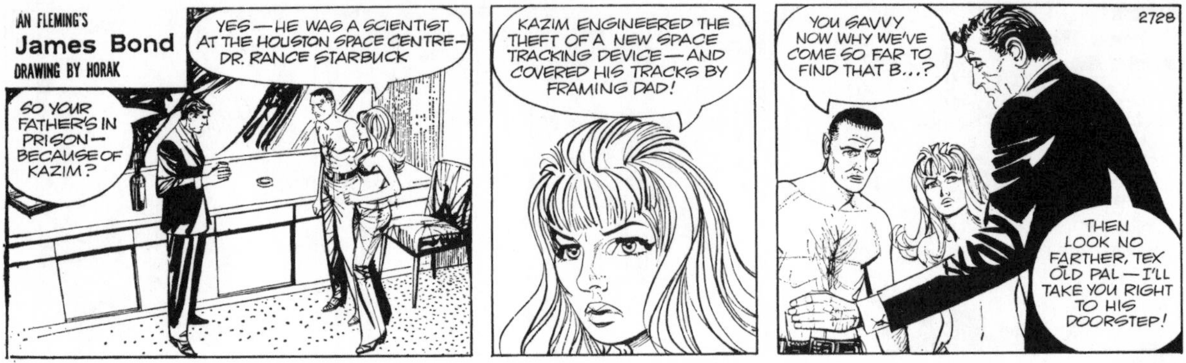
IAN FLEMING'S
James Bond
DRAWING BY HORAK
SO YOUR FATHER'S IN PRISON— BECAUSE OF KAZIM?
YES—HE WAS A SCIENTIST AT THE HOUSTON SPACE CENTRE— DR. RANCE STARBUCK
KAZIM ENGINEERED THE THEFT OF A NEW SPACE TRACKING DEVICE—AND COVERED HIS TRACKS BY FRAMING DAD!
2728
YOU SAVVY NOW WHY WE'VE COME SO FAR TO FIND THAT B...?
THEN LOOK NO FARTHER, TEX OLD PAL—I'LL TAKE YOU RIGHT TO HIS DOORSTEP!

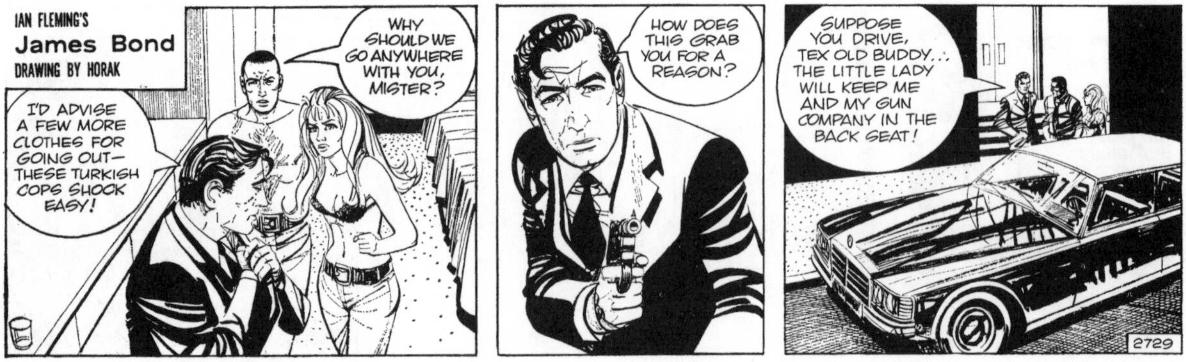
IAN FLEMING'S
James Bond
DRAWING BY HORAK
I'D ADVISE A FEW MORE CLOTHES FOR GOING OUT— THESE TURKISH COPS SHOCK EASY!
WHY SHOULD WE GO ANYWHERE WITH YOU, MISTER?
HOW DOES THIS GRAB YOU FOR A REASON?
SUPPOSE YOU DRIVE, TEX OLD BUDDY... THE LITTLE LADY WILL KEEP ME AND MY GUN COMPANY IN THE BACK SEAT!
2729

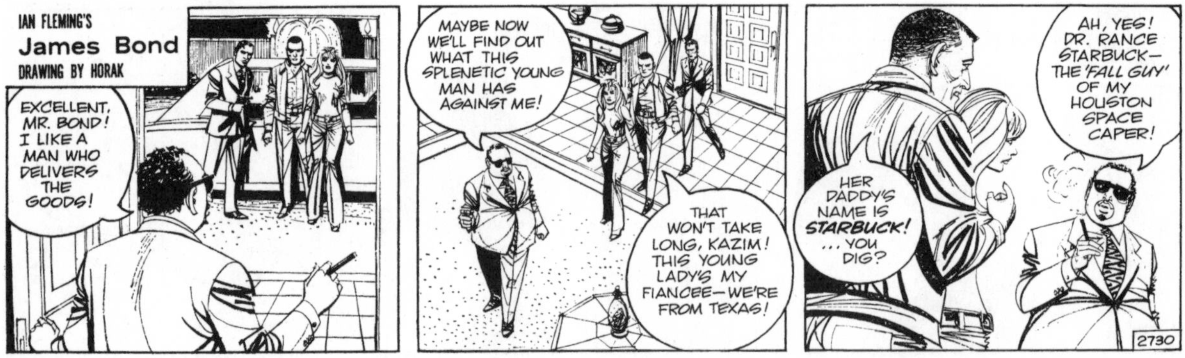
IAN FLEMING'S
James Bond
DRAWING BY HORAK
EXCELLENT, MR. BOND! I LIKE A MAN WHO DELIVERS THE GOODS!
MAYBE NOW WE'LL FIND OUT WHAT THIS SPLENETIC YOUNG MAN HAS AGAINST ME!
THAT WON'T TAKE LONG, KAZIM! THIS YOUNG LADY'S MY FIANCEE—WE'RE FROM TEXAS!
HER DADDY'S NAME IS STARBUCK! ...YOU DIG?
AH, YES! DR. RANCE STARBUCK— THE 'FALL GUY' OF MY HOUSTON SPACE CAPER!
2730

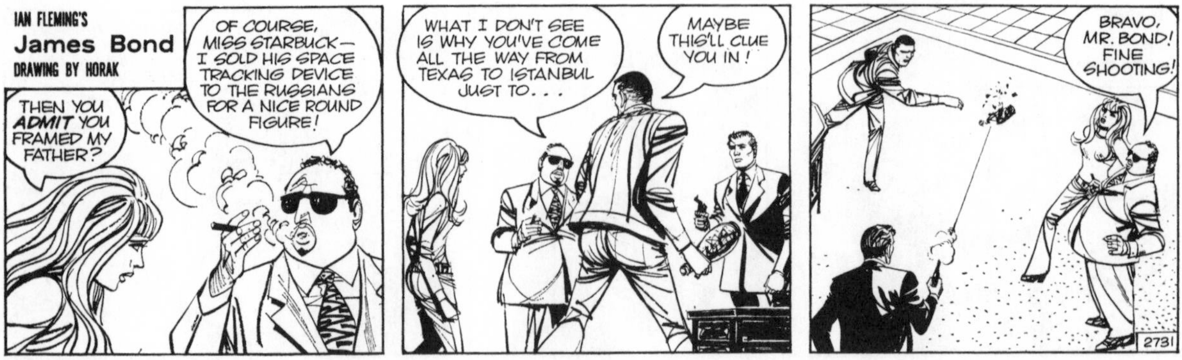
IAN FLEMING'S
James Bond
DRAWING BY HORAK
THEN YOU ADMIT YOU FRAMED MY FATHER?
OF COURSE, MISS STARBUCK— I SOLD HIS SPACE TRACKING DEVICE TO THE RUSSIANS FOR A NICE ROUND FIGURE!
WHAT I DON'T SEE IS WHY YOU'VE COME ALL THE WAY FROM TEXAS TO ISTANBUL JUST TO...
MAYBE THIS'LL CLUE YOU IN!
BRAVO, MR. BOND! FINE SHOOTING!
2731

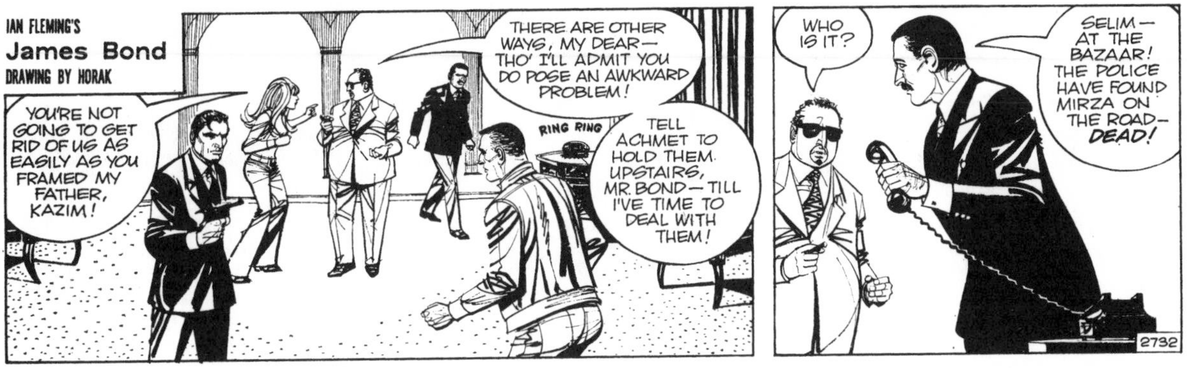
IAN FLEMING'S
James Bond
DRAWING BY HORAK
YOU'RE NOT GOING TO GET RID OF US AS EASILY AS YOU FRAMED MY FATHER, KAZIM!
THERE ARE OTHER WAYS, MY DEAR— THO' I'LL ADMIT YOU DO POSE AN AWKWARD PROBLEM!
RING RING
TELL ACHMET TO HOLD THEM UPSTAIRS, MR. BOND—TILL I'VE TIME TO DEAL WITH THEM!
WHO IS IT?
SELIM— AT THE BAZAAR! THE POLICE HAVE FOUND MIRZA ON THE ROAD— DEAD!
2732

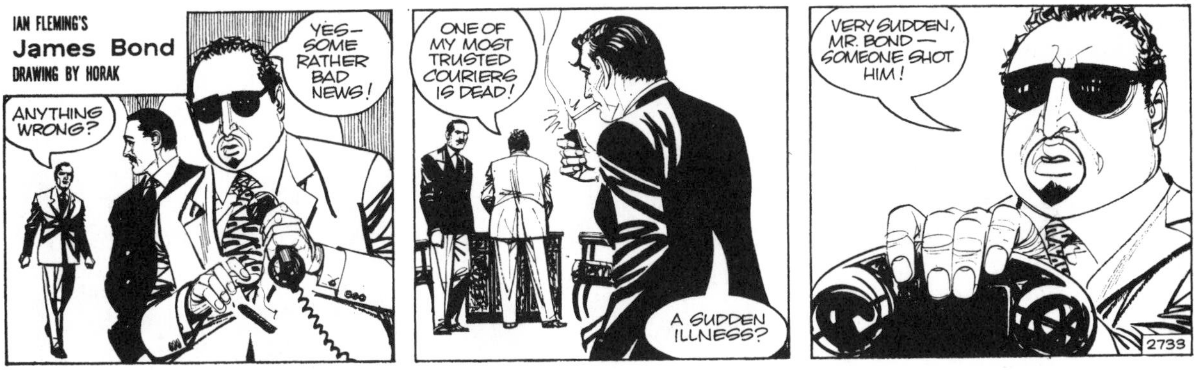
IAN FLEMING'S
James Bond
DRAWING BY HORAK
ANYTHING WRONG?
YES— SOME RATHER BAD NEWS!
ONE OF MY MOST TRUSTED COURIERS IS DEAD!
A SUDDEN ILLNESS?
VERY SUDDEN, MR. BOND— SOMEONE SHOT HIM!
2733

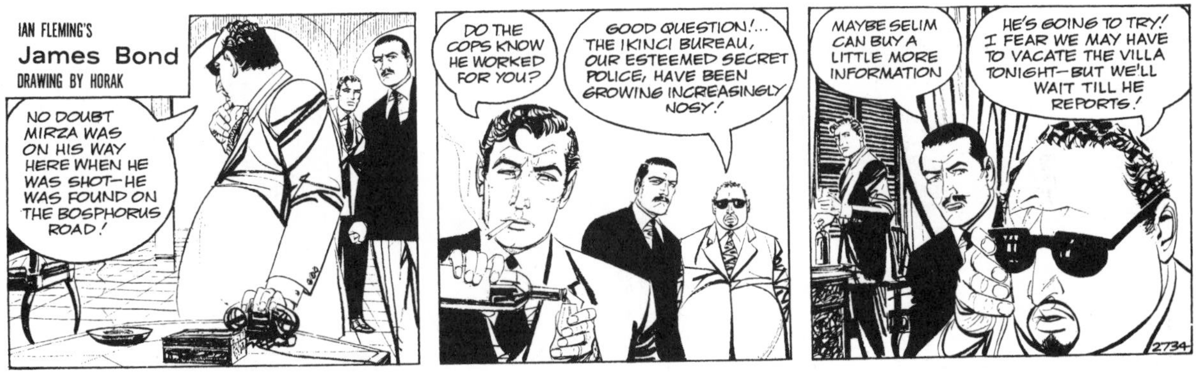
IAN FLEMING'S
James Bond
DRAWING BY HORAK
NO DOUBT MIRZA WAS ON HIS WAY HERE WHEN HE WAS SHOT—HE WAS FOUND ON THE BOSPHORUS ROAD!
DO THE COPS KNOW HE WORKED FOR YOU?
GOOD QUESTION!... THE IKINCI BUREAU, OUR ESTEEMED SECRET POLICE, HAVE BEEN GROWING INCREASINGLY NOSY!
MAYBE SELIM CAN BUY A LITTLE MORE INFORMATION
HE'S GOING TO TRY! I FEAR WE MAY HAVE TO VACATE THE VILLA TONIGHT—BUT WE'LL WAIT TILL HE REPORTS!
2734

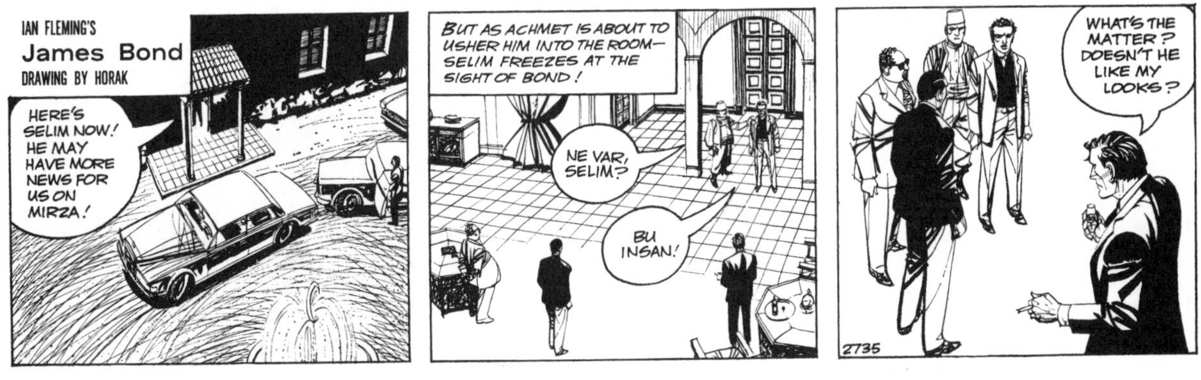
IAN FLEMING'S
James Bond
DRAWING BY HORAK
HERE'S SELIM NOW! HE MAY HAVE MORE NEWS FOR US ON MIRZA!
BUT AS ACHMET IS ABOUT TO USHER HIM INTO THE ROOM— SELIM FREEZES AT THE SIGHT OF BOND!
NE VAR, SELIM?
BU INSAN!
2735
WHAT'S THE MATTER? DOESN'T HE LIKE MY LOOKS?

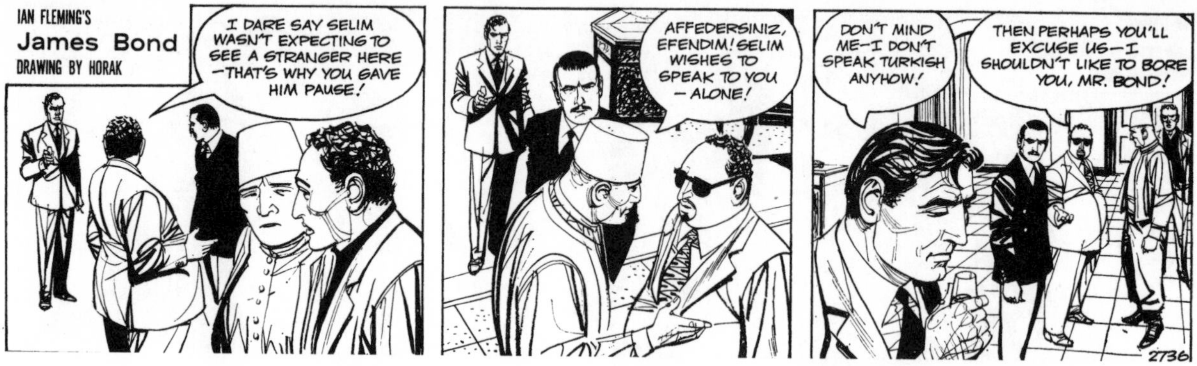
IAN FLEMING'S
James Bond
DRAWING BY HORAK
I DARE SAY SELIM WASN'T EXPECTING TO SEE A STRANGER HERE —THAT'S WHY YOU GAVE HIM PAUSE!
AFFEDERSINIZ, EFENDIM! SELIM WISHES TO SPEAK TO YOU —ALONE!
DON'T MIND ME—I DON'T SPEAK TURKISH ANYHOW!
THEN PERHAPS YOU'LL EXCUSE US—I SHOULDN'T LIKE TO BORE YOU, MR. BOND!
2736

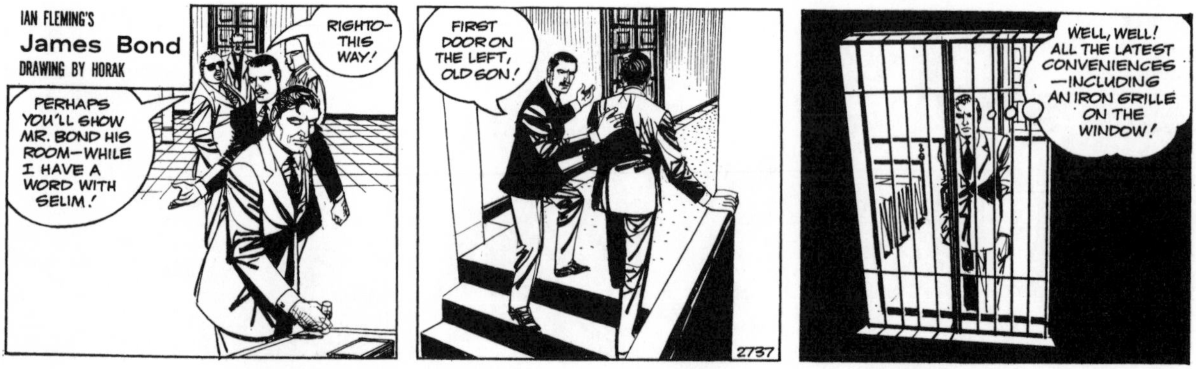
IAN FLEMING'S
James Bond
DRAWING BY HORAK
PERHAPS YOU'LL SHOW MR. BOND HIS ROOM—WHILE I HAVE A WORD WITH SELIM!
RIGHTO— THIS WAY!
FIRST DOOR ON THE LEFT, OLD SON!
2737
WELL, WELL! ALL THE LATEST CONVENIENCES —INCLUDING AN IRON GRILLE ON THE WINDOW!

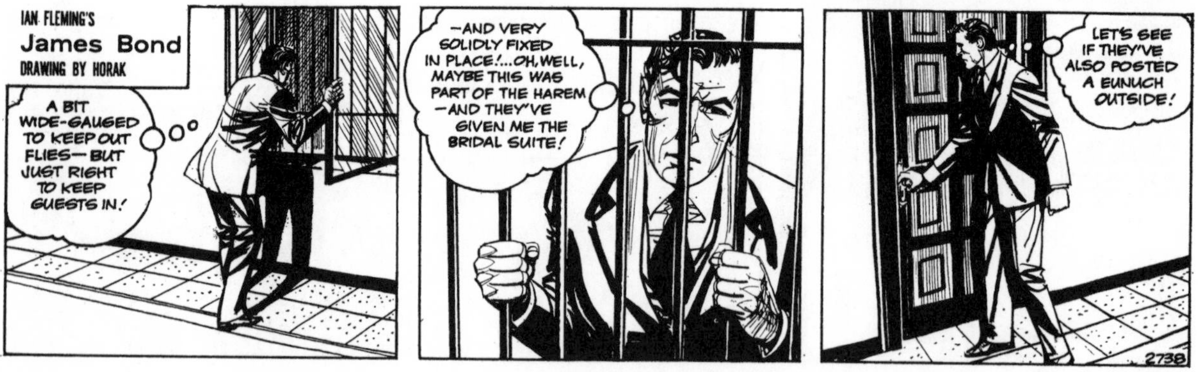
IAN FLEMING'S
James Bond
DRAWING BY HORAK
A BIT WIDE-GAUGED TO KEEP OUT FLIES—BUT JUST RIGHT TO KEEP GUESTS IN!
—AND VERY SOLIDLY FIXED IN PLACE!...OH, WELL, MAYBE THIS WAS PART OF THE HAREM —AND THEY'VE GIVEN ME THE BRIDAL SUITE!
LET'S SEE IF THEY'VE ALSO POSTED A EUNUCH OUTSIDE!
2738

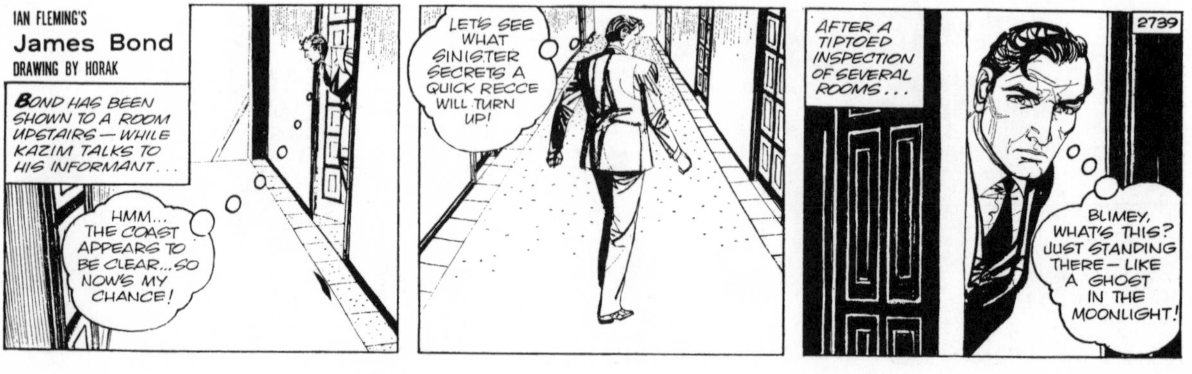
IAN FLEMING'S
James Bond
DRAWING BY HORAK
BOND HAS BEEN SHOWN TO A ROOM UPSTAIRS — WHILE KAZIM TALKS TO HIS INFORMANT...
HMM... THE COAST APPEARS TO BE CLEAR... SO NOW'S MY CHANCE!
LET'S SEE WHAT SINISTER SECRETS A QUICK RECCE WILL TURN UP!
AFTER A TIPTOED INSPECTION OF SEVERAL ROOMS...
2739
BLIMEY, WHAT'S THIS? JUST STANDING THERE— LIKE A GHOST IN THE MOONLIGHT!

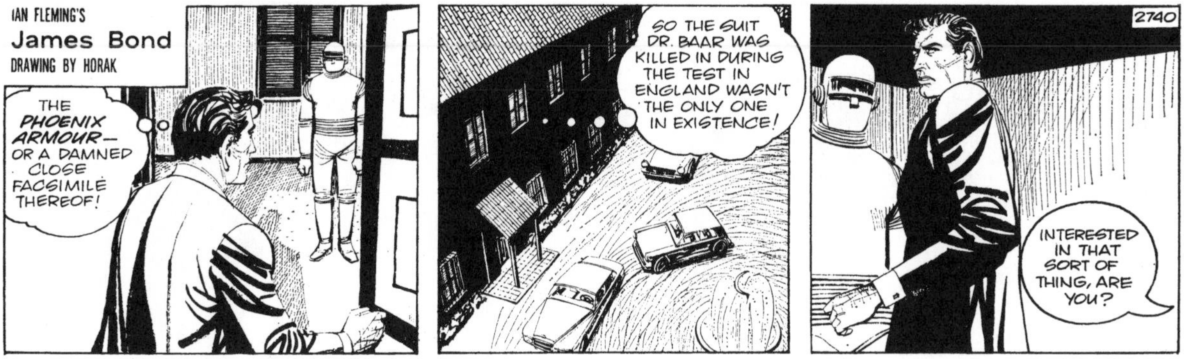
IAN FLEMING'S
James Bond
DRAWING BY HORAK
THE PHOENIX ARMOUR— OR A DAMNED CLOSE FACSIMILE THEREOF!
SO THE SUIT DR. BAAR WAS KILLED IN DURING THE TEST IN ENGLAND WASN'T THE ONLY ONE IN EXISTENCE!
2740
INTERESTED IN THAT SORT OF THING, ARE YOU?

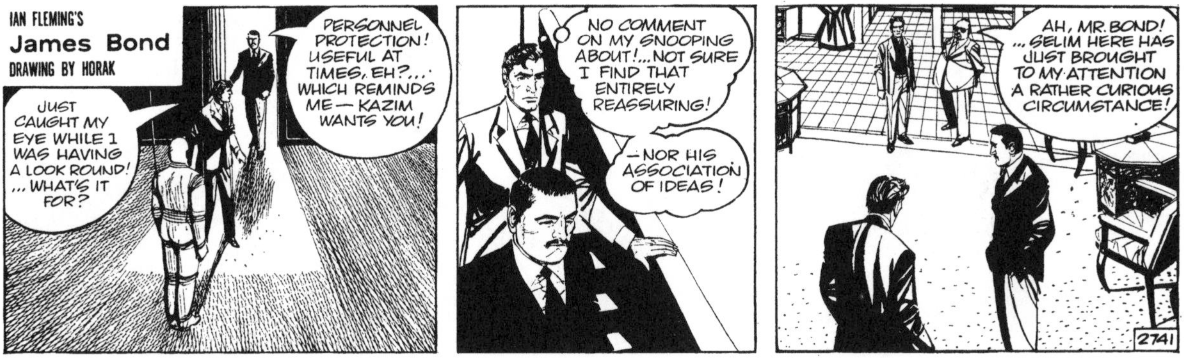
IAN FLEMING'S
James Bond
DRAWING BY HORAK
JUST CAUGHT MY EYE WHILE I WAS HAVING A LOOK ROUND! ... WHAT'S IT FOR?
PERSONNEL PROTECTION! USEFUL AT TIMES, EH?... WHICH REMINDS ME — KAZIM WANTS YOU!
NO COMMENT ON MY SNOOPING ABOUT!... NOT SURE I FIND THAT ENTIRELY REASSURING!
— NOR HIS ASSOCIATION OF IDEAS!
AH, MR. BOND! ... SELIM HERE HAS JUST BROUGHT TO MY ATTENTION A RATHER CURIOUS CIRCUMSTANCE!
2741

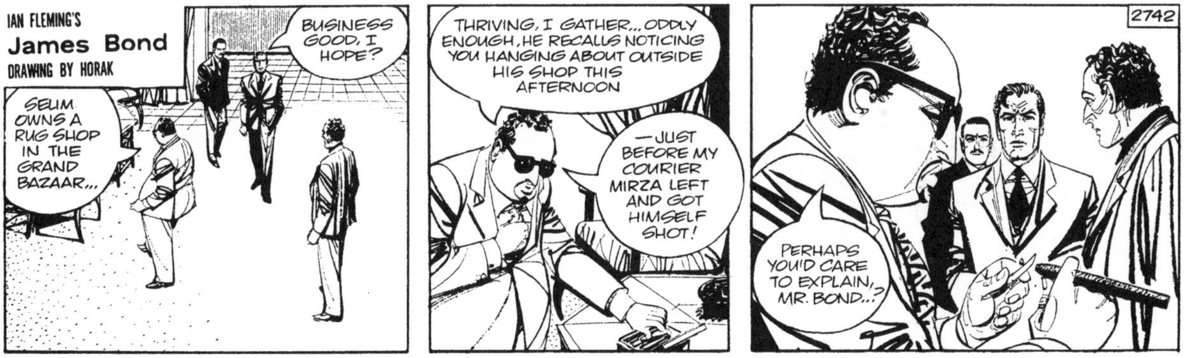
IAN FLEMING'S
James Bond
DRAWING BY HORAK
SELIM OWNS A RUG SHOP IN THE GRAND BAZAAR...
BUSINESS GOOD, I HOPE?
THRIVING, I GATHER... ODDLY ENOUGH, HE RECALLS NOTICING YOU HANGING ABOUT OUTSIDE HIS SHOP THIS AFTERNOON
— JUST BEFORE MY COURIER MIRZA LEFT AND GOT HIMSELF SHOT!
2742
PERHAPS YOU'D CARE TO EXPLAIN, MR. BOND...?

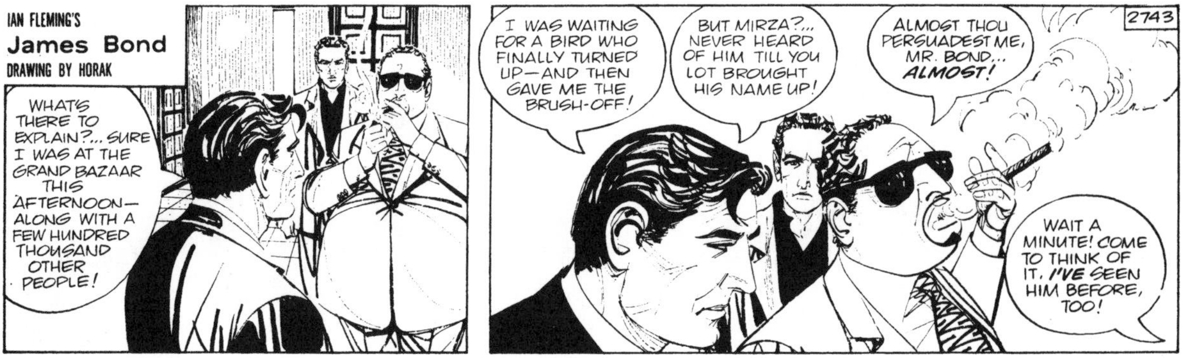
IAN FLEMING'S
James Bond
DRAWING BY HORAK
WHAT'S THERE TO EXPLAIN?... SURE I WAS AT THE GRAND BAZAAR THIS AFTERNOON— ALONG WITH A FEW HUNDRED THOUSAND OTHER PEOPLE!
I WAS WAITING FOR A BIRD WHO FINALLY TURNED UP—AND THEN GAVE ME THE BRUSH-OFF!
BUT MIRZA?... NEVER HEARD OF HIM TILL YOU LOT BROUGHT HIS NAME UP!
ALMOST THOU PERSUADEST ME, MR. BOND... ALMOST!
2743
WAIT A MINUTE! COME TO THINK OF IT, I'VE SEEN HIM BEFORE, TOO!

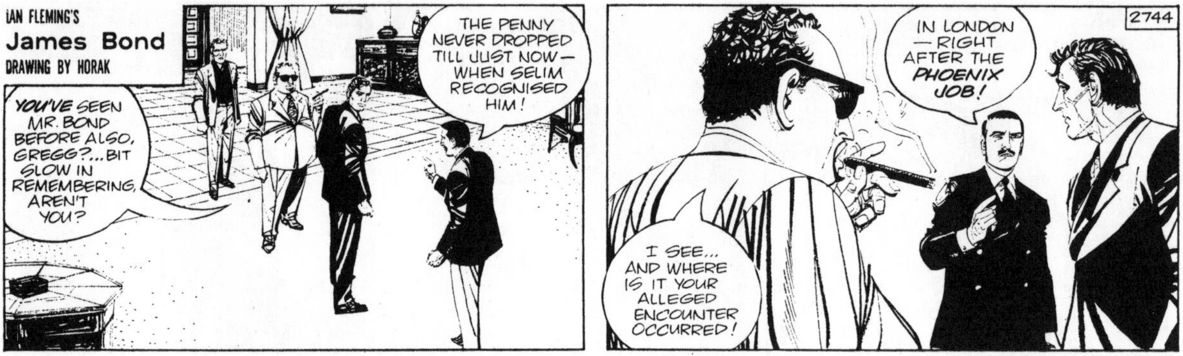
IAN FLEMING'S
James Bond
DRAWING BY HORAK
YOU'VE SEEN MR. BOND BEFORE ALSO, GREGG?... BIT SLOW IN REMEMBERING, AREN'T YOU?
THE PENNY NEVER DROPPED TILL JUST NOW — WHEN SELIM RECOGNISED HIM!
2744
I SEE... AND WHERE IS IT YOUR ALLEGED ENCOUNTER OCCURRED!
IN LONDON — RIGHT AFTER THE PHOENIX JOB!

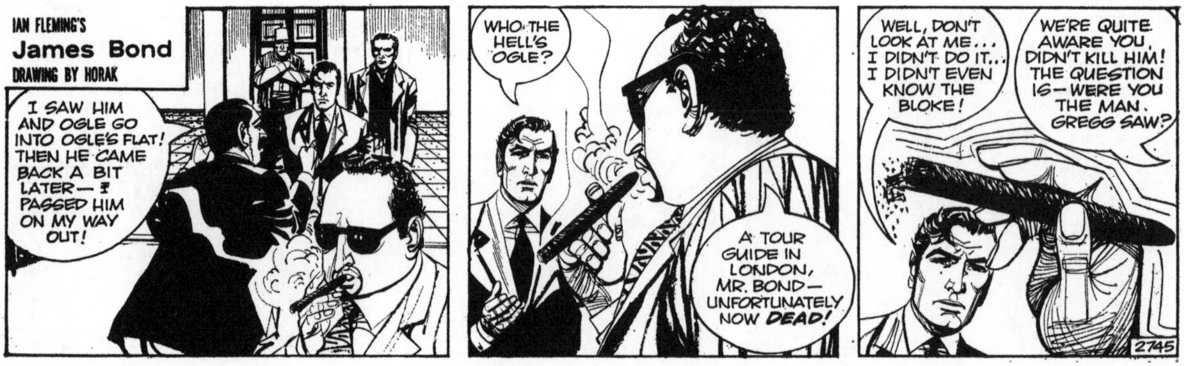
IAN FLEMING'S
James Bond
DRAWING BY HORAK
I SAW HIM AND OGLE GO INTO OGLE'S FLAT! THEN HE CAME BACK A BIT LATER — I PASSED HIM ON MY WAY OUT!
WHO THE HELL'S OGLE?
A TOUR GUIDE IN LONDON, MR. BOND — UNFORTUNATELY NOW DEAD!
WELL, DON'T LOOK AT ME... I DIDN'T DO IT... I DIDN'T EVEN KNOW THE BLOKE!
WE'RE QUITE AWARE YOU DIDN'T KILL HIM! THE QUESTION IS — WERE YOU THE MAN GREGG SAW?
2745

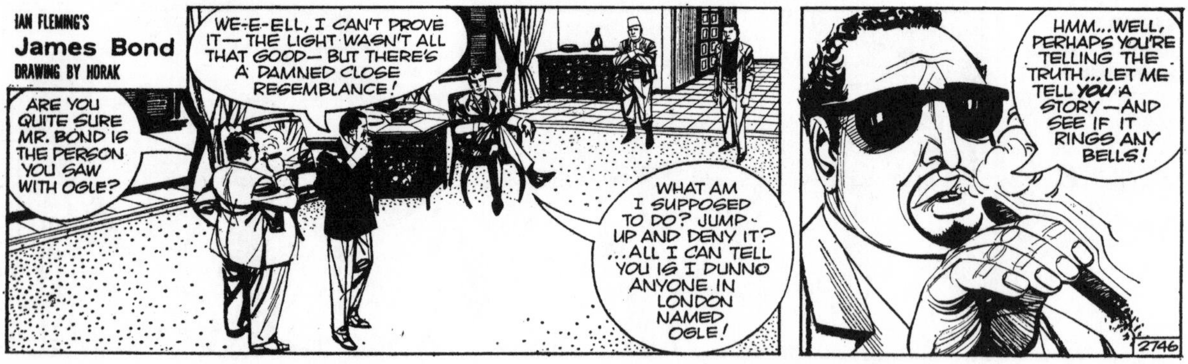
IAN FLEMING'S
James Bond
DRAWING BY HORAK
ARE YOU QUITE SURE MR. BOND IS THE PERSON YOU SAW WITH OGLE?
WE-E-ELL, I CAN'T PROVE IT — THE LIGHT WASN'T ALL THAT GOOD — BUT THERE'S A DAMNED CLOSE RESEMBLANCE!
WHAT AM I SUPPOSED TO DO? JUMP UP AND DENY IT? ...ALL I CAN TELL YOU IS I DUNNO ANYONE IN LONDON NAMED OGLE!
HMM... WELL, PERHAPS YOU'RE TELLING THE TRUTH... LET ME TELL YOU A STORY — AND SEE IF IT RINGS ANY BELLS!
2746

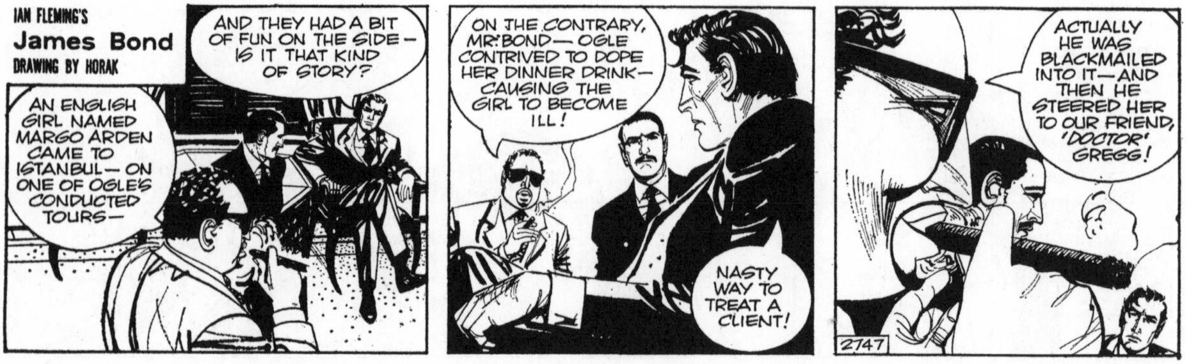
IAN FLEMING'S
James Bond
DRAWING BY HORAK
AN ENGLISH GIRL NAMED MARGO ARDEN CAME TO ISTANBUL — ON ONE OF OGLE'S CONDUCTED TOURS —
AND THEY HAD A BIT OF FUN ON THE SIDE — IS IT THAT KIND OF STORY?
ON THE CONTRARY, MR. BOND — OGLE CONTRIVED TO DOPE HER DINNER DRINK — CAUSING THE GIRL TO BECOME ILL!
NASTY WAY TO TREAT A CLIENT!
2747
ACTUALLY HE WAS BLACKMAILED INTO IT — AND THEN HE STEERED HER TO OUR FRIEND, 'DOCTOR' GREGG!

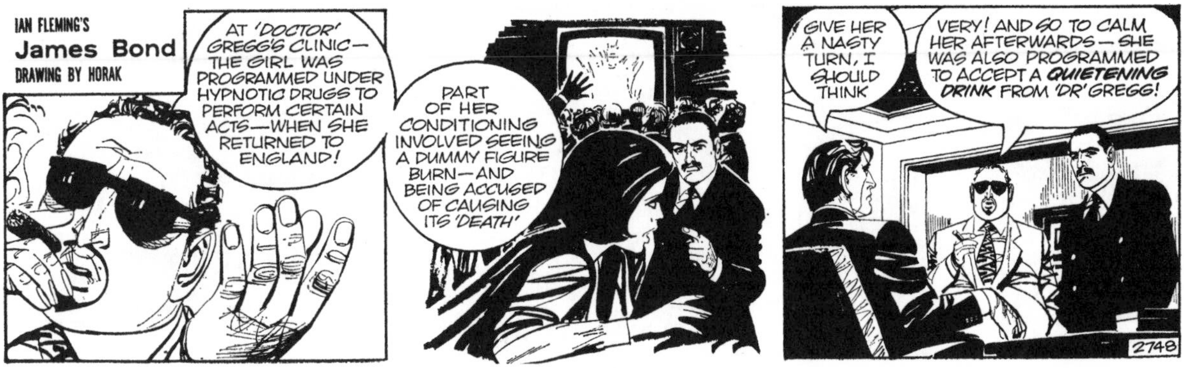
IAN FLEMING'S
James Bond
DRAWING BY HORAK
AT 'DOCTOR' GREGG'S CLINIC—THE GIRL WAS PROGRAMMED UNDER HYPNOTIC DRUGS TO PERFORM CERTAIN ACTS—WHEN SHE RETURNED TO ENGLAND!
PART OF HER CONDITIONING INVOLVED SEEING A DUMMY FIGURE BURN—AND BEING ACCUSED OF CAUSING ITS 'DEATH'
GIVE HER A NASTY TURN, I SHOULD THINK
VERY! AND SO TO CALM HER AFTERWARDS—SHE WAS ALSO PROGRAMMED TO ACCEPT A QUIETENING DRINK FROM 'DR' GREGG!
2748

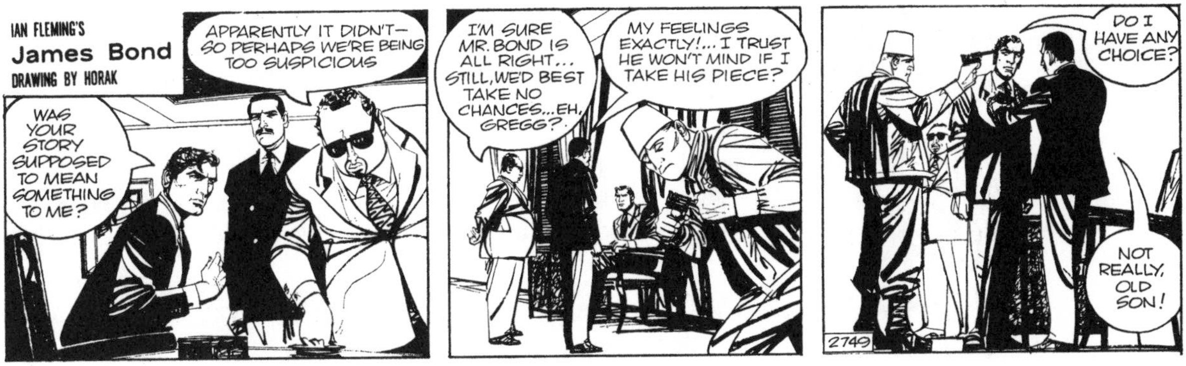
IAN FLEMING'S
James Bond
DRAWING BY HORAK
APPARENTLY IT DIDN'T—SO PERHAPS WE'RE BEING TOO SUSPICIOUS
WAS YOUR STORY SUPPOSED TO MEAN SOMETHING TO ME?
I'M SURE MR. BOND IS ALL RIGHT... STILL, WE'D BEST TAKE NO CHANCES...EH, GREGG?
MY FEELINGS EXACTLY!... I TRUST HE WON'T MIND IF I TAKE HIS PIECE?
DO I HAVE ANY CHOICE?
NOT REALLY, OLD SON!
2749

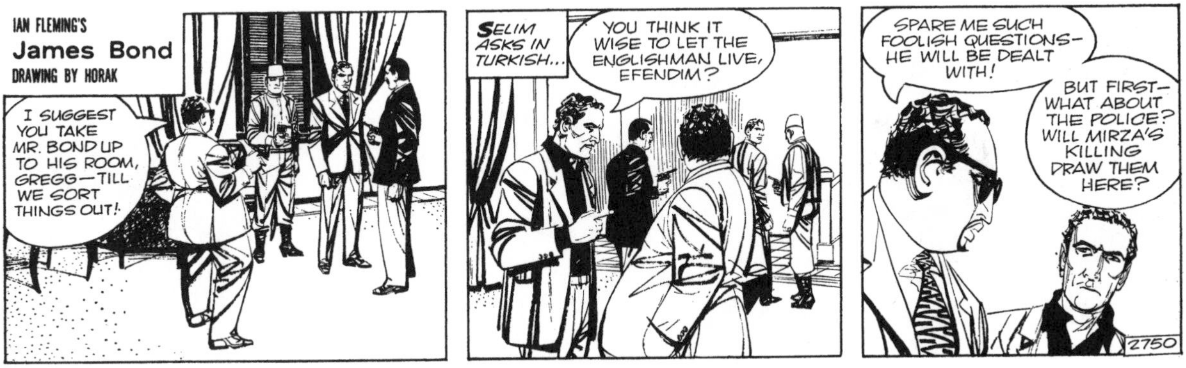
IAN FLEMING'S
James Bond
DRAWING BY HORAK
I SUGGEST YOU TAKE MR. BOND UP TO HIS ROOM, GREGG—TILL WE SORT THINGS OUT!
SELIM ASKS IN TURKISH...
YOU THINK IT WISE TO LET THE ENGLISHMAN LIVE, EFENDIM?
SPARE ME SUCH FOOLISH QUESTIONS—HE WILL BE DEALT WITH!
BUT FIRST—WHAT ABOUT THE POLICE? WILL MIRZA'S KILLING DRAW THEM HERE?
2750

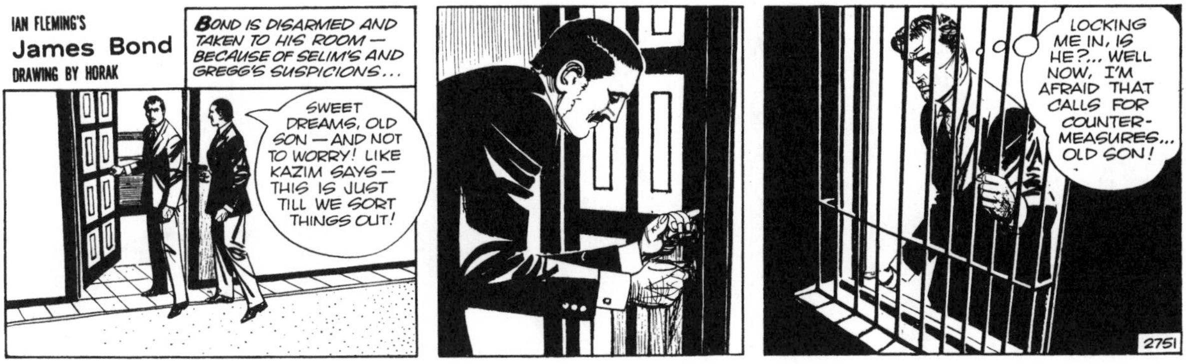
IAN FLEMING'S
James Bond
DRAWING BY HORAK
BOND IS DISARMED AND TAKEN TO HIS ROOM—BECAUSE OF SELIM'S AND GREGG'S SUSPICIONS...
SWEET DREAMS, OLD SON—AND NOT TO WORRY! LIKE KAZIM SAYS—THIS IS JUST TILL WE SORT THINGS OUT!
LOCKING ME IN, IS HE?... WELL NOW, I'M AFRAID THAT CALLS FOR COUNTER-MEASURES... OLD SON!
2751

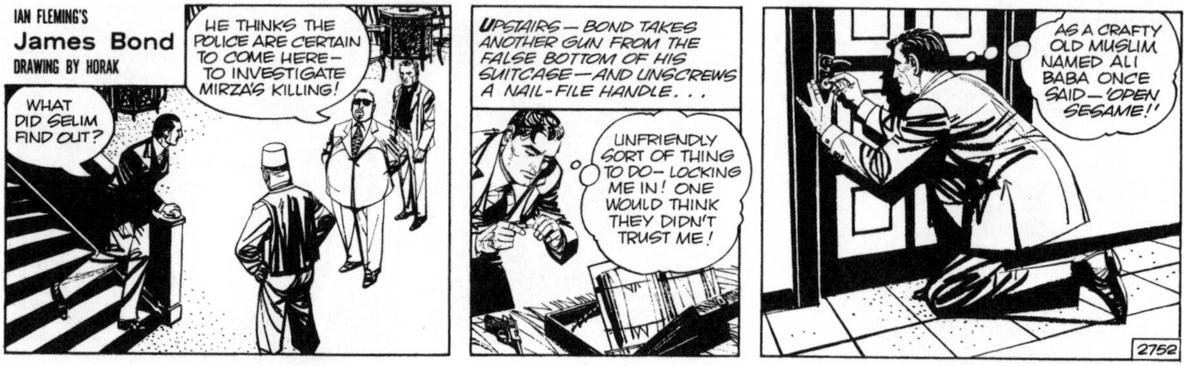
IAN FLEMING'S
James Bond
DRAWING BY HORAK
WHAT DID SELIM FIND OUT?
HE THINKS THE POLICE ARE CERTAIN TO COME HERE- TO INVESTIGATE MIRZA'S KILLING!
UPSTAIRS — BOND TAKES ANOTHER GUN FROM THE FALSE BOTTOM OF HIS SUITCASE — AND UNSCREWS A NAIL-FILE HANDLE . . .
UNFRIENDLY SORT OF THING TO DO- LOCKING ME IN! ONE WOULD THINK THEY DIDN'T TRUST ME!
AS A CRAFTY OLD MUSLIM NAMED ALI BABA ONCE SAID — 'OPEN SESAME!'
2752

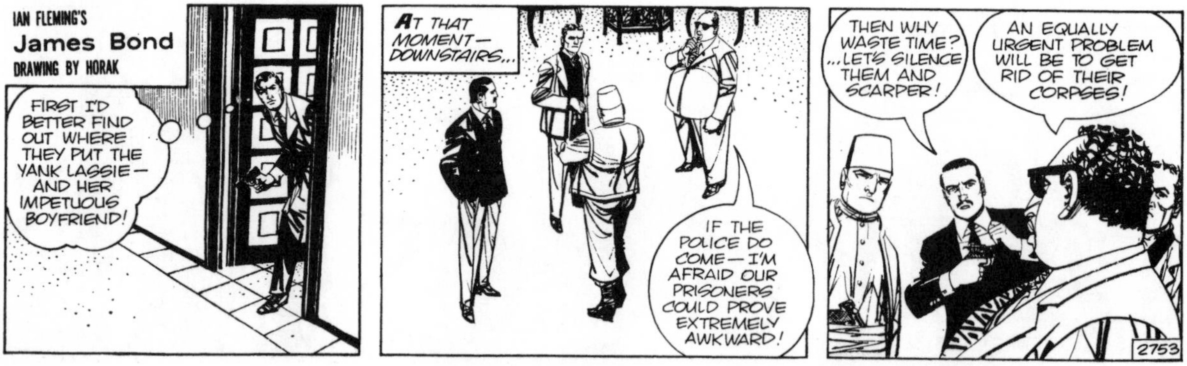
IAN FLEMING'S
James Bond
DRAWING BY HORAK
FIRST I'D BETTER FIND OUT WHERE THEY PUT THE YANK LASSIE — AND HER IMPETUOUS BOYFRIEND!
AT THAT MOMENT— DOWNSTAIRS...
IF THE POLICE DO COME — I'M AFRAID OUR PRISONERS COULD PROVE EXTREMELY AWKWARD!
THEN WHY WASTE TIME? ...LET'S SILENCE THEM AND SCARPER!
AN EQUALLY URGENT PROBLEM WILL BE TO GET RID OF THEIR CORPSES!
2753

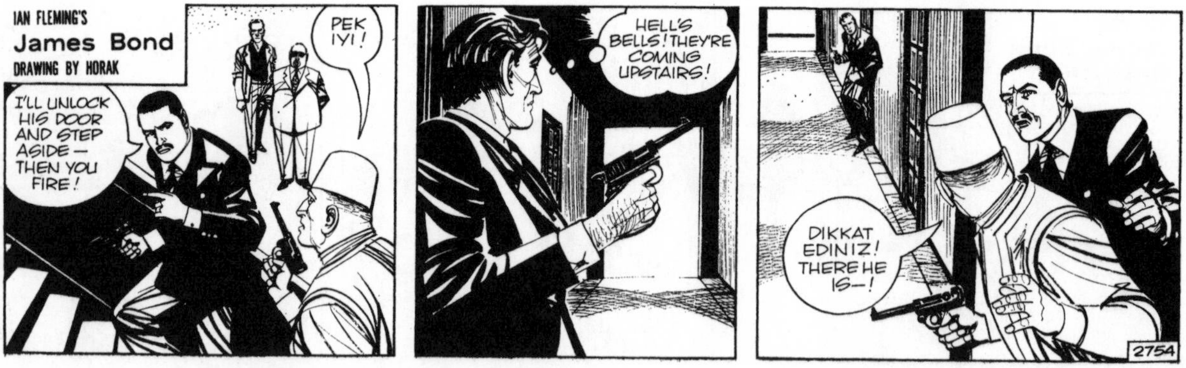
IAN FLEMING'S
James Bond
DRAWING BY HORAK
I'LL UNLOCK HIS DOOR AND STEP ASIDE — THEN YOU FIRE!
PEK IYI!
HELL'S BELLS! THEY'RE COMING UPSTAIRS!
DIKKAT EDINIZ! THERE HE IS—!
2754

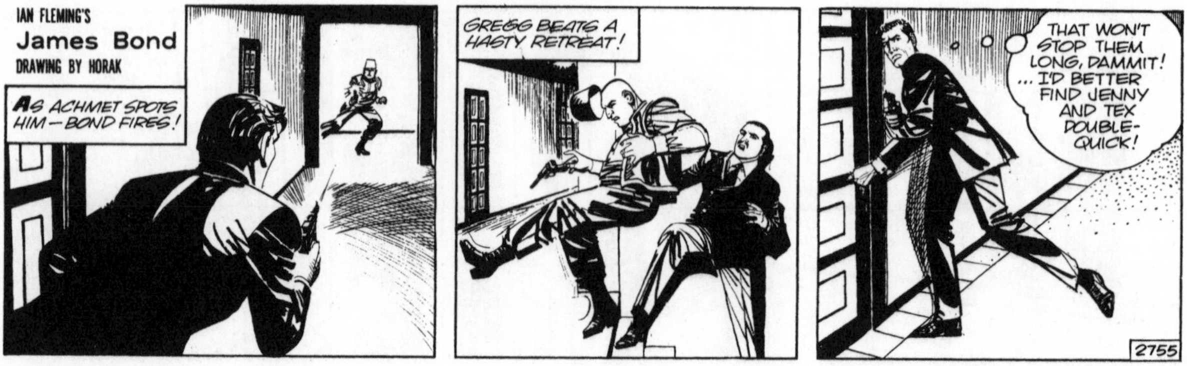
IAN FLEMING'S
James Bond
DRAWING BY HORAK
AS ACHMET SPOTS HIM — BOND FIRES!
GREGG BEATS A HASTY RETREAT!
THAT WON'T STOP THEM LONG, DAMMIT! ... I'D BETTER FIND JENNY AND TEX DOUBLE-QUICK!
2755

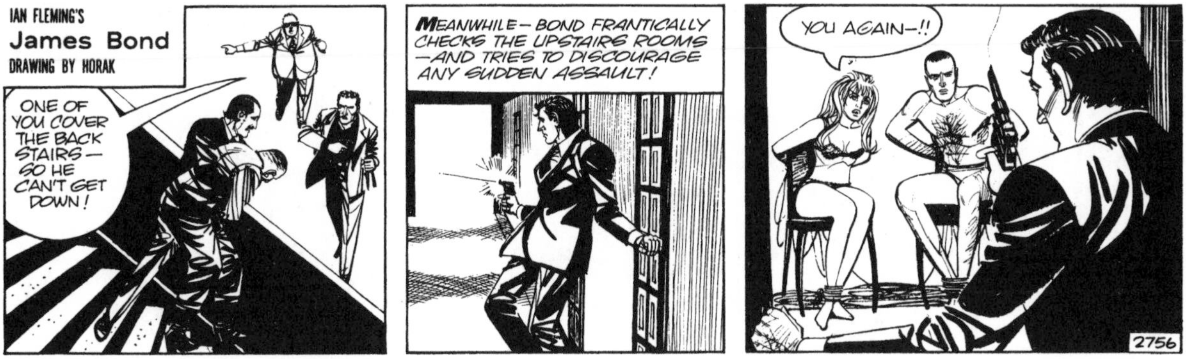
IAN FLEMING'S
James Bond
DRAWING BY HORAK
ONE OF YOU COVER THE BACK STAIRS— SO HE CAN'T GET DOWN!
MEANWHILE— BOND FRANTICALLY CHECKS THE UPSTAIRS ROOMS —AND TRIES TO DISCOURAGE ANY SUDDEN ASSAULT!
YOU AGAIN—!!
2756

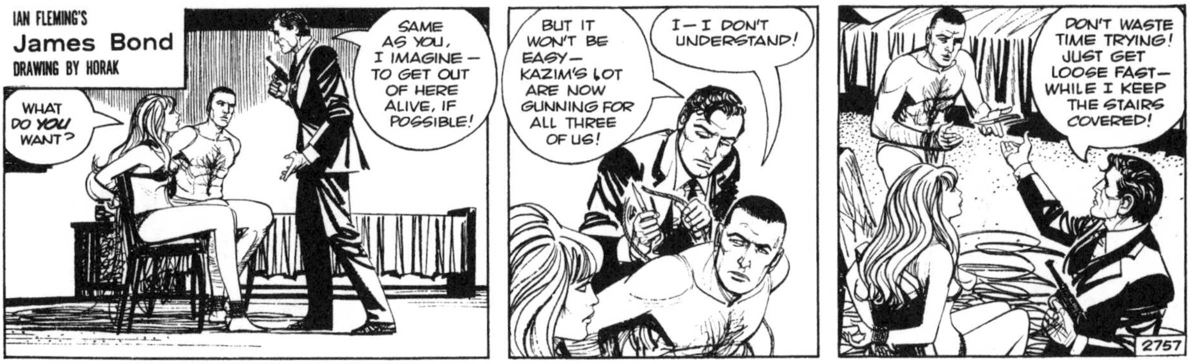
IAN FLEMING'S
James Bond
DRAWING BY HORAK
WHAT DO YOU WANT?
SAME AS YOU, I IMAGINE— TO GET OUT OF HERE ALIVE, IF POSSIBLE!
BUT IT WON'T BE EASY— KAZIM'S LOT ARE NOW GUNNING FOR ALL THREE OF US!
I— I DON'T UNDERSTAND!
DON'T WASTE TIME TRYING! JUST GET LOOSE FAST— WHILE I KEEP THE STAIRS COVERED!
2757

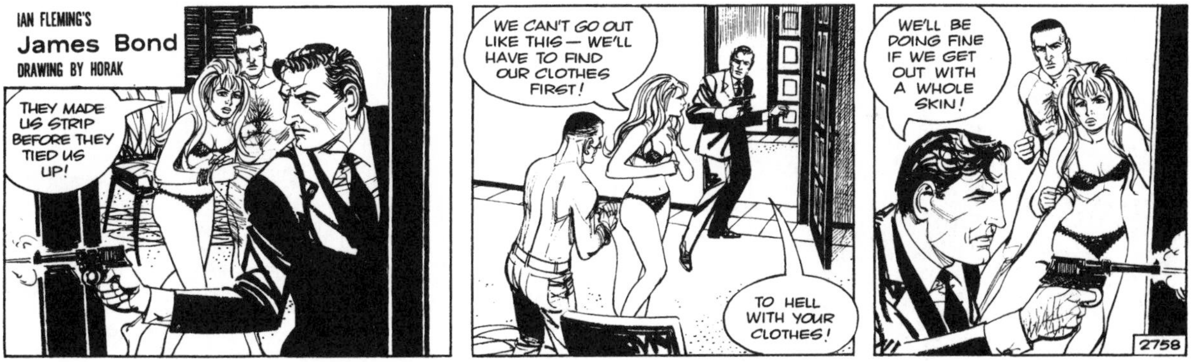
IAN FLEMING'S
James Bond
DRAWING BY HORAK
THEY MADE US STRIP BEFORE THEY TIED US UP!
WE CAN'T GO OUT LIKE THIS— WE'LL HAVE TO FIND OUR CLOTHES FIRST!
TO HELL WITH YOUR CLOTHES!
WE'LL BE DOING FINE IF WE GET OUT WITH A WHOLE SKIN!
2758

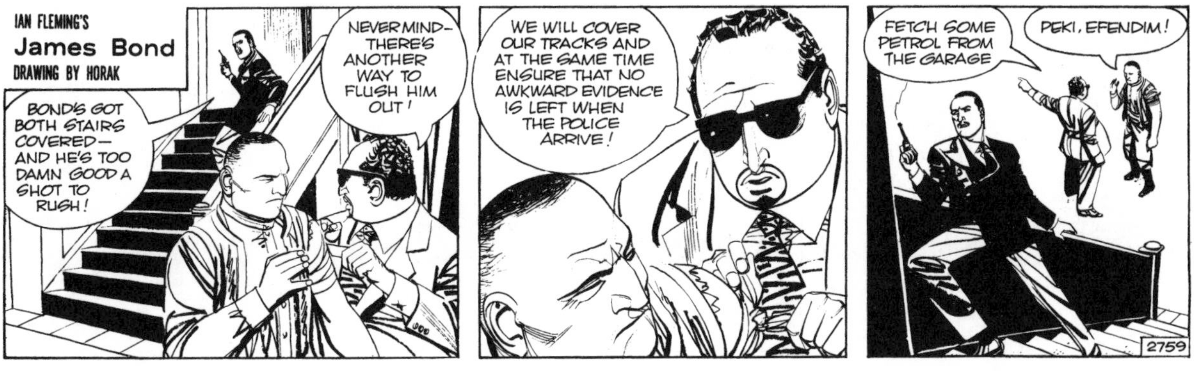
IAN FLEMING'S
James Bond
DRAWING BY HORAK
BOND'S GOT BOTH STAIRS COVERED— AND HE'S TOO DAMN GOOD A SHOT TO RUSH!
NEVERMIND— THERE'S ANOTHER WAY TO FLUSH HIM OUT!
WE WILL COVER OUR TRACKS AND AT THE SAME TIME ENSURE THAT NO AWKWARD EVIDENCE IS LEFT WHEN THE POLICE ARRIVE!
FETCH SOME PETROL FROM THE GARAGE
PEKI, EFENDIM!
2759

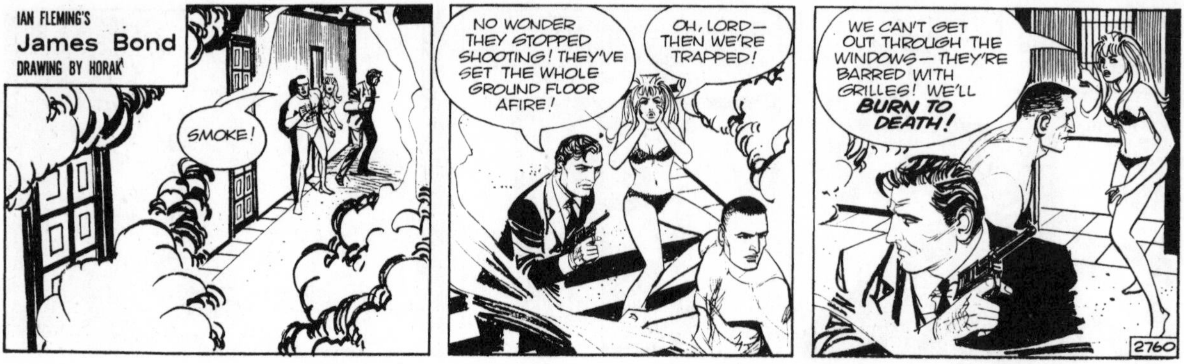
IAN FLEMING'S
James Bond
DRAWING BY HORAK
SMOKE!
NO WONDER THEY STOPPED SHOOTING! THEY'VE SET THE WHOLE GROUND FLOOR AFIRE!
OH, LORD— THEN WE'RE TRAPPED!
WE CAN'T GET OUT THROUGH THE WINDOWS— THEY'RE BARRED WITH GRILLES! WE'LL **BURN TO DEATH!**
2760

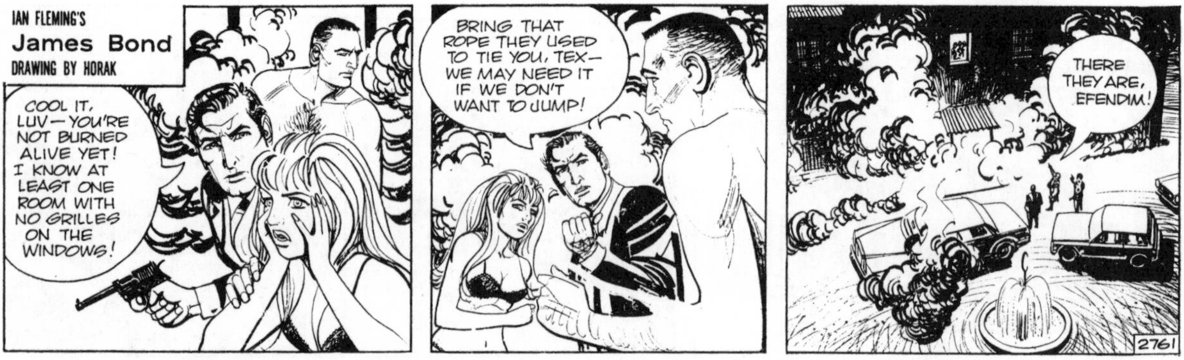
IAN FLEMING'S
James Bond
DRAWING BY HORAK
COOL IT, LUV— YOU'RE NOT BURNED ALIVE YET! I KNOW AT LEAST ONE ROOM WITH NO GRILLES ON THE WINDOWS!
BRING THAT ROPE THEY USED TO TIE YOU, TEX— WE MAY NEED IT IF WE DON'T WANT TO JUMP!
THERE THEY ARE, EFENDIM!
2761

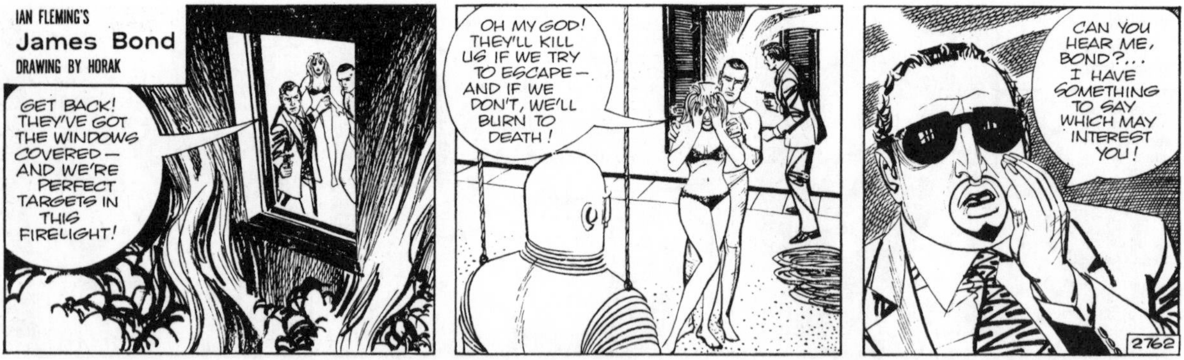
IAN FLEMING'S
James Bond
DRAWING BY HORAK
GET BACK! THEY'VE GOT THE WINDOWS COVERED— AND WE'RE PERFECT TARGETS IN THIS FIRELIGHT!
OH MY GOD! THEY'LL KILL US IF WE TRY TO ESCAPE— AND IF WE DON'T, WE'LL BURN TO DEATH!
CAN YOU HEAR ME, BOND?... I HAVE SOMETHING TO SAY WHICH MAY INTEREST YOU!
2762

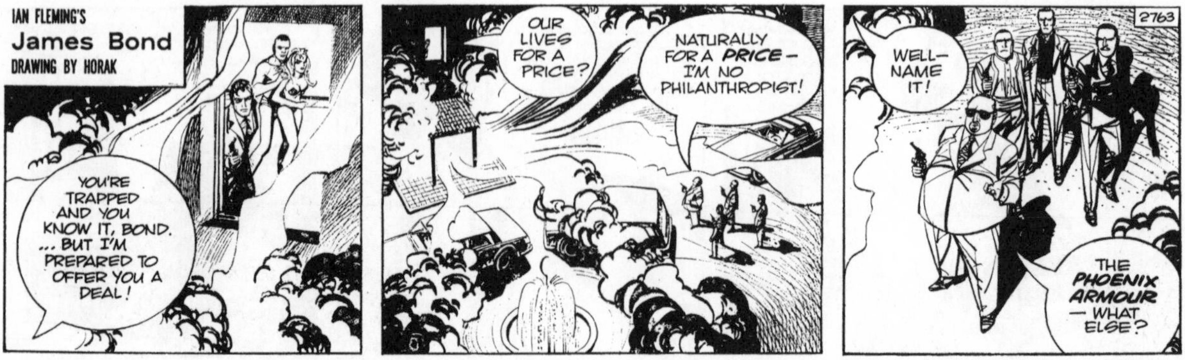
IAN FLEMING'S
James Bond
DRAWING BY HORAK
YOU'RE TRAPPED AND YOU KNOW IT, BOND. ... BUT I'M PREPARED TO OFFER YOU A DEAL!
OUR LIVES FOR A PRICE?
NATURALLY FOR A **PRICE**— I'M NO PHILANTHROPIST!
2763
WELL— NAME IT!
THE ***PHOENIX ARMOUR*** — WHAT ELSE?

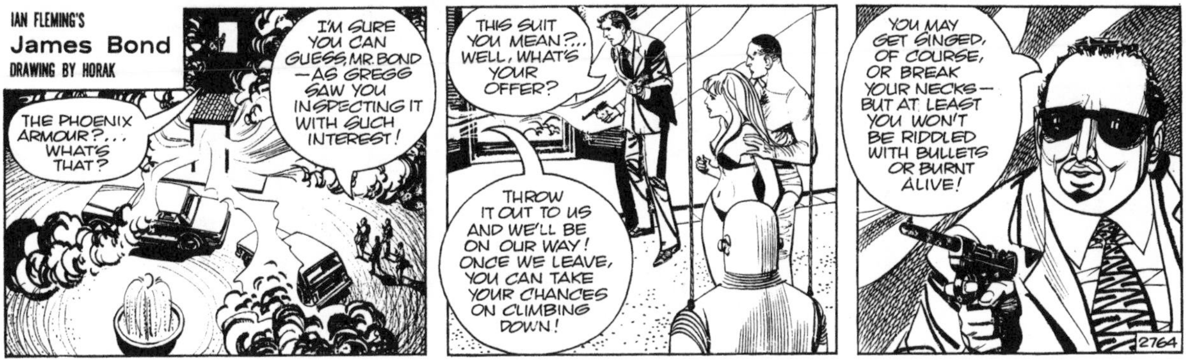
IAN FLEMING'S
James Bond
DRAWING BY HORAK
THE PHOENIX ARMOUR?... WHAT'S THAT?
I'M SURE YOU CAN GUESS, MR. BOND —AS GREGG SAW YOU INSPECTING IT WITH SUCH INTEREST!
THIS SUIT YOU MEAN?... WELL, WHAT'S YOUR OFFER?
THROW IT OUT TO US AND WE'LL BE ON OUR WAY! ONCE WE LEAVE, YOU CAN TAKE YOUR CHANCES ON CLIMBING DOWN!
YOU MAY GET SINGED, OF COURSE, OR BREAK YOUR NECKS— BUT AT LEAST YOU WON'T BE RIDDLED WITH BULLETS OR BURNT ALIVE!
2764

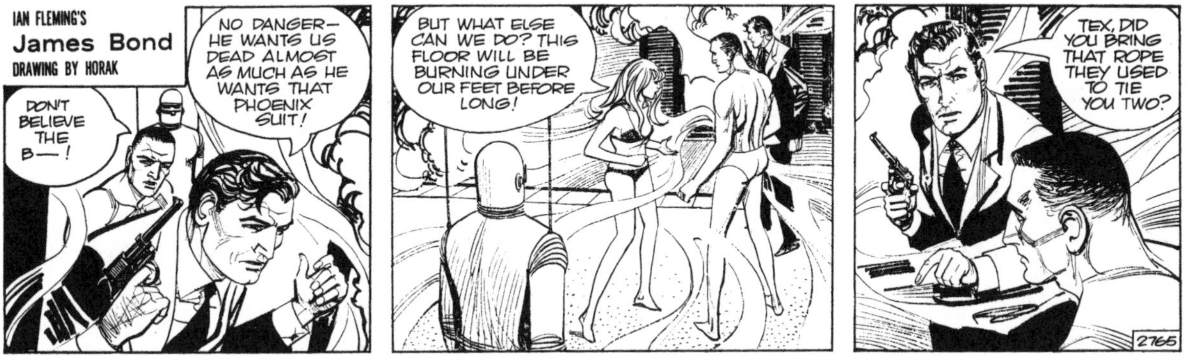
IAN FLEMING'S
James Bond
DRAWING BY HORAK
DON'T BELIEVE THE B—!
NO DANGER— HE WANTS US DEAD ALMOST AS MUCH AS HE WANTS THAT PHOENIX SUIT!
BUT WHAT ELSE CAN WE DO? THIS FLOOR WILL BE BURNING UNDER OUR FEET BEFORE LONG!
TEX, DID YOU BRING THAT ROPE THEY USED TO TIE YOU TWO?
2765

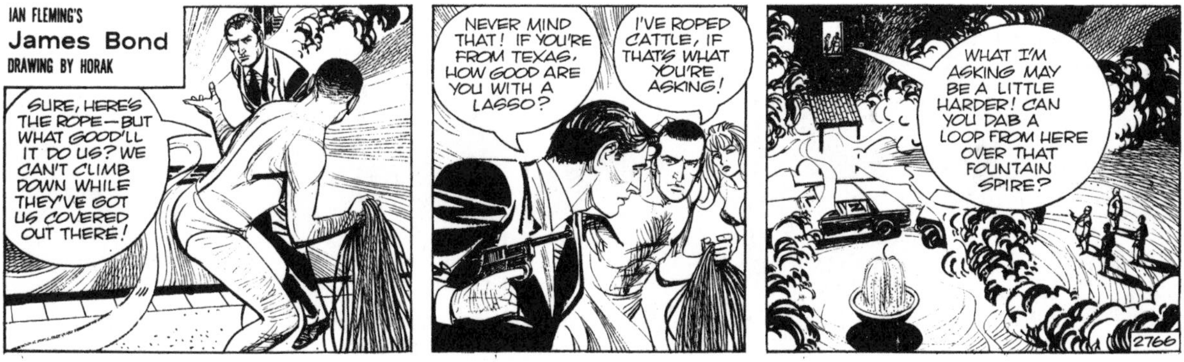
IAN FLEMING'S
James Bond
DRAWING BY HORAK
SURE, HERE'S THE ROPE—BUT WHAT GOOD'LL IT DO US? WE CAN'T CLIMB DOWN WHILE THEY'VE GOT US COVERED OUT THERE!
NEVER MIND THAT! IF YOU'RE FROM TEXAS, HOW GOOD ARE YOU WITH A LASSO?
I'VE ROPED CATTLE, IF THAT'S WHAT YOU'RE ASKING!
WHAT I'M ASKING MAY BE A LITTLE HARDER! CAN YOU DAB A LOOP FROM HERE OVER THAT FOUNTAIN SPIRE?
2766

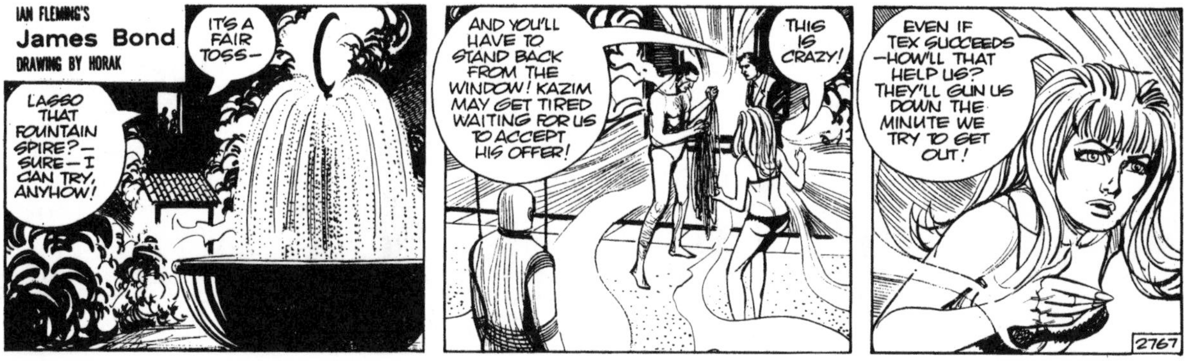
IAN FLEMING'S
James Bond
DRAWING BY HORAK
LASSO THAT FOUNTAIN SPIRE?— SURE— I CAN TRY, ANYHOW!
IT'S A FAIR TOSS—
AND YOU'LL HAVE TO STAND BACK FROM THE WINDOW! KAZIM MAY GET TIRED WAITING FOR US TO ACCEPT HIS OFFER!
THIS IS CRAZY!
EVEN IF TEX SUCCEEDS —HOW'LL THAT HELP US? THEY'LL GUN US DOWN THE MINUTE WE TRY TO GET OUT!
2767

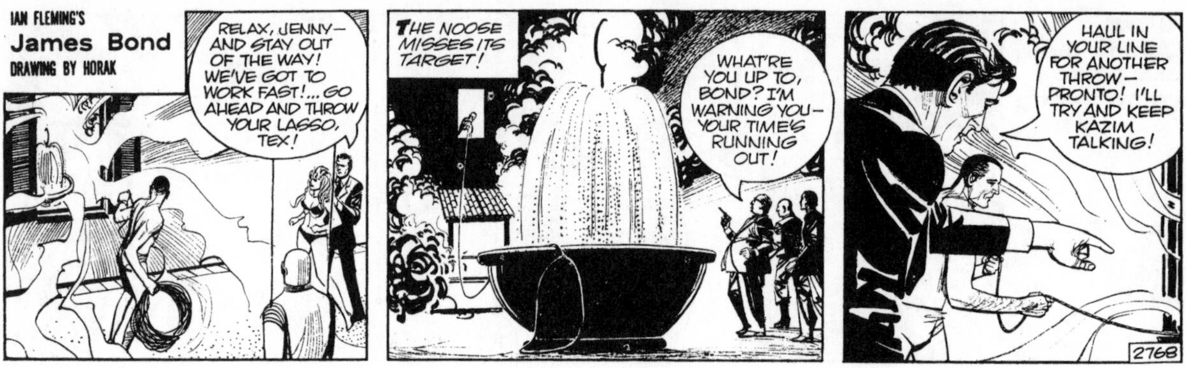
IAN FLEMING'S
James Bond
DRAWING BY HORAK
RELAX, JENNY— AND STAY OUT OF THE WAY! WE'VE GOT TO WORK FAST!... GO AHEAD AND THROW YOUR LASSO, TEX!
THE NOOSE MISSES ITS TARGET!
WHAT'RE YOU UP TO, BOND? I'M WARNING YOU— YOUR TIME'S RUNNING OUT!
HAUL IN YOUR LINE FOR ANOTHER THROW— PRONTO! I'LL TRY AND KEEP KAZIM TALKING!
2768

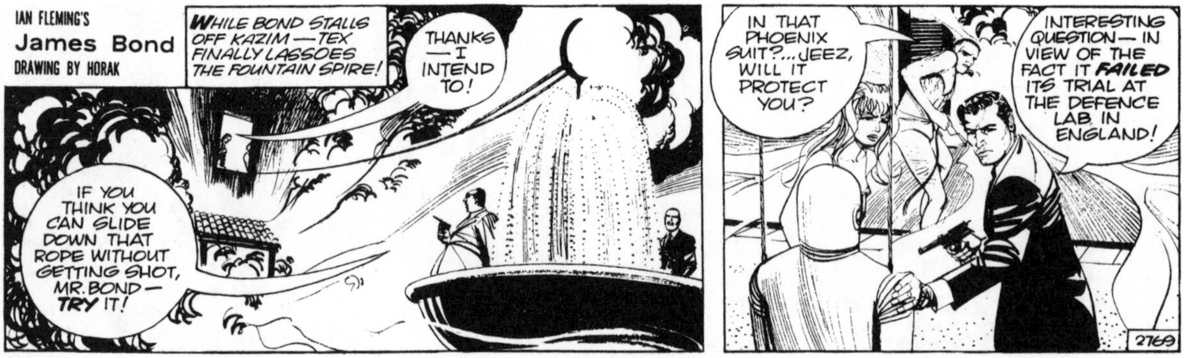
IAN FLEMING'S
James Bond
DRAWING BY HORAK
WHILE BOND STALLS OFF KAZIM —TEX FINALLY LASSOES THE FOUNTAIN SPIRE!
IF YOU THINK YOU CAN SLIDE DOWN THAT ROPE WITHOUT GETTING SHOT, MR. BOND— TRY IT!
THANKS —I INTEND TO!
IN THAT PHOENIX SUIT?... JEEZ, WILL IT PROTECT YOU?
INTERESTING QUESTION— IN VIEW OF THE FACT IT FAILED ITS TRIAL AT THE DEFENCE LAB IN ENGLAND!
2769

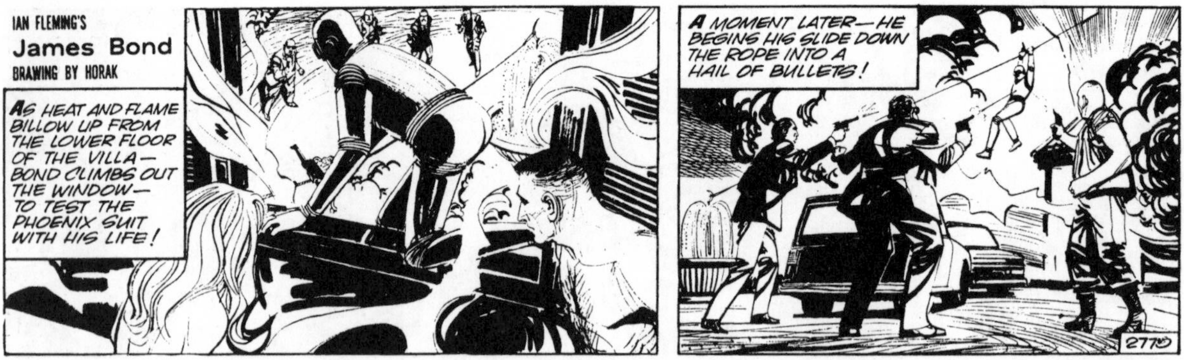
IAN FLEMING'S
James Bond
DRAWING BY HORAK
AS HEAT AND FLAME BILLOW UP FROM THE LOWER FLOOR OF THE VILLA— BOND CLIMBS OUT THE WINDOW— TO TEST THE PHOENIX SUIT WITH HIS LIFE!
A MOMENT LATER— HE BEGINS HIS SLIDE DOWN THE ROPE INTO A HAIL OF BULLETS!
2770

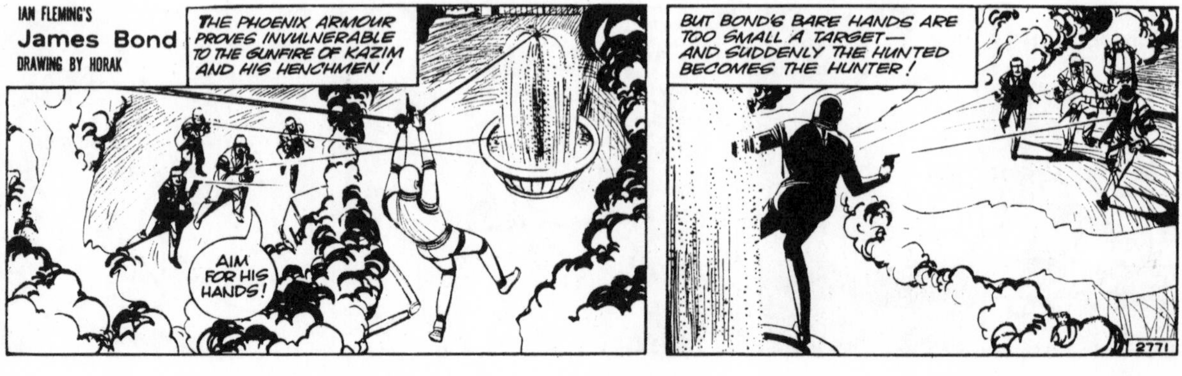
IAN FLEMING'S
James Bond
DRAWING BY HORAK
THE PHOENIX ARMOUR PROVES INVULNERABLE TO THE GUNFIRE OF KAZIM AND HIS HENCHMEN!
AIM FOR HIS HANDS!
BUT BOND'S BARE HANDS ARE TOO SMALL A TARGET— AND SUDDENLY THE HUNTED BECOMES THE HUNTER!
2771

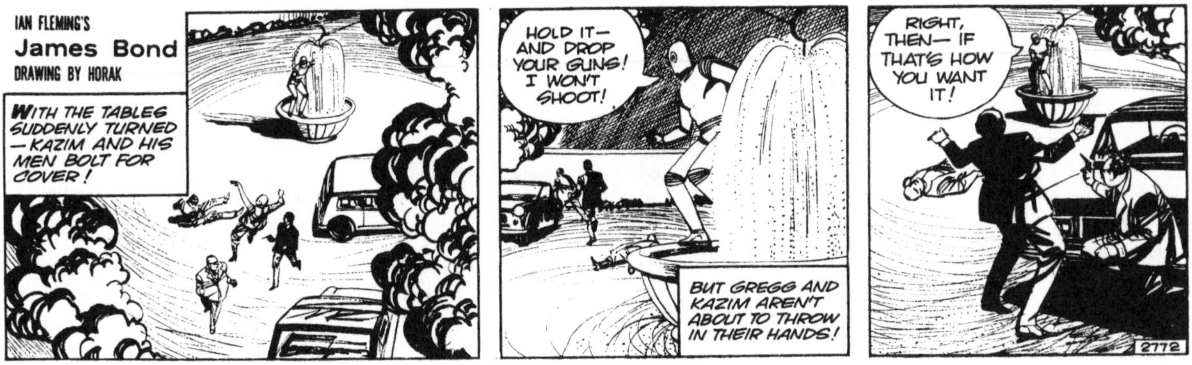
IAN FLEMING'S
James Bond
DRAWING BY HORAK
WITH THE TABLES SUDDENLY TURNED —KAZIM AND HIS MEN BOLT FOR COVER!
HOLD IT— AND DROP YOUR GUNS! I WON'T SHOOT!
BUT GREGG AND KAZIM AREN'T ABOUT TO THROW IN THEIR HANDS!
RIGHT, THEN— IF THAT'S HOW YOU WANT IT!
2772

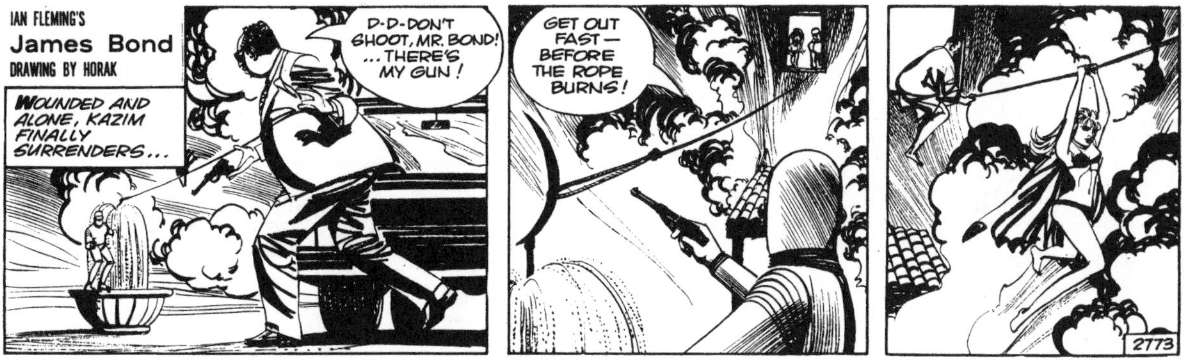
IAN FLEMING'S
James Bond
DRAWING BY HORAK
WOUNDED AND ALONE, KAZIM FINALLY SURRENDERS...
D-D-DON'T SHOOT, MR. BOND! ...THERE'S MY GUN!
GET OUT FAST— BEFORE THE ROPE BURNS!
2773

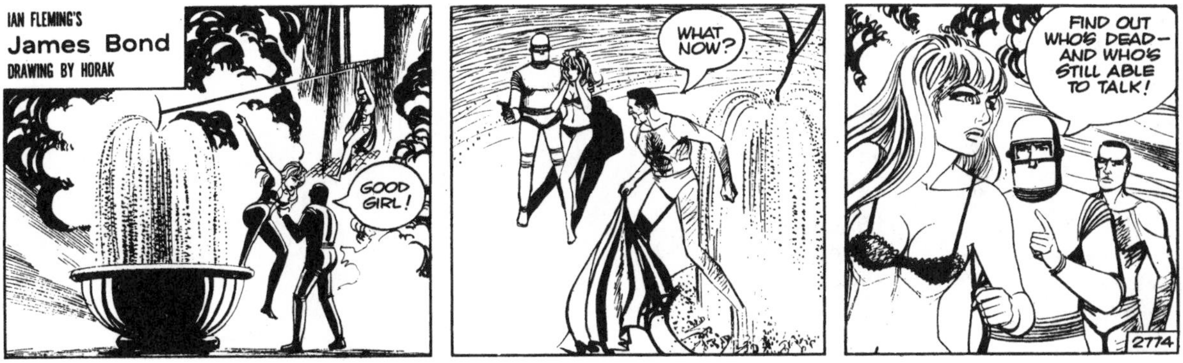
IAN FLEMING'S
James Bond
DRAWING BY HORAK
GOOD GIRL!
WHAT NOW?
FIND OUT WHO'S DEAD— AND WHO'S STILL ABLE TO TALK!
2774

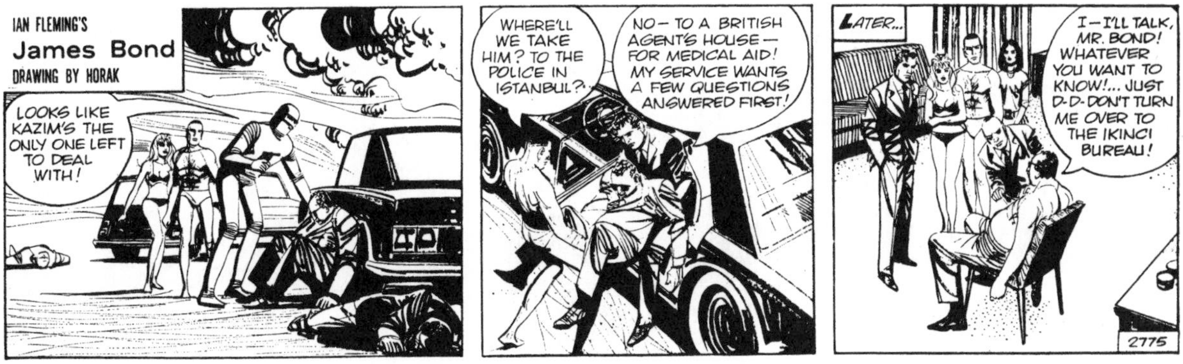
IAN FLEMING'S
James Bond
DRAWING BY HORAK
LOOKS LIKE KAZIM'S THE ONLY ONE LEFT TO DEAL WITH!
WHERE'LL WE TAKE HIM? TO THE POLICE IN ISTANBUL?
NO— TO A BRITISH AGENT'S HOUSE— FOR MEDICAL AID! MY SERVICE WANTS A FEW QUESTIONS ANSWERED FIRST!
LATER...
I—I'LL TALK, MR. BOND! WHATEVER YOU WANT TO KNOW!... JUST D-D-DON'T TURN ME OVER TO THE IKINCI BUREAU!
2775

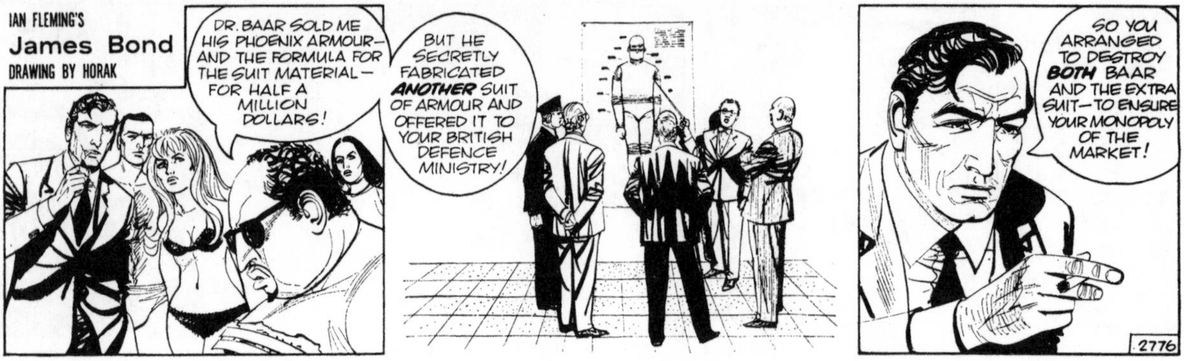
IAN FLEMING'S
James Bond
DRAWING BY HORAK
DR. BAAR SOLD ME HIS PHOENIX ARMOUR— AND THE FORMULA FOR THE SUIT MATERIAL— FOR HALF A MILLION DOLLARS!
BUT HE SECRETLY FABRICATED ANOTHER SUIT OF ARMOUR AND OFFERED IT TO YOUR BRITISH DEFENCE MINISTRY!
SO YOU ARRANGED TO DESTROY BOTH BAAR AND THE EXTRA SUIT—TO ENSURE YOUR MONOPOLY OF THE MARKET!
2776

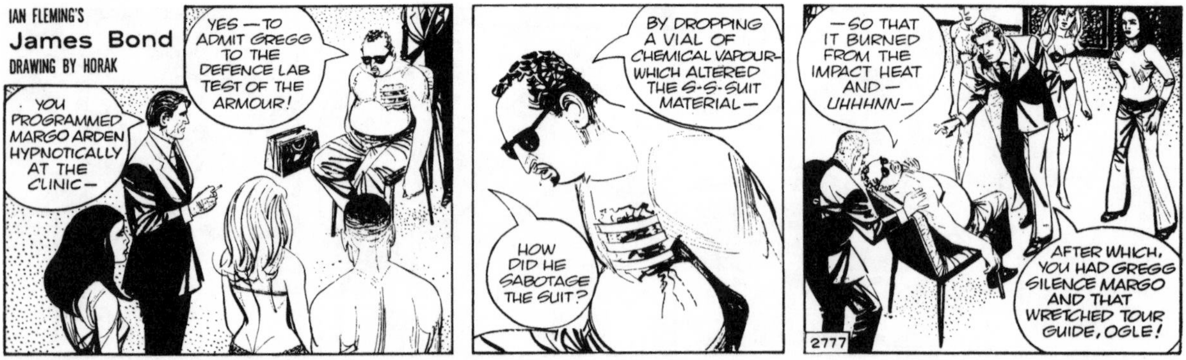
IAN FLEMING'S
James Bond
DRAWING BY HORAK
YES — TO ADMIT GREGG TO THE DEFENCE LAB TEST OF THE ARMOUR!
YOU PROGRAMMED MARGO ARDEN HYPNOTICALLY AT THE CLINIC—
BY DROPPING A VIAL OF CHEMICAL VAPOUR— WHICH ALTERED THE S-S-SUIT MATERIAL—
HOW DID HE SABOTAGE THE SUIT?
—SO THAT IT BURNED FROM THE IMPACT HEAT AND— UHHHNN—
AFTER WHICH, YOU HAD GREGG SILENCE MARGO AND THAT WRETCHED TOUR GUIDE, OGLE!
2777

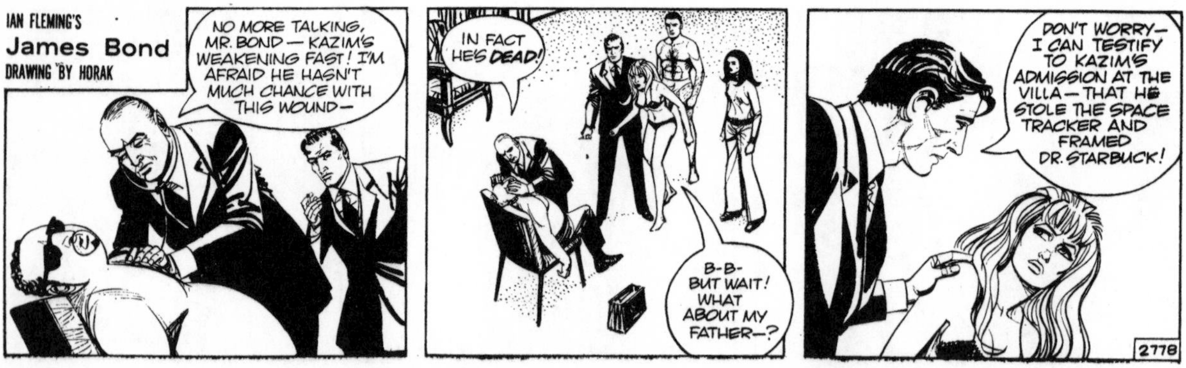
IAN FLEMING'S
James Bond
DRAWING BY HORAK
NO MORE TALKING, MR. BOND — KAZIM'S WEAKENING FAST! I'M AFRAID HE HASN'T MUCH CHANCE WITH THIS WOUND—
IN FACT HE'S DEAD!
B-B-BUT WAIT! WHAT ABOUT MY FATHER—?
DON'T WORRY— I CAN TESTIFY TO KAZIM'S ADMISSION AT THE VILLA—THAT HE STOLE THE SPACE TRACKER AND FRAMED DR. STARBUCK!
2778

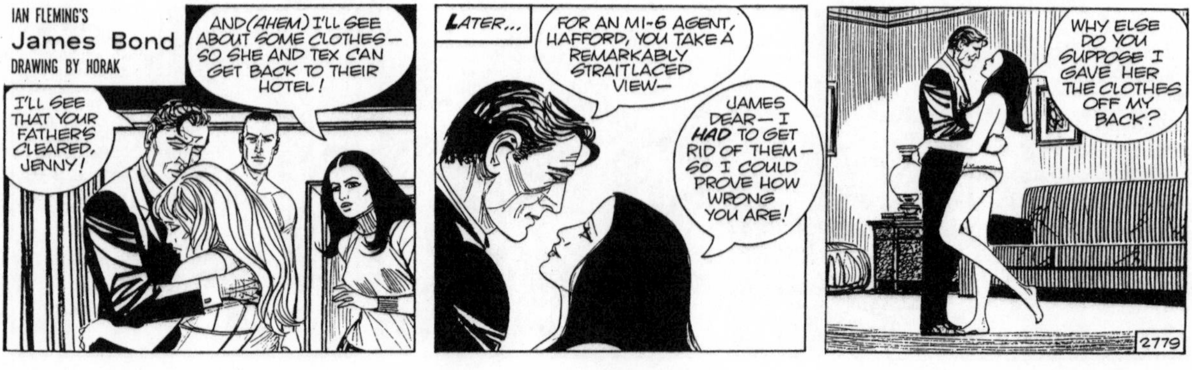
IAN FLEMING'S
James Bond
DRAWING BY HORAK
I'LL SEE THAT YOUR FATHER'S CLEARED, JENNY!
AND (AHEM) I'LL SEE ABOUT SOME CLOTHES— SO SHE AND TEX CAN GET BACK TO THEIR HOTEL!
LATER...
FOR AN MI-6 AGENT, HAFFORD, YOU TAKE A REMARKABLY STRAITLACED VIEW—
JAMES DEAR— I HAD TO GET RID OF THEM— SO I COULD PROVE HOW WRONG YOU ARE!
WHY ELSE DO YOU SUPPOSE I GAVE HER THE CLOTHES OFF MY BACK?
2779

IAN FLEMING'S
James Bond
DRAWING BY HORAK
TURK H
HOW CAN I EVER THANK YOU?
MI-6'S BEEN ON TO WASHINGTON— YOUR FATHER WILL BE FREE BY THE TIME YOU LAND BACK IN THE STATES!
THAT LOOKS LIKE A GOOD START!
LET'S NOT MAKE IT TOO GOOD— OR WE'LL MISS OUR TAKEOFF!
HE'S RIGHT, JAMES— I WOULDN'T WANT YOU TO MISS MY TAKEOFF!
2780
END OF STORY

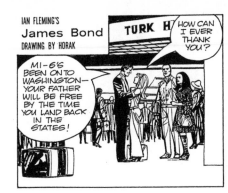

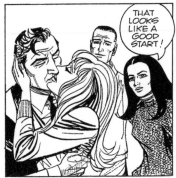

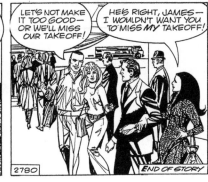

# THE BLACK RUBY CAPER

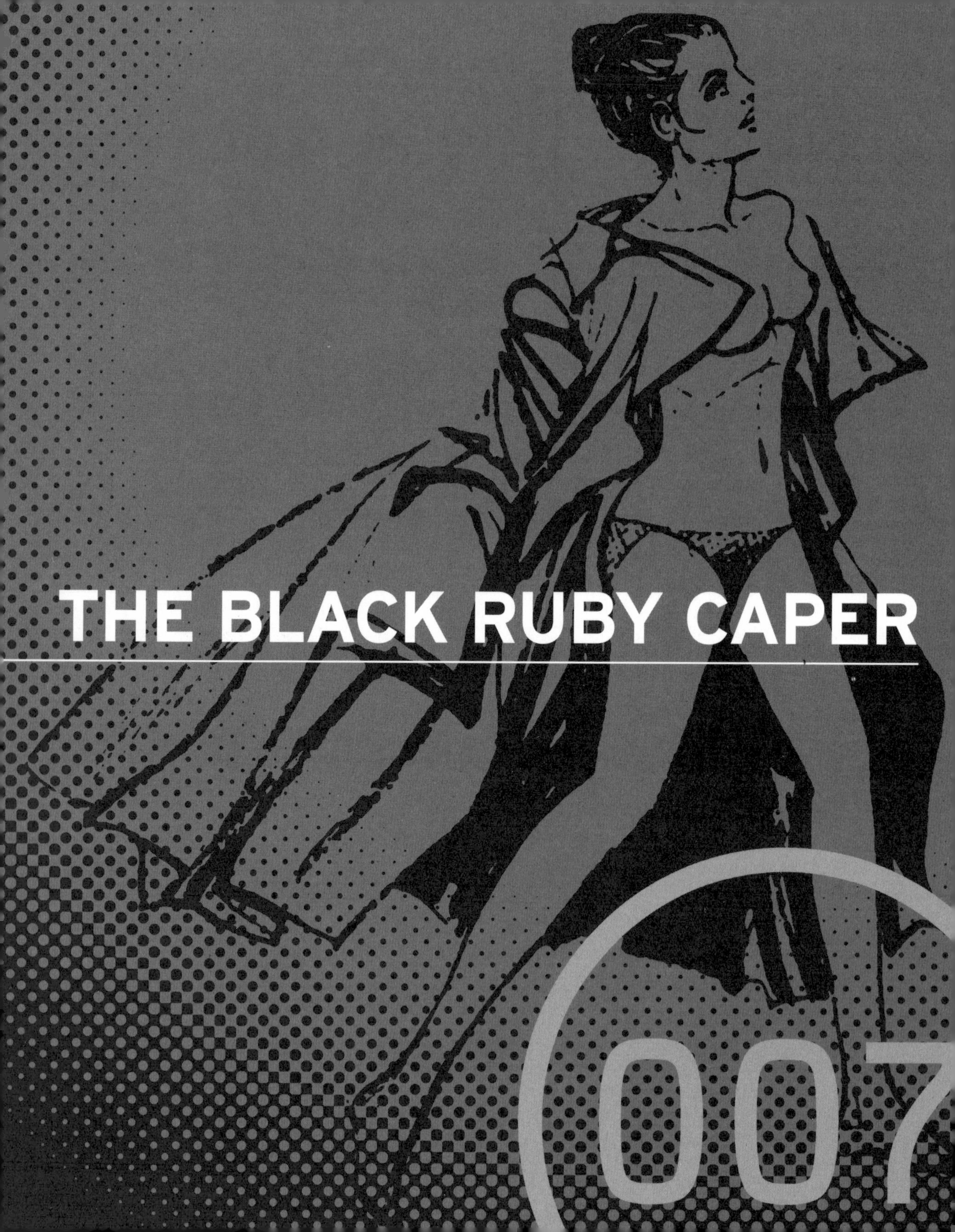
007

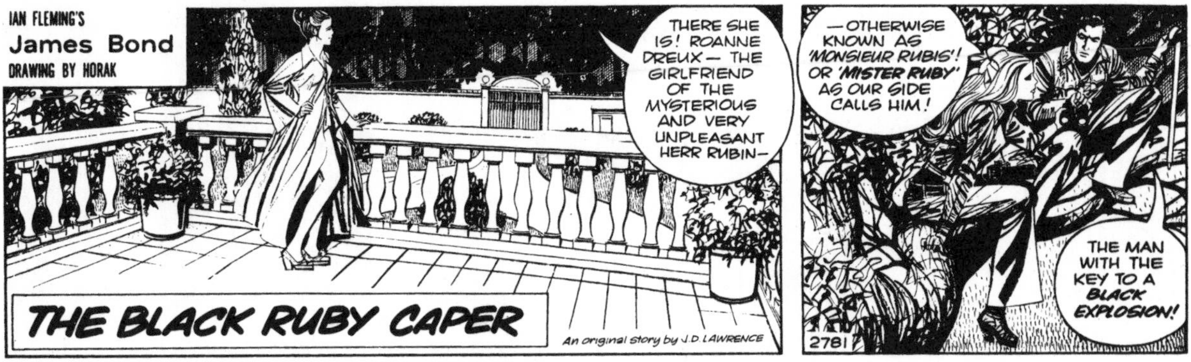
IAN FLEMING'S
James Bond
DRAWING BY HORAK
THERE SHE IS! ROANNE DREUX — THE GIRLFRIEND OF THE MYSTERIOUS AND VERY UNPLEASANT HERR RUBIN—
THE BLACK RUBY CAPER
An original story by J.D. LAWRENCE
—OTHERWISE KNOWN AS 'MONSIEUR RUBIS'! OR 'MISTER RUBY' AS OUR SIDE CALLS HIM!
THE MAN WITH THE KEY TO A BLACK EXPLOSION!
2781

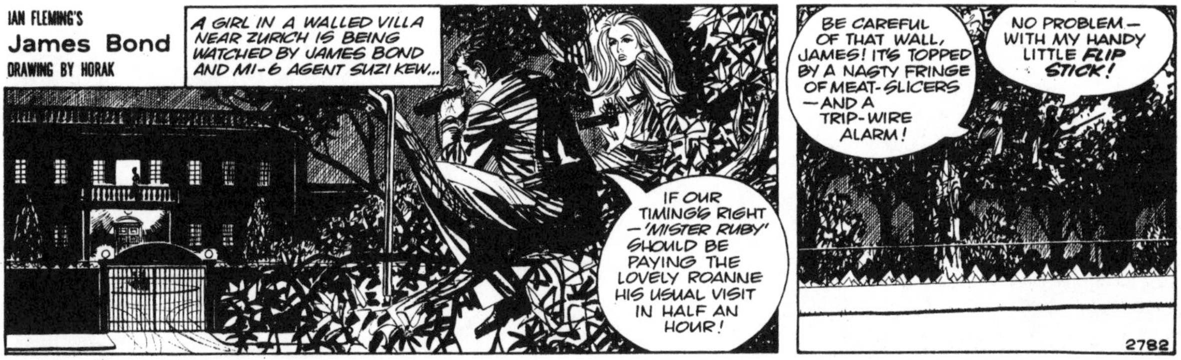
IAN FLEMING'S
James Bond
DRAWING BY HORAK
A GIRL IN A WALLED VILLA NEAR ZURICH IS BEING WATCHED BY JAMES BOND AND MI-6 AGENT SUZI KEW...
IF OUR TIMING'S RIGHT —'MISTER RUBY' SHOULD BE PAYING THE LOVELY ROANNE HIS USUAL VISIT IN HALF AN HOUR!
BE CAREFUL OF THAT WALL, JAMES! IT'S TOPPED BY A NASTY FRINGE OF MEAT-SLICERS —AND A TRIP-WIRE ALARM!
NO PROBLEM — WITH MY HANDY LITTLE FLIP STICK!
2782

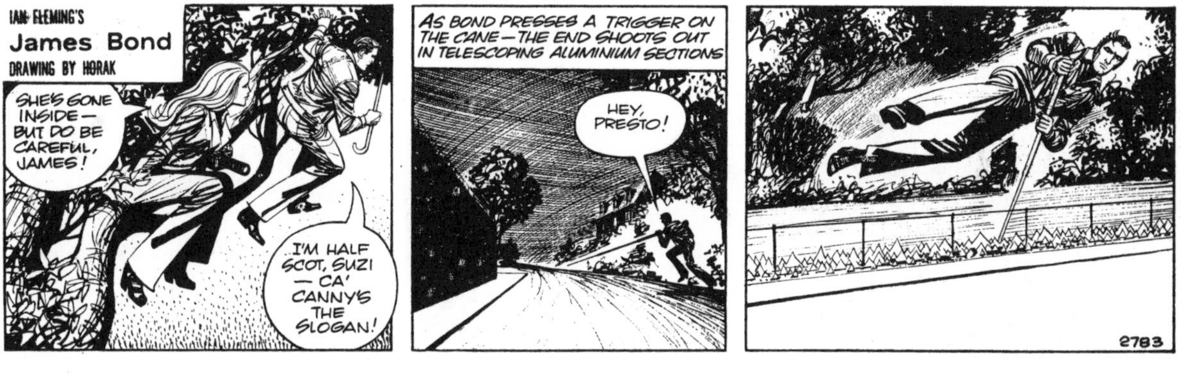
IAN FLEMING'S
James Bond
DRAWING BY HORAK
SHE'S GONE INSIDE — BUT DO BE CAREFUL, JAMES!
I'M HALF SCOT, SUZI — CA' CANNY'S THE SLOGAN!
AS BOND PRESSES A TRIGGER ON THE CANE — THE END SHOOTS OUT IN TELESCOPING ALUMINIUM SECTIONS
HEY, PRESTO!
2783

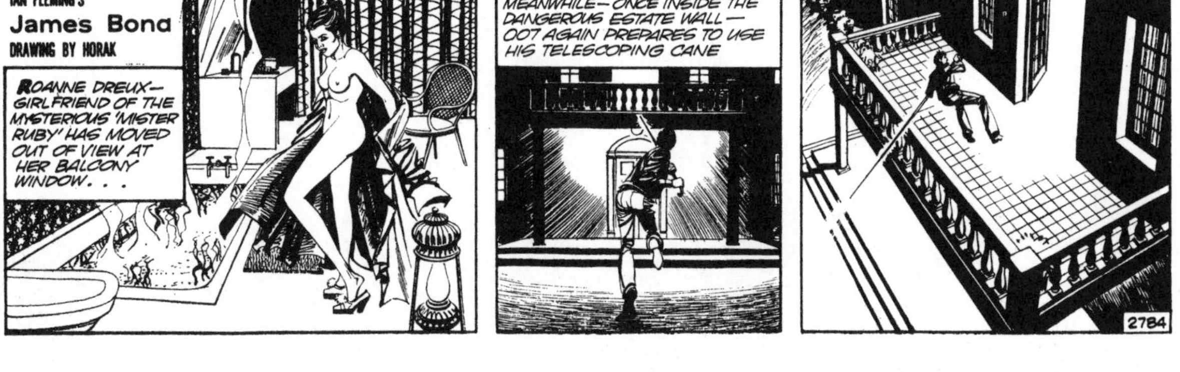
IAN FLEMING'S
James Bond
DRAWING BY HORAK
ROANNE DREUX— GIRLFRIEND OF THE MYSTERIOUS 'MISTER RUBY' HAS MOVED OUT OF VIEW AT HER BALCONY WINDOW. . .
MEANWHILE— ONCE INSIDE THE DANGEROUS ESTATE WALL — 007 AGAIN PREPARES TO USE HIS TELESCOPING CANE
2784

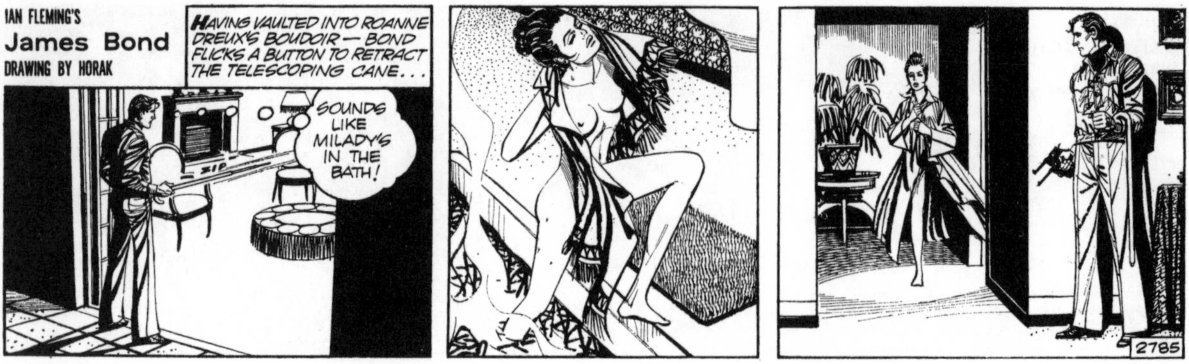
IAN FLEMING'S
James Bond
DRAWING BY HORAK
HAVING VAULTED INTO ROANNE DREUX'S BOUDOIR — BOND FLICKS A BUTTON TO RETRACT THE TELESCOPING CANE . . .
SOUNDS LIKE MILADY'S IN THE BATH!
2785

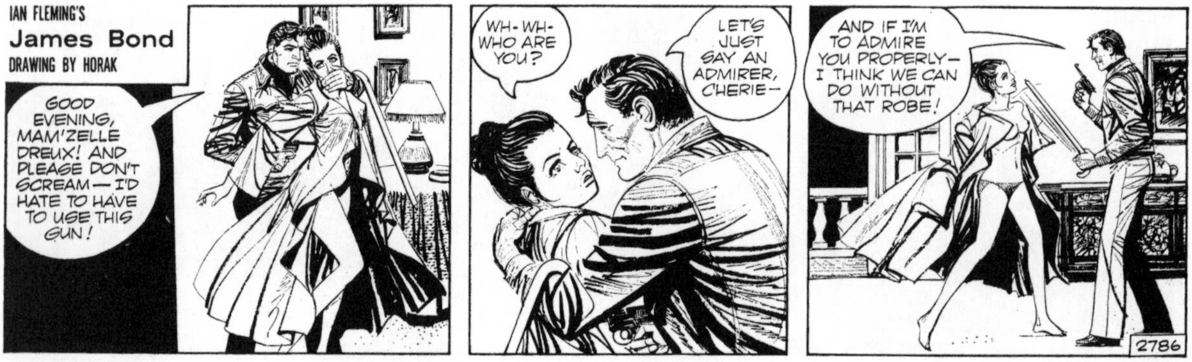
IAN FLEMING'S
James Bond
DRAWING BY HORAK
GOOD EVENING, MAM'ZELLE DREUX! AND PLEASE DON'T SCREAM — I'D HATE TO HAVE TO USE THIS GUN!
WH-WH-WHO ARE YOU?
LET'S JUST SAY AN ADMIRER, CHERIE —
AND IF I'M TO ADMIRE YOU PROPERLY — I THINK WE CAN DO WITHOUT THAT ROBE!
2786

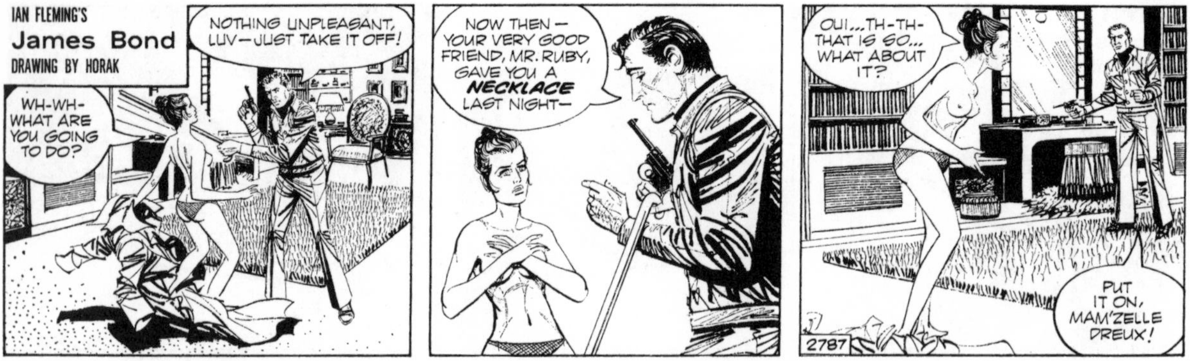
IAN FLEMING'S
James Bond
DRAWING BY HORAK
NOTHING UNPLEASANT, LUV — JUST TAKE IT OFF!
WH-WH-WHAT ARE YOU GOING TO DO?
NOW THEN — YOUR VERY GOOD FRIEND, MR. RUBY, GAVE YOU A NECKLACE LAST NIGHT —
OUI...TH-TH-THAT IS SO... WHAT ABOUT IT?
PUT IT ON, MAM'ZELLE DREUX!
2787

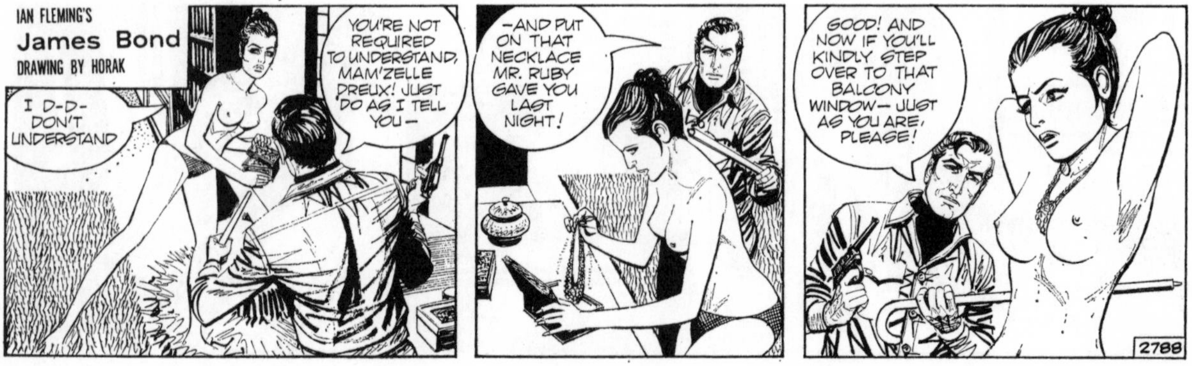
IAN FLEMING'S
James Bond
DRAWING BY HORAK
I D-D-DON'T UNDERSTAND
YOU'RE NOT REQUIRED TO UNDERSTAND, MAM'ZELLE DREUX! JUST DO AS I TELL YOU —
— AND PUT ON THAT NECKLACE MR. RUBY GAVE YOU LAST NIGHT!
GOOD! AND NOW IF YOU'LL KINDLY STEP OVER TO THAT BALCONY WINDOW — JUST AS YOU ARE, PLEASE!
2788

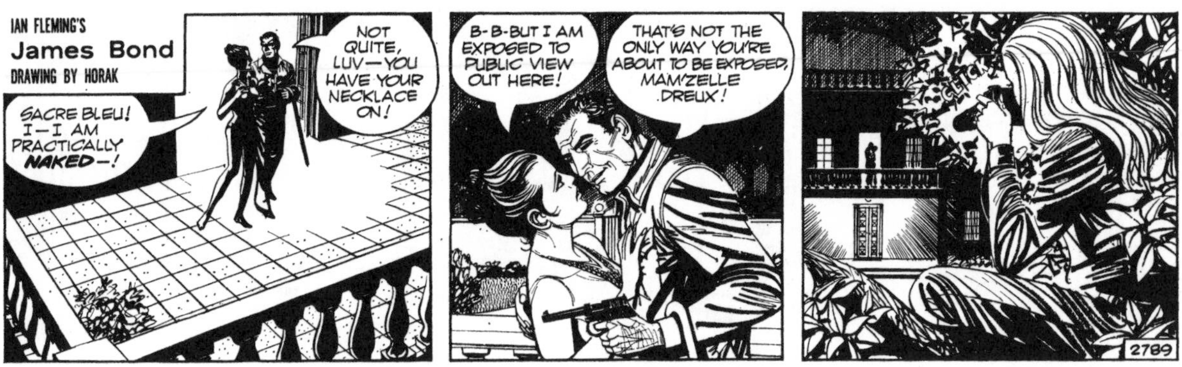
IAN FLEMING'S
James Bond
DRAWING BY HORAK
SACRE BLEU! I—I AM PRACTICALLY NAKED—!
NOT QUITE, LUV—YOU HAVE YOUR NECKLACE ON!
B-B-BUT I AM EXPOSED TO PUBLIC VIEW OUT HERE!
THAT'S NOT THE ONLY WAY YOU'RE ABOUT TO BE EXPOSED, MAM'ZELLE DREUX!
CLICK
2789

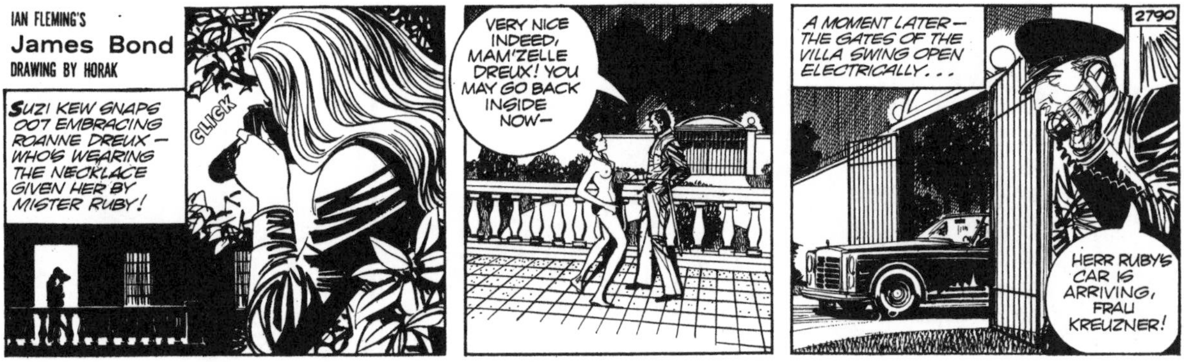
IAN FLEMING'S
James Bond
DRAWING BY HORAK
SUZI KEW SNAPS 007 EMBRACING ROANNE DREUX—WHO'S WEARING THE NECKLACE GIVEN HER BY MISTER RUBY!
CLICK
VERY NICE INDEED, MAM'ZELLE DREUX! YOU MAY GO BACK INSIDE NOW—
2790
A MOMENT LATER—THE GATES OF THE VILLA SWING OPEN ELECTRICALLY...
HERR RUBY'S CAR IS ARRIVING, FRAU KREUZNER!

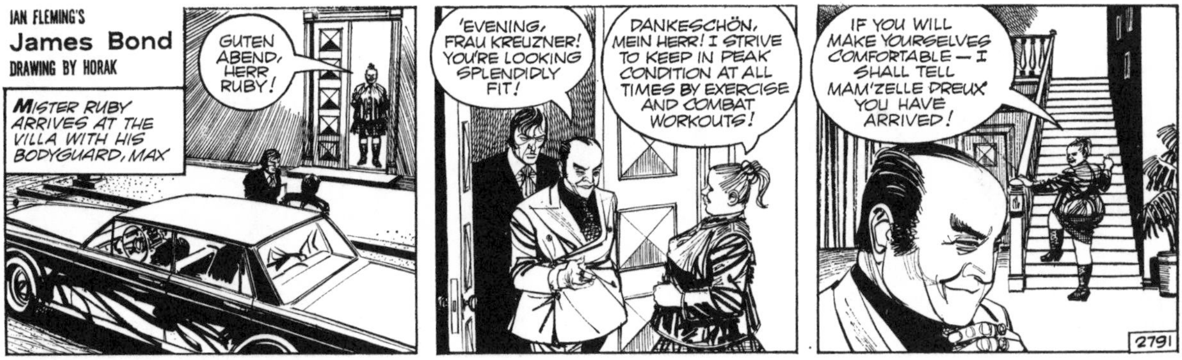
IAN FLEMING'S
James Bond
DRAWING BY HORAK
MISTER RUBY ARRIVES AT THE VILLA WITH HIS BODYGUARD, MAX
GUTEN ABEND, HERR RUBY!
'EVENING, FRAU KREUZNER! YOU'RE LOOKING SPLENDIDLY FIT!
DANKESCHÖN, MEIN HERR! I STRIVE TO KEEP IN PEAK CONDITION AT ALL TIMES BY EXERCISE AND COMBAT WORKOUTS!
IF YOU WILL MAKE YOURSELVES COMFORTABLE—I SHALL TELL MAM'ZELLE DREUX YOU HAVE ARRIVED!
2791

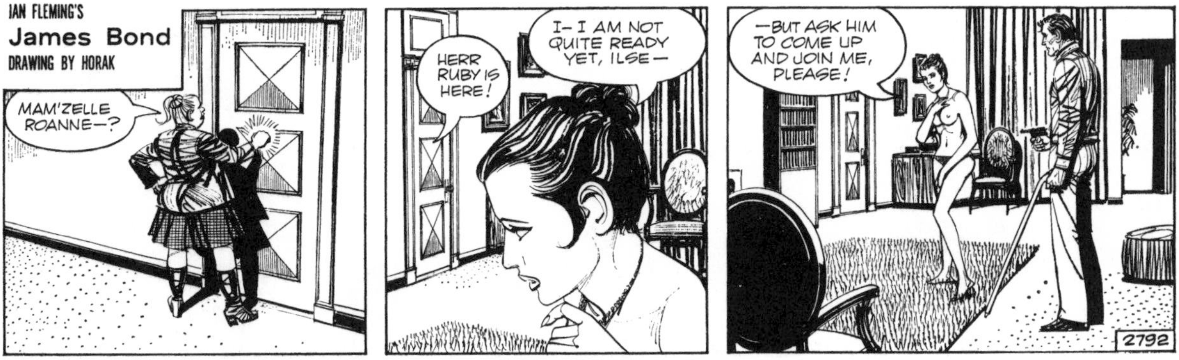
IAN FLEMING'S
James Bond
DRAWING BY HORAK
MAM'ZELLE ROANNE—?
HERR RUBY IS HERE!
I—I AM NOT QUITE READY YET, ILSE—
—BUT ASK HIM TO COME UP AND JOIN ME, PLEASE!
2792

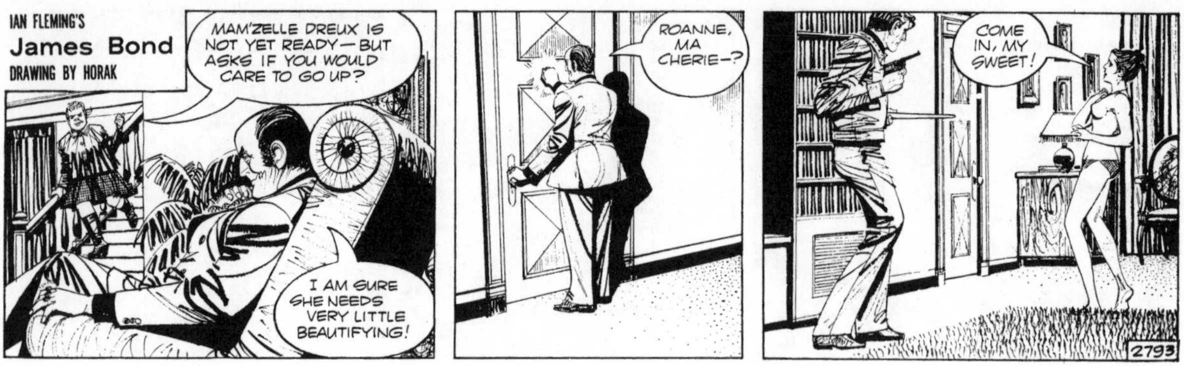
IAN FLEMING'S
James Bond
DRAWING BY HORAK
MAM'ZELLE DREUX IS NOT YET READY—BUT ASKS IF YOU WOULD CARE TO GO UP?
I AM SURE SHE NEEDS VERY LITTLE BEAUTIFYING!
ROANNE, MA CHERIE—?
COME IN, MY SWEET!
2793

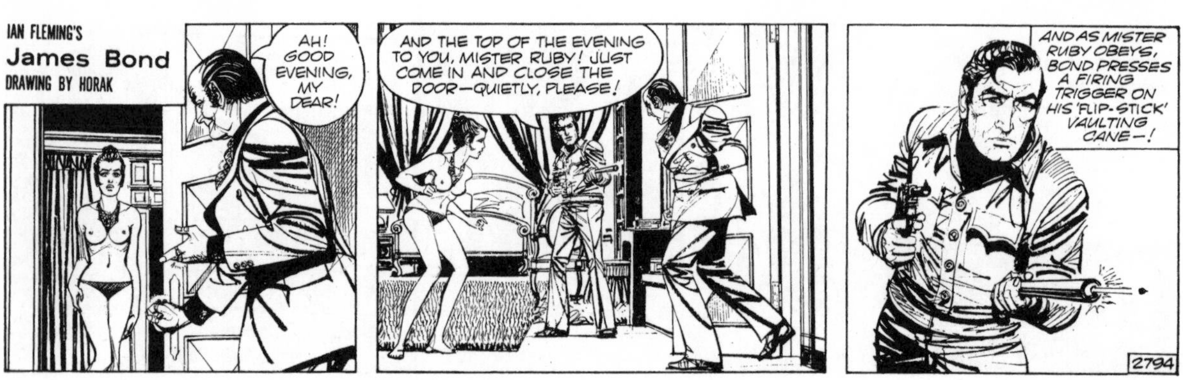
IAN FLEMING'S
James Bond
DRAWING BY HORAK
AH! GOOD EVENING, MY DEAR!
AND THE TOP OF THE EVENING TO YOU, MISTER RUBY! JUST COME IN AND CLOSE THE DOOR—QUIETLY, PLEASE!
AND AS MISTER RUBY OBEYS, BOND PRESSES A FIRING TRIGGER ON HIS 'FLIP-STICK' VAULTING CANE—!
2794

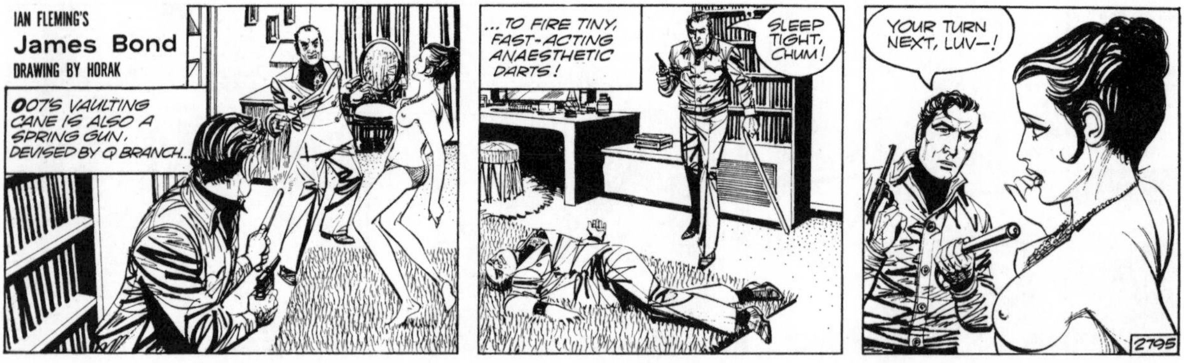
IAN FLEMING'S
James Bond
DRAWING BY HORAK
007'S VAULTING CANE IS ALSO A SPRING GUN, DEVISED BY Q BRANCH...
...TO FIRE TINY, FAST-ACTING ANAESTHETIC DARTS!
SLEEP TIGHT, CHUM!
YOUR TURN NEXT, LUV—!
2795

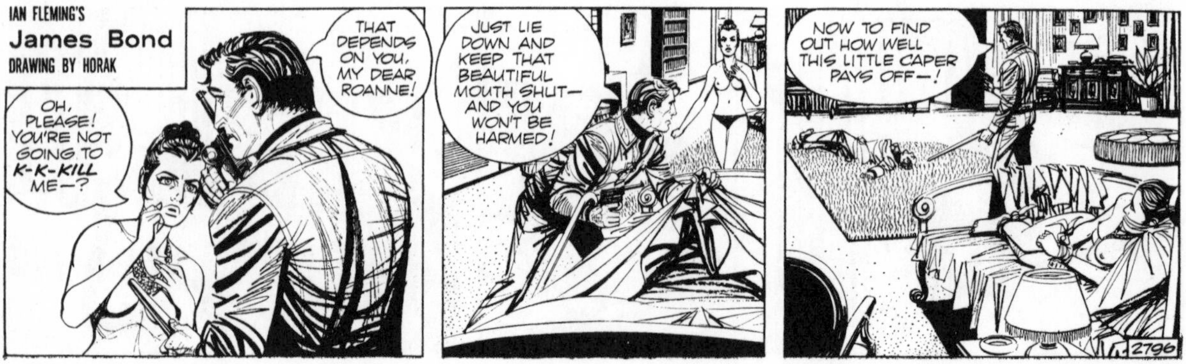
IAN FLEMING'S
James Bond
DRAWING BY HORAK
OH, PLEASE! YOU'RE NOT GOING TO K-K-KILL ME—?
THAT DEPENDS ON YOU, MY DEAR ROANNE!
JUST LIE DOWN AND KEEP THAT BEAUTIFUL MOUTH SHUT—AND YOU WON'T BE HARMED!
NOW TO FIND OUT HOW WELL THIS LITTLE CAPER PAYS OFF—!
2796

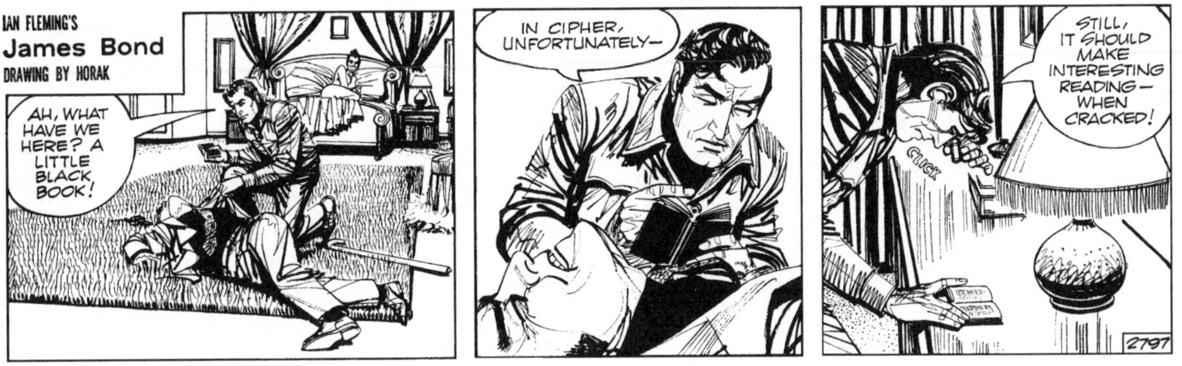
IAN FLEMING'S
James Bond
DRAWING BY HORAK
AH, WHAT HAVE WE HERE? A LITTLE BLACK BOOK!
IN CIPHER, UNFORTUNATELY—
STILL, IT SHOULD MAKE INTERESTING READING—WHEN CRACKED!
CLICK
2797

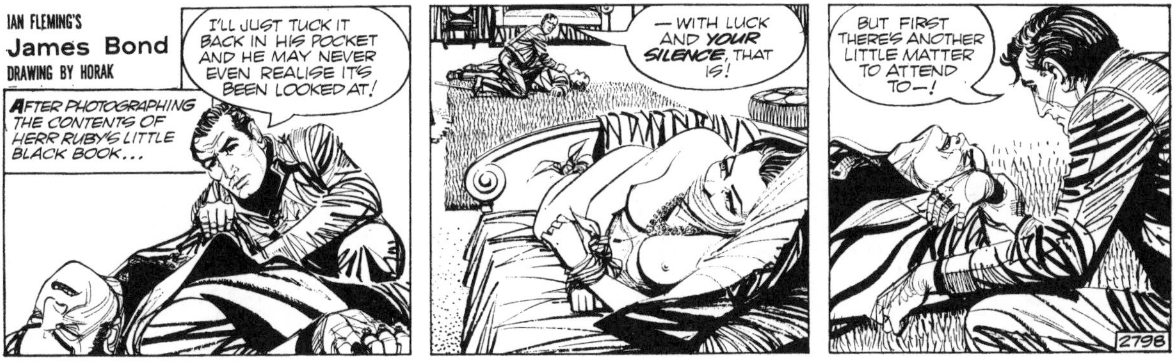
IAN FLEMING'S
James Bond
DRAWING BY HORAK
AFTER PHOTOGRAPHING THE CONTENTS OF HERR RUBY'S LITTLE BLACK BOOK...
I'LL JUST TUCK IT BACK IN HIS POCKET AND HE MAY NEVER EVEN REALISE IT'S BEEN LOOKED AT!
—WITH LUCK AND YOUR SILENCE, THAT IS!
BUT FIRST THERE'S ANOTHER LITTLE MATTER TO ATTEND TO—!
2798

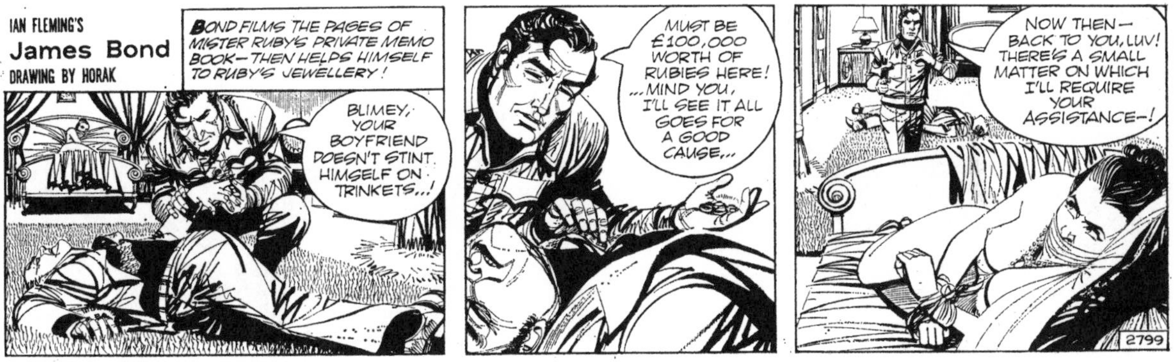
IAN FLEMING'S
James Bond
DRAWING BY HORAK
BOND FILMS THE PAGES OF MISTER RUBY'S PRIVATE MEMO BOOK—THEN HELPS HIMSELF TO RUBY'S JEWELLERY!
BLIMEY, YOUR BOYFRIEND DOESN'T STINT HIMSELF ON TRINKETS...!
MUST BE £100,000 WORTH OF RUBIES HERE! ...MIND YOU, I'LL SEE IT ALL GOES FOR A GOOD CAUSE,..
NOW THEN—BACK TO YOU, LUV! THERE'S A SMALL MATTER ON WHICH I'LL REQUIRE YOUR ASSISTANCE—!
2799

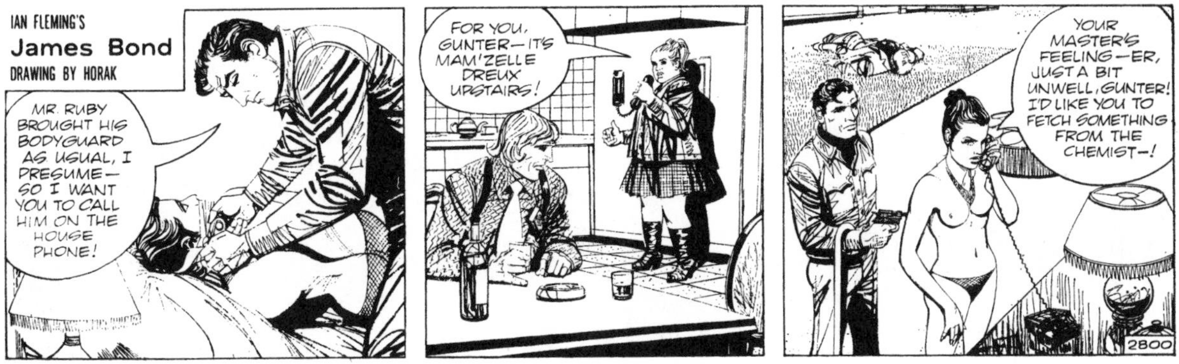
IAN FLEMING'S
James Bond
DRAWING BY HORAK
MR. RUBY BROUGHT HIS BODYGUARD AS USUAL, I PRESUME—SO I WANT YOU TO CALL HIM ON THE HOUSE PHONE!
FOR YOU, GUNTER—IT'S MAM'ZELLE DREUX UPSTAIRS!
YOUR MASTER'S FEELING—ER, JUST A BIT UNWELL, GUNTER! I'D LIKE YOU TO FETCH SOMETHING FROM THE CHEMIST—!
2800

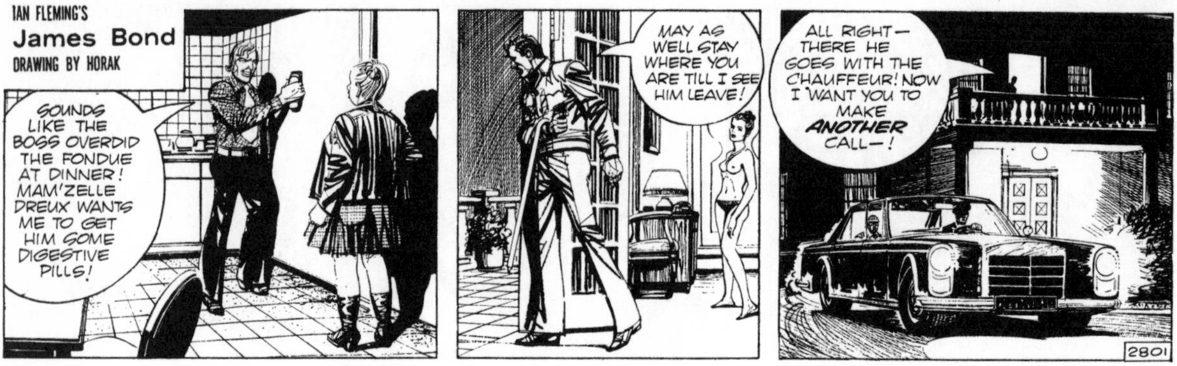
IAN FLEMING'S
James Bond
DRAWING BY HORAK
SOUNDS LIKE THE BOSS OVERDID THE FONDUE AT DINNER! MAM'ZELLE DREUX WANTS ME TO GET HIM SOME DIGESTIVE PILLS!
MAY AS WELL STAY WHERE YOU ARE TILL I SEE HIM LEAVE!
ALL RIGHT— THERE HE GOES WITH THE CHAUFFEUR! NOW I WANT YOU TO MAKE ANOTHER CALL—!
2801

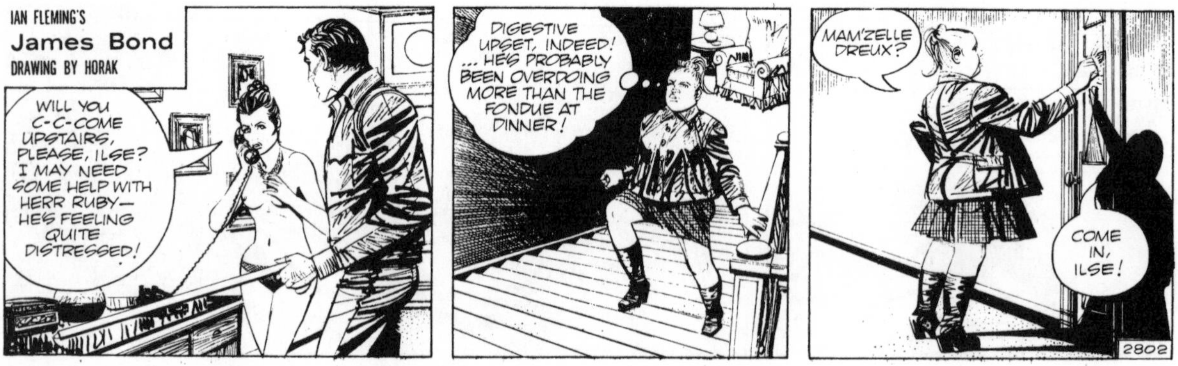
IAN FLEMING'S
James Bond
DRAWING BY HORAK
WILL YOU C-C-COME UPSTAIRS, PLEASE, ILSE? I MAY NEED SOME HELP WITH HERR RUBY— HE'S FEELING QUITE DISTRESSED!
DIGESTIVE UPSET, INDEED! ... HE'S PROBABLY BEEN OVERDOING MORE THAN THE FONDUE AT DINNER!
MAM'ZELLE DREUX?
COME IN, ILSE!
2802

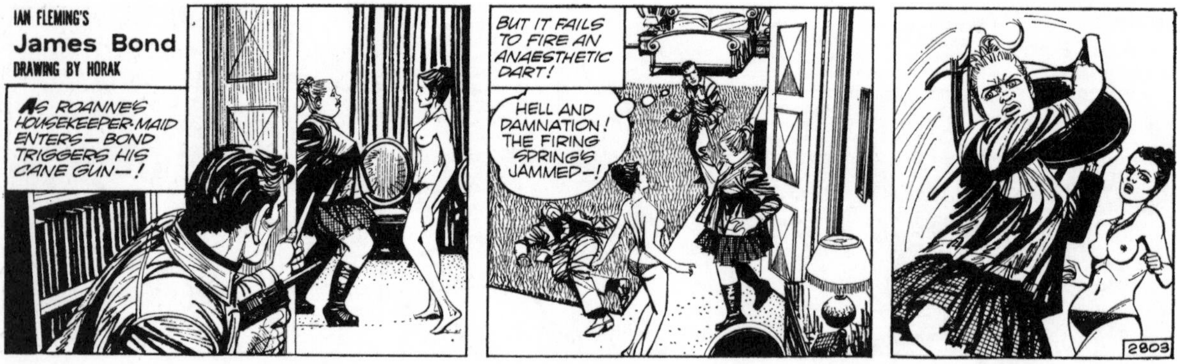
IAN FLEMING'S
James Bond
DRAWING BY HORAK
AS ROANNE'S HOUSEKEEPER-MAID ENTERS—BOND TRIGGERS HIS CANE GUN—!
BUT IT FAILS TO FIRE AN ANAESTHETIC DART!
HELL AND DAMNATION! THE FIRING SPRING'S JAMMED—!
2803

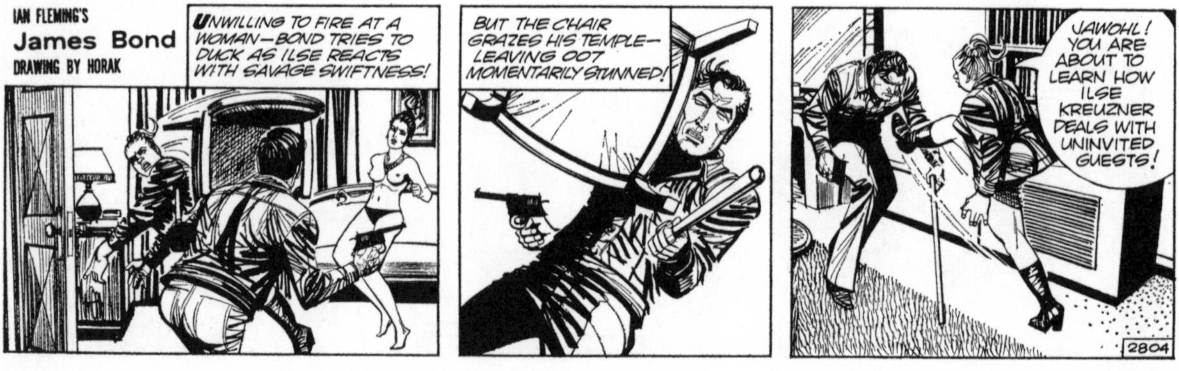
IAN FLEMING'S
James Bond
DRAWING BY HORAK
UNWILLING TO FIRE AT A WOMAN—BOND TRIES TO DUCK AS ILSE REACTS WITH SAVAGE SWIFTNESS!
BUT THE CHAIR GRAZES HIS TEMPLE— LEAVING 007 MOMENTARILY STUNNED!
JAWOHL! YOU ARE ABOUT TO LEARN HOW ILSE KREUZNER DEALS WITH UNINVITED GUESTS!
2804

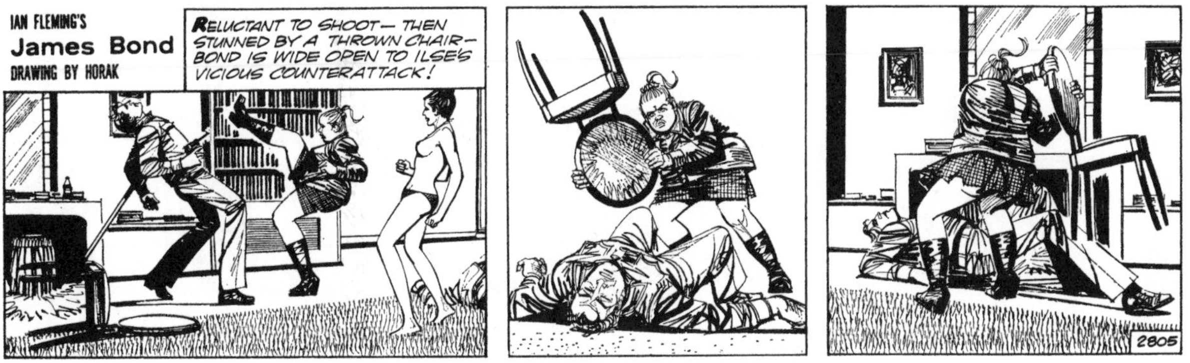
IAN FLEMING'S
James Bond
DRAWING BY HORAK
RELUCTANT TO SHOOT— THEN STUNNED BY A THROWN CHAIR— BOND IS WIDE OPEN TO ILSE'S VICIOUS COUNTERATTACK!
2805

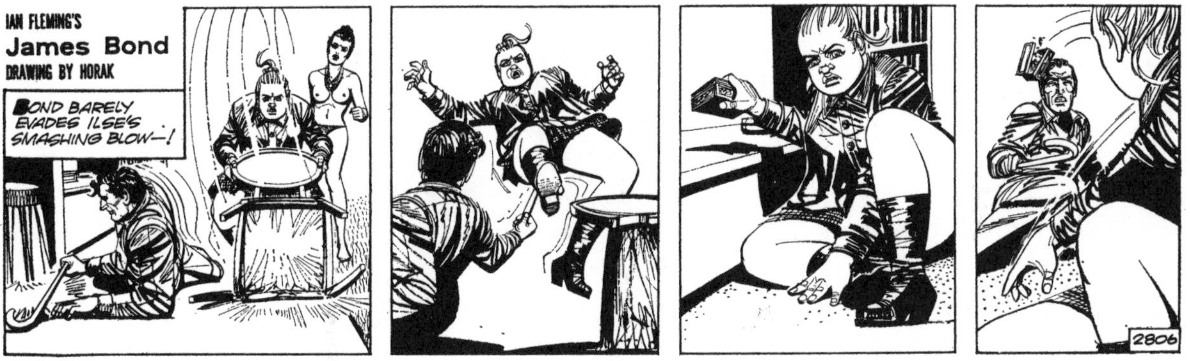
IAN FLEMING'S
James Bond
DRAWING BY HORAK
BOND BARELY EVADES ILSE'S SMASHING BLOW—!
2806

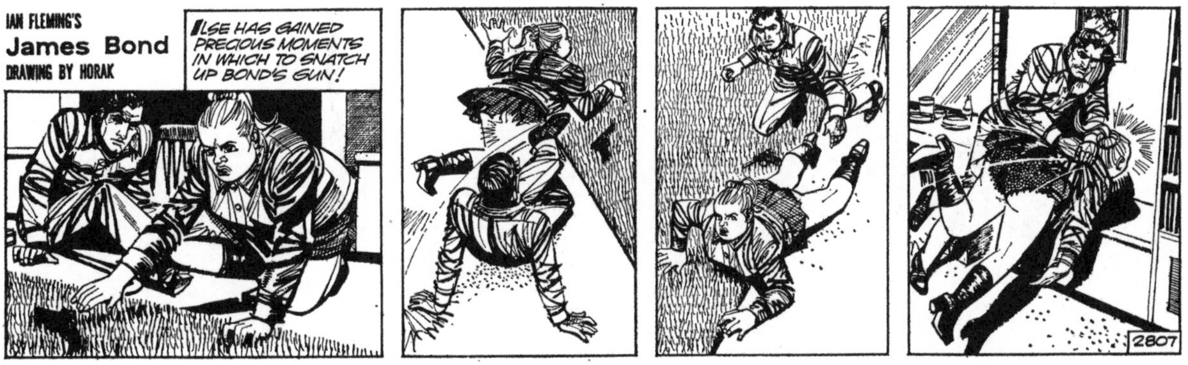
IAN FLEMING'S
James Bond
DRAWING BY HORAK
ILSE HAS GAINED PRECIOUS MOMENTS IN WHICH TO SNATCH UP BOND'S GUN!
2807

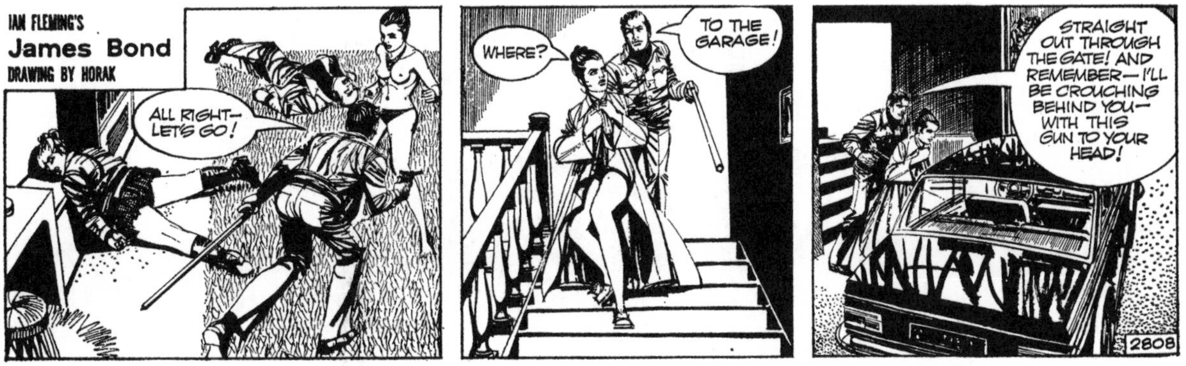
IAN FLEMING'S
James Bond
DRAWING BY HORAK
ALL RIGHT— LET'S GO!
WHERE?
TO THE GARAGE!
STRAIGHT OUT THROUGH THE GATE! AND REMEMBER— I'LL BE CROUCHING BEHIND YOU— WITH THIS GUN TO YOUR HEAD!
2808

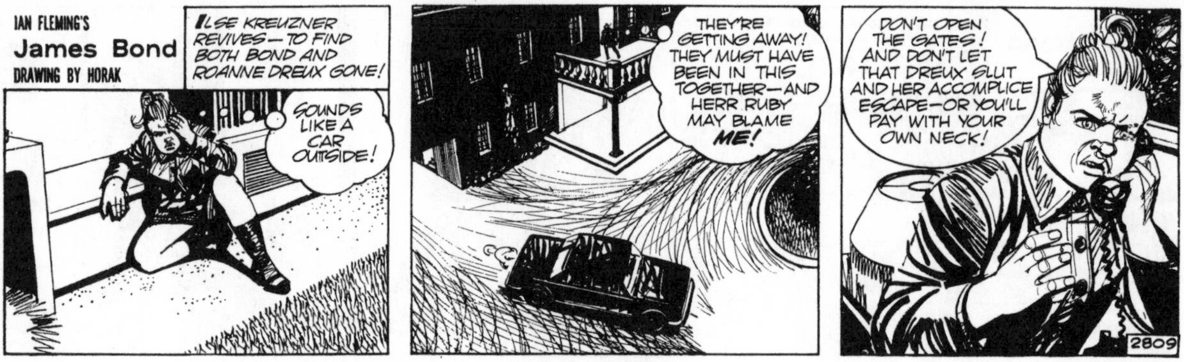
IAN FLEMING'S
James Bond
DRAWING BY HORAK
ILSE KREUZNER REVIVES—TO FIND BOTH BOND AND ROANNE DREUX GONE!
SOUNDS LIKE A CAR OUTSIDE!
THEY'RE GETTING AWAY! THEY MUST HAVE BEEN IN THIS TOGETHER—AND HERR RUBY MAY BLAME ME!
DON'T OPEN THE GATES! AND DON'T LET THAT DREUX SLUT AND HER ACCOMPLICE ESCAPE—OR YOU'LL PAY WITH YOUR OWN NECK!
2809

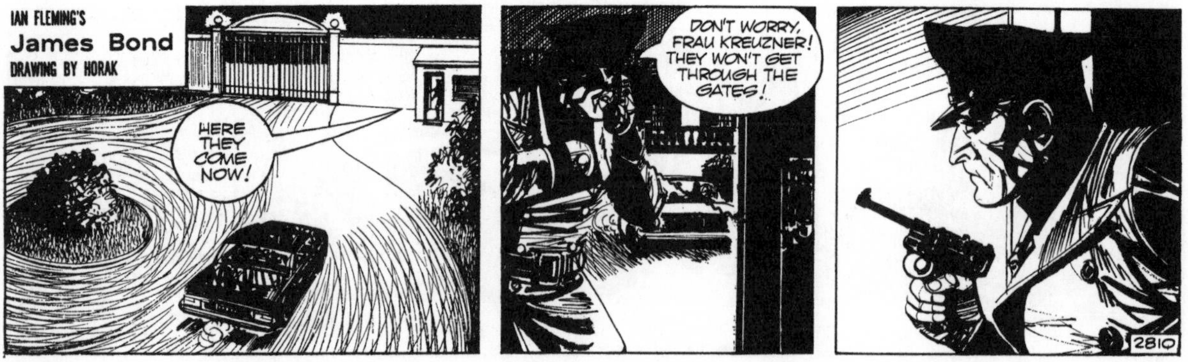
IAN FLEMING'S
James Bond
DRAWING BY HORAK
HERE THEY COME NOW!
DON'T WORRY, FRAU KREUZNER! THEY WON'T GET THROUGH THE GATES!
2810

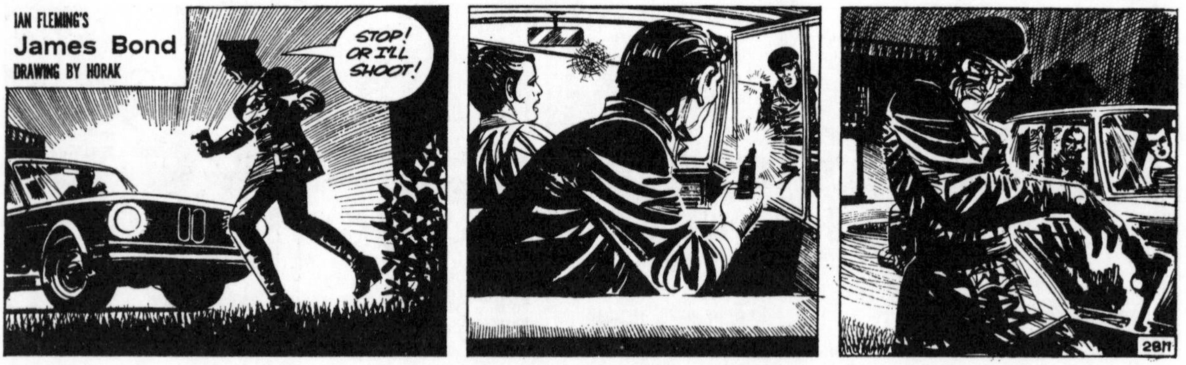
IAN FLEMING'S
James Bond
DRAWING BY HORAK
STOP! OR I'LL SHOOT!
2811

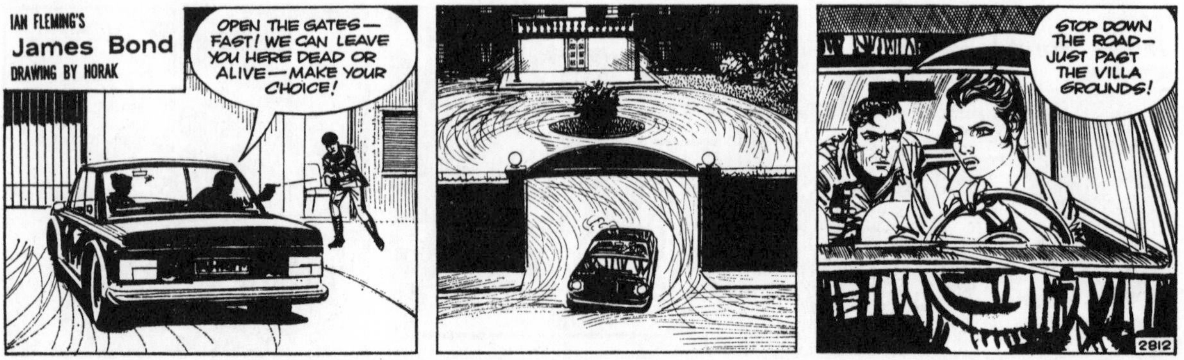
IAN FLEMING'S
James Bond
DRAWING BY HORAK
OPEN THE GATES—FAST! WE CAN LEAVE YOU HERE DEAD OR ALIVE—MAKE YOUR CHOICE!
STOP DOWN THE ROAD—JUST PAST THE VILLA GROUNDS!
2812

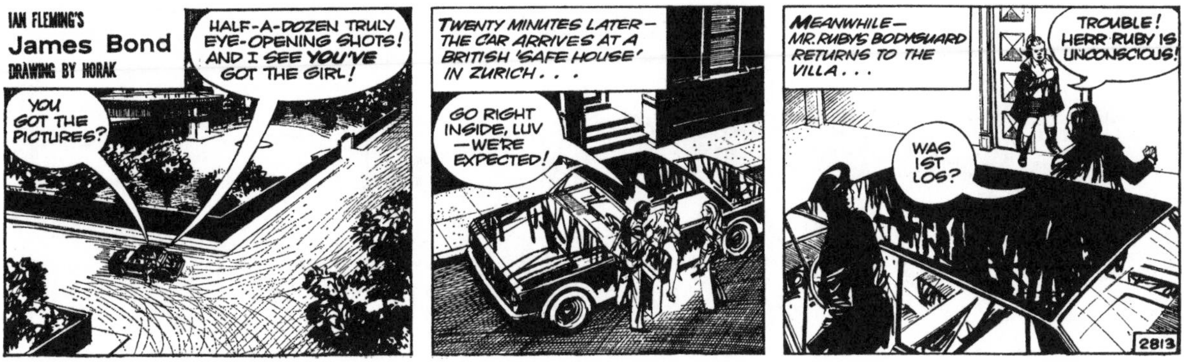
IAN FLEMING'S
James Bond
DRAWING BY HORAK
HALF-A-DOZEN TRULY EYE-OPENING SHOTS! AND I SEE YOU'VE GOT THE GIRL!
YOU GOT THE PICTURES?
TWENTY MINUTES LATER— THE CAR ARRIVES AT A BRITISH 'SAFE HOUSE' IN ZURICH . . .
GO RIGHT INSIDE, LUV —WE'RE EXPECTED!
MEANWHILE— MR. RUBY'S BODYGUARD RETURNS TO THE VILLA . . .
TROUBLE! HERR RUBY IS UNCONSCIOUS!
WAS IST LOS?
2813

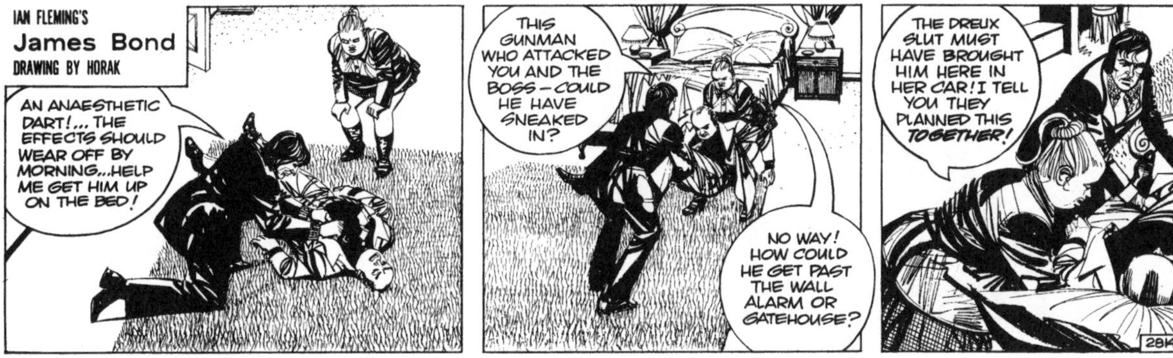
IAN FLEMING'S
James Bond
DRAWING BY HORAK
AN ANAESTHETIC DART!... THE EFFECTS SHOULD WEAR OFF BY MORNING...HELP ME GET HIM UP ON THE BED!
THIS GUNMAN WHO ATTACKED YOU AND THE BOSS—COULD HE HAVE SNEAKED IN?
NO WAY! HOW COULD HE GET PAST THE WALL ALARM OR GATEHOUSE?
THE DREUX SLUT MUST HAVE BROUGHT HIM HERE IN HER CAR! I TELL YOU THEY PLANNED THIS TOGETHER!
2814

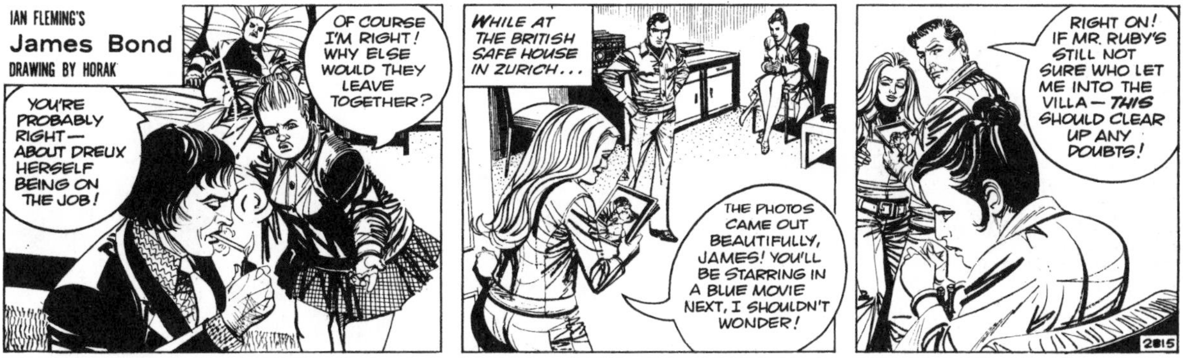
IAN FLEMING'S
James Bond
DRAWING BY HORAK
YOU'RE PROBABLY RIGHT— ABOUT DREUX HERSELF BEING ON THE JOB!
OF COURSE I'M RIGHT! WHY ELSE WOULD THEY LEAVE TOGETHER?
WHILE AT THE BRITISH SAFE HOUSE IN ZURICH . . .
THE PHOTOS CAME OUT BEAUTIFULLY, JAMES! YOU'LL BE STARRING IN A BLUE MOVIE NEXT, I SHOULDN'T WONDER!
RIGHT ON! IF MR. RUBY'S STILL NOT SURE WHO LET ME INTO THE VILLA—THIS SHOULD CLEAR UP ANY DOUBTS!
2815

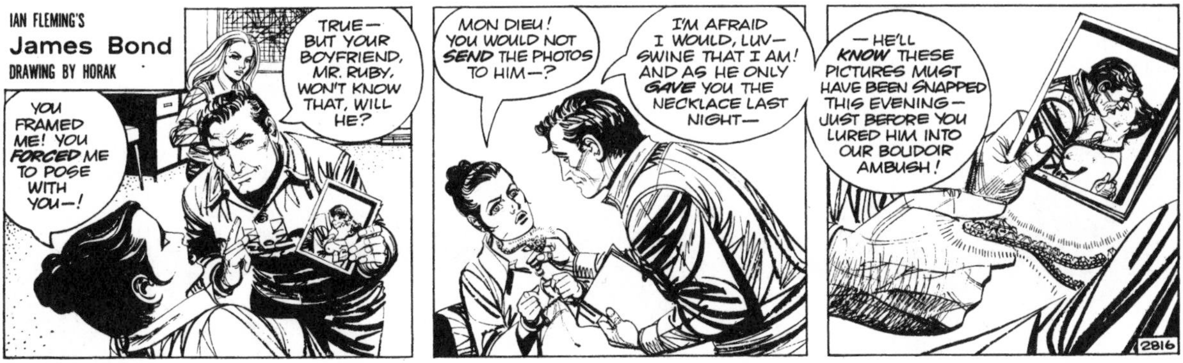
IAN FLEMING'S
James Bond
DRAWING BY HORAK
YOU FRAMED ME! YOU FORCED ME TO POSE WITH YOU—!
TRUE— BUT YOUR BOYFRIEND, MR. RUBY, WON'T KNOW THAT, WILL HE?
MON DIEU! YOU WOULD NOT SEND THE PHOTOS TO HIM—?
I'M AFRAID I WOULD, LUV— SWINE THAT I AM! AND AS HE ONLY GAVE YOU THE NECKLACE LAST NIGHT—
—HE'LL KNOW THESE PICTURES MUST HAVE BEEN SNAPPED THIS EVENING— JUST BEFORE YOU LURED HIM INTO OUR BOUDOIR AMBUSH!
2816

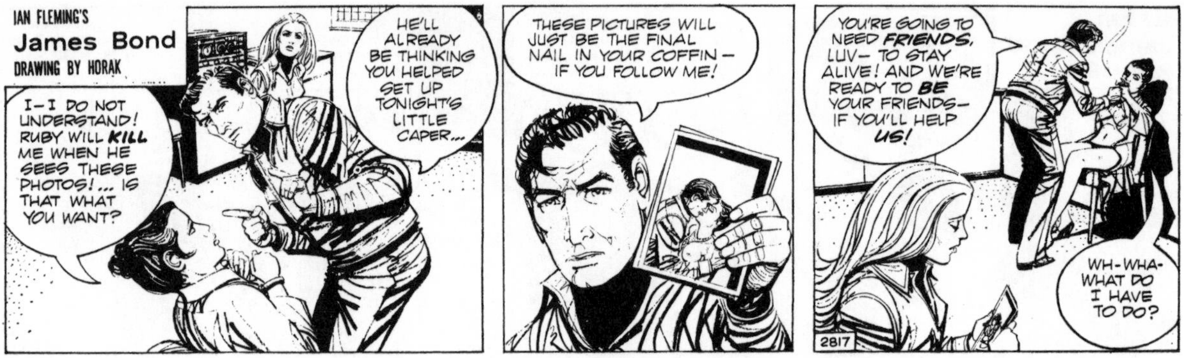
IAN FLEMING'S
James Bond
DRAWING BY HORAK
I-I DO NOT UNDERSTAND! RUBY WILL KILL ME WHEN HE SEES THESE PHOTOS!... IS THAT WHAT YOU WANT?
HE'LL ALREADY BE THINKING YOU HELPED SET UP TONIGHT'S LITTLE CAPER...
THESE PICTURES WILL JUST BE THE FINAL NAIL IN YOUR COFFIN— IF YOU FOLLOW ME!
YOU'RE GOING TO NEED FRIENDS, LUV— TO STAY ALIVE! AND WE'RE READY TO BE YOUR FRIENDS— IF YOU'LL HELP US!
WH-WHA-WHAT DO I HAVE TO DO?
2817

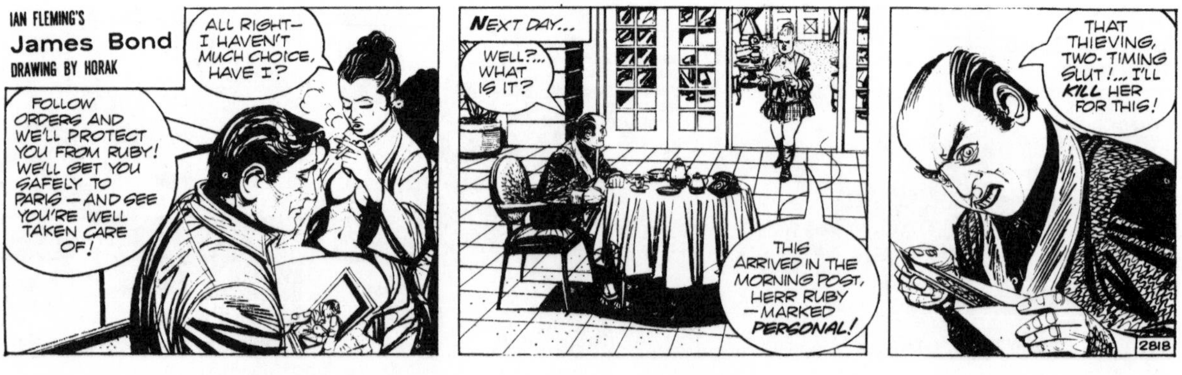
IAN FLEMING'S
James Bond
DRAWING BY HORAK
ALL RIGHT— I HAVEN'T MUCH CHOICE, HAVE I?
FOLLOW ORDERS AND WE'LL PROTECT YOU FROM RUBY! WE'LL GET YOU SAFELY TO PARIS —AND SEE YOU'RE WELL TAKEN CARE OF!
NEXT DAY...
WELL?... WHAT IS IT?
THIS ARRIVED IN THE MORNING POST, HERR RUBY —MARKED PERSONAL!
THAT THIEVING, TWO-TIMING SLUT!... I'LL KILL HER FOR THIS!
2818

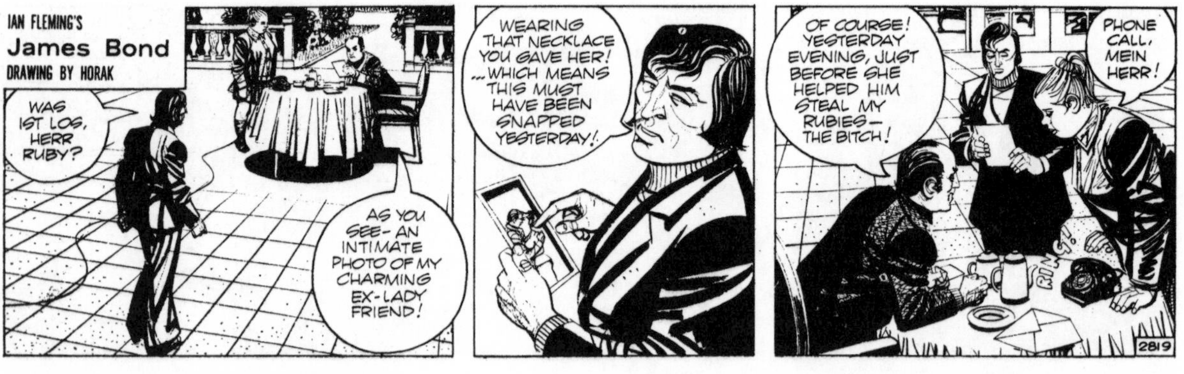
IAN FLEMING'S
James Bond
DRAWING BY HORAK
WAS IST LOS, HERR RUBY?
AS YOU SEE—AN INTIMATE PHOTO OF MY CHARMING EX-LADY FRIEND!
WEARING THAT NECKLACE YOU GAVE HER! ...WHICH MEANS THIS MUST HAVE BEEN SNAPPED YESTERDAY!
OF COURSE! YESTERDAY EVENING, JUST BEFORE SHE HELPED HIM STEAL MY RUBIES— THE BITCH!
PHONE CALL, MEIN HERR!
2819

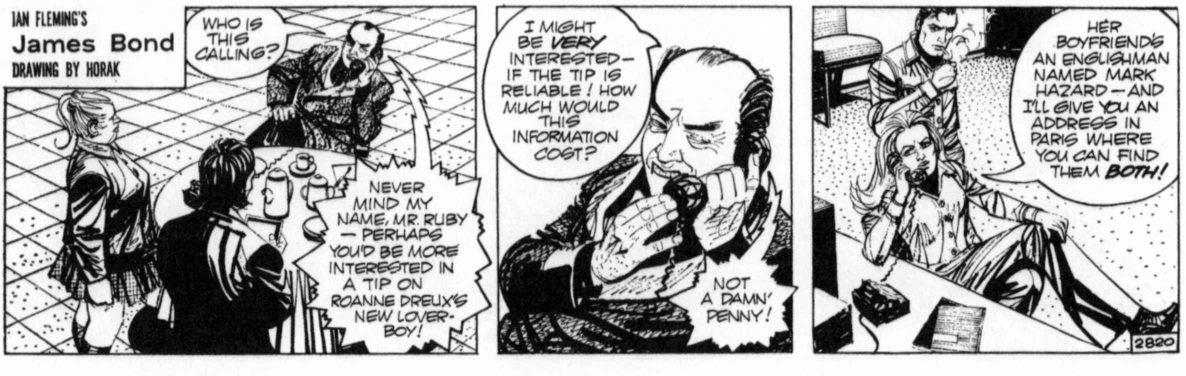
IAN FLEMING'S
James Bond
DRAWING BY HORAK
WHO IS THIS CALLING?
NEVER MIND MY NAME, MR. RUBY —PERHAPS YOU'D BE MORE INTERESTED IN A TIP ON ROANNE DREUX'S NEW LOVER-BOY!
I MIGHT BE VERY INTERESTED— IF THE TIP IS RELIABLE! HOW MUCH WOULD THIS INFORMATION COST?
NOT A DAMN' PENNY!
HER BOYFRIEND'S AN ENGLISHMAN NAMED MARK HAZARD—AND I'LL GIVE YOU AN ADDRESS IN PARIS WHERE YOU CAN FIND THEM BOTH!
2820

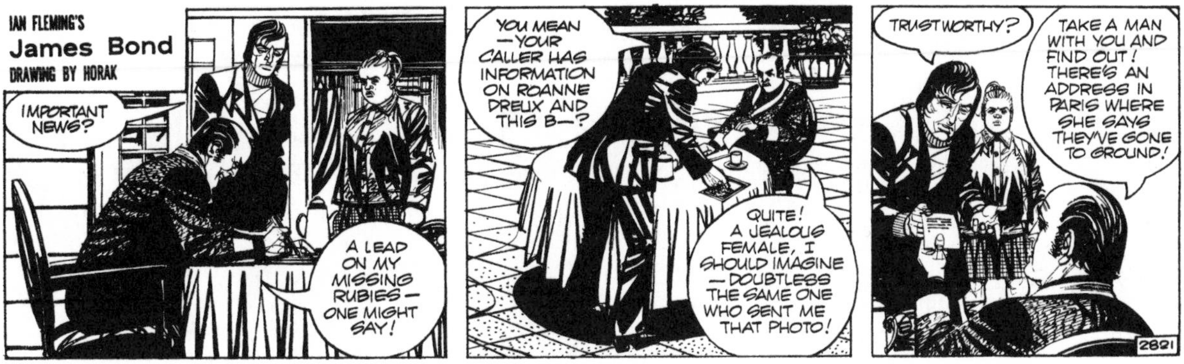
IAN FLEMING'S
James Bond
DRAWING BY HORAK
IMPORTANT NEWS?
A LEAD ON MY MISSING RUBIES — ONE MIGHT SAY!
YOU MEAN — YOUR CALLER HAS INFORMATION ON ROANNE DREUX AND THIS B—?
QUITE! A JEALOUS FEMALE, I SHOULD IMAGINE — DOUBTLESS THE SAME ONE WHO SENT ME THAT PHOTO!
TRUSTWORTHY?
TAKE A MAN WITH YOU AND FIND OUT! THERE'S AN ADDRESS IN PARIS WHERE SHE SAYS THEY'VE GONE TO GROUND!
2821

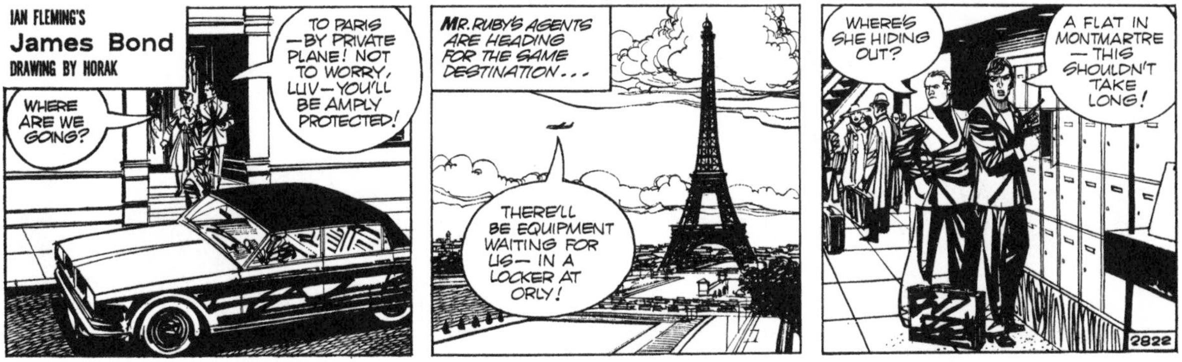
IAN FLEMING'S
James Bond
DRAWING BY HORAK
WHERE ARE WE GOING?
TO PARIS — BY PRIVATE PLANE! NOT TO WORRY, LUV — YOU'LL BE AMPLY PROTECTED!
MR. RUBY'S AGENTS ARE HEADING FOR THE SAME DESTINATION . . .
THERE'LL BE EQUIPMENT WAITING FOR US — IN A LOCKER AT ORLY!
WHERE'S SHE HIDING OUT?
A FLAT IN MONTMARTRE — THIS SHOULDN'T TAKE LONG!
2822

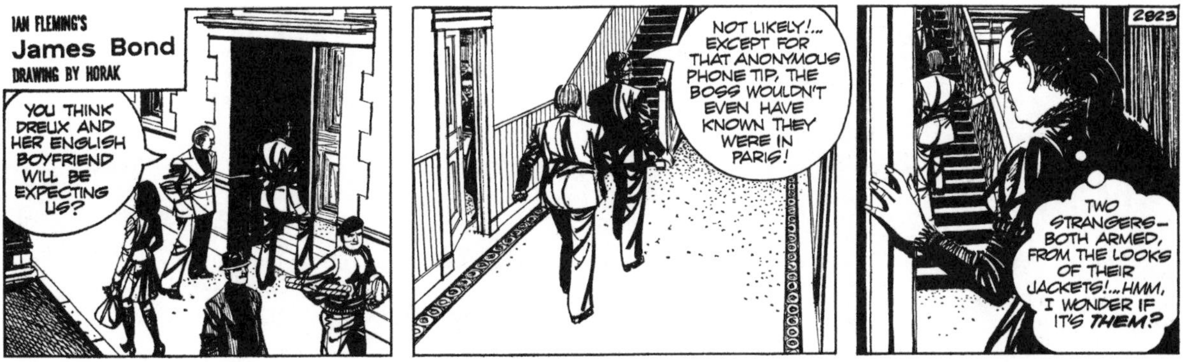
IAN FLEMING'S
James Bond
DRAWING BY HORAK
YOU THINK DREUX AND HER ENGLISH BOYFRIEND WILL BE EXPECTING US?
NOT LIKELY!... EXCEPT FOR THAT ANONYMOUS PHONE TIP, THE BOSS WOULDN'T EVEN HAVE KNOWN THEY WERE IN PARIS!
2823
TWO STRANGERS — BOTH ARMED, FROM THE LOOKS OF THEIR JACKETS!... HMM, I WONDER IF IT'S THEM?

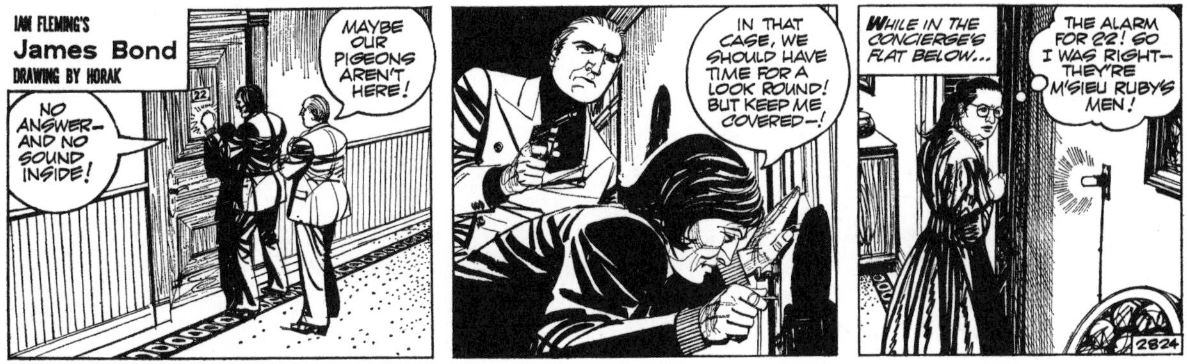
IAN FLEMING'S
James Bond
DRAWING BY HORAK
NO ANSWER — AND NO SOUND INSIDE!
MAYBE OUR PIGEONS AREN'T HERE!
IN THAT CASE, WE SHOULD HAVE TIME FOR A LOOK ROUND! BUT KEEP ME COVERED—!
WHILE IN THE CONCIERGE'S FLAT BELOW...
THE ALARM FOR 22! SO I WAS RIGHT — THEY'RE M'SIEU RUBY'S MEN!
2824

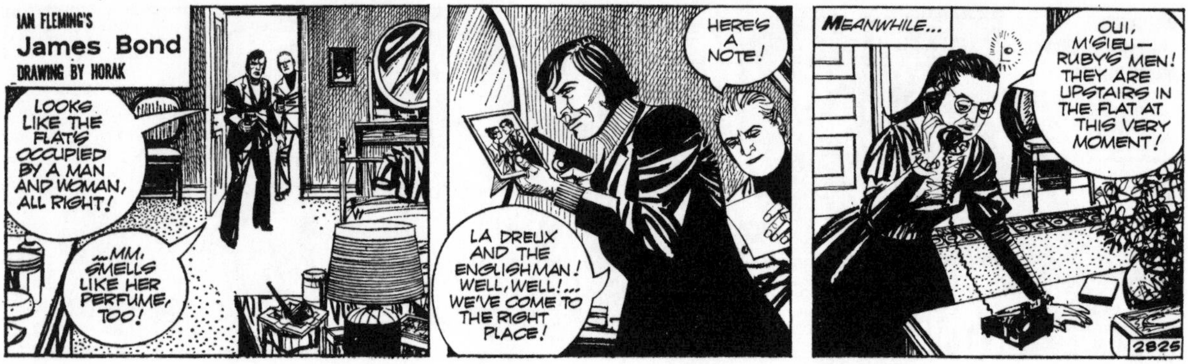
IAN FLEMING'S
James Bond
DRAWING BY HORAK
LOOKS LIKE THE FLAT'S OCCUPIED BY A MAN AND WOMAN, ALL RIGHT!
...MM. SMELLS LIKE HER PERFUME, TOO!
HERE'S A NOTE!
LA DREUX AND THE ENGLISHMAN! WELL, WELL!... WE'VE COME TO THE RIGHT PLACE!
MEANWHILE...
OUI, M'SIEU— RUBY'S MEN! THEY ARE UPSTAIRS IN THE FLAT AT THIS VERY MOMENT!
2825

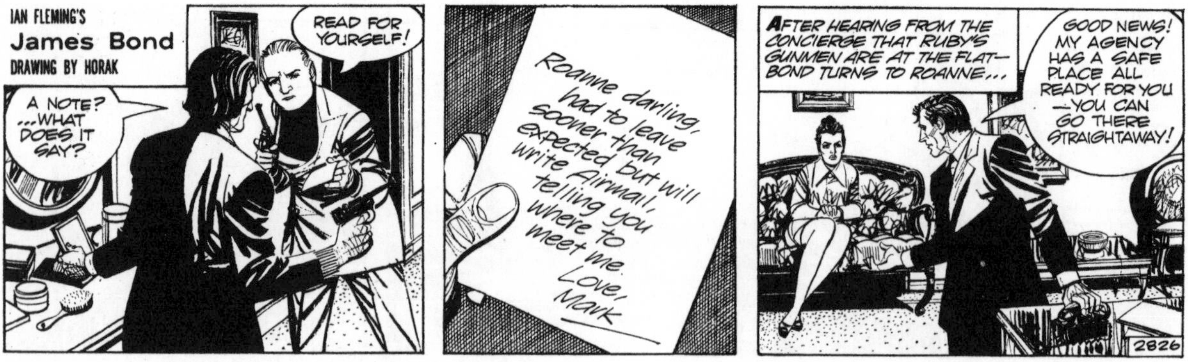
IAN FLEMING'S
James Bond
DRAWING BY HORAK
READ FOR YOURSELF!
A NOTE? ...WHAT DOES IT SAY?
Roanne darling, had to leave sooner than expected but will write Airmail, telling you where to meet me. Love, Mark
AFTER HEARING FROM THE CONCIERGE THAT RUBY'S GUNMEN ARE AT THE FLAT— BOND TURNS TO ROANNE...
GOOD NEWS! MY AGENCY HAS A SAFE PLACE ALL READY FOR YOU —YOU CAN GO THERE STRAIGHTAWAY!
2826

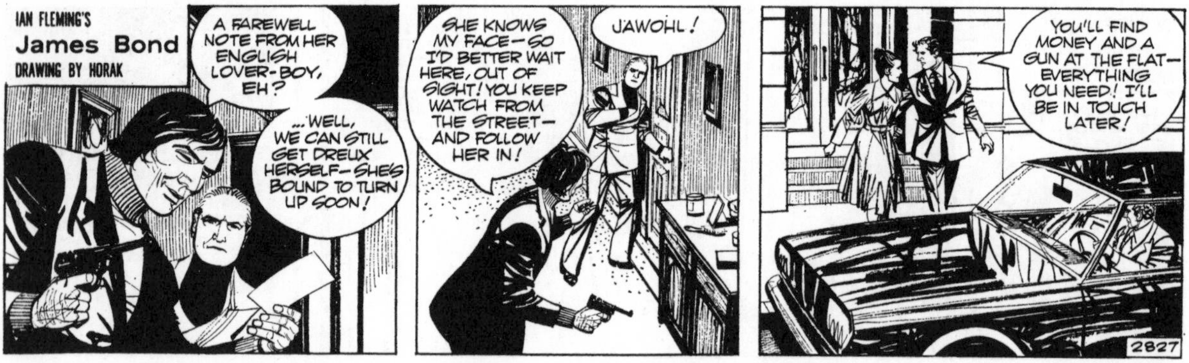
IAN FLEMING'S
James Bond
DRAWING BY HORAK
A FAREWELL NOTE FROM HER ENGLISH LOVER-BOY, EH?
...WELL, WE CAN STILL GET DREUX HERSELF—SHE'S BOUND TO TURN UP SOON!
SHE KNOWS MY FACE—SO I'D BETTER WAIT HERE, OUT OF SIGHT! YOU KEEP WATCH FROM THE STREET— AND FOLLOW HER IN!
JAWOHL!
YOU'LL FIND MONEY AND A GUN AT THE FLAT— EVERYTHING YOU NEED! I'LL BE IN TOUCH LATER!
2827

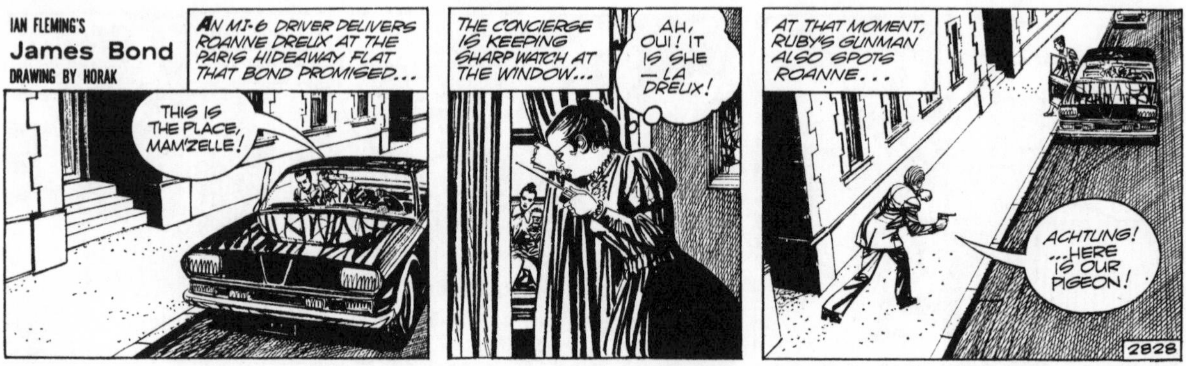
IAN FLEMING'S
James Bond
DRAWING BY HORAK
AN MI-6 DRIVER DELIVERS ROANNE DREUX AT THE PARIS HIDEAWAY FLAT THAT BOND PROMISED...
THIS IS THE PLACE, MAM'ZELLE!
THE CONCIERGE IS KEEPING SHARP WATCH AT THE WINDOW...
AH, OUI! IT IS SHE —LA DREUX!
AT THAT MOMENT, RUBY'S GUNMAN ALSO SPOTS ROANNE...
ACHTUNG! ...HERE IS OUR PIGEON!
2828

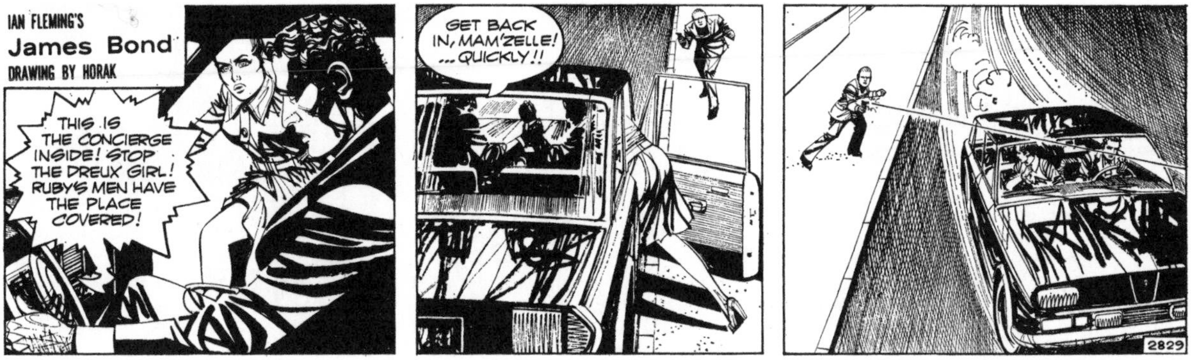
IAN FLEMING'S
James Bond
DRAWING BY HORAK
THIS IS THE CONCIERGE INSIDE! STOP THE DREUX GIRL! RUBY'S MEN HAVE THE PLACE COVERED!
GET BACK IN, MAM'ZELLE! ...QUICKLY!!
2829

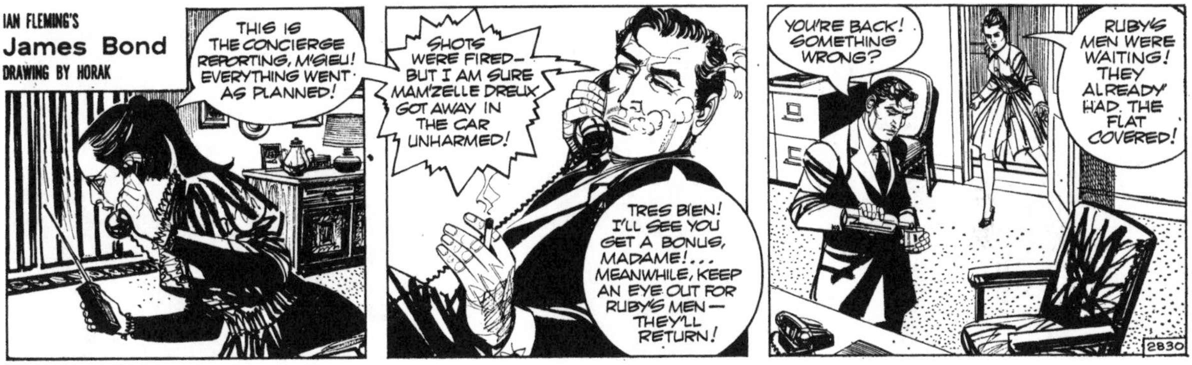
IAN FLEMING'S
James Bond
DRAWING BY HORAK
THIS IS THE CONCIERGE REPORTING, M'SIEU! EVERYTHING WENT AS PLANNED!
SHOTS WERE FIRED— BUT I AM SURE MAM'ZELLE DREUX GOT AWAY IN THE CAR UNHARMED!
TRES BIEN! I'LL SEE YOU GET A BONUS, MADAME!... MEANWHILE, KEEP AN EYE OUT FOR RUBY'S MEN— THEY'LL RETURN!
YOU'RE BACK! SOMETHING WRONG?
RUBY'S MEN WERE WAITING! THEY ALREADY HAD THE FLAT COVERED!
2830

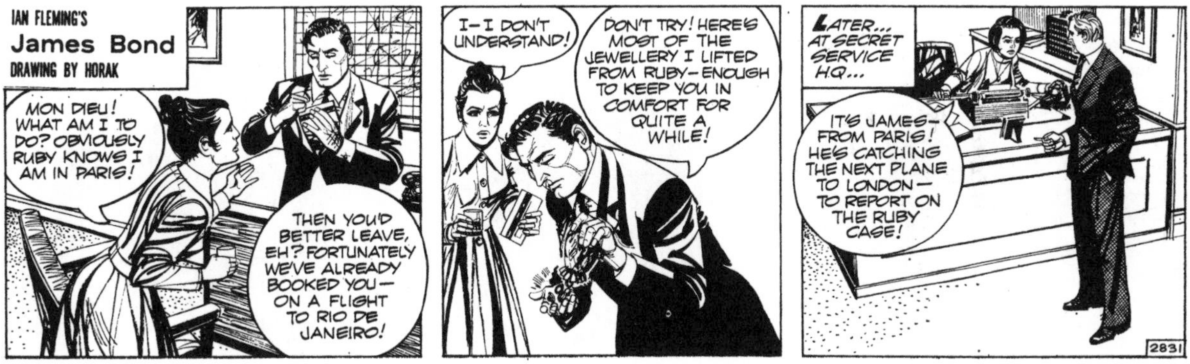
IAN FLEMING'S
James Bond
DRAWING BY HORAK
MON DIEU! WHAT AM I TO DO? OBVIOUSLY RUBY KNOWS I AM IN PARIS!
THEN YOU'D BETTER LEAVE, EH? FORTUNATELY WE'VE ALREADY BOOKED YOU— ON A FLIGHT TO RIO DE JANEIRO!
I—I DON'T UNDERSTAND!
DON'T TRY! HERE'S MOST OF THE JEWELLERY I LIFTED FROM RUBY— ENOUGH TO KEEP YOU IN COMFORT FOR QUITE A WHILE!
LATER... AT SECRET SERVICE HQ...
IT'S JAMES— FROM PARIS! HE'S CATCHING THE NEXT PLANE TO LONDON— TO REPORT ON THE RUBY CASE!
2831

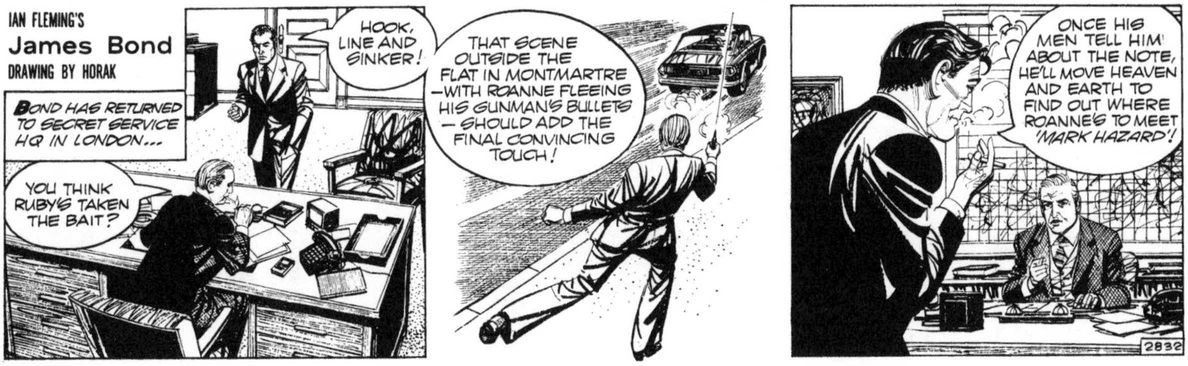
IAN FLEMING'S
James Bond
DRAWING BY HORAK
BOND HAS RETURNED TO SECRET SERVICE HQ IN LONDON...
YOU THINK RUBY'S TAKEN THE BAIT?
HOOK, LINE AND SINKER!
THAT SCENE OUTSIDE THE FLAT IN MONTMARTRE —WITH ROANNE FLEEING HIS GUNMAN'S BULLETS —SHOULD ADD THE FINAL CONVINCING TOUCH!
ONCE HIS MEN TELL HIM ABOUT THE NOTE, HE'LL MOVE HEAVEN AND EARTH TO FIND OUT WHERE ROANNE'S TO MEET 'MARK HAZARD'!
2832

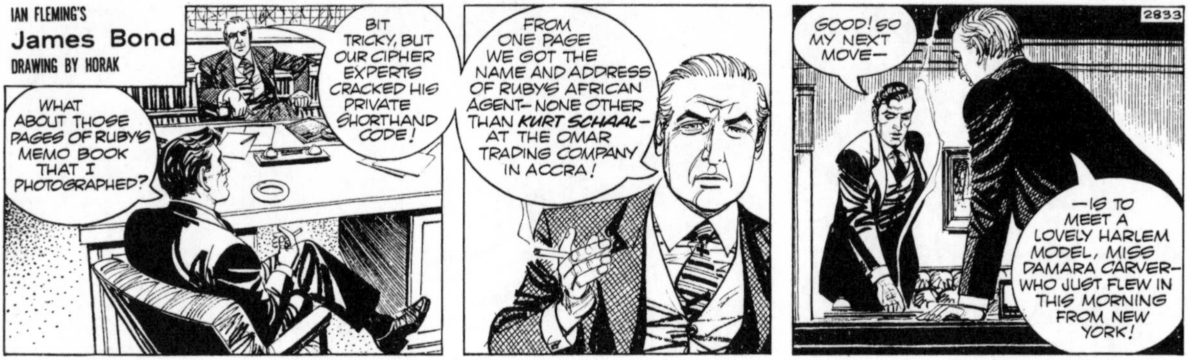
IAN FLEMING'S
James Bond
DRAWING BY HORAK
WHAT ABOUT THOSE PAGES OF RUBY'S MEMO BOOK THAT I PHOTOGRAPHED?
BIT TRICKY, BUT OUR CIPHER EXPERTS CRACKED HIS PRIVATE SHORTHAND CODE!
FROM ONE PAGE WE GOT THE NAME AND ADDRESS OF RUBY'S AFRICAN AGENT– NONE OTHER THAN KURT SCHAAL– AT THE OMAR TRADING COMPANY IN ACCRA!
2833
GOOD! SO MY NEXT MOVE–
–IS TO MEET A LOVELY HARLEM MODEL, MISS DAMARA CARVER– WHO JUST FLEW IN THIS MORNING FROM NEW YORK!

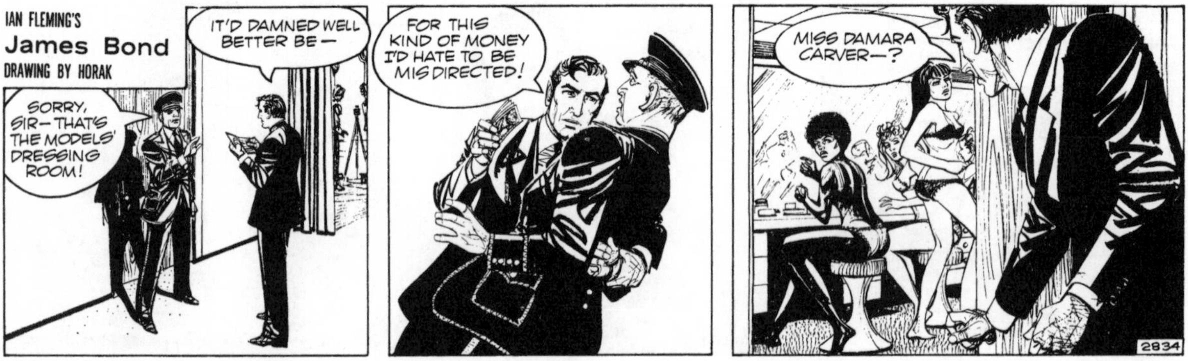
IAN FLEMING'S
James Bond
DRAWING BY HORAK
SORRY, SIR– THAT'S THE MODELS' DRESSING ROOM!
IT'D DAMNED WELL BETTER BE –
FOR THIS KIND OF MONEY I'D HATE TO BE MISDIRECTED!
MISS DAMARA CARVER–?
2834

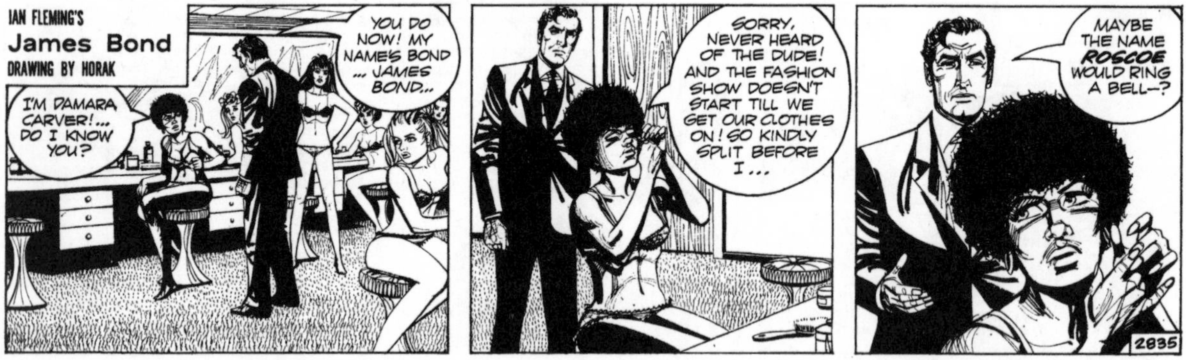
IAN FLEMING'S
James Bond
DRAWING BY HORAK
I'M DAMARA CARVER!... DO I KNOW YOU?
YOU DO NOW! MY NAME'S BOND ... JAMES BOND...
SORRY, NEVER HEARD OF THE DUDE! AND THE FASHION SHOW DOESN'T START TILL WE GET OUR CLOTHES ON! SO KINDLY SPLIT BEFORE I ...
MAYBE THE NAME ROSCOE WOULD RING A BELL–?
2835

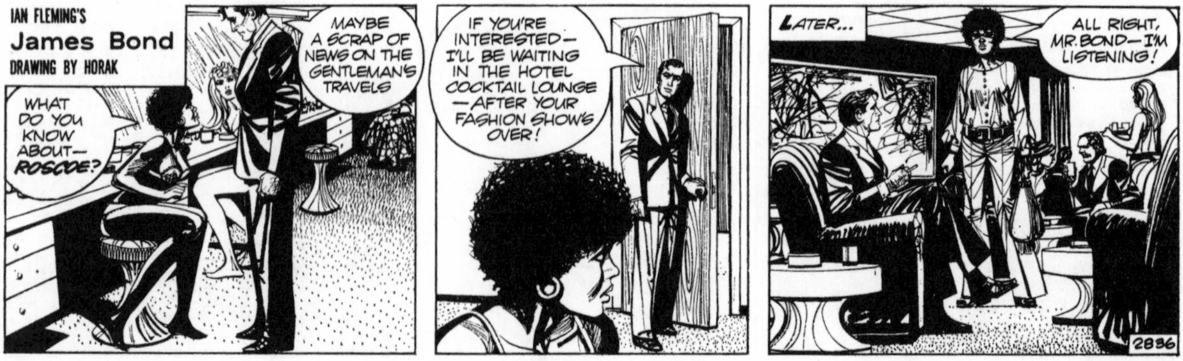
IAN FLEMING'S
James Bond
DRAWING BY HORAK
WHAT DO YOU KNOW ABOUT– ROSCOE?
MAYBE A SCRAP OF NEWS ON THE GENTLEMAN'S TRAVELS
IF YOU'RE INTERESTED– I'LL BE WAITING IN THE HOTEL COCKTAIL LOUNGE –AFTER YOUR FASHION SHOW'S OVER!
LATER...
ALL RIGHT, MR. BOND– I'M LISTENING!
2836

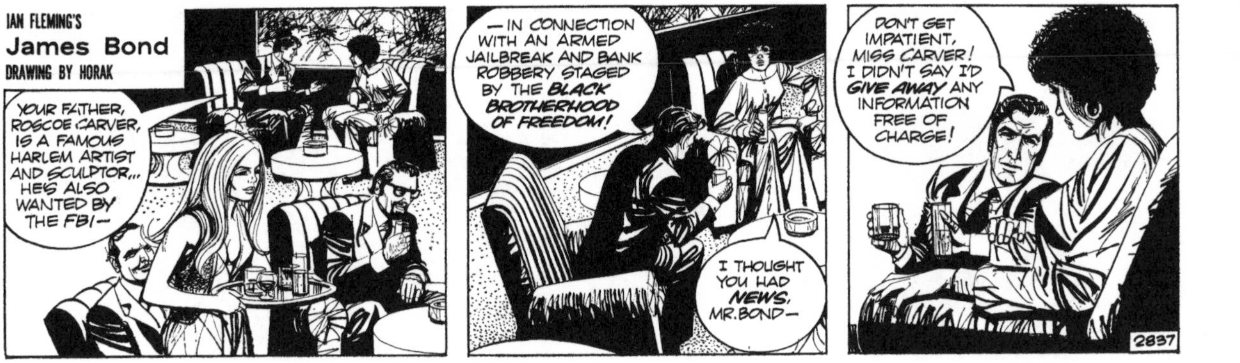
IAN FLEMING'S
James Bond
DRAWING BY HORAK
YOUR FATHER, ROSCOE CARVER, IS A FAMOUS HARLEM ARTIST AND SCULPTOR... HE'S ALSO WANTED BY THE FBI—
—IN CONNECTION WITH AN ARMED JAILBREAK AND BANK ROBBERY STAGED BY THE BLACK BROTHERHOOD OF FREEDOM!
I THOUGHT YOU HAD NEWS, MR. BOND—
DON'T GET IMPATIENT, MISS CARVER! I DIDN'T SAY I'D GIVE AWAY ANY INFORMATION FREE OF CHARGE!
2837

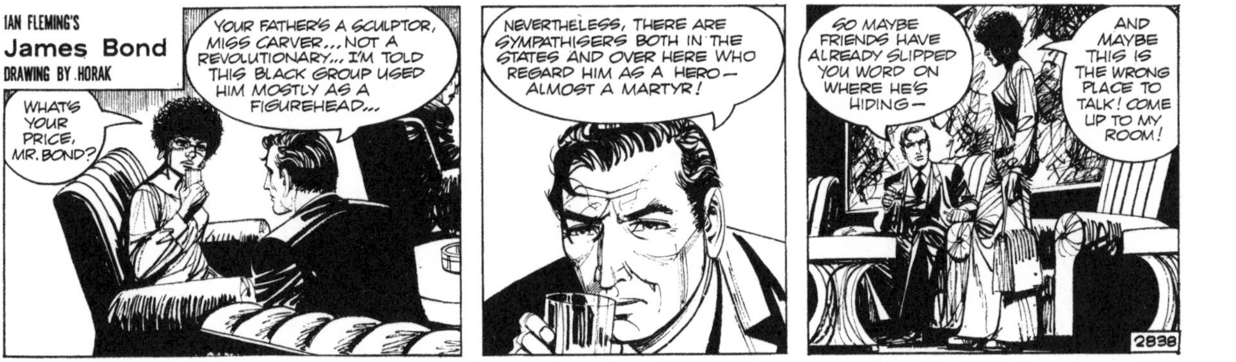
IAN FLEMING'S
James Bond
DRAWING BY HORAK
WHAT'S YOUR PRICE, MR. BOND?
YOUR FATHER'S A SCULPTOR, MISS CARVER... NOT A REVOLUTIONARY... I'M TOLD THIS BLACK GROUP USED HIM MOSTLY AS A FIGUREHEAD...
NEVERTHELESS, THERE ARE SYMPATHISERS BOTH IN THE STATES AND OVER HERE WHO REGARD HIM AS A HERO—ALMOST A MARTYR!
SO MAYBE FRIENDS HAVE ALREADY SLIPPED YOU WORD ON WHERE HE'S HIDING—
AND MAYBE THIS IS THE WRONG PLACE TO TALK! COME UP TO MY ROOM!
2838

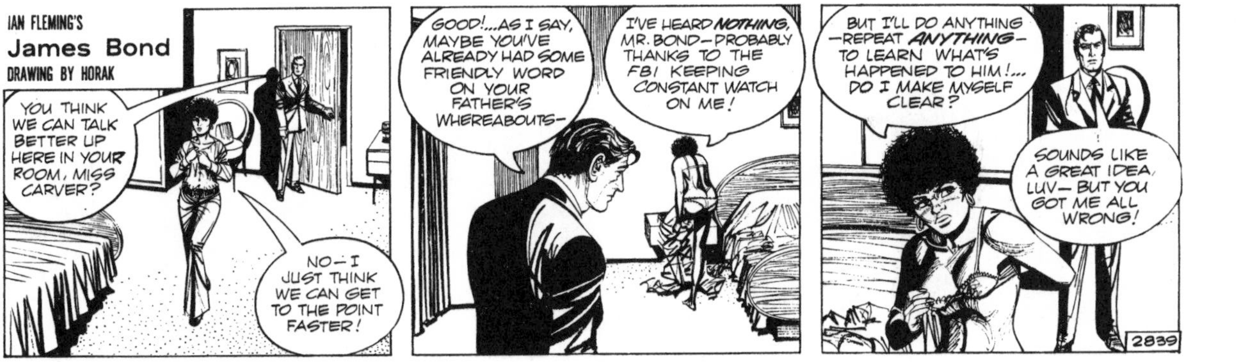
IAN FLEMING'S
James Bond
DRAWING BY HORAK
YOU THINK WE CAN TALK BETTER UP HERE IN YOUR ROOM, MISS CARVER?
NO—I JUST THINK WE CAN GET TO THE POINT FASTER!
GOOD!... AS I SAY, MAYBE YOU'VE ALREADY HAD SOME FRIENDLY WORD ON YOUR FATHER'S WHEREABOUTS—
I'VE HEARD NOTHING, MR. BOND—PROBABLY THANKS TO THE FBI KEEPING CONSTANT WATCH ON ME!
BUT I'LL DO ANYTHING —REPEAT ANYTHING— TO LEARN WHAT'S HAPPENED TO HIM!... DO I MAKE MYSELF CLEAR?
SOUNDS LIKE A GREAT IDEA, LUV—BUT YOU GOT ME ALL WRONG!
2839

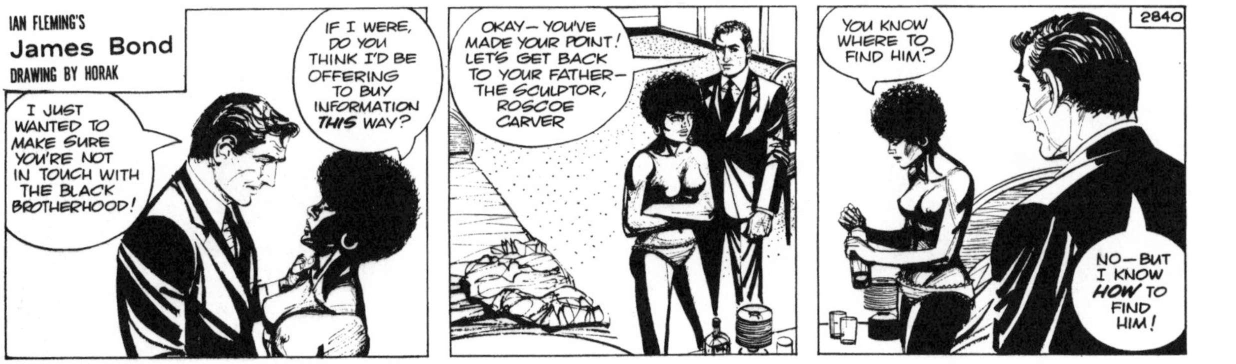
IAN FLEMING'S
James Bond
DRAWING BY HORAK
I JUST WANTED TO MAKE SURE YOU'RE NOT IN TOUCH WITH THE BLACK BROTHERHOOD!
IF I WERE, DO YOU THINK I'D BE OFFERING TO BUY INFORMATION THIS WAY?
OKAY—YOU'VE MADE YOUR POINT! LET'S GET BACK TO YOUR FATHER—THE SCULPTOR, ROSCOE CARVER
2840
YOU KNOW WHERE TO FIND HIM?
NO—BUT I KNOW HOW TO FIND HIM!

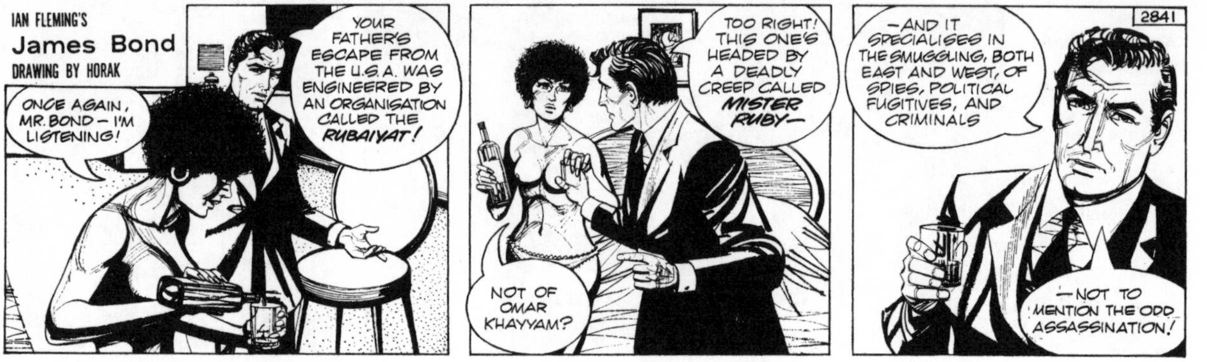
IAN FLEMING'S
James Bond
DRAWING BY HORAK
ONCE AGAIN, MR. BOND — I'M LISTENING!
YOUR FATHER'S ESCAPE FROM THE U.S.A. WAS ENGINEERED BY AN ORGANISATION CALLED THE RUBAIYAT!
NOT OF OMAR KHAYYAM?
TOO RIGHT! THIS ONE'S HEADED BY A DEADLY CREEP CALLED MISTER RUBY—
2841
—AND IT SPECIALISES IN THE SMUGGLING, BOTH EAST AND WEST, OF SPIES, POLITICAL FUGITIVES, AND CRIMINALS
—NOT TO MENTION THE ODD ASSASSINATION!

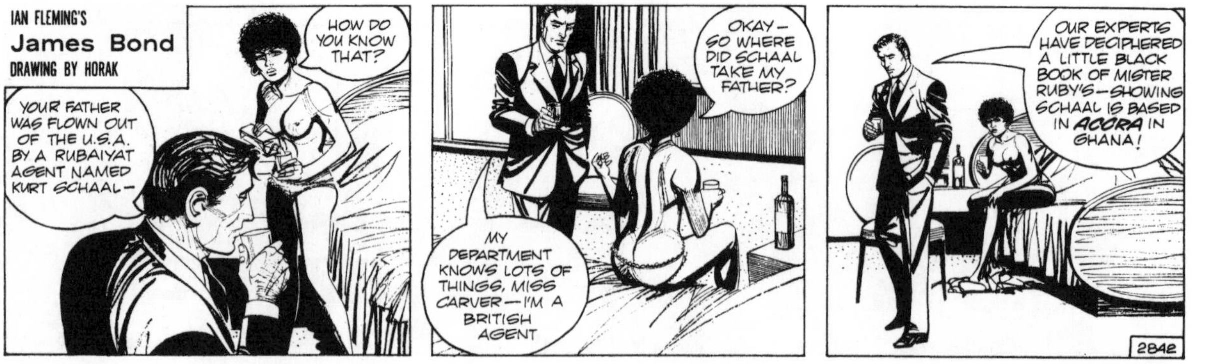
IAN FLEMING'S
James Bond
DRAWING BY HORAK
YOUR FATHER WAS FLOWN OUT OF THE U.S.A. BY A RUBAIYAT AGENT NAMED KURT SCHAAL—
HOW DO YOU KNOW THAT?
MY DEPARTMENT KNOWS LOTS OF THINGS, MISS CARVER — I'M A BRITISH AGENT
OKAY — SO WHERE DID SCHAAL TAKE MY FATHER?
OUR EXPERTS HAVE DECIPHERED A LITTLE BLACK BOOK OF MISTER RUBY'S — SHOWING SCHAAL IS BASED IN ACCRA IN GHANA!
2842

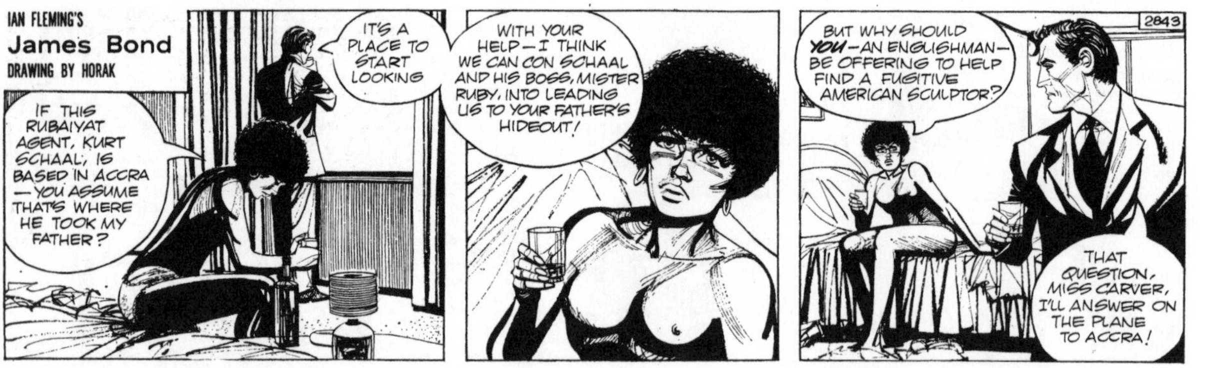
IAN FLEMING'S
James Bond
DRAWING BY HORAK
IF THIS RUBAIYAT AGENT, KURT SCHAAL, IS BASED IN ACCRA — YOU ASSUME THAT'S WHERE HE TOOK MY FATHER?
IT'S A PLACE TO START LOOKING
WITH YOUR HELP — I THINK WE CAN CON SCHAAL AND HIS BOSS, MISTER RUBY, INTO LEADING US TO YOUR FATHER'S HIDEOUT!
2843
BUT WHY SHOULD YOU — AN ENGLISHMAN — BE OFFERING TO HELP FIND A FUGITIVE AMERICAN SCULPTOR?
THAT QUESTION, MISS CARVER, I'LL ANSWER ON THE PLANE TO ACCRA!

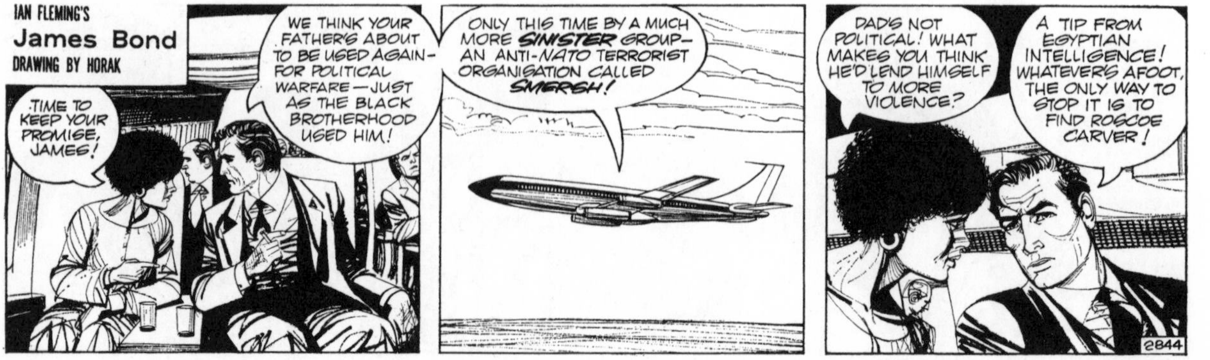
IAN FLEMING'S
James Bond
DRAWING BY HORAK
TIME TO KEEP YOUR PROMISE, JAMES!
WE THINK YOUR FATHER'S ABOUT TO BE USED AGAIN — FOR POLITICAL WARFARE — JUST AS THE BLACK BROTHERHOOD USED HIM!
ONLY THIS TIME BY A MUCH MORE SINISTER GROUP — AN ANTI-NATO TERRORIST ORGANISATION CALLED SMERSH!
DAD'S NOT POLITICAL! WHAT MAKES YOU THINK HE'D LEND HIMSELF TO MORE VIOLENCE?
A TIP FROM EGYPTIAN INTELLIGENCE! WHATEVER'S AFOOT, THE ONLY WAY TO STOP IT IS TO FIND ROSCOE CARVER!
2844

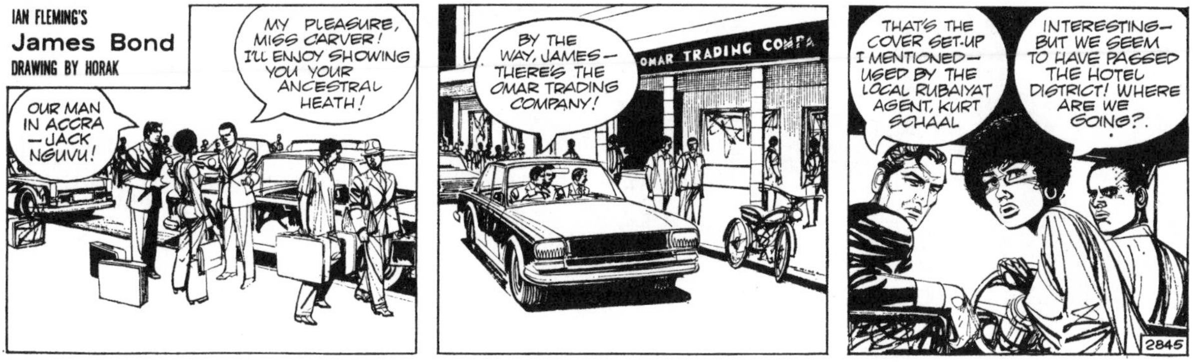
IAN FLEMING'S
James Bond
DRAWING BY HORAK
OUR MAN IN ACCRA —JACK NGUVU!
MY PLEASURE, MISS CARVER! I'LL ENJOY SHOWING YOU YOUR ANCESTRAL HEATH!
BY THE WAY, JAMES— THERE'S THE OMAR TRADING COMPANY!
OMAR TRADING COMPA
THAT'S THE COVER SET-UP I MENTIONED— USED BY THE LOCAL RUBAIYAT AGENT, KURT SCHAAL
INTERESTING— BUT WE SEEM TO HAVE PASSED THE HOTEL DISTRICT! WHERE ARE WE GOING?
2845

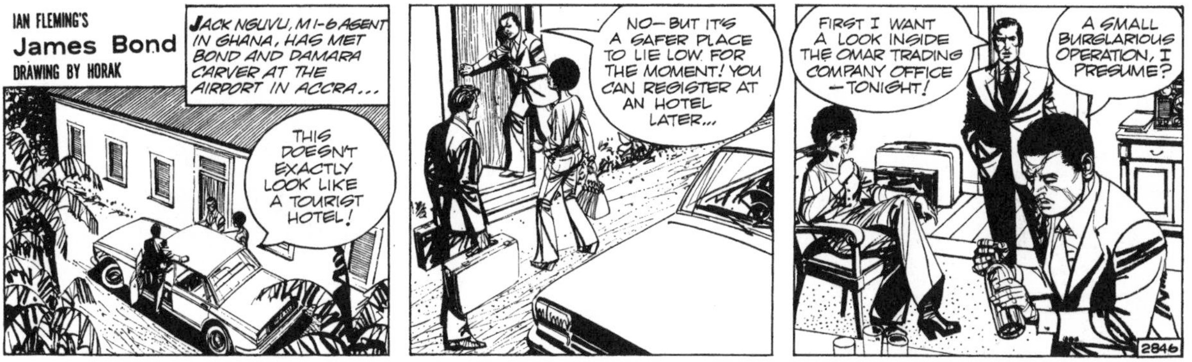
IAN FLEMING'S
James Bond
DRAWING BY HORAK
JACK NGUVU, MI-6 AGENT IN GHANA, HAS MET BOND AND DAMARA CARVER AT THE AIRPORT IN ACCRA...
THIS DOESN'T EXACTLY LOOK LIKE A TOURIST HOTEL!
NO— BUT IT'S A SAFER PLACE TO LIE LOW FOR THE MOMENT! YOU CAN REGISTER AT AN HOTEL LATER...
FIRST I WANT A LOOK INSIDE THE OMAR TRADING COMPANY OFFICE —TONIGHT!
A SMALL BURGLARIOUS OPERATION, I PRESUME?
2846

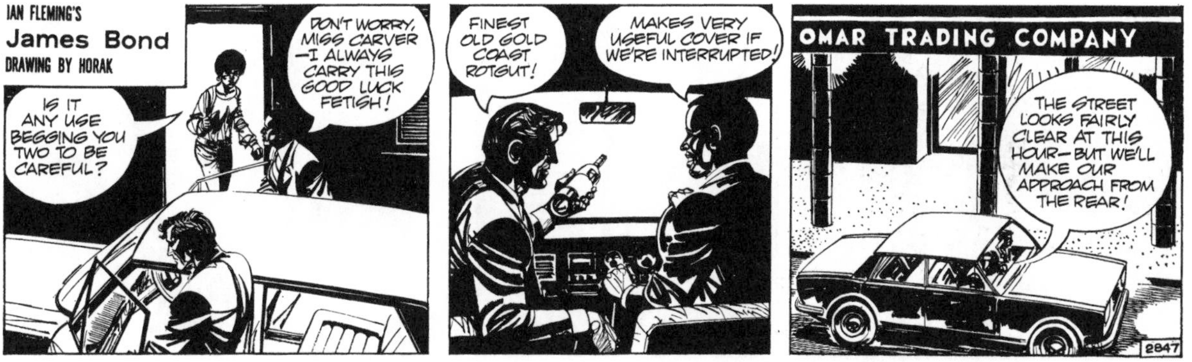
IAN FLEMING'S
James Bond
DRAWING BY HORAK
IS IT ANY USE BEGGING YOU TWO TO BE CAREFUL?
DON'T WORRY, MISS CARVER —I ALWAYS CARRY THIS GOOD LUCK FETISH!
FINEST OLD GOLD COAST ROTGUT!
MAKES VERY USEFUL COVER IF WE'RE INTERRUPTED!
OMAR TRADING COMPANY
THE STREET LOOKS FAIRLY CLEAR AT THIS HOUR— BUT WE'LL MAKE OUR APPROACH FROM THE REAR!
2847

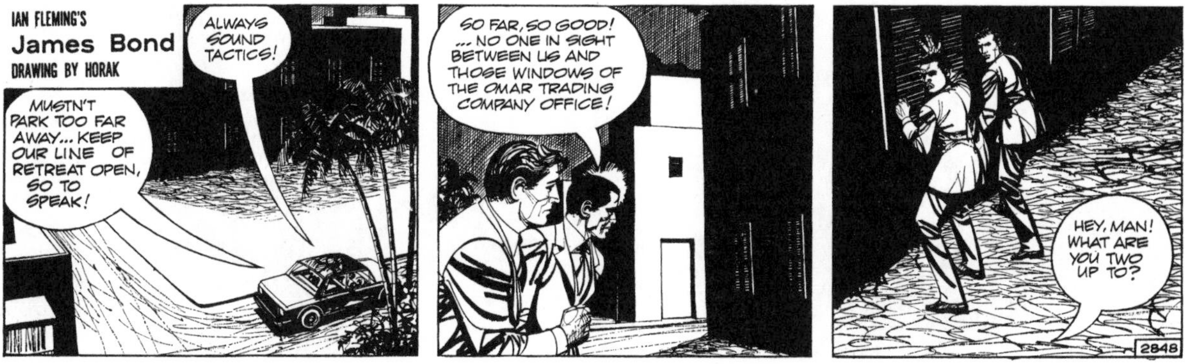
IAN FLEMING'S
James Bond
DRAWING BY HORAK
ALWAYS SOUND TACTICS!
MUSTN'T PARK TOO FAR AWAY... KEEP OUR LINE OF RETREAT OPEN, SO TO SPEAK!
SO FAR, SO GOOD! ... NO ONE IN SIGHT BETWEEN US AND THOSE WINDOWS OF THE OMAR TRADING COMPANY OFFICE!
HEY, MAN! WHAT ARE YOU TWO UP TO?
2848

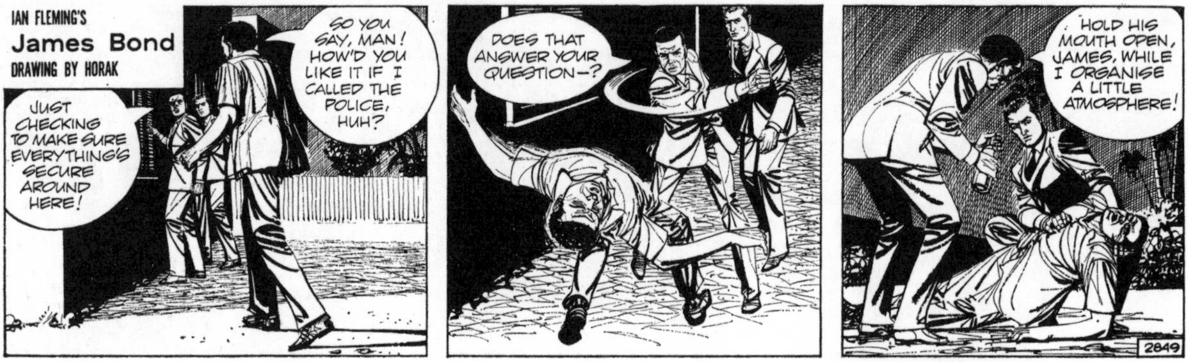
IAN FLEMING'S
James Bond
DRAWING BY HORAK
JUST CHECKING TO MAKE SURE EVERYTHING'S SECURE AROUND HERE!
SO YOU SAY, MAN! HOW'D YOU LIKE IT IF I CALLED THE POLICE, HUH?
DOES THAT ANSWER YOUR QUESTION—?
HOLD HIS MOUTH OPEN, JAMES, WHILE I ORGANISE A LITTLE ATMOSPHERE!
2849

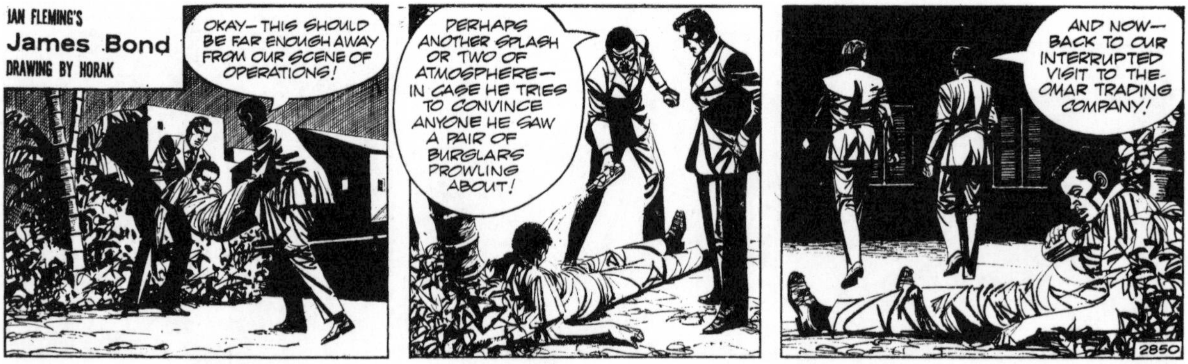
IAN FLEMING'S
James Bond
DRAWING BY HORAK
OKAY—THIS SHOULD BE FAR ENOUGH AWAY FROM OUR SCENE OF OPERATIONS!
PERHAPS ANOTHER SPLASH OR TWO OF ATMOSPHERE—IN CASE HE TRIES TO CONVINCE ANYONE HE SAW A PAIR OF BURGLARS PROWLING ABOUT!
AND NOW—BACK TO OUR INTERRUPTED VISIT TO THE OMAR TRADING COMPANY!
2850

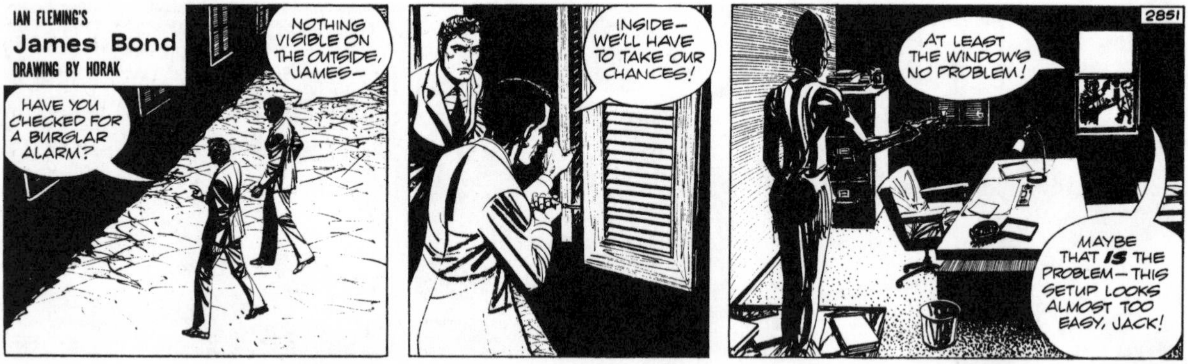
IAN FLEMING'S
James Bond
DRAWING BY HORAK
HAVE YOU CHECKED FOR A BURGLAR ALARM?
NOTHING VISIBLE ON THE OUTSIDE, JAMES—
INSIDE—WE'LL HAVE TO TAKE OUR CHANCES!
2851
AT LEAST THE WINDOW'S NO PROBLEM!
MAYBE THAT IS THE PROBLEM—THIS SETUP LOOKS ALMOST TOO EASY, JACK!

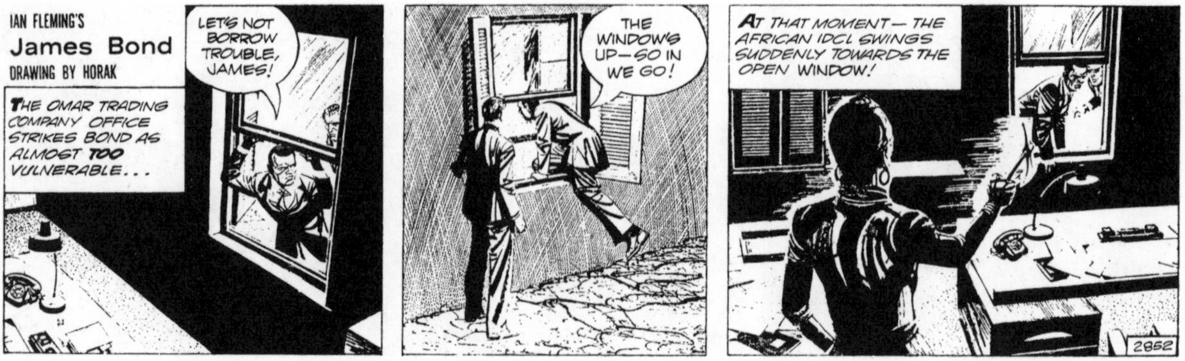
IAN FLEMING'S
James Bond
DRAWING BY HORAK
THE OMAR TRADING COMPANY OFFICE STRIKES BOND AS ALMOST TOO VULNERABLE...
LET'S NOT BORROW TROUBLE, JAMES!
THE WINDOW'S UP—SO IN WE GO!
AT THAT MOMENT— THE AFRICAN IDCL SWINGS SUDDENLY TOWARDS THE OPEN WINDOW!
2852

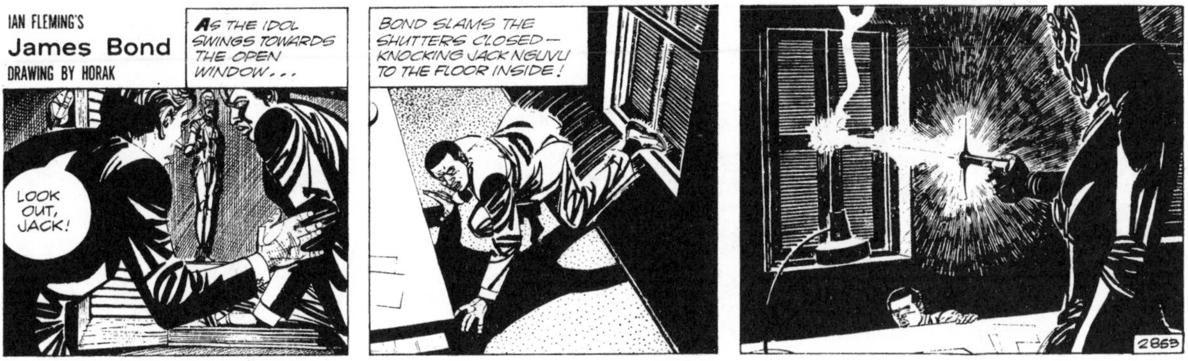
IAN FLEMING'S
James Bond
DRAWING BY HORAK
AS THE IDOL SWINGS TOWARDS THE OPEN WINDOW . . .
LOOK OUT, JACK!
BOND SLAMS THE SHUTTERS CLOSED— KNOCKING JACK NGUVU TO THE FLOOR INSIDE!
2853

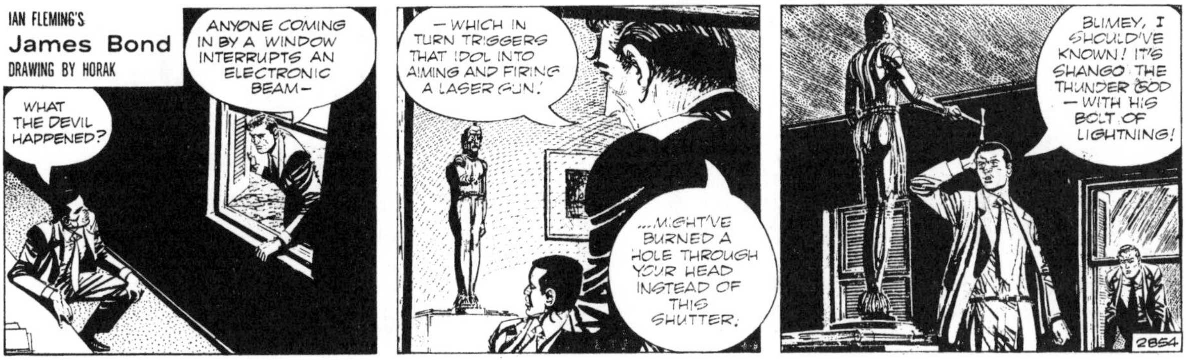
IAN FLEMING'S
James Bond
DRAWING BY HORAK
WHAT THE DEVIL HAPPENED?
ANYONE COMING IN BY A WINDOW INTERRUPTS AN ELECTRONIC BEAM—
—WHICH IN TURN TRIGGERS THAT IDOL INTO AIMING AND FIRING A LASER GUN!
...MIGHT'VE BURNED A HOLE THROUGH YOUR HEAD INSTEAD OF THIS SHUTTER!
BLIMEY, I SHOULD'VE KNOWN! IT'S SHANGO THE THUNDER GOD —WITH HIS BOLT OF LIGHTNING!
2854

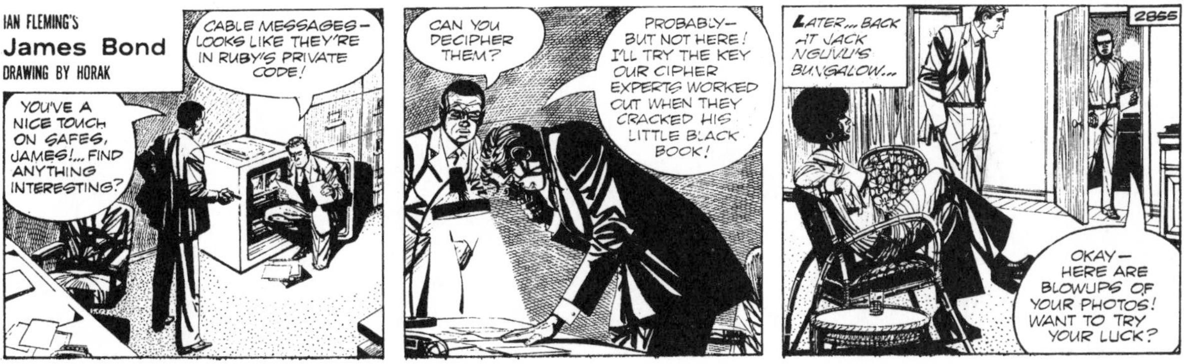
IAN FLEMING'S
James Bond
DRAWING BY HORAK
YOU'VE A NICE TOUCH ON SAFES, JAMES!... FIND ANYTHING INTERESTING?
CABLE MESSAGES— LOOKS LIKE THEY'RE IN RUBY'S PRIVATE CODE!
CAN YOU DECIPHER THEM?
PROBABLY— BUT NOT HERE! I'LL TRY THE KEY OUR CIPHER EXPERTS WORKED OUT WHEN THEY CRACKED HIS LITTLE BLACK BOOK!
LATER... BACK AT JACK NGUVU'S BUNGALOW...
2855
OKAY— HERE ARE BLOWUPS OF YOUR PHOTOS! WANT TO TRY YOUR LUCK?

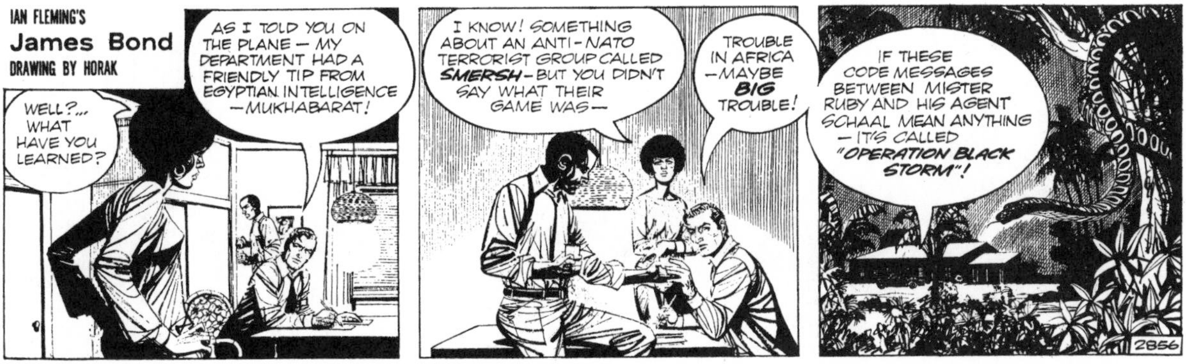
IAN FLEMING'S
James Bond
DRAWING BY HORAK
WELL?... WHAT HAVE YOU LEARNED?
AS I TOLD YOU ON THE PLANE — MY DEPARTMENT HAD A FRIENDLY TIP FROM EGYPTIAN INTELLIGENCE —MUKHABARAT!
I KNOW! SOMETHING ABOUT AN ANTI-NATO TERRORIST GROUP CALLED SMERSH—BUT YOU DIDN'T SAY WHAT THEIR GAME WAS—
TROUBLE IN AFRICA —MAYBE BIG TROUBLE!
IF THESE CODE MESSAGES BETWEEN MISTER RUBY AND HIS AGENT SCHAAL MEAN ANYTHING —IT'S CALLED "OPERATION BLACK STORM"!
2856

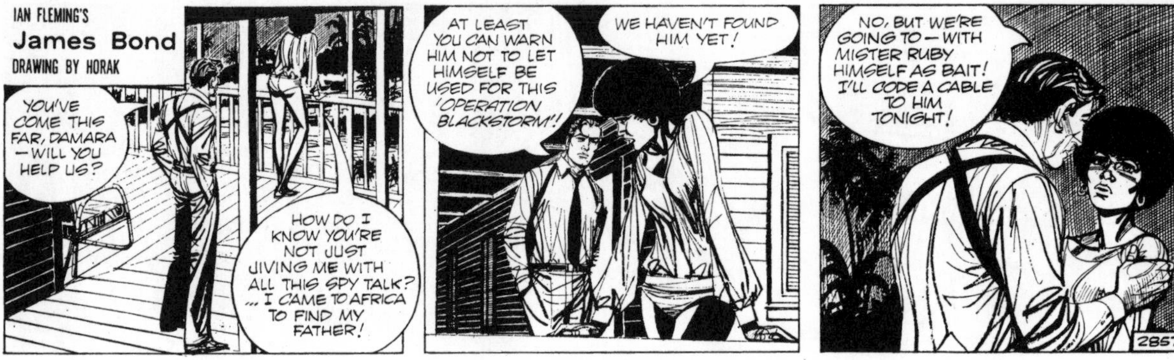
IAN FLEMING'S
James Bond
DRAWING BY HORAK
YOU'VE COME THIS FAR, DAMARA — WILL YOU HELP US?
HOW DO I KNOW YOU'RE NOT JUST JIVING ME WITH ALL THIS SPY TALK? ... I CAME TO AFRICA TO FIND MY FATHER!
AT LEAST YOU CAN WARN HIM NOT TO LET HIMSELF BE USED FOR THIS 'OPERATION BLACKSTORM'!
WE HAVEN'T FOUND HIM YET!
NO, BUT WE'RE GOING TO — WITH MISTER RUBY HIMSELF AS BAIT! I'LL CODE A CABLE TO HIM TONIGHT!
2857

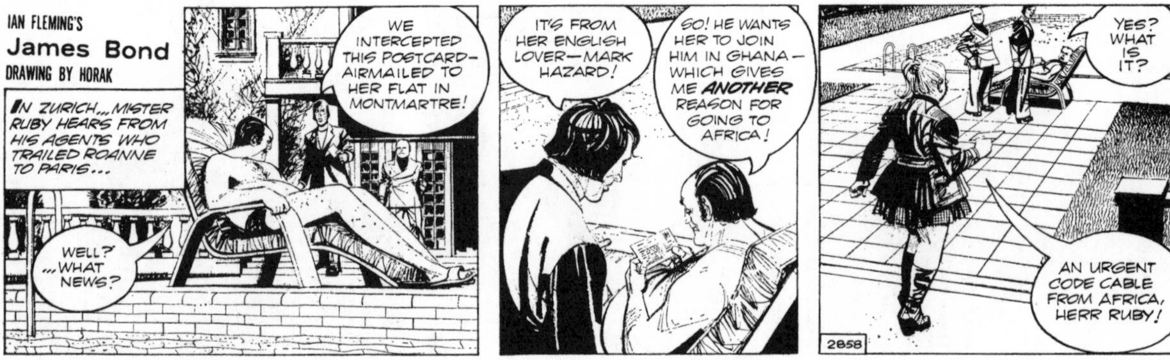
IAN FLEMING'S
James Bond
DRAWING BY HORAK
IN ZURICH... MISTER RUBY HEARS FROM HIS AGENTS WHO TRAILED ROANNE TO PARIS...
WELL? ...WHAT NEWS?
WE INTERCEPTED THIS POSTCARD — AIRMAILED TO HER FLAT IN MONTMARTRE!
IT'S FROM HER ENGLISH LOVER — MARK HAZARD!
SO! HE WANTS HER TO JOIN HIM IN GHANA — WHICH GIVES ME ANOTHER REASON FOR GOING TO AFRICA!
2858
YES? WHAT IS IT?
AN URGENT CODE CABLE FROM AFRICA, HERR RUBY!

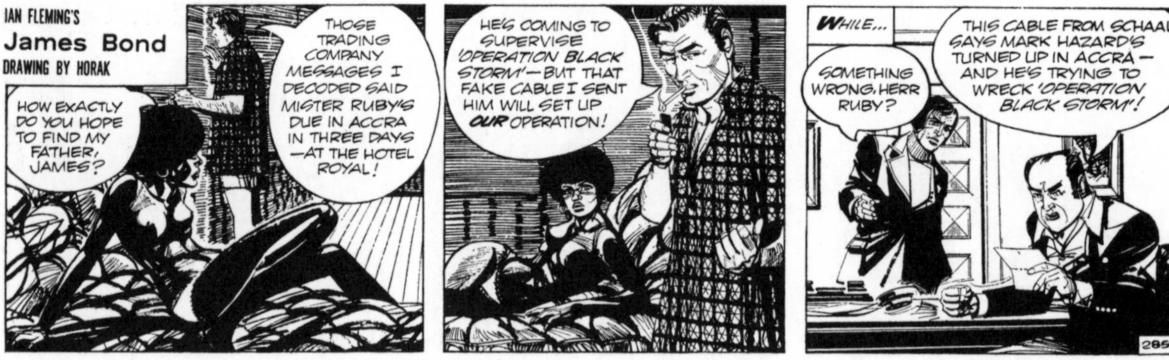
IAN FLEMING'S
James Bond
DRAWING BY HORAK
HOW EXACTLY DO YOU HOPE TO FIND MY FATHER, JAMES?
THOSE TRADING COMPANY MESSAGES I DECODED SAID MISTER RUBY'S DUE IN ACCRA IN THREE DAYS — AT THE HOTEL ROYAL!
HE'S COMING TO SUPERVISE 'OPERATION BLACK STORM' — BUT THAT FAKE CABLE I SENT HIM WILL SET UP OUR OPERATION!
WHILE...
SOMETHING WRONG, HERR RUBY?
THIS CABLE FROM SCHAAL SAYS MARK HAZARD'S TURNED UP IN ACCRA — AND HE'S TRYING TO WRECK 'OPERATION BLACK STORM'!
2859

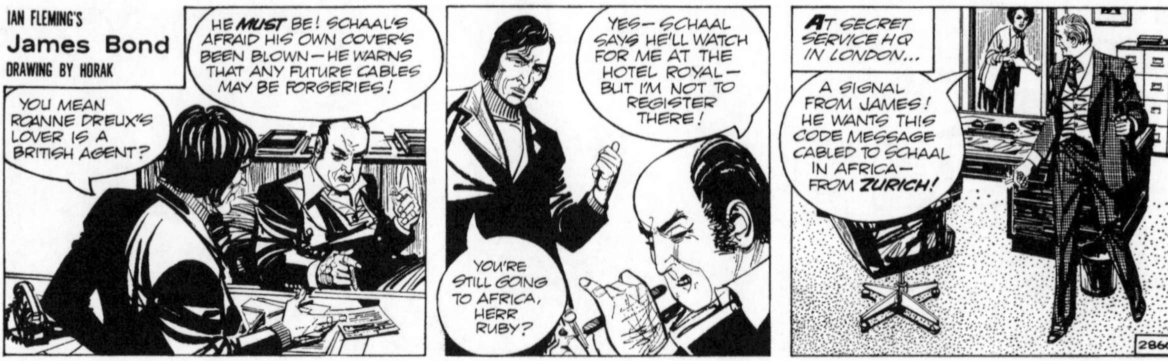
IAN FLEMING'S
James Bond
DRAWING BY HORAK
YOU MEAN ROANNE DREUX'S LOVER IS A BRITISH AGENT?
HE MUST BE! SCHAAL'S AFRAID HIS OWN COVER'S BEEN BLOWN — HE WARNS THAT ANY FUTURE CABLES MAY BE FORGERIES!
YES — SCHAAL SAYS HE'LL WATCH FOR ME AT THE HOTEL ROYAL — BUT I'M NOT TO REGISTER THERE!
YOU'RE STILL GOING TO AFRICA, HERR RUBY?
AT SECRET SERVICE HQ IN LONDON...
A SIGNAL FROM JAMES! HE WANTS THIS CODE MESSAGE CABLED TO SCHAAL IN AFRICA — FROM ZURICH!
2860

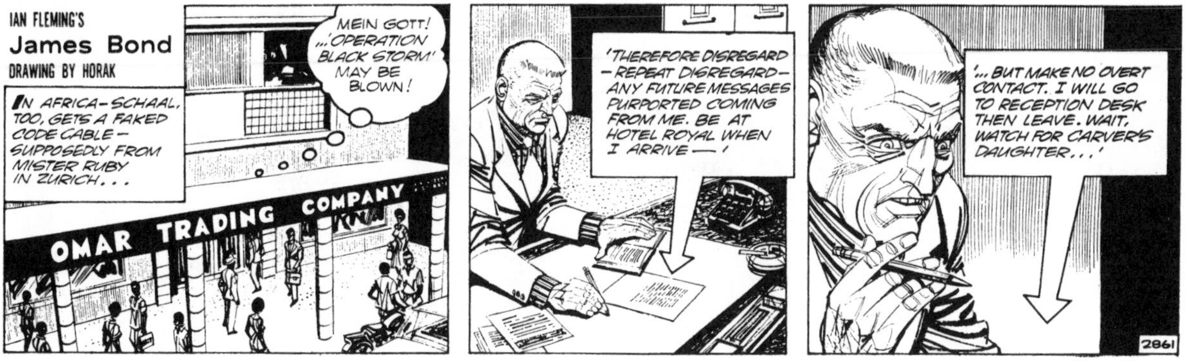
IAN FLEMING'S
James Bond
DRAWING BY HORAK
IN AFRICA–SCHAAL, TOO, GETS A FAKED CODE CABLE–SUPPOSEDLY FROM MISTER RUBY IN ZURICH . . .
MEIN GOTT! ...'OPERATION BLACK STORM' MAY BE BLOWN!
OMAR TRADING COMPANY
'THEREFORE DISREGARD –REPEAT DISREGARD– ANY FUTURE MESSAGES PURPORTED COMING FROM ME. BE AT HOTEL ROYAL WHEN I ARRIVE—'
'... BUT MAKE NO OVERT CONTACT. I WILL GO TO RECEPTION DESK THEN LEAVE. WAIT. WATCH FOR CARVER'S DAUGHTER . . .'
2861

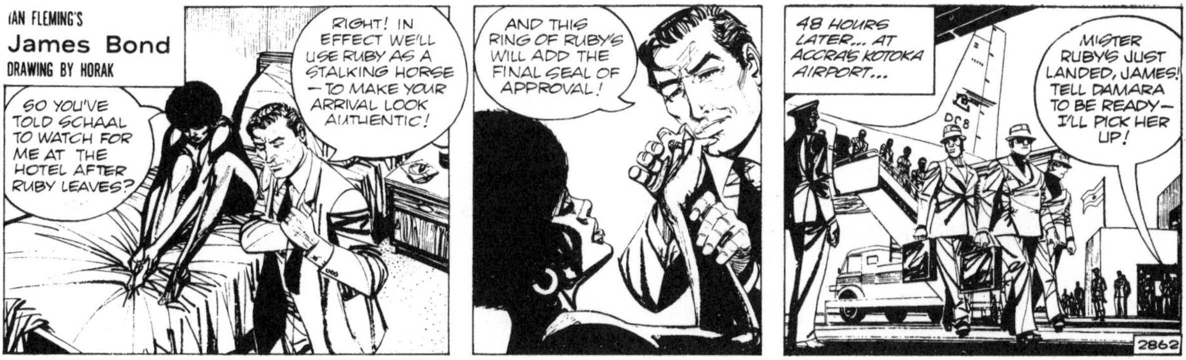
IAN FLEMING'S
James Bond
DRAWING BY HORAK
SO YOU'VE TOLD SCHAAL TO WATCH FOR ME AT THE HOTEL AFTER RUBY LEAVES?
RIGHT! IN EFFECT WE'LL USE RUBY AS A STALKING HORSE –TO MAKE YOUR ARRIVAL LOOK AUTHENTIC!
AND THIS RING OF RUBY'S WILL ADD THE FINAL SEAL OF APPROVAL!
48 HOURS LATER... AT ACCRA'S KOTOKA AIRPORT...
MISTER RUBY'S JUST LANDED, JAMES! TELL DAMARA TO BE READY– I'LL PICK HER UP!
DC8
2862

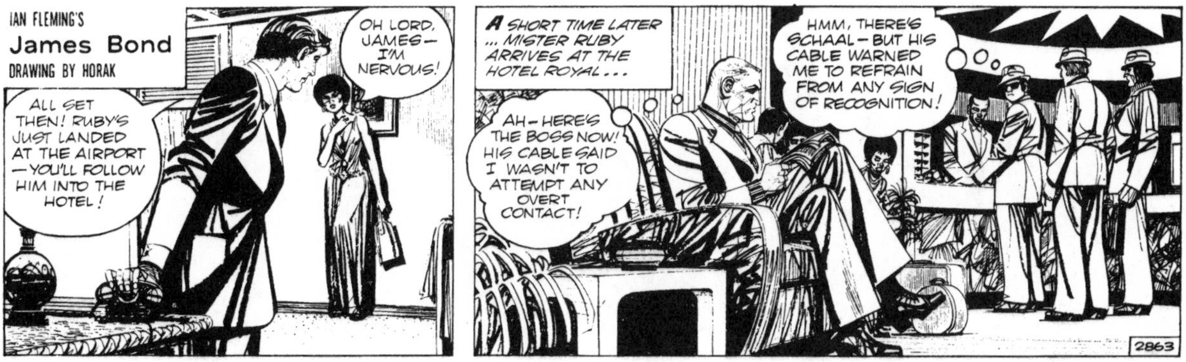
IAN FLEMING'S
James Bond
DRAWING BY HORAK
ALL SET THEN! RUBY'S JUST LANDED AT THE AIRPORT –YOU'LL FOLLOW HIM INTO THE HOTEL!
OH LORD, JAMES– I'M NERVOUS!
A SHORT TIME LATER ... MISTER RUBY ARRIVES AT THE HOTEL ROYAL . . .
HMM, THERE'S SCHAAL– BUT HIS CABLE WARNED ME TO REFRAIN FROM ANY SIGN OF RECOGNITION!
AH–HERE'S THE BOSS NOW! HIS CABLE SAID I WASN'T TO ATTEMPT ANY OVERT CONTACT!
2863

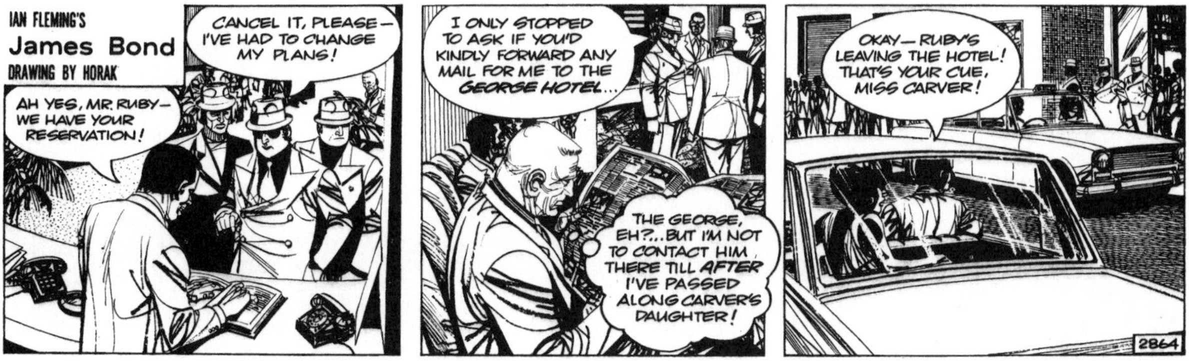
IAN FLEMING'S
James Bond
DRAWING BY HORAK
AH YES, MR. RUBY– WE HAVE YOUR RESERVATION!
CANCEL IT, PLEASE– I'VE HAD TO CHANGE MY PLANS!
I ONLY STOPPED TO ASK IF YOU'D KINDLY FORWARD ANY MAIL FOR ME TO THE GEORGE HOTEL...
THE GEORGE, EH?... BUT I'M NOT TO CONTACT HIM THERE TILL AFTER I'VE PASSED ALONG CARVER'S DAUGHTER!
OKAY– RUBY'S LEAVING THE HOTEL! THAT'S YOUR CUE, MISS CARVER!
2864

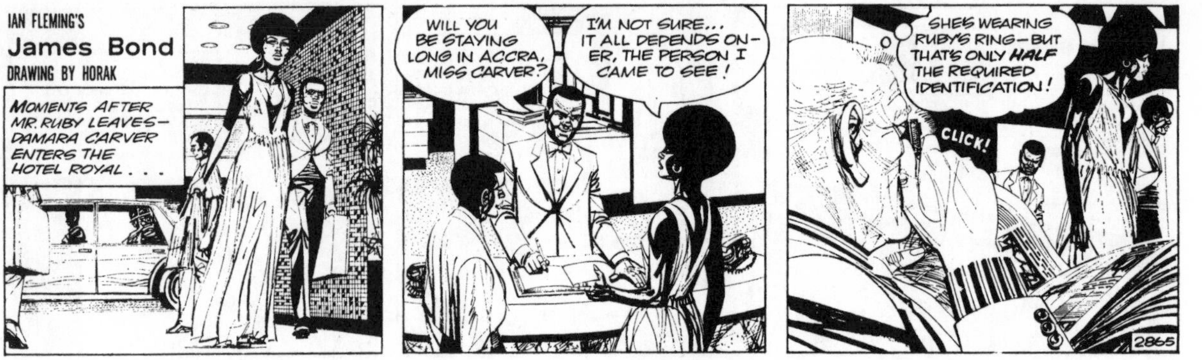
IAN FLEMING'S
James Bond
DRAWING BY HORAK
MOMENTS AFTER MR. RUBY LEAVES— DAMARA CARVER ENTERS THE HOTEL ROYAL . . .
WILL YOU BE STAYING LONG IN ACCRA, MISS CARVER?
I'M NOT SURE... IT ALL DEPENDS ON— ER, THE PERSON I CAME TO SEE!
SHE'S WEARING RUBY'S RING—BUT THAT'S ONLY HALF THE REQUIRED IDENTIFICATION!
CLICK!
2865

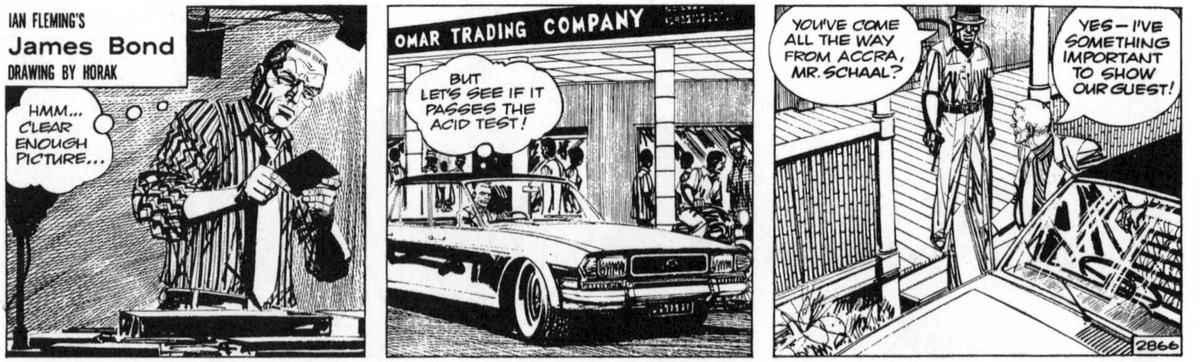
IAN FLEMING'S
James Bond
DRAWING BY HORAK
HMM... CLEAR ENOUGH PICTURE...
OMAR TRADING COMPANY
BUT LET'S SEE IF IT PASSES THE ACID TEST!
YOU'VE COME ALL THE WAY FROM ACCRA, MR. SCHAAL?
YES—I'VE SOMETHING IMPORTANT TO SHOW OUR GUEST!
2866

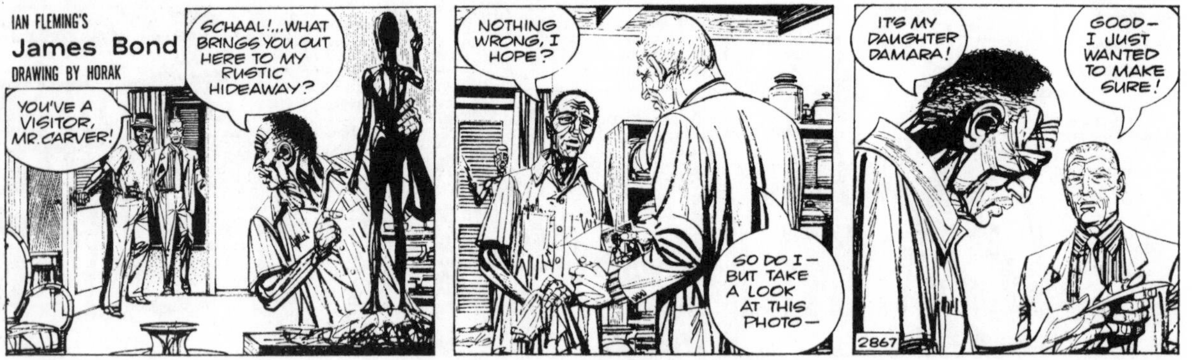
IAN FLEMING'S
James Bond
DRAWING BY HORAK
YOU'VE A VISITOR, MR. CARVER!
SCHAAL!...WHAT BRINGS YOU OUT HERE TO MY RUSTIC HIDEAWAY?
NOTHING WRONG, I HOPE?
SO DO I— BUT TAKE A LOOK AT THIS PHOTO—
IT'S MY DAUGHTER DAMARA!
GOOD— I JUST WANTED TO MAKE SURE!
2867

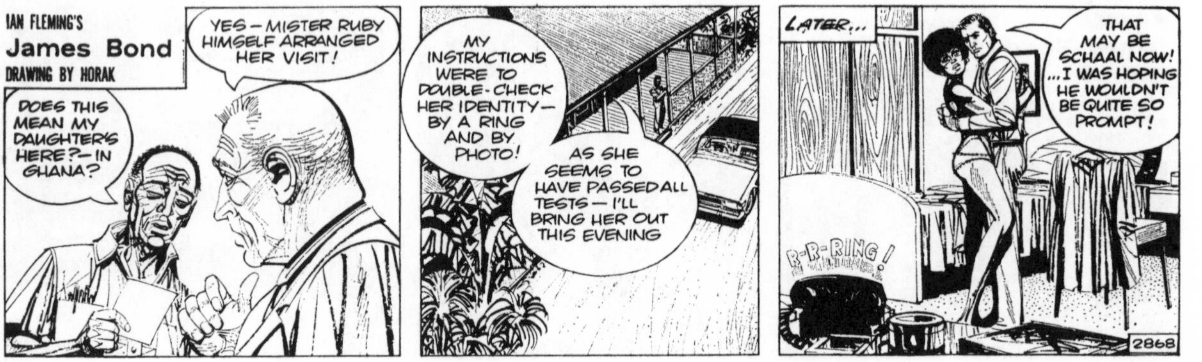
IAN FLEMING'S
James Bond
DRAWING BY HORAK
DOES THIS MEAN MY DAUGHTER'S HERE?—IN GHANA?
YES—MISTER RUBY HIMSELF ARRANGED HER VISIT!
MY INSTRUCTIONS WERE TO DOUBLE-CHECK HER IDENTITY— BY A RING AND BY PHOTO!
AS SHE SEEMS TO HAVE PASSED ALL TESTS—I'LL BRING HER OUT THIS EVENING
LATER...
THAT MAY BE SCHAAL NOW! ...I WAS HOPING HE WOULDN'T BE QUITE SO PROMPT!
R-R-RING!
2868

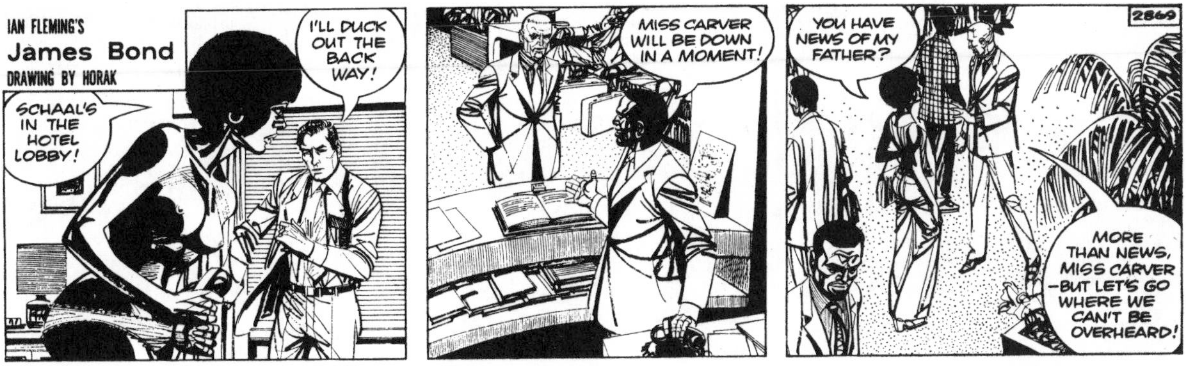
IAN FLEMING'S
James Bond
DRAWING BY HORAK
SCHAAL'S IN THE HOTEL LOBBY!
I'LL DUCK OUT THE BACK WAY!
MISS CARVER WILL BE DOWN IN A MOMENT!
YOU HAVE NEWS OF MY FATHER?
MORE THAN NEWS, MISS CARVER —BUT LET'S GO WHERE WE CAN'T BE OVERHEARD!
2869

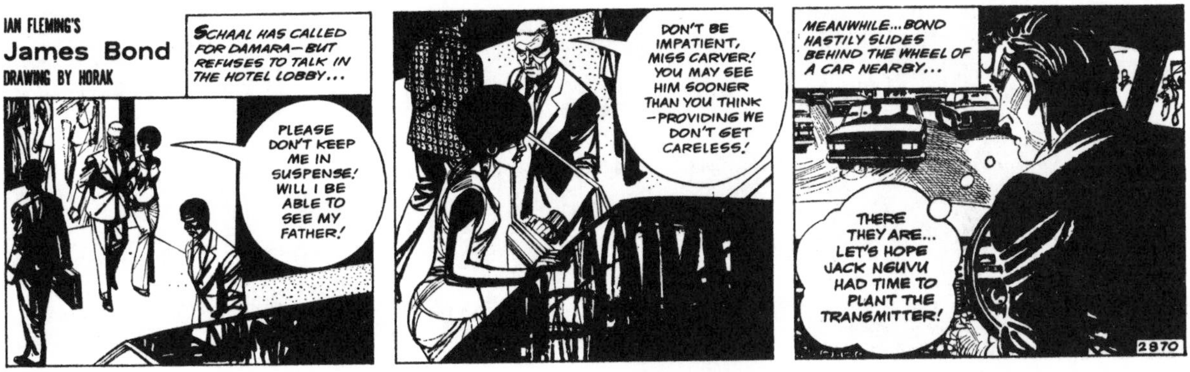
IAN FLEMING'S
James Bond
DRAWING BY HORAK
SCHAAL HAS CALLED FOR DAMARA—BUT REFUSES TO TALK IN THE HOTEL LOBBY...
PLEASE DON'T KEEP ME IN SUSPENSE! WILL I BE ABLE TO SEE MY FATHER!
DON'T BE IMPATIENT, MISS CARVER! YOU MAY SEE HIM SOONER THAN YOU THINK —PROVIDING WE DON'T GET CARELESS!
MEANWHILE...BOND HASTILY SLIDES BEHIND THE WHEEL OF A CAR NEARBY...
THERE THEY ARE... LET'S HOPE JACK NGUVU HAD TIME TO PLANT THE TRANSMITTER!
2870

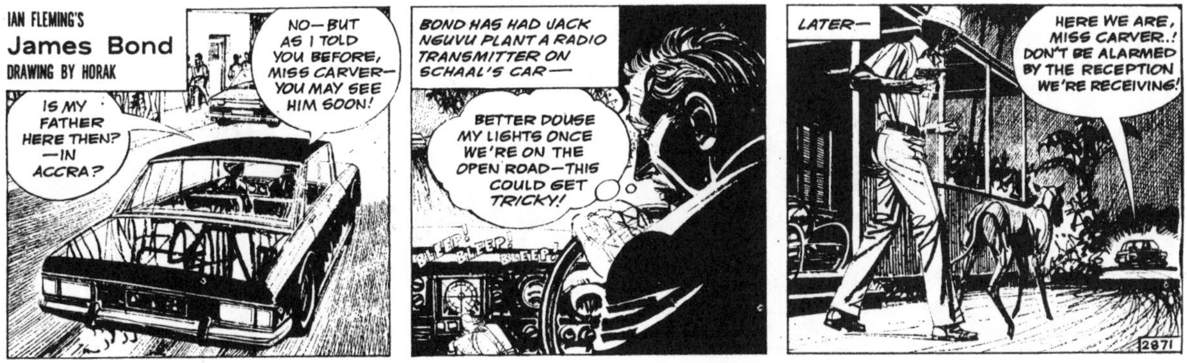
IAN FLEMING'S
James Bond
DRAWING BY HORAK
IS MY FATHER HERE THEN? —IN ACCRA?
NO—BUT AS I TOLD YOU BEFORE, MISS CARVER— YOU MAY SEE HIM SOON!
BOND HAS HAD JACK NGUVU PLANT A RADIO TRANSMITTER ON SCHAAL'S CAR—
BETTER DOUSE MY LIGHTS ONCE WE'RE ON THE OPEN ROAD—THIS COULD GET TRICKY!
BLEEP! BLEEP! BLEEP!
LATER—
HERE WE ARE, MISS CARVER..! DON'T BE ALARMED BY THE RECEPTION WE'RE RECEIVING!
2871

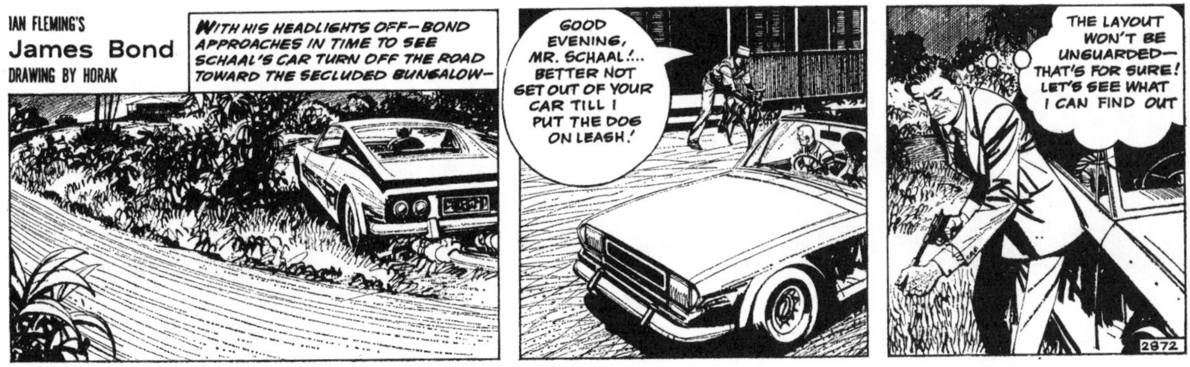
IAN FLEMING'S
James Bond
DRAWING BY HORAK
WITH HIS HEADLIGHTS OFF—BOND APPROACHES IN TIME TO SEE SCHAAL'S CAR TURN OFF THE ROAD TOWARD THE SECLUDED BUNGALOW—
GOOD EVENING, MR. SCHAAL!... BETTER NOT GET OUT OF YOUR CAR TILL I PUT THE DOG ON LEASH!
THE LAYOUT WON'T BE UNGUARDED— THAT'S FOR SURE! LET'S SEE WHAT I CAN FIND OUT
2872

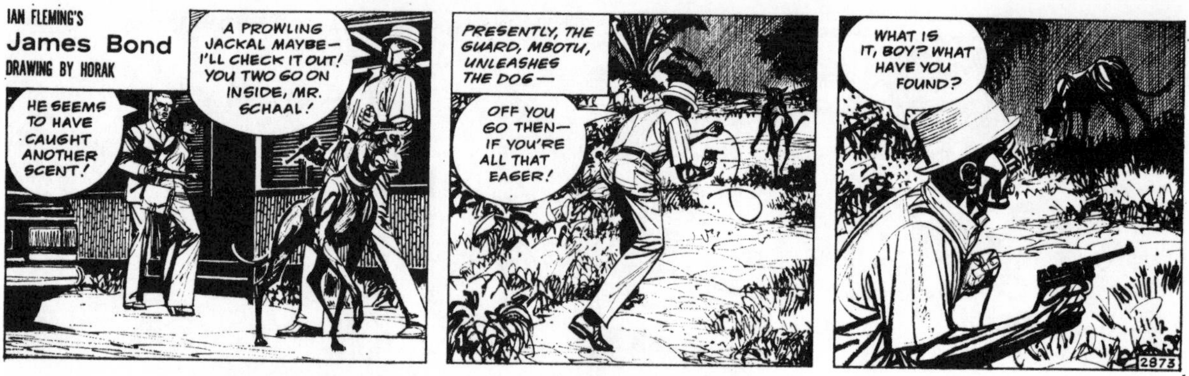
IAN FLEMING'S
James Bond
DRAWING BY HORAK
HE SEEMS TO HAVE CAUGHT ANOTHER SCENT!
A PROWLING JACKAL MAYBE—I'LL CHECK IT OUT! YOU TWO GO ON INSIDE, MR. SCHAAL!
PRESENTLY, THE GUARD, MBOTU, UNLEASHES THE DOG—
OFF YOU GO THEN—IF YOU'RE ALL THAT EAGER!
WHAT IS IT, BOY? WHAT HAVE YOU FOUND?
2873

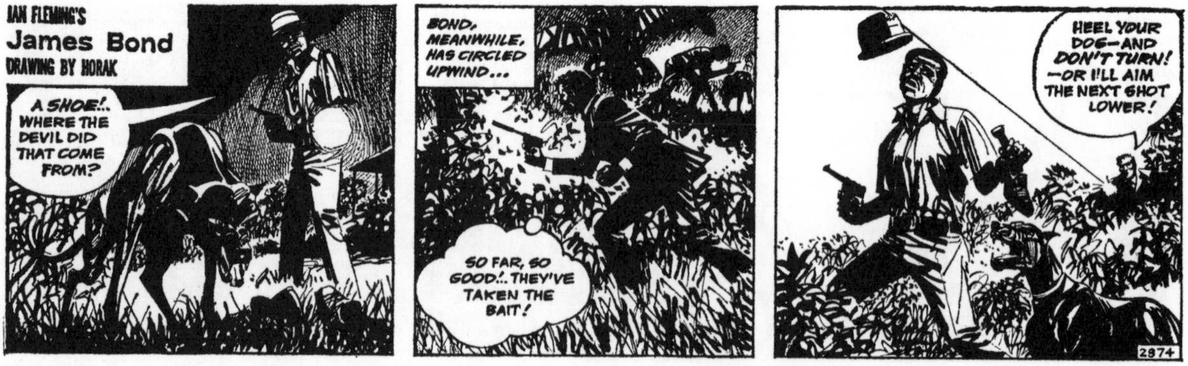
IAN FLEMING'S
James Bond
DRAWING BY HORAK
A SHOE!.. WHERE THE DEVIL DID THAT COME FROM?
BOND, MEANWHILE, HAS CIRCLED UPWIND...
SO FAR, SO GOOD!.. THEY'VE TAKEN THE BAIT!
HEEL YOUR DOG—AND DON'T TURN! —OR I'LL AIM THE NEXT SHOT LOWER!
2874

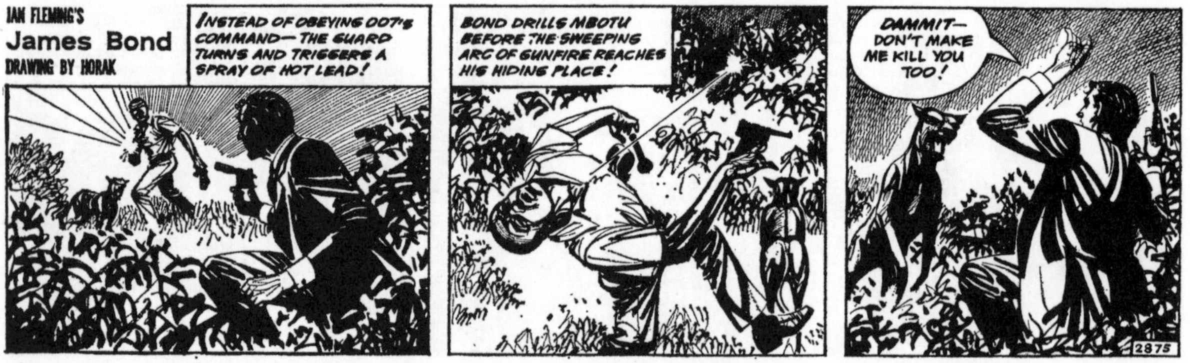
IAN FLEMING'S
James Bond
DRAWING BY HORAK
INSTEAD OF OBEYING DOT'S COMMAND—THE GUARD TURNS AND TRIGGERS A SPRAY OF HOT LEAD!
BOND DRILLS MBOTU BEFORE THE SWEEPING ARC OF GUNFIRE REACHES HIS HIDING PLACE!
DAMMIT—DON'T MAKE ME KILL YOU TOO!
2875

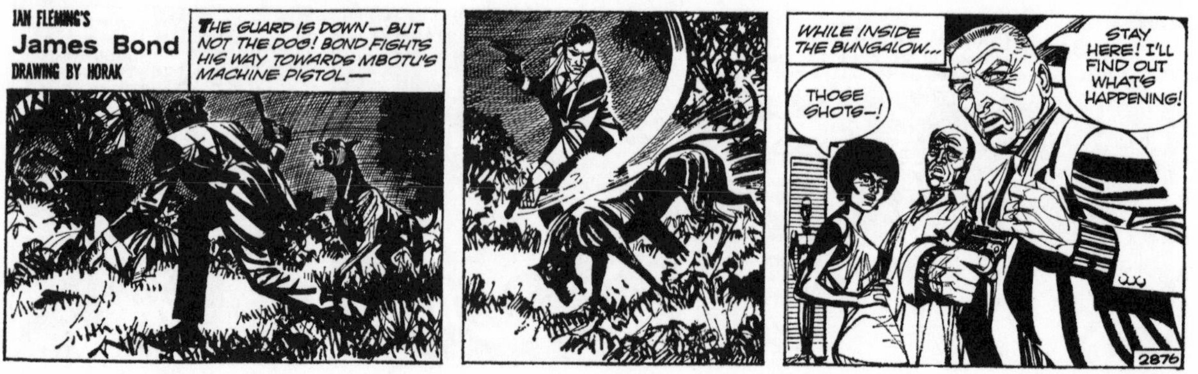
IAN FLEMING'S
James Bond
DRAWING BY HORAK
THE GUARD IS DOWN—BUT NOT THE DOG! BOND FIGHTS HIS WAY TOWARDS MBOTU'S MACHINE PISTOL—
WHILE INSIDE THE BUNGALOW...
THOSE SHOTS—!
STAY HERE! I'LL FIND OUT WHAT'S HAPPENING!
2876

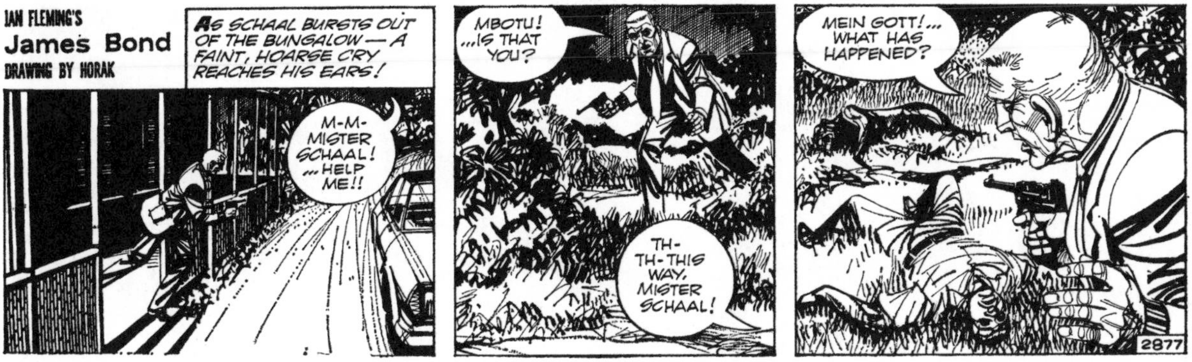
IAN FLEMING'S
James Bond
DRAWING BY HORAK
AS SCHAAL BURSTS OUT OF THE BUNGALOW — A FAINT, HOARSE CRY REACHES HIS EARS!
M-M-MISTER SCHAAL! ...HELP ME!!
MBOTU! ...IS THAT YOU?
TH-TH-THIS WAY, MISTER SCHAAL!
MEIN GOTT!... WHAT HAS HAPPENED?
2877

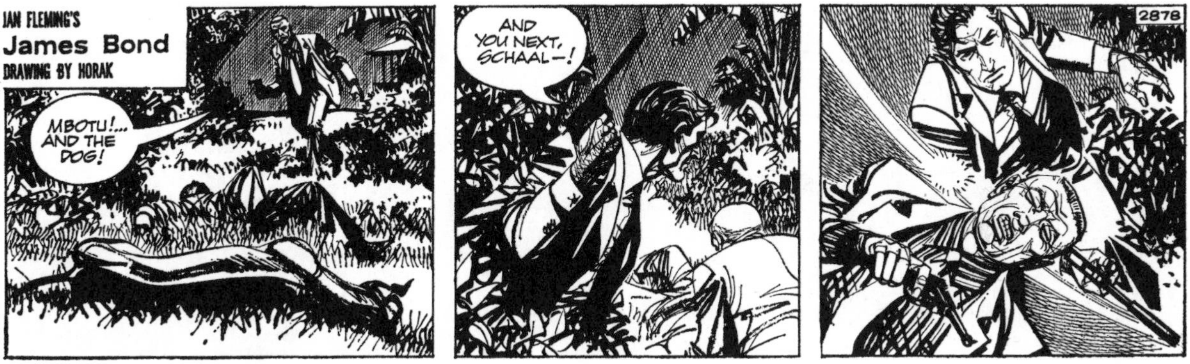
IAN FLEMING'S
James Bond
DRAWING BY HORAK
MBOTU!... AND THE DOG!
AND YOU NEXT, SCHAAL—!
2878

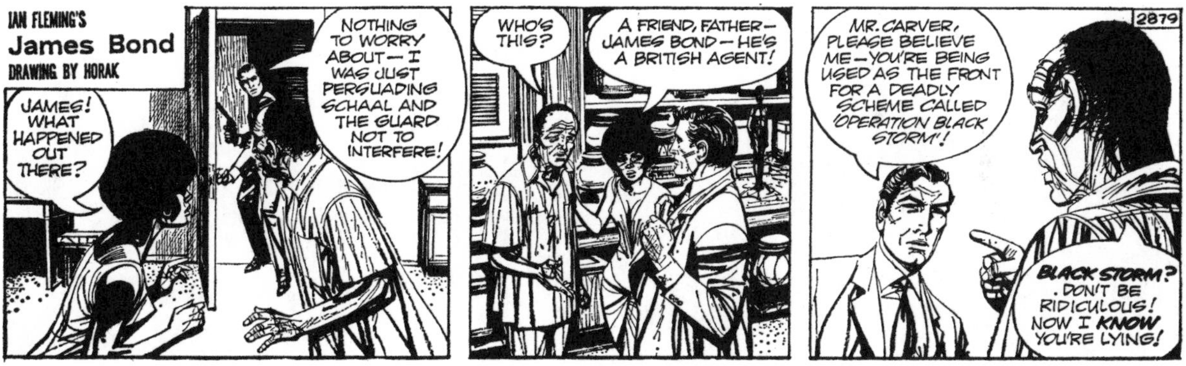
IAN FLEMING'S
James Bond
DRAWING BY HORAK
JAMES! WHAT HAPPENED OUT THERE?
NOTHING TO WORRY ABOUT—I WAS JUST PERSUADING SCHAAL AND THE GUARD NOT TO INTERFERE!
WHO'S THIS?
A FRIEND, FATHER—JAMES BOND—HE'S A BRITISH AGENT!
2879
MR. CARVER, PLEASE BELIEVE ME—YOU'RE BEING USED AS THE FRONT FOR A DEADLY SCHEME CALLED 'OPERATION BLACK STORM'!
BLACK STORM? DON'T BE RIDICULOUS! NOW I KNOW YOU'RE LYING!

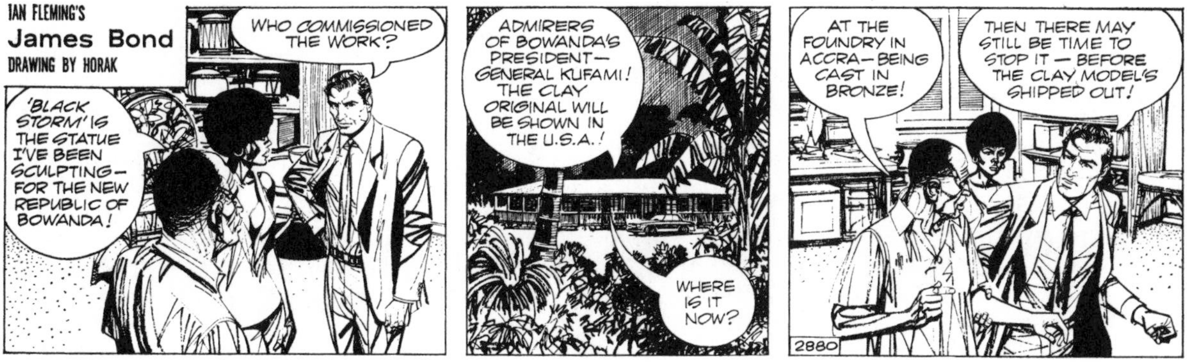
IAN FLEMING'S
James Bond
DRAWING BY HORAK
'BLACK STORM' IS THE STATUE I'VE BEEN SCULPTING—FOR THE NEW REPUBLIC OF BOWANDA!
WHO COMMISSIONED THE WORK?
ADMIRERS OF BOWANDA'S PRESIDENT—GENERAL KUFAMI! THE CLAY ORIGINAL WILL BE SHOWN IN THE U.S.A.!
WHERE IS IT NOW?
AT THE FOUNDRY IN ACCRA—BEING CAST IN BRONZE!
THEN THERE MAY STILL BE TIME TO STOP IT — BEFORE THE CLAY MODEL'S SHIPPED OUT!
2880

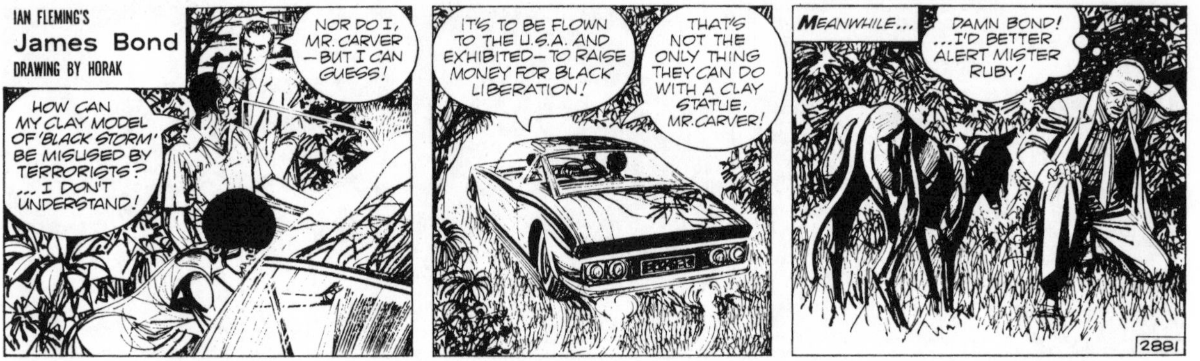
IAN FLEMING'S
James Bond
DRAWING BY HORAK
NOR DO I, MR. CARVER — BUT I CAN GUESS!
HOW CAN MY CLAY MODEL OF 'BLACK STORM' BE MISUSED BY TERRORISTS? ... I DON'T UNDERSTAND!
IT'S TO BE FLOWN TO THE U.S.A. AND EXHIBITED — TO RAISE MONEY FOR BLACK LIBERATION!
THAT'S NOT THE ONLY THING THEY CAN DO WITH A CLAY STATUE, MR. CARVER!
MEANWHILE...
DAMN BOND! ... I'D BETTER ALERT MISTER RUBY!
2881

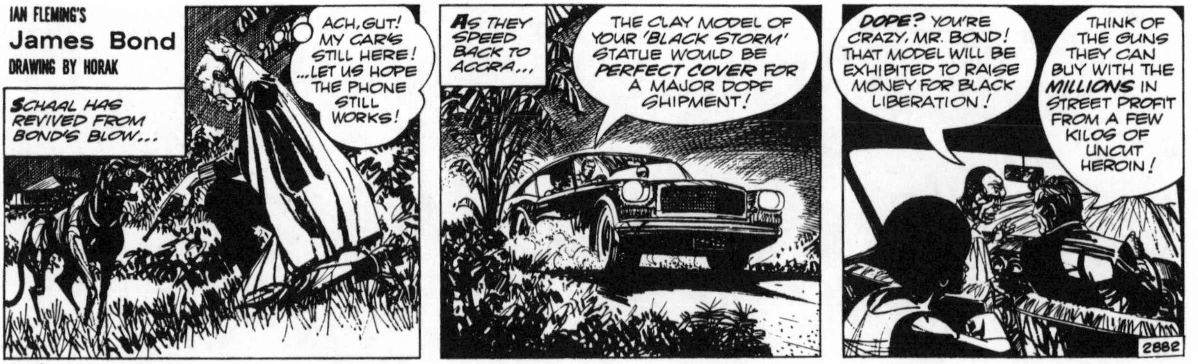
IAN FLEMING'S
James Bond
DRAWING BY HORAK
SCHAAL HAS REVIVED FROM BOND'S BLOW...
ACH, GUT! MY CAR'S STILL HERE! ...LET US HOPE THE PHONE STILL WORKS!
AS THEY SPEED BACK TO ACCRA...
THE CLAY MODEL OF YOUR 'BLACK STORM' STATUE WOULD BE PERFECT COVER FOR A MAJOR DOPE SHIPMENT!
DOPE? YOU'RE CRAZY, MR. BOND! THAT MODEL WILL BE EXHIBITED TO RAISE MONEY FOR BLACK LIBERATION!
THINK OF THE GUNS THEY CAN BUY WITH THE MILLIONS IN STREET PROFIT FROM A FEW KILOS OF UNCUT HEROIN!
2882

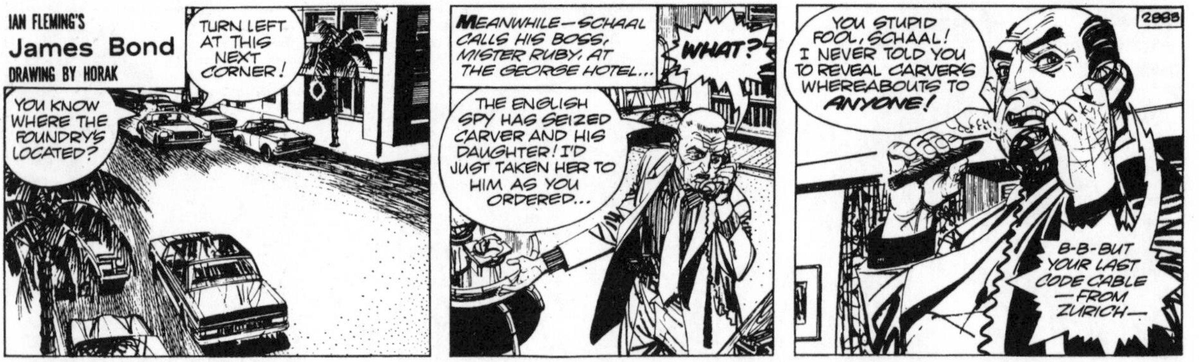
IAN FLEMING'S
James Bond
DRAWING BY HORAK
YOU KNOW WHERE THE FOUNDRY'S LOCATED?
TURN LEFT AT THIS NEXT CORNER!
MEANWHILE — SCHAAL CALLS HIS BOSS, MISTER RUBY, AT THE GEORGE HOTEL...
WHAT?
THE ENGLISH SPY HAS SEIZED CARVER AND HIS DAUGHTER! I'D JUST TAKEN HER TO HIM AS YOU ORDERED...
2883
YOU STUPID FOOL, SCHAAL! I NEVER TOLD YOU TO REVEAL CARVER'S WHEREABOUTS TO ANYONE!
B-B-BUT YOUR LAST CODE CABLE — FROM ZURICH —

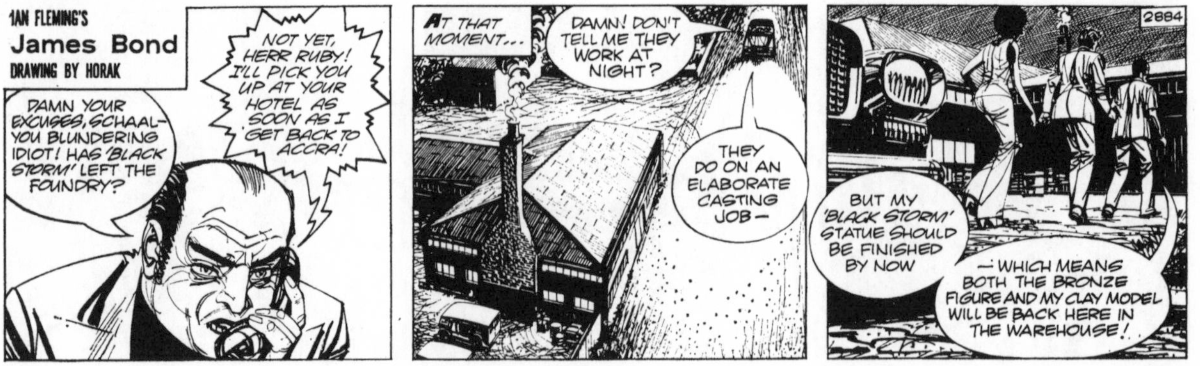
IAN FLEMING'S
James Bond
DRAWING BY HORAK
DAMN YOUR EXCUSES, SCHAAL — YOU BLUNDERING IDIOT! HAS 'BLACK STORM' LEFT THE FOUNDRY?
NOT YET, HERR RUBY! I'LL PICK YOU UP AT YOUR HOTEL AS SOON AS I GET BACK TO ACCRA!
AT THAT MOMENT...
DAMN! DON'T TELL ME THEY WORK AT NIGHT?
THEY DO ON AN ELABORATE CASTING JOB —
2884
BUT MY 'BLACK STORM' STATUE SHOULD BE FINISHED BY NOW
— WHICH MEANS BOTH THE BRONZE FIGURE AND MY CLAY MODEL WILL BE BACK HERE IN THE WAREHOUSE!

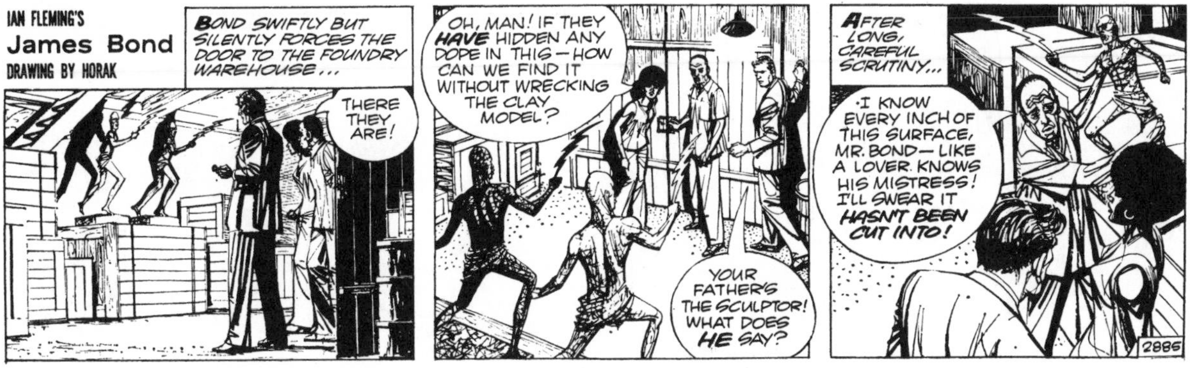
IAN FLEMING'S
James Bond
DRAWING BY HORAK
BOND SWIFTLY BUT SILENTLY FORCES THE DOOR TO THE FOUNDRY WAREHOUSE...
THERE THEY ARE!
OH, MAN! IF THEY HAVE HIDDEN ANY DOPE IN THIS—HOW CAN WE FIND IT WITHOUT WRECKING THE CLAY MODEL?
YOUR FATHER'S THE SCULPTOR! WHAT DOES HE SAY?
AFTER LONG, CAREFUL SCRUTINY...
I KNOW EVERY INCH OF THIS SURFACE, MR. BOND—LIKE A LOVER KNOWS HIS MISTRESS! I'LL SWEAR IT HASN'T BEEN CUT INTO!
2885

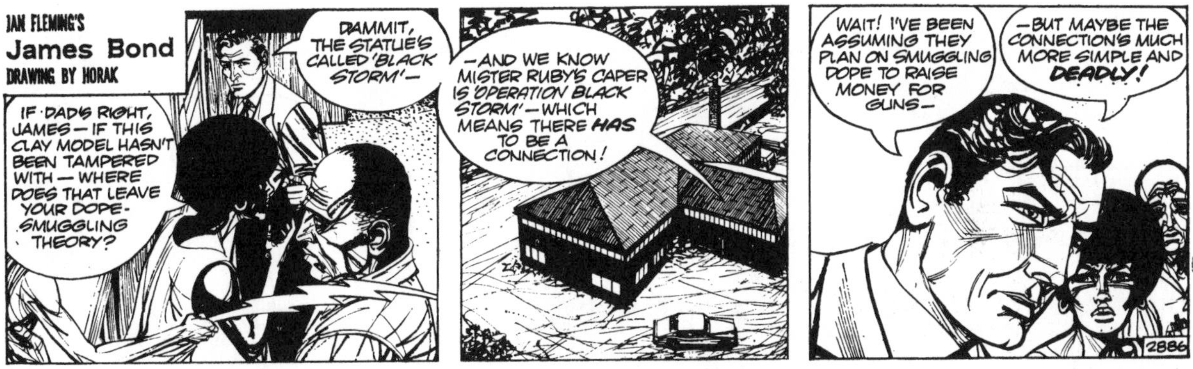
IAN FLEMING'S
James Bond
DRAWING BY HORAK
DAMMIT, THE STATUE'S CALLED 'BLACK STORM'—
IF DAD'S RIGHT, JAMES—IF THIS CLAY MODEL HASN'T BEEN TAMPERED WITH—WHERE DOES THAT LEAVE YOUR DOPE-SMUGGLING THEORY?
—AND WE KNOW MISTER RUBY'S CAPER IS 'OPERATION BLACK STORM'—WHICH MEANS THERE HAS TO BE A CONNECTION!
WAIT! I'VE BEEN ASSUMING THEY PLAN ON SMUGGLING DOPE TO RAISE MONEY FOR GUNS—
—BUT MAYBE THE CONNECTION'S MUCH MORE SIMPLE AND DEADLY!
2886

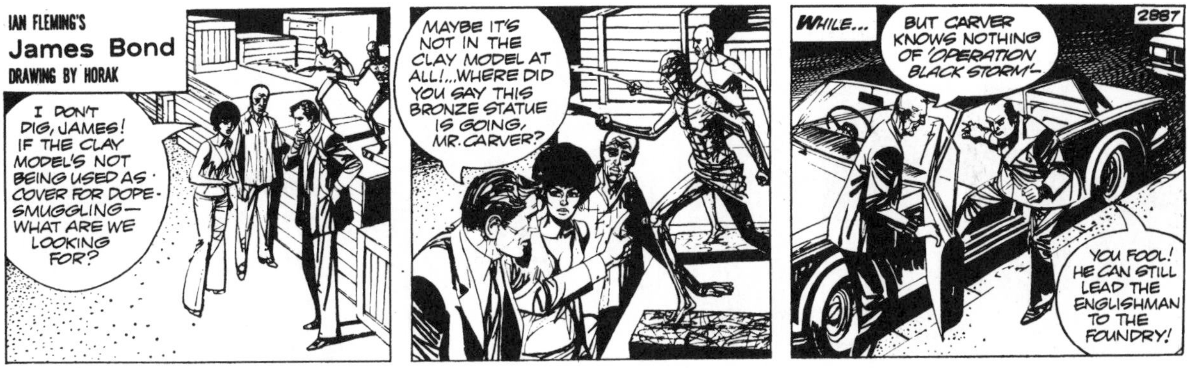
IAN FLEMING'S
James Bond
DRAWING BY HORAK
I DON'T DIG, JAMES! IF THE CLAY MODEL'S NOT BEING USED AS COVER FOR DOPE-SMUGGLING—WHAT ARE WE LOOKING FOR?
MAYBE IT'S NOT IN THE CLAY MODEL AT ALL!...WHERE DID YOU SAY THIS BRONZE STATUE IS GOING, MR. CARVER?
2887
WHILE...
BUT CARVER KNOWS NOTHING OF 'OPERATION BLACK STORM'—
YOU FOOL! HE CAN STILL LEAD THE ENGLISHMAN TO THE FOUNDRY!

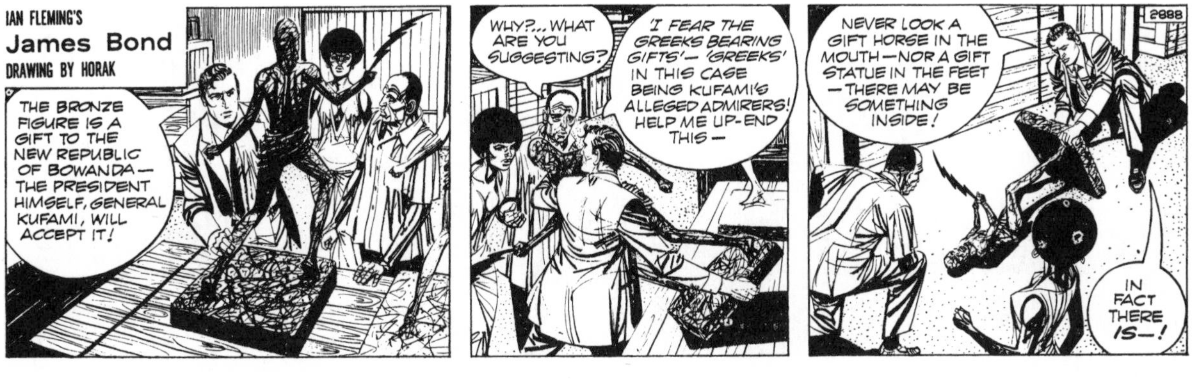
IAN FLEMING'S
James Bond
DRAWING BY HORAK
THE BRONZE FIGURE IS A GIFT TO THE NEW REPUBLIC OF BOWANDA—THE PRESIDENT HIMSELF, GENERAL KUFAMI, WILL ACCEPT IT!
WHY?...WHAT ARE YOU SUGGESTING?
'I FEAR THE GREEKS BEARING GIFTS'—'GREEKS' IN THIS CASE BEING KUFAMI'S ALLEGED ADMIRERS! HELP ME UP-END THIS—
2888
NEVER LOOK A GIFT HORSE IN THE MOUTH—NOR A GIFT STATUE IN THE FEET—THERE MAY BE SOMETHING INSIDE!
IN FACT THERE IS—!

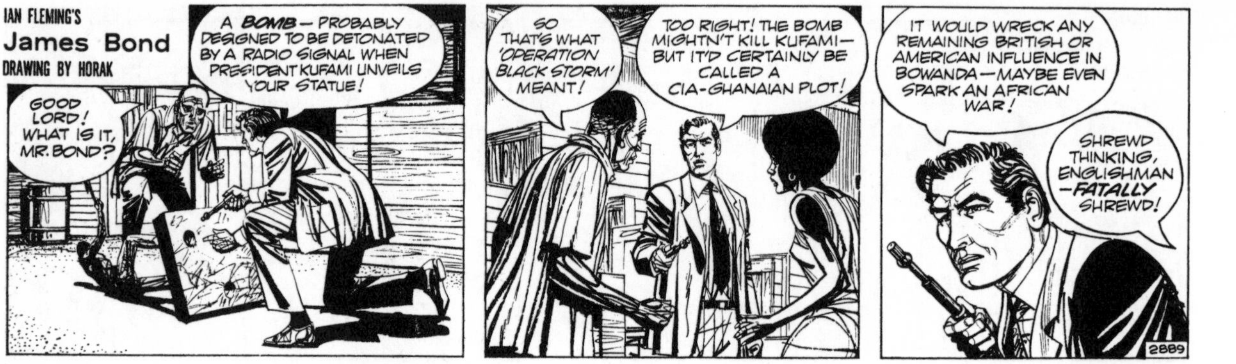
IAN FLEMING'S
James Bond
DRAWING BY HORAK
A BOMB — PROBABLY DESIGNED TO BE DETONATED BY A RADIO SIGNAL WHEN PRESIDENT KUFAMI UNVEILS YOUR STATUE!
GOOD LORD! WHAT IS IT, MR. BOND?
SO THAT'S WHAT 'OPERATION BLACK STORM' MEANT!
TOO RIGHT! THE BOMB MIGHTN'T KILL KUFAMI — BUT IT'D CERTAINLY BE CALLED A CIA-GHANAIAN PLOT!
IT WOULD WRECK ANY REMAINING BRITISH OR AMERICAN INFLUENCE IN BOWANDA — MAYBE EVEN SPARK AN AFRICAN WAR!
SHREWD THINKING, ENGLISHMAN — FATALLY SHREWD!
2889

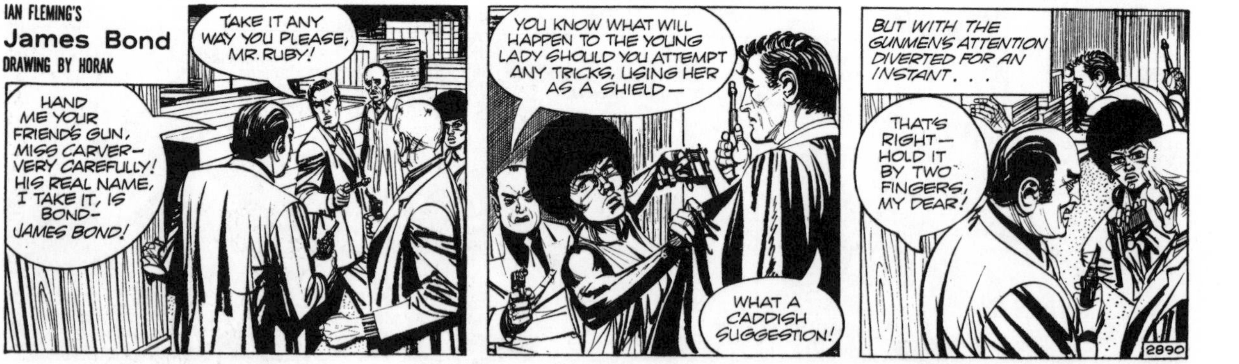
IAN FLEMING'S
James Bond
DRAWING BY HORAK
TAKE IT ANY WAY YOU PLEASE, MR. RUBY!
HAND ME YOUR FRIEND'S GUN, MISS CARVER — VERY CAREFULLY! HIS REAL NAME, I TAKE IT, IS BOND — JAMES BOND!
YOU KNOW WHAT WILL HAPPEN TO THE YOUNG LADY SHOULD YOU ATTEMPT ANY TRICKS, USING HER AS A SHIELD —
WHAT A CADDISH SUGGESTION!
BUT WITH THE GUNMEN'S ATTENTION DIVERTED FOR AN INSTANT . . .
THAT'S RIGHT — HOLD IT BY TWO FINGERS, MY DEAR!
2890

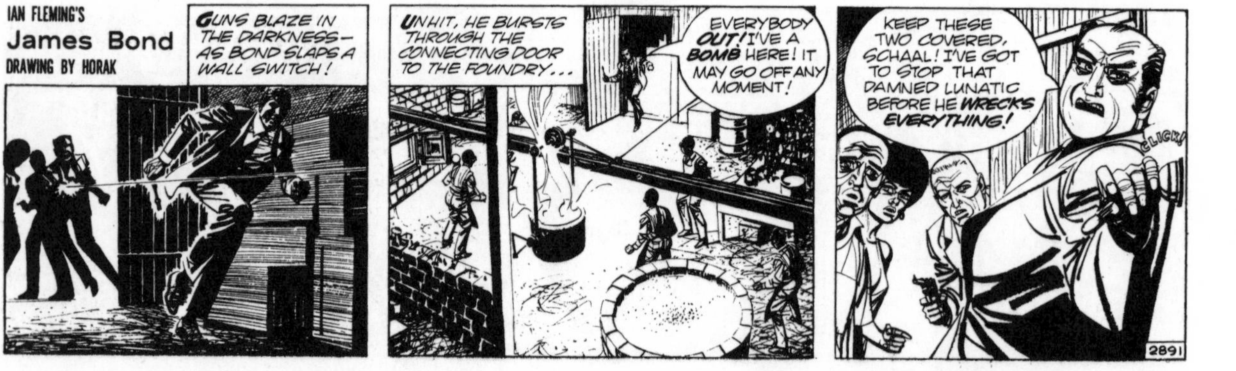
IAN FLEMING'S
James Bond
DRAWING BY HORAK
GUNS BLAZE IN THE DARKNESS — AS BOND SLAPS A WALL SWITCH!
UNHIT, HE BURSTS THROUGH THE CONNECTING DOOR TO THE FOUNDRY...
EVERYBODY OUT! I'VE A BOMB HERE! IT MAY GO OFF ANY MOMENT!
KEEP THESE TWO COVERED, SCHAAL! I'VE GOT TO STOP THAT DAMNED LUNATIC BEFORE HE WRECKS EVERYTHING!
CLICK!
2891

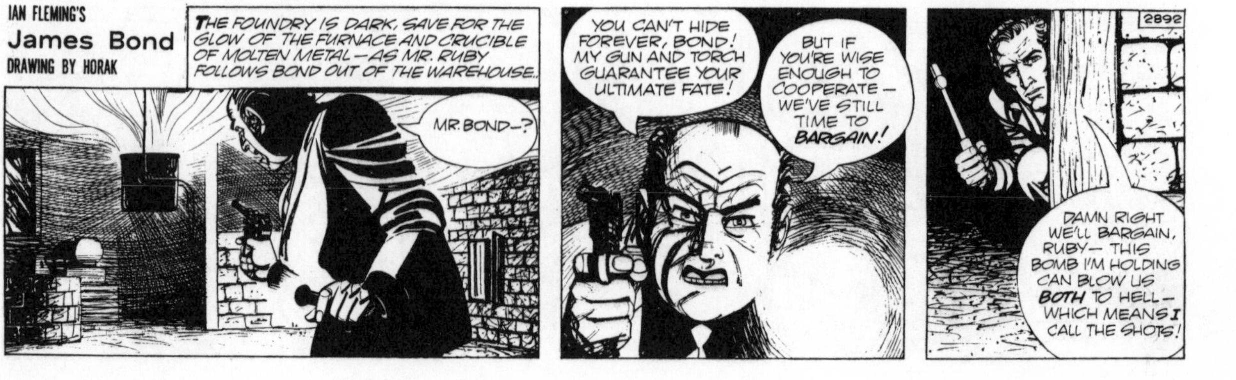
IAN FLEMING'S
James Bond
DRAWING BY HORAK
THE FOUNDRY IS DARK, SAVE FOR THE GLOW OF THE FURNACE AND CRUCIBLE OF MOLTEN METAL — AS MR. RUBY FOLLOWS BOND OUT OF THE WAREHOUSE..
MR. BOND —?
YOU CAN'T HIDE FOREVER, BOND! MY GUN AND TORCH GUARANTEE YOUR ULTIMATE FATE!
BUT IF YOU'RE WISE ENOUGH TO COOPERATE — WE'VE STILL TIME TO BARGAIN!
2892
DAMN RIGHT WE'LL BARGAIN, RUBY — THIS BOMB I'M HOLDING CAN BLOW US BOTH TO HELL — WHICH MEANS I CALL THE SHOTS!

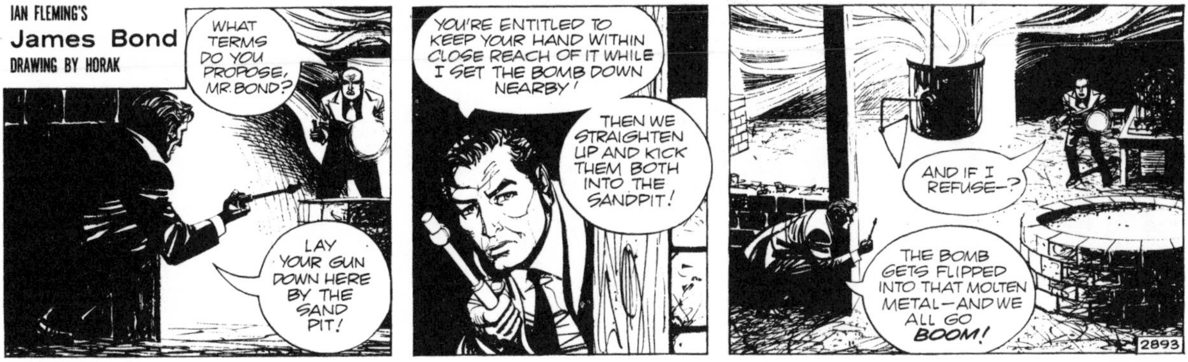
IAN FLEMING'S
James Bond
DRAWING BY HORAK
WHAT TERMS DO YOU PROPOSE, MR. BOND?
LAY YOUR GUN DOWN HERE BY THE SAND PIT!
YOU'RE ENTITLED TO KEEP YOUR HAND WITHIN CLOSE REACH OF IT WHILE I SET THE BOMB DOWN NEARBY!
THEN WE STRAIGHTEN UP AND KICK THEM BOTH INTO THE SANDPIT!
AND IF I REFUSE—?
THE BOMB GETS FLIPPED INTO THAT MOLTEN METAL—AND WE ALL GO BOOM!
2893

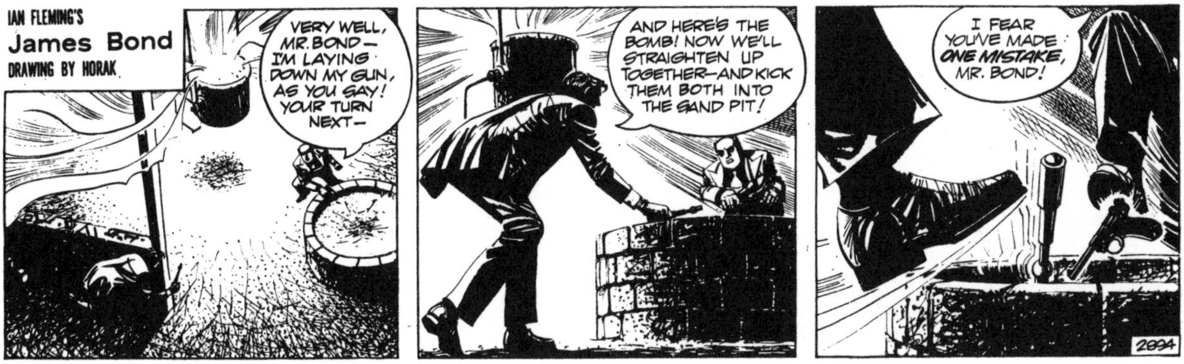
IAN FLEMING'S
James Bond
DRAWING BY HORAK
VERY WELL, MR. BOND—I'M LAYING DOWN MY GUN, AS YOU SAY! YOUR TURN NEXT—
AND HERE'S THE BOMB! NOW WE'LL STRAIGHTEN UP TOGETHER—AND KICK THEM BOTH INTO THE SAND PIT!
I FEAR YOU'VE MADE ONE MISTAKE, MR. BOND!
2894

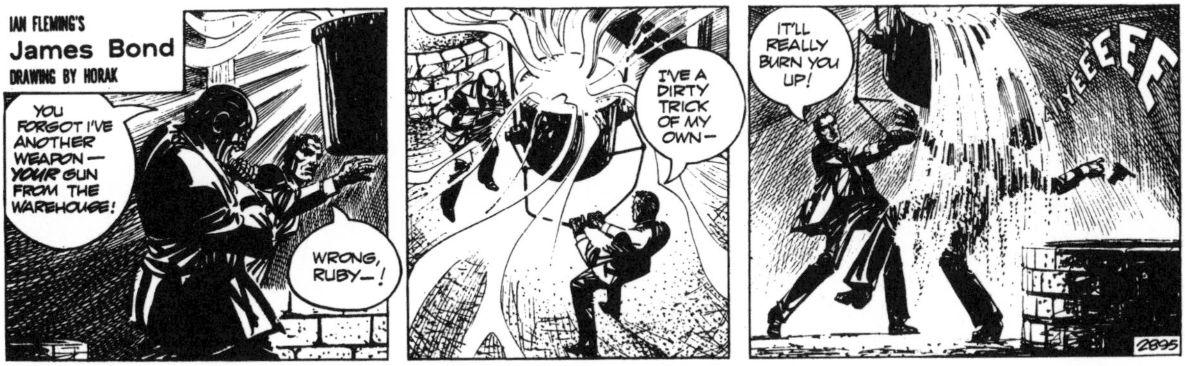
IAN FLEMING'S
James Bond
DRAWING BY HORAK
YOU FORGOT I'VE ANOTHER WEAPON—YOUR GUN FROM THE WAREHOUSE!
WRONG, RUBY—!
I'VE A DIRTY TRICK OF MY OWN—
IT'LL REALLY BURN YOU UP!
AYEEEEE
2895

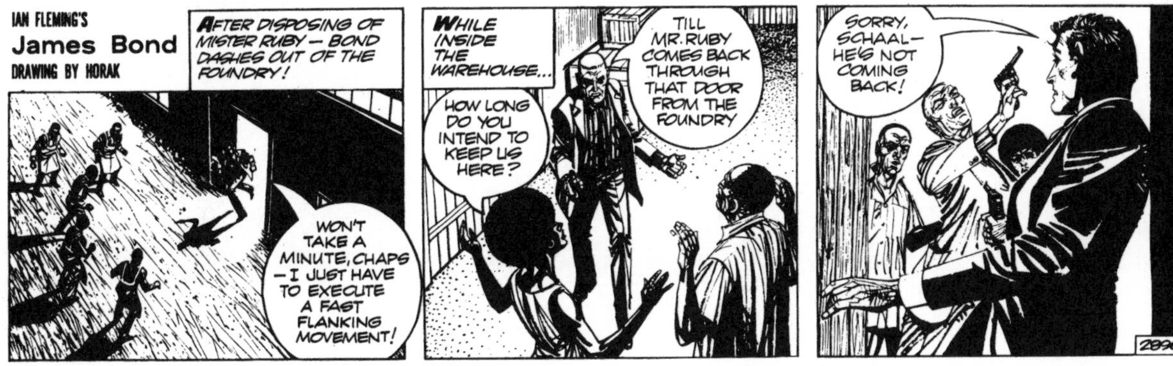
IAN FLEMING'S
James Bond
DRAWING BY HORAK
AFTER DISPOSING OF MISTER RUBY — BOND DASHES OUT OF THE FOUNDRY!
WON'T TAKE A MINUTE, CHAPS —I JUST HAVE TO EXECUTE A FAST FLANKING MOVEMENT!
WHILE INSIDE THE WAREHOUSE...
HOW LONG DO YOU INTEND TO KEEP US HERE?
TILL MR. RUBY COMES BACK THROUGH THAT DOOR FROM THE FOUNDRY
SORRY, SCHAAL—HE'S NOT COMING BACK!
2896

IAN FLEMING'S
James Bond
DRAWING BY HORAK
YOUR FATHER'S QUITE THE LION OF THE HOUR, DAMARA– EVEN IN THE EYES OF THE CIA!
FOR HELPING TO STOP 'OPERATION BLACK STORM' YOU TWO'LL PROBABLY RATE A HEROES' WELCOME IN THE STATES!
NOT ME! I'M STAYING ON HERE A WHILE— THAT IS, IF YOU'LL STICK AROUND TOO, JAMES!
JUST WHAT DID YOU HAVE IN MIND?
CALL IT A CULTURAL EXCHANGE PROGRAMME! LATER ON AT THE HOTEL, WE CAN LAY OUT ALL THE SPECIFICS IN BLACK AND WHITE!.
2897

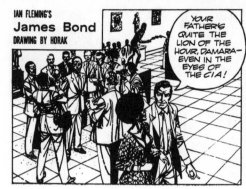

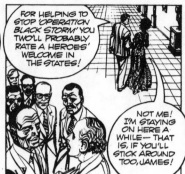

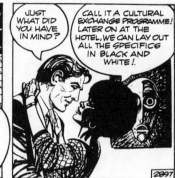